"*The man who fights for his ideals is the man who is alive.*"

CERVANTES
author of
DON QUIXOTE

Mac
Taylor

WAR AND PEACE

WAR AND PEACE

A NOVEL BY COUNT LEO TOLSTOY

>>>

TRANSLATED FROM THE RUSSIAN

BY CONSTANCE GARNETT

>>

THE MODERN LIBRARY

NEW YORK

THE MODERN LIBRARY

is published by RANDOM HOUSE, INC.

Manufactured in the United States of America by H. Wolff

WAR AND PEACE

PART ONE

I

"**W**ELL, PRINCE, Genoa and Lucca are now no more than private estates of the Bonaparte family. No, I warn you, that if you do not tell me we are at war, if you again allow yourself to palliate all the infamies and atrocities of this Antichrist (upon my word, I believe he is), I don't know you in future, you are no longer my friend, no longer my faithful slave, as you say. There, how do you do, how do you do? I see I'm scaring you, sit down and talk to me."

These words were uttered in July 1805 by Anna Pavlovna Scherer, a distinguished lady of the court, and confidential maid-of-honour to the Empress Marya Fyodorovna. It was her greeting to Prince Vassily, a man high in rank and office, who was the first to arrive at her *soirée*. Anna Pavlovna had been coughing for the last few days; she had an attack of *la grippe,* as she said—*grippe* was then a new word only used by a few people. In the notes she had sent round in the morning by a footman in red livery, she had written to all indiscriminately:

"If you have nothing better to do, count (or prince), and if the prospect of spending an evening with a poor invalid is not too alarming to you, I shall be charmed to see you at my house between 7 and 10. Annette Scherer."

"Heavens! what a violent outburst!" the prince responded, not in the least disconcerted at such a reception. He was wearing an embroidered court uniform, stockings and slippers, and had stars on his breast, and a bright smile on his flat face.

He spoke in that elaborately choice French, in which our forefathers not only spoke but thought, and with those slow, patronising intonations peculiar to a man of importance who has grown old in court society. He went up to Anna Pavlovna, kissed her hand, presenting her with a view of his perfumed, shining bald head, and complacently settled himself on the sofa.

"First of all, tell me how you are, dear friend. Relieve a friend's anxiety," he said, with no change of his voice and tone, in which indifference, and even irony, was perceptible through the veil of courtesy and sympathy.

"How can one be well when one is in moral suffering? How can one help being worried in these times, if one has any feeling?" said Anna Pavlovna. "You'll spend the whole evening with me, I hope?"

"And the fête at the English ambassador's? To-day is Wednesday. I must put in an appearance there," said the prince. "My daughter is coming to fetch me and take me there."

1

"I thought to-day's fête had been put off. I confess that all these festivities and fireworks are beginning to pall."

"If they had known that it was your wish, the fête would have been put off," said the prince, from habit, like a wound-up clock, saying things he did not even wish to be believed.

"Don't tease me. Well, what has been decided in regard to the Novosiltsov dispatch? You know everything."

"What is there to tell?" said the prince in a tired, listless tone. "What has been decided? It has been decided that Bonaparte has burnt his ships, and I think that we are about to burn ours."

Prince Vassily always spoke languidly, like an actor repeating his part in an old play. Anna Pavlovna Scherer, in spite of her forty years, was on the contrary brimming over with excitement and impulsiveness. To be enthusiastic had become her pose in society, and at times even when she had, indeed, no inclination to be so, she was enthusiastic so as not to disappoint the expectations of those who knew her. The affected smile which played continually about Anna Pavlovna's face, out of keeping as it was with her faded looks, expressed a spoilt child's continual consciousness of a charming failing of which she had neither the wish nor the power to correct herself, which, indeed, she saw no need to correct.

In the midst of a conversation about politics, Anna Pavlovna became greatly excited.

"Ah, don't talk to me about Austria! I know nothing about it, perhaps, but Austria has never wanted, and doesn't want war. She is betraying us. Russia alone is to be the saviour of Europe. Our benefactor knows his lofty destiny, and will be true to it. That's the one thing I have faith in. Our good and sublime emperor has the greatest part in the world to play, and he is so virtuous and noble that God will not desert him, and he will fulfil his mission—to strangle the hydra of revolution, which is more horrible than ever now in the person of this murderer and miscreant. . . . Whom can we reckon on, I ask you? . . . England with her commercial spirit will not comprehend and cannot comprehend all the loftiness of soul of the Emperor Alexander. She has refused to evacuate Malta. She tries to detect, she seeks a hidden motive in our actions. What have they said to Novosiltsov? Nothing. They didn't understand, they're incapable of understanding the self-sacrifice of our emperor, who desires nothing for himself, and everything for the good of humanity. And what have they promised? Nothing. What they have promised even won't come to anything! Prussia has declared that Bonaparte is invincible, and that all Europe can do nothing against him. . . . And I don't believe a single word of what was said by Hardenberg or Haugwitz. That famous Prussian neutrality is a mere snare. I have no faith but in God and the lofty destiny of our adored emperor. He will save Europe!" She stopped short abruptly, with a smile of amusement at her own warmth.

"I imagine," said the prince, smiling, "that if you had been sent instead of our dear Wintsengerode, you would have carried the Prussian king's consent by storm,—you are so eloquent. Will you give me some tea?"

"In a moment. By the way," she added, subsiding into calm again, "there are two very interesting men to be here to-night, the vicomte de Mortemart; he is connected with the Montmorencies through the Rohans, one of the best families in France. He is one of the good emigrants, the real ones. Then Abbé Morio; you know that profound intellect? He has been received by the emperor. Do you know him?"

"Ah! I shall be delighted," said the prince. "Tell me," he added, as though he had just recollected something, speaking with special nonchalance, though the question was the chief motive of his visit: "is it true that the dowager empress desires the appointment of Baron Funke as first secretary to the Vienna legation? He is a poor creature, it appears, that baron." Prince Vassily would have liked to see his son appointed to the post, which people were trying, through the Empress Marya Fyodorovna, to obtain for the baron.

Anna Pavlovna almost closed her eyes to signify that neither she nor any one else could pass judgment on what the empress might be pleased or see fit to do.

"Baron Funke has been recommended to the empress-mother by her sister," was all she said in a dry, mournful tone. When Anna Pavlovna spoke of the empress her countenance suddenly assumed a profound and genuine expression of devotion and respect, mingled with melancholy, and this happened whenever she mentioned in conversation her illustrious patroness. She said that her Imperial Majesty had been graciously pleased to show great esteem to Baron Funke, and again a shade of melancholy passed over her face. The prince preserved an indifferent silence. Anna Pavlovna, with the adroitness and quick tact of a courtier and a woman, felt an inclination to chastise the prince for his temerity in referring in such terms to a person recommended to the empress, and at the same time to console him.

"But about your own family," she said, "do you know that your daughter, since she has come out, charms everybody? People say she is as beautiful as the day."

The prince bowed in token of respect and acknowledgment.

"I often think," pursued Anna Pavlovna, moving up to the prince and smiling cordially to him, as though to mark that political and worldly conversation was over and now intimate talk was to begin: "I often think how unfairly the blessings of life are sometimes apportioned. Why has fate given you two such splendid children—I don't include Anatole, your youngest—him I don't like" (she put in with a decision admitting of no appeal, raising her eyebrows)—"such charming children? And you really seem to appreciate them less than any one, and so you don't deserve them."

And she smiled her ecstatic smile.

"What would you have? Lavater would have said that I have not the bump of paternity," said the prince.

"Don't keep on joking. I wanted to talk to you seriously. Do you know I'm not pleased with your youngest son. Between ourselves" (her face took its mournful expression), "people have been talking about him to her majesty and commiserating you . . ."

The prince did not answer, but looking at him significantly, she waited in silence for his answer. Prince Vassily frowned.

"What would you have me do?" he said at last. "You know I have done everything for their education a father could do, and they have both turned out *des imbéciles*. Ippolit is at least a quiet fool, while Anatole's a fool that won't keep quiet, that's the only difference," he said, with a smile, more unnatural and more animated than usual, bringing out with peculiar prominence something surprisingly brutal and unpleasant in the lines about his mouth.

"Why are children born to men like you? If you weren't a father, I could find no fault with you," said Anna Pavlovna, raising her eyes pensively.

"I am your faithful slave and to you alone I can confess. My children are the bane of my existence. It's the cross I have to bear, that's how I explain it to myself. What would you have?" . . . He broke off with a gesture expressing his resignation to a cruel fate. Anna Pavlovna pondered a moment.

"Have you never thought of marrying your prodigal son Anatole? People say," she said, "that old maids have a mania for matchmaking. I have never been conscious of this failing before, but I have a little person in my mind, who is very unhappy with her father, a relation of ours, the young Princess Bolkonsky."

Prince Vassily made no reply, but with the rapidity of reflection and memory characteristic of worldly people, he signified by a motion of the head that he had taken in and was considering what she said.

"No, do you know that that boy is costing me forty thousand roubles a year?" he said, evidently unable to restrain the gloomy current of his thoughts. He paused. "What will it be in five years if this goes on? These are the advantages of being a father. . . . Is she rich, your young princess?"

"Her father is very rich and miserly. He lives in the country. You know that notorious Prince Bolkonsky, retired under the late emperor, and nicknamed the 'Prussian King.' He's a very clever man, but eccentric and tedious. The poor little thing is as unhappy as possible. Her brother it is who has lately been married to Liza Meinen, an adjutant of Kutuzov's. He'll be here this evening."

"Listen, dear Annette," said the prince, suddenly taking his companion's hand, and for some reason bending it downwards. "Arrange this matter for me and I am your faithful slave for ever and ever. She's of good family and well off. That's all I want."

And with the freedom, familiarity, and grace that distinguished him, he took the maid-of-honour's hand, kissed it, and as he kissed it waved her hand, while he stretched forward in his low chair and gazed away into the distance.

"Wait," said Anna Pavlovna, considering. "I'll talk to Lise (the wife of young Bolkonsky) this very evening, and perhaps it can be arranged I'll try my prentice hand as an old maid in your family."

II

ANNA PAVLOVNA's drawing-room gradually began to fill. The people of the highest distinction in Petersburg were there, people very different in ages and characters, but alike in the set in which they moved. The daughter of Prince Vassily, the beauty, Ellen, came to fetch her father and go with him to the ambassador's fête. She was wearing a ball-dress with an imperial badge on it. The young Princess Bolkonsky was there, celebrated as the most seductive woman in Petersburg. She had been married the previous winter, and was not now going out into the great world on account of her interesting condition, but was still to be seen at small parties. Prince Ippolit, the son of Prince Vassily, came too with Mortemart, whom he introduced. The Abbé Morio was there too, and many others.

"Have you not yet seen, or not been introduced to *ma tante*?" Anna Pavlovna said to her guests as they arrived, and very seriously she led them up to a little old lady wearing tall bows, who had sailed in out of the next room as soon as the guests began to arrive. Anna Pavlovna mentioned their names, deliberately turning her eyes from the guest to *ma tante*, and then withdrew. All the guests performed the ceremony of greeting the aunt, who was unknown, uninteresting and unnecessary to every one. Anna Pavlovna with mournful, solemn sympathy, followed these greetings, silently approving them. *Ma tante* said to each person the same words about his health, her own health, and the health of her majesty, who was, thank God, better to-day. Every one, though from politeness showing no undue haste, moved away from the old lady with a sense of relief at a tiresome duty accomplished, and did not approach her again all the evening. The young Princess Bolkonsky had come with her work in a gold-embroidered velvet bag. Her pretty little upper lip, faintly darkened with down, was very short over her teeth, but was all the more charming when it was lifted, and still more charming when it was at times drawn down to meet the lower lip. As is always the case with perfectly charming women, her defect—the shortness of the lip and the half-opened mouth—seemed her peculiar, her characteristic beauty. Every one took delight in watching the pretty creature full of life and gaiety, so soon to be a mother, and so lightly bearing her burden. Old men and bored, depressed young men gazing at her felt as though they were becoming like her, by being with her and talking a little while to her. Any man who spoke to her, and at every word saw her bright little smile and shining white teeth, gleaming continually, imagined that he was being particularly successful this evening. And this each thought in turn.

The little princess, moving with a slight swing, walked with rapid little steps round the table with her work-bag in her hand, and gaily ar-

ranging the folds of her gown, sat down on a sofa near the silver samovar; it seemed as though everything she did was a festival for herself
and all around her.

"I have brought my work," she said, displaying her reticule, and addressing the company generally. "Mind, Annette, don't play me a nasty
trick," she turned to the lady of the house; "you wrote to me that it was
quite a little gathering. See how I am got up."

And she flung her arms open to show her elegant grey dress, trimmed
with lace and girt a little below the bosom with a broad sash.

"Never mind, Lise, you will always be prettier than any one else,"
answered Anna Pavlovna.

"You know my husband is deserting me," she went on in just the same
voice, addressing a general; "he is going to get himself killed. Tell me
what this nasty war is for," she said to Prince Vassily, and without waiting for an answer she turned to Prince Vassily's daughter, the beautiful
Ellen.

"How delightful this little princess is!" said Prince Vassily in an undertone to Anna Pavlovna.

Soon after the little princess, there walked in a massively built, stout
young man in spectacles, with a cropped head, light breeches in the
mode of the day, with a high lace ruffle and a ginger-coloured coat. This
stout young man was the illegitimate son of a celebrated dandy of the
days of Catherine, Count Bezuhov, who was now dying at Moscow. He
had not yet entered any branch of the service; he had only just returned
from abroad, where he had been educated, and this was his first appearance in society. Anna Pavlovna greeted him with a nod reserved
for persons of the very lowest hierarchy in her drawing-room. But, in
spite of this greeting, Anna Pavlovna's countenance showed signs on
seeing Pierre of uneasiness and alarm, such as is shown at the sight of
something too big and out of place. Though Pierre certainly was somewhat bigger than any of the other men in the room, this expression could
only have reference to the clever, though shy, observant and natural look
that distinguished him from every one else in the drawing-room.

"It is very kind of you, M. Pierre, to have come to see a poor invalid,"
Anna Pavlovna said to him, exchanging anxious glances with her aunt,
to whom she was conducting him.

Pierre murmured something unintelligible, and continued searching
for something with his eyes. He smiled gleefully and delightedly, bowing
to the little princess as though she were an intimate friend, and went up
to the aunt. Anna Pavlovna's alarm was not without grounds, for Pierre
walked away from the aunt without waiting to the end of her remarks
about her majesty's health. Anna Pavlovna stopped him in dismay with
the words: "You don't know Abbé Morio? He's a very interesting man,"
she said.

"Yes, I have heard of his scheme for perpetual peace, and it's very
interesting, but hardly possible . . ."

"You think so?" said Anna Pavlovna in order to say something and to
get away again to her duties as hostess, but Pierre committed the oppo-

site incivility. Just now he had walked off without listening to the lady who was addressing him; now he detained by his talk a lady who wanted to get away from him. With head bent and legs planted wide apart, he began explaining to Anna Pavlovna why he considered the abbé's scheme chimerical.

"We will talk of it later," said Anna Pavlovna, smiling.

And getting rid of this unmannerly young man she returned to her duties, keeping her eyes and ears open, ready to fly to the assistance at any point where the conversation was flagging. Just as the foreman of a spinning-mill settles the work-people in their places, walks up and down the works, and noting any stoppage or unusual creaking or too loud a whir in the spindles, goes up hurriedly, slackens the machinery and sets it going properly, so Anna Pavlovna, walking about her drawing-room, went up to any circle that was pausing or too loud in conversation and by a single word or change of position set the conversational machine going again in its regular, decorous way. But in the midst of these cares a special anxiety on Pierre's account could still be discerned in her. She kept an anxious watch on him as he went up to listen to what was being said near Mortemart, and walked away to another group where the abbé was talking. Pierre had been educated abroad, and this party at Anna Pavlovna's was the first at which he had been present in Russia. He knew all the intellectual lights of Petersburg gathered together here, and his eyes strayed about like a child's in a toy-shop. He was afraid at every moment of missing some intellectual conversation which he might have heard. Gazing at the self-confident and refined expressions of the personages assembled here, he was continually expecting something exceptionally clever. At last he moved up to Abbé Morio. The conversation seemed interesting, and he stood still waiting for an opportunity of expressing his own ideas, as young people are fond of doing.

III

ANNA PAVLOVNA's *soirée* was in full swing. The spindles kept up their regular hum on all sides without pause. Except the aunt, beside whom was sitting no one but an elderly lady with a thin, careworn face, who seemed rather out of her element in this brilliant society, the company was broken up into three groups. In one of these, the more masculine, the centre was the abbé; in the other, the group of young people, the chief attractions were the beautiful Princess Ellen, Prince Vassily's daughter, and the little Princess Bolkonsky, with her rosy prettiness, too plump for her years. In the third group were Mortemart and Anna Pavlovna.

The vicomte was a pretty young gentleman with soft features and manners, who obviously regarded himself as a celebrity, but with good-breeding modestly allowed the company the benefit of his society. Anna Pavlovna unmistakably regarded him as the chief entertainment she was giving her guests. As a clever *maître d'hôtel* serves as something superla-

tively good the piece of beef which no one would have cared to eat seeing
it in the dirty kitchen, Anna Pavlovna that evening served up to her
guests—first, the vicomte and then the abbé, as something superlatively
subtle. In Mortemart's group the talk turned at once on the execution of
the duc d'Enghien. The vicomte said that the duc d'Enghien had been
lost by his own magnanimity and that there were special reasons for
Bonaparte's bitterness again him.

"Ah, come! Tell us about that, vicomte," said Anna Pavlovna gleefully, feeling that the phrase had a peculiarly Louis Quinze note about
it: *"Contez-nous cela, vicomte."*

The vicomte bowed and smiled courteously in token of his readiness
to obey. Anna Pavlovna made a circle round the vicomte and invited
every one to hear his story.

"The vicomte was personally acquainted with his highness," Anna
Pavlovna whispered to one. "The vicomte tells a story perfectly," she
said to another. "How one sees the man of quality," she said to a third,
and the vicomte was presented to the company in the most elegant and
advantageous light, like the roast-beef on the hot dish garnished with
green parsley.

The vicomte was about to begin his narrative, and he smiled subtly.

"Come over here, *chère Hélène,*" said Anna Pavlovna to the young
beauty who was sitting a little way off, the centre of another group.

Princess Ellen smiled. She got up with the same unchanging smile of
the acknowledged beauty with which she had entered the drawing-room.
Her white ball-dress adorned with ivy and moss rustled lightly; her
white shoulders, glossy hair, and diamonds glittered, as she passed between the men who moved apart to make way for her. Not looking
directly at any one, but smiling at every one, as it were courteously allowing to all the right to admire the beauty of her figure, her full shoulders, her bosom and back, which were extremely exposed in the mode of
the day, she moved up to Anna Pavlovna, seeming to bring with her the
brilliance of the ballroom. Ellen was so lovely that she was not merely
free from the slightest shade of coquetry, she seemed on the contrary
ashamed of the too evident, too violent and all-conquering influence of
her beauty. She seemed to wish but to be unable to soften the effect of
her beauty.

"What a beautiful woman!" every one said on seeing her. As though
struck by something extraordinary, the vicomte shrugged his shoulders
and dropped his eyes, when she seated herself near him and dazzled him
too with the same unchanging smile.

"Madame, I doubt my abilities before such an audience," he said,
bowing with a smile.

The princess leaned her plump, bare arm on the table and did not
find it necessary to say anything. She waited, smiling. During the
vicomte's story she sat upright, looking from time to time at her beautiful, plump arm, which lay with its line changed by pressure on the table,
then at her still lovelier bosom, on which she set straight her diamond
necklace. Several times she settled the folds of her gown, and when the

narrative made a sensation upon the audience, she glanced at Anna Pavlovna and at once assumed the expression she saw on the maid-of-honour's face, then she relapsed again into her unvarying smile. After Ellen the little princess too moved away from the tea-table.

"Wait for me, I will take my work," she said. "Come, what are you thinking of?" she said to Prince Ippolit. "Bring me my reticule."

The little princess, smiling and talking to every one, at once effected a change of position, and settling down again, gaily smoothed out her skirts.

"Now I'm comfortable," she said, and begging the vicomte to begin, she took up her work. Prince Ippolit brought her reticule, moved to her side, and bending close over her chair, sat beside her.

Le charmant Hippolyte struck every one as extraordinarily like this sister, and, still more, as being, in spite of the likeness, strikingly ugly. His features were like his sister's, but in her, everything was radiant with joyous life, with the complacent, never-failing smile of youth and life and an extraordinary antique beauty of figure. The brother's face on the contrary was clouded over by imbecility and invariably wore a look of aggressive fretfulness, while he was thin and feebly built. His eyes, his nose, his mouth—everything was, as it were, puckered up in one vacant, bored grimace, while his arms and legs always fell into the most grotesque attitudes.

"It is not a ghost story," he said, sitting down by the princess and hurriedly fixing his eyeglass in his eye, as though without that instrument he could not begin to speak.

"Why, no, my dear fellow," said the astonished vicomte, with a shrug.

"Because I detest ghost stories," said Prince Ippolit in a tone which showed that he uttered the words before he was aware of their meaning.

From the self-confidence with which he spoke, no one could tell whether what he said was very clever or very stupid. He was dressed in a dark-green frock coat, breeches of the colour of the *cuisse de nymphe effrayée*, as he called it, stockings and slippers. The vicomte very charmingly related the anecdote then current, that the duc d'Enghien had secretly visited Paris for the sake of an interview with the actress, Mlle. Georges, and that there he met Bonaparte, who also enjoyed the favours of the celebrated actress, and that, meeting the duc, Napoleon had fallen into one of the fits to which he was subject and had been completely in the duc's power, how the duc had not taken advantage of it, and Bonaparte had in the sequel avenged his magnanimity by the duc's death.

The story was very charming and interesting, especially at the point when the rivals suddenly recognise each other and the ladies seemed to be greatly excited by it. *"Charmant!"* said Anna Pavlovna, looking inquiringly at the little princess. "Charming!" whispered the little princess, sticking her needle into her work as an indication that the interest and charm of the story prevented her working. The vicomte appreciated this silent homage, and smiling gratefully, resumed his narrative. But meanwhile Anna Pavlovna, still keeping a watch on the dreadful young man, noticed that he was talking too loudly and too warmly with the abbé and hurried to the spot of danger. Pierre had in fact succeeded in getting into a political conversation with the abbé on the balance of power, and the abbé, evidently interested by the simple-hearted fervour of the young man, was unfolding to him his cherished idea. Both were listening and talking too eagerly and naturally, and Anna Pavlovna did not like it.

"The means?—the balance of power in Europe and the rights of the people," said the abbé. "One powerful state like Russia—with the prestige of barbarism—need only take a disinterested stand at the head of the alliance that aims at securing the balance of power in Europe, and it would save the world!" "How are you going to get such a balance of power?" Pierre was beginning; but at that moment Anna Pavlovna came up, and glancing severely at Pierre, asked the Italian how he was supporting the climate. The Italian's face changed instantly and assumed the look of offensive, affected sweetness, which was evidently its habitual expression in conversation with women. "I am so enchanted by the wit and culture of the society—especially of the ladies—in which I have had the happiness to be received, that I have not yet had time to think of the climate," he said. Not letting the abbé and Pierre slip out of her grasp, Anna Pavlovna, for greater convenience in watching them, made them join the bigger group.

At that moment another guest walked into the drawing-room. This was the young Prince Andrey Bolkonsky, the husband of the little princess. Prince Bolkonsky was a very handsome young man, of medium height, with clear, clean-cut features. Everything in his appearance, from his weary, bored expression to his slow, measured step, formed the most striking contrast to his lively little wife. Obviously all the people in the drawing-room were familiar figures to him, and more than that, he was unmistakably so sick of them that even to look at them and to listen to them was a weariness to him. Of all the wearisome faces the face of his pretty wife seemed to bore him most. With a grimace that distorted his handsome face he turned away from her. He kissed Anna Pavlovna's hand, and with half-closed eyelids scanned the whole company.

"You are enlisting for the war, prince?" said Anna Pavlovna.

"General Kutuzov has been kind enough to have me as an aide-de-camp," said Bolkonsky.

"And Lise, your wife?——"

"She is going into the country."

"Isn't it too bad of you to rob us of your charming wife?"

"*André*," said his wife, addressing her husband in exactly the same coquettish tone in which she spoke to outsiders, "the vicomte has just told us such a story about Mlle. Georges and Bonaparte!"

Prince Andrey scowled and turned away. Pierre, who had kept his eyes joyfully and affectionately fixed on him ever since he came in, went up to him and took hold of his arm. Prince Andrey, without looking round, twisted his face into a grimace of annoyance at any one's touching him, but seeing Pierre's smiling face, he gave him a smile that was unexpectedly sweet and pleasant.

"Why, you! . . . And in such society too," he said to Pierre.

"I knew you would be here," answered Pierre. "I'm coming to supper with you," he added in an undertone, not to interrupt the vicomte who was still talking. "Can I?"

"Oh no, impossible," said Prince Andrey, laughing, with a squeeze of his hand giving Pierre to understand that there was no need to ask. He would have said something more, but at that instant Prince Vassily and his daughter got up and the two young men rose to make way for them.

"Pardon me, my dear vicomte," said Prince Vassily in French, gently pulling him down by his sleeve to prevent him from getting up from his seat. "This luckless fête at the ambassador's deprives me of a pleasure and interrupts you. I am very sorry to leave your enchanting party," he said to Anna Pavlovna.

His daughter, Princess Ellen, lightly holding the folds of her gown, passed between the chairs, and the smile glowed more brightly than ever on her handsome face. Pierre looked with rapturous, almost frightened eyes at this beautiful creature as she passed them.

"Very lovely!" said Prince Andrey.

"Very," said Pierre.

As he came up to them, Prince Vassily took Pierre by the arm, and addressing Anna Pavlovna:

"Get this bear into shape for me," he said. "Here he has been staying with me for a month, and this is the first time I have seen him in society. Nothing's so necessary for a young man as the society of clever women."

IV

ANNA PAVLOVNA smiled and promised to look after Pierre, who was, she knew, related to Prince Vassily on his father's side. The elderly lady, who had been till then sitting by the aunt, got up hurriedly, and over-took Prince Vassily in the hall. All the affectation of interest she had assumed till now vanished. Her kindly, careworn face expressed nothing but anxiety and alarm.

"What have you to tell me, prince, of my Boris?" she said, catching him in the hall. "I can't stay any longer in Petersburg. Tell me what news am I to take to my poor boy?"

Although Prince Vassily listened reluctantly and almost uncivilly to the elderly lady and even showed signs of impatience, she gave him an ingratiating and appealing smile, and to prevent his going away she took him by the arm. "It is nothing for you to say a word to the Em-peror, and he will be transferred at once to the Guards," she implored.

"Believe me, I will do all I can, princess," answered Prince Vassily; "but it's not easy for me to petition the Emperor. I should advise you to apply to Rumyantsov, through Prince Galitsin; that would be the wisest course."

The elderly lady was a Princess Drubetskoy, one of the best families in Russia; but she was poor, had been a long while out of society, and had lost touch with her former connections. She had come now to try and obtain the appointment of her only son to the Guards. It was simply in order to see Prince Vassily that she had invited herself and come to Anna Pavlovna's party, simply for that she had listened to the vicomte's story. She was dismayed at Prince Vassily's words; her once handsome face showed exasperation, but that lasted only one moment. She smiled again and grasped Prince Vassily's arm more tightly.

"Hear what I have to say, prince," she said. "I have never asked you a favour, and never will I ask one; I have never reminded you of my father's affection for you. But now, for God's sake, I beseech you, do this for my son, and I shall consider you my greatest benefactor," she added hurriedly. "No, don't be angry, but promise me. I have asked Galitsin; he has refused. Be as kind as you used to be," she said, trying to smile, though there were tears in her eyes.

"Papa, we are late," said Princess Ellen, turning her lovely head on her statuesque shoulders as she waited at the door.

But influence in the world is a capital, which must be carefully guarded if it is not to disappear. Prince Vassily knew this, and having once for all reflected that if he were to beg for all who begged him to do so, he would soon be unable to beg for himself, he rarely made use of his influence. In Princess Drubetskoy's case, however, he felt after her new appeal something akin to a conscience-prick. She had reminded him of the truth; for his first step upwards in the service he had been indebted to her father. Besides this, he saw from her manner that she was one of those women—especially mothers—who having once taken an idea into their heads will not give it up till their wishes are fulfilled, and till then are prepared for daily, hourly persistence, and even for scenes. This last consideration made him waver.

"*Chère* Anna Mihalovna," he said, with his invariable familiarity and boredom in his voice, "it's almost impossible for me to do what you wish; but to show you my devotion to you, and my reverence for your dear father's memory, I will do the impossible—your son shall be transferred to the Guards; here is my hand on it. Are you satisfied?"

"My dear prince, you are our benefactor. I expected nothing less indeed; I know how good you are——" He tried to get away. "Wait a moment, one word. Once in the Guards . . ." She hesitated. "You are on friendly terms with Mihail Ilarionovitch Kutuzov, recommend Boris as his adjutant. Then my heart will be set at rest, then indeed . . ."

Prince Vassily smiled. "That I can't promise. You don't know how Kutuzov has been besieged ever since he has been appointed commander-in-chief. He told me himself that all the Moscow ladies were in league together to give him all their offspring as adjutants."

"No, promise me; I can't let you off, kind, good friend, benefactor . . ."

"Papa," repeated the beauty in the same tone, "we are late."

"Come, *au revoir*, good-bye. You see how it is."

"To-morrow then you will speak to the Emperor?"

"Certainly; but about Kutuzov I can't promise."

"Yes; do promise, promise, *Basile*," Anna Mihalovna said, pursuing him with the smile of a coquettish girl, once perhaps characteristic, but now utterly incongruous with her careworn face. Evidently she had forgotten her age and from habit was bringing out every feminine resource. But as soon as he had gone out her face assumed once more the frigid, artificial expression it had worn all the evening. She went back to the group in which the vicomte was still talking, and again affected to be listening, waiting for the suitable moment to get away, now that her object had been attained.

"And what do you think of this latest farce of the coronation at Milan?" said Anna Pavlovna. "And the new comedy of the people of Lucca and Genoa coming to present their petitions to Monsieur Buonaparte. Monsieur Buonaparte sitting on a throne and granting the petitions of nations! Adorable! Why, it is enough to drive one out of one's senses! It seems as though the whole world had lost its head."

Prince Andrey smiled sarcastically, looking straight into Anna Pavlovna's face.

"God gives it me; let man beware of touching it," he said (Bonaparte's words uttered at the coronation). "They say that he was very fine as he spoke those words," he added, and he repeated the same words in Italian: *"Dio me l'ha data, e quai a chi la tocca."*

"I hope that at last," pursued Anna Pavlovna, "this has been the drop of water that will make the glass run over. The sovereigns cannot continue to endure this man who is a threat to everything."

"The sovereigns! I am not speaking of Russia," said the vicomte, deferentially and hopelessly. "The sovereigns! . . . Madame! What did they do for Louis the Sixteenth, for the queen, for Madame Elisabeth? Nothing," he went on with more animation; "and believe me, they are undergoing the punishment of their treason to the Bourbon cause. The sovereigns! . . . They are sending ambassadors to congratulate the usurper."

And with a scornful sigh he shifted his attitude again. Prince Ippolit, who had for a long time been staring through his eyeglass at the vicomte, at these words suddenly turned completely round, and bending over the little princess asked her for a needle, and began showing her the coat-of-arms of the Condé family, scratching it with the needle on the table. He explained the coat-of-arms with an air of gravity, as though the princess had asked him about it. "Staff, gules; engrailed with gules of azure—house of Condé," he said. The princess listened smiling.

"If Bonaparte remains another year on the throne of France," resumed the vicomte, with the air of a man who, being better acquainted with the subject than any one else, pursues his own train of thought without listening to other people, "things will have gone too far. By intrigue and violence, by exiles and executions, French society—I mean good society—will have been destroyed for ever, and then . . ."

He shrugged his shoulders, and made a despairing gesture with his hand. Pierre wanted to say something—the conversation interested him —but Anna Pavlovna, who was keeping her eye on him, interposed.

"And the Emperor Alexander," she said with the pathetic note that always accompanied all her references to the imperial family, "has declared his intention of leaving it to the French themselves to choose their own form of government. And I imagine there is no doubt that the whole nation, delivered from the usurper, would fling itself into the arms of its lawful king," said Anna Pavlovna, trying to be agreeable to an *émigré* and loyalist.

"That's not certain," said Prince Andrey. "*M. le vicomte* is quite right in supposing that things have gone too far by now. I imagine it would not be easy to return to the old régime."

"As far as I could hear," Pierre, blushing, again interposed in the conversation, "almost all the nobility have gone over to Bonaparte."

"That's what the Bonapartists assert," said the vicomte without looking at Pierre. "It's a difficult matter now to find out what public opinion is in France."

"Bonaparte said so," observed Prince Andrey with a sarcastic smile. It was evident that he did not like the vicomte, and that though he was not looking at him, he was directing his remarks against him.

" 'I showed them the path of glory; they would not take it,' " he said after a brief pause, again quoting Napoleon's words. " 'I opened my anterooms to them; they crowded in.' . . . I do not know in what degree he had a right to say so."

"None!" retorted the vicomte. "Since the duc's murder even his warmest partisans have ceased to regard him as a hero. If indeed some people made a hero of him," said the vicomte addressing Anna Pavlovna, "since the duke's assassination there has been a martyr more in heaven, and a hero less on earth."

Anna Pavlovna and the rest of the company hardly had time to smile their appreciation of the vicomte's words, when Pierre again broke into the conversation, and though Anna Pavlovna had a foreboding he would say something inappropriate, this time she was unable to stop him.

"The execution of the duc d'Enghien," said Monsieur Pierre, "was a political necessity, and I consider it a proof of greatness of soul that Napoleon did not hesitate to take the whole responsibility of it upon himself."

"*Dieu! mon Dieu!*" moaned Anna Pavlovna, in a terrified whisper.

"What, Monsieur Pierre! you think assassination is greatness of soul?" said the little princess, smiling and moving her work nearer to her.

"Ah! oh!" cried different voices.

"Capital!" Prince Ippolit said in English, and he began slapping his knee. The vicomte merely shrugged his shoulders.

Pierre looked solemnly over his spectacles at his audience.

"I say so," he pursued desperately, "because the Bourbons ran away from the Revolution, leaving the people to anarchy; and Napoleon alone was capable of understanding the Revolution, of overcoming it, and so for the public good he could not stop short at the life of one man."

"Won't you come over to this table?" said Anna Pavlovna. But Pierre went on without answering her.

"Yes," he said, getting more and more eager, "Napoleon is great because he has towered above the Revolution, and subdued its evil tendencies, preserving all that was good—the equality of all citizens, and freedom of speech and of the press, and only to that end has he possessed himself of supreme power."

"Yes, if on obtaining power he had surrendered it to the lawful king, instead of making use of it to commit murder," said the vicomte, "then I might have called him a great man."

"He could not have done that. The people gave him power simply for him to rid them of the Bourbons, and that was just why the people believed him to be a great man. The Revolution was a grand fact," pursued Monsieur Pierre, betraying by this desperate and irrelevantly provocative statement his extreme youth and desire to give full expression to everything.

"Revolution and regicide a grand fact? . . . What next? . . . but won't you come to this table?" repeated Anna Pavlovna.

"*Contrat social,*" said the vicomte with a bland smile.

"I'm not speaking of regicide. I'm speaking of the idea."

"The idea of plunder, murder, and regicide!" an ironical voice put in.

"Those were extremes, of course; but the whole meaning of the Revolution did not lie in them, but in the rights of man, in emancipation from conventional ideas, in equality; and all these Napoleon has maintained in their full force."

"Liberty and equality," said the vicomte contemptuously, as though he had at last made up his mind to show this youth seriously all the folly of his assertions: "all high-sounding words, which have long since been debased. Who does not love liberty and equality? Our Saviour indeed preached liberty and equality. Have men been any happier since the Revolution? On the contrary. We wanted liberty, but Bonaparte has crushed it."

Prince Andrey looked with a smile first at Pierre, then at the vicomte, then at their hostess.

For the first minute Anna Pavlovna had, in spite of her social adroitness, been dismayed by Pierre's outbreak; but when she saw that the vicomte was not greatly discomposed by Pierre's sacrilegious utterances, and had convinced herself that it was impossible to suppress them, she rallied her forces and joined the vicomte in attacking the orator.

"*Mais, mon cher Monsieur Pierre,*" said Anna Pavlovna, "what have you to say for a great man who was capable of executing the duc—or simply any human being—guiltless and untried?"

"I should like to ask," said the vicomte, "how *monsieur* would explain the 18th of Brumaire? Was not that treachery?"

"It was a juggling trick, not at all like a great man's way of acting."

"And the wounded he killed in Africa?" said the little princess; "that was awful!" And she shrugged her shoulders.

"He's a plebeian, whatever you may say," said Prince Ippolit.

Monsieur Pierre did not know which to answer. He looked at them all and smiled. His smile was utterly unlike the half-smile of all the others. When he smiled, suddenly, instantaneously, his serious, even rather sullen, face vanished completely, and a quite different face appeared, childish, good-humoured, even rather stupid, that seemed to beg indulgence. The vicomte, who was seeing him for the first time, saw clearly that this Jacobin was by no means so formidable as his words. Every one was silent.

"How is he to answer every one at once?" said Prince Andrey. "Besides, in the actions of a statesman, one must distinguish between his acts as a private person and as a general or an emperor. So it seems to me."

"Yes, yes, of course," put in Pierre, delighted at the assistance that had come to support him.

"One must admit," pursued Prince Andrey, "that Napoleon as a man was great at the bridge of Arcola, or in the hospital at Jaffa, when he gave his hand to the plague-stricken, but . . . but there are other actions it would be hard to justify."

Prince Andrey, who obviously wished to relieve the awkwardness of Pierre's position, got up to go, and made a sign to his wife.

Suddenly Prince Ippolit got up, and with a wave of his hands stopped every one, and motioning to them to be seated, began:

"Ah, I heard a Moscow story to-day; I must entertain you with it. You will excuse me, vicomte, I must tell it in Russian. If not, the point of the story will be lost." And Prince Ippolit began speaking in Russian, using the sort of jargon Frenchmen speak after spending a year in Russia. Every one waited expectant; Prince Ippolit had so eagerly, so insistently called for the attention of all for his story.

"In Moscow there is a lady, *une dame*. And she is very stingy. She wanted to have two footmen behind her carriage. And very tall footmen. That was her taste. And she had a lady's maid, also very tall. She said . . ."

Here Prince Ippolit paused and pondered, apparently collecting his ideas with difficulty.

"She said . . . yes, she said: 'Girl,' to the lady's maid, 'put on *livrée*, and get up behind the carriage, to pay calls.'"

Here Prince Ippolit gave a loud guffaw, laughing long before any of his audience, which created an impression by no means flattering to him. Several persons, among them the elderly lady and Anna Pavlovna, did smile, however.

"She drove off. Suddenly there was a violent gust of wind. The girl lost her hat, and her long hair fell down . . ."

At this point he could not restrain himself, and began laughing violently, articulating in the middle of a loud guffaw, "And all the world knew . . ."

There the anecdote ended. Though no one could understand why he had told it, and why he had insisted on telling it in Russian, still Anna Pavlovna and several other people appreciated the social breeding of Prince Ippolit in so agreeably putting a close to the disagreeable and ill-bred outbreak of Monsieur Pierre. The conversation after this episode broke up into small talk of no interest concerning the last and the approaching ball, the theatre, and where and when one would meet so-and-so again.

V

THANKING Anna Pavlovna for her *charmante soirée*, the guests began to take leave.

Pierre was clumsy, stout and uncommonly tall, with huge red hands; he did not, as they say, know how to come into a drawing-room and still less how to get out of one, that is, how to say something particularly agreeable on going away. Moreover, he was dreamy. He stood up, and picking up a three-cornered hat with the plume of a general in it instead of his own, he kept hold of it, pulling the feathers till the general asked him to restore it. But all his dreaminess and his inability to enter a drawing-room or talk properly in it were atoned for by his expression of good-nature, simplicity and modesty. Anna Pavlovna turned to him, and with Christian meekness signifying her forgiveness for his misbehaviour, she nodded to him and said:

"I hope I shall see you again, but I hope too you will change your opinions, my dear Monsieur Pierre."

He made no answer, simply bowed and displayed to every one once more his smile, which said as plainly as words: "Opinions or no opinions, you see what a nice, good-hearted fellow I am." And Anna Pavlovna and every one else instinctively felt this. Prince Andrey had gone out into the hall and turning his shoulders to the footman who was ready to put his cloak on him, he listened indifferently to his wife's chatter with Prince Ippolit, who had also come out into the hall. Prince Ippolit stood close to the pretty princess, so soon to be a mother, and stared persistently straight at her through his eyeglass.

"Go in, Annette, you'll catch cold," said the little princess, saying good-bye to Anna Pavlovna. "It is settled," she added in a low voice.

Anna Pavlovna had managed to have a few words with Liza about the match she was planning between Anatole and the sister-in-law of the little princess.

"I rely on you, my dear," said Anna Pavlovna, also in an undertone; "you write to her and tell me how the father will view the matter. *Au revoir!*" And she went back out of the hall.

Prince Ippolit went up to the little princess and, bending his face down close to her, began saying something to her in a half whisper.

Two footmen, one the princess's, the other his own, stood with shawl and redingote waiting till they should finish talking, and listened to their

French prattle, incomprehensible to them, with faces that seemed to say that they understood what was being said but would not show it. The princess, as always, talked with a smile and listened laughing.

"I'm very glad I didn't go to the ambassador's," Prince Ippolit was saying: "such a bore. . . . A delightful evening it has been, hasn't it? delightful."

"They say the ball will be a very fine one," answered the little princess, twitching up her downy little lip. "All the pretty women are to be there."

"Not all, since you won't be there; not all," said Prince Ippolit, laughing gleefully; and snatching the shawl from the footman, shoving him aside as he did so, he began putting it on the little princess. Either from awkwardness or intentionally—no one could have said which—he did not remove his arms for a long while after the shawl had been put on, as it were holding the young woman in his embrace.

Gracefully, but still smiling, she moved away, turned round and glanced at her husband. Prince Andrey's eyes were closed: he seemed weary and drowsy.

"Are you ready?" he asked his wife, avoiding her eyes.

Prince Ippolit hurriedly put on his redingote, which in the latest mode hung down to his heels, and stumbling over it, ran out on to the steps after the princess, whom the footman was assisting into the carriage.

"*Princesse, au revoir,*" he shouted, his tongue tripping like his legs.

The princess, picking up her gown, seated herself in the darkness of the carriage; her husband was arranging his sabre; Prince Ippolit, under the pretence of assisting, was in every one's way.

"Allow me, sir," Prince Andrey said in Russian drily and disagreeably to Prince Ippolit, who prevented his passing.

"I expect you, Pierre," the same voice called in warm and friendly tones.

The postillion started at a trot, and the carriage rumbled away. Prince Ippolit gave vent to a short, jerky guffaw, as he stood on the steps waiting for the vicomte, whom he had promised to take home.

"Well, my dear fellow, your little princess is very good-looking, very good-looking," said the vicomte, as he sat in the carriage with Ippolit. "Very good-looking indeed;" he kissed his finger tips. "And quite French."

Ippolit snorted and laughed.

"And, do you know, you are a terrible fellow with that little innocent way of yours," pursued the vicomte. "I am sorry for the poor husband, that officer boy who gives himself the airs of a reigning prince."

Ippolit guffawed again, and in the middle of a laugh articulated:

"And you said that the Russian ladies were not equal to the French ladies. You must know how to take them."

Pierre, arriving first, went to Prince Andrey's study, like one of the household, and at once lay down on the sofa, as his habit was, and taking up the first book he came upon in the shelf (it was Cæsar's *Commen-*

taries) he propped himself on his elbow, and began reading it in the middle.

"What a shock you gave Mlle. Scherer! She'll be quite ill now," Prince Andrey said, as he came into the study rubbing his small white hands.

Pierre rolled his whole person over so that the sofa creaked, turned his eager face to Prince Andrey, smiled and waved his hand to him.

"Oh, that abbé was very interesting, only he's got a wrong notion about it. . . . To my thinking, perpetual peace is possible, but I don't know how to put it. . . . Not by means of the balance of political power. . . ."

Prince Andrey was obviously not interested in these abstract discussions.

"One can't always say all one thinks everywhere, *mon cher.* Come tell me, have you settled on anything at last? Are you going into the cavalry or the diplomatic service?" asked Prince Andrey, after a momentary pause.

Pierre sat on the sofa with his legs crossed under him.

"Can you believe it, I still don't know. I don't like either."

"But you must decide on something; you know your father's expecting it."

At ten years old Pierre had been sent with an abbé as tutor to be educated abroad, and there he remained till he was twenty. When he returned to Moscow, his father had dismissed the tutor and said to the young man: "Now you go to Petersburg, look about you and make your choice. I agree to anything. Here is a letter to Prince Vassily and here is money. Write and tell me everything; I will help you in everything." Pierre had been three months already choosing a career and had not yet made his choice. It was of this choice Prince Andrey spoke to him now. Pierre rubbed his forehead.

"But he must be a freemason," he said, meaning the abbé he had seen that evening.

"That's all nonsense," Prince Andrey pulled him up again; "we'd better talk of serious things. Have you been to the Horse Guards?"

"No, I haven't; but this is what struck me and I wanted to talk to you about it. This war now is against Napoleon. If it were a war for freedom, I could have understood it, I would have been the first to go into the army; but to help England and Austria against the greatest man in the world—that's not right."

Prince Andrey simply shrugged his shoulders at Pierre's childish words. He looked as though one really could not answer such absurdities. But in reality it was hard to find any answer to this naïve question other than the answer Prince Andrey made. "If every one would only fight for his own convictions, there'd be no war," he said.

"And a very good thing that would be too," said Pierre.

Prince Andrey smiled ironically. "Very likely it would be a good thing, but it will never come to pass . . ."

"Well, what are you going to the war for?" asked Pierre.

"What for? I don't know. Because I have to. Besides, I'm going . . ." he stopped. "I'm going because the life I lead here, this life is—not to my taste!"

VI

THERE was the rustle of a woman's dress in the next room. Prince Andrey started up, as it were pulling himself together, and his face assumed the expression it had worn in Anna Pavlovna's drawing-room. Pierre dropped his legs down off the sofa. The princess came in. She had changed her gown, and was wearing a house dress as fresh and elegant as the other had been. Prince Andrey got up and courteously set a chair for her.

"Why is it, I often wonder," she began in French as always, while she hurriedly and fussily settled herself in the low chair, "why is it Annette never married? How stupid you gentlemen all are not to have married her. You must excuse me, but you really have no sense about women. What an argumentative person you are, Monsieur Pierre!"

"I'm still arguing with your husband; I can't make out why he wants to go to the war," said Pierre, addressing the princess without any of the affectation so common in the attitude of a young man to a young woman.

The princess shivered. Clearly Pierre's words touched a tender spot.

"Ah, that's what I say," she said. "I can't understand, I simply can't understand why men can't get on without war. Why is it we women want nothing of the sort? We don't care for it. Come, you shall be the judge. I keep saying to him: here he is uncle's adjutant, a most brilliant position. He's so well known, so appreciated by every one. The other day at the Apraxins' I heard a lady ask: 'So that is the famous Prince André? Upon my word!'" She laughed. "He's asked everywhere. He could very easily be a flügel-adjutant. You know the Emperor has spoken very graciously to him. Annette and I were saying it would be quite easy to arrange it. What do you think?"

Pierre looked at Prince Andrey, and, noticing that his friend did not like this subject, made no reply.

"When are you starting?" he asked.

"Ah, don't talk to me about that going away; don't talk about it. I won't even hear it spoken of," said the princess in just the capriciously playful tone in which she had talked to Ippolit at the *soirée*, a tone utterly incongruous in her own home circle, where Pierre was like one of the family. "This evening when I thought all these relations so precious to me must be broken off. . . . And then, you know, André?" She looked significantly at her husband. "I'm afraid! I'm afraid!" she whispered, twitching her shoulder. Her husband looked at her as though he were surprised to observe that there was some one in the room besides himself and Pierre, and with frigid courtesy he addressed an inquiry to his wife.

"What are you afraid of, Liza? I don't understand," he said.

"See what egoists all men are; they are all, all egoists! Of his own accord, for his own whim, for no reason whatever, he is deserting me, shutting me up alone in the country."

"With my father and sister, remember," said Prince Andrey quietly.

"It's just the same as alone, without my friends. . . . And he doesn't expect me to be afraid." Her tone was querulous now, her upper lip was lifted, giving her face not a joyous expression, but a wild-animal look, like a squirrel. She paused as though feeling it indecorous to speak of her condition before Pierre, though the whole gist of the matter lay in that.

"I still don't understand what you are afraid of," Prince Andrey said deliberately, not taking his eyes off his wife. The princess flushed red, and waved her hands despairingly.

"No, André, I say you are so changed, so changed . . ."

"Your doctor's orders were that you were to go to bed earlier," said Prince Andrey. "It's time you were asleep."

The princess said nothing, and suddenly her short, downy lip began to quiver; Prince Andrey got up and walked about the room, shrugging his shoulders.

Pierre looked over his spectacles in naïve wonder from him to the princess, and stirred uneasily as though he too meant to get up, but had changed his mind.

"What do I care if Monsieur Pierre is here," the little princess said suddenly, her pretty face contorted into a tearful grimace; "I have long wanted to say to you, Andrey, why are you so changed to me? What have I done? You go away to the war, you don't feel for me. Why is it?"

"Liza!" was all Prince Andrey said, but in that one word there was entreaty and menace, and, most of all, conviction that she would herself regret her words; but she went on hurriedly.

"You treat me as though I were ill, or a child. I see it all. You weren't like this six months ago."

"Liza, I beg you to be silent," said Prince Andrey, still more expressively.

Pierre, who had been growing more and more agitated during this conversation, got up and went to the princess. He seemed unable to endure the sight of her tears, and was ready to weep himself.

"Please don't distress yourself, princess. You only fancy that because . . . I assure you, I've felt so myself . . . because . . . through . . . Oh, excuse me, an outsider has no business . . . Oh, don't distress yourself . . . good-bye."

Prince Andrey held his hand and stopped him.

"No, stay a little, Pierre. The princess is so good, she would not wish to deprive me of the pleasure of spending an evening with you."

"No, he thinks of nothing but himself," the princess declared, not attempting to check her tears of anger.

"Liza," said Prince Andrey drily, raising his voice to a pitch that showed his patience was exhausted.

All at once the angry squirrel expression of the princess's lovely little face changed to an attractive look of terror that awakened sympathy. She glanced from under her brows with lovely eyes at her husband, and her face wore the timorous, deprecating look of a dog when it faintly but rapidly wags its tail in penitence.

"*Mon Dieu! mon Dieu!*" murmured the princess, and holding her gown with one hand, she went to her husband and kissed him on the forehead.

"Good-night, Liza," said Prince Andrey, getting up and kissing her hand courteously, as though she were a stranger.

The friends were silent. Neither of them began to talk. Pierre looked at Prince Andrey; Prince Andrey rubbed his forehead with his small hand.

"Let us go and have supper," he said with a sigh, getting up and going to the door.

They went into the elegantly, newly and richly furnished dining-room. Everything from the dinner-napkins to the silver, the china and the glass, wore that peculiar stamp of newness that is seen in the household belongings of newly married couples. In the middle of supper Prince Andrey leaned on his elbow, and like a man who has long had something on his mind, and suddenly resolves on giving it utterance, he began to speak with an expression of nervous irritation which Pierre had never seen in his friend before.

"Never, never marry, my dear fellow; that's my advice to you; don't marry till you have faced the fact that you have done all you're capable of doing, and till you cease to love the woman you have chosen, till you see her plainly, or else you will make a cruel mistake that can never be set right. Marry when you're old and good for nothing . . . Or else everything good and lofty in you will be done for. It will all be frittered away over trifles. Yes, yes, yes! Don't look at me with such surprise. If you expect anything of yourself in the future you will feel at every step that for you all is over, all is closed up except the drawing-room, where you will stand on the same level with the court lackey and the idiot . . . And why!" . . . He made a vigorous gesture.

Pierre took off his spectacles, which transformed his face, making it look even more good-natured, and looked wonderingly at his friend.

"My wife," pursued Prince Andrey, "is an excellent woman. She is one of those rare women with whom one can feel quite secure of one's honour; but, my God! what wouldn't I give now not to be married! You are the first and the only person I say this to, because I like you."

As Prince Andrey said this he was less than ever like the Bolkonsky who had sat lolling in Anna Pavlovna's drawing-room with half-closed eyelids, filtering French phrases through his teeth. His dry face was quivering with nervous excitement in every muscle; his eyes, which had seemed lustreless and lifeless, now gleamed with a full, vivid light. It

seemed that the more lifeless he was at ordinary times, the more ener
getic he became at such moments of morbid irritability.

"You can't understand why I say this," he went on. "Why, the whole
story of life lies in it. You talk of Bonaparte and his career," he said,
though Pierre had not talked of Bonaparte; "you talk of Bonaparte, but
Bonaparte when he was working his way up, going step by step straight
to his aim, he was free; he had nothing except his aim and he attained
it. But tie yourself up with a woman, and, like a chained convict, you
lose all freedom. And all the hope and strength there is in you is only a
drag on you, torturing you with regret. Drawing-rooms, gossip, balls,
vanity, frivolity—that's the enchanted circle I can't get out of. I am setting off now to the war, the greatest war there has ever been, and I know
nothing, and am good for nothing. I am very agreeable and sarcastic,"
pursued Prince Andrey, "and at Anna Pavlovna's every one listens to
me. And this imbecile society without which my wife can't exist, and
these women . . . If you only knew what these society women are, and,
indeed, women generally! My father's right. Egoism, vanity, silliness,
triviality in everything—that's what women are when they show themselves as they really are. Looking at them in society, one fancies there's
something in them, but there's nothing, nothing, nothing. No, don't
marry, my dear fellow, don't marry!" Prince Andrey concluded.

"It seems absurd to me," said Pierre, "that *you, you* consider *yourself*
a failure, your life wrecked. You have everything, everything before you.
And *you* . . ."

He did not say *why you*, but his tone showed how highly he thought
of his friend, and how much he expected of him in the future.

"How can he say that?" Pierre thought.

Pierre regarded Prince Andrey as a model of all perfection, because
Prince Andrey possessed in the highest degree just that combination of
qualities in which Pierre was deficient, and which might be most nearly
expressed by the idea of strength of will. Pierre always marvelled at
Prince Andrey's faculty for dealing with people of every sort with perfect composure, his exceptional memory, his wide knowledge (he had
read everything, knew everything, had some notion of everything), and
most of all at his capacity for working and learning. If Pierre were frequently struck in Andrey by his lack of capacity for dreaming and philosophising (to which Pierre was himself greatly given), he did not regard this as a defect but as a strong point. Even in the very warmest,
friendliest, and simplest relations, flattery or praise is needed just as
grease is needed to keep wheels going round.

"I am a man whose day is done," said Prince Andrey. "Why talk of
me? let's talk about you," he said after a brief pause, smiling at his own
reassuring thoughts. The smile was instantly reflected on Pierre's face.

"Why, what is there to say about me?" said Pierre, letting his face
relax into an easy-going, happy smile. "What am I? I am a bastard."
And he suddenly flushed crimson. Apparently it was a great effort to
him to say this. "With no name, no fortune. . . . And after all, really
. . ." He did not finish. "Meanwhile, I am free though and I'm content.

Only I don't know in the least what to set about doing. I meant to ask your advice in earnest."

Prince Andrey looked at him with kindly eyes. But in his eyes, friendly and kind as they were, there was yet a consciousness of his own superiority.

"You are dear to me just because you are the one live person in all our society. You're lucky. Choose what you will, that's all the same. You'll always be all right, but there's one thing: give up going about with the Kuragins and leading this sort of life. It's not the right thing for you at all; all this riotous living and dissipation and all . . ."

"What would you have, my dear fellow?" said Pierre, shrugging his shoulders; "women, my dear fellow, women."

"I can't understand it," answered Andrey. "Ladies, that's another matter, but Kuragin's women, women and wine, I can't understand!"

Pierre was living at Prince Vassily Kuragin's, and sharing in the dissipated mode of life of his son Anatole, the son whom they were proposing to marry to Prince Andrey's sister to reform him.

"Do you know what," said Pierre, as though a happy thought had suddenly occurred to him; "seriously, I have been thinking so for a long while. Leading this sort of life I can't decide on anything, or consider anything properly. My head aches and my money's all gone. He invited me to-night, but I won't go."

"Give me your word of honour that you will give up going."

"On my honour!"

It was past one o'clock when Pierre left his friend's house. It was a cloudless night, a typical Petersburg summer night. Pierre got into a hired coach, intending to drive home. But the nearer he got, the more he felt it impossible to go to bed on such a night, more like evening or morning. It was light enough to see a long way in the empty streets. On the way Pierre remembered that all the usual gambling set were to meet at Anatole Kuragin's that evening, after which there usually followed a drinking-bout, winding up with one of Pierre's favourite entertainments.

"It would be jolly to go to Kuragin's," he thought. But he immediately recalled his promise to Prince Andrey not to go there again.

But, as so often happens with people of weak character, as it is called, he was at once overcome with such a passionate desire to enjoy once more this sort of dissipation which had become so familiar to him, that he determined to go. And the idea at once occurred to him that his promise was of no consequence, since he had already promised Prince Anatole to go before making the promise to Andrey. Finally he reflected that all such promises were merely relative matters, having no sort of precise significance, especially if one considered that to-morrow one might be dead or something so extraordinary might happen that the distinction between honourable and dishonourable would have ceased to exist. Such reflections often occurred to Pierre, completely nullifying all his resolutions and intentions. He went to Kuragin's.

Driving up to the steps of a big house in the Horse Guards' barracks, where Anatole lived, he ran up the lighted steps and the staircase and went in at an open door. There was no one in the ante-room; empty bottles, cloaks, and over-shoes were lying about in disorder: there was a strong smell of spirits; in the distance he heard talking and shouting.

The card-playing and the supper were over, but the party had not broken up. Pierre flung off his cloak, and went into the first room, where there were the remnants of supper, and a footman who, thinking himself unobserved, was emptying the half-full glasses on the sly. In the third room there was a great uproar of laughter, familiar voices shouting, and a bear growling. Eight young men were crowding eagerly about the open window. Three others were busy with a young bear, one of them dragging at its chain and frightening the others with it.

"I bet a hundred on Stevens!" cried one.

"Mind there's no holding him up!" shouted another.

"I'm for Dolohov!" shouted a third. "Hold the stakes, Kuragin."

"I say, let Mishka be, we're betting."

"All at a go or the wager's lost!" cried a fourth.

"Yakov, give us a bottle, Yakov!" shouted Anatole himself, a tall, handsome fellow, standing in the middle of the room, in nothing but a thin shirt, open over his chest. "Stop, gentlemen. Here he is, here's Petrusha, the dear fellow." He turned to Pierre.

A man of medium height with bright blue eyes, especially remarkable from looking sober in the midst of the drunken uproar, shouted from the window: "Come here. I'll explain the bets!" This was Dolohov, an officer of the Semenov regiment, a notorious gambler and duellist, who was living with Anatole. Pierre smiled, looking good-humouredly about him.

"I don't understand. What's the point?"

"Wait a minute, he's not drunk. A bottle here," said Anatole; and taking a glass from the table he went up to Pierre.

"First of all, you must drink."

Pierre began drinking off glass after glass, looking from under his brows at the drunken group, who had crowded about the window again, and listening to their talk. Anatole kept his glass filled and told him that Dolohov had made a bet with an Englishman, Stevens, a sailor who was staying here, that he, Dolohov, would drink a bottle of rum sitting in the third story window with his legs hanging down outside.

"Come, empty the bottle," said Anatole, giving Pierre the last glass, "or I won't let you go!"

"No, I don't want to," said Pierre, shoving Anatole away; and he went up to the window.

Dolohov was holding the Englishman's hand and explaining distinctly the terms of the bet, addressing himself principally to Anatole and Pierre.

Dolohov was a man of medium height, with curly hair and clear blue eyes. He was five-and-twenty. Like all infantry officers he wore no moustache, so that his mouth, the most striking feature in his face, was not concealed. The lines of that mouth were extremely delicately chiselled. The upper lip closed vigorously in a sharp wedge-shape on the firm lower one, and at the corners the mouth always formed something like two smiles, one at each side, and altogether, especially in conjunction with the resolute, insolent, shrewd look of his eyes, made such an impression that it was impossible to overlook his face. Dolohov was a man of small means and no connections. And yet though Anatole was spending ten thousand a year, Dolohov lived with him and succeeded in so regulating the position that Anatole and all who knew them respected Dolohov more than Anatole. Dolohov played at every sort of game, and almost always won. However much he drank, his brain never lost its clearness. Both Kuragin and Dolohov were at that time notorious figures in the fast and dissipated world in Petersburg.

The bottle of rum was brought: the window-frame, which hindered any one sitting on the outside sill of the window, was being broken out by two footmen, obviously flurried and intimidated by the shouts and directions given by the gentlemen around them.

Anatole with his swaggering air came up to the window. He was longing to break something. He shoved the footmen aside and pulled at the frame, but the frame did not give. He smashed a pane.

"Now then, you're the strong man," he turned to Pierre. Pierre took hold of the cross beam, tugged, and with a crash wrenched the oak frame out.

"All out, or they'll think I'm holding on," said Dolohov.

"The Englishman's bragging . . . it's a fine feat . . . eh?" said Anatole.

"Fine," said Pierre, looking at Dolohov, who with the bottle in his hand had gone up to the window, from which the light of the sky could be seen and the glow of morning and of evening melting into it. Dolohov jumped up on to the window, holding the bottle of rum in his hand. "Listen!" he shouted, standing on the sill and facing the room. Every one was silent.

"I take a bet" (he spoke in French that the Englishman might hear him, and spoke it none too well) . . . "I take a bet for fifty imperials— like to make it a hundred?" he added, turning to the Englishman.

"No, fifty," said the Englishman.

"Good, for fifty imperials, that I'll drink off a whole bottle of rum without taking it from my lips. I'll drink it sitting outside the window, here on this place" (he bent down and pointed to the sloping projection of the wall outside the window) . . . "and without holding on to anything. . . . That right?"

"All right," said the Englishman.

Anatole turned to the Englishman and taking him by the button of his coat, and looking down at him (the Englishman was a short man), he began repeating the terms of the wager in English.

"Wait a minute!" shouted Dolohov, striking the bottle on the window to call attention. "Wait a minute, Kuragin; listen: if any one does the same thing, I'll pay him a hundred imperials. Do you understand?"

The Englishman nodded without making it plain whether he intended to take this new bet or not.

Anatole persisted in keeping hold of the Englishman, and although the latter, nodding, gave him to understand that he comprehended fully, Anatole translated Dolohov's words into English. A thin, youthful hussar, who had been losing at cards that evening, slipped up to the window, poked his head out and looked down.

"Oo! . . . oo! . . . oo!" he said looking out of window at the pavement below.

"Shut up!" cried Dolohov, and he pushed the officer away, so that, tripping over his spurs, he went skipping awkwardly into the room.

Setting the bottle on the window-sill, so as to have it within reach, Dolohov climbed slowly and carefully into the window. Lowering his legs over, with both hands spread open on the window-ledge, he tried the position, seated himself, let his hands go, moved a little to the right, and then to the left, and took the bottle. Anatole brought two candles, and set them on the window-ledge, so that it was quite light. Dolohov's back in his white shirt and his curly head were lighted up on both sides. All crowded round the window. The Englishman stood in front. Pierre smiled, and said nothing. One of the party, rather older than the rest, suddenly came forward with a scared and angry face, and tried to clutch Dolohov by his shirt.

"Gentlemen, this is idiocy; he'll be killed," said this more sensible man.

Anatole stopped him.

"Don't touch him; you'll startle him and he'll be killed. Eh? . . . What then, eh?"

Dolohov turned, balancing himself, and again spreading his hands out

"If any one takes hold of me again," he said, letting his words drop one by one through his thin, tightly compressed lips, "I'll throw him down from here. Now . . ."

Saying "now," he turned again, let his hands drop, took the bottle and put it to his lips, bent his head back and held his disengaged hand upwards to keep his balance. One of the footmen who had begun clearing away the broken glass, stopped still in a stooping posture, his eyes fixed on the window and Dolohov's back. Anatole stood upright, with wide-open eyes. The Englishman stared from one side, pursing up his lips. The man who had tried to stop it, had retreated to the corner of the room, and lay on the sofa with his face to the wall. Pierre hid his face, and a smile strayed forgotten upon it, though it was full of terror and fear. All were silent. Pierre took his hands from his eyes; Dolohov was still sitting in the same position, only his head was so far bent back that his curls touched his shirt collar, and the hand with the bottle rose higher and higher, trembling with evident effort. Evidently the bottle was nearly empty, and so was tipped higher, throwing the head back. "Why is it so long?" thought Pierre. It seemed to him that more than half an hour had passed. Suddenly Dolohov made a backward movement of the spine, and his arm trembled nervously; this was enough to displace his whole body as he sat on the sloping projection. He moved all over, and his arm and head trembled still more violently with the strain. One hand rose to clutch at the window-ledge, but it dropped again. Pierre shut his eyes once more, and said to himself that he would never open them again. Suddenly he was aware of a general stir about him. He glanced up, Dolohov was standing on the window-ledge, his face was pale and full of merriment.

"Empty!"

He tossed the bottle to the Englishman, who caught it neatly. Dolohov jumped down from the window. He smelt very strongly of rum.

"Capital! Bravo! That's something like a bet. You're a devil of a ellow!" came shouts from all sides.

The Englishman took out his purse and counted out the money. Dolohov frowned and did not speak. Pierre dashed up to the window.

"Gentlemen. Who'll take a bet with me? I'll do the same!" he shouted suddenly. "I don't care about betting; see here, tell them to give me a bottle. I'll do it. . . . Tell them to give it here."

"Let him, let him!" said Dolohov, smiling.

"What, are you mad? No one would let you. Why, you turn giddy going downstairs," various persons protested.

"I'll drink it; give me the bottle of rum," roared Pierre, striking the table with a resolute, drunken gesture, and he climbed into the window. They clutched at his arms; but he was so strong that he shoved every one far away who came near him.

"No, there's no managing him like that," said Anatole. "Wait a bit, I'll get round him. . . . Listen, I'll take your bet, but for to-morrow, for we're all going on now to . . ."

"Yes, come along," shouted Pierre, "come along. . . . And take Mishka with us." . . . And he caught hold of the bear, and embracing it and lifting it up, began waltzing round the room with it.

VII

PRINCE VASSILY kept the promise he had made at Anna Pavlovna's *soirée* to Princess Drubetskoy, who had petitioned him in favour of her only son Boris. His case had been laid before the Emperor, and though it was not to be a precedent for others, he received a commission as sub-lieutenant in the Guards of the Semenovsky regiment. But the post of an adjutant or *attaché* in Kutuzov's service was not to be obtained for Boris by all Anna Mihalovna's efforts and entreaties. Shortly after the gathering at Anna Pavlovna's, Anna Mihalovna went back to Moscow, to her rich relatives the Rostovs, with whom she stayed in Moscow. It was with these relations that her adored Borinka, who had only recently entered a regiment of the line, and was now at once transferred to the Guards as a sub-lieutenant, had been educated from childhood and had lived for years. The Guards had already left Petersburg on the 10th of August, and her son, who was remaining in Moscow to get his equipment, was to overtake them on the road to Radzivilov.

The Rostovs were keeping the name-day of the mother and the younger daughter, both called Natalya. Ever since the morning, coaches with six horses had been incessantly driving to and from the Countess Rostov's big house in Povarsky, which was known to all Moscow. The countess and her handsomest eldest daughter were sitting in the drawing-room with their visitors, who came in continual succession to present their congratulations to the elder lady.

The countess was a woman with a thin face of Oriental cast, forty-five years old, and obviously exhausted by child-bearing. She had had twelve children. The deliberate slowness of her movements and conversation, arising from weak health, gave her an air of dignity which inspired respect. Princess Anna Mihalovna Drubetskoy, as an intimate friend of the family, sat with them assisting in the work of receiving and entertaining their guests. The younger members of the family were in the back rooms, not seeing fit to take part in receiving visitors. The count met his visitors and escorted them to the door, inviting all of them to dinner.

"I am very, very grateful to you, *mon cher*" or "*ma chère*," he said to every one without exception (making not the slightest distinction between persons of higher or of lower standing than his own), "for myself and my two dear ones whose name-day we are keeping. Mind you come to dinner. I shall be offended if you don't, *mon cher*. I beg you most sincerely from all the family, my dear." These words, invariably accompanied by the same expression on his full, good-humoured, clean-shaven face, and the same warm pressure of the hand, and repeated short bows, he said to all without exception or variation. When he had escorted one guest to the hall, the count returned to the gentleman or lady who was still in the drawing-room. Moving up a chair, and with the air of a man fond of society and at home in it, he would sit down, his legs jauntily apart, and his hands on his knees, and sway to and fro with dignity as he proffered surmises upon the weather, gave advice about health, sometimes in Russian, sometimes in very bad but complacent French. Then again he would get up, and with the air of a man weary but resolute in the performance of his duty, he would escort guests out, stroking up his grey hair over his bald patch, and again he would urge them to come to dinner. Sometimes on his way back from the hall, he would pass through the conservatory and the butler's room into a big room with a marble floor, where they were setting a table for eighty guests; and looking at the waiters who were bringing in the silver and china, setting out tables and unfolding damask tablecloths, he would call up Dmitry Vassilyevitch, a young man of good family, who performed the duties of a steward in his household, and would say: "Now then, Mitenka, mind everything's right. That's it, that's it," he would say, looking round with pleasure at the immense table opened out to its full extent; "the great thing is the service. So, so." . . . And he went off again with a sigh of satisfaction to the drawing-room.

"Marya Lvovna Karagin and her daughter," the countess's huge foot-

man announced in a deep bass at the drawing-room door. The countess
thought a moment, and took a pinch from a golden snuff-box with her
husband's portrait on it.

"I'm worn out with these callers," she said; "well, this is the last one
I'll see. She's so affected. Show her up," she said in a dejected tone, as
though she were saying, "Very well, finish me off entirely!"

A tall, stout, haughty-looking lady and her round-faced, smiling
daughter walked with rustling skirts into the drawing-room.

"Dear countess, it is such a long time . . . she has been laid up, poor
child . . . at the Razumovskys' ball, and the Countess Apraxin . . . I
was so glad," feminine voices chattered briskly, interrupting one another
and mingling with the sound of rustling skirts and the scraping of chairs.
Conversation began of the sort which is kept up just long enough for
the caller to get up at the first pause, rustling her skirts and with a
murmur of "I am so charmed; mamma's health . . . and the Countess
Apraxin . . ." walk out again with the same rustle to the hall to put on
cloak or overcoat and drive away. The conversation touched on the chief
items of news in the town, on the illness of the wealthy old Count
Bezuhov, a man who had been renowned for his personal beauty in the
days of Catherine, and on his illegitimate son, Pierre, who had behaved
so improperly at a *soirée* at Anna Pavlovna's. "I am very sorry for the
poor count," declared the visitor; "his health in such a precarious state,
and now this distress caused him by his son; it will be the death of
him!"

"Why, what has happened?" asked the countess, as though she did
not know what was meant, though she had heard about the cause of
Count Bezuhov's distress fifteen times already.

"This is what comes of modern education! When he was abroad," the
visitor pursued, "this young man was left to his own devices, and now in
Petersburg, they say, he has been doing such atrocious things that he
has been sent away under police escort."

"Really!" said the countess.

"He has made a bad choice of his companions," put in Princess Anna
Mihalovna. "Prince Vassily's son—he and a young man called Dolohov,
they say—God only knows the dreadful things they've been doing. And
both have suffered for it. Dolohov has been degraded to the rank of a
common soldier, while Bezuhov's son has been banished to Moscow. As
to Anatole Kuragin . . . his father managed to hush it up somehow.
But he has been sent out of Petersburg too."

"Why, what did they do?" asked the countess.

"They're perfect ruffians, especially Dolohov," said the visitor. "He's
the son of Marya Ivanovna Dolohov, such a worthy woman, you know,
but there! Only fancy, the three of them had got hold of a bear somewhere, put it in a carriage with them, and were taking it to some actress's. The police ran up to stop them. They took the police officer,
tied him back to back to the bear, and dropped the bear into the Moika:
the bear swam with the police officer on him."

"A pretty figure he must have looked, *ma chère*," cried the count, helpless with laughter.

"Ah, such a horror! What is there to laugh at in it, count?"

But the ladies could not help laughing at it themselves.

"It was all they could do to rescue the unlucky man," the visitor went on. "And that's the intellectual sort of amusement the son of Count Kirill Vladimirovitch Bezuhov indulges in!" she added. "And people said he was so well educated and clever. That's how foreign education turns out. I hope no one will receive him here, in spite of his great wealth. They tried to introduce him to me. I gave an absolute refusal: I have daughters."

"What makes you say the young man is so wealthy?" asked the countess, turning away from the girls, who at once looked as though they did not hear. "He has none but illegitimate children. I believe that . . . Pierre too is illegitimate."

The visitor waved her hand. "He has a score of them, I suppose."

Princess Anna Mihalovna interposed, obviously wishing to show her connections and intimate knowledge with every detail in society.

"This is how the matter stands," she said meaningly, speaking in a half whisper. "Count Kirill Vladimirovitch's reputation we all know. . . . He has lost count of his own children, indeed, but this Pierre was his favourite."

"How handsome the old man was," said the countess, "only last year! A finer-looking man I have never seen."

"Now he's very much altered," said Anna Mihalovna. "Well, I was just saying," she went on, "the direct heir to all the property is Prince Vassily through his wife, but the father is very fond of Pierre, has taken trouble over his education, and he has written to the Emperor . . . so that no one can tell, if he dies (he's so ill that it's expected any moment, and Lorrain has come from Petersburg), whom that immense property will come to, Pierre or Prince Vassily. Forty thousand serfs and millions of money. I know this for a fact, for Prince Vassily himself told me so. And indeed Kirill Vladimirovitch happens to be a third cousin of mine on my mother's side, and he's Boris's godfather too," she added, apparently attaching no importance to this circumstance.

"Prince Vassily arrived in Moscow yesterday. He's coming on some inspection business, so I was told," said the visitor.

"Yes, between ourselves," said the princess, "that's a pretext; he has come simply to see Prince Kirill Vladimirovitch, hearing he was in such a serious state."

"But, really, *ma chère*, that was a capital piece of fun," said the count; and seeing that the elder visitor did not hear him, he turned to the young ladies. "A funny figure the police officer must have looked; I can just fancy him."

And showing how the police officer waved his arms about, he went off again into his rich bass laugh, his sides shaking with mirth, as people do laugh who always eat and, still more, drink well. "Then do, please, come to dinner with us," he said.

VIII

A SILENCE followed. The countess looked at her guest, smiling affably, but still not disguising the fact that she would not take it at all amiss now if the guest were to get up and go. The daughter was already fingering at the folds of her gown and looking interrogatively at her mother, when suddenly they heard in the next room several girls and boys running to the door, and the grating sound of a chair knocked over and a girl of thirteen ran in, hiding something in her short muslin petticoat, and stopped short in the middle of the room. She had evidently bounded so far by mistake, unable to stop in her flight. At the same instant there appeared in the doorway a student with a crimson band on his collar, a young officer in the Guards, a girl of fifteen, and a fat, rosy-cheeked boy in a child's smock.

The prince jumped up, and swaying from side to side, held his arms out wide round the little girl.

"Ah, here she is!" he cried, laughing. "Our little darling on her fête day!"

"My dear, there is a time for everything," said the countess, affecting severity. "You're always spoiling her, *Elie*," she added to her husband.

"*Bonjour, ma chère, je vous félicite*," said the visitor. "*Quelle délicieuse enfant!*" she added, turning to her mother.

The dark-eyed little girl, plain, but full of life, with her wide mouth, her childish bare shoulders, which shrugged and panted in her bodice from her rapid motion, her black hair brushed back, her slender bare arms and little legs in lace-edged long drawers and open slippers, was at that charming stage when the girl is no longer a child, while the child is not yet a young girl. Wriggling away from her father, she ran up to her mother, and taking no notice whatever of her severe remarks, she hid her flushed face in her mother's lace kerchief and broke into laughter. As she laughed she uttered some incoherent phrases about the doll, which was poking out from her petticoat.

"Do you see? . . . My doll . . . Mimi . . . you see . . ." And Natasha could say no more, it all seemed to her so funny. She sank on her mother's lap, and went off into such a loud peal of laughter that every one, even the prim visitor, could not help laughing too.

"Come, run along, run along with your monstrosity!" said her mother, pushing her daughter off with a pretence of anger. "This is my younger girl," she said to the visitor. Natasha, pulling her face away from her mother's lace kerchief for a minute, peeped down at her through tears of laughter, and hid her face again.

The visitor, forced to admire this domestic scene, thought it suitable to take some part in it.

"Tell me, my dear," she said, addressing Natasha, "how did you come by your Mimi? Your daughter, I suppose?"

Natasha did not like the tone of condescension to childish things with which the visitor had spoken to her. She made no answer, but stared solemnly at her.

Meanwhile all the younger generation, Boris, the officer, Anna Mihalovna's son; Nikolay, the student, the count's elder son; Sonya, the count's niece; and little Petya, his younger son, had all placed themselves about the drawing-room, and were obviously trying to restrain within the bounds of decorum the excitement and mirth which was brimming over in their faces. Clearly in the back part of the house, from which they had dashed out so impetuously, the conversation had been more amusing than the small-talk in the drawing-room of the scandal of the town, the weather, and Countess Apraxin. Now and then they glanced at one another and could hardly suppress their laughter.

The two young men, the student and the officer, friends from childhood, were of the same age, and both good-looking, but not like each other. Boris was a tall, fair-haired lad with delicate, regular features, and a look of composure on his handsome face. Nikolay was a curly-headed youth, not tall, with an open expression. On his upper lip there were already signs of a black moustache coming, and his whole face expressed impulsiveness and enthusiasm. Nikolay flushed red as he came into the drawing-room. He was unmistakably trying to find something to say, and unable to find anything. Boris, on the contrary, was at home immediately and talked easily and playfully of the doll Mimi, saying that he had known her as a young girl before her nose was broken, and she had grown older during the five years he remembered her, and how her head was cracked right across the skull. As he said this he looked at Natasha. Natasha turned away from him, glanced at her younger brother, who, with a scowl on his face, was shaking with noiseless laughter, and unable to restrain herself, she skipped up and flew out of the room as quickly as her swift little legs could carry her. Boris did not laugh.

"You were meaning to go out, mamma, weren't you? Do you want the carriage?" he said, addressing his mother with a smile.

"Yes, go along and tell them to get it ready," she said, smiling. Boris walked slowly to the door and went after Natasha. The stout boy ran wrathfully after them, as though resenting the interruption of his pursuits.

IX

OF the young people, not reckoning the countess's elder daughter (who was four years older than her sister and behaved quite like a grown-up person) and the young lady visitor, there were left in the drawing-room Nikolay and Sonya, the niece. Sonya was a slender, miniature brunette, with soft eyes shaded by long lashes, thick black hair twisted in two coils round her head, and a skin of a somewhat sallow tint, particularly marked on her bare, thin, but shapely, muscular arms and neck. The smoothness of her movements, the softness and flexibility of her little limbs, and something of slyness and reserve in her manner, suggested a lovely half-grown kitten, which would one day be a charming cat. Apparently she thought it only proper to show an interest in the general conversation and to smile. But against her own will, her eyes turned under their thick, long lashes to her cousin, who was going away into the army, with such girlish, passionate adoration, that her smile could not for one moment impose upon any one, and it was clear that the kitten had only perched there to skip off more energetically than ever and to play with her cousin as soon as they could, like Boris and Natasha, get out of the drawing-room.

"Yes, *ma chère*," said the old count, addressing the visitor and pointing to his Nikolay; "here his friend Boris has received his commission as an officer, and he's so fond of him he doesn't want to be left behind, and is giving up the university and his poor old father to go into the army, *ma chère*. And there was a place all ready for him in the archives department, and all. Isn't that friendship now?" said the count interrogatively.

"But they do say that war has been declared, you know," said the visitor.

"They've been saying so a long while," said the count. "They'll say so again and again, and so it will remain. There's friendship for you, *ma chère*!" he repeated. "He's going into the hussars."

The visitor, not knowing what to say, shook her head.

"It's not from friendship at all," answered Nikolay, flushing hotly, and denying it as though it were some disgraceful imputation. "Not friendship at all, but simply I feel drawn to the military service."

He looked round at his cousin and the young lady visitor; both looked at him with a smile of approval.

"Schubert's dining with us to-night, the colonel of the Pavologradsky regiment of hussars. He has been here on leave, and is taking him with him. There's no help for it," said the count, shrugging his shoulders and speaking playfully of what evidently was a source of much distress to him.

"I've told you already, papa," said his son, "that if you're unwilling to let me go, I'll stay. But I know I'm no good for anything except in the army. I'm not a diplomatist, or a government clerk. I'm not clever at disguising my feelings," he said, glancing repeatedly with the coquetry of handsome youth at Sonya and the young lady.

The kitten, her eyes riveted on him, seemed on the point of breaking into frolic, and showing her cat-like nature.

"Well, well, it's all right!" said the old count; "he always gets so hot. Bonaparte's turned all their heads; they're all dreaming of how he rose from a lieutenant to be an emperor. Well, and so may it turn out again, please God," he added, not noticing the visitor's sarcastic smile.

While their elders began talking about Bonaparte, Julie, Madame Karagin's daughter, turned to young Rostov.

"What a pity you weren't at the Arharovs' on Thursday. I was so dull without you," she said, giving him a tender smile. The youth, highly flattered, moved with a coquettish smile nearer her, and entered into a conversation apart with the smiling Julie, entirely unaware that his unconscious smile had dealt a jealous stab to the heart of Sonya, who was flushing crimson and assuming a forced smile. In the middle of his talk with Julie he glanced round at her. Sonya gave him an intensely furious look, and, hardly able to restrain her tears, though there was still a constrained smile on her lips, she got up and went out of the room. All Nikolay's animation was gone. He waited for the first break in the conversation, and, with a face of distress, walked out of the room to look for Sonya.

"How all the young things wear their hearts on their sleeves!" said Anna Mihalovna, pointing to Nikolay's retreating figure. *"Cousinage, dangereux voisinage,"* she added.

"Yes," said the countess, when the sunshine that had come into the drawing-room with the young people had vanished. She was, as it were, replying to a question which no one had put to her, but which was always in her thoughts: "What miseries, what anxieties one has gone through for the happiness one has in them now! And even now one feels really more dread than joy over them. One's always in terror! At this age particularly when there are so many dangers both for girls and boys."

"Everything depends on bringing up," said the visitor.

"Yes, you are right," the countess went on. "So far I have been, thank God, my children's friend and have enjoyed their full confidence," said the countess, repeating the error of so many parents, who imagine their children have no secrets from them. "I know I shall always be first in my children's confidence, and that Nikolay, if, with his impulsive character, he does get into mischief (boys will be boys) it won't be like these Petersburg young gentlemen."

"Yes, they're capital children, capital children," assented the count, who always solved all perplexing questions by deciding that everything was capital. "Fancy now, his taking it into his head to be an hussar! But what can one expect, *ma chère?*"

"What a sweet little thing your younger girl is!" said the visitor. "Full of fun and mischief!"

"Yes, that she is," said the count. "She takes after me! And such a voice; though she's my daughter, it's the truth I'm telling you, she'll be a singer, another Salomini. We've engaged an Italian to give her lessons."

"Isn't it too early? They say it injures the voice to train it at that age."

"Oh, no! Too early!" said the count. "Why, our mothers used to be married at twelve and thirteen."

"Well, she's in love with Boris already! What do you say to that?" said the countess, smiling softly and looking at Boris's mother. And apparently in reply to the question that was always in her mind, she went on: "Why, you know, if I were strict with her, if I were to forbid her . . . God knows what they might not be doing in secret" (the countess

meant that they might kiss each other), "but as it is I know every word
she utters. She'll come to me this evening and tell me everything of herself. I spoil her, perhaps, but I really believe it's the best way. I brought
my elder girl up more strictly."

"Yes, I was brought up quite differently," said the elder girl, the
handsome young Countess Vera; and she smiled. But the smile did not
improve Vera's face; on the contrary her face looked unnatural, and
therefore unpleasing. Vera was good-looking; she was not stupid, was
clever at her lessons, and well educated; she had a pleasant voice, and
what she said was true and appropriate. But, strange to say, every one—
both the visitor and the countess—looked at her, as though wondering
why she had said it, and conscious of a certain awkwardness.

"People are always too clever with their elder children; they try to
do something exceptional with them," said the visitor.

"We won't conceal our errors, *ma chère*! My dear countess was too
clever with Vera," said the count. "But what of it? she has turned out
capitally all the same," he added, with a wink of approval to Vera.

The guests got up and went away, promising to come to dinner.

"What manners! Staying on and on!" said the countess, when she had
seen her guests out.

X

WHEN Natasha ran out of the drawing-room she only ran as far as the
conservatory. There she stopped listening to the talk in the drawing-
room, and waiting for Boris to come out. She was beginning to get impatient, and stamping her foot was almost ready to cry at his not coming
at once, when she heard the young man's footsteps coming out discreetly, not too slowly nor too quickly. Natasha darted swiftly away
and hid among the tubs of shrubs.

Boris stood still in the middle of the room, looked round him, brushed
a speck of dirt off the sleeve of his uniform, and going up to the looking-
glass examined his handsome face. Natasha, keeping quiet, peeped out
of her hiding-place, waiting to see what he would do. He stood a little
while before the glass, smiled at his reflection, and walked towards the
other door. Natasha was on the point of calling to him, but she changed
her mind. "Let him look for me," she said to herself. Boris had only just
gone out, when at the other door Sonya came in, flushed and muttering
something angrily through her tears. Natasha checked her first impulse
to run out to her, and remained in her hiding-place, as it were under the
invisible cap, looking on at what was going on in the world. She began
to feel a peculiar novel sort of enjoyment in it. Sonya was murmuring
something as she looked towards the drawing-room door. The door
opened and Nikolay came in.

"Sonya! what is the matter? how can you?" said Nikolay, running up
to her.

"Nothing, nothing, leave me alone!" Sonya was sobbing.

"No, I know what it is."

"Very well, you do, so much the better then, and you can go back to her."

"So-o-onya! one word! How can you torture me and yourself for a mere fancy?" said Nikolay, taking her hand. Sonya did not pull her hand away, and left off crying.

Natasha, not stirring and hardly breathing, looked with shining eyes from her hiding-place. "What's coming now?" she thought.

"Sonya! I care for nothing in the whole world! You're everything to me," said Nikolay. "I'll prove it to you."

"I don't like you to talk like that."

"Well, I won't then; come, forgive me, Sonya." He drew her to him and kissed her.

"Oh, that's nice," thought Natasha, and when Sonya and Nikolay had gone out of the room she followed them and called Boris to her.

"Boris, come here," she said with a sly and significant look. "I've something I want to tell you. Here, here," she said, and she led him into the conservatory, to the place where she had hidden between the tubs. Boris followed her, smiling.

"What is the *something*?" he inquired. She was a little embarrassed; she looked round her, and seeing her doll flung down on a tub she picked it up.

"Kiss the doll," she said. Boris looked with observant, affectionate eyes at her eager face and made no answer. "Don't you want to? Well, then come here," she said, and went further in among the shrubs and tossed away the doll. "Closer, closer!" she whispered. She caught hold of the young officer's arms above the cuff, and her flushed face had a look of solemnity and awe.

"Would you like to kiss me?" she whispered, hardly audibly, peeping up at him from under her eyelids, smiling and almost crying with excitement.

Boris reddened. "How absurd you are!" he said, bending down to her, flushing redder still, but doing nothing, waiting what would come next. Suddenly she jumped on to a tub, so that as she stood she was taller than he, flung both arms round him so that her slender, bare arms clasped him above his neck, and flinging back her hair with a toss of her head, she kissed him just on his lips.

She slipped away among the flower-pots on the other side, and stood with hanging head.

"Natasha," he said, "you know I love you, but— —"

"You're in love with me," Natasha broke in.

"Yes I am, but, please, don't let us do like that. . . . In another four years . . . Then I shall ask for your hand." Natasha pondered a moment.

"Thirteen, fourteen, fifteen, sixteen . . ." she said, counting on her thin little fingers.

"Very well. Then it's settled?" And her excited face beamed with a smile of delight and relief.

"Settled!" said Boris.

"For ever?" said the little girl. "Till death?" And taking his arm, with a happy face she walked quietly beside him into the next room.

XI

THE countess was so tired from seeing visitors that she gave orders that she would see no one else, and the doorkeeper was told to be sure and invite to dinner every one who should call with congratulations. The countess was longing for a *tête-à-tête* talk with the friend of her childhood, Anna Mihalovna, whom she had not seen properly since she had arrived from Petersburg. Anna Mihalovna, with her tear-worn and amiable face, moved closer up to the countess's easy-chair.

"With you I will be perfectly open," said Anna Mihalovna. "We haven't many old friends left. That's how it is I value your friendship so."

Anna Mihalovna looked at Vera and stopped. The countess pressed her friend's hand.

"Vera," said the countess to her eldest daughter, unmistakably not her favourite, "how is it you have no notion about anything? Don't you feel that you're not wanted here? Go to your sister or . . ."

The handsome young countess smiled scornfully, apparently not in the least mortified.

"If you had told me, mamma, I would have gone away long ago," she said, and went off towards her own room. But passing through the divan-room, she noticed two couples sitting symmetrically in the two windows. She stopped and smiled contemptuously at them. Sonya was sitting close beside Nikolay, who was copying out some verses for her, the first he had ever written. Boris and Natasha were sitting in the other window, and were silent when Vera came in. Sonya and Natasha looked at Vera with guilty, happy faces.

It was an amusing and touching sight to see these little girls in love, but the sight of them did not apparently arouse any agreeable feeling in Vera. "How often have I asked you," she said, "not to take my things? You have a room of your own." She took the inkstand away from Nikolay.

"One minute, one minute," he said, dipping his pen in.

"You always manage to do things just at the wrong moment," said Vera. "First you burst into the drawing-room so that every one was ashamed of you." Although or just because what she said was perfectly true, no one answered; all the four simply looked at one another. She lingered in the room with the inkstand in her hand. "And what sort of secrets can you have at your age, Natasha and Boris, and you two!— it's all simply silly nonsense!"

"Well, what has it to do with you, Vera?" Natasha said in defence, speaking very gently. She was evidently more good-humoured and affectionate than usual that day with every one.

"It's very silly," said Vera; "I am ashamed of you. What sort of secret . . ."

"Every one has secrets. We don't interfere with you and Berg," said Natasha, getting warmer.

"I should think you didn't interfere," said Vera, "because there could be no harm in any conduct of mine. But I shall tell mamma how you behave with Boris."

"Natalya Ilyinishna behaves very well to me," said Boris. "I have nothing to complain of," he said.

"Leave off, Boris, you're such a diplomatist" (the word *diplomatist* was much in use among the children in the special sense they attached to the word). "It's tiresome, really," said Natasha, in a mortified and shaking voice; "why does she set upon me?"

"You'll never understand it," she said, addressing Vera, "because you've never cared for any one; you've no heart; you're simply Madame de Genlis" (this nickname, considered most offensive, had been given to Vera by Nikolay), "and your greatest delight is in getting other people into trouble. You can flirt with Berg, as much as you like," she said quickly.

"Well, I'm not likely to run after a young man before visitors. . . ."

"Well, she has gained her object!" Nikolay put in; "she has said something nasty to every one, and upset everybody. Let's go into the nursery."

All four rose, like a flock of scared birds, and went out of the room.

"You've said nasty things to me, and I said nothing to any one," said Vera.

"Madame de Genlis! Madame de Genlis!" cried laughing voices through the door.

The handsome girl who produced such an irritating and unpleasant effect on every one smiled; and, obviously unaffected by what had been said to her, she went up to the looking-glass and put her scarf and her hair tidy. Looking at her handsome face, she seemed to become colder and more composed than ever.

In the drawing-room the conversation was still going on.

"*Ah, chère,*" said the countess, "in my life, too, everything is not rose-coloured. Do you suppose I don't see that, in the way we are going on, our fortune can't last long? And it's all the club and his good-nature. When we're in the country we have no rest from it,—it's nothing but theatricals, hunting parties, and God knows what. But we won't talk of me. Come, tell me how you managed it all. I often wonder at you, Annette, the way you go racing off alone, at your age, to Moscow, and to Petersburg, to all the ministers, and all the great people, and know how to get round them all too. I admire you, really! Well, how was it arranged? Why, I could never do it."

"Ah, my dear!" answered Princess Anna Mihalovna, "God grant that you never know what it is to be left a widow, with no one to support you, and a son whom you love to distraction. One learns how to do anything," she said with some pride. "My lawsuit trained me to it. If I want to see one of these great people, I write a note: 'Princess so-and-so wishes to see so-and-so,' and I go myself in a hired cab two or three times—four, if need be—till I get what I want. I don't mind what they think of me."

"Well, tell me, then, whom did you interview for Borinka?" asked the countess. "Here's your boy an officer in the Guards, while my Nikolinka's going as an ensign. There's no one to manage things for him. Whose help did you ask?"

"Prince Vassily's. He was so kind. Agreed to do everything immediately; put the case before the Emperor," said Princess Anna Mihalovna enthusiastically, entirely forgetting all the humiliation she had been through to attain her object.

"And how is he? beginning to get old, Prince Vassily?" inquired the countess. "I have never seen him since our theatricals at the Rumyantsovs', and I dare say he has forgotten me. He paid me attentions," the countess recalled with a smile.

"He's just the same," answered Anna Mihalovna, "so affable, brimming over. Greatness has not turned his head. 'I am sorry I can do so little for you, Princess,' he said to me; 'I'm at your command.' Yes, he's a splendid man, and very good to his relatives. But you know, Natalie, my love for my boy. I don't know what I would not do to make him happy. And my means are so scanty," pursued Anna Mihalovna, dropping her voice mournfully, "that now I am in a most awful position. My wretched lawsuit is eating up all I have, and making no progress. I have not, can you conceive it, literally, not sixpence in the world, and I don't know how to get Boris's equipment." She took out her handkerchief and shed tears. "I must have five hundred roubles, and I have only a twenty-five rouble note. I'm in such a position. . . . My one hope now is in Prince Kirill Vladimirovitch Bezuhov. If he will not come to the help of his godson—you know he is Boris's godfather—and allow him something for his maintenance, all my efforts will have been in vain; I shall have nothing to get his equipment with."

The countess deliberated in tearful silence.

"I often think—perhaps it's a sinful thought," said the princess—"but I often think: here is Prince Kirill Vladimirovitch Bezuhov living all alone . . . that immense fortune . . . and what is he living for? Life is a burden to him, while Boris is only just beginning life."

"He will be sure to leave something to Boris," said the countess.

"God knows, *chère amie*! These wealthy grand people are such egoists. But still I'm going to see him at once with Boris, and I will tell him plainly the state of the case. People may think what they choose of me, I really don't care, when my son's fate depends on it." The princess got up. "It's now two o'clock, and you dine at four. I shall have time to drive there and back."

And with the air of a Petersburg lady, used to business, and knowing how to make use of every moment, Anna Mihalovna sent for her son, and with him went out into the hall.

"Good-bye, my dear," she said to the countess, who accompanied her to the door. "Wish me good-luck," she added in a whisper unheard by her son.

"You're going to Prince Kirill Vladimirovitch's, *ma chère?*" said the count, coming out of the dining-room into the hall. "If he's better, invite Pierre to dine with us. He has been here; used to dance with the children. Be sure you invite him, *ma chère.* Now do come and look how Taras has surpassed himself to-day. He says Count Orlov never had such a dinner as we're going to have to-day."

XII

"*Mon cher Boris,*" said Anna Mihalovna as the Countess Rostov's carriage drove along the street strewn with straw and into the wide courtyard of Count Kirill Vladimirovitch Bezuhov's house. "*Mon cher Boris,*" said the mother, putting her hand out from under her old mantle, and laying it on her son's hand with a timid, caressing movement, "be nice, be attentive. Count Kirill Vladimirovitch is after all your godfather, and your future depends on him. Remember that, *mon cher,* be charming, as you know so well how to be. . . ."

"If I knew anything would come of it but humiliation," her son answered coldly. "But I have promised, and I will do it for your sake."

Although the carriage was standing at the entrance, the hall-porter, scanning the mother and son (they had not sent in their names, but had walked straight in through the glass doors between two rows of statues in niches), and looking significantly at the old mantle, inquired whom they wanted, the princesses or the count; and hearing that they wanted to see the count, said that his excellency was worse to-day, and his excellency could see no one.

"We may as well go away," the son said in French.

"*Mon ami!*" said the mother in a voice of entreaty, again touching her son's hand, as though the contact might soothe or rouse him. Boris said no more, but without taking off his overcoat, looked inquiringly at his mother.

"My good man," Anna Mihalovna said ingratiatingly, addressing the hall-porter, "I know that Count Kirill Vladimirovitch is very ill . . . that is why I am here. . . . I am a relation. . . . I shall not disturb him, my good man. . . . I need only see Prince Vassily Sergyevitch; he's staying here, I know. Announce us, please."

The hall-porter sullenly pulled the bell-rope that rang upstairs and turned away.

"Princess Drubetskoy to see Prince Vassily Sergyevitch," he called to a footman in stockings, slippers and a frockcoat, who ran down from above, and looked down from the turn in the staircase.

The mother straightened out the folds of her dyed silk gown, looked at herself in the full-length Venetian looking-glass on the wall, and boldly walked up on the stair carpet in her shabby, shapeless shoes.

"My dear, you promised me," she turned again to her son, rousing him by a touch on his arm. The son, with his eyes on the floor, walked submissively after her.

They went into a large room, from which a door led to the apartments that had been assigned to Prince Vassily.

At the moment when the mother and son reached the middle of the room and were about to ask their way of an old footman, who had darted out at their entrance, the bronze handle of one of the doors turned, and Prince Vassily, dressed in a house jacket of velvet, with one star, came out, accompanying a handsome, black-haired man. This man was the celebrated Petersburg doctor, Lorrain.

"It is positive, then?" said the Prince.

"Prince, *errare est humanum*," answered the doctor, lisping, and pronouncing the Latin words with a French accent.

"Very well, very well . . ."

Perceiving Anna Mihalovna and her son, Prince Vassily dismissed the doctor with a bow, and in silence, with an air of inquiry, advanced to meet them. The son noticed how an expression of intense grief came at once into his mother's eyes, and he smiled slightly.

"Yes, in what distressing circumstances we were destined to meet again, prince. . . . Tell me how is our dear patient?" she said, apparently not observing the frigid, offensive glance that was fixed on her. Prince Vassily stared at her, then at Boris with a look of inquiry that amounted to perplexity. Boris bowed politely. Prince Vassily, without acknowledging his bow, turned away to Anna Mihalovna, and to her question he replied by a movement of the head and lips, indicative of the worst fears for the patient.

"Is it possible?" cried Anna Mihalovna. "Ah, this is terrible! It is dreadful to think . . . This is my son," she added, indicating Boris. "He wanted to thank you in person."

Boris once more made a polite bow.

"Believe me, prince, a mother's heart will never forget what you have done for us."

"I am glad I have been able to do you any service, my dear Anna Mihalovna," said Prince Vassily, pulling his lace frill straight, and in voice and manner manifesting here in Moscow, before Anna Mihalovna, who was under obligation to him, an even greater sense of his own dignity than in Petersburg at Anna Pavlovna's *soirée*.

"Try to do your duty in the service, and to be worthy of it," he added, turning severely to him. "I am glad . . . you are here on leave?" he asked in his expressionless voice.

"I am awaiting orders, your excellency, to join my new regiment," answered Boris, showing no sign either of resentment at the prince's abrupt manner, nor of desire to get into conversation, but speaking with such respectful composure that the prince looked at him attentively.

"You are living with your mother?"

"I am living at Countess Rostov's," said Boris, again adding: "your excellency."

"The Ilya Rostov, who married Natalie Shinshin," said Anna Mihalovna.

"I know, I know," said Prince Vassily in his monotonous voice. "I
have never been able to understand how Natalie Shinshin could make
up her mind to marry that unlicked bear. A completely stupid and
ridiculous person. And a gambler too, I am told."

"But a very worthy man, prince," observed Anna Mihalovna, with a
pathetic smile, as though she too recognised that Count Rostov deserved
this criticism, but begged him not to be too hard on the poor old fellow.
"What do the doctors say?" asked the princess, after a brief pause, and
again the expression of deep distress reappeared on her tear-worn face.

"There is little hope," said the prince.

"And, I was so longing to thank uncle once more for all his kindness
to me and to Boris. He is his godson," she added in a tone that suggested
that Prince Vassily would be highly delighted to hear this fact.

Prince Vassily pondered and frowned. Anna Mihalovna saw he was
afraid of finding in her a rival with claims on Count Bezuhov's will. She
hastened to reassure him. "If it were not for my genuine love and devotion for uncle," she said, uttering the last word with peculiar assurance
and carelessness, "I know his character,—generous, upright; but with
only the princesses about him. . . . They are young. . . ." She bent
her head and added in a whisper: "Has he performed his last duties,
prince? How priceless are these last moments! He is as bad as he could
be, it seems; it is absolutely necessary to prepare him, if he is so ill. We
women, prince," she smiled tenderly, "always know how to say these
things. I absolutely must see him. Hard as it will be for me, I am used
to suffering."

The prince evidently understood, and understood, too, as he had at
Anna Pavlovna's, that it was no easy task to get rid of Anna Mihalovna.

"Would not this interview be trying for him, *chère* Anna Mihalovna?"
he said. "Let us wait till the evening; the doctors have predicted a
crisis."

"But waiting's out of the question, prince, at such a moment. Think,
it is a question of saving his soul. Ah! how terrible, the duties of a
Christian. . . ."

The door from the inner rooms opened, and one of the count's nieces
entered with a cold and forbidding face, and a long waist strikingly out
of proportion with the shortness of her legs.

Prince Vassily turned to her. "Well, how is he?"

"Still the same. What can you expect with this noise? . . ." said the
princess, scanning Anna Mihalovna, as a stranger.

"Ah, dear, I did not recognise you," said Anna Mihalovna, with a
delighted smile, and she ambled lightly up to the count's niece. "I have
just come, and I am at your service to help in nursing my uncle. I
imagine what you have been suffering," she added, sympathetically turning her eyes up.

The princess made no reply, she did not even smile, but walked
straight away. Anna Mihalovna took off her gloves, and entrenched her-

self as it were in an armchair, inviting Prince Vassily to sit down beside
her.

"Boris!" she said to her son, and she smiled at him, "I am going in
to the count, to poor uncle, and you can go to Pierre, *mon ami*, meanwhile, and don't forget to give him the Rostovs' invitation. They ask
him to dinner. I suppose he won't go?" she said to the prince.

"On the contrary," said the prince, visibly cast down. "I should be
very glad if you would take that young man off my hands. . . . He
sticks on here. The count has not once asked for him."

He shrugged his shoulders. A footman conducted the youth downstairs and up another staircase to the apartments of Pyotr Kirillovitch.

XIII

PIERRE had not succeeded in fixing upon a career in Petersburg, and
really had been banished to Moscow for disorderly conduct. The story
told about him at Count Rostov's was true. Pierre had assisted in tying
the police officer to the bear. He had arrived a few days previously,
stopping as he always did at his father's house. Though he had assumed
that his story would be already known at Moscow, and that the ladies
who were about his father, always unfavourably disposed to him, would
profit by this opportunity of turning the count against him, he went on
the day of his arrival to his father's part of the house. Going into the
drawing-room, where the princesses usually sat, he greeted the ladies,
two of whom were sitting at their embroidery frames, while one read
aloud. There were three of them. The eldest, a trim, long-waisted, severe
maiden-lady, the one who had come out to Anna Mihalovna, was reading. The younger ones, both rosy and pretty, were only to be distinguished by the fact that one of them had a little mole which made her
much prettier. They were both working at their embroidery frames.
Pierre was received like a man risen from the dead or stricken with
plague. The eldest princess paused in her reading and stared at him in
silence with dismay in her eyes. The second assumed precisely the same
expression. The youngest, the one with the mole, who was of a mirthful
and laughing disposition, bent over her frame, to conceal a smile, probably evoked by the amusing scene she foresaw coming. She pulled her
embroidery wool out below, and bent down as though examining the
pattern, hardly able to suppress her laughter.

"Good morning, cousin," said Pierre. "You don't know me?"

"I know you only too well, only too well."

"How is the count? Can I see him?" Pierre asked, awkwardly as always, but not disconcerted.

"The count is suffering both physically and morally, and your only
anxiety seems to be to occasion him as much suffering as possible."

"Can I see the count?" repeated Pierre.

"Hm . . . if you want to kill him, to kill him outright, you can see him. Olga, go and see if uncle's broth is ready—it will soon be time for it," she added, to show Pierre they were busy, and busy in seeing after his father's comfort, while he was obviously only busy in causing him discomfort.

Olga went out. Pierre stood still a moment, looked at the sisters and bowing said: "Then I will go to my room. When I can see him, you will tell me." He went away and heard the ringing but not loud laugh of the sister with the mole behind him.

The next day Prince Vassily had come and settled in the count's house. He sent for Pierre and said to him:

"My dear fellow, if you behave here as you did at Petersburg, you will come to a very bad end; that's all I have to say to you. The count is very, very ill; you must not see him."

Since then Pierre had not been disturbed, and he spent the whole day alone in his room upstairs.

At the moment when Boris came in, Pierre was walking up and down his room, stopping now and then in the corners, making menacing gestures at the wall, as though thrusting some invisible enemy through with a lance, then he gazed sternly over his spectacles, then pacing up and down again, murmuring indistinct words, shrugging his shoulders and gesticulating.

"England's day is over!" he said, scowling and pointing at some one with his finger. "Mr. Pitt, as a traitor to the nation and to the rights of man, is condemned . . ." he had not time to deliver Pitt's sentence, imagining himself at that moment Napoleon, and having in the person of his hero succeeded in the dangerous crossing of the Channel and in the conquest of London, when he saw a graceful, handsome young officer come in. He stood still. Pierre had seen Boris last as a boy of fourteen, and did not remember him in the least. But in spite of that he took his hand in his characteristically quick and warm-hearted manner, and smiled cordially at him.

"You remember me?" Boris said calmly with a pleasant smile. "I have come with my mother to see the count, but it seems he is not quite well."

"Yes, he is ill, it seems. People are always bothering him," answered Pierre, trying to recall who this youth might be.

Boris perceived that Pierre did not know him, but did not think fit to make himself known, and without the slightest embarrassment looked him straight in the face.

"Count Rostov asks you to come to dinner with him to-day," he said, after a rather long silence somewhat disconcerting for Pierre.

"Ah, Count Rostov," began Pierre, delighted. "So you are his son, Ilya? Can you believe it, for the first moment I did not recognise you. Do you remember how we used to slide on the Sparrow Hills with Madame Jacquot . . . long ago?"

"You are mistaken," said Boris, deliberately, with a bold and rather sarcastic smile. "I am Boris, the son of Princess Anna Mihalovna Drubetskoy. It is the father of the Rostovs who is called Ilya, the son's Nikolay. And I don't know any Madame Jacquot."

Pierre shook his hands and head, as though flies or bees were swarming upon him.

"Ah, how is it! I've mixed it all up. There are such a lot of relatives in Moscow! You are Boris . . . yes. Well, now, we have got it clear. Tell me, what do you think of the Boulogne expedition? Things will go badly with the English, you know, if Napoleon gets across the Channel. I believe that the expedition is very possible. If only Villeneuve doesn't make a mess of it!"

Boris knew nothing at all about the Boulogne expedition, and it was the first time he had heard of Villeneuve.

"Here in Moscow we are more interested in dinner parties and scandal than in politics," he said in his self-possessed, sarcastic tone. "I know nothing and think nothing about it. Moscow's more engrossed in scandal than anything," he went on. "Just now they are all talking about you and about the count."

Pierre smiled his kindly smile, as though afraid for his companion's sake that he might say something he would regret. But Boris spoke distinctly, clearly and drily, looking straight into Pierre's face.

"There's nothing else to do in Moscow but talk scandal," he went on. "Every one's absorbed in the question whom the count will leave his fortune to, though perhaps he will outlive us all, as I sincerely hope he may."

"Yes, all that's very horrid," Pierre interposed, "very horrid." Pierre was still afraid this officer would inadvertently drop into some remark disconcerting for himself.

"And it must seem to you," said Boris, flushing slightly, but not changing his voice or attitude, "it must seem to you that every one's thinking of nothing but getting something from him."

"That's just it," thought Pierre.

"And that's just what I want to say to you to prevent misunderstandings, that you are very much mistaken if you reckon me and my mother among those people. We are very poor, but I—at least I speak for myself—just because your father is rich, I don't consider myself a relation of his, and neither I nor my mother would ever ask him for anything or take anything from him."

It was a long while before Pierre understood, but, when he did understand, he jumped up from the sofa, seized Boris's hand with his characteristic quickness and awkwardness, and blushing far more than Boris, began speaking with a mixed sensation of shame and annoyance.

"Well, this is strange! Do you suppose I . . . how you could think . . . I know very well . . ."

But Boris again interrupted him.

"I am glad I have told you everything frankly. Perhaps you dislike it: you must excuse me," he said, trying to put Pierre at his ease instead of being put at his ease by him; "but I hope I have not offended you. I make it a rule to say everything quite plainly. . . . Then what message am I to take? You will come to dinner at the Rostovs'?" And Boris, with an evident sense of having discharged an onerous duty, having extricated himself from an awkward position, and put somebody else into one became perfectly pleasant again.

"No, let me tell you," said Pierre, regaining his composure, "you are a wonderful person. What you have just said was very fine, very fine. Of course you don't know me, it's so long since we've seen each other . . . we were children. . . . You might suppose I should . . . I understand, I quite understand. I shouldn't have done it, I shouldn't have had the courage, but it's splendid. I'm very glad I have made your acquaintance. A queer idea," he added, pausing and smiling, "you must have had of me." He laughed. "But what of it? Let us know each other better, please!" He pressed Boris's hand. "Do you know I've not once seen the count? He has not sent for me . . . I am sorry for him, as a man . . . But what can one do?"

"And so you think Napoleon will succeed in getting his army across?" Boris queried, smiling.

Pierre saw that Boris was trying to change the conversation, and so he began explaining the advantages and difficulties of the Boulogne expedition.

A footman came in to summon Boris to the princess. The princess was going. Pierre promised to come to dinner in order to see more of Boris, and pressed his hand warmly at parting, looking affectionately into his face over his spectacles.

When he had gone, Pierre walked for some time longer up and down his room, not thrusting at an unseen foe, but smiling at the recollection of that charming, intelligent, and resolute young man.

As so often happens with young people, especially if they are in a position of loneliness, he felt an unreasonable tenderness for this youth, and he firmly resolved to become friends with him.

Prince Vassily accompanied the princess to the hall. The princess was holding her handkerchief to her eyes, and her face was tearful.

"It is terrible, terrible!" she said; "but whatever it costs me, I will do my duty. I will come to stay the night. He can't be left like this. Every minute is precious. I can't understand why his nieces put it off. Maybe God will help me to find a way to prepare him. Adieu, prince, may God support you . . ."

"Adieu, my kind friend," answered Prince Vassily, turning away from her.

"Oh, he is in an awful position!" said the mother to her son, when they were sitting in the carriage again. "He scarcely knows any one."

"I don't understand, mamma, what his attitude is as regards Pierre."

"The will will make all that plain, my dear; our fate, too, hangs upon it . . ."

"But what makes you think he will leave us anything?"

"Oh, my dear! He is so rich, and we are so poor."

"Well, that's hardly a sufficient reason, mamma."

"Oh, my God, how ill he is, how ill he is!" cried his mother.

XIV

WHEN Anna Mihalovna had driven off with her son to Count Kirill Vladimirovitch Bezuhov's, Countess Rostov sat a long while alone, putting her handkerchief to her eyes. At last she rang the bell.

"What does it mean?" she said angrily to the maid, who had kept her waiting a few minutes; "don't you care for my service, eh? I'll find you another place, if so."

The countess was distressed at the troubles and degrading poverty of her friend, and so out of humour, which always found expression in such remarks to her servants.

"I'm very sorry," said the maid.

"Ask the count to come to me."

The count came waddling in to see his wife, looking, as usual, rather guilty.

"Well, little countess! What a *sauté* of woodcocks and Madeira we're to have, *ma chère*! I've tried it; I did well to give a thousand roubles for Taras. He's worth it!"

He sat down by his wife, setting his elbow jauntily on his knee, and ruffling up his grey hair. "What are your commands, little countess?"

"It's this, my dear—why, what is this mess on you here?" she said, pointing to his waistcoat. "It's the *sauté*, most likely," she added, smiling. "It's this, my dear, I want some money." Her face became gloomy.

"Ah, little countess! . . ." And the count fidgeted about, pulling out his pocket-book.

"I want a great deal, count. I want five hundred roubles." And taking out her cambric handkerchief she wiped her husband's waistcoat.

"This minute, this minute. Hey, who's there?" he shouted, as men only shout who are certain that those they call will run headlong at their summons. "Send Mitenka to me!"

Mitenka, the young man of noble family who had been brought up in the count's house, and now had charge of all his money affairs, walked softly into the room.

"Here, my dear boy," said the count to the young man, who came up respectfully. "Bring me," he thought a moment, "yes, seven hundred roubles, yes. And mind, don't bring me such torn and dirty notes as last time; nice ones now, for the countess."

"Yes, Mitenka, clean ones, please," said the countess with a depressed sigh.

"Your excellency, when do you desire me to get the money?" said Mitenka. "Your honour ought to know . . . But don't trouble," he added, noticing that the count was beginning to breathe rapidly and heavily, which was always the sign of approaching anger. "I was forgetting . . . This minute do you desire me to bring them?"

"Yes, yes, just so, bring them. Give them to the countess. What a treasure that Mitenka is," added the count, smiling, when the young man had gone out. "He doesn't know the meaning of impossible. That's a thing I can't bear. Everything's possible."

"Ah, money, count, money, what a lot of sorrow it causes in the world!" said the countess. "This money I am in great need of."

"You are a terrible spendthrift, little countess, we all know," said the count, and kissing his wife's hand he went away again to his own room.

When Anna Mihalovna came back from the Bezuhovs', the money was already on the countess's little table, all in new notes, under her pocket-handkerchief. Anna Mihalovna noticed that the countess was fluttered about something.

"Well, my dear?" queried the countess.

"Ah, he is in a terrible condition! One would not recognise him, he is so ill, so ill; I was there only a minute, and did not say two words."

"Annette, for God's sake don't refuse me," the countess said suddenly with a blush, which was strangely incongruous with her elderly, thin, and dignified face, taking the money from under her handkerchief. Anna Mihalovna instantly grasped the situation, and was already bending over to embrace the countess at the appropriate moment.

"This is for Boris, from me, for his equipment . . ."

Anna Mihalovna was already embracing her and weeping. The countess wept too. They wept because they were friends, and because they were soft-hearted, and that they, who had been friends in youth, should have to think of anything so base as money, and that their youth was over. . . . But the tears of both were sweet to them. . . .

XV

COUNTESS ROSTOV, with her daughters and the greater number of the guests, was sitting in the drawing-room. The count led the gentlemen of the party to his room, calling their attention to his connoisseur's collection of Turkish pipes. Now and then he went out and inquired, had she come yet? They were waiting for Marya Dmitryevna Ahrosimov, known in society as *le terrible dragon*, a lady who owed her renown not to her wealth or her rank, but to her mental directness and her open, unconventional behaviour. Marya Dmitryevna was known to the imperial family; she was known to all Moscow and all Petersburg, and both cities, while they marvelled at her, laughed in their sleeves at her rudeness, and told good stories about her, nevertheless, all without exception respected and feared her.

In the count's room, full of smoke, there was talk of the war, which had been declared in a manifesto, and of the levies of troops. The manifesto no one had yet read, but every one knew of its appearance. The count was sitting on an ottoman with a man smoking and talking on each side of him. The count himself was neither smoking nor talking, but, with his head cocked first on one side and then on the other, gazed with evident satisfaction at the smokers, and listened to the argument he had got up between his two neighbours.

One of these two was a civilian with a thin, wrinkled, bilious, close-shaven face, a man past middle age, though dressed like the most fashionable young man. He sat with his leg up on the ottoman, as though he were at home, and with the amber mouthpiece in the side of his mouth, he smoked spasmodically, puckering up his face. This was an old bachelor, Shinshin, a cousin of the countess's, famed in Moscow drawing-rooms for his biting wit. He seemed supercilious in his manner to his companion, a fresh, rosy officer of the Guards, irreproachably washed and brushed and buttoned. He held his pipe in the middle of his mouth, and drawing in a little smoke, sent it coiling in rings out of his fine red lips. He was the Lieutenant Berg, an officer in the Semenovsky regiment with whom Boris was to go away, and about whom Natasha had taunted Vera, calling Berg her suitor. The count sat between these two listening intently to them. The count's favourite entertainment, next to playing boston, of which he was very fond, was that of listening to conversation, especially when he had succeeded in getting up a dispute between two talkative friends.

"Come, how is it, *mon très honorable* Alphonse Karlitch," said Shinshin, chuckling, and using a combination of the most popular Russian colloquialisms and the most *recherchès* French expressions, which constituted the peculiarity of his phraseology. "You reckon you'll get an income from the government, and you want to get a little something from your company too?"

"No, Pyotr Nikolaitch, I only want to show that in the cavalry the advantages are few as compared with the infantry. Consider my position now, for instance, Pyotr Nikolaitch." Berg talked very precisely, serenely, and politely. All he said was always concerning himself. He always maintained a serene silence when any subject was discussed that had no direct bearing on himself. And he could be silent in that way for several hours at a time, neither experiencing nor causing in others the slightest embarrassment. But as soon as the conversation concerned him personally, he began to talk at length and with visible satisfaction.

"Consider my position, Pyotr Nikolaitch: if I were in the cavalry, I should get no more than two hundred roubles every four months, even at the rank of lieutenant, while as it is I get two hundred and thirty," he explained with a beaming, friendly smile, looking at Shinshin and the count as though he had no doubt that his success would always be the chief goal of all other people's wishes. "Besides that, Pyotr Nikolaitch, exchanging into the Guards, I'm so much nearer the front," pursued Berg, "and vacancies occur so much more frequently in the infantry guards. Then you can fancy how well I can manage on two hundred and thirty roubles. Why, I'm putting by and sending some off to my father too," he pursued, letting off a ring of smoke.

"There is a balance. A German will thrash wheat out of the head of an axe, as the Russian proverb has it," said Shinshin, shifting his pipe to the other side of his mouth and winking to the count.

The count chuckled. The other visitors seeing that Shinshin was talking came up to listen. Berg, without perceiving either their sneers or

their lack of interest, proceeded to explain how by exchanging into the
guards he had already gained a step in advance of his old comrades in
the corps; how in war-time the commander of a company may so easily
be killed, and he as next in command might very easily succeed him, and
how every one in the regiment liked him, and how pleased his father was
with him. Berg was unmistakably enjoying himself as he told all this,
and seemed never to suspect that other people too might have their
own interests. But all he said was so nice, so sedate, the naïveté of his
youthful egoism was so undisguised, that he disarmed his listeners.

"Well, my good fellow, whether you're in the infantry or in the
cavalry, you'll always get on all right, that I venture to predict," said
Shinshin, patting him on the shoulder, and setting his feet down off the
ottoman. Berg smiled gleefully. The count and the guests after him went
into the drawing-room.

It was that interval just before a dinner when the assembled guests
do not care to enter on a lengthy conversation, expecting to be summoned to the dining-room; while they feel it incumbent on them to
move about and not to be silent, so as to show that they are not impatient to sit down to table. The host and hostess look towards the door,
and occasionally at one another. The guests try from these glances to
divine whom or what they are waiting for; some important relation late
in arriving, or some dish which is not ready.

Pierre arrived just at dinner-time, and awkwardly sat down in the
middle of the drawing-room in the first easy-chair he came across, blocking up the way for every one. The countess tried to make him talk, but
he looked naïvely round him over his spectacles as though he were
looking for some one, and replied in monosyllables to all the countess's
questions. He was in the way, and was the only person unaware of it.
The greater number of the guests, knowing the story of the bear, looked
inquisitively at this big, stout, inoffensive-looking person, puzzled to
think how such a spiritless and staid young man could have played such
a prank.

"You have only lately arrived?" the countess asked him.

"*Oui, madame.*"

"You have not seen my husband?"

"*Non, madame.*" He smiled very inappropriately.

"You have lately been in Paris, I believe? I suppose it's very interesting."

"Very interesting."

The countess exchanged glances with Anna Mihalovna. Anna Mihalovna saw that she was asked to undertake the young man, and sitting
down by him she began talking of his father. But to her as to the
countess he replied only in monosyllables. The other guests were all
busily engaged together. "The Razumovskys . . . It was very charming . . . You are so kind . . . Countess Apraxin . . ." rose in murmurs on all sides. The countess got up and went into the reception hall.

"Marya Dmitryevna?" her voice was heard asking from there.

"Herself," a rough voice was heard in reply, and immediately after, Marya Dmitryevna walked into the room. All the girls and even the ladies, except the very old ones, got up. Marya Dmitryevna, a stout woman of fifty, stopped in the doorway, and holding her head with its grey curls erect, she looked down at the guests and as though tucking up her cuffs, she deliberately arranged the wide sleeves of her gown. Marya Dmitryevna always spoke Russian.

"Health and happiness to the lady whose name-day we are keeping and to her children," she said in her loud, rich voice that dominated all other sounds. "Well, you old sinner," she turned to the count who was kissing her hand, "I suppose you are tired of Moscow—nowhere to go out with the dogs? Well, my good man, what's to be done? these nestlings will grow up. . . ." She pointed to the girls. "Willy-nilly, you must look out for young men for them."

"Well, my Cossack?" (Marya Dmitryevna used to call Natasha a Cossack) she said, stroking the hand of Natasha, who came up to kiss her hand gaily without shyness. "I know you're a wicked girl, but I like you."

She took out of her huge reticule some amber earrings with drops, and giving them to Natasha, whose beaming birthday face flushed rosy red, she turned away immediately and addressed Pierre.

"Ay, ay! come here, sir!" she said in an intentionally quiet and gentle voice. "Come here, sir . . ." And she tucked her sleeve up higher in an ominous manner.

Pierre went up, looking innocently at her over his spectacles.

"Come along, come along, sir! I was the only person that told your father the truth when he was in high favour, and in your case it is a sacred duty." She paused. Every one was mutely expectant of what was to follow, feeling that this was merely a prelude. "A pretty fellow, there's no denying! a pretty fellow! . . . His father is lying on his deathbed, and he's amusing himself, setting a police-constable astride on a bear! For shame, sir, for shame! You had better have gone to the war."

She turned away and gave her hand to the count, who could hardly keep from laughing.

"Well, I suppose dinner's ready, eh?" said Marya Dmitryevna. The count led the way with Marya Dmitryevna, then followed the countess, taken in by a colonel of hussars, a person of importance, as Nikolay was to travel in his company to join the regiment; then Anna Mihalovna with Shinshin. Berg gave his arm to Vera, Julie Karagin walked in smiling with Nikolay. They were followed by a string of other couples, stretching right across the hall, and behind all, the children with their tutors and governesses trooped in, walked singly. There was a bustle among the waiters and a creaking of chairs; the orchestra began playing, as the guests took their places. Then the strains of the count's household band were succeeded by the clatter of knives and forks, the conversation of the guests, and the subdued tread of the waiters. The countess presided at one end of the table. On her right was Marya Dmitryevna;

on her left Anna Mihalovna and the other ladies of the party. At the other end sat the count, with the colonel of hussars on his left, and on his right Shinshin and the other guests of the male sex. On one side of the large table sat the more grown-up of the young people: Vera beside Berg, Pierre beside Boris. On the other side were the children with their tutors and governesses. The count peeped from behind the crystal of the decanters and fruit-dishes at his wife and her high cap with blue ribbons, and zealously poured out wine for his neighbours, not overlooking himself. The countess, too, while mindful of her duties as hostess, cast significant glances from behind the pineapples at her husband, whose face and bald head struck her as looking particularly red against his grey hair. At the ladies' end there was a rhythmic murmur of talk, but at the other end of the table the men's voices grew louder and louder, especially the voice of the colonel of hussars, who, getting more and more flushed, ate and drank so much that the count held him up as a pattern to the rest. Berg with a tender smile was telling Vera that love was an emotion not of earth but of heaven. Boris was telling his new friend Pierre the names of the guests, while he exchanged glances with Natasha sitting opposite him. Pierre said little, looked about at the new faces, and ate a great deal. Of the two soups he chose à la tortue, and from that course to the fish-pasties and the grouse, he did not let a single dish pass, and took every sort of wine that the butler offered him, as he mysteriously poked a bottle wrapped in a napkin over his neighbour's shoulder, murmuring, "Dry Madeira," or "Hungarian," or "Rhine wine." Pierre took a wine-glass at random out of the four crystal glasses engraved with the count's crest that were set at each place, and drank with relish, staring at the guests with a countenance that became more and more amiable as the dinner went on. Natasha, who sat opposite him, gazed at Boris as girls of thirteen gaze at the boy whom they have just kissed for the first time, and with whom they are in love. This gaze sometimes strayed to Pierre, and at the look on the funny, excited little girl's face, he felt an impulse to laugh himself without knowing why.

Nikolay was sitting a long way from Sonya, beside Julie Karagin, and again smiling the same unconscious smile, he was talking to her. Sonya wore a company smile, but she was visibly in agonies of jealousy; at one moment she turned pale, then she crimsoned, and all her energies were concentrated on listening to what Nikolay and Julie were saying. The governess looked nervously about her, as though preparing to resent any slight that might be offered to the children. The German tutor was trying to learn by heart a list of all the kinds of dishes, desserts, and wines, in order to write a detailed description of them to the folks at home in Germany, and was greatly mortified that the butler with the bottle in the napkin had passed him over. The German knitted his brows, and tried to look as though he would not have cared to take that wine, but he was mortified because no one would understand that he had not wanted the wine to quench his thirst, or through greed, but from a conscientious desire for knowledge.

XVI

At the men's end of the table the conversation was becoming more and more lively. The colonel was asserting that the proclamation of the declaration of war had already been issued in Petersburg, and that a copy, which he had seen himself, had that day been brought by a courier to the commander-in-chief.

"And what evil spirit must make us go to war with Bonaparte?" said Shinshin. "He has already made Austria take a back seat. I am afraid it may be our turn this time."

The colonel was a stout, tall, and plethoric German, evidently a zealous officer and good patriot. He resented Shinshin's words.

"The reason why, my good sir," he said, speaking with a German accent, "is just that the emperor knows that. In his proclamation he says that he cannot behold with equanimity the danger threatening Russia, and the security of the empire, its dignity, and the sacredness of its *alliances*." He laid a special emphasis on the word *alliances*, as though the gist of the matter lay in that word. And with the unfailing memory for official matters that was peculiar to him, he repeated the introductory words of the proclamation . . . "and the desire, which constitutes the Sovereign's sole and immutable aim, to establish peace on a secure foundation, have determined him to despatch now a part of the troops abroad, and to make dispositions for carrying out this new project. That is the reason why, my dear sir," he concluded, tossing off a glass of wine in edifying fashion, and looking towards the count for encouragement.

"Do you know the proverb, 'Erema, Erema, you'd better stay at home and mind your spindle'?" said Shinshin, frowning and smiling. "That suits us to a hair. Why, Suvorov even was defeated hollow, and where are our Suvorovs nowadays? I just ask you that," he said, continually shifting from Russian to French and back again.

"We ought to fight to the last drop of our blood," said the colonel, thumping the table, "and to die for our emperor, and then all will be well. And to discuss it as little as possible," he concluded, turning again to the count, and drawling out the word "possible." "That's how we old hussars look at it; that's all we have to say. And how do you look at it, young man and young hussar?" he added, addressing Nikolay, who, catching that it was the war they were discussing, had dropped his conversation with Julie, and was all eyes and all ears, intent on the colonel.

"I perfectly agree with you," answered Nikolay, growing hot all over, twisting his plate round, and changing the places of the glasses with a face as desperate and determined as though he were exposed to great danger at that actual moment. "I am convinced that the Russians must die or conquer," he said. He was himself, like the rest of the party, conscious after the words were uttered that he had spoken with an enthusiasm and fervour out of keeping with the occasion, and so he was embarrassed.

"That was very fine, what you just said," Julie sitting beside him said breathlessly. Sonya trembled all over and crimsoned to her ears, and behind her ears, and down her neck and shoulders, while Nikolay was speaking. Pierre listened to the colonel's remarks, and nodded his head approvingly.

"That's capital," said he.

"You're a true hussar, young man," the colonel shouted, thumping on the table again.

"What are you making such a noise about over there?" Marya Dmitryevna's bass voice was suddenly heard asking across the table. "What are you thumping the table for?" she addressed the colonel. "Whom are you so hot against? You imagine, I suppose, that the French are before you?"

"I speak the truth," said the hussar, smiling.

"It's all about the war," the count shouted across the table. "My son's going, you see, Marya Dmitryevna, my son's going."

"And I've four sons in the army, but I don't grieve. All's in God's hands; one may die in one's bed, and in battle God may spare," Marya Dmitryevna's deep voice boomed back, speaking without the slightest effort from the further end of the table.

"That's true."

And the conversation concentrated into two groups again, one at the ladies' end, and one at the men's.

"You don't dare to ask!" said her little brother to Natasha, "and you won't ask!"

"I will ask," answered Natasha. Her face suddenly glowed, expressing a desperate and mirthful resolution. She rose in her seat, her eyes inviting Pierre to listen, and addressed her mother.

"Mamma!" her childish contralto rang out over the table.

"What is it?" the countess asked in dismay; but seeing from her daughter's face that it was mischief, she shook her hand at her sternly, with a threatening and forbidding movement of her head.

All conversation was hushed.

"Mamma! what pudding will there be?" Natasha's little voice rang out still more resolutely and deliberately.

The countess tried to frown, but could not. Marya Dmitryevna shook her fat finger.

"Cossack!" she said menacingly.

Most of the guests looked at the parents, not knowing how they were to take this sally.

"I'll give it to you," said the countess.

"Mamma! what pudding will it be?" Natasha cried, with bold and saucy gaiety, feeling sure that her prank would be taken in the right spirit. Sonya and fat little Petya were hiding their giggles. "You see I did ask," Natasha whispered to her little brother and Pierre, at whom she glanced again.

"Ice-pudding, only you are not to have any," said Marya Dmitryevna.

Natasha saw there was nothing to be afraid of, and so she was not frightened at Marya Dmitryevna even.

"Marya Dmitryevna! what sort of ice-pudding? I don't like ice-cream."

"Carrot-ices."

"No, what sort, Marya Dmitryevna, what sort?" she almost shrieked. "I want to know." Marya Dmitryevna and the countess burst out laughing, and all the party followed their example. They all laughed, not at Marya Dmitryevna's answer, but at the irrepressible boldness and smartness of the little girl, who had the pluck and the wit to tackle Marya Dmitryevna in this fashion.

Natasha only desisted when she had been told it was to be pineapple ice. Before the ices, champagne was passed round. Again the band struck up, the count kissed the countess, and the guests getting up from the table congratulated the countess, and clinked glasses across the table with the count, the children, and one another. Again the waiters darted about, chairs grated on the floor, and in the same order, but with flushed faces, the guests returned to the drawing-room and the count's study.

XVII

THE card-tables were opened, parties were made up for boston, and the count's guests settled themselves in the two drawing-rooms, the divan room, and the library.

The count, holding his cards in a fan, with some difficulty kept himself from dropping into his customary after-dinner nap, and laughed at everything. The young people, at the countess's suggestion, gathered about the clavichord and the harp. Julie was first pressed by every one to perform, and played a piece with variations on the harp. Then she joined the other young ladies in begging Natasha and Nikolay, who were noted for their musical talents, to sing something Natasha, who was treated by every one as though she were grown-up, was visibly very proud of it, and at the same time made shy by it.

"What are we to sing?" she asked.

"The 'Spring,' " answered Nikolay.

"Well, then, let's make haste. Boris, come here," said Natasha. "But where's Sonya?" She looked round, and seeing that her friend was not in the room, she ran off to find her.

After running to Sonya's room, and not finding her there, Natasha ran to the nursery: Sonya was not there either. Natasha knew that she must be on the chest in the corridor. The chest in the corridor was the scene of the woes of the younger feminine generation of the house of Rostov. Yes, Sonya was on the chest, lying face downwards, crushing her gossamer pink frock on their old nurse's dirty striped feather-bed. Her face hidden in her fingers, she was sobbing, and her little bare shoulders were heaving. Natasha's birthday face that had been festive and excited all day, changed at once; her eyes wore a fixed look, then her broad neck quivered, and the corners of her lips drooped.

"Sonya! what is it? . . . what's the matter with you? Oo-oo-oo! . . ." and Natasha, letting her big mouth drop open and becoming quite ugly, wailed like a baby, not knowing why, simply because Sonya was crying. Sonya tried to lift up her head, tried to answer, but could not, and buried her face more than ever. Natasha cried, sitting on the edge of the blue feather-bed and hugging her friend. Making an effort, Sonya got up, began to dry her tears and to talk.

"Nikolinka's going away in a week, his . . . paper . . . has come . . . he told me himself. . . . But still I shouldn't cry . . ." (she showed a sheet of paper she was holding in her hand; on it were verses written by Nikolay). "I shouldn't have cried; but you can't . . . no one can understand . . . what a soul he has."

And again she fell to weeping at the thought of how noble his soul was.

"It's all right for you . . . I'm not envious . . . I love you and Boris too," she said, controlling herself a little; "he's so nice . . . there are no difficulties in your way. But Nikolay's my cousin . . . the metropolitan chief priest himself . . . has to . . . or else it's impossible. And so, if mamma's told" (Sonya looked on the countess and addressed her as a mother), "she'll say that I'm spoiling Nikolay's career, that I have no heart, that I'm ungrateful, though really . . . in God's name" (she made the sign of the cross) "I love her so, and all of you, only Vera . . . Why is it? What have I done to her? I am so grateful to you that I would be glad to sacrifice everything for you, but I have nothing. . . ."

Sonya could say no more, and again she buried her head in her hands and the feather-bed. Natasha tried to comfort her, but her face showed that she grasped all the gravity of her friend's trouble.

"Sonya!" she said all at once, as though she had guessed the real cause of her cousin's misery, "of course Vera's been talking to you since dinner? Yes?"

"Yes, these verses Nikolay wrote himself, and I copied some others; and she found them on my table, and said she should show them to mamma, and she said too that I was ungrateful, and that mamma would never allow him to marry me, but that he would marry Julie. You see how he has been with her all day . . . Natasha! why is it?"

And again she sobbed more bitterly than ever. Natasha lifted her up, hugged her, and, smiling through her tears, began comforting her.

"Sonya, don't you believe her, darling; don't believe her. Do you remember how we talked with Nikolay, all three of us together, in the divan-room, do you remember, after supper? Why, we settled how it should all be. I don't quite remember now, but do you remember, it was all right and all possible. Why, uncle Shinshin's brother is married to his first cousin, and we're only second cousins, you know. And Boris said that it's quite easily arranged. You know I told him all about it. He's so clever and so good," said Natasha. . . . "Don't cry, Sonya, darling, sweet one, precious, Sonya," and she kissed her, laughing. "Vera's spiteful; never mind her! and it will all come right and she won't tell mamma. Nikolinka will tell her himself, and he's never thought of Julie."

And she kissed her on the head. Sonya got up, and the kitten revived; its eyes sparkled, and it was ready, it seemed, to wag its tail, spring on its soft paws and begin to play with a ball, in its own natural, kittenish way.

"Do you think so? Really? Truly?" she said rapidly, smoothing her frock and her hair.

"Really, truly," answered Natasha, putting back a stray coil of rough hair on her friend's head; and they both laughed. "Well, come along and sing the 'Spring.'"

"Let's go, then."

"And do you know that fat Pierre, who was sitting opposite me, he's so funny!" Natasha said suddenly, stopping. "I am enjoying myself so," and Natasha ran along the corridor.

Brushing off the feather fluff from her frock, and thrusting the verses into her bodice next her little throat and prominent breast-bones, Sonya ran with flushed face and light, happy steps, following Natasha along the corridor to the divan room. At the request of their guests the young people sang the quartette the "Spring," with which every one was delighted; then Nikolay sang a song he had lately learnt.

> "How sweet in the moon's kindly ray,
> In fancy to thyself to say,
> That earth holds still one dear to thee!
> Whose thoughts, whose dreams are all of thee!
> That her fair fingers as of old
> Stray still upon the harp of gold,
> Making sweet, passionate harmony,
> That to her side doth summon thee!
> To-morrow and thy bliss is near!
> Alas! all's past! she is not here!"

And he had hardly sung the last words when the young people were getting ready to dance in the big hall, and the musicians began stamping with their feet and coughing in the orchestra.

Pierre was sitting in the drawing-room, where Shinshin had started a conversation with him on the political situation, as a subject likely to be of interest to any one who had just come home from abroad, though it did not in fact interest Pierre. Several other persons joined in the conversation. When the orchestra struck up, Natasha walked into the drawing-room, and going straight up to Pierre, laughing and blushing, she said, "Mamma told me to ask you to dance."

"I'm afraid of muddling the figures," said Pierre, "but if you will be my teacher . . ." and he gave his fat hand to the slim little girl, putting his arm low down to reach her level.

While the couples were placing themselves and the musicians were tuning up, Pierre sat down with his little partner. Natasha was perfectly happy; she was dancing with a grown-up person, with a man who had just come from abroad. She was sitting in view of every one and talking to him like a grown-up person. She had in her hand a fan, which some lady had given her to hold, and taking the most modish pose (God knows where and when she had learnt it), fanning herself and smiling all over her face, she talked to her partner.

"What a girl! Just look at her, look at her!" said the old countess, crossing the big hall and pointing to Natasha. Natasha coloured and laughed.

"Why, what do you mean, mamma? Why should you laugh? Is there anything strange about it?"

In the middle of the third écossaise there was a clatter of chairs in the drawing-room, where the count and Marya Dmitryevna were playing, and the greater number of the more honoured guests and elderly people stretching themselves after sitting so long, put their pocket-books and purses in their pockets and came out to the door of the big hall. In front of all came Marya Dmitryevna and the count, both with radiant faces. The count gave his arm, curved into a hoop, to Marya Dmitryevna with playfully exaggerated ceremony, like a ballet-dancer. He drew himself up, and his face beamed with a peculiar, jauntily-knowing smile, and as soon as they had finished dancing the last figure of the écossaise, he clapped his hands to the orchestra, and shouted to the first violin: "Semyon! do you know 'Daniel Cooper'?"

That was the count's favourite dance that he had danced in his youth. (Daniel Cooper was the name of a figure of the anglaise.)

"Look at papa!" Natasha shouted to all the room (entirely forgetting that she was dancing with a grown-up partner), and ducking down till her curly head almost touched her knees, she went off into her ringing laugh that filled the hall. Every one in the hall was, in fact, looking with a smile of delight at the gleeful old gentleman. Standing beside his majestic partner, Marya Dmitryevna, who was taller than he was, he curved his arms, swaying them in time to the music, moved his shoulders, twirled with his legs, lightly tapping with his heels, and with a broadening grin on his round face, prepared the spectators for what was to come. As soon as the orchestra played the gay, irresistible air of Daniel Cooper, somewhat like a livelier Russian *trepak*, all the doorways of the big hall were suddenly filled with the smiling faces of the house-serfs—men on one side, and women on the other—come to look at their master making merry.

"Our little father! An eagle he is!" the old nurse said out loud at one door.

The count danced well and knew that he did, but his partner could not dance at all, and did not care about dancing well. Her portly figure stood erect, with her mighty arms hanging by her side (she had handed her reticule to the countess). It was only her stern, but comely face that danced. What was expressed by the whole round person of the count, was expressed by Marya Dmitryevna in her more and more beaming countenance and puckered nose. While the count, with greater and greater expenditure of energy, enchanted the spectators by the unexpectedness of the nimble pirouettes and capers of his supple legs, Marya Dmitryevna with the slightest effort in the movement of her shoulders or curving of her arms, when they turned or marked the time with their feet, produced no less impression from the contrast, which every one appreciated, with her portliness and her habitual severity of demeanour. The dance grew more and more animated. The *vis-à-vis* could not obtain one moment's attention, and did not attempt to do so. All attention was absorbed by the count and Marya Dmitryevna. Natasha pulled at the sleeve or gown of every one present, urging them to look at papa, though they never took their eyes off the dancers. In the pauses in the dance the count drew a deep breath, waved his hands and shouted to the musician to play faster. More and more quickly, more and more nimbly the count pirouetted, turning now on his toes and now on his heels, round Marya Dmitryevna. At last, twisting his lady round to her place, he executed the last steps, kicking his supple legs up behind him, and bowing his perspiring head and smiling face, with a round sweep of his right arm, amidst a thunder of applause and laughter, in which Natasha's laugh was loudest. Both partners stood still, breathing heavily, and mopping their faces with their batiste handkerchiefs.

"That's how they used to dance in our day, *ma chère*," said the count.

"Bravo, Daniel Cooper!" said Marya Dmitryevna, tucking up her sleeves and drawing a deep, prolonged breath.

XVIII

WHILE in the Rostovs' hall they were dancing the sixth anglaise, while the weary orchestra played wrong notes, and the tired footmen and cooks were getting the supper, Count Bezuhov had just had his sixth stroke. The doctors declared that there was no hope of recovery; the sick man received absolution and the sacrament while unconscious. Preparations were being made for administering extreme unction, and the house was full of the bustle and thrill of suspense usual at such moments. Outside the house undertakers were crowding beyond the gates, trying to escape the notice of the carriages that drove up, but eagerly anticipating a good order for the count's funeral. The governor of Moscow, who had been constantly sending his adjutants to inquire after the count's condition, came himself that evening to say good-bye to the renowned grandee of Catherine's court, Count Bezuhov.

The magnificent reception-room was full. Every one stood up respectfully when the governor, after being half an hour alone with the sick man, came out of the sick-room. Bestowing scanty recognition on the bows with which he was received, he tried to escape as quickly as possible from the gaze of the doctors, ecclesiastical personages, and relations. Prince Vassily, who had grown paler and thinner during the last few days, escorted the governor out, and softly repeated something to him several times over.

After seeing the governor, Prince Vassily sat down on a chair in the hall alone, crossing one leg high over the other, leaning his elbow on his knee, and covering his eyes with his hand. After sitting so for some time he got up, and with steps more hurried than his wont, he crossed the long corridor, looking round him with frightened eyes, and went to the back part of the house to the apartments of the eldest princess.

The persons he had left in the dimly lighted reception-room, next to the sick-room, talked in broken whispers among themselves, pausing, and looking round with eyes full of suspense and inquiry whenever the door that led into the dying man's room creaked as some one went in or came out.

"Man's limitation," said a little man, an ecclesiastic of some sort, to a lady, who was sitting near him listening naïvely to his words—"his limitation is fixed, there is no overstepping it."

"I wonder if it won't be late for extreme unction?" inquired the lady, using his clerical title, and apparently having no opinion of her own on the matter.

"It is a great mystery, ma'am," answered the clerk, passing his hands over his bald head, on which lay a few tresses of carefully combed, half grey hair.

"Who was that? was it the governor himself?" they were asking at the other end of the room. "What a young-looking man!"

"And he's over sixty! . . . What, do they say, the count does not know any one? Do they mean to give extreme unction?"

"I knew a man who received extreme unction seven times."

The second princess came out of the sick-room with tearful eyes, and sat down beside Doctor Lorrain, who was sitting in a graceful pose under the portrait of Catherine, with his elbow on the table.

"Very fine," said the doctor in reply to a question about the weather; "very fine, princess, and besides, at Moscow, one might suppose oneself in the country."

"Might one not?" said the princess, sighing. "So may he have something to drink?" Lorrain thought a moment.

"He has taken his medicine?"

"Yes."

The doctor looked at his memoranda.

"Take a glass of boiled water and put in a pinch" (he showed with his delicate fingers what was meant by a pinch) "of cream of tartar."

"There has never been a case," said the German doctor to the adjutant, speaking broken Russian, "of recovery after having a third stroke."

"And what a vigorous man he was!" said the adjutant. "And to whom will this great wealth go?" he added in a whisper.

"Candidates will be found," the German replied, smiling. Every one looked round again at the door; it creaked, and the second princess having made the drink according to Lorrain's direction, carried it into the sick-room. The German doctor went up to Lorrain.

"Can it drag on till to-morrow morning?" asked the German, with a vile French accent.

Lorrain, with compressed lips and a stern face, moved his finger before his nose to express a negative.

"To-night, not later," he said softly, and with a decorous smile of satisfaction at being able to understand and to express the exact position of the sick man, he walked away.

Meanwhile Prince Vassily had opened the door of the princess's room.

It was half dark in the room; there were only two lamps burning before the holy pictures, and there was a sweet perfume of incense and flowers. The whole room was furnished with miniature furniture, little sideboards, small bookcases, and small tables. Behind a screen could be seen the white coverings of a high feather-bed. A little dog barked.

"Ah, is that you, *mon cousin?*"

She got up and smoothed her hair, which was always, even now, so extraordinarily smooth that it seemed as though made out of one piece with her head and covered with varnish.

"Has anything happened?" she asked. "I am in continual dread."

"Nothing, everything is unchanged. I have only come to have a little talk with you, Katish, about business," said the prince, sitting down wearily in the low chair from which she had just risen. "How warm it is here, though," he said. "Come, sit here; let us talk."

"I wondered whether anything had happened," said the princess, and with her stonily severe expression unchanged, she sat down opposite the prince, preparing herself to listen. "I have been trying to get some sleep, *mon cousin*, but I can't."

"Well, my dear?" said Prince Vassily, taking the princess's hand, and bending it downwards as his habit was.

It was plain that this "well?" referred to much that they both comprehended without mentioning it in words.

The princess, with her spare, upright figure, so disproportionately long in the body, looked straight at the prince with no sign of emotion in her prominent grey eyes. She shook her head, and sighing looked towards the holy pictures. Her gesture might have been interpreted as an expression of grief and devotion, or as an expression of weariness and the hope of a speedy release. Prince Vassily took it as an expression of weariness.

"And do you suppose it's any easier for me?" he said. "I am as worn out as a post horse. I must have a little talk with you, Katish, and a very serious one."

Prince Vassily paused, and his cheeks began twitching nervously, first on one side, then on the other, giving his face an unpleasant expression such as was never seen on his countenance when he was in drawingrooms. His eyes, too, were different from usual: at one moment they stared with a sort of insolent jocoseness, at the next they looked round furtively.

The princess, pulling her dog on her lap with her thin, dry hands, gazed intently at the eyes of Prince Vassily, but it was evident that she would not break the silence, if she had to sit silent till morning.

"You see, my dear princess and cousin, Katerina Semyonovna," pursued Prince Vassily, obviously with some inner conflict bracing himself to go on with what he wanted to say, "at such moments as the present, one has to think of everything. One must think of the future, of you . . . I care for all of you as if you were my own children; you know that."

The princess looked at him with the same dull immovable gaze.

"Finally, we have to think of my family too," continued Prince Vassily, angrily pushing away a little table and not looking at her: "you know, Katish, that you three Mamontov sisters and my wife,—we are the only direct heirs of the count. I know, I know how painful it is for you to speak and think of such things. And it's as hard for me; but, my dear, I am a man over fifty, I must be ready for anything. Do you know that I have sent for Pierre, and that the count, pointing straight at his portrait, has asked for him?"

Prince Vassily looked inquiringly at the princess, but he could not make out whether she was considering what he had said, or was simply staring at him.

"I pray to God for one thing only continually, *mon cousin,*" she replied, "that He may have mercy upon him, and allow his noble soul to leave this . . ."

"Yes, quite so," Prince Vassily continued impatiently, rubbing his bald head and again wrathfully moving the table towards him that he had just moved away, "but in fact . . . in fact the point is, as you are yourself aware, that last winter the count made a will by which, passing over his direct heirs and us, he bequeathed all his property to Pierre."

"He may have made ever so many wills!" the princess said placidly; "but he can't leave it to Pierre. Pierre is illegitimate."

"*Ma chère,*" said Prince Vassily suddenly, pushing the table against him, growing more earnest and beginning to speak more rapidly: "but what if a letter has been written to the Emperor, and the count has petitioned him to legitimise Pierre? You understand, that the count's services would make his petition carry weight . . ."

The princess smiled, as people smile who believe that they know much more about the subject than those with whom they are talking.

"I can say more," Prince Vassily went on, clasping her hand; "that letter has been written, though it has not been sent off, and the Emperor has heard about it. The question only is whether it has been destroyed or not. If not, as soon as all is over," Prince Vassily sighed, giving her thereby to understand what he meant precisely by the words "all is over," "and they open the count's papers, the will with the letter will be given to the Emperor, and his petition will certainly be granted. Pierre, as the legitimate son, will receive everything."

"What about our share?" the princess inquired, smiling ironically as though anything but that might happen.

"Why, my poor Katish, it is as clear as daylight. He will then be the only legal heir of all, and you won't receive as much as this, see. You ought to know, my dear, whether the will and the petition were written, and whether they have been destroyed, and if they have somehow been overlooked, then you ought to know where they are and to find them, because . . ."

"That would be rather too much!" the princess interrupted him, smiling sardonically, with no change in the expression of her eyes. "I am a woman, and you think we are all silly; but I do know so much, that an illegitimate son can't inherit . . . *Un bâtard*," she added, supposing that by this translation of the word she was conclusively proving to the prince the groundlessness of his contention.

"How can you not understand, Katish, really! You are so intelligent; how is it you don't understand that if the count has written a letter to the Emperor, begging him to recognise his son as legitimate, then Pierre will not be Pierre but Count Bezuhov, and then he will inherit everything under the will? And if the will and the letter have not been destroyed, then except the consolation of having been dutiful and of all that results from having done your duty, nothing is left for you. That's the fact."

"I know that the will was made, but I know, too, that it is invalid, and you seem to take me for a perfect fool, *mon cousin*," said the princess, with the air with which women speak when they imagine they are saying something witty and biting.

"My dear princess, Katerina Semyonovna!" Prince Vassily began impatiently, "I have come to you not to provoke you, but to talk to you as a kinswoman, a good, kind-hearted, true kinswoman, of your own interests. I tell you for the tenth time that if the letter to the Emperor and the will in Pierre's favour are among the count's papers, you, my dear girl, and your sisters are not heiresses. If you don't believe me, believe people who know; I have just been talking to Dmitry Onufritch" (this was the family solicitor); "he said the same."

There was obviously some sudden change in the princess's ideas; her thin lips turned white (her eyes did not change), and when she began to speak, her voice passed through transitions, which she clearly did not herself anticipate.

"That would be a pretty thing," she said. "I wanted nothing, and I want nothing." She flung her dog off her lap and smoothed out the folds of her skirt.

"That's the gratitude, that's the recognition people get who have sacrificed everything for him," she said. "Very nice! Excellent! I don't want anything, prince."

"Yes, but you are not alone, you have sisters," answered Prince Vassily. But the princess did not heed him.

"Yes, I knew it long ago, but I'd forgotten that I could expect nothing in this house but baseness, deceit, envy, scheming, nothing but ingratitude, the blackest ingratitude . . ."

"Do you or do you not know where that will is?" asked Prince Vassily, the twitching of his cheeks more marked than ever.

"Yes, I have been foolish; I still kept faith in people, and cared for them and sacrificed myself. But no one succeeds except those who are base and vile. I know whose plotting this is."

The princess would have risen, but the prince held her by the arm. The princess had the air of a person who has suddenly lost faith in the whole human race. She looked viciously at her companion.

"There is still time, my dear. Remember, Katish, that all this was done heedlessly, in a moment of anger, of illness, and then forgotten. Our duty, my dear girl, is to correct his mistake, to soften his last moments by not letting him commit this injustice, not letting him die with the thought that he has made miserable those . . ."

"Those who have sacrificed everything for him," the princess caught him up; and she made an impulsive effort again to stand up, but the prince would not let her, "a sacrifice he has never known how to appreciate. No, *mon cousin*," she added, with a sigh, "I will remember that one can expect no reward in this world, that in this world there is no honour, no justice. Cunning and wickedness is what one wants in this world."

"Come, *voyons*, calm yourself; I know your noble heart."

"No, I have a wicked heart."

"I know your heart," repeated the prince. "I value your affection, and I could wish you had the same opinion of me. Calm yourself and let us talk sensibly while there is time—perhaps twenty-four hours, perhaps one. Tell me all you know about the will, and what's of most consequence, where it is; you must know. We will take it now at once and show it to the count. He has no doubt forgotten about it and would wish to destroy it. You understand that my desire is to carry out his wishes religiously. That is what I came here for. I am only here to be of use to him and to you."

"Now I see it all. I know whose plotting this is. I know," the princess was saying.

"That's not the point, my dear."

"It's all your precious Anna Mihalovna, your *protégée* whom I wouldn't take as a housemaid, the nasty creature."

"Do not let us waste time."

"Oh, don't talk to me! Last winter she forced her way in here and told such a pack of vile, mean tales to the count about all of us, especially Sophie—I can't repeat them—that it made the count ill, and he wouldn't see us for a fortnight. It was at that time, I know, he wrote that hateful, infamous document, but I thought it was of no consequence."

"There we are. Why didn't you tell us about it before?"

"It's in the inlaid portfolio that he keeps under his pillow. Now I know," said the princess, making no reply. "Yes, if I have a sin to my account, a great sin, it's my hatred of that infamous woman," almost shrieked the princess, utterly transformed. "And why does she force herself in here? But I'll have it out with her. The time will come!"

XIX

At the time that these conversations were taking place in the reception-room and the princess's room, a carriage with Pierre (who had been sent for) and Anna Mihalovna (who had thought fit to come with him) in it was driving into the court of Count Bezuhov's mansion. When the sound of the carriage wheels was muffled by the straw in the street, Anna Mihalovna turned with words of consolation to her companion, discovered that he was asleep in his corner of the carriage, and waked him up. Rousing himself, Pierre followed Anna Mihalovna out of the carriage, and only then began to think of the interview with his dying father that awaited him. He noticed that they had driven not up to the visitors' approach, but to the back entrance. As he got down from the carriage step, two men in the dress of tradesmen hastily scurried away from the entrance into the shadow of the wall. Pierre, as he stood waiting, noticed several other similar persons standing in the shadow of the house on both sides. But neither Anna Mihalovna nor the footman and coachman, who must have seen these people, took any notice of them. So it must be all right, Pierre decided, and he followed Anna Mihalovna. With hurrying footsteps Anna Mihalovna walked up the dimly lighted, narrow stone staircase, urging on Pierre, who lagged behind. Though Pierre had no notion why he had to go to the count at all, and still less why he had to go by the back stairs, yet, impressed by Anna Mihalovna's assurance and haste, he made up his mind that it was undoubtedly necessary for him to do so. Half-way up the stairs they were almost knocked over by some men with pails, who ran down towards them, tramping loudly with their big boots. These men huddled up against the wall to let Pierre and Anna Mihalovna pass, and showed not the slightest surprise at seeing them.

"Is this the princess's side of the house?" Anna Mihalovna asked of one of them . . .

"Yes, it is," answered the footman in a bold, loud voice, as though anything were permissible at such a time; "the door on the left, ma'am."

"Perhaps the count has not asked for me," said Pierre, as he reached the landing. "I had better go to my own room." Anna Mihalovna stopped for Pierre to catch her up.

"*Ah, mon ami*," she said, touching his hand with just the same gesture as she had used in the morning with her son. "Believe me, I am suffering as much as you; but be a man."

"Really, had I not better go?" Pierre asked affectionately, looking at her over his spectacles.

"Ah, *mon ami*, forget the wrong that may have been done you, think that it is your father . . . and perhaps in his death agony," she sighed. "I have loved you like a son from the first. Trust in me, Pierre. I shall not forget your interests."

Pierre did not understand a word. Again he felt more strongly than before that all this had to be so, and he obediently followed Anna Mihal-ovna, who was already opening the door. The door led into the vestibule of the back stairs. In the corner sat the princess's old man-servant knit-ting stockings. Pierre had never been in this part of the house, and had not even suspected the existence of these apartments. A maid-servant carrying a tray with a decanter overtook them, and Anna Mihalovna (calling her "my dear" and "my good girl") asked her after the prin-cesses' health, and drew Pierre further along the stone corridor. The first door to the left led out of the corridor into the princesses' living rooms. The maid with the decanter was in a hurry (everything seemed to be done in a hurry at that moment in the house), and she did not close the door after her. Pierre and Anna Mihalovna, as they passed by, glanced unconsciously into the room where the eldest princess and Prince Vassily were sitting close together talking. On catching sight of their passing fig-ures, Prince Vassily made an impatient movement and drew back, the princess jumped up, and with a despairing gesture she closed the door, slamming it with all her might. This action was so unlike the princess's habitual composure, the dismay depicted on the countenance of Prince Vassily was so out of keeping with his dignity, that Pierre stopped short and looked inquiringly over his spectacles at his guide. Anna Mihalovna manifested no surprise; she simply smiled a little and sighed, as though to show that she had anticipated all that.

"Be a man, *mon ami,* I am looking after your interests," she said in response to his look of inquiry, and she walked more quickly along the corridor.

Pierre had no notion what was going on, and no inkling of what was meant by watching over his interests. But he felt that all this had had to be so. From the corridor they went into the half-lighted hall adjoining the count's reception-room. This was one of the cold, sumptuously fur-nished rooms which Pierre knew, leading from the visitors' staircase. But even in this apartment there was an empty bath standing in the middle of the floor, and water had been spilt on the carpet. They were met here by a servant and a church attendant with a censer, who walked on tiptoe and took no notice of them. They went into the reception-room opening into the winter garden, a room Pierre knew well, with its two Italian windows, its big bust and full-length portrait of Catherine. The same persons were all sitting almost in the same positions exchanging whispers in the reception-room. All ceased speaking and looked round at Anna Mihalovna, as she came in with her pale, tear-stained face, and at the big, stout figure of Pierre, as with downcast head he followed her sub-missively.

The countenance of Anna Mihalovna showed a consciousness that the crucial moment had arrived. With the air of a Petersburg lady of ex-perience, she walked into the room even more boldly than in the morn-ing, keeping Pierre at her side. She felt that as she was bringing the per-son the dying man wanted to see, she might feel secure as to her recep-tion. With a rapid glance, scanning all the persons in the room, and ob-serving the count's spiritual adviser, she did not precisely bow down,

but seemed somehow suddenly to shrink in stature, and with a tripping
amble swam up to the priest and reverentially received a blessing first
from one and then from another ecclesiastic.

"Thank God that we are in time," she said to the priest; "all of us,
his kinsfolk, have been in such alarm. This young man is the count's
son," she added more softly, "It is a terrible moment."

Having uttered these words she approached the doctor.

"Dear doctor," she said to him, "this young man is the count's son. Is
there any hope?"

The doctor did not speak but rapidly shrugged his shoulders and
turned up his eyes. With precisely the same gesture Anna Mihalovna
moved her shoulders and eyes, almost closing her eyelids, sighed and
went away from the doctor to Pierre. She addressed Pierre with peculiar
deference and tender melancholy.

"Have faith in His mercy," she said to him, and indicating a sofa for
him to sit down and wait for her, she went herself with inaudible steps
towards the door, at which every one was looking, and after almost
noiselessly opening it, she vanished behind it.

Pierre, having decided to obey his monitress in everything, moved
towards the sofa she had pointed out to him. As soon as Anna Mihalovna
had disappeared, he noticed that the eyes of all the persons in the room
were fixed upon him with something more than curiosity and sympathy
in their gaze. He noticed that they were all whispering together, looking
towards him with something like awe and even obsequious deference.
They showed him a respect such as had never been shown him before.
A lady, a stranger to him, the one who had been talking to the priest,
got up and offered him her place. An adjutant picked up the glove Pierre
had dropped and handed it to him. The doctors respectfully paused in
their talk when he passed by them and moved aside to make way for
him. Pierre wanted at first to sit somewhere else, so as not to trouble
the lady; he would have liked to pick up the glove himself and to walk
round the doctors, who were really not at all in the way. But he felt all
at once that to do so would be improper; he felt that he was that night
a person who had to go through a terrible ceremony which every one
expected of him, and that for that reason he was bound to accept service
from every one. He took the glove from the adjutant in silence, sat down
in the lady's place, laying his big hands on his knees, sitting in the
naïvely symmetrical pose of an Egyptian statue, and decided mentally
that it must all inevitably be like this, and that to avoid losing his head
and doing something stupid, he must for that evening not act on his own
ideas, but abandon himself wholly to the will of those who were guiding
him.

Two minutes had not elapsed before Prince Vassily came majestically
into the room, wearing his coat with three stars on it, and carrying his
head high. He looked as though he had grown thinner since the morning.
His eyes seemed larger than usual as he glanced round the room, and
caught sight of Pierre. He went up to him, took his hand (a thing he had

never done before), and drew it downwards, as though he wanted to try its strength.

"Courage, courage, *mon ami*. He has asked to see you, that is well . . ." and he would have gone on, but Pierre thought it fitting to ask: "How is . . . ?" He hesitated, not knowing whether it was proper for him to call the dying man "the count"; he felt ashamed to call him "father."

"He has had another stroke half-an-hour ago. Courage, *mon ami*."

Pierre was in a condition of such mental confusion that the word stroke aroused in his mind the idea of a blow from some heavy body. He looked in perplexity at Prince Vassily, and only later grasped that an attack of illness was called a stroke. Prince Vassily said a few words to Lorrain as he passed and went to the door on tiptoe. He could not walk easily on tiptoe, and jerked his whole person up and down in an ungainly fashion. He was followed by the eldest princess, then by the clergy and church attendants; some servants too went in at the door. Through that door a stir could be heard, and at last Anna Mihalovna, with a face still pale but resolute in the performance of duty, ran out and, touching Pierre on the arm, said:

"The goodness of heaven is inexhaustible; it is the ceremony of extreme unction which they are beginning. Come."

Pierre went in, stepping on to the soft carpet, and noticed that the adjutant and the unknown lady and some servants too, all followed him in, as though there were no need now to ask permission to enter that room.

XX

PIERRE KNEW well that great room, divided by columns and an arch, and carpeted with Persian rugs. The part of the room behind the columns, where on one side there stood a high mahogany bedstead with silken hangings, and on the other a huge case of holy pictures, was brightly and decoratively lighted up, as churches are lighted for evening service. Under the gleaming ornamentation of the case stood a long invalid chair, and in the chair, on snow-white, uncrumpled, freshly changed pillows, covered to the waist with a bright green quilt, Pierre recognised the majestic figure of his father, Count Bezuhov, with the grey shock of hair like a lion's mane over his broad forehead, and the characteristically aristocratic, deep lines on his handsome, reddish-yellow face. He was lying directly under the holy pictures: both his great stout arms were lying on the quilt. In his right hand, which lay with the palm downwards, a wax candle had been thrust between the thumb and forefinger, and an old servant bending down over the chair held it in it. About the chair stood the clergy in their shining ceremonial vestments, with their long hair pulled out over them. They held lighted candles in their hands, and were performing the service with deliberate solemnity. A little behind them stood the two younger princesses holding handkerchiefs to their eyes, and in front of them the eldest, Katish, stood with a vindictive and determined air, never for an instant taking her eyes off the holy image, as though she were declaring to all that she would not answer for herself, if she were to look around. Anna Mihalovna with a countenance of meek sorrow and forgiveness stood at the door with the unknown lady. Prince Vassily was standing close to the invalid chair on the other side of the door. He had drawn a carved, velvet chair up to him, and was leaning on the back of it with his left hand, in which he held a candle, while with his right he crossed himself, turning his eyes upwards every time as he put his finger to his forehead. His face expressed quiet piety and submission to the will of God. 'If you don't understand such feelings, so much the worse for you,' his face seemed to say.

Behind him stood the adjutant, the doctors, and the men-servants; the men and the women had separated as though they were in church. All were silently crossing themselves, nothing was audible but the reading of the service, the subdued, deep bass singing, and in the intervals of silence sighs could be heard and the shuffling of feet. With a significant air, which showed she knew what she was about, Anna Mihalovna walked right across the room to Pierre and gave him a candle. He lighted it, and absorbed in watching the people around him, he absent-mindedly crossed himself with the hand in which he held the candle. The youngest princess, Sophie, the rosy, laughing one with the mole, was looking at him. She smiled, hid her face in her handkerchief, and for a long while did not uncover it. But looking at Pierre again, again she laughed. She was apparently unable to look at him without laughing, but could not resist looking at him, and to be out of temptation, she softly moved behind a column. In the middle of the service the voices of the priests suddenly ceased, and they whispered something to one another. The old servant, who was holding the count's hand, got up and turned to the ladies. Anna Mihalovna stepped forward and, stooping over the sick man, she beckoned behind her back to Lorrain. The French doctor had been leaning against the column without a candle, in the respectful attitude of the foreigner, who would show that in spite of the difference of religion he comprehends all the solemnity of the ceremony and even approves of it. With the noiseless steps of a man in full vigour of his age, he went up to the sick man. His delicate, white fingers lifted his disengaged hand from the quilt, and turning away, the doctor began feeling the pulse in absorbed attention. They gave the sick man some drink; there was a slight bustle around him, then all went back to their places and the service was continued. During this break in the proceedings Pierre noticed that Prince Vassily moved away from his chair-back, and with that same air of being quite sure of what he was about, and of its being so much the worse for others, if they failed to understand it, he did not go up to the sick man, but passed by him and joined the eldest princess. Then together they went away to the further end of the room to the high bedstead under the silk canopy. When they moved away from the bed the prince and princess disappeared together by the further door, but before the end of the service they returned one after the other to their places Pierre paid no more attention to this circumstance than to all the rest, having once for all made up his mind that all that he saw taking place that evening must inevitably be as it was.

The sounds of the church singing ceased and the voice of the chief ecclesiastic was heard, respectfully congratulating the sick man on his reception of the mystery. The dying man lay as lifeless and immovable as before. Every one was moving about him, there was the sound of footsteps and of whispers, Anna Mihalovna's whisper rising above the rest.

Pierre heard her say: "Undoubtedly he must be moved on to the bed; it's impossible . . ."

The sick man was so surrounded by the doctors, the princesses and the servants, that Pierre could no longer see the reddish-yellow face with the grey mane, which he had never lost sight of for one instant during the ceremony, even though he had been watching other people too. Pierre guessed from the cautious movements of the people about the chair that they were lifting the dying man up and moving him.

"Hold on to my arm; you'll drop him so," he heard the frightened whisper of one of the servants. "Lower down . . . another one here," said voices. And their heavy breathing and hurried tread seemed to show that the weight they carried was too heavy for them.

As they passed him—Anna Mihalovna among them—the young man caught a glimpse over people's backs and necks of the great muscular open chest, the grey, curly, leonine head, and the massive shoulders of the sick man, which were pushed up, as he was supported under the armpits. His head, with its extraordinarily broad brow and cheek-bones, its beautiful sensual mouth, and haughty, cold eyes, was not disfigured by the proximity of death. It was just the same as Pierre had seen it three months before, when his father had been sending him off to Petersburg. But the head swayed helplessly with the jerky steps of the bearers, and the cold, apathetic eyes did not know on what to rest.

They were busy for several minutes round the high bed; then the people, who had moved the count, dispersed. Anna Mihalovna touched Pierre's arm and said, "Come along." With her Pierre approached the bed, on which the sick man had been laid in a ceremonial position in keeping with the sacred rite that had just been performed. He was lying with his head propped high on the pillows. His hands were laid symmetrically on the green silk quilt with the palms turned downwards. When Pierre came up, the count looked straight at him, but he looked at him with a gaze the intent and significance of which no man could fathom. Either these eyes said nothing, but simply looked because as eyes they must look at something, or they said too much. Pierre stopped, not knowing what he was to do, and looked inquiringly at his monitress. Anna Mihalovna gave him a hurried glance, with a gesture indicating the sick man's hand and with her lips wafting towards it a phantom kiss. Pierre did as he was bid, and carefully craning his neck to avoid entanglement with the quilt, kissed the broad-boned, muscular hand. There was not the faintest stir in the hand, nor in any muscle of the count's face. Pierre again looked inquiringly at Anna Mihalovna to learn what he was to do now. Anna Mihalovna glanced towards the armchair that stood beside the bed. Pierre proceeded obediently to sit down there, his eyes still inquiring whether he had done the right thing. Anna Mihalovna nodded approvingly. Again Pierre fell into the naïvely symmetrical pose of an Egyptian statue, obviously distressed that his ungainly person took up so much room, and doing his utmost to look as small as possible. He looked at the count. The count still gazed at the spot where Pierre's face had been, when he was standing up. Anna Mihalovna's attitude evinced her consciousness of the touching gravity of this last meeting between father and son. It lasted for two minutes, which seemed to Pierre an hour. Suddenly a shudder passed over the thick muscles and furrows of the count's face. The shudder grew more intense; the beautiful mouth was contorted (it was only then that Pierre grasped how near death his father was) and from the contorted mouth there came a husky, muffled sound. Anna Mihalovna looked intently at the sick man's mouth, and trying to guess what he wanted, pointed first to Pierre, then to some drink, then in an inquiring whisper she mentioned the name of Prince Vassily, then pointed to the quilt. The eyes and face of the sick man showed impatience. He made an effort to glance at the servant, who never moved away from the head of his bed.

"His excellency wants to be turned over on the other side," whispered the servant, and he got up to turn the heavy body of the count facing the wall.

Pierre stood up to help the servant.

While the count was being turned over, one of his arms dragged helplessly behind, and he made a vain effort to pull it after him. Whether the count noticed the face of horror with which Pierre looked at that lifeless arm, or whether some other idea passed through his dying brain, he looked at the refractory arm, at the expression of horror on Pierre's face, again at his arm, and a smile came on his face, strangely out of keeping with its features; a weak, suffering smile, which seemed mocking at his own helplessness. Suddenly, at the sight of that smile, Pierre felt a lump in his throat and a tickling in his nose, and tears dimmed his eyes. The sick man was turned towards the wall. He sighed.

"He has fallen into a doze," said Anna Mihalovna, noticing the princess coming to take her turn by the bedside. "Let us go."

Pierre went out.

XXI

THERE WAS by now no one in the reception-room except Prince Vassily and the eldest princess, who were in eager conversation together, sitting under the portrait of Catherine. They were mute at once on seeing Pierre and his companion, and the princess concealed something as Pierre fancied and murmured: "I can't stand the sight of that woman."

"Katish has had tea served in the little drawing-room," Prince Vassily said to Anna Mihalovna. "Go, my poor Anna Mihalovna, take something or you will not hold out."

To Pierre he said nothing; he simply pressed his arm sympathetically. Pierre and Anna Mihalovna went on into the little drawing-room.

"There is nothing so reviving as a cup of this excellent Russian tea, after a sleepless night," said Lorrain with an air of restrained briskness, sipping it out of a delicate china cup without a handle, as he stood in the little circular drawing-room close to a table laid with tea-things and cold supper-dishes. All who were in Count Bezuhov's house on that night had, with a view to fortifying themselves, gathered around the table. Pierre remembered well that little circular drawing-room with its mirrors and little tables. When there had been balls in the count's house, Pierre, who could not dance, had liked sitting in that little room full of mirrors, watching the ladies in ball-dresses with pearls and diamonds on their bare shoulders, as they crossed that room and looked at themselves in the brightly lighted mirrors that repeated their reflections several times. Now the same room was dimly lighted with two candles, and in the middle of the night the tea-set and supper-dishes stood in disorder on one of the little tables, and heterogeneous, plainly dressed persons were sitting at it, whispering together, and showing in every word that no one could forget what was passing at that moment and what was still to come in the bedroom. Pierre did not eat anything, though he felt very much inclined to. He looked round inquiringly towards his monitress, and perceived that she had gone out again on tiptoe into the reception-room where Prince Vassily had remained with the eldest princess. Pierre supposed that this too was an inevitable part of the proceedings, and, after a little delay, he followed her. Anna Mihalovna was standing beside the princess, and they were both talking at once in excited tones.

"Allow me, madam, to know what is and what is not to be done," said the princess, who was apparently in the same exasperated temper as she had been when she slammed the door of her room.

"But, dear princess," Anna Mihalovna was saying mildly and persuasively, blocking up the way towards the bedroom and not letting the princess pass. "Would that not be too great a tax on poor uncle at such a moment, when he needs repose? At such moments to talk of worldly matters when his soul is already prepared . . ."

Prince Vassily was sitting in a low chair in his habitual attitude, with one leg crossed high above the other. His cheeks were twitching violently, and when they relaxed, they looked heavier below; but he wore the air of a man little interested in the two ladies' discussion.

"No, my dear Anna Mihalovna, let Katish act on her own discretion. You know how the count loves her."

"I don't even know what is in this document," said the princess, addressing Prince Vassily, and pointing to the inlaid portfolio which she held in her hand. "All I know is that the real will is in the bureau, and this is a paper that has been forgotten. . . ."

She tried to get round Anna Mihalovna, but the latter, with another little skip, barred her way again.

"I know, dear, sweet princess," said Anna Mihalovna, taking hold of the portfolio, and so firmly that it was clear she would not readily let go of it again. "Dear princess, I beg you, I beseech you, spare him. I entreat you."

The princess did not speak. All that was heard was the sound of a scuffle over the portfolio. There could be no doubt that if she were to speak, she would say nothing complimentary to Anna Mihalovna. The latter kept a tight grip, but in spite of that her voice retained all its sweet gravity and softness.

"Pierre, come here, my dear boy. He will not be one too many, I should imagine, in a family council; eh, prince?"

"Why don't you speak, *mon cousin?*" the princess shrieked all of a sudden, so loudly that they heard her voice, and were alarmed by it in the drawing-room. "Why don't you speak when here a meddling outsider takes upon herself to interfere, and make a scene on the very threshold of a dying man's room? Scheming creature," she muttered viciously, and tugged at the portfolio with all her might, but Anna Mihalovna took a few steps forward so as not to lose her grasp of it and changed hands.

"Ah," said Prince Vassily, in reproachful wonder. He got up. "It is ridiculous. Come, let go. I tell you." The princess let go.

"And you."

Anna Mihalovna did not heed him.

"Let go, I tell you. I will take it all upon myself. I will go and ask him. I . . . you let it alone."

"But, prince," said Anna Mihalovna, "after this solemn sacrament, let him have a moment's peace. Here, Pierre, tell me your opinion," she turned to the young man, who going up to them was staring in surprise at the exasperated face of the princess, which had thrown off all appearance of decorum, and the twitching cheeks of Prince Vassily.

"Remember that you will have to answer for all the consequences," said Prince Vassily sternly; "you don't know what you are doing."

"Infamous woman," shrieked the princess, suddenly pouncing on Anna Mihalovna and tearing the portfolio from her. Prince Vassily bowed his head and flung up his hands.

At that instant the door, the dreadful door at which Pierre had gazed so long, and which had opened so softly, was flung rapidly, noisily open, banging against the wall, and the second princess ran out wringing her hands.

"What are you about?" she said, in despair. "He is passing away, and you leave me alone."

The eldest princess dropped the portfolio. Swiftly Anna Mihalovna stooped and, snatching up the object of dispute, ran into the bedroom. The eldest princess and Prince Vassily recovering themselves followed her. A few minutes later the eldest princess came out again with a pale, dry face, biting her underlip. At the sight of Pierre her face expressed irrepressible hatred.

"Yes, now you can give yourself airs," she said, "you have got what you wanted." And breaking into sobs, she hid her face in her handkerchief and ran out of the room.

The next to emerge was Prince Vassily. He staggered to the sofa, on which Pierre was sitting, and sank on to it, covering his eyes with his hand. Pierre noticed that he was pale, and that his lower jaw was quivering and working as though in ague.

"Ah, my dear boy," he said, taking Pierre by the elbow—and there was a sincerity and a weakness in his voice that Pierre had never observed in him before—"what sins, what frauds we commit, and all for what? I'm over fifty, my dear boy. . . . I too. . . . It all ends in death, all. Death is awful." He burst into tears.

Anna Mihalovna was the last to come out. She approached Pierre with soft, deliberate steps. "Pierre," she said. Pierre looked inquiringly at her. She kissed the young man on the forehead, wetting him with her tears. She did not speak for a while.

"He is no more. . . ."

Pierre gazed at her over his spectacles.

"Come. I will take you back. Try to cry. Nothing relieves like tears."

She led him into the dark drawing-room, and Pierre was glad that no one could see his face. Anna Mihalovna left him, and when she came back he was fast asleep with his arm under his head.

The next morning Anna Mihalovna said to Pierre: "Yes, my dear boy, it is a great loss for us all. I do not speak of you. But God will uphold you; you are young, and now you are at the head of an immense fortune, I hope. The will has not been opened yet. I know you well enough to know that this will not turn your head, but it will impose duties upon you and you must be a man."

Pierre did not speak.

"Perhaps, later, I may tell you, my dear boy, that if I had not been there God knows what would have happened. You know, my uncle promised me, only the day before yesterday, not to forget Boris. But he had no time. I hope, dear friend, that you will fulfil your father's desire."

Pierre did not understand a word, and colouring shyly, looked dumbly at Anna Mihalovna. After talking to him, Anna Mihalovna drove to the Rostovs', and went to bed. On waking in the morning, she told the Rostovs and all her acquaintances the details of Count Bezuhov's death. She said that the count had died, as she would wish to die herself, that his end had been not simply touching, but edifying; that the last interview of the father and son had been so touching that she could not recall it without tears; and that she did not know which had behaved more nobly in those terrible moments: the father, who had remembered everything and every one so well at the last, and had said such moving words to his son; or Pierre, whom it was heartbreaking to see, so utterly crushed was he, though he yet tried to conceal his grief, so as not to distress his dying father. "It is painful, but it does one good; it uplifts the soul to see such men as the old count and his worthy son," she said. She told them about the action of the princess and Prince Vassily too, but in great secrecy, in whispers, and with disapproval.

XXII

AT BLEAK HILLS, the estate of Prince Nikolay Andreivitch Bolkonsky, the arrival of young Prince Andrey and his wife was daily expected. But this expectation did not disturb the regular routine in which life moved in the old prince's household. Prince Nikolay Andreivitch, once a commander-in-chief, known in the fashionable world by the nickname of "the Prussian king," had been exiled to his estate in the reign of Paul, and had remained at Bleak Hills ever since with his daughter, Princess Marya, and her companion, Mademoiselle Bourienne. Even in the new reign, though he had received permission to return to the capital, he had never left his home in the country, saying that if any one wanted to see him, he could travel the hundred and fifty versts from Moscow to Bleak Hills, and, for his part, he wanted nobody and nothing. He used to maintain that human vices all sprang from only two sources—idleness and superstition, and that there were but two virtues—energy and intelligence. He had himself undertaken the education of his daughter; and to develop in her these important qualities, he continued giving her lessons in algebra and geometry up to her twentieth year, and mapped out her whole life in uninterrupted occupation. He was himself always occupied in writing his memoirs, working out problems in higher mathematics, turning snuff-boxes on his lathe, working in his garden, or looking after the erection of farm buildings which were always being built on his estate. Since the great thing for enabling one to get through work is regularity, he had carried regularity in his manner of life to the highest point of exactitude. His meals were served in a fixed and invariable manner, and not only at a certain hour, but at a certain minute. With those about him, from his daughter to his servants, the count was sharp and invariably exacting, and so, without being cruel, he inspired a degree of respect and awe that the most cruel man could not readily have commanded. In spite of the fact that he was now on the retired list, and had no influence whatever in political circles, every high official in the province in which was the prince's estate felt obliged to call upon him, and had, just like the architect, the gardener, or Princess Marya, to wait till the regular hour at which the prince always made his appearance in the lofty waiting-room. And every one in the waiting-room felt the same veneration, and even awe, when the immensely high door of the study opened and showed the small figure of the old man in a powdered wig, with his little withered hands and grey, overhanging eyebrows, that, at times when he scowled, hid the gleam in his shrewd, youthful-looking eyes.

On the day that the young people were expected to arrive, Princess Marya went as usual at the fixed hour in the morning into the waiting-room to say good-morning to her father, and with dread in her heart crossed herself and mentally repeated a prayer. Every day she went in to her father in the same way, and every day she prayed that her interview with her father might pass off well that day. The old man-servant, wearing powder, softly got up from his seat in the waiting-room and whispered: "Walk in."

Through the door came the regular sounds of the lathe. The princess kept timidly hold of the door, which opened smoothly and easily, and stood still in the doorway. The prince was working at his lathe, and glancing round, he went on with what he was doing.

The immense room was filled with things obviously in constant use. The large table, on which lay books and plans, the high bookcases with keys in the glass-covered doors, the high table for the prince to write at, standing up, with an open manuscript-book upon it, the carpenter's lathe, with tools ranged about it and shavings scattered around, all suggested continual, varied, and orderly activity. The movements of the prince's small foot in its Tatar, silver-embroidered boot, the firm pressure of his sinewy, lean hand, showed the strength of vigorous old age still strong-willed and wiry. After making a few more turns, he took his foot from the pedal of the lathe, wiped the plane, dropped it into a leather pouch attached to the lathe, and going up to the table called his daughter. He never gave the usual blessing to his children; he simply offered her his scrubby, not yet shaved cheek, and said sternly and yet at the same time with intense tenderness, as he looked her over: "Quite well? . . . All right, then, sit down!" He took a geometry exercise-book written by his own hand, and drew his chair up with his leg.

"For to-morrow," he said quickly, turning to the page and marking it from one paragraph to the next with his rough nail. The princess bent over the exercise-book. "Stop, there's a letter for you," the old man said suddenly, pulling out of a pocket hanging over the table an envelope addressed in a feminine hand, and putting it on the table.

The princess's face coloured red in patches at the sight of the letter. She took it hurriedly and bent over it.

"From Heloise?" asked the prince, showing his still strong, yellow teeth in a cold smile.

"Yes, from Julie," said the princess, glancing timidly at him, and timidly smiling.

"Two more letters I'll let pass, but the third I shall read," said the prince severely; "I'm afraid you write a lot of nonsense. The third I shall read."

"Read this one, father," answered the princess, colouring still more and handing him the letter.

"The third, I said the third," the prince cried shortly; pushing away the letter and leaning his elbow on the table, he drew up to him the book with the figures of geometry in it.

"Now, madam," began the old man, bending over the book close to his daughter, and laying one arm on the back of the chair she was sitting on, so that the princess felt herself surrounded on all sides by the peculiar acrid smell of old age and tobacco, which she had so long associated with her father. "Come, madam, these triangles are equal: kindly look; the angle A B C . . . ."

The princess glanced in a sacred way at her father's eyes gleaming close beside her. The red patches overspread her whole face, and it was evident-that she did not understand a word, and was so frightened that terror prevented her from understanding all the subsequent explanations her father offered her, however clear they might be. Whether it was the teacher's fault or the pupil's, every day the same scene was repeated. The princess's eyes grew dim; she could see and hear nothing; she could feel nothing but the dry face of her stern father near her, his breath and the smell of him, and could think of nothing but how to escape as soon as possible from the study and to make out the problem in freedom in her room. The old man lost his temper; with a loud, grating noise he pushed back and drew up again the chair he was sitting on, made an effort to control himself, not to fly into a rage, and almost every time did fly into a rage, and scold, and sometimes flung the book away.

The princess answered a question wrong.

"Well, you are too stupid!" cried the prince, pushing away the book, and turning sharply away. But he got up immediately, walked up and down, laid his hand on the princess's hair, and sat down again. He drew himself up to the table and continued his explanations. "This won't do; it won't do," he said, when Princess Marya, taking the exercise-book with the lesson set her, and shutting it, was about to leave the room: "mathematics is a grand subject, madam. And to have you like the common run of our silly misses is what I don't want at all. Patience, and you'll get to like it." He patted her on the cheek. "It will drive all the nonsense out of your head." She would have gone; he stopped her with a gesture, and took a new, uncut book from the high table.

"Here's a book, too, your Heloise sends you some sort of Key to the Mystery. Religious. But I don't interfere with any one's belief. . . . I have looked at it. Take it. Come, run along, run along."

He patted her on the shoulder, and himself closed the door after her.

Princess Marya went back to her own room with that dejected, scared expression that rarely left her, and made her plain, sickly face even plainer. She sat down at her writing-table, which was dotted with miniature portraits, and strewn with books and manuscripts. The princess was as untidy as her father was tidy. She put down the geometry exercise-book and impatiently opened the letter. The letter was from the princess's dearest friend from childhood; this friend was none other than Julie Karagin, who had been at the Rostov's name-day party.

Julie wrote in French:

"DEAR AND EXCELLENT FRIEND,—What a terrible and frightful thing is absence! I say to myself that half of my existence and of my happiness is in you, that notwithstanding the distance that separates us, our hearts are united by invisible bonds; yet mine rebels against destiny, and in spite of the pleasures and distractions around me, I cannot overcome a certain hidden sadness which I feel in the bottom of my heart since our separation. Why are we not together as we were this summer in your great study, on the blue sofa, the confidential sofa? Why can I not, as I did three months ago, draw new moral strength from that gentle, calm, penetrating look of yours, a look that I loved so well and that I seem to see before me as I write to you."

When she reached this passage, Princess Marya sighed and looked round into the pier-glass that stood on her right. The glass reflected a feeble, ungraceful figure and a thin face. The eyes, always melancholy, were looking just now with a particularly hopeless expression at herself in the looking-glass. She flatters me, thought the princess, and she turned away and went on reading. But Julie did not flatter her friend: the princess's eyes—large, deep, and luminous (rays of warm light seemed at times to radiate in streams from them), were really so fine, that very often in spite of the plainness of the whole face her eyes were more attractive than beauty. But the princess had never seen the beautiful expression of her eyes; the expression that came into them when she was not thinking of herself. As is the case with every one, her face assumed an affected, unnatural, ugly expression as soon as she looked in the looking-glass.

She went on reading:

"All Moscow talks of nothing but war. One of my two brothers is already abroad, the other is with the Guards, who are starting on the march to the frontier. Our dear Emperor has left Petersburg, and, people declare, intends to expose his precious existence to the risks of war. God grant that the Corsican monster who is destroying the peace of Europe may be brought low by the angel whom the Almighty in His mercy has given us as sovereign. Without speaking of my brothers, this war has deprived me of one of my heart's dearest alliances. I mean the young Nicholas Rostov, whose enthusiasm could not endure inaction, and who has left the university to go and join the army. Well, dear Marie, I will own to you that, in spite of his extreme youth, his departure for the army has been a great grief to me. This young man, of whom I spoke to you in the summer, has so much nobility, so much real youthfulness, rarely to be met with in our age, among our old men of twenty. Above all, he has so much openness and so much heart. He is so pure and poetic that my acquaintance with him, though so transient, has been one of the dearest joys known by my poor heart, which has already had so much suffering. Some day I will tell you about our farewells and all that we said to each other as we parted. As yet, all that is too fresh. Ah, dear friend, you are fortunate in not knowing these joys and these pains which are so poignant. You are fortunate, because the latter are generally stronger! I know very well that Count Nicholas is too young ever to become more to me than a friend, but this sweet friendship, this poetic and pure intimacy have fulfilled a need of my heart. No more of this. The great news of the day, with which all Moscow is taken up, is the death of old Count Bezuhov, and his inheritance. Fancy, the three princesses have hardly got anything, Prince Vassily nothing, and everything has been left to M. Pierre, who has been acknowledged as a legitimate son into the bargain, so that he is Count Bezuhov and has the finest fortune in Russia. People say that Prince Vassily behaved very badly in all these matters and that he has gone back to Petersburg quite cast down.

"I own that I understand very little about all these details of legacies and wills; what I know is that since the young man whom we all used to know as plain M. Pierre has become Count Bezuhov and owner of one of the largest fortunes in Russia, I am much amused to observe the change in the tone and the manners of mammas burdened with marriageable daughters and of those young ladies themselves, towards that individual—who I may say in passing has always seemed to me a poor creature. As people have amused themselves for the last two years in giving me husbands whom I don't know, the matrimonial gossip of Moscow generally makes me Countess Bezuhov. But you, I am sure, feel that I have no desire to become so. About marriage, by the by, do you know that the *universal aunt,* Anna Mihalovna, has confided to me, under the seal of the deepest secrecy, a marriage scheme for you. It is no one more or less than Prince Vassily's son, Anatole, whom they want to settle by marrying him to some one rich and distinguished, and the choice of his relations has fallen on you. I don't know what view you will take of the matter, but I thought it my duty to let you know beforehand. He is said to be very handsome and very wild; that is all I have been able to find out about him.

"But enough of gossip. I am finishing my second sheet and mamma is sending for me to go and dine with the Apraxins. Read the mystical book which I send you, and which is the rage here. Though there are things in this book, difficult for our human conceptions to attain to, it is an admirable book, and reading it calms and elevates the soul. Farewell. My respects to your father and my compliments to Mlle. Bourienne. I embrace you as I love you.   JULIE.

"*P.S.*—Let me hear news of your brother and his charming little wife."

Princess Marya thought a minute, smiling dreamily (her face, lighted up by her luminous eyes, was completely transformed). Suddenly getting up, she crossed over to the table, treading heavily. She got out a sheet of paper and her hand began rapidly moving over it. She wrote the following answer:

"DEAR AND EXCELLENT FRIEND,—Your letter of the 13th gave me great delight. So you still love me, my poetic Julie. So, absence, which you so bitterly denounce, has not had its usual effect upon you. You complain of absence—what might I say, if I ventured to complain, I, deprived of all who are dear to me? Ah, if we had not religion to console us, life would be very sad. Why do you suppose that I should look severe when you tell me of your affection for that young man? In such matters I am hard upon no one but myself. I understand such feelings in other people, and if, never having felt them, I cannot express approval, I do not condemn them. Only it seems to me that Christian love, the love of our neighbour, the love of our enemies, is more meritorious, sweeter and more beautiful than those feelings that may be inspired in a poetic and loving young girl like you, by the fine eyes of a young man.

"The news of Count Bezuhov's death reached us before your letter, and affected my father very much. He says that the count was the last representative but one of the great century and that it is his turn now; but that he will do his best to have his turn come as late as possible. May God save us from that terrible misfortune. I cannot agree with you about Pierre, whom I knew as a child. He always appeared to me to have an excellent heart, and that is the quality that I most esteem in people. As to his inheritance and Prince Vassily's behaviour about it, it is very sad for both. Ah, my dear friend, our divine Saviour's word, that it is easier for a camel to pass through the eye of a needle than for a rich man to enter into the kingdom of Heaven is a terribly true saying; I pity Prince Vassily, and I am yet more sorry for Pierre. So young and burdened with this wealth, to what temptations he will be exposed! If I were asked what I wished most in the world, it would be to be poorer than the poorest beggar. A thousand thanks, dear friend, for the work you send me, and which is all the rage where you are. As, however, you tell me that amid many good things there are others to which our weak human understanding cannot attain, it seems to me rather useless to busy oneself in reading an unintelligible book, since for that very reason it cannot yield any profit. I have never been able to comprehend the passion which some people have for confusing their minds by giving themselves to the study of mystical books which only awaken their doubts, inflaming their imagination, and giving them a disposition to exaggeration altogether contrary to Christian simplicity. Let us read the Apostles and the Gospel. Do not let us seek to penetrate what is mysterious in these, for how can we dare presume, miserable sinners as we are, to enter into the terrible and sacred secrets of Providence, while we wear this carnal husk that raises an impenetrable veil between us and the Eternal? Let us rather confine ourselves to studying those sublime principles which our divine Saviour has left us as guides for our conduct here below; let us seek to conform ourselves to those and follow them; let us persuade ourselves that the less range we give to our weak human understanding, the more agreeable it will be to God, who rejects all knowledge that does not come from Him; that the less we seek to dive into that which He has pleased to hide from our knowledge the sooner will He discover it to us by means of His divine Spirit.

"My father has not spoken to me of the suitor, but has only told me that he has received a letter, and was expecting a visit from Prince Vassily. In regard to a marriage-scheme concerning myself, I will tell you, my dear and excellent friend, that to my mind marriage is a divine institution to which we must conform. However painful it may be to me, if the Almighty should ever impose upon me the duties of a wife and mother, I shall try to fulfil them as faithfully as I can, without disquieting myself by examining my feelings in regard to him whom He may give me for a husband.

"I have received a letter from my brother, who announces his coming to Bleak Hills with his wife. It will be a pleasure of brief duration, since he is leaving us to take part in this unhappy war into which we have been drawn, God knows how and why. It is not only with you, in the centre of business and society, that people talk of nothing except war, for here also, amid those rustic labours and that calm of nature, which townspeople generally imagine in the country, rumours of war are heard and are felt painfully. My father talks of nothing but marches and counter-marches, things of which I understand nothing; and the day before yesterday, taking my usual walk in the village street, I witnessed a heartrending scene. . . . It was a convoy of recruits that had been enrolled in our district, and were being sent away to the army. You should have seen the state of the mothers, wives and children of the men who were going, and have heard the sobs on both sides. It seems as though humanity had forgotten the laws of its divine Saviour, Who preached love and the forgiveness of offences, and were making the greatest merit to consist in the art of killing one another.

"Adieu, dear and good friend: may our divine Saviour and His most Holy Mother keep you in their holy and powerful care.   MARIE."

"Ah, you are sending off your letters, princess. I have already finished mine. I have written to my poor mother," said Mademoiselle Bourienne quickly in her agreeable, juicy voice, with a roll of the *r*'s. She came in, all smiles, bringing into the intense, melancholy, gloomy atmosphere of the Princess Marya an alien world of gay frivolity and self-satisfaction. "Princess, I must warn you," she added, dropping her voice, "the prince has had an altercation," she said, with a peculiar roll of the *r*, seeming to listen to herself with pleasure. "An altercation with Mihail Ivanov. He is in a very ill humour, very morose. Be prepared, you know."

"Ah, *chère amie*," answered Princess Marya, "I have begged you never to tell me beforehand in what humour I shall find my father. I do not permit myself to judge him and I would not have others do so."

The princess glanced at her watch, and seeing that it was already five minutes later than the hour fixed for her practice on the clavichord, she went with a face of alarm into the divan-room. In accordance with the rules by which the day was mapped out, the prince rested from twelve to two, while the young princess practised on the clavichord.

XXIII

THE GREY-HAIRED valet was sitting in the waiting-room dozing and listening to the prince's snoring in his immense study. From a far-off part of the house there came through closed doors the sound of difficult passages of a sonata of Dusseck's repeated twenty times over.

At that moment a carriage and a little cart drove up to the steps, and Prince Andrey got out of the carriage, helped his little wife out and let her pass into the house before him. Grey Tihon in his wig, popping out at the door of the waiting-room, informed him in a whisper that the prince was taking a nap and made haste to close the door. Tihon knew that no extraordinary event, not even the arrival of his son, would be permitted to break through the routine of the day. Prince Andrey was apparently as well aware of the fact as Tihon. He looked at his watch as though to ascertain whether his father's habits had changed during the time he had not seen him, and satisfying himself that they were unchanged, he turned to his wife.

"He will get up in twenty minutes. Let's go to Marie," he said.

The little princess had grown stouter during this time, but her short upper lip, with a smile and the faint moustache on it, rose as gaily and charmingly as ever when she spoke.

"Why, it is a palace," she said to her husband, looking round her with exactly the expression with which people pay compliments to the host at a ball. "Come, quick, quick!" As she looked about her, she smiled at Tihon and at her husband, and at the footman who was showing them in.

"It is Marie practising? Let us go quietly, we must surprise her." Prince Andrey followed her with a courteous and depressed expression.

"You're looking older, Tihon," he said as he passed to the old man, who was kissing his hand.

Before they had reached the room, from which the sounds of the clavichord were coming, the pretty, fair-haired Frenchwoman emerged from a side-door. Mademoiselle Bourienne seemed overwhelmed with delight.

"Ah, what a pleasure for the princess!" she exclaimed. "At last! I must tell her."

"No, no, please not" . . . said the little princess, kissing her. "You are Mademoiselle Bourienne; I know you already through my sister-in-law's friendship for you. She does not expect us!"

They went up to the door of the divan-room, from which came the sound of the same passage repeated over and over again. Prince Andrey stood still frowning as though in expectation of something unpleasant.

The little princess went in. The passage broke off in the middle; he heard an exclamation, the heavy tread of Princess Marya, and the sound of kissing. When Prince Andrey went in, the two ladies, who had only seen each other once for a short time at Prince Andrey's wedding, were clasped in each other's arms, warmly pressing their lips to the first place each had chanced upon. Mademoiselle Bourienne was standing near them, her hands pressed to her heart; she was smiling devoutly, apparently equally ready to weep and to laugh. Prince Andrey shrugged his shoulders, and scowled as lovers of music scowl when they hear a false note. The two ladies let each other go; then hastened again, as though each afraid of being remiss, to hug each other, began kissing each other's hands and pulling them away, and then fell to kissing each other on the face again. Then they quite astonished Prince Andrey by both suddenly bursting into tears and beginning the kissing over again. Mademoiselle Bourienne cried too. Prince Andrey was unmistakably ill at ease. But to the two women it seemed such a natural thing that they should weep; it seemed never to have occurred to them that their meeting could have taken place without tears.

"*Ah, ma chère!* . . . *Ah, Marie!*" . . . both the ladies began talking at once, and they laughed. "I had a dream last night. Then you did not expect us? O Marie, you have got thinner."

"And you are looking better . . ."

"I recognized the princess at once," put in Mademoiselle Bourienne.

"And I had no idea!" . . . cried Princess Marya. "Ah, Andrey, I did not see you."

Prince Andrey and his sister kissed each other's hands, and he told her she was just as great a cry-baby as she always had been. Princess Marya turned to her brother, and through her tears, her great, luminous eyes, that were beautiful at that instant, rested with a loving, warm and gentle gaze on Prince Andrey's face. The little princess talked incessantly. The short, downy upper lip was continually flying down to meet the rosy, lower lip when necessary, and parting again in a smile of gleaming teeth and eyes. The little princess described an incident that had occurred to them on Spasskoe hill, and might have been serious for her in her condition. And immediately after that she communicated the intelligence that she had left all her clothes in Petersburg, and God knew what she would have to go about in here, and that Andrey was quite changed, and that Kitty Odintsov had married an old man, and that a suitor had turned up for Princess Marya, "who was a suitor worth having," but that they would talk about that later. Princess Marya was still gazing mutely at her brother, and her beautiful eyes were full of love and melancholy. It was clear that her thoughts were following a train of their own, apart from the chatter of her sister-in-law. In the middle of the latter's description of the last fête-day at Petersburg, she addressed her brother.

"And is it quite settled that you are going to the war, Andrey?" she said, sighing. Liza sighed too.

"Yes, and to-morrow too," answered her brother.

"He is deserting me here, and Heaven knows why, when he might have had promotion . . ." Princess Marya did not listen to the end, but following her own train of thought, she turned to her sister-in-law, letting her affectionate eyes rest on her waist.

"Is it really true?" she said.

The face of her sister-in-law changed. She sighed.

"Yes, it's true," she said. "Oh! It's very dreadful . . ."

Liza's lip drooped. She put her face close to her sister-in-law's face, and again she unexpectedly began to cry.

"She needs rest," said Prince Andrey, frowning. "Don't you, Liza? Take her to your room, while I go to father. How is he—just the same?"

"The same, just the same; I don't know what you will think," Princess Marya answered joyfully.

"And the same hours, and the walks about the avenues, and the lathe?" asked Prince Andrey with a scarcely perceptible smile, showing that, in spite of all his love and respect for his father, he recognised his weaknesses.

"The same hours and the lathe, mathematics too, and my geometry lessons," Princess Marya answered gaily, as though those lessons were one of the most delightful events of her life.

When the twenty minutes had elapsed, and the time for the old prince to get up had come, Tihon came to call the young man to his father. The old man made a departure from his ordinary routine in honour of his son's arrival. He directed that he should be admitted into his apartments during his time for dressing, before dinner. The old prince used to wear the old-fashioned dress, the kaftan and powder. And when Prince An-drey—not with the disdainful face and manners with which he walked into drawing-rooms, but with the eager face with which he had talked to Pierre—went in to his father's room, the old gentleman was in his dressing-room sitting in a roomy morocco chair in a *peignoir*, with his head in the hands of Tihon.

"Ah! the warrior! So you want to fight Bonaparte?" said the old man, shaking his powdered head as far as his plaited tail, which was in Tihon's hands, would permit him.

"Mind you look sharp after him, at any rate, or he'll soon be putting us on the list of his subjects. How are you?"

And he held out his cheek to him.

The old gentleman was in excellent humour after his nap before dinner. (He used to say that sleep after dinner was silver, but before dinner it was golden.) He took delighted, sidelong glances at his son from under his thick, overhanging brows. Prince Andrey went up and kissed his father on the spot indicated for him. He made no reply on his father's favourite topic—jesting banter at the military men of the period, and particularly at Bonaparte.

"Yes, I have come to you, father, bringing a wife with child," said Prince Andrey, with eager and reverential eyes watching every move-ment of his father's face. "How is your health?"

"None but fools, my lad, and profligates are unwell, and you know me; busy from morning till night and temperate, so of course I'm well."

"Thank God," said his son, smiling.

"God's not much to do with the matter. Come, tell me," the old man went on, going back to his favourite hobby, "how have the Germans trained you to fight with Bonaparte on their new scientific method—strategy as they call it?"

Prince Andrey smiled.

"Give me time to recover myself, father," he said, with a smile that showed that his father's failings did not prevent his respecting and lov-ing him. "Why, I have only just got here."

"Nonsense, nonsense," cried the old man, shaking his tail to try whether it were tightly plaited, and taking his son by the hand. "The house is ready for your wife. Marie will look after her and show her everything, and talk nineteen to the dozen with her too. That's their feminine way. I'm glad to have her. Sit down, talk to me. Miheison's army, I understand, Tolstoy's too . . . a simultaneous expedition . . . but what's the army of the South going to do? Prussia, her neutrality . . . I know all that. What of Austria?" he said, getting up from his chair and walking about the room, with Tihon running after him, giving him various articles of his apparel. "What about Sweden? How will they cross Pomerania?"

Prince Andrey, seeing the urgency of his father's questions, began explaining the plan of operations of the proposed campaign, speaking at first reluctantly, but becoming more interested as he went on, and unconsciously from habit passing from Russian into French. He told him how an army of ninety thousand troops was to threaten Prussia so as to drive her out of her neutrality and draw her into the war, how part of these troops were to join the Swedish troops at Strahlsund, how two hundred and twenty thousand Austrians were to combine with a hundred thousand Russians in Italy and on the Rhine, and how fifty thousand Russians and fifty thousand English troops were to meet at Naples, and how the army, forming a total of five hundred thousand, was to attack the French on different sides at once. The old prince did not manifest the slightest interest in what he told him. He went on dressing, as he walked about, apparently not listening, and three times he unexpectedly interrupted him. Once he stopped him and shouted: "the white one! the white one!"

This meant that Tihon had not given him the waistcoat he wanted. Another time, he stood still, asked: "And will she be confined soon?" and shook his head reproachfully: "That's bad! Go on, go on."

The third time was when Prince Andrey was just finishing his description. The old man hummed in French, in his falsetto old voice: "Malbrook goes off to battle, God knows when he'll come back."

His son only smiled.

"I don't say that this is a plan I approve of," he said; "I'm only telling you what it is. Napoleon has made a plan by now as good as this one."

"Well, you have told me nothing new." And thoughtfully the old man repeated, speaking quickly to himself: "God knows when he'll come back. Go into the dining-room."

XXIV

At the exact hour, the prince, powdered and shaven, walked into the dining-room, where there were waiting for him his daughter-in-law, Princess Marya, Mademoiselle Bourienne, and the prince's architect, who, by a strange whim of the old gentleman's, dined at his table, though being an insignificant person of no social standing, he would not naturally have expected to be treated with such honour. The prince, who was in practice a firm stickler for distinctions of rank, and rarely admitted to his table even important provincial functionaries, had suddenly pitched on the architect Mihail Ivanovitch, blowing his nose in a check pocket-handkerchief in the corner, to illustrate the theory that all men are equal, and had more than once impressed upon his daughter that Mihail Ivanovitch was every whit as good as himself and her. At table the prince addressed his conversation to the taciturn architect more often than to any one.

In the dining-room, which, like all the other rooms in the house, was immensely lofty, the prince's entrance was awaited by all the members of his household and the footmen, standing behind each chair. The butler with a table-napkin on his arm scanned the setting of the table, making signs to the footmen, and continually he glanced uneasily from the clock on the wall to the door, by which the prince was to enter. Prince Andrey stood at an immense golden frame on the wall that was new to him. It contained the genealogical tree of Bolkonskys, and hanging opposite it was a frame, equally immense, with a badly painted representation (evidently the work of some household artist) of a reigning prince in a crown, intended for the descendant of Rurik and founder of the family of the Bolkonsky princes. Prince Andrey looked at this genealogical tree shaking his head, and he laughed.

"There you have him all over!" he said to Princess Marya as she came up to him.

Princess Marya looked at her brother in surprise. She did not know what he was smiling at. Everything her father did inspired in her a reverence that did not admit of criticism.

"Every one has his weak spot," Prince Andrey went on; "with *his* vast intellect to condescend to such triviality!"

Princess Marya could not understand the boldness of her brother's criticism and was making ready to protest, when the step they were all listening for was heard coming from the study. The prince walked in with a quick, lively step, as he always walked, as though intentionally contrasting the elasticity of his movements with the rigidity of the routine of the house. At that instant the big clock struck two, and another clock in the drawing-room echoed it in thinner tones. The prince stood still; his keen, stern eyes gleaming under his bushy, overhanging brows scanned all the company and rested on the little princess. The little princess experienced at that moment the sensation that courtiers know on the entrance of the Tsar, that feeling of awe and veneration that this old man inspired in every one about him. He stroked the little princess on the head, and then with an awkward movement patted her on her neck.

"I'm glad, glad to see you," he said, and looking intently into her eyes he walked away and sat down in his place. "Sit down, sit down, Mihail Ivanovitch, sit down."

He pointed his daughter-in-law to a seat beside him. The footman moved a chair back for her.

"Ho, ho!" said the old man, looking at her rounded figure. "You've not lost time; that's bad!" He laughed a dry, cold, unpleasant laugh, laughing as he always did with his lips, but not with his eyes. "You must have exercise, as much exercise as possible, as much as possible," he said.

The little princess did not hear or did not care to hear his words. She sat dumb and seemed disconcerted. The prince asked after her father, and she began to talk and to smile. He asked her about common acquaintances; the princess became more and more animated, and began talking away, giving the prince greetings from various people and retailing the gossip of the town.

"Poor Countess Apraxin has lost her husband; she has quite cried her eyes out, poor dear," she said, growing more and more lively.

As she became livelier, the prince looked more and more sternly at her, and all at once, as though he had studied her sufficiently and had formed a clear idea of her, he turned away and addressed Mihail Ivanovitch:

"Well, Mihail Ivanovitch, our friend Bonaparte is to have a bad time of it. Prince Andrey" (this was how he always spoke of his son) "has been telling me what forces are being massed against him! While you and I have always looked upon him as a very insignificant person."

Mihail Ivanovitch, utterly at a loss to conjecture when "you and I" had said anything of the sort about Bonaparte, but grasping that he was wanted for the introduction of the prince's favourite subject, glanced in wonder at the young prince, not knowing what was to come next.

"He's a great tactician!" said the prince to his son, indicating the architect, and the conversation turned again on the war, on Bonaparte, and the generals and political personages of the day. The old prince was, it seemed, convinced that all the public men of the period were mere babes who had no idea of the A B C of military and political matters; while Bonaparte, according to him, was an insignificant Frenchman, who had met with success simply because there were no Potyomkins and Suvorovs to oppose him. He was even persuaded firmly that there were no political difficulties in Europe, that there was no war indeed, but only a sort of marionette show in which the men of the day took part, pretending to be doing the real thing. Prince Andrey received his father's jeers at modern people gaily, and with obvious pleasure drew his father out and listened to him.

"Does everything seem good that was done in the past?" he said; "why, didn't Suvorov himself fall into the trap Moreau laid for him, and wasn't he unable to get out of it too?"

"Who told you that? Who said so?" cried the prince. "Suvorov!" And he flung away his plate, which Tihon very neatly caught. "Suvorov! . . . Think again, Prince Andrey. There were two men—Friedrich and Suvorov . . . Moreau! Moreau would have been a prisoner if Suvorov's hands had been free, but his hands were tied by the Hofskriegswurst-schnappsrath; the devil himself would have been in a tight place. Ah, you'll find out what these Hofskriegswurstschnappsraths are like! Suvorov couldn't get the better of them, so how is Mihail Kutuzov going to do it? No, my dear," he went on; "so you and your generals

aren't able to get round Bonaparte; you must needs call in Frenchmen
—set a thief to catch a thief! The German, Pahlen, has been sent to
New York in America to get the Frenchman Moreau," he said, alluding
to the invitation that had that year been made to Moreau to enter the
Russian service. "A queer business! . . . Why the Potyomkins, the
Suvorovs, the Orlovs, were they Germans? No, my lad, either you have
all lost your wits, or I have outlived mine. God help you, and we shall
see. Bonaparte's become a great military leader among them! H'm! . . ."

"I don't say at all that all those plans are good," said Prince Andrey;
"only I can't understand how you can have such an opinion of Bonaparte. Laugh, if you like, but Bonaparte is any way a great general!"

"Mihail Ivanovitch!" the old prince cried to the architect, who, absorbed in the roast meat, hoped they had forgotten him. "Didn't I tell
you Bonaparte was a great tactician? Here he says so too."

"To be sure, your excellency," replied the architect. The prince
laughed again his frigid laugh.

"Bonaparte was born with a silver spoon in his mouth. He has splendid soldiers. And he attacked the Germans first too. And any fool can
beat the Germans. From the very beginning of the world every one has
beaten the Germans. And they've never beaten any one. They only conquer each other. He made his reputation fighting against them."

And the prince began analysing all the blunders that in his opinion
Bonaparte had committed in his wars and even in politics. His son did
not protest, but it was evident that whatever arguments were advanced
against him, he was as little disposed to give up his opinion as the old
prince himself. Prince Andrey listened and refrained from replying. He
could not help wondering how this old man, living so many years alone
and never leaving the country, could know all the military and political
events in Europe of the last few years in such detail and with such accuracy, and form his own judgment on them.

"You think I'm an old man and don't understand the actual position
of affairs?" he wound up. "But I'll tell you I'm taken up with it! I don't
sleep at nights. Come, where has this great general of yours proved himself to be such?"

"That would be a long story," answered his son.

"You go along to your Bonaparte. Mademoiselle Bourienne, here is
another admirer of your blackguard of an emperor!" he cried in excellent French.

"You know that I am not a Bonapartist, prince."

"God knows when he'll come back . . ." the prince hummed in falsetto, laughed still more falsetto, and got up from the table.

The little princess had sat silent during the whole discussion and the
rest of the dinner, looking in alarm first at Princess Marya and then at
her father-in-law. When they left the dinner-table, she took her sister-in-
law's arm and drew her into another room.

"What a clever man your father is," she said; "perhaps that is why
I am afraid of him."

"Oh, he is so kind!" said Princess Marya.

XXV

PRINCE ANDREY was leaving the following evening. The old prince, not departing from his regular routine, went away to his own room after dinner. The little princess was with her sister-in-law. Prince Andrey, having changed his dress and put on a traveling-coat without epaulettes, had been packing with his valet in the rooms set apart for him. After himself inspecting the coach and the packing of his trunks on it, he gave orders for the horses to be put to. Nothing was left in the room but the things that Prince Andrey always carried with him: a travelling-case, a big silver wine-case, two Turkish pistols and a sabre, a present from his father, brought back from his campaign under Otchakov. All Prince Andrey's belongings for the journey were in good order; everything was new and clean, in cloth covers, carefully fastened with tape.

At moments of starting off and beginning a different life, persons given to deliberating on their actions are usually apt to be in a serious frame of mind. At such moments one reviews the past and forms plans for the future. The face of Prince Andrey was very dreamy and tender. Clasping his hands behind him, he walked rapidly up and down the room from corner to corner, looking straight before him and dreamily shaking his head. Whether he felt dread at going to the war, or grief at forsaking his wife—or possibly something of both—he evidently did not care to be seen in that mood, for, catching the sound of footsteps in the outer room, he hastily unclasped his hands, stood at the table, as though engaged in fastening the cover of the case, and assumed his habitual calm and impenetrable expression. It was the heavy step of Princess Marya.

"They told me you had ordered the horses to be put in," she said, panting (she had evidently been running), "and I did so want to have a little more talk with you alone. God knows how long we shall be parted again. You're not angry with me for coming? You're very much changed, Andryusha," she added, as though to explain the question.

She smiled as she uttered the word "Andryusha." It was obviously strange to her to think that this stern, handsome man was the same as the thin, mischievous boy, the Andryusha who had been the companion of her childhood.

"And where's Liza?" he asked, only answering her question by a smile.

"She was so tired that she fell asleep on the sofa in my room. Oh Andrey, what a treasure of a wife you have," she said, sitting down on the sofa, facing her brother. "She is a perfect child; such a sweet, merry child. I like her so much." Prince Andrey did not speak, but the princess noticed the ironical and contemptuous expression that came into his face.

"But one must be indulgent to little weaknesses. Who is free from them, Andrey? You mustn't forget that she has grown up and been educated in society. And then her position is not a very cheerful one. One must put oneself in every one's position. To understand everything is to forgive everything. Only think what it must be for her, poor girl, after the life she has been used to, to part from her husband and be left alone in the country, and in her condition too. It's very hard."

Prince Andrey smiled, looking at his sister as we smile listening to people whom we fancy we see through.

"You live in the country and think the life so awful?" he said.

"I—that's a different matter. Why bring me in? I don't wish for any other life, and indeed I can't wish for anything different, for I know no other sort of life. But only think, Andrey, what it is for a young woman used to fashionable society to be buried for the best years of her life in the country, alone, because papa is always busy, and I . . . you know me . . . I am not a cheerful companion for women used to the best society. Mademoiselle Bourienne is the only person . . ."

"I don't like her at all, your Bourienne," said Prince Andrey.

"Oh, no! she's a very good and sweet girl, and what's more, she's very much to be pitied. She has nobody, nobody. To tell the truth, she is of no use to me, but only in my way. I have always, you know, been a solitary creature, and now I'm getting more and more so. I like to be alone . . . *Mon père* likes her very much. She and Mihail Ivanovitch are the two people he is always friendly and good-tempered with, be-cause he has been a benefactor to both of them; as Sterne says: 'We don't love people so much for the good they have done us as for the good we have done them.' *Mon père* picked her up an orphan in the streets, and she's very good-natured. And *mon père* likes her way of reading. She reads aloud to him in the evenings. She reads very well."

"Come, tell me the truth, Marie, you suffer a good deal, I expect, sometimes from our father's character?" Prince Andrey asked suddenly. Princess Marya was at first amazed, then aghast at the question.

"Me? . . . me? . . . me suffer!" she said.

"He was always harsh, but he's growing very tedious, I should think," said Prince Andrey, speaking so slightingly of his father with an unmis-takable intention either of puzzling or of testing his sister.

"You are good in every way, Andrey, but you have a sort of pride of intellect," said the princess, evidently following her own train of thought rather than the thread of the conversation, "and that's a great sin. Do you think it right to judge our father? But if it were right, what feeling but *vénération* could be aroused by such a man as *mon père*? And I am so contented and happy with him. I could only wish you were all as happy as I am."

Her brother shook his head incredulously.

"The only thing that troubles me,—I'll tell you the truth, Andrey,—is our father's way of thinking in religious matters. I can't understand how a man of such immense intellect can fail to see what is as clear as day, and can fall into such error. That is the one thing that makes me unhappy. But even in this I see a slight change for the better of late.

Lately his jeers have not been so bitter, and there is a monk whom he received and talked to a long time."

"Well, my dear, I'm afraid you and your monk are wasting your powder and shot," Prince Andrey said ironically but affectionately.

"*Ah, mon ami!* I can only pray to God and trust that He will hear me. Andrey," she said timidly after a minute's silence, "I have a great favour to ask of you."

"What is it, dear?"

"No; promise me you won't refuse. It will be no trouble to you, and there is nothing beneath you in it. Only it will be a comfort to me. Promise, Andryusha," she said, putting her hand into her reticule and holding something in it, but not showing it yet, as though what she was holding was the object of her entreaty, and before she received a promise to grant it, she could not take that something out of her reticule. She looked timidly with imploring eyes at her brother.

"Even if it were a great trouble . . ." answered Prince Andrey, seeming to guess what the favour was.

"You may think what you please about it. I know you are like *mon père*. Think what you please, but do this for my sake. Do, please. The father of my father, our grandfather, always wore it in all his wars . . ." She still did not take out what she was holding in her reticule. "You promise me, then?"

"Of course, what is it?"

"Andrey, I am blessing you with the holy image, and you must promise me you will never take it off. . . . You promise?"

"If it does not weigh a ton and won't drag my neck off . . . To please you," said Prince Andrey. The same second he noticed the pained expression that came over his sister's face at this jest, and felt remorseful. "I am very glad, really very glad, dear," he added.

"Against your own will He will save and will have mercy on you and turn you to Himself, because in Him alone is truth and peace," she said in a voice shaking with emotion, and with a solemn gesture holding in both hands before her brother an old-fashioned, little, oval holy image of the Saviour with a black face in a silver setting, on a little silver chain of delicate workmanship. She crossed herself, kissed the image, and gave it to Andrey.

"Please, Andrey, for my sake."

Rays of kindly, timid light beamed from her great eyes. Those eyes lighted up all the thin, sickly face and made it beautiful. Her brother would have taken the image, but she stopped him. Andrey understood, crossed himself, and kissed the image. His face looked at once tender (he was touched) and ironical.

"*Merci, mon ami.*" She kissed him on the forehead and sat down again on the sofa. Both were silent.

"So as I was telling you, Andrey, you must be kind and generous as you always used to be. Don't judge Liza harshly," she began; "she is so sweet, so good-natured, and her position is a very hard one just now."

"I fancy I have said nothing to you, Masha, of my blaming my wife for anything or being dissatisfied with her. What makes you say all this to me?"

Princess Marya coloured in patches, and was mute, as though she felt guilty.

"I have said nothing to you, but you have been *talked to*. And that makes me sad."

The red patches grew deeper on the forehead and neck and cheeks of Princess Marya. She would have said something, but could not utter the words. Her brother had guessed right: his wife had shed tears after dinner. had said that she had a presentiment of a bad confinement, that she was afraid of it, and had complained of her hard lot, of her father-in-law and her husband. After crying she had fallen asleep. Prince Andrey felt sorry for his sister.

"Let me tell you one thing, Masha, I can't reproach *my wife* for anything, I never have and I never shall, nor can I reproach myself for anything in regard to her, and that shall always be so in whatever circumstances I may be placed. But if you want to know the truth . . . if you want to know if I am happy. No. Is she happy? No. Why is it so? I don't know."

As he said this, he went up to his sister, and stooping over her kissed her on the forehead. His fine eyes shone with an unaccustomed light of intelligence and goodness. But he was not looking at his sister, but towards the darkness of the open door, over her head.

"Let us go to her; I must say good-bye. Or you go alone and wake her up, and I'll come in a moment. Petrushka!" he called to his valet, "come here and take away these things. This is to go in the seat and this on the right side."

Princess Marya got up and moved toward the door. She stopped. "Andrey, if you had faith, you would have appealed to God, to give you the love that you do not feel, and your prayer would have been granted."

"Yes, perhaps so," said Prince Andrey. "Go, Masha, I'll come immediately."

On the way to his sister's room, in the gallery that united one house to the other, Prince Andrey encountered Mademoiselle Bourienne smiling sweetly. It was the third time that day that with an innocent and enthusiastic smile she had thrown herself in his way in secluded passages.

"Ah, I thought you were in your own room," she said, for some reason blushing and casting down her eyes. Prince Andrey looked sternly at her. A sudden look of wrathful exasperation came into his face. He said nothing to her, but stared at her forehead and her hair, without looking at her eyes, with such contempt that the Frenchwoman crimsoned and went away without a word. When he reached his sister's room, the little princess was awake and her gay little voice could be heard through the open door, hurrying one word after another. She talked as though, after being long restrained, she wanted to make up for lost time, and, as always, she spoke French.

"No, but imagine the old Countess Zubov, with false curls and her mouth full of false teeth as though she wanted to defy the years. *Ha, ha, ha, Marie!"*

Just the same phrase about Countess Zubov and just the same laugh Prince Andrey had heard five times already from his wife before outsiders. He walked softly into the room. The little princess, plump and rosy, was sitting in a low chair with her work in her hands, trotting out her Petersburg reminiscences and phrases. Prince Andrey went up, stroked her on the head, and asked if she had got over the fatigue of the journey. She answered him and went on talking.

The coach with six horses stood at the steps. It was a dark autumn night. The coachman could not see the shafts of the carriage. Servants with lanterns were running to and fro on the steps. The immense house glared with its great windows lighted up. The house-serfs were crowding in the outer hall, anxious to say good-bye to their young prince. In the great hall within stood all the members of the household: Mihail Ivanovitch, Mademoiselle Bourienne, Princess Marya, and the little princess. Prince Andrey had been summoned to the study of his father, who wanted to take leave of him alone. All were waiting for him to come out again. When Prince Andrey went into the study, the old prince was in his old-age spectacles and his white dressing-gown, in which he never saw any one but his son. He was sitting at the table writing. He looked round.

"Going?" And he went on writing again.

"I have come to say good-bye."

"Kiss me here," he touched his cheek; "thanks, thanks!"

"What are you thanking me for?"

"For not lingering beyond your fixed time, for not hanging about a woman's petticoats. Duty before everything. Thanks, thanks!" And he went on writing, so that ink spurted from the scratching pen.

"If you want to say anything, say it. I can do these two things at once," he added.

"About my wife . . . I'm ashamed as it is to leave her on your hands. . . ."

"Why talk nonsense? Say what you want."

"When my wife's confinement is due, send to Moscow for an *accoucheur* . . . Let him be here."

The old man stopped and stared with stern eyes at his son, as though not understanding.

"I know that no one can be of use, if nature does not assist," said Prince Andrey, evidently confused. "I admit that out of a million cases only one goes wrong, but it's her fancy and mine. They've been telling her things; she's had a dream and she's frightened."

"H'm . . . h'm . . ." the old prince muttered to himself, going on with his writing. "I will do so." He scribbled his signature, and suddenly turned quickly to his son and laughed.

"It's a bad business, eh?"

"What's a bad business, father?"

"Wife!" the old prince said briefly and significantly.

"I don't understand," said Prince Andrey.

"But there's no help for it, my dear boy," said the old prince; "they're all like that, and there's no getting unmarried again. Don't be afraid, I won't say a word to any one, but you know it yourself."

He grasped his hand with his thin, little, bony fingers, shook it, looked straight into his son's face with his keen eyes, that seemed to see right through any one, and again he laughed his frigid laugh.

The son sighed, acknowledging in that sigh that his father understood him. The old man, still busy folding and sealing the letters with his habitual rapidity, snatched up and flung down again the wax, the seal, and the paper.

"It can't be helped. She's pretty. I'll do everything. Set your mind at rest," he said jerkily, as he sealed the letter.

Andrey did not speak; it was both pleasant and painful to him that his father understood him. The old man got up and gave his son the letter.

"Listen," said he. "Don't worry about your wife; what can be done shall be done. Now, listen; give this letter to Mihail Ilarionovitch. I write that he is to make use of you on good work, and not to keep you long an adjutant; a vile duty! Tell him I remember him and like him. And write to me how he receives you. If he's all right, serve him. The son of Nikolay Andreitch Bolkonsky has no need to serve under any man as a favour. Now, come here."

He spoke so rapidly that he did not finish half of his words, but his son was used to understanding him. He led his son to the bureau, opened it, drew out a drawer, and took out of it a manuscript book filled with his bold, big, compressed handwriting.

"I am sure to die before you. See, here are my notes, to be given to the Emperor after my death. Now here, see, is a bank note and a letter: this is a prize for any one who writes a history of Suvorov's wars. Send it to the academy. Here are my remarks, read them after I am gone for your own sake; you will find them profitable."

Andrey did not tell his father that he probably had many years before him. He knew there was no need to say that.

"I will do all that, father," he said.

"Well, now, good-bye!" He gave his son his hand to kiss and embraced him. "Remember one thing, Prince Andrey, if you are killed, it will be a grief to me in my old age . . ." He paused abruptly, and all at once in a shrill voice went on: "But if I learn that you have not behaved like the son of Nikolay Bolkonsky, I shall be . . . ashamed," he shrilled.

"You needn't have said that to me, father," said his son, smiling.

The old man did not speak.

"There's another thing I wanted to ask you," went on Prince Andrey; "if I'm killed, and if I have a son, don't let him slip out of your hands, as I said to you yesterday; let him grow up with you . . . please."

"Not give him up to your wife?" said the old man, and he laughed. They stood mutually facing each other. The old man's sharp eyes were fixed on his son's eyes. A quiver passed over the lower part of the old prince's face.

"We have said good-bye . . . go along!" he said suddenly. "Go along!" he cried in a loud and wrathful voice, opening the study door.

"What is it, what's the matter?" asked the two princesses on seeing Prince Andrey, and catching a momentary glimpse of the figure of the old man in his white dressing-gown, wearing his spectacles and no wig, and shouting in a wrathful voice.

Prince Andrey sighed and made no reply.

"Now, then," he said, turning to his wife, and that "now then" sounded like a cold sneer, as though he had said, "Now, go through your little performance."

"Andrey? Already!" said the little princess, turning pale and looking with dismay at her husband. He embraced her. She shrieked and fell swooning on his shoulder.

He cautiously withdrew the shoulder, on which she was lying, glanced into her face and carefully laid her in a low chair.

"Good-bye, Masha," he said gently to his sister, and they kissed one another's hands, then with rapid steps he walked out of the room.

The little princess lay in the arm-chair; Mademoiselle Bourienne rubbed her temples. Princess Marya, supporting her sister-in-law, still gazed with her fine eyes full of tears at the door by which Prince Andrey had gone, and she made the sign of the cross at it. From the study she heard like pistol shots the repeated and angry sounds of the old man blowing his nose. Just after Prince Andrey had gone, the door of the study was flung open, and the stern figure of the old man in his white dressing-gown peeped out.

"Gone? Well, and a good thing too!" he said, looking furiously at the fainting princess. He shook his head reproachfully and slammed the door.

PART TWO

I

IN THE October of 1805 the Russian troops were occupying the towns and villages of the Austrian archduchy, and fresh regiments kept arriving from Russia and encamping about the fortress of Braunau, burdening the inhabitants on whom they were billeted. Braunau was the chief headquarters of the commander-in-chief, Kutuzov.

On the 11th of October 1805, one of the infantry regiments that had just reached Braunau had halted half a mile from the town, awaiting the inspection of the commander-in-chief. In spite of the un-Russian character of the country and the environment (the fruit gardens, the stone walls, the tiled roofs, the mountains in the distance, the foreign peasants, who looked with curiosity at the Russian soldiers), the regiment looked exactly as every Russian regiment always looks when it is getting ready for inspection anywhere in the heart of Russia. In the evening, on the last stage of the march, the order had been received that the commander-in-chief would inspect the regiment on the march. Though the wording of the order did not seem quite clear to the general in command of the regiment, and the question arose whether they were to take it to mean, in marching order or not, it was decided on a consultation between the majors to present the regiment in parade order on the ground, since, as the saying is, it is better to bow too low than not to bow low enough. And the soldiers after a twenty-five mile march had not closed their eyes, but had spent the night mending and cleaning, while the adjutants and officers had been reckoning up and calculating. And by the morning the regiment, instead of the straggling, disorderly crowd it had been on the last march, the previous evening, presented the spectacle of an organised mass of two thousand men, of whom every one knew his part and his duty, and had every button and every strap in its proper position, and shining with cleanliness. It was not only the outside that was in good order; if the commander-in-chief should think fit to peep below the uniform, he would see on every man alike a clean shirt, and in every knapsack he would find the regulation number of articles. There was only one circumstance which no one could feel comfortable about. That was their foot-gear. More than half the soldiers had holes in their boots. But this deficiency was not due to any shortcoming on the part of their commanding officer, since in spite of his repeated demands the boots had not yet been granted him by the Austrian authorities, and the regiment had marched nearly a thousand miles.

The commander of the regiment was a sanguine-looking general past middle age, with grey whiskers and eyebrows, broad and thick-set, and thicker through from the chest to the back than across the shoulders. He wore a brand-new uniform with the creases still in it where it had been folded, and rich gold epaulettes, which seemed to stand up instead of lying down on his thick shoulders. The general had the air of a man who has successfully performed one of the most solemn duties of his life. He walked about in front of the line, and quivered as he walked, with a slight jerk of his back at each step. The general was unmistakably admiring his regiment, and happy in it, and it was evident that his whole brain was engrossed by the regiment. But for all that, his quivering strut seemed to say that, apart from his military interests, he had plenty of warmth in his heart for the attractions of social life and the fair sex.

"Well, Mihail Mitritch, sir," he said, addressing a major (the major came forward smiling; they were evidently in excellent spirits).

"We have had our hands full all night . . . But it'll do, I fancy; the regiment's not so bad as some . . . eh?"

The major understood this good-humoured irony and laughed.

"Even on the Tsaritsyn review ground they wouldn't be turned off."

"Eh?" said the commander.

At that moment two figures on horseback came into sight on the road from the town, where sentinels had been posted to give the signal. They were an adjutant, and a Cossack riding behind him.

The adjutant had been sent by the commander-in-chief to confirm to the commander what had not been clearly stated in the previous order, namely, that the commander-in-chief wished to inspect the regiment exactly in the order in which it had arrived—wearing their overcoats, and carrying their baggage, and without any sort of preparation. A member of the Hofkriegsrath from Vienna had been with Kutuzov the previous day, proposing and demanding that he should move on as quickly as possible to effect a junction with the army of Archduke Ferdinand and Mack; and Kutuzov, not considering this combination advisable, had intended, among other arguments in support of his view, to point out to the Austrian general the pitiable condition in which were the troops that had arrived from Russia. It was with this object, indeed, that he had meant to meet the regiment, so that the worse the condition of the regiment, the better pleased the commander-in-chief would be with it. Though the adjutant did not know these details, he gave the general in command of the regiment the message that the commander-in-chief absolutely insisted on the men being in their overcoats and marching order, and that, if the contrary were the case, the commander-in-chief would be displeased.

On hearing this the general's head sank; he shrugged his shoulders, and flung up his hands with a choleric gesture.

"Here's a mess we've made of it," he said. "Why, didn't I tell you, Mihail Mitritch, that on the march meant in their overcoats," he said reproachfully to the major. "Ah, my God!" he added, and stepped resolutely forward. "Captains of the companies!" he shouted in a voice used to command. "Sergeants! . . . Will his excellency be coming soon?" he said, turning to the adjutant with an expression of respectful deference, that related obviously only to the person he was speaking of.

"In an hour's time, I believe."

"Have we time to change clothes?"

"I can't say, general. . . ."

The general, going himself among the ranks, gave orders for the men to change back to their overcoats. The captains ran about among the companies, the sergeants bustled to and fro (the overcoats were not quite up to the mark), and instantaneously the squadrons, that had been in regular order and silent, were heaving to and fro, straggling apart and humming with talk. The soldiers ran backwards and forwards in all directions, stooping with their shoulders thrown back, drawing their knapsacks off over their heads, taking out their overcoats and lifting their arms up to thrust them into the sleeves.

Half an hour later everything was in its former good order again, only the squadrons were now grey instead of black. The general walked in front of the regiment again with his quivering strut, and scanned it from some distance.

"What next? what's this!" he shouted, stopping short. "Captain of the third company!"

"The captain of the third company to the general! The captain to the general of the third company to the captain!" . . . voices were heard along the ranks, and an adjutant ran to look for the tardy officer. When the sound of the officious voices, varying the command, and, by now, crying, "the general to the third company," reached their destination, the officer called for emerged from behind his company, and, though he was an elderly man and not accustomed to running, he moved at a quick trot towards the general, stumbling awkwardly over the toes of his boots. The captain's face showed the uneasiness of a schoolboy who is called up to repeat an unlearnt lesson. Patches came out on his red nose (unmistakably due to intemperance), and he did not know how to keep his mouth steady. The general looked the captain up and down as he ran panting up, slackening his pace as he drew nearer.

"You'll soon be dressing your men in petticoats! What's the meaning of it?" shouted the general, thrusting out his lower jaw and pointing in the ranks of the third division to a soldier in an overcoat of a colour different from the rest. "Where have you been yourself? The commander-in-chief is expected, and you're not in your place? Eh? . . . I'll teach you to rig your men out in dressing-gowns for inspection! . . . Eh?"

The captain, never taking his eyes off his superior officer, pressed the peak of his cap more and more tightly with his two fingers, as though he saw in this compression his only hope of safety.

"Well, why don't you speak? Who's that dressed up like a Hungarian?" the general jested bitterly.

"Your excellency . . ."

"Well, what's your excellency? Your excellency! Your excellency! But what that means, your excellency, nobody knows."

"Your excellency, that's Dolohov, the degraded officer," the captain said softly.

"Well, is he degraded to be a field-marshal, or a common soldier? If he's a soldier, then he must be dressed like all the rest, according to regulation."

"Your excellency, you gave him leave yourself on the march."

"Gave him leave? There, you're always like that, you young men," said the general, softening a little. "Gave him leave? If one says a word to you, you go and . . ." The general paused. "One says a word to you, and you go and . . . Eh?" he said with renewed irritation. "Be so good as to clothe your men decently. . . ."

And the general, looking round at the adjutant, walked with his quivering strut towards the regiment. It was obvious that he was pleased with his own display of anger, and that, walking through the regiment, he was trying to find a pretext for wrath. Falling foul of one officer for an unpolished ensign, of another for the unevenness of the rank, he approached the third company.

"How are you standing? Where is your leg? Where is your leg?" the general shouted with a note of anguish in his voice, stopping five men off Dolohov, who was wearing his blue overcoat. Dolohov slowly straightened his bent leg, and looked with his clear, insolent eyes straight in the general's face.

"Why are you in a blue coat? Off with it! . . . Sergeant! change his coat . . . the dir . . ." Before he had time to finish the word—

"General, I am bound to obey orders, but I am not bound to put up with . . ." Dolohov hastened to say.

"No talking in the ranks! . . . No talking, no talking!"

"Not bound to put up with insults," Dolohov went on, loudly and clearly. The eyes of the general and the soldier met. The general paused, angrily pulling down his stiff scarf.

"Change your coat, if you please," he said as he walked away.

II

"Coming!" the sentinel shouted at that moment. The general, turning red, ran to his horse, with trembling hands caught at the stirrup, swung himself up, settled himself in the saddle, drew out his sword, and with a pleased and resolute face opened his mouth on one side, in readiness to shout. The regiment fluttered all over, like a bird preening its wings, and subsided into stillness.

"Silence!" roared the general, in a soul-quaking voice, expressing at once gladness on his own account, severity as regards the regiment, and welcome as regards the approaching commander-in-chief.

A high, blue Vienna coach with several horses was driving at a smart trot, rumbling on its springs, along the broad unpaved high-road, with trees planted on each side of it. The general's suite and an escort of Croats galloped after the coach. Beside Kutuzov sat an Austrian general in a white uniform, that looked strange among the black Russian ones. The coach drew up on reaching the regiment. Kutuzov and the Austrian general were talking of something in low voices, and Kutuzov smiled slightly as, treading heavily, he put his foot on the carriage step, exactly as though those two thousand men gazing breathlessly at him and at their general, did not exist at all.

The word of command rang out, again the regiment quivered with a clanking sound as it presented arms. In the deathly silence the weak voice of the commander-in-chief was audible. The regiment roared: "Good health to your Ex . . lency . . lency . . lency!" And again all was still. At first Kutuzov stood in one spot, while the regiment moved; then Kutuzov began walking on foot among the ranks, the white general beside him, followed by his suite.

From the way that the general in command of the regiment saluted the commander-in-chief, fixing his eyes intently on him, rigidly respectful and obsequious, from the way in which, craning forward, he followed the generals through the ranks, with an effort restraining his quivering strut, and darted up at every word and every gesture of the commander-in-chief,—it was evident that he performed his duties as a subordinate with even greater zest than his duties as a commanding officer. Thanks to the strictness and assiduity of its commander, the regiment was in excellent form as compared with the others that had arrived at Braunau at the same time. The sick and the stragglers left behind only numbered two hundred and seventeen, and everything was in good order except the soldiers' boots.

Kutuzov walked through the ranks, stopping now and then, and saying a few friendly words to officers he had known in the Turkish war, and sometimes to the soldiers. Looking at their boots, he several times shook his head dejectedly, and pointed them out to the Austrian general, with an expression as much as to say that he blamed no one for it, but he could not help seeing what a bad state of things it was. The general in command of the regiment, on every occasion such as this, ran forward, afraid of missing a single word the commander-in-chief might utter regarding the regiment. Behind Kutuzov, at such a distance that every word, even feebly articulated, could be heard, followed his suite, consisting of some twenty persons. These gentlemen were talking among themselves, and sometimes laughed. Nearest of all to the commander-in-chief walked a handsome adjutant. It was Prince Bolkonsky. Beside him was his comrade Nesvitsky, a tall staff-officer, excessively stout, with a good-natured, smiling, handsome face, and moist eyes. Nesvitsky could hardly suppress his mirth, which was excited by a swarthy officer of hussars walking near him. This officer, without a smile or a change in the expression of his fixed eyes, was staring with a serious face at the commanding officer's back, and mimicking every movement he made. Every time the commanding officer quivered and darted forward, the officer of hussars quivered and darted forward in precisely the same way. Nesvitsky laughed, and poked the others to make them look at the mimic.

Kutuzov walked slowly and listlessly by the thousands of eyes which were almost rolling out of their sockets in the effort to watch him. On reaching the third company, he suddenly stopped. The suite, not foreseeing this halt, could not help pressing up closer to him.

"Ah, Timohin!" said the commander-in-chief, recognising the captain with the red nose who had got into trouble over the blue overcoat.

One would have thought it impossible to stand more rigidly erect than Timohin had done when the general in command of the regiment had made his remarks to him; but at the instant when the commander-in-chief addressed him, the captain stood with such erect rigidity that it seemed that, were the commander-in-chief to remain for some time looking at him, the captain could hardly sustain the ordeal, and for that reason Kutuzov, realising his position, and wishing him nothing but good, hurriedly turned away. A scarcely perceptible smile passed over Kutuzov's podgy face, disfigured by the scar of a wound.

"Another old comrade at Ismail!" he said. "A gallant officer! Are you satisfied with him?" Kutuzov asked of the general in command.

And the general, all unconscious that he was being reflected as in a mirror in the officer of hussars behind him, quivered, pressed forward, and answered: "Fully, your most high excellency."

"We all have our weaknesses," said Kutuzov, smiling and walking away from him. "He had a predilection for Bacchus."

The general in command was afraid that he might be to blame for this, and made no answer. The officer of hussars at that instant noticed the face of the captain with the red nose, and the rigidly drawn-in stomach, and mimicked his face and attitude in such a life-like manner that Nesvitsky could not restrain his laughter. Kutuzov turned round. The officer could apparently do anything he liked with his face; at the instant Kutuzov turned round, the officer had time to get in a grimace before assuming the most serious, respectful, and innocent expression.

The third company was the last, and Kutuzov seemed pondering, as though trying to recall something. Prince Andrey stepped forward and said softly in French: "You told me to remind you of the degraded officer, Dolohov, serving in the ranks in this regiment."

"Where is Dolohov?" asked Kutuzov.

Dolohov, attired by now in the grey overcoat of a private soldier, did not wait to be called up. The slender figure of the fair-haired soldier, with his bright blue eyes, stepped out of the line. He went up to the commander-in-chief and presented arms.

"A complaint to make?" Kutuzov asked with a slight frown.

"This is Dolohov," said Prince Andrey.

"Ah!" said Kutuzov. "I hope this will be a lesson to you, do your duty thoroughly. The Emperor is gracious. And I shall not forget you, if you deserve it."

The bright blue eyes looked at the commander-in-chief just as impudently as at the general of his regiment, as though by his expression tearing down the veil of convention that removed the commander-in-chief so far from the soldier.

"The only favour I beg of your most high excellency," he said in his firm, ringing, deliberate voice, "is to give me a chance to atone for my offence, and to prove my devotion to his majesty the Emperor, and to Russia."

Kutuzov turned away. There was a gleam in his eyes of the same smile with which he had turned away from Captain Timohin. He turned away and frowned, as though to express that all Dolohov had said to him and all he could say, he had known long, long ago, that he was sick to death long ago of it, and that it was not at all what was wanted. He turned away and went towards the coach.

The regiment broke into companies and went towards the quarters assigned them at no great distance from Braunau, where they hoped to find boots and clothes, and to rest after their hard marches.

"You won't bear me a grudge, Proho Ignatitch?" said the commanding general, overtaking the third company and riding up to Captain Timohin, who was walking in front of it. The general's face beamed with a delight he could not suppress after the successful inspection. "It's in the Tsar's service . . . can't be helped . . . sometimes one has to be a little sharp at inspection. I'm the first to apologise; you know me. . . . He was very much pleased." And he held out his hand to the captain.

"Upon my word, general, as if I'd make so bold," answered the captain, his nose flushing redder. He smiled, and his smile revealed the loss of two front teeth, knocked out by the butt-end of a gun at Ismail.

"And tell Dolohov that I won't forget him; he can be easy about that. And tell me, please, what about him, how's he behaving himself . . . I've been meaning to inquire . . ."

"He's very exact in the discharge of his duties, your excellency . . . but he's a character . . ." said Timohin.

"Why, what sort of a character?" asked the general.

"It's different on different days, your excellency," said the captain; "at one time he's sensible and well-educated and good-natured. And then he'll be like a wild beast. In Poland, he all but killed a Jew, if you please. . . ."

"Well, well," said the general, "still one must feel for a young man in trouble. He has great connections, you know. . . . So you . . ."

"Oh, yes, your excellency," said Timohin, with a smile that showed he understood his superior officer's wish in the matter.

"Very well, then, very well."

The general sought out Dolohov in the ranks and pulled up his horse. "In the first action you may win your epaulettes," he said to him.

Dolohov looked round and said nothing. There was no change in the lines of his ironically-smiling mouth.

"Well, that's all right then," the general went on. "A glass of brandy to every man from me," he added, so that the soldiers could hear. "I thank you all. God be praised!" And riding round the company, he galloped off to another.

"Well, he's really a good fellow, one can get on very well under him," said Timohin to the subaltern officer walking beside him.

"The king of hearts, that's the only word for him," the subaltern said, laughing. (The general was nicknamed the king of hearts.)

The cheerful state of mind of the officers after the inspection was shared by the soldiers. The companies went along merrily. Soldiers' voices could be heard on all sides chatting away.

"Why, don't they say Kutuzov's blind in one eye?"

"To be sure he is. Quite blind of one eye."

"Nay . . . lads, he's more sharp-eyed than you are. See how he looked at our boots and things." . . .

"I say, mate, when he looked at my legs . . . well, thinks I . . ."

"And the other was an Austrian with him, that looked as if he'd been chalked all over. As white as flour. I bet they rub him up as we rub up our guns."

"I say, Fedeshou . . . did he say anything as to when the battles are going to begin? You stood nearer. They did say Bonaparte himself was in Brunovo."

"Bonaparte! What nonsense the fellow talks! What won't you know next! Now it's the Prussian that's revolting. The Austrian, do you see, is pacifying him. When he's quiet, then the war will begin with Bonaparte. And he talks of Bonaparte's being in Brunovo! It's plain the fellow's a fool. You'd better keep your ears open."

"Those devils of quartermasters! . . . The fifth company's turned into the village by now, and they're cooking their porridge, and we're not there yet."

"Give us a biscuit, old man."

"And did you give me tobacco yesterday? All right, my lad. Well, well, God be with you."

"They might have made a halt, or we'll have to do another four miles with nothing to eat."

"I say, it was fine how those Germans gave us carriages. One drove along, something like."

"But here, lads, the folks are regularly stripped bare. There it was all Poles of some sort, all under the Russian crown, but now we've come to the regular Germans, my boy."

"Singers to the front," the captain called. And from the different ranks about twenty men advanced to the front. The drummer, who was their leader, turned round facing the chorus and waving his arm, struck up a soldier's song, beginning: "The sun was scarcely dawning," and ending with the words: "So, lads, we'll march to glory with Father Kamensky." . . . This song had been composed in Turkey, and now was sung in Austria, the only change being the substitution of the words "Father Kutuzov" for "Father Kamensky."

Jerking out the last words in soldierly fashion and waving his arms, as though he were flinging something on the ground, the drummer, a lean, handsome soldier of forty, looked sternly at the soldier-chorus and frowned. Then, having satisfied himself that all eyes were fixed upon him, he gesticulated, as though he were carefully lifting some unseen precious object over his head in both hands, holding it there some seconds, and all at once with a desperate movement flinging it away.

> "Ah, the threshold of my cottage,
> My new cottage."

Here twenty voices caught up the refrain, and the castanet player, in spite of the weight of his weapon and knapsack, bounded nimbly forward, and walked backwards facing the company, shaking his shoulders, and seeming to menace some one with the castanets. The soldiers stepped out in time to the song, swinging their arms and unconsciously falling into step. Behind the company came the sound of wheels, the rumble of springs, and the tramp of horses. Kutuzov and his suite were going back to the town. The commander-in-chief made a sign for the soldiers to go on freely, and he and all his suite looked as though they took pleasure in the sound of the singing, and the spectacle of the dancing soldier and the gaily, smartly marching men. In the second row from the right flank, beside which the carriage passed, they could not help noticing the blue-eyed soldier, Dolohov, who marched with a special jauntiness and grace in time to the song, and looked at the faces of the persons driving by with an expression that seemed to pity every one who was not at that moment marching in the ranks. The cornet of hussars, the officer of Kutuzov's suite, who had mimicked the general, fell back from the carriage and rode up to Dolohov.

The cornet of hussars, Zherkov, had at one time belonged to the fast set in Petersburg, of which Dolohov had been the leader. Zherkov had met Dolohov abroad as a common soldier, and had not seen fit to recognise him. But now, after Kutuzov's conversation with the degraded officer, he addressed him with all the cordiality of an old friend.

"Friend of my heart, how are you?" he said, through the singing, making his horse keep pace with the marching soldiers.

"How am I?" Dolohov answered coldly. "As you see." The lively song gave a peculiar flavour to the tone of free-and-easy gaiety, with which Zherkov spoke, and the studied coldness of Dolohov's replies.

"Well, how do you get on with your officers?" asked Zherkov.

"All right; they're good fellows. How did you manage to poke yourself on to the staff?"

"I was attached; I'm on duty."

They were silent.

> "My gay goshawk I took with me,
> From my right sleeve I set him free,"

said the song, arousing an involuntary sensation of courage and cheerfulness. Their conversation would most likely have been different, if they had not been talking while the song was singing.

"Is it true, the Austrians have been beaten?" asked Dolohov.

"Devil knows; they say so."

"I'm glad," Dolohov made a brief, sharp reply, as was required to fit in with the tune.

"I say, come round to us some evening; we'll have a game of faro," said Zherkov.

"Is money so plentiful among you?"

"Do come."

"I can't; I've sworn not to. I won't drink or play till I'm promoted."

"Well, but in the first action . . ."

"Then we shall see." Again they paused.

"You come, if you want anything; one can always be of use on the staff. . . ."

Dolohov grinned. "Don't trouble yourself. What I want, I'm not going to ask for; I take it for myself."

"Oh, well, I only . . ."

"Well, and I only."

"Good-bye."

"Good-bye."

> "And far and free
> To his own country."

Zherkov put spurs to his horse, which three times picked up its legs excitedly, not knowing which to start from, then galloped off round the company, and overtook the carriage, keeping time too to the song.

III

ON returning from the review, Kutuzov, accompanied by the Austrian general, went to his private room, and calling his adjutant, told him to give him certain papers, relating to the condition of the newly arrived troops, and letters, received from Archduke Ferdinand, who was in command of the army at the front. Prince Andrey Bolkonsky came into the commander-in-chief's room with the papers he had asked for. Kutuzov and the Austrian member of the Hofkriegsrath were sitting over a plan that lay unfolded on the table.

"Ah!" . . . said Kutuzov, looking round at Bolkonsky; and inviting his adjutant, as it were, by his word to wait, he went on in French with the conversation.

"I have only one thing to say, general," said Kutuzov, with an agreeable elegance of expression and intonation, that forced one to listen for each deliberately uttered word. It was evident that Kutuzov himself listened to his voice with pleasure. "I can only say one thing, that if the matter depended on my personal wishes, the desire of his majesty, the Emperor Francis, should long ago have been accomplished; I should long ago have joined the archduke. And, upon my honour, believe me that for me personally to hand over the chief command of the army to more experienced and skilful generals—such as Austria is so rich in— and to throw off all this weighty responsibility, for me personally would

be a relief. But circumstances are too strong for us, general." And Kutuzov smiled with an expression that seemed to say: "You are perfectly
at liberty not to believe me, and indeed it's a matter of perfect indifference to me whether you believe me or not, but you have no grounds
for saying so. And that's the whole point." The Austrian general looked
dissatisfied, but he had no choice but to answer Kutuzov in the same
tone.

"On the contrary," he said in a querulous and irritated voice, that
contrasted with the flattering intention of the words he uttered; "on the
contrary, the participation of your most high excellency in common
action is highly appreciated by his majesty. But we imagine that the
present delay robs the gallant Russian troops and their commander-in-
chief of the laurels they are accustomed to winning in action," he concluded a phrase he had evidently prepared beforehand.

Kutuzov bowed, still with the same smile.

"But I am convinced of this, and relying on the last letter with which
his Highness the Archduke Ferdinand has honoured me, I imagine that
the Austrian troops under the command of so talented a leader as General Mack, have by now gained a decisive victory and have no longer
need of our aid," said Kutuzov.

The general frowned. Though there was no positive news of the
defeat of the Austrians, there were too many circumstances in confirmation of the unfavourable reports; and so Kutuzov's supposition in regard
to an Austrian victory sounded very much like a sneer. But Kutuzov
smiled blandly, still with the same expression, which seemed to say that
he had a right to suppose so. And in fact the last letter he had received
from the army of General Mack had given him news of victory, and
of the most favourable strategical position of the army.

"Give me that letter," said Kutuzov, addressing Prince Andrey.
"Here, if you will kindly look"—and Kutuzov, with an ironical smile
about the corners of his mouth, read in German the following passage
from the letter of the Archduke Ferdinand:

"We have a force, perfectly kept together, of nearly 70,000 men, in
order to attack and defeat the enemy if they should pass the Lech. As
we are masters of Ulm, we cannot lose the advantage of remaining masters also of both sides of the Danube; and moreover able, should the
enemy not cross the Lech, to pass over the Danube at any moment,
throw ourselves upon their line of communications, recross the Danube
lower down, and entirely resist the enemy's aim if they should attempt
to turn their whole force upon our faithful ally. In this way we shall
await courageously the moment when the Imperial Russian is ready, and
shall then, in conjunction, easily find a possibility of preparing for the
foe that fate which he so richly deserves."

Kutuzov concluded this period with a heavy sigh and looked intently
and genially at the member of the Hofkriegsrath.

"But you know, your excellency, the sage precept to prepare for the worst," said the Austrian general, obviously wishing to have done with jests and to come to business. He could not help glancing round at the adjutant.

"Excuse me, general," Kutuzov interrupted him, and he, too, turned to Prince Andrey. "Here, my dear boy, get all the reports from our scouts from Kozlovsky. Here are two letters from Count Nostits, here is a letter from his Highness the Archduke Ferdinand, here is another," he said, giving him several papers. "And of all this make out clearly in French a memorandum showing all the information we have had of the movements of the Austrian Army. Well, do so, and then show it to his excellency."

Prince Andrey bowed in token of understanding from the first word not merely what had been said, but also what Kutuzov would have liked to have said to him. He gathered up the papers, and making a comprehensive bow, stepped softly over the carpet and went out into the reception-room.

Although so short a time had passed since Prince Andrey had left Russia, he had changed greatly during that time. In the expression of his face, in his gestures, in his gait, there was scarcely a trace to be seen now of his former affectation, ennui, and indolence. He had the air of a man who has not time to think of the impression he is making on others, and is absorbed in work, both agreeable and interesting. His face showed more satisfaction with himself and those around him. His smile and his glance were more light-hearted and attractive.

Kutuzov, whom he had overtaken in Poland, had received him very cordially, had promised not to forget him, had marked him out among the other adjutants, had taken him with him to Vienna and given him the more serious commissions. From Vienna, Kutuzov had written to his old comrade, Prince Andrey's father.

"Your son," he wrote, "gives promise of becoming an officer, who will make his name by his industry, firmness, and conscientiousness. I consider myself lucky to have such an assistant at hand."

On Kutuzov's staff, among his fellow-officers, and in the army generally, Prince Andrey had, as he had had in Petersburg society, two quite opposite reputations. Some, the minority, regarded Prince Andrey as a being different from themselves and from all other men, expected great things of him, listened to him, were enthusiastic in his praise, and imitated him, and with such people Prince Andrey was frank and agreeable. Others, the majority, did not like Prince Andrey, and regarded him as a sulky, cold, and disagreeable person. But with the latter class, too, Prince Andrey knew how to behave so that he was respected and even feared by them.

Coming out of Kutuzov's room into the reception-room, Prince Andrey went in with his papers to his comrade, the adjutant on duty, Kozlovsky, who was sitting in the window with a book.

"What is it, prince?" queried Kozlovsky.

"I am told to make a note of the reason why we are not moving forward."

"And why aren't we?"

Prince Andrey shrugged his shoulders.

"No news from Mack?" asked Kozlovsky.

"No."

"If it were true that he had been beaten, news would have come."

"Most likely," said Prince Andrey, and he moved towards the door to go out. But he was met on the way by a tall man who at that instant walked into the reception-room, slamming the door. The stranger, who had obviously just arrived, was an Austrian general in a long coat, with a black kerchief tied round his head, and the order of Maria Theresa on his neck. Prince Andrey stopped short.

"Commander-in-chief Kutuzov?" the general asked quickly, speaking with a harsh German accent. He looked about him on both sides, and without a pause walked to the door of the private room.

"The commander-in-chief is engaged," said Kozlovsky, hurriedly going up to the unknown general and barring his way to the door. "Whom am I to announce?"

The unknown general looked disdainfully down at the short figure of Kozlovsky, as though surprised that they could be ignorant of his identity.

"The commander-in-chief is engaged," Kozlovsky repeated tranquilly.

The general's face contracted, his lips twitched and quivered. He took out a notebook, hurriedly scribbled something in pencil, tore out the leaf, handed it to Kozlovsky, and with rapid steps walked to the window, dropped on to a chair and looked round at the persons in the room, as though asking what they were looking at him for. Then the general lifted his head, craned his neck forward as though intending to say something, but immediately, as though carelessly beginning to hum to himself, uttered a strange sound which broke off at once. The door of the private room opened, and Kutuzov appeared in the doorway.

The general with the bandaged head, bent forward as though fleeing from danger, strode towards Kutuzov, his thin legs moving swiftly.

"You see the unfortunate Mack," he articulated in French in a break-ing voice.

The face of Kutuzov, as he stood in the doorway, remained for sev-eral instants perfectly unmoved. Then a frown seemed to run over his face, like a wave, leaving his forehead smooth again; he bowed his head respectfully, closed his eyes, ushered Mack in before him without a word, and closed the door behind him.

The report, which had been in circulation before this, of the defeat of the Austrians and the surrender of the whole army at Ulm, turned out to be the truth. Within half an hour adjutants had been despatched in various directions with orders. It was evident that the Russian troops which had hitherto been inactive, were destined soon to meet the enemy.

Prince Andrey was one of those rare staff-officers whose interests were concentrated on the general progress of the war. On seeing Mack and learning the details of his overthrow, he grasped the fact that half the campaign was lost; he perceived all the difficulty of the position of the

Russian troops, and vividly pictured to himself what lay before the army, and the part he would have to play in the work in store for them. He could not help feeling a rush of joyful emotion at the thought of the humiliation of self-confident Austria, and the prospect within a week, perhaps, of seeing and taking part in the meeting of the Russians with the French, the first since Suvorov's day. But he was afraid of the genius of Bonaparte, which might turn out to be more powerful than all the bravery of the Russian troops; and at the same time he could not bear to entertain the idea of the disgrace of his favourite hero.

Excited and irritated by these ideas, Prince Andrey went towards his own room to write to his father, to whom he wrote every day. In the corridor he met Nesvitsky, the comrade with whom he shared a room, and the comic man, Zherkov. They were, as usual, laughing at some joke.

"What are you looking so dismal about?" asked Nesvitsky, noticing Prince Andrey's pale face and gleaming eyes.

"There's nothing to be gay about," answered Bolkonsky.

Just as Prince Andrey met Nesvitsky and Zherkov, there came towards them from the other end of the corridor Strauch, an Austrian general, who was on Kutuzov's staff in charge of the provisioning of the Russian army, and the member of the Hofkriegsrath, who had arrived the previous evening. There was plenty of room in the wide corridor for the generals to pass the three officers easily. But Zherkov, pulling Nesvitsky back by the arm, cried in a breathless voice:

"They are coming! . . . they are coming! . . . move aside, make way! please, make way."

The generals advanced with an air of wishing to avoid burdensome honours. The face of the comic man, Zherkov, suddenly wore a stupid smile of glee, which he seemed unable to suppress.

"Your Excellency," he said in German, moving forward and addressing the Austrian general, "I have the honour to congratulate you." He bowed, and awkwardly, as children do at dancing-lessons, he began scraping first with one leg and then with the other. The member of the Hofkriegsrath looked severely at him, but seeing the seriousness of his stupid smile, he could not refuse him a moment's attention. He screwed up his eyes and showed that he was listening.

"I have the honour to congratulate you. General Mack has arrived, quite well, only slightly wounded here," he added, pointing with a beaming smile to his head.

The general frowned, turned away and went on.

"*Gott, wie naïv!*" he said angrily, when he was a few steps away.

Nesvitsky with a chuckle threw his arms round Prince Andrey, but Bolkonsky, turning even paler, pushed him away with a furious expression, and turned to Zherkov. The nervous irritability, into which he had been thrown by the sight of Mack, the news of his defeat and the thought of what lay before the Russian army, found a vent in anger at the misplaced jest of Zherkov.

"If you, sir," he began cuttingly, with a slight trembling in his lower jaw, "like to be a *clown*, I can't prevent your being so, but if you *dare* to play the fool another time in my presence, I'll teach you how to behave."

Nesvitsky and Zherkov were so astounded at this outburst that they gazed at Bolkonsky with open eyes.

"Why, I only congratulated them," said Zherkov.

"I am not jesting with you; be silent, please!" shouted Bolkonsky, and taking Nesvitsky's arm, he walked away from Zherkov, who could not find any reply.

"Come, what is the matter, my dear boy?" said Nesvitsky, trying to soothe him.

"What's the matter?" said Prince Andrey, standing still from excitement. "Why, you ought to understand that we're either officers, who serve their Tsar and their country and rejoice in the success, and grieve at the defeat of the common cause, or we're hirelings, who have no interest in our master's business. Forty thousand men massacred and the army of our allies destroyed, and you find something in that to laugh at," he said, as though by this French phrase he were strengthening his view. "It is all very well for a worthless fellow like that individual of whom you have made a friend, but not for you, not for you. None but *schoolboys* can find amusement in such jokes," Prince Andrey added in Russian, uttering the word with a French accent. He noticed that Zherkov could still hear him, and waited to see whether the cornet would not reply. But the cornet turned and went out of the corridor.

IV

The Pavlogradsky regiment of hussars was stationed two miles from Braunau. The squadron in which Nikolay Rostov was serving as ensign was billeted on a German village, Salzeneck. The officer in command of the squadron, Captain Denisov, known through the whole cavalry division under the name of Vaska Denisov, had been assigned the best quarters in the village. Ensign Rostov had been sharing his quarters, ever since he overtook the regiment in Poland.

On the 8th of October, the very day when at headquarters all was astir over the news of Mack's defeat, the routine of life was going on as before among the officers of this squadron.

Denisov, who had been losing all night at cards, had not yet returned home, when Rostov rode back early in the morning from a foraging expedition. Rostov, in his ensign's uniform, rode up to the steps, with a jerk to his horse, swung his leg over with a supple, youthful action, stood a moment in the stirrup as though loath to part from the horse, at last sprang down and called the orderly.

"Ah, Bondarenko, friend of my heart," he said to the hussar who rushed headlong up to his horse. "Walk him up and down, my dear fellow," he said, with that gay and brotherly cordiality with which good-hearted young people behave to every one, when they are happy.

"Yes, your excellency," answered the Little Russian, shaking his head good-humouredly.

"Mind now, walk him about well!"

Another hussar rushed up to the horse too, but Bondarenko had already hold of the reins.

It was evident that the ensign was liberal with his tips, and that his service was a profitable one. Rostov stroked the horse on the neck and then on the haunch, and lingered on the steps.

"Splendid! What a horse he will be!" he said to himself, and smiling and holding his sword, he ran up the steps, clanking his spurs. The German, on whom they were billeted, looked out of the cowshed, wearing a jerkin and a pointed cap, and holding a fork, with which he was clearing out the dung. The German's face brightened at once when he saw Rostov. He smiled good-humouredly and winked. "Good-morning, good-morning!" he repeated, apparently taking pleasure in greeting the young man.

"At work already!" said Rostov, still with the same happy, fraternal smile that was constantly on his eager face. "Long live the Austrians! Long live the Russians! Hurrah for the Emperor Alexander!" he said, repeating phrases that had often been uttered by the German. The German laughed, came right out of the cowshed, pulled off his cap, and waving it over his head, cried:

"And long live all the world!"

Rostov too, like the German, waved his cap over his head, and laughing cried: "And hurrah for all the world!" Though there was no reason for any special rejoicing either for the German, clearing out his shed, or for Rostov, coming back from foraging for hay, both these persons gazed at one another in delighted ecstasy and brotherly love, wagged their heads at each other in token of their mutual affection, and parted with smiles, the German to his cowshed, and Rostov to the cottage he shared with Denisov.

"Where's your master?" he asked of Lavrushka, Denisov's valet, well known to all the regiment as a rogue.

"His honour's not been in since the evening. He's been losing, for sure," answered Lavrushka. "I know by now, if he wins, he'll come home early to boast of his luck; but if he's not back by morning, it means that he's lost,—he'll come back in a rage. Shall I bring coffee?"

"Yes, bring it."

Ten minutes later, Lavrushka brought in the coffee.

"He's coming!" said he; "now for trouble!"

Rostov glanced out of the window and saw Denisov returning home. Denisov was a little man with a red face, sparkling black eyes, tousled black whiskers and hair. He was wearing an unbuttoned tunic, wide breeches that fell in folds, and on the back of his head a crushed hussar's cap. Gloomily, with downcast head, he drew near the steps.

"Lavrushka," he shouted, loudly and angrily, lisping the *r*, "come, take it off, blockhead!"

"Well, I am taking it off," answered Lavrushka's voice.

"Ah! you are up already," said Denisov, coming into the room.

"Long ago," said Rostov; "I've been out already after hay, and I have seen Fräulein Mathilde."

"Really? And I've been losing, my boy, all night, like the son of a dog," cried Denisov, not pronouncing his *r's*. "Such ill-luck! such ill-luck! . . . As soon as you left, my luck was gone. Hey, tea?"

Denisov, puckering up his face as though he were smiling, and showing his short, strong teeth, began with his short-fingered hands ruffling up his thick, black hair, that was tangled like a forest.

"The devil was in me to go to that rat" (the nickname of an officer), he said, rubbing his brow and face with both hands. "Only fancy, he didn't deal me one card, not one, not one card!" Denisov took the lighted pipe that was handed to him, gripped it in his fist, and scattering sparks, he tapped it on the floor, still shouting.

"He lets me have the simple, and beats the parole; lets me get the simple, and beats the parole."

He scattered the sparks, broke the pipe, and threw it away. Then Denisov paused, and all at once he glanced brightly at Rostov with his gleaming black eyes.

"If there were only women. But here, except drinking, there's nothing to do. If only we could get to fighting soon. . . . Hey, who's there?" he called towards the door, catching the sounds of thick boots and clanking spurs that came to a stop, and of a respectful cough.

"The sergeant!" said Lavrushka. Denisov puckered up his face more than ever.

"That's a nuisance," he said, flinging down a purse with several gold coins in it. "Rostov, count, there's a dear boy, how much is left, and put the purse under the pillow," he said, and he went out to the sergeant. Rostov took the money and mechanically sorting and arranging in heaps the old and new gold, he began counting it over.

"Ah, Telyanin! Good-morning! I was cleaned out last night," he heard Denisov's voice saying from the other room.

"Where was that? At Bykov's? At the rat's? . . . I knew it," said a thin voice, and thereupon there walked into the room Lieutenant Telyanin, a little officer in the same squadron.

Rostov put the purse under the pillow, and shook the damp little hand that was offered him. Telyanin had for some reason been transferred from the guards just before the regiment set out. He had behaved very well in the regiment, but he was not liked, and Rostov, in particular, could not endure him, and could not conceal his groundless aversion for this officer.

"Well, young cavalryman, how is my Rook doing for you?" (Rook was a riding-horse Telyanin had sold to Rostov.) The lieutenant never looked the person he was speaking to in the face. His eyes were continually flitting from one object to another. "I saw you riding to-day . . ."

"Oh, he's all right; a good horse," answered Rostov, though the horse, for which he had paid seven hundred roubles, was not worth half that sum. "He's begun to go a little lame in the left foreleg . . ." he added.

"The hoof cracked! That's no matter. I'll teach you, I'll show you the sort of thing to put on it."

"Yes, please do," said Rostov.

"I'll show you, I'll show you; it's not a secret. But you'll be grateful to me for that horse."

"Then I'll have the horse brought round," said Rostov, anxious to be rid of Telyanin. He went out to order the horse to be brought round.

In the outer room Denisov was squatting on the threshold with a pipe, facing the sergeant, who was giving him some report. On seeing Rostov, Denisov screwed up his eyes, and pointing over his shoulder with his thumb to the room where Telyanin was sitting, he frowned and shook his head with an air of loathing.

"Ugh! I don't like the fellow," he said, regardless of the presence of the sergeant.

Rostov shrugged his shoulders as though to say, "Nor do I, but what's one to do?" And having given his order, he went back to Telyanin.

The latter was still sitting in the same indolent pose in which Rostov had left him, rubbing his little white hands.

"What nasty faces there are in this world!" thought Rostov as he went into the room.

"Well, have you given orders for the horse to be fetched out?" said Telyanin, getting up and looking carelessly about him.

"Yes."

"Well, you come along yourself. I only came round to ask Denisov about yesterday's order. Have you got it, Denisov?"

"Not yet. But where are you off to?"

"I'm going to show this young man here how to shoe a horse," said Telyanin.

They went out down the steps and into the stable. The lieutenant showed how to put on the remedy, and went away to his own quarters.

When Rostov went back there was a bottle of vodka and some sausage on the table. Denisov was sitting at the table, and his pen was squeaking over the paper. He looked gloomily into Rostov's face.

"I am writing to her," he said. He leaned his elbow on the table with the pen in his hand, and obviously rejoiced at the possibility of saying by word of mouth all he meant to write, he told the contents of his letter to Rostov. "You see, my dear boy," he said, "we are plunged in slumber, we are the children of dust and ashes, until we love . . . but love, and you are a god, you are pure, as on the first day of creation . . . Who's that now? Send him to the devil! I've no time!" he shouted to Lavrushka, who, not in the slightest daunted, went up to him.

"Why, who should it be? You told him to come yourself. The sergeant has come for the money."

Denisov frowned, seemed about to shout some reply, but did not speak.

"It's a nuisance," he said to himself. "How much money was there left there in the purse?" he asked Rostov.

"Seven new and three old gold pieces."

"Oh, it's a nuisance! Well, why are you standing there, you mummy? Send the sergeant!" Denisov shouted to Lavrushka.

"Please, Denisov, take the money from me; I've plenty," said Rostov, blushing.

"I don't like borrowing from my own friends; I dislike it," grumbled Denisov.

"But if you won't take money from me like a comrade, you'll offend me. I've really got it," repeated Rostov.

"Oh, no." And Denisov went to the bed to take the purse from under the pillow.

"Where did you put it, Rostov?"

"Under the lower pillow."

"But it's not there." Denisov threw both the pillows on the floor, There was no purse. "Well, that's a queer thing."

"Wait a bit, haven't you dropped it?" said Rostov, picking the pillows up one at a time and shaking them. He took off the quilt and shook it. The purse was not there.

"Could I have forgotten? No, for I thought that you keep it like a secret treasure under your head," said Rostov. "I laid the purse here. Where is it?" He turned to Lavrushka.

"I never came into the room. Where you put it, there it must be."

"But it isn't."

"You're always like that; you throw things down anywhere and for-get them. Look in your pockets."

"No, if I hadn't thought of its being a secret treasure," said Rostov, "but I remember where I put it."

Lavrushka ransacked the whole bed, glanced under it and under the table, ransacked the whole room and stood still in the middle of the room. Denisov watched Lavrushka's movements in silence, and when Lavrushka flung up his hands in amazement to signify that it was no-where, he looked round at Rostov.

"Rostov, none of your schoolboy jokes."

Rostov, feeling Denisov's eyes upon him, lifted his eyes and in-stantly dropped them again. All his blood, which felt as though it had been locked up somewhere below his throat, rushed to his face and eyes. He could hardly draw his breath.

"And there's been no one in the room but the lieutenant and your-selves. It must be here somewhere," said Lavrushka.

"Now then, you devil's puppet, bestir yourself and look for it!" Denisov shouted suddenly, turning purple and dashing at the valet with a threatening gesture. "The purse is to be found, or I'll flog you! I'll flog you all!"

Rostov, his eyes avoiding Denisov, began buttoning up his jacket, fastening on his sword, and putting on his forage-cap.

"I tell you the purse is to be found," roared Denisov, shaking the orderly by the shoulders and pushing him against the wall.

"Denisov, let him be; I know who has taken it," said Rostov, going towards the door without raising his eyes.

Denisov stopped, thought a moment, and evidently understanding Rostov's hint, he clutched him by the arm.

"Nonsense!" he roared so that the veins stood out on his neck and forehead like cords. "I tell you, you've gone out of your mind; I won't allow it. The purse is here; I'll flay the skin off this rascal, and it will be here."

"I know who has taken it," repeated Rostov, in a shaking voice, and he went to the door.

"And I tell you, you're not to dare to do it," shouted Denisov, making a dash at the ensign to detain him. But Rostov pulled his arm away, lifted his eyes, and looked directly and resolutely at Denisov with as much fury as if he had been his greatest enemy.

"Do you understand what you're saying?" he said in a trembling voice; "except me, there has been no one else in the room. So that, if it's not so, why then . . ."

He could not utter the rest, and ran out of the room.

"Oh, damn you and all the rest," were the last words Rostov heard.

Rostov went to Telyanin's quarters.

"The master's not at home, he's gone to the staff," Telyanin's orderly told him. "Has something happened?" the orderly added, wondering at the ensign's troubled face.

"No, nothing."

"You've only just missed him," said the orderly.

The staff quarters were two miles and a half from Salzeneck. Not having found him at home, Rostov took his horse and rode to the quarters of the staff. In the village, where the staff was quartered, there was a restaurant which the officers frequented. Rostov reached the restaurant and saw Telyanin's horse at the entry.

In the second room the lieutenant was sitting over a dish of sausages and a bottle of wine.

"Ah, you have come here too, young man," he said, smiling and lifting his eyebrows.

"Yes," said Rostov, speaking as though the utterance of the word cost him great effort; and he sat down at the nearest table.

Both were silent; there were two Germans and a Russian officer in the room. Every one was mute, and the only sounds audible were the clatter of knives on the plates and the munching of the lieutenant. When Telyanin had finished his lunch, he took out of his pocket a double purse; with his little white fingers, that were curved at the tips, he parted the rings, took out some gold, and raising his eyebrows, gave the money to the attendant.

"Make haste, please," he said.

The gold was new. Rostov got up and went to Telyanin.

"Let me look at the purse," he said in a low voice, scarcely audible.

With shifting eyes, but eyebrows still raised, Telyanin gave him the purse.

"Yes, it's a pretty purse . . . yes . . ." he said, and suddenly he turned white. "You can look at it, young man," he added.

Rostov took the purse in his hand and looked both at it and at the money in it, and also at Telyanin. The lieutenant looked about him, as his way was, and seemed suddenly to have grown very good-humoured.

"If we go to Vienna, I suspect I shall leave it all there, but now there's nowhere to spend our money in these wretched little places," he said. "Come, give it me, young man; I'm going."

Rostov did not speak.

"What are you going to do? have lunch too? They give you decent food," Telyanin went on. "Give it me." He put out his hand and took hold of the purse. Rostov let go of it. Telyanin took the purse and began carelessly dropping it into the pocket of his riding trousers, while his eyebrows were carelessly lifted and his mouth stood a little open, as though he would say: "Yes, yes, I'm putting my purse in my pocket, and that's a very simple matter, and no one has anything to do with it."

"Well, young man?" he said with a sign, and from under his lifted eyebrows he glanced into Rostov's eyes. A kind of gleam passed with the swiftness of an electric flash from Telyanin's eyes to the eyes of Rostov, and back again and back again and again, all in one instant.

"Come here," said Rostov, taking Telyanin by the arm. He almost dragged him to the window. "That's Denisov's money; you took it . . ." he whispered in his ear.

"What? . . . what? . . . How dare you? What?" . . . said Telyanin. But the words sounded like a plaintive, despairing cry and prayer for forgiveness. As soon as Rostov heard the sound of his voice, a great weight of suspense, like a stone, rolled off his heart. He felt glad, and at the same instant he pitied the luckless creature standing before him, but he had to carry the thing through to the end.

"God knows what the people here may think," muttered Telyanin, snatching up his forage-cap and turning towards a small empty room. "You must explain . . ."

"I know that, and I'll prove it," said Rostov.

"I . . ."

The terrified, white face of Telyanin began twitching in every muscle; his eyes still moved uneasily, but on the ground, never rising to the level of Rostov's face, and tearful sobs could be heard.

"Count! . . . don't ruin a young man . . . here is the wretched money, take it." . . . He threw it on the table. "I've an old father and mother!" . . .

Rostov took the money, avoiding Telyanin's eyes, and without uttering a word, he went out of the room. But in the doorway he stopped and turned back.

"My God!" he said, with tears in his eyes, "how could you do it?"

"Count," said Telyanin, coming nearer to the ensign.

"Don't touch me," said Rostov, drawing back. "If you're in need, take the money."

He thrust a purse on him and ran out of the restaurant.

V

IN the evening of the same day a lively discussion was taking place in Denisov's quarters between some officers of the squadron.

"But I tell you, Rostov, that you must apologise to the colonel," the tall staff-captain was saying, addressing Rostov, who was crimson with excitement. The staff-captain, Kirsten, a man with grizzled hair, immense whiskers, thick features and a wrinkled face, had been twice degraded to the ranks for affairs of honour, and had twice risen again to holding a commission.

"I permit no one to tell me I'm lying!" cried Rostov. "He told me I was lying and I told him he was lying. And there it rests. He can put me on duty every day, he can place me under arrest, but no one can compel me to apologise, because if he, as the colonel, considers it beneath his dignity to give me satisfaction, then . . ."

"But you wait a bit, my good fellow; you listen to me," interrupted the staff-captain in his bass voice, calmly stroking his long whiskers. "You tell the colonel in the presence of other officers that an officer has stolen——"

"I'm not to blame for the conversation being in the presence of other officers. Possibly I ought not to have spoken before them, but I'm not a diplomatist. That's just why I went into the hussars; I thought that here I should have no need of such finicky considerations, and he tells me I'm a liar . . . so let him give me satisfaction."

"That's all very fine, no one imagines that you're a coward; but that's not the point. Ask Denisov if it's not utterly out of the question for an ensign to demand satisfaction of his colonel?"

Denisov was biting his moustache with a morose air, listening to the conversation, evidently with no desire to take part in it. To the captain's question, he replied by a negative shake of the head.

"You speak to the colonel in the presence of other officers of this dirty business," pursued the staff-captain. "Bogdanitch" (Bogdanitch was what they called the colonel) "snubbed you . . ."

"No, he didn't. He said I was telling an untruth."

"Quite so, and you talked nonsense to him, and you must apologise."

"Not on any consideration!" shouted Rostov.

"I shouldn't have expected this of you," said the staff-captain seriously and severely. "You won't apologise, but, my good sir, it's not only him, but all the regiment, all of us, that you've acted wrongly by; you're to blame all round. Look here; if you'd only thought it over, and taken advice how to deal with the matter, but you must go and blurt it all straight out before the officers. What was the colonel to do then? Is he to bring the officer up for trial and disgrace the whole regiment? On account of one scoundrel is the whole regiment to be put to shame? Is that the thing for him to do, to your thinking? It is not to our thinking. And Bogdanitch did the right thing. He told you that you were telling an untruth. It's unpleasant, but what could he do? you brought it on yourself. And now when they try to smooth the thing over, you're so high and mighty, you won't apologise, and want to have the whole story out. You're huffy at being put on duty, but what is it for you to apologise to an old and honourable officer! Whatever Bogdanitch may be, any way he's an honourable and gallant old colonel; you're offended at that, but disgracing the regiment's nothing to you." The staff-captain's voice began to quaver. "You, sir, have been next to no time in the regiment; you're here to-day, and to-morrow you'll be passed on somewhere as an adjutant; you don't care a straw for people saying: 'There are thieves among the Pavlograd officers!' But we do care! Don't we, Denisov? Do we care?"

Denisov still did not speak or stir; his gleaming black eyes glanced now and then at Rostov.

"Your pride is dear to you, you don't want to apologise," continued the staff-captain, "but we old fellows, as we grew up in the regiment and, please God, we hope to die in it, it's the honour of the regiment is dear to us, and Bogdanitch knows that. Ah, isn't it dear to us! But this isn't right; it's not right! You may take offence or not; but I always speak the plain truth. It's not right!"

And the staff-captain got up and turned away from Rostov.

"That's the truth, damn it!" shouted Denisov, jumping up. "Come, Rostov, come!"

Rostov, turning crimson and white again, looked first at one officer and then at the other.

"No, gentlemen, no . . . you mustn't think . . . I quite understand, you're wrong in thinking that of me . . . I . . . for me . . . for the honour of the regiment I'd . . . but why talk? I'll prove that in action and for me the honour of the flag . . . well, never mind, it's true, I'm to blame!" . . . There were tears in his eyes. "I'm wrong, wrong all round! Well, what more do you want?" . . .

"Come, that's right, count," cried the staff-captain, turning round and clapping him on the shoulder with his big hand.

"I tell you," shouted Denisov, "he's a capital fellow."

"That's better, count," repeated the captain, beginning to address him by his title as though in acknowledgment of his confession. "Go and apologise, your excellency."

"Gentlemen, I'll do anything, no one shall hear a word from me," Rostov protested in an imploring voice, "but I can't apologise, by God, I can't, say what you will! How can I apologise, like a little boy begging pardon!"

Denisov laughed.

"It'll be the worse for you, if you don't. Bogdanitch doesn't forget things; he'll make you pay for your obstinacy," said Kirsten.

"By God, it's not obstinacy! I can't describe the feeling it gives me. I can't do it."

"Well, as you like," said the staff-captain. "What has the scoundrel done with himself?" he asked Denisov.

"He has reported himself ill; to-morrow the order's given for him to be struck off," said Denisov.

"It is an illness, there's no other way of explaining it," said the staff-captain.

"Whether it's illness or whether it's not, he'd better not cross my path —I'd kill him," Denisov shouted bloodthirstily.

Zherkov walked into the room.

"How do you come here?" the officers cried to the newcomer at once.

"To the front, gentlemen. Mack has surrendered with his whole army."

"Nonsense!"

"I've seen him myself."

"What? Seen Mack alive, with all his arms and legs?"

"To the front! to the front! Give him a bottle for such news. How did you come here?"

"I've been dismissed back to the regiment again on account of that devil, Mack. The Austrian general complained of me. I congratulated him on Mack's arrival. . . . What is it, Rostov, you look as if you'd just come out of a hot bath?"

"We've been in such a mess these last two days, old boy."

The regimental adjutant came in and confirmed the news brought by Zherkov. They were under orders to advance next day.

"To the front, gentlemen!"

"Well, thank God! we've been sticking here too long."

VI

KUTUZOV fell back to Vienna, destroying behind him the bridges over the river Inn (in Braunau) and the river Traun (in Linz). On the 23rd of October the Russian troops crossed the river Enns. The Russian baggage-waggons and artillery and the columns of troops were in the middle of that day stretching in a long string across the town of Enns on both sides of the bridge. The day was warm, autumnal, and rainy. The wide view that opened out from the heights where the Russian batteries stood guarding the bridge was at times narrowed by the slanting rain that shut it in like a muslin curtain, then again widened out, and in the bright sunlight objects could be distinctly seen in the distance, looking as if covered with a coat of varnish. The little town could be seen below with its white houses and its red roofs, its cathedral and its bridge, on both sides of which streamed masses of Russian troops, crowded together. At the bend of the Danube could be seen ships and the island and a castle with a park, surrounded by the waters formed by the Enns falling into the Danube, and the precipitous left bank of the Danube, covered with pine forest, with a mysterious distance of green tree-tops and bluish gorges. Beyond the pine forest, that looked wild and untouched by the hand of man, rose the turrets of a nunnery; and in the far distance in front, on the hill on the further side of the Enns, could be seen the scouts of the enemy.

Between the cannons on the height stood the general in command of the rear-guard and an officer of the suite scanning the country through a field-glass. A little behind them, there sat on the trunk of a cannon, Nesvitsky, who had been despatched by the commander-in-chief to the rear-guard. The Cossack who accompanied Nesvitsky had handed him over a knapsack and a flask, and Nesvitsky was regaling the officers with pies and real doppel-kümmel. The officers surrounded him in a delighted circle, some on their knees, some sitting cross-legged, like Turks, on the wet grass.

"Yes, there was some sense in that Austrian prince who built a castle here. It's a magnificent spot. Why aren't you eating, gentlemen?" said Nesvitsky.

"Thank you very much, prince," answered one of the officers, enjoying the opportunity of talking to a staff-official of such importance. "It's a lovely spot. We marched right by the park; we saw two deer and such a splendid house!"

"Look, prince," said another, who would dearly have liked to take another pie, but was ashamed to, and therefore affected to be gazing at the countryside; "look, our infantry have just got in there. Over there, near the meadow behind the village, three of them are dragging something. They will clean out that palace nicely," he said, with evident approval.

"No doubt," said Nesvitsky. "No; but what I should like," he added, munching a pie in his moist, handsome mouth, "would be to slip in there." He pointed to the turreted nunnery that could be seen on the mountainside. He smiled, his eyes narrowing and gleaming. "Yes, that would be first-rate, gentlemen!" The officers laughed.

"One might at least scare the nuns a little. There are Italian girls, they say, among them. Upon my word, I'd give five years of my life for it!"

"They must be bored, too," said an officer who was rather bolder, laughing.

Meanwhile the officer of the suite, who was standing in front, pointed something out to the general; the general looked through the field-glass.

"Yes, so it is, so it is," said the general angrily, taking the field-glass away from his eye and shrugging his shoulders; "they are going to fire at them at the crossing of the river. And why do they linger so?"

With the naked eye, looking in that direction, one could discern the enemy and their batteries, from which a milky-white smoke was rising. The smoke was followed by the sound of a shot in the distance, and our troops were unmistakably hurrying to the place of crossing.

Nesvitsky got up puffing and went up to the general, smiling.

"Wouldn't your excellency take some lunch?" he said.

"It's a bad business," said the general, without answering him; "our men have been too slow."

"Shouldn't I ride over, your excellency?" said Nesvitsky.

"Yes, ride over, please," said the general, repeating an order that had already once before been given in detail; "and tell the hussars that they are to cross last and to burn the bridge, as I sent orders, and that they're to overhaul the burning materials on the bridge."

"Very good," answered Nesvitsky. He called the Cossack with his horse, told him to pick up the knapsack and flask, and lightly swung his heavy person into the saddle.

"Upon my word, I am going to pay a visit to the nuns," he said to the officers who were watching him, smiling, and he rode along the winding path down the mountain.

"Now then, captain, try how far it'll carry," said the general, turning to the artillery officer. "Have a little fun to pass the time."

"Men, to the guns!" commanded the officer, and in a moment the gunners ran gaily from the camp fires and loaded the big guns.

"One!" they heard the word of command. Number one bounded back nimbly. The cannon boomed with a deafening metallic sound, and whistling over the heads of our men under the mountainside, the grenade flew across, and falling a long way short of the enemy showed by the rising smoke where it had fallen and burst.

The faces of the soldiers and officers lightened up at the sound. Every one got up and busily watched the movements of our troops below, which could be seen as in the hollow of a hand, and the movements of the advancing enemy. At the same instant, the sun came out fully from behind the clouds, and the full note of the solitary shot and the brilliance of the bright sunshine melted into a single inspiriting impression of light-hearted gaiety.

VII

OVER the bridge two of the enemy's shots had already flown and there was a crush on the bridge. In the middle of the bridge stood Nesvitsky. He had dismounted and stood with his stout person jammed against the railings. He looked laughingly back at his Cossack, who was standing several paces behind him holding the two horses by their bridles. Every time Nesvitsky tried to move on, the advancing soldiers and waggons bore down upon him and shoved him back against the railings. There was nothing for him to do but to smile.

"Hi there, my lad," said the Cossack to a soldier in charge of a waggon-load who was forcing his way through the foot-soldiers that pressed right up to his wheels and his horses; "what are you about? No, you wait a bit; you see the general wants to pass."

But the convoy soldier, taking no notice of the allusion to the general, bawled to the soldiers who blocked the way: "Hi! fellows, keep to the left! wait a bit!" But the fellows, shoulder to shoulder, with their bayonets interlocked, moved over the bridge in one compact mass. Looking down over the rails, Prince Nesvitsky saw the noisy, rapid, but not high waves of the Enns, which, swirling in eddies round the piles of the bridge, chased one another down stream. Looking on the bridge he saw the living waves of the soldiers, all alike as they streamed by: shakoes with covers on them, knapsacks, bayonets, long rifles, and under the shakoes broad-jawed faces, sunken cheeks, and looks of listless weariness, and legs moving over the boards of the bridge, that were coated with sticky mud. Sometimes among the monotonous streams of soldiers, like a crest of white foam on the waves of the Enns, an officer forced his way through, in a cloak, with a face of a different type from the soldiers. Sometimes, like a chip whirling on the river, there passed over the bridge among the waves of infantry a dismounted hussar, an orderly, or an inhabitant of the town. Sometimes, like a log floating down the river, there moved over the bridge, hemmed in on all sides, a baggage-waggon, piled up high and covered with leather covers.

"Why, they're like a river bursting its banks," said the Cossack, stopping hopelessly. "Are there many more over there?"

"A million, all but one!" said a cheerful soldier in a torn coat, winking, as he passed out of sight; after him came another soldier, an older man.

"If *he*" (*he* meant the enemy) "starts popping at the bridge just now," said the old soldier dismally, addressing his companion, "you'll forget to scratch yourself." And he passed on. After him came another soldier riding on a waggon.

"Where the devil did you put the leg-wrappers?" said an orderly, running after the waggon and fumbling in the back part of it. And he too passed on with the waggon.

Then came some hilarious soldiers, who had unmistakably been drinking.

"And didn't he up with the butt end of his gun and give him one right in the teeth," one soldier was saying gleefully with a wide sweep of his arm.

"It just was a delicious ham," answered the other with a chuckle. And they passed on, so that Nesvitsky never knew who had received the blow in his teeth, and what the ham had to do with it.

"Yes, they're in a hurry now! When *he* let fly a bit of cold lead, one would have thought they were all being killed," said an under officer, angrily and reproachfully.

"When it whizzed by me, uncle, the bullet," said a young soldier with a huge mouth, scarcely able to keep from laughing, "I turned fairly numb. Upon my soul, wasn't I in a fright, to be sure!" said the soldier, making a sort of boast of his terror.

He, too, passed on. After him came a waggon unlike all that had passed over before. It was a German *Vorspann* with two horses, loaded, it seemed, with the goods of a whole household. The horses were led by a German, and behind was fastened a handsome, brindled cow with an immense udder. On piled-up feather-beds sat a woman with a small baby, an old woman, and a good-looking, rosy-cheeked German girl. They were evidently country people, moving, who had been allowed through by special permit. The eyes of all the soldiers were turned upon the women, and, while the waggon moved by, a step at a time, all the soldiers' remarks related to the two women. Every face wore almost the same smile, reflecting indecent ideas about the women.

"Hey, the sausage, he's moving away!"

"Sell us your missis," said another soldier, addressing the German, who strode along with downcast eyes, looking wrathful and alarmed.

"See how she's dressed herself up! Ah, you devils!"

"I say, wouldn't you like to be billeted on them, Fedotov!"

"I know a thing or two, mate!"

"Where are you going?" asked the infantry officer, who was eating an apple. He too was half smiling and staring at the handsome girl. The German, shutting his eyes, signified that he did not understand.

"Take it, if you like," said the officer, giving the girl an apple. The girl smiled and took it. Nesvitsky, like all the men on the bridge, never took his eyes off the women till they had passed by. When they had passed by, again there moved by the same soldiers, with the same talk, and at last all came to a standstill. As often happens, the horses in a convoy-waggon became unmanageable at the end of the bridge, and the whole crowd had to wait.

"What are they standing still for? There's no order kept!" said the soldiers. "Where are you shoving?" "Damn it!" "Can't you wait a little?" "It'll be a bad look-out if *he* sets light to the bridge."

"Look, there's an officer jammed in too," the soldiers said in different parts of the stationary crowd, as they looked about them and kept pressing forward to the end of the bridge. Looking round at the waters of the Enns under the bridge, Nesvitsky suddenly heard a sound new to him, the sound of something rapidly coming nearer . . . something big, and then a splash in the water.

"Look where it reaches to!" a soldier standing near said sternly, looking round at the sound.

"He's encouraging us to get on quicker," said another uneasily. The crowd moved again. Nesvitsky grasped that it was a cannon ball.

"Hey, Cossack, give me my horse!" he said. "Now then, stand aside! stand aside! make way!"

With a mighty effort he succeeded in getting to his horse. Shouting continually, he moved forward. The soldiers pressed together to make way for him, but jammed upon him again, so that they squeezed his leg, and those nearest him were not to blame, for they were pressed forward even more violently from behind.

"Nesvitsky! Nesvitsky! You, old chap!" he heard a husky voice shouting from behind at that instant.

Nesvitsky looked round and saw, fifteen paces away, separated from him by a living mass of moving infantry, the red and black and tousled face of Vaska Denisov with a forage-cap on the back of his head, and a pelisse swung jauntily over his shoulder.

"Tell them to make way, the damned devils!" roared Denisov, who was evidently in a great state of excitement. He rolled his flashing, coal-black eyes, showing the bloodshot whites, and waved a sheathed sword, which he held in a bare hand as red as his face.

"Eh! Vaska!" Nesvitsky responded joyfully. "But what are you about?"

"The squadron can't advance!" roared Vaska Denisov, viciously showing his white teeth, and spurring his handsome, raven thorough-bred "Bedouin," which, twitching its ears at the bayonets against which it pricked itself, snorting and shooting froth from its bit, tramped with metallic clang on the boards of the bridge, and seemed ready to leap over the railings, if its rider would let it.

"What next! like sheep! for all the world like sheep; back . . . make way! . . . Stand there! go to the devil with the waggon! I'll cut you down with my sword!" he roared, actually drawing his sword out of the sheath and beginning to brandish it.

The soldiers, with terrified faces, squeezed together, and Denisov joined Nesvitsky.

"How is it you're not drunk to-day?" said Nesvitsky, when he came up.

"They don't even give us time to drink!" answered Vaska Denisov. "They've been dragging the regiment to and fro the whole day. Fighting's all very well, but who the devil's to know what this is!"

"How smart you are to-day!" said Nesvitsky, looking at his new pelisse and fur saddle-cloth.

Denisov smiled, pulled out of his sabretache a handkerchief that diffused a smell of scent, and put it to Nesvitsky's nose.

"To be sure, I'm going into action! I've shaved, and cleaned my teeth and scented myself!"

Nesvitsky's imposing figure, accompanied by his Cossack, and the determination of Denisov, waving his sword and shouting desperately, produced so much effect that they stopped the infantry and got to the other end of the bridge. Nesvitsky found at the entry the colonel, to whom he had to deliver the command, and having executed his commission he rode back.

Having cleared the way for him, Denisov stopped at the entrance of the bridge. Carelessly holding in his horse, who neighed to get to his companions, and stamped with its foot, he looked at the squadron moving towards him. The clang of the hoofs on the boards of the bridge sounded as though several horses were galloping, and the squadron, with the officers in front, drew out four men abreast across the bridge and began emerging on the other side.

The infantry soldiers, who had been forced to stop, crowding in the trampled mud of the bridge, looked at the clean, smart hussars, passing them in good order, with that special feeling of aloofness and irony with which different branches of the service usually meet.

"They're a smart lot! They ought to be on the Podnovinsky!"

"They're a great deal of use! They're only for show!" said another.

"Infantry, don't you kick up a dust!" jested a hussar, whose horse, prancing, sent a spurt of mud on an infantry soldier.

"I should like to see you after two long marches with the knapsack on your shoulder. Your frogs would be a bit shabby," said the foot-soldier, rubbing the mud off his face with his sleeve; "perched up there you're more like a bird than a man!"

"Wouldn't you like to be popped on a horse, Zikin; you'd make an elegant rider," jested a corporal at a thin soldier, bowed down by the weight of his knapsack.

"Put a stick between your legs and you'd have a horse to suit you," responded the hussar.

VIII

THE rest of the infantry pressed together into a funnel shape at the entrance of the bridge, and hastily marched across it. At last all the baggage-waggons had passed over; the crush was less, and the last battalion were stepping on to the bridge. Only the hussars of Denisov's squadron were left on the further side of the river facing the enemy. The enemy, visible in the distance from the opposite mountain, could not yet be seen from the bridge below, as, from the valley, through which the river flowed, the horizon was bounded by rising ground not more than half a mile away. In front lay a waste plain dotted here and there with handfuls of our scouting Cossacks. Suddenly on the road, where it ran up the rising ground opposite, troops came into sight wearing blue tunics and accompanied by artillery. They were the French. A scouting party of Cossacks trotted away down the hillside. Though the officers and the men of Denisov's squadron tried to talk of other things, and to look in other directions, they all thought continually of nothing else but what was there on the hillside, and kept constantly glancing towards the dark patches they saw coming into sight on the sky-line, and recognised as the enemy's forces. The weather had cleared again after midday, and the sun shone brilliantly as it began to go down over the Danube and the dark mountains that encircle it. The air was still, and from the hillside there floated across from time to time the sound of bugles and of the shouts of the enemy. Between the squadron and the enemy there was no one now but a few scouting parties. An empty plain, about six hundred yards across, separated them from the hostile troops. The enemy had ceased firing, and that made even more keenly felt the stern menace of that inaccessible, unassailable borderland that was the dividing-line between the two hostile armies.

"One step across that line, that suggests the line dividing the living from the dead, and unknown sufferings and death. And what is there? and who is there? there, beyond that field and that tree and the roofs with the sunlight on them? No one knows, and one longs to know and dreads crossing that line, and longs to cross it, and one knows that sooner or later one will have to cross it and find out what there is on the other side of the line, just as one must inevitably find out what is on

the other side of death. Yet one is strong and well and cheerful and nervously excited, and surrounded by men as strong in the same irritable
excitement." That is how every man, even if he does not think, feels in
the sight of the enemy, and that feeling gives a peculiar brilliance and
delightful keenness to one's impressions of all that takes place at such
moments.

On the rising ground occupied by the enemy, there rose the smoke of
a shot, and a cannon ball flew whizzing over the heads of the squadron
of hussars. The officers, who had been standing together, scattered in
different directions. The hussars began carefully getting their horses
back into line. The whole squadron subsided into silence. All the men
were looking at the enemy in front and at the commander of the squadron, expecting an order to be given. Another cannon ball flew by them,
and a third. There was no doubt that they were firing at the hussars.
But the cannon balls, whizzing regularly and rapidly, flew over the
heads of the hussars and struck the ground beyond them. The hussars
did not look round, but at each sound of a flying ball, as though at the
word of command, the whole squadron, with their faces so alike, through
all their dissimilarity, rose in the stirrups, holding their breath, as the
ball whizzed by, then sank again. The soldiers did not turn their heads,
but glanced out of the corners of their eyes at one another, curious to
see the effect on their comrades. Every face from Denisov down to the
bugler showed about the lips and chin the same lines of conflict and
nervous irritability and excitement. The sergeant frowned, looking the
soldiers up and down, as though threatening them with punishment.
Ensign Mironov ducked at the passing of each cannon ball. On the left
flank, Rostov on his Rook—a handsome beast, in spite of his unsound
legs—had the happy air of a schoolboy called up before a large audience
for an examination in which he is confident that he will distinguish
himself. He looked serenely and brightly at every one, as though calling
upon them all to notice how unconcerned he was under fire. But into his
face too there crept, against his will, that line about the mouth that
betrayed some new and strenuous feeling.

"Who's bobbing up and down there? Ensign Mironov! Not the thing!
look at me!" roared Denisov, who could not keep still in one place, but
galloped to and fro before the squadron.

The snub-nosed, black, hairy face of Vaska Denisov, and his little,
battered figure, and the sinewy, short-fingered hand in which he held the
hilt of his naked sword—his whole figure was just as it always was,
especially in the evening after he had drunk a couple of bottles. He was
only rather redder in the face than usual, and tossing back his shaggy
head, as birds do when they drink, his little legs mercilessly driving the
spurs into his good horse Bedouin, he galloped to the other flank of the
squadron, looking as though he were falling backwards in the saddle,
and shouted in a husky voice to the men to look to their pistols. He rode
up to Kirsten. The staff-captain on his stout, steady charger rode at a
walking pace to meet him. The staff-captain's face with its long whiskers
was serious, as always, but his eyes looked brighter than usual.

"Well," he said to Denisov, "it won't come to a fight. You'll see, we shall retreat again."

"Devil knows what they're about!" growled Denisov. "Ah, Rostov!" he called to the ensign, noticing his beaming face. "Well, you've not had long to wait." And he smiled approvingly, unmistakably pleased at the sight of the ensign. Rostov felt perfectly blissful. At that moment the colonel appeared at the bridge. Denisov galloped up to him.

"Your excellency, let us attack! we'll settle them."

"Attack, indeed!" said the colonel in a bored voice, puckering his face up as though at a teasing fly. "And what are you stopping here for? You see the flanks are retreating. Lead the squadron back."

The squadron crossed the bridge and passed out of range of the enemy's guns without losing a single man. It was followed by the second squadron, and the Cossacks last of all crossed, leaving the further side of the river clear.

The two squadrons of the Pavlograd regiment, after crossing the bridge, rode one after the other up the hill. Their colonel, Karl Bogdanitch Schubert, had joined Denisov's squadron, and was riding at a walking pace not far from Rostov, taking no notice of him, though this was the first time they had met since the incident in connection with Telyanin. Rostov, feeling himself at the front in the power of the man towards whom he now admitted that he had been to blame, never took his eyes off the athletic back, and flaxen head and red neck of the colonel. It seemed to Rostov at one time that Bogdanitch was only feigning inattention, and that his whole aim was now to test the ensign's pluck; and he drew himself up and looked about him gaily. Then he fancied that Bogdanitch was riding close by him on purpose to show off his own valour. Then the thought struck him that his enemy was now sending the squadron to a hopeless attack on purpose to punish him, Rostov. Then he dreamed of how after the attack he would go up to him as he lay wounded, and magnanimously hold out his hand in reconciliation. The high-shouldered figure of Zherkov, who was known to the Pavlograd hussars, as he had not long before left their regiment, rode up to the colonel. After Zherkov had been dismissed from the staff of the commander-in-chief, he had not remained in the regiment, saying that he was not such a fool as to go to hard labour at the front when he could get more pay for doing nothing on the staff, and he had succeeded in getting appointed an orderly on the staff of Prince Bagration. He rode up to his old colonel with an order from the commander of the rear guard.

"Colonel," he said, with his gloomy seriousness, addressing Rostov's enemy, and looking round at his comrades, "there's an order to go back and burn the bridge."

"An order, *who to*?" asked the colonel grimly.

"Well, I don't know, colonel, *who to*." answered the cornet, seriously, "only the prince commanded me: 'Ride and tell the colonel the hussars are to make haste back and burn the bridge.'"

Zherkov was followed by an officer of the suite, who rode up to the colonel with the same command. After the officer of the suite the stout figure of Nesvitsky was seen riding up on a Cossack's horse, which had some trouble to gallop with him.

"Why, colonel," he shouted, while still galloping towards him, "I told you to burn the bridge, and now some one's got it wrong; they're all frantic over there, there's no making out anything."

The colonel in a leisurely way stopped the regiment and turned to Nesvitsky.

"You told me about burning materials," he said; "but about burning it, you never said a word."

"Why, my good man," said Nesvitsky, as he halted, taking off his forage-cap and passing his plump hand over his hair, which was drenched with sweat, "what need to say the bridge was to be burnt when you put burning materials to it?"

"I'm not your 'good man,' M. le staff-officer, and you never told me to set fire to the bridge! I know my duty, and it's my habit to carry out my orders strictly. You said the bridge will be burnt, but who was going to burn it I couldn't tell."

"Well, that's always the way," said Nesvitsky, with a wave of his arm. "How do you come here?" he added, addressing Zherkov.

"Why, about the same order. You're sopping though, you want to be rubbed down."

"You said, M. le staff-officer . . ." pursued the colonel in an aggrieved tone.

"Colonel," interposed the officer of the suite, "there is need of haste, or the enemy will have moved up their grape-shot guns."

The colonel looked dumbly at the officer of the suite, at the stout staff-officer, at Zherkov, and scowled.

"I will burn the bridge," he said in a solemn tone, as though he would express that in spite of everything they might do to annoy him, he would still do what he ought.

Beating his long muscular legs against his horse, as though he were to blame for it all, the colonel moved forward and commanded the second squadron, the one under Denisov's command, in which Rostov was serving, to turn back to the bridge.

"Yes, it really is so," thought Rostov, "he wants to test me!" His heart throbbed and the blood rushed to his face. "Let him see whether I'm a coward!" he thought.

Again all the light-hearted faces of the men of the squadron wore that grave line, which had come upon them when they were under fire. Rostov looked steadily at his enemy, the colonel, trying to find confirmation of his suppositions on his face. But the colonel never once glanced at Rostov, and looked, as he always did at the front, stern and solemn. The word of command was given.

"Look sharp! look sharp!" several voices repeated around him.

Their swords catching in the reins and their spurs jingling, the hussars dismounted in haste, not knowing themselves what they were to do. The soldiers crossed themselves. Rostov did not look at the colonel now;

he had no time. He dreaded, with a sinking heart he dreaded, being left behind by the hussars. His hand trembled as he gave his horse to an orderly, and he felt that the blood was rushing to his heart with a thud. Denisov, rolling backwards, and shouting something, rode by him. Rostov saw nothing but the hussars running around him, clinking spurs and jingling swords.

"Stretchers!" shouted a voice behind him. Rostov did not think of the meaning of the need of stretchers. He ran along, trying only to be ahead of all. But just at the bridge, not looking at his feet, he got into the slippery, trodden mud, and stumbling fell on his hands. The others outstripped him.

"On both sides, captain," he heard shouted by the colonel, who, riding on ahead, had pulled his horse up near the bridge, with a triumphant and cheerful face.

Rostov, rubbing his muddy hands on his riding-breeches, looked round at his enemy, and would have run on further, imagining that the forwarder he went the better it would be. But though Bogdanitch was not looking, and did not recognise Rostov, he shouted to him.

"Who will go along the middle of the bridge? On the right side? Ensign, back!" he shouted angrily, and he turned to Denisov, who with swaggering bravado rode on horseback on to the planks of the bridge.

"Why run risks, captain? You should dismount," said the colonel.

"Eh! it'll strike the guilty one," said Vaska Denisov, turning in his saddle.

Meanwhile Nesvitsky, Zherkov, and the officer of the suite were standing together out of range of the enemy, watching the little group of men in yellow shakoes, dark-green jackets, embroidered with frogs, and blue riding-breeches, swarming about the bridge, and on the other side of the river the blue tunics and the groups with horses, that might so easily be taken for guns, approaching in the distance.

"Will they burn the bridge or not? Who'll get there first? Will they run there and burn it, or the French train their grape-shot on them and kill them?" These were the questions that, with a sinking of the heart, each man was asking himself in the great mass of troops overlooking the bridge. In the brilliant evening sunshine they gazed at the bridge and the hussars and at the blue tunics, with bayonets and guns, moving up on the other side.

"Ugh! The hussars will be caught," said Nesvitsky. "They're not out of range of grape-shot now."

"He did wrong to take so many men," said the officer of the suite.

"Yes, indeed," said Nesvitsky. "If he'd sent two bold fellows it would have done as well."

"Ah, your excellency," put in Zherkov, his eyes fixed on the hussars, though he still spoke with his naïve manner, from which one could not guess whether he were speaking seriously or not. "Ah, your excellency. How you look at things. Send two men, but who would give us the Vladimir and ribbon then? But as it is, even if they do pepper them, one can represent the squadron and receive the ribbon oneself. Our good friend Bogdanitch knows the way to do things."

"I say," said the officer of the suite, "that's grape-shot."

He pointed to the French guns, which had been taken out of the gun-carriages, and were hurriedly moving away.

On the French side, smoke rose among the groups that had cannons. One puff, a second and a third almost at the same instant; and at the very moment when they heard the sound of the first shot, there rose the smoke of a fourth; two booms came one after another, then a third.

"Oh, oh!" moaned Nesvitsky, clutching at the hand of the officer of the suite, as though in intense pain. "Look, a man has fallen, fallen, fallen!"

"Two, I think."

"If I were Tsar, I'd never go to war," said Nesvitsky, turning away.

The French cannons were speedily loaded again. The infantry in their blue tunics were running towards the bridge. Again the puffs of smoke rose at different intervals, and the grape-shot rattled and cracked on the bridge. But this time Nesvitsky could not see what was happening at the bridge. A thick cloud of smoke had risen from it. The hussars had succeeded in setting fire to the bridge, and the French batteries were firing at them now, not to hinder them, but because their guns had been brought up and they had some one to fire at.

The French had time to fire three volleys of grape-shot before the hussars got back to their horses. Two were badly aimed, and the shot flew over them, but the last volley fell in the middle of the group of hussars and knocked down three men.

Rostov, absorbed by his relations with Bogdanitch, stepped on the bridge, not knowing what he had to do. There was no one to slash at with his sword (that was how he always pictured a battle to himself), and he could be of no use in burning the bridge, because he had not brought with him any wisps of straw, like the other soldiers. He stood and looked about him, when suddenly there was a rattle on the bridge, like a lot of nuts being scattered, and one of the hussars, the one standing nearest him, fell with a groan on the railing. Rostov ran up to him with the others. Again some one shouted. "Stretchers!" Four men took hold of the hussar and began lifting him up. "Oooo! . . . Let me be, for Christ's sake!" shrieked the wounded man, but still they lifted him up and laid him on a stretcher. Nikolay Rostov turned away, and began staring into the distance, at the waters of the Danube, at the sky, at the sun, as though he were searching for something. How fair that sky seemed, how blue and calm and deep. How brilliant and triumphant seemed the setting sun. With what an enticing glimmer shone the water of the far-away Danube. And fairer still were the far-away mountains that showed blue beyond the Danube, the nunnery, the mysterious gorges, the pine forests, filled with mist to the tree-tops . . . there all was peace and happiness. . . . "There is nothing, nothing I could wish for, if only I were there," thought Rostov. "In myself alone and in that sunshine there is so much happiness, while here . . . groans, agonies, and this uncertainty, this hurry. . . . Here they are shouting something again and again, all of them are running back somewhere, and I'm running with them, and here is *it, it,* death hanging over me, all round me. . . . One instant, and I shall never see that sunshine, that water, that mountain gorge again. . . ." At that moment the sun went behind the clouds; more stretchers came into view ahead of Rostov. And the terror of death and of the stretchers, and the loss of the sunshine and life, all blended into one sensation of sickening fear.

"Good God, Thou who art in that sky, save and forgive, and protect me," Rostov whispered to himself.

The hussars ran back to their horses; their voices grew louder and more assured; the stretchers disappeared from sight.

"Well, lad, so you've had a sniff of powder!" Vaska Denisov shouted in his ear.

"It's all over, but I am a coward, yes, I am a coward," thought Rostov, and with a heavy sigh he took his Rook, who had begun to go lame of one leg, from the man who held him and began mounting.

"What was that—grape-shot?" he asked of Denisov.

"Yes, and something like it too," cried Denisov; "they worked their guns in fine style. But it's a nasty business. A cavalry attack's a pleasant thing—slash away at the dogs; but this is for all the devil like aiming at a target."

And Denisov rode away to a group standing not far from Rostov, consisting of the colonel, Nesvitsky, Zherkov, and the officer of the suite.

"It seems as if no one noticed it, though," Rostov thought to himself. And indeed no one had noticed it at all, for every one was familiar with the feeling that the ensign, never before under fire, was experiencing for the first time.

"Now you'll have something to talk about," said Zherkov; "they'll be promoting me a sub-lieutenant before I know where I am, eh?"

"Inform the prince that I have burnt the bridge," said the colonel, in a cheerful and triumphant tone.

"And if he inquires with what losses?"

"Not worth mentioning," boomed the colonel; "two hussars wounded, and one stark dead on the spot," he said, with undisguised cheerfulness. The German was unable to repress a smile of satisfaction as he sonorously enunciated the idiomatic Russian colloquialism of the last phrase.

IX

PURSUED by the French army of a hundred thousand men under the command of Bonaparte, received with hostility by the inhabitants, losing confidence in their allies, suffering from shortness of supplies, and forced to act under circumstances unlike anything that had been foreseen, the Russian army of thirty-five thousand men, under the command of Kutuzov, beat a hasty retreat to the lower ground about the Danube.

There they halted, and were overtaken by the enemy, and fought a few rear-guard skirmishes, avoiding an engagement, except in so far as it was necessary to secure a retreat without the loss of their baggage and guns. There were actions at Lambach, at Amsteten, and at Melk; but in spite of the courage and stubbornness—acknowledged even by the enemy—with which the Russians fought, the only consequence of these engagements was a still more rapid retreat. The Austrian troops that had escaped being taken at Ulm, and had joined Kutuzov's forces at Braunau, now parted from the Russian army, and Kutuzov was left unsupported with his weak and exhausted forces. The defence of Vienna could no longer be dreamed of. Instead of the elaborately planned campaign of attack, in accordance with the principles of the modern science of strategy, the plan of which had been communicated to Kutuzov during his sojourn in Vienna by the Austrian Hofkriegsrath, the sole aim— almost a hopeless one—that remained now for Kutuzov was to avoid losing his army, like Mack at Ulm, and to effect a junction with the fresh troops marching from Russia.

On the 28th of October, Kutuzov took his army across to the left bank of the Danube, and then for the first time halted, leaving the Danube between his army and the greater part of the enemy's forces. On the 30th he attacked Mortier's division, which was on the left bank of the Danube, and defeated it. In this action for the first time trophies were taken—a flag, cannons, and two of the enemy's generals. For the first time, after retreating for a fortnight, the Russian troops had halted, and after fighting had not merely kept the field of battle, but had driven the French off it. Although the troops were without clothing and exhausted, and had lost a third of their strength in wounded, killed, and missing; although they had left their sick and wounded behind on the other side of the Danube, with a letter from Kutuzov commending them to the humanity of the enemy; although the great hospitals and houses in Krems could not contain all the sick and wounded,—in spite of all that, the halt before Krems and the victory over Mortier had greatly raised the spirits of the troops. Throughout the whole army, and also at headquarters, there were the most cheerful but groundless rumours of the near approach of the columns from Russia, of some victory gained by the Austrians, and of the retreat of Bonaparte panic-stricken.

Prince Andrey had been during the engagement in attendance on the Austrian general Schmidt, who was killed in the battle. His horse had been wounded under him, and he had himself received a slight wound on his arm from a bullet. As a mark of special favour on the part of the commander-in-chief, he was sent with the news of this victory to the Austrian court, now at Brünn, as Vienna was threatened by the French. On the night of the battle, excited, but not weary (though Prince Andrey did not look robustly built, he could bear fatigue better than very strong men), he had ridden with a despatch from Dohturov to Krems to Kutuzov. The same night he had been sent on with a special despatch to Brünn. This commission, apart from its reward, meant an important step in promotion.

The night was dark and starlit; the road looked black in the white snow that had fallen on the day of the battle. With his mind filled with impressions of the battle, joyful anticipations of the effect that would be produced by the news of the victory, and recollections of the farewells of the commander-in-chief and his comrades, Prince Andrey trotted along in a light posting cart, with the sensations of a man who, after long waiting, has at last attained the first instalment of some coveted happiness. As soon as he closed his eyes, the firing of guns and cannons was echoing in his ears, and that sound blended with the rattle of the wheels and the sensation of victory. At one moment he would begin to dream that the Russians were flying, that he was himself slain; but he waked up in haste, and with fresh happiness realised anew that that was all unreal, and that it was the French, on the contrary, who were put to flight. He recalled again all the details of the victory, his own calm manliness during the battle, and, reassured, he began to doze. . . . The dark, starlit night was followed by a bright and sunny morning. The snow was thawing in the sun, the horses galloped quickly, and new and different-looking forests, fields, and trees flew by on both sides of the road alike.

At one of the stations he overtook a convoy of Russian wounded. The Russian officer in charge of the transport lay lolling back in the foremost cart, and was shouting coarse abuse at a soldier. In each of the long German *Vorspanns* six or more pale, bandaged, and dirty wounded men were being jolted over the stony roads. Some of them were talking (he caught the sound of Russian words), others were eating bread; the most severely wounded gazed dumbly at the posting cart trotting by, with the languid interest of sick children.

Prince Andrey told the driver to stop, and asked a soldier in what battle they had been wounded.

"The day before yesterday on the Danube," answered the soldier. Prince Andrey took out his purse and gave the soldier three gold pieces.

"For all," he added, addressing the officer as he came up. "Get well, lads," he said to the soldiers, "there's a lot to do yet."

"What news?" asked the officer, evidently anxious to get into conversation.

"Good news! Forward!" he called to the driver, and galloped on.

It was quite dark when Prince Andrey rode into Brünn, and saw himself surrounded by high houses, lighted shops, the lighted windows of houses, and street lamps, handsome carriages noisily rolling over the pavement, and all that atmosphere of a great town full of life, which is so attractive to a soldier after camp. In spite of the rapid drive and sleepless night, Prince Andrey felt even more alert, as he drove up to the palace, than he had on the previous evening. Only his eyes glittered with a feverish brilliance, and his ideas followed one another with extreme rapidity and clearness. He vividly pictured again all the details of the battle, not in confusion, but definitely, in condensed shape, as he meant to present them to the Emperor Francis. He vividly imagined the casual questions that might be put to him, and the answers he would make to them. He imagined that he would be at once presented to the Emperor. But at the chief entrance of the palace an official ran out to meet him, and learning that he was a special messenger, led him to another entrance.

"Turning to the right out of the corridor, *Euer Hochgeboren*, you will find the adjutant on duty," the official said to him. "He will conduct you to the minister of war."

The adjutant on duty, meeting Prince Andrey, asked him to wait, and went into the war minister. Five minutes later the adjutant returned, and with marked courtesy, bowing and ushering Prince Andrey before him, he led him across the corridor to the private room of the war minister. The adjutant, by his elaborately formal courtesy, seemed to wish to guard himself from any attempt at familiarity on the part of the Russian adjutant. The joyous feeling of Prince Andrey was considerably damped as he approached the door of the minister's room. He felt slighted, and the feeling of being slighted passed instantaneously—without his being aware of it himself—into a feeling of disdain, which was quite uncalled for. His subtle brain at the same instant supplied him with the point of view from which he had the right to feel disdain both of the adjutant and the minister of war. "No doubt it seems to them a very simple matter to win victories, never having smelt powder!" he thought. His eyelids drooped disdainfully; he walked with peculiar deliberateness into the war minister's room. This feeling was intensified when he saw the minister of war sitting at a big table, and for the first two minutes taking no notice of his entrance. The minister of war had his bald head, with grey curls on the temple, held low between two wax candles; he was reading some papers, and marking them with a pencil. He went on reading to the end, without raising his eyes at the opening of the door and the sound of footsteps.

"Take this and give it him," said the minister of war to his adjutant, handing him the papers, and taking no notice of the Russian attaché.

Prince Andrey felt that either the minister of war took less interest in the doings of Kutuzov's army than in any other subject demanding his attention, or that he wanted to make the Russian attaché feel this. "But that's a matter of complete indifference to me," thought he. The minister of war put the other remaining papers together, making their edges level, and lifted his head. He had an intellectual and characteristic head. But the instant he turned to Prince Andrey, the shrewd and determined expression of the war minister's face changed in a manner evidently conscious and habitual. On his face was left the stupid smile—hypocritical, and not disguising its hypocrisy—of a man who receives many petitioners, one after another.

"From General—Field Marshal Kutuzov?" he queried. "Good news, I hope? Has there been an engagement with Mortier? A victory? It was high time!"

He took the despatch, which was addressed to him, and began to read it with a mournful expression.

"Ah! My God! my God! Schmidt!" he said in German. "What a

calamity! what a calamity!" Skimming through the despatch, he laid it on the table and glanced at Prince Andrey, visibly meditating on something.

"Ah, what a calamity! So the action, you say, was a decisive one?" ("Mortier was not taken, however," he reflected.) "Very glad you have brought good news, though the death of Schmidt is a costly price for the victory. His majesty will certainly wish to see you, but not to-day. I thank you; you must need repose. To-morrow, be at the levée after the review. But I will let you know."

The stupid smile, which had disappeared while he was talking, reappeared on the war minister's face.

"*Au revoir*, I thank you indeed. His majesty the Emperor will most likely wish to see you," he repeated, and he bowed his head.

As Prince Andrey left the palace, he felt that all the interest and happiness that had been given him by this victory had been left behind by him now in the indifferent hands of the minister and the formal adjutant. The whole tenor of his thoughts had instantaneously changed. The battle figured in his mind as a remote, far-away memory.

X

Prince Andrey stayed at Brünn with a Russian of his acquaintance in the diplomatic service, Bilibin.

"Ah, my dear prince, there's no one I could have been more pleased to see," said Bilibin, coming to meet Prince Andrey. "Franz, take the prince's things to my bedroom," he said to the servant, who was ushering Bolkonsky in. "What, a messenger of victory? That's capital. I'm kept indoors ill, as you see."

After washing and dressing, Prince Andrey came into the diplomat's luxurious study and sat down to the dinner prepared for him. Bilibin was sitting quietly at the fireplace.

Not his journey only, but all the time he had spent with the army on the march, deprived of all the conveniences of cleanliness and the elegancies of life, made Prince Andrey feel now an agreeable sense of repose among the luxurious surroundings to which he had been accustomed from childhood. Moreover, after his Austrian reception, he was glad to speak—if not in Russian, for they talked French—at least to a Russian, who would, he imagined, share the general Russian dislike (which he felt particularly keenly just then) for the Austrians.

Bilibin was a man of five-and-thirty, a bachelor, of the same circle as Prince Andrey. They had been acquainted in Petersburg, but had become more intimate during Prince Andrey's last stay at Vienna with Kutuzov. Just as Prince Andrey was a young man, who promised to rise high in a military career, Bilibin promised to do even better in diplomacy. He was still a young man, but not a young diplomat, as he had been in the service since he was sixteen. He had been in Paris and in

Copenhagen; and now in Vienna he filled a post of considerable importance. Both the foreign minister and our ambassador at Vienna knew him and valued him. He was not one of that great multitude of diplomats whose qualification is limited to the possession of negative qualities, who need simply avoid doing certain things and speak French in order to be very good diplomats. He was one of those diplomats who like work and understand it, and in spite of his natural indolence, he often spent nights at his writing-table. He worked equally well whatever the object of his work might be. He was interested not in the question "Why?" but in the question "How?" What constituted his diplomatic work, he did not mind, but to draw up a circular, a memorandum, or a report subtly, pointedly, and elegantly, was a task which gave him great pleasure. Apart from such labours, Bilibin's merits were esteemed the more from his ease in moving and talking in the higher spheres.

Bilibin enjoyed conversation just as he enjoyed work, only when the conversation could be elegantly witty. In society he was continually watching for an opportunity of saying something striking, and did not enter into conversation except under such circumstances. Bilibin's conversation was continually sprinkled with original, epigrammatic, polished phrases of general interest. These phrases were fashioned in the inner laboratory of Bilibin's mind, as though intentionally, of portable form, so that insignificant persons could easily remember them and carry them from drawing-room to drawing-room. And Bilibin's good things were hawked about in Viennese drawing-rooms and afterwards had an influence on so-called great events.

His thin, lean, yellow face was all covered with deep creases, which always looked as clean and carefully washed as the tips of one's fingers after a bath. The movement of these wrinkles made up the chief play of expression of his countenance. At one moment his forehead wrinkled up in broad furrows, and his eyebrows were lifted, at another moment his eyebrows drooped again and deep lines creased his cheeks. His deep-set, small eyes looked out frankly and good-humouredly.

"Come, now, tell us about your victories," he said. Bolkonsky in the most modest fashion, without once mentioning himself in connection with it, described the engagement, and afterwards his reception by the war minister.

"They received me and my news like a dog in a game of skittles," he concluded.

Bilibin grinned, and the creases in his face disappeared.

"All the same, my dear fellow," he said, gazing from a distance at his finger-nails, and wrinkling up the skin over his left eye, "notwithstanding my high esteem for the holy Russian armament, I own that your victory is not so remarkably victorious."

He went on talking in French, only uttering in Russian those words to which he wished to give a contemptuous intonation.

"Why?" with the whole mass of your army you fell upon the unlucky Mortier with one division, and Mortier slipped through your fingers? Where's the victory?"

"Seriously speaking, though," answered Prince Andrey, "we can at least say without boasting that it's rather better than Ulm . . ."

"Why didn't you capture us one, at least, one marshal?"

"Because everything isn't done as one expects it will be, and things are not as regular as on parade. We had expected, as I told you, to attack the enemy in the rear at seven o'clock in the morning, but we did not arrive at it until five o'clock in the evening."

"But why didn't you do it at seven in the morning? You ought to have done it at seven in the morning," said Bilibin, smiling; "you ought to have done it at seven in the morning."

"Why didn't you succeed in impressing on Bonaparte by diplomatic methods that he had better leave Genoa alone?" said Prince Andrey in the same tone.

"I know," broke in Bilibin, "you are thinking that it's very easy to capture marshals, sitting on the sofa by one's fireside. That's true, but still why didn't you capture him? And you needn't feel surprised if the most august Emperor and King Francis, like the war minister, is not very jubilant over your victory. Why, even I, a poor secretary of the Russian Embassy, feel no necessity to testify my rejoicing by giving my Franz a thaler and sending him out for a holiday to disport himself with his Liebchen on the Prater . . . though it's true there is no Prater here . . ." He looked straight at Prince Andrey and suddenly let the creases drop out of his puckered forehead.

"Now it's my turn to ask you 'why,' my dear boy," said Bolkonsky. "I must own that I don't understand it; perhaps there are diplomatic subtleties in it that are beyond my feeble intellect; but I can't make it out. Mack loses a whole army, Archduke Ferdinand and Archduke Karl give no sign of life and make one blunder after another; Kutuzov alone gains at last a decisive victory, breaks the prestige of invincibility of the French, and the minister of war does not even care to learn the details!"

"For that very reason, my dear boy, don't you see! Hurrah for the Tsar, for Russia, for the faith! That's all very nice; but what have we, I mean the Austrian court, to do with your victories? You bring us good news of a victory of Archduke Karl of Ferdinand—one archduke's as good as the other, as you know—if it's only a victory over a fire brigade of Bonaparte, and it will be another matter, it will set the cannons booming. But this can only tantalise us, as if it were done on purpose. Archduke Karl does nothing, Archduke Ferdinand covers himself with disgrace, you abandon Vienna, give up its defence, as though you would say to us, God is with us, and the devil take you and your capital. One general, whom we all loved, Schmidt, you put in the way of a bullet, and then congratulate us on your victory! . . . You must admit that anything more exasperating than the news you have brought could not be conceived. It's as though it were done on purpose, done on purpose. But apart from that, if you were to gain a really brilliant victory, if Archduke Karl even were to win a victory, what effect could it have on the general course of events? It's too late now, when Vienna is occupied by the French forces."

"Occupied? Vienna occupied?"

"Not only is Vienna occupied, but Bonaparte is at Schönbrunn, and the count—our dear Count Urbna—is setting off to receive his orders."

After the fatigues and impressions of his journey and his reception, and even more after the dinner he had just eaten, Bolkonsky felt that he could not take in all the significance of the words he had just heard.

"Count Lichtenfels was here this morning," pursued Bilibin, "and he showed me a letter containing a full description of the parade of the French at Vienna. Prince Murat and all the rest of it . . . You see that your victory is not a great matter for rejoicing, and that you can't be received as our deliverer . . ."

"Really, I don't care about that, I don't care in the slightest!" said Prince Andrey, beginning to understand that his news of the battle before Krems was really of little importance in view of such an event as the taking of the capital of Austria. "How was Vienna taken? And its bridge and its famous fortifications, and Prince Auersperg? We heard rumours that Prince Auersperg was defending Vienna," said he.

"Prince Auersperg is stationed on this side—our side—and is defending us; defending us very ineffectually, I imagine, but any way he is defending us. But Vienna's on the other side of the river. No, the bridge has not been taken, and I hope it won't be taken, because it is mined and orders have been given to blow it up. If it were not so, we should have long ago been in the mountains of Bohemia, and you and your army would have spent a bad quarter of an hour between two fires."

"But still that doesn't mean that the campaign is over," said Prince Andrey.

"But I believe that it is over. And so do all the big-wigs here, though they don't dare to say so. It will be as I said at the beginning of the campaign, that the matter will not be settled by your firing before Dürenstein, not by gunpowder, but by those who invented it," said Bilibin, repeating one of his *mots*, letting the creases run out of his forehead and pausing. "The only question is what the meeting of the Emperor Alexander and the Prussian king may bring forth. If Prussia enters the alliance, they will force Austria's hand and there will be war. If not, the only point will be to arrange where to draw up the articles of the new Campo Formio."

"But what an extraordinary genius!" cried Prince Andrey suddenly, clenching his small hand and bringing it down on the table. "And what luck the man has!"

"Buonaparte?" said Bilibin interrogatively, puckering up his forehead and so intimating that a *mot* was coming. "Buonaparte?" he said, with special stress on the *u*. "I think, though, that now when he is dictating laws to Austria from Schönbrunn, we must let him off the *u*. I shall certainly adopt the innovation, and call him simply Bonaparte."

"No, joking apart," said Prince Andrey, "do you really believe the campaign is over?"

"I'll tell you what I think. Austria has been made a fool of, and she is not used to that. And she'll avenge it. And she has been made a fool of because in the first place her provinces have been pillaged (they say the Holy Russian armament is plundering them cruelly), her army has been destroyed, her capital has been taken, and all this for the sweet sake of his Sardinian Majesty. And so between ourselves, my dear boy, my instinct tells me we are being deceived; my instinct tells me of negotiations with France and projects of peace, a secret peace, concluded separately."

"Impossible!" said Prince Andrey. "That would be too base."

"Time will show," said Bilibin, letting the creases run off his forehead again in token of being done with the subject.

When Prince Andrey went to the room that had been prepared for him, and lay down in the clean linen on the feather-bed and warmed and fragrant pillows, he felt as though the battle of which he brought tidings was far, far away from him. The Prussian alliance, the treachery of Austria, the new triumph of Bonaparte, the levée and parade and the audience of Emperor Francis next day, engrossed his attention. He closed his eyes and instantly his ears were ringing with the cannonade, the firing of muskets, and the creaking of wheels, and again he saw the long line of musketeers running down-hill and the French firing, and he felt his heart beating and saw himself galloping in front of the lines with Schmidt, and, the bullets whizzing merrily around him, and he knew that sense of intensified joy in living that he had not experienced since childhood. He waked up.

"Yes, that all happened!" . . . he said, with a happy, childlike smile to himself. And he fell into the deep sleep of youth.

XI

Next day he waked up late. Going over the impressions of the past, what he recalled most vividly was that he was to be presented to the Emperor Francis; he remembered the minister of war, the ceremonious adjutant, Bilibin, and the conversation of the previous evening. He dressed for his attendance at court in full court-dress, which he had not worn for a long time, and fresh, eager, and handsome, he walked into Bilibin's room with his arm in a sling. Four gentlemen of the diplomatic corps were already there. With Prince Ippolit Kuragin, who was a secretary to the embassy, Bolkonsky was already acquainted; Bilibin introduced him to the others.

The gentlemen calling on Bilibin were a set of fashionable, wealthy, and lively young men, who here, as at Vienna, made up a circle apart, a circle which Bilibin, its leader, spoke of as *les nôtres*. This circle, consisting almost exclusively of diplomatists, evidently had its own interests —quite apart from the war and politics—interests, that revolved round the fashionable world, relations with certain women and the formal side of the service. They gave Prince Andrey an unmistakably cordial recep‚ tion, as one of themselves (a distinction they allowed to few). From civility and to break the ice they asked him a few questions about the army and the battle, and the conversation slipped back again to disconnected, good-humoured jests and gossip.

"But what was so particularly nice," said one, relating a disaster that had befallen a colleague, "was that the minister told him in so many words that his appointment to London was a promotion and that that was how he ought to regard it. Can you fancy his figure at the moment?" . . .

"But the worst of all is to come, gentlemen. I'm going to betray Kuragin—here is this Don Juan going to profit by his misfortune; he's a shocking fellow!"

Prince Ippolit lounged in a reclining chair, with his legs over the arm. He laughed.

"Tell me about that," said he.

"O Don Juan! O serpent!" cried the voices.

"You're not aware, I dare say, Bolkonsky," said Bilibin, turning to Prince Andrey, "that all the atrocities of the French army (I was almost saying of the Russian) are nothing in comparison with the exploits of this fellow among the ladies."

"Woman . . . is the companion of man," Prince Ippolit enunciated, and he stared through his eyeglass at his elevated legs.

Bilibin and *les nôtres* roared, looking Ippolit straight in the face. Prince Andrey saw that this Ippolit, of whom—he could not disguise it from himself—he had been almost jealous on his wife's account, was the butt of this set.

"No, I must entertain you with a specimen of Kuragin," said Bilibin aside to Bolkonsky. "He's exquisite, when he airs his views upon politics; you must see his gravity."

He sat down by Ippolit, and, wrinkling up his forehead, began talking to him about politics. Prince Andrey and the others stood round the two.

"The Berlin cabinet cannot express a feeling of alliance," Ippolit began, looking consequentially round at all of them, "without expressing . . . as in its last note . . . you understand . . . you understand . . . and besides, if his Majesty the Emperor does not give up the principle of our alliance."

"Wait, I have not finished," he said to Prince Andrey, taking him by the arm. "I suppose that intervention will be stronger than non-intervention. And . . ." He paused. "Our dispatch of the 28th of November cannot be reckoned as an exception. That is how it will all end." And he dropped Bolkonsky's arm as a sign that he had now quite concluded.

"Demosthenes, I recognise you by the pebble that you hide in your golden mouth," said Bilibin, whose thick thatch of hair moved forward on his head from the puckering of his brows with delight.

Every one laughed. Ippolit laughed louder than any. He was visibly distressed; he breathed painfully, but he could not help breaking into a savage laugh, that convulsed his usually impassive face.

"Well now, gentlemen," said Bilibin, "Bolkonsky is my guest here in Brünn and I want to show him, as far as I can, all the attractions of our life here. If we were in Vienna, it would be easy enough; but here, in this vile Moravian hole, it is more difficult, and I beg you all for assistance. We must do him the honour of Brünn. You undertake the theatre and I will undertake society; you, Ippolit, of course, the ladies."

"We ought to let him see Amélie; she's exquisite!" said one of *les nôtres*, kissing his finger-tips.

"Altogether," said Bilibin, "we must turn this bloodthirsty man to more humane interests."

"I fear I can hardly take advantage of your hospitality, gentlemen; it's time I was off even now," said Bolkonsky, glancing at his watch.

"Where to?"

"To the Emperor!"

"Oh! oh! oh!"

"Well, *au revoir*, Bolkonsky! *Au revoir*, prince! Come early to dinner," said voices. "We reckon upon you."

"Try to make the most of the good discipline of the troops, in the provisioning of supplies and on the lines of march, when you talk to the Emperor," said Bilibin, accompanying Bolkonsky to the hall.

"I should like to speak well of it, but as far as my observation goes, I can't," answered Bolkonsky, smiling.

"Well, talk as much as you can, any way. Audiences are his passion, but he doesn't like talking himself, and can't talk either, as you will see."

XII

At the levée the Emperor Francis only looked intently into Prince Andrey's face, and nodded his long head to him as he stood in the place assigned him among the Austrian officers. But after the levée the adjutant of the previous evening ceremoniously communicated to Bolkonsky the Emperor's desire to give him an audience. The Emperor Francis received him, standing in the middle of the room. Prince Andrey was struck by the fact that before beginning the conversation, the Emperor seemed embarrassed, didn't know what to say, and reddened.

"Tell me when the battle began," he asked hurriedly. Prince Andrey answered. The question was followed by others, as simple: "Was Kutuzov well?" "How long was it since he left Krems?" and so on. The Emperor spoke as though his sole aim was to put a certain number of questions. The answers to these questions, as was only too evident, could have no interest for him.

"At what o'clock did the battle begin?" asked the Emperor.

"I cannot inform your majesty at what o'clock the battle began in the front lines, but at Dürenstein, where I was, the troops began the attack about six in the evening," said Bolkonsky, growing more eager, and conceiving that now there was a chance for him to give an accurate descrip-

tion, just as he had it ready in his head, of all he knew and had seen.
But the Emperor smiled and interrupted him:

"How many miles?"

"From where to where, your majesty?"

"From Dürenstein to Krems?"

"Three and a half miles, your majesty."

"The French abandoned the left bank?"

"As our scouts reported, the last crossed the river on rafts in the
night."

"Have you enough provisions at Krems?"

"Provisions have not been furnished to the amount . . ."

The Emperor interrupted him:

"At what o'clock was General Schmidt killed?"

"At seven o'clock, I think."

"At seven o'clock? Very sad! very sad!"

The Emperor said that he thanked him, and bowed. Prince Andrey
withdrew, and was at once surrounded by courtiers on all sides. Everywhere he saw friendly eyes gazing at him, and heard friendly voices addressing him. The adjutant of the preceding evening reproached him for
not having stopped at the palace, and offered him his own house. The
minister of war came up and congratulated him on the Order of Maria
Theresa of the third grade, with which the Emperor was presenting him.
The Empress's chamberlain invited him to her majesty. The archduchess, too, wished to see him. He did not know whom to answer, and
for a few seconds he was trying to collect his ideas. The Russian ambassador took him by the shoulder, led him away to a window, and began
to talk to him.

Contrary to Bilibin's prognostications, the news he brought was received with rejoicing. A thanksgiving service was arranged. Kutuzov was
decorated with the great cross of Maria Theresa, and rewards were bestowed on the whole army. Bolkonsky received invitations on all hands,
and had to spend the whole morning paying visits to the principal personages in the Austrian Government. After paying his visits, Prince Andrey, at five o'clock in the evening, was returning homewards to Bilibin's, mentally composing a letter to his father about the battle and his
reception at Brünn. At the steps of Bilibin's house stood a cart packed
half full of things, and Franz, Bilibin's servant, came out of the doorway, with difficulty dragging a travelling-trunk.

Before going back to Bilibin's Prince Andrey had driven to a book-
seller's to lay in a stock of books for the campaign, and had spent some
time in the shop.

"What is it?" asked Bolkonsky.

"Ah, your excellency!" said Franz, with some exertion rolling the
trunk on the cart. "We are to move on still farther. The scoundrel is
already at our heels again!"

"Eh? what?" queried Prince Andrey.

Bilibin came out to meet Bolkonsky. His ordinarily composed face
looked excited.

"No, no, confess that this is charming," he said, "this story of the bridge of Tabor. They have crossed it without striking a blow."

Prince Andrey could not understand.

"Why, where do you come from not to know what every coachman in the town knows by now?"

"I come from the archduchess. I heard nothing there."

"And didn't you see that people are packing up everywhere?"

"I have seen nothing . . . But what's the matter?" Prince Andrey asked impatiently.

"What's the matter? The matter is that the French have crossed the bridge that Auersperg was defending, and they haven't blown up the bridge, so that Murat is at this moment running along the road to Brünn, and to-day or to-morrow they'll be here."

"Here? But how is it the bridge wasn't blown up, since it was mined?"

"Why, that's what I ask you. No one—not Bonaparte himself—can tell why." Bolkonsky shrugged his shoulders.

"But if they have crossed the bridge, then it will be all over with the army; it will be cut off," he said.

"That's the whole point," answered Bilibin. "Listen. The French enter Vienna, as I told you. Everything is satisfactory. Next day, that is yesterday, *Messieurs les Maréchaux*, Murat, Lannes, and Beliard get on their horses and ride off to the bridge. (Remark that all three are Gascons.) 'Gentlemen,' says one, 'you know that the Tabor bridge has been mined and countermined, and is protected by a formidable fortification and fifteen thousand troops, who have orders to blow up the bridge and not to let us pass. But our gracious Emperor Napoleon will be pleased if we take the bridge. Let us go us three and take it.' 'Yes, let us go,' say the others; and they start off and take the bridge, cross it, and now with their whole army on this side of the Danube, they are coming straight upon us, and upon you and your communications."

"Leave off jesting," said Prince Andrey, with mournful seriousness. The news grieved Prince Andrey, and yet it gave him pleasure. As soon as he heard that the Russian army was in such a hopeless position, the idea struck him that he was the very man destined to extricate the Russian army from that position, and that it had come—the Toulon—that would lift him for ever from out of the ranks of unknown officers, and open the first path to glory for him! As he listened to Bilibin, he was already considering how, on reaching the army, he would, at a council of war, give the opinion that alone could save the army, and how he would be entrusted alone to execute the plan.

"Leave off joking," he said.

"I'm not joking," Bilibin went on. "Nothing could be more truthful or more melancholy. These three gentlemen advance to the bridge alone and wave white handkerchiefs; they declare that it's a truce, and that they, the marshals, are come for a parley with Prince Auersperg. The officer on duty lets them into the *tête du pont*. They tell him a thousand Gascon absurdities; say that the war is over, that Emperor Francis has arranged a meeting with Bonaparte, that they desire to see Prince Auersperg, and so on. The officer sends for Auersperg. These Gascon gentlemen embrace the officers, make jokes, and sit about on the cannons, while a French battalion meantime advances unnoticed on the bridge, flings the sacks of inflammable material into the river, and marches up to the *tête du pont*. Finally the lieutenant-general himself appears, our dear Prince Auersperg von Mautern. 'My dear enemy! Flower of Austrian chivalry! hero of the Turkish war! Hostility is at end, we can take each other's hands . . . the Emperor Napoleon burns with impatience to make the acquaintance of Prince Auersperg.' In a word, these gentlemen —not Gascons for nothing—so bewilder Auersperg with fair words—he is so flattered at this speedy intimacy with French marshals, so dazzled by the spectacle of their cloaks, and of the ostrich feathers of Murat— that their fire gets into his eyes and makes him forget that he ought to be firing on the enemy" (in spite of the interest of his story, Bilibin did not omit to pause after this *mot*, to give time for its appreciation). "A French battalion runs into the *tête du pont*, spikes the cannons, and the bridge is taken. No, but really the best part of the whole episode," he went on, his excitement subsiding under the interest of his own story, "is that the sergeant in charge of the cannon which was to give the signal for firing the mines and blowing up the bridge, this sergeant seeing the French troops running on to the bridge wanted to fire, but Lannes pulled his arm away. The sergeant, who seems to have been sharper than his general, goes up to Auersperg and says: 'Prince, they're deceiving you, here are the French!' Murat sees the game is up if he lets the sergeant have his say. With an affectation of surprise (a true Gascon!) he addresses Auersperg: 'Is this the Austrian discipline so highly extolled all over the world,' says he, 'do you let a man of low rank speak to you like this?' It was a stroke of genius. The Prince of Auersperg is touched in his honour and has the sergeant put under arrest. No, but confess that all this story of the bridge of Tabor is charming. It is neither stupidity, nor cowardice . . ."

"It is treason, perhaps," said Prince Andrey, vividly picturing to himself grey overcoats, wounds, the smoke and sound of firing, and the glory awaiting him.

"Not that either. This puts the court into a pretty pickle," pursued Bilibin. "It is not treason, nor cowardice, nor stupidity; it is just as it was at Ulm . . ." He seemed to ponder, seeking the phrase, "it is . . . *c'est du Mack. Nous sommes mackés*," he said, feeling he was uttering *un mot*, and a fresh one, one that would be repeated. His creased-up brows let the puckers smooth out quickly in sign of satisfaction, and with a faint smile he fell to scrutinizing his finger-nails.

"Where are you off to?" he said, suddenly turning to Prince Andrey, who had got up and was going to his room.

"I must start."

"Where to?"

"To the army."

"But you meant to stay another two days?"

"But now I am going at once"; and Prince Andrey, after a few words arranging about his journey, went to his room.

"Do you know, my dear boy," said Bilibin, coming into his room, "I have been thinking about you. What are you going for?" And in support of the irrefutability of his arguments on the subject, all the creases ran off his face.

Prince Andrey looked inquiringly at him and made no reply.

"Why are you going? I know you consider that it's your duty to gallop off to the army now that the army is in danger. I understand that, my boy, it's heroism."

"Nothing of the kind," said Prince Andrey.

"But you are *un philosophe*, be one fully, look at things from the other side, and you will see that it is your duty, on the contrary, to take care of yourself. Leave that to others who are no good for anything else . . . You have received no orders to go back, and you are not dismissed from here, so that you can remain and go with us, where our ill-luck takes us. They say they are going to Olmütz. And Olmütz is a very charming town. And we can travel there comfortably together in my carriage."

"That's enough joking, Bilibin," said Bolkonsky.

"I am speaking to you sincerely as a friend. Consider where are you going and with what object now, when you can stay here. You have two alternatives before you" (he puckered up the skin of his left temple) "either you won't reach the army before peace will be concluded, or you will share the defeat and disgrace with Kutuzov's whole army." And Bilibin let his brow go smooth again, feeling that his dilemma was beyond attack.

"That I can't enter into," said Prince Andrey coldly, but he thought: "I am going to save the army."

"My dear fellow, you are a hero," said Bilibin.

XIII

The same night, after taking leave of the minister of war, Bolkonsky set off to join the army, not knowing where he should find it, at the risk of being caught by the French on the way to Krems.

At Brünn all the court and every one connected with it was packing up, and the heavy baggage was already being despatched to Olmütz. Near Esselsdorf, Prince Andrey came out on the road along which the Russian army was moving in the utmost haste and in the greatest disorder. The road was so obstructed with baggage-waggons that it was impossible to get by in a carriage. Prince Andrey procured a horse and a Cossack from the officer in command of the Cossacks, and hungry and weary he threaded his way in and out between the waggons and rode in search of the commander-in-chief and his own luggage. The most sinister rumours as to the position of the army reached him on the road, and the appearance of the army fleeing in disorder confirmed these rumours.

"As for that Russian army which English gold has brought from the ends of the universe, we are going to inflict upon it the same fate (the fate of the army of Ulm)"; he remembered the words of Bonaparte's address to his army at the beginning of the campaign, and these words aroused in him simultaneously admiration for the genius of his hero, a feeling of mortified pride, and the hope of glory. "And if there's nothing left but to die?" he thought. "Well, if it must be! I will do it no worse than others."

Prince Andrey looked disdainfully at the endless, confused mass of companies, of baggage-waggons, parks of artillery, and again store-waggons, carts, and waggons of every possible form, pursuing one another and obstructing the muddy road three and four abreast. On every side, behind and before, as far as the ear could reach in every direction there was the rumble of wheels, the rattle of carts, of waggons, and of gun-carriages, the tramp of horses, the crack of whips, the shouts of drivers, the swearing of soldiers, of orderlies, and officers. At the sides of the roads he saw fallen horses, and sometimes their skinned carcases, broken-down waggons, with solitary soldiers sitting on them, waiting for something, detached groups of soldiers strayed from their companies, starting off to neighbouring villages, or dragging back from them fowls, sheep, hay, or sacks of stores of some sort. Where the road went uphill or downhill the crush became greater, and there was an uninterrupted roar of shouts. The soldiers floundering knee-deep in the mud clutched the guns and clung to the waggons in the midst of cracking whips, slipping hoofs, breaking traces and throat-splitting yells. The officers superintending their movements rode to and fro in front and behind the convoys. Their voices were faintly audible in the midst of the general uproar, their faces betrayed that they despaired of the possibility of checking the disorder.

"*Voilà le cher* holy armament," thought Bolkonsky, recalling Bilibin's words.

He rode up to a convoy, intending to ask of some one of these men where he could find the commander-in-chief. Directly opposite to him came a strange vehicle, with one horse, obviously rigged up by soldiers with the resources at their disposal, and looking like something between a cart, a cabriolet, and a coach. A soldier was driving it, and under the leathern tilt behind a cover sat a woman, muffled up in shawls. Prince Andrey rode up and was just addressing a question to the soldier, when his attention was taken off by the despairing shrieks of the woman in this conveyance. The officer, directing the traffic, aimed a blow at the soldier who sat in the coachman's seat, for trying to push in ahead of others, and the lash fell on the cover of the equipage. The woman shrieked shrilly. On catching sight of Prince Andrey, she looked out from under the cover and putting her thin arms out from the shawls and waving them, she screamed:

"Adjutant! sir! . . . For God's sake! . . . protect me. . . . What will happen to us? . . . I am the wife of the doctor of the Seventh Chasseurs . . . they won't let us pass, we have dropped behind, lost our own people. . . ."

"I'll thrash you into mincemeat! turn back!" shouted the exasperated officer to the soldier: "turn back with your hussy!"

"Sir, protect us. What does it mean?" screamed the doctor's wife.

"Kindly let this cart get through. Don't you see that it is a woman?" said Prince Andrey, riding up to the officer.

The officer glanced at him, and without making any reply turned again to the soldier. "I'll teach you how to push in. . . . Back! . . ."

"Let it pass, I tell you," repeated Prince Andrey, setting his lips tightly.

"And who are you?" cried the officer, turning upon him suddenly with drunken fury. "Who are you? Are *you*" (he put a peculiarly offensive intonation into the word) "in command, pray? I'm commanding officer here, not you. Back you go," he repeated, "or I'll lash you into mincemeat." The expression evidently pleased the officer.

"A nice snub he gave the little adjutant," said a voice in the background.

Prince Andrey saw that the officer was in that stage of drunken unreasoning fury, when men do not remember what they say. He saw that his championship of the doctor's wife in the queer conveyance was exposing him to what he dreaded more than anything else in the world, what is called in French *ridicule*, but his instinct said something else. The officer had hardly uttered the last words when Prince Andrey rode up to him with a face distorted by frenzied anger, and raised his riding-whip: "Let—them—pass!"

The officer flourished his arm and hurriedly rode away.

"It's all their doing, these staff-officers, all the disorder," he grumbled. "Do as you like."

Prince Andrey, without lifting his eyes, made haste to escape from the doctor's wife, who called him her deliverer. And dwelling on the minutest detail of this humiliating scene with loathing, he galloped on towards the village, where he was told that the commander-in-chief was.

On reaching the village, he got off his horse, and went into the first house with the intention of resting for a moment at least, eating something, and getting all the mortifying impressions that were torturing him into some clear shape. "This is a mob of scoundrels, not an army," he thought, going up to the window of the first house, when a familiar voice called him by his name.

He looked round. Out of a little window was thrust the handsome face of Nesvitsky. Nesvitsky, munching something in his moist mouth and beckoning to him, called him in.

"Bolkonsky! Bolkonsky! Don't you hear, eh? Make haste," he shouted.

Going into the house, Prince Andrey found Nesvitsky and another adjutant having a meal. They hastily turned to Bolkonsky with the inquiry, had he any news? On their familiar faces Prince Andrey read alarm and uneasiness. That expression was particularly noticeable in Nesvitsky's face, usually so full of laughter.

"Where is the commander-in-chief?" asked Bolkonsky.

"Here in this house," answered the adjutant.

"Well, is it true, about the peace and capitulation?" asked Nesvitsky.

"I ask you. I know nothing except that I have had great difficulty in getting through to you."

"And the things that have been going on, my boy! Awful! I was wrong to laugh at Mack; there's worse in store for us," said Nesvitsky. "But sit down, have something to eat."

"You won't find your baggage or anything now, prince, and God knows what's become of your Pyotr," said the other adjutant.

"Where are the headquarters?"

"We shall spend the night in Znaim."

"Well, I got everything I wanted packed up on two horses," said Nesvitsky; "and capital packs they made for me, fit to scamper as far as the Bohemian mountains at least. Things are in a bad way, my boy. But, I say, you must be ill, shivering like that?" Nesvitsky queried, noticing how Prince Andrey shuddered, as though in contact with a galvanic battery.

"No; I'm all right," answered Prince Andrey. He had recalled at that instant the incident with the doctor's wife and the transport officer.

"What is the commander-in-chief doing here?" he asked.

"I can't make out anything," said Nesvitsky.

"I know one thing, that it's all loathsome, loathsome, loathsome," said Prince Andrey, and he went into the house where the commander-in-chief was stopping.

Passing by Kutuzov's carriage, the exhausted saddle-horses of his suite, and the Cossacks talking loudly together, Prince Andrey went into the outer room. Kutuzov himself was, as Prince Andrey had been told, in the inner room of the hut with Prince Bagration and Weierother. The latter was the Austrian general, who had taken Schmidt's place. In the outer room little Kozlovsky was squatting on his heels in front of a copying-clerk. The latter was sitting on a tub turned upside down, he was writing rapidly with the cuffs of his uniform tucked up. Kozlovsky's face was careworn; he too looked as if he had not slept all night. He glanced at Prince Andrey, and did not even nod to him.

"The second line. . . . Ready?" he went on, dictating to the clerk: "the Kiev Grenadiers, the Podolsky . . ."

"Don't be in such a hurry, your honour," the clerk answered rudely and angrily, looking at Kozlovsky. Through the door he heard at that moment Kutuzov's voice, eager and dissatisfied, and other unfamiliar voices interrupting him. The sound of those voices, the inattention with which Kozlovsky glanced at him, the churlishness of the harassed clerk, the fact that the clerk and Kozlovsky were sitting round a tub on the floor at so little distance from the commander-in-chief, and that the Cossacks holding the horses laughed so loudly at the window—all made Prince Andrey feel that some grave calamity was hanging over them.

Prince Andrey turned to Kozlovsky with urgent questions.

"In a minute, prince," said Kozlovsky. "The disposition of Bagration's troops . . ."

"What about capitulation?"

"Nothing of the sort; arrangements have been made for a battle!"

Prince Andrey went towards the door from which the sound of voices came. But at the moment when he was going to open the door, the voices in the room paused, the door opened of itself, and Kutuzov with his eagle nose and podgy face appeared in the doorway. Prince Andrey was standing exactly opposite Kutuzov; but from the expression of the commander-in-chief's one seeing eye it was evident that thought and anxiety so engrossed him as to veil, as it were, his vision. He looked straight into his adjutant's face and did not recognise him.

"Well, have you finished?" he addressed Kozlovsky.

"In a second, your Excellency."

Bagration, a short lean man, not yet elderly, with a resolute and impassive face of oriental type, came out after the commander-in-chief.

"I have the honour to report myself," Prince Andrey said for the second time, rather loudly, as he handed Kutuzov an envelope.

"Ah, from Vienna? Very good! Later, later!" Kutuzov went out to the steps with Bagration.

"Well, prince, good-bye," he said to Bagration. "Christ be with you! May my blessing bring you a great victory!" Kutuzov's face suddenly softened, and there were tears in his eyes. With his left arm he drew Bagration to him, while with his right hand, on which he wore a ring, he crossed him with a gesture evidently habitual. He offered him his podgy cheek, but Bagration kissed him on the neck. "Christ be with you!" repeated Kutuzov, and he went towards his carriage. "Get in with me," he said to Bolkonsky.

"Your Most High Excellency, I should have liked to be of use here. Allow me to remain in Prince Bagration's detachment."

"Get in," said Kutuzov, and noticing that Bolkonsky still delayed: "I have need of good officers myself, myself."

They took their seats in the carriage and drove for some minutes in silence.

"There is a great deal, a great deal of everything still before us," he said, with an expression of old-age clairvoyance, as though he saw all that was passing in Bolkonsky's heart. "If one-tenth part of his detachment comes in, I shall thank God," added Kutuzov, as though talking to himself.

Prince Andrey glanced at Kutuzov, and unconsciously his eyes were caught by the carefully washed seams of the scar on his temple, where the bullet had gone through his head at Ismail, and the empty eyesocket, not a yard from him. "Yes, he has the right to speak so calmly of the destruction of these men," thought Bolkonsky.

"That's why I ask you to send me to that detachment," he said.

Kutuzov made no reply. He seemed to have forgotten what was said to him, and sat plunged in thought. Five minutes later, swaying easily in the soft carriage springs, Kutuzov addressed Prince Andrey. There was no trace of emotion on his face now. With delicate irony he questioned Prince Andrey about the details of his interview with the Emperor, about the comments he had heard at Court on the Krems engagement, and about ladies of their common acquaintance.

XIV

KUTUZOV had, on the 1st of November, received from one of his spies information that showed the army he commanded to be in an almost hopeless position. The spy reported that the French, after crossing the bridge at Vienna, were moving in immense force on Kutuzov's line of communications with the reinforcements marching from Russia. If Kutuzov were to determine to remain at Krems, Napoleon's army of a hundred and fifty thousand men would cut him off from all communications, and would surround his exhausted army of forty thousand, and he would find himself in the position of Mack before Ulm. If Kutuzov decided to leave the road leading to a junction with the Russian reinforcements, he would have to make his way with no road through unknown country to the mountains of Bohemia, pursued by the cream of the enemy's forces, and to give up all hope of effecting a junction with Buxhevden. If Kutuzov decided to march by the road from Krems to Olmütz to join the forces from Russia he ran the risk of finding the French, who had crossed the Vienna bridge, in advance of him on this road, and so being forced to give battle on the march, encumbered with all his stores and transport, with an enemy three times as numerous and hemming him in on both sides. Kutuzov chose the last course.

The French, after crossing the river, had, as the spy reported, set off at a quick march toward Znaim, which lay on Kutuzov's line of route, more than a hundred versts in front of him. To reach Znaim before the French offered the best hopes of saving the army. To allow the French to get to Znaim before him would mean exposing the whole army to a disgrace like that of the Austrians at Ulm, or to complete destruction. But to arrive there before the French with the whole army was impossible. The road of the French army from Vienna to Znaim was shorter and better than the Russians' road from Krems to Znaim.

On the night of receiving the news Kutuzov sent Bagration's advance guard of four thousand soldiers to the right over the mountains from the Krems-Znaim road to the Vienna and Znaim road. Bagration was to make a forced march, to halt facing towards Vienna and with his back to Znaim, and if he succeeded in getting on the road in advance of the French, he was to delay them as long as he could. Kutuzov himself with all the transport was making straight for Znaim.

Bagration marched forty-five versts, by night in stormy weather, through the mountains, with no road, and with hungry, barefoot soldiers. Leaving a third of his men straggling behind him, Bagration reached Hollabrunn, on the Vienna and Znaim road, a few hours before the French, who marched upon Hollabrunn from Vienna. Kutuzov needed fully another twenty-four hours to get to Znaim with all the transport, and so to save the army Bagration would have had, with his four thousand hungry and exhausted soldiers, to have kept at bay the whole army of the enemy confronting him at Hollabrunn for four-and-twenty hours, and this was obviously impossible. But a freak of fate made the impossible possible. The success of the trick that had given the Vienna bridge into the hands of the French encouraged Murat to try and take in Kutuzov too. Murat, on meeting Bagration's weak detachment on the Znaim road, supposed it to be the whole army of Kutuzov. To give this army a final and crushing defeat he waited for the troops still on the road from Vienna, and to that end he proposed a truce for three days, on the condition that neither army should change its position nor stir from where it was. Murat averred that negotiations for peace were now proceeding, and that he proposed a truce therefore to avoid useless bloodshed. The Austrian general, Nostits, who was in charge of the advance posts, believed the statements of Murat's messengers and retired, leaving Bagration's detachment unprotected. The other messengers rode off to the Russian line to make the same announcement about peace negotiations, and to propose a truce of three days to the Russian troops. Bagration replied that he was not authorised to accept or to decline a truce, and sent his adjutant to Kutuzov with a report of the proposition made to him.

A truce gave Kutuzov the only possibility of gaining time, of letting Bagration's exhausted forces rest, and of getting the transport and heavy convoys (the movement of which was concealed from the French) a further stage on their journey. The offer of a truce gave the one—and totally unexpected—chance of saving the army. On receiving information of it, Kutuzov promptly despatched the general-adjutant, Winzengerode, who was with him, to the enemy's camp. Winzengerode was instructed not only to accept the truce, but to propose terms of capitulation, while Kutuzov meanwhile sent his adjutants back to hasten to the utmost the transport of the luggage of the whole army along the Krems and Znaim road. Bagration's hungry and exhausted detachment alone was to cover the movements of the transport and of the whole army, by remaining stationary in face of an enemy eight times stronger numerically.

Kutuzov's anticipations were correct both as to the proposals of capitulation, which bound him to nothing, giving time for part of the transport to reach Znaim, and as to Murat's blunder being very quickly discovered. As soon as Bonaparte, who was at Schönbrunn, only twenty-five versts from Hollabrunn, received Murat's despatch and projects of truce and capitulation, he detected the deception and despatched the following letter to Murat:

To Prince Murat.

Schönbrunn, 25 Brumaire, year 1805,
at 8 o'clock in the morning.

"It is impossible to find terms in which to express to you my displeasure. You only command my advance guard and you have no right to make any truce without my order. You are causing me to lose the results of a campaign. Break the truce immediately and march upon the enemy. You must make a declaration to them that the general who signed this capitulation had no right to do so, and that only the Emperor of Russia has that right.

"Whenever the Emperor of Russia ratifies the aforesaid convention, however, I will ratify it; but it is only a stratagem. March on, destroy the Russian army . . . you are in a position to take its baggage and artillery.

"The Emperor of Russia's aide-de-camp is a . . . Officers are nothing when they have not powers; this one had none. . . . The Austrians let themselves be tricked about the crossing of the bridge of Vienna, you are letting yourself be tricked by one of the Emperor's aides-de-camp.

"NAPOLEON."

Bonaparte's adjutant dashed off at full gallop with this menacing letter to Murat. Not trusting his generals, Bonaparte himself advanced to the field of battle with his whole guard, fearful of letting the snared victim slip through his fingers. Meanwhile the four thousand men of Bagration's detachment, merrily lighting camp-fires, dried and warmed themselves, and cooked their porridge for the first time for three days, and not one among them knew or dreamed of what was in store for them.

XV

BEFORE four o'clock in the afternoon Prince Andrey, who had persisted in his petition to Kutuzov, reached Grunte, and joined Bagration. Bonaparte's adjutant had not yet reached Murat's division, and the battle had not yet begun. In Bagration's detachment, they knew nothing of the progress of events. They talked about peace, but did not believe in its possibility. They talked of a battle, but did not believe in a battle's being close at hand either.

Knowing Bolkonsky to be a favourite and trusted adjutant, Bagration received him with a commanding officer's special graciousness and condescension. He informed him that there would probably be an engagement that day or the next day, and gave him full liberty to remain in attendance on him during the battle, or to retire to the rear-guard to watch over the order of the retreat, also a matter of great importance.

"To-day, though, there will most likely be no action," said Bagration, as though to reassure Prince Andrey.

"If this is one of the common run of little staff dandies, sent here to win a cross, he can do that in the rear-guard, but if he wants to be with me, let him . . . he'll be of use, if he's a brave officer," thought Bagration. Prince Andrey, without replying, asked the prince's permission to ride round the position and find out the disposition of the forces, so that, in case of a message, he might know where to take it. An officer

on duty, a handsome and elegantly dressed man, with a diamond ring
on his forefinger, who spoke French badly, but with assurance, was summoned to conduct Prince Andrey.

On all sides they saw officers drenched through, with dejected faces,
apparently looking for something, and soldiers dragging doors, benches,
and fences from the village.

"Here we can't put a stop to these people," said the staff-officer, pointing to them. "Their commanders let their companies get out of hand.
And look here," he pointed to a canteen-keeper's booth, "they gather
here, and here they sit. I drove them all out this morning, and look, it's
full again. I must go and scare them, prince. One moment."

"Let us go together, and I'll get some bread and cheese there," said
Prince Andrey, who had not yet had time for a meal.

"Why didn't you mention it, prince? I would have offered you something."

They got off their horses and went into the canteen-keeper's booth.
Several officers, with flushed and exhausted faces, were sitting at the
tables, eating and drinking.

"Now what does this mean, gentlemen?" said the staff-officer, in the
reproachful tone of a man who has repeated the same thing several
times. "You mustn't absent yourselves like this. The prince gave orders
that no one was to leave his post. Come, really, captain," he remon-
strated with a muddy, thin little artillery officer, who in his stockings (he
had given his boots to the canteen-keeper to dry) stood up at their entrance, smiling not quite naturally.

"Now aren't you ashamed, Captain Tushin?" pursued the staff-officer.
"I should have thought you as an artillery officer ought to set an example, and you have no boots on. They'll sound the alarm, and you'll be
in a pretty position without your boots on." (The staff-officer smiled.)
"Kindly return to your posts, gentlemen, all, all," he added in a tone
of authority.

Prince Andrey could not help smiling as he glanced at Captain Tushin.
Smiling, without a word, Tushin shifted from one bare foot to the other,
looking inquiringly, with his big, shrewd, and good-natured eyes, from
Prince Andrey to the staff-officer.

"The soldiers say it's easier barefoot," said Captain Tushin, smiling
shyly, evidently anxious to carry off his awkward position in a jesting
tone. But before he had uttered the words, he felt that his joke would
not do and had not come off. He was in confusion.

"Kindly go to your places," said the staff-officer, trying to preserve
his gravity.

Prince Andrey glanced once more at the little figure of the artillery
officer. There was something peculiar about it, utterly unsoldierly, rather
comic, but very attractive.

The staff-officer and Prince Andrey got on their horses and rode on.

Riding out beyond the village, continually meeting or overtaking
soldiers and officers of various ranks, they saw on the left earthworks
being thrown up, still red with the freshly dug clay. Several battalions

of soldiers, in their shirt-sleeves, in spite of the cold wind were toiling like white ants at these entrenchments; from the trench they saw spadefuls of red clay continually being thrown out by unseen hands. They rode up to the entrenchment, examined it, and were riding on further. Close behind the entrenchment they came upon dozens of soldiers continually running to and from the earthworks, and they had to hold their noses and put their horses to a gallop to get by the pestilential atmosphere of this improvised sewer.

"*Voilà l'agrément des camps, monsieur le prince,*" said the staff-officer. They rode up the opposite hill. From that hill they had a view of the French. Prince Andrey stopped and began looking closer at what lay before them.

"You see here is where our battery stands," said the staff-officer, pointing to the highest point, "commanded by that queer fellow sitting without his boots; from there you can see everything; let us go there, prince."

"I am very grateful to you, I'll go on alone now," said Prince Andrey, anxious to be rid of the staff-officer; "don't trouble yourself further, please."

The staff-officer left him, and Prince Andrey rode on alone.

The further forward and the nearer to the enemy he went, the more orderly and cheerful he found the troops. The greatest disorder and depression had prevailed in the transport forces before Znaim, which Prince Andrey had passed that morning, ten versts from the French. At Grunte too a certain alarm and vague dread could be felt. But the nearer Prince Andrey got to the French line, the more self-confident was the appearance of our troops. The soldiers, in their great-coats, stood ranged in lines with their sergeant, and the captain was calling over the men, poking the last soldier in the line in the ribs, and telling him to hold up his hand. Soldiers were dotted all over the plain, dragging logs and brushwood, and constructing shanties, chatting together, and laughing good-humouredly. They were sitting round the fires, dressed and stripped, drying shirts and foot-gear. Or they thronged round the porridge-pots and cauldrons, brushing their boots and their coats. In one company dinner was ready, and the soldiers, with greedy faces, watched the steaming pots, and waited for the sample, which was being taken in a wooden bowl to the commissariat officer, sitting on a piece of wood facing his shanty.

In another company—a lucky one, for not all had vodka—the soldiers stood in a group round a broad-shouldered, pock-marked sergeant, who was tilting a keg of vodka, and pouring it into the covers of the canteens held out to him in turn. The soldiers, with reverential faces, lifted the covers to their mouths, drained them, and licking their lips and rubbing them with the sleeves of their coats, they walked away looking more good-humoured than before. Every face was as serene as though it were all happening not in sight of the enemy, just before an action in which at least half of the detachment must certainly be left on the field, but somewhere at home in Russia, with every prospect of a quiet halting-place. Prince Andrey rode by the Chasseur regiment, and as he advanced into the ranks of the Kiev Grenadiers, stalwart fellows all engaged in the same peaceful pursuits, not far from the colonel's shanty, standing higher than the rest, he came upon a platoon of grenadiers, before whom lay a man stripped naked. Two soldiers were holding him, while two others were brandishing supple twigs and bringing them down at regular intervals on the man's bare back. The man shrieked unnaturally. A stout major was walking up and down in front of the platoon, and regardless of the screams, he kept saying: "It's a disgrace for a soldier to steal; a soldier must be honest, honourable, and brave, and to steal from a comrade, he must be without honour indeed, a monster. Again, again!"

And still he heard the dull thuds and the desperate but affected scream.

"Again, again," the major was saying.

A young officer, with an expression of bewilderment and distress in his face, walked away from the flogging, looking inquiringly at the adjutant.

Prince Andrey, coming out to the foremost line, rode along in front of it. Our line and the enemy's were far from one another at the left and also at the right flank; but in the centre, at the spot where in the morning the messengers had met, the lines came so close that the soldiers of the two armies could see each other's faces and talk together. Besides these soldiers, whose place was in that part of the line, many others had gathered there from both sides, and they were laughing, as they scrutinised the strange and novel dress and aspect of their foes.

Since early morning, though it was forbidden to go up to the line, the commanding officers could not keep the inquisitive soldiers back. The soldiers, whose post was in that part of the line, like showmen exhibiting some curiosity, no longer looked at the French, but made observations on the men who came up to look, and waited with a bored face to be relieved. Prince Andrey stopped to look carefully at the French.

"Look'ee, look'ee," one soldier was saying to a comrade, pointing to a Russian musketeer, who had gone up to the lines with an officer and was talking warmly and rapidly with a French grenadier. "I say, doesn't he jabber away fine! I bet the Frenchy can't keep pace with him. Now, then, Sidorov?"

"Wait a bit; listen. Aye, it's fine!" replied Sidorov, reputed a regular scholar at talking French.

The soldier, at whom they had pointed laughing, was Dolohov. Prince Andrey recognised him and listened to what he was saying. Dolohov, together with his captain, had come from the left flank, where his regiment was posted.

"Come, again, again!" the captain urged, craning forward and trying not to lose a syllable of the conversation, though it was unintelligible to him. "Please, go on. What's he saying?"

Dolohov did not answer the captain; he had been drawn into a hot dispute with the French grenadier. They were talking, as was to be expected, of the campaign. The Frenchman, mixing up the Austrians and the Russians, was maintaining that the Russians had been defeated and had been fleeing all the way from Ulm. Dolohov declared that the Russians had never been defeated, but had beaten the French.

"We have orders to drive you away from here, and we shall too," said Dolohov.

"You had better take care you are not all captured with all your Cossacks," said the French grenadier.

Spectators and listeners on the French side laughed.

"We shall make you dance, as you danced in Suvorov's day" (*on vous fera danser*), said Dolohov.

"What is he prating about?" said a Frenchman.

"Ancient history," said another, guessing that the allusion was to former wars. "The Emperor will show your Suvorov, like the others. . . ."

"Bonaparte . . ." Dolohov was beginning, but the Frenchman interrupted him.

"Not Bonaparte. He is the Emperor! *Sacré nom* . . ." he said angrily.

"Damnation to him, your Emperor!"

And Dolohov swore a coarse soldier's oath in Russian, and, shouldering his gun, walked away.

"Come along, Ivan Lukitch," he said to his captain.

"So that's how they talk French," said the soldiers in the line. "Now then, you, Sidorov." Sidorov winked, and, turning to the French, he fell to gabbling disconnected syllables very rapidly.

"*Kari-ma-la-ta-fa-sa-fi-mu-ter-kess-ka*," he jabbered, trying to give the most expressive intonation to his voice.

"Ho, ho, ho! ha ha! ha ha! Oh! oo!" the soldiers burst into a roar of such hearty, good-humoured laughter, in which the French line too could not keep from joining, that after it it seemed as though they must unload their guns, blow up their ammunition, and all hurry away back to their homes. But the guns remained loaded, the port-holes in the houses and earthworks looked out as menacingly as ever, and the cannons, taken off their platforms, confronted one another as before.

XVI

After making a circuit round the whole line of the army, from the right flank to the left, Prince Andrey rode up to that battery from which the staff-officer told him that the whole field could be seen. Here he dismounted and stood by the end of one of the four cannons, which had been taken off their platforms. An artilleryman on sentinel duty in front of the cannons was just confronting the officer, but at a sign being made to him, he renewed his regular, monotonous pacing. Behind the cannons stood their platforms, and still further behind, the picket-ropes and camp-fires of the artillerymen. To the left, not far from the end cannon, was a little newly rigged-up shanty, from which came the sounds of officers' voices in eager conversation. From the battery there was in fact a view of almost the whole disposition of the Russian forces, and the greater part of the enemy's. Directly facing the battery on the skyline of the opposite hill could be seen the village of Schöngraben; to the left and to the right could be discerned in three places through the smoke of the camp-fires masses of the French troops, of which the greater number were undoubtedly in the village itself and behind the hill. To the left of the village there was something in the smoke that looked like a battery, but it could not be made out clearly by the naked eye. Our right flank was stationed on a rather steep eminence, which dominated the French position. About it were disposed our infantry regiments, and on the very ridge could be seen dragoons. In the centre, where was placed Tushin's battery, from which Prince Andrey was surveying the position, there was the most sloping and direct descent to the stream that separated us from Schöngraben. On the left our troops were close to a copse, where there was the smoke of the camp-fires of our infantry, chopping wood in it. The French line was wider than ours, and it was obviously easy for the French to outflank us on both sides. Behind our position was a precipitous and deep ravine, down which it would be difficult to retreat with artillery and cavalry. Prince Andrey leaned his elbow on the cannon, and taking out a note-book, sketched for himself a plan of the disposition of the troops. In two places he made notes with a pencil, intending to speak on the points to Bagration. He meant to suggest first concentrating all the artillery in the centre, and secondly drawing the cavalry back to the further side of the ravine. Prince Andrey, who was constantly in attendance on the commander-in-chief, watching the movements of masses of men and manœuvring of troops, and also continually studying the historical accounts of battles, could not help viewing the course of the military operations that were to come only in their general features. His imagination dwelt on the broad possibilities, such as the following: "If the enemy makes the right flank the point of attack," he said to himself, "the Kiev grenadiers and Podolosky Chasseurs will have to defend their position, till the reserves from the centre come to their support. In that case the dragoons can get them in the flank and drive them back. In case of an attack on the centre, we station on this height the central battery, and under its cover we draw off the left flank and retreat to the ravine by platoons," he reasoned. . . . All the while he was on the cannon, he heard, as one often does, the sounds of the voices of the officers talking in the shanty, but he did not take in a single word of what they were saying. Suddenly a voice from the shanty impressed him by a tone of such earnestness that he could not help listening.

"No, my dear fellow," said a pleasant voice that seemed somehow familiar to Prince Andrey. "I say that if one could know what will happen after death, then not one of us would be afraid of death. That's so, my dear fellow."

Another younger voice interrupted him: "But afraid or not afraid, there's no escaping it."

"Why, you're always in fear! Fie on you learned fellows," said a

third, a manly voice, interrupting both. "To be sure, you artillerymen are clever fellows, because you can carry everything with you to eat and to drink."

And the owner of the manly voice, apparently an infantry officer, laughed.

"Still one is in fear," pursued the first voice, the one Prince Andrey knew. "One's afraid of the unknown, that's what it is. It's all very well to say the soul goes to heaven . . . but this we do know, that there is no heaven, but only atmosphere."

Again the manly voice interrupted.

"Come, give us a drop of your herb-brandy, Tushin," it said.

"Oh, it's the captain, who had his boots off in the booth," thought Prince Andrey, recognising with pleasure the agreeable philosophising voice.

"Herb-brandy by all means," said Tushin; "but still to conceive of a future life . . ." He did not finish his sentence.

At that moment there was a whiz heard in the air: nearer, nearer, faster and more distinctly, and faster it came; and the cannon-ball, as though not uttering all it had to say, thudded into the earth not far from the shanty, tearing up the soil with superhuman force. The earth seemed to moan at the terrible blow. At the same instant there dashed out of the shanty, before any of the rest, little Tushin with his short pipe in his mouth; his shrewd, good-humoured face was rather pale. After him emerged the owner of the manly voice, a stalwart infantry officer, who ran off to his company, buttoning his coat as he ran.

XVII

PRINCE ANDREY mounted his horse but lingered at the battery, looking at the smoke of the cannon from which the ball had flown. His eyes moved rapidly over the wide plain. He only saw that the previously immobile masses of the French were heaving to and fro, and that it really was a battery on the left. The smoke still clung about it. Two Frenchmen on horseback, doubtless adjutants, were galloping on the hill. A small column of the enemy, distinctly visible, were moving downhill, probably to strengthen the line. The smoke of the first shot had not cleared away, when there was a fresh puff of smoke and another shot. The battle was beginning. Prince Andrey turned his horse and galloped back to Grunte to look for Prince Bagration. Behind him he heard the cannonade becoming louder and more frequent. Our men were evidently beginning to reply. Musket shots could be heard below at the spot where the lines were closest. Lemarrois had only just galloped to Murat with Napoleon's menacing letter, and Murat, abashed and anxious to efface his error, at once moved his forces to the centre and towards both flanks, hoping before evening and the arrival of the Emperor to destroy the insignificant detachment before him.

"It has begun! Here it comes!" thought Prince Andrey, feeling the blood rush to his heart. "But where? What form is my Toulon to take?" he wondered.

Passing between the companies that had been eating porridge and drinking vodka a quarter of an hour before, he saw everywhere nothing but the same rapid movements of soldiers forming in ranks and getting their guns, and on every face he saw the same eagerness that he felt in his heart. "It has begun! Here it comes! Terrible and delightful!" said the face of every private and officer. Before he reached the earthworks that were being thrown up, he saw in the evening light of the dull autumn day men on horseback crossing towards him. The foremost, wearing a cloak and an Astrachan cap, was riding on a white horse. It was Prince Bagration. Prince Andrey stopped and waited for him to come up. Prince Bagration stopped his horse, and recognising Prince Andrey nodded to him. He still gazed on ahead while Prince Andrey told him what he had been seeing.

The expression: "It has begun! it is coming!" was discernible even on Prince Bagration's strong, brown face, with his half-closed, lustreless, sleepy-looking eyes. Prince Andrey glanced with uneasy curiosity at that impassive face, and he longed to know: Was that man thinking and feeling, and what was he thinking and feeling at that moment? "Is there anything at all there behind that impassive face?" Prince Andrey wondered, looking at him. Prince Bagration nodded in token of his assent to Prince Andrey's words, and said: "Very good," with an expression that seemed to signify that all that happened, and all that was told him, was exactly what he had foreseen. Prince Andrey, panting from his rapid ride, spoke quickly. Prince Bagration uttered his words in his Oriental accent with peculiar deliberation, as though impressing upon him that there was no need of hurry. He did, however, spur his horse into a gallop in the direction of Tushin's battery. Prince Andrey rode after him with his suite. The party consisted of an officer of the suite, Bagration's private adjutant, Zherkov, an orderly officer, the staff-officer on duty, riding a beautiful horse of English breed, and a civilian official, the auditor, who had asked to be present from curiosity to see the battle. The auditor, a plump man with a plump face, looked about him with a naïve smile of amusement, swaying about on his horse, and cutting a queer figure in his cloak on his saddle among the hussars, Cossacks, and adjutants.

"This gentleman wants to see a battle," said Zherkov to Bolkonsky, indicating the auditor, "but has begun to feel queer already."

"Come, leave off," said the auditor, with a beaming smile at once naïve and cunning, as though he were flattered at being the object of Zherkov's jests, and was purposely trying to seem stupider than he was in reality.

"It's very curious, *mon Monsieur Prince*," said the staff-officer on duty. (He vaguely remembered that the title *prince* was translated in some peculiar way in French, but could not get it quite right.) By this time they were all riding up to Tushin's battery, and a ball struck the ground before them.

"What was that falling?" asked the auditor, smiling naïvely.

"A French pancake," said Zherkov.

"That's what they hit you with, then?" asked the auditor. "How awful!" And he seemed to expand all over with enjoyment. He had hardly uttered the words when again there was a sudden terrible whiz, which ended abruptly in a thud into something soft, and flop—a Cossack, riding a little behind and to the right of the auditor, dropped from his horse to the ground. Zherkov and the staff-officer bent forward over their saddles and turned their horses away. The auditor stopped facing the Cossack, and looking with curiosity at him. The Cossack was dead, the horse was still struggling.

Prince Bagration dropped his eyelids, looked round, and seeing the cause of the delay, turned away indifferently, seeming to ask, "Why notice these trivial details?" With the ease of a first-rate horseman he stopped his horse, bent over a little and disengaged his sabre, which had caught under his cloak. The sabre was an old-fashioned one, unlike what are worn now. Prince Andrey remembered the story that Suvorov had given his sabre to Bagration in Italy, and the recollection was particularly pleasant to him at that moment. They had ridden up to the very battery from which Prince Andrey had surveyed the field of battle.

"Whose company?" Prince Bagration asked of the artilleryman standing at the ammunition boxes.

He asked in words: "Whose company?" but what he was really asking was, "You're not in a panic here?" And the artilleryman understood that.

"Captain Tushin's, your excellency," the red-haired, freckled artilleryman sang out in a cheerful voice, as he ducked forward.

"To be sure, to be sure," said Bagration, pondering something, and he rode by the platforms up to the end cannon. Just as he reached it, a shot boomed from the cannon, deafening him and his suite, and in the smoke that suddenly enveloped the cannon the artillerymen could be seen hauling at the cannon, dragging and rolling it back to its former position. A broad-shouldered, gigantic soldier, gunner number one, with a mop, darted up to the wheel and planted himself, his legs wide apart; while number two, with a shaking hand, put the charge into the cannon's mouth; a small man with stooping shoulders, the officer Tushin, stumbling against the cannon, dashed forward, not noticing the general, and looked out, shading his eyes with his little hand.

"Another two points higher, and it will be just right," he shouted in a shrill voice, to which he tried to give a swaggering note utterly out of keeping with his figure. "Two!" he piped. "Smash away, Medvyedev!"

Bagration called to the officer, and Tushin went up to the general, putting three fingers to the peak of his cap with a timid and awkward gesture, more like a priest blessing some one than a soldier saluting. Though Tushin's guns had been intended to cannonade the valley, he

was throwing shells over the village of Schöngraben, in part of which
immense masses of French soldiers were moving out.

No one had given Tushin instructions at what or with what to fire,
and after consulting his sergeant, Zaharchenko, for whom he had a great
respect, he had decided that it would be a good thing to set fire to the
village. "Very good!" Bagration said, on the officer's submitting that he
had done so, and he began scrutinising the whole field of battle that lay
unfolded before him. He seemed to be considering something. The
French had advanced nearest on the right side. In the hollow where the
stream flowed, below the eminence on which the Kiev regiment was stationed, could be heard a continual roll and crash of guns, the din of
which was overwhelming. And much further to the right, behind the
dragoons, the officer of the suite pointed out to Bagration a column of
French outflanking our flank. On the left the horizon was bounded by
the copse close by. Prince Bagration gave orders for two battalions from
the centre to go to the right to reinforce the flank. The officer of the
suite ventured to observe to the prince that the removal of these battalions would leave the cannon unprotected. Prince Bagration turned to
the officer of the suite and stared at him with his lustreless eyes in
silence. Prince Andrey thought that the officer's observation was a very
just one, and that really there was nothing to be said in reply. But at
that instant an adjutant galloped up with a message from the colonel of
the regiment in the hollow that immense masses of the French were
coming down upon them, that his men were in disorder and retreating
upon the Kiev grenadiers. Prince Bagration nodded to signify his assent
and approval. He rode at a walking pace to the right, and sent an adjutant to the dragoons with orders to attack the French. But the adjutant
returned half an hour later with the news that the colonel of the
dragoons had already retired beyond the ravine, as a destructive fire had
been opened upon him, and he was losing his men for nothing, and so
he had concentrated his men in the wood.

"Very good!" said Bagration.

Just as he was leaving the battery, shots had been heard in the wood
on the left too; and as it was too far to the left flank for him to go
himself, Prince Bagration despatched Zherkov to tell the senior general
—the general whose regiment had been inspected by Kutuzov at Braunau—to retreat as rapidly as possible beyond the ravine, as the right
flank would probably not long be able to detain the enemy. Tushin, and
the battalion that was to have defended his battery, was forgotten.
Prince Andrey listened carefully to Prince Bagration's colloquies with
the commanding officers, and to the orders he gave them, and noticed, to
his astonishment, that no orders were really given by him at all, but that
Prince Bagration confined himself to trying to appear as though everything that was being done of necessity, by chance, or at the will of individual officers, was all done, if not by his order, at least in accordance with his intentions. Prince Andrey observed, however, that, thanks
to the tact shown by Prince Bagration, notwithstanding that what was
done was due to chance, and not dependent on the commander's will,

his presence was of the greatest value. Commanding officers, who rode up to Bagration looking distraught, regained their composure; soldiers and officers greeted him cheerfully, recovered their spirits in his pres· ence, and were unmistakably anxious to display their pluck before him,

XVIII

AFTER riding up to the highest point of our right flank, Prince Bagration began to go downhill, where a continuous roll of musketry was heard and nothing could be seen for the smoke. The nearer they got to the hollow the less they could see, and the more distinctly could be felt the nearness of the actual battlefield. They began to meet wounded men. Two soldiers were dragging one along, supporting him on each side. His head was covered with blood; he had no cap, and was coughing and spitting. The bullet had apparently entered his mouth or throat. Another one came towards them, walking pluckily alone without his gun, groaning aloud and wringing his hands from the pain of a wound from which the blood was flowing, as though from a bottle, over his greatcoat. His face looked more frightened than in pain. He had been wounded only a moment before. Crossing the road, they began going down a deep descent, and on the slope they saw several men lying on the ground. They were met by a crowd of soldiers, among them some who were not wounded. The soldiers were hurrying up the hill, gasping for breath, and in spite of the general's presence, they were talking loudly together and gesticulating with their arms. In the smoke ahead of them they could see now rows of grey coats, and the commanding officer, seeing Bagration, ran after the group of retreating soldiers, calling upon them to come back. Bagration rode up to the ranks, along which there was here and there a rapid snapping of shots drowning the talk of the soldiers and the shouts of the officers. The whole air was reeking with smoke. The soldiers' faces were all full of excitement and smudged with powder. Some were plugging with their ramrods, others were putting powder on the touch-pans, and getting charges out of their pouches, others were firing their guns. But it was impossible to see at whom they were firing from the smoke, which the wind did not lift. The pleasant hum and whiz of the bullets was repeated pretty rapidly. "What is it?" wondered Prince Andrey, as he rode up to the crowd of soldiers. "It can't be the line, for they are all crowded together; it can't be an attacking party, for they are not moving; it can't be a square, they are not standing like one."

A thin, weak-looking colonel, apparently an old man, with an amiable smile, and eyelids that half-covered his old-looking eyes and gave him a mild air, rode up to Prince Bagration and received him as though he were welcoming an honoured guest into his house. He announced to Prince Bagration that his regiment had had to face a cavalry attack of the French, that though the attack had been repulsed, the regiment had lost more than half of its men. The colonel said that the attack had been repulsed, supposing that to be the• proper military term for what had happened; but he did not really know himself what had been taking place during that half hour in the troops under his command, and could not have said with any certainty whether the attack had been repelled or his regiment had been beaten by the attack. All he knew was that at the beginning of the action balls and grenades had begun flying all about his regiment, and killing men, that then some one had shouted "cavalry," and our men had begun firing. And they were firing still, though not now at the cavalry, who had disappeared, but at the French infantry, who had made their appearance in the hollow and were firing at our men. Prince Bagration nodded his head to betoken that all this was exactly what he had desired and expected. Turning to an adjutant, he commanded him to bring down from the hill the two battalions of the Sixth Chasseurs, by whom they had just come. Prince Andrey was struck at that instant by the change that had come over Prince Bagration's face. His face wore the look of concentrated and happy determination, which may be seen in a man who in a hot day takes the final run before a header into the water. The lustreless, sleepy look in the eyes, the affectation of profound thought had gone. The round, hard, eagle eyes looked ecstatically and rather disdainfully before him, obviously not resting on anything, though there was still the same deliberation in his measured movements.

The colonel addressed a protest to Prince Bagration, urging him to go back, as there it was too dangerous for him. "I beg of you, your excellency, for God's sake!" he kept on saying, looking for support to the officer of the suite, who only turned away from him.

"Only look, your excellency!" He called his attention to the bullets which were continually whizzing, singing, and hissing about them. He spoke in the tone of protest and entreaty with which a carpenter speaks to a gentleman who has picked up a hatchet. "We are used to it, but you may blister your fingers." He talked as though these bullets could not kill him, and his half-closed eyes gave a still more persuasive effect to his words. The staff-officer added his protests to the colonel, but Bagration made them no answer. He merely gave the order to cease firing, and to form so as to make room for the two battalions of reinforcements. Just as he was speaking the cloud of smoke covering the hollow was lifted as by an unseen hand and blown by the rising wind from right to left, and the opposite hill came into sight with the French moving across it. All eyes instinctively fastened on that French column moving down upon them and winding in and out over the ups and downs of the ground. Already they could see the fur caps of the soldiers, could distinguish officers from privates, could see their flag flapping against its staff.

"How well they're marching," said some one in Bagration's suite.

The front part of the column was already dipping down into the hollow. The engagement would take place then on the nearer side of the slope . . .

The remnants of the regiment that had already been in action, forming hurriedly, drew off to the right; the two battalions of the Sixth Chasseurs marched up in good order, driving the last stragglers before them. They had not yet reached Bagration, but the heavy, weighty tread could be heard of the whole mass keeping step. On the left flank, nearest of all to Bagration, marched the captain, a round-faced imposing-looking man, with a foolish and happy expression of face. It was the same infantry officer who had run out of the shanty after Tushin. He was obviously thinking of nothing at the moment, but that he was marching before his commander in fine style. With the complacency of a man on parade, he stepped springing on his muscular legs, drawing himself up without the slightest effort, as though he were swinging, and this easy elasticity was a striking contrast to the heavy tread of the soldiers keeping step with him. He wore hanging by his leg an unsheathed, slender, narrow sword (a small bent sabre, more like a toy than a weapon), and looking about him, now at the commander, now behind, he turned his whole powerful frame round without getting out of step. It looked as though all the force of his soul was directed to marching by his commander in the best style possible. And conscious that he was accomplishing this, he was happy. "Left . . . left . . . left . . ." he seemed to be inwardly repeating at each alternate step. And the wall of soldierly figures, weighed down by their knapsacks and guns, with their faces all grave in different ways, moved by in the same rhythm, as though each of the hundreds of soldiers were repeating mentally at each alternate step, "Left . . . left . . . left . . ." A stout major skirted a bush on the road, puffing and shifting his step. A soldier, who had dropped behind, trotted after the company, looking panic-stricken at his own defection. A cannon ball, whizzing through the air, flew over the heads of Prince Bagration and his suite, and in time to the same rhythm, "Left . . . left . . ." it fell into the column.

"Close the ranks!" rang out the jaunty voice of the captain. The soldiers marched in a half circle round something in the place where the ball had fallen, and an old cavalryman, an under officer, lingered behind near the dead, and overtaking his line, changed feet with a hop, got into step, and looked angrily about him. "Left . . . left . . . left . . ." seemed to echo out of the menacing silence and the monotonous sound of the simultaneous tread of the feet on the ground.

"Well done, lads!" said Prince Bagration.

"For your ex . . . slen, slen, slency!" rang out along the ranks. A surly-looking soldier, marching on the left, turned his eyes on Bagration as he shouted, with an expression that seemed to say, "We know that without telling." Another, opening his mouth wide, shouted without glancing round, and marched on, as though afraid of letting his attention stray. The order was given to halt and take off their knapsacks.

Bagration rode round the ranks of men who had marched by him, and then dismounted from his horse. He gave the reins to a Cossack, took off his cloak and handed it to him, stretched his legs and set his cap straight on his head. The French column with the officers in front came into sight under the hill.

"With God's help!" cried Bagration in a resolute, sonorous voice. He turned for one instant to the front line, and swinging his arms a little, with the awkward, lumbering gait of a man always on horseback, he walked forward over the uneven ground. Prince Andrey felt that some unseen force was drawing him forward, and he had a sensation of great happiness.[1]

The French were near. Already Prince Andrey, walking beside Bagration, could distinguish clearly the sashes, the red epaulettes, even the faces of the French. (He saw distinctly one bandy-legged old French officer, wearing Hessian boots, who was getting up the hill with difficulty, taking hold of the bushes.) Prince Bagration gave no new command, and still marched in front of the ranks in the same silence. Suddenly there was the snap of a shot among the French, another and a third . . . and smoke rose and firing rang out in all the broken-up ranks of the enemy. Several of our men fell, among them the round-faced officer, who had been marching so carefully and complacently. But at the very instant of the first shot, Bagration looked round and shouted, "Hurrah!" "Hurra . . . a . . . a . . . ah!" rang out along our lines in a prolonged roar, and out-stripping Prince Bagration and one another, in no order, but in an eager and joyous crowd, our men ran downhill after the routed French.

XIX

THE attack of the Sixth Chasseurs covered the retreat of the right flank. In the centre Tushin's forgotten battery had succeeded in setting fire to Schöngraben and delaying the advance of the French. The French stayed to put out the fire, which was fanned by the wind, and this gave time for the Russians to retreat. The retreat of the centre beyond the ravine was hurried and noisy; but the different companies kept apart. But the left flank, which consisted of the Azovsky and Podolosky infantry and the Pavlograd hussars, was simultaneously attacked in front and surrounded by the cream of the French army under Lannes, and was thrown into disorder. Bagration had sent Zherkov to the general in command of the left flank with orders to retreat immediately.

Zherkov, keeping his hand still at his cap, had briskly started his horse and galloped off. But no sooner had he ridden out of Bagration's sight than his courage failed him. He was overtaken by a panic he could not contend against, and he could not bring himself to go where there was danger.

After galloping some distance towards the troops of the left flank, he rode not forward where he heard firing, but off to look for the general and the officers in a direction where they could not by any possibility be; and so it was that he did not deliver the message.

The command of the left flank belonged by right of seniority to the general of the regiment in which Dolohov was serving—the regiment

---

[1] This was the attack of which Thiers says: "The Russians behaved valiantly and, which is rare in warfare, two bodies of infantry marched resolutely upon each other, neither giving way before the other came up." And Napoleon on St. Helena said: "Some Russian battalions showed intrepidity."

which Kutuzov had inspected before Braunau. But the command of the extreme left flank had been entrusted to the colonel of the Pavlograd hussars, in which Rostov was serving. Hence arose a misunderstanding. Both commanding officers were intensely exasperated with one another, and at a time when fighting had been going on a long while on the right flank, and the French had already begun their advance on the left, these two officers were engaged in negotiations, the sole aim of which was the mortification of one another. The regiments—cavalry and infantry alike —were by no means in readiness for the engagement. No one from the common soldier to the general expected a battle; and they were all calmly engaged in peaceful occupations—feeding their horses in the cavalry, gathering wood in the infantry.

"He is my senior in rank, however," said the German colonel of the hussars, growing very red and addressing an adjutant, who had ridden up. "So let him do as he likes. I can't sacrifice my hussars. Bugler! Sound the retreat!"

But things were becoming urgent. The fire of cannon and musketry thundered in unison on the right and in the centre, and the French tunics of Lannes's sharpshooters had already passed over the milldam, and were forming on this side of it hardly out of musket-shot range.

The infantry general walked up to his horse with his quivering strut, and mounting it and drawing himself up very erect and tall, he rode up to the Pavlograd colonel. The two officers met with affable bows and concealed fury in their hearts.

"Again, colonel," the general said, "I cannot leave half my men in the wood. I *beg* you, I *beg* you," he repeated, "to occupy the *position*, and prepare for an attack."

"And I beg you not to meddle in what's not your business," answered the colonel, getting hot. "If you were a cavalry officer . . ."

"I am not a cavalry officer, colonel, but I am a Russian general, and if you are unaware of the fact . . ."

"I am fully aware of it, your excellency," the colonel screamed suddenly, setting his horse in motion and becoming purple in the face. "If you care to come to the front, you will see that this position cannot be held. I don't want to massacre my regiment for your satisfaction."

"You forget yourself, colonel. I am not considering my own satisfaction, and I do not allow such a thing to be said."

Taking the colonel's proposition as a challenge to his courage, the general squared his chest and rode scowling beside him to the front line, as though their whole difference would inevitably be settled there under the enemy's fire. They reached the line, several bullets flew by them, and they stood still without a word. To look at the front line was a useless proceeding, since from the spot where they had been standing before, it was clear that the cavalry could not act, owing to the bushes and the steep and broken character of the ground, and that the French were outflanking the left wing. The general and the colonel glared sternly and significantly at one another, like two cocks preparing for a fight, seeking in vain for a symptom of cowardice. Both stood the test without flinching. Since there was nothing to be said, and neither was willing to give the other grounds for asserting that he was the first to withdraw from under fire, they might have remained a long while standing there, mutually testing each other's pluck, if there had not at that moment been heard in the copse, almost behind them, the snap of musketry and a confused shout of voices. The French were attacking the soldiers gathering wood in the copse. The hussars could not now retreat, nor could the infantry. They were cut off from falling back on the left by the French line. Now, unfavourable as the ground was, they must attack to fight a way through for themselves.

The hussars of the squadron in which Rostov was an ensign had hardly time to mount their horses when they were confronted by the enemy. Again, as on the Enns bridge, there was no one between the squadron and the enemy, and between them lay that terrible border-line of uncertainty and dread, like the line dividing the living from the dead. All the soldiers were conscious of that line, and the question whether they would cross it or not, and how they would cross it, filled them with excitement.

The colonel rode up to the front, made some angry reply to the questions of the officers, and, like a man desperately insisting on his rights, gave some command. No one said anything distinctly, but through the whole squadron there ran a vague rumour of attack. The command to form in order rang out, then there was the clank of sabres being drawn out of their sheaths. But still no one moved. The troops of the left flank, both the infantry and the hussars, felt that their commanders themselves did not know what to do, and the uncertainty of the commanders infected the soldiers.

"Make haste, if only they'd make haste," thought Rostov, feeling that at last the moment had come to taste the joys of the attack, of which he had heard so much from his comrades.

"With God's help, lads," rang out Denisov's voice, "forward, quick, gallop!"

The horses' haunches began moving in the front line. Rook pulled at the reins and set off of himself.

On the right Rostov saw the foremost lines of his own hussars, and still further ahead he could see a dark streak, which he could not distinguish clearly, but assumed to be the enemy. Shots could be heard, but at a distance.

"Quicker!" rang out the word of command, and Rostov felt the drooping of Rook's hindquarters as he broke into a gallop. He felt the joy of the gallop coming, and was more and more lighthearted. He noticed a solitary tree ahead of him. The tree was at first in front of him, in the middle of that border-land that had seemed so terrible. But now they had crossed it and nothing terrible had happened, but he felt more lively and excited every moment. "Ah, won't I slash at him!" thought Rostov, grasping the hilt of his sabre tightly. "Hur . . . r . . . a . . . a!" roared voices.

"Now, let him come on, whoever it may be," thought Rostov, driving the spurs into Rook, and outstripping the rest, he let him go at full gallop. Already the enemy could be seen in front. Suddenly something swept over the squadron like a broad broom. Rostov lifted his sabre, making ready to deal a blow, but at that instant the soldier Nikitenko galloped ahead and left his side, and Rostov felt as though he were in a dream being carried forward with supernatural swiftness and yet remaining at the same spot. An hussar, Bandartchuk, galloped up from behind close upon him and looked angrily at him. Bandartchuk's horse started aside, and he galloped by.

"What's the matter? I'm not moving? I've fallen, I'm killed . . ." Rostov asked and answered himself all in one instant. He was alone in the middle of the field. Instead of the moving horses and the hussars' backs, he saw around him the motionless earth and stubblefield. There was warm blood under him.

"No, I'm wounded, and my horse is killed." Rook tried to get up on his forelegs, but he sank again, crushing his rider's leg under his leg. Blood was flowing from the horse's head. The horse struggled, but could not get up. Rostov tried to get up, and fell down too. His sabretache had caught in the saddle. Where were our men, where were the French, he did not know. All around him there was no one.

Getting his leg free, he stood up. "Which side, where now was that line that had so sharply divided the two armies?" he asked himself, and could not answer. "Hasn't something gone wrong with me? Do such things happen, and what ought one to do in such cases?" he wondered as he was getting up. But at that instant he felt as though something superfluous was hanging on his benumbed left arm. The wrist seemed not to belong to it. He looked at his hand, carefully searching for blood on it. "Come, here are some men," he thought joyfully, seeing some men running towards him. "They will help me!" In front of these men ran a single figure in a strange shako and a blue coat, with a swarthy sunburnt face and a hooked nose. Then came two men, and many more were running up behind. One of them said some strange words, not Russian. Between some similar figures in similar shakoes behind stood a Russian hussar. He was being held by the arms; behind him they were holding his horse too.

"It must be one of ours taken prisoner. . . . Yes. Surely they couldn't take me too? What sort of men are they?" Rostov was still wondering, unable to believe his own eyes. "Can they be the French?" He gazed at the approaching French, and although only a few seconds before he had been longing to get at these Frenchmen and to cut them down, their being so near seemed to him now so awful that he could not believe his eyes. "Who are they? What are they running for? Can it be to me? Can they be running to me? And what for? To kill me? *Me,* whom every one's so fond of?" He recalled his mother's love, the love of his family and his friends, and the enemy's intention of killing him seemed impossible. "But they may even kill me." For more than ten seconds he stood, not moving from the spot, nor grasping his position. The foremost Frenchman with the hook nose was getting so near that he could see the expression of his face. And the excited, alien countenance of the man, who was running so lightly and breathlessly towards him, with his bayonet lowered, terrified Rostov. He snatched up his pistol, and instead of firing with it, flung it at the Frenchman and ran to the bushes with all his might. Not with the feeling of doubt and conflict with which he had moved at the Enns bridge, did he now run, but with the feeling of a hare fleeing from the dogs. One unmixed feeling of fear for his young, happy life took possession of his whole being. Leaping rapidly over the hedges with the same impetuosity with which he used to run when he played games, he flew over the field, now and then turning his pale, good-natured, youthful face, and a chill of horror ran down his spine. "No, better not to look," he thought, but as he got near to the bushes he looked round once more. The French had given it up, and just at the moment when he looked round the foremost man was just dropping from a run into a walk, and turning round to shout something loudly to a comrade behind. Rostov stopped. "There's some mistake," he thought; "it can't be that they meant to kill me." And meanwhile his left arm was as heavy as if a hundred pound weight were hanging on it. He could run no further. The Frenchman stopped too and took aim. Rostov frowned and ducked. One bullet and then another flew hissing by him; he took his left hand in his right, and with a last effort ran as far as the bushes. In the bushes there were Russian sharpshooters.

XX

THE infantry, who had been caught unawares in the copse, had run away, and the different companies all confused together had retreated in disorderly crowds. One soldier in a panic had uttered those words— terrible in war and meaningless: "Cut off!" and those words had infected the whole mass with panic.

"Outflanked! Cut off! Lost!" they shouted as they ran.

When their general heard the firing and the shouts in the rear he had grasped at the instant that something awful was happening to his regiment; and the thought that he, an exemplary officer, who had served so many years without ever having been guilty of the slightest shortcoming, might be held responsible by his superiors for negligence or lack of discipline, so affected him that, instantly oblivious of the insubordinate cavalry colonel and his dignity as a general, utterly oblivious even of danger and of the instinct of self-preservation, he clutched at the crupper of his saddle, and spurring his horse, galloped off to the regiment under a perfect hail of bullets that luckily missed him. He was possessed by the one desire to find out what was wrong, and to help and correct the mistake whatever it might be, if it were a mistake on his part, so that after twenty-two years of exemplary service, without incurring a reprimand for anything, he might avoid being responsible for this blunder.

Galloping successfully between the French forces, he reached the field behind the copse across which our men were running downhill, not heeding the word of command. That moment had come of moral vacillation which decides the fate of battles. Would these disorderly crowds of soldiers hear the voice of their commander, or, looking back at him, run on further? In spite of the despairing yell of the commander, who had once been so awe-inspiring to his soldiers, in spite of his infuriated, purple face, distorted out of all likeness to itself, in spite of his brandished sword, the soldiers still ran and talked together, shooting into the air and not listening to the word of command. The moral balance which decides the fate of battle was unmistakably falling on the side of panic.

The general was choked with screaming and gunpowder-smoke, and he stood still in despair. All seemed lost; but at that moment the French, who had been advancing against our men, suddenly, for no apparent reason, ran back, vanished from the edge of the copse, and Russian sharpshooters appeared in the copse. This was Timohin's division, the only one that had retained its good order in the copse, and hiding in ambush in the ditch behind the copse, had suddenly attacked the French. Timohin had rushed with such a desperate yell upon the French, and with such desperate and drunken energy had he dashed at the enemy with only a sword in his hand, that the French flung down their weapons and fled without pausing to recover themselves. Dolohov, running beside Timohin, killed one French soldier at close quarters, and was the first to seize by the collar an officer who surrendered. The fleeing Russians came back; the battalions were brought together; and the French, who had been on the point of splitting the forces of the left flank into two parts, were for the moment held in check. The reserves had time to join the main forces, and the runaways were stopped. The general stood with Major Ekonomov at the bridge, watching the retreating companies go by, when a soldier ran up to him, caught hold of his stirrup, and almost clung on to it. The soldier was wearing a coat of blue fine cloth, he had no knapsack nor shako, his head was bound up, and across his shoulders was slung a French cartridge case. In his hand he held an officer's sword. The soldier was pale, his blue eyes looked impudently into the general's face, but his mouth was smiling. Although the general was engaged in giving instructions to Major Ekonomov, he could not help noticing this soldier.

"Your excellency, here are two trophies," said Dolohov, pointing to the French sword and cartridge case. "An officer was taken prisoner by me. I stopped the company." Dolohov breathed hard from weariness; he spoke in jerks. "The whole company can bear me witness. I beg you to remember me, your excellency!"

"Very good, very good," said the general, and he turned to Major Ekonomov. But Dolohov did not leave him; he undid the bandage, and showed the blood congealed on his head.

"A bayonet wound; I kept my place in the front. Remember me, your excellency."

Tushin's battery had been forgotten, and it was only at the very end of the action that Prince Bagration, still hearing the cannonade in the centre, sent the staff-officer on duty and then Prince Andrey to command the battery to retire as quickly as possible. The force which had been stationed near Tushin's cannons to protect them had by somebody's orders retreated in the middle of the battle. But the battery still kept up its fire, and was not taken by the French simply because the enemy could not conceive of the reckless daring of firing from four cannons that were quite unprotected. The French supposed, on the contrary, judging from the energetic action of the battery, that the chief forces of the Russians were concentrated here in the centre, and twice attempted to attack that point, and both times were driven back by the grapeshot fired on them from the four cannons which stood in solitude on the heights. Shortly after Prince Bagration's departure, Tushin had succeeded in setting fire to Schöngraben.

"Look, what a fuss they're in! It's flaming! What a smoke! Smartly done! First-rate! The smoke! the smoke!" cried the gunners, their spirits reviving.

All the guns were aimed without instructions in the direction of the conflagration. The soldiers, as though they were urging each other on, shouted at every volley: "Bravo! That's something like now! Go it! . . . First-rate!" The fire, fanned by the wind, soon spread. The French columns, who had marched out beyond the village, went back, but as though in revenge for this mischance, the enemy stationed ten cannons a little to the right of the village, and began firing from them on Tushin.

In their childlike glee at the conflagration of the village, and the excitement of their successful firing on the French, our artillerymen only noticed this battery when two cannon-balls and after them four more fell among their cannons, and one knocked over two horses and another tore off the foot of a gunner. Their spirits, however, once raised, did not flag; their excitement simply found another direction. The horses were replaced by others from the ammunition carriage; the wounded were removed, and the four cannons were turned facing the ten of the enemy's battery. The other officer, Tushin's comrade, was killed at the beginning of the action, and after an hour's time, of the forty gunners of the battery, seventeen were disabled, but they were still as merry and as eager as ever. Twice they noticed the French appearing below close to them, and they sent volleys of grapeshot at them.

The little man with his weak, clumsy movements, was continually asking his orderly *for just one more pipe for that stroke,* as he said, and scattering sparks from it, he kept running out in front and looking from under his little hand at the French.

"Smash away, lads!" he was continually saying, and he clutched at the cannon wheels himself and unscrewed the screws. In the smoke, deafened by the incessant booming of the cannons that made him shudder every time one was fired, Tushin ran from one cannon to the other, his short pipe never out of his mouth. At one moment he was taking aim, then reckoning the charges, then arranging for the changing and unharnessing of the killed and wounded horses, and all the time shouting in his weak, shrill, hesitating voice. His face grew more and more eager. Only when men were killed and wounded he knitted his brows, and turning away from the dead man, shouted angrily to the men, slow, as they always are, to pick up a wounded man or a dead body. The soldiers, for the most part fine, handsome fellows (a couple of heads taller than their officer and twice as broad in the chest, as they mostly are in the artillery), all looked to their commanding officer like children in a difficult position, and the expression they found on his face was invariably reflected at once on their own.

Owing to the fearful uproar and noise and the necessity of attention and activity, Tushin experienced not the slightest unpleasant sensation of fear; and the idea that he might be killed or badly wounded never entered his head. On the contrary, he felt more and more lively. It seemed to him that the moment in which he had first seen the enemy and had fired the first shot was long, long ago, yesterday perhaps, and that the spot of earth on which he stood was a place long familiar to him, in which he was quite at home. Although he thought of everything, considered everything, did everything the very best officer could have done in his position, he was in a state of mind akin to the delirium of fever or the intoxication of a drunken man.

The deafening sound of his own guns on all sides, the hiss and thud of the enemy's shells, the sight of the perspiring, flushed gunners hurrying about the cannons, the sight of the blood of men and horses, and of the puffs of smoke from the enemy on the opposite side (always followed by a cannon-ball that flew across and hit the earth, a man, a horse, or a cannon)—all these images made up for him a fantastic world of his own, in which he found enjoyment at the moment. The enemy's cannons in his fancy were not cannons, but pipes from which an invisible smoker blew puffs of smoke at intervals.

"There he's puffing away again," Tushin murmured to himself as a cloud of smoke rolled downhill, and was borne off by the wind in a wreath to the left. "Now, your ball—throw it back."

"What is it, your honour?" asked a gunner who stood near him, and heard him muttering something.

"Nothing, a grenade . . ." he answered. "Now for it, our Matvyevna," he said to himself. Matvyevna was the name his fancy gave to the big cannon, cast in an old-fashioned mould, that stood at the end. The French seemed to be ants swarming about their cannons. The handsome, drunken soldier, number one gunner of the second cannon, was in his dreamworld "uncle"; Tushin looked at him more often than at any of the rest, and took delight in every gesture of the man. The sound—dying away, then quickening again—of the musketry fire below the hill seemed to him like the heaving of some creature's breathing. He listened to the ebb and flow of these sounds.

"Ah, she's taking another breath again," he was saying to himself. He himself figured in his imagination as a mighty man of immense stature, who was flinging cannon balls at the French with both hands.

"Come, Matvyevna, old lady, stick by us!" he was saying, moving back from the cannon, when a strange, unfamiliar voice called over his head. "Captain Tushin! Captain!"

Tushin looked round in dismay. It was the same staff-officer who had turned him out of the booth at Grunte. He was shouting to him in a breathless voice:

"I say, are you mad? You've been commanded twice to retreat, and you . . ."

"Now, what are they pitching into me for?" . . . Tushin wondered, looking in alarm at the superior officer.

"I . . . don't . . ." he began, putting two fingers to the peak of his cap. "I . . ."

But the staff-officer did not say all he had meant to. A cannon ball flying near him made him duck down on his horse. He paused, and was just going to say something more, when another ball stopped him. He turned his horse's head and galloped away.

"Retreat! All to retreat!" he shouted from a distance.

The soldiers laughed. A minute later an adjutant arrived with the same message. This was Prince Andrey. The first thing he saw, on reaching the place where Tushin's cannons were stationed, was an unharnessed horse with a broken leg, which was neighing beside the harnessed horses. The blood was flowing in a perfect stream from its leg. Among the platforms lay several dead men. One cannon ball after another flew over him as he rode up, and he felt a nervous shudder running down his spine. But the very idea that he was afraid was enough to rouse him again. "I can't be frightened," he thought, and he deliberately dismounted from his horse between the cannons. He gave his message, but he did not leave the battery. He decided to stay and assist in removing the cannons from the position and getting them away. Stepping over the corpses, under the fearful fire from the French, he helped Tushin in getting the cannons ready.

"The officer that came just now ran off quicker than he came," said a gunner to Prince Andrey, "not like your honour."

Prince Andrey had no conversation with Tushin. They were both so busy that they hardly seemed to see each other. When they had got the two out of the four cannons that were uninjured on to the platforms and were moving downhill (one cannon that had been smashed and a howitzer were left behind), Prince Andrey went up to Tushin.

"Well, good-bye till we meet again," said Prince Andrey, holding out his hand to Tushin.

"Good-bye, my dear fellow," said Tushin, "dear soul! good-bye, my dear fellow," he said with tears, which for some unknown reason started suddenly into his eyes.

XXI

THE wind had sunk, black storm-clouds hung low over the battlefield, melting on the horizon into the clouds of smoke from the powder. Dark-

ness had come, and the glow of conflagrations showed all the more distinctly in two places. The cannonade had grown feebler, but the snapping of musketry-fire in the rear and on the right was heard nearer and
more often. As soon as Tushin with his cannons, continually driving
round the wounded and coming upon them, had got out of fire and were
descending the ravine, he was met by the staff, among whom was the
staff-officer and Zherkov, who had twice been sent to Tushin's battery,
but had not once reached it. They all vied with one another in giving him
orders, telling him how and where to go, finding fault and making criticisms. Tushin gave no orders, and in silence, afraid to speak because at
every word he felt, he could not have said why, ready to burst into tears,
he rode behind on his artillery nag. Though orders were given to abandon the wounded, many of them dragged themselves after the troops and
begged for a seat on the cannons. The jaunty infantry-officer—the one
who had run out of Tushin's shanty just before the battle—was laid on
Matvyevna's carriage with a bullet in his stomach. At the bottom of the
hill a pale ensign of hussars, holding one arm in the other hand, came up
to Tushin and begged for a seat.

"Captain, for God's sake. I've hurt my arm," he said timidly. "For
God's sake. I can't walk. For God's sake!" It was evident that this was
not the first time the ensign had asked for a lift, and that he had been
everywhere refused. He asked in a hesitating and piteous voice, "Tell
them to let me get on, for God's sake!"

"Let him get on, let him get on," said Tushin. "Put a coat under him,
you, uncle." He turned to his favourite soldier. "But where's the
wounded officer?"

"We took him off; he was dead," answered some one.

"Help him on. Sit down, my dear fellow, sit down. Lay the coat there,
Antonov."

The ensign was Rostov. He was holding one hand in the other. He was
pale and his lower jaw was trembling as though in a fever. They put him
on Matvyevna, the cannon from which they had just removed the dead
officer. There was blood on the coat that was laid under him, and Rostov's riding-breeches and arm were smeared with it.

"What, are you wounded, my dear?" said Tushin, going up to the
cannon on which Rostov was sitting.

"No; it's a sprain."

"How is it there's blood on the frame?" asked Tushin.

"That was the officer, your honour, stained it," answered an artilleryman, wiping the blood off with the sleeve of his coat, and as it were
apologising for the dirty state of the cannon.

With difficulty, aided by the infantry, they dragged the cannon uphill, and halted on reaching the village of Guntersdorf. It was by now so
dark that one could not distinguish the soldiers' uniforms ten paces
away, and the firing had begun to subside. All of a sudden there came
the sound of firing and shouts again close by on the right side. The flash
of the shots could be seen in the darkness. This was the last attack of the
French. It was met by the soldiers in ambush in the houses of the village.

All rushed out of the village again, but Tushin's cannons could not move, and the artillerymen, Tushin, and the ensign looked at on another in anticipation of their fate. The firing on both sides began to subside, and some soldiers in lively conversation streamed out of a side street.

"Not hurt, Petrov?" inquired one.

"We gave it them hot, lads. They won't meddle with us now," another was saying.

"One couldn't see a thing. Didn't they give it to their own men! No seeing for the darkness, mates. Isn't there something to drink?"

The French had been repulsed for the last time. And again, in the complete darkness, Tushin's cannons moved forward, surrounded by the infantry, who kept up a hum of talk.

In the darkness they flowed on like an unseen, gloomy river always in the same direction, with a buzz of whisper and talk and the thud of hoofs and rumble of wheels. Above all other sounds, in the confused uproar, rose the moans and cries of the wounded, more distinct than anything in the darkness of the night. Their moans seemed to fill all the darkness surrounding the troops. Their moans and the darkness seemed to melt into one. A little later a thrill of emotion passed over the moving crowd. Some one followed by a suite had ridden by on a white horse, and had said something as he passed.

"What did he say? Where we are going now? to halt, eh? Thanked us, what?" eager questions were heard on all sides, and the whole moving mass began to press back on itself (the foremost, it seemed, had halted), and a rumour passed through that the order had been given to halt. All halted in the muddy road, just where they were.

Fires were lighted and the talk became more audible. Captain Tushin, after giving instructions to his battery, sent some of his soldiers to look for an ambulance or a doctor for the ensign, and sat down by the fire his soldiers had lighted by the roadside. Rostov too dragged himself to the fire. His whole body was trembling with fever from the pain, the cold, and the damp. He was dreadfully sleepy, but he could not go to sleep for the agonising pain in his arm, which ached and would not be easy in any position. He closed his eyes, then opened them to stare at the fire, which seemed to him dazzling red, and then at the stooping, feeble figure of Tushin, squatting in Turkish fashion near him. The big, kindly, and shrewd eyes of Tushin were fixed upon him with sympathy and commiseration. He saw that Tushin wished with all his soul to help him, but could do nothing for him.

On all sides they heard the footsteps and the chatter of the infantry going and coming and settling themselves round them. The sounds of voices, of steps, and of horses' hoofs tramping in the mud, the crackling firewood far and near, all melted into one fluctuating roar of sound. It was not now as before an unseen river flowing in the darkness, but a gloomy sea subsiding and still agitated after a storm. Rostov gazed vacantly and listened to what was passing before him and around him. An infantry soldier came up to the fire, squatted on his heels, held his hands to the fire, and turned his face.

"You don't mind, your honour?" he said, looking inquiringly at Tushin. "Here I've got lost from my company, your honour; I don't know myself where I am. It's dreadful!"

With the soldier an infantry officer approached the fire with a bandaged face. He asked Tushin to have the cannon moved a very little, so as to let a store waggon pass by. After the officer two soldiers ran up to the fire. They were swearing desperately and fighting, trying to pull a boot from one another.

"No fear! you picked it up! that's smart!" one shouted in a husky voice.

Then a thin, pale soldier approached, his neck bandaged with a blood-stained rag. With a voice of exasperation he asked the artillerymen for water.

"Why, is one to die like a dog?" he said.

Tushin told them to give him water. Next a good-humoured soldier ran up, to beg for some red-hot embers for the infantry.

"Some of your fire for the infantry! Glad to halt, lads. Thanks for the loan of the firing; we'll pay it back with interest," he said, carrying some glowing firebrands away into the darkness.

Next four soldiers passed by, carrying something heavy in an over-coat. One of them stumbled.

"Ay, the devils, they've left firewood in the road," grumbled one.

"He's dead; why carry him?" said one of them.

"Come on, you!" And they vanished into the darkness with their burden.

"Does it ache, eh?" Tushin asked Rostov in a whisper.

"Yes, it does ache."

"Your honour's sent for to the general. Here in a cottage he is," said a gunner, coming up to Tushin.

"In a minute, my dear." Tushin got up and walked away from the fire, buttoning up his coat and setting himself straight.

In a cottage that had been prepared for him not far from the artillery-men's fire, Prince Bagration was sitting at dinner, talking with several commanding officers, who had gathered about him. The little old colonel with the half-shut eyes was there, greedily gnawing at a mutton-bone, and the general of twenty-two years' irreproachable service, flushed with a glass of vodka and his dinner, and the staff-officer with the signet ring, and Zherkov, stealing uneasy glances at every one, and Prince Andrey, pale with set lips and feverishly glittering eyes.

In the corner of the cottage room stood a French flag, that had been captured, and the auditor with the naïve countenance was feeling the stuff of which the flag was made, and shaking his head with a puzzled air, possibly because looking at the flag really interested him, or possibly because he did not enjoy the sight of the dinner, as he was hungry and no place had been laid for him. In the next cottage there was the French colonel, who had been taken prisoner by the dragoons. Our officers were flocking in to look at him. Prince Bagration thanked the several commanding officers, and inquired into details of the battle and of the losses.

The general, whose regiment had been inspected at Braunau, submitted to the prince that as soon as the engagement began, he had fallen back from the copse, mustered the men who were cutting wood, and letting them pass by him, had made a bayonet charge with two battalions and repulsed the French.

"As soon as I saw, your excellency, that the first battalion was thrown into confusion, I stood in the road and thought, 'I'll let them get through and then open fire on them'; and that's what I did."

The general had so longed to do this, he had so regretted not having succeeded in doing it, that it seemed to him now that this was just what had happened. Indeed might it not actually have been so? Who could make out in such confusion what did and what did not happen?

"And by the way I ought to note, your excellency," he continued, recalling Dolohov's conversation with Kutuzov and his own late interview with the degraded officer, "that the private Dolohov, degraded to the ranks, took a French officer prisoner before my eyes and particularly distinguished himself."

"I saw here, your excellency, the attack of the Pavlograd hussars," Zherkov put in, looking uneasily about him. He had not seen the hussars at all that day, but had only heard about them from an infantry officer. "They broke up two squares, your excellency."

When Zherkov began to speak, several officers smiled, as they always did, expecting a joke from him. But as they perceived that what he was saying all redounded to the glory of our arms and of the day, they assumed a serious expression, although many were very well aware that what Zherkov was saying was a lie utterly without foundation. Prince Bagration turned to the old colonel.

"I thank you all, gentlemen; all branches of the service behaved heroically—infantry, cavalry, and artillery. How did two cannons come to be abandoned in the centre?" he inquired, looking about for some one. (Prince Bagration did not ask about the cannons of the left flank; he knew that all of them had been abandoned at the very beginning of the action.) "I think it was you I sent," he added, addressing the staff-officer.

"One had been disabled," answered the staff-officer, "but the other, I can't explain; I was there all the while myself, giving instructions, and I had scarcely left there. . . . It was pretty hot, it's true," he added modestly.

Some one said that Captain Tushin was close by here in the village, and that he had already been sent for.

"Oh, but you went there," said Prince Bagration, addressing Prince Andrey.

"To be sure, we rode there almost together," said the staff-officer, smiling affably to Bolkonsky.

"I had not the pleasure of seeing you," said Prince Andrey, coldly and abruptly. Every one was silent.

Tushin appeared in the doorway, timidly edging in behind the generals' backs. Making his way round the generals in the crowded hut, embarrassed as he always was before his superior officers, Tushin did not see the flag-staff and tumbled over it. Several of the officers laughed.

"How was it a cannon was abandoned?" asked Bagration, frowning, not so much at the captain as at the laughing officers, among whom Zherkov's laugh was the loudest. Only now in the presence of the angry-looking commander, Tushin conceived in all its awfulness the crime and disgrace of his being still alive when he had lost two cannons. He had been so excited that till that instant he had not had time to think of that. The officers' laughter had bewildered him still more. He stood before Bagration, his lower jaw quivering, and could scarcely articulate: "I don't know . . . your excellency . . . I hadn't the men, your excellency."

"You could have got them from the battalions that were covering your position!" That there were no battalions there was what Tushin did not say, though it was the fact. He was afraid of getting another officer into trouble by saying that, and without uttering a word he gazed straight into Bagration's face, as a confused schoolboy gazes at the face of an examiner.

The silence was rather a lengthy one. Prince Bagration, though he had no wish to be severe, apparently found nothing to say; the others did not venture to intervene. Prince Andrey was looking from under his brows at Tushin and his fingers moved nervously.

"Your excellency," Prince Andrey broke the silence with his abrupt voice, "you sent me to Captain Tushin's battery. I went there and found two-thirds of the men and horses killed, two cannons disabled and no forces near to defend them."

Prince Bagration and Tushin looked now with equal intensity at Bolkonsky, as he went on speaking with suppressed emotion.

"And if your excellency will permit me to express my opinion," he went on, "we owe the success of the day more to the action of that battery and the heroic steadiness of Captain Tushin and his men than to anything else," said Prince Andrey, and he got up at once and walked away from the table, without waiting for a reply.

Prince Bagration looked at Tushin and, apparently loath to express his disbelief in Bolkonsky's off-handed judgment, yet unable to put complete faith in it, he bent his head and said to Tushin that he could go. Prince Andrey walked out after him.

"Thanks, my dear fellow, you got me out of a scrape," Tushin said to him.

Prince Andrey looked at Tushin, and walked away without uttering a word. Prince Andrey felt bitter and melancholy. It was all so strange, so unlike what he had been hoping for.

"Who are they? Why are they here? What do they want? And when will it all end?" thought Rostov, looking at the shadowy figures that kept flitting before his eyes. The pain in his arm became even more agonising. He was heavy with sleep, crimson circles danced before his eyes, and the impression of these voices and these faces and the sense of his loneliness all blended with the misery of the pain. It was they, these soldiers, wounded and unhurt alike, it was they crushing and weighing upon him, and twisting his veins and burning the flesh in his sprained arm and shoulder. To get rid of them he closed his eyes.

He dozed off for a minute, but in that brief interval he dreamed of innumerable things. He saw his mother and her large, white hand; he saw Sonya's thin shoulders, Natasha's eyes and her laugh, and Denisov with his voice and his whiskers, and Telyanin, and all the affair with Telyanin and Bogdanitch. All that affair was inextricably mixed up with this soldier with the harsh voice, and that affair and this soldier here were so agonisingly, so ruthlessly pulling, crushing, and twisting his arm always in the same direction. He was trying to get away from them, but they would not let go of his shoulder for a second. It would not ache, it would be all right if they wouldn't drag at it; but there was no getting rid of them.

He opened his eyes and looked upwards. The black pall of darkness hung only a few feet above the light of the fire. In the light fluttered tiny flakes of falling snow. Tushin had not returned, the doctor had not come. He was alone, only a soldier was sitting now naked on the other side of the fire, warming his thin, yellow body.

"Nobody cares for me!" thought Rostov. "No one to help me, no one to feel sorry for me. And I too was once at home, and strong, and happy and loved," he sighed, and with the sigh unconsciously he moaned.

"In pain, eh?" asked the soldier, shaking his shirt out before the fire, and without waiting for an answer, he added huskily: "Ah, what a lot of fellows done for to-day—awful!"

Rostov did not hear the soldier. He gazed at the snowflakes whirling over the fire and thought of the Russian winter with his warm, brightly lighted home, his cosy fur cloak, his swift sledge, his good health, and all the love and tenderness of his family. "And what did I come here for!" he wondered.

On the next day, the French did not renew the attack and the remnant of Bagration's detachment joined Kutuzov's army.

PART THREE

I

PRINCE VASSILY used not to think over his plans. Still less did he think of doing harm to others for the sake of his own interest. He was simply a man of the world, who had been successful in the world, and had formed a habit of being so. Various plans and calculations were continually forming in his mind, arising from circumstances and the persons he met, but he never deliberately considered them, though they constituted the whole interest of his life. Of such plans and calculations he had not one or two, but dozens in train at once, some of them only beginning to occur to him, others attaining their aim, others again coming to nothing. He never said to himself, for instance: "That man is now in power, I must secure his friendship and confidence, and through him obtain a grant from the Single-Assistance Fund"; nor, "Now Pierre is a wealthy man, I must entice him to marry my daughter and borrow the forty thousand I need." But the man in power met him, and at the instant his instinct told him that that man might be of use, and Prince Vassily made friends with him, and at the first opportunity by instinct, without previous consideration, flattered him, became intimate with him, and told him of what he wanted.

Pierre was ready at hand in Moscow, and Prince Vassily secured an appointment as gentleman of the bedchamber for him, a position at that time reckoned equal in status to that of a councillor of state, and insisted on the young man's travelling with him to Petersburg, and staying at his house. Without apparent design, but yet with unhesitating conviction that it was the right thing, Prince Vassily did everything to ensure Pierre's marrying his daughter. If Prince Vassily had definitely reflected upon his plans beforehand, he could not have been so natural in his behaviour and so straightforward and familiar in his relations with every one, of higher and of lower rank than himself. Something drew him infallibly towards men richer or more powerful than himself, and he was endowed with a rare instinct for hitting on precisely the moment when he should and could make use of such persons.

Pierre, on unexpectedly becoming rich and Count Bezuhov, after his lonely and careless manner of life, felt so surrounded, so occupied, that he never succeeded in being by himself except in his bed. He had to sign papers, to present himself at legal institutions, of the significance of which he had no definite idea, to make some inquiry of his chief steward, to visit his estate near Moscow, and to receive a great number of persons, who previously had not cared to be aware of his existence, but now would have been hurt and offended if he had not chosen to see them. All these various people, business men, relations, acquaintances, were all equally friendly and well disposed towards the young heir. They were all obviously and unhesitatingly convinced of Pierre's noble qualities. He was continually hearing phrases, such as, "With your exceptionally kindly disposition"; or, "Considering your excellent heart"; or, "You are so pure-minded yourself, count . . ." or, "If he were as clever as you," and so on, so that he was beginning genuinely to believe in his own exceptional goodness and his own exceptional intelligence, the more so, as at the bottom of his heart it had always seemed to him that he really was very good-natured and very intelligent. Even people, who had before been spiteful and openly hostile to him, became tender and affectionate. The hitherto ill-tempered, eldest princess, with the long waist and the hair plastered down like a doll, had gone into Pierre's room after the funeral. Dropping her eyes and repeatedly turning crimson, she said that she very much regretted the misunderstanding that had arisen between them, and that now she felt she had no right to ask him for anything except permission, after the blow that had befallen her, to remain for a few weeks longer in the house which she was so fond of, and in which she had made such sacrifices. She could not control herself, and wept at these words. Touched at seeing the statue-like princess so changed, Pierre took her by the hand and begged her pardon, though he could not have said what for. From that day the princess began knitting a striped scarf for Pierre, and was completely changed towards him.

"Do this for my sake, my dear boy; she had to put up with a great deal from the deceased, any way," Prince Vassily said to him, giving him some deed to sign for the princess's benefit. Prince Vassily reflected that this note of hand for thirty thousand was a sop worth throwing to the poor princess, that it might not occur to her to gossip about Prince Vassily's part in the action taken with the inlaid portfolio. Pierre signed the note, and from that time the princess became even more amiable. The younger sisters became as affectionate too, especially the youngest one, the pretty one with the mole, who often disconcerted Pierre with her smiles and her confusion at the sight of him.

To Pierre it seemed so natural that every one should be fond of him, it would have seemed to him so unnatural if any one had not liked him, that he could not help believing in the sincerity of the people surrounding him. Besides, he had no time to doubt their sincerity or insincerity. He never had a moment of leisure, and felt in a continual state of mild and agreeable intoxication. He felt as though he were the centre of some important public function, felt that something was continually being expected of him; that if he did this and that, all would be well, and he did what was expected of him, but still that happy result loomed in the future.

In these early days Prince Vassily, more than all the rest, took control of Pierre's affairs, and of Pierre himself. On the death of Count Bezuhov he did not let Pierre slip out of his hands. Prince Vassily had the air of a man weighed down by affairs, weary, worried, but from sympathetic feeling, unable in the last resort to abandon this helpless lad, the son, after all, of his friend, and the heir to such an immense fortune, to leave him to his fate to become a prey to plotting knaves. During the few days he had stayed on in Moscow after Count Bezuhov's death, he had invited Pierre to him, or had himself gone to see Pierre, and had dictated to him what he was to do in a tone of weariness and certainty which seemed to be always saying: "You know that I am overwhelmed with business and that it is out of pure charity that I concern myself with you, and moreover you know very well that what I propose to you is the only feasible thing."

"Well, my dear boy, to-morrow we are off at last," he said one day, closing his eyes, drumming his fingers on his elbow, and speaking as though the matter had long ago been settled between them, and could not be settled in any other way.

"To-morrow we set off; I'll give you a place in my coach. I'm very glad. Here all our important business is settled. And I ought to have been back long ago. Here, I have received this from the chancellor. I petitioned him in your favour, and you are put on the diplomatic corps, and created a gentleman of the bedchamber. Now a diplomatic career lies open to you."

Notwithstanding the effect produced on him by the tone of weariness and certainty with which these words were uttered, Pierre, who had so long been pondering over his future career, tried to protest. But Prince Vassily broke in on his protest in droning, bass tones, that precluded all possibility of interrupting the flow of his words; it was the resource he fell back upon when extreme measures of persuasion were needed.

"But, my dear boy, I have done it for my own sake, for my conscience' sake, and there is no need to thank me. No one has ever complained yet of being too much loved; and then you are free, you can give it all up to-morrow. You'll see for yourself in Petersburg. And it is high time you were getting away from these terrible associations." Prince Vassily sighed. "So that's all settled, my dear fellow. And let my valet go in your coach. Ah, yes, I was almost forgetting," Prince Vassily added. "You know, my dear boy, I had a little account to settle with your father, so as I have received something from the Ryazan estate, I'll keep that; you don't want it. We'll go into accounts later."

What Prince Vassily called "something from the Ryazan estate" was several thousands of roubles paid in lieu of service by the peasants, and this sum he kept for himself.

In Petersburg, Pierre was surrounded by the same atmosphere of affection and tenderness as in Moscow. He could not decline the post, or rather the title (for he did nothing) that Prince Vassily had obtained for him, and acquaintances, invitations, and social duties were so numerous that Pierre was even more than in Moscow conscious of the feeling of stupefaction, hurry and continued expectation of some future good which was always coming and was never realised.

Of his old circle of bachelor acquaintances there were not many left in Petersburg. The Guards were on active service, Dolohov had been degraded to the ranks; Anatole had gone into the army and was somewhere in the provinces; Prince Andrey was abroad; and so Pierre had not the opportunity of spending his nights in the way he had so loved spending them before, nor could he open his heart in intimate talk with the friend who was older than himself and a man he respected. All his time was spent at dinners and balls, or at Prince Vassily's in the society of the fat princess, his wife, and the beauty, his daughter Ellen.

Like every one else, Anna Pavlovna Scherer showed Pierre the change that had taken place in the attitude of society towards him.

In former days, Pierre had always felt in Anna Pavlovna's presence that what he was saying was unsuitable, tactless, not the right thing; that the phrases, which seemed to him clever as he formed them in his mind, became somehow stupid as soon as he uttered them aloud, and that, on the contrary, Ippolit's most pointless remarks had the effect of being clever and charming. Now everything he said was always "delightful." Even if Anna Pavlovna did not say so, he saw she was longing to say so, and only refraining from doing so from regard for his modesty.

At the beginning of the winter, in the year 1805, Pierre received one of Anna Pavlovna's customary pink notes of invitation, in which the words occurred: "You will find the fair Hélène at my house, whom one never gets tired of seeing."

On reading that passage, Pierre felt for the first time that there was being formed between himself and Ellen some sort of tie, recognised by other people, and this idea at once alarmed him, as though an obligation were being laid upon him which he could not fulfil, and pleased him as an amusing supposition.

Anna Pavlovna's evening party was like her first one, only the novel attraction which she had provided for her guests was not on this occasion Mortemart, but a diplomat, who had just arrived from Berlin, bringing the latest details of the Emperor Alexander's stay at Potsdam, and of the inviolable alliance the two exalted friends had sworn together, to maintain the true cause against the enemy of the human race. Pierre was welcomed by Anna Pavlovna with a shade of melancholy, bearing unmistakable reference to the recent loss sustained by the young man in the death of Count Bezuhov (every one felt bound to be continually assuring Pierre that he was greatly afflicted at the death of his father, whom he had hardly known). Her melancholy was of precisely the same kind as that more exalted melancholy she always displayed at any allusion to Her Most August Majesty the Empress Marya Fyodorovna. Pierre felt flattered by it. Anna Pavlovna had arranged the groups in her drawing-room with her usual skill. The larger group, in which were Prince Vassily and some generals, had the benefit of the diplomat. Another group gathered about the tea-table. Pierre would have liked to join the first group, but Anna Pavlovna, who was in the nervous excitement of a general on the battlefield, that mental condition in which numbers of brilliant new ideas occur to one that one has hardly time to put into execution—Anna Pavlovna, on seeing Pierre, detained him with a finger on his coat sleeve: "Wait, I have designs on you for this evening."

She looked round at Ellen and smiled at her.

"My dear Hélène, you must show charity to my poor aunt, who has an adoration for you. Go and keep her company for ten minutes. And that you may not find it too tiresome, here's our dear count, who certainly won't refuse to follow you."

The beauty moved away towards the old aunt; but Anna Pavlovna still detained Pierre at her side, with the air of having still some last and essential arrangement to make with him.

"She is exquisite, isn't she?" she said to Pierre, indicating the majestic beauty swimming away from them. "And how she carries herself! For such a young girl, what tact, what a finished perfection of manner. It comes from the heart. Happy will be the man who wins her. The most unworldly of men would take a brilliant place in society as her husband. That's true, isn't it? I only wanted to know your opinion," and Anna Pavlovna let Pierre go.

Pierre was perfectly sincere in giving an affirmative answer to her question about Ellen's perfection of manner. If ever he thought of Ellen, it was either of her beauty that he thought, or of her extraordinary capacity for serene, dignified silence in society.

The old aunt received the two young people in her corner, but appeared anxious to conceal her adoration of Ellen, and rather to show her fear of Anna Pavlovna. She glanced at her niece, as though to inquire what she was to do with them. Anna Pavlovna again laid a finger on Pierre's sleeve and said: "I hope you will never say in future that people are bored at my house," and glanced at Ellen. Ellen smiled with an air, which seemed to say that she did not admit the possibility of any one's seeing her without being enchanted. The old aunt coughed, swallowed the phlegm, and said in French that she was very glad to see Ellen; then she addressed Pierre with the same greeting and the same grimace. In the middle of a halting and tedious conversation, Ellen looked round at Pierre and smiled at him with the bright, beautiful smile with which she smiled at every one. Pierre was so used to this smile, it meant so little to him, that he did not even notice it. The aunt was speaking at that moment of a collection of snuff-boxes belonging to Pierre's father, Count Bezuhov, and she showed them her snuff-box. Princess Ellen asked to look at the portrait of the aunt's husband, which was on the snuff-box.

"It's probably the work of Vines," said Pierre, mentioning a celebrated miniature painter. He bent over the table to take the snuff-box, listening all the while to the conversation going on in the larger group. He got up to move towards it, but the aunt handed him the snuff-box, passing it across Ellen, behind her back. Ellen bent forward to make room, and looked round smiling. She was, as always in the evening, wearing a dress cut in the fashion of the day, very low in the neck both in front and behind. Her bust, which had always to Pierre looked like marble, was so close to his short-sighted eyes that he could discern all the living charm of her neck and shoulders, and so near his lips that he need scarcely have stooped to kiss it. He felt the warmth of her body, the fragrance of scent, and heard the creaking of her corset as she moved. He saw not her marble beauty making up one whole with her gown; he saw and felt all the charm of her body, which was only veiled by her clothes. And having once seen this, he could not see it otherwise, just as we cannot return to an illusion that has been explained.

"So you have never noticed till now that I am lovely?" Ellen seemed to be saying. "You haven't noticed that I am a woman? Yes, I am a woman, who might belong to any one—to you, too," her eyes said. And at that moment Pierre felt that Ellen not only could, but would become his wife, that it must be so.

He knew it at that moment as surely as he would have known it, standing under the wedding crown beside her. How would it be? and when? He knew not, knew not even if it would be a good thing (he had a feeling, indeed, that for some reason it would not), but he knew it would be so.

Pierre dropped his eyes, raised them again, and tried once more to see her as a distant beauty, far removed from him, as he had seen her every day before. But he could not do this. He could not, just as a man who has been staring in a fog at a blade of tall steppe grass and taking it for a tree cannot see a tree in it again, after he has once recognised it as a blade of grass. She was terribly close to him. Already she had power over him. And between him and her there existed no barriers of any kind, but the barrier of his own will.

"Very good, I will leave you in your little corner. I see you are very comfortable there," said Anna Pavlovna's voice. And Pierre, trying panic-stricken to think whether he had done anything reprehensible, looked about him, crimsoning. It seemed to him as though every one knew, as well as he did, what was passing in him. A little later, when he went up to the bigger group, Anna Pavlovna said to him:

"I am told you are making improvements in your Petersburg house." (This was the fact: the architect had told him it was necessary, and Pierre, without knowing with what object, was having his immense house in Petersburg redecorated.) "That is all very well, but do not move from Prince Vassily's. It is a good thing to have such a friend as the prince," she said, smiling to Prince Vassily. "I know something about that. Don't I? And you are so young. You need advice. You mustn't be angry with me for making use of an old woman's privileges." She paused, as women always do pause, in anticipation of something, after speaking of their age. "If you marry, it's a different matter." And she united them in one glance. Pierre did not look at Ellen, nor she at him. But she was still as terribly close to him.

He muttered something and blushed.

After Pierre had gone home, it was a long while before he could get to sleep; he kept pondering on what was happening to him. What was happening? Nothing. Simply he had grasped the fact that a woman, whom he had known as a child, of whom he had said, without giving her a thought, "Yes, she's nice-looking," when he had been told she was a beauty, he had grasped the fact that that woman might belong to him.

"But she's stupid, I used to say myself that she was stupid," he thought. "There is something nasty in the feeling she excites in me, something not legitimate. I have been told that her brother, Anatole, was in love with her, and she in love with him, that there was a regular scandal, and that's why Anatole was sent away. Her brother is Ippolit. . . . Her father is Prince Vassily. . . . That's bad," he mused; and at the very moment that he was reflecting thus (the reflections were not followed out to the end) he caught himself smiling, and became conscious that another series of reflections had risen to the surface across the first, that he was at the same time meditating on her worthlessness, and dreaming of how she would be his wife, how she might love him, how she might become quite different, and how all he had thought and heard about her might be untrue. And again he saw her, not as the daughter of Prince Vassily, but saw her whole body, only veiled by her grey gown. "But, no, why didn't that idea ever occur to me before?" And again he told himself that it was impossible, that there would be something nasty, unnatural, as it seemed to him, and dishonourable in this marriage. He recalled her past words and looks, and the words and looks of people, who had seen them together. He remembered the words and looks of Anna Pavlovna, when she had spoken about his house, he recollected thousands of such hints from Prince Vassily and other people, and he was overwhelmed with terror that he might have bound himself in some way to do a thing obviously wrong, and not what he ought to do. But at the very time that he was expressing this to himself, in another part of his mind her image floated to the surface in all its womanly beauty.

II

In the November of 1805 Prince Vassily was obliged to go on a tour of inspection through four provinces. He had secured this appointment for himself, in order to be able at the same time to visit his estates, which were in a neglected state. He intended to pick up his son, Anatole, on the way (where his regiment was stationed), and to pay a visit to Prince Nikolay Andreivitch Bolkonsky, with a view to marrying his son to the rich old man's daughter. But before going away and entering on these new affairs, Prince Vassily wanted to settle matters with Pierre, who had, it was true, of late spent whole days at home, that is, at Prince Vassily's, where he was staying, and was as absurd, as agitated, and as stupid in Ellen's presence, as a young man in love should be, but still made no offer.

"This is all very fine, but the thing must come to a conclusion," Prince Vassily said to himself one morning, with a melancholy sigh, recognising that Pierre, who was so greatly indebted to him (But there! God bless the fellow!), was not behaving quite nicely to him in the matter. "Youth . . . frivolity . . . well, God be with him," thought Prince Vassily, enjoying the sense of his own goodness of heart, "but the thing must come to a conclusion. The day after to-morrow is Ellen's name-day, I'll invite some people, and if he doesn't understand what he's to do, then it will be my affair to see to it. Yes, my affair. I'm her father."

Six weeks after Anna Pavlovna's party, and the sleepless and agitated night after it, in which Pierre had made up his mind that a marriage with Ellen would be a calamity, and that he must avoid her and go away; six weeks after that decision Pierre had still not left Prince Vassily's, and felt with horror that every day he was more and more connected with her in people's minds, that he could not go back to his former view of her, that he could not tear himself away from her even, that it would be an awful thing, but that he would have to unite his life to hers. Perhaps he might have mastered himself, but not a day passed without a party at Prince Vassily's (where receptions had not been frequent), and Pierre was bound to be present if he did not want to disturb the general satisfaction and disappoint every one. At the rare moments when Prince Vassily was at home, he took Pierre's hand if he passed him, carelessly offered him his shaven, wrinkled cheek for a kiss, and said, "till to-morrow," or "be in to dinner, or I shan't see you," or "I shall stay at home on your account," or some such remark. But although, when Prince Vassily did stay at home for Pierre (as he said), he never spoke two words to him, Pierre did not feel equal to disappointing him. Every day he said the same thing over and over to himself. "I must really understand her and make up my mind, what she is. Was I mistaken before, or am I mistaken now? No, she's not stupid; no, she's a good girl," he said to himself sometimes. "She never makes a mistake, nor has said anything stupid. She says very little, but what she does say is always simple and clear. So she's not stupid. She has never been abashed, and she is not abashed now. So she isn't a bad woman." It often happened that he began to make reflections, to think aloud in her company, and every time she had replied either by a brief, but appropriate remark, that showed she was not interested in the matter, or by a mute smile and glance, which more palpably than anything proved to Pierre her superiority. She was right in regarding all reflections as nonsense in comparison with that smile.

She always addressed him now with a glad, confiding smile—a smile having reference to him alone, and full of something more significant than the society smile that always adorned her face. Pierre knew that every one was only waiting for him to say one word, to cross a certain line, and he knew that sooner or later he would cross it. But a kind of uncomprehended horror seized upon him at the mere thought of this fearful step. A thousand times in the course of those six weeks, during which he felt himself being drawn on further and further toward the abyss that horrified him, Pierre had said to himself: "But what does it mean? I must act with decision! Can it be that I haven't any?" He tried to come to a decision, but felt with dismay that he had not in this case the strength of will which he had known in himself and really did possess. Pierre belonged to that class of persons who are only strong when they feel themselves perfectly pure. And ever since the day when he had been overcome by the sensation of desire, that he had felt stooping over the snuff-box at Anna Pavlovna's, an unconscious sense of the sinfulness of that impulse paralysed his will.

On Ellen's name-day, Prince Vassily was giving a little supper party of just their own people, as his wife said, that is, of friends and relations. All these friends and relations were made to feel that the day was to be a momentous one in the young lady's life. The guests were seated at supper. Princess Kuragin, a massive woman of imposing presence, who had once been beautiful, sat in the hostess' place, with the most honoured guests on each side of her—an old general and his wife, and Anna Pavlovna Scherer. Towards the bottom of the table sat the less elderly and less honoured guests, and there too sat as members of the family Pierre and Ellen, side by side. Prince Vassily did not take supper. He moved to and fro about the table, in excellent spirits, sitting down beside one guest after another. To every one he dropped a few careless and agreeable words, except to Pierre and Ellen, whose presence he seemed not to notice. Prince Vassily enlivened the whole company. The wax candles burned brightly, there was a glitter of silver and crystal on the table, of ladies' ornaments and the gold and silver of epaulettes. The servants threaded their way in and out round the table in their red coats. There was a clatter of knives, glasses, and plates, and the sound of eager talk from several separate conversations round the table. The old kammerherr at one end could be heard asseverating to an elderly baroness his ardent love for her, while she laughed. At the other end an anecdote was being told of the ill-success of some Marya Viktorovna. In the centre Prince Vassily concentrated the attention on himself. With a playful smile on his lips, he was telling the ladies about the last Wednesday's session of the privy council, at which Sergey Kuzmitch Vyazmitinov, the new military governor-general of Petersburg, had received and read a rescript—much talked of at the time—from the Emperor Alexander Pavlovitch. The Emperor, writing from the army to Sergey Kuzmitch, had said that on all sides he was receiving proofs of the devotion of his people, and that the testimony from Petersburg was particularly gratifying to him, that he was proud of the honour of being at the head of such a people, and would do his best to be worthy of it. This rescript began with the words: "Sergey Kuzmitch. From all sides reports reach me," etc.

"So that he never got further with it than 'Sergey Kuzmitch'?" one lady asked.

"No, no, not a syllable," Prince Vassily answered laughing. " 'Sergey Kuzmitch . . . from all sides.' 'From all sides . . . Sergey Kuzmitch. . . .' Poor Vyazmitinov could not get any further. Several times he started upon the letter again, but no sooner did he utter 'Sergey,' . . . than a sniff . . . 'Kuz . . . mi . . . itch'—tears . . . and 'from all sides' is smothered in sobs, and he can get no further. And again the handkerchief and again 'Sergey Kuzmitch from all sides' and tears, . . . so that we begged some one else to read it. . . ."

" 'Kuzmitch . . . from all sides' . . . and tears. . . ." some one repeated, laughing.

"Don't be naughty," said Anna Pavlovna, from the other end of the
table, shaking her finger at him. "He is such a worthy, excellent man,
our good Vyazmitinov."

Every one laughed heartily. At the upper end of the table, the place
of honour, every one seemed in good spirits, under the influence of
various enlivening tendencies. Only Pierre and Ellen sat mutely side by
side almost at the bottom of the table. The faces of both wore a restrained but beaming smile that had no connection with Sergey Kuzmitch—the smile of bashfulness at their own feelings. Gaily as the others
laughed and talked and jested, appetising as were the Rhine wine, the
sauté, and the ices they were discussing, carefully as they avoided glancing at the young couple, heedless and unobservant as they seemed of
them, yet it was somehow perceptible from the glances stolen at times
at them, that the anecdote about Sergey Kuzmitch, and the laughter and
the dishes, were all affectation, and that the whole attention of all the
party was really concentrated simply on that pair—Pierre and Ellen.
Prince Vassily mimicked the sniffs of Sergey Kuzmitch, and at the same
time avoided glancing at his daughter, and at the very time that he was
laughing, his expression seemed to say: "Yes, yes, it's all going well, it
will all be settled to-day." Anna Pavlovna shook her finger at him for
laughing at "our good Vyazmitinov," but in her eyes, which at that
second flashed a glance in Pierre's direction, Prince Vassily read con-
gratulation on his future son-in-law and his daughter's felicity. Old Princess Kuragin, offering wine to the lady next her with a pensive sigh,
looking angrily at her daughter, seemed in that sigh to be saying: "Yes,
there's nothing left for you and me now, my dear, but to drink sweet
wine, now that the time has come for the young people to be so in-
decently, provokingly happy!" "And what stupid stuff it all is that I'm
talking about, as though it interested me," thought the diplomat, glancing at the happy faces of the lovers. "That's happiness!"

Into the midst of the petty trivialities, the conventional interests,
which made the common tie uniting that company, had fallen the simple
feeling of the attraction of two beautiful and healthy young creatures to
one another. And this human feeling dominated everything and tri-
umphed over all their conventional chatter. The jests fell flat, the news
was not interesting, the liveliness was unmistakably forced. Not the
guests only, but the footmen waiting at table seemed to feel the same
and forget their duties, glancing at the lovely Ellen with her radiant face
and the broad, red, happy and uneasy face of Pierre. The very light of
the candles seemed concentrated on those two happy faces.

Pierre felt that he was the centre of it all, and this position both
pleased him and embarrassed him. He was like a man absorbed in some
engrossing occupation. He had no clear sight, nor hearing; no understanding of anything. Only from time to time disconnected ideas and
impressions of the reality flashed unexpectedly into his mind.

"So it is all over!" he thought. "And how has it all been done? So quickly! Now I know that not for her sake, nor for my sake alone, but for every one *it* must inevitably come to pass. They all expect it so, they are all so convinced that it will be, that I cannot, I cannot, disappoint them. But how will it be? I don't know, but it will be infallibly, it will be!" mused Pierre, glancing at the dazzling shoulders that were so close to his eyes.

Then he suddenly felt a vague shame. He felt awkward at being the sole object of the general attention, at being a happy man in the eyes of others, with his ugly face being a sort of Paris in possession of a Helen. "But, no doubt, it's always like this, and must be so," he consoled himself. "And yet what have I done to bring it about? When did it begin? I came here from Moscow with Prince Vassily, then there was nothing. Afterwards what reason was there for not staying with him? Then I played cards with her and picked up her reticule, and went skating with her. When did it begin, when did it all come about?" And here he was sitting beside her as her betrothed, hearing, seeing, feeling her closeness, her breathing, her movements, her beauty. Then it suddenly seemed to him that it was not she, but he who was himself extraordinarily beautiful, that that was why they were looking at him so, and he, happy in the general admiration, was drawing himself up, lifting his head and rejoicing in his happiness. All at once he heard a voice, a familiar voice, addressing him for the second time.

But Pierre was so absorbed that he did not understand what was said to him.

"I'm asking you, when you heard last from Bolkonsky," Prince Vassily repeated a third time. "How absent-minded you are, my dear boy." Prince Vassily smiled, and Pierre saw that every one, every one was smiling at him and at Ellen.

"Well, what of it, since you all know," Pierre was saying to himself. "What of it? it's the truth," and he smiled himself his gentle, childlike smile, and Ellen smiled.

"When did you get a letter? From Olmütz?" repeated Prince Vassily, who wanted to know in order to settle some disputed question.

"How can people talk and think of such trifles?" thought Pierre.

"Yes, from Olmütz," he answered with a sigh.

Pierre took his lady in behind the rest from supper to the drawing-room. The guests began to take leave, and several went away without saying good-bye to Ellen. As though unwilling to take her away from a serious occupation, several went up to her for an instant and made haste to retire again, refusing to let her accompany them out. The diplomat went out of the drawing-room in dumb dejection. He felt vividly all the vanity of his diplomatic career by comparison with Pierre's happiness. The old general growled angrily at his wife when she inquired how his leg was. "The old fool," he thought. "Look at Elena Vassilyevna; she'll be beautiful at fifty."

"I believe I may congratulate you," Anna Pavlovna whispered to

Princess Kuragin, as she kissed her warmly. "If I hadn't a headache, I would stay on." The princess made no answer; she was tormented by envy of her daughter's happiness.

While the guests were taking leave, Pierre was left a long while alone with Ellen in the little drawing-room, where they were sitting. Often before, during the last six weeks he had been left alone with Ellen, but he had never spoken of love to her. Now he felt that this was inevitable, but he could not make up his mind to this final step. He felt ashamed; it seemed to him that here at Ellen's side he was filling some other man's place. "This happiness is not for you," some inner voice said to him. "This happiness is for those who have not in them what you have within you." But he had to say something, and he began to speak. He asked her whether she had enjoyed the evening. With her habitual directness in replying, she answered that this name-day had been one of the pleasantest she had ever had.

A few of the nearest relations were still lingering on. They were sitting in the big drawing-room. Prince Vassily walked with languid steps towards Pierre. Pierre rose and observed that it was getting late. Prince Vassily levelled a look of stern inquiry upon him, as though what he had said was so strange that one could not believe one's ears. But the expression of severity immediately passed away, and Prince Vassily taking Pierre's hand drew him down into a seat and smiled affectionately.

"Well, Ellen?" he said at once, addressing his daughter in that careless tone of habitual tenderness which comes natural to parents who have petted their children from infancy, but in Prince Vassily's case was only arrived at by imitation of other parents. And he turned to Pierre again: "'Sergey Kuzmitch on all sides,'" he repeated, unbuttoning the top button of his waistcoat.

Pierre smiled, but his smile betrayed that he understood that it was not the anecdote of Sergey Kuzmitch that interested Prince Vassily at that moment, and Prince Vassily knew that Pierre knew it. Prince Vassily all at once muttered something and went away. It seemed to Pierre that Prince Vassily was positively disconcerted. The sight of the discomfiture of this elderly man of the world touched Pierre; he looked round at Ellen—and she, he fancied, was disconcerted too, and her glance seemed to say: "Well, it's your own fault."

"I must inevitably cross the barrier, but I can't, I can't," thought Pierre, and he began again speaking of extraneous subjects, of Sergey Kuzmitch, inquiring what was the point of the anecdote, as he had not caught it all. Ellen, with a smile, replied that she did not know it either.

When Prince Vassily went into the drawing-room, the princess was talking in subdued tones with an elderly lady about Pierre.

"Of course it is a very brilliant match, but happiness, my dear . . ."

"Marriages are made in heaven," responded the elderly lady.

Prince Vassily walked to the furthest corner and sat down on a sofa, as though he had not heard the ladies. He closed his eyes and seemed to doze. His head began to droop, and he roused himself.

"Aline," he said to his wife, "go and see what they are doing."

The princess went up to the door, walked by it with a countenance full of meaning and affected nonchalance, and glanced into the little drawing-room. Pierre and Ellen were sitting and talking as before.

"Just the same," she said in answer to her husband. Prince Vassily frowned, twisting his mouth on one side, his cheeks twitched with the unpleasant, brutal expression peculiar to him at such moments. He shook himself, got up, flung his head back, and with resolute steps passed the ladies and crossed over to the little drawing-room. He walked quickly, joyfully up to Pierre. The prince's face was so extraordinarily solemn that Pierre got up in alarm on seeing him.

"Thank God!" he said. "My wife has told me all about it." He put one arm round Pierre, the other round his daughter. "My dear boy! Ellen! I am very, very glad." His voice quavered. "I loved your father . . . and she will make you a good wife . . . God's blessing on you! . . ." He embraced his daughter, then Pierre again, and kissed him with his elderly lips. Tears were actually moist on his cheeks. "Aline, come here," he called.

The princess went in and wept too. The elderly lady also put her handkerchief to her eye. They kissed Pierre, and he several times kissed the hand of the lovely Ellen. A little later they were again left alone.

"All this had to be so and could not have been otherwise," thought Pierre, "so that it's no use to inquire whether it was a good thing or not. It's a good thing because it's definite, and there's none of the agonising suspense there was before." Pierre held his betrothed's hand in silence, and gazed at the heaving and falling of her lovely bosom.

"Ellen!" he said aloud, and stopped. "There's something special is said on these occasions," he thought; but he could not recollect precisely what it was that was said on these occasions. He glanced into her face. She bent forward closer to him. Her face flushed rosy red.

"Ah, take off those . . . those . . ." she pointed to his spectacles.

Pierre took off his spectacles, and there was in his eyes besides the strange look people's eyes always have when they remove spectacles, a look of dismay and inquiry. He would have bent over her hand and have kissed it. But with an almost brutal movement of her head, she caught at his lips and pressed them to her own. Pierre was struck by the transformed, the unpleasantly confused expression of her face.

"Now it's too late, it's all over, and besides I love her," thought Pierre.

"I love you!" he said, remembering what had to be said on these occasions. But the words sounded so poor that he felt ashamed of himself.

Six weeks later he was married, and the lucky possessor of a lovely wife and millions of money, as people said; he took up his abode in the great, newly decorated Petersburg mansion of the Counts Bezuhov.

III

In the December of 1805, the old Prince Nikolay Andreitch Bolkonsky received a letter from Prince Vassily, announcing that he intended to visit him with his son. ("I am going on an inspection tour, and of course a hundred versts is only a step out of the way for me to visit you, my deeply-honoured benefactor," he wrote. "My Anatole is accompanying me on his way to the army, and I hope you will permit him to express to you in person the profound veneration that, following his father's example, he entertains for you.")

"Well, there's no need to bring Marie out, it seems; suitors come to us of themselves," the little princess said heedlessly on hearing of this. Prince Nikolay Andreitch scowled and said nothing.

A fortnight after receiving the letter, Prince Vassily's servants arrived one evening in advance of him, and the following day he came himself with his son.

Old Bolkonsky had always had a poor opinion of Prince Vassily's character, and this opinion had grown stronger of late since Prince Vassily had, under the new reigns of Paul and Alexander, advanced to high rank and honours. Now from the letter and the little princess's hints, he saw what the object of the visit was, and his poor opinion of Prince Vassily passed into a feeling of ill-will and contempt in the old prince's heart. He snorted indignantly whenever he spoke of him. On the day of Prince Vassily's arrival, the old prince was particularly discontented and out of humour. Whether he was out of humour because Prince Vassily was coming, or whether he was particularly displeased at Prince Vassily's coming because he was out of humour, no one can say. But he was out of humour, and early in the morning Tihon had dissuaded the architect from going to the prince with his report.

"Listen how he's walking," said Tihon, calling the attention of the architect to the sound of the prince's footsteps. "Stepping flat on his heels . . . then we know . . ."

At nine o'clock, however, the old prince went out for a walk, as usual, wearing his short, velvet, fur-lined cloak with a sable collar and a sable cap. There had been a fall of snow on the previous evening. The path along which Prince Nikolay Andreitch walked to the conservatory had been cleared; there were marks of a broom in the swept snow, and a spade had been left sticking in the crisp bank of snow that bordered the path on both sides. The prince walked through the conservatories, the servants' quarters, and the out-buildings, frowning and silent.

"Could a sledge drive up?" he asked the respectful steward, who was escorting him to the house, with a countenance and manners like his own.

"The snow is deep, your excellency. I gave orders for the avenue to be swept too."

The prince nodded, and was approaching the steps. "Glory to Thee, O Lord!" thought the steward, "the storm has passed over!"

"It would have been hard to drive up, your excellency," added the steward. "So I hear, your excellency, there's a minister coming to visit your excellency?" The prince turned to the steward and stared with scowling eyes at him.

"Eh? A minister? What minister? Who gave you orders?" he began in his shrill, cruel voice. "For the princess my daughter, you do not clear the way, but for the minister you do! For me there are no ministers!"

"Your excellency, I supposed . . ."

"You supposed," shouted the prince, articulating with greater and greater haste and incoherence. "You supposed . . . Brigands! blackguards! . . . I'll teach you to suppose," and raising his stick he waved it at Alpatitch, and would have hit him, had not the steward instinctively shrunk back and escaped the blow. "You supposed . . . Blackguards! . . ." he still cried hurriedly. But although Alpatitch, shocked at his own insolence in dodging the blow, went closer to the prince, with his bald head bent humbly before him, or perhaps just because of this, the prince did not lift the stick again, and still shouting, "Blackguards! . . . fill up the road . . ." he ran to his room.

Princess Marya and Mademoiselle Bourienne stood, waiting for the old prince before dinner, well aware that he was out of temper. Mademoiselle Bourienne's beaming countenance seemed to say, "I know nothing about it, I am just the same as usual," while Princess Marya stood pale and terrified with downcast eyes. What made it harder for Princess Marya was that she knew that she ought to act like Mademoiselle Bourienne at such times, but she could not do it. She felt, "If I behave as if I did not notice it, he'll think I have no sympathy with him. If I behave as if I were depressed and out of humour myself, he'll say (as indeed often happened) that I'm sulky . . ." and so on.

The prince glanced at his daughter's scared face and snorted.

"Stuff!" or perhaps "stupid!" he muttered. "And the other is not here! they've been telling tales to her already," he thought, noticing that the little princess was not in the dining-room.

"Where's Princess Liza?" he asked. "In hiding?"

"She's not quite well," said Mademoiselle Bourienne with a bright smile; "she is not coming down. In her condition it is only to be expected."

"H'm! h'm! kh! kh!" growled the prince, and he sat down to the table. He thought his plate was not clean: he pointed to a mark on it and threw it away. Tihon caught it and handed it to a footman. The little princess was quite well, but she was in such overwhelming terror of the prince, that on hearing he was in a bad temper, she had decided not to come in.

"I am afraid for my baby," she said to Mademoiselle Bourienne; "God knows what might not be the result of a fright."

The little princess, in fact, lived at Bleak Hills in a state of continual terror of the old prince, and had an aversion for him, of which she was herself unconscious, so completely did terror overbear every other feeling. There was the same aversion on the prince's side, too; but in his case it was swallowed up in contempt. As she went on staying at Bleak Hills, the little princess became particularly fond of Mademoiselle Bourienne; she spent her days with her, begged her to sleep in her room, and often talked of her father-in-law, and criticised him to her.

"We have company coming, prince," said Mademoiselle Bourienne, her rosy fingers unfolding her dinner-napkin. "His excellency Prince

Kuragin with his son, as I have heard say?" she said in a tone of inquiry.

"H'm! . . his *excellence* is an upstart. I got him his place in the college," the old prince said huffily. "And what his son's coming for, I can't make out. Princess Lizaveta Karlovna and Princess Marya can tell us, maybe; I don't know what he's bringing this son here for. I don't want him." And he looked at his daughter, who turned crimson.

"Unwell, eh? Scared of the minister, as that blockhead Alpatitch called him to-day?"

"*Non, mon père.*"

Unsuccessful as Mademoiselle Bourienne had been in the subject she had started, she did not desist, but went on prattling away about the conservatories, the beauty of a flower that had just opened, and after the soup the prince subsided.

After dinner he went to see his daughter-in-law. The little princess was sitting at a little table gossiping with Masha, her maid. She turned pale on seeing her father-in-law.

The little princess was greatly changed. She looked ugly rather than pretty now. Her cheeks were sunken, her lip was drawn up, and her eyes were hollow.

"Yes, a sort of heaviness," she said in answer to the prince's inquiry how she felt.

"Isn't there anything you need?"

"*Non, merci, mon père.*"

"Oh, very well then, very well."

He went out and into the waiting-room. Alpatitch was standing there with downcast head.

"Filled up the road again?"

"Yes, your excellency; for God's sake, forgive me, it was simply a blunder."

The prince cut him short with his unnatural laugh.

"Oh, very well, very well." He held out his hand, which Alpatitch kissed, and then he went to his study.

In the evening Prince Vassily arrived. He was met on the way by the coachmen and footmen of the Bolkonskys, who with shouts dragged his carriages and sledge to the lodge, over the road, which had been purposely obstructed with snow again.

Prince Vassily and Anatole were conducted to separate apartments. Taking off his tunic, Anatole sat with his elbows on the table, on a corner of which he fixed his handsome, large eyes with a smiling, unconcerned stare. All his life he had looked upon as an uninterrupted entertainment, which some one or other was, he felt, somehow bound to provide for him. In just the same spirit he had looked at his visit to the cross old gentleman and his rich and hideous daughter. It might all, according to his anticipations, turn out very jolly and amusing. "And why not get married, if she has such a lot of money? That never comes amiss," thought Anatole.

He shaved and scented himself with the care and elegance that had become habitual with him, and with his characteristic expression of

all-conquering good-humour, he walked into his father's room, holding
his head high. Two valets were busily engaged in dressing Prince Vassily; he was looking about him eagerly, and nodded gaily to his son, as
he entered with an air that said, "Yes, that's just how I wanted to see
you looking."

"Come, joking apart, father, is she so hideous? Eh?" he asked in
French, as though reverting to a subject more than once discussed on the
journey.

"Nonsense! The great thing for you is to try and be respectful and
sensible with the old prince."

"If he gets nasty, I'm off," said Anatole. "I can't stand those old
gentlemen. Eh?"

"Remember that for you everything depends on it."

Meanwhile, in the feminine part of the household not only the arrival
of the minister and his son was already known, but the appearance of
both had been minutely described. Princess Marya was sitting alone in
her room doing her utmost to control her inner emotion.

"Why did they write, why did Liza tell me about it? Why, it cannot
be!" she thought, looking at herself in the glass. "How am I to go into
the drawing-room? Even if I like him, I could never be myself with him
now." The mere thought of her father's eyes reduced her to terror. The
little princess and Mademoiselle Bourienne had already obtained all
necessary information from the maid, Masha; they had learned what a
handsome fellow the minister's son was, with rosy cheeks and black
eyebrows; how his papa had dragged his legs upstairs with difficulty,
while he, like a young eagle, had flown up after him three steps at a
time. On receiving these items of information, the little princess and
Mademoiselle Bourienne, whose eager voices were audible in the corridor, went into Princess Marya's room.

"They are come, Marie, do you know?" said the little princess, waddling in and sinking heavily into an armchair. She was not wearing the
gown in which she had been sitting in the morning, but had put on one
of her best dresses. Her hair had been carefully arranged, and her face
was full of an eager excitement, which did not, however, conceal its
wasted and pallid look. In the smart clothes which she had been used
to wear in Petersburg in society, the loss of her good looks was even more
noticeable. Mademoiselle Bourienne, too, had put some hardly perceptible finishing touches to her costume, which made her fresh, pretty face
even more attractive.

"What, and you are staying just as you are, dear princess. They will
come in a minute to tell us the gentlemen are in the drawing-room," she
began. "We shall have to go down, and you are doing nothing at all to
your dress."

The little princess got up from her chair, rang for the maid, and hurriedly and eagerly began to arrange what Princess Marya was to wear,
and to put her ideas into practice. Princess Marya's sense of personal
dignity was wounded by her own agitation at the arrival of her suitor,
and still more was she mortified that her two companions should not

even conceive that she ought not to be so agitated. To have told them how ashamed she was of herself and of them would have been to betray her own excitement. Besides, to refuse to be dressed up, as they suggested, would have been exposing herself to reiterated raillery and insistence. She flushed; her beautiful eyes grew dim; her face was suffused with patches of crimson; and with the unbeautiful, victimised expression which was the one most often seen on her face, she abandoned herself to Mademoiselle Bourienne and Liza. Both women exerted themselves with *perfect sincerity* to make her look well. She was so plain that the idea of rivalry with her could never have entered their heads. Consequently it was with perfect sincerity, in the naïve and unhesitating conviction women have that dress can make a face handsome, that they set to work to attire her.

"No, really, *ma bonne amie*, that dress isn't pretty," said Liza, looking sideways at Princess Marya from a distance; "tell her to put on you your maroon velvet there. Yes, really! Why, you know, it may be the turning-point in your whole life. That one's too light, it's not right, no, it's not!"

It was not the dress that was wrong, but the face and the whole figure of the princess, but that was not felt by Mademoiselle Bourienne and the little princess. They still fancied that if they were to put a blue ribbon in her hair, and do it up high, and to put the blue sash lower on the maroon dress and so on, then all would be well. They forgot that the frightened face and figure of Princess Marya could not be changed, and therefore, however presentable they might make the setting and decoration of the face, the face itself would still look piteous and ugly. After two or three changes, to which Princess Marya submitted passively, when her hair had been done on the top of her head (which completely changed and utterly disfigured her), and the blue sash and best maroon velvet dress had been put on, the little princess walked twice round, and with her little hand stroked out a fold here and pulled down the sash there, and gazed at her with her head first on one side and then on the other.

"No, it won't do," she said resolutely, throwing up her hands. "No, Marie, decidedly that does not suit you. I like you better in your little grey everyday frock. No, please do that for me. Katya," she said to the maid, "bring the princess her grey dress, and look, Mademoiselle Bourienne, how I'll arrange it," she said, smiling with a foretaste of artistic pleasure. But when Katya brought the dress, Princess Marya was still sitting motionless before the looking-glass, looking at her own face, and in the looking-glass she saw that there were tears in her eyes and her mouth was quivering, on the point of breaking into sobs.

"Come, dear princess," said Mademoiselle Bourienne, "one more little effort."

The little princess, taking the dress from the hands of the maid, went up to Princess Marya.

"Now, we'll try something simple and charming," she said. Her voice and Mademoiselle Bourienne's and the giggle of Katya blended into a sort of gay babble like the twitter of birds.

"No, leave me alone," said the princess; and there was such serious-ness and such suffering in her voice that the twitter of the birds ceased at once. They looked at the great, beautiful eyes, full of tears and of thought, looking at them imploringly and they saw that to insist was useless and even cruel.

"At least alter your hair," said the little princess. "I told you," she said reproachfully to Mademoiselle Bourienne, "there were faces which that way of doing the hair does not suit a bit. Not a bit, not a bit, please alter it."

"Leave me alone, leave me alone, all that is nothing to me," answered a voice scarcely able to struggle with tears.

Mademoiselle Bourienne and the little princess could not but admit to themselves that Princess Marya was very plain in this guise, far worse than usual, but it was too late. She looked at them with an expression they knew well, an expression of deep thought and sadness. That expression did not inspire fear. (That was a feeling she could never have inspired in any one.) But they knew that when that expression came into her face, she was mute and inflexible in her resolutions.

"You will alter it, won't you?" said Liza, and when Princess Marya made no reply, Liza went out of the room.

Princess Marya was left alone. She did not act upon Liza's wishes, she did not re-arrange her hair, she did not even glance into the looking-glass. Letting her eyes and her hands drop helplessly, she sat mentally dreaming. She pictured her husband, a man, a strong, masterful, and inconceivably attractive creature, who would bear her away all at once into an utterly different, happy world of his own. A child, *her own*, like the baby she had seen at her old nurse's daughter's, she fancied at her own breast. The husband standing, gazing tenderly at her and the child. "But no, it can never be, I am too ugly," she thought.

"Kindly come to tea. The prince will be going in immediately," said the maid's voice at the door. She started and was horrified at what she had been thinking. And before going downstairs she went into the oratory, and fixing her eyes on the black outline of the great image of the Saviour, she stood for several minutes before it with clasped hands. Princess Marya's soul was full of an agonising doubt. Could the joy of love, of earthly love for a man, be for her? In her reveries of marriage, Princess Marya dreamed of happiness in a home and children of her own, but her chief, her strongest and most secret dream was of earthly love. The feeling became the stronger the more she tried to conceal it from others, and even from herself. "My God," she said, "how am I to subdue in my heart these temptations of the devil? How am I to renounce for ever all evil thoughts, so as in peace to fulfil Thy will?" And scarcely had she put this question than God's answer came to her in her own heart. "Desire nothing for thyself, be not covetous, anxious, envious. The future of men and thy destiny too must be unknown for thee; but

live that thou mayest be ready for all. If it shall be God's will to prove
thee in the duties of marriage, be ready to obey His will." With this
soothing thought (though still she hoped for the fulfilment of that forbidden earthly dream) Princess Marya crossed herself, sighing, and
went downstairs, without thinking of her dress nor how her hair was
done, of how she would go in nor what she would say. What could all
that signify beside the guidance of Him, without Whose will not one
hair falls from the head of man?

IV

WHEN Princess Marya went into the room, Prince Vassily and his son
were already in the drawing-room, talking to the little princess and Mademoiselle Bourienne. When she walked in with her heavy step, treading
on her heels, the gentlemen and Mademoiselle Bourienne rose, and the
little princess, with a gesture indicating her to the gentlemen, said:
"Here is Marie!" Princess Marya saw them all and saw them in detail.
She saw the face of Prince Vassily, growing serious for an instant at the
sight of her, and then hastily smiling, and the face of the little princess,
scanning the faces of the guests with curiosity to detect the impression
Marie was making on them. She saw Mademoiselle Bourienne, too, with
her ribbon and her pretty face, turned towards *him* with a look of more
eagerness than she had ever seen on it. But *him* she could not see, she
could only see something large, bright-coloured, and handsome moving
towards her, as she entered the room. Prince Vassily approached her
first; and she kissed his bald head, as he bent over to kiss her hand, and
in reply to his words said, that on the contrary, she remembered him
very well. Then Anatole went up to her. She still could not see him. She
only felt a soft hand taking her hand firmly, and she touched with her
lips a white forehead, over which there was beautiful fair hair, smelling
of pomade. When she glanced at him, she was impressed by his beauty.
Anatole was standing with the thumb of his right hand at a button of
his uniform, his chest squared and his spine arched; swinging one foot,
with his head a little on one side, he was gazing in silence with a beaming face on the princess, obviously not thinking of her at all. Anatole
was not quick-witted, he was not ready, not eloquent in conversation,
but he had that faculty, so invaluable for social purposes, of composure
and imperturbable assurance. If a man of no self-confidence is dumb at
first making acquaintance, and betrays a consciousness of the impro-
priety of this dumbness and an anxiety to find something to say, the effect will be bad. But Anatole was dumb and swung his leg, as he watched
the princess's hair with a radiant face. It was clear that he could be
silent with the same serenity for a very long while. "If anybody feels
silence awkward, let him talk, but I don't care about it," his demeanour
seemed to say. Moreover, in his manner to women, Anatole had that air,
which does more than anything else to excite curiosity, awe, and even
love in women, the air of supercilious consciousness of his own superior-

ity. His manner seemed to say to them: "I know you, I know, but why trouble my head about you? You'd be pleased enough, of course!" Possibly he did not think this on meeting women (it is probable, indeed, that he did not, for he thought very little at any time), but that was the effect of his air and his manner. Princess Marya felt it, and as though to show him she did not even venture to think of inviting his attention, she turned to his father. The conversation was general and animated, thanks to the voice and the little downy lip, that flew up and down over the white teeth of the little princess. She met Prince Vassily in that playful tone so often adopted by chatty and lively persons, the point of which consists in the assumption that there exists a sort of long-established series of jokes and amusing, partly private, humorous reminiscences between the persons so addressed and oneself, even when no such reminiscences are really shared, as indeed was the case with Prince Vassily and the little princess. Prince Vassily readily fell in with this tone; the little princess embellished their supposed common reminiscences with all sorts of droll incidents that had never occurred, and drew Anatole too into them, though she had scarcely known him. Mademoiselle Bourienne too succeeded in taking a part in them, and even Princess Marya felt with pleasure that she was being made to share in their gaiety.

"Well, anyway, we shall take advantage of you to the utmost now we have got you, dear prince," said the little princess, in French, of course, to Prince Vassily. "Here it is not as it used to be at our evenings at Annette's, where you always ran away. Do you remember our dear Annette?"

"Ah yes, but then you mustn't talk to me about politics, like Annette!"

"And our little tea-table?"

"Oh yes!"

"Why is it you never used to be at Annette's?" the little princess asked of Anatole. "Ah, I know, I know," she said, winking; "your brother, Ippolit, has told me tales of your doings. Oh!" She shook her finger at him. "I know about your exploits in Paris too!"

"But he, Ippolit, didn't tell you, did he?" said Prince Vassily (addressing his son and taking the little princess by the arm, as though she would have run away and he were just in time to catch her); "he didn't tell you how he, Ippolit himself, was breaking his heart over our sweet princess, and how she turned him out of doors."

"Oh! she is the pearl of women, princess," he said, addressing Princess Marya. Mademoiselle Bourienne on her side, at the mention of Paris, did not let her chance slip for taking a share in the common stock of recollections.

She ventured to inquire if it were long since Anatole was in Paris, and how he had liked that city. Anatole very readily answered the Frenchwoman, and smiling and staring at her, he talked to her about her native country. At first sight of the pretty Mademoiselle, Anatole had decided that even here at Bleak Hills he should not be dull. "Not half bad-looking," he thought, scrutinising her, "she's not half bad-looking, that companion! I hope she'll bring her along when we're married," he mused; "she is a nice little thing."

The old prince was dressing deliberately in his room, scowling and ruminating on what he was to do. The arrival of these visitors angered him. "What's Prince Vassily to me, he and his son? Prince Vassily is a braggart, an empty-headed fool, and a nice fellow the son is, I expect," he growled to himself. What angered him was that this visit revived in his mind the unsettled question, continually thrust aside, the question in regard to which the old prince always deceived himself. That question was whether he would ever bring himself to part with his daughter and give her to a husband. The prince could never bring himself to put this question directly to himself, knowing beforehand that if he did he would have to answer it justly, but against justice in this case was ranged more than feeling, the very possibility of life. Life without Princess Marya was unthinkable to the old prince, little as in appearance he prized her. "And what is she to be married for?" he thought; "to be unhappy, beyond a doubt. Look at Liza with Andrey (and a better husband, I should fancy, it would be difficult to find nowadays), but she's not satisfied with her lot. And who would marry her for love? She's plain and ungraceful. She'd be married for her connections, her wealth. And don't old maids get on well enough? They are happier really!" So Prince Nikolay Andreivitch mused, as he dressed, yet the question constantly deferred demanded an immediate decision. Prince Vassily had brought his son obviously with the intention of making an offer, and probably that day or the next he would ask for a direct answer. The name, the position in the world, was suitable. "Well, I'm not against it," the prince kept saying to himself, "only let him be worthy of her. That's what we shall see. That's what we shall see," he said aloud, "that's what we shall see," and with his usual alert step he walked into the drawing-room, taking in the whole company in a rapid glance. He noticed the change in the dress of the little princess and Mademoiselle Bourienne's ribbon, and the hideous way in which Princess Marya's hair was done, and the smiles of the Frenchwoman and Anatole, and the isolation of his daughter in the general talk. "She's decked herself out like a fool!" he thought, glancing vindictively at his daughter. "No shame in her; while he doesn't care to speak to her!"

He went up to Prince Vassily.

"Well, how d'ye do, how d'ye do, glad to see you."

"For a friend that one loves seven versts is close by," said Prince Vassily, quoting the Russian proverb, and speaking in his usual rapid, self-confident, and familiar tone. "This is my second, I beg you to love him and welcome him, as they say."

Prince Nikolay Andreivitch scrutinised Anatole.

"A fine fellow, a fine fellow!" he said. "Well, come and give me a kiss," and he offered him his cheek. Anatole kissed the old man, and looked at him with curiosity and perfect composure, waiting for some instance of the eccentricity his father had told him to expect.

The old prince sat down in his customary place in the corner of the sofa, moved up an armchair for Prince Vassily, pointed to it, and began questioning him about political affairs and news. He seemed to be listening with attention to what Prince Vassily was saying, but glanced continually at Princess Marya.

"So they're writing from Potsdam already?" He repeated Prince Vassily's last words, and suddenly getting up, he went up to his daughter.

"So it was for visitors you dressed yourself up like this, eh?" he said. "Nice of you, very nice. You do your hair up in some new fashion before visitors, and before visitors, I tell you, never dare in future to change your dress without my leave."

"It was my fault . . ." stammered the little princess, flushing.

"You are quite at liberty," said the old prince, with a scrape before his daughter-in-law, "but she has no need to disfigure herself—she's ugly enough without that." And he sat down again in his place, taking no further notice of his daughter, whom he had reduced to tears.

"On the contrary, that coiffure is extremely becoming to the princess," said Prince Vassily.

"Well, my young prince, what's your name?" said the old prince, turning to Anatole. "Come here, let us talk to you a little and make your acquaintance."

"Now the fun's beginning," thought Anatole, and with a smile he sat down by the old prince.

"That's it; they tell me, my dear boy, you have been educated abroad. Not taught to read and write by the deacon, like your father and me. Tell me, are you serving now in the Horse Guards?" asked the old man, looking closely and intently at Anatole.

"No, I have transferred into the line," answered Anatole, with difficulty restraining his laughter.

"Ah! a good thing. So you want to serve your Tsar and your country, do you? These are times of war. Such a fine young fellow ought to be on service, he ought to be on service. Ordered to the front, eh?"

"No, prince, our regiment has gone to the front. But I'm attached. What is it I'm attached to, papa?" Anatole turned to his father with a laugh.

"He is a credit to the service, a credit. What is it I'm attached to! Ha-ha-ha!" laughed the old prince, and Anatole laughed still louder. Suddenly the old prince frowned. "Well, you can go," he said to Anatole. With a smile Anatole returned to the ladies.

"So you had him educated abroad, Prince Vassily? Eh?" said the old prince to Prince Vassily.

"I did what I could, and I assure you the education there is far better than ours."

"Yes, nowadays everything's different, everything's new-fashioned. A fine fellow! a fine fellow! Well, come to my room." He took Prince Vassily's arm and led him away to his study.

Left alone with the old prince, Prince Vassily promptly made known to him his wishes and his hopes.

"Why, do you imagine," said the old prince wrathfully, "that I keep her, that I can't part with her? What an idea!" he protested angrily. "I am ready for it to-morrow! Only, I tell you, I want to know my future son-in-law better. You know my principles: everything open! To-morrow I will ask her in your presence; if she wishes it, let him stay on. Let him stay on, and I'll see." The prince snorted. "Let her marry, it's nothing to me," he screamed in the piercing voice in which he had screamed at saying good-bye to his son.

"I will be frank with you," said Prince Vassily in the tone of a crafty man, who is convinced of the uselessness of being crafty with so penetrating a companion. "You see right through people, I know. Anatole is not a genius, but a straightforward, good-hearted lad, good as a son or a kinsman."

"Well, well, very good, we shall see."

As is always the case with women who have for a long while been living a secluded life apart from masculine society, on the appearance of Anatole on the scene, all the three women in Prince Nikolay Andreivitch's house felt alike that their life had not been real life till then. Their powers of thought, of feeling, of observation, were instantly redoubled. It seemed as though their life had till then been passed in darkness, and was all at once lighted up by a new brightness that was full of significance.

Princess Marya did not remember her face and her coiffure. The handsome, open face of the man who might, perhaps, become her husband, absorbed her whole attention. She thought him kind, brave, resolute, manly, and magnanimous. She was convinced of all that. Thousands of dreams of her future married life were continually floating into her imagination. She drove them away and tried to disguise them.

"But am I not too cold with him?" thought Princess Marya. "I try to check myself, because at the bottom of my heart I feel myself too close to him. But of course he doesn't know all I think of him, and may imagine I don't like him."

And she tried and knew not how to be cordial to him.

"The poor girl is devilish ugly," Anatole was thinking about her.

Mademoiselle Bourienne, who had also been thrown by Anatole's arrival into a high state of excitement, was absorbed in reflections of a different order. Naturally, a beautiful young girl with no defined position in society, without friends or relations, without even a country of her own, did not look forward to devoting her life to waiting on Prince Nikolay Andreivitch, to reading him books and being a friend to Princess Marya. Mademoiselle Bourienne had long been looking forward to the Russian prince, who would have the discrimination to discern her superiority to the ugly, badly dressed, ungainly Russian princesses—who would fall in love with her and bear her away. And now this Russian prince at last had come. Mademoiselle Bourienne knew a story she had heard from her aunt, and had finished to her own taste, which she loved to go over in her own imagination. It was the story of how a girl had been seduced, and her poor mother (*sa pauvre mère*) had appeared to her and reproached her for yielding to a man's allurements without marriage. Mademoiselle was often touched to tears, as in imagination she told "*him*," her seducer, this tale. Now this "*he*," a real Russian prince, had appeared. He would elope with her, then "my poor mother" would come on the scene, and he would marry her. This was how all her future history shaped itself in Mademoiselle Bourienne's brain at the very moment when she was talking to him of Paris. Mademoiselle Bourienne was not guided by calculations (she did not even consider for one instant what she would do), but it had all been ready within her long before, and now it all centred about Anatole as soon as he appeared, and she wished and tried to attract him as much as possible.

The little princess, like an old warhorse hearing the blast of the trumpet, was prepared to gallop off into a flirtation as her habit was, unconsciously forgetting her position, with no ulterior motive, no struggle, nothing but simple-hearted, frivolous gaiety in her heart.

Although in feminine society Anatole habitually took up the attitude of a man weary of the attentions of women, his vanity was agreeably flattered by the spectacle of the effect he produced on these three women. Moreover, he was beginning to feel towards the pretty and provocative Mademoiselle Bourienne that violent, animal feeling, which was apt to come upon him with extreme rapidity, and to impel him to the coarsest and most reckless actions.

After tea the party moved into the divan-room, and Princess Marya was asked to play on the clavichord. Anatole leaned on his elbow facing her, and near Mademoiselle Bourienne, and his eyes were fixed on Princess Marya, full of laughter and glee. Princess Marya felt his eyes upon her with troubled and joyful agitation. Her favourite sonata bore her away to a world of soul-felt poetry, and the feeling of his eyes upon her added still more poetry to that world. The look in Anatole's eyes, though they were indeed fixed upon her, had reference not to her, but to the movements of Mademoiselle's little foot, which he was at that very time touching with his own under the piano. Mademoiselle Bourienne too was gazing at Princess Marya, and in her fine eyes, too, there was an expression of frightened joy and hope that was new to the princess.

"How she loves me!" thought Princess Marya. "How happy I am now and how happy I may be with such a friend and such a husband! Can he possibly be my husband?" she thought, not daring to glance at his face, but still feeling his eyes fastened upon her.

When the party broke up after supper, Anatole kissed Princess Marya's hand. She was herself at a loss to know how she had the hardihood, but she looked straight with her short-sighted eyes at the handsome face as it came close to her. After the princess, he bent over the hand of Mademoiselle Bourienne (it was a breach of etiquette, but he did everything with the same ease and simplicity) and Mademoiselle Bourienne crimsoned and glanced in dismay at the princess.

"*Quelle délicatesse!*" thought Princess Marya. "Can Amélie" (Mademoiselle's name) "suppose I could be jealous of her, and fail to appreciate her tenderness and devotion to me?" She went up to Mademoiselle Bourienne and kissed her warmly. Anatole went to the little princess.

"No, no, no! When your father writes me word that you are behaving well, I will give you my hand to kiss." And shaking her little finger at him, she went smiling out of the room.

V

THEY all went to their rooms, and except Anatole, who fell asleep the instant he got into bed, no one could get to sleep for a long while that night. "Can he possibly be—my husband, that stranger, that handsome, kind man; yes, he is certainly kind," thought Princess Marya, and a feeling of terror, such as she scarcely ever felt, came upon her. She was afraid to look round; it seemed to her that there was some one there— the devil, and he was that man with his white forehead, black eyebrows, and red lips.

She rang for her maid and asked her to sleep in her room.

Mademoiselle Bourienne walked up and down the winter garden for a long while that evening, in vain expectation of some one; at one moment she was smiling at that some one, the next, moved to tears by an imaginary reference to *ma pauvre mère* reproaching her for her fall.

The little princess kept grumbling to her maid that her bed had not been properly made. She could not lie on her side nor on her face. She felt uncomfortable and ill at ease in every position. Her burden oppressed her, oppressed her more than ever that night, because Anatole's presence had carried her vividly back to another time when it was not so, and she had been light and gay. She sat in a low chair in her nightcap and dressing-jacket. Katya, sleepy and dishevelled, for the third time beat and turned the heavy feather bed, murmuring something.

"I told you it was all in lumps and hollows," the little princess repeated; "I should be glad enough to go to sleep, so it's not my fault." And her voice quivered like a child's when it is going to cry.

The old prince too could not sleep. Tihon, half asleep, heard him pacing angrily up and down and blowing his nose. The old prince felt as though he had been insulted through his daughter. The insult was the more bitter because it concerned not himself, but another, his daughter, whom he loved more than himself. He said to himself that he would think the whole matter over thoroughly and decide what was right and what must be done, but instead of doing so, he only worked up his irritation more and more.

"The first stray comer that appears! and father and all forgotten, and she runs upstairs, and does up her hair, and rigs herself out, and doesn't know what she's doing! She's glad to abandon her father! And she knew I should notice it. Fr . . . fr . . . fr . . . And don't I see the fool has no eyes but for Bourienne (must get rid of her). And how can she have so little pride, as not to see it? If not for her own sake, if she has no pride, at least for mine. I must show her that the blockhead doesn't give her a thought, and only looks at Bourienne. She has no pride, but I'll make her see it . . ."

By telling his daughter that she was making a mistake, that Anatole was getting up a flirtation with Mademoiselle Bourienne, the old prince knew that he would wound her self-respect, and so his object (not to be parted from his daughter) would be gained, and so at this reflection he grew calmer. He called Tihon and began undressing.

"The devil brought them here!" he thought, as Tihon slipped his nightshirt over his dried-up old body and his chest covered with grey hair.

"I didn't invite them. They come and upset my life. And there's not much of it left. Damn them!" he muttered, while his head was hidden in the nightshirt. Tihon was used to the prince's habit of expressing his thoughts aloud, and so it was with an unmoved countenance that he met the wrathful and inquiring face that emerged from the nightshirt.

"Gone to bed?" inquired the prince.

Tihon, like all good valets, indeed, knew by instinct the direction of his master's thoughts. He guessed that it was Prince Vassily and his son who were meant.

"Their honours have gone to bed and put out their lights, your excellency."

"They had no reason, no reason . . ." the prince articulated rapidly, and slipping his feet into his slippers and his arms into his dressing-gown, he went to the couch on which he always slept.

Although nothing had been said between Anatole and Mademoiselle Bourienne, they understood each other perfectly so far as the first part of the romance was concerned, the part previous to the *pauvre mère* episode. They felt that they had a great deal to say to each other in private, and so from early morning they sought an opportunity of meeting alone. While the princess was away, spending her hour as usual with her father, Mademoiselle Bourienne was meeting Anatole in the winter garden.

That day it was with even more than her usual trepidation that Princess Marya went to the door of the study. It seemed to her not only that every one was aware that her fate would be that day decided, but that all were aware of what she was feeling about it. She read it in Tihon's face and in the face of Prince Vassily's valet, who met her in the corridor with hot water, and made her a low bow.

The old prince's manner to his daughter that morning was extremely affectionate, though strained. That strained expression Princess Marya knew well. It was the expression she saw in his face at the moments when his withered hands were clenched with vexation at Princess Marya's not understanding some arithmetical problem, and he would get up and walk away from her, repeating the same words several times in a low voice.

He came to the point at once and began talking. "A proposal has been made to me on your behalf," he said, with an unnatural smile. "I dare say, you have guessed," he went on "that Prince Vassily has not come here and brought his protégé" (for some unknown reason the old prince elected to refer to Anatole in this way) "for the sake of my charms. Yesterday, they made me a proposal on your behalf. And as you know my principles, I refer the matter to you."

"How am I to understand you, *mon père*?" said the princess, turning pale and red.

"How understand me!" cried her father angrily. "Prince Vassily finds you to his taste as a daughter-in-law, and makes you a proposal for his protégé. That's how to understand it. How understand it! . . . Why, I ask you."

"I don't know how you, *mon père* . . ." the princess articulated in a whisper.

"I? I? what have I to do with it? leave me out of the question. I am not going to be married. What do you say? that's what it's desirable to learn."

The princess saw that her father looked with ill-will on the project, but at that instant the thought had occurred to her that now or never the fate of her life would be decided. She dropped her eyes so as to avoid the gaze under which she felt incapable of thought, and capable of nothing but her habitual obedience: "My only desire is to carry out your wishes," she said; "if I had to express my own desire . . ."

She had not time to finish. The prince cut her short. "Very good, then!" he shouted. "He shall take you with your dowry, and hook on Mademoiselle Bourienne into the bargain. She'll be his wife, while you . . ." The prince stopped. He noticed the effect of these words on his daughter. She had bowed her head and was beginning to cry.

"Come, come, I was joking, I was joking," he said. "Remember one thing, princess; I stick to my principles, that a girl has a full right to choose. And I give you complete freedom. Remember one thing; the happiness of your life depends on your decision. No need to talk about me."

"But I don't know . . . father."

"No need for talking! He's told to, and he's ready to marry any one, but you are free to choose. . . . Go to your own room, think it over, and come to me in an hour's time and tell me in his presence: yes or no. I know you will pray over it. Well, pray if you like. Only you'd do better to think. You can go."

"Yes or no, yes or no, yes or no!" he shouted again as the princess went out of the room, reeling in a sort of fog. Her fate was decided, and decided for happiness. But what her father had said about Mademoiselle Bourienne, that hint was horrible. It was not true, of course, but still it was horrible; she could not help thinking of it. She walked straight forward through the winter garden, seeing and hearing nothing, when all of a sudden she was roused by the familiar voice of Mademoiselle Bourienne. She lifted her eyes, and only two paces before her she saw Anatole with his arms round the Frenchwoman, whispering something to her. With a terrible expression on his handsome face, Anatole looked round at Princess Marya, and did not for the first second let go the waist of Mademoiselle Bourienne, who had not seen her.

"Who's there? What do you want? Wait a little!" was what Anatole's face expressed. Princess Marya gazed blankly at them. She could not believe her eyes. At last Mademoiselle Bourienne shrieked and ran away. With a gay smile Anatole bowed to Princess Marya, as though inviting her to share his amusement at this strange incident, and with a shrug of his shoulders he went to the door that led to his apartment.

An hour later Tihon came to summon Princess Marya to the old prince, and added that Prince Vassily was with him. When Tihon came to her, Princess Marya was sitting on the sofa in her own room holding in her arms the weeping Mademoiselle Bourienne. Princess Marya was softly stroking her head. Her beautiful eyes had regained all their luminous peace, and were gazing with tender love and commiseration at the pretty little face of Mademoiselle Bourienne.

"Oh, princess, I am ruined for ever in your heart," Mademoiselle Bourienne was saying.

"Why? I love you more than ever," said Princess Marya, "and I will try to do everything in my power for your happiness."

"But you despise me, you who are so pure, you will never understand this frenzy of passion. Ah, it is only my poor mother . . ."

"I understand everything," said Princess Marya, smiling mournfully. "Calm yourself, my dear. I am going to my father," she said, and she went out.

When the princess went in, Prince Vassily was sitting with one leg crossed high over the other, and a snuff-box in his hand. There was a smile of emotion on his face, and he looked as though moved to such an extreme point that he could but regret and smile at his own sensibility. He took a hasty pinch of snuff.

"Ah, my dear, my dear!" he said, getting up and taking her by both hands. He heaved a sigh, and went on: "My son's fate is in your hands. Decide, my good dear, sweet Marie, whom I have always loved like a daughter." He drew back. There was a real tear in his eye.

"Fr . . . ffr . . ." snorted the old prince. "The prince in his protégé's . . . his son's name makes you a proposal. Are you willing or not to be the wife of Prince Anatole Kuragin? You say: yes or no," he shouted, "and then I reserve for myself the right to express my opinion. Yes, my opinion, and nothing but my opinion," added the old prince, to Prince Vassily in response to his supplicating expression, "Yes or no!"

"My wish, *mon père*, is never to leave you; never to divide my life from yours. I do not wish to marry," she said resolutely, glancing with her beautiful eyes at Prince Vassily and at her father.

"Nonsense, fiddlesticks! Nonsense, nonsense!" shouted the old prince, frowning. He took his daughter's hand, drew her towards him and did not kiss her, but bending over, touched her forehead with his, and wrung the hand he held so violently that she winced and uttered a cry. Prince Vassily got up.

"My dear, let me tell you that this is a moment I shall never forget, never; but, dear, will you not give us a little hope of touching so kind and generous a heart. Say that perhaps. . . . The future is so wide. . . . Say: perhaps."

"Prince, what I have said is all that is in my heart. I thank you for the honor you do me, but I shall never be your son's wife."

"Well, then it's all over, my dear fellow. Very glad to have seen you, very glad to have seen you. Go to your room, princess; go along now," said the old prince. "Very, very glad to have seen you," he repeated, embracing Prince Vassily.

"My vocation is a different one," Princess Marya was thinking to herself; "my vocation is to be happy in the happiness of others, in the happiness of love and self-sacrifice. And at any cost I will make poor Amélie happy. She loves him so passionately. She is so passionately penitent. I will do everything to bring about their marriage. If he is not rich I will give her means, I will beg my father, I will beg Andrey. I shall be so happy when she is his wife. She is so unhappy, a stranger, solitary and helpless! And, my God, how passionately she must love him to be able to forget herself so. Perhaps I might have done the same! . . ." thought Princess Marya.

VI

It was a long while since the Rostovs had had news of their Nikolushka. But in the middle of the winter a letter was handed to Count Rostov, on the envelope of which he recognised his son's handwriting. On receiving the letter the count, in alarm and in haste, ran on tiptoe to his room, trying to escape notice, shut himself in and read the letter. Anna Mihalovna had learned (as she always did learn all that passed in the house) that he had received a letter, and treading softly, she went in to the count and found him with the letter in his hand, sobbing and laughing at once. Anna Mihalovna, though her fortunes had been looking up, was still an inmate of the Rostov household.

"My dear friend?" Anna Mihalovna brought out in a voice of melancholy inquiry, equally ready for sympathy in any direction. The count sobbed more violently.

"Nikolushka . . . letter . . . wounded . . . he would . . . my dear . . . wounded . . . my darling boy . . . the little countess . . . promoted . . . thank God . . . how are we to tell the little countess?"

Anna Mihalovna sat down by his side, with her own handkerchief wiped the tears from his eyes and from the letter, then dried her own tears, read the letter, soothed the count, and decided that before dinner and before tea she would prepare the countess; and after tea, with God's help, tell her all. During dinner Anna Mihalovna talked of the rumours from the war, of dear Nikolay, inquired twice when his last letter had been received, though she knew perfectly well, and observed that they might well be getting a letter from him to-day. Every time that the countess began to be uneasy under these hints and looked in trepidation from the count to Anna Mihalovna, the latter turned the conversation in the most unnoticeable way to insignificant subjects. Natasha, who was of all the family the one most gifted with the faculty of catching the shades of intonations, of glances, and expressions, had been on the alert from the beginning of dinner, and was certain that there was some secret between her father and Anna Mihalovna, and that it had something to do with her brother, and that Anna Mihalovna was paving the way for it. Natasha knew how easily upset her mother was by any references to news from Nikolushka, and in spite of all her recklessness she did not venture at dinner to ask a question. But she was too much excited to eat any dinner and kept wriggling about on her chair, regardless of the protests of her governess. After dinner she rushed headlong to overtake Anna Mihalovna, and in the divan-room dashed at her and flung herself on her neck: "Auntie, darling, do tell me what it is."

"Nothing, my dear."

"No, darling, sweet, precious peach, I won't leave off; I know you know something."

Anna Mihalovna shook her head. "You are sharp, my child!" she said.

"A letter from Nikolinka? I'm sure of it!" cried Natasha, reading an affirmative answer on the face of Anna Mihalovna.

"But, for God's sake, be more careful; you know what a shock it may be to your mamma."

"I will be, I will, but tell me about it. You won't? Well, then, I'll run and tell her this minute."

Anna Mihalovna gave Natasha a brief account of what was in the letter, on condition that she would not tell a soul.

"On my word of honour," said Natasha, crossing herself, "I won't tell any one," and she ran at once to Sonya. "Nikolinka . . . wounded . . . a letter . . ." she proclaimed in gleeful triumph.

"Nikolinka!" was all Sonya could articulate, instantly turning white. Natasha seeing the effect of the news of her brother's wound on Sonya, for the first time felt the painful aspect of the news.

She rushed at Sonya, hugged her, and began to cry. "A little wounded, but promoted to be an officer; he's all right now, he writes himself," she said through her tears.

"One can see all you women are regular cry-babies," said Petya, striding with resolute steps up and down the room; "I'm very glad, really very glad, that my brother has distinguished himself so. You all start blubbering! you don't understand anything about it." Natasha smiled through her tears.

"You haven't read the letter?" asked Sonya.

"No; but she told me it was all over, and that he's an officer now . . ."

"Thank God," said Sonya, crossing herself. "But perhaps she was deceiving you. Let us go to mamma."

Petya had been strutting up and down in silence.

"If I were in Nikolinka's place, I'd have killed a lot more of those Frenchmen," he said, "they're such beasts! I'd have killed them till there was a regular heap of them." Petya went on.

"Hold your tongue, Petya, what a silly you are! . . ."

"I'm not a silly; people are silly who cry for trifles," said Petya.

"Do you remember him?" Natasha asked suddenly, after a moment's silence. Sonya smiled.

"Do I remember Nikolinka?"

"No, Sonya, but do you remember him so as to remember him thoroughly, to remember him quite," said Natasha with a strenuous gesture, as though she were trying to put into her words the most earnest meaning. "And I do remember Nikolinka, I remember him," she said. "But I don't remember Boris. I don't remember him a bit . . ."

"What? You don't remember Boris?" Sonya queried with surprise.

"I don't mean I don't remember him. I know what he's like, but not as I remember Nikolinka. I shut my eyes and I can see him, but not Boris" (she shut her eyes), "no, nothing!"

"Ah, Natasha!" said Sonya, looking solemnly and earnestly at her friend, as though she considered her unworthy to hear what she meant to say, and was saying it to some one else with whom joking was out of the question. "I have come to love your brother once for all, and whatever were to happen to him and to me, I could never cease to love him all my life."

With inquisitive, wondering eyes, Natasha gazed at Sonya, and she did not speak. She felt that what Sonya was saying was the truth, that there was love such as Sonya was speaking of. But Natasha had never known anything like it. She believed that it might be so, but she did not understand it.

"Shall you write to him?" she asked. Sonya sank into thought. How she should write to Nikolay, and whether she ought to write to him, was a question that worried her. Now that he was an officer, and a wounded hero, would it be nice on her part to remind him of herself, and as it were of the obligations he had taken on himself in regard to her. "I don't know. I suppose if he writes to me I shall write," she said, blushing.

"And you won't be ashamed to write to him?"

Sonya smiled.

"No."

"And I should be ashamed to write to Boris, and I'm not going to write."

"But why should you be ashamed?"

"Oh, I don't know. I feel awkward, ashamed."

"I know why she'd be ashamed," said Petya, offended at Natasha's previous remark, "because she fell in love with that fat fellow in spectacles" (this was how Petya used to describe his namesake, the new Count Bezuhov); "and now she's in love with that singing fellow" (Petya meant Natasha's Italian singing-master), "that's why she's ashamed."

"Petya, you're a stupid," said Natasha.

"No stupider than you, ma'am," said nine-year-old Petya, exactly as though he had been an elderly brigadier.

The countess had been prepared by Anna Mihalovna's hints during dinner. On returning to her room she had sat down in a low chair with her eyes fixed on the miniature of her son, painted on the lid of her snuff-box, and the tears started into her eyes. Anna Mihalovna, with the letter, approached the countess's room on tiptoe, and stood still at the door.

"Don't come in," she said to the old count, who was following her; "later," and she closed the door after her. The count put his ear to the keyhole, and listened.

At first he heard the sound of indifferent talk, then Anna Mihalovna's voice alone, uttering a long speech, then a shriek, then silence, then both voices talking at once with joyful intonations, then there were steps, and Anna Mihalovna opened the door. Her face wore the look of pride of an operator who has performed a difficult amputation, and invites the public in to appreciate his skill.

"It is done," she said to the count triumphantly, motioning him to the countess, who was holding in one hand the snuff-box with the portrait, in the other the letter, and pressing her lips first to one and then to the other. On seeing the count, she held out her arms to him, embraced his bald head, and looked again over the bald head at the letter and the portrait, and in order again to press them to her lips, slightly repelled the bald head from her. Vera, Natasha, Sonya, and Petya came into the room, and the reading of the letter began. The letter briefly described the march and the two battles in which Nikolushka had taken part, and the receiving of his commission, and said that he kissed the hands of his mamma and papa, begging their blessing, and sent kisses to Vera, Natasha, and Petya. He sent greetings, too, to Monsieur Schelling and Madame Schoss, and his old nurse, and begged them to kiss for him his darling Sonya, whom he still loved and thought of the same as ever. On hearing this, Sonya blushed till the tears came into her eyes. And unable to stand the eyes fixed upon her, she ran into the big hall, ran about with a flushed and smiling face, whirled round and round and ducked down, making her skirts into a balloon. The countess was crying.

"What are you crying about, mamma?" said Vera. "From all he writes, we ought to rejoice instead of crying."

This was perfectly true, but the count and the countess and Natasha all looked at her reproachfully. "And who is it that she takes after!" thought the countess.

Nikolushka's letter was read over hundreds of times, and those who were considered worthy of hearing it had to come in to the countess, who did not let it go out of her hands. The tutors went in, the nurses, Mitenka, and several acquaintances, and the countess read the letter every time with fresh enjoyment and every time she discovered from it new virtues in her Nikolushka. How strange, extraordinary, and joyful, it was to her to think that her son—the little son, whose tiny limbs had faintly stirred within her twenty years ago, for whose sake she had so often quarrelled with the count, who would spoil him, the little son, who had first learnt to say *grusha,* and then had learnt to say *baba*—that that son was now in a foreign land, in strange surroundings, a manly warrior, alone without help or guidance, doing there his proper manly work. All

the world-wide experience of ages, proving that children do imperceptibly from the cradle grow up into men, did not exist for the countess.
The growth of her son had been for her at every stage of his growth just
as extraordinary as though millions of millions of men had not grown up
in the same way. Just as, twenty years before, she could not believe that
the little creature that was lying somewhere under her heart, would one
day cry and suck her breast and learn to talk, now she could not believe
that the same little creature could be that strong, brave man, that para-
gon of sons and of men that, judging by this letter, he was now.

"What *style*, how charmingly he describes everything!" she said, reading over the descriptions in the letter. "And what soul! Of himself not a
word . . . not a word! A great deal about a man called Denisov, though
he was himself, I dare say, braver than any one. He doesn't write a word
about his sufferings. What a heart! How like him it is! How he thinks
of every one! No one forgotten. I always, always said, when he was no
more than that high, I always used to say . . ."

For over a week they were hard at work preparing a letter to Nikolushka from all the household, writing out rough copies, copying out fair
copies. With the watchful care of the countess, and the fussy solicitude
of the count, all sorts of necessary things were got together, and money,
too, for the equipment and the uniform of the young officer. Anna
Mihalovna, practical woman, had succeeded in obtaining special patronage for herself and her son in the army, that even extended to their correspondence. She had opportunities of sending her letters to the Grand
Duke Konstantin Pavlovitch, who was in command of the guards. The
Rostovs assumed that "The Russian Guards Abroad," was quite a sufficiently definite address, and that if a letter reached the grand duke in
command of the guards, there was no reason why it should not reach
the Pavlograd regiment, who were presumably somewhere in the same
vicinity. And so it was decided to send off their letters, and money by
the special messenger of the grand duke to Boris, and Boris would have
to forward them to Nikolushka. There were letters from the count, the
countess, Petya, Vera, Natasha, and Sonya, a sum of six thousand
roubles for his equipment, and various other things which the count was
sending to his son.

VII

On the 12th of November, Kutuzov's army, encamped near Olmütz, was
preparing to be reviewed on the following day by the two Emperors—
the Russian and the Austrian. The guards, who had only just arrived
from Russia, spent a night fifteen versts from Olmütz, and at ten o'clock
the next morning went straight to be reviewed in the Olmütz plain.

That day Nikolay Rostov had received a note from Boris informing
him that the Ismailovsky regiment was quartered for the night fifteen
versts from Olmütz, and that he wanted to see him to give him a letter
and some money. The money Rostov particularly needed just now, when

the troops after active service were stationed near Olmütz, and the camp swarmed with well-equipped canteen keepers and Austrian Jews, offering all kinds of attractions. The Pavlograd hussars had been keeping up a round of gaiety, fêtes in honour of the promotions received in the field, and excursions to Olmütz to a certain Caroline la Hongroise, who had recently opened a restaurant there with girls as waiters. Rostov had just been celebrating his commission as a cornet; he had bought Denisov's horse Bedouin, too, and was in debt all round to his comrades and the canteen keepers. On getting the note from Boris, Rostov rode into Olmütz with a comrade, dined there, drank a bottle of wine, and rode on alone to the guards' camp to find the companion of his childhood. Rostov had not yet got his uniform. He was wearing a shabby ensign's jacket with a private soldier's cross, equally shabby riding-trousers lined with worn leather, and an officer's sabre with a sword-knot. The horse he was riding was of the Don breed, bought of a Cossack on the march. A crushed hussars' cap was stuck jauntily back on one side of his head. As he rode up to the camp of the Ismailovsky regiment, he was thinking of how he would impress Boris and all his comrades in the guards by looking so thoroughly a hussar who has been under fire and roughed it at the front.

The guards had made their march as though it were a pleasure excursion, priding themselves on their smartness and discipline. They moved by short stages, their krapsacks were carried in the transport waggons, and at every halt the Austrian government provided the officers with excellent dinners. The regiments made their entry into towns and their exit from them with bands playing, and, according to the grand duke's order, the whole march had (a point on which the guards prided themselves) been performed by the soldiers in step, the officers too walking in their proper places. Boris had throughout the march walked and stayed with Berg, who was by this time a captain. Berg, who had received his company on the march, had succeeded in gaining the confidence of his superior officers by his conscientiousness and accuracy, and had established his financial position on a very satisfactory basis. Boris had during the same period made the acquaintance of many persons likely to be of use to him, and by means of a letter of recommendation brought from Pierre, had made the acquaintance of Prince Andrey Bolkonsky, through whom he had hopes of obtaining a post on the staff of the commander-in-chief. Berg and Boris, who had rested well after the previous day's march, were sitting smartly and neatly dressed, in the clean quarters assigned them, playing draughts at a round table. Berg was holding between his knees a smoking pipe. Boris, with his characteristic nicety, was building the draughts into a pyramid with his delicate, white fingers, while he waited for Berg to play. He was watching his partner's face, obviously thinking of the game, his attention concentrated, as it always was, on what he was engaged in.

"Well, how are you going to get out of that?" he said.

"I am going to try," answered Berg, touching the pieces, and taking his hand away again.

At that instant the door opened.

"Here he is at last!" shouted Rostov. "And Berg too. *Ah, petisanfan, alley cooshey dormir!*" he cried, repeating the saying of their old nurse's that had once been a joke with him and Boris.

"Goodness, how changed you are!" Boris got up to greet Rostov, but as he rose, he did not forget to hold the board, and to put back the falling pieces. He was about to embrace his friend, but Nikolay drew back from him. With that peculiarly youthful feeling of fearing beaten tracks, of wanting to avoid imitation, to express one's feelings in some new way of one's own, so as to escape the forms often conventionally used by one's elders, Nikolay wanted to do something striking on meeting his friend. He wanted somehow to give him a pinch, to give Berg a shove, anything rather than to kiss, as people always did on such occasions. Boris, on the contrary, embraced Rostov in a composed and friendly manner, and gave him three kisses.

It was almost six months since they had seen each other. And being at the stage when young men take their first steps along the path of life, each found immense changes in the other, quite new reflections of the different society in which they had taken those first steps. Both had changed greatly since they were last together, and both wanted to show as soon as possible what a change had taken place.

"Ah, you damned floor polishers! Smart and clean, as if you'd been enjoying yourselves; not like us poor devils at the front," said Rostov, with martial swagger, and with baritone notes in his voice that were new to Boris. He pointed to his mud-stained riding-breeches. The German woman of the house popped her head out of a door at Rostov's loud voice.

"A pretty woman, eh?" said he, winking.

"Why do you shout so? You are frightening them," said Boris. "I didn't expect you to-day," he added. "I only sent the note off to you yesterday—through an adjutant of Kutuzov's, who's a friend of mine—Bolkonsky. I didn't expect he would send it to you so quickly. Well, how are you? Been under fire already?" asked Boris.

Without answering, Rostov, in soldierly fashion, shook the cross of St. George that hung on the cording of his uniform, and pointing to his arm in a sling, he glanced at Berg.

"As you see," he said.

"To be sure, yes, yes," said Boris, smiling, "and we have had a capital march here too. You know his Highness kept all the while with our regiment, so that we had every convenience and advantage. In Poland, the receptions, the dinners, the balls!—I can't tell you. And the Tsare-vitch was very gracious to all our officers." And both the friends began describing; one, the gay revels of the hussars and life at the front; the other, the amenities and advantages of service under the command of royalty.

"Oh, you guards," said Rostov. "But, I say, send for some wine."

Boris frowned.

"If you really want some," he said. And he went to the bedstead, took a purse from under the clean pillows, and ordered some wine. "Oh, and I have a letter and money to give you," he added.

Rostov took the letter, and flinging the money on the sofa, put both his elbows on the table and began reading it. He read a few lines, and looked wrathfully at Berg. Meeting his eyes, Rostov hid his face with the letter.

"They sent you a decent lot of money, though," said Berg, looking at the heavy bag, that sank into the sofa. "But we manage to scrape along on our pay, count, I can tell you in my own case. . . ."

"I say, Berg, my dear fellow," said Rostov; "when you get a letter from home and meet one of your own people, whom you want to talk everything over with, and I'm on the scene, I'll clear out at once, so as not to be in your way. Do you hear, be off, please, anywhere, anywhere . . . to the devil!" he cried, and immediately seizing him by the shoulder, and looking affectionately into his face, evidently to soften the rudeness of his words, he added: "you know, you're not angry, my dear fellow, I speak straight from the heart to an old friend like you."

"Why, of course, count, I quite understand," said Berg, getting up and speaking in his deep voice.

"You might go and see the people of the house; they did invite you," added Boris.

Berg put on a spotless clean coat, brushed his lovelocks upwards before the looking-glass, in the fashion worn by the Tsar Alexander Pavlovitch, and having assured himself from Rostov's expression that his coat had been observed, he went out of the room with a bland smile.

"Ah, what a beast I am, though," said Rostov, as he read the letter. "Oh, why?"

"Ah, what a pig I've been, never once to have written and to have given them such a fright. Ah, what a pig I am!" he repeated, flushing all at once. "Well, did you send Gavrila for some wine? That's right, let's have some!" said he.

With the letters from his family there had been inserted a letter of recommendation to Prince Bagration, by Anna Mihalovna's advice, which Countess Rostov had obtained through acquaintances, and had sent to her son, begging him to take it to its address, and to make use of it.

"What nonsense! Much use to me," said Rostov, throwing the letter under the table.

"What did you throw that away for?" asked Boris.

"It's a letter of recommendation of some sort; what the devil do I want with a letter like that!"

"What the devil do you want with it?" said Boris, picking it up and reading the address; "that letter would be of great use to you."

"I'm not in want of anything, and I'm not going to be an adjutant to anybody."

"Why not?" asked Boris.

"A lackey's duty."

"You are just as much of an idealist as ever, I see," said Boris, shaking his head.

"And you're just as much of a diplomat. But that's not the point. . . . Come, how are you?" asked Rostov.

"Why, as you see. So far everything's gone well; but I'll own I should be very glad to get a post as adjutant, and not to stay in the line."

"What for?"

"Why, because if once one goes in for a military career, one ought to try to make it as successful a career as one can."

"Oh, that's it," said Rostov, unmistakably thinking of something else. He looked intently and inquiringly into his friend's eyes, apparently seeking earnestly the solution of some question.

Old Gavrila brought in the wine.

"Shouldn't we send for Alphonse Karlitch now?" said Boris. "He'll drink with you, but I can't."

"Send for him, send for him. Well, how do you get on with the Teuton?" said Rostov, with a contemptuous smile.

"He's a very, very nice, honest, and pleasant fellow," said Boris.

Rostov looked intently into Boris's face once more and he sighed. Berg came back, and over the bottle the conversation between the three officers became livelier. The guardsmen told Rostov about their march and how they had been fêted in Russia, in Poland, and abroad. They talked of the sayings and doings of their commander, the Grand Duke, and told anecdotes of his kind-heartedness and his irascibility. Berg was silent, as he always was, when the subject did not concern him personally, but à propos of the irascibility of the Grand Duke he related with gusto how he had had some words with the Grand Duke in Galicia, when his Highness had inspected the regiments and had flown into a rage over some irregularity in their movements. With a bland smile on his face he described how the Grand Duke had ridden up to him in a violent rage, shouting "Arnauts," ("Arnauts" was the Tsarevitch's favourite term of abuse when he was in a passion), and how he had asked for the captain. "Would you believe me, count, I wasn't in the least alarmed, because I knew I was right. Without boasting, you know, count, I may say I know all the regimental drill-book by heart, and the standing orders, too, I know as I know 'Our Father that art in Heaven.' And so that's how it is, count, there's never the slightest detail neglected in my company. So my conscience was at ease. I came forward." (Berg stood up and mimicked how he had come forward with his hand to the beak of his cap. It would certainly have been difficult to imagine more respectfulness and more self-complacency in a face.) "Well, he scolded, and scolded, and rated at me, and shouted his 'Arnauts,' and damns, and 'to Siberia,'" said Berg, with a subtle smile. "I knew I was right, and so I didn't speak; how could I, count? 'Why are you dumb?' he shouted. Still I held my tongue, and what do you think, count? Next day there was nothing about it in the orders of the day; that's what comes of keeping one's head. Yes, indeed, count," said Berg, pulling at his pipe and letting off rings of smoke.

"Yes, that's capital," said Rostov, smiling; but Boris, seeing that Rostov was disposed to make fun of Berg, skilfully turned the conversation. He begged Rostov to tell them how and where he had been wounded. That pleased Rostov, and he began telling them, getting more and more eager as he talked. He described to them his battle at Schöngraben exactly as men who have taken part in battles always do describe them, that is, as they would have liked them to be, as they have heard them described by others, and as sounds well, but not in the least as it really had been. Rostov was a truthful young man; he would not have intentionally told a lie. He began with the intention of telling everything precisely as it had happened, but imperceptibly, unconsciously, and inevitably he passed into falsehood. If he had told the truth to his listeners, who, like himself, had heard numerous descriptions of cavalry charges, and had formed a definite idea of what a charge was like and were expecting a similar description, either they would not have believed him, or worse still, would have assumed that Rostov was himself to blame for not having performed the exploits usually performed by those who describe cavalry charges. He could not tell them simply that they had all been charging full gallop, that he had fallen off his horse, sprained his arm, and run with all his might away from the French into the copse. And besides, to tell everything exactly as it happened, he would have had to exercise considerable self-control in order to tell nothing beyond what happened. To tell the truth is a very difficult thing; and young people are rarely capable of it. His listeners expected to hear how he had been all on fire with excitement, had forgotten himself, had flown like a tempest on the enemy's square, had cut his way into it, hewing men down right and left, how a sabre had been thrust into his flesh, how he had fallen unconscious, and so on. And he described all that. In the middle of his tale, just as he was saying: "You can't fancy what a strange frenzy takes possession of one at the moment of the charge," there walked into the room Prince Andrey Bolkonsky, whom Boris was expecting. Prince Andrey liked to encourage and assist younger men, he was flattered at being applied to for his influence, and well disposed to Boris, who had succeeded in making a favourable impression on him the previous day; he was eager to do for the young man what he desired. Having been sent with papers from Kutuzov to the Tsarevitch, he called upon Boris, hoping to find him alone. When he came into the room and saw the hussar with his soldierly swagger describing his warlike exploits (Prince Andrey could not endure the kind of men who are fond of doing so), he smiled cordially to Boris, but frowned and dropped his eyelids as he turned to Rostov with a slight bow. Wearily and languidly he sat down on the sofa, regretting that he had dropped into such undesirable society. Rostov, perceiving it, grew hot, but he did not care; this man was nothing to him. Glancing at Boris, he saw, however, that he too seemed ashamed of the valiant hussar. In spite of Prince Andrey's unpleasant, ironical manner, in spite of the disdain with which Rostov, from his point of view of a fighting man in the regular army, regarded the whole race of staff-adjutants in general—the class to which the new-comer unmistakably belonged—he yet felt abashed, reddened, and subsided into silence. Boris inquired what news there was on the staff and whether he could not without indiscretion tell them something about our plans.

"Most likely they will advance," answered Bolkonsky, obviously unwilling to say more before outsiders. Berg seized the opportunity to inquire with peculiar deference whether the report was true, as he had heard, that the allowance of forage to captains of companies was to be doubled. To this Prince Andrey replied with a smile that he could not presume to offer an opinion on state questions of such gravity, and Berg laughed with delight.

"As to your business," Prince Andrey turned back to Boris, "we will talk of it later," and he glanced at Rostov. "You come to me after the review, and we'll do what we can." And looking round the room he addressed Rostov, whose childish, uncontrollable embarrassment, passing now into anger, he did not think fit to notice: "You were talking, I think, about the Schöngraben action? Were you there?"

"I was there," Rostov said in a tone of exasperation, which he seemed to intend as an insult to the adjutant. Bolkonsky noticed the hussar's state of mind, and it seemed to amuse him. He smiled rather disdainfully.

"Ah! there are a great many stories now about that engagement."

"Yes, stories!" said Rostov loudly, looking from Boris to Bolkonsky with eyes full of sudden fury, "a great many stories, I dare say, but our stories are the stories of men who have been under the enemy's fire, our stories have some weight, they're not the tales of little staff upstarts, who draw pay for doing nothing."

"The class to which you assume me to belong," said Prince Andrey, with a calm and particularly amiable smile.

A strange feeling of exasperation was mingled in Rostov's heart with respect for the self-possession of this person.

"I'm not talking about you," he said; "I don't know you, and, I'll own, I don't want to. I'm speaking of staff-officers in general."

"Let me tell you this," Prince Andrey cut him short in a tone of quiet authority, "you are trying to insult me, and I'm ready to agree with you that it is very easy to do so, if you haven't sufficient respect for yourself. But you will agree that the time and place is ill-chosen for this squabble. In a day or two we have to take part in a great and more serious duel, and besides, Drubetskoy, who tells me he is an old friend of yours, is in no way to blame because my physiognomy is so unfortunate as to displease you. However," he said, getting up, "you know my name, and know where to find me; but don't forget," he added, "that I don't consider either myself or you insulted, and my advice, as a man older than you, is to let the matter drop. So on Friday, after the review, I shall "expect you, Drubetskoy; good-bye till then," cried Prince Andrey, and he went out, bowing to both.

Rostov only bethought him of what he ought to have answered when he had gone. And he was more furious still that he had not thought of saying it. He ordered his horse to be brought round at once, and taking leave of Boris coldly, he rode back. Whether to ride to-morrow to headquarters and challenge that conceited adjutant, or whether really to let the matter drop, was the question that worried him all the way. At one moment he thought vindictively how he would enjoy seeing the fright that feeble, little, conceited fellow would be in, facing his pistol, at the next he was feeling with surprise that, of all the men he knew, there was no one he would be more glad to have for his friend than that detested little adjutant.

VIII

The day after Rostov's visit to Boris, the review took place of the Austrian and Russian troops, both the reinforcements freshly arrived from Russia and the troops that had been campaigning with Kutuzov. Both Emperors, the Russian Emperor with the Tsarevitch, and the Austrian with the archduke, were to assist at this review of the allied forces, making up together an army of eighty thousand men. From early morning the troops, all smart and clean, had been moving about the plain before the fortress. Thousands of legs and bayonets moved with flags waving, and halted at the word of command, turned and formed at regular intervals, moving round other similar masses of infantry in different uniforms. With the rhythmic tramp of hoofs, the smartly dressed cavalry in blue, and red, and green laced uniforms rode jingling by on black and chestnut and grey horses, the bandsmen in front covered with embroidery. Between the infantry and the cavalry the artillery, in a long line of polished, shining cannons quivering on their carriages, crawled slowly by with their heavy, brazen sound, and their peculiar smell from the linstocks, and ranged themselves in their places. Not only the generals in their full parade uniform, wearing scarves and all their decorations, with waists, portly and slim alike, pinched in to the uttermost, and red necks squeezed into stiff collars, not only the pomaded, dandified officers, but every soldier, with his clean, washed, and shaven face, and weapons polished to the utmost possibility of glitter, every horse rubbed down till its coat shone like satin, and every hair in its moistened mane lay in place—all alike felt it no joking matter, felt that something grave and solemn was going forward. Every general and every soldier was conscious of his own significance, feeling himself but a grain of sand in that ocean of humanity, and at the same time was conscious of his might, feeling himself a part of that vast whole. There had been strenuous exertion and bustle since early morning, and by ten o'clock everything was in the required order. The rows of soldiers were

standing on the immense plain. The whole army was drawn out in three
lines. In front was the cavalry; behind, the artillery; still further back,
the infantry.

Between each two ranks of soldiery there was as it were a street. The
army was sharply divided into three parts: Kutuzov's army (on the
right flank of which stood the Pavlograd hussars in the front line), the
regiments of the line and the guards that had arrived from Russia, and
the Austrian troops. But all stood in one line, under one command, and
in similar order.

Like a wind passing over the leaves, the excited whisper fluttered over
the plain: "They are coming! they are coming!" There was a sound of
frightened voices, and the hurried men's fuss over the last finishing
touches ran like a wave over the troops.

A group came into sight moving towards them from Olmütz in front
of them. And at the same moment, though there had been no wind, a
faint breeze fluttered over the army, and stirred the streamers on the
lances, and sent the unfurled flags flapping against their flag-staffs. It
looked as though in this slight movement the army itself were expressing
its joy at the approach of the Emperors. One voice was heard saying:
"Steady!" Then like cocks at sunrise, voices caught up and repeated the
sound in different parts of the plain. And all sank into silence.

In the deathlike stillness, the only sound was the tramp of hoofs. It
was the Emperors' suite. The Emperors rode towards the flank, and the
trumpets of the first cavalry regiment began playing a march. It seemed
as though the sound did not come from the trumpeters, but that the
army itself was naturally giving forth this music in its delight at the
Emperors' approach. Through the music could be distinctly heard one
voice, the genial, youthful voice of the Emperor Alexander. He uttered
some words of greeting, and the first regiment boomed out: "Hurrah!"
with a shout so deafening, so prolonged, so joyful, that the men themselves felt awestruck at the multitude and force of the mass they made
up.

Rostov, standing in the foremost ranks of Kutuzov's army, which the
Tsar approached first of all, was possessed by the feeling, common to
every man in that army—a feeling of self-oblivion, of proud consciousness of their might and passionate devotion to the man who was the
centre of that solemn ceremony.

He felt that at one word from that man all that vast mass (and he, an
insignificant atom bound up with it) would rush through fire and water,
to crime, to death, or to the grandest heroism, and so he could not but
thrill and tremble at the sight of the man who was the embodiment of
that word.

"Hurrah! hurrah! hurrah!" thundered on all sides, and one regiment
after another greeted the Tsar with the strains of the march, then hurrah! . . . then the march, and again hurrah! and hurrah! which growing stronger and fuller, blended into a deafening roar.

Before the Tsar had reached it, each regiment in its speechless immobility seemed like a lifeless body. But as soon as the Tsar was on

a level with it, each regiment broke into life and noise, which joined with the roar of all the line, by which the Tsar had passed already. In the terrific, deafening uproar of those voices, between the square masses of troops, immobile as though turned to stone, moved carelessly, but symmetrically and freely, some hundreds of men on horseback, the suite, and in front of them two figures—the Emperors. Upon these was entirely concentrated the repressed, passionate attention of all that mass of men.

The handsome, youthful Emperor Alexander, in the uniform of the Horse Guards, in a triangular hat with the base in front, attracted the greater share of attention with his pleasant face and sonorous, low voice.

Rostov was standing near the trumpeters, and with his keen eyes he recognised the Tsar from a distance and watched him approaching. When the Tsar was only twenty paces away, and Nikolay saw clearly in every detail the handsome, young, and happy face of the Emperor, he experienced a feeling of tenderness and ecstasy such as he had never known before. Everything in the Tsar—every feature, every movement —seemed to him full of charm.

Halting before the Pavlograd regiment, the Tsar said something in French to the Austrian Emperor and smiled.

Seeing that smile, Rostov unconsciously began to smile himself and felt an even stronger rush of love for his Emperor. He longed to express his love for the Tsar in some way. He knew it was impossible, and he wanted to cry. The Tsar called up the colonel of the regiment and said a few words to him.

"By God! what would happen to me if the Emperor were to address me!" thought Rostov; "I should die of happiness."

The Tsar addressed the officers, too.

"All of you, gentlemen" (every word sounded to Rostov like heavenly music), "I thank you with all my heart."

How happy Rostov would have been if he could have died on the spot for his Emperor.

"You have won the flags of St. George and will be worthy of them."

"Only to die, to die for him!" thought Rostov.

The Tsar said something more which Rostov did not catch, and the soldiers, straining their lungs, roared "hurrah!"

Rostov, too, bending over in his saddle, shouted with all his might, feeling he would like to do himself some injury by this shout, if only he could give full expression to his enthusiasm for the Tsar.

The Tsar stood for several seconds facing the hussars, as though he were hesitating.

"How could the Emperor hesitate?" Rostov wondered; but then, even that hesitation seemed to him majestic and enchanting, like all the Tsar did.

The Tsar's hesitation lasted only an instant. The Tsar's foot, in the narrow-pointed boot of the day, touched the belly of the bay English thoroughbred he was riding. The Tsar's hand in its white glove gathered up the reins and he moved off, accompanied by the irregularly heaving sea of adjutants. Further and further he rode away, stopping at the other regiments, and at last the white plume of his hat was all that Rostov could see above the suite that encircled the Emperors.

Among the gentlemen of the suite, Rostov noticed Bolkonsky, sitting his horse in a slack, indolent pose. Rostov remembered his quarrel with him on the previous day and his doubt whether he ought or ought not to challenge him. "Of course, I ought not," Rostov reflected now. . . . "And is it worth thinking and speaking of it at such a moment as the present? At the moment of such a feeling of love, enthusiasm, and self-sacrifice, what are all our slights and squabbles? I love every one, I forgive every one at this moment," thought Rostov.

When the Tsar had made the round of almost all the regiments, the troops began to file by him in a parade march, and Rostov on Bedouin, which he had lately bought from Denisov, was the officer at the rear, that is, had to pass last, alone, and directly in view of the Tsar.

Before he reached the Tsar, Rostov, who was a capital horseman, set spurs twice to his Bedouin, and succeeded in forcing him into that frantic form of gallop into which Bedouin always dropped when he was excited. Bending his foaming nose to his chest, arching his tail, and seeming to skim through the air without touching the earth, Bedouin, as though he, too, were conscious of the Tsar's eye upon him, flew by in superb style, with a graceful high action of his legs.

Rostov himself drew back his legs and drew in his stomach, and feeling himself all of a piece with his horse, rode by the Tsar with a frowning but blissful face, looking a regular devil, as Denisov used to say.

"Bravo, Pavlograds!" said the Tsar.

"My God! shouldn't I be happy if he bade me fling myself into fire this instant," thought Rostov.

When the review was over, the officers, both of the reinforcements and of Kutuzov's army, began to gather together in groups. Conversations sprang up about the honours that had been conferred, about the Austrians and their uniforms, and their front line, about Bonaparte and the bad time in store for him now, especially when Essen's corps, too, should arrive, and Prussia should take our side. But the chief subject of conversation in every circle was the Emperor Alexander; every word he had uttered, every gesture was described and expatiated upon with enthusiasm.

There was but one desire in all: under the Emperor's leadership to face the enemy as soon as possible. Under the command of the Emperor himself they would not fail to conquer any one whatever: so thought Rostov and most of the officers after the review.

After the review they all felt more certain of victory than they could have been after two decisive victories.

IX

THE day after the review Boris Drubetskoy put on his best uniform, and accompanied by his comrade Berg's good wishes for his success, rode to Olmütz to see Bolkonsky, in the hope of profiting by his friendliness to obtain a better position, especially the position of an adjutant in attendance on some personage of importance, a post which seemed to him particularly alluring.

"It's all very well for Rostov, whose father sends him ten thousand at a time, to talk about not caring to cringe to any one, and not being a lackey to any man. But I, with nothing of my own but my brains, have my career to make, and mustn't let opportunities slip, but must make the most of them."

He did not find Prince Andrey at Olmütz that day. But the sight of Olmütz—where were the headquarters and the diplomatic corps, and where both Emperors with their suites, their households, and their court, were staying—only strengthened his desire to belong to this upper world.

He knew no one; and in spite of his smart guardsman's uniform, all these exalted persons, racing to and fro about the streets in their elegant carriages, plumes, ribbons, and orders, courtiers and military alike, all seemed to be so immeasurably above him, a little officer in the Guards, as to be not simply unwilling, but positively unable to recognise his existence. At the quarters of the commander-in-chief, Kutuzov, where he asked for Bolkonsky, all the adjutants and even the orderlies looked at him as though they wished to impress on him that a great many officers of his sort came hanging about here, and that they were all heartily sick of seeing them. In spite of this, or rather in consequence of it, he went again the following day, the 15th, after dinner, to Olmütz, and going into the house occupied by Kutuzov, asked for Bolkonsky. Prince Andrey was at home, and Boris was ushered into a large room, probably at some time used for dancing. Now there were five bedsteads in it and furniture of various kinds: a table, chairs, a clavichord. One adjutant was sitting in a Persian dressing-gown writing at a table near the door. Another, the stout, red-faced Nesvitsky, was lying on a bed, his arms under his head, laughing with an officer sitting by the bedside. A third was playing a Vienna waltz on the clavichord, while a fourth lay on the clavichord, humming to the tune. Bolkonsky was not in the room. Not one of these gentlemen changed his position on observing Boris. The one who was writing, on being applied to by Boris, turned round with an air of annoyance, and told him that Bolkonsky was the adjutant on duty, and that he should go to the door to the left, into the reception-room, if he wanted to see him. Boris thanked him, and went to the reception-room. There he found some ten officers and generals.

At the moment when Boris entered, Prince Andrey dropping his eye-lids disdainfully (with that peculiar air of courteous weariness which so distinctly says, "If it were not my duty, I would not stay talking to you for a minute"), was listening to an old Russian general with many decorations, who, rigidly erect, almost on tiptoe, was laying some matter before Prince Andrey with the obsequious expression of a common soldier on his purple face.

"Very good, be so kind as to wait a moment," he said to the general in Russian, with that French accent with which he always spoke when he meant to speak disdainfully, and noticing Boris, Prince Andrey took no further notice of the general (who ran after him with entreaties, begging him to hear something more), but nodded to Boris with a bright smile, as he turned towards him. At that moment Boris saw distinctly what he had had an inkling of before, that is, that quite apart from that subordination and discipline, which is written down in the drill-book, and recognised in the regiment and known to him, there was in the army another and more actual subordination, that which made this rigid, purple-faced general wait respectfully while Prince Andrey—of captain's rank— found it more in accordance with his pleasure to talk to Lieutenant Drubetskoy. Boris felt more than ever determined to follow in future the guidance not of the written code laid down in the regulations, but of this unwritten code. He felt now that simply because he had been recommended to Prince Andrey, he had become at one step superior to the general, who in other circumstances, at the front, could annihilate a mere lieutenant in the guards like him. Prince Andrey went up to him and shook hands.

"Very sorry you didn't find me in yesterday. I was busy the whole day with the Germans. We went with Weierother to survey the disposition. When Germans start being accurate, there's no end to it!"

Boris smiled, as though he understood, as a matter of common knowledge, what Prince Andrey was referring to. But it was the first time he had heard the name of Weierother, or even the word "disposition" used in that sense.

"Well, my dear boy, you still want an adjutant's post? I have been thinking about you since I saw you."

"Yes," said Boris, involuntarily flushing for some reason, "I was thinking of asking the commander-in-chief; he has had a letter about me from Prince Kuragin; and I wanted to ask him simply because," he added, as though excusing himself, "I am afraid the guards won't be in action."

"Very good, very good! we will talk it over later," said Prince Andrey, "only let me report on this gentleman's business and I am at your disposal." While Prince Andrey was away reporting to the commander-in-chief on the business of the purple-faced general, that general, who apparently did not share Boris's views as to the superior advantages of the unwritten code, glared at the insolent lieutenant, who had hindered his having his say out, so that Boris began to be uncomfortable. He turned away and waited with impatience for Prince Andrey to come out of the commander-in-chief's room.

"Well, my dear fellow, I have been thinking about you," said Prince Andrey, when they had gone into the big room with the clavichord in it.

"It's no use your going to the commander-in-chief; he will say a lot of polite things to you, will ask you to dine with him" ("that wouldn't come amiss in the service of that unwritten code," thought Boris), "but nothing more would come of it; we shall soon have a complete battalion of adjutants and orderly officers. But I tell you what we will do: I have a friend, a general adjutant and an excellent fellow, Prince Dolgorukov. And though you may not be aware of it, the fact is that Kutuzov and his staff and all of us are just now of no account at all. Everything now is concentrated about the Emperor, so we'll go together to Dolgorukov. I have to go to see him, and I have already spoken of you to him. So we can see whether he may not think it possible to find a post for you on his staff, or somewhere there nearer to the sun."

Prince Andrey was always particularly keen over guiding a young man and helping him to attain worldly success. Under cover of this help for another, which he would never have accepted for himself, he was brought into the circle which bestowed success, and which attracted him. He very readily took up Boris's cause, and went with him to Prince Dolgorukov.

It was late in the evening as they entered the palace at Olmütz, occupied by the Emperors and their retinues.

There had been on that same day a council of war, at which all the members of the Hofkriegsrath and the two Emperors had been present. At the council it had been decided, contrary to the advice of the elder generals, Kutuzov and Prince Schwarzenberg, to advance at once and to fight a general engagement with Bonaparte. The council of war was only just over when Prince Andrey, accompanied by Boris, went into the palace in search of Prince Dolgorukov. Every one at headquarters was still under the spell of the victory gained that day by the younger party at the council of war. The voices of those who urged delay, and counselled waiting for something and not advancing, had been so unanimously drowned and their arguments had been confuted by such indubitable proofs of the advantages of advancing, that what had been discussed at the council, the future battle and the victory certain to follow it, seemed no longer future but past. All the advantages were on our side. Our immense forces, undoubtedly superior to those of Napoleon, were concentrated in one place; the troops were encouraged by the presence of the two Emperors, and were eager for battle. The strategic position on which they were to act was to the minutest detail known to the Austrian general Weierother, who was at the head of the troops (as a lucky chance would have it, the Austrian troops had chosen for their manœuvres the very fields in which they had now to fight the French). Every detail of the surrounding neighbourhood was known and put down on maps, while Bonaparte, apparently growing feebler, was taking no measures.

Dolgorukov, who had been one of the warmest advocates of attack, had just come back from the council, weary, exhausted, but eager and proud of the victory he had gained. Prince Andrey presented the officer for whom he was asking his influence, but Prince Dolgorukov, though he shook hands politely and warmly, said nothing to Boris. Obviously unable to restrain himself from uttering the thoughts which were engrossing him at that moment, he addressed Prince Andrey in French.

"Well, my dear fellow, what a battle we have won! God only grant that the one which will be the result of it may be as victorious. I must own, though, my dear fellow," he said jerkily and eagerly, "my shortcomings compared with the Austrians and especially Weierother. What accuracy, what minuteness, what knowledge of the locality, what foresight of every possibility, every condition, of every minutest detail! No, my dear boy, anything more propitious than the circumstance we are placed in could not have been found, if one had arranged it purposely. The union of Austrian exactitude with Russian valour—what could you wish for more?"

"So an attack has been finally decided upon?" said Bolkonsky.

"And do you know, I fancy, Bonaparte really has lost his head. You know that a letter came from him to-day to the Emperor." Dolgorukov smiled significantly.

"You don't say so! What does he write?" asked Bolkonsky.

"What can he write? Tradi-ri-di-ra—all simply to gain time. I tell you he's in our hands; that's the fact! But the most amusing part of it all," he said, breaking all at once into a good-natured laugh, "is that they couldn't think how to address an answer to him. If not 'consul,' and of course not 'emperor,' it should be 'general' Bonaparte, it seemed to me."

"But between not recognising him as emperor and calling him General Bonaparte, there's a difference," said Bolkonsky.

"That's just the point," Dolgorukov interrupted quickly, laughing. "You know Bilibin, he's a very clever fellow; he suggested addressing it, 'To the Usurper and Enemy of the Human Race,' " Dolgorukov chuckled merrily.

"And nothing more?" observed Bolkonsky.

"But still it was Bilibin who found the suitable form of address in earnest. He's both shrewd and witty . . ."

"How was it?"

"To the Chief of the French Government: *au chef du gouvernement français*," Dolgorukov said seriously and with satisfaction. "That was the right thing, wasn't it?"

"It was all right, but he will dislike it extremely," observed Bolkonsky.

"Oh, extremely! My brother knows him; he's dined more than once with him—nowadays the emperor—in Paris, and used to tell me that he'd never seen a subtler and more crafty diplomat; you know, a combination of French adroitness and the Italian actor-faculty! You know the anecdote about Bonaparte and Count Markov? Count Markov was the only person who knew how to treat him. You know the story of the handkerchief? It's a gem!" And the talkative Dolgorukov turning from Boris to Prince Andrey told the story of how Bonaparte, to test Markov, our ambassador, had purposely dropped his handkerchief before him, and had stood looking at him, probably expecting Markov to pick it up for him, and how Markov promptly dropped his own beside it, and had picked up his own without touching Bonaparte's.

"Capital," said Bolkonsky. "But, prince, I have come to you as a petitioner in behalf of this young friend. You see . . ." But before Prince Andrey could finish, an adjutant came into the room to summon Prince Dolgorukov to the Emperor.

"Ah, how annoying!" said Dolgorukov, getting up hurriedly and shaking hands with Prince Andrey and Boris. "You know I shall be very glad to do all that depends on me both for you and for this charming young man." Once more he shook hands with Boris with an expression of good-natured, genuine, heedless gaiety. "But you see . . . another time!"

Boris was excited by the thought of being so close to the higher powers, as he felt himself to be at that instant. He was conscious here of being in contact with the springs that controlled all those vast movements of the masses, of which in his regiment he felt himself a tiny, humble, and insignificant part. They followed Prince Dolgorukov out into the corridor and met (coming out of the door of the Tsar's room at which Dolgorukov went in) a short man in civilian dress with a shrewd face and a sharply projecting lower jaw, which, without spoiling his face, gave him a peculiar alertness and shiftiness of expression. This short man nodded to Dolgorukov, as if he were an intimate friend, and stared with an intently cold gaze at Prince Andrey, walking straight towards him and apparently expecting him to bow or move out of his way. Prince Andrey did neither; there was a vindictive look on his face, and the short young man turned away and walked at the side of the corridor.

"Who's that?" asked Boris.

"That's one of the most remarkable men—and the most unpleasant to me. The minister of foreign affairs, Prince Adam Tchartorizhsky."

"Those are the men," added Bolkonsky with a sigh which he could not suppress, as they went out of the palace, "those are the men who decide the fates of nations."

Next day the troops set off on the march, and up to the time of the battle of Austerlitz, Boris did not succeed in seeing Bolkonsky or Dolgorukov again, and remained for a while in the Ismailov regiment.

X

At dawn on the 16th, Denisov's squadron, in which Nikolay Rostov was serving, and which formed part of Prince Bagration's detachment, moved on from its halting place for the night—to advance into action, as was said. After about a mile's march, in the rear of other columns, it was brought to a standstill on the high-road. Rostov saw the Cossacks, the first and second squadrons of hussars, and the infantry battalions with the artillery pass him and march on ahead; he also saw the Generals Bagration and Dolgorukov ride by with their adjutants. All the panic he had felt, as before, at the prospect of battle, all the inner conflict by means of which he had overcome that panic, all his dreams of distinguishing himself in true hussar style in this battle—all were for nothing. His squadron was held back in reserve, and Nikolay Rostov spent a tedious and wretched day. About nine o'clock in the morning he heard firing ahead of him, and shouts of hurrah, saw the wounded being brought back (there were not many of them), and finally saw a whole detachment of French cavalry being brought away in the midst of a company of Cossacks. Obviously the action was over, and the action had, obviously, been a small one, but successful. The soldiers and officers as they came back were talking of a brilliant victory, of the taking of the town of Vishau, and a whole French squadron taken prisoners. The day was bright and sunny after a sharp frost at night, and the cheerful brightness of the autumn day was in keeping with the news of victory, which was told not only by the accounts of those who had taken part in it, but by the joyful expression of soldiers, officers, generals, and adjutants, who rode to and fro by Rostov. All the greater was the pang in Nikolay's heart that he should have suffered the dread that goes before the battle for nothing, and have spent that happy day in inactivity.

"Rostov, come here, let's drink 'begone, dull care!' " shouted Denisov, sitting at the roadside before a bottle and some edibles. The officers gathered in a ring, eating and talking, round Denisov's wine-case.

"Here they're bringing another!" said one of the officers, pointing to a French prisoner, a dragoon, who was being led on foot by two Cossacks. One of them was leading by the bridle the prisoner's horse, a tall and beautiful French beast.

"Sell the horse?" Denisov called to the Cossacks.

"If you will, your honour."

The officers got up and stood round the Cossacks and the prisoner. The French dragoon was a young fellow, an Alsatian who spoke French with a German accent. He was breathless with excitement, his face was red, and hearing French spoken he began quickly speaking to the officers, turning from one to another. He said that they wouldn't have taken him, that it wasn't his fault he was taken, but the fault of the corporal, who had sent him to get the horsecloths, that he had told him the Russians were there. And at every word he added: "But don't let anybody hurt my little horse," and stroked his horse. It was evident that he did not quite grasp where he was. At one moment he was excusing himself for having been taken prisoner, at the next, imagining himself before his superior officers, he was trying to prove his soldierly discipline and zeal for the service. He brought with him in all its freshness into our rearguard the atmosphere of the French army, so alien to us.

The Cossacks sold the horse for two gold pieces, and Rostov, being the richest of the officers since he had received money from home, bought it.

"Be good to the little horse!" the Alsatian said with simple-hearted good-nature to Rostov, when the horse was handed to the hussar.

Rostov smiling, soothed the dragoon, and gave him money.

"Alley. Alley," said the Cossack, touching the prisoner's arm to make him go on.

"The Emperor! the Emperor!" was suddenly heard among the hussars. Everything was bustle and hurry, and Rostov saw behind them on the road several horsemen riding up with white plumes in their hats. In a single moment all were in their places and eagerly expectant.

Rostov had no memory and no consciousness of how he ran to his post and got on his horse. Instantly his regret at not taking part in the battle, his humdrum mood among the men he saw every day—all was gone; instantly all thought of self had vanished. He was entirely absorbed in the feeling of happiness at the Tsar's being near. His nearness alone made up to him by itself, he felt, for the loss of the whole day. He was happy, as a lover is happy when the moment of the longed-for meeting has come. Not daring to look round from the front line, by an ecstatic instinct without looking round, he felt his approach. And he felt it not only from the sound of the tramping hoofs of the approaching cavalcade, he felt it because as the Tsar came nearer everything grew brighter, more joyful and significant, and more festive. Nearer and nearer moved this sun, as he seemed to Rostov, shedding around him rays of mild and majestic light, and now he felt himself enfolded in that radiance, he heard his voice—that voice caressing, calm, majestic, and yet so simple. A deathlike silence had come—as seemed to Rostov fitting —and in that silence he heard the sound of the Tsar's voice.

"The Pavlograd hussars?" he was saying interrogatively.

"The reserve, sire," replied a voice—such a human voice, after the superhuman voice that had said: *"Les hussards de Pavlograd?"*

The Tsar was on a level with Rostov, and he stood still there. Alexander's face was even handsomer than it had been at the review three days before. It beamed with such gaiety and youth, such innocent youthfulness, that suggested the playfulness of a boy of fourteen, and yet it was still the face of the majestic Emperor. Glancing casually along the squadron, the Tsar's eyes met the eyes of Rostov, and for not more than two seconds rested on them. Whether it was that the Tsar saw what was passing in Rostov's soul (it seemed to Rostov that he saw everything), any way he looked for two seconds with his blue eyes into Rostov's face. (A soft, mild radiance beamed from them.) Then all at once he raised his eyebrows, struck his left foot sharply against his horse, and galloped on.

The young Emperor could not restrain his desire to be present at the battle, and in spite of the expostulations of his courtiers, at twelve o'clock, escaping from the third column which he had been following, he galloped to the vanguard. Before he reached the hussars, several adjutants met him with news of the successful issue of the engagement.

The action, which had simply consisted in the capture of a squadron of the French, was magnified into a brilliant victory over the enemy, and so the Tsar and the whole army believed, especially while the smoke still hung over the field of battle, that the French had been defeated, and had been forced to retreat against their will. A few minutes after the Tsar had galloped on, the division of the Pavlograd hussars received orders to move forward. In Vishau itself, a little German town, Rostov saw the Tsar once more. In the market-place of the town where there had been rather a heavy firing before the Tsar's arrival, lay several dead and wounded soldiers, whom there had not been time to pick up. The Tsar, surrounded by his suite of officers and courtiers, was mounted on a different horse from the one he had ridden at the review, a chestnut English thoroughbred. Bending on one side with a graceful gesture, holding a gold field-glass to his eyes, he was looking at a soldier lying on his face with a blood-stained and uncovered head. The wounded soldier was an object so impure, so grim, and so revolting, that Rostov was shocked at his being near the Emperor. Rostov saw how the Tsar's stooping shoulders shuddered, as though a cold shiver had passed over them, how his left foot convulsively pressed the spur into the horse's side, and how the trained horse looked round indifferently and did not stir. An adjutant dismounting lifted the soldier up under his arms, and began laying him on a stretcher that came up. The soldier groaned.

"Gently, gently, can't you do it more gently?" said the Tsar, apparently suffering more than the dying soldier, and he rode away.

Rostov saw the tears in the Tsar's eyes, and heard him say in French to Tchartorizhsky, as he rode off: "What an awful thing war is, what an awful thing!"

The forces of the vanguard were posted before Vishau in sight of the enemy's line, which had been all day retreating before us at the slightest exchange of shots. The Tsar's thanks were conveyed to the vanguard, rewards were promised, and a double allowance of vodka was served out to the men. Even more gaily than on the previous night the bivouac fires crackled, and the soldiers sang their songs. Denisov on that night celebrated his promotion to major, and, towards the end of the carousal, after a good deal of drinking, Rostov proposed a toast to the health of the Emperor, but "not our Sovereign the Emperor, as they say at official dinners," said he, "but to the health of the Emperor, the good, enchanting, great man, let us drink to his health, and to a decisive victory over the French!"

"If we fought before," said he, "and would not yield an inch before the French, as at Schöngraben, what will it be now when he is at our head? We will all die, we will gladly die for him. Eh, gentlemen? Perhaps I'm not saying it right. I've drunk a good deal, but that's how I feel, and you do too. To the health of Alexander the First! Hurrah!"

"Hurrah!" rang out the cheery voices of the officers. And the old captain Kirsten shouted no less heartily and sincerely than Rostov, the boy of twenty.

When the officers had drunk the toast and smashed their glasses, Kirsten filled some fresh ones, and in his shirt-sleeves and riding-breeches went out to the soldiers' camp-fires, glass in hand, and waving his hand in the air stood in a majestic pose, with his long grey whiskers and his white chest visible through the open shirt in the light of the camp-fire.

"Lads, to the health of our Sovereign the Emperor, to victory over our enemies, hurrah!" he roared in his stalwart old soldier's baritone. The hussars thronged about him and responded by a loud shout in unison.

Late at night, when they had all separated, Denisov clapped his short hand on the shoulder of his favourite Rostov. "To be sure he'd no one to fall in love with in the field, so he's fallen in love with the Tsar," he said.

"Denisov, don't joke about that," cried Rostov, "it's such a lofty, such a sublime feeling, so . . ."

"I believe you, I believe you, my dear, and I share the feeling and approve . . ."

"No, you don't understand!" And Rostov got up and went out to wander about among the camp-fires, dreaming of what happiness it would be to die—not saving the Emperor's life—(of that he did not even dare to dream), but simply to die before the Emperor's eyes. He really was in love with the Tsar and the glory of the Russian arms and the hope of coming victory. And he was not the only man who felt thus in those memorable days that preceded the battle of Austerlitz: nine-tenths of the men in the Russian army were at that moment in love, though less ecstatically, with their Tsar and the glory of the Russian arms.

XI

THE following day the Tsar stayed in Vishau. His medical attendant, Villier, was several times summoned to him. At headquarters and among the troops that were nearer, the news circulated that the Tsar was un-well. He was eating nothing and had slept badly that night, so those about him reported. The cause of this indisposition was the too violent shock given to the sensitive soul of the Tsar by the sight of the killed and wounded.

At dawn on the 17th, a French officer was conducted from our out-posts into Vishau. He came under a flag of truce to ask for an interview with the Russian Emperor. This officer was Savary. The Tsar had only just fallen asleep, and so Savary had to wait. At midday he was admitted to the Emperor, and an hour later he rode away accompanied by Prince Dolgorukov to the outposts of the French army. Savary's mission was, so it was rumoured, to propose a meeting between Alexander and Napoleon. A personal interview was, to the pride and rejoicing of the whole army, refused, and instead of the Tsar, Prince Dolgorukov, the general victori-ous in the action at Vishau, was despatched with Savary to undertake negotiations with Napoleon, if these negotiations—contrary to expecta-tion—were founded on a real desire for peace. In the evening Dolgoru-kov came back, went straight to the Tsar and remained a long while alone with him.

On the 18th and 19th the troops moved forward two days' march, and the enemy's outposts, after a brief interchange of shots, retired. In the higher departments of the army an intense, bustling excitement and activity prevailed from midday of the 19th till the morning of the following day, the 20th of November, on which was fought the memorable battle of Austerlitz. Up to midday of the 19th the activity, the eager talk, the bustle, and the despatching of adjutants was confined to the headquarters of the Emperors; after midday the activity had reached the headquarters of Kutuzov and the staff of the commanding officers of the columns. By evening this activity had been carried by the adjutants in all directions into every part of the army, and in the night of the 19th the multitude of the eighty thousands of the allied army rose from its halting-place, and with a hum of talk moved on, a heaving mass nine versts long.

The intense activity that had begun in the morning in the headquarters of the Emperors, and had given the impetus to all the activity in remoter parts, was like the first action in the centre wheel of a great tower clock. Slowly one wheel began moving, another began turning, and a third, and more and more rapidly, levers, wheels, and blocks began to revolve, chimes began playing, figures began to pop out, and the hands began moving rhythmically, as a result of that activity.

Just as in the mechanism of the clock, in the mechanism of the military machine too, once the impetus given, it was carried on to the last results, and just as unsympathetically stationary were the parts of the machinery which the impulse had not yet reached. Wheels creak on their axles, and teeth bite into cogs, and blocks whir in rapid motion, while the next wheel stands as apathetic and motionless as though it were ready to stand so for a hundred years. But the momentum reaches it— the lever catches, and the wheel, obeying the impulse, creaks and takes its share in the common movement, the result and aim of which are beyond its ken.

Just as in the clock, the result of the complex action of countless different wheels and blocks is only the slow, regular movement of the hand marking the time, so the result of all the complex human movement of those 160,000 Russians and Frenchmen—of all the passions, hopes, regrets, humiliations, sufferings, impulses of pride, of fear, and of enthusiasm of those men—was only the loss of the battle of Austerlitz, the so-called battle of the three Emperors, that is, the slow shifting of the registering hand on the dial of the history of mankind.

Prince Andrey was on duty that day, and in close attendance on the commander-in-chief. At six o'clock in the evening Kutuzov visited the headquarters of the Emperors, and after a brief interview with the Tsar, went in to see the Ober-Hofmarschall Count Tolstoy.

Bolkonsky took advantage of this interval to go in to Dolgorukov to try and learn details about the coming action. Prince Andrey felt that Kutuzov was disturbed and displeased about something, and that they were displeased with him at headquarters, and that all the persons at the Emperor's headquarters took the tone with him of people who knew something other people are not aware of; and for that reason he wanted to have some talk with Dolgorukov.

"Oh, good evening, my dear boy," said Dolgorukov, who was sitting at tea with Bilibin. "The fête's for to-morrow. How's your old fellow? out of humour?"

"I won't say he's out of humour, but I fancy he would like to get a hearing."

"But he did get a hearing at the council of war, and he will get a hearing when he begins to talk sense. But to delay and wait about now when Bonaparte fears a general engagement more than anything—is out of the question."

"Oh yes, you have seen him," said Prince Andrey. "Well, what did you think of Bonaparte? What impression did he make on you?"

"Yes, I saw him, and I'm persuaded he fears a general engagement more than anything in the world," repeated Dolgorukov, who evidently attached great value to this general deduction he had made from his interview with Napoleon. "If he weren't afraid of an engagement what reason has he to ask for this interview, to open negotiations, and, above all, to retreat, when retreat is contrary to his whole method of conducting warfare? Believe me, he's afraid, afraid of a general engagement; his hour has come, mark my words."

"But tell me what was he like, how did he behave?" Prince Andrey still insisted.

"He's a man in a grey overcoat, very anxious to be called 'your majesty,' but disappointed at not getting a title of any kind out of me. That's the sort of man he is, that's all," answered Dolgorukov, looking round with a smile at Bilibin.

"In spite of my profound respect for old Kutuzov," he pursued, "a pretty set of fools we should be to wait about and let him have a chance to get away or cheat us, when as it is he's in our hands for certain. No, we mustn't forget Suvorov and his rule—never to put oneself in a position to be attacked, but to make the attack oneself. Believe me, the energy of young men is often a safer guide in warfare than all the experience of the old cunctators."

"But in what position are you going to attack him? I have been at the outposts to-day, and there was no making out where his chief forces are concentrated," said Prince Andrey. He was longing to explain to Dolgorukov his own idea, the plan of attack he had formed.

"Ah, that's a matter of no consequence whatever," Dolgorukov said quickly, getting up and unfolding a map on the table. "Every contingency has been provided for; if he is concentrated at Brünn. . . ." And Prince Dolgorukov gave a rapid and vague account of Weierother's plan of a flank movement.

Prince Andrey began to make objections and to explain his own plan, which may have been as good as Weierother's, but had the fatal disadvantage that Weierother's plan had already been accepted. As soon as Prince Andrey began to enlarge on the drawbacks of the latter and the advantages of his own scheme, Prince Dolgorukov ceased to attend, and looked without interest not at the map, but at Prince Andrey's face.

"There is to be a council of war at Kutuzov's to-night, though; you can explain all that then," said Dolgorukov.

"That's what I am going to do," said Prince Andrey, moving away from the map.

"And what are you worrying yourselves about, gentlemen?" said Bilibin, who had till then been listening to their talk with a beaming smile, but now unmistakably intended to make a joke. "Whether there is victory or defeat to-morrow, the glory of the Russian arms is secure. Except your Kutuzov, there's not a single Russian in command of a column. The commanders are: Herr General Wimpfen, le comte de Langeron, le prince de Lichtenstein, le prince de Hohenlohe and Prishprshiprsh, or some such Polish name."

"Hold your tongue, backbiter," said Dolgorukov. "It's not true, there are two Russians: Miloradovitch and Dohturov, and there would have been a third, Count Araktcheev, but for his weak nerves."

"Mihail Ilarionovitch has come out, I think," said Prince Andrey. "Good luck and success to you, gentlemen," he added, and went out, after shaking hands with Dolgorukov and Bilibin.

On returning home Prince Andrey could not refrain from asking Kutuzov, who sat near him in silence, what he thought about the coming battle. Kutuzov looked sternly at his adjutant, and after a pause, answered: "I think the battle will be lost, and I said so to Count Tolstoy and asked him to give that message to the Tsar. And what do you suppose was the answer he gave me? '*Eh, mon cher général, je me mêle de riz et de côtelettes, mêlez-vous des affaires de la guerre.*' Yes. . . . That's the answer I got!"

XII

AT ten o'clock in the evening, Weierother with his plans rode over to Kutuzov's quarters, where the council of war was to take place. All the commanders of columns were summoned to the commander-in-chief's, and with the exception of Prince Bagration, who declined to come, all of them arrived at the hour fixed.

Weierother, who was entirely responsible for all the arrangements for the proposed battle, in his eagerness and hurry, was a striking contrast to the ill-humoured and sleepy Kutuzov, who reluctantly played the part of president and chairman of the council of war. Weierother obviously felt himself at the head of the movement that had been set going and could not be stopped. He was like a horse in harness running downhill with a heavy load behind him. Whether he were pulling it or it were pushing him, he could not have said, but he was flying along at full speed with no time to consider where this swift motion would land him. Weierother had been twice that evening to make a personal inspection up to the enemy's line, and twice he had been with the Emperors, Russian and

Austrian, to report and explain, and to his office, where he had dictated the disposition of the German troops. He came now, exhausted, to Kutuzov's.

He was evidently so much engrossed that he even forgot to be respectful to the commander-in-chief. He interrupted him, talked rapidly and indistinctly, without looking at the person he was addressing, failed to answer questions that were put to him, was spattered with mud, and had an air pitiful, exhausted, distracted, and at the same time self-confident and haughty.

Kutuzov was staying in a small nobleman's castle near Austerlitz. In the drawing-room, which had been made the commander-in-chief's study, were gathered together: Kutuzov himself, Weierother, and the members of the council of war. They were drinking tea. They were only waiting for Prince Bagration to open the council. Presently Bagration's orderly officer came with a message that the prince could not be present. Prince Andrey came in to inform the commander-in-chief of this; and, profiting by the permission previously given him by Kutuzov to be present at the council, he remained in the room.

"Well, since Prince Bagration isn't coming, we can begin," said Weierother, hastily getting up from his place and approaching the table, on which an immense map of the environs of Brünn lay unfolded.

Kutuzov, his uniform unbuttoned, and his fat neck as though set free from bondage, bulging over the collar, was sitting in a low chair with his podgy old hands laid symmetrically on the arms; he was almost asleep.

At the sound of Weierother's voice, he made an effort and opened his solitary eye.

"Yes, yes, please, it's late as it is," he assented, and nodding his head, he let it droop and closed his eyes again.

If the members of the council had at first believed Kutuzov to be shamming sleep, the nasal sounds to which he gave vent during the reading that followed, proved that the commander-in-chief was concerned with something of far greater consequence than the desire to show his contempt for their disposition of the troops or anything else whatever; he was concerned with the satisfaction of an irresistible human necessity —sleep. He was really asleep. Weierother, with the gesture of a man too busy to lose even a minute of his time, glanced at Kutuzov and satisfying himself that he was asleep, he took up a paper and in a loud, monotonous tone began reading the disposition of the troops in the approaching battle under a heading, which he also read.

"Disposition for the attack of the enemy's position behind Kobelnitz and Sokolnitz, November 20, 1805."

The disposition was very complicated and intricate.

"As the enemy's left wing lies against the wooded hills and their right wing is advancing by way of Kobelnitz and Sokolnitz behind the swamps that lie there, while on the other hand our left wing stretches far beyond their right, it will be advantageous to attack this last-named wing, especially if we have possession of the villages of Sokolnitz and Kobelnitz, by which means we can at once fall on them in the rear, and pursue them in the open between Schlapanitz and the Thuerassa-Wald, thereby avoiding the defiles of Schlapanitz and Bellowitz, which are covered by the enemy's front. With this ultimate aim it will be necessary . . . The first column marches . . . The second column marches . . . The third column marches" . . . read Weierother.

The generals seemed to listen reluctantly to the intricate account of the disposition of the troops. The tall, fair-haired general, Buxhevden, stood leaning his back against the wall, and fixing his eyes on a burning candle, he seemed not to be listening, not even to wish to be thought to be listening. Exactly opposite to Weierother, with his bright, wide-open eyes fixed upon him was Miloradovitch, a ruddy man, with whiskers and shoulders turned upwards, sitting in a military pose with his hands on his knees and his elbows bent outwards. He sat in obstinate silence, staring into Weierother's face, and only taking his eyes off him when the Austrian staff-commander ceased speaking. Then Miloradovitch looked round significantly at the other generals. But from that significant glance it was impossible to tell whether he agreed or disagreed, was pleased or displeased, at the arrangements. Next to Weierother sat Count Langeron, with a subtle smile that never left his Southern French face during the reading; he gazed at his delicate fingers as he twisted round a golden snuff-box with a portrait on it. In the middle of one of the lengthy paragraphs he stopped the rotatory motion of the snuff-box, lifted his head, and with hostile courtesy lurking in the corners of his thin lips, interrupted Weierother and would have said something. But the Austrian general, continuing to read, frowned angrily with a motion of the elbows that seemed to say: "Later, later, you shall give your opinion, now be so good as to look at the map and listen." Langeron turned up his eyes with a look of bewilderment, looked round at Miloradovitch, as though seeking enlightenment, but meeting the significant gaze of Miloradovitch, that signified nothing, he dropped his eyes dejectedly, and fell to twisting his snuff-box again.

"A geography lesson," he murmured as though to himself, but loud enough to be heard.

Przhebyshevsky, with respectful but dignified courtesy, put his hand up to his ear on the side nearest Weierother, with the air of a man absorbed in attention. Dohturov, a little man, sat opposite Weierother with a studious and modest look on his face. Bending over the map, he was conscientiously studying the arrangement of the troops and the unfamiliar locality. Several times he asked Weierother to repeat words and difficult names of villages that he had not caught. Weierother did so, and Dohturov made a note of them.

When the reading, which lasted more than an hour, was over, Langeron, stopping his twisting snuff-box, began to speak without looking at Weierother or any one in particular. He pointed out how difficult it was to carry out such a disposition, in which the enemy's position was assumed to be known, when it might well be uncertain seeing that the enemy was in movement. Langeron's objections were well founded, yet it was evident that their principal object was to make Weierother, who had read his plans so conceitedly, as though to a lot of schoolboys, feel that he had to deal not with fools, but with men who could teach him something in military matters.

When the monotonous sound of Weierother's voice ceased, Kutuzov opened his eyes, as the miller wakes up at any interruption in the droning of the mill-wheels, listened to what Langeron was saying, and as though saying to himself: "Oh, you're still at the same nonsense!" made haste to close his eyes again, and let his head sink still lower.

Langeron, trying to deal the most malignant thrusts possible at Weierother's military vanity as author of the plan, showed that Bonaparte might easily become the attacking party instead of waiting to be attacked, and so render all this plan of the disposition of the troops utterly futile. Weierother met all objections with a confident and contemptuous smile, obviously prepared beforehand for every objection, regardless of what they might say to him.

"If he could have attacked us, he would have done so to-day," he said.

"You suppose him, then, to be powerless?" said Langeron.

"I doubt if he has as much as forty thousand troops," answered Weierother with the smile of a doctor to whom the sick-nurse is trying to expound her own method of treatment.

"In that case, he is going to meet his ruin in awaiting our attack," said Langeron with a subtle, ironical smile, looking round again for support to Miloradovitch near him. But Miloradovitch was obviously thinking at that instant of anything in the world rather than the matter in dispute between the generals.

"*Ma foi*," he said, "to-morrow we shall see all that on the field of battle."

Weierother smiled again, a smile that said that it was comic and queer for *him* to meet with objections from Russian generals and to have to give proofs to confirm what he was not simply himself convinced of, but had thoroughly convinced their majesties the Emperors of too.

"The enemy have extinguished their fires and a continual noise has been heard in their camp," he said. "What does that mean? Either they are retreating—the only thing we have to fear, or changing their position" (he smiled ironically). "But even if they were to take up their position at Turas, it would only be saving us a great deal of trouble, and all our arrangements will remain unchanged in the smallest detail."

"How can that be? . . ." said Prince Andrey, who had a long while been looking out for an opportunity of expressing his doubts. Kutuzov waked up, cleared his throat huskily, and looked round at the generals.

"Gentlemen, the disposition for to-morrow, for to-day indeed (for it's going on for one o'clock), can't be altered now," he said. "You have heard it, and we will all do our duty. And before a battle nothing is of so much importance . . ." (he paused) "as a good night's rest."

He made a show of rising from his chair. The generals bowed themselves out. It was past midnight. Prince Andrey went out.

The council of war at which Prince Andrey had not succeeded in expressing his opinion, as he had hoped to do, had left on him an impression of uncertainty and uneasiness. Which was right—Dolgorukov and Weierother, or Kutuzov and Langeron and the others, who did not approve of the plan of attack—he did not know. But had it really been impossible for Kutuzov to tell the Tsar his views directly? Could it not have been managed differently? On account of personal and court considerations were tens of thousands of lives to be risked—"and my life, *mine?*" he thought.

"Yes, it may well be that I shall be killed to-morrow," he thought.

And all at once, at that thought of death, a whole chain of memories, the most remote and closest to his heart, rose up in his imagination. He recalled his last farewell to his father and his wife; he recalled the early days of his love for her, thought of her approaching motherhood; and he felt sorry for her and for himself, and in a nervously overwrought and softened mood he went out of the cottage at which he and Nesvitsky were putting up, and began to walk to and fro before it. The night was foggy, and the moonlight glimmered mysteriously through the mist. "Yes, to-morrow, to-morrow!" he thought. "To-morrow, maybe, all will be over for me, all these memories will be no more, all these memories will have no more meaning for me. To-morrow, perhaps—for certain, indeed—to-morrow, I have a presentiment, I shall have for the first time to show all I can do." And he pictured the engagement, the loss of it, the concentration of the fighting at one point, and the hesitation of all the commanding officers. And then the happy moment—that Toulon he had been waiting for so long—at last comes to him. Resolutely and clearly he speaks his opinion to Kutuzov and Weierother, and the Emperors. All are struck by the justness of his view, but no one undertakes to carry it into execution, and behold, he leads the regiment, only making it a condition that no one is to interfere with his plans, and he leads his division to the critical point and wins the victory alone. "And death and agony!" said another voice. But Prince Andrey did not answer that voice, and went on with his triumphs. The disposition of the battle that ensues is all his work alone. Nominally, he is an adjutant on the staff of Kutuzov, but he does everything alone. The battle is gained by him alone. Kutuzov is replaced, he is appointed. . . . "Well, and then?" said the other voice again, "what then, if you do a dozen times over escape being wounded, killed, or deceived before that; well, what then?" "Why, then . . ." Prince Andrey answered himself, "I don't know what will come then, I can't know, and don't want to; but if I want that, if I want glory, want to be known to men, want to be loved by them, it's not my fault that I want it, that it's the only thing I care for, the only thing I live for. Yes, the only thing! I shall never say to any one, but, my God! what am I to do, if I care for nothing but glory, but men's love? Death, wounds, the loss of my family—nothing has terrors for me. And dear and precious as many people are to me: father, sister, wife—the people dearest to me; yet dreadful and unnatural as it seems, I would give them all up for a moment of glory, of triumph over men, of love from men whom I don't know, and shall never know, for the love of those people there," he thought, listening to the talk in the courtyard of Kutuzov's house. He could hear the voices of the officers' servants packing up; one of them, probably a coachman, was teasing Kutuzov's old cook, a man called Tit, whom Prince Andrey knew. He kept calling him and making a joke on his name.

"Tit, hey, Tit?" he said.

"Well?" answered the old man.

"*Tit, stupay molotit*" ("Tit, go a thrashing"), said the jester.

"Pooh, go to the devil, do," he heard the cook's voice, smothered in the laughter of the servants.

"And yet, the only thing I love and prize is triumph over all of them, that mysterious power and glory which seems hovering over me in this mist!"

XIII

ROSTOV had been sent that night with a platoon on picket duty to the line of outposts in the foremost part of Bagration's detachment. His hussars were scattered in couples about the outposts; he himself rode about the line of the outposts trying to struggle against the sleepiness which kept overcoming him. Behind him could be seen the immense expanse of the dimly burning fires of our army; before him was the misty darkness. However intently Rostov gazed into this misty distance, he could see nothing; at one moment there seemed something greyish, at the next something blackish, then something like the glimmer of a fire over there where the enemy must be, then he fancied the glimmer had been only in his own eyes. His eyes kept closing, and there floated before his mind the image of the Emperor, then of Denisov, and Moscow memories, and again he opened his eyes and saw close before him the head and ears of the horse he was riding, and sometimes black figures of hussars, when he rode within six paces of them, but in the distance still the same misty darkness. "Why? it may well happen," mused Rostov, "that the Emperor will meet me and give me some commission, as he might to any officer; he'll say, "Go and find out what's there." There are a lot of stories of how quite by chance he has made the acquaintance of officers and given them some place close to him too. Oh, if he were to give me a place in attendance on him! Oh, what care I would take of him, how I would tell him the whole truth, how I would unmask all who deceive him!" And to picture his love and devotion to the Tsar more vividly, Rostov imagined some enemy or treacherous German, whom he would with great zest not simply kill, but slap in the face before the Tsar's eyes. All at once a shout in the distance roused Rostov. He started and opened his eyes. "Where am I? Yes, in the picket line; the pass and watchword —shaft, Olmütz. How annoying that our squadron will be in reserve . . ." he thought. "I'll ask to go to the front. It may be my only chance of seeing the Emperor. And now it's not long before I'm off duty. I'll ride round once more, and as I come back, I'll go to the general and ask him." He sat up straight in the saddle and set off to ride once more round his hussars. It seemed to him that it was lighter. On the left side he could see a sloping descent that looked lighted up and a black knoll facing it that seemed steep as a wall. On this knoll was a white patch which Rostov could not understand; was it a clearing in the wood, lighted up by the moon, or the remains of snow, or white horses? It seemed to him indeed that something was moving over that white spot. "It must be snow —that spot: a spot—*une tache*," Rostov mused dreamily. "But that's not a *tache* . . . Na . . . tasha, my sister, her black eyes. Na . . . tasha (won't she be surprised when I tell her how I've seen the Emperor!) Natasha . . . tasha . . . sabretache. . . ." "Keep to the right, your honour, there are bushes here," said the voice of an hussar, by whom Rostov was riding as he fell asleep. Rostov lifted his head, which had dropped on to his horse's mane, and pulled up beside the hussar. He could not shake off the youthful, childish drowsiness that overcame him. "But, I say, what was I thinking? I mustn't forget. How I am going to speak to the Emperor? No, not that—that's to-morrow. Yes, yes! Natasha, attacks, tacks us,—whom? The hussars. Ah, the hussars with their moustaches . . . Along the Tversky boulevard rode that hussar with the moustaches, I was thinking of him too just opposite Guryev's house. . . . Old Guryev. . . . Ah, a fine fellow, Denisov! But that's all nonsense. The great thing is that the Emperor's here now. How he looked at me and longed to say something, but he did not dare. . . . No, it was I did not dare. But that's nonsense, and the great thing is not to forget something important I was thinking of, yes. Natasha, attacks us, yes, yes, yes. That's right." And again he dropped with his head on his horse's neck. All at once it seemed to him that he was being fired at. "What? what? . . . Cut them down! What?" Rostov was saying, as he wakened up. At the instant that he opened his eyes, Rostov heard in front, over where the enemy were, the prolonged shouting of thousands of voices. His horse and the horse of the hussar near him pricked up their ears at these shouts. Over where the shouts came from, a light was lighted and put out, then another, and all along the line of the French troops on the hillside fires were lighted and the shouts grew louder and louder. Rostov heard the sound of French words though he could not distinguish them. He could only hear: aaaa! and rrrr!

"What is it? What do you think?" Rostov said to the hussar near him. "That's in the enemy's camp surely?"

The hussar made no reply.

"Why, don't you hear it?" Rostov asked again, after waiting some time for a reply.

"Who can tell, your honour?" the hussar answered reluctantly.

"From the direction it must be the enemy," Rostov said again.

"May be 'tis, and may be not," said the hussar; "it's dark. Now! steady," he shouted to his horse, who fidgeted. Rostov's horse too was restless, and pawed the frozen ground as it listened to the shouts and looked at the lights. The shouting grew louder and passed into a mingled roar that could only be produced by an army of several thousands. The lights stretched further and further probably along the line of the French camp. Rostov was not sleepy now. The gay, triumphant shouts in the enemy's army had a rousing effect on him. *"Vive l'Empereur! l'Empereur!"* Rostov could hear distinctly now.

"Not far off, beyond the stream it must be," he said to the hussar near him.

The hussar merely sighed without replying, and cleared his throat angrily. They heard the thud of a horse trotting along the line of hussars, and there suddenly sprang up out of the night mist, looking huge as an elephant, the figure of a sergeant of hussars.

"Your honour, the generals!" said the sergeant, riding up to Rostov. Rostov, still looking away towards the lights and shouts, rode with the sergeant to meet several men galloping along the line. One was on a white horse. Prince Bagration with Prince Dolgorukov and his adjutant had ridden out to look at the strange demonstration of lights and shouts in the enemy's army. Rostov, going up to Bagration, reported what he had heard and seen to him, and joined the adjutants, listening to what the generals were saying.

"Take my word for it," Prince Dolgorukov was saying to Bagration, "it's nothing but a trick; they have retreated and ordered the rearguard to light fires and make a noise to deceive us."

"I doubt it," said Bagration; "since evening I have seen them on that knoll; if they had retreated, they would have withdrawn from there too. Monsieur l'officier," Prince Bagration turned to Rostov, "are the enemy's pickets still there?"

"They were there this evening, but now I can't be sure, your excellency. Shall I go with some hussars and see?" said Rostov.

Bagration stood still, and before answering, tried to make out Rostov's face in the mist.

"Well, go and see," he said after a brief pause.

"Yes, sir."

Rostov put spurs to his horse, called up the sergeant Fedtchenko, and two other hussars, told them to ride after him, and trotted off downhill in the direction of the shouting, which still continued. Rostov felt both dread and joy in riding alone with three hussars into that mysterious and dangerous, misty distance, where no one had been before him. Bagration shouted to him from the hill not to go beyond the stream, but Rostov made as though he had not heard his words, and rode on without stopping, further and further, continually mistaking bushes for trees and ravines for men, and continually discovering his mistakes. As he galloped downhill he lost sight both of our men and the enemy, but more loudly and distinctly he heard the shouts of the French. In the valley he saw ahead of him something that looked like a river, but when he had ridden up to it, he found out it was a road. As he got out on the road he pulled up his horse, hesitating whether to go along it or to cut across it, and ride over the black field up the hillside. To follow the road, which showed lighter in the mist, was more dangerous, because figures could be more easily descried upon it. "Follow me," he said; "cut across the road," and began galloping up the hill towards the point where the French picket had been in the evening.

"Your honour, here he is!" said one of the hussars behind; and before Rostov had time to make out something that rose up suddenly black in the mist, there was a flash of light, the crack of a shot and a bullet, that seemed whining a complaint, whizzed high in the air and flew away out of hearing. Another shot missed fire, but there was a flash in the pan. Rostov turned his horse's head and galloped back. He heard four more shots at varying intervals, and four more bullets whistled in varying tones somewhere in the mist. Rostov held in his horse, who seemed inspirited, as he was himself by the shots, and rode back at a walking-pace. "Now, then, some more; now then, more!" a sort of light-hearted voice murmured in his soul. But there were no more shots. Only as he approached Bagration, Rostov put his horse into a gallop again, and with his hand to his cap, rode up to him.

Dolgorukov was still insisting on his opinion that the French were retreating, and had only lighted fires to mislead them. "What does it prove?" he was saying, as Rostov rode up to them. "They might have retreated and left pickets."

"It's clear they have not all retired, prince," said Bagration. "We must wait till morning; to-morrow we shall know all about it."

"The picket's on the hill, your excellency, still where it was in the evening," Rostov announced, his hand to his cap, unable to restrain the smile of delight that had been called up by his expedition and the whiz of the bullets.

"Very good, very good," said Bagration, "I thank you, monsieur l'officier."

"Your excellency," said Rostov, "may I ask a favour?"

"What is it?"

"To-morrow our squadron is ordered to the rear; may I beg you to attach me to the first squadron?"

"What's your name?"

"Count Rostov."

"Ah, very good! You may stay in attendance on me."

"Ilya Andreitch's son?" said Dolgorukov. But Rostov made him no reply.

"So I may reckon on it, your excellency."

"I will give the order."

"To-morrow, very likely, they will send me with some message to the Emperor," he thought. "Thank God!"

The shouts and lights in the enemy's army had been due to the fact that while Napoleon's proclamation had been read to the troops, the Emperor had himself ridden among the bivouacs. The soldiers on seeing the Emperor had lighted wisps of straw and run after him, shouting, "Vive l'empereur!" Napoleon's proclamation was as follows:—

"Soldiers! The Russian army is coming to meet you, to avenge the Austrian army, the army of Ulm. They are the forces you have defeated at Hollabrunn, and have been pursuing ever since up to this place. The

position we occupy is a powerful one, and while they will march to out-
flank me on the right, they will expose their flank to me! Soldiers! I will
myself lead your battalions. I will keep out of fire, if you, with your
habitual bravery, carry defeat and disorder into the ranks of the enemy.
But if victory is for one moment doubtful, you will see your Emperor
exposed to the enemy's hottest attack, for there can be no uncertainty
of victory, especially on this day, when it is a question of the honour of
the French infantry, on which rests the honour of our nation. Do not,
on the pretext of removing the wounded, break the order of the ranks!
Let every man be fully penetrated by the idea that we must subdue these
minions of England, who are inspired by such hatred of our country.
This victory will conclude our campaign, and we can return to winter
quarters, where we shall be reinforced by fresh forces now being formed
in France; and then the peace I shall conclude will be one worthy of
my people, of you and me.   "NAPOLEON."

XIV

AT five o'clock in the morning it was still quite dark. The troops of the
centre, of the reserves, and of Bagration's right flank, were still at rest.
But on the left flank the columns of the infantry, cavalry, and artillery,
destined to be the first to descend from the heights, so as to attack the
French right flank, and, according to Weierother's plan, to drive it back
to the Bohemian mountains, were already up and astir. The smoke from
the camp-fires, into which they were throwing everything superfluous,
made the eyes smart. It was cold and dark. The officers were hurriedly
drinking tea and eating breakfast; the soldiers were munching biscuits,
stamping their feet rhythmically, while they gathered about the fires
warming themselves, and throwing into the blaze remains of shanties,
chairs, tables, wheels, tubs, everything superfluous that they could not
take away with them. Austrian officers were moving in and out among
the Russian troops, coming everywhere as heralds of their advance. As
soon as an Austrian officer appeared near a commanding officer's quarters, the regiment began to bestir themselves; the soldiers ran from the
fires, thrust pipes into boot-legs, bags into waggons, saw to their muskets,
and formed into ranks. The officers buttoned themselves up, put on their
sabres and pouches, and moved up and down the ranks shouting. The
commissariat men and officers' servants harnessed the horses, packed and
tied up the waggons. The adjutants and the officers in command of regiments and battalions got on their horses, crossed themselves, gave final
orders, exhortations and commissions to the men who remained behind
with the baggage, and the monotonous thud of thousands of feet began.
The columns moved, not knowing where they were going, and unable
from the crowds round them, the smoke, and the thickening fog, to see
either the place which they were leaving, or that into which they were
advancing.

The soldier in movement is as much shut in, surrounded, drawn along

by his regiment, as the sailor is by his ship. However great a distance he
traverses, however strange, unknown, and dangerous the regions to
which he penetrates, all about him, as the sailor has the deck and masts
and rigging of his ship, he has always everywhere the same comrades, the
same ranks, the same sergeant Ivan Mitritch, the same regimental dog
Zhutchka, the same officers. The soldier rarely cares to know into what
region his ship has sailed; but on the day of battle—God knows how or
whence it comes—there may be heard in the moral world of the troops
a sterner note that sounds at the approach of something grave and
solemn, and rouses them to a curiosity unusual in them. On days of battle, soldiers make strenuous efforts to escape from the routine of their
regiment's interests, they listen, watch intently, and greedily inquire
what is being done around them.

The fog had become so thick that though it was growing light, they
could not see ten steps in front of them. Bushes looked like huge trees,
level places looked like ravines and slopes. Anywhere, on any side, they
might stumble upon unseen enemies ten paces from them. But for a long
while the columns marched on in the same fog, going downhill and uphill, passing gardens and fences, in new and unknown country, without
coming upon the enemy anywhere. On the contrary, the soldiers became
aware that in front, behind, on all sides, were the Russian columns moving in the same direction. Every soldier felt cheered at heart by knowing
that where he was going, to that unknown spot were going also many,
many more of our men.

"I say, the Kurskies have gone on," they were saying in the ranks.

"Stupendous, my lad, the forces of our men that are met together!
Last night I looked at the fires burning, no end of them. A regular
Moscow!"

Though not one of the officers in command of the columns rode up
to the ranks nor talked to the soldiers (the commanding officers, as we
have seen at the council of war, were out of humour, and displeased with
the plans that had been adopted, and so they simply carried out their
orders without exerting themselves to encourage the soldiers), yet the
soldiers marched on in good spirits, as they always do when advancing
into action, especially when on the offensive.

But after they had been marching on for about an hour in the thick
fog, a great part of the troops had to halt, and an unpleasant impression
of mismanagement and misunderstanding spread through the ranks. In
what way that impression reached them it is very difficult to define. But
there is no doubt that it did reach them, and with extraordinary correctness and rapidity, and spread imperceptibly and irresistibly, like water
flowing over a valley. Had the Russian army been acting alone, without
allies, possibly it would have taken a long time for this impression of
mismanagement to become a general conviction. But as it was, it was so
particularly pleasant and natural to ascribe the mismanagement to the
senseless Germans, and all believed that there was some dangerous
muddle due to a blunder on the part of the sausage-makers.

"What are they stopping for? Blocked up the way, eh? Or hit upon the French at last?"

"No, not heard so. There'd have been firing. After hurrying us to march off, and we've marched off—to stand in the middle of a field for no sense—all the damned Germans making a muddle of it. The senseless devils! I'd have sent them on in front. But no fear, they crowd to the rear. And now one's to stand with nothing to eat."

"I say, will they be quick there?"

"The cavalry is blocking up the road, they say," said an officer.

"Ah, these damned Germans, they don't know their own country," said another.

"Which division are you?" shouted an adjutant, riding up.

"Eighteenth."

"Then why are you here? You ought to have been in front long ago; you won't get there now before evening."

"The silly fools' arrangements, they don't know themselves what they're about," said the officer, and he galloped away. Then a general trotted up, and shouted something angrily in a foreign tongue.

"*Ta-fa-la-fa,* and no making out what he's jabbering," said a soldier, mimicking the retreating general. "I'd like to shoot the lot of them, the blackguards!"

"Our orders were to be on the spot before ten o'clock, and we're not halfway there. That's a nice way of managing things!" was repeated on different sides, and the feeling of energy with which the troops had started began to turn to vexation and anger against the muddled arrangements and the Germans.

The muddle originated in the fact that while the Austrian cavalry were in movement, going to the left flank, the chief authorities had come to the conclusion that our centre was too far from the right flank, and all the cavalry had received orders to cross over to the right. Several thousands of mounted troops had to cross in front of the infantry, and the infantry had to wait till they had gone by.

Ahead of the troops a dispute had arisen between the Austrian officer and the Russian general. The Russian general shouted a request that the cavalry should stop. The Austrian tried to explain that he was not responsible, but the higher authorities. The troops meanwhile stood, growing listless and dispirited. After an hour's delay the troops moved on at last, and began going downhill. The fog, that overspread the hill, lay even more densely on the low ground to which the troops were descending. Ahead in the fog they heard one shot, and another, at first at random, at irregular intervals; tratta-tat, then growing more regular and frequent, and the skirmish of the little stream, the Holdbach, began.

Not having reckoned on meeting the enemy at the stream, and coming upon them unexpectedly in the fog, not hearing a word of encouragement from their commanding officers, with a general sense of being too late, and seeing nothing before or about them in the fog, the Russians fired slowly and languidly at the enemy, never receiving a command in time from the officers and adjutants, who wandered about in the fog in an unknown country, unable to find their own divisions. This was how the battle began for the first, the second, and the third columns, who had gone down into the low-lying ground. The fourth column, with which Kutuzov was, was still on the plateau of Pratzen.

The thick fog still hung over the low ground where the action was beginning; higher up it was beginning to clear, but still nothing could be seen of what was going on in front. Whether all the enemy's forces were, as we had assumed, ten versts away from us, or whether they were close by in that stretch of fog, no one knew till nine o'clock.

Nine o'clock came. The fog lay stretched in an unbroken sea over the plain, but at the village of Schlapanitz on the high ground where Napoleon was, surrounded by his marshals, it was now perfectly clear. There was bright blue sky over his head, and the vast orb of the sun, like a huge, hollow, purple float, quivered on the surface of the milky sea of fog. Not the French troops only, but Napoleon himself with his staff were not on the further side of the streams, and the villages of Sokolnitz and Schlapanitz, beyond which we had intended to take up our position and begin the attack, but were on the nearer side, so close indeed to our forces that Napoleon could distinguish a cavalry man from a foot soldier in our army with the naked eye. Napoleon was standing a little in front of his marshals, on a little grey Arab horse, wearing the same blue overcoat he had worn through the Italian campaign. He was looking intently and silently at the hills, which stood up out of the sea of mist, and the Russian troops moving across them in the distance, and he listened to the sounds of firing in the valley. His face—still thin in those days—did not stir a single muscle; his gleaming eyes were fixed intently on one spot. His forecasts were turning out correct. Part of the Russian forces were going down into the valley towards the ponds and lakes, while part were evacuating the heights of Pratzen, which he regarded as the key of the position, and had intended to take. He saw through the fog, in the dip between two hills near the village of Pratzen, Russian columns with glittering bayonets moving always in one direction towards the valleys, and vanishing one after another into the mist. From information he had received over night, from the sounds of wheels and footsteps he had heard in the night at the outposts, from the loose order of the march of the Russian columns, from all the evidence, he saw clearly that the allies believed him to be a long way in front of the, that the columns moving close to Pratzen constituted the centre of the Russian army, and that the centre was by this time too much weakened to be able to attack him successfully. But still he delayed beginning the battle.

That day was for him a day of triumph—the anniversary of his coronation. He had slept for a few hours in the early morning, and feeling fresh, and in good health and spirits, in that happy frame of mind in which everything seems possible and everything succeeds, he got on his horse and rode out. He stood without stirring, looking at the heights that rose out of the fog, and his cold face wore that peculiar shade of confident, self-complacent happiness, seen on the face of a happy boy in love. The marshals stood behind him, and did not venture to distract his attention. He looked at the heights of Pratzen, then at the sun floating up out of the mist.

When the sun had completely emerged from the fog, and was glittering with dazzling brilliance over the fields and the mist (as though he had been waiting for that to begin the battle), he took his glove off his handsome white hand, made a signal with it to his marshals, and gave orders for the battle to begin. The marshals, accompanied by adjutants, galloped in various directions, and in a few minutes the chief forces of the French army were moving towards those heights of Pratzen, which were left more and more exposed by the Russian troops as the latter kept moving to the left towards the valley.

XV

AT eight o'clock Kutuzov rode out to Pratzen at the head of Miloradovitch's fourth column, the one which was to occupy the place left vacant by the columns of Przhebyshevsky and Langeron, who had by this time gone down to the plain. He greeted the men of the foremost regiment, and gave them the command to march, showing thereby that he meant to lead that column himself. On reaching the village of Pratzen he halted. Prince Andrey was behind among the immense number of persons who made up the commander-in-chief's suite. Prince Andrey was in a state of excitement, of irritation, and at the same time of repressed calm, as a man often is on attaining a long-desired moment. He was firmly convinced that to-day would be the day of his Toulon or his bridge of Arcola. How it would come to pass he knew not, but he was firmly convinced that it would be so. The locality and the position of our troops he had mastered to the minutest detail, so far as they could be known to any one in our army. His own strategic plan, which obviously could not conceivably be carried out now, was forgotten by him. Throwing himself into Weierother's plan, Prince Andrey was now deliberating over the contingencies that might arise, and inventing new combinations, in which his rapidity of resource and decision might be called for.

On the left, below in the fog, could be heard firing between unseen forces. There, it seemed to Prince Andrey, the battle would be concentrated, there "the difficulty would arise, and there I shall be sent," he thought, "with a brigade or a division, and there, flag in hand, I shall march forward and shatter all before me."

Prince Andrey could not look unmoved upon the flags of the passing battalions. Looking at the flag, he kept thinking; perhaps it is that very flag with which I shall have to lead the men. Towards morning nothing was left of the fog on the heights but a hoar frost passing into dew, but in the valleys the fog still lay in a milky-white sea. Nothing could be seen in the valley to the left into which our troops had vanished, and from which sounds of firing were coming. Above the heights stood a clear, dark blue sky, and on the right the vast orb of the sun. In the distance in front, on the coast of that sea of mist, rose up the wooded hills, on which the enemy's army should have been, and something could be descried there. On the right there was the tramp of hoofs and rumble of wheels, with now and then the gleam of bayonets, as the guards plunged into the region of mist; on the left, behind the village, similar masses of cavalry were moving and disappearing into the sea of fog. In front and behind were the marching infantry. The commander-in-chief was standing at the end of the village, letting the troops pass before him. Kutuzov seemed exhausted and irritable that morning. The infantry marching by him halted without any command being given, apparently because something in front blocked up the way.

"Do tell the men to form in battalion columns and go round the village," said Kutuzov angrily to a general who rode up. "How is it you don't understand, my dear sir, that it's out of the question to let them file through the defile of the village street, when we are advancing to meet the enemy."

"I had proposed forming beyond the village, your most high excellency," replied the general.

Kutuzov laughed bitterly.

"A nice position you'll be in, deploying your front in sight of the enemy—very nice."

"The enemy is a long way off yet, your most high excellency. According to the disposition. . . ."

"The disposition!" Kutuzov cried with bitter spleen; "but who told you so? . . . Kindly do as you are commanded."

"Yes, sir."

"My dear boy," Nesvitsky whispered to Prince Andrey, "the old fellow is in a vile temper."

An Austrian officer wearing a white uniform and green plumes in his hat, galloped up to Kutuzov and asked him in the Emperor's name: Had the fourth column started?

Kutuzov turned away without answering, and his eye fell casually on Prince Andrey, who was standing near him. Seeing Bolkonsky, Kutuzov let his vindictive and bitter expression soften, as though recognising that his adjutant was not to blame for what was being done. And still not answering the Austrian adjutant, he addressed Bolkonsky.

"Go and see, my dear fellow, whether the third division has passed the village. Tell them to stop and wait for my orders."

Prince Andrey had scarcely started when he stopped him.

"And ask whether the sharpshooters are posted," he added. "What they are doing, what they are doing!" he murmured to himself, still making no reply to the Austrian.

Prince Andrey galloped off to do his bidding. Overtaking all the advancing battalions, he stopped the third division and ascertained that there actually was no line of sharpshooters in advance of our columns. The officer in command of the foremost regiment was greatly astounded on the order being brought him from the commander-in-chief to send a flying line of sharpshooters in advance. The officer had been resting in the full conviction that there were other troops in front of him, and that the enemy could not be less than ten versts away. In reality there was nothing in front of him but an empty stretch of ground, sloping down-hill and covered with fog. Giving him the commander-in-chief's order to rectify the omission, Prince Andrey galloped back. Kutuzov was still at the same spot; his bulky frame drooped in the saddle with the lassitude of old age, and he was yawning wearily with closed eyes. The troops had not yet moved on, but were standing at attention.

"Good, good," he said to Prince Andrey, and he turned to the general who, watch in hand, was saying that it was time they started, as all the columns of the left flank had gone down already.

"We have plenty of time yet, your excellency," Kutuzov interpolated between his yawns. "Plenty of time!" he repeated.

At that moment in the distance behind Kutuzov there were sounds of regiments saluting; the shouts came rapidly nearer along the whole drawn-out line of the advancing Russian columns. Clearly he who was the object of these greetings was riding quickly. When the soldiers of the regiment, in front of which Kutuzov was standing, began to shout, he rode off a little on one side, and wrinkling up his face, looked round. Along the road from Pratzen, galloped what looked like a whole squad-ron of horsemen of different colours. Two of them galloped side by side ahead of the rest. One was in a black uniform with a white plume, on a chestnut English thoroughbred, the other in a white uniform on a black horse. These were the two Emperors and their suites. With a sort of affectation of the manner of an old soldier at the head of his regiment, Kutuzov gave the command, "Steady," to the standing troops and rode up to the Emperors, saluting. His whole figure and manner were sud-denly transformed. He assumed the air of a subordinate, a man who accepts without criticism. With an affectation of respectfulness which unmistakably made an unpleasant impression on Alexander, he rode up and saluted him.

The unpleasant impression, like the traces of fog in a clear sky, merely flitted across the young and happy face of the Emperor and vanished. He looked that day rather thinner after his illness than he had been at the review of Olmütz, where Bolkonsky had seen him for the first time abroad. But there was the same bewitching combination of majesty and mildness in his fine, grey eyes, and on his delicate lips the same possi-bility of varying expressions and the predominant expression of noble-hearted, guileless youth.

At the Olmütz review he had been more majestic, here he was livelier and more energetic. He was flushed a little from the rapid three-verst gallop, and as he pulled up his horse, he breathed a sigh of relief, and looked round at those among the faces of his suite that were as young and eager as his own. Behind the Tsar were Tchartorizhsky, and Novo-siltsov, and Prince Bolkonsky, and Stroganov, and the rest, all richly dressed, gay young men on splendid, well-groomed, fresh horses, slightly heated from the gallop. The Emperor Francis, a rosy, long-faced young man, sat excessively erect on his handsome sable horse, casting deliberate and anxious looks around him. He beckoned one of his white adjutants and asked him a question. "Most likely at what o'clock they started," thought Prince Andrey, watching his old acquaintance with a smile, which he could not repress, as he remembered his audience with him. With the Emperors' suite were a certain number of fashionable young aristocrats—Russians and Austrians—selected from the regiments of the guards and the line. Among them were postillions leading extra horses, beautiful beasts from the Tsar's stables, covered with embroidered horse-cloths.

Like a breath of fresh country air rushing into a stuffy room through an open window was the youth, energy, and confidence of success that the cavalcade of brilliant young people brought with them into Kutuzov's cheerless staff.

"Why aren't you beginning, Mihail Larionovitch?" the Emperor Alexander said hurriedly, addressing Kutuzov, while he glanced courteously towards the Emperor Francis.

"I am waiting to see, your majesty," Kutuzov answered, bowing reverentially.

The Emperor turned his ear towards him, with a slight frown and an air of not having caught his words.

"I'm waiting to see, your majesty," repeated Kutuzov (Prince Andrey noticed that Kutuzov's upper lip quivered unnaturally as he uttered that: "I'm waiting"). "Not all the columns are massed yet, your majesty."

The Tsar heard him, but the answer apparently did not please him; he shrugged his sloping shoulders, and glanced at Novosiltsov, who stood near, with a look that seemed to complain of Kutuzov.

"We are not on the Tsaritsin field, you know, Mihail Larionovitch, where the parade is not begun till all the regiments are ready," said the Tsar, glancing again at the Emperor Francis as though inviting him, if not to take part, at least to listen to what he was saying. But the Emperor Francis still gazed away and did not listen.

"That's just why I'm not beginning, sire," said Kutuzov in a resounding voice, as though foreseeing a possibility his words might be ignored, and once more there was a quiver in his face. "That's why I am not beginning, sire; because we are not on parade and not on the Tsaritsin field," he articulated clearly and distinctly.

All in the Tsar's suite exchanged instantaneous glances with one another, and every face wore an expression of regret and reproach. "However old he may be, he ought not, he ought never to speak like that," the faces expressed.

The Tsar looked steadily and attentively into Kutuzov's face, waiting to see if he were not going to say more. But Kutuzov too on his side, bending his head respectfully, seemed to be waiting. The silence lasted about a minute.

"However, if it's your majesty's command," said Kutuzov, lifting his head and relapsing into his former affectation of the tone of a stupid, uncritical general, who obeys orders. He moved away, and beckoning the commanding officer of the column, Miloradovitch, gave him the command to advance.

The troops began to move again, and two battalions of the Novgorod regiment and a battalion of the Apsheron regiment passed before the Tsar.

While the Apsheron battalion was marching by, Miloradovitch, a red-faced man, wearing a uniform and orders, with no overcoat, and a turned-up hat with huge plumes stuck on one side, galloped ahead of them, and saluting in gallant style, reined up his horse before the Tsar.

"With God's aid, general," said the Tsar.

"*Ma foi*, sire, we will do whatever is in our power to do," he answered gaily, arousing none the less an ironical smile among the gentlemen of the Tsar's suite by his bad French accent. Miloradovitch wheeled his horse round sharply, and halted a few steps behind the Tsar. The Apsheron men, roused by the presence of the Tsar, stepped out gallantly as they marched by the Emperors and their suites.

"Lads!" shouted Miloradovitch in his loud, self-confident, and cheery voice. He was apparently so excited by the sounds of the firing, the anticipation of battle, and the sight of the gallant Apsheron men, his old comrades with Suvorov, that he forgot the Tsar's presence. "Lads! it's not the first village you've had to take!" he shouted.

"Glad to do our best," roared the soldiers. The Tsar's horse reared at the unexpected sound. This horse, who had carried the Tsar at reviews in Russia, bore his rider here on the field of Austerlitz, patiently enduring the heedless blows of his left foot, and pricked up his ears at the sound of shots as he had done on the review ground with no comprehension of the significance of these sounds, nor of the nearness of the raven horse of Emperor Francis, nor of all that was said and thought and felt that day by the man who rode upon his back.

The Tsar turned with a smile to one of his courtiers, pointing to the gallant-looking Apsheron regiment, and said something to him.

XVI

KUTUZOV, accompanied by his adjutants, followed the carabineers at a walking pace.

After going on for half a mile at the tail of the column, he stopped at a solitary, deserted house (probably once an inn), near the branching of two roads. Both roads led downhill, and troops were marching along both.

The fog was beginning to part, and a mile and a half away the enemy's troops could be indistinctly seen on the opposite heights. On the left below, the firing became more distinct. Kutuzov stood still in conversation with an Austrian general. Prince Andrey standing a little behind watched them intently, and turned to an adjutant, meaning to ask him for a field-glass.

"Look, look!" this adjutant said, looking not at the troops in the distance, but down the hill before him. "It's the French!"

The two generals and the adjutant began snatching at the field-glass, pulling it from one another. All their faces suddenly changed, and horror was apparent in them all. They had supposed the French to be over a mile and a half away, and here they were all of a sudden confronting us.

"Is it the enemy? . . . No. . . . But, look, it is . . . for certain. . . . What does it mean?" voices were heard saying.

With the naked eye Prince Andrey saw to the right, below them, a dense column of French soldiers coming up towards the Apsheron regiment, not over five hundred paces from where Kutuzov was standing.

"Here it is, it is coming, the decisive moment! My moment has come," thought Prince Andrey, and slashing his horse, he rode up to Kutuzov.

"We must stop the Apsheron regiment," he shouted, "your most high excellency."

But at that instant everything was lost in a cloud of smoke, there was a sound of firing close by, and a voice in naïve terror cried not two paces from Prince Andrey: "Hey, mates, it's all up!" And this voice was like a command. At that voice there was a general rush, crowds, growing larger every moment, ran back in confusion to the spot where five minutes before they had marched by the Emperors. It was not simply difficult to check this rushing crowd, it was impossible not to be carried back with the stream oneself. Bolkonsky tried only not to be left behind by it, and looked about him in bewilderment, unable to grasp what was taking place. Nesvitsky, with an exasperated, crimson face, utterly unlike himself, was shouting to Kutuzov that if he didn't get away at once he'd be taken prisoner to a certainty. Kutuzov was standing in the same place: he was taking out his handkerchief, and did not answer. The blood was flowing from his cheek. Prince Andrey forced his way up to him.

"You are wounded?" he asked, hardly able to control the quivering of his lower jaw.

"The wound's not here, but there, see!" said Kutuzov, pressing the handkerchief to his wounded cheek, and pointing to the running soldiers.

"Stop them!" he shouted, and at the same time convinced that it was impossible to stop them, he lashed his horse and rode to the right. A fresh rush of flying crowds caught him up with it and carried him back.

The troops were running in such a dense multitude, that once getting into the midst of the crowd, it was a hard matter to get out of it. One was shouting: "Get on! what are you lagging for?" Another was turning round to fire in the air; another striking the very horse on which Kutuzov was mounted. Getting out with an immense effort from the stream on the left, Kutuzov, with his suite diminished to a half, rode towards the sounds of cannon close by. Prince Andrey, trying not to be left behind by Kutuzov, saw, as he got out of the racing multitude, a Russian battery still firing in the smoke on the hillside and the French running towards it. A little higher up stood Russian infantry, neither moving forward to

the support of the battery, nor back in the same direction as the runaways. A general on horseback detached himself from the infantry and
rode towards Kutuzov. Of Kutuzov's suite only four men were left. They
were all pale and looking at one another dumbly.

"Stop those wretches!" Kutuzov gasped to the officer in command of
the regiment, pointing to the flying soldiers. But at the same instant, as
though in revenge for the words, the bullets came whizzing over the
regiment and Kutuzov's suite like a flock of birds. The French were attacking the battery, and catching sight of Kutuzov, they were shooting
at him. With this volley the general clutched at his leg; several soldiers
fell, and the second lieutenant standing with the flag let it drop out of
his hands. The flag tottered and was caught on the guns of the nearest
soldiers. The soldiers had begun firing without orders.

"Ooogh!" Kutuzov growled with an expression of despair, and he
looked round him. "Bolkonsky," he whispered in a voice shaking with
the consciousness of his old age and helplessness. "Bolkonsky," he whispered, pointing to the routed battalion and the enemy, "what's this?"

But before he had uttered the words, Prince Andrey, feeling the tears
of shame and mortification rising in his throat, was jumping off his horse
and running to the flag.

"Lads, forward!" he shrieked in a voice of childish shrillness. "Here, it
is come!" Prince Andrey thought, seizing the staff of the flag, and hearing with relief the whiz of bullets, unmistakably aimed at him. Several
soldiers dropped.

"Hurrah!" shouted Prince Andrey, and hardly able to hold up the
heavy flag in both his hands, he ran forward in the unhesitating conviction that the whole battalion would run after him. And in fact it was
only for a few steps that he ran alone. One soldier started, then another,
and then the whole battalion with a shout of "hurrah!" was running forward and overtaking him. An under-officer of the battalion ran up and
took the flag which tottered from its weight in Prince Andrey's hands,
but he was at once killed. Prince Andrey snatched up the flag again, and
waving it by the staff, ran on with the battalion. In front of him he saw
our artillery men, of whom some were fighting, while others had abandoned their cannons and were running towards him. He saw French infantry soldiers, too, seizing the artillery horses and turning the cannons
round. Prince Andrey and the battalion were within twenty paces of the
cannons. He heard the bullets whizzing over him incessantly, and continually the soldiers moaned and fell to the right and left of him. But he
did not look at them; his eyes were fixed on what was going on in front
of him—at the battery. He could now see distinctly the figure of the
red-haired artilleryman, with a shako crushed on one side, pulling a mop
one way, while a French soldier was tugging it the other way. Prince
Andrey could see distinctly now the distraught, and at the same time
exasperated expression of the faces of the two men, who were obviously
quite unconscious of what they were doing.

"What are they about?" wondered Prince Andrey, watching them;
"why doesn't the red-haired artilleryman run, since he has no weapon?

Why doesn't the Frenchman stab him? He won't have time to run away before the Frenchman will think of his gun, and knock him on the head." Another Frenchman did, indeed, run up to the combatants with his gun almost overbalancing him, and the fate of the red-haired artilleryman, who still had no conception of what was awaiting him, and was pulling the mop away in triumph, was probably sealed. But Prince Andrey did not see how it ended. It seemed to him as though a hard stick were swung full at him by some soldier near, dealing him a violent blow on the head. It hurt a little, but the worst of it was that the pain distracted his attention, and prevented him from seeing what he was looking at.

"What's this? am I falling? my legs are giving way under me," he thought, and fell on his back. He opened his eyes, hoping to see how the struggle of the French soldiers with the artilleryman was ending, and eager to know whether the red-haired artilleryman was killed or not, whether the cannons had been taken or saved. But he saw nothing of all that. Above him there was nothing but the sky—the lofty sky, not clear, but still immeasurably lofty, with grey clouds creeping quietly over it. "How quietly, peacefully, and triumphantly, and not like us running, shouting, and fighting, not like the Frenchman and artilleryman dragging the mop from one another with frightened and frantic faces, how differently are those clouds creeping over that lofty, limitless sky. How was it I did not see that lofty sky before? And how happy I am to have found it at last. Yes! all is vanity, all is a cheat, except that infinite sky. There is nothing, nothing but that. But even that is not, there is nothing but peace and stillness. And thank God! . . ."

XVII

On the right flank in Bagration's detachment, at nine o'clock the battle had not yet begun. Not caring to assent to Dolgorukov's request that he should advance into action, and anxious to be rid of all responsibility, Prince Bagration proposed to Dolgorukov to send to inquire of the commander-in-chief. Bagration was aware that as the distance between one flank and the other was almost eight miles, if the messenger sent were not killed (which was highly probable), and if he were to succeed in finding the commander-in-chief (which would be very difficult), he would hardly succeed in making his way back before the evening.

Bagration looked up and down his suite with his large, expressionless, sleepy eyes, and the childish face of Rostov, unconsciously all a-quiver with excitement and hope, was the first that caught his eye. And he sent him.

"And if I meet his majesty before the commander-in-chief, your excellency?" said Rostov, with his hand to the peak of his cap.

"You can give the message to his majesty," said Dolgorukov, hurriedly interposing before Bagration.

On being relieved from picket duty, Rostov had managed to get a few hours' sleep before morning, and felt cheerful, bold, and resolute, with a peculiar springiness in his movements, and confidence in his luck, and in that frame of mind in which everything seems easy and possible.

All his hopes had been fulfilled that morning: there was to be a general engagement, he was taking part in it; more than that, he was in attendance on the bravest general; more than that, he was being sent on a commission to Kutuzov, perhaps even to the Tsar himself. It was a fine morning, he had a good horse under him, his heart was full of joy and happiness. On receiving his orders, he spurred his horse and galloped along the line. At first he rode along the line of Bagration's troops which had not yet advanced into action, and were standing motionless, then he rode into the region occupied by Uvarov's cavalry, and here he began to observe activity and signs of preparation for battle. After he had passed Uvarov's cavalry, he could distinctly hear the sound of musket-fire and the booming of cannons ahead of him. The firing grew louder and more intense.

The sound that reached him in the fresh morning air was not now, as before, the report of two or three shots at irregular intervals, and then one or two cannons booming. Down the slopes of the hillsides before Pratzen, he could hear volleys of musketry, interspersed with such frequent shots of cannon that sometimes several booming shots could not be distinguished from one another, but melted into one mingled roar of sound.

He could see the puffs of musket smoke flying down the hillsides, as though racing one another, while the cannon smoke hung in clouds, that floated along and melted into one another. He could see, from the gleam of bayonets in the smoke, that masses of infantry were moving down, and narrow lines of artillery with green caissons.

On a hillock Rostov stopped his horse to try and make out what was going on. But however much he strained his attention, he could not make out and understand what he saw; there were men of some sort moving about there in the smoke, lines of troops were moving both backwards and forwards; but what for? Who? where were they going? it was impossible to make out. This sight, and these sounds, so far from exciting any feeling of depression or timidity in him, only increased his energy and determination.

"Come, fire away, at them again!" was his mental response to the sounds he heard. Again he galloped along the line, penetrating further and further into the part where the troops were already in action.

"How it will be there, I don't know, but it will all be all right!" thought Rostov.

After passing Austrian troops of some sort, Rostov noticed that the next part of the forces (they were the guards) had already advanced into action.

"So much the better! I shall see it close," he thought.

He was riding almost along the front line. A body of horsemen came galloping towards him. They were a troop of our Uhlans returning in disorder from the attack. Rostov, as he passed them, could not help noticing one of them covered with blood, but he galloped on.

"That's no affair of mine!" he thought.

He had not ridden on many hundred paces further when there came into sight, on his left, across the whole extent of the field, an immense mass of cavalry on black horses, in dazzling white uniforms, trotting straight towards him, cutting off his advance. Rostov put his horse to his utmost speed to get out of the way of these cavalrymen, and he would have cleared them had they been advancing at the same rate, but they kept increasing their pace, so that several horses broke into a gallop. More and more loudly Rostov could hear the thud of their horses' hoofs, and the jingle of their weapons, and more and more distinctly he could see their horses, their figures, and even their faces. These were our horse-guards, charging to attack the French cavalry, who were advancing to meet them.

The cavalry guards were galloping, though still holding in their horses. Rostov could see their faces now, and hear the word of command, "Charge!" uttered by an officer, as he let his thoroughbred go at full speed. Rostov, in danger of being trampled underfoot or carried away to attack the French, galloped along before their line as fast as his horse could go, and still he was not in time to escape them.

The last of the line of cavalry, a pock-marked man of immense stature, scowled viciously on seeing Rostov just in front of him, where he must inevitably come into collision with him. This horse-guard would infallibly have overturned Rostov and his Bedouin (Rostov felt himself so little and feeble beside these gigantic men and horses) if he had not bethought himself of striking the horse-guard's horse in the face with his riding-whip. The heavy, black, high horse twitched its ears and reared, but its pock-marked rider brought it down with a violent thrust of the spurs into its huge sides, and the horse, lashing its tail and dragging its neck, flew on faster than ever. The horse-guard had hardly passed Rostov when he heard their shout, "Hurrah!" and looking round saw their foremost ranks mixed up with some strange cavalry, in red epaulettes, probably French. He could see nothing more, for immediately after cannons were fired from somewhere, and everything was lost in the smoke.

At the moment when the horse-guards passing him vanished into the smoke, Rostov hesitated whether to gallop after them or to go on where he had to go. This was the brilliant charge of the horse-guards of which the French themselves expressed their admiration. Rostov was appalled to hear afterwards that of all that mass of huge, fine men, of all those brilliant, rich young officers and ensigns who had galloped by him on horses worth thousands of roubles, only eighteen were left after the charge.

"I have no need to envy them, my share won't be taken from me, and may be I shall see the Emperor in a minute!" thought Rostov, and he galloped on.

When he reached the infantry of the guards, he noticed that cannon

balls were flying over and about them, not so much from the sound of the
cannon balls, as from the uneasiness he saw in the faces of the soldiers
and the unnatural, martial solemnity on the faces of the officers.

As he rode behind one of the lines of the regiments of footguards, he
heard a voice calling him by name: "Rostov!"

"Eh?" he called back, not recognising Boris.

"I say, we've been in the front line! Our regiment marched to the attack!" said Boris, smiling that happy smile that is seen in young men
who have been for the first time under fire. Rostov stopped.

"Really!" he said. "Well, how was it?"

"We beat them!" said Boris, growing talkative in his eagerness. "You
can fancy . . ." And Boris began describing how the guards having taken
up their position, and seeing troops in front of them had taken them for
Austrians, and all at once had found out from the cannon balls aimed at
them from those troops that they were in the front line, and had quite
unexpectedly to advance to battle. Rostov set his horse moving without
waiting to hear Boris to the end.

"Where are you off to?" asked Boris.

"To his majesty with a commission."

"Here he is!" said Boris, who had not caught what Rostov said, and
thinking it was the grand duke he wanted, he pointed him out, standing
a hundred paces from them, wearing a helmet and a horse-guard's white
elk tunic, with his high shoulders and scowling brows, shouting something to a pale, white-uniformed Austrian officer.

"Why, that's the grand duke, and I must see the commander-in-chief
or the Emperor," said Rostov, and he was about to start again.

"Count, count!" shouted Berg, running up on the other side, as eager
as Boris. "I was wounded in my right hand" (he pointed to his blood-
stained hand, bound up with a pocket-handkerchief), "and I kept my
place in the front. Count, I held my sabre in my left hand. All my family, count, the Von Bergs, have been knights." Berg would have said
more, but Rostov rode on without listening.

After riding by the guards, and on through an empty space, Rostov
rode along the line of the reserves for fear of getting in the way of the
front line, as he had done in the charge of the horse-guards, and made a
wide circuit round the place where he heard the hottest musket-fire and
cannonade. All of a sudden, in front of him and behind our troops, in a
place where he could never have expected the enemy to be, he heard the
sound of musket-fire quite close.

"What can it be?" thought Rostov. "The enemy in the rear of our
troops? It can't be," thought Rostov, but a panic of fear for himself and
for the issue of the whole battle came over him all at once. "Whatever
happens, though," he reflected, "it's useless to try and escape now. It's
my duty to seek the commander-in-chief here, and if everything's lost,
it's my duty to perish with all the rest."

The foreboding of evil that had suddenly come upon Rostov grew
stronger and stronger the further he advanced into the region behind the
village of Pratzen, which was full of crowds of troops of all sorts.

"What does it mean? What is it? Whom are they firing at? Who is firing?" Rostov kept asking, as he met Austrian and Russian soldiers running in confused crowds across his path.

"Devil knows! Killed them all! Damn it all," he was answered in Russian, in German, and in Czech, by the hurrying rabble, who knew no more than he what was being done.

"Kill the Germans!" shouted one.

"To hell with them—the traitors."

"*Zum Henker diese Russen,*" muttered a German.

Several wounded were among the crowds on the road. Shouts, oaths, moans were mingled in the general hubbub. The firing began to subside, and, as Rostov found out later, the Russian and Austrian soldiers had been firing at one another.

"My God! how can this be?" thought Rostov. "And here, where any minute the Emperor may see them. . . . No, these can only be a few wretches. It will soon be over, it's not the real thing, it can't be," he thought. "Only to make haste, make haste, and get by them."

The idea of defeat and flight could not force its way into Rostov's head. Though he saw the French cannons and troops precisely on Pratzen hill, the very spot where he had been told to look for the commander-in-chief, he could not and would not believe in it.

XVIII

NEAR the village of Pratzen Rostov had been told to look for Kutuzov and the Emperor. But there they were not, nor was there a single officer to be found in command, nothing but disorderly crowds of troops of different sorts. He urged on his weary horse to hasten through this rabble, but the further he went the more disorderly the crowds became. The high road along which he rode, was thronged with carriages, with vehicles of all sorts, and Austrian and Russian soldiers of every kind, wounded and unwounded. It was all uproar and confused bustle under the sinister whiz of the flying cannon balls from the French batteries stationed on the heights of Pratzen.

"Where's the Emperor? Where's Kutuzov?" Rostov kept asking of every one he could stop, and from no one could he get an answer.

At last clutching a soldier by the collar, he forced him to answer him.

"Aye! brother! they've all bolted long ago!" the soldier said to Rostov, laughing for some reason as he pulled himself away. Letting go that soldier, who must, he thought, be drunk, Rostov stopped the horse of a groom or postillion of some personage of consequence, and began to cross-question him. The groom informed Rostov that an hour before the Tsar had been driven at full speed in a carriage along this very road, and that the Tsar was dangerously wounded.

"It can't be," said Rostov; "probably some one else."

"I saw him myself," said the groom with a self-satisfied smirk; "it's high time I should know the Emperor, I should think, after the many times I've seen him in Petersburg; I saw him as it might be here. Pale, deadly pale, sitting in the carriage. The way they drove the four raven horses! my goodness, didn't they dash by us! It would be strange, I should think, if I didn't know the Tsar's horses and Ilya Ivanitch; why, Ilya never drives any one else but the Tsar."

Rostov let go of the horse and would have gone on. A wounded officer passing by addressed him. "Why, who is it you want?" asked the officer, "the commander-in-chief? Oh, he was killed by a cannon ball, struck in the breast before our regiment."

"Not killed—wounded," another officer corrected him.

"Who? Kutuzov?" asked Rostov.

"Not Kutuzov, but what's his name—well, it's all the same, there are not many left alive. Go that way, over there to that village, all the commanding officers are there," said the officer, pointing to the village of Gostieradeck, and he walked on.

Rostov rode on at a walking pace, not knowing to whom and with what object he was going now. The Tsar was wounded, the battle was lost. There was no refusing to believe in it now. Rostov rode in the direction which had been pointed out to him, and saw in the distance turrets and a church. What had he to hasten for now? What was he to say now to the Tsar or to Kutuzov, even if they were alive and not wounded?

"Go along this road, your honour, that way you will be killed in a trice!" a soldier shouted to him. "You'll be killed that way!"

"Oh! what nonsense!" said another. "Where is he to go? That way's nearest." Rostov pondered, and rode off precisely in the direction in which he had been told he would be killed.

"Now, nothing matters; if the Emperor is wounded, can I try and save myself?" he thought. He rode into the region where more men had been killed than anywhere, in fleeing from Pratzen. The French had not yet taken that region, though the Russians—those who were slightly wounded or unhurt—had long abandoned it. All over the field, like ridges of dung on well-kept plough-land, lay the heaps of dead and wounded, a dozen or fifteen bodies to every three acres. The wounded were crawling two or three together, and their shrieks and groans had a painful and sometimes affected sound, it seemed to Rostov. Rostov put his horse to a trot to avoid the sight of all those suffering people, and he felt afraid. He was afraid of losing not his life, but his pluck, which he needed so much, which he knew would not stand the sight of those luckless wretches. The French had ceased firing at this field that was dotted over with dead and wounded, because there seemed no one living upon it, but seeing an adjutant trotting across it, they turned a cannon upon him and shot off several cannon balls. The sense of those whizzing, fearful sounds, and of the dead bodies all round him melted into a single impression of horror and pity for himself in Rostov's heart. He thought of his mother's last letter. "What would she be feeling now," he thought, "if she could see me here now on this field with cannons aimed at me?"

In the village of Gostieradeck there were Russian troops, in some confusion indeed, but in far better discipline, who had come from the field of battle. Here they were out of range of the French cannons, and the sounds of firing seemed far away. Here every one saw clearly that the battle was lost, and all were talking of it. No one to whom Rostov applied could tell him where was the Tsar, or where was Kutuzov. Some said that the rumour of the Tsar's wound was correct, others said not, and explained this widely spread false report by the fact that the Ober-Hofmarschall Tolstoy, who had come out with others of the Emperor's suite to the field of battle, had been seen pale and terrified driving back at full gallop in the Tsar's carriage. One officer told Rostov that, behind the village to the left, he had seen some one from headquarters, and Rostov rode off in that direction, with no hope now of finding any one, but simply to satisfy his conscience. After going about two miles and passing the last of the Russian troops, Rostov saw, near a kitchen-garden enclosed by a ditch, two horsemen standing facing the ditch. One with a white plume in his hat seemed somehow a familiar figure to Rostov, the other, a stranger on a splendid chestnut horse (the horse Rostov fancied he had seen before) rode up to the ditch, put spurs to his horse, and lightly leaped over the ditch into the garden. A little earth from the bank crumbled off under his horse's hind hoofs. Turning the horse sharply, he leaped the ditch again and deferentially addressed the horseman in the white plume, apparently urging him to do the same. The rider, whose figure seemed familiar to Rostov had somehow riveted his attention, made a gesture of refusal with his head and his hand, and in that gesture Rostov instantly recognised his lamented, his idolised sovereign.

"But it can't be he, alone, in the middle of this empty field," thought Rostov. At that moment Alexander turned his head and Rostov saw the beloved features so vividly imprinted on his memory. The Tsar was pale, his cheeks looked sunken, and his eyes hollow, but the charm, the mildness of his face was only the more striking. Rostov felt happy in the certainty that the report of the Emperor's wound was false. He was happy that he was seeing him. He knew that he might, that he ought, indeed, to go straight to him and to give him the message he had been commanded to give by Dolgorukov.

But, as a youth in love trembles and turns faint and dares not utter what he has spent nights in dreaming of, and looks about in terror, seeking aid or a chance of delay or flight, when the moment he has longed for comes and he stands alone at her side, so Rostov, now when he was attaining what he had longed for beyond everything in the world, did not know how to approach the Emperor, and thousands of reasons why it was unsuitable, unseemly, and impossible came into his mind.

"What! it's as though I were glad to take advantage of his being alone and despondent. It may be disagreeable and painful to him, perhaps, to see an unknown face at such a moment of sadness; besides, what can I say to him now, when at the mere sight of him my heart is throbbing and leaping into my mouth?" Not one of the innumerable speeches he had addressed to the Tsar in his imagination recurred to his mind now. These speeches for the most part were appropriate to quite other circumstances; they had been uttered for the most part at moments of victory and triumph, and principally on his deathbed when, as he lay dying of his wounds, the Emperor thanked him for his heroic exploits, and he gave expression as he died to the love he had proved in deeds. "And then, how am I to ask the Emperor for his instructions to the right flank when it's four o'clock in the afternoon and the battle is lost? No, certainly I ought not to ride up to him, I ought not to break in on his sorrow. Better die a thousand deaths than that he should give me a glance, a thought of disapproval," Rostov decided, and with grief and despair in his heart he rode away, continually looking back at the Tsar, who still stood in the attitude of indecision.

While Rostov was making these reflections and riding mournfully away from the Tsar, Captain Von Toll happened to ride up to the same spot, and seeing the Emperor, went straight up to him, offered him his services, and assisted him to cross the ditch on foot. The Tsar, feeling unwell and in need of rest, sat down under an apple-tree, and Von Toll remained standing by his side. Rostov from a distance saw with envy and remorse how Von Toll talked a long while warmly to the Emperor, how the Emperor, apparently weeping, hid his face in his hand, and pressed Von Toll's hand.

"And it might have been I in his place?" Rostov thought, and hardly restraining his tears of sympathy for the Tsar, he rode away in utter despair, not knowing where and with what object he was going now.

His despair was all the greater from feeling that it was his own weakness that was the cause of his regret.

He might ... not only might, but ought to have gone up to the Emperor. And it was a unique chance of showing his devotion to the Emperor. And he had not made use of it.... "What have I done?" he thought. And he turned his horse and galloped back to the spot where he had seen the Emperor; but there was no one now beyond the ditch. There were only transport waggons and carriages going by. From one carrier Rostov learned that Kutuzov's staff were not far off in the village towards which the transport waggons were going. Rostov followed them.

In front of him was Kutuzov's postillion leading horses in horsecloths. A baggage waggon followed the postillion, and behind the waggon walked an old bandy-legged servant in a cap and a cape.

"Tit, hey. Tit!" said the postillion.

"Eh," responded the old man absent-mindedly.

"Tit! Stupay molotit!" ("Tit, go a thrashing!")

"Ugh, the fool, pugh!" said the old man, spitting angrily. A short interval of silence followed, and then the same joke was repeated.

By five o'clock in the evening the battle had been lost at every point More than a hundred cannons were in the possession of the French. Przhebyshevsky and his corps had surrendered. The other columns had retreated, with the loss of half their men, in confused, disorderly masses. All that were left of Langeron's and Dohturov's forces were crowded together in hopeless confusion on the dikes and banks of the ponds near the village of Augest.

At six o'clock the only firing still to be heard was a heavy cannonade on the French side from numerous batteries ranged on the slope of the table-land of Pratzen, and directed at our retreating troops.

In the rearguard Dohturov and the rest, rallying their battalions, had been firing at the French cavalry who were pursuing them. It was beginning to get dark. On the narrow dam of Augest, where the old miller in his peaked cap had sat for so many years with his fishing tackle, while his grandson, with tucked-up shirt-sleeves, turned over the silvery, floundering fish in the net; on that dam where the Moravians, in their shaggy caps and blue jackets, had for so many years peacefully driven their horses and waggons, loaded with wheat, to the mill and driven back over the same dam, dusty with flour that whitened their waggons—on that narrow dam men, made hideous by the terror of death, now crowded together, amid army waggons and cannons, under horses' feet and between carriage-wheels, crushing each other, dying, stepping over the dying, and killing each other, only to be killed in the same way a few steps further on.

Every ten seconds a cannon ball flew lashing the air and thumped down, or a grenade burst in the midst of that dense crowd, slaying men and splashing blood on those who stood near. Dolohov, wounded in the hand, with some dozen soldiers of his company on foot (he was already an officer) and his general on horseback, were the sole representatives of a whole regiment. Carried along by the crowd, they were squeezed in the approach to the dam and stood still, jammed in on all sides because a horse with a cannon had fallen, and the crowd were dragging it away. A cannon ball killed some one behind them, another fell in front of them and spurted the blood upon Dolohov. The crowd moved forward desperately, was jammed, moved a few steps and was stopped again. "Only to get over these hundred steps and certain safety: stay here two minutes and death to a certainty," each man was thinking.

Dolohov standing in the centre of the crowd, forced his way to the edge of the dam, knocking down two soldiers, and ran on to the slippery ice that covered the millpond.

"Turn this way!" he shouted, bounding over the ice, which cracked under him. "Turn this way!" he kept shouting to the cannon. "It bears! ..." The ice bore him, but swayed and cracked, and it was evident that, not to speak of a cannon or a crowd of people, it would give way in a moment under him alone. Men gazed at him and pressed to the bank, unable to bring themselves to step on to the ice. The general of his regiment on horseback at the end of the dam lifted his hand and opened his mouth to speak to Dolohov. Suddenly one of the cannon balls flew so low over the heads of the crowd that all ducked. There was a wet splash, as the general fell from his horse into a pool of blood. No one glanced at the general, no one thought of picking him up.

"On to the ice! Get on the ice! Get on! turn! don't you hear! Get on!" innumerable voices fell to shouting immediately after the ball had struck the general, not knowing themselves what and why they were shouting.

One of the hindmost cannons that had been got on to the dam was turned off upon the ice. Crowds of soldiers began running from the dam

on to the frozen pond. The ice cracked under one of the foremost sol¬
diers, and one leg slipped into the water. He tried to right himself and
floundered up to his waist. The soldiers nearest tried to draw back, the
driver of the cannon pulled up his horse, but still the shouts were heard
from behind: "Get on to the ice, why are you stopping? go on! go on!"
And screams of terror were heard in the crowd. The soldiers near the
cannon waved at the horses, and lashed them to make them turn and go
on. The horses moved from the dam's edge. The ice that had held under
the foot-soldiers broke in a huge piece, and some forty men who were on
it dashed, some forwards, some backwards, drowning one another.

Still the cannon balls whizzed as regularly and thumped on to the ice,
into the water, and most often into the crowd that covered the dam, the
pond and the bank.

XIX

PRINCE ANDREY BOLKONSKY was lying on the hill of Pratzen, on the spot
where he had fallen with the flagstaff in his hands. He was losing blood,
and kept moaning a soft, plaintive, childish moan, of which he himself
knew nothing. Towards evening he ceased moaning and became perfectly
still. He did not know how long his unconsciousness lasted. Suddenly he
felt again that he was alive and suffering from a burning, lacerating pain
in his head.

"Where is it, that lofty sky that I knew not till now and saw to-day?"
was his first thought. "And this agony I did not know either," he
thought. "Yes, I knew nothing, nothing till now. But where am I?"

He fell to listening, and caught the sound of approaching hoofs and
voices speaking French. He opened his eyes. Above him was again the
same lofty sky, with clouds higher than ever floating over it, and between
them stretches of blue infinity. He did not turn his head and did not see
the men who, judging from the voices and the thud of hoofs, had ridden
up to him and stopped.

They were Napoleon and two adjutants escorting him. Bonaparte,
making a tour of the field of battle, had been giving his last instructions
for the strengthening of the battery firing at the Augest dam, and was
inspecting the dead and wounded on the field of battle.

"Fine men!" said Napoleon, looking at a dead Russian grenadier, who
with his face thrust into the earth and blackened neck lay on his stomach, one stiff arm flung wide.

"The field-guns have exhausted their ammunition," said an adjutant,
arriving that moment from the battery that was firing at Augest.

"Bring up more from the reserve," said Napoleon, and riding a few
steps away stood still, looking at Prince Andrey, who lay on his back
with the abandoned flagstaff beside him (the flag had been taken by the
French as a trophy).

"That's a fine death!" said Napoleon, looking at Bolkonsky. Prince
Andrey knew that it was said of him, and that it was Napoleon saying it.
He heard the speaker of those words addressed as "your majesty." But

he heard the words as he heard the buzzing of flies. It was not merely that he took no interest in them, but he did not attend to them and at once forgot them. There was a burning pain in his head; he felt he was losing blood, and he saw above him the high, far-away, everlasting sky. He knew it was Napoleon—his hero—but at that moment Napoleon seemed to him such a small, insignificant creature in comparison with what was passing now between his soul and that lofty, limitless sky with the clouds flying over it. It meant nothing to him at that moment who was standing over him, what was being said of him. He was only glad that people were standing over him, and his only desire was that these people should help him and bring him back to life, which seemed to him so good, because he saw it all quite differently now. He made a supreme effort to stir and utter some sound. He moved his leg faintly, and uttered a weak, sickly moan that touched himself. "Ah, he's alive," said Napoleon. "Pick up this young man and carry him to an ambulance!" Saying this, Napoleon rode on to meet Marshal Lannes, who rode up to meet the conqueror, smiling, taking off his hat and congratulating him on his victory.

Prince Andrey remembered nothing more; he lost consciousness from the excruciating pain caused by being laid on the stretcher, the jolting while he was being moved, and the sounding of his wound at the ambulance. He only regained consciousness towards the end of the day when with other Russian officers, wounded and prisoners, he was being taken to the hospital. On this journey he felt a little stronger, and could look about him and even speak.

The first words he heard on coming to himself were from a French convoy officer who was saying hurriedly: "They must stop here; the Emperor will be here directly; it will be a pleasure for him to see these prisoners."

"There are such a lot of prisoners to-day, almost the whole of the Russian army, that he is probably weary of seeing them," said another officer.

"Well, but this one, they say, is the commander of all the Emperor Alexander's guards," said the first speaker, pointing to a wounded Russian officer in the white uniform of the horse-guards. Bolkonsky recognised Prince Repnin, whom he had met in Petersburg society. Beside him stood another officer of the horse-guards, a lad of nineteen, also wounded.

Bonaparte rode up at a gallop and pulled up, "Who is the senior officer?" he said, on seeing the prisoners.

They named the colonel, Prince Repnin.

"Are you the commander of the regiment of Emperor Alexander's horse-guards?" asked Napoleon.

"I was in command of a squadron," replied Repnin.

"Your regiment did its duty honourably," said Napoleon.

"The praise of a great general is a soldier's best reward," said Repnin.

"I bestow it upon you with pleasure," said Napoleon. "Who is this young man beside you?" Prince Repnin gave his name, Lieutenant Suhtelen.

Looking at him, Napoleon said with a smile: "He has come very young to meddle with us."

"Youth is no hindrance to valour," said Suhtelen in a breaking voice.

"A fine answer," said Napoleon; "young man, you will go far."

Prince Andrey, who had been thrust forward under the Emperor's eyes to complete the show of prisoners, could not fail to attract his notice. Napoleon apparently remembered seeing him on the field, and addressing him he used the same epithet, "young man," with which his first sight of Bolkonsky was associated in his memory.

"And you, young man," he said to him, "how are you feeling, *mon brave?*"

Although five minutes previously Prince Andrey had been able to say a few words to the soldiers who were carrying him, he was silent now, with his eyes fastened directly upon Napoleon. So trivial seemed to him at that moment all the interests that were engrossing Napoleon, so petty seemed to him his hero, with his paltry vanity and glee of victory, in comparison with that lofty, righteous, and kindly sky which he had seen and comprehended, that he could not answer him. And all indeed seemed to him so trifling and unprofitable beside the stern and solemn train of thought aroused in him by weakness from loss of blood, by suffering and the nearness of death. Gazing into Napoleon's eyes, Prince Andrey mused on the nothingness of greatness, on the nothingness of life, of which no one could comprehend the significance, and on the nothingness —still more—of death, the meaning of which could be understood and explained by none of the living.

The Emperor, after vainly pausing for a reply, turned away and said to one of the officers in command—

"See that they look after these gentlemen and take them to my bivouac; let my doctor Larrey attend to their wounds. *Au revoir,* Prince Repnin," and he galloped away.

His face was radiant with happiness and self-satisfaction.

The soldiers, who had been carrying Prince Andrey, had come across the golden relic Princess Marya had hung upon her brother's neck, and taken it off him, but seeing the graciousness the Emperor had shown to the prisoners, they made haste to restore the holy image.

Prince Andrey did not see who put it on him again, nor how it was replaced, but all at once he found the locket on its delicate gold chain on his chest outside his uniform.

"How good it would be," thought Prince Andrey, as he glanced at the image which his sister had hung round his neck with such emotion and reverence, "how good it would be if all were as clear and simple as it seems to Marie. How good to know where to seek aid in this life and what to expect after it, there, beyond the grave!"

"How happy and at peace I should be, if I could say now, 'Lord, have mercy on me! . . .' But to whom am I to say that? Either a Power infinite, inconceivable, to which I cannot appeal, which I cannot even put into words, the great whole, or nothing," he said to himself, "or that God, who has been sewn up here in this locket by Marie? There is nothing, nothing certain but the nothingness of all that is comprehensible to us, and the grandeur of something incomprehensible, but more important!"

The stretchers began to be moved. At every jolt he felt intolerable pain again. The fever became higher, and he fell into delirium. Visions of his father, his wife, his sister, and his future son, and the tenderness he had felt for them on the night before the battle, the figure of that little, petty Napoleon, and over all these the lofty sky, formed the chief substance of his delirious dreams. The quiet home life and peaceful happiness of Bleak Hills passed before his imagination. He was enjoying that happiness when suddenly there appeared that little Napoleon with his callous, narrow look of happiness in the misery of others, and there came doubts and torments, and only the sky promised peace. Towards morning all his dreams mingled and melted away in the chaos and darkness of unconsciousness and oblivion, far more likely, in the opinion of Napoleon's doctor, Larrey, to be ended by death than by recovery.

"He is a nervous, bilious subject," said Larrey; "he won't recover."

Prince Andrey, with the rest of the hopeless cases, was handed over to the care of the inhabitants of the district.

PART FOUR

I

AT THE beginning of the year 1806, Nikolay Rostov was coming home on leave. Denisov, too, was going home to Voronezh, and Rostov persuaded him to go with him to Moscow and to pay him a visit there. Denisov met his comrade at the last posting station but one, drank three bottles of wine with him, and, in spite of the jolting of the road on the journey to Moscow, slept soundly lying at the bottom of the posting sledge beside Rostov, who grew more and more impatient, as they got nearer to Moscow.

"Will it come soon? Soon? Oh, these insufferable streets, bunshops, street lamps, and sledge drivers!" thought Rostov, when they had presented their papers at the town gates and were driving into Moscow.

"Denisov, we're here! Asleep!" he kept saying, flinging his whole person forward as though by that position he hoped to hasten the progress of the sledge. Denisov made no response.

"Here's the corner of the cross-roads, where Zahar the sledge-driver used to stand; and here is Zahar, too, and still the same horse. And here's the little shop where we used to buy cakes. Make haste! Now!"

"Which house is it?" asked the driver.

"Over there, at the end, the big one; how is it you don't see it? That's our house," Rostov kept saying; "that's our house, of course."

"Denisov! Denisov! we shall be there in a minute."

Denisov raised his head, cleared his throat, and said nothing.

"Dmitry," said Rostov to his valet on the box, "surely that light is home?"

"To be sure it is; it's the light in your papa's study, too."

"They've not gone to bed yet? Eh? What do you think?"

"Mind now, don't forget to get me out my new tunic," added Rostov, fingering his new moustaches.

"Come, get on," he shouted to the driver. "And do wake up, Vasya," he said to Denisov, who had begun nodding again.

"Come, get on, three silver roubles for vodka—get on!" shouted Rostov, when they were only three houses from the entrance. It seemed to him that the horses were not moving. At last the sledge turned to the right into the approach, Rostov saw the familiar cornice with the broken plaster overhead, the steps, the lamp-post. He jumped out of the sledge while it was moving and ran into the porch. The house stood so inhospitably, as though it were no concern of its who had come into it. There was no one in the porch. "My God! is everything all right?" wondered Rostov, stopping for a moment with a sinking heart, and then running on again along the porch and up the familiar, crooked steps. Still the same door handle, the dirtiness of which so often angered the countess, turned in the same halting fashion. In the hall there was a single tallow candle burning.

Old Mihailo was asleep on his perch.

Prokofy, the footman, a man so strong that he had lifted up a carriage, was sitting there in his list shoes. He glanced towards the opening door and his expression of sleepy indifference was suddenly transformed into one of frightened ecstasy.

"Merciful Heavens! The young count!" he cried, recognising his young master. "Can it be? my darling?" And Prokofy, shaking with emotion, made a dash towards the drawing-room door, probably with the view of announcing him; but apparently he changed his mind, for he came back and fell on his young master's shoulder.

"All well?" asked Rostov, pulling his hand away from him.

"Thank God, yes! All, thank God! Only just finished supper! Let me have a look at you, your excellency!"

"Everything perfectly all right?"

"Thank God, yes, thank God!"

Rostov, completely forgetting Denisov, flung off his fur coat and, anxious that no one should prepare the way for him, he ran on tip-toe into the big, dark reception-hall. Everything was the same, the same card-tables, the same candelabra with a cover over it, but some one had already seen the young master, and he had not reached the drawing-room when from a side door something swooped headlong, like a storm upon him, and began hugging and kissing him. A second and a third figure dashed in at a second door and at a third; more huggings, more kisses, more outcries and tears of delight. He could not distinguish where and which was papa, which was Natasha, and which was Petya. All were screaming and talking and kissing him at the same moment. Only his mother was not among them, that he remembered.

"And I never knew ... Nikolenka ... my darling!"

"Here he is ... our boy ... my darling Kolya. . . . Isn't he changed! Where are the candles? Tea!"

"Kiss me too!"

"Dearest . . . and me too."

Sonya, Natasha, Petya, Anna Mihalovna, Vera, and the old count were all hugging him; and the servants and the maids flocked into the room with talk and outcries.

Petya hung on his legs.

"Me too!" he kept shouting.

Natasha, after pulling him down to her and kissing his face all over, skipped back from him and, keeping her hold of his jacket, pranced like a goat up and down in the same place, uttering shrill shrieks of delight.

All round him were loving eyes shining with tears of joy, all round were lips seeking kisses.

Sonya too, as red as crimson baize, clung to his arm and beamed all over, gazing blissfully at his eyes for which she had so long been waiting.

Sonya was just sixteen and she was very pretty, especially at this moment of happy, eager excitement. She gazed at him, unable to take her
eyes off him, smiling and holding her breath. He glanced gratefully at
her; but still he was expectant and looking for some one, and the old
countess had not come in yet. And now steps were heard at the door.
The steps were so rapid that they could hardly be his mother's footsteps.

But she it was in a new dress that he did not know, made during his
absence. All of them let him go, and he ran to her. When they came
together, she sank on his bosom, sobbing. She could not lift up her face,
and only pressed it to the cold braiding of his hussar's jacket. Denisov,
who had come into the room unnoticed by any one, stood still looking at
them and rubbing his eyes.

"Vassily Denisov, your son's friend," he said, introducing himself to
the count, who looked inquiringly at him.

"Very welcome. I know you, I know you," said the count, kissing and
embracing Denisov. "Nikolenka wrote to us ... Natasha, Vera, here he
is, Denisov."

The same happy, ecstatic faces turned to the tousled figure of Denisov
and surrounded him.

"Darling Denisov," squealed Natasha, and, beside herself with delight,
she darted up to him, hugging and kissing him. Every one was disconcerted by Natasha's behaviour. Denisov too reddened, but he smiled,
took Natasha's hand and kissed it.

Denisov was conducted to the room assigned him, while the Rostovs
all gathered about Nikolenka in the divan-room.

The old countess sat beside him, keeping tight hold of his hand, which
she was every minute kissing. The others thronged round them, gloating
over every movement, every glance, every word he uttered, and never
taking their enthusiastic and loving eyes off him. His brother and sisters
quarrelled and snatched from one another the place nearest him and disputed over which was to bring him tea, a handkerchief, a pipe.

Rostov was very happy in the love they showed him. But the first
minute of meeting them had been so blissful that his happiness now
seemed a little thing, and he kept expecting something more and more
and more.

Next morning after his journey he slept on till ten o'clock.

The adjoining room was littered with swords, bags, sabretaches, open
trunks, and dirty boots. Two pairs of cleaned boots with spurs had just
been stood against the wall. The servants brought in wash-hand basins,
hot water for shaving, and their clothes well brushed. The room was full
of a masculine odour and reeked of tobacco.

"Hi, Grishka, a pipe!" shouted the husky voice of Vaska Denisov.
"Rostov, get up!"

Rostov, rubbing his eyelids that seemed glued together, lifted his
tousled head from the warm pillow.

"Why, is it late?"

"It is late, nearly ten," answered Natasha's voice, and in the next
room they heard the rustle of starched skirts and girlish laughter. The

door was opened a crack, and there was a glimpse of something blue, of ribbons, black hair and merry faces. Natasha with Sonya and Petya had come to see if he were not getting up.

"Nikolenka, get up!" Natasha's voice was heard again at the door.

"At once!" Meanwhile in the outer room Petya had caught sight of the swords and seized upon them with the rapture small boys feel at the sight of a soldier brother, and regardless of its not being the proper thing for his sisters to see the young men undressed, he opened the bedroom door.

"Is this your sword?" he shouted.

The girls skipped away. Denisov hid his hairy legs under the bedclothes, looking with a scared face to his comrade for assistance. The door admitted Petya and closed after him. A giggle was heard from outside.

"Nikolenka, come out in your dressing-gown," cried Natasha's voice.

"Is this your sword?" asked Petya, "or is it yours?" he turned with deferential respect to the swarthy, whiskered Denisov.

Rostov made haste to get on his shoes and stockings, put on his dressing-gown and went out. Natasha had put on one spurred boot and was just getting into the other. Sonya was "making cheeses," and had just whirled her skirt into a balloon and was ducking down, when he came in. They were dressed alike in new blue frocks, both fresh, rosy, and good-humoured. Sonya ran away, but Natasha, taking her brother's arm, led him into the divan-room, and a conversation began between them. They had not time to ask and answer all the questions about the thousand trifling matters which could only be of interest to them. Natasha laughed at every word he said and at every word she said, not because what they said was amusing, but because she was in high spirits and unable to contain her joy, which brimmed over in laughter.

"Ah, isn't it nice, isn't it splendid!" she kept saying every moment. Under the influence of the warm sunshine of love, Rostov felt that for the first time for a year and a half his soul and his face were expanding in that childish smile, he had not once smiled since he left home.

"No, I say," she said, "you're quite a man now, eh? I'm awfully glad you're my brother." She touched his moustache. "I do want to know what sort of creatures you men are. Just like us? No."

"Why did Sonya run away?" asked Rostov.

"Oh, there's a lot to say about that! How are you going to speak to Sonya? Shall you call her 'thou' or 'you'?"

"As it happens," said Rostov.

"Call her 'you,' please; I'll tell you why afterwards."

"But why?"

"Well, I'll tell you now. You know that Sonya's my friend, such a friend that I burnt my arm for her sake. Here, look." She pulled up her muslin sleeve and showed him on her long, thin, soft arm above the elbow near the shoulder (on the part which is covered even in a ball-dress) a red mark.

"I burnt that to show her my love. I simply heated a ruler in the fire and pressed it on it."

Sitting in his old schoolroom on the sofa with little cushions on the arms, and looking into Natasha's wildly eager eyes, Rostov was carried back into that world of home and childhood which had no meaning for any one else but gave him some of the greatest pleasures in his life. And burning one's arm with a ruler as a proof of love did not strike him as pointless; he understood it, and was not surprised at it.

"Well, is that all?" he asked.

"Well, we are such friends, such great friends! That's nonsense—the ruler; but we are friends for ever. If she once loves any one, it's for ever; I don't understand that, I forget so quickly."

"Well, what then?"

"Yes, so she loves me and you." Natasha suddenly flushed. "Well, you remember before you went away . . . She says you are to forget it all . . . She said, I shall always love him, but let him be free. That really is splendid, noble! Yes, yes; very noble? Yes?" Natasha asked with such seriousness and emotion that it was clear that what she was saying now she had talked of before with tears. Rostov thought a little.

"I never take back my word," he said. "And besides, Sonya's so charming that who would be such a fool as to renounce his own happiness?"

"No, no," cried Natasha. "She and I have talked about that already. We knew that you'd say that. But that won't do, because, don't you see, if you say that—if you consider yourself bound by your word, then it makes it as though she had said that on purpose. It makes it as though you were, after all, obliged to marry her, and it makes it all wrong."

Rostov saw that it had all been well thought over by them. On the previous day, Sonya had struck him by her beauty; in the glimpse he had caught of her to-day, she seemed even prettier. She was a charming girl of sixteen, obviously passionately in love with him (of that he could not doubt for an instant). "Why should he not love her now, even if he did not marry her," mused Rostov, "but . . . just now he had so many other joys and interests!"

"Yes, that's a very good conclusion on their part," he thought; "I must remain free."

"Well, that's all right, then," he said; "we'll talk about it later on. Ah, how glad I am to be back with you!" he added. "Come, tell me, you've not been false to Boris?"

"That's nonsense!" cried Natasha, laughing. "I never think of him nor of any one else, and don't want to."

"Oh, you don't, don't you! Then what do you want?"

"I?" Natasha queried, and her face beamed with a happy smile. "Have you seen Duport?"

"No."

"Not seen Duport, the celebrated dancer? Oh, well then, you won't understand. I—that's what I am." Curving her arms, Natasha held out her skirt, as dancers do, ran back a few steps, whirled round, executed a pirouette, bringing her little feet together and standing on the very tips of her toes, moved a few steps forward.

"You see how I stand? there, like this," she kept saying; but she could not keep on her toes. "So that's what I'm going to be! I'm never going to be married to any one; I'm going to be a dancer. Only, don't tell anybody."

Rostov laughed so loudly and merrily that Denisov in his room felt envious, and Natasha could not help laughing with him.

"No, isn't it all right?" she kept saying.

"Oh, quite. So you don't want to marry Boris now?"

Natasha got hot.

"I don't want to marry any one. I'll tell him so myself when I see him."

"Oh, will you?" said Rostov.

"But that's all nonsense," Natasha prattled on. "And, I say, is Denisov nice?" she asked.

"Yes, he's nice."

"Well, good-bye, go and dress. Is he a dreadful person—Denisov?"

"How, dreadful?" asked Nikolay. "No, Vaska's jolly."

"You call him Vaska? . . . that's funny. Well, is he very nice?"

"Very nice."

"Make haste and come to tea, then. We are all going to have it together."

And Natasha rose on to her toes and stepped out of the room, as dancers do, but smiling as only happy girls of fifteen can smile. Rostov reddened on meeting Sonya in the drawing-room. He did not know how to behave with her. Yesterday they had kissed in the first moment of joy at meeting, but to-day they felt that out of the question. He felt that every one, his mother and his sisters, were looking inquiringly at him, and wondering how he would behave with her. He kissed her hand, and called her *you* and *Sonya*. But their eyes when they met spoke more fondly and kissed tenderly. Her eyes asked his forgiveness for having dared, by Natasha's mediation, to remind him of his promise, and thanked him for his love. His eyes thanked her for offering him his freedom, and told her that whether so, or otherwise, he should never cease to love her, because it was impossible not to love her.

"How queer it is, though," said Vera, selecting a moment of general silence, "that Sonya and Nikolenka meet now and speak like strangers."

Vera's observation was true, as were all her observations; but like most of her observations it made every one uncomfortable—not Sonya, Nikolay, and Natasha only crimsoned; the countess, too, who was afraid of her son's love for Sonya as a possible obstacle to his making a brilliant marriage, blushed like a girl.

To Rostov's surprise, Denisov in his new uniform, pomaded and perfumed, was quite as dashing a figure in a drawing-room as on the field of battle, and was polite to the ladies and gentlemen as Rostov had never expected to see him.

II

On his return to Moscow from the army, Nikolay Rostov was received by his family as a hero, as the best of sons, their idolised Nikolenka; by his relations, as a charming, agreeable, and polite young man; by his acquaintances as a handsome lieutenant of hussars, a good dancer, and one of the best matches in Moscow.

All Moscow was acquainted with the Rostovs; the old count had plenty of money that year, because all his estates had been mortgaged, and so Nikolenka, who kept his own racehorse, and wore the most fashionable riding-breeches of a special cut, unlike any yet seen in Moscow, and the most fashionable boots, with extremely pointed toes, and little silver spurs, was able to pass his time very agreeably. After the first brief interval of adapting himself to the old conditions of life, Rostov felt very happy at being home again. He felt that he had grown up and become a man. His despair at failing in a Scripture examination, his borrowing money from Gavrilo for his sledge-drivers, his stolen kisses with Sonya—all that he looked back upon as childishness from which he was now immeasurably remote. Now he was a lieutenant of hussars with a silver-braided jacket, and a soldier's cross of St. George, he had a horse in training for a race, and kept company with well-known racing men, elderly and respected persons. He had struck up an acquaintance, too, with a lady living in a boulevard, whom he used to visit in the evening. He led the mazurka at the Arharovs' balls, talked to Field-Marshal Kamensky about the war, and used familiar forms of address to a colonel of forty, to whom he had been introduced by Denisov.

His passion for the Tsar flagged a little in Moscow, as he did not see him, and had no chance of seeing him all that time. But still he often used to talk about the Emperor and his love for him, always with a suggestion in his tone that he was not saying all that there was in his feeling for the Emperor, something that every one could not understand; and with his whole heart he shared the general feeling in Moscow of adoration for the Emperor Alexander Pavlovitch, who was spoken of at that time in Moscow by the designation of the "angel incarnate."

During this brief stay in Moscow, before his return to the army, Rostov did not come nearer to Sonya, but on the contrary drifted further away from her. She was very pretty and charming, and it was obvious that she was passionately in love with him. But he was at that stage of youth when there seems so much to do, that one has not time to pay attention to love, and a young man dreads being bound, and prizes his liberty, which he wants for so much else. When he thought about Sonya during this stay at Moscow, he said to himself: "Ah! there are many, many more like her to come, and there are many of them somewhere now, though I don't know them yet. There's plenty of time before me to think about love when I want to, but I have not the time now." Moreover, it seemed to him that feminine society was somewhat beneath his manly dignity. He went to balls, and into ladies' society with an affection of doing so against his will. Races, the English club, carousals with Denisov, and the nocturnal visits that followed—all that was different, all that was the correct thing for a dashing young hussar.

At the beginning of March the old count, Ilya Andreivitch Rostov, was very busily engaged in arranging a dinner at the English Club, to be given in honour of Prince Bagration.

The count, in his dressing-gown, was continually walking up and down in the big hall, seeing the club manager, the celebrated Feoktista, and the head cook, and giving them instructions relative to asparagus, fresh cucumbers, strawberries, veal, and fish, for Prince Bagration's dinner. From the day of its foundation, the count had been a member of the club, and was its steward. He had been entrusted with the organisation of the banquet to Bagration by the club, because it would have been hard to find any one so well able to organise a banquet on a large and hospitable scale, and still more hard to find any one so able and willing to advance his own money, if funds were needed, for the organisation of the fête. The cook and the club manager listened to the count's orders with good-humoured faces, because they knew that with no one better than with him could one make a handsome profit out of a dinner costing several thousands.

"Well, then, mind there are scallops, scallops in pie-crust, you know."

"Cold *entrées*, I suppose—three? . . ." questioned the cook.

The count pondered.

"Couldn't do with less, three . . . *mayonnaise*, one," he said, crooking his finger.

"Then it's your excellency's order to take the big sturgeons?" asked the manager.

"Yes; it can't be helped, we must take them, if they won't knock the price down. Ah, mercy on us, I was forgetting. Of course we must have another *entrée* on the table. Ah, good heavens!" he clutched at his head. "And who's going to get me the flowers? Mitenka! Hey, Mitenka! You gallop, Mitenka," he said to the steward who came in at his call, "you gallop off to the Podmoskovny estate" (the count's property in the environs of Moscow), "and tell Maksimka the gardener to set the serfs to work to get decorations from the greenhouses. Tell him everything from his conservatories is to be brought here, and is to be packed in felt. And that I'm to have two hundred pots here by Friday."

After giving further and yet further directions of all sorts, he was just going off to the countess to rest from his labours, but he recollected something else, turned back himself, brought the cook and manager back, and began giving orders again. They heard in the doorway a light, manly tread and a jingling of spurs, and the young count came in, handsome and rosy, with his darkening moustache, visibly sleeker and in better trim for his easy life in Moscow.

"Ah, my boy! my head's in a whirl," said the old gentleman, with a somewhat shamefaced smile at his son. "You might come to my aid! We have still the singers to get, you see. The music is all settled, but shouldn't we order some gypsy singers? You military gentlemen are fond of that sort of thing."

"Upon my word, papa, I do believe that Prince Bagration made less fuss over getting ready for the battle of Schöngraben than you are making now," said his son, smiling.

The old count pretended to be angry.

"Well, you talk, you try!" And the count turned to the cook, who with a shrewd and respectful face looked observantly and sympathetically from father to son.

"What are the young people coming to, eh, Feoktista?" said he; "they laugh at us old fellows!"

"To be sure, your excellency, all they have to do is to eat a good dinner, but to arrange it all and serve it up, that's no affair of theirs!"

"True, true!" cried the count; and gaily seizing his son by both hands, he cried: "Do you know now I've got hold of you! Take a sledge and pair this minute and drive off to Bezuhov, and say that Count Ilya Andreivitch has sent, say, to ask him for strawberries and fresh pineapples. There's no getting them from any one else. If he's not at home himself, you go in and give the message to the princesses; and, I say, from there you drive off to the Gaiety—Ipatka the coachman knows the place—and look up Ilyushka there, the gypsy who danced at Count Orlov's, do you remember, in a white Cossack dress, and bring him here to me."

"And bring his gypsy girls here with him?" asked Nikolay, laughing.

"Come, come! . . ."

At this moment Anna Mihalovna stepped noiselessly into the room with that air of Christian meekness, mingled with practical and anxious preoccupation that never left her face. Although Anna Mihalovna came upon the count in his dressing-gown every day, he was invariably disconcerted at her doing so, and apologised for his costume.

"Don't mention it, my dear count," she said, closing her eyes meekly. "I am just going to see Bezuhov," she said. "Young Bezuhov has arrived, and now we shall get all we want, count, from his greenhouses. I was wanting to see him on my own account, too. He has forwarded me a letter from Boris. Thank God, Boris is now on the staff."

The count was overjoyed at Anna Mihalovna's undertaking one part of his commissions, and gave orders for the carriage to be brought round for her.

"Tell Bezuhov to come. I'll put his name down. Brought his wife with him?" he asked.

Anna Mihalovna turned up her eyes, and an expression of profound sadness came into her face.

"Ah, my dear, he's very unhappy," she said. "If it's true what we have been hearing, it's awful. How little did we think of this when we were rejoicing in happiness! and such a lofty, angelic nature, that young Bezuhov! Yes, I pity him from my soul, and will do my utmost to give him any consolation in my power."

"Why, what is the matter?" inquired both the Rostovs, young and old together.

Anna Mihalovna heaved a deep sigh.

"Dolohov, Marya Ivanovna's son," she said in a mysterious whisper, "has, they say, utterly compromised her. He brought him forward, invited him to his house in Petersburg, and now this! . . . She has come here, and that scapegrace has come after her," said Anna Mihalovna. She wished to express nothing but sympathy with Pierre, but in her involuntary intonations and half smile, she betrayed her sympathy with the scapegrace, as she called Dolohov. "Pierre himself, they say, is utterly crushed by his trouble."

"Well, any way, tell him to come to the club—it will divert his mind. It will be a banquet on a grand scale."

On the next day, the 3rd of March, at about two in the afternoon, the two hundred and fifty members of the English Club and fifty of their guests were awaiting the arrival of their honoured guest, the hero of the Austrian campaign, Prince Bagration.

On receiving the news of the defeat of Austerlitz, all Moscow had at first been thrown into bewilderment. At that period the Russians were so used to victories, that on receiving news of a defeat, some people were simply incredulous, while others sought an explanation of so strange an event in exceptional circumstances of some kind. At the English Club, where every one of note, every one who had authentic information and weight gathered together, during December, when the news began to arrive, not a word was said about the war and about the last defeat; it was as though all were in a conspiracy of silence. The men who took the lead in conversation at the club, such as Count Rostoptchin, Prince Yury Vladimirovitch Dolgoruky, Valuev, Count Markov, and Prince Vyazemsky, did not put in an appearance at the club, but met together in their intimate circles at each other's houses.

That section of Moscow society which took its opinions from others (to which, indeed, Count Ilya Andreivitch Rostov belonged) remained for a short time without leaders and without definite views upon the progress of the war. People felt in Moscow that something was wrong, and that it was difficult to know what to think of the bad news, and so better to be silent. But a little later, like jurymen coming out of their consultation room, the leaders reappeared to give their opinion in the club, and a clear and definite formula was found. Causes had been discovered to account for the fact—so incredible, unheard-of, and impossible—that the Russians had been beaten, and all became clear, and the same version was repeated from one end of Moscow to the other. These causes were: the treachery of the Austrians; the defective commissariat; the treachery of the Pole Przhebyshevsky and the Frenchman Langeron; the incapacity of Kutuzov; and (this was murmured in subdued tones) the youth and inexperience of the Emperor, who had put faith in men of no character and ability. But the army, the Russian army, said every one, had been extraordinary, and had performed miracles of valour. The soldiers, the officers, the generals—all were heroes. But the hero among heroes was Prince Bagration, who had distinguished himself in his Schöngraben engagement and in the retreat from Austerlitz, where he alone had withdrawn his column in good order, and had succeeded in repelling during the whole day an enemy twice as numerous. What contributed to Bagration's being chosen for the popular hero at Moscow was the fact that he was an outsider, that he had no connections in Moscow. In his person they could do honour to the simple fighting Russian soldier, unsupported by connections and intrigues, and still associated by memories of the Italian campaign with the name of Suvorov. And besides, bestowing upon him such honours was the best possible way of showing their dislike and disapproval of Kutuzov.

"If there had been no Bagration, somebody would have to invent him," said the wit, Shinshin, parodying the words of Voltaire.

Of Kutuzov people did not speak at all, or whispered abuse of him, calling him the court weathercock and the old satyr.

All Moscow was repeating the words of Prince Dolgorukov: "Chop down trees enough and you're bound to cut your finger," which in our defeat suggested a consolatory reminder of former victories, and the saying of Rostoptchin, that French soldiers have to be excited to battle by high-sounding phrases; that Germans must have it logically proved to them that it is more dangerous to run away than to go forward; but that all Russian soldiers need is to be held back and urged not to be too reckless! New anecdotes were continually to be heard on every side of individual feats of gallantry performed by our officers and men at Austerlitz. Here a man had saved a flag, another had killed five Frenchmen, another had kept five cannons loaded single-handed. The story was told of Berg, by those who did not know him, that wounded in his right hand, he had taken his sword in his left and charged on the enemy. Nothing was said about Bolkonsky, and only those who had known him intimately regretted that he had died so young, leaving a wife with child, and his queer old father.

III

On the 3rd of March all the rooms of the English Club were full of the hum of voices, and the members and guests of the club, in uniforms and frock-coats, some even in powder and Russian kaftans, were standing meeting, parting, and running to and fro like bees swarming in spring. Powdered footmen in livery, wearing slippers and stockings, stood at every door, anxiously trying to follow every movement of the guests and club members, so as to proffer their services. The majority of those present were elderly and respected persons, with broad, self-confident faces, fat fingers, and resolute gestures and voices. Guests and members of this class sat in certain habitual places, and met together in certain habitual circles. A small proportion of those present were casual guests —chiefly young men, among them Denisov, Rostov, and Dolohov, who was now an officer in the Semyonovsky regiment again. The faces of the younger men, especially the officers, wore that expression of condescending deference to their elders which seems to say to the older generation, "Respect and deference we are prepared to give you, but remember all the same the future is for us." Nesvitsky, an old member of the club, was there too. Pierre, who at his wife's command had let his hair grow and left off spectacles, was walking about the rooms dressed in the height of the fashion, but looking melancholy and depressed. Here, as everywhere, he was surrounded by the atmosphere of people paying homage to his wealth, and he behaved to them with the careless, contemptuous air of sovereignty that had become habitual with him.

In years, he belonged to the younger generation, but by his wealth and connections he was a member of the older circles, and so he passed from one set to the other. The most distinguished of the elder members formed the centres of circles, which even strangers respectfully approached to listen to the words of well-known men. The larger groups were formed round Count Rostoptchin, Valuev, and Naryshkin. Rostoptchin was describing how the Russians had been trampled underfoot by the fleeing Austrians, and had had to force a way with the bayonet through the fugitives. Valuev was confidentially informing his circle that Uvarov had been sent from Petersburg to ascertain the state of opinion in Moscow in regard to Austerlitz.

In the third group Naryshkin was repeating the tale of the meeting of the Austrian council of war, at which, in reply to the stupidity of the Austrian general, Suvorov crowed like a cock. Shinshin, who stood near, tried to make a joke, saying that Kutuzov, it seemed, had not even been able to learn from Suvorov that not very difficult art—of crowing like a cock—but the elder club members looked sternly at the wit, giving him thereby to understand that even such a reference to Kutuzov was out of place on that day.

Count Ilya Andreitch Rostov kept anxiously hurrying in his soft boots to and fro from the dining-room to the drawing-room, giving hasty greetings to important and unimportant persons, all of whom he knew, and all of whom he treated alike, on an equal footing. Now and then his eyes sought out the graceful, dashing figure of his young son, rested gleefully on him, and winked to him. Young Rostov was standing at the window with Dolohov, whose acquaintance he had lately made, and greatly prized. The old count went up to them, and shook hands with Dolohov.

"I beg you will come and see us; so you're a friend of my youngster's . . . been together, playing the hero together out there. . . . Ah! Vassily Ignatitch . . . a good day to you, old man," he turned to an old gentleman who had just come in, but before he had time to finish his greetings to him there was a general stir, and a footman running in with an alarmed countenance, announced: "He has arrived!"

Bells rang; the stewards rushed forward; the guests, scattered about the different rooms, gathered together in one mass, like rye shaken together in a shovel, and waited at the door of the great drawing-room.

At the door of the ante-room appeared the figure of Bagration, without his hat or sword, which, in accordance with the club custom, he had left with the hall porter. He was not wearing an Astrachan cap, and had not a riding-whip over his shoulder, as Rostov had seen him on the night before the battle of Austerlitz, but wore a tight new uniform with Russian and foreign orders and the star of St. George on the left side of his chest. He had, obviously with a view to the banquet, just had his hair cut and his whiskers clipped, which changed his appearance for the worse. He had a sort of naïvely festive air, which, in conjunction with his determined, manly features, gave an expression positively rather comic to his face. Bekleshov and Fyodor Petrovitch Uvarov, who had come with him, stood still in the doorway trying to make him, as the guest of most importance, precede them. Bagration was embarrassed, and unwilling to avail himself of their courtesy; there was a hitch in the proceedings at the door, but finally Bagration did, after all, enter first. He walked shyly and awkwardly over the parquet of the reception-room, not knowing what to do with his hands. He would have been more at home and at his ease walking over a ploughed field under fire, as he had walked at the head of the Kursk regiment at Schöngraben. The stewards met him at the first door, and saying a few words of their pleasure at seeing such an honoured guest, they surrounded him without waiting for an answer, and, as it were, taking possession of him, led him off to the drawing-room. There was no possibility of getting in at the drawing-room door from the crowds of members and guests, who were crushing one another in their efforts to get a look over each other's shoulders at Bagration, as if he were some rare sort of beast. Count Ilya Andreitch laughed more vigorously than any one, and continually repeating, "Make way for him, my dear boy, make way, make way," shoved the crowd aside, led the guests into the drawing-room, and seated them on the sofa in the middle of it. The great men, and the more honoured members of the club, surrounded the newly arrived guests. Count Ilya Andreitch, shoving his way again through the crowd, went out of the drawing-room, and reappeared a minute later with another steward carrying a great silver dish, which he held out to Prince Bagration. On the dish lay a poem, composed and printed in the hero's honour. Bagration, on seeing the dish, looked about him in dismay, as though seeking assistance. But in all eyes he saw the expectation that he would submit. Feeling himself in their power, Bagration resolutely took the dish in both hands, and looked angrily and reproachfully at the count, who had brought it. Some one officiously took the dish from Bagration (or he would, it seemed, have held it so till nightfall, and have carried it with him to the table), and drew his attention to the poem. "Well I'll read it then," Bagration seemed to say, and fixing his weary eyes on the paper, he began reading it with a serious and concentrated expression. The author of the verses took them, and began to read them aloud himself. Prince Bagration bowed his head and listened.

> "Be thou the pride of Alexander's reign!
> And save for us our Titus on the throne!
> Be thou our champion and our country's stay!
> A noble heart, a Cæsar in the fray!
> Napoleon in the zenith of his fame
> Learns to his cost to fear Bagration's name,
> Nor dares provoke a Russian foe again," etc. etc.

But he had not finished the poem, when the butler boomed out sono rously: "Dinner is ready!" The door opened, from the dining-room thun dered the strains of the Polonaise: "Raise the shout of victory, valiant Russian, festive sing," and Count Ilya Andreitch, looking angrily at the author, who still went on reading his verses, bowed to Bagration as a signal to go in. All the company rose, feeling the dinner of more impor tance than the poem, and Bagration, again preceding all the rest, went in to dinner. In the place of honour between two Alexanders—Bekleshov and Naryshkin—(this, too, was intentional, in allusion to the name of the Tsar) they put Bagration: three hundred persons were ranged about the tables according to their rank and importance, those of greater con sequence, nearer to the distinguished guest—as naturally as water flows to find its own level.

Just before dinner, Count Ilya Andreitch presented his son to the prince. Bagration recognised him, and uttered a few words, awkward and incoherent, as were indeed all he spoke that day. Count Ilya Andreitch looked about at every one in gleeful pride while Bagration was speaking to his son.

Nikolay Rostov, with Denisov and his new acquaintance Dolohov, sat together almost in the middle of the table. Facing them sat Pierre with Prince Nesvitsky. Count Ilya Andreitch was sitting with the other stewards facing Bagration, and, the very impersonation of Moscow hos pitality, did his utmost to regale the prince.

His labours had not been in vain. All the banquet—the meat dishes and the Lenten fare alike—was sumptuous, but still he could not be per fectly at ease till the end of dinner. He made signs to the carver, gave whispered directions to the footmen, and not without emotion awaited the arrival of each anticipated dish. Everything was capital. At the sec ond course, with the gigantic sturgeon (at the sight of which Ilya An dreitch flushed with shamefaced delight), the footman began popping corks and pouring out champagne. After the fish, which made a certain sensation, Count Ilya Andreitch exchanged glances with the other stew ards. "There will be a great many toasts, it's time to begin!" he whis pered, and, glass in hand, he got up. All were silent, waiting for what he would say.

"To the health of our sovereign, the Emperor!" he shouted, and at the moment his kindly eyes grew moist with tears of pleasure and en thusiasm. At that instant they began playing: "Raise the shout of vic tory!" All rose from their seats and shouted "Hurrah!" And Bagration shouted "Hurrah!" in the same voice in which he had shouted it in the field at Schöngraben. The enthusiastic voice of young Rostov could be heard above the three hundred other voices. He was on the very point of tears. "The health of our sovereign, the Emperor," he roared, "hurrah!" Emptying his glass at one gulp, he flung it on the floor. Many followed his example. And the loud shouts lasted for a long while. When the up roar subsided, the footmen cleared away the broken glass, and all began settling themselves again; and smiling at the noise they had made, began talking. Count Ilya Andreitch rose once more, glanced at a note that lay beside his plate, and proposed a toast to the health of the hero of our last campaign, Prince Pyotr Ivanovitch Bagration, and again the count's blue eyes were dimmed with tears. "Hurrah!" was shouted again by the three hundred voices of the guests, and instead of music this time a chorus of singers began to sing a cantata composed by Pavel Ivanovitch Kutuzov:

> "No hindrance bars a Russian's way,
> Valour's the pledge of victory,
> We have our Bagrations.
> Our foes will all be at our feet," etc. etc.

As soon as the singers had finished, more and more toasts followed, at which Count Ilya Andreitch became more and more moved, and more glass was broken and even more uproar was made. They drank to the health of Bekleshov, of Naryshkin, of Uvarov, of Dolgorukov, of Apraxin, of Valuev, to the health of the stewards, to the health of the committee, to the health of all the club members, to the health of all the guests of the club, and finally and separately to the health of the organiser of the banquet, Count Ilya Andreitch. At that toast the count took out his handkerchief and, hiding his face in it, fairly broke down.

IV

PIERRE was sitting opposite Dolohov and Nikolay Rostov. He ate greedily and drank heavily, as he always did. But those who knew him slightly could see that some great change was taking place in him that day. He was silent all through dinner, and blinking and screwing up his eyes, looked about him, or letting his eyes rest on something with an air of complete absent-mindedness, rubbed the bridge of his nose with his finger. His face was depressed and gloomy. He seemed not to be seeing or hearing what was passing about him and to be thinking of some one thing, something painful and unsettled.

This unsettled question that worried him was due to the hints dropped by the princess, his cousin, at Moscow in regard to Dolohov's close intimacy with his wife, and to an anonymous letter he had received that morning, which, with the vile jocoseness peculiar to all anonymous letters, had said that he didn't seem to see clearly through his spectacles, and that his wife's connection with Dolohov was a secret from no one but himself. Pierre did not absolutely believe either the princess's hints, or the anonymous letter, but he was afraid now to look at Dolohov, who sat opposite him. Every time his glance casually met Dolohov's handsome, insolent eyes, Pierre felt as though something awful, hideous was rising up in his soul, and he made haste to turn away. Involuntarily recalling all his wife's past and her attitude to Dolohov, Pierre saw clearly that what was said in the letter might well be true, might at least appear to be the truth, if only it had not related to *his wife*. Pierre could not help recalling how Dolohov, who had been completely reinstated, had returned to Petersburg and come to see him. Dolohov had taken advantage

of his friendly relations with Pierre in their old rowdy days, had come
straight to his house, and Pierre had established him in it and lent him
money. Pierre recalled how Ellen, smiling, had expressed her dissatisfaction at Dolohov's staying in their house, and how cynically Dolohov had
praised his wife's beauty to him, and how he had never since left them
up to the time of their coming to Moscow.

"Yes, he is very handsome," thought Pierre, "and I know him. There
would be a particular charm for him in disgracing my name and turning
me into ridicule, just because I have exerted myself in his behalf, have
befriended him and helped him. I know, I understand what zest that
would be sure to give to his betrayal of me, if it were true. Yes, if it were
true, but I don't believe it. I have no right to and I can't believe it." He
recalled the expression on Dolohov's face in his moments of cruelty,
such as when he was tying the police officer on to the bear and dropping
him into the water, or when he had utterly without provocation challenged a man to a duel or killed a sledge-driver's horse with a shot from
his pistol. That expression often came into Dolohov's face when he was
looking at him. "Yes, he's a duelling bully," thought Pierre; "to him it
means nothing to kill a man, it must seem to him that every one's afraid
of him. He must like it. He must think I am afraid of him. And, in fact,
I really am afraid of him," Pierre mused; and again at these thoughts
he felt as though something terrible and hideous were rising up in his
soul. Dolohov, Denisov, and Rostov were sitting facing Pierre and
seemed to be greatly enjoying themselves. Rostov talked away merrily
to his two friends, of whom one was a dashing hussar, the other a notorious duellist and scapegrace, and now and then cast ironical glances at
Pierre, whose appearance at the dinner was a striking one, with his preoccupied, absent-minded, massive figure. Rostov looked with disfavour
upon Pierre. In the first place, because Pierre, in the eyes of the smart
hussar, was a rich civilian, and husband of a beauty, was altogether, in
fact, an old woman. And secondly, because Pierre in his preoccupation
and absent-mindedness had not recognised Rostov and had failed to respond to his bow. When they got up to drink the health of the Tsar,
Pierre, plunged in thought, did not rise nor take up his glass.

"What are you about?" Rostov shouted to him, looking at him with
enthusiastic and exasperated eyes. "Don't you hear: the health of our
sovereign the Emperor!"

Pierre with a sigh obeyed, got up, emptied his glass, and waiting till all
were seated again, he turned with his kindly smile to Rostov. "Why, I
didn't recognise you," he said. But Rostov had no thoughts for him, he
was shouting "Hurrah!"

"Why don't you renew the acquaintance?" said Dolohov to Rostov.

"Oh, bother him, he's a fool," said Rostov.

"One has to be sweet to the husbands of pretty women," said Denisov.
Pierre did not hear what they were saying, but he knew they were talking of him. He flushed and turned away. "Well, now to the health of
pretty women," said Dolohov, and with a serious expression, though a
smile lurked in the corners of his mouth, he turned to Pierre.

"To the health of pretty women, Petrusha, and their lovers too," he said.

Pierre, with downcast eyes, sipped his glass, without looking at Dolohov or answering him. The footman, distributing copies of Kutuzov's cantata, laid a copy by Pierre, as one of the more honoured guests. He would have taken it, but Dolohov bent forward, snatched the paper out of his hands and began reading it. Pierre glanced at Dolohov, and his eyes dropped; something terrible and hideous, that had been torturing him all through the dinner, rose up and took possession of him. He bent the whole of his ungainly person across the table. "Don't you dare to take it!" he shouted.

Hearing that shout and seeing to whom it was addressed, Nesvitsky and his neighbour on the right side turned in haste and alarm to Bezuhov.

"Hush, hush, what are you about?" whispered panic-stricken voices. Dolohov looked at Pierre with his clear, mirthful, cruel eyes, still with the same smile, as though he were saying: "Come now, this is what I like."

"I won't give it up," he said distinctly.

Pale and with quivering lips, Pierre snatched the copy.

"You . . . you . . . blackguard! . . . I challenge you," he said, and moving back his chair, he got up from the table. At the second Pierre did this and uttered these words he felt that the question of his wife's guilt, that had been torturing him for the last four and twenty hours, was finally and incontestably answered in the affirmative. He hated her and was severed from her for ever. In spite of Denisov's entreaties that Rostov would have nothing to do with the affair, Rostov agreed to be Dolohov's second, and after dinner he discussed with Nesvitsky, Bezuhov's second, the arrangements for the duel. Pierre had gone home, but Rostov with Dolohov and Denisov stayed on at the club listening to the gypsies and the singers till late in the evening.

"So good-bye till to-morrow, at Sokolniky," said Dolohov, as he parted from Rostov at the club steps.

"And do you feel quite calm?" asked Rostov.

Dolohov stopped.

"Well, do you see, in a couple of words I'll let you into the whole secret of duelling. If, when you go to a duel, you make your will and write long letters to your parents, if you think that you may be killed, you're a fool and certain to be done for. But go with the firm intention of killing your man, as quickly and as surely as may be, then everything will be all right. As our bear-killer from Kostroma used to say to me: 'A bear,' he'd say, 'why, who's not afraid of one? but come to see one and your fear's all gone, all you hope is he won't get away!' Well, that's just how I feel. *A demain, mon cher.*"

Next day at eight o'clock in the morning, Pierre and Nesvitsky reached the Sokolniky copse, and found Dolohov, Denisov, and Rostov already there. Pierre had the air of a man absorbed in reflections in no way connected with the matter in hand. His face looked hollow and yellow. He had not slept all night. He looked about him absent-mindedly, and screwed up his eyes, as though in glaring sunshine. He was exclusively absorbed by two considerations: the guilt of his wife, of which after a sleepless night he had not a vestige of doubt, and the guiltlessness of Dolohov, who was in no way bound to guard the honour of a man, who was nothing to him. "Maybe I should have done the same in his place," thought Pierre. "For certain, indeed, I should have done the same; then why this duel, this murder? Either I shall kill him, or he will shoot me in the head, in the elbow, or the knee. To get away from here, to run, to bury myself somewhere," was the longing that came into his mind. But precisely at the moments when such ideas were in his mind, he would turn with a peculiarly calm and unconcerned face, which inspired respect in the seconds looking at him, and ask: "Will it be soon?" or "Aren't we ready?"

When everything was ready, the swords stuck in the snow to mark the barrier, and the pistols loaded, Nesvitsky went up to Pierre.

"I should not be doing my duty, count," he said in a timid voice, "nor justifying the confidence and the honour you have done me in choosing me for your second, if at this grave moment, this very grave moment, I did not speak the whole truth to you. I consider that the quarrel has not sufficient grounds and is not worth shedding blood over. . . . You were not right, not quite in the right; you lost your temper. . . ."

"Oh, yes, it was awfully stupid," said Pierre.

"Then allow me to express your regret, and I am convinced that our opponents will agree to accept your apology," said Nesvitsky (who, like the others assisting in the affair, and every one at such affairs, was unable to believe that the quarrel would come to an actual duel). "You know, count, it is far nobler to acknowledge one's mistake than to push things to the irrevocable. There was no great offence on either side. Permit me to convey . . ."

"No, what are you talking about?" said Pierre; "it doesn't matter. . . . Ready then?" he added. "Only tell me how and where I am to go, and what to shoot at?" he said with a smile unnaturally gentle. He took up a pistol, and began inquiring how to let it off, as he had never had a pistol in his hand before, a fact he did not care to confess. "Oh, yes, of course, I know, I had only forgotten," he said.

"No apologies, absolutely nothing," Dolohov was saying to Denisov, who for his part was also making an attempt at reconciliation, and he too went up to the appointed spot.

The place chosen for the duel was some eighty paces from the road, on which their sledges had been left, in a small clearing in the pine wood, covered with snow that had thawed in the warmer weather of the last few days. The antagonists stood forty paces from each other at the further edge of the clearing. The seconds, in measuring the paces, left tracks in the deep, wet snow from the spot where they had been standing to the swords of Nesvitsky and Denisov, which had been thrust in the ground ten paces from one another to mark the barrier. The thaw and mist persisted; forty paces away nothing could be seen. In three

minutes everything was ready, but still they delayed beginning. Every
one was silent.

V

"WELL, let us begin," said Dolohov.

"To be sure," said Pierre, still with the same smile.

A feeling of dread was in the air. It was obvious that the affair that
had begun so lightly could not now be in any way turned back, that it
was going forward of itself, independently of men's will, and must run
its course. Denisov was the first to come forward to the barrier and pronounce the words:

"Since the antagonists refuse all reconciliation, would it not be as
well to begin? Take your pistols, and at the word 'three' begin to advance together. O . . . one! Two! Three! . . ." Denisov shouted angrily, and he walked away from the barrier. Both walked along the
trodden tracks closer and closer together, beginning to recognise one
another in the mist. The combatants had the right to fire when they
chose as they approached the barrier. Dolohov walked slowly, not lifting
his pistol, and looking intently with his clear, shining eyes into the face
of his antagonist. His mouth wore, as always, the semblance of a smile.

"So when I like, I can fire," said Pierre, and at the word *three*, he
walked with rapid steps forward, straying off the beaten track and stepping over the untrodden snow. Pierre held his pistol at full length in his
right hand, obviously afraid of killing himself with that pistol. His left
arm he studiously held behind him, because he felt inclined to use it to
support his right arm, and he knew that was not allowed. After advancing six paces, and getting off the track into the snow, Pierre looked about
under his feet, glancing rapidly again at Dolohov, and stretching out his
finger, as he had been shown, fired. Not at all expecting so loud a report,
Pierre started at his own shot, then smiled at his own sensation and
stood still. The smoke, which was made thicker by the fog, hindered
him from seeing for the first moment; but the other shot that he was
expecting did not follow. All that could be heard were Dolohov's rapid
footsteps, and his figure came into view through the smoke. With one
hand he was clutching at his left side, the other was clenched on the
lower pistol. His face was pale. Rostov was running up and saying
something to him.

"N . . . no," Dolohov muttered through his teeth, "no, it's not
over"; and struggling on a few sinking, staggering steps up to the sword,
he sank on to the snow beside it. His left hand was covered with blood,
he rubbed it on his coat and leaned upon it. His face was pale, frowning
and trembling.

"Co . . ." Dolohov began, but he could not at once articulate the
words: "come up," he said, with an effort. Pierre, hardly able to restrain
his sobs, ran towards Dolohov, and would have crossed the space that
separated the barriers, when Dolohov cried: "To the barrier!" and

Pierre, grasping what was wanted, stood still just at the sword. Only ten paces divided them. Dolohov putting his head down, greedily bit at the snow, lifted his head again, sat up, tried to get on his legs and sat down, trying to find a secure centre of gravity. He took a mouthful of the cold snow, and sucked it; his lips quivered, but still he smiled; his eyes glittered with the strain and exasperation of the struggle with his failing forces. He raised the pistol and began taking aim.

"Sideways, don't expose yourself to the pistol," said Nesvitsky.

"Don't face it!" Denisov could not help shouting, though it was to an antagonist.

With his gentle smile of sympathy and remorse, Pierre stood with his legs and arms straddling helplessly, and his broad chest directly facing Dolohov, and looked at him mournfully. Denisov, Rostov, and Nesvitsky screwed up their eyes. At the same instant they heard a shot and Dolohov's wrathful cry.

"Missed!" shouted Dolohov, and he dropped helplessly, face downwards, in the snow. Pierre clutched at his head, and turning back, walked into the wood, off the path in the snow, muttering aloud incoherent words.

"Stupid . . . stupid! Death . . . lies . . ." he kept repeating, scowling. Nesvitsky stopped him and took him home.

Rostov and Denisov got the wounded Dolohov away.

Dolohov lay in the sledge with closed eyes, in silence, and uttered not a word in reply to questions addressed to him. But as they were driving into Moscow, he suddenly came to himself, and lifting his head with an effort, he took the hand of Rostov, who was sitting near him. Rostov was struck by the utterly transformed and unexpectedly passionately tender expression on Dolohov's face.

"Well? How do you feel?" asked Rostov.

"Bad! but that's not the point. My friend," said Dolohov, in a breaking voice, "where are we? We are in Moscow, I know. I don't matter, but I have killed her, killed her. . . . She won't get over this. She can't bear . . ."

"Who?" asked Rostov.

"My mother. My mother, my angel, my adored angel, my mother," and squeezing Rostov's hand, Dolohov burst into tears. When he was a little calmer, he explained to Rostov that he was living with his mother, that if his mother were to see him dying, she would not get over the shock. He besought Rostov to go to her and prepare her.

Rostov drove on ahead to carry out his wish, and to his immense astonishment he learned that Dolohov, this bully, this noted duellist Dolohov, lived at Moscow with his old mother and a hunchback sister, and was the tenderest son and brother.

VI

PIERRE had of late rarely seen his wife alone. Both at Petersburg and at Moscow their house had been constantly full of guests. On the night following the duel he did not go to his bedroom, but spent the night, as he often did, in his huge study, formerly his father's room, the very room indeed in which Count Bezuhov had died.

He lay down on the couch and tried to go to sleep, so as to forget all that had happened to him, but he could not do so. Such a tempest of feelings, thoughts, and reminiscences suddenly arose in his soul, that, far from going to sleep, he could not even sit still in one place, and was forced to leap up from the couch and pace with rapid steps about the room. At one moment he had a vision of his wife, as she was in the first days after their marriage, with her bare shoulders, and languid, passionate eyes; and then immediately by her side he saw the handsome, impudent, hard, and ironical face of Dolohov, as he had seen it at the banquet, and again the same face of Dolohov, pale, quivering, in agony, as it had been when he turned and sank in the snow.

"What has happened?" he asked himself; "I have killed *her lover*; yes, killed the lover of my wife. Yes, that has happened. Why was it? How have I come to this?" "Because you married her," answered an inner voice.

"But how am I to blame?" he asked. "For marrying without loving her, for deceiving yourself and her." And vividly he recalled that minute after supper at Prince Vassily's when he had said those words he found so difficult to utter: "I love you." "It has all come from that. Even then I felt it," he thought; "I felt at the time that it wasn't the right thing, that I had no right to do it. And so it has turned out." He recalled the honeymoon, and blushed at the recollection of it. Particularly vivid, humiliating, and shameful was the memory of how one day soon after his marriage he had come in his silk dressing-gown out of his bedroom into his study at twelve o'clock in the day, and in his study had found his head steward, who had bowed deferentially, and looking at Pierre's face and his dressing-gown, had faintly smiled, as though to express by that smile his respectful sympathy with his patron's happiness. "And how often I have been proud of her, proud of her majestic beauty, her social tact," he thought; "proud of my house, in which she received all Petersburg, proud of her unapproachability and beauty. So this was what I prided myself on. I used to think then that I did not understand her. How often, reflecting on her character, I have told myself that I was to blame, that I did not understand her, did not understand that everlasting composure and complacency, and the absence of all preferences and desires, and the solution of the whole riddle lay in that fearful word, that she is a dissolute woman; I have found that fearful word, and all has become clear.

"Anatole used to come to borrow money of her, and used to kiss her on her bare shoulders. She didn't give him money; but she let herself be kissed. Her father used to try in joke to rouse her jealousy; with a serene smile she used to say she was not fool enough to be jealous. Let him do as he likes, she used to say about me. I asked her once if she felt no symptoms of pregnancy. She laughed contemptuously, and said she was not such a fool as to want children, and that she would never have a child by me."

Then he thought of the coarseness, the bluntness of her ideas, and the vulgarity of the expressions that were characteristic of her, although she had been brought up in the highest aristocratic circles. "Not quite such a fool . . . you just try it on . . . you clear out of this," she would say. Often, watching the favourable impression she made on young and old, on men and women, Pierre could not understand why it was he did not love her. "Yes; I never loved her," Pierre said to himself; "I knew she was a dissolute woman," he repeated to himself; "but I did not dare own it to myself.

"And now Dolohov: there he sits in the snow and forces himself to smile; and dies with maybe some swaggering affectation on his lips in answer to my remorse."

Pierre was one of those people who in spite of external weakness of character—so-called—do not seek a confidant for their sorrows. He worked through his trouble alone.

"She, she alone is to blame for everything," he said to himself; "but what of it? Why did I bind myself to her; why did I say to her that 'I love you,' which was a lie, and worse than a lie," he said to himself; "I am to blame, and ought to bear . . . What? The disgrace to my name, the misery of my life? Oh, that's all rubbish," he thought, "disgrace to one's name and honour, all that's relative, all that's apart from myself.

"Louis XVI was executed because *they* said he was dishonourable and a criminal" (the idea crossed Pierre's mind), "and they were right from their point of view just as those were right too who died a martyr's death for his sake, and canonised him as a saint. Then Robespierre was executed for being a tyrant. Who is right, who is wrong? No one. But live while you live, to-morrow you die, as I might have died an hour ago. And is it worth worrying oneself, when life is only one second in comparison with eternity?" But at the moment when he believed himself soothed by reflections of that sort, he suddenly had a vision of *her*, and of her at those moments when he had most violently expressed his most insincere love to her, and he felt a rush of blood to his heart, and had to jump up again, and move about and break and tear to pieces anything that his hands came across. "Why did I say to her 'I love you'?" he kept repeating to himself. And as he repeated the question for the tenth time the saying of Molière came into his head: "But what the devil was he doing in that galley?" and he laughed at himself.

In the night he called for his valet and bade him pack up to go to Petersburg. He could not conceive how he was going to speak to her now. He resolved that next day he would go away, leaving her a letter, in which he would announce his intention of parting from her for ever.

In the morning when the valet came into the study with his coffee, Pierre was lying on an ottoman asleep with an open book in his hand.

He woke up and looked about him for a long while in alarm, unable to grasp where he was.

"The countess sent to inquire if your excellency were at home," said the valet.

But before Pierre had time to make up his mind what answer he would send, the countess herself walked calmly and majestically into the room. She was wearing a white satin dressing-gown embroidered with silver, and had her hair in two immense coils wound like a coronet round her exquisite head. In spite of her calm, there was a wrathful line on her rather prominent, marble brow. With her accustomed self-control and composure she did not begin to speak till the valet had left the room. She knew of the duel and had come to talk of it. She waited till the valet had set the coffee and gone out. Pierre looked timidly at her over his spectacles, and as the hare, hemmed in by dogs, goes on lying with its ears back in sight of its foes, so he tried to go on reading. But he felt that this was senseless and impossible, and again he glanced timidly at her. She did not sit down, but stood looking at him with a disdainful smile, waiting for the valet to be gone.

"What's this about now? What have you been up to? I'm asking you," she said sternly.

"I? I? what?" said Pierre.

"You going in for deeds of valour! Now, answer me, what does this duel mean? What did you want to prove by it? Eh! I ask you the question." Pierre turned heavily on the sofa, opened his mouth but could not answer.

"If you won't answer, I'll tell you . . ." Ellen went on. "You believe everything you're told. You were told . . ." Ellen laughed, "that Dolohov was my lover," she said in French, with her coarse plainness of speech, uttering the word *"amant"* like any other word, "and you believed it! But what have you proved by this? What have you proved by this duel? That you're a fool; but every one knew that as it was. What does it lead to? Why, that I'm made a laughing-stock to all Moscow; that every one's saying that when you were drunk and didn't know what you were doing, you challenged a man of whom you were jealous without grounds," Ellen raised her voice and grew more and more passionate; "who's a better man than you in every respect. . . ."

"Hem . . . hem . . ." Pierre growled, wrinkling up his face, and neither looking at her nor stirring a muscle.

"And how came you to believe that he's my lover? . . . Eh? Because I like his society? If you were cleverer and more agreeable, I should prefer yours."

"Don't speak to me . . . I beseech you," Pierre muttered huskily.

"Why shouldn't I speak? I can speak as I like, and I tell you boldly that it's not many a wife who with a husband like you wouldn't have taken a lover, but I haven't done it," she said. Pierre tried to say something, glanced at her with strange eyes, whose meaning she did not comprehend, and lay down again. He was in physical agony at that moment; he felt a weight on his chest so that he could not breathe. He knew that he must do something to put an end to this agony but what he wanted to do was too horrible.

"We had better part," he articulated huskily.

"Part, by all means, only if you give me a fortune," said Ellen. . . . "Part—that's a threat to frighten me!"

Pierre leaped up from the couch and rushed staggering towards her.

"I'll kill you!" he shouted, and snatching up a marble slab from a table with a strength he had not known in himself till then, he made a step towards her and waved it at her.

Ellen's face was terrible to see; she shrieked and darted away from him. His father's nature showed itself in him. Pierre felt the abandonment and the fascination of frenzy. He flung down the slab, shivering it into fragments, and with open arms swooping down upon Ellen, screamed "Go!" in a voice so terrible that they heard it all over the house with horror. God knows what Pierre would have done at that moment if Ellen had not run out of the room.

A week later Pierre had made over to his wife the revenue from all his estates in Great Russia, which made up the larger half of his property, and had gone away alone to Petersburg.

VII

Two months had passed since the news of the defeat of Austerlitz and the loss of Prince Andrey had reached Bleak Hills. In spite of all researches and letters through the Russian embassy, his body had not been found, nor was he among the prisoners. What made it worst of all for his father and sister was the fact that there was still hope that he might have been picked up on the battlefield by the people of the country, and might perhaps be lying, recovering, or dying somewhere alone, among strangers, incapable of giving any account of himself. The newspapers, from which the old prince had first heard of the defeat at Austerlitz, had, as always, given very brief and vague accounts of how the Russians had been obliged after brilliant victories to retreat and had made their withdrawal in perfect order. The old prince saw from this official account that our army had been defeated. A week after the newspaper that had brought news of the defeat of Austerlitz, came a letter from Kutuzov, who described to the old prince the part taken in it by his son.

"Before my eyes," wrote Kutuzov, "your son with the flag in his hands, at the head of a regiment, fell like a hero, worthy of his father and his fatherland. To my regret and the general regret of the whole army it has not been ascertained up to now whether he is alive or dead. I comfort myself and you with the hope that your son is living, as, otherwise, he would have been mentioned among the officers found on the field of battle, a list of whom has been given me under flag of truce."

After receiving this letter, late in the evening when he was alone in his study, the old prince went for his morning walk as usual next day. But he was silent with the bailiff, the gardener, and the architect, and though he looked wrathful, said nothing to them. When Princess Marya went in to him at the usual hour, he was standing at the lathe and went on turning as usual, without looking round at her. "Ah? Princess Marya!" he said suddenly in an unnatural voice, and he let the lathe go. (The wheel swung round from the impetus. Long after, Princess Marya remembered the dying creak of the wheel, which was associated for her with what followed.)

Princess Marya went up to him; she caught sight of his face, and something seemed suddenly to give way within her. Her eyes could not see clearly. From her father's face—not sad nor crushed, but vindictive and full of unnatural conflict—she saw that there was hanging over her, coming to crush her, a terrible calamity, the worst in life, a calamity she had not known till then, a calamity irrevocable, irremediable, the death of one beloved.

"Father! Andrey? . . ." said the ungainly, awkward princess with such unutterable beauty of sorrow and self-forgetfulness that her father could not bear to meet her eyes and turned away sobbing.

"I have had news. Not among the prisoners, not among the killed, Kutuzov writes," he screamed shrilly, as though he would drive his daughter away with that shriek. "Killed!"

The princess did not swoon, she did not fall into a faint. She was pale, but when she heard those words her face was transformed, and there was a radiance of something in her beautiful, luminous eyes. Something like joy, an exalted joy, apart from the sorrows and joys of this world, flooded the bitter grief she felt within her. She forgot all her terror of her father, went up to him, took him by the hand, drew him to her, and put her arm about his withered, sinewy neck.

"Father," she said, "do not turn away from me, let us weep for him together."

"Blackguards, scoundrels!" screamed the old man, turning his face away from her. "Destroying the army, destroying men! What for? Go, go and tell Liza."

Princess Marya sank helplessly into an armchair beside her father and burst into tears. She could see her brother now at the moment when he parted from her and from Liza with his tender and at the same time haughty expression. She saw him at the moment when tenderly and ironically he had put the image on. "Did he believe now? Had he repented of his unbelief? Was he there now? There in the realm of eternal peace and blessedness?" she wondered. "Father, tell me how it was," she asked through her tears.

"Go away, go,—killed in a defeat into which they led the best men of Russia and the glory of Russia to ruin. Go away, Princess Marya. Go and tell Liza. I will come." When Princess Marya went back from her father, the little princess was sitting at her work, and she looked up with that special inward look of happy calm that is peculiar to women with child. It was clear that her eyes were not seeing Princess Marya, but looking deep within herself, at some happy mystery that was being accomplished within her.

"Marie," she said, moving away from the embroidery frame and leaning back, "give me your hand." She took her sister-in-law's hand and laid it below her waist. Her eyes smiled, expectant, her little dewy lip was lifted and stayed so in childlike rapture. Princess Marya knelt down before her, and hid her face in the folds of her sister-in-law's dress. "There—there—do you feel it? I feel so strange. And do you know, Marie, I am going to love him very much," said Liza, looking at her sister-in-law with shining, happy eyes. Princess Marya could not lift her head; she was crying.

"What's the matter with you, Marie?"

"Nothing . . . only I felt sad . . . sad about Andrey," she said, brushing away the tears on the folds of her sister-in-law's dress. Several times in the course of the morning Princess Marya began trying to prepare her sister-in-law's mind, and every time she began to weep. These tears, which the little princess could not account for, agitated her, little as she was observant in general. She said nothing, but looked about her uneasily, as though seeking for something. Before dinner the old prince, of whom she was always afraid, came into her room, with a particularly restless and malignant expression, and went out without uttering a word. She looked at Princess Marya with that expression of attention concentrated within herself that is only seen in women with child, and suddenly she burst into tears.

"Have you heard news from Andrey?" she said.

"No; you know news could not come yet; but father is uneasy, and I feel frightened."

"Then you have heard nothing?"

"Nothing," said Princess Marya, looking resolutely at her with her luminous eyes. She had made up her mind not to tell her, and had persuaded her father to conceal the dreadful news from her till her confinement, which was expected before many days. Princess Marya and the old prince, in their different ways, bore and hid their grief. The old prince refused to hope; he made up his mind that Prince Andrey had been killed, and though he sent a clerk to Austria to seek for traces of his son, he ordered a monument for him in Moscow and intended to put it up in his garden, and he told every one that his son was dead. He tried to keep up his old manner of life unchanged, but his strength was failing him: he walked less, ate less, slept less, and every day he grew weaker. Princess Marya went on hoping. She prayed for her brother, as living, and every moment she expected news of his return.

VIII

"*Ma bonne amie,*" said the little princess, after breakfast, on the morning of the 19th of March, and her little downy lip was lifted as of old;

but as in that house since the terrible news had come, smiles, tones of voice, movements even bore the stamp of mourning, so now the smile of the little princess, who was influenced by the general temper without knowing its cause, was such that more than all else it was eloquent of the common burden of sorrow.

"My dear, I am afraid that this morning's *fruschtique* (as Foka calls it) has disagreed with me."

"What is the matter with you, my darling? You look pale. Oh, you are very pale," said Princess Marya in alarm, running with her soft, ponderous tread up to her sister-in-law.

"Shouldn't we send for Marya Bogdanovna, your excellency?" said one of the maids who was present. Marya Bogdanovna was a midwife from a district town, who had been for the last fortnight at Bleak Hills.

"Yes, truly," assented Princess Marya, "perhaps it is really that. I'll go and get her. Courage, my angel." She kissed Liza and was going out of the room.

"Oh, no, no!" And besides her pallor, the face of the little princess expressed a childish terror at the inevitable physical suffering before her.

"No, it is indigestion, say it is indigestion, say so, Marie, say so!" And the little princess began to cry, wringing her little hands with childish misery and capriciousness and affected exaggeration too. Princess Marya ran out of the room to fetch Marya Bogdanovna.

"*Mon Dieu! mon Dieu!* Oh!" she heard behind her. The midwife was already on her way to meet her, rubbing her plump, small white hands, with a face of significant composure.

"Marya Bogdanovna! I think it has begun," said Princess Marya, looking with wide-open, frightened eyes at the midwife.

"Well, I thank God for it," said Marya Bogdanovna, not hastening her step. "You young ladies have no need to know anything about it."

"But how is it the doctor has not come from Moscow yet?" said the princess. (In accordance with the wishes of Liza and Prince Andrey, they had sent to Moscow for a doctor, and were expecting him every minute.)

"It's no matter, princess, don't be uneasy," said Marya Bogdanovna; "we shall do very well without the doctor."

Five minutes later the princess from her room heard something heavy being carried by. She peeped out; the footmen were for some reason moving into the bedroom the leather sofa which stood in Prince Andrey's study. There was a solemn and subdued look on the men's faces.

Princess Marya sat alone in her room, listening to the sounds of the house, now and then opening the door when any one passed by and looking at what was taking place in the corridor. Several women passed to and fro treading softly; they glanced at the princess and turned away from her. She did not venture to ask questions, and going back to her room closed the door and sat still in an armchair, or took up her prayer-book, or knelt down before the shrine. To her distress and astonishment she felt that prayer did not soothe her emotion. All at once the door of her room was softly opened, and she saw on the threshold her old nurse,

Praskovya Savvishna, with a kerchief over her head. The old woman hardly ever, owing to the old prince's prohibition, came into her room.

"I've come to sit a bit with thee, Mashenka," said the nurse; "and here I've brought the prince's wedding candles to light before his saint, my angel," she said, sighing.

"Ah, how glad I am, nurse!"

"God is merciful, my darling." The nurse lighted the gilt candles before the shrine, and sat down with her stocking near the door. Princess Marya took a book and began reading. Only when they heard steps or voices, the princess and the nurse looked at one another, one with alarmed inquiry, the other with soothing reassurance in her face. The feeling that Princess Marya was experiencing as she sat in her room had overpowered the whole house and taken possession of every one. Owing to the belief that the fewer people know of the sufferings of a woman in labour, the less she suffers, every one tried to affect to know nothing of it; no one talked about it, but over and above the habitual staidness and respectfulness of good manners that always reigned in the prince's household, there was apparent in all a sort of anxiety, a softening of the heart, and a consciousness of some great, unfathomable mystery being accomplished at that moment. There was no sound of laughter in the big room where the maids sat. In the waiting-room the men all sat in silence, as it were on the alert. Torches and candles were burning in the serfs' quarters, and no one slept. The old prince walked about his study, treading on his heels, and sent Tihon to Marya Bogdanovna to ask what news.

"Only say: the prince has sent to ask, what news and come and tell me what she says."

"Inform the prince that the labour has commenced," said Marya Bogdanovna, looking significantly at the messenger. Tihon went and gave the prince that information.

"Very good," said the prince, closing the door behind him, and Tihon heard not the slightest sound in the study after that. After a short interval Tihon went into the study, as though to attend to the candles. Seeing the prince lying on the couch, Tihon looked at him, looked at his perturbed face, shook his head, and went up to him dumbly and kissed him on the shoulder, then went out without touching the candles or saying why he had come. The most solemn mystery in the world was being accomplished. Evening passed, night came on. And the feeling of suspense and softening of the heart before the unfathomable did not wane, but grew more intense. No one slept.

It was one of those March nights when winter seems to regain its sway, and flings its last snows and storms with malignant desperation. A relay of horses had been sent to the high-road for the German doctor who was expected every minute, and men were despatched on horseback with lanterns to the turning at the cross-roads to guide him over the holes and treacherous places in the ice.

Princess Marya had long abandoned her book; she sat in silence, her luminous eyes fixed on the wrinkled face of her old nurse (so familiar to her in the minutest detail), on the lock of grey hair that had escaped from the kerchief, on the baggy looseness of the skin under her chin.

The old nurse, with her stocking in her hand, talked away in a soft voice, not hearing it herself nor following the meaning of her own words; telling, as she had told hundreds of times before, how the late princess had been brought to bed of Princess Marya at Kishinyov, and had only a Moldavian peasant woman instead of a midwife.

"God is merciful, doctors are never wanted," she said.

Suddenly a gust of wind blew on one of the window-frames (by the prince's decree the double frames were always taken out of every window when the larks returned), and flinging open a badly fastened window bolt, set the stiff curtain fluttering; and the chill, snowy draught blew out the candle. Princess Marya shuddered; the nurse, putting down her stocking, went to the window, and putting her head out tried to catch the open frame. The cold wind flapped the ends of her kerchief and the grey locks of her hair.

"Princess, my dearie, there's some one driving up the avenue!" she said, holding the window-frame and not closing it. "With lanterns; it must be the doctor. . . ."

"Ah, my God! Thank God!" said the Princess Marya. "I must go and meet him; he does not know Russian."

Princess Marya flung on a shawl and ran to meet the stranger. As she passed through the ante-room, she saw through the window a carriage and lanterns standing at the entrance. She went out on to the stairs. At the post of the balustrade stood a tallow-candle guttering in the draught. The footman Filipp, looking scared, stood below on the first landing of the staircase, with another candle in his hand. Still lower down, at the turn of the winding stairs, steps in thick overshoes could be heard coming up. And a voice—familiar it seemed to Princess Marya—was saying something.

"Thank God!" said the voice. "And father?"

"He has gone to bed," answered the voice of the butler, Demyan, who was below.

Then the voice said something more, Demyan answered something, and the steps in thick overshoes began approaching more rapidly up the unseen part of the staircase.

"It is Andrey!" thought Princess Marya. "No, it cannot be, it would be too extraordinary," she thought; and at the very instant she was thinking so, on the landing where the footman stood with a candle, there came into sight the face and figure of Prince Andrey, in a fur coat, with a deep collar covered with snow. Yes, it was he, but pale and thin, and with a transformed, strangely softened, agitated expression on his face. He went up the stairs and embraced his sister.

"You did not get my letter, then?" he asked; and not waiting for an answer, which he would not have received, for the princess could not speak, he turned back, and with the doctor who was behind him (they had met at the last station), he ran again rapidly upstairs and again embraced his sister.

"What a strange fate!" he said, "Masha, darling!" And flinging off his fur coat and overboots, he went towards the little princess's room.

IX

THE little princess was lying on the pillows in her white nightcap (the agony had only a moment left her). Her black hair lay in curls about her swollen and perspiring cheeks; her rosy, charming little mouth, with the downy lip, was open, and she was smiling joyfully. Prince Andrey went into the room, and stood facing her at the foot of the bed on which she lay. The glittering eyes, staring in childish terror and excitement, rested on him with no change in their expression. "I love you all, I have done no one any harm; why am I suffering? help me," her face seemed to say. She saw her husband, but she did not take in the meaning of his appearance now before her. Prince Andrey went round the bed and kissed her on the forehead.

"My precious," he said, a word he had never used speaking to her before. "God is merciful. . . ." She stared at him with a face of inquiry, of childish reproach.

"I hoped for help from you, and nothing, nothing, you too!" her eyes said. She was not surprised at his having come; she did not understand that he had come. His coming had nothing to do with her agony and its alleviation. The pains began again, and Marya Bogdanovna advised Prince Andrey to go out of the room.

The doctor went into the room. Prince Andrey came out, and, meeting Princess Marya, went to her again. They talked in whispers, but every moment their talk was hushed. They were waiting and listening.

"Go, *mon ami*," said Princess Marya. Prince Andrey went again to his wife and sat down in the adjoining room, waiting. A woman ran out of the bedroom with a frightened face, and was disconcerted on seeing Prince Andrey. He hid his face in his hands and sat so for some minutes. Piteous, helpless, animal groans came from the next room. Prince Andrey got up, went to the door, and would have opened it. Some one was holding the door.

"Can't come in, can't!" a frightened voice said from within. He began walking about the room. The screams ceased; several seconds passed. Suddenly a fearful scream—not her scream, could she scream like that? —came from the room. Prince Andrey ran to the door; the scream ceased; he heard the cry of a baby.

"What have they taken a baby in there for?" Prince Andrey wondered for the first second. "A baby? What baby? . . . Why a baby there? Or is the baby born?"

When he suddenly realised all the joyful significance of that cry, tears

choked him, and leaning both elbows on the window-sill he cried, sobbing as children cry. The door opened. The doctor with his shirt sleeves
tucked up, and no coat on, came out of the room, pale, and his lower
jaw twitching. Prince Andrey addressed him, but the doctor, looking at
him in a distracted way, passed by without uttering a word. A woman
ran out, and, seeing Prince Andrey, stopped hesitating in the door. He
went into his wife's room. She was lying dead in the same position in
which he had seen her five minutes before, and in spite of the fixed gaze
and white cheeks, there was the same expression still on the charming
childish face with the little lip covered with fine dark hair. "I love you
all, and have done no harm to any one, and what have you done to me?"
said her charming, piteous, dead face. In a corner of the room was something red and tiny, squealing and grunting in the trembling white hands
of Marya Bogdanovna.

Two hours later Prince Andrey went with soft steps into his father's
room. The old man knew everything already. He was standing near the
door, and, as soon as it opened, his rough old arms closed like a vice
round his son's neck, and without a word he burst into sobs like a child.

Three days afterwards the little princess was buried, and Prince
Andrey went to the steps of the tomb to take his last farewell of her.
Even in the coffin the face was the same, though the eyes were closed.
"Ah, what have you done to me?" it still seemed to say; and Prince
Andrey felt that something was being torn out of his soul, that he was
guilty of a crime that he could never set right nor forget. He could not
weep. The old man, too, went in and kissed the little waxen hand that
lay so peacefully crossed over the other, and to him, too, her face said:
"Ah, what have you done to me, and why?" And the old man turned
angrily away, when he caught sight of the face.

In another five days there followed the christening of the young
prince, Nikolay Andreitch. The nurse held the swaddling clothes up to
her chin, while the priest with a goose feather anointed the baby's red,
wrinkled hands and feet.

His grandfather, who was his godfather, trembling and afraid of dropping the baby, carried him round the battered tin font, and handed him
over to the godmother, Princess Marya. Faint with terror that they
would let the baby drown in the font, Prince Andrey sat in an adjoining
room, waiting for the conclusion of the ceremony. He looked joyfully at
the baby when the nurse brought him out, and nodded approvingly
when the nurse told him that a bit of wax with the baby's hairs in it,
thrown into the font, had not sunk in the water but floated on the
surface.

X

ROSTOV'S share in the duel between Dolohov and Bezuhov had been
hushed up by the efforts of the old count, and instead of being degraded

to the ranks, as Nikolay had expected, he had been appointed an adjutant to the governor of Moscow. In consequence of this, he could not go to the country with the rest of the family, but was kept by his new duties all the summer in Moscow. Dolohov recovered, and Rostov became particularly friendly with him during his convalescence. Dolohov lay ill in the house of his mother, who was tenderly and passionately devoted to him. Marya Ivanovna, who had taken a fancy to Rostov, seeing his attachment to her Fedya, often talked to him about her son.

"Yes, count, he is too noble, too pure-hearted," she would say, "for the corrupt society of our day. Virtue is in favour with no one; it is apt to be a reproach to everybody. Come, tell me, count, was it right, was it honourable on Bezuhov's part? Fedya in his noble-hearted way loved him, and even now he never says a word against him. In Petersburg those pranks with the police constables, those practical jokes they played there, didn't they do everything together? And Bezuhov got nothing for it, while Fedya took all the blame on his shoulders. What he has had to go through! He has been reinstated, I know, but how could they help reinstating him? I don't suppose there were many such gallant, true sons of their fatherland out there! And now, what?—this duel! Is there any feeling, any honour left in men? Knowing he was the only son, to call him out and aim so straight at him! We may be thankful God has been merciful to us. And what was it all for? Why, who hasn't intrigues nowadays? Why, if he were so jealous—I can understand it—he ought to have let it be seen long before, you know, and it had been going on for a year. And then to call him out, reckoning on Fedya's not fighting him because he was indebted to him. What baseness! What vileness! I know you understand Fedya, my dear count, and that's why I love you, believe me, from my heart. Few do understand him. His is such a lofty, heavenly nature!"

Dolohov himself, during his convalescence, often said to Rostov things which could never have been expected from him.

"People think me a wicked man, I know," he would say; "and they're welcome to think so. I don't care to know any one except those whom I love. But those I do love, I love in such a way that I would give my life for them, and all the rest I will crush if they get in my way. I have a precious and adored mother, and two or three friends, you among them; and as to the rest, I only pay attention to them in so far as they are useful or mischievous. And almost all are mischievous, especially the women. Yes, my dear," he went on, "men I have met who were loving, noble, and lofty-minded. But women that were not cattle for sale—countesses and cooks, they're all alike—I have not come across yet. I have not yet met the angelic purity and devotion which I look for in woman. If I could find such a woman, I would give my life for her! But these creatures! . . ." He made a gesture of contempt. "But believe me, if I still care for life, I care for it because I still hope to meet such a heavenly creature, who would regenerate and purify and elevate me. But you don't understand that."

"Yes, I quite understand," answered Rostov, who was very much under the influence of his new friend.

In the autumn the Rostov family returned to Moscow. At the beginning of the winter Denisov too came back and stayed again with the Rostovs. The early part of the winter of 1806 spent by Nikolay Rostov in Moscow, was one of the happiest and liveliest periods for him and all the family. Nikolay brought a lot of young men about him into his parents' house. Vera was a handsome girl of twenty; Sonya, a girl of sixteen, with all the charm of an opening flower; Natasha, half grown up, half a child, at one time childishly absurd, and at another fascinating with the charm of a young girl.

The Rostovs' house was at that time full of a sort of peculiar atmosphere of love-making, as commonly happens in a household where there are very young and very charming girls. Among those young girls' faces, impressionable and always smiling (probably at their own happiness), in that whirl of eager bustle, amid that young feminine chatter, so inconsequent, but so friendly to every one, so ready for anything, so full of hope, and the inconsequent sound of singing and of music, any young man who came into the house felt the same sensation of readiness to fall in love and longing for happiness, that the younger members of the Rostov household were feeling themselves.

Among the young men Rostov brought to the house, one of the foremost was Dolohov, who was liked by every one in the house except Natasha. She almost had a quarrel with her brother over Dolohov. She persisted that he was a spiteful man; that in the duel with Bezuhov, Pierre had been in the right and Dolohov in the wrong, and that he was horrid and not natural.

"I know nothing about it, indeed," Natasha would cry with self-willed obstinacy; "he's spiteful and heartless. Your Denisov now, you see, I like; he's a rake, and all that, but still I like him, so I do understand. I don't know how to tell you; with him everything is done on a plan, and I don't like that. Denisov, now . . ."

"Oh, Denisov's another matter," answered Nikolay, in a tone that implied that in comparison with Dolohov even Denisov was not of much account. "One must understand what soul there is in that Dolohov; one must see him with his mother; such a noble heart!"

"I know nothing about that, but I don't feel at home with him. And do you know he's falling in love with Sonya?"

"What nonsense!"

"I am sure, you will see he is."

Natasha's prediction was fulfilled. Dolohov, who did not as a rule care for ladies, began to come often to the house; and the question, for whose sake he came, was soon (though no one spoke of it) decided—it was on Sonya's account. And though Sonya would never have ventured to say so, she knew it, and blushed scarlet every time Dolohov made his appearance.

Dolohov often dined at the Rostovs', never missed a performance at which they were to be present, and attended Iogel's balls "for the boys and girls," at which the Rostovs were always to be found. He showed marked attention to Sonya, and looked at her with such an expression in his eyes that Sonya could not bear his eyes on her without turning crimson, and even the old countess and Natasha blushed when they saw that look.

It was evident that this strong, strange man could not shake off the impression made on him by the dark, graceful young girl, who was in love with another man.

Rostov noticed something new between Dolohov and Sonya, but he did not define to himself precisely what that new attitude was. "They are all in love with some one," he thought of Sonya and Natasha. But he did not feel quite at his ease as before with Sonya and Dolohov, and he began to be less often at home.

In the autumn of 1806 every one was beginning to talk again of war with Napoleon, and with even greater fervour than in the previous year. A levy was decreed, not only of ten recruits for active service, but of nine militiamen for the reserve as well, from every thousand of the population. Everywhere Bonaparte was anathematised, and the only thing talked of in Moscow was the impending war. To the Rostov family the interest of these preparations for war was entirely centered in the fact that Nikolushka refused to remain longer in Moscow, and was only waiting for the end of Denisov's leave to rejoin his regiment with him after the holidays. His approaching departure, far from hindering him from enjoying himself, gave an added zest to his pleasures. The greater part of his time he spent away from home, at dinners, parties, and balls.

XI

On the third day after Christmas Nikolay dined at home, which he had rarely done of late. This was a farewell dinner in Nikolay's honour, as he was to set off with Denisov after the baptism festival to rejoin his regiment. Twenty persons were dining, among them Dolohov and Denisov.

Never had the love in the air of the Rostovs' house, never had the atmosphere of being in love, made itself so strongly felt as during those Christmas holidays. "Seize the moment of happiness, love and be loved! That is the only thing real in the world; the rest is all nonsense. And that is the one thing we are interested in here," was the sentiment that atmosphere was eloquent of.

After exhausting two pairs of horses, as he did every day without having been everywhere he ought to have been, and everywhere he had been invited, Nikolay reached home just at dinner-time. As soon as he went in he felt that intense atmosphere of love in the house, but in addition to that he became conscious of a strange embarrassment that seemed to prevail between certain persons in the company. Sonya seemed particularly disturbed, so did Dolohov and the old countess, and in a lesser degree Natasha. Nikolay saw that something must have passed before dinner between Sonya and Dolohov, and with the delicate instinct characteristic of him, he was very sympathetic and wary with both of them during dinner. On that evening there was to be one of the dances given by Iogel, the dancing-master, during the holidays to his pupils.

"Nikolenka, are you going to Iogel's? Please, do go," said Natasha; "he particularly begged you to, and Vassily Dmitritch" (this was Denisov) "is going."

"Where would I not go at the countess's commands!" said Denisov, who had jestingly taken up the rôle of Natasha's knight in the Rostov household. "I am ready to dance the *pas de châle*."

"If I have time! I promised the Arharovs; they have a party," said Nikolay.

"And you? . . ." he turned to Dolohov. And as soon as he had asked the question, he saw that he should not have asked it.

"Yes, possibly . . ." Dolohov answered coldly and angrily, glancing at Sonya; and he glanced again, scowling at Nikolay with exactly the same look with which he had looked at Pierre at the club dinner.

"There's something wrong," thought Nikolay; and he was still more confirmed in that surmise, when immediately after dinner Dolohov went away. He beckoned Natasha, and asked her what had happened.

"I was looking for you," said Natasha, running out to him. "I told you so, and still you wouldn't believe me," she said triumphantly; "he has made Sonya an offer."

Little as Nikolay had been thinking of Sonya of late, he felt as if something were being torn from him when he heard this. Dolohov was a good, and in some respects a brilliant, match for the portionless orphan Sonya. From the point of view of the countess and of society it was out of the question for her to refuse him. And so Nikolay's first feeling when he heard of it was one of exasperation against Sonya. He braced himself up to say, "And a capital thing, too; of course she must forget her childish promises and accept the offer"; but he had not succeeded in saying this when Natasha said:

"Only fancy! she has refused him, absolutely refused him! She says she loves some one else," she added after a brief pause.

"Yes, my Sonya could not do otherwise!" thought Nikolay.

"Mamma begged her ever so many times not to, but she refused; and I know she won't change, if she has said a thing. . . ."

"And mamma begged her not to!" Nikolay said reproachfully.

"Yes," said Natasha. "Do you know, Nikolenka—don't be angry— but I know you won't marry her. I know—I don't know why—but I know for certain that you won't marry her."

"Well, you can't know that," said Nikolay; "but I want to talk to her. How charming Sonya is!" he added, smiling.

"Yes, she is so charming! I'll send her in to you." And Natasha kissed her brother and ran away.

A minute later Sonya came in, looking frightened, distraught, and guilty. Nikolay went up to her and kissed her hand. It was the first time since his return that they had talked alone and of their love.

"Sophie," he said to her, at first timidly, but more and more boldly as he went on, "if you were simply refusing a brilliant, an advantageous match—but he's a splendid, noble fellow . . . he's my friend . . ."

Sonya interrupted him.

"I have refused him," she said hastily.

"If you are refusing him for my sake, I am afraid that I . . ."

Sonya again cut him short. With frightened, imploring eyes she looked at him.

"Nikolenka, don't say that to me," she said.

"No, I must. Perhaps it's *suffisance* on my part, but still it's better to say it. If you are refusing him on my account, I ought to tell you the whole truth. I love you, I believe, more than any one . . ."

"That's enough for me," said Sonya, flushing crimson.

"No; but I have been in love a thousand times, and I shall fall in love again, though such a feeling of affection, confidence and love I have for no one as for you. Then I am young. Mamma does not wish it. Well —in fact—I can make no promise. And I beg you to consider the offer of Dolohov," he said, with an effort articulating the name of his friend.

"Don't speak to me of it. I want nothing. I love you as a brother, and shall always love you, and I want nothing more."

"You are an angel; I'm not worthy of you, but I am only afraid of deceiving you."

Nikolay kissed her hand once more.

XII

IOGEL's were the most enjoyable balls in Moscow. So the mammas said as they looked at their boys and girls executing the steps they had only lately learnt. So too said the boys and girls themselves, who danced till they were ready to drop; so too said the grown-up girls and young men, who came to those dances in a spirit of condescension, and found in them the greatest enjoyment. That year two matches had been made at those dances. The two pretty young princesses Gortchakov had found suitors there, and had been married, and this had given the dances even greater vogue than before. What distinguished these dances from others was the absence of host and hostess, and the presence of the good-humoured Iogel, who had sold tickets for lessons to all his guests, and fluttered about like a feather, bowing and scraping in accordance with the rules of his art. Another point of difference, too, was that none came to these dances but those who really wanted to dance and enjoy themselves, in the way that girls of thirteen and fourteen do, putting on long dresses for the first time. All with rare exceptions were or looked pretty, so ecstatically they smiled and so rapturously their eyes sparkled. The *pas de châle* even was sometimes danced by the best pupils, among whom Natasha was the best of all, and conspicuous for her gracefulness. But at this last ball they only danced ecossaises, anglaises, and a mazurka that was just coming into fashion. A great hall had been taken by Iogel in the house of Bezuhov, and the ball, as every one said, was a great success. There were many pretty girls, and the Rostov girls were among the prettiest. They were both particularly happy and gay. That evening Sonya, elated by Dolohov's offer, her refusal, and her interview with Nikolay, had kept whirling round at home, not letting her maid have a chance of doing her hair, and now at the dance she was transparently radiant with impulsive happiness.

Natasha, no less elated at being for the first time at a real ball in a long skirt, was even happier. Both the girls wore white muslin dresses with pink ribbons.

Natasha fell in love the moment she walked into the ballroom. She was not in love with any one in particular, but in love with every one. Whomever she looked at, for the moment that she was looking at him, she was in love with.

"Oh, how nice it is!" she kept saying, running up to Sonya.

Nikolay and Denisov walked about the room and looked with friendly patronage at the dancers.

"How sweet she is; she will be a beauty," said Denisov.

"Who?"

"Countess Natasha," answered Denisov.

"And how she dances; what grace!" he said again, after a short pause.

"Of whom are you speaking?"

"Why, of your sister," cried Denisov angrily.

Rostov laughed.

"My dear count, you are one of my best pupils, you must dance," said little Iogel, coming up to Nikolay. "Look at all these pretty young ladies!" He turned with the same request to Denisov, who had also at one time been his pupil.

"No, my dear fellow, I will be a wallflower," said Denisov. "Don't you remember how little credit I did to your teaching?"

"Oh no!" said Iogel, hastening to reassure him. "You were only inattentive, but you had talent, you had talent."

They began to play the new mazurka. Nikolay could not refuse Iogel, and asked Sonya to dance. Denisov sat down by the elderly ladies, and leaning his elbow on his sword, and beating time with his foot, he began telling something amusing and making the old ladies laugh, while he watched the young ones dancing. Iogel was dancing in the first couple with Natasha, his best pupil and his pride. With soft and delicate move-ments of his little slippered feet, Iogel first flew across the room with Natasha—shy, but conscientiously executing her steps. Denisov did not take his eyes off her, and beat time with his sword with an air that be-trayed, that if he were not dancing it was because he would not, and not because he could not, dance. In the middle of a figure he beckoned Rostov to him.

"That's not the right thing a bit," he said. "Is that the Polish ma-zurka? But she does dance splendidly."

Knowing that Denisov had been renowned even in Poland for his fine dancing of the Polish mazurka, Nikolay ran up to Natasha.

"Go and choose Denisov. He does dance. It's a marvel!" he said.

When it was Natasha's turn again, she got up, and tripping rapidly in her ribbon-trimmed dancing-shoes, she timidly ran alone across the room to the corner where Denisov was sitting. She saw that every one was looking at her, waiting to see what she would do. Nikolay saw that Denisov and Natasha were carrying on a smiling dispute, and that Denisov was refusing, though his face wore a delighted smile. He ran up.

"Please do, Vassily Dmitritch," Natasha was saying; "come please."

"Oh, have mercy on me, countess," Denisov was saying jocosely.

"Come now, nonsense, Vaska," said Nikolay.

"They coax me like the pussy-cat Vaska," said Denisov good-humouredly.

"I'll sing to you a whole evening," said Natasha.

"The little witch, she can do anything with me!" said Denisov; and he unhooked his sword. He came out from behind the chairs, clasped his partner firmly by the hand, raised his head and stood with one foot behind the other, waiting for the time. It was only on horseback and in the mazurka that Denisov's low stature was not noticeable, and that he looked the dashing hero he felt himself to be. At the right bar in the time he glanced sideways with a triumphant and amused air at his partner, and making an unexpected tap with one foot he bounded springily like a ball from the floor and flew round, whirling his partner round with him. He flew inaudibly across the hall with one leg forward, and seemed not to see the chairs standing before him, darting straight at them; but all at once with a clink of his spurs and a flourish of his foot he stopped short on his heels, stood so a second, with a clanking of spurs stamped with both feet, whirled rapidly round, and clapping the left foot against the right, again he flew round. Natasha's instinct told her what he was going to do, and without herself knowing how she did it, she followed his lead, abandoning herself to him. At one moment he spun her round, first on his right arm, then on his left arm, then falling on one knee, twirled her round him and again galloped, dashing forward with such vehemence that he seemed to intend to race through the whole suite of rooms without taking breath. Then he stopped suddenly again and executed new and unexpected steps in the dance. When after spinning his partner round before her seat he drew up smartly with a clink of his spurs, bowing to her, Natasha did not even make him a curtsey. She looked at him smiling with a puzzled face, as though she did not recognise him.

"What does it mean?" she said.

Although Iogel would not acknowledge this mazurka as the real one, every one was enchanted with Denisov's dancing of it, and he was continually being chosen as partner; while the old gentlemen, smiling, talked about Poland and the good old days. Denisov, flushed with his exertions and mopping his face with his handkerchief, sat by Natasha and would not leave her side all the rest of the ball.

XIII

FOR two days after the dance, Rostov had not seen Dolohov at his people's house nor found him at home; on the third day he received a note from him.

"As I do not intend to be at your house again owing to causes of which you are aware, and am going to rejoin the regiment, I am giving a farewell supper to my friends—come to the English Hotel." On the day fixed Rostov went at about ten o'clock, from the theatre where he had been with his family and Denisov, to the English Hotel. He was at once conducted to the best room in the hotel, which Dolohov had taken for the occasion.

Some twenty men were gathered about a table before which Dolohov was sitting between two candles. On the table lay money and notes, and Dolohov was keeping the bank. Nikolay had not seen him again since his offer and Sonya's refusal, and he felt uneasy at the thought of meeting him.

Dolohov's clear, cold glance met Rostov in the doorway as though he had been expecting him a long while.

"It's a long while since we've met," said he; "thanks for coming. I'll just finish dealing here, and Ilyushka will make his appearance with his chorus."

"I did go to see you," said Rostov, flushing.

Dolohov made him no reply.

"You might put down a stake," he said.

Rostov recalled at that instant a strange conversation he once had with Dolohov. "None but fools trust to luck in play," Dolohov had said then. "Or are you afraid to play with me?" Dolohov said now, as though divining Rostov's thought; and he smiled. Behind his smile Rostov saw in him that mood which he had seen in him at the club dinner and at other times, when Dolohov seemed, as it were, weary of the monotony of daily life, and felt a craving to escape from it by some strange, for the most part cruel, act.

Rostov felt ill at ease; he racked his brain and could not find in it a joke in which to reply to Dolohov's words. But before he had time to do so, Dolohov, looking straight into Rostov's face, said to him slowly and deliberately so that all could hear: "Do you remember, I was talking to you about play . . . he's a fool who trusts to luck in play; one must play a sure game, and I want to try."

"Try his luck, or try to play a sure game?" wondered Rostov.

"Indeed, and you'd better not play," he added; and throwing down a pack he had just torn open, he said, "Bank, gentlemen!"

Moving the money forward, Dolohov began dealing.

Rostov sat near him, and at first he did not play. Dolohov glanced at him.

"Why don't you play?" said Dolohov. And strange to say, Nikolay felt that he could not help taking up a card, staking a trifling sum on it, and beginning to play.

"I have no money with me," said Rostov.

"I'll trust you!"

Rostov staked five roubles on a card and lost it, staked again and again lost. Dolohov "killed," that is, beat ten cards in succession from Rostov.

"Gentlemen," he said, after dealing again for a little while, "I beg you to put the money on the cards or else I shall get muddled over the reckoning."

One of the players said that he hoped he could trust him.

"I can trust you, but I'm afraid of making mistakes; I beg you to lay the money on the cards," answered Dolohov. "You needn't worry, we'll settle our accounts," he added to Rostov.

The play went on; a footman never ceased carrying round champagne.

All Rostov's cards were beaten, and the sum of eight hundred roubles was scored against him. He wrote on a card eight hundred roubles, but while champagne was being poured out for him, he changed his mind and again wrote down the usual stake, twenty roubles.

"Leave it," said Dolohov, though he did not seem to be looking at Rostov; "you'll win it back all the sooner. I lose to the rest, while I win from you. Or perhaps you are afraid of me," he repeated.

Rostov excused himself, left the stake of eight hundred and laid down the seven of hearts, a card with a corner torn, which he had picked up from the ground. Well he remembered that card afterwards. He laid down the seven of hearts, wrote on it with a broken piece of chalk 800 in bold round figures; he drank the glass of warmed champagne that had been given him, smiled at Dolohov's words, and with a sinking at his heart, waiting for the seven of hearts, he watched Dolohov's hands that held the pack. The loss or gain of that card meant a great deal for Rostov. On the previous Sunday Count Ilya Andreitch had given his son two thousand roubles, and though he never liked speaking of money difficulties, he told him that this money was the last they would get till May, and so he begged him to be a little more careful. Nikolay said that that was too much really for him, and that he would give him his word of honour not to come for more before May. Now there was only twelve hundred out of that two thousand left. So that on the seven of hearts there hung not merely the loss of sixteen hundred roubles, but the consequent inevitable betrayal of his word. With a sinking heart he watched Dolohov's hands and thought: "Well, make haste and deal me that card, and I'll take my cap and drive home to supper with Denisov, Natasha, and Sonya, and I'm sure I'll never take a card in my hand again." At that moment his home life, his jokes with Petya, his talks with Sonya, his duets with Natasha, his game of picquet with his father, even his comfortable bed in the house in Povarsky, rose before his imagination with such vividness, such brightness, and such charm, that it seemed as though it were all some long past, lost, and hitherto unappreciated happiness. He could not conceive that a stupid chance, leading the seven to the right rather than to the left, could deprive him of all that happiness

felt now with new comprehension and seen in a new radiance, could hurl
him into the abyss of unknown and undefined misery. It could not be;
but yet it was with a thrill of dread that he waited for the movement of
Dolohov's hands. Those broad-boned, reddish hands, with hairs visible
under the shirt-cuffs, laid down the pack of cards and took up the glass
and pipe that had been handed him.

"So you're not afraid to play with me?" repeated Dolohov; and as
though he were about to tell a good story, he laid down the cards, leaned
back in his chair, and began deliberately with a smile:

"Yes, gentlemen, I have been told there's a story going about Moscow
that I'm too sharp with cards, so I advise you to be a little on your
guard with me."

"Come, deal away!" said Rostov.

"Ugh, these Moscow gossips!" said Dolohov, and he took up the cards
with a smile.

"Aaah!" Rostov almost screamed, putting both his hands up to his
hair. The seven he needed was lying uppermost, the first card in the
pack. He had lost more than he could pay.

"Don't swim beyond your depth, though," said Dolohov, with a passing glance at Rostov, and he went on.

XIV

WITHIN an hour and a half the greater number of the players were no
longer seriously interested in their own play.

The whole interest of the game was concentrated on Rostov. Instead
of a mere loss of sixteen hundred roubles he had by now scored against
him a long column of figures, which he had added up to the tenth thousand, though he vaguely supposed that by now it had risen to fifteen
thousand. In reality the score already exceeded twenty thousand roubles.
Dolohov was not now listening to stories, or telling them, he followed
every movement of Rostov's hands, and from time to time took a cursory
survey of his score with him. He had resolved to keep the play up till
that score had reached forty-three thousand. He had fixed on that number because it represented the sum of his and Sonya's ages. Rostov sat
with his head propped in both hands, before the wine-stained table
scrawled over with scorings and littered with cards. One torturing sensation never left him; those broad-boned, reddish hands, with the hairs
visible under the shirt-cuffs, those hands which he loved and hated, held
him in their power.

"Six hundred roubles, ace, corner, nine; winning it back's out of the
question! . . . And how happy I should be at home. . . . The knave
double or quits, it can't be! . . . And why is he doing this to me? . . ."
Rostov pondered and thought. Sometimes he put a higher stake on a
card; but Dolohov refused it and fixed the stake himself. Nikolay submitted to him, and at one moment he was praying to God, as he had
prayed under fire on the bridge of Amschteten; at the next he tried his

fortune on the chance that the card that he would first pick up among
the heap of crumpled ones under the table would save him; then he
reckoned up the rows of braidings on his coat, and tried staking the
whole amount of his losses on a card of that number, then he looked
round for help to the others playing, or stared into Dolohov's face, which
looked quite cold now, and tried to penetrate into what was passing
within him.

"He knows, of course, what this loss means to me. Surely he can't
want me to be ruined? Why, he was my friend. I loved him. . . . But,
indeed, it's not his fault; what's he to do, if he has all the luck? And it's
not my fault," he kept saying to himself. "I have done nothing wrong. I
haven't murdered or hurt any one, or wished any one harm, have I?
What is this awful calamity for? And when did it begin? Such a little
while ago I came to this table with the idea of winning a hundred
roubles, and buying mamma that little casket for her name-day, and going home. I was so happy, so free, so light-hearted. And I didn't even
know then how happy I was. When did all that end, and when did this
new awful state of things begin? What was the outward token of that
change? I still went on sitting in the same place at this table, and in the
same way picking out cards and putting them forward, and watching
those deft, broad-boned hands. When did it come to pass, and what has
come to pass? I am strong and well, and still the same, and still in the
same place. No; it cannot be. It will all be sure to end in nothing."

He was all red and in a sweat though the room was not hot. And his
face was painful and piteous to see, particularly from its helpless efforts
to seem calm.

The score reached the fateful number of forty-three thousand roubles.
Rostov already had the card ready which he meant to stake for double
or quits on the three thousand, that had just been put down to his score,
when Dolohov slapped the pack of cards down on the table, pushed it
away, and taking the chalk began rapidly in his clear, strong hand, writing down the total of Rostov's losses, breaking the chalk as he did so.

"Supper, supper-time. And here are the gypsies." And some swarthy
men and women did in fact come in from the cold outside, saying something with their gypsy accent. Nikolay grasped that it was all over; but
he said in an indifferent voice:

"What, won't you go on? And I have such a nice little card all ready."
As though what chiefly interested him was the game itself.

"It's all over, I'm done for," he thought. "Now a bullet through the
head's the only thing left for me," and at the same time he was saying in
a cheerful voice:

"Come, just one more card."

"Very good," answered Dolohov, finishing his addition. "Very good.
Twenty-one roubles . . . done," he said, pointing to the figure 21, over
and above the round sum of forty-three thousand, and taking a pack,
he made ready to deal, Rostov submissively turned down the corner, and
instead of the 8000 he had meant to write, noted down 21.

"It's all the same to me," he said; "only it's interesting to me to know whether you will win on that ten or let me have it."

Dolohov began seriously dealing. Oh, how Rostov hated at that moment those reddish hands, with their short fingers and the hairs visible under the shirt sleeves, those hands that held him in their clutches. . . . The ten was not beaten. Forty-three thousand to your score, count," said Dolohov, and he got up from the table stretching. "One does get tired sitting so long," he said.

"Yes, I'm tired too," said Rostov.

Dolohov cut him short, as though to warn him it was not for him to take a light tone.

"When am I to receive the money, count?"

Rostov flushing hotly drew Dolohov away into the other room.

"I can't pay it all at once, you must take an I.O.U.," said he.

"Listen, Rostov," said Dolohov, smiling brightly, and looking straight into Nikolay's eyes, "you know the saying: 'Lucky in love, unlucky at cards.' Your cousin is in love with you. I know it."

"Oh! this is awful to feel oneself in this man's power like this," thought Rostov. He knew the shock the news of this loss would be to his father and mother; he knew what happiness it would be to be free of it all, and felt that Dolohov knew that he could set him free from this shame and grief, and wanted now to play cat and mouse with him.

"Your cousin . . ." Dolohov would have said, but Nikolay cut him short.

"My cousin has nothing to do with the matter, and there is no need to mention her!" he cried, with fury.

"Then, when am I to receive it?" asked Dolohov.

"To-morrow," said Rostov, and went out of the room.

XV

To say "to-morrow," and maintain the right tone was not difficult; but to arrive home alone, to see his sisters and brother, his mother and father, to confess and beg for money to which he had no right after giving his word of honour, was terrible.

At home they had not yet gone to bed. The younger members of the family after coming home from the theatre had had supper, and were now in a group about the clavichord. As soon as Nikolay entered the hall, he felt himself enfolded in the poetic atmosphere of love which dominated their household that winter; and now, since Dolohov's proposal and Iogel's ball, seemed to have grown thicker about Sonya and Natasha, like the air before a storm. Sonya and Natasha, wearing the light blue dresses they had put on for the theatre, stood at the clavichord, pretty and conscious of being so, happy and smiling. Vera was playing draughts with Shinshin in the drawing-room. The old countess, waiting for her son and her husband to come in, was playing patience an an old gentlewoman, who was one of their household. Denisov, with shining eyes and ruffled hair, was sitting with one leg behind him at the clavichord. He was striking chords with his short fingers, and rolling his eyes, as he sang in his small, husky, but true voice a poem of his own composition, "The Enchantress," to which he was trying to fit music.

> "Enchantress, say what hidden fire
> Draws me to my forsaken lyre?
> What rapture thrills my fingers slow,
> What passion sets my heart aglow?"

he sang in his passionate voice, his black, agate eyes gleaming at the frightened and delighted Natasha.

"Splendid, capital!" Natasha cried. "Another couplet," she said, not noticing Nikolay.

"Everything's just the same with them," thought Nikolay, peeping into the drawing-room, where he saw Vera and his mother and the old lady playing patience with her.

"Ah, and here's Nikolenka." Natasha ran up to him. "Is papa at home?" he asked.

"How glad I am that you have come," said Natasha, not answering his question, "we are having such fun. Vassily Dmitritch is staying a day longer for me, do you know?"

"No, papa has not come in yet," answered Sonya.

"Kolya, you there? Come to me, darling," said the voice of the countess from the drawing-room. Nikolay went up to his mother, kissed her hand, and sitting down by her table, began silently watching her hands as they dealt the cards. From the hall he kept hearing the sound of laughter and merry voices, persuading Natasha to do something.

"Oh, very well, very well!" Denisov cried; "now it's no use crying off, it's your turn to sing the barcarolle, I entreat you."

The countess looked round at her silent son.

"What's the matter?" his mother asked Nikolay.

"Oh, nothing," he said, as though sick of being continually asked the same question: "Will papa soon be in?"

"I expect so."

"Everything's the same with them. They know nothing about it. What am I to do with myself?" thought Nikolay, and he went back to the hall, where the clavichord was.

Sonya was sitting at the clavichord, playing the prelude of the barcarolle that Denisov particularly liked. Natasha was preparing to sing. Denisov was watching her with impassioned eyes.

Nikolay began walking to and fro in the room.

"What can induce her to want to sing? What can she sing? And there's nothing to be so happy about in it," thought Nikolay.

Sonya struck the first chord of the prelude. "My God, I'm ruined, I'm a dishonoured man. Bullet through my head, that's the only thing left for me, and not singing," he thought. "Go away? But where? It makes no difference, let them sing."

Still walking about the room, Nikolay glanced gloomily at Denisov and the girls, avoiding their eyes.

"Nikolenka, what's the matter?" Sonya's eyes asked, looking intently at him. She saw at once that something had happened to him.

Nikolay turned away from her. Natasha, too, with her quick instinct instantly detected her brother's state of mind. She noticed him, but she was herself in such high spirits at that moment, she was so far from sorrow, from sadness, from reproaches, that purposely she deceived herself (as young people so often do). "No, I'm too happy just now to spoil my enjoyment by sympathy with any one's sorrow," she felt, and she said to herself: "No, I'm most likely mistaken, he must be happy, just as I am."

"Come, Sonya," she said. walking into the very middle of the room, where to her mind the resonance was best of all. Holding her head up, letting her arms hang lifelessly as dancers do, Natasha, with a vigorous turn from her heel on to her toe, walked over to the middle of the room and stood still.

"Behold me, here I am!" she seemed to say, in response to the enthusiastic gaze with which Denisov followed her. "And what can she find to be so pleased at!" Nikolay wondered, looking at his sister. "How is it she isn't feeling dull and ashamed!" Natasha took the first note, her throat swelled, her bosom heaved, a serious expression came into her face. She was thinking of no one and of nothing at that moment, and from her smiling mouth poured forth notes, those notes that any one can produce at the same intervals, and hold for the same length of time, yet a thousand times they leave us cold, and the thousand and first time they set us thrilling and weeping.

Natasha had for the first time begun that winter to take singing seriously, especially since Denisov had been so enthusiastic over her singing. She did not now sing like a child; there was not now in her singing that comical childish effort which used to be perceptible in it. But she did not yet sing well, said the musical connoisseurs who heard her. "Not trained: a fine voice, it must be trained," every one said. But this was usually said a good while after her voice was hushed. While that untrained voice, with its irregular breathing and its strained transitions sounded, even connoisseurs said nothing, and simply enjoyed that untrained voice, and simply longed to hear it again. Her voice had a virginal purity, an ignorance of its capacities, and an unlaboured velvety softness, so closely connected with its lack of art in singing, that it seemed as though nothing could be changed in that voice without spoiling it.

"How is it?" thought Nikolay, hearing her voice and opening his eyes wide; "what has happened to her? How she is singing to-day!" he thought. And all at once the whole world was for him concentrated into anticipations of the next note, the next bar, and everything in the world seemed divided up into three motives: "*Oh, mio crudele affetto* . . . One, two, three . . . one . . . *Oh, mio crudele affetto* . . . One, two, three . . . one. Ugh, this senseless life of ours!" thought Nikolay. "All that, this calamity, and money, and Dolohov, and anger, and honour— it's all nonsense . . . and this is what's the real thing . . . Now, Na-

tasha! now, darling! now, my girl! . . . how will she take that *si*?
taken it! thank God!" and without being conscious that he was singing,
he himself sung a second to support her high note. "My God! how fine!
Can I have taken that note? how glorious!" he thought.

Oh, how that note had thrilled, and how something better that was in
Rostov's soul began thrilling too. And that something was apart from
everything in the world, and above everything in the world. What were
losses, and Dolohovs, and honour beside it! . . . All nonsense! One
might murder, and steal, and yet be happy. . . .

XVI

It was long since Rostov had derived such enjoyment from music as on
that day. But as soon as Natasha had finished her barcarolle, the reality
forced itself upon his mind again. Saying nothing, he went out, and went
down stairs to his own room. A quarter of an hour later, the old prince
came in, good-humoured and satisfied from his club. Nikolay heard him
come in, and went in to him.

"Well, had a good time?" said Ilya Andreivitch. smiling proudly and
joyfully to his son. Nikolay tried to say "Yes," but could not; he was
on the point of sobbing. The count was lighting his pipe, and did not
notice his son's condition.

"Ugh, it's inevitable!" thought Nikolay, for the first and last time.
And all at once, as though he were asking for the carriage to drive into
town, he said to his father in the most casual tone, that made him feel
vile to himself:

"Papa, I have come to you on a matter of business I was almost forgetting. I want some money."

"You don't say so?" said his father, who happened to be in particularly good spirits. "I told you that we shouldn't be having any. Do you
want a large sum?"

"Very large," said Nikolay, flushing and smiling a stupid, careless
smile, for which long after he could not forgive himself. "I have lost a
little at cards, that is, a good deal, really, a great deal, forty-three thousand."

"What! To whom? . . . You're joking!" cried the count, flushing, as
old people flush, an apoplectic red over his neck and the back of his
head.

"I have promised to pay it to-morrow," said Nikolay.

"Oh!" . . . said the count, flinging up his arms; and he dropped
helplessly on the sofa.

"It can't be helped! It happens to every one," said his son in a free
and easy tone, while in his heart he was feeling himself a low scoundrel,
whose whole life could not atone for his crime. He would have liked to
kiss his father's hands, to beg his forgiveness on his knees, while carelessly, rudely even, he was telling him that it happened to every one.

Count Ilya Andreivitch dropped his eyes when he heard those words from his son, and began moving hurriedly, as though looking for something.

"Yes, yes," he brought out, "it will be difficult, I fear, difficult to raise . . . happens to every one! yes, it happens to every one . . ." And the count cast a fleeting glance at his son's face and walked out of the room. . . . Nikolay had been prepared to face resistance, but he had not expected this.

"Papa! pa . . . pa!" he cried after him, sobbing; "forgive me!" And clutching at his father's hand, he pressed it to his lips and burst into tears.

While the father and son were having this interview, another, hardly less important, was taking place between the mother and daughter. Natasha, in great excitement, had run in to her mother.

"Mamma! . . . Mamma! . . . he has made me . . ."

"Made you what?"

"He's made, made an offer. Mamma! Mamma!" she kept crying.

The countess could not believe her ears. Denisov had made an offer . . . to whom? . . . To this chit of a girl Natasha, who had only just given up playing with dolls, and was still having lessons.

"Natasha, enough of this silliness!" she said, hoping it was a joke.

"Silliness indeed! I am telling you the fact," said Natasha angrily. "I have come to ask you what to do, and you talk to me of 'silliness' . . ."

The countess shrugged her shoulders.

"If it is true that Monsieur Denisov has made you an offer, then tell him he is a fool, that's all."

"No, he's not a fool," said Natasha, resentfully and seriously.

"Well, what would you have, then? You are all in love, it seems, nowadays. Oh, well, if you're in love with him, better marry him," said the countess, laughing angrily, "and God bless you."

"No, mamma, I'm not in love with him. I suppose I'm not in love with him."

"Well, then, tell him so."

"Mamma, are you cross? Don't be cross, darling; it's not my fault, is it?"

"No, but upon my word, my dear, if you like, I will go and tell him so," said the countess, smiling.

"No, I'll do it myself; only tell me how to say it. Everything comes easy to you," she added, responding to her smile. "And if you could have seen how he said it to me! I know he did not mean to say it, but said it by accident."

"Well, any way you must refuse him."

"No, I mustn't. I feel so sorry for him! He's so nice."

"Oh, well, accept his proposal, then. High time you were married, I suppose," said her mother angrily and ironically.

"No, mamma, but I'm so sorry for him. I don't know how to say it."

"Well, there's no need for you to say anything. I'll speak to him

myself," said the countess, indignant that any one should have dared
to treat this little Natasha as grown up.

"No, not on any account; I'll go myself, and you listen at the door,"—
and Natasha ran across the drawing-room to the hall, where Denisov, his
face in his hands, was still sitting in the same chair at the clavichord. He
jumped up at the sound of her light footsteps.

"Natalie," he said, moving with rapid steps towards her, "decide my
fate. It is in your hands!"

"Vassily Dmitritch, I'm so sorry for you! . . . No, but you are so
nice . . . but it won't do . . . that . . . but I shall always love you
as I do now."

Denisov bent over her, and she heard strange sounds that she did not
understand. She kissed his tangled curly black head. At that moment
they heard the hurried rustle of the countess's skirts. She came up to
them.

"Vassily Dmitritch, I thank you for the honour you do us," said the
countess, in an embarrassed voice, which sounded severe to Denisov,
"but my daughter is so young, and I should have thought that as my
son's friend you would have come first to me. In that case you would
not have forced me to make this refusal."

"Countess! . . ." said Denisov, with downcast eyes and a guilty face;
he tried to say more, and stammered.

Natasha could not see him in such a piteous plight without emotion.
She began to whimper loudly.

"Countess, I have acted wrongly," Denisov went on in a breaking
voice, "but believe me, I so adore your daughter and all your family that
I'd give my life twice over . . ." He looked at the countess and noticed
her stern face. . . . "Well, good-bye, countess," he said, kissing her
hand, and without glancing at Natasha he walked with rapid and resolute steps out of the room.

Next day Rostov saw Denisov off, as he was unwilling to remain another day in Moscow. All his Moscow friends gave him a farewell entertainment at the Gypsies', and he had no recollection of how they got
him into his sledge, or of the first three stations he passed.

After Denisov's departure Rostov spent another fortnight in Moscow,
waiting for the money to pay his debt, which the count was unable to
raise all at once. He hardly left the house, and spent most of his time
in the young girls' room.

Sonya was more affectionate and devoted to him then ever. She seemed
to want to show him that his loss at cards was an exploit for which she
loved him more than ever. But now Nikolay regarded himself as unworthy of her.

He copied music for the girls, and wrote verses in their albums, and
after at last sending off all the forty-three thousand roubles, and receiving Dolohov's receipt for it, he left Moscow towards the end of November without taking leave of any of his acquaintances, and overtook his
regiment, which was already in Poland.

PART FIVE

I

AFTER HIS interview with his wife, Pierre had set off for Petersburg. At the station of Torzhok there were no horses, or the overseer was unwilling to let him have them. Pierre had to wait. Without removing his outdoor things, he lay down on a leather sofa, in front of a round table, put up his big feet in their thick overboots on this table and sank into thought.

"Shall I bring in the trunks? Make up a bed? Will you take tea?" the valet kept asking.

Pierre made no reply, for he heard nothing and said nothing. He had been deep in thought since he left the last station, and still went on thinking of the same thing—of something so important that he did not notice what was passing around him. Far from being concerned whether he reached Petersburg sooner or later, or whether there would or would not be a place for him to rest in at this station, in comparison with the thoughts that engrossed him now, it was a matter of utter indifference to him whether he spent a few hours or the rest of his life at that station.

The overseer and his wife, his valet, and a peasant woman with Torzhok embroidery for sale, came into the room, offering their services. Without changing the position of his raised feet, Pierre gazed at them over his spectacles, and did not understand what they could want and how they all managed to live, without having solved the questions that absorbed him. These same questions had possessed his mind ever since that day when he had come back after the duel from Sokolniky and had spent that first agonising, sleepless night. But now in the solitude of his journey they seized upon him with special force. Of whatever he began thinking he came back to the same questions, which he could not answer, and from which he could not escape. It was as though the chief screw in his brain upon which his whole life rested were loose. The screw moved no forwarder, no backwarder, but still it turned, catching on nothing, always in the same groove, and there was no making it cease turning.

The overseer came in and began humbly begging his excellency to wait only a couple of hours, after which he would (come what might of it) let his excellency have the special mail service horses. The overseer was unmistakably lying, with the sole aim of getting an extra tip from the traveller. "Was that good or bad?" Pierre wondered. "For me good, for the next traveller bad, and for himself inevitable because he has nothing to eat; he said that an officer had thrashed him for it. And the officer thrashed him because he had to travel in haste. And I shot

Dolohov because I considered myself injured. Louis XVI. was executed because they considered him to be a criminal, and a year later his judges were killed too for something. What is wrong? What is right? What must one love, what must one hate? What is life for, and what am I? What is life? What is death? What force controls it all?" he asked himself. And there was no answer to one of these questions, except one illogical reply that was in no way an answer to any of them. That reply was: "One dies and it's all over. One dies and finds it all out or ceases asking." But dying too was terrible.

The Torzhok pedlar woman in a whining voice proffered her wares, especially some goatskin slippers. "I have hundreds of roubles I don't know what to do with, and she's standing in her torn cloak looking timidly at me," thought Pierre. "And what does she want the money for? As though the money could give her one hairsbreadth of happiness, of peace of soul. Is there anything in the world that can make her and me less enslaved to evil and to death? Death, which ends all, and must come to-day or to-morrow—which beside eternity is the same as an instant's time." And again he turned the screw that did not bite in anything, and the screw still went on turning in the same place.

His servant handed him a half-cut volume of a novel in the form of letters by Madame Suza. He began reading of the sufferings and the virtuous struggles of a certain "Amélie de Mansfeld." "And what did she struggle against her seducer for?" he thought, "when she loved him. God could not have put in her heart an impulse that was against His will. My wife—as she was once—didn't struggle, and perhaps she was right. Nothing has been discovered," Pierre said to himself again, "nothing has been invented. We can only know that we know nothing. And that's the highest degree of human wisdom."

Everything within himself and around him struck him as confused, meaningless, and loathsome. But in this very loathing of everything surrounding him Pierre found a sort of tantalising satisfaction.

"I make bold to beg your excellency to make room the least bit for this gentleman here," said the overseer, coming into the room and ushering in after him another traveller, brought to a standstill from lack of horses. The traveller was a thickset, square-shouldered, yellow, wrinkled old man, with grey eyelashes overhanging gleaming eyes of an indefinite grey colour.

Pierre took his feet off the table, stood up and went to lie down on the bed that had been made ready for him, glancing now and then at the newcomer, who, without looking at Pierre, with an air of surly fatigue was wearily taking off his outer wraps with the aid of his servant. The traveller, now clothed in a shabby nankin-covered sheepskin coat with felt highboots on his thin bony legs, sat down on the sofa, and leaning on its back his close-cropped head, which was very large and broad across the temples, he glanced at Bezuhov. The stern, shrewd, and penetrating expression in that glance impressed Pierre. He felt disposed to speak to the traveller, but by the time he had ready a question about the road with which to address him, the traveller had closed his eyes, and folded his wrinkled old hands, on one finger of which there was a large iron ring with a seal representing the head of Adam. He sat without stirring, either resting or sunk, as it seemed to Pierre, in profound and calm meditation. The newcomer's servant was also a yellow old man, covered with wrinkles. He had neither moustache nor beard, not because he was shaved, but obviously had never had any. The old servant was active in unpacking a travelling-case, in setting the tea-table, and in bringing in a boiling samovar. When everything was ready, the traveller opened his eyes, moved to the table, and pouring out a glass of tea for himself, poured out another for the beardless old man and gave it him. Pierre began to feel an uneasiness and a sense of the necessity, of the inevitability of entering into conversation with the traveller.

The servant brought back his empty glass turned upside down with an unfinished piece of nibbled sugar beside it, and asked if anything were wanted.

"Nothing. Give me my book," said the traveller. The servant gave him a book, which seemed to Pierre to be of a devotional character, and the traveller became absorbed in its perusal. Pierre looked at him. All at once the stranger laid down the book, and putting a mark in it, shut it up. Then closing his eyes and leaning his arms on the back of the sofa, he fell back into his former attitude. Pierre stared at him, and had not time to look away when the old man opened his eyes and bent his resolute and stern glance upon Pierre. Pierre felt confused and tried to turn away from that glance, but the gleaming old eyes drew him irresistibly to them.

II

"I HAVE the pleasure of speaking to Count Bezuhov, if I am not mistaken," said the stranger, in a loud deliberate voice. Pierre looked in silence and inquiringly over his spectacles at the speaker. "I have heard of you," continued the stranger, "and I have heard, sir, of what has happened to you, of your misfortune." He underlined, as it were, the last word, as though to say: "Yes, misfortune, whatever you call it, I know that what happened to you in Moscow was a misfortune."

"I am very sorry for it, sir." Pierre reddened, and hurriedly dropping his legs over the edge of the bed, he bent forward towards the old man, smiling timidly and unnaturally.

"I have not mentioned this to you, sir, from curiosity, but from graver reasons." He paused, not letting Pierre escape from his gaze, and moved aside on the sofa, inviting him by this movement to sit beside him. Pierre disliked entering into conversation with this old man, but involuntarily submitting to him, he came and sat down beside him.

"You are unhappy, sir," he went on, "you are young, and I am old. I should like, as far as it is in my power, to help you."

"Oh, yes," said Pierre, with an unnatural smile. "Very much obliged to you . . . where have you been travelling from?" The stranger's face was not cordial, it was even cold and severe, but in spite of that, both the speech and the face of his new acquaintance were irresistibly attractive to Pierre.

"But if for any reason you dislike conversing with me," said the old man, "then you say so, sir." And suddenly he smiled a quite unexpected smile of fatherly kindliness.

"Oh, no, not at all; on the contrary, I am very glad to make your acquaintance," said Pierre, and glancing once more at the stranger's hands, he examined the ring more closely. He saw the head of Adam, the token of masonry.

"Allow me to inquire," he said, "are you a mason?"

"Yes, I belong to the brotherhood of the freemasons," said the stranger, looking now more searchingly into Pierre's eyes. "And from myself and in their name I hold out to you a brotherly hand."

"I am afraid," said Pierre, smiling and hesitating between the confidence inspired in him by the personality of the freemason and the habit of ridiculing the articles of the masons' creed; "I am afraid that I am very far from a comprehension—how shall I say—I am afraid that my way of thinking in regard to the whole theory of the universe is so opposed to yours that we shall not understand one another."

"I am aware of your way of thinking," said the freemason, "and that way of thinking of which you speak, which seems to you the result of your own thought, is the way of thinking of the majority of men, and is the invariable fruit of pride, indolence, and ignorance. Excuse my saying, sir, that if I had not been aware of it, I should not have addressed you. Your way of thinking is a melancholy error."

"Just as I may take for granted that you are in error," said Pierre, faintly smiling.

"I would never be so bold as to say I know the truth," said the mason, the definiteness and decision of whose manner of speaking impressed Pierre more and more. "No one alone can attain truth; only stone upon stone, with the co-operation of all, by the millions of generations from our first father Adam down to our day is that temple being reared that should be a fitting dwelling-place of the Great God," said the freemason, and he shut his eyes.

"I ought to tell you that I don't believe, don't . . . believe in God," said Pierre regretfully and with effort, feeling it essential to speak the whole truth.

The freemason looked intently at Pierre and smiled as a rich man, holding millions in his hands, might smile to a poor wretch, who should say to him that he, the poor man, has not five roubles that would secure his happiness.

"Yes, you do not know Him, sir," said the freemason. "You cannot know Him. You know not Him, that is why you are unhappy."

"Yes, yes, I am unhappy," Pierre assented; "but what am I to do?"

"You know not Him, sir, and that's why you are very unhappy. You know not Him, but He is here, He is within me, He is in my words, He is in thee, and even in these scoffing words that thou hast just uttered," said the mason in a stern, vibrating voice.

He paused and sighed, evidently trying to be calm.

"If He were not," he said softly, "we should not be speaking of Him, sir. Of what, of whom were we speaking? Whom dost thou deny?" he said all at once, with enthusiastic austerity and authority in his voice. "Who invented Him, if He be not? How came there within thee the conception that there is such an incomprehensible Being? How comes it that thou and all the world have assumed the existence of such an inconceivable Being, a Being all powerful, eternal and infinite in all His qualities? . . ." He stopped and made a long pause.

Pierre could not and would not interrupt this silence.

"He exists, but to comprehend Him is hard," the mason began again, not looking into Pierre's face, but straight before him, while his old hands, which could not keep still for inward emotion, turned the leaves of the book. "If it had been a man of whose existence thou hadst doubts, I could have brought thee the man, taken him by the hand, and shown him thee. But how am I, an insignificant mortal, to show all the power, all the eternity, all the blessedness of Him to one who is blind, or to one who shuts his eyes that he may not see, may not understand Him, and may not see, and not understand all his own vileness and viciousness." He paused. "Who art thou? What art thou? Thou dreamest that thou art wise because thou couldst utter those scoffing words," he said, with a gloomy and scornful irony, "while thou art more foolish and artless than a little babe, who, playing with the parts of a cunningly fashioned watch, should rashly say that because he understands not the use of that watch, he does not believe in the maker who fashioned it. To know Him is a hard matter. For ages, from our first father Adam to our day, have we been striving for this knowledge, and are infinitely far from the attainment of our aim; but in our lack of understanding we see only our own weakness and His greatness . . ."

Pierre gazed with shining eyes into the freemason's face, listening with a thrill at his heart to his words; he did not interrupt him, nor ask questions, but with all his soul he believed what this strange man was telling him. Whether he believed on the rational grounds put before him by the freemason, or believed, as children do, through the intonations, the conviction, and the earnestness, of the mason's words, the quiver in his voice that sometimes almost broke his utterance, or the gleaming old eyes that had grown old in that conviction, or the calm, the resolution, and the certainty of his destination, which were conspicuous in the whole personality of the old man, and struck Pierre with particular force, beside his own abjectness and hopelessness,—any way, with his whole soul he longed to believe, and believed and felt a joyful sense of soothing, of renewal, and of return to life.

"It is not attained by the reason, but by life," said the mason.

"I don't understand," said Pierre, feeling with dismay that doubt was stirring within him. He dreaded obscurity and feebleness in the freemason's arguments, he dreaded being unable to believe in him. "I don't understand," he said, "in what way human reason cannot attain that knowledge of which you speak."

The freemason smiled his mild, fatherly smile.

"The highest wisdom and truth is like the purest dew, which we try to hold within us," said he. "Can I hold in an impure vessel that pure dew and judge of its purity? Only by the inner purification of myself can I bring that dew contained within me to some degree of purity."

"Yes, yes; that's so," Pierre said joyfully.

"The highest wisdom is founded not on reason only, not on those worldly sciences, of physics, history, chemistry, etc., into which knowledge of the intellect is divided. The highest wisdom is one. The highest wisdom knows but one science—the science of the whole, the science that explains the whole creation and the place of man in it. To instil this science into one's soul, it is needful to purify and renew one's inner man, and so, before one can know, one must believe and be made perfect. And for the attainment of these aims there has been put into our souls the light of God, called the conscience."

"Yes, yes," Pierre assented.

"Look with the spiritual eye into thy inner man, and ask of thyself whether thou art content with thyself. What hast thou attained with the guidance of the intellect alone? What art thou? You are young, you are wealthy, you are cultured, sir. What have you made of all the blessings vouchsafed you? Are you satisfied with yourself and your life?"

"No, I hate my life," said Pierre, frowning.

"Thou hatest it; then change it, purify thyself, and as thou art purified, thou wilt come to know wisdom. Look at your life, sir. How have you been spending it? In riotous orgies and debauchery, taking everything from society and giving nothing in return. You have received wealth. How have you used it? What nave you done for your neighbour? Have you given a thought to the tens of thousands of your slaves, have you succoured them physically and morally? No. You have profited by their toil to lead a dissipated life. That's what you have done. Have you chosen a post in the service where you might be of use to your neighbour? No. You have spent your life in idleness. Then you married, sir, took upon yourself the responsibility of guiding a young woman in life, and what have you done? You have not helped her, sir, to find the path of truth, but have cast her into an abyss of deception and misery. A man injured you, and you have killed him, and you say you do not know God, and that you hate your life. There is no wisdom in all that, sir."

After these words the freemason leaned his elbow again on the back of the sofa and closed his eyes, as though weary of prolonged talking. Pierre gazed at that stern, immovable, old, almost death-like face, and moved his lips without uttering a sound. He wanted to say, "Yes, a vile, idle, vicious life," and he dared not break the silence. The freemason cleared his throat huskily, as old men do, and called his servant.

"How about horses?" he asked, without looking at Pierre.

"They have brought round some that were given up," answered the old man. "You won't rest?"

"No, tell them to harness them."

"Can he really be going away and leaving me all alone, without tell-

ing me everything and promising me help?" thought Pierre, getting up
with downcast head, beginning to walk up and down the room, casting a
glance from time to time at the freemason. "Yes, I had not thought of
it, but I have led a contemptible, dissolute life, but I did not like it,
and I didn't want to," thought Pierre, "and this man knows the truth,
and if he liked he could reveal it to me." Pierre wanted to say this to the
freemason and dared not. After packing his things with his practised old
hands, the traveller buttoned up his sheepskin. On finishing these preparations, he turned to Bezuhov, and in a polite, indifferent tone, said to
him:

"Where are you going now, sir?"

"I? . . . I'm going to Petersburg," answered Pierre in a tone of childish indecision. "I thank you. I agree with you in everything. But do not
suppose that I have been so bad. With all my soul I have desired to be
what you would wish me to be; but I have never met with help from
any one. . . . Though I was myself most to blame for everything. Help
me, instruct me, and perhaps I shall be able . . ."

Pierre could not say more; his voice broke and he turned away.

The freemason was silent, obviously pondering something.

"Help comes only from God," he said, "but such measure of aid as it
is in the power of our order to give you, it will give you, sir. You go to
Petersburg, and give this to Count Villarsky" (he took out his notebook
and wrote a few words on a large sheet of paper folded into four). "One
piece of advice let me give you. When you reach the capital, devote
your time at first there to solitude and to self-examination, and do not
return to your old manner of life. Therewith I wish you a good journey,
sir," he added, noticing that his servant had entered the room, "and all
success . . ."

The stranger was Osip Alexyevitch Bazdyev, as Pierre found out from
the overseer's book. Bazdyev had been one of the most well-known freemasons and Martinists even in Novikov's day. For a long while after he
had gone, Pierre walked about the station room, neither lying down to
sleep nor asking for horses. He reviewed his vicious past, and with an
ecstatic sense of beginning anew, pictured to himself a blissful, irreproachably virtuous future, which seemed to him easy of attainment. It
seemed to him that he had been vicious, simply because he had accidentally forgotten how good it was to be virtuous. There was left in his
soul not a trace of his former doubts. He firmly believed in the possibility of the brotherhood of man, united in the aim of supporting one
another in the path of virtue. And freemasonry he pictured to himself
as such a brotherhood.

III

ON reaching Petersburg, Pierre let no one know of his arrival, went out
to see nobody, and spent whole days in reading Thomas à Kempis, a
book which had been sent him, he did not know from whom. One thing,

and one thing only, Pierre thoroughly understood in reading that book;
he understood what he had hitherto known nothing of, all the bliss of
believing in the possibility of attaining perfection, and in the possibility
of brotherly and active love between men, revealed to him by Osip
Alexyevitch. A week after his arrival, the young Polish count, Villarsky,
whom Pierre knew very slightly in Petersburg society, came one evening
into his room with the same official and ceremonious air with which
Dolohov's second had called on him. Closing the door behind him, and
assuring himself that there was nobody in the room but Pierre, he addressed him:

"I have come to you with a message and a suggestion, count," he said
to him, not sitting down. "A personage of very high standing in our
brotherhood has been interceding for you to be admitted into our
brotherhood before the usual term, and has asked me to be your sponsor.
I regard it as a sacred duty to carry out that person's wishes. Do you
wish under my sponsorship to enter the brotherhood of freemasons?"

Pierre was impressed by the cold and austere tone of this man, whom
he had almost always seen before at balls wearing an agreeable smile,
in the society of the most brilliant women.

"Yes, I do wish it," said Pierre.

Villarsky bent his head.

"One more question, count," he said, "to which I beg you, not as a
future mason, but as an honest man (*galant homme*) to answer me in all
sincerity: have you renounced your former convictions? do you believe
in God?"

Pierre thought a moment.

"Yes . . . yes, I do believe in God," he said.

"In that case . . ." Villarsky was beginning, but Pierre interrupted
him.

"Yes, I believe in God," he said once more.

"In that case, we can go," said Villarsky. "My carriage is at your
disposal."

Throughout the drive Villarsky was silent. In answer to Pierre's inquiries, what he would have to do, and how he would have to answer,
Villarsky simply said that brothers, more worthy than he, would prove
him, and that Pierre need do nothing but tell the truth.

They drove in at the gates of a large house, where the lodge had its
quarters, and, passing up a dark staircase, entered a small, lighted ante-
room, where they took off their overcoats without the assistance of
servants. From the ante-room they walked into another room. A man in
strange attire appeared at the door. Villarsky, going in to meet him, said
something to him in French in a low voice, and went up to a small cupboard, where Pierre noticed garments unlike any he had seen before.
Taking a handkerchief from the cupboard, Villarsky put it over Pierre's
eyes and tied it in a knot behind, catching his hair painfully in the knot.
Then he drew him towards himself, kissed him, and taking him by the
hand led him away somewhere. Pierre had been hurt by his hair being
pulled in the knot: he puckered up his face from the pain, and smiled

with vague shame. His huge figure with his arms hanging at his sides, and his face puckered up and smiling, moved after Villarsky with timid and uncertain steps.

After leading him for about ten steps, Villarsky stopped.

"Whatever happens to you," said he, "you must endure all with good courage if you are firmly resolved to enter our brotherhood." (Pierre answered affirmatively by an inclination of his head.) "When you hear a knock at the door, you may uncover your eyes," added Villarsky; "I wish you good courage and success," and, pressing Pierre's hand, Villarsky went away.

When he was left alone, Pierre still went on smiling in the same way. Twice he shrugged his shoulders and raised his hand to the handkerchief, as though he would have liked to take it off, but he let it drop again. The five minutes he had spent with his eyes bandaged seemed to him an hour. His arms felt numb, his legs tottered, he felt as though he were tired out. He was aware of the most complex and conflicting feelings. He was afraid of what would be done to him, and still more afraid of showing fear. He felt inquisitive to know what was coming, what would be revealed to him; but above everything, he felt joy that the moment had come when he would at last enter upon that path of regeneration and of an actively virtuous life, of which he had been dreaming ever since his meeting with Osip Alexyevitch.

There came loud knocks at the door. Pierre took off the bandage and looked about him. It was black darkness in the room; only in one spot there was a little lamp burning before something white. Pierre went nearer and saw that the little lamp stood on a black table, on which there lay an open book. The book was the gospel: the white thing in which the lamp was burning was a human skull with its eyeholes and teeth. After reading the first words of the gospel, "In the beginning was the Word and the Word was with God," Pierre went round the table and caught sight of a large open box filled with something. It was a coffin full of bones. He was not in the least surprised by what he saw. Hoping to enter upon a completely new life, utterly unlike the old life, he was ready for anything extraordinary, more extraordinary indeed than what he was seeing. The skull, the coffin, the gospel—it seemed to him that he had been expecting all that; had been expecting more, indeed. He tried to stir up a devotional feeling in himself; he looked about him. "God, death, love, the brotherhood of man," he kept saying to himself, associating with those words vague but joyful conceptions of some sort. The door opened and some one came in. In the faint light, in which Pierre could, however, see a little by this time, a short man approached. Apparently dazed by coming out of the light into the darkness, the man stopped, then with cautious steps moved again towards the table, and laid on it both his small hands covered with leather gloves.

This short man was wearing a white leather apron, that covered his chest and part of his legs; upon his neck could be seen something like a necklace, and a high white ruffle stood up from under the necklace, framing his long face, on which the light fell from below.

"For what are you come hither?" asked the newcomer, turning towards Pierre at a faint rustle made by the latter. "For what are you, an unbeliever in the truth of the light, who have not seen the light, for what are you come here? What do you seek from us? Wisdom, virtue, enlightenment?"

At the moment when the door opened and the unknown person came in, Pierre had a sensation of awe and reverence, such as he had felt in childhood at confession; he felt himself alone with a man who was in the circumstances of life a complete stranger, and yet through the brotherhood of men so near. With a beating heart that made him gasp for breath, Pierre turned to the *rhetor*, as in the phraseology of freemasonry the man is called who prepares the *seeker* for entering the brotherhood. Going closer, Pierre recognised in the rhetor a man he knew, Smolyaninov, but it was mortifying to him to think that the newcomer was a familiar figure; he was to him only a brother and a guide in the path of virtue. For a long while Pierre could not utter a word, so that the rhetor was obliged to repeat his question.

"Yes; I . . . I . . . wish to begin anew," Pierre articulated with difficulty.

"Very good," said Smolyaninov, and went on at once.

"Have you any idea of the means by which our holy order will assist you in attaining your aim? . . ." said the rhetor calmly and rapidly.

"I . . . hope for . . . guidance . . . for help . . . in renewing . . ." said Pierre, with a tremble in his voice and a difficulty in utterance due both to emotion and to being unaccustomed to speak of abstract subjects in Russian.

"What idea have you of freemasonry?"

"I assume that freemasonry is the *fraternité* and equality of men with virtuous aims," said Pierre, feeling ashamed as he spoke of the incongruity of his words with the solemnity of the moment. "I assume . . ."

"Very good," said the rhetor hastily, apparently quite satisfied with the reply. "Have you sought the means of attaining your aim in religion?"

"No; I regarded it as untrue and have not followed it," said Pierre, so softly that the rhetor did not catch it, and asked him what he was saying. "I was an atheist," answered Pierre.

"You seek the truth in order to follow its laws in life; consequently, you seek wisdom and virtue, do you not?" said the rhetor, after a moment's pause.

"Yes, yes," assented Pierre.

The rhetor cleared his throat, folded his gloved hands across his chest, and began speaking.

"Now I must reveal to you the chief aim of our order," he said, "and if that aim coincides with yours, you may with profit enter our brotherhood. The first and greatest aim and united basis of our order, on which it is established and which no human force can destroy, is the preservation and handing down to posterity of a certain important mystery . . . that has come down to us from the most ancient times, even from the first man—a mystery upon which, perhaps, the fate of the human race depends. But since this mystery is of such a kind that no one can know it and profit by it if he has not been prepared by a prolonged and diligent self-purification, not every one can hope to attain it quickly. Hence we have a second aim, which consists in preparing our members, as far as possible reforming their hearts, purifying and enlightening their intelligence by those means which have been revealed to us by tradition from men who have striven to attain this mystery, and thereby to render them fit for the reception of it. Purifying and regenerating our members, we endeavor, thirdly, to improve the whole human race, offering it in our members an example of piety and virtue, and thereby we strive with all our strength to combat the evil that is paramount in the world. Ponder on these things, and I will come again to you," he said, and went out of the room.

"To combat the evil that is paramount in the world . . ." Pierre repeated, and a mental image of his future activity in that direction rose before him. He seemed to see men such as he had been himself a fortnight ago, and he was mentally addressing an edifying exhortation to them. He pictured to himself persons vicious and unhappy, whom he would help in word and in deed; he pictured oppressors whose victims he would rescue. Of the three aims enumerated by the rhetor the last—the reformation of the human race—appealed particularly to Pierre. The great mystery of which the rhetor had made mention, though it excited his curiosity, did not strike his imagination as a reality; while the second aim, the purification and regeneration of himself, had little interest for him, because at that moment he was full of a blissful sense of being completely cured of all his former vices, and being ready for nothing but goodness.

Half an hour later the rhetor returned to enumerate to the seeker the seven virtues corresponding to the seven steps of the temple of Solomon, in which every freemason must train himself. Those virtues were: (1) discretion, the keeping of the secrets of the order; (2) obedience to the higher authorities of the order; (3) morality; (4) love for mankind; (5) courage; (6) liberality; and (7) love of death.

"Seventhly, strive," said the rhetor, "by frequent meditation upon death to bring yourself to feel it not an enemy to be dreaded, but a friend . . . which delivers the soul grown weary in the labours of virtue from this distressful life and leads it to its place of recompense and peace."

"Yes, that's as it should be," thought Pierre, when the rhetor after these words left him again to solitary reflection; "that's as it ought to be, but I'm still so weak as to love this life, the meaning of which is only now by degrees being revealed to me." But the other five virtues which Pierre recalled, reckoning them on his fingers, he felt already in his soul; courage and liberality, morality and love for mankind, and above all, obedience, which seemed to him not to be a virtue, indeed, but a happiness. (It was such a joy to him now to be escaping from the guidance of his own caprice, and to be submitting his will to those who knew the absolute truth.) The seventh virtue Pierre had forgotten, and he could not recall it.

The third time the rhetor came back sooner, and asked Pierre whether he were still resolute in his intention, and whether he were prepared to submit to everything that would be demanded of him.

"I am ready for anything," said Pierre.

"I must inform you further," said the rhetor, "that our order promulgates its doctrine not by word only, but by certain means which have perhaps on the true seeker after wisdom and virtue a more potent effect than merely verbal explanations. This temple, with what you see therein, should shed more light on your heart, if it is sincere, than any words can do. You will see, maybe, a like method of enlightenment in the further rites of your admittance. Our order follows the usage of ancient societies which revealed their doctrine in hieroglyphs. A hieroglyph," said the rhetor, "is the name given to a symbol of some object, imperceptible to the senses and possessing qualities similar to those of the symbol."

Pierre knew very well what a hieroglyph was, but he did not venture to say so. He listened to the rhetor in silence, feeling from everything he said that his ordeal was soon to begin.

"If you are resolved, I must proceed to your initiation," said the rhetor, coming closer to Pierre. "In token of liberality I beg you to give me everything precious you have."

"But I have nothing with me," said Pierre, supposing he was being asked to give up all his possessions.

"What you have with you: watch, money, rings . . ."

Pierre made haste to get out his purse and his watch, and was a long time trying to get his betrothal ring off his fat finger. When this had been done, the freemason said:

"In token of obedience I beg you to undress." Pierre took off his coat and waistcoat and left boot at the rhetor's instructions. The mason opened his shirt over the left side of his chest and pulled up his breeches on the left leg above the knee. Pierre would hurriedly have taken off the right boot and tucked up the trouser-leg, to save this stranger the trouble of doing so, but the mason told him this was not necessary and gave him a slipper to put on his left foot. With a childish smile of embarrassment, of doubt, and of self-mockery, which would come into his face in spite of himself, Pierre stood with his legs wide apart and his hands hanging at his sides, facing the rhetor and awaiting his next commands.

"And finally, in token of candour, I beg you to disclose to me your chief temptation," he said.

"My temptation! I *had* so many," said Pierre.

"The temptation which does more than all the rest to make you stumble on the path of virtue," said the freemason.

Pierre paused, seeking a reply.

"Wine? gluttony? frivolity? laziness? hasty temper? anger? women?" he went through his vices, mentally balancing them, and not knowing to which to give the pre-eminence.

"Women," said Pierre in a low, hardly audible voice. The freemason

did not speak nor stir for a long while after that reply. At last he moved
up to Pierre, took the handkerchief that lay on the table, and again tied
it over his eyes.

"For the last time I say to you: turn all your attention upon yourself,
put a bridle on your feelings, and seek blessedness not in your passions,
but in your own heart. The secret of blessing is not without but within
us. . . ."

Pierre had for a long while been conscious of this refreshing fount of
blessing within him that now flooded his heart with joy and emotion.

IV

SHORTLY after this, there walked into the dark temple to fetch Pierre,
not the rhetor, but his sponsor Villarsky, whom he recognised by his
voice. In reply to fresh inquiries as to the firmness of his resolve, Pierre
answered:

"Yes, yes, I agree," and with a beaming, childlike smile he walked
forward, stepping timidly and unevenly with one booted and one slippered foot, while Villarsky held a sword pointed at his fat, uncovered
chest. He was led out of the room along corridors, turning backwards
and forwards, till at last he was brought to the doors of the lodge. Villarsky coughed; he was answered by masonic taps with hammers; the
door opened before them. A bass voice (Pierre's eyes were again bandaged) put questions to him, who he was, where and when he was born,
and so on. Then he was again led away somewhere with his eyes still
bandaged, and as he walked they spoke to him in allegories of the toils
of his pilgrimage, and of holy love, of the Eternal Creator of the world,
of the courage with which he was to endure toils and dangers. During
this time Pierre noticed that he was called sometimes the *seeker*, sometimes the *sufferer*, and sometimes the *postulant*, and that they made
various tapping sounds with hammers and with swords. While he was
being led up to some object, he noticed that there was hesitation and
uncertainty among his conductors. He heard a whispered dispute among
the people round him, and one of them insisting that he should be made
to cross a certain carpet. After this they took his right hand, laid it on
something, while they bade him with the left hold a compass to his left
breast, while they made him repeat after some one who read the words
aloud, the oath of fidelity to the laws of the order. Then the candles were
extinguished and spirit was lighted, as Pierre knew from the smell of it,
and he was told that he would see the lesser light. The bandage was
taken off his eyes, and in the faint light of the burning spirit Pierre saw,
as though it were in a dream, several persons who stood facing him in
aprons like the rhetor's, and held swords pointed at his breast. Among
them stood a man in a white shirt stained with blood. On seeing this,
Pierre moved with his chest forward towards the swords, meaning them
to stab him. But the swords were drawn back, and the bandage was at
once replaced on his eyes.

"Now you have seen the lesser light," said a voice. Then again they lighted the candles, told him that he had now to see the full light, and again removed the bandage, and more than ten voices said all at once: "*Sic transit gloria mundi.*"

Pierre gradually began to regain his self-possession, and to look about at the room and the people in it. Round a long table covered with black were sitting some dozen men, all in the same strange garment that he had seen before. Several of them Pierre knew in Petersburg society. In the president's chair sat a young man, with a peculiar cross on his neck, whom he did not know. On his right hand sat the Italian abbé whom Pierre had seen two years before at Anna Pavlovna's. There were among them a dignitary of very high standing and a Swiss tutor, who had once been in the Kuragin family. All preserved a solemn silence, listening to the president, who held a hammer in his hand. In the wall was carved a blazing star; on one side of the table was a small rug with various figures worked upon it; on the other was something like an altar with the gospel and a skull on it. Round the table stood seven big ecclesiastical-looking candlesticks. Two of the brothers led Pierre up to the altar, set his feet at right angles and bade him lie down, saying that he would be casting himself down at the gates of the temple.

"He ought first to receive the spade," said one of the brothers in a whisper.

"Oh! hush, please," said another.

Pierre did not obey, but with uneasy short-sighted eyes looked about him, and suddenly doubt came over him. "Where am I? What am I doing? Aren't they laughing at me? Shan't I be ashamed to remember this?" But this doubt only lasted a moment. Pierre looked round at the serious faces of the people round him, thought of all he had just been through, and felt that there was no stopping half-way. He was terrified at his own hesitation, and trying to arouse in himself his former devotional feeling, he cast himself down at the gates of the temple. And the devotional feeling did in fact come more strongly than ever upon him. When he had lain there some time, he was told to get up, and a white leather apron such as the others wore was put round him, and a spade and three pairs of gloves were put in his hands; then the grand master addressed him. He told him that he must try never to stain the whiteness of that apron, which symbolised strength and purity. Then of the unexplained spade he told him to toil with it at clearing his heart from vice, and with forbearing patience smoothing the way in the heart of his neighbour. Then of the first pair of gloves he said that he could not know yet their significance, but must treasure them; of the second pair he said that he must put them on at meetings; and finally of the third pair—they were women's gloves—he said:

"Dear brother, and these woman's gloves are destined for you too. Give them to the woman whom you shall honour beyond all others. That gift will be a pledge of your purity of heart to her whom you select as a worthy helpmeet in masonry." After a brief pause, he added: "But beware, dear brother, that these gloves never deck hands that are impure."

While the grand master uttered the last words it seemed to Pierre that he was embarrassed. Pierre was even more embarrassed; he blushed to the point of tears, as children blush, looking about him uneasily, and an awkward silence followed.

This silence was broken by one of the brothers who, leading Pierre to the rug, began reading out of a manuscript book the interpretation of all the figures delineated upon it: the sun, the moon, the hammer, the balance, the spade, the rough stone and the shaped stone, the post, the three windows, etc. Then Pierre was shown his appointed place, he was shown the signs of the lodge, told the password, and at last permitted to sit down. The grand master began reading the exhortation. The exhortation was very long, and Pierre in his joy, his emotion, and his embarrassment was hardly in a condition to understand what was read. He only grasped the last words of the exhortation, which stuck in his memory.

"In our temples we know of no distinctions," read the grand master, "but those between virtue and vice. Beware of making any difference that may transgress against equality. Fly to the succour of a brother whoever he may be, exhort him that goeth astray, lift up him that falleth, and cherish not malice nor hatred against a brother. Be thou friendly and courteous. Kindle in all hearts the fire of virtue. Share thy happiness with thy neighbour, and never will envy trouble that pure bliss. Forgive thy enemy, revenge not thyself on him but by doing him good. Fulfilling in this wise the highest law, thou wilt regain traces of the ancient grandeur thou hadst lost," he concluded, and getting up he embraced Pierre and kissed him.

Pierre looked round with tears of joy in his eyes, not knowing how to answer the congratulations and greetings from acquaintances with which he was surrounded. He did not recognise any acquaintances; in all these men he saw only brothers, and he burned with impatience to get to work with them. The grand master tapped with his hammer, all sat down in their places, and one began reading a sermon on the necessity of meekness.

The grand master proposed that the last duty be performed, and the great dignitary whose duty it was to collect the alms began making the round of all the brothers. Pierre would have liked to give to the list of alms all the money he had in the world, but he feared thereby to sin by pride, and only wrote down the same sum as the others.

The sitting was over, and it seemed to Pierre on returning home that he had come back from a long journey on which he had spent dozens of years, and had become utterly changed, and had renounced his old habits and manner of life.

V

THE day after his initiation at the Lodge, Pierre was sitting at home reading a book, and trying to penetrate to the significance of the square, which symbolised by one of its sides, God, by another the moral, by the

third the physical, by the fourth the nature of both mingled. Now and
then he broke off from the book and the symbolic square, and in his
imagination shaped his new plan of life. On the previous day he had
been told at the lodge that the rumour of the duel had reached the
Emperor's ears, and that it would be more judicious for him to withdraw
from Petersburg. Pierre proposed going to his estates in the south, and
there occupying himself with the care of his peasants. He was joyfully
dreaming of this new life when Prince Vassily suddenly walked into his
room.

"My dear fellow, what have you been about in Moscow? What have
you been quarrelling over with Ellen, my dear boy? You have been
making a mistake," said Prince Vassily, as he came into the room. "I
have heard all about it; I can tell you for a fact that Ellen is as innocent in her conduct towards you as Christ was to the Jews."

Pierre would have answered, but he interrupted him.

"And why didn't you come simply and frankly to me as to a friend?
I know all about it; I understand it all," said he. "You have behaved as
was proper for a man who valued his honour, too hastily, perhaps, but
we won't go into that. One thing you must think of, the position you are
placing her and me in, in the eyes of society and even of the court," he
added, dropping his voice. "She is in Moscow, while you are here. Think
of it, my dear boy." He drew him down by the arm. "It's simply a misunderstanding; I expect you feel it so yourself. Write a letter with me
now at once, and she'll come here, and everything will be explained, or
else, I tell you plainly, my dear boy, you may very easily have to suffer
for it."

Prince Vassily looked significantly at Pierre.

"I have learned from excellent sources that the Dowager Empress is
taking a keen interest in the whole affair. You know she is very graciously disposed to Ellen."

Several times Pierre had prepared himself to speak, but on one hand
Prince Vassily would not let him, and on the other hand Pierre himself
was loath to begin to speak in the tone of resolute refusal and denial, in
which he was firmly resolved to answer his father-in-law. Moreover the
words of the masonic precept: "Be thou friendly and courteous," recurred to his mind. He blinked and blushed, got up and sank back again,
trying to force himself to do what was for him the hardest thing in life—
to say an unpleasant thing to a man's face, to say what was not expected
by that man, whoever he might be. He was so much in the habit of submitting to that tone of careless authority in which Prince Vassily spoke,
that even now he felt incapable of resisting it. But he felt, too, that on
what he said now all his future fate would depend; that it would decide
whether he continued along the old way of his past life, or advanced
along the new path that had been so attractively pointed out to him by
the masons, and that he firmly believed would lead him to regeneration
in a new life.

"Come, my dear boy," said Prince Vassily playfully, "simply say 'yes,' and I'll write on my own account to her, and we'll kill the fatted calf." But before Prince Vassily had finished uttering his playful words, Pierre not looking at him, but with a fury in his face that made him like his father, whispered, "Prince, I did not invite you here: go, please, go!" He leaped up and opened the door to him. "Go!" he repeated, amazed at himself and enjoying the expression of confusion and terror in the countenance of Prince Vassily.

"What's the matter with you? are you ill?"

"Go!" the quivering voice repeated once more. And Prince Vassily had to go, without receiving a word of explanation.

A week later Pierre went away to his estates, after taking leave of his new friends, the freemasons, and leaving large sums in their hands for alms. His new brethren gave him letters for Kiev and Odessa, to masons living there, and promised to write to him and guide him in his new activity.

VI

PIERRE'S duel with Dolohov was smoothed over, and in spite of the Tsar's severity in regard to duels at that time, neither the principals nor the seconds suffered for it. But the scandal of the duel, confirmed by Pierre's rupture with his wife, made a great noise in society. Pierre had been looked upon with patronising condescension when he was an illegitimate son; he had been made much of and extolled for his virtues while he was the wealthiest match in the Russian empire; but after his marriage, when young ladies and their mothers had nothing to hope from him, he had fallen greatly in the opinion of society, especially as he had neither the wit nor the wish to ingratiate himself in public favour. Now the blame of the whole affair was thrown on him; it was said that he was insanely jealous, and subject to the same fits of bloodthirsty fury as his father had been. And when, after Pierre's departure, Ellen returned to Petersburg, she was received by all her acquaintances not only cordially, but with a shade of deference that was a tribute to her distress. When the conversation touched upon her husband, Ellen assumed an expression of dignity, which her characteristic tact prompted her to adopt, though she had no conception of its significance. That expression suggested that she had resolved to bear her affliction without complaint, and that her husband was a cross God had laid upon her. Prince Vassily expressed his opinion more openly. He shrugged his shoulders when the conversation turned upon Pierre, and pointing to his forehead, said:

"Crackbrained, I always said so."

"I used to say so even before," Anna Pavlovna would say of Pierre, "at the time I said at once and before every one" (she insisted on her priority) "that he was an insane young man, corrupted by the dissolute ideas of the age. I used to say so at the time when every one was in such ecstasies over him; and he had only just come home from abroad, and do you remember at one of my *soirées* he thought fit to pose as a sort of Marat? And how has it ended? Even then I was against this marriage, and foretold all that has come to pass."

Anna Pavlovna used still to give *soirées* on her free days as before, *soirées* such as only she had the gift of arranging, *soirées* at which were gathered "the cream of really good society, the flower of the intellectual essence of Petersburg society," as Anna Pavlovna herself used to say. Besides this fine sifting of the society, Anna Pavlovna's *soirées* were further distinguished by some new interesting person, secured by the hostess on every occasion for the entertainment of the company. Moreover, the point on the political thermometer, at which the temperature of loyal court society stood in Petersburg, was nowhere so clearly and unmistakably marked as at these *soirées*.

Towards the end of the year 1806, when all the melancholy details of Napoleon's destruction of the Prussian army at Jena and Auerstadt, and the surrender of the greater number of the Prussian forts, had arrived, when our troops were already entering Prussia, and our second war with Napoleon was beginning, Anna Pavlovna was giving one of her *soirées*. "The cream of really good society" consisted of the fascinating and unhappy Ellen, abandoned by her husband; of Mortemart; of the fascinating Prince Ippolit, who had just come home from Vienna; of two diplomats, of the old aunt; of a young man, always referred to in that society by the designation, "a man of a great deal of merit . . ."; of a newly appointed maid of honour and her mother, and several other less noteworthy persons.

The novelty Anna Pavlovna was offering her guests for their entertainment that evening was Boris Drubetskoy, who had just arrived as a special messenger from the Prussian army, and was in the suite of a personage of very high rank.

What the political thermometer indicated at that *soirée* was something as follows: All the European rulers and generals may do their utmost to flatter Bonaparte with the object of causing *me* and *us* generally these annoyances and mortifications, but our opinion in regard to Bonaparte can undergo no change. We do not cease giving undisguised expression to our way of thinking on the subject, and can only say to the Prussian king and others: "So much the worse for you." *"Tu l'as voulu, George Dandin,"* that's all we can say. This was what the political thermometer indicated at Anna Pavlovna's *soirée*. When Boris, who was to be offered up to the guests, came into the drawing-room, almost all the company had assembled, and the conversation, guided by Anna Pavlovna, was of our diplomatic relations with Austria, and the hope of an alliance with her.

Boris, fresh, rosy, and manlier looking, walked easily into the drawing-room, wearing the elegant uniform of an adjutant. He was duly conducted to pay his respects to the aunt, and then joined the general circle.

Anna Pavlovna gave him her shrivelled hand to kiss, introduced him to several persons whom he did not know, and gave him a whispered description of each of them. "Prince Ippolit Kuragin, M Krug, *chargé d'affaires* from Copenhagen, a profound intellect and simple, M. Shitov, a man of a great deal of merit . . ." this of the young man always so spoken of.

Thanks to the efforts of Anna Mihalovna, his own tastes and the peculiarities of his reserved character, Boris had succeeded by that time in getting into a very advantageous position in the service. He was an adjutant in the suite of a personage of very high rank, he had received a very important commission in Prussia, and had only just returned thence as a special messenger. He had completely assimilated that unwritten code which had so pleased him at Olmütz, that code in virtue of which a lieutenant may stand infinitely higher than a general, and all that is needed for success in the service is not effort, not work, not gallantry, not perseverance, but simply the art of getting on with those who have the bestowal of promotion, and he often himself marvelled at the rapidity of his own progress, and that others failed to grasp the secret of it. His whole manner of life, all his relations with his old friends, all his plans for the future were completely transformed in consequence of this discovery. He was not well off, but he spent his last copeck to be better dressed than others. He would have deprived himself of many pleasures rather than have allowed himself to drive in an inferior carriage, or to be seen in the streets of Petersburg in an old uniform. He sought the acquaintance and cultivated the friendship only of persons who were in a higher position, and could consequently be of use to him. He loved Petersburg and despised Moscow. His memories of the Rostov household and his childish passion for Natasha were distasteful to him, and he had not once been at the Rostovs' since he had entered the army. In Anna Pavlovna's drawing-room, his entry into which he looked upon as an important step upward in the service, he at once took his cue, and let Anna Pavlovna make the most of what interest he had to offer, while himself attentively watching every face and appraising the advantages and possibilities of intimacy with every one of the persons present. He sat on the seat indicated to him beside the fair Ellen and listened to the general conversation.

"Vienna considers the bases of the proposed treaty so unattainable that not even a continuance of the most brilliant successes would put them within reach, and doubts whether any means could gain them for us. These are the actual words of the ministry in Vienna," said the Danish *chargé d'affaires*.

"It is polite of them to doubt," said the man of profound intellect with a subtle smile.

"We must distinguish between the ministry in Vienna and the Emperor of Austria," said Mortemart. "The Emperor of Austria can never have thought of such a thing; it is only the ministers who say it."

"Ah, my dear vicomte," put in Anna Pavlovna; "Europe will never be our sincere ally."

Then Anna Pavlovna turned the conversation upon the courage and firmness of the Prussian king, with the object of bringing Boris into action.

Boris listened attentively to the person who was speaking, and waited
for his turn, but meanwhile he had leisure to look round several times
at the fair Ellen, who several times met the handsome young adjutant's
eyes with a smile.

Very naturally, speaking of the position of Prussia, Anna Pavlovna
asked Boris to describe his journey to Glogau, and the position in which
he had found the Prussian army. Boris in his pure, correct French, told
them very deliberately a great many interesting details about the armies,
and the court, studiously abstaining from any expression of his own
opinion in regard to the facts he was narrating. For some time Boris
engrossed the whole attention of the company, and Anna Pavlovna felt
that the novelty she was serving her guests was being accepted by them
all with pleasure. Of all the party, the person who showed most interest
in Boris's description was Ellen. She asked him several questions about
his expedition, and seemed to be extremely interested in the position
of the Prussian army. As soon as he had finished, she turned to him with
her habitual smile.

"You absolutely must come and see me," she said in a tone that suggested that for certain considerations, of which he could have no knowledge, it was absolutely essential. "On Tuesday between eight and nine.
It will give me great pleasure."

Boris promised to do so, and was about to enter into conversation with
her, when Anna Pavlovna drew him aside on the pretext that her aunt
wished to hear his story.

"You know her husband, of course?" said Anna Pavlovna, dropping
her eyelids, and with a melancholy gesture indicating Ellen. "Ah, such
an unhappy and exquisite woman! Don't speak of him before her; pray,
don't speak of him. It's too much for her!"

VII

WHEN Boris and Anna Pavlovna returned to the rest, Prince Ippolit
was in possession of the ear of the company. Bending forward in his low
chair, he was saying:

"The King of Prussia!" and as he said it, he laughed. Every one
turned towards him. "The King of Prussia," Ippolit said interrogatively,
and again he laughed and again settled himself placidly and seriously in
the depths of his big, low chair. Anna Pavlovna paused a little for him,
but as Ippolit seemed quite certainly not intending to say more, she
began to speak of how the godless Bonaparte had at Potsdam carried
off the sword of Frederick the Great.

"It is the sword of Frederick the Great, which I . . ." she was beginning, but Ippolit interrupted her with the words:

"The King of Prussia . . ." and again as soon as all turned to listen
to him, he excused himself and said no more. Anna Pavlovna frowned.
Mortemart, Ippolit's friend, addressed him with decision:

"Come, what are you after with your King of Prussia?"

Ippolit laughed as though he were ashamed of his own laughter.

"No, it's nothing. I only meant . . ." (He had intended to repeat a joke that he had heard in Vienna and had been trying all the evening to get in.) "I only meant that we are wrong to make war for the King of Prussia." [1]

Boris smiled circumspectly, a smile that might do duty either for a sneer or a tribute to the jest, according to the way it was received. Every one laughed.

"It is too bad, your joke, very witty but unjust," said Anna Pavlovna, shaking her little wrinkled finger at him. "We are not making war for the sake of the King of Prussia, but for the sake of right principles. Ah, *le méchant, ce Prince Hippolyte!*" she said.

The conversation did not flag all the evening, and turned principally upon the political news. Towards the end of the evening it became particularly eager, when the rewards bestowed by the Tsar were the subjects of discussion.

"Why, last year N. N. received the snuff-box with the portrait," said the man of profound intellect. "Why shouldn't S. S. receive the same reward?"

"I beg your pardon, a snuff-box with the Emperor's portrait is a reward, but not a distinction," said a diplomatist. "A present, rather."

"There are precedents. I would instance Schwartzenberg."

"It is impossible," retorted another.

"A bet on it. The ribbon of the order is different."

When every one got up to take leave, Ellen, who had said very little all the evening, turned to Boris again with a request, and a caressing, impressive command that he would come to her on Tuesday.

"It is of great importance to me," she said with a smile, looking round at Anna Pavlovna, and Anna Pavlovna, with the same mournful smile with which she accompanied any reference to her royal patroness, gave her support to Ellen's wishes. It appeared that from some words Boris had uttered that evening about the Prussian army Ellen had suddenly discovered the absolute necessity of seeing him. She seemed to promise him that when he came on Tuesday she would disclose to him that necessity. When Boris entered Ellen's magnificent reception-room on Tuesday evening he received no clear explanation of the urgent reasons for his visit. Other guests were present, the countess talked little to him, and only as he kissed her hand at taking leave, with a strangely unsmiling face, she whispered to him unexpectedly:

"Come to dinner to-morrow . . . in the evening . . . you must come . . . come."

During that stay in Petersburg Boris was constantly at the house of the Countess Bezuhov on a footing of the closest intimacy.

---

[1] *"Faire queique chose pour le roi de Prusse,"* is a French idiom meaning to do anything for insufficient reason or in vain.

VIII

WAR had broken out and the theatre of it was closer to the borders of Russia. On all sides could be heard curses upon the enemy of the human race, Bonaparte; in the villages there were levies of recruits and reserve men, and from the theatre of war came news of the most conflicting kind, false as usual, and hence variously interpreted.

The life of the old Prince Bolkonsky, of Prince Andrey, and of Princess Marya was greatly changed since the year 1805.

In 1806 the old prince had been appointed one of the eight commanders-in-chief, created at that time for the equipment of the militia throughout all Russia. In spite of his weakness and age, which had been particularly noticeable during the time when he believed his son to have been killed, the old prince did not think it right to refuse a duty to which he had been appointed by the Emperor himself, and this new field for his activity gave him fresh energy and strength. He was continually away on tours about the three provinces that were put under his command; he was punctilious to pedantry in the performance of his duties, severe to cruelty with his subordinates, and entered into the minutest details of the work himself. Princess Marya no longer took lessons in mathematics from her father, and only went into her father's room on the mornings when he was at home, accompanied by the wet nurse and little Prince Nikolay (as his grandfather called him). The baby, Prince Nikolay, with his wet nurse and the old nurse Savishna, occupied the rooms that had been his mother's, and Princess Marya spent most of her time in the nursery taking a mother's place to her little nephew, to the best of her powers. Mademoiselle Bourienne, too, appeared to be passionately fond of the child, and Princess Marya often sacrificed herself by giving up to her friend the pleasure of dandling and playing with the little *angel* (as she called the baby).

Near the altar of the church at Bleak Hills was a little chapel over the tomb of the little princess, and in the chapel had been placed a marble monument brought from Italy, representing an angel with its wings parted about to take flight for heaven. The angel had the upper lip lifted as though about to smile, and one day Prince Andrey and Princess Marya, as they came out of the chapel, confessed to one another that, strange to say, the face of the angel reminded them of the face of the little princess. But what was stranger, though this Prince Andrey did not confess to his sister, was that in the expression the sculptor had chanced to put into the angel's face, Prince Andrey read the same words of reproach which he had read then on the face of his dead wife: "Ah, why have you done this to me? . . ."

Soon after Prince Andrey's return, the old prince made over a part of the property to him, giving him Bogutcharovo, a large estate about thirty miles from Bleak Hills. Partly to escape the painful memories associated with Bleak Hills, partly because Prince Andrey did not always feel equal to bearing with his father's peculiarities, and partly from a craving for solitude, Prince Andrey made use of Bogutcharovo, established himself there and spent the greater part of his time there.

After the Austerlitz campaign, Prince Andrey had grimly resolved never to serve again in the army. And when war broke out and all were bound to serve, he took service under his father in the levying of the militia, so as to escape active service. Since the campaign of 1805 the old prince and his son had as it were exchanged parts. The old prince, stimulated by activity, expected the best results from the present campaign. Prince Andrey, on the contrary, taking no part in the war, and secretly regretting his inaction, saw in it nothing but what was bad.

On the 26th of February, 1807 the old prince set off on a tour of inspection. Prince Andrey was staying at Bleak Hills, as he usually did in his father's absence. Little Nikolushka had been ill for the last three days. The coachman, who had driven the old prince away, returned bringing papers and letters from the town for Prince Andrey. The valet with the letters not finding the young prince in his study, went to Princess Marya's apartments, but he was not there either. The valet was told that the prince had gone to the nursery. "If you please, your excellency, Petrusha has come with some papers," said one of the nursery maids, addressing Prince Andrey, who was sitting on a child's little chair. Screwing up his eyes, he was with trembling hands pouring drops from a medicine bottle into a glass half full of water.

"What is it?" he said angrily, and his hand shaking, he accidentally poured too many drops from the bottle into the glass. He tipped the medicine out of the glass on to the floor and asked for some more water. The maid gave it him.

In the room were a couple of armchairs, a child's crib, a table and a child's table and a little chair, on which Prince Andrey was sitting. The windows were curtained, and on the table a single candle was burning, screened by a note-book, so that the light did not fall on the crib.

"My dear," said Princess Marya, turning to her brother from beside the crib where she was standing, "it would be better to wait a little . . . later."

"Oh, please, do as I say, what nonsense you keep talking; you have kept putting things off, and see what's come of it!" said Prince Andrey in an exasperated whisper, evidently meaning to wound his sister.

"My dear, it's really better not to wake him, he has fallen asleep," said the princess in a voice of entreaty.

Prince Andrey got up and went on tiptoe to the crib with the glass in his hand.

"Should we really not wake him?" he said, hesitating.

"As you think—really . . . I believe so . . . but as you think," said Princess Marya, obviously intimidated and ashamed that her opinion should triumph. She drew her brother's attention to the maid, who was summoning him in a whisper.

It was the second night that they had been without sleep looking after the baby who was feverish. Mistrusting their own household doctor and expecting the doctor they had sent from the town, they had spent all that time trying first one remedy and then another. Agitated and worn out by sleeplessness, they vented their anxiety on each other, found fault with each other, and quarrelled.

"Petrusha with papers from your papa," whispered the maid. Prince Andrey went out.

"Damn them all!" he commented angrily, and after listening to the verbal instructions sent him from his father, and taking the correspondence and his father's letter, he went back to the nursery. "Well?" queried Prince Andrey.

"No change, wait a little, for God's sake. Karl Ivanitch always says sleep is better than anything," Princess Marya whispered with a sigh. Prince Andrey went up to the baby and felt him. He was burning hot. "Bother you and your Karl Ivanitch!" He took the glass with the drops of medicine in it and again went up to the crib.

"Andryusha, you shouldn't!" said Princess Marya. But he scowled at her with an expression of anger and at the same time of anguish, and bent over the child with the glass.

"But I wish it," he said. "Come, I beg you, give it him . . ."

Princess Marya shrugged her shoulders, but obediently she took the glass, and calling the nurse, began giving the child the medicine. The baby screamed and wheezed. Prince Andrey, scowling and clutching at his head, went out of the room and sat down on the sofa in the adjoining one.

The letters were still in his hand. Mechanically he opened them and began to read. The old prince in his big, sprawling hand, making use of occasional abbreviations, wrote on blue paper as follows:

"I have this moment received, through a special messenger, very joyful news, if it's not a falsehood. Bennigsen has gained it seems a complete victory over Bonaparte near Eylau. In Petersburg every one's jubilant and rewards have been sent to the army without stint. Though he's a German—I congratulate him. Commander in Kortchevo, a certain Handrikov, I can't make out what he's about; full contingent of men and regulation provision not yet arrived. Gallop over at once and say I'll have his head off if it's not all here within the week. I have a letter too about the Prussian battle at Preussisch-Eylau from Petenka, he took part in it,—it's true. If people don't meddle who've no business to meddle, even a German beats Bonaparte. They say he's running away in great disorder. Mind you gallop over to Kortchevo and do the business without delay!"

Prince Andrey sighed and broke open the other letter. It was a letter from Bilibin, two sheets covered with fine handwriting. He folded it up without reading it, and read through once more his father's letter, ending with the words: "Mind you gallop over to Kortchevo and do the business without delay!"

"No, excuse me, I'm not going now till the child is better," he thought, and going to the door he glanced into the nursery. Princess Marya was still standing at the crib, softly rocking the baby. "Oh, and what was the other unpleasant thing he writes about?" Prince Andrey thought of the contents of his father's letter. "Yes. Our troops have gained a victory over Bonaparte precisely when I'm not in the army. Yes, yes, everything mocks at me . . . well and welcome too . . ." and he began reading the letter in French from Bilibin. He read, not understanding half of it, read simply to escape for one moment from thinking of what he had too long, too exclusively and too anxiously been dwelling upon.

IX

BILIBIN was now in a diplomatic capacity at the headquarters of the army, and though he wrote in French, with French jests, and French turns of speech, he described the whole campaign with an impartial self-criticism and self-mockery exclusively Russian. Bilibin wrote that the obligation of diplomatic discretion was a torture to him, and that he was happy to have in Prince Andrey a trustworthy correspondent to whom he could pour out all the spleen that had been accumulating in him at the sight of what was going on in the army. The letter was dated some time back, before the battle of Eylau.

"Since our great success at Austerlitz, you know, my dear prince," wrote Bilibin, "that I have not left headquarters. Decidedly I have acquired a taste for warfare, and it is just as well for me. What I have seen in these three months is incredible.

"I will begin *ab ovo*. 'The enemy of the human race,' as you know, is attacking the Prussians. The Prussians are our faithful allies, who have only deceived us three times in three years. We stand up for them. But it occurs that the enemy of the human race pays no attention to our fine speeches, and in his uncivil and savage way flings himself upon the Prussians without giving them time to finish the parade that they had begun, and by a couple of conjuring tricks thrashes them completely, and goes to take up his quarters in the palace of Potsdam.

" 'I most earnestly desire,' writes the King of Prussia to Bonaparte, 'that your majesty may be received and treated in my palace in a manner agreeable to you, and I have hastened to take all the measures to that end which circumstances allowed. May I have succeeded!' The Prussian generals pride themselves on their politeness towards the French, and lay down their arms at the first summons.

"The head of the garrison at Glogau, who has ten thousand men, asks the King of Prussia what he is to do if he is summoned to surrender. . . . All these are actual facts.

"In short, hoping only to produce an effect by our military attitude, we find ourselves at war in good earnest, and, what is more, at war on our own frontiers *with and for the King of Prussia*. Everything is fully ready, we only want one little thing, that is the commander-in-chief. As it is thought that the successes at Austerlitz might have been more decisive if the commander-in-chief had not been so young, the men of eighty have been passed in review, and of Prosorovsky and Kamensky the lat-

ter is preferred. The general comes to us in a *kibik* after the fashion of
Suvorov, and is greeted with acclamations of joy and triumph.

"On the 4th comes the first post from Petersburg. The mails are taken
to the marshal's room, for he likes to do everything himself. I am called
to sort the letters and take those meant for us. The marshal looks on
while we do it, and waits for the packets addressed to him. We seek—
there are none. The marshal gets impatient, sets to work himself, and
finds letters from the Emperor for Count T., Prince V., and others. Then
he throws himself into one of his furies. He rages against everybody,
snatches hold of the letters, opens them, and reads those from the Emperor to other people.

" 'Ah, so that's how I'm being treated! No confidence in me! Oh,
ordered to keep an eye on me, very well; get along with you!'

"And then he writes the famous order of the day to General Bennigsen:

" 'I am wounded, I cannot ride on horseback, consequently cannot
command the army. You have led your corps d'armée defeated to Pultusk! Here it remains exposed and destitute of wood and of forage, and
in need of assistance, and so, as you reported yourself to Count Buxhevden yesterday, you must think of retreat to our frontier, and so do
to-day.'

" 'All my expeditions on horseback,' he writes to the Emperor, 'have
given me a saddle sore, which, after my former journeys, quite prevents
my sitting a horse, and commanding an army so widely scattered; and
therefore I have handed over the said command to the general next in
seniority to me, Count Buxhevden, having despatched to him all my
suite and appurtenances of the same, advising him, if bread should run
short, to retreat further into the interior of Prussia, seeing that bread
for one day's rations only is left, and some regiments have none, as the
commanders Osterman and Sedmoretsky have reported, and the peasantry of the country have had everything eaten up. I shall myself remain
in the hospital at Ostrolenka till I am cured. In regard to which I must
humbly submit the report that if the army remains another fortnight in
its present bivouac, by spring not a man will be left in health.

" 'Graciously discharge from his duty an old man who is sufficiently
disgraced by his inability to perform the great and glorious task for
which he was chosen. I shall await here in the hospital your most gracious acceptance of my retirement, that I may not have to act the part
of a secretary rather than a commander. My removal is not producing
the slightest sensation—a blind man is leaving the army, that is all.
More like me can be found in Russia by thousands!'

"The marshal is angry with the Emperor and punishes all of us; isn't
it logical!

"That is the first act. In the next the interest and the absurdity rise,
as they ought. After the marshal has departed it appears that we are
within sight of the enemy and shall have to give battle. Buxhevden is
commanding officer by right of seniority, but General Bennigsen is not

of that opinion, the rather that it is he and his corps who face the enemy, and he wants to seize the opportunity to fight a battle 'on his own hand,' as the Germans say. He fights it. It is the battle of Pultusk, which is counted a great victory, but which in my opinion is nothing of the kind. We civilians, you know, have a very ugly way of deciding whether battles are lost or won. The side that retreats after the battle has lost, that is what we say, and according to that we lost the battle of Pultusk. In short, we retreat after the battle, but we send a message to Petersburg with news of a victory, and the general does not give up the command to Buxhevden, hoping to receive from Petersburg the title of commander-in-chief in return for his victory. During this interregnum we begin an excessively interesting and original scheme of manœuvres. The aim does not, as it should, consist in avoiding or attacking the enemy, but solely in avoiding General Buxhevden, who by right of seniority should be our commanding officer. We pursue this object with so much energy that even when we cross a river which is not fordable we burn the bridges in order to separate ourselves from our enemy, who, at the moment, is not Bonaparte but Buxhevden. General Buxhevden was nearly attacked and taken by a superior force of the enemy, in consequence of one of our fine manœuvres which saved us from him. Buxhevden pursues us; we scuttle. No sooner does he cross to our side of the river than we cross back to the other. At last our enemy Buxhevden catches us and attacks us. The two generals quarrel. There is even a challenge on Buxhevden's part and an epileptic fit on Bennigsen's. But at the critical moment the messenger who carried the news of our Pultusk victory brings us from Petersburg our appointment as commander-in-chief, and the first enemy, Buxhevden, being overthrown, we are able to think of the second, Bonaparte. But what should happen at that very moment but the rising against us of a third enemy, which is the 'holy armament' fiercely crying out for bread, meat, biscuits, hay, and I don't know what else! The storehouses are empty, the roads impassable. The 'holy armament' sets itself to pillage, and that in a way of which the last campaign can give you no notion. Half the regiments have turned themselves into free companies, and are overrunning the country with fire and sword. The inhabitants are totally ruined, the hospitals are overflowing with sick, and famine is everywhere. Twice over the headquarters have been attacked by bands of marauders, and the commander-in-chief himself has had to ask for a battalion to drive them off. In one of these attacks my empty trunk and my dressing-gown were carried off. The Emperor proposes to give authority to all the commanders of divisions to shoot marauders, but I greatly fear this will oblige one half of the army to shoot the other."

Prince Andrey at first read only with his eyes, but unconsciously what he read (though he knew how much faith to put in Bilibin) began to interest him more and more. When he reached this passage, he crumpled up the letter and threw it away. It was not what he read that angered him; he was angry that the far-away life out there—in which he had no part—could trouble him. He closed his eyes, rubbed his forehead with his hand, as though to drive out all interest in what he had been reading, and listened to what was passing in the nursery. Suddenly he fancied a strange sound through the door. A panic seized him; he was afraid something might have happened to the baby while he was reading the letter. He went on tiptoe to the door of the nursery and opened it.

At the instant that he went in, he saw that the nurse was hiding something from him with a scared face, and Princess Marya was no longer beside the crib.

"My dear," he heard behind him Princess Marya whisper—in a tone of despair it seemed to him. As so often happens after prolonged sleeplessness and anxiety, he was seized by a groundless panic; the idea came into his mind that the baby was dead. All he saw and heard seemed a confirmation of his terror.

"All is over," he thought, and a cold sweat came out on his forehead. He went to the crib, beside himself, believing that he would find it empty, that the nurse had been hiding the dead baby. He opened the curtains, and for a long while his hurrying, frightened eyes could not find the baby. At last he saw him. The red-cheeked child lay stretched across the crib, with its head lower than the pillow; and it was making a smacking sound with its lips in its sleep and breathing evenly.

Prince Andrey rejoiced at seeing the child, as though he had already lost him. He bent down and tried with his lips whether the baby was feverish, as his sister had shown him. The soft forehead was moist; he touched the head with his hand—even the hair was wet: the child was in such a thorough perspiration. He was not dead; on the contrary, it was evident that the crisis was over and he was better. Prince Andrey longed to snatch up, to squeeze, to press to his heart that little helpless creature; he did not dare to do so. He stood over him, gazing at his head and his little arms and legs that showed beneath the quilt. He heard a rustle beside him, and a shadow seemed to come under the canopy of the crib. He did not look round, and still gazing at the baby's face, listened to his regular breathing. The dark shadow was Princess Marya, who with noiseless steps had approached the crib, lifted the canopy, and let it fall again behind her. Prince Andrey knew it was she without looking round, and held out his hand to her. She squeezed his hand.

"He is in a perspiration," said Prince Andrey.

"I was coming to tell you so."

The baby faintly stirred in its sleep, smiled and rubbed its forehead against the pillow.

Prince Andrey looked at his sister. In the even half light under the hanging of the crib, Princess Marya's luminous eyes shone more than usual with the happy tears that stood in them. She bent forward to her brother and kissed him, her head catching in the canopy of the crib. They shook their fingers at one another, and still stood in the twilight of the canopy, as though unwilling to leave that seclusion where they three were alone, shut off from all the world. Prince Andrey, ruffling his hair

against the muslin hangings, was the first to move away. "Yes, that is
the one thing left me now," he said with a sigh.

X

SHORTLY after his reception into the brotherhood of the freemasons,
Pierre set off to the Kiev province, where were the greater number of his
peasants, with full instructions written for his guidance in doing his
duty on his estates.

On reaching Kiev, Pierre sent for all his stewards to his head counting-house, and explained to them his intentions and his desires. He told
them that steps would very shortly be taken for the complete liberation
of his peasants from serfdom, that till that time his peasants were not
to be overburdened with labour, that the women with children were not
to be sent out to work, that assistance was to be given to the peasants,
that wrong-doing was to be met with admonishment, and not with corporal punishment; and that on every estate there must be founded hospitals, almshouses, and schools. Several of the stewards (among them
were some bailiffs barely able to read and write) listened in dismay,
supposing the upshot of the young count's remarks to be that he was dissatisfied with their management and embezzlement of his money. Others,
after the first shock of alarm, derived amusement from Pierre's lisp and
the new words he used that they had not heard before. Others again
found a simple satisfaction in hearing the sound of their master's voice.
But some, among them the head steward, divined from this speech how
to deal with their master for the attainment of their own ends.

The head steward expressed great sympathy with Pierre's projects;
but observed that, apart from these innovations, matters were in a bad
way and needed thoroughly going into.

In spite of Count Bezuhov's enormous wealth, Pierre ever since he
had inherited it, and had been, as people said, in receipt of an annual income of five hundred thousand, had felt much less rich than when he
had been receiving an allowance of ten thousand from his father. In
general outlines he was vaguely aware of the following budget. About
eighty thousand was being paid into the Land Bank as interest on mort-
gages on his estates. About thirty thousand went to the maintenance of
his estate in the suburbs of Moscow, his Moscow house, and his cousins,
the princesses. About fifteen thousand were given in pensions, and as
much more to benevolent institutions. One hundred and fifty thousand
were sent to his countess for her maintenance. Some seventy thousand
were paid away as interest on debts. The building of a new church had
for the last two years been costing about ten thousand. The remainder—
some one hundred thousand—was spent—he hardly knew how—and
almost every year he was forced to borrow. Moreover every year the
head steward wrote to him of conflagrations, or failures of crops, or of
the necessity of rebuilding factories or workshops. And so the first duty

with which Pierre was confronted was the one for which he had the least capacity and inclination—attention to practical business.

Every day Pierre *went into* things with the head steward. But he felt that what he was doing did not advance matters one inch. He felt that all he did was quite apart from the reality, that his efforts had no grip on the business, and would not set it in progress. On one side the head steward put matters in their worst light, proving to Pierre the necessity of paying his debts, and entering upon new undertakings with the labour of his serf peasants, to which Pierre would not agree. On the other side, Pierre urged their entering upon the work of liberation, to which the head steward objected the necessity of first paying off the loans from the Land Bank, and the consequent impossibility of haste in the matter. The head steward did not say that this was utterly impossible; he proposed as the means for attaining this object, the sale of the forests in the Kostroma province, the sale of the lands on the lower Volga, and of the Crimean estate. But all these operations were connected in the head steward's talk with such a complexity of processes, the removal of certain prohibitory clauses, the obtaining of certain permissions, and so on, that Pierre lost the thread, and could only say: "Yes, yes, do so then."

Pierre had none of that practical tenacity, which would have made it possible for him to undertake the business himself, and so he did not like it, and only tried to keep up a pretence of going into business before the head steward. The steward too kept up a pretence before the count of regarding his participation in it as of great use to his master, and a great inconvenience to himself.

In Kiev he had acquaintances: persons not acquaintances made haste to become so, and gave a warm welcome to the young man of fortune, the largest landowner of the province, who had come into their midst. The temptations on the side of Pierre's besetting weakness, the one to which he had given the first place at his initiation into the lodge, were so strong that he could not resist them. Again whole days, weeks, and months of his life were busily filled up with parties, dinners, breakfasts, and balls, giving him as little time to think as at Petersburg. Instead of the new life Pierre had hoped to lead, he was living just the same old life only in different surroundings.

Of the three precepts of freemasonry, Pierre had to admit that he had not fulfilled that one which prescribes for every mason the duty of being a model of moral life; and of the seven virtues he was entirely without two—morality and love of death. He comforted himself by reflecting that, on the other hand, he was fulfilling the other precept—the improvement of the human race; and had other virtues, love for his neighbour and liberality.

In the spring of 1807, Pierre made up his mind to go back again to Petersburg. On the way back he intended to make the tour of all his estates, and to ascertain personally what had been done of what had been prescribed by him, and in what position the people now were who had been entrusted to him by God, and whom he had been striving to benefit.

The head steward, who regarded all the young count's freaks as almost insanity—disastrous to him, to himself, and to his peasants—made concessions to his weaknesses. While continuing to represent the liberation of his serfs as impracticable, he made arrangements on all his estates for the building of schools, hospitals, and asylums on a large scale to be begun ready for the master's visit, prepared everywhere for him to be met, not with ceremonious processions, which he knew would not be to Pierre's taste, but with just the devotionally grateful welcomes, with holy images and bread and salt, such as would, according to his understanding of the count, impress him and delude him.

The southern spring, the easy, rapid journey in his Vienna carriage, and the solitude of the road, had a gladdening influence on Pierre. The estates, which he had not before visited, were one more picturesque than the other; the peasantry seemed everywhere thriving, and touchingly grateful for the benefits conferred on them. Everywhere he was met by welcomes, which though they embarrassed Pierre, yet at the bottom of his heart rejoiced him. At one place the peasants had brought him bread and salt and the images of Peter and Paul, and begged permission in honour of his patron saints, Peter and Paul, and in token of love and gratitude for the benefits conferred on them, to erect at their own expense a new chapel in the church. At another place he was welcomed by women with babies in their arms, who came to thank him for being released from the obligation of heavy labour. In a third place he was met by a priest with a cross, surrounded by children, whom by the favour of the count he was instructing in reading and writing and religion. On all his estates Pierre saw with his own eyes stone buildings erected, or in course of erection, all on one plan, hospitals, schools, and almshouses, which were in short time to be opened. Everywhere Pierre saw the steward's reckoning of service due to him diminished in comparison with the past, and heard touching thanks for what was remitted from deputations of peasants in blue, full-skirted coats.

But Pierre did not know that where they brought him bread and salt and were building a chapel of Peter and Paul there was a trading village, and a fair on St. Peter's day, that the chapel had been built long ago by wealthy peasants of the village, and that nine-tenths of the peasants of that village were in the utmost destitution. He did not know that since by his orders nursing mothers were not sent to work on their master's land, those same mothers did even harder work on their own bit of land. He did not know that the priest who met him with the cross oppressed the peasants with his exactions, and that the pupils gathered around him were yielded up to him with tears and redeemed for large sums by their parents. He did not know that the stone buildings were being raised by his labourers, and increased the forced labour of his peasants, which was only less upon paper. He did not know that where the steward pointed out to him in the account book the reduction of rent to one-third in accordance with his will, the labour exacted had been raised by one half. And so Pierre was enchanted by his journey over his estates, and came back completely to the philanthropic frame of mind in which he had left Petersburg, and wrote enthusiastic letters to his preceptor and brother, as he called the grand master.

"How easy it is, how little effort is needed to do so much good," thought Pierre, "and how little we trouble ourselves to do it!"

He was happy at the gratitude shown him, but abashed at receiving it. That gratitude reminded him how much more he could do for those simple, good-hearted people.

The head steward, a very stupid and crafty man, who thoroughly understood the clever and naïve count, and played with him like a toy, seeing the effect produced on Pierre by these carefully arranged receptions, was bolder in advancing arguments to prove the impossibility, and even more, the uselessness of liberating the peasants, who were so perfectly happy without that.

In the recesses of his own heart, Pierre agreed with the steward that it was difficult to imagine people happier, and that there was no knowing what their future would be in freedom. But though reluctantly, he stuck to what he thought the right thing. The steward promised to use every effort to carry out the count's wishes, perceiving clearly that the count would never be in a position to verify whether every measure had been taken for the sale of the forests and estates for the repayment of loans from the bank, would never probably even inquire, and would certainly never find out that the buildings, when finished, stood empty, and that the peasants were giving in labour and money just what they gave with other masters, that is, all that could be got out of them.

XI

RETURNING from his southern tour in the happiest frame of mind, Pierre carried out an intention he had long had, of visiting his friend Bolkonsky, whom he had not seen for two years.

Bogutcharovo lay in a flat, ugly part of the country, covered with fields and copses of fir and birch-trees, in parts cut down. The manor house was at the end of the straight village that ran along each side of the high road, behind an overflowing pond newly dug, and still bare of grass on its banks in the midst of a young copse, with several large pines standing among the smaller trees.

The homestead consisted of a threshing floor, serfs' quarters, stables, bath-houses, lodges, and a large stone house with a semicircular façade, still in course of erection. Round the house a garden had been newly laid out. The fences and gates were solid and new; under a shed stood two fire-engines and a tub painted green. The paths were straight, the bridges were strong and furnished with stone parapets. Everything had an air of being cared for and looked after. The house serfs on the way, in reply to inquiries where the prince was living, pointed to a small new lodge at the very edge of the pond. Prince Andrey's old body-servant, Anton, after assisting Pierre out of his carriage, said that the prince was at home, and conducted him into a clean little lobby.

Pierre was struck by the modesty of this little, clean house, after the splendid surroundings in which he had last seen his friend in Petersburg.

He went hurriedly into the little parlour, still unplastered and smelling of pine wood, and would have gone further, but Anton ran ahead on tip-toe and knocked at the door.

"What is it?" he heard a harsh, unpleasant voice.

"A visitor," answered Anton.

"Ask him to wait"; and there was the sound of a chair being pushed back.

Pierre went with rapid steps to the door, and came face to face with Prince Andrey, who came out frowning and looking older. Pierre embraced him, and taking off his spectacles, kissed him and looked close at him.

"Well, I didn't expect you; I am glad," said Prince Andrey.

Pierre said nothing; he was looking in wonder at his friend, and could not take his eyes off him. He was struck by the change in Prince Andrey. His words were warm, there was a smile on the lips and the face, but there was a lustreless, dead look in his eyes, into which, in spite of his evident desire to seem glad, Prince Andrey could not throw a gleam of happiness. It was not only that his friend was thinner, paler, more manly looking, but the look in his eyes and the line on his brow, that expressed prolonged concentration on some one subject, struck Pierre and repelled him till he got used to it.

On meeting after a long separation, the conversation, as is always the case, did not for a long while rest on one subject. They asked questions and gave brief replies about things of which they knew themselves they must talk at length. At last the conversation began gradually to revolve more slowly about the questions previously touched only in passing, their life in the past, their plans for the future, Pierre's journeys, and what he had been doing, the war, and so on. The concentrated and crushed look which Pierre had noticed in Prince Andrey's eyes was still more striking now in the smile with which he listened to him, especially when he was telling him with earnestness and delight of his past or his future. It was as though Prince Andrey would have liked to take interest in what he was telling him, but could not. Pierre began to feel that to express enthusiasm, ideals, and hopes of happiness and goodness was unseemly before Prince Andrey. He felt ashamed of giving expression to all the new ideas he had gained from the masons, which had been revived and strengthened in him by his last tour. He restrained himself, afraid of seeming naïve. At the same time he felt an irresistible desire to show his friend at once that he was now a quite different Pierre, better than the one he had known in Petersburg.

"I can't tell you how much I have passed through during this time I shouldn't know my old self."

"Yes, you are very, very much changed since those days," said Prince Andrey.

"Well, and what of you?" asked Pierre. "What are your plans?"

"Plans?" repeated Prince Andrey ironically. "My plans?" he repeated, as though wondering what was the meaning of such a word. "Why, you see, I am building; I want next year to settle in here altogether . . ."

Pierre looked silently and intently into the face of Prince Andrey, which had grown so much older.

"No, I'm asking about . . ." Pierre began, but Prince Andrey interrupted him.

"But why talk about me . . . talk to me, and tell me about your journey, about everything you have been doing on your estates."

Pierre began describing what he had been doing on his estates, trying as far as he could to disguise his share in the improvements made on them. Prince Andrey several times put in a few words before Pierre could utter them, as though all Pierre's doings were an old, familiar story, and he were hearing it not only without interest, but even as it were a little ashamed of what was told him.

Pierre began to feel awkward and positively wretched in his friend's company. He relapsed into silence.

"I tell you what, my dear fellow," said Prince Andrey, who was unmistakably dreary and ill at ease with his visitor, "I'm simply bivouacking here; I only came over to have a look at things. I'm going back again to my sister to-day. I will introduce you to her. But I think you know her, though," he added, obviously trying to provide entertainment for his guest, with whom he now found nothing in common. "We will set off after dinner. And now would you care to see my place?" They went out and walked about till dinner time, talking of political news and common acquaintances, like people not very intimate. The only thing of which Prince Andrey now spoke with some eagerness and interest was the new buildings and homestead he was building; but even in the middle of a conversation on this subject, on the scaffolding, when Prince Andrey was describing to Pierre the plan of the house, he suddenly stopped. "There's nothing interesting in that, though, let us go in to dinner and set off."

At dinner the conversation fell on Pierre's marriage.

"I was very much surprised when I heard of it," said Prince Andrey.

Pierre blushed as he always did at any reference to his marriage, and said hurriedly: "I'll tell you one day how it all happened. But you know that it's all over and for ever."

"For ever?" said Prince Andrey; "nothing's for ever."

"But do you know how it all ended? Did you hear of the duel?"

"Yes, you had to go through that too!"

"The one thing for which I thank God is that I didn't kill that man," said Pierre.

"Why so?" said Prince Andrey. "To kill a vicious dog is a very good thing to do, really."

"No, to kill a man is bad, wrong . . ."

"Why is it wrong?" repeated Prince Andrey; "what's right and wrong is a question it has not been given to men to decide. Men are for ever

in error, and always will be in error, and in nothing more than in what
they regard as right and wrong."

"What does harm to another man is wrong," said Pierre, feeling with
pleasure that for the first time since his arrival Prince Andrey was
roused and was beginning to speak and eager to give expression to what
had made him what he now was.

"And who has told you what is harm to another man?" he asked.

"Harm? harm?" said Pierre; "we all know what harms ourselves."

"Yes, we know that, but it's not the same harm we know about for
ourselves that we do to another man," said Prince Andrey, growing more
and more eager, and evidently anxious to express to Pierre his new view
of things. He spoke in French. "I only know two very real ills in life, remorse and sickness. There is no good except the absence of those ills,
To live for myself so as to avoid these two evils: that's the sum of my
wisdom now."

"And love for your neighbour, and self-sacrifice?" began Pierre. "No,
I can't agree with you! To live with the sole object of avoiding doing
evil, so as not to be remorseful, that's very little. I used to live so, I used
to live for myself, and I spoilt my life. And only now, when I'm living,
at least trying to live" (modesty impelled Pierre to correct himself) "for
others, only now I have learnt to know all the happiness of life. No, I
don't agree with you, and indeed, you don't believe what you're saying
yourself."

Prince Andrey looked at Pierre without speaking, and smiled ironically. "Well, you'll see my sister Marie. You will get on with her," said
he. "Perhaps you are right for yourself," he added, after a brief pause,
"but every one lives in his own way; you used to live for yourself, and
you say that by doing so you almost spoiled your life, and have only
known happiness since you began to live for others. And my experience
has been the reverse. I used to live for glory. (And what is glory? The
same love for others, the desire to do something for them, the desire of
their praise.) In that way I lived for others, and not almost, but quite
spoilt my life. And I have become more peaceful since I live only for
myself."

"But how are you living only for yourself?" Pierre asked, getting hot.
"What of your son, your sister, your father?"

"Yes, but that's all the same as myself, they are not others," said
Prince Andrey; "but others, one's neighbours, as you and Marie call
them, they are the great source of error and evil. One's neighbours are
those—your Kiev peasants—whom one wants to do good to."

And he looked at Pierre with a glance of ironical challenge. He unmistakably meant to draw him on.

"You are joking," said Pierre, getting more and more earnest. "What
error and evil can there be in my wishing (I have done very little and
done it very badly), but still wishing to do good, and doing indeed something any way? Where can be the harm if unhappy people, our peasants,
people just like ourselves growing up and dying with no other idea of

God and the truth, but a senseless prayer and ceremony, if they are instructed in the consoling doctrines of a future life, of retribution, and recompense and consolation? What harm and error can there be in my giving them doctors, and a hospital, and a refuge for the aged, when men are dying of disease without help, and it is so easy to give them material aid? And isn't there palpable, incontestable good, when the peasants and the women with young children have no rest day or night, and I give them leisure and rest? . . ." said Pierre, talking hurriedly and lisping. "And I have done that; badly it's true, and too little of it, but I have done something towards it, and you'll not only fail to shake my conviction that I have done well, you'll not even shake my conviction that you don't believe that yourself. And the great thing," Pierre continued, "is that I know this—and know it for a certainty—that the enjoyment of doing this good is the only real happiness in life."

"Oh, if you put the question like that, it's a different matter," said Prince Andrey. "I'm building a house and laying out a garden, while you are building hospitals. Either occupation may serve to pass the time. But as to what's right and what's good—leave that to one who knows all to judge; it's not for us to decide. Well, you want an argument," he added; "all right, let us have one." They got up from the table and sat out on the steps in default of a balcony. "Come, let us argue the matter," said Prince Andrey. "You talk of schools," he went on, crooking one finger, "instruction, and so forth, that is, you want to draw him" (he pointed to a peasant who passed by them taking off his cap), "out of his animal condition and to give him spiritual needs, but it seems to me that the only possible happiness is animal happiness, and you want to deprive him of it. I envy him, while you are trying to make him into me, without giving him my circumstances. Another thing you speak of is lightening his toil. But to my notions, physical labour is as much a necessity for him, as much a condition of his existence, as intellectual work is for me and for you. You can't help thinking. I go to bed at three o'clock, thoughts come into my mind, and I can't go to sleep; I turn over, and can't sleep till morning, because I'm thinking, and I can't help thinking, just as he can't help ploughing and mowing. If he didn't, he would go to the tavern, or become ill. Just as I could not stand his terrible physical labour, but should die of it in a week, so he could not stand my physical inactivity, he would grow fat and die. The third thing—what was it you talked about?"

Prince Andrey crooked his third finger.

"Oh, yes, hospitals, medicine. He has a fit and dies, but you have him bled and cure him. He will drag about an invalid for ten years, a burden to every one. It would be ever so much simpler and more comfortable for him to die. Others are born, and there are always plenty. If you grudge losing a labourer—that's how I look at him—but you want to cure him from love for him. But he has no need of that. And besides, what a notion that medicine has ever cured any one! Killed them— yes!" he said, scowling and turning away from Pierre.

Prince Andrey gave such clear and precise utterance to his ideas that it was evident he had thought more than once of this already, and he talked rapidly and eagerly, as a man does who has long been silent. His eyes grew keener, the more pessimistic were the views he expressed.

"Oh, this is awful, awful!" said Pierre. "I don't understand how one can live with such ideas. I have had moments of thinking like that; it was not long ago at Moscow and on a journey, but then I become so abject that I don't live at all, everything's hateful to me . . . myself, most of all. Then I don't eat, I don't wash . . . how can you go on? . . ."

"Why not wash, that's not clean," said Prince Andrey; "on the contrary, one has to try and make one's life more agreeable as far as one can. I'm alive, and it's not my fault that I am, and so I have to try without hurting others to get on as well as I can till death."

"But what impulse have you to live with such ideas? You would sit still without stirring, taking no part in anything. . . ."

"Life won't leave you in peace even so. I should be glad to do nothing, but here you see on one side, the local nobility have done me the honour of electing me a marshal; it was all I could do to get out of it. They could not understand that I haven't what's needed, haven't that good-natured, fussy vulgarity we all know so well, that's needed for it. Then there's this house here, which had to be built that I might have a nook of my own where I could be quiet. Now there's the militia."

"Why aren't you serving in the army?"

"After Austerlitz!" said Prince Andrey gloomily. "No, thank you; I swore to myself that I would never serve in the Russian army again. And I will not, if Bonaparte were stationed here at Smolensk, threatening Bleak Hills! even then I wouldn't serve in the Russian army. Well, so I was saying," Prince Andrey went on, regaining his composure. "Now, there's the militia; my father's commander-in-chief of the third circuit, and the only means for me to escape from active service is to serve under him."

"So you are in the service, then?"

"Yes." He was silent for a while.

"Then why do you serve?"

"I'll tell you why. My father is one of the most remarkable men of his time. But he's grown old, and he's not cruel exactly, but he's of too energetic a character. He's terrible from his habit of unlimited power, and now with this authority given him by the Emperor as a commander-in-chief in the militia. If I had been two hours later a fortnight ago, he would have hanged the register-clerk at Yuhnovo," said Prince Andrey with a smile. "So I serve under him now because no one except me has any influence over my father, and I sometimes save him from an act which would be a source of misery to him afterwards."

"Ah, there you see!"

"Yes, it is not as you think," Prince Andrey continued. "I didn't, and I don't wish well in the slightest to that scoundrelly register-clerk who had stolen boots or something from the militiamen; indeed, I would have been very glad to see him hanged, but I feel for my father, that is again myself."

Prince Andrey grew more and more eager. His eyes glittered feverishly, as he tried to prove to Pierre that there was never the slightest
desire to do good to his neighbour in his actions.

"Well, you want to liberate your serfs, too," he pursued; "that's a
very good thing, but not for you—I expect you have never flogged a
man nor sent one to Siberia—and still less for your peasants. If a peasant is beaten, flogged, sent to Siberia, I dare say he's not a bit the worse
for it. In Siberia he can lead the same brute existence; the stripes on
the body heal, and he's as happy as before. But it's needed for the people
who are ruined morally, who are devoured by remorse, who stifle that
remorse and grow callous from being able to inflict punishment all
round them. Perhaps you have not seen it, but I have seen good men,
brought up in the traditions of unlimited power with years, as they grew
more irritable, become cruel and brutal, conscious of it, and unable to
control themselves, and growing more and more miserable."

Prince Andrey spoke with such earnestness that Pierre could not help
thinking those ideas were suggested to him by his father. He made him
no reply.

"So that's what I grieve for—for human dignity, for peace of conscience, for purity, and not for their backs or their heads, which always
remain just the same backs and heads, however you thrash or shave
them."

"No, no, a thousand times no! I shall never agree with you," said
Pierre.

XII

IN the evening Prince Andrey and Pierre got into the coach and drove
to Bleak Hills. Prince Andrey watched Pierre and broke the silence from
time to time with speeches that showed he was in a good humour.

Pointing to the fields, he told him of the improvements he was making in the management of his land.

Pierre preserved a gloomy silence, replying only by monosyllables,
and apparently plunged in his own thoughts.

Pierre was reflecting that Prince Andrey was unhappy, that he was
in error, that he did not know the true light, and that he ought to come
to his aid, enlighten him and lift him up. But as soon as he began to
deliberate on what he would say, he foresaw that Prince Andrey with
one word, one argument, would annihilate everything in his doctrine;
and he was afraid to begin, afraid of exposing his most cherished and
holiest to possible ridicule.

"No, what makes you think so?" Pierre began all at once, lowering
his head and looking like a butting bull; "what makes you think so?
You ought not to think so."

"Think so, about what?" asked Prince Andrey in surprise.

"About life. About the destination of man. It can't be so. I used to
think like that, and I have been saved, do you know by what?—freemasonry. No, you must not smile. Freemasonry is not a religious sect,

nor mere ceremonial rites, as I used to suppose; freemasonry is the
best, the only expression of the highest, eternal aspects of humanity."
And he began expounding to Prince Andrey freemasonry, as he understood it.

He said that freemasonry is the teaching of Christianity, freed from
its political and religious fetters; the teaching of equality, fraternity,
and love.

"Our holy brotherhood is the only thing that has real meaning in life;
all the rest is a dream," said Pierre. "You understand, my dear fellow,
that outside this brotherhood all is filled with lying and falsehood, and
I agree with you that there's nothing left for an intelligent and good-
hearted man but, like you, to get through his life, only trying not to hurt
others. But make our fundamental convictions your own, enter into our
brotherhood, give yourself up to us, let us guide you, and you will at
once feel yourself, as I felt, a part of a vast, unseen chain, the origin of
which is lost in the skies," said Pierre, looking straight before him.

Prince Andrey listened to Pierre's words in silence. Several times he
did not catch words from the noise of the wheels, and he asked Pierre
to repeat what he had missed. From the peculiar light that glowed in
Prince Andrey's eyes, and from his silence, Pierre saw that his words
were not in vain, that Prince Andrey would not interrupt him nor laugh
at what he said.

They reached a river that had overflowed its banks, and had to cross
it by a ferry. While the coach and horses waited they crossed on the
ferry. Prince Andrey with his elbow on the rail gazed mutely over the
stretch of water shining in the setting sun.

"Well, what do you think about it?" asked Pierre. "Why are you
silent?"

"What do I think? I have heard what you say. That's all right," said
Prince Andrey. "But you say, enter into our brotherhood, and we will
show you the object of life and the destination of man, and the laws that
govern the universe. But who are we?—men? How do you know it all?
Why is it I alone don't see what you see? You see on earth the dominion
of good and truth, but I don't see it."

Pierre interrupted him. "Do you believe in a future life?" he asked.

"In a future life?" repeated Prince Andrey.

But Pierre did not give him time to answer, and took this repetition
as a negative reply, the more readily as he knew Prince Andrey's atheis-
tic views in the past. "You say that you can't see the dominion of good
and truth on the earth. I have not seen it either, and it cannot be seen
if one looks upon our life as the end of everything. On earth, this earth
here" (Pierre pointed to the open country), "there is no truth—all is
deception and wickedness. But in the world, the whole world, there is a
dominion of truth, and we are now the children of earth, but eternally
the children of the whole universe. Don't I feel in my soul that I am a
part of that vast, harmonious whole? Don't I feel that in that vast, innumerable multitude of beings, in which is made manifest the Godhead,
the higher power—what you choose to call it—I constitute one grain,

one step upward from lower beings to higher ones? If I see, see clearly that ladder that rises up from the vegetable to man, why should I suppose that ladder breaks off with me and does not go on further and further? I feel that I cannot disappear as nothing does disappear in the universe, that indeed I always shall be and always have been. I feel that beside me, above me, there are spirits, and that in their world there is truth."

"Yes, that's Herder's theory," said Prince Andrey. "But it's not that, my dear boy, convinces me; but life and death are what have convinced me. What convinces me is seeing a creature dear to me, and bound up with me, to whom one has done wrong, and hoped to make it right" (Prince Andrey's voice shook and he turned away), "and all at once that creature suffers, is in agony, and ceases to be. . . . What for? It cannot be that there is no answer! And I believe there is. . . . That's what convinces, that's what has convinced me," said Prince Andrey.

"Just so, just so," said Pierre; "isn't that the very thing I'm saying?"

"No. I only say that one is convinced of the necessity of a future life, not by argument, but when one goes hand-in-hand with some one, and all at once that some one slips away *yonder into nowhere,* and you are left facing that abyss and looking down into it. And I have looked into it . . ."

"Well, that's it then! You know there is a *yonder* and there is *some one. Yonder* is the future life; *Some One* is God."

Prince Andrey did not answer. The coach and horses had long been taken across to the other bank, and had been put back into the shafts, and the sun had half sunk below the horizon, and the frost of evening was starring the pools at the fording-place; but Pierre and Andrey, to the astonishment of the footmen, coachmen, and ferrymen, still stood in the ferry and were still talking.

"If there is God and there is a future life, then there is truth and there is goodness; and the highest happiness of man consists in striving for their attainment. We must live, we must love, we must believe," said Pierre, "that we are not only living to-day on this clod of earth, but have lived and will live for ever there in everything" (he pointed to the sky). Prince Andrey stood with his elbow on the rail of the ferry, and as he listened to Pierre he kept his eyes fixed on the red reflection of the sun on the bluish stretch of water. Pierre ceased speaking. There was perfect stillness. The ferry had long since come to a standstill, and only the eddies of the current flapped with a faint sound on the bottom of the ferry boat. It seemed to Prince Andrey that the lapping of the water kept up a refrain to Pierre's words: "It's the truth, believe it."

Prince Andrey sighed, and with a radiant, childlike, tender look in his eyes glanced at the face of Pierre—flushed and triumphant, though still timidly conscious of his friend's superiority.

"Yes, if only it were so!" he said. "Let us go and get in, though," added Prince Andrey, and as he got out of the ferry he looked up at the sky, to which Pierre had pointed him, and for the first time since Austerlitz he saw the lofty, eternal sky, as he had seen it lying on the field of Austerlitz, and something that had long been slumbering, something better that had been in him, suddenly awoke with a joyful, youthful feeling in his soul. That feeling vanished as soon as Prince Andrey returned again to the habitual conditions of life, but he knew that that feeling—though he knew not how to develop it—was still within him. Pierre's visit was for Prince Andrey an epoch, from which there began. though outwardly unchanged, a new life in his inner world.

XIII

It was dark by the time Prince Andrey and Pierre drove up to the principal entrance of the house at Bleak Hills. While they were driving in, Prince Andrey with a smile drew Pierre's attention to a commotion that was taking place at the back entrance. A bent little old woman with a wallet on her back, and a short man with long hair, in a black garment, ran back to the gate on seeing the carriage driving up. Two women ran out after them, and all the four, looking round at the carriage with scared faces, ran in at the back entrance.

"Those are Masha's God's folk," said Prince Andrey. "They took us for my father. It's the one matter in which she does not obey him. He orders them to drive away these pilgrims, but she receives them."

"But what are God's folk?" asked Pierre.

Prince Andrey had not time to answer him. The servants came out to meet them, and he inquired where the old prince was and whether they expected him home soon. The old prince was still in the town, and they were expecting him every minute.

Prince Andrey led Pierre away to his own suite of rooms, which were always in perfect readiness for him in his father's house, and went off himself to the nursery.

"Let us go to my sister," said Prince Andrey, coming back to Pierre; "I have not seen her yet, she is in hiding now, sitting with her God's folk. Serve her right; she will be put to shame, and you will see God's folk. It's curious, upon my word."

"What are 'God's folk'?" asked Pierre.

"You shall see."

Princess Marya certainly was disconcerted, and reddened in patches when they went in. In her snug room, with lamps before the holy picture stand, there was sitting, behind the samovar, on the sofa beside her, a young lad with a long nose and long hair, wearing a monk's cassock. In a low chair near sat a wrinkled, thin, old woman, with a meek expression on her childlike face.

"Andrey, why did you not let me know?" she said with mild reproach, standing before her pilgrims like a hen before her chickens.

"Delighted to see you. I am very glad to see you," she said to Pierre, as he kissed her hand. She had known him as a child, and now his friendship with Andrey, his unhappy marriage, and above all, his kindly.

simple face, disposed her favourably to him. She looked at him with her
beautiful, luminous eyes, and seemed to say to him: "I like you very
much, but, please, don't laugh at my friends."

After the first phrases of greeting, they sat down.

"Oh, and Ivanushka's here," said Prince Andrey with a smile, indicating the young pilgrim.

"Andryusha!" said Princess Marya imploringly.

"You must know, it is a woman," said Andrey to Pierre in French.

"Andrey, for heaven's sake!" repeated Princess Marya.

It was plain that Prince Andrey's ironical tone to the pilgrims, and
Princess Marya's helpless championship of them, were their habitual,
long-established attitudes on the subject.

"Why, my dear girl," said Prince Andrey, "you ought to be obliged to
me, on the contrary, for explaining your intimacy with this young man
to Pierre."

"Indeed?" said Pierre, looking with curiosity and seriousness (for
which Princess Marya felt particularly grateful to him) at the face of
Ivanushka, who, seeing that he was the subject under discussion, looked
at all of them with his crafty eyes.

Princess Marya had not the slightest need to feel embarrassment on
her friends' account. They were quite at their ease. The old woman cast
down her eyes, but stole sidelong glances at the new-comers, and turning
her cup upside down in the saucer, and laying a nibbled lump of sugar
beside it, sat calmly without stirring in her chair, waiting to be offered
another cup. Ivanushka, sipping out of the saucer, peeped from under
his brows with his sly, feminine eyes at the young men.

"Where have you been, in Kiev?" Prince Andrey asked the old
woman.

"I have, good sir," answered the old woman, who was conversationally
disposed; "just at the Holy Birth I was deemed worthy to be a partaker
in holy, heavenly mysteries from the saints. And now, good sir, from
Kolyazin a great blessing has been revealed."

"And Ivanushka was with you?"

"I go alone by myself, benefactor," said Ivanushka, trying to speak
in a bass voice. "It was only at Yuhnovo I joined Pelageyushka . . ."

Pelageyushka interrupted her companion; she was evidently anxious
to tell of what she had seen. "In Kolyazin, good sir, great is the blessing
revealed."

"What, new relics?" asked Prince Andrey.

"Hush, Andrey," said Princess Marya. "Don't tell us about it, Pelageyushka."

"Not . . . nay, ma'am, why not tell him? I like him. He's a good
gentleman, chosen of God, he's my benefactor; he gave me ten roubles,
I remember. When I was in Kiev, Kiryusha, the crazy pilgrim, tells me
—verily a man of God, winter and summer he goes barefoot—why are
you not going to your right place, says he; go to Kolyazin, there a wonder-working ikon, a holy Mother of God has been revealed. On these
words I said good-bye to the holy folk and off I went . . ."

All were silent, only the pilgrim woman talked on in her measured voice, drawing her breath regularly. "I came, good sir, and folks say to me: a great blessing has been vouchsafed, drops of myrrh trickle from the cheeks of the Holy Mother of God . . ."

"Come, that will do, that will do; you shall tell me later," said Princess Marya, flushing.

"Let me ask her a question," said Pierre. "Did you see it yourself?" he asked.

"To be sure, good sir, I myself was found worthy. Such a brightness overspread the face, like the light of heaven, and from the Holy Mother's cheeks drops like this and like this . . ."

"Why, but it must be a trick," said Pierre naïvely, after listening attentively to the old woman.

"Oh, sir, what a thing to say!" said Pelageyushka with horror, turning to Princess Marya for support.

"They impose upon the people," he repeated.

"Lord Jesus Christ!" said the pilgrim woman, crossing herself. "Oh, don't speak so, sir. There was a general did not believe like that, said 'the monks cheat,' and as he said it, he was struck blind. And he dreamed a dream, the holy mother of Petchersky comes to him and says: 'Believe in me and I will heal thee.' And so he kept beseeching them: 'Take me to her, take me to her.' It's the holy truth I'm telling you, I've seen it myself. They carried him, blind as he was, to her; he went up, fell down, and said: 'Heal me! I will give thee,' says he, 'what the Tsar bestowed on me.' I saw it myself—a sort of star carved in it. Well—he regained his sight! It's a sin to speak so. God will punish you," she said admonishingly to Pierre.

"How? Was the star in the holy image?" asked Pierre.

"And didn't they make the holy mother a general?" said Prince Andrey, smiling.

Pelageyushka turned suddenly pale and flung up her hands.

"Sir, sir, it's a sin of you, you've a son!" she said, suddenly turning from white to dark red. "Sir, for what you have said, God forgive you." She crossed herself. "Lord, forgive him. Lady, what's this? . . ." she turned to Princess Marya. She got up, and almost crying began gathering up her wallet. Plainly she was both frightened and ashamed at having accepted bounty in a house where they could say such things, and sorry that she must henceforth deprive herself of the bounty of that house.

"What did you want to do this for?" said Princess Marya. "Why did you come to me? . . ."

"No, I was joking really, Pelageyushka," said Pierre. "*Princess, ma parole, je n'ai pas voulu l'offenser*. I said it, meaning nothing. Don't think of it, I was joking," he said, smiling timidly and trying to smooth over his crime. "It was all my fault; but he didn't mean it, he was joking."

Pelageyushka remained mistrustful, but Pierre's face wore a look of such genuine penitence, and Prince Andrey looked so mildly from Pela-geyushka to Pierre, that she was gradually reassured.

XIV

THE pilgrim woman was appeased, and being drawn into conversation again, told them a long story again of Father Amfilohey, who was of so holy a life that his hands smelt of incense, and how some monks of her acquaintance had, on her last pilgrimage to Kiev, given her the keys of the catacombs, and how taking with her some dry bread she had spent two days and nights in the catacombs with the saints. "I pray a bit in one, chant a hymn, and go into another. I fall asleep, again I go and kiss the holy relics; and such peace, ma'am, such blessedness, that one has no wish to come out into God's world again."

Pierre listened to her attentively and seriously. Prince Andrey went out of the room. And leaving God's folk to finish their tea, Princess Marya followed him with Pierre to the drawing-room. "You are very kind," she said to him.

"Ah, I really didn't mean to hurt her feelings; I so well understand those feelings, and prize them so highly."

Princess Marya looked mutely at him, and smiled affectionately.

"I have known you for a long time, you see, and I love you like a brother," she said. "How do you think Andrey is looking?" she asked hurriedly, not letting him have time to say anything in reply to her affectionate words. "He makes me very uneasy. His health was better in the winter, but last spring the wound reopened, and the doctor says he ought to go away for proper treatment. And I feel afraid for him mor-ally. He has not a character like us women, to suffer and find relief for sorrow in tears. He keeps it all within him. To-day he is lively and in good spirits. But that's the effect of your being with him; he is not often like this. If only you could persuade him to go abroad. He needs activity, and this quiet, regular life is bad for him. Others don't notice it, but I see it."

Towards ten o'clock the footmen rushed to the steps, hearing the bells of the old prince's carriage approaching. Prince Andrey and Pierre, too, went out on to the steps.

"Who's that?" asked the old prince, as he got out of the carriage and saw Pierre.

"Ah! very glad! kiss me!" he said, on learning who the young stranger was.

The old prince was in good humour and very cordial to Pierre.

Before supper, Prince Andrey, on coming back into his father's study, found the old prince in hot dispute with Pierre. The latter was maintain-ing that a time would come when there would be no more war. The old prince was making fun of him, but with good humour. "Let off blood from men's veins and fill them up with water, then there'll be no more war. Old women's nonsense, old women's nonsense," he was saying, but still he slapped Pierre affectionately on the shoulder, and went up to the table where Prince Andrey, evidently not caring to take part in the conversation, was looking through the papers the old prince had brought from the town. The old prince went up to him and began to talk of business.

"The marshal, a Count Rostov, hasn't sent half his contingent. Came to the town and thought fit to invite me to dinner—a pretty dinner I gave him; . . . And here, look at this. . . . Well, my boy," said the old prince to his son, clapping Pierre on the shoulder, "your friend is a capital fellow; I like him! He warms me up. Other people will talk sense and one doesn't care to listen, and he talks nonsense, but it does an old man like me good. There, run along," he said; "maybe I'll come and sit with you at your supper. We'll have another dispute. Make friends with my dunce, Princess Marya," he shouted to Pierre from the door.

It was only now on his visit to Bleak Hills that Pierre appreciated fully all the charm of his friendship with Prince Andrey. The charm was not so manifest in his relations with his friend himself as in his relations with all his family and household. Though he had hardly known them, Pierre felt at once like an old friend both with the harsh old prince and the gentle, timid Princess Marya. They all liked him. Not only Princess Marya, who had been won by his kindliness with the pilgrims, looked at him with her most radiant expression, little Prince Nikolay, as the old prince called the year-old baby, smiled at Pierre and went to him. Mihail Ivanitch and Mademoiselle Bourienne looked at him with smiles when he talked to the old prince.

The old prince came in to supper; it was obviously on Pierre's account. He was extremely warm with him both days of his stay at Bleak Hills, and asked him to come and stay with him again.

When Pierre had gone, and all the members of the family were met together, they began to criticise him, as people always do after a new guest has left, and as rarely happens, all said nothing but good of him.

XV

On returning this time from his leave, Rostov for the first time felt and recognised how strong was the tie that bound him to Denisov and all his regiment.

When Rostov reached the regiment, he experienced a sensation akin to what he had felt on reaching his home at Moscow. When he caught sight of the first hussar in the unbuttoned uniform of his regiment, when he recognised red-haired Dementyev, and saw the picket ropes of the chestnut horses, when Lavrushka gleefully shouted to his master, "The count has come!" and Denisov, who had been asleep on his bed, ran all dishevelled out of the mud-hut, and embraced him, and the officers gathered around to welcome the newcomer—Rostov felt the same sensation as when his mother had embraced him, and his father and sisters, and the tears of joy that rose in his throat prevented his speaking. The regiment was a home, too, and a home as unchangeably dear and precious as the parental home.

After reporting himself to his colonel, being assigned to his own squadron, and serving on orderly duty and going for forage, after entering into all the little interests of the regiment, and feeling himself deprived of liberty and nailed down within one narrow, unchangeable framework, Rostov had the same feeling of peace and of moral support and the same sense of being at home here, and in his proper place, as he had once felt under his father's roof. Here was none of all that confusion of the free world, where he did not know his proper place, and made mistakes in exercising free choice. There was no Sonya, with whom one ought or ought not to have a clear understanding. There was no possibility of going to one place or to another. There were not twenty-four hours every day which could be used in so many different ways. There were not those innumerable masses of people of whom no one was nearer or further from one. There were none of those vague and undefined money relations with his father; no memories of his awful loss to Dolohov. Here in the regiment everything was clear and simple. The whole world was divided into two unequal parts: one, our Pavlograd regiment, and the other—all the remainder. And with all that great remainder one had no concern. In the regiment everything was well known: this man was a lieutenant, that one a captain; this was a good fellow and that one was not; but most of all, every one was a comrade. The canteen-keeper would give him credit, his pay would come every four months. There was no need of thought or of choice; one had only to do nothing that was considered low in the Pavlograd regiment, and when occasion came, to do what was clear and distinct, defined and commanded; and all would be well.

On becoming subject again to the definite regulations of regimental life, Rostov had a sense of pleasure and relief, such as a weary man feels in lying down to rest. The regimental life was the greater relief to Rostov on this campaign, because after his loss to Dolohov (for which, in spite of his family's efforts to console him, he could not forgive himself), he had resolved not to serve as before, but to atone for his fault by good conduct, and by being a thoroughly good soldier and officer, that is a good man, a task so difficult in the *world,* but so possible in the regiment.

Rostov had determined to repay his gambling debt to his parents in the course of five years. He had been sent ten thousand a year; now he had made up his mind to take only two thousand, and to leave the remainder to repay the debt to his parents.

After continual retreats, advances, and engagements at Pultusk and Preussisch-Eylau, our army was concentrated about Bartenstein. They were waiting for the arrival of the Tsar and the beginning of a new campaign.

The Pavlograd regiment, belonging to that part of the army which had been in the campaign of 1805, had stayed behind in Russia to make up its full complement of men, and did not arrive in time for the first actions of the campaign. It took no part in the battles of Pultusk and of Preussisch-Eylau, and joining the army in the field, in the second half of the campaign, was attached to Platov's detachment.

Platov's detachment was acting independently of the main army. Several times the Pavlograd hussars had taken part in skirmishes with the enemy, had captured prisoners, and on one occasion had even carried off the carriages of Marshal Oudinot. In April the Pavlograd hussars had for several weeks been encamped near an utterly ruined, empty German village, and had not stirred from that spot.

It was thawing, muddy, and cold, the ice had broken upon the river, the roads had become impassable; for several days there had been neither provender for the horses nor provisions for the men. Seeing that the transport of provisions was impossible, the soldiers dispersed about the abandoned and desert villages to try and find potatoes, but very few were to be found even of these.

Everything had been eaten up, and all the inhabitants of the district had fled; those that remained were worse than beggars, and there was nothing to be taken from them; indeed, the soldiers, although little given to compassion, often gave their last ration to them.

The Pavlograd regiment had only lost two men wounded in action, but had lost almost half its men from hunger and disease. In the hospitals they died so invariably, that soldiers sick with fever or the swelling that came from bad food, preferred to remain on duty, to drag their feeble limbs in the ranks, rather than to go to the hospitals. As spring came on, the soldiers found a plant growing out of the ground, like asparagus, which for some reason they called Mary's sweet-root, and they wandered about the fields and meadows seeking this Mary's sweet-root (which was very bitter). They dug it up with their swords and ate it, in spite of all prohibition of this noxious root being eaten. In the spring a new disease broke out among the soldiers, with swelling of the hands, legs, and face, which the doctors attributed to eating this root. But in spite of the prohibition, the soldiers of Denisov's squadron in particular ate a great deal of the Mary's sweet-root, because they had been for a fortnight eking out the last biscuits, giving out only half a pound a man, and the potatoes in the last lot of stores were sprouting and rotten.

The horses, too, had for the last fortnight been fed on the thatched roofs of the houses; they were hideously thin, and still covered with their shaggy, winter coats, which were coming off in tufts.

In spite of their destitute condition, the soldiers and officers went on living exactly as they always did. Just as always, though now with pale and swollen faces and torn uniforms, the hussars were drawn up for calling over, went out to collect forage, cleaned down their horses, and rubbed up their arms, dragged in straw from the thatched roofs in place of fodder, and assembled for dinner round the cauldrons, from which they rose up hungry, making jokes over their vile food and their hunger. Just as ever, in their spare time off duty the soldiers lighted camp-fires, and warmed themselves naked before them, smoked, picked out, and baked the sprouting, rotten potatoes, and told and heard either stories of Potyomkin's and Suvorov's campaigns or popular legends of cunning Alyoshka, and of the priests' workman, Mikolka.

The officers lived as usual in twos and threes in the roofless, broken-down houses. The senior officers were busily engaged in trying to get hold of straw and potatoes, and the means of sustenance for the soldiers generally, while the younger ones spent their time as they always did, some over cards (money was plentiful, though there was nothing to eat), others over more innocent games, a sort of quoits and skittles. Of the general cause of the campaign little was said, partly because nothing certain was known, partly because there was a vague feeling that the war was not going well.

Rostov lived as before with Denisov, and the bond of friendship between them had become still closer since their furlough. Denisov never spoke of any of Rostov's family, but from the tender affection the senior officer showed his junior, Rostov felt that the older hussar's luckless passion for Natasha had something to do with the strengthening of their friendship. There was no doubt that Denisov tried to take care of Rostov, and to expose him as rarely as possible to danger, and after action it was with unmistakable joy that he saw him return safe and sound. On one of his foraging expeditions in a deserted and ruined village to which he had come in search of provisions, Rostov found an old Pole and his daughter with a tiny baby. They were without clothes or food; they had not the strength to go away on foot, and had no means of getting driven away. Rostov brought them to his camp, installed them in his own quarters, and maintained them for several weeks till the old man was better. One of Rostov's comrades, talking of women, began to rally him on the subject, declaring that he was the slyest fellow of the lot, and that he ought to be ashamed not to have introduced his comrades, too, to the pretty Polish woman he had rescued. Rostov took the jest as an insult, and firing up, said such unpleasant things to the officer, that Denisov had much ado to prevent a duel. When the officer had gone away, and Denisov, who knew nothing himself of Rostov's relations with the Polish woman, began to scold him for his hastiness, Rostov said to him: "Say what you like. . . . She was like a sister to me, and I can't tell you how sick it made me . . . because . . . well, just because . . ."

Denisov slapped him on the shoulder, and fell to walking rapidly up and down the room not looking at Rostov, which was what he always did at moments of emotional excitement. "What a jolly lot of fools all you Rostovs are," he said, and Rostov saw tears in Denisov's eyes.

XVI

In April the army was excited by the news of the arrival of the Tsar. Rostov did not succeed in being present at the review the Tsar held at

Bartenstein; the Pavlograd hussars were at the advance posts, a long way in front of Bartenstein.

They were bivouacking. Denisov and Rostov were living in a mud hut dug out by the soldiers for them, and roofed with branches and turf. The hut was made after a pattern that had just come into fashion among the soldiers. A trench was dug out an ell and a half in breadth, two ells in depth, and three and a half in length. At one end of the trench steps were scooped out, and these formed the entrance and the approach. The trench itself was the room, and in it the lucky officers, such as the captain, had a plank lying on piles at the further end away from the steps—this was the table. On both sides of the trench the earth had been thrown up, and these mounds made the two beds and the sofa. The roof was so constructed that one could stand upright in the middle, and on the beds it was possible to sit, if one moved up close to the table. Denisov, who always fared luxuriously, because the soldiers of his squadron were fond of him, had a board nailed up in the front part of the roof, and in the board a broken but cemented window pane. When it was very cold, they used to bring red-hot embers from the soldiers' camp-fires in a bent sheet of iron and set them near the steps (in the drawing-room, as Denisov called that part of the hut), and this made it so warm that the officers, of whom there were always a number with Denisov and Rostov, used to sit with nothing but their shirts on.

In April Rostov had been on duty. At eight o'clock in the morning, on coming home after a sleepless night, he sent for hot embers, changed his rain-soaked underclothes, said his prayers, drank some tea, warmed himself, put things tidy in his corner and on the table, and with a wind-beaten, heated face, and with only his shirt on, lay down on his back, folding his hands behind his head. He was engaged in agreeable meditations, reflecting that he would be sure to be promoted for the last reconnoitring expedition, and was expecting Denisov to come in. He wanted to talk to him.

Behind the hut he heard the resounding roar of Denisov, unmistakably irritated. Rostov moved to the window to see to whom he was speaking, and saw the quartermaster, Toptcheenko.

"I told you not to let them stuff themselves with that root—Mary's what do you call it!" Denisov was roaring. "Why, I saw it myself, Lazartchuk was pulling it up in the field."

"I did give the order, your honour; they won't heed it," answered the quartermaster.

Rostov lay down again on his bed, and thought contentedly: "Let him see to things now; he's fussing about while I have done my work, and I am lying here—it's splendid!" Through the wall he could hear now some one besides the quartermaster speaking. Lavrushka, Denisov's smart rogue of a valet, was telling him something about some transports, biscuits and oxen, he had seen, while on the look-out for provisions.

Again he heard Denisov's shout from further away, and the words: "Saddle! second platoon!"

"Where are they off to?" thought Rostov.

Five minutes later Denisov came into the hut, clambered with muddy feet on the bed, angrily lighted his pipe, scattered about all his belongings, put on his riding-whip and sword, and was going out of the hut. In reply to Rostov's question, where was he going? he answered angrily and vaguely that he had business to see after.

"God be my judge, then, and our gracious Emperor!" said Denisov, as he went out. Outside the hut Rostov heard the hoofs of several horses splashing through the mud. Rostov did not even trouble himself to find out where Denisov was going. Getting warm through in his corner, he fell asleep, and it was only towards evening that he came out of the hut. Denisov had not yet come back. The weather had cleared; near the next hut two officers were playing quoits, with a laugh sticking big radishes for pegs in the soft muddy earth. Rostov joined them. In the middle of a game the officers saw transport waggons driving up to them, some fifteen hussars on lean horses rode behind them. The transport waggons, escorted by the hussars, drove up to the picket ropes, and a crowd of hussars surrounded them.

"There, look! Denisov was always fretting about it," said Rostov; "here are provisions come at last."

"High time, too!" said the officers. "Won't the soldiers be pleased!"

A little behind the hussars rode Denisov, accompanied by two infantry officers, with whom he was in conversation. Rostov went to meet them.

"I warn you, captain," one of the officers was saying, a thin, little man, visibly wrathful.

"Well, I have told you, I won't give them up," answered Denisov.

"You will have to answer for it, captain. It's mutiny—carrying off transports from your own army! Our men have had no food for two days."

"Mine have had nothing for a fortnight," answered Denisov.

"It's brigandage; you will answer for it, sir!" repeated the infantry officer, raising his voice.

"But why do you keep pestering me? Eh?" roared Denisov, suddenly getting furious. "It's I will have to answer for it, and not you; and you'd better not cry out till you're hurt. Be off!" he shouted at the officers.

"All right!" the little officer responded, not the least intimidated, and not moving away. "It's robbery, so I tell you. . . ."

"Go to the devil, quick march, while you're safe and sound." And Denisov moved towards the officer.

"All right, all right," said the officer threateningly; and he turned his horse and trotted away, swaying in the saddle.

"A dog astride a fence, a dog astride a fence to the life!" Denisov called after him—the bitterest insult a cavalry man can pay an infantry man on horseback; and riding up to Rostov he broke into a guffaw.

"Carried off the transports, carried them off from the infantry by force!" he said. "Why, am I to let the men die of hunger?"

The stores carried off by the hussars had been intended for an infan-

try regiment, but learning from Lavrushka that the transport was un-
escorted, Denisov and his hussars had carried off the stores by force.
Biscuits were dealt out freely to the soldiers; they even shared them
with the other squadrons.

Next day the colonel sent for Denisov, and putting his fingers held
apart before his eyes, he said to him: "I look at the matter like this;
see, I know nothing, and will take no steps; but I advise you to ride
over to the staff, and there, in the commissariat department, to smooth
the thing over, and if possible give a receipt for so much stores. If not,
and a claim is entered for the infantry regiments, there will be a fuss,
and it may end unpleasantly."

Denisov went straight from the colonel to the staff with a sincere
desire to follow his advice.

In the evening he came back to his hut in a condition such as Rostov
had never seen his friend in before. Denisov could not speak, and was
gasping for breath. When Rostov asked him what was wrong with him,
he could only in a faint and husky voice utter incoherent oaths and
threats.

Alarmed at Denisov's condition, Rostov suggested he should undress,
drink some water, and sent for the doctor.

"Me to be court-martialled for brigandage—oh! some more water!—
Let them court-martial me; I will, I always will, beat blackguards, and
I'll tell the Emperor.—Ice," he kept saying.

The regimental doctor said it was necessary to bleed him. A deep
saucer of black blood was drawn from Denisov's hairy arm, and only
then did he recover himself sufficiently to relate what had happened.

"I got there," Denisov said. " 'Well, where are your chief's quarters?'
I asked. They showed me. 'Will you please to wait?' 'I have come on
business, and I have come over thirty versts, I haven't time to wait; announce me.' Very good; but the over-thief appears; he, too, thought fit
to lecture me. 'This is robbery!' says he. 'The robber,' said I, 'is not
the man who takes the stores to feed his soldiers, but the man who takes
them to fill his pockets.' 'Will you please to be silent?' Very good.
'Give a receipt,' says he, 'to the commissioner, but the affair will be
reported at headquarters.' I go before the commissioner. I go in. Sitting
at the table . . . Who? No, think of it! . . . Who is it that's starving
us to death?" roared Denisov, bringing the fist of his lanced arm down
so violently that the table almost fell over, and the glasses jumped on it.
"Telyanin! . . . 'What, it's you that's starving us to death?' said I,
and I gave him one on the snout, and well it went home, and then another, so . . . 'Ah! . . . you so-and-so . . .' and I gave him a thrashing. But I did have a bit of fun, though, I can say that," cried Denisov,
his white teeth showing in a smile of malignant glee under his black
moustaches. "I should have killed him, if they hadn't pulled me off."

"But why are you shouting; keep quiet," said Rostov; "it's bleeding
again. Stay, it must be bound up."

Denisov was bandaged up and put to bed. Next day he waked up calm
and in good spirits.

But at midday the adjutant of the regiment came with a grave and gloomy face to the hut shared by Denisov and Rostov, and regretfully showed them a formal communication to Major Denisov from the colonel, in which inquiries were made about the incidents of the previous day. The adjutant informed them that the affair seemed likely to take a very disastrous turn; that a court-martial was to be held; and that, with the strictness now prevailing as regards pillaging and breach of discipline, it would be a lucky chance if it ended in being degraded to the ranks.

The case, as presented by the offended parties, was that Major Denisov, after carrying off the transports, had without any provocation come in a drunken condition to the chief commissioner of the commissariat, had called him a thief, threatened to beat him; and, when he was led out, had rushed into the office, attacked two officials, and sprained the arm of one of them.

In response to further inquiries from Rostov, Denisov said, laughing, that it did seem certainly as though some other fellow had been mixed up in it, but that it was all stuff and nonsense; that he would never dream of being afraid of courts of any sort, and that if the scoundrels dared to pick a quarrel with him, he would give them an answer they wouldn't soon forget.

Denisov spoke in this careless way of the whole affair. But Rostov knew him too well not to detect that in his heart (though he hid it from others) he was afraid of a court-martial, and was worrying over the matter, which was obviously certain to have disastrous consequences. Documents began to come every day, and notices from the court, and Denisov received a summons to put his squadron under the command of the officer next in seniority, and on the first of May to appear before the staff of the division for an investigation into the row in the commissariat office. On the previous day Platov undertook a reconnaissance of the enemy with two regiments of Cossacks and two squadrons of hussars. Denisov, with his usual swaggering gallantry, rode in the front of the line. One of the bullets fired by the French sharpshooters struck him in the fleshy upper part of the leg. Possibly at any other time Denisov would not have left the regiment for so slight a wound, but now he took advantage of it to excuse himself from appearing before the staff, and went into the hospital.

XVII

In the month of June was fought the battle of Friedland, in which the Pavlograd hussars did not take part. It was followed by a truce. Rostov, who sorely felt his friend's absence, and had had no news of him since he left, was uneasy about his wound and the course his difficulties might be taking, and he took advantage of the truce to get leave to visit Denisov at the hospital.

The hospital was in a little Prussian town, which had twice been sacked by Russian and French troops. In the summer weather, when the country looked so pleasant, this little town presented a strikingly melancholy contrast, with its broken roofs and fences, its foul streets and ragged inhabitants, and the sick and drunken soldiers wandering about it.

The hospital was a stone house with remnants of fence torn up in the yard, and window frames and panes partly broken. Several soldiers bandaged up, and with pale and swollen faces, were walking or sitting in the sunshine in the yard.

As soon as Rostov went in at the door, he was conscious of the stench of hospital and putrefying flesh all about him. On the stairs he met a Russian army doctor with a cigar in his mouth. He was followed by a Russian trained assistant.

"I can't be everywhere at once," the doctor was saying; "come in the evening to Makar Alexyevitch's, I shall be there." The assistant asked some further question. "Oh! do as you think best! What difference will it make?"

The doctor caught sight of Rostov mounting the stairs.

"What are you here for, your honour?" said the doctor. "What are you here for? Couldn't you meet with a bullet that you want to pick up typhus? This is a pest-house, my good sir."

"How so?" asked Rostov.

"Typhus, sir. It's death to any one to go in. It's only we two, Makeev and I" (he pointed to the assistant) "who are still afoot here. Five of us, doctors, have died here already. As soon as a new one comes, he's done for in a week," said the doctor with evident satisfaction. "They have sent for Prussian doctors, but our allies aren't fond of the job."

Rostov explained that he wanted to see Major Denisov of the hussars, who was lying wounded here.

"I don't know, can't tell you, my good sir. Only think, I have three hospitals to look after alone—over four hundred patients. It's a good thing the Prussian charitable ladies send us coffee and lint—two pounds a month—or we should be lost." He laughed. "Four hundred, sir; and they keep sending me in fresh cases. It is four hundred, isn't it? Eh?" He turned to the assistant.

The assistant looked worried. He was unmistakably in a hurry for the talkative doctor to be gone, and was waiting with vexation.

"Major Denisov," repeated Rostov; "he was wounded at Moliten."

"I believe he's dead. Eh, Makeev?" the doctor queried of the assistant carelessly.

The assistant did not, however, confirm the doctor's words.

"Is he a long, red-haired man?" asked the doctor.

Rostov described Denisov's appearance.

"He was here, he was," the doctor declared, with a sort of glee. "He must be dead, but still I'll see. I have lists. Have you got them, Makeev?"

"The lists are at Makar Alexyevitch's," said the assistant. "But go to the officers' ward, there you'll see for yourself," he added, turning to Rostov.

"Ah, you'd better not, sir!" said the doctor, "or you may have to stay here yourself." But Rostov bowed himself away from the doctor, and asked the assistant to show him the way.

"Don't blame me afterwards, mind!" the doctor shouted up from the stairs below.

Rostov and the assistant went into the corridor. The hospital stench was so strong in that dark corridor that Rostov held his nose, and was obliged to pause to recover his energy to go on. A door was opened on the right, and there limped out on crutches a thin yellow man with bare feet, and nothing on but his underlinen. Leaning against the doorpost, he gazed with glittering, anxious eyes at the persons approaching. Rostov glanced in at the door and saw that the sick and wounded were lying there on the floor, on straw and on overcoats.

"Can one go in and look?" asked Rostov.

"What is there to look at?" said the assistant. But just because the assistant was obviously disinclined to let him go in, Rostov went into the soldiers' ward. The stench, to which he had grown used a little in the corridor, was stronger here. Here the stench was different; it was more intense; and one could smell that it was from here that it came. In the long room, brightly lighted by the sun in the big window, lay the sick and wounded in two rows with their heads to the wall, leaving a passage down the middle. The greater number of them were unconscious, and took no notice of the entrance of outsiders. Those who were conscious got up or raised their thin, yellow faces, and all gazed intently at Rostov, with the same expression of hope of help, of reproach, and envy of another man's health. Rostov went into the middle of the room, glanced in at the open doors of adjoining rooms, and on both sides saw the same thing. He stood still, looking round him speechless. He had never expected to see anything like this. Just before him lay right across the empty space down the middle, on the bare floor, a sick man, probably a Cossack, for his hair was cut round in basin shape. This Cossack lay on his back, his huge arms and legs outstretched. His face was of a purple red, his eyes were quite sunk in his head so that only the whites could be seen, and on his legs and on his hands, which were still red, the veins stood out like cords. He was knocking his head against the floor, and he uttered some word and kept repeating it. Rostov listened to what he was saying, and distinguished the word he kept repeating. That word was "drink—drink—drink!" Rostov looked about for some one who could lay the sick man in his place and give him water.

"Who looks after the patients here?" he asked the assistant. At that moment a commissariat soldier, a hospital orderly, came in from the adjoining room, and, marching in drill step, drew himself up before him.

"Good day, your honour!" bawled this soldier, rolling his eyes at Rostov, and obviously mistaking him for one in authority.

"Take him away, give him water," said Rostov, indicating the Cossack.

"Certainly, your honour," the soldier replied complacently, rolling his eyes more strenuously than ever. and drawing himself up, but not budging to do so.

"No, there's no doing anything here," thought Rostov, dropping his eyes; and he wanted to get away, but he was aware of a significant look bent upon him from the right side, and he looked round at it. Almost in the corner there was, sitting on a military overcoat, an old soldier with a stern yellow face, thin as a skeleton's, and an unshaved grey beard. He was looking persistently at Rostov. The man next the old soldier was whispering something to him, pointing to Rostov. Rostov saw the old man wanted to ask him something. He went closer and saw that the old man had only one leg bent under him, the other had been cut off above the knee. On the other side of the old man, at some distance from him, there lay with head thrown back the motionless figure of a young soldier with a waxen pallor on his snub-nosed and still freckled face, and eyes sunken under the lids. Rostov looked at the snub-nosed soldier and a shiver ran down his back.

"Why, that one seems to be . . ." he said to the assistant.

"We've begged and begged, your honour," said the old soldier with a quiver in his lower jaw. "He died early in the morning. We're men, too, not dogs. . . ."

"I'll see to it directly; they shall take him, they shall take him away,' said the assistant hurriedly. "Come, your honour."

"Let us go, let us go," said Rostov hastily; and dropping his eyes and shrinking together, trying to pass unnoticed through the lines of those reproachful and envious eyes fastened upon him, he went out of the room.

XVIII

THE assistant walked along the corridor and led Rostov to the officers' wards, three rooms with doors opening between them. In these rooms there were bedsteads; the officers were sitting and lying upon them. Some were walking about the room in hospital dressing-gowns. The first person who met Rostov in the officers' ward was a thin little man who had lost one arm. He was walking about the first room in a nightcap and hospital dressing-gown, with a short pipe between his teeth. Rostov, looking intently at him, tried to recall where he had seen him.

"See where it was God's will for us to meet again," said the little man. "Tushin, Tushin, do you remember I brought you along after Schöngraben? They have sliced a bit off me, see, . . ." said he smiling, and showing the empty sleeve of his dressing-gown. "Is it Vassily Dmitryevitch Denisov you are looking for—a fellow-lodger here?" he said, hearing who it was Rostov wanted. "Here, here," and he led him into the next room, from which there came the sound of several men laughing.

"How can they live in this place even, much less laugh?" thought Rostov, still aware of that corpse-like smell that had been so overpowering in the soldiers' ward, and still seeing around him those envious eyes following him on both sides, and the face of that young soldier with the sunken eyes.

Denisov, covered up to his head with the quilt, was still in bed, though it was twelve o'clock in the day.

"Ah, Rostov! How are you, how are you?" he shouted, still in the same voice as in the regiment. But Rostov noticed with grief, behind this habitual briskness and swagger, some new, sinister, smothered feeling that peeped out in the words and intonations and the expression of the face of Denisov.

His wound, trifling as it was, had still not healed, though six weeks had passed since he was wounded. His face had the same swollen pallor as all the faces in the hospital. But that was not what struck Rostov: what struck him was that Denisov did not seem pleased to see him, and his smile was forced. Denisov asked him nothing either of the regiment or of the general progress of the war. When Rostov talked of it, Denisov did not listen.

Rostov even noticed that Denisov disliked all reference to the regiment, and to that other free life going on outside the hospital walls. He seemed to be trying to forget that old life, and to be interested only in his quarrel with the commissariat officials. In reply to Rostov's inquiry as to how this matter was going, he promptly drew from under his pillow a communication he had received from the commissioner, and a rough copy of his answer. He grew more eager as he began to read his answer, and specially called Rostov's attention to the biting sarcasm with which he addressed his foes. Denisov's companions in the hospital, who had gathered round Rostov, as a person newly come from the world of freedom outside, gradually began to move away as soon as Denisov began reading his answer. From their faces Rostov surmised that all these gentlemen had more than once heard the whole story, and had had time to be bored with it. Only his nearest neighbour, a stout Uhlan, sat on his pallet-bed, scowling gloomily and smoking a pipe, and little one-armed Tushin still listened, shaking his head disapprovingly. In the middle of the reading the Uhlan interrupted Denisov.

"What I say is," he said, turning to Rostov, "he ought simply to petition the Emperor for pardon. Just now, they say, there will be great rewards given and they will surely pardon."

"Me petition the Emperor!" said Denisov in a voice into which he tried to throw his old energy and fire, but which sounded like the expression of impotent irritability. "What for? If I had been a robber, I'd beg for mercy; why, I'm being called up for trying to show up robbers. Let them try me, I'm not afraid of any one; I have served my Tsar and my country honestly, and I'm not a thief! And degrade me to the ranks and . . . Listen, I tell them straight out, see, I write to them, 'If I had been a thief of government property . . .'"

"It's neatly put, no question about it," said Tushin. "But that's not the point, Vassily Dmitritch," he too turned to Rostov, "one must submit, and Vassily Dmitritch here won't do it. The auditor told you, you know, that it looks serious for you."

"Well, let it be serious," said Denisov.

"The auditor wrote a petition for you," Tushin went on, "and you ought to sign it and despatch it by this gentleman. No doubt he" (he indicated Rostov) "has influence on the staff too. You won't find a better opportunity."

"But I have said I won't go cringing and fawning," Denisov interrupted, and he went on reading his answer.

Rostov did not dare to try and persuade Denisov, though he felt instinctively that the course proposed by Tushin and the other officers was the safest. He would have felt happy if he could have been of assistance to Denisov, but he knew his stubborn will and straightforward hasty temper.

When the reading of Denisov's biting replies, which lasted over an hour, was over, Rostov said nothing, and in the most dejected frame of mind spent the rest of the day in the society of Denisov's companions, who had again gathered about him. He told them what he knew, and listened to the stories told by others. Denisov maintained a gloomy silence the whole evening.

Late in the evening, when Rostov was about to leave, he asked Denisov if he had no commission for him.

"Yes, wait a bit," said Denisov. He looked round at the officers, and taking his papers from under his pillow, he went to the window where there was an inkstand, and sat down to write.

"It seems it's no good knocking one's head against a stone wall," said he, coming from the window and giving Rostov a large envelope. It was the petition addressed to the Emperor that had been drawn up by the auditor. In it Denisov, making no reference to the shortcoming of the commissariat department, simply begged for mercy. "Give it, it seems . . ." He did not finish, and smiled a forced and sickly smile.

XIX

AFTER going back to the regiment and reporting to the colonel the position of Denisov's affairs, Rostov rode to Tilsit with the letter to the Emperor.

On the 13th of June the French and Russian Emperors met at Tilsit. Boris Drubetskoy had asked the personage of high rank on whom he was in attendance to include him in the suite destined to be staying at Tilsit.

"I should like to see the great man," he said, meaning Napoleon, whom he had hitherto, like every one else, always spoken of as Bonaparte.

"You are speaking of Buonaparte?" the general said to him, smiling.

Boris looked inquiringly at his general, and immediately saw that this was a playful test.

"I am speaking, prince, of the Emperor Napoleon," he replied. With a smile the general clapped him on the shoulder.

"You will get on," said he, and he took him with him. Boris was among the few present at Niemen on the day of the meeting of the Emperors. He saw the raft with the royal monograms, saw Napoleon's progress through the French guards along the further bank, saw the pensive face of the Emperor Alexander as he sat silent in the inn on the bank of the Niemen waiting for Napoleon's arrival. He saw both the Emperors get into boats, and Napoleon reaching the raft first, walked rapidly forward, and meeting Alexander, gave him his hand; then both the Emperors disappeared into a pavilion. Ever since he had entered these higher spheres, Boris had made it his habit to keep an attentive watch on what was passing round him, and to note it all down. During the meeting of the Emperors at Tilsit, he asked the names of the persons accompanying Napoleon, inquired about the uniforms they were wearing, and listened carefully to the utterances of persons of consequence. When the Emperors went into the pavilion, he looked at his watch, and did not forget to look at it again when Alexander came out. The interview had lasted an hour and fifty-three minutes; he noted this down that evening among other facts, which he felt were of historical importance. As the Emperors' suite were few in number, to be present at Tilsit at the meeting of the Emperors was a matter of great consequence for a man who valued success in the service, and Boris, when he succeeded in obtaining this privilege, felt that his position was henceforth perfectly secure. He was not simply known, he had become an observed and familiar figure. On two occasions he had been sent with commissions to the Emperor himself, so that the Emperor knew him personally, and all the court no longer held aloof from him, as they had done at first, considering him a new man, and would even have noticed his absence with surprise if he had been away.

Boris was lodging with another adjutant, the Polish count, Zhilinsky. Zhilinsky, a Pole educated in Paris, was a wealthy man, devotedly attached to the French, and almost every day of their stay in Tilsit, French officers of the Guards and of the French head staff were dining and breakfasting with Zhilinsky and Boris.

On the 24th of June Zhilinsky, with whom Boris shared quarters, was giving a supper to his French acquaintances. At this supper there were present one of Napoleon's adjutants—the guest of honour—several officers of the French Guards, and a young lad of an aristocratic old French family, a page of Napoleon's. On the same evening Rostov, taking advantage of the darkness to pass through unrecognised, came to Tilsit in civilian dress, and went to the quarters of Zhilinsky and Boris.

Rostov, like the whole army indeed, was far from having passed through that revolution of feeling in regard to Napoleon and the French —transforming them from foes into friends—that had taken place at headquarters and in Boris. In the army every one was still feeling the same mingled hatred, fear, and contempt for Bonaparte and the French. Only recently Rostov had argued with an officer of Platov's Cossacks the question whether if Napoleon was taken prisoner he was to be treated as an emperor or as a criminal. Only a little while previously Rostov had met a wounded French colonel on the road, and had maintained to him with heat that there could be no peace concluded between a legitimate emperor and the criminal Bonaparte. Consequently it struck Rostov as strange to see French officers in Boris's quarters wearing the uniforms at which he was used to looking with very different eyes from the line of pickets. As soon as he caught sight of a French officer, that feeling of war, of hostility, which he always experienced at the sight of the enemy, came upon him at once. He stood still on the threshold and asked in Russian whether Drubetskoy lived there. Boris, hearing a strange voice in the passage, went out to meet him. For the first moment when he recognised Rostov, his face betrayed his annoyance.

"Ah, that's you, very glad, very glad to see you," he said, however, smiling and moving towards him. But Rostov had detected his first impulse.

"I have come at a bad time, it seems," said he; "I shouldn't have come, but it's on a matter of importance," he said coldly. . . .

"No, I was only surprised at your getting away from the regiment. I will be with you in a moment," he said in reply to a voice calling him.

"I see I have come at a bad time," repeated Rostov.

The expression of annoyance had by now vanished from Boris's face; evidently having reflected and made up his mind how to act, he took him by both hands with marked composure and led him into the next room. Boris's eyes, gazing serenely and unflinchingly at Rostov, seemed as it were veiled by something, as though a sort of screen—the blue spectacles of conventional life—had been put over them. So it seemed to Rostov.

"Oh, please, don't talk nonsense, as if you could come at a wrong time," said Boris. Boris led him into a room where supper was laid, introduced him to his guests, mentioning his name, and explaining that he was not a civilian, but an officer in the hussars, and his old friend. "Count Zhilinsky, Count N. N., Captain S. S.," he said, naming his guests. Rostov looked frowning at the Frenchmen, bowed reluctantly, and was mute.

Zhilinsky was obviously not pleased to receive this unknown Russian outsider into his circle, and said nothing to Rostov. Boris appeared not to notice the constraint produced by the newcomer, and with the same amiable composure and the same veiled look in his eyes with which he had welcomed Rostov, he endeavoured to enliven the conversation. With characteristic French courtesy one of the French officers turned to Rostov, as he sat in stubborn silence, and said to him that he had probably come to Tilsit to see the Emperor.

"No, I came on business," was Rostov's short reply. Rostov had been out of humour from the moment when he detected the dissatisfaction on the face of Boris, and as is always the case with persons who are ill-humoured, it seemed to him that every one looked at him with hostile eyes, and that he was in every one's way. And in fact he was in every one's way, and he was the only person left out of the general conversation, as it sprang up again. And what is he sitting on here for? was the question asked by the eyes of the guests turned upon him. He got up and went up to Boris.

"I'm in your way, though," he said to him in an undertone; "let us have a talk about my business, and I'll go away."

"Oh, no, not the least," said Boris. "But if you are tired, come to my room and lie down and rest."

"Well, really . . ."

They went into the little room where Boris slept. Rostov, without sitting down, began speaking at once with irritation—as though Boris were in some way to blame in the matter. He told him of Denisov's scrape, asking whether he would and could through his general intercede with the Emperor in Denisov's favour, and through him present the letter. When they were alone together, Rostov was for the first time distinctly aware that he felt an awkwardness in looking Boris in the face. Boris crossing one leg over the other, and stroking the slender fingers of his right hand with his left, listened to Rostov, as a general listens to a report presented by a subordinate, at one time looking away, at the next looking Rostov straight in the face with the same veiled look in his eyes. Every time he did so, Rostov felt ill at ease, and dropped his eyes.

"I have heard of affairs of the sort, and I know that the Emperor is very severe in such cases. I think it had better not be taken before his majesty. To my mind, it would be better to apply directly to the commander of the corps. . . . But generally speaking, I believe . . ."

"Then you don't care to do anything, so say so!" Rostov almost shouted, not looking Boris in the face.

Boris smiled.

"On the contrary, I will do what I can, only I imagine . . ."

At that moment they heard the voice of Zhilinsky at the door, calling Boris.

"Well, go along, go, go . . ." said Rostov, and refusing supper and remaining alone in the little room, he walked up and down for a long while, listening to the light-hearted French chatter in the next room.

XX

Rostov had arrived at Tilsit on the day least suitable for interceding in Denisov's behalf. It was out of the question for him to go himself to the general in attendance, since he was wearing civilian dress, and had come to Tilsit without permission to do so, and Boris, even had he been willing, could not have done so on the day following Rostov's arrival. On that day, the 27th of June, the preliminaries of peace were signed. The Emperors exchanged orders: Alexander received the Legion of Honour. and Napoleon the Order of St. Andrey of the first degree, and that day had been fixed for the dinner to be given by a battalion of French guards to the Preobrazhensky battalion. The Emperors were to be present at this banquet. Rostov felt so uncomfortable and ill at ease with Boris, that when the latter peeped in at him after supper he pretended to be asleep, and the next day he left early in the morning to avoid seeing him. In a frock coat and round hat, Nikolay strolled about the town, staring at the French and their uniforms, examining the streets and the houses where the Russian and the French Emperors were staying. In the market-place he saw tables set out and preparations for the banquet; in the streets he saw draperies hung across with flags of the Russian and French colours, and huge monograms of A and N. In the windows of the houses, too, there were flags and monograms.

"Boris doesn't care to help me, and I don't care to apply to him. That question's closed," thought Nikolay; "everything's over between us, but I'm not going away from here without having done all I can for Denisov, and, above all, getting the letter given to the Emperor. To the Emperor? . . . He is here!" thought Rostov, who had unconsciously gone back to the house occupied by Alexander.

Saddle horses were standing at the entrance, and the suite were riding up, evidently getting ready for the Emperor to come out.

"Any minute I may see him," thought Rostov. "If only I could give him the letter directly, and tell him all . . . could they really arrest me for my frock coat? Impossible. He would understand on which side the truth lay. He understands everything, he knows everything. Who can be juster and more magnanimous than he? Besides, even if they were to arrest me for being here, what would it matter?" he thought, looking at an officer who was going into the house. "Why, people go in, I see. Oh! it's all nonsense. I'll go and give the letter to the Emperor myself; so much the worse for Drubetskoy who has driven me to it." And all at once, with a decision he would never have expected of himself, Rostov, fingering the letter in his pocket, went straight into the house where the Emperor was staying.

"No, this time I won't miss my opportunity as I did after Austerlitz," he thought, expecting every minute to meet the Emperor, and feeling a rush of blood to the heart at the idea. "I will fall at his feet and will beseech him. He will lift me up, hear me out, and thank me too. 'I am happy when I can do good, but to cancel injustice is the greatest happiness,'" Rostov fancied the Emperor would say to him. And he passed up the stairs regardless of the inquisitive eyes that were turned upon him. The broad staircase led straight upwards from the entry; on the right was a closed door. Below, under the stairs, was a door to the rooms on the ground floor.

"Whom are you looking for?" some one asked him.

"To give a letter, a petition, to his majesty," said Nikolay, with a quiver in his voice.

"A petition—to the officer on duty, this way; please" (he was motioned to the door below). "Only it won't receive attention."

Hearing this indifferent voice, Rostov felt panic-stricken at what he was doing; the idea that he might meet the Emperor at any minute was so fascinating and consequently so terrible, that he was ready to fly; but an attendant meeting him opened the door to the officer's room for him, and Rostov went in.

A short, stout man of about thirty in white breeches, high boots, and in a batiste shirt, apparently only just put on, was standing in this room. A valet was buttoning behind him some fine-looking, new, silk-embroidered braces, which for some reason attracted Rostov's notice. The stout man was conversing with some one in the adjoining room.

"A good figure and in her first bloom," he was saying, but seeing Rostov he broke off and frowned.

"What do you want? A petition? . . ."

"What is it?" asked some one in the next room.

"Another petition," answered the man in the braces.

"Tell him to come later. He'll be coming out directly; we must go.'

"Later, later, to-morrow. It's too late. . . ."

Rostov turned away and would have gone out, but the man in the braces stopped him.

"From whom is it? Who are you?"

"From Major Denisov," answered Rostov.

"Who are you—an officer?"

"A lieutenant, Count Rostov."

"What audacity! Send it through the proper channel. And go along with you, go. . . ." And he began putting on the uniform the valet handed him.

Rostov went out into the hall again, and noticed that by this time there were a great many officers and generals in full dress, and he had to pass through their midst.

Cursing his temerity, ready to faint at the thought that he might any minute meet the Emperor and be put to shame before him and placed under arrest, fully aware by now of all the indecorum of his action, and regretting it, Rostov was making his way out of the house with downcast eyes, through the crowd of the gorgeously dressed suite, when a familiar voice called to him, and a hand detained him.

"Well, sir, what are you doing here in a frock coat?" asked the bass voice

It was a cavalry general who had won the Emperor's special favour during this campaign, and had formerly been in command of the division in which Rostov was serving.

Rostov began in dismay to try and excuse himself, but seeing the good-naturedly jocose face of the general, he moved on one side, and in an excited voice told him of the whole affair, begging him to intercede for Denisov, whom the general knew.

The general on hearing Rostov's story shook his head gravely. "I'm sorry, very sorry for the gallant fellow; give me the letter."

Rostov had scarcely time to give him the letter and tell him all about Denisov's scrape, when the clank of rapid footsteps with spurs was heard on the stairs, and the general left his side and moved up to the steps. The gentlemen of the Emperor's suite ran downstairs and went to their horses. The postillion, the same one who had been at Austerlitz, led up the Emperor's horse, and on the stairs was heard a light footstep, which Rostov knew at once. Forgetting the danger of being recognised, Rostov moved right up to the steps together with some curious persons from the town; and again after two years he saw the features he adored: the same face, the same glance, the same walk, the same combination of majesty and mildness. . . . And the feeling of enthusiasm and devotion to the Emperor rose up again in Rostov's heart with all its old force. The Emperor wore the uniform of the Preobrazhensky regiment, white elkskin breeches and high boots, and a star which Rostov did not recognise (it was the star of the Legion of Honour). He came out on the steps, holding his hat under his arm, and putting on his glove. He stopped, looking round and seeming to shed brightness around him with his glance. To some one of the generals he said a few words. He recognised, too, the former commander of Rostov's division, smiled to him, and summoned him to him.

All the suite stood back, and Rostov saw the general talking at some length to the Emperor.

The Emperor said a few words to him, and took a step towards his horse. Again the crowd of the suite and the street gazers, among whom was Rostov, moved up closer to the Emperor. Standing still with his hand on the saddle, the Emperor turned to the cavalry general and said aloud with the obvious intention of being heard by all: "I cannot, general, and I cannot because the law is mightier than I am," and he put his foot in the stirrup. The general bent his head respectfully; the Emperor took his seat and galloped up the street. Rostov, wild with enthusiasm, ran after him with the crowd.

XXI

In the public square towards which the Tsar rode there stood, facing each other, the battalion of the Preobrazhensky regiment on the right, and the battalion of the French guards in bearskin caps on the left.

While the Emperor was riding up to one flank of the battalions, who presented arms, another crowd of horsemen was galloping up to the opposite flank, and at the head of them Rostov recognised Napoleon. That figure could be no one else. He galloped up, wearing a little hat, the ribbon of St. Andrey across his shoulder, and a blue uniform open over a white vest. He was riding a grey Arab horse of extremely fine breed, with a crimson, gold-embroidered saddle-cloth. Riding up to Alexander, he raised his hat, and at that moment Rostov, with his cavalryman's eye, could not help noticing that Napoleon had a bad and uncertain seat on horseback. The battalions shouted hurrah, and *vive l'Empereur!* Napoleon said something to Alexander. Both Emperors dismounted from their horses and took each other by the hands. Napoleon's face wore an unpleasantly hypocritical smile. Alexander was saying something to him with a cordial expression.

In spite of the kicking of the horses of the French gendarmes, who were keeping back the crowd, Rostov watched every movement of the Emperor Alexander and of Bonaparte, and never took his eyes off them. What struck him as something unexpected and strange was that Alexander behaved as though Bonaparte were his equal, and that Bonaparte in his manner to the Russian Tsar seemed perfectly at ease, as though this equal and intimate relation with a monarch were something natural and customary with him.

Alexander and Napoleon, with a long tail of suite, moved towards the right flank of the Preobrazhensky battalion, close up to the crowd which was standing there. The crowd found itself unexpectedly so close to the Emperors, that Rostov, who stood in the front part of it, began to be afraid he might be recognised.

"Sire, I ask your permission to give the Legion of Honour to the bravest of your soldiers," said a harsh, precise voice, fully articulating every letter.

It was little Bonaparte speaking, looking up straight into Alexander's eyes. Alexander listened attentively to what was said to him, and bending his head smiled amiably.

"To him who bore himself most valiantly in this last war," added Napoleon, emphasising each syllable, and with an assurance and composure, revolting to Rostov, scanning the rows of Russian soldiers drawn up before him, all presenting arms, and all gazing immovably at the face of their own Emperor.

"Will your majesty allow me to ask the opinion of the colonel?" said Alexander, and he took a few hurried steps towards Prince Kozlovsky, the commander of the battalion. Bonaparte was meanwhile taking the glove off his little white hand, and, tearing it, he threw it away. An adjutant, rushing hurriedly forward from behind, picked it up. "Give it to whom?" the Emperor Alexander asked of Kozlovsky in Russian, in a low voice.

"As your majesty commands."

The Emperor frowned, with a look of displeasure, and, looking round, said: "Well, we must give him an answer."

Kozlovsky scanned the ranks with a resolute air, taking in Rostov, too, in that glance.

"Won't it be me!" thought Rostov.

"Lazarev!" the colonel called with a scowling face; and Lazarev, the soldier who was the best shot in firing at the range, stepped smartly forward.

"Where are you off to? Stand still!" voices whispered to Lazarev, who did not know where he was to go. Lazarev stopped short, with a sidelong scared look at his colonel, and his face quivered, as one so often sees in soldiers called up in front of the ranks.

Napoleon gave a slight backward turn of his head, and a slight motion of his little fat hand, as though seeking something with it. The members of his suite, who guessed the same second what was wanted, were all in a bustle; they whispered together, passing something from one to another, and a page—the same one Rostov had seen the previous evening at Boris's quarters—ran forward, and respectfully bowing over the outstretched hand and not keeping it one instant waiting, put in it an order on a red ribbon. Napoleon, without looking at it, pressed two fingers together; the order was between them. Napoleon approached Lazarev, who stood rolling his eyes, and still gazing obstinately at his own Emperor only. Napoleon looked round at the Emperor Alexander, as though to show that what he was doing now he was doing for the sake of his ally. The little white hand, with the order in it, just touched the button of the soldier Lazarev. It was as though Napoleon knew that it was enough for his, Napoleon's, hand to deign to touch the soldier's breast, for that soldier to be happy, rewarded, and distinguished from every one in the world. Napoleon merely laid the cross on Lazarev's breast, and, dropping his hand, turned to Alexander, as though he knew that cross would be sure to stick on Lazarev's breast. The cross did, in fact, stick on.

Officious hands, Russian and French, were instantaneously ready to support it, to fasten it to his uniform.

Lazarev looked darkly at the little man with white hands who was doing something to him, and still standing rigidly, presenting arms, he looked again straight into Alexander's face, as though he were asking him: "Was he to go on standing there, or was it his pleasure for him to go now, or perhaps to do something else?" But no order was given him, and he remained for a good while still in the same rigid position.

The Emperors mounted their horses and rode away. The Preobrazhensky battalion broke up, and, mingling with the French guards, sat down to the tables prepared for them.

Lazarev was put in the place of honour. French and Russian officers embraced him, congratulated him, and shook hands with him. Crowds of officers and common people flocked up simply to look at Lazarev. There was a continual hum of laughter and French and Russian chatter round the tables in the square. Two officers with flushed faces passed by Rostov, looking cheerful and happy.

"What do you say to the banquet, my boy? All served on silver," one was saying. "Seen Lazarev?"

"Yes."

"They say the Preobrazhenskies are to give them a dinner to-morrow."

"I say, what luck for Lazarev! Twelve hundred francs pension for life."

"Here's a cap, lads!" cried a Preobrazhensky soldier, putting on a French soldier's fur cap.

"It's awfully nice, first-rate!"

"Have you heard the watchword?" said an officer of the guards to another. "The day before yesterday it was 'Napoléon, France, bra-

voure'; to-day it's *'Alexandre, Russie, grandeur.'* One day our Emperor gives it, and next day Napoleon. To-morrow the Emperor is to
send the St. George to the bravest of the French guards. Can't be
helped! Must respond in the same way."

Boris, with his comrade Zhilinsky, had come too to look at the banquet. On his way back Boris noticed Rostov, who was standing at the
corner of a house. "Rostov! good day; we haven't seen each other," he
said, and could not refrain from asking him what was the matter, so
strangely gloomy and troubled was the face of Rostov.

"Nothing, nothing," answered Rostov.

"Are you coming in?"

"Yes."

Rostov stood a long while in the corner, looking at the fête from a
distance. His brain was seething in an agonising confusion, which he
could not work out to any conclusion. Horrible doubts were stirring in
his soul. He thought of Denisov with his changed expression, his submission, and all the hospital with torn-off legs and arms, with the filth
and disease. So vividly he recalled that hospital smell of corpse that he
looked round to ascertain where the stench came from. Then he thought
of that self-satisfied Bonaparte, with his white hands—treated now with
cordiality and respect by the Emperor Alexander. For what, then, had
those legs and arms been torn off, those men been killed? Then he
thought of Lazarev rewarded, and Denisov punished and unpardoned.
He caught himself in such strange reflections that he was terrified at
them.

Hunger and the savoury smell of the Preobrazhensky dinner roused
him from this mood; he must get something to eat before going away.
He went to an hotel which he had seen in the morning. In the hotel he
found such a crowd of people, and of officers who had come, as he had,
in civilian dress, that he had difficulty in getting dinner. Two officers of
his own division joined him at table. The conversation naturally turned
on the peace. The two officers, Rostov's comrades, like the greater part
of the army, were not satisfied with the peace concluded after Friedland.
They said that had they kept on a little longer it would have meant
Napoleon's downfall; that his troops had neither provisions nor ammunition. Nikolay ate in silence and drank heavily. He finished two
bottles of wine by himself. The inward ferment working within him still
fretted him, and found no solution. He dreaded giving himself up to his
thoughts, and could not get away from them. All of a sudden, on one of
the officers saying that it was humiliating to look at the French, Rostov
began shouting with a violence that was quite unprovoked, and consequently greatly astounded the officers.

"And how can you judge what would be best!" he shouted, with his
face suddenly suffused with a rush of blood. "How can you judge of the
action of the Emperor? What right have we to criticise him? We cannot
comprehend the aims or the actions of the Emperor!"

"But I didn't say a word about the Emperor," the officer said in justification of himself, unable to put any other interpretation on Rostov's violence than that he was drunk.

But Rostov did not heed him.

"We are not diplomatic clerks, we are soldiers, and nothing more," he went on. "Command us to die—then we die. And if we are punished, it follows we're in fault; it's not for us to judge. If it's his majesty the Emperor's pleasure to recognise Bonaparte as emperor, and to conclude an alliance with him, then it must be the right thing. If we were once to begin criticising and reasoning about everything, nothing would be left holy to us. In that way we shall be saying there is no God, nothing," cried Nikolay, bringing his fist down on the table. His remarks seemed utterly irrelevant to his companions, but followed quite consistently from the train of his own ideas. "It's our business to do our duty, to hack them to pieces, and not to think; that's all about it," he shouted.

"And to drink," put in one of the officers, who had no desire to quarrel.

"Yes, and to drink," assented Nikolay. "Hi, you there! Another bottle!" he roared.

PART SIX

I

IN THE year 1808 the Emperor Alexander visited Erfurt for another interview with the Emperor Napoleon; and in the highest Petersburg society a great deal was said of the great significance of this meeting.

In 1809 the amity between the two sovereigns of the world, as Napoleon and Alexander used to be called, had become so close that when Napoleon declared war that year with Austria, a Russian corps crossed the frontier to co-operate with their old enemy Bonaparte against their old ally, the Austrian Emperor; so close that in the highest society there was talk of a possible marriage between Napoleon and one of the sisters of the Emperor Alexander. But, apart from foreign policy, the attention of Russian society was at that time drawn with special interest to the internal changes taking place in all departments of the government.

Life meanwhile, the actual life of men with their real interests of health and sickness, labour and rest, with their interests of thought, science, poetry, music, love, affection, hatred, passion, went its way, as always, independently, apart from the political amity or enmity of Napoleon Bonaparte, and apart from all possible reforms.

Prince Andrey had spent two years without a break in the country. All those projects which Pierre had attempted on his estates, and changing continually from one enterprise to another, had never carried out to any real result—all those projects had been carried out by Prince Andrey without display to any one and without any perceptible exertion. He possessed in the highest degree the quality Pierre lacked, that practical tenacity which, without fuss or any great effort on his part, set things in working order.

On one estate of his, three hundred serfs were transformed into free cultivators (it was one of the first examples in Russia), in others forced labour was replaced by payment of rent. On Bogutcha)vo a trained midwife had been engaged at his expense to assist the peasant-women in childbirth, and a priest, at a fixed salary, was teaching the children of the peasants and house servants to read and write.

Half his time Prince Andrey spent at Bleak Hills with his father and his son, who was still in the nursery. The other half he passed at his Bogutcharovo retreat, as his father called his estate. In spite of the indifference to all the external events of the world that he had shown to Pierre, he studiously followed them, received many books, and, to his own surprise, when people coming fresh from Petersburg, the very vor-

384

tex of life, visited him or his father, he noticed that those people, in knowledge of all that was passing in home and foreign politics, were far behind him, though he had never left the country.

Besides looking after his estates, and much general reading of the most varied kind, Prince Andrey was busily engaged at this time upon a critical survey of our two late disastrous campaigns and the composition of a proposal for reforms in our army rules and regulations.

In the spring of 1809 Prince Andrey set off to visit the Ryazan estates, the heritage of his son, whose trustee he was.

Warmed by the spring sunshine he sat in the carriage, looking at the first grass, the first birch leaves and the first flecks of white spring clouds floating over the bright blue of the sky. He was thinking of nothing, but looking about him, light-hearted and thoughtless.

They crossed the ford where he had talked with Pierre a year before. They drove through a muddy village, by threshing floors, and patches of green corn; down hill by a drift of snow still lying near the bridge, up hill along a clay road hollowed out by the rain, by strips of stubble-field, with copse turning green here and there; and drove at last into a birch forest that lay on both sides of the road. In the forest it was almost hot, the wind could not be felt. The birches, all studded with sticky, green leaves, did not stir, and lilac-coloured flowers and the first grass lifted the last year's leaves and peeped out green from under them. Tiny fir-trees, dotted here and there among the birches, brought a jarring reminder of winter with their coarse, unchanging green. The horses neighed as they entered the forest and were visibly heated.

Pyotr the footman said something to the coachman; the coachman assented. But apparently the coachman's sympathy was not enough for Pyotr. He turned round on the box to his master.

"Your excellency, how soft it is!" he said, smiling respectfully.

"Eh?"

"It is soft, your excellency."

"What does he mean?" wondered Prince Andrey. "Oh, the weather, most likely," he thought, looking from side to side. "And, indeed, everything's green already . . . how soon! And the birch and the wild cherry and the alder beginning to come out. . . . But I haven't noticed the oak. Yes, here he is, the oak!"

At the edge of the wood stood an oak. Probably ten times the age of the birch-trees that formed the bulk of the forest, it was ten times the thickness and twice the height of any birch-tree. It was a huge oak, double a man's span, with branches broken off, long ago it seemed, and with bark torn off, and seared with old scars. With its huge, uncouth, gnarled arms and fingers sprawling unsymmetrically, it stood an aged, angry, and scornful monster among the smiling birches. Only the few dead-looking, evergreen firs dotted about the forest, and this oak, refused to yield to the spell of spring, and would see neither spring nor sunshine.

"Spring and love and happiness!" that oak seemed to say. "Are you not sick of that ever-same, stupid, and meaningless cheat? Always the same, and always a cheat! There is no spring, nor sunshine, nor happiness. See yonder stand the cramped, dead fir-trees, ever the same, and here I have flung my torn and broken fingers wherever they have grown out of my back or my sides. As they have grown, so I stand, and I put no faith in your hopes and deceptions."

Prince Andrey looked round several times at that oak as though he expected something from it. There were flowers and grass under the oak too, but still it stood, scowling, rigid, weird and grim, among them.

"Yes, he's right, a thousand times right, the old oak," thought Prince Andrey. "Others, young creatures, may be caught anew by that deception, but we know life—our life is over!" A whole fresh train of ideas, hopeless, but mournfully sweet, stirred up in Prince Andrey's soul in connection with that oak. During this journey he thought over his whole life as it were anew, and came to the same hopeless but calming conclusion, that it was not for him to begin anything fresh, that he must live his life, content to do no harm, dreading nothing and desiring nothing.

II

PRINCE ANDREY's duties as trustee of his son's Ryazan estates necessitated an interview with the marshal of the district. This marshal was Count Ilya Andreivitch Rostov, and in the middle of May Prince Andrey went to see him.

It was by now the hot period of spring. The forest was already in full leaf. It was dusty, and so hot that at the sight of water one longed to bathe.

Prince Andrey drove along the avenue leading to the Rostovs' house at Otradnoe, depressed and absorbed in considering what questions he must ask the marshal about his business. Behind some trees on the right he heard merry girlish cries, and caught sight of a party of girls running across the avenue along which his coach was driving. In front of all the rest there ran towards the coach a black-haired, very slender, strangely slender, black-eyed girl in a yellow cotton gown. On her head was a white pocket-handkerchief, from under which strayed locks of her loose hair. The girl was shouting something, but perceiving a stranger, she ran back laughing, without glancing at him.

Prince Andrey for some reason felt a sudden pang. The day was so lovely, the sun so bright, everything around him so gay, and that slim and pretty girl knew nothing of his existence, and cared to know nothing, and was content and happy in her own life—foolish doubtless—but gay and happy and remote from him. What was she so glad about? What was she thinking of? Not of army regulations; not of the organisation of the Ryazan rent-paying peasants. "What is she thinking about, and why is she so happy?" Prince Andrey could not help wondering with interest.

Count Ilya Andreivitch was living in the year 1809 at Otradnoe, exactly as he had always done in previous years; that is to say, entertaining almost the whole province with hunts, theatricals, dinner parties and concerts. He was delighted to see Prince Andrey, as he always was to see any new guest, and quite forced him to stay the night.

Prince Andrey spent a tedious day, entertained by his elderly host and hostess and the more honoured among the guests, of whom the count's house was full in honour of an approaching name-day. Several times in the course of it, Bolkonsky glanced at Natasha, continually laughing and full of gaiety among the younger members of the company, and asked himself each time, "What is she thinking of? What is she so glad about?"

In the evening, alone in a new place, he was for a long while unable to sleep. He read for a time, then put out his candle, and afterwards lighted it again. It was hot in the bedroom with the shutters closed on the inside. He felt irritated with this foolish old gentleman (so he mentally called Count Rostov) who had detained him, declaring that the necessary deeds had not yet come from the town, and he was vexed with himself for staying.

Prince Andrey got up and went to the window to open it. As soon as he opened the shutter, the moonlight broke into the room as though it had been waiting a long while outside on the watch for this chance. He opened the window. The night was fresh and bright and still. Just in front of the window stood a row of pollard-trees, black on one side, silvery bright on the other. Under the trees were rank, moist, bushy, growing plants of some kind, with leaves and stems touched here and there with silver. Further away, beyond the black trees, was the roof of something glistening with dew; to the right was a great, leafy tree, with its trunk and branches brilliantly white, and above it the moon, almost full, in a clear, almost starless, spring sky. Prince Andrey leaned his elbow on the window, and his eyes rested on that sky.

His room was on the second story; there were people in the room over his head, and awake too. He heard girls' chatter overhead.

"Only this once more," said a girlish voice, which Prince Andrey recognised at once.

"But when are you coming to bed?" answered another voice.

"I'm not coming! I can't sleep; what's the use? Come, for the last time. . . ."

Two feminine voices sang a musical phrase, the finale of some song.

"Oh, it's exquisite! Well, now go to sleep, and there's an end of it."

"You go to sleep, but I can't," responded the first voice, coming nearer to the window. She was evidently leaning right out of the window, for he could hear the rustle of her garments and even her breathing. All was hushed and stonily still, like the moon and its lights and shadows. Prince Andrey dared not stir for fear of betraying his unintentional presence.

"Sonya! Sonya!" he heard the first voice again. "Oh, how can you sleep! Do look how exquisite! Oh, how exquisite! Do wake up, Sonya!"

she said, almost with tears in her voice. "Do you know such an exquisite night has never, never been before."

Sonya made some reluctant reply.

"No, do look what a moon! . . . Oh, how lovely it is! Do come here. Darling, precious, do come here. There, do you see? One has only to squat on one's heels like this—see—and to hold one's knees—as tight, as tight as one can—give a great spring and one would fly away. . . . Like this—see!"

"Mind, you'll fall."

He heard sounds of a scuffle and Sonya's voice in a tone of vexation: "Why, it's past one o'clock."

"Oh, you only spoil it all for me. Well, go to bed then, go along."

All was hushed again; but Prince Andrey knew she was still sitting there. He heard at times a soft rustle, and at times a sigh.

"O my God! my God! what does it mean?" she cried suddenly. "To bed then, if it must be so!" and she closed the window with a slam.

"And nothing to do with my existence!" thought Prince Andrey while he had been listening to her talk, for some reason hoping and dreading she might say something about him. "And she again! As though it were on purpose!" he thought. All at once there stirred within his soul such a wholly unexpected medley of youthful hopes and ideas, running counter to the whole tenor of his life, that he made haste to fall asleep, feeling incapable of seeing clearly into his own state of mind.

III

NEXT day Prince Andrey took leave of the count alone and set off on his way home, without waiting for the ladies to appear.

It was the beginning of June when Prince Andrey, on his return journey, drove again into the birch forest, in which the old, gnarled oak had made upon him so strange and memorable an impression. The ringing of the bells did not carry so far now in the forest as six weeks before. Everything was fully out, thick, and shut in. And the young firs, dotted about the forest, did not break the general beauty, but, subdued to the same character as the rest, were softly green with their feathery bunches of young needles.

The whole day had been hot; a storm was gathering, but only a small rain-cloud had sprinkled the dust of the road and the sappy leaves. The left side of the forest was dark, lying in shadow. The right side, glistening with the raindrops, gleamed in the sunlight, faintly undulating in the wind. Everything was in flower, the nightingales twittered and carolled, now close, now far away.

"Yes, it was here, in this forest, I saw that oak, with whom I was in sympathy," thought Prince Andrey. "But where is he?" he thought again as he gazed at the left side of the road, and, all unaware and unrecognising, he was admiring the very oak he was seeking. The old oak, utterly transformed, draped in a tent of sappy dark green, basked faintly, undulating in the rays of the evening sun. Of the knotted fingers, the gnarled excrescences, the aged grief and mistrust—nothing was to be seen. Through the rough, century-old bark, where there were no twigs, leaves had burst out so sappy, so young, that it was hard to believe that aged creature had borne them.

"Yes, that is the same tree," thought Prince Andrey, and all at once there came upon him an irrational, spring feeling of joy and of renewal. All the best moments of his life rose to his memory at once. Austerlitz, with that lofty sky, and the dead, reproachful face of his wife, and Pierre on the ferry, and the girl, thrilled by the beauty of the night, and that night and moon—it all rushed at once into his mind.

"No, life is not over at thirty-one," Prince Andrey decided all at once, finally and absolutely. "It's not enough for me to know all there is in me, every one must know it too; Pierre and that girl, who wanted to fly away into the sky; every one must know me so that my life may not be spent only on myself; they must not live so apart from my life, it must be reflected in all of them and they must all share my life with me!"

On getting home after his journey, Prince Andrey made up his mind to go to Petersburg in the autumn, and began inventing all sorts of reasons for this decision. A whole chain of sensible, logical reasons, making it essential for him to visit Petersburg, and even to re-enter the service, was at every moment ready at his disposal. He could not indeed comprehend now how he could ever have doubted of the necessity of taking an active share in life, just a month before he could not have understood how the idea of leaving the country could ever occur to him. It seemed clear to him that all his experience of life would be wasted and come to naught, if he did not apply it in practice and take an active part in life again. He could not understand indeed how on a basis of such poor arguments it could have seemed so incontestable to him that he would be lowering himself, if after the lessons he had received from life, he were to put faith again in the possibility of being useful and in the possibility of happiness and of love. Reason now gave its whole support to the other side. After his journey to Ryazan, Prince Andrey began to weary of life in the country; his former pursuits ceased to interest him, and often sitting alone in his study, he got up, went to the looking-glass and gazed a long while at his own face. Then he turned away to the portrait of Liza, who, with her curls tied up *à la grecque*, looked gaily and tenderly out of the gold frame at him. She did not say those terrible words to him; she looked curiously and merrily at him. And, clasping his hands behind him, Prince Andrey would walk a long while up and down his room, frowning and smiling by turns, as he brooded over those irrational ideas, that could not be put into words, and were secret as a crime—the ideas connected with Pierre, with glory, with the girl at the window, with the oak, with woman's beauty, and love, which had changed the whole current of his life. And if any one came into his room at such moments, he would be particularly short, severely decided and disagreeably logical.

"*Mon cher,*" Princess Marya would say coming in at such a moment, 'Nikolushka cannot go out for a walk to-day; it is very cold."

"If it were hot," Prince Andrey would answer his sister with peculiar dryness on such occasions, "then he would go out with only his smock on; but as it is cold, you must put on him warm clothes that have been designed for that object. That's what follows from its being cold, and not staying at home when the child needs fresh air," he would say, with an exaggerated logicality, as it were punishing some one for that secret, illogical element working within him.

On such occasions Princess Marya thought what a chilling effect so much intellectual work had upon men.

IV

PRINCE ANDREY arrived in Petersburg in the August of 1809. It was the period when the young Speransky was at the zenith of his fame and his reforms were being carried out with the utmost vigour. In that very month the Tsar was thrown out of his carriage, hurt his foot, and was laid up for three weeks at Peterhof, seeing Speransky every day and no one else. At that period there were in preparation the two famous decrees that so convulsed society, abolishing the bestowal of grades by court favour and establishing examinations for obtaining the ranks of collegiate assessors and state councillors. But besides these reforms, a whole political constitution was under discussion destined to transform the whole legal, administrative and financial system of government from the Privy Council to the district tribunals. At this time the vague, liberal ideals with which the Emperor Alexander had ascended the throne were taking shape and being carried into practice. Those ideals he had striven to realise with the aid of Tchartorizhsky, Novosiltsov, Kotchubey, and Stroganov, whom he used himself to call in fun his "*comité du salut publique.*" Now all were replaced by Speransky on the civil side and Araktcheev on the military.

Soon after his arrival, Prince Andrey, as a kammerherr, presented himself at court and at a levée. The Tsar, meeting him on two occasions, did not deign to bestow a single word upon him. Prince Andrey had fancied even before then that he was antipathetic to the Tsar; that the Tsar disliked his face and his whole personality. In the cold, repellent glance with which the Tsar looked at him, Prince Andrey found further confirmation of this supposition. Courtiers explained the Tsar's slight to Prince Andrey by saying that his majesty was displeased at Bolkonsky's having retired from active service since 1805.

"I know myself that one has no control over one's likes and dislikes," thought Prince Andrey, "and so it is of no use to think of presenting my note on army reform in person to the Tsar, but the thing will speak for itself." He sent word about his note to an old field-marshal, a friend of his father's. The field-marshal fixed an hour to see him, received him cordially, and promised to lay it before the Tsar. A few days later,

Prince Andrey received notice that he was to call upon the minister of war, Count Araktcheev.

At nine o'clock in the morning on the day appointed, Prince Andrey entered Count Araktcheev's reception-room.

Prince Andrey did not know Araktcheev personally and had never seen him, but all that he knew about him had inspired him with little respect for the man.

"He is the minister of war, a person the Tsar trusts, and no one need have any concern with his personal qualities; he has been commissioned to look at my note, consequently he is the only person who can get it adopted," thought Prince Andrey, as he waited among many persons of importance and unimportance in Count Araktcheev's anteroom.

During the years of his service—for the most part as an adjutant— Prince Andrey had seen the anterooms of many great personages, and the various characteristic types of such anterooms were very readily recognised by him. Count Araktcheev's anteroom had quite a special character. The faces of the persons of no consequence who were await-ing their turns for an audience with Count Araktcheev betrayed a feel-ing of humiliation and servility; the faces of those of superior rank all wore an expression of general discomfort, concealed under a mask of ease and ridicule, of themselves and their position and the person they were waiting to see. Some of them walked up and down plunged in thought; others were laughing and whispering together, and Prince An-drey caught the nickname *Sila Andreitch* (Sila meaning Force or Vio-lence), and the words "the governor'll give it you," referring to Count Araktcheev. One general (a person of great consequence), unmistakably chagrined at being kept waiting so long, sat with crossed legs, disdain-fully smiling to himself.

But as soon as the door opened, all faces instantly betrayed one feel-ing only—terror.

Prince Andrey asked the adjutant on duty to mention his name again, but he received a sarcastic stare, and was told his turn would come in due course. After several persons had been let in and let out of the min-ister's room by the adjutant, an officer was admitted at the dreadful door, whose abject and panic-stricken face had struck Prince Andrey. The officer's audience lasted a long while. Suddenly the roar of a harsh voice was heard through the door, and the officer, with a white face and trembling lips, came out, and clutching at his head, crossed the ante-room. After that, Prince Andrey was conducted to the door, and the ad-jutant in a whisper said: "To the right, at the window."

Prince Andrey went into a plain, neat study, and saw at the table a man of forty with a long waist, with a long, closely-cropped head, deep wrinkles, scowling brows over brown-green, dull eyes, and a red, over-hanging nose. Araktcheev turned his head towards him, without looking at him.

"What is it you are petitioning for?" asked Araktcheev.

"There is nothing that I am . . . petitioning for, your excellency," Prince Andrey pronounced softly. Araktcheev's eyes turned to him.

"Sit down," said Araktcheev. "Prince Bolkonsky?"

"I have no petition to make, but his majesty the Tsar has graciously sent to your excellency a note submitted by me——"

"Be so good as to see, my dear sir; I have read your note," Araktcheev interrupted, uttering only the first words civilly, again looking away from him, and relapsing more and more into a tone of grumbling contempt. "Is it new army regulations you propose? There are regulations in plenty; no one will carry out the old ones. Nowadays every one's drawing up regulations; it's easier writing than doing."

"I have come by the desire of his majesty the Tsar to learn from your excellency how you propose to deal with my project," said Prince Andrey courteously.

"I have proposed a resolution in regard to your note, and have forwarded it to the committee. I do *not* approve," said Araktcheev, getting up and taking a paper out of the writing-table. "Here." He gave it to Prince Andrey. Right across the note had been scrawled, without punctuation or capital letters and with words misspelt: "Superficially compiled seeing that it's drawn up in imitation of the French army regulations and needlessly departing from the standing orders."

"To what committee has the note been referred?" asked Prince Andrey.

"To the Committee on Army Regulations, and I have proposed your honour being enrolled among its members. Only without salary."

Prince Andrey smiled.

"I am not seeking a salary."

"A member without salary," repeated Araktcheev. "I wish you good day. Hey! call! who's the next?" he shouted, as he bowed to Prince Andrey.

V

WHILE awaiting the announcement of his name having been put on the committee, Prince Andrey looked up old acquaintances, especially among those persons whom he knew to be in power, and so able to be of use to him. He experienced now in Petersburg a sensation akin to what he had known on the eve of a battle, when he was fretted by restless curiosity and irresistibly attracted to those higher spheres, where the future was in preparation, that future on which hung the fate of millions. From the angry irritability of the elder generation, from the curiosity of the uninitiated and the reserve of the initiated, from the hurry and anxious absorption of every one, from the multiplicity of committees and commissions—he was learning of new ones every day—he felt that now, in the year 1809, there was in preparation here in Petersburg some vast political contest, and the commander-in-chief in it was a mysterious personage whom he did not know, but imagined to be a man of genius—Speransky.

And this movement of reform, of which he knew vaguely, and Speransky, the moving spirit of it, began to interest him so keenly that his proposed reform of the army regulations very soon fell into a subordinate position in his mind.

Prince Andrey happened to be most favourably placed for obtaining a good reception in the highest and most various circles of the Petersburg society of that day. The reforming party welcomed him warmly, and sought him out, in the first place, because he had the reputation of being clever and very well read, and secondly because he had already gained the reputation of being a liberal by the emancipation of his serfs. The party of the dissatisfied older generation welcomed him simply as the son of his father, and reckoned upon his sympathy in their disapproval of the reforms. The feminine world, *society*, received him cordially because he was a wealthy match of high rank, and a person almost new, encircled by a halo of romance from his narrow escape from death and the tragic loss of his young wife. Moreover the general verdict of all who had known him previously was that he had greatly changed for the better during the last five years, had grown softer and more manly; that he had lost his old affectation, pride, and sarcastic irony, and had gained the serenity that comes with years. People talked of him, were interested in him, and eager to see him.

The day after his interview with Count Araktcheev, Prince Andrey was at a *soirée* at Count Kotchubey's. He described to the latter his interview with *Sila Andreitch*. (This was the name by which Kotchubey spoke of Araktcheev with that vague note of jeering in his voice which Prince Andrey had noticed in the anteroom of the minister of war.)

"*Mon cher*, even in this affair you can't do without Mihail Mihalovitch. He has a hand in everything. I'll speak to him. He promised to come in the evening . . ."

"But what has Speransky to do with the army regulations?" asked Prince Andrey.

Kotchubey shook his head, smiling, as though wondering at Bolkonsky's simplicity.

"We were talking to him about you the other day," Kotchubey continued; "about your free cultivators . . ."

"Yes, so it was you, prince, who freed your serfs?" said an old gentleman of Catherine's court, turning disdainfully to Bolkonsky.

"The little estate brought me no income as it was," answered Bolkonsky, trying to minimise what he had done to the old gentleman, to avoid irritating him needlessly.

"You are afraid of being late," said the old gentleman, looking at Kotchubey.

"There's one thing I don't understand," pursued the old gentleman. "Who is to till the land if they are set free? It's easy to pass laws, but hard work to govern. It's just the same as now; I ask you, count, who will preside over the courts when all have to pass examinations?"

"Those who pass the examinations, I suppose," answered Kotchubey, crossing his legs and looking about him.

"Here I have Pryanitchnikov in my department, a capital man, a priceless man, but he is sixty; how is he to go in for examinations? . . ."

"Yes, that's a difficult question, considering that education is so restricted, but . . ."

Count Kotchubey did not finish his sentence; he got up, and taking Prince Andrey by the arm, went to meet a tall, bald, fair-haired man of forty, who had just come in. He had a large, open forehead, and his long face was of a strange, exceptional whiteness; he wore a blue frock coat and had a cross at his neck and a star on the left side of his breast. It was Speransky. Prince Andrey recognised him at once, and that thrill passed through him that comes at the great moments of one's life. Whether it was a thrill of respect, of envy, of anticipation, he did not know. Speransky's whole figure had a peculiar character by which he could be distinguished immediately. Never in any one of the circles in which Prince Andrey had moved had he seen such calm and self-confidence as was manifest in this man's heavy and ungainly movements. Never in any one had he seen a glance so resolute, and yet so soft, as now in those half-closed and moist-looking eyes; never had he seen such firmness as in that smile that meant nothing. Never had he heard a voice so delicate, smooth, and soft; but what struck him most of all was the tender whiteness of the face, and still more the hands, which were rather broad, but extremely plump, soft, and white. Such whiteness and softness Prince Andrey had seen only in the faces of soldiers who had been a long while in hospital.

This was Speransky, the secretary of state, the Tsar's confidential adviser, who had accompanied him to Erfurt, and there had more than once seen and talked with Napoleon. Speransky's eyes did not shift from one face to another, as one's eyes unconsciously do on first coming into a large company, and he was in no hurry to speak. He spoke slowly, with conviction that he would be listened to, and looked only at the person to whom he was speaking. Prince Andrey watched every word and gesture of Speransky's with peculiar intentness. As is often the case with men, particularly with those who criticise their fellows severely, Prince Andrey on meeting a new person, especially one like Speransky, whom he knew by reputation, had always a hope of finding in him a full perfection of human qualities.

Speransky said to Kotchubey that he was sorry that he had not been able to come earlier, because he had been detained at the palace. He did not say that the Tsar had kept him. And this affectation of modesty did not escape Prince Andrey. When Kotchubey mentioned Prince Andrey's name to him, Speransky slowly transferred his eyes to Bolkonsky, with the same smile on his face, and gazed for a moment at him in silence.

"I am very glad to make your acquaintance; I have heard of you, as every one has," said he.

Kotchubey said a few words about the reception Araktcheev had given Bolkonsky. Speransky's smile broadened.

"The chairman of the Committee of Army Regulations is a friend of mine—M. Magnitsky," he said, articulating fully every word and every syllable, "and, if you wish it, I can make you acquainted_with him."

(He paused at the full stop.) "I expect that you would meet with sympathy in him and a desire to assist in anything reasonable."

A circle formed at once round Speransky, and the same old gentleman, who had talked of his clerk, Pryanitchnikov, addressed a question to Speransky.

Taking no part in the conversation, Prince Andrey watched every gesture of Speransky—this man, only a little time before an insignificant divinity student, who now held in his hands—those plump white hands—the fate of Russia, as Bolkonsky thought. Prince Andrey was struck by the extraordinary contemptuous composure with which Speransky answered the old gentleman. He seemed to drop him his condescending words from an immeasurable height above him. When the old gentleman began talking too loud, Speransky smiled and said that he could not judge of the advantage or disadvantage of what the Tsar saw fit to command.

After talking for a little while in the general circle, Speransky got up, and going to Prince Andrey, drew him away to the other end of the room. It was evident that he thought it well to interest himself in Bolkonsky.

"I have not had time for a word with you, prince, in the engrossing conversation into which I was dragged by that excellent old gentleman," he said, with a smile of bland contempt, by which he seemed to take for granted that Prince Andrey and himself were at one in recognising the insignificance of the people with whom he had just been talking. This flattered Prince Andrey. "I have known you for a long while: first from your action with the serfs, the first instance of the kind among us, an example which one would desire to find many following; and, secondly, from your being one of those kammerherrs who have not considered themselves wronged by the new decree in regard to promotion by court favour, that has provoked so much criticism and censure."

"Yes," said Prince Andrey, "my father did not care for me to take advantage of that privilege; I began the service from the lower grades."

"Your father, a man of the older generation, is undoubtedly above the level of our contemporaries, who condemn this measure, though it is simply an act of natural justice."

"I imagine there is some basis though even for that condemnation," said Prince Andrey, trying to resist the influence of Speransky, of which he began to be aware. He disliked agreeing with him in everything; he tried to oppose him. Prince Andrey, who usually spoke so well and so readily, felt a difficulty even in expressing himself as he talked with Speransky. He was too much occupied in observing the personality of the celebrated man.

"In the interests of personal ambition perhaps," Speransky slowly put in his word.

"And to some extent in the interests of the state," said Prince Andrey.

"How do you mean? . . ." said Speransky slowly, dropping his eyes.

"I am an admirer of Montesquieu," said Prince Andrey. "And his theory that the principle of monarchies is honour seems to me incon-

testable. Certain rights and privileges of the nobility appear to me to be
means of maintaining that sentiment."

The smile vanished from Speransky's white face, and his countenance
gained greatly by its absence. Probably Prince Andrey's idea seemed to
him an interesting one.

"If you look at the question from that point of view," he began, pronouncing French with obvious difficulty, and speaking even more deliberately than he had done when speaking Russian, but still with perfect composure. He said that honour, *l'honneur*, cannot be supported by
privileges prejudicial to the working of the government; that honour,
l'honneur, is either a negative concept of avoidance of reprehensible
actions or a certain source of emulation in obtaining the commendation
and rewards in which it finds expression.

His arguments were condensed, simple, and clear. "The institution
that best maintains that honour, the source of emulation, is an institution akin to the Legion of Honour of the great Emperor Napoleon,
which does not detract from but conduces to the successful working of
the government service, and not a class or court privilege."

"I do not dispute that, but there is no denying that the court privileges did attain the same object," said Prince Andrey. "Every courtier
thought himself bound to do credit to his position."

"But you did not care to profit by it, prince," said Speransky, showing with a smile that he wished to conclude with civility an argument
embarrassing for his companion. "If you will do me the honour to call
on Wednesday, then I shall have seen Magnitsky, and shall have something to tell you that may interest you, and besides I shall have the
pleasure of more conversation with you." Closing his eyes, he bowed,
and trying to escape unnoticed, he went out of the drawing-room without saying good-bye, *à la française*.

VI

During the first part of his stay in Petersburg, Prince Andrey found
all the habits of thought he had formed in his solitary life completely
obscured by the trifling cares which engrossed him in Petersburg.

In the evening on returning home he noted down in his memorandum-
book four or five unavoidable visits or appointments for fixed hours.
The mechanism of life, the arrangement of his day, so as to be in time
everywhere, absorbed the greater part of his vital energy. He did nothing, thought of nothing even, and had no time to think, but only talked,
and talked successfully, of what he had had time to think about in the
past in the country.

He sometimes noticed with dissatisfaction that it happened to him to
repeat the same remarks on the same day to different audiences. But he
was so busy for whole days together that he had no time to reflect that
he was thinking of nothing. Just as at their first meeting at Kotchubey's,
Speransky had a long and confidential talk with Prince Andrey on

Wednesday at his own home, where he received Bolkonsky alone and made a great impression on him.

Prince Andrey regarded the immense mass of men as contemptible and worthless creatures, and he had such a longing to find in some other man the living pattern of that perfection after which he strove himself, that he was ready to believe that in Speransky he had found this ideal of a perfectly rational and virtuous man. Had Speransky belonged to the same world as Prince Andrey, had he been of the same breeding and moral traditions, Bolkonsky would soon have detected the weak, human, unheroic sides of his character; but this logical turn of mind was strange to him and inspired him with the more respect from his not fully understanding it. Besides this, Speransky, either because he appreciated Prince Andrey's abilities or because he thought it as well to secure his adherence, showed off his calm, impartial sagacity before Prince Andrey, and flattered him with that delicate flattery that goes hand in hand with conceit, and consists in a tacit assumption that one's companion and oneself are the only people capable of understanding all the folly of the rest of the world and the sagacity and profundity of their own ideas.

In the course of their long conversation on Wednesday evening Speransky said more than once: "Among *us* everything that is out of the common rut of tradition is looked at," . . . or with a smile: "But *we* want the wolves to be well fed and the sheep to be unhurt." . . . or: "*They* can't grasp that" . . . and always with an expression that said: "We, you and I, we understand what *they* are and who *we* are."

This first long conversation with Speransky only strengthened the feeling with which Prince Andrey had seen him for the first time. He saw in him a man of vast intellect and sober, accurate judgment, who had attained power by energy and persistence, and was using it for the good of Russia only. In Prince Andrey's eyes Speransky was precisely the man—finding a rational explanation for all the phenomena of life, recognising as of importance only what was rational and capable of applying the standard of reason to everything—that he would have liked to be himself. Everything took a form so simple, so clear in Speransky's exposition of it that Prince Andrey could not help agreeing with him on every subject. If he argued and raised objections it was simply with the express object of being independent and not being entirely swayed by Speransky's ideas. Everything was right, everything was as it should be, yet one thing disconcerted Prince Andrey. That was the cold, mirror-like eye of Speransky, which seemed to refuse all admittance to his soul, and his flabby, white hand, at which Prince Andrey instinctively looked, as one usually does look at the hands of men who have power. That mirror-like eye and that flabby hand vaguely irritated Prince Andrey. He was disagreeably struck too by the excessive contempt for other people that he observed in Speransky, and by the variety of the lines of argument he employed in support of his views. He made use of every possible weapon of thought, except analogy, and his transitions from one line of defence to another seemed to Prince Andrey too violent. At one time he took his stand as a practical man and found fault with idealists, then he took a satirical line and jeered sarcastically at his opponents, then maintained a strictly logical position, or flew off into the domain of metaphysics. (This last resource was one he was particularly fond of using in argument.) He raised the question into the loftiest region of metaphysics, passed to definitions of space, of time, and of thought, and carrying off arguments to confute his opponent, descended again to the plane of the original discussion. What impressed Prince Andrey as the leading characteristic of Speransky's mind was his unhesitating, unmovable faith in the power and authority of the reason. It was plain that Speransky's brain could never admit the idea—so common with Prince Andrey—that one can never after all express all one thinks. It had never occurred to him to doubt whether all he thought and all he believed might not be meaningless nonsense. And that peculiarity of Speransky's mind was what attracted Prince Andrey most.

During the first period of his acquaintance with Speransky, Prince Andrey had a passionate and enthusiastic admiration for him, akin to what he had once felt for Bonaparte. The very fact that Speransky was the son of a priest, which enabled many foolish persons to regard him with vulgar contempt, as a member of a despised class, made Prince Andrey peculiarly delicate in dealing with his own feeling for Speransky, and unconsciously strengthened it in him.

On that first evening that Bolkonsky spent with him, they talked of the commission for the revision of the legal code; and Speransky described ironically to Prince Andrey how the commission had been sitting for one hundred and fifty years, had cost millions, and had done nothing, and how Rosenkampf had pasted labels on all the various legislative codes.

"And that's all the state has got for the millions it has spent!" said he. "We want to give new judicial powers to the Senate, and we have no laws. That's why it is a sin for men like you, prince, not to be in the government."

Prince Andrey observed that some education in jurisprudence was necessary for such work, and that he had none.

"But no one has, so what would you have? It's a *circulus viciosus*, which one must force some way out of."

Within a week Prince Andrey was a member of the committee for the reconstruction of the army regulations, and—a thing he would never have expected—he was also chairman of a section of the commission for the revision of the legal code. At Speransky's request he took the first part of the civil code under revision; and with the help of the Napoleonic Code and the Code of Justinian he worked at the revision of the section on Personal Rights.

VII

Two years before, at the beginning of 1808, Pierre had returned to Petersburg from his visits to his estates, and by no design of his own had taken a leading position among the freemasons in Petersburg. He organised dining and funeral lodges, enrolled new members, took an active part in the formation of different lodges, and the acquisition of authentic acts. He spent his money on the construction of temples, and, to the best of his powers, made up the arrears of alms, a matter in which the majority of members were niggardly and irregular. At his own expense, almost unaided, he maintained the poorhouse built by the order in Petersburg.

Meanwhile his life ran on in the old way, yielding to the same temptations and the same laxity. He liked a good dinner and he liked strong drink; and, though he thought it immoral and degrading to yield to them, he was unable to resist the temptations of the bachelor society in which he moved.

Yet even in the whirl of his active work and his dissipations, Pierre began, after the lapse of a year, to feel more and more as though the ground of freemasonry on which he had taken his stand was slipping away under his feet the more firmly he tried to rest on it. At the same time he felt that the further the ground slipped from under his feet, the more close was his bondage to the order. When he had entered the brotherhood he had felt like a man who confidently puts his foot down on the smooth surface of a bog. Having put one foot down, he had sunk in; and to convince himself of the firmness of the ground on which he stood, he had put the other foot down on it too, and had sunk in further, had stuck in the mud, and now was against his own will struggling knee-deep in the bog.

Osip Alexyevitch was not in Petersburg. (He had withdrawn from all participation in the affairs of the Petersburg lodge, and now never left Moscow.) All the brothers who were members of the lodge were people Pierre knew in daily life, and it was difficult for him to see in them simply brothers in freemasonry, and not Prince B., nor Ivan Vasilyevitch D., whom he knew in private life mostly as persons of weak and worthless character. Under their masonic aprons and emblems he could not help seeing the uniforms and the decorations they were striving after in mundane life. Often after collecting the alms and reckoning up twenty to thirty roubles promised—and for the most part left owing—from some ten members, of whom half were as well-off as Pierre himself, he thought of the masonic vow by which every brother promised to give up all his belongings for his neighbour; and doubts stirred in his soul from which he tried to escape.

He divided all the brothers he knew into four classes. In the first class he reckoned brothers who took no active interest in the affairs of the lodges nor in the service of humanity, but were occupied exclusively with the scientific secrets of the order, with questions relating to the threefold designation of God, or the three first elements of things— sulphur, mercury, and salt—or the significance of the square and all the figures of the Temple of Solomon. Pierre respected this class of masons, to which the elder brothers principally belonged—in it Pierre reckoned Osip Alexyevitch—but he did not share their interests. His heart was not in the mystic side of freemasonry.

In the second class Pierre included himself, and brothers like himself, wavering, seeking, and not yet finding in freemasonry a straight and fully understood path for themselves, but still hoping to find it.

In the third class he reckoned brothers—they formed the majority— who saw in freemasonry nothing but an external form and ceremonial, and valued the strict performance of that external form without troubling themselves about its import or significance. Such were Villarsky, and the Grand Master of the lodge indeed.

The fourth class, too, included a great number of the brothers especially among those who had entered the brotherhood of late. These were men who, as far as Pierre could observe, had no belief in anything, nor desire of anything, but had entered the brotherhood simply for the sake of getting into touch with the wealthy young men, powerful through their connections or their rank, who were numerous in the lodge.

Pierre began to feel dissatisfied with what he was doing. Freemasonry, at least as he knew it here, seemed to him sometimes to rest simply upon formal observances. He never dreamed of doubting of freemasonry itself, but began to suspect that Russian freemasonry had got on to a false track, and was deviating from its original course. And so towards the end of the year Pierre went abroad to devote himself to the higher mysteries of the order.

It was in the summer of 1809 that Pierre returned to Petersburg. From the correspondence that passed between freemasons in Russia and abroad, it was known that Bezuhov had succeeded in gaining the confidence of many persons in high positions abroad; that he had been initiated into many mysteries, had been raised to a higher grade, and was bringing back with him much that would conduce to the progress of freemasonry in Russia. The Petersburg freemasons all came to see him, tried to ingratiate themselves with him, and all fancied that he had something in reserve that he was preparing for them.

A solemn assembly of the lodge of the second order was arranged, at which Pierre promised to communicate the message he had to give the Petersburg brothers from the highest leaders of the order abroad. The assembly was a full one. After the usual ceremonies Pierre got up and began to speak:

"Dear brothers," he began, blushing and hesitating, with a written speech in his hand, "it is not enough to guard our secrets in the seclusion of the lodge,—what is needed is to act . . . to act. . . . We are falling into slumber, and we need to act."

Pierre opened his manuscript and began to read.

"For the propagation of the pure truth and the attainment of virtue," he read, "we must purify men from prejudice, diffuse principles in harmony with the spirit of the times, undertake the education of the younger generation, ally ourselves by indissoluble ties with the most enlightened men, boldly, and at the same time prudently, overcome superstition, infidelity, and folly, and form of those devoted to us men linked together by a common aim and possessed of power and authority.

"For the attainment of this aim we must secure to virtue the preponderance over vice; we must strive that the honest man may obtain his eternal reward even in this world. But in those great projects we are very gravely hindered by existing political institutions. What is to be done in the existing state of affairs? Are we to welcome revolutions, to overthrow everything, to repel violence by violence? . . . No, we are very far from that. Every reform by violence is to be deprecated, because it does little to correct the evil while men remain as they are, and because wisdom has no need of violence.

"The whole plan of our order should be founded on the training of men of character and virtue, bound together by unity of conviction and aim,—the aim of suppressing vice and folly everywhere by every means, and protecting talent and virtue, raising deserving persons out of the dust and enrolling them in our brotherhood. Only then will our order obtain the power insensibly to tie the hands of the promoters of disorder, and to control them without their being aware of it. In a word, we want to found a form of government holding universal sway, which should be diffused over the whole world without encroaching on civil obligations; under which all other governments could continue in their ordinary course and do all, except what hinders the great aim of our order, that is, the triumph of virtue over vice. This aim is that of Christianity itself. It has taught men to be holy and good, and for their own profit to follow the precept and example of better and wiser men.

"In times when all was plunged in darkness, exhortation alone was of course enough; the novelty of truth gave it peculiar force, but nowadays far more powerful means are necessary for us. Now a man guided by his senses needs to find in virtue a charm palpable to the senses. The passions cannot be uprooted; we must only attempt to direct them to a noble object, and so every one should be able to find satisfaction for his passions within the bounds of virtue, and our order should provide means to that end. As soon as we have a certain number of capable men in every state, each of them training again two others, and all keeping in close cooperation, then everything will be possible for our order, which has already done much in secret for the good of humanity."

This speech did not merely make a great impression, it produced a thrill of excitement in the lodge. The majority of the brothers, seeing in this speech dangerous projects of "illuminism," to Pierre's surprise received it coldly. The Grand Master began to raise objections to it; Pierre began to expound his own views with greater and greater heat. It was long since there had been so stormy a meeting. The lodge split up into parties; one party opposed Pierre, accusing him of "illuminism"; the other supported him. Pierre was for the first time at this meeting impressed by the endless multiplicity of men's minds, which leads to no truth being ever seen by two persons alike.

Even those among the members who seemed to be on his side interpreted him in their own way, with limitations and variations, to which he could not agree. What Pierre chiefly desired was always to transmit his thought to another exactly as he conceived it himself.

At the conclusion of the sitting, the Grand Master spoke with ill-will and irony to Bezuhov of his hasty temper; and observed that it was not love of virtue alone, but a passion for strife, that had guided him in the discussion.

Pierre made him no reply, but briefly inquired whether his proposal would be accepted. He was told that it would not be; and without waiting for the usual formalities, he left the lodge and went home.

VIII

AGAIN Pierre was overtaken by that despondency he so dreaded. For three days after the delivery of his speech at the lodge he lay on a sofa at home, seeing no one, and going nowhere.

At this time he received a letter from his wife who besought him to see her, wrote of her unhappiness on his account, and her desire to devote her whole life to him.

At the end of the letter she informed him that in a day or two she would arrive in Petersburg from abroad.

The letter was followed up by one of the freemasons whom Pierre respected least bursting in upon his solitude. Turning the conversation upon Pierre's matrimonial affairs, he gave him, by way of brotherly counsel, his opinion that his severity to his wife was wrong, and that Pierre was departing from the first principles of freemasonry in not forgiving the penitent. At the same time his mother-in-law, Prince Vassily's wife, sent to him, beseeching him to visit her, if only for a few minutes, to discuss a matter of great importance. Pierre saw there was a conspiracy against him, that they meant to reconcile him with his wife, and he did not even dislike this in the mood in which he then was. Nothing mattered to him; Pierre regarded nothing in life as a matter of great consequence, and under the influence of the despondency which had taken possession of him, he attached no significance either to his own freedom or to having his own way by punishing his wife.

"No one is right, no one is to blame, and so she, too, is not to blame," he thought. If Pierre did not at once give his consent to being reunited to his wife, it was simply because in the despondent state into which he had lapsed, he was incapable of taking any line of action. Had his wife come to him, he could not now have driven her away. Could it matter, beside the questions that were absorbing Pierre, whether he lived with his wife or not?

Without answering either his wife or his mother-in-law, Pierre at once set off late in the evening, and drove to Moscow to see Osip Alexyevitch.

This is what Pierre wrote in his diary.

"*Moscow, November* 17.—I have only just come from seeing my benefactor, and I hasten to note down all I have been feeling. Osip Alexyevitch lives in poverty, and has been for three years past suffering from a painful disease of the bladder. No one has ever heard from him a groan or a word of complaint. From morning till late at night, except at the times when he partakes of the very plainest food, he is working at science. He received me graciously, and made me sit down on the bed on which he was lying. I made him the sign of the Knights of the East and of Jerusalem; he responded with the same, and asked me with a gentle smile what I had learned and gained in the Prussian and Scottish lodges. I told him everything as best I could, repeating to him the principles of action I had proposed in our Petersburg lodge, and telling him of the unfavourable reception given me, and the rupture between me and the brothers. Osip Alexyevitch, after some silent thought, laid all his own views of the subject before me, which immediately threw light on all the past and all the course that lies before me. He surprised me by asking whether I remembered the threefold aim of the order—(1) the preservation and study of the holy mystery; (2) the purification and reformation of self for its reception; and (3) the improvement of the human race through striving for such purification. Which, he asked, was the first and greatest of those three aims? Undoubtedly self-reformation and self-purification. It is only towards that aim that we can always strive independently of all circumstances. But at the same time it is just that aim which requires of us the greatest effort, and therefore, led astray by pride, we let that aim drop, and either strive to penetrate to the mystery which we are unworthy in our impurity to receive, or seek after the reformation of the human race, while we are ourselves setting an example of vice and abomination. 'Illuminism' is not a pure doctrine precisely because it is seduced by worldly activity and puffed up with pride. On this ground Osip Alexyevitch censured my speech and all I am doing. At the bottom of my heart I agreed with him. Talking of my domestic affairs, he said to me: 'The first duty of a mason, as I have told you, is the perfection of himself. But often we imagine that by removing all the difficulties of our life, we may better attain this aim. It is quite the contrary, sir,' he said to me: 'it is only in the midst of the cares of the world that we can reach the three great aims—(1) self-knowledge, for a man can know himself only by comparison; (2) greater perfection, which can only be obtained by conflict; and (3) the attainment of the chief virtue—love of death. Only the corruptions of life can show us all its vanity, and strengthen our innate love for death, or rather regeneration into new life.' These words were the more remarkable as Osip Alexyevitch, in spite of his grievous physical sufferings, is never weary of life, though he loves death, for which he does not, in spite of all the purity and loftiness of his inner man, yet feel himself prepared. Then my benefactor explained to me fully the significance of the great square of creation, and pointed out that the third and the seventh number are the basis of everything. He counselled me not to

withdraw from co-operation with the Petersburg brothers, and while
undertaking duties only of the second order in the lodge, to endeavour
to draw the brothers away from the seductions of pride, and to turn
them into the true path of self-knowledge and self-perfection. Moreover,
for myself personally, he advised me first of all to keep a watch over
myself, and with that aim he gave me a manuscript-book, the one in
which I am writing now, and am to note down all my actions in the
future."

"*Petersburg, November* 23.—I am reconciled with my wife. My
mother-in-law came to me in tears, and said that Ellen was here, and
that she besought me to hear her; that she was innocent, that she was
miserable at my desertion of her, and a great deal more. I knew that if
I once let myself see her, I should not be able to refuse to accede to her
wishes. In my uncertainty, I did not know to whose help and advice to
have recourse. If my benefactor had been here, he would have told me
what to do. I retired to my own room, read over the letters of Osip
Alexyevitch, recalled my conversations with him, and from all that I
reached the conclusion that I ought not to refuse a suppliant, and ought
to hold out a helping hand to every one, and, above all, to a person so
closely connected with me, and that I must bear my cross. But if I forgive her for the sake of doing right, at least let my reunion with her
have a spiritual end only. So I decided, and so I wrote to Osip Alexyevitch. I said to my wife that I begged her to forget all the past, that I
begged her to forgive whatever wrong I might have done her, and that
I had nothing to forgive her. It was a joy to me to tell her that. May she
never know how painful it was to me to see her again! I have installed
myself in the upper rooms in this great house, and I am conscious of a
happy feeling of beginning anew."

IX

At that time, as always indeed, the exalted society that met at court
and at the great balls was split up into several circles, each of which
had its special tone. The largest among them was the French circle—
supporting the Napoleonic alliance—the circle of Count Rumyantsev
and Caulaincourt. In this circle Ellen took a leading position, as soon
as she had established herself in her husband's house in Petersburg. She
received the members of the French embassy, and a great number of
people, noted for their wit and their politeness, and belonging to that
political section.

Ellen had been at Erfurt at the time of the famous meeting of the
Emperors; and had there formed close ties with all the notable figures
in Europe belonging to the Napoleonic circle. In Erfurt she had been
brilliantly successful. Napoleon himself, seeing her at the theatre, had
asked who she was, and admired her beauty. Her triumphs in the character of a beautiful and elegant woman did not surprise Pierre, for with
years she had become even more beautiful than before. But what did

surprise him was that during the last two years his wife had succeeded in gaining a reputation as "a charming woman, as witty as she is beautiful," as was said of her. The distinguished Prince de Ligne wrote her letters of eight pages. Bilibin treasured up his *mots* to utter them for the first time before Countess Bezuhov. To be received in Countess Bezuhov's salon was looked upon as a certificate of intellect. Young men read up subjects before one of Ellen's *soirées*, so as to be able to talk of something in her salon, and secretaries of the embassy, and even ambassadors, confided diplomatic secrets to her, so that Ellen was in a way a power. It was with a strange feeling of perplexity and alarm that Pierre, who knew she was very stupid, sometimes at her dinners and *soirées*, listened to conversation about politics, poetry, and philosophy. At these *soirées* he experienced a sensation such as a conjuror must feel who expects every moment that his trick will be discovered. But either because stupidity was just what was needed for the successful management of such a salon, or because those who were deceived took pleasure in the deception, the cheat was not discovered, and the reputation of "a charming woman" clung so persistently to Elena Vassilyevna Bezuhov, that she could utter the vulgarest and stupidest speeches, and every one was just as enthusiastic over every word, and eagerly found in it a profound meaning of which she did not dream herself.

Pierre was exactly the husband needed by this brilliant society woman. He was that absent-minded, eccentric, grand seigneur of a husband, who got in nobody's way and far from spoiling the general impression of the highest tone in her drawing-room, formed by his contrast with his wife's elegance and tact an advantageous foil to her. Pierre's continual concentration on immaterial interests during the last two years, and his genuine contempt for everything else, gave him in his wife's circle, which did not interest him, that tone of unconcern, indifference, and benevolence towards all alike, which cannot be acquired artificially, and for that reason commands involuntary respect. He entered his wife's drawing-room as though it were a theatre, was acquainted with every one, equally affable to all, and to all equally indifferent. Sometimes he took part in conversation on some subject that interested him, and then, without any consideration whether the "gentlemen of the embassy" were present or not, he mumbled out his opinions, which were by no means always in harmony with the received catchwords of the time. But the public estimate of the eccentric husband of "the most distinguished woman in Petersburg" was now so well established that no one took his sallies seriously.

Among the numerous young men, who were daily to be seen in Ellen's house, Boris Drubetskoy, who had by now achieved marked success in the service, was, after Ellen's return from Erfurt, the most intimate friend of the Bezuhov household. Ellen used to call him *"mon page,"* and treated him like a child. Her smile for him was the same smile she bestowed on all, but it was sometimes distasteful to Pierre to see that smile. Boris behaved to Pierre with a marked, dignified, and mournful respectfulness. This shade of respectfulness too disturbed Pierre. He had suffered so much three years before from the mortification caused him by his wife, that now he secured himself from all possibility of similar mortification; in the first place, by being his wife's husband only in name, and secondly, by not allowing himself to suspect anything. "No, now she has become a blue-stocking, she has renounced for ever her former errors," he said to himself. "There has never been an instance of a blue-stocking giving way to tender passions," he repeated to himself; a maxim he had picked up somewhere and implicitly believed. But, strange to say, the presence of Boris in his wife's drawing-room (and he was almost always there) had a physical effect on Pierre; it seemed to make all his limbs contract, and destroyed the unconsciousness and freedom of his movement.

"Such a strange antipathy," thought Pierre; "and at one time I really liked him very much."

In the eyes of the world, Pierre was a great lord, the rather blind and absurd husband of a distinguished wife; a clever eccentric, who did nothing but who was no trouble to any one, a good-natured, capital fellow. In Pierre's soul all this while a complex and laborious process of inner development was going on that revealed much to him and led him to many spiritual doubts and joys.

X

He kept up his diary and this was what he was writing in it at that time:

"*November* 24.—I got up at eight o'clock, read the Scriptures, then went to my duties" (Pierre by the advice of Osip Alexyevitch was serving on one of the government committees), "came back to dinner, dined alone (the countess had a lot of guests whom I did not care for), ate and drank with moderation, and after dinner copied out passages for the brothers. In the evening I went down to the countess, and told a ridiculous story about B., and only bethought myself that I ought not to have done so, when every one was laughing loudly at it.

"I went to bed with a calm and happy spirit. Great Lord, help me to walk in Thy paths: (1) to flee anger by gentleness and deliberation; (2) to flee lust by self-restraint and loathing, (3) to escape from the turmoil of the world without cutting myself off from (*a*) the duties of my political work, (*b*) the cares of my household, (*c*) relations with my friends, and (*d*) the management of my finances."

"*November* 27.—I got up late and lay a long while in bed after I was awake, giving way to sloth. My God, help me and strengthen me that I may walk in Thy ways. Read the Scriptures, but without proper feeling. Brother Urusov came: talked of the cares of this world. He told me of the Tsar's new projects. I was beginning to criticise them, but remembered my principles and the words of my benefactor, that a true mason ought to be zealous in working for the state, when his aid is required, but should look on quietly at what he is not called upon to assist in. My tongue is my enemy. Brothers G. V. and O. visited me; there was a con-

versation preliminary to the reception of a new brother. They lay upon
me the duty of rhetor. I feel weak and unworthy. Then there was talk
of the interpretation of the seven pillars and steps of the Temple, of the
seven sciences, the seven virtues, the seven vices, the seven gifts of the
Holy Spirit. Brother O. was very eloquent. In the evening the reception
took place. The new decoration of the building added a good deal to the
magnificence of the spectacle. Boris Drubetskoy was admitted. I had
proposed him, and I was the rhetor. A strange feeling troubled me all
the time I was with him in the dark temple. I detected in myself a feeling of hatred, which I studiously strove to overcome. And I could sincerely have desired to save him from evil and to lead him into the way
of truth, but evil thoughts of him never left me. The thought came to
me that his object in entering the brotherhood was simply to gain the
intimacy and favour of men in our lodge. Apart from the fact that he
several times asked me whether N. or S. were not members of our lodge
(a question I could not answer), he is incapable, so far as my observation goes, of feeling a reverence for our holy order, and is too much
occupied, and too well satisfied with the outer man, to care much for
the improvement of the spiritual man. I had no grounds for doubting of
him, but he seemed to me insincere; and all the time I stood face to face
with him in the dark temple I kept fancying he was smiling contemptuously at my words, and I should have liked really to stab his bare
chest with the sword I held pointed at it. I could not be eloquent, and
could not sincerely communicate my doubts to the brothers and the
Grand Master. O Great Architect of Nature, help me to find the true
path that leads out of the labyrinth of falsehood!"

After this three pages of the diary were left blank, and then had been
written:

"I had a long and instructive conversation with brother V., who advised me not to abandon brother A. Much was revealed to me, unworthy
as I am. Adonai is the name of the creator of worlds. Elohim is the name
of the ruler of all. The third name, the name unutterable, has the significance of the All. Talks with brother V. strengthen and refresh me and
confirm me in the path of virtue. In his presence there is no room for
doubt. I see clearly the distinction between the poor doctrine of mundane science and our sacred, all-embracing teaching. Human sciences
dissect everything to understand it, and destroy everything to analyse
it. In the sacred science of our order all is one, all is known for its combination and life. The trinity—the three elements of things—are sulphur, mercury, and salt. Sulphur is of an oily and fiery nature; in its
combination with salt by its fiery quality it arouses a craving in it, by
means of which it attracts mercury, fastens upon it, holds it, and in
combination with it forms various substances. Mercury is the unsub-
stantial, floating, spiritual essence—Christ, the Holy Ghost, Him."

"*December 3.*—I waked up late, read the Scripture, but was unmoved
by it. Afterwards I went down and walked up and down the big hall.
I tried to meditate; but instead of that my imagination brought before
me an incident which occurred four years ago. Dolohov, meeting me

after my duel in Moscow, said to me that he hoped I was now enjoying complete mental peace in spite of my wife's absence. At the time I made him no answer. Now I recalled all the details of that interview, and in my mind made him the most vindictive and biting retorts. I recovered myself and drove away that idea, only when I had caught myself in a passion of anger; but I did not repent of it sufficiently. Afterwards Boris Drubetskoy came and began describing various incidents. The moment he came in I felt amazed at his visit and said something horrid to him. He retorted. I got hot, and said a great deal to him that was disagreeable and even rude. He did not reply, and I checked myself only when it was too late. My God, I cannot get on with him at all. It is myself too that is to blame for it. I set myself above him, and so I become far inferior to him, for he is lenient to my rudeness, while I nourish a contempt for him. My God, grant me that in his presence I may see more clearly my own vileness and act so that it may be profitable to him too. After dinner I went to sleep, and just as I was falling asleep, I distinctly heard a voice saying in my left ear: 'Thy day.'

"I dreamed I was walking along in the dark and was all of a sudden surrounded by dogs, but I went on undismayed; all at once one small dog seized me by the thigh with its teeth and would not let go. I tried to strangle it with my hands. And as soon as I tore it off, another, a bigger one, began to bite me. I lifted it up, and the more I lifted it up, the bigger and heavier it became. And suddenly brother A. came up, and taking me by the arm, led me away with him and brought me into a building, to enter which we had to pass over a narrow plank. I stepped on it, and the plank bent and gave way, and I began clambering on the fence, which I just managed to get hold of with my hands. After great efforts I dragged my body up, so that my legs were hanging over on one side and my body on the other. I looked round and saw brother A. standing on the fence and pointing out to me a great avenue and garden, and in the garden a great and beautiful building. I waked up. Lord, Great Architect of Nature, help me to tear away these dogs—my evil passions and especially the last—that unites in itself the violence of all the former ones, and aid me to enter that temple of virtue, of which I was vouchsafed a vision in my sleep."

"*December* 7.—I dreamed that Osip Alexyevitch was sitting in my house, and I was very glad to see him and eager to entertain him. But in my dream I kept chattering away incessantly with other people, and all at once I bethought myself that this could not be to his liking and I wanted to come close to him and to embrace him. But as soon as I approached him, I saw that his face was transformed, and had grown young, and he said something to me softly, some doctrine of our order, but so softly that I could not catch it. Then we all seemed to go out of the room, and something strange happened. We were sitting or lying on the floor. He was telling me something. But in my dream I longed to show him my devotional feeling, and, not listening to his words, I began picturing to myself the state of my own inner man, and the grace of God sanctifying me. And tears came into my eyes, and I was glad that he noticed it. But he glanced at me with vexation, and jumped up, breaking off his conversation with me. I was abashed and asked him whether what he had been saying did not concern me. But he made no reply, but gave me a friendly look, and then all of a sudden we found ourselves in my bedroom, where stood a big double bed. He lay down on the edge of it, and I seemed to be filled with a desire to embrace him and to lie down too. And in my dream he asked me, 'Tell me the truth, what is your chief temptation? Do you know it? I believe that you do know it.' Abashed at this question, I answered that sloth was my besetting temptation. He shook his head incredulously. And even more abashed, I told him that though I was living here with my wife, I was not living with her as a husband. To this he replied that I had no right to deprive my wife of my embraces, and gave me to understand that this was my duty. But I answered that I should be ashamed of it, and suddenly everything vanished. And I waked up, and in my mind there was the text of scripture: 'And the life was the light of man, and the light shineth in the darkness, and the darkness comprehendeth it not.'

"The face of Osip Alexyevitch had been youthful and bright-looking. That day I received a letter from my benefactor, in which he wrote to me of my conjugal duties.

"*December* 9.—I had a dream from which I waked up with a throbbing heart. I dreamed I was in Moscow in my own house, in the big divan-room, and Osip Alexyevitch came out of the drawing-room. I dreamed that I knew at once that the process of regeneration had begun in him, and I rushed to meet him. I kissed his face and his hands, while he said: 'Do you notice that my face is different?' I looked at him, still holding him in my arms, and I dreamed that I saw that his face was young, but he had no hair on his head and his features were quite different. And I dreamed that I said to him: 'I should have recognised you if I had met you by chance'; and thought as I said it, 'Am I telling the truth?' And all at once I saw him lying like a dead body; then he gradually came to himself again and went with me into the big study, holding a big folio book of manuscript. And I dreamed I said: 'I wrote that.' And he answered me by an inclination of the head. I opened the book, and on all the pages were fine drawings. And in my dream I knew that these pictures depicted the soul's love adventures with its beloved. And I saw a beautiful presentment of a maiden in transparent garments and with a transparent body flying up to the clouds. And I seemed to know that this maiden was nothing else but the figure of the Song of Songs. And in my dream, as I looked at these pictures, I felt I was doing wrong and could not tear myself away from them. Lord, help me! My God, if Thy forsaking me is Thy doing, then Thy will be done; but if I am myself the cause, teach me what I am to do. I perish from my vileness as though Thou wast utterly forsaking me."

XI

THE Rostovs' pecuniary position had not improved during the two years they had spent in the country. Although Nikolay Rostov had kept firmly to his resolution, and was still living in a modest way in an obscure regiment, spending comparatively little, the manner of life at Otradnoe, and still more Mitenka's management of affairs, were such that debts went on unchecked, growing bigger every year. The sole resource that presented itself to the old count as the obvious thing to do was to enter the government service, and he had come to Petersburg to seek a post, and at the same time, as he said, to let his poor wenches enjoy themselves for the last time.

Soon after the Rostovs' arrival in Petersburg, Berg made Vera an offer, and his offer was accepted. Although in Moscow the Rostovs belonged to the best society—themselves unaware of the fact, and never troubling themselves to consider what society they belonged to—yet in Petersburg their position was an uncertain and indefinite one. In Petersburg they were provincials; and were not visited by the very people who in Moscow had dined at the Rostovs' expense without their inquiring to what society they belonged.

The Rostovs kept open house in Petersburg, just as they used to do in Moscow; and at their suppers people of the most diverse sorts could be seen together—country neighbours, old and not well-to-do country gentlemen with their daughters, and the old-maid-of-honour, Madame Peronsky, Pierre Bezuhov, and the son of their district postmaster, who was in an office in Petersburg. Of the men who were constantly at the Rostovs' house in Petersburg, the most intimate friends of the family were very soon Boris, Pierre, who had been met in the street by the old count and dragged home by him, and Berg, who spent whole days with the Rostovs, and paid the elder of the young countesses, Vera, every attention a young man can pay who intends to make a proposal.

Not in vain had Berg shown everybody his right hand that had been wounded at Austerlitz, and the sword quite unnecessarily held in his left. He had related this episode to everybody so persistently and with such an air of importance, that every one had come to believe in the utility and merit of the feat, and Berg had received two decorations for Austerlitz.

In the war in Finland, too, he had succeeded in distinguishing himself. He had picked up a fragment of a grenade, by which an adjutant had been killed close to the commander-in-chief, and had carried this fragment to his commander. Again, as after Austerlitz, he talked to every one at such length and with such persistency about this incident that people ended by believing that this, too, was something that ought to have been done, and Berg received two decorations for the Finnish war too. In 1809 he was a captain in the guards with decorations on his breast, and was filling some particularly profitable posts in Petersburg.

Though there were some sceptics who smiled when Berg's merits were mentioned before them, it could not be denied that Berg was a gallant officer, punctual in the discharge of his duties, in excellent repute with the authorities, and a conscientious young man with a brilliant career before him and a secure position, indeed, in society.

Four years before, on meeting a German comrade in the *parterre* of a Moscow theatre, Berg had pointed out to him Vera Rostov, and said to him in German, "That girl will be my wife." From that moment he had made up his mind to marry her. Now in Petersburg, after duly considering the Rostovs' position and his own, he decided that the time had come and made his offer.

Berg's proposal was received at first with a hesitation by no means flattering for him. It seemed a strange idea at first that the son of an obscure Livonian gentleman should propose for the hand of a Countess Rostov. But Berg's leading characteristic was an egoism so naïve and good-natured that the Rostovs unconsciously began to think that it must be a good thing since he was himself so firmly convinced that it would be a good thing, and indeed a very good thing. The Rostovs were, moreover, seriously embarrassed in their pecuniary affairs, a fact of which the suitor could not but be aware; and what was the chief consideration, Vera was now four-and-twenty, and had been brought out everywhere; and, in spite of the fact that she was undeniably good-looking and sensible, no one had hitherto made her an offer. The offer was accepted.

"You see," Berg said to a comrade, whom he called his friend—only because he knew all people do have friends—"you see, I have taken everything into consideration, and I should not have got married if I had not thought it well over, or if it had been unsuitable in any way. But at present my papa and mamma are well provided for, I have secured them the lease of that place in the Ostsee district, and I can live in Petersburg with my pay and her fortune and my careful habits. We can get along nicely. I'm not marrying for money, I consider that ungentlemanly, but the wife ought to bring her share and the husband his. I have my position in the service; she has connections and some small means. That's worth something nowadays, isn't it? And what's the chief consideration, she's a handsome, estimable girl, and she loves me. . . ."

Berg blushed and smiled.

"And I love her because she has a character that is reasonable and very nice. Her sister now—though they are of the same family—is utterly different, and her character is disagreeable, and she has none of that intelligence, but something you know . . . I don't like. . . . But my betrothed . . . You must come and see us; come to . . ." Berg went on; he was going to say "to dinner," but on second thoughts he said "to tea," and putting out his tongue he blew a little ring of tobacco smoke that embodied for him all his dreams of happiness.

The first feeling of hesitation aroused in the parents by Berg's proposal had been followed by the festivity and rejoicing in the family usual on such occasions, but the rejoicing was apparent and not genuine. A certain embarrassment and shamefacedness could be detected in the feelings of the relations in regard to this marriage. It was as though their conscience smote them for not having been very fond of Vera and of being so ready now to get her off their hands. The old count was more disconcerted over it than any one. He would most likely have been unable to say what made him feel so, but his financial difficulties were at the root of the matter. He absolutely did not know what he had, how much his debts amounted to, and what he would be in a position to give for Vera's dowry. Each of his daughters had at their birth been assigned a portion, consisting of an estate with three hundred serfs on it. But one of those estates had by now been sold, and the other had been mortgaged, and the interest was so much in arrears that it would have to be sold, so that to give this estate was impossible. There was no money either.

Berg had been betrothed more than a month, and it was only a week before the date fixed for the wedding, but the count was still unable to come to a decision on the subject of the dowry, and had not spoken of it to his wife. At one time the count thought of making over the Ryazan estate to Vera, then he thought of selling his forest, then of borrowing money on a note of hand.

A few days before the wedding, Berg went early in the morning into the count's study, and with an agreeable smile, respectfully invited his father-in-law to let him know what fortune would be given with the Countess Vera. The count was so much disconcerted by this long-foreseen inquiry that, without thinking, he said the first thing that came into his head.

"I like your being businesslike about it, I like it; you will be quite satisfied . . ."

And clapping Berg on the shoulder, he got up, intending to cut short the conversation. But Berg, smiling blandly, announced that if he were not to know for certain what would be given with Vera, and to receive at least part of the dowry in advance, he would be obliged to break off the marriage. "Because, you must consider, count, if I were to allow myself to marry now without having a definite security for the maintenance of my wife I should be acting like a scoundrel . . ."

The conversation ended by the count, in his anxiety to be generous and to avoid further requests, saying that he would give him a note of hand for eighty thousand. Berg smiled gently, kissed the count on the shoulder, and said that he was very grateful, but could not make his arrangements in his new life without receiving thirty thousand in ready money. "Twenty thousand at least, count," he added, "and then a note of hand simply for sixty thousand."

"Yes, yes, very good," said the count hurriedly. "Only excuse me, my dear boy, I'll give you twenty thousand and the note of hand for eighty thousand as well. That's all right, kiss me."

XII

NATASHA was sixteen, and it was the year 1809, that year to which she had reckoned up on her fingers with Boris, after she had kissed him four years before. Since then she had not once seen him. When Boris was mentioned she would speak quite freely of it before Sonya and her mother, treating it as a settled thing that all that had passed between them was childish nonsense, not worth talking of and long ago forgotten. But in the most secret recesses of her soul the question whether her engagement to Boris were really a mere jest or a solemn, binding promise worried her.

Ever since Boris had left Moscow in 1805 to go into the army he had not once seen the Rostovs. Several times he had been in Moscow, and in travelling had passed not far from Otradnoe, but he had not once been at the Rostovs'.

It had sometimes occurred to Natasha that he did not want to see her, and her surmises had been confirmed by the mournful tone in which he was referred to by her elders.

"Old friends are soon forgotten nowadays," the countess would say after Boris had been mentioned.

Anna Mihalovna had taken in these latter days to seeing less of the Rostovs. There was a marked dignity, too, in her manner with them, and she spoke on every occasion with thankfulness and enthusiasm of her son's great abilities and brilliant career. When the Rostovs arrived in Petersburg Boris came to call on them.

It was not without emotion that he came to see them. His reminiscences of Natasha were Boris's most poetic memories. But at the same time he came to call on them firmly resolved to make her and her relations feel that the childish vows between Natasha and him could have no binding force for her or for him. He had a brilliant position in society, thanks to his intimacy with Countess Bezuhov; a brilliant position in the service, thanks to the protection of a great person whose confidence he had completely won; and he was beginning to make plans for marrying one of the richest heiresses in Petersburg, plans which might very easily be realised. When Boris went into the Rostovs' drawing-room, Natasha was in her own room. On hearing of his arrival she almost ran with a flushed face into the drawing-room, radiant with a smile that was more than cordial.

Boris had thought of Natasha as the little girl he had known four years before in a short frock, with black eyes glancing under her curls, and a desperate, childish giggle; and so, when a quite different Natasha came in, he was taken aback and his face expressed surprise and admiration. His expression delighted Natasha.

"Well, would you know your mischievous little playmate?" said the countess. Boris kissed Natasha's hand, and said he was surprised at the change in her.

"How pretty you have grown!"

"I should hope so!" was the answer in Natasha's laughing eyes.

"And does papa look older?" she asked.

Natasha sat still, taking no part in the talk between Boris and her mother. Silently and minutely she scrutinised the young man who had been her suitor in her childhood. He felt oppressed by that persistent, friendly gaze, and glanced once or twice at her.

The uniform, the spurs, the tie, the way Boris had brushed his hair,— it was all fashionable and *comme il faut*. That Natasha noticed at once. He sat a little sideways on a low chair beside the countess, with his right hand smacking the exquisitely clean and perfectly fitting glove on his left. He talked with a peculiar, refined compression of the lips about the divisions of the best society in Petersburg; with faint irony referred to old days in Moscow and old Moscow acquaintances. Not unintentionally, as Natasha felt, he mentioned some of the highest aristocracy, alluded to the ambassador's ball, at which he had been present, and to invitations from N. N. and from S. S.

Natasha sat the whole time without speaking, looking up from under her brows at him. Her eyes made Boris more and more uneasy and embarrassed. He looked round more frequently at Natasha, and broke off in his sentences. After staying no more than ten minutes he got up and took leave. Still the same curious, challenging, and rather ironical eyes gazed at him. After his first visit, Boris said to himself that Natasha was as attractive to him as she had been in the past, but that he must not give way to his feelings, because to marry her—a girl almost without fortune—would be the ruin of his career, and to renew their old relations without any intention of marriage would be dishonourable. Boris resolved to avoid meeting Natasha; but in spite of this resolution he came a few days later, and began to come often, and to spend whole days at the Rostovs'. He fancied that it was essential for him to have a frank explanation with Natasha, to tell her that all the past must be forgotten, that in spite of everything . . . she could not be his wife, that he had no means, and that they would never consent to her marrying him. But he always failed to do so, and felt an awkwardness in approaching the subject. Every day he became more and more entangled. Natasha—so her mother and Sonya judged—seemed to be in love with Boris, as in the past. She sang for him her favourite songs, showed him her album, made him write in it, would not let him refer to the past, making him feel how delightful she considered the present; and every day he went home in a whirl without having said what he meant to say, not knowing what he was doing, why he had come, and how it would end. Boris gave up visiting Ellen, received reproachful notes every day from her, and still spent whole days together at the Rostovs'.

XIII

ONE evening the old countess in her bed-jacket, without her false curls, and with only one poor wisp of hair peeping out from under her white cotton nightcap, was bowing down on the carpet, sighing and moaning as she repeated her evening prayers. Her door creaked, and Natasha, also in a bed-jacket, ran in, bare-legged, with her feet in slippers, and her hair in curl papers. The countess looked round and frowned. She was repeating her last prayer. "Can it be this couch will be my bier?" Her devotional mood was dispelled. Natasha, flushed and eager, stopped sud-denly short in her rapid movement as she saw her mother at her prayers. She half-sat down and unconsciously put out her tongue at herself. See-ing that her mother was still praying, she ran on tiptoe to the bed; and rapidly slipping one little foot against the other, pushed off her slippers and sprang on to that couch which the countess in her prayer feared might become her bier. That couch was a high feather-bed, with five pillows, each smaller than the one below. Natasha skipped in, sank into the feather-bed, rolled over towards the side, and began snuggling up under the quilt, tucking herself up, bending her knees up to her chin, kicking out and giving a faintly audible giggle as she alternately hid her face under the quilt and peeped out at her mother. The countess had finished her prayers, and was approaching her bed with a stern face, but seeing that Natasha was playing bo-peep with her she smiled her good-natured, weak smile.

"Come, come, come!" said the mother.

"Mamma, may I speak; yes?" said Natasha. "Come, under the chin, one, and now another, and enough." And she clutched at her mother's neck and kissed her favourite place on her chin. In Natasha's behaviour to her mother there was a superficial roughness of manner, but she had a natural tact and knack of doing things, so that, however she snatched her mother in her arms, she always managed so that she was not hurt, nor uncomfortable, nor displeased by it.

"Well, what is it to-night?" said her mother, settling herself in the pillows and waiting for Natasha, who had already rolled over twice, to lie down by her side under the bedclothes, to put out her arms and assume a serious expression.

These visits of Natasha to her mother at night before the count came home from the club were one of the greatest pleasures both of mother and daughter.

"What is it to-night? And I want to talk to you . . ." Natasha put her hand on her mother's lips.

"About Boris . . . I know," she said seriously; "that's what I have come about. Don't say it; I know. No, do say it!" She took her hand away. "Say it, mamma! He's nice, eh?"

"Natasha, you are sixteen! At your age I was married. You say Boris is nice. He is very nice, and I love him like a son! But what do you want? . . . What are you thinking about? You have quite turned his head, I can see that . . ."

As she said this, the countess looked round at her daughter. Natasha was lying, looking steadily straight before her at one of the mahogany sphinxes carved on a corner of the bedstead, so that the countess could only see her daughter's face in profile. Her face impressed the countess by its strikingly serious and concentrated expression.

Natasha was listening and considering.

"Well, so what then?" she said.

"You have completely turned his head, and what for? What do you want of him? You know you can't marry him."

"Why not?" said Natasha, with no change in her attitude.

"Because he's so young, because he's poor, because he's a relation . . . because you don't care for him yourself."

"How do you know that?"

"I know. It's not right, my darling."

"But if I want to . . ." said Natasha.

"Leave off talking nonsense," said the countess.

"But if I want to . . ."

"Natasha, I am serious . . ."

Natasha did not let her finish; she drew the countess's large hand to her, and kissed it on the upper side, and then on the palm, then turned it over again and began kissing it on the knuckle of the top joint of the finger, then on the space between the knuckles, then on a knuckle again, whispering: "January, February, March, April, May."

"Speak, mamma; why are you silent? Speak," she said, looking round at her mother, who was gazing tenderly at her daughter, and apparently in gazing at her had forgotten all she meant to say.

"This won't do, my dear. It's not every one who will understand your childish feelings for one another, and seeing him on such intimate terms with you may prejudice you in the eyes of other young men who visit us, and what is of more consequence, it's making him wretched for nothing. He had very likely found a match that would suit him, some wealthy girl, and now he's half-crazy."

"Half-crazy?" repeated Natasha.

"I'll tell you what happened in my own case. I had a cousin . . ."

"I know—Kirilla Matveitch; but he's old."

"He was not always old. But I tell you what, Natasha, I'll speak to Boris. He mustn't come so often . . ."

"Why mustn't he, if he wants to?"

"Because I know it can't come to anything."

"How do you know? No, mamma, don't speak to him. What nonsense!" said Natasha, in the tone of a man being robbed of his property. "Well, I won't marry him, so let him come, if he enjoys it and I enjoy it." Natasha looked at her mother, smiling. "Not to be married, but—just so," she repeated.

"How so, my dear?"

"Oh, just *so*. I see it's very necessary I shouldn't marry him, but . . . just *so*."

"Just so, just so," repeated the countess, and shaking all over, she went off into a good-natured, unexpectedly elderly laugh.

"Don't laugh, stop," cried Natasha; "you're shaking all the bed. You're awfully like me, just another giggler . . . Stop . . ." She snatched both the countess's hands, kissed one knuckle of the little finger, for June, and went on kissing—July, August—on the other hand. "Mamma, is he very much in love? What do you think? Were men as much in love with you? And he's very nice, very, very nice! Only not quite to my liking—he's so narrow, somehow, like a clock on the wall. . . . Don't you understand? . . . Narrow, you know, grey, light-coloured . . ."

"What nonsense you talk!" said the countess.

Natasha went on:

"Don't you really understand? Nikolenka would understand . . . Bezuhov now—he's blue, dark blue and red, and he's quadrangular."

"You're flirting with him, too," said the countess, laughing.

"No, he's a freemason, I have heard. He's jolly, dark blue and red; how am I to explain to you . . ."

"Little countess," they heard the count's voice through the door, "you're not asleep?" Natasha skipped up, snatched up her slippers, and ran barefoot to her own room. For a long while she could not go to sleep. She kept musing on no one's being able to understand all she understood and all that was in her.

"Sonya?" she wondered, looking at her friend asleep, curled up like a kitten with her great mass of hair. "No, how could she! She's virtuous. She's in love with Nikolenka and doesn't care to know anything more. Mamma, even she doesn't understand. It's wonderful how clever I am and how . . . she is charming," she went on, speaking of herself in the third person, and fancying that it was some very clever, the very cleverest and finest of men, who was saying it of her . . . "There is everything, everything in her," this man continued, "extraordinarily clever, charming and then pretty, extraordinarily pretty, graceful. She swims, rides capitally, and a voice!—a marvellous voice, one may say!" She hummed her favourite musical phrase from an opera of Cherubini, flung herself into bed, laughed with delight at the thought that she would soon be asleep, called to Dunyasha to blow out the candle; and before Dunyasha had left her room she had already passed into another still happier world of dreams, where everything was as easy and as beautiful as in reality, and was only better because it was all different.

Next day the countess sent for Boris, and talked to him, and from that day he gave up visiting at the Rostovs'.

XIV

On the 31st of December, on the eve of the new year 1810, a ball was given by a grand personage who had been a star of the court of Catherine. The Tsar and the diplomatic corps were to be present at this ball.

The well-known mansion of this grandee in the English Embankment was illuminated by innumerable lights. The police were standing at the lighted entry, laid with red baize; and not merely policemen, but a police commander was at the entrance, and dozens of officers of the police. Carriages kept driving away, and fresh ones kept driving up, with grooms in red livery and grooms in plumed hats. From the carriages emerged men wearing uniforms, stars, and ribbons; while ladies in satin and ermine stepped carefully out on the carriage steps, that were let down with a bang, and then walked hurriedly and noiselessly over the baize of the entry.

Almost every time a new carriage drove up, a whisper ran through the crowd and hats were taken off. "The Emperor? . . . No, a minister . . . prince . . . ambassador . . . Don't you see the plumes? . . ." was audible in the crowd. One person, better dressed than the rest, seemed to know every one, and mentioned by name all the most celebrated personages of the day.

A third of the guests had already arrived at this ball, while the Rostovs, who were to be present at it, were still engaged in hurried preparations.

Many had been the discussions and the preparations for that ball in the Rostov family; many the fears that an invitation might not arrive, that the dresses would not be ready, and that everything would not be arranged as it ought to be.

The Rostovs were to be accompanied by Marya Ignatyevna Peronsky, a friend and relation of the countess, a thin and yellow maid-of-honour of the old court, who was acting as a guide to the provincial Rostovs in the higher circles of Petersburg society.

At ten o'clock the Rostovs were to drive to Tavritchesky Garden to call for the maid-of-honour. Meantime it was five minutes to ten, and the young ladies were not yet dressed.

Natasha was going to her first great ball. She had got up at eight o'clock that morning, and had spent the whole day in feverish agitation and activity. All her energies had since morning been directed to the one aim of getting herself, her mother, and Sonya as well dressed as possible. Sonya and her mother put themselves entirely in her hands. The countess was to wear a dark red velvet dress; the two girls white tulle dresses over pink silk slips, and roses on their bodices. They were to wear their hair *à la grecque*.

All the essentials were ready. Feet, arms, necks, and ears had been washed, scented, and powdered with peculiar care in readiness for the ball. Openwork silk stockings and white satin shoes with ribbons had been put on. The hairdressing was almost accomplished. Sonya was finishing dressing, so was the countess; but Natasha, who had been busily looking after every one, was behindhand. She was still sitting before the looking-glass with a *peignoir* thrown over her thin shoulders. Sonya, already dressed, stood in the middle of the room, and was trying to fasten in a last ribbon, hurting her little finger as she pressed the pin with a scrooping sound into the silk.

"Not like that, Sonya, not like that!" said Natasha, turning her head, and clutching her hair in both hands, as the maid arranging it was not quick enough in letting it go. "The ribbon mustn't go like that; come here." Sonya squatted down. Natasha pinned the ribbon in her own way.

"Really, miss, you mustn't do so," said the maid, holding Natasha's hair.

"Oh, my goodness! Afterwards! There, that's right, Sonya."

"Will you soon be ready?" they heard the countess's voice. "It will be ten in a minute."

"Immediately, immediately. . . . And are you ready, mamma?"

"Only my cap to fasten on."

"Don't do it without me," shouted Natasha; "you don't know how to!"

"But its ten o'clock already."

It had been arranged to be at the ball at half-past ten, and Natasha still had to dress, and they had to drive to Tavritchesky Garden.

When her coiffure was finished, Natasha, in her mother's dressing-jacket and a short petticoat under which her dancing-shoes could be seen, ran up to Sonya, looked her over, and then ran to her mother. Turning her head round, she pinned on her cap, and hurriedly kissing her grey hair, ran back to the maids who were shortening her skirt.

All attention was now centred on Natasha's skirt, which was too long. Two maids were running it up round the edge, hurriedly biting off the threads. A third one, with pins in her teeth and lips, was running from the countess to Sonya; a fourth was holding up the whole tulle dress in her arms.

"Mavrushka, quicker, darling!"

"Give me that thimble, miss."

"Will you be quick?" said the count from outside the door, coming in. "Here are your smelling-salts. Madame Peronsky must be tired of waiting."

"Ready, miss," said the maid, lifting up the shortened tulle skirt on two fingers, blowing something off it, and giving it a shake to show her appreciation of the transparency and purity of what she had in her hands.

Natasha began putting on the dress.

"In a minute, in a minute, don't come in, papa," she shouted to her father at the door, from under the tulle of the dress that concealed all her face. Sonya slammed the door. A minute later the count was admitted. He was wearing a blue frock coat, stockings, and dancing-shoes, and was perfumed and pomaded.

"Ah, papa, how nice you look, lovely!" said Natasha, standing in the middle of the room, stroking out the folds of her tulle.

"If you please, miss, if you please . . ." said a maid, pulling up the skirt and turning the pins from one corner of her mouth to the other with her tongue.

"Say what you like!" cried Sonya, with despair in her voice, as she gazed at Natasha's skirt, "say what you like!—it's too long still!"

Natasha walked a little further off to look at herself in the pierglass. The skirt was too long.

"My goodness, madam, it's not a bit too long," said Mavrushka, creeping along the floor on her knees after her young lady.

"Well, if it's long, we'll tack it up, in one minute, we'll tack it up," said Dunyasha, a resolute character. And taking a needle out of the kerchief on her bosom she set to work again on the floor.

At that moment the countess in her cap and velvet gown walked shyly with soft steps into the room.

"Oo-oo! my beauty!" cried the count. "She looks nicer than any of you!" . . . He would have embraced her, but, flushing, she drew back to avoid being crumpled.

"Mamma, the cap should be more on one side," said Natasha. "I'll pin it fresh," and she darted forward. The maids turning up her skirt, not prepared for her hasty movement, tore off a piece of the tulle.

"Oh, mercy! What was that? Really it's not my fault . . ."

"It's all right, I'll run it up, it won't show," said Dunyasha.

"My beauty, my queen!" said the old nurse coming in at the doorway. "And Sonyushka, too; ah, the beauties! . . ."

At a quarter past ten they were at last seated in their carriage and driving off. But they still had to drive to Tavritchesky Garden.

Madame Peronsky was ready and waiting. In spite of her age and ugliness, just the same process had been going on with her as with the Rostovs, not with flurry, for with her it was a matter of routine. Her elderly and unprepossessing person had been also washed and scented and powdered; she had washed as carefully behind her ears, and like the Rostovs' nurse, her old maid had enthusiastically admired her mistress's attire, when she came into the drawing-room in her yellow gown adorned with her badge of a maid-of-honour. Madame Peronsky praised the Rostovs' costumes, and they praised her attire and her taste. Then, careful of their coiffures and their dresses, at eleven o'clock they settled themselves in the carriages and drove off.

XV

NATASHA had not had a free moment all that day, and had not once had time to think of what lay before her.

In the damp, chill air, in the closeness and half dark of the swaying carriage, she pictured to herself for the first time what was in store for her there, at the ball, in the brightly lighted halls—music, flowers, dancing, the Tsar, all the brilliant young people of Petersburg. The prospect before her was so splendid that she could not even believe that it would come to pass: so incongruous it seemed with the chilliness, darkness, and closeness of the carriage. She could only grasp all that awaited her when, walking over the red cloth, she went into the vestibule, took off her cloak, and walked beside Sonya in front of her mother between the flowers up the lighted staircase. Only then she remembered how she must behave at a ball, and tried to assume the majestic manner that she considered indispensable for a girl at a ball. But luckily she felt that there was a mist before her eyes; she could see nothing clearly, her pulse beat a hundred times a minute, and the blood throbbed at her heart. She was unable to assume the manner that would have made her absurd; and moved on, thrilling with excitement, and trying with all her might simply to conceal it. And it was just in this mood that she looked her best. In front and behind them walked guests dressed in similar ball-dresses and conversing in similarly subdued tones. The looking-glasses on the staircases reflected ladies in white, blue, and pink dresses, with diamonds and pearls on their bare arms and necks.

Natasha looked into the looking-glasses and could not distinguish herself from the rest. All was mingled into one brilliant procession. At the entrance into the first room, the regular hum of voices, footsteps, greetings, deafened Natasha; the light and brilliance dazzled her still more. The host and hostess who had been already standing at the door for half an hour, saying exactly the same words to every guest on arrival, *Charmé de vous voir,* gave the same greeting to the Rostovs and Madame Peronsky. The two young girls in their white dresses, with roses alike in their black hair, made curtsies just alike, but unconsciously the hostess's eyes rested longer on the slender figure of Natasha. She looked at her, and smiled at her a smile that was something more than the smile of welcome she had for all. Looking at her, the hostess was reminded perhaps of her golden days of girlhood, gone never to return, of her own first ball. The host too followed Natasha with his eyes, and asked the count which of the girls was his daughter.

"Charming!" he said, kissing his own finger-tips.

In the ballroom, guests stood crowding about the entry in expectation of the Tsar. The countess took up her position in the front row of this crowd. Natasha heard and felt that several voices were asking who she was, that many pairs of eyes were fixed on her. She knew that she was making a good impression on those who noticed her, and this observation calmed her somewhat.

"There are some like ourselves, and some not as good," she thought.

Madame Peronsky was pointing out to the countess the most distinguished persons at the ball.

"That is the Dutch ambassador, do you see, the grey-haired man," Madame Peronsky was saying, indicating an old man with a profusion of silver-grey curls, who was surrounded by ladies laughing at some story he was telling. "And here she comes, the queen of Petersburg society, Countess Bezuhov," she said, pointing to Ellen who had just come in.

"How lovely! She's quite equal to Marya Antonovna. Look how attentive all the men are to her, young and old alike. She's both lovely and clever. . . . They say Prince So-and-So is wild about her. And you see these two, though they are not good-looking, they are even more run after."

She pointed out a lady who was crossing the room accompanied by a very ugly daughter.

"That's the heiress of a million," said Madame Peronsky. "And, look, here come her suitors. . . . That's Countess Bezuhov's brother, Anatole Kuragin," she said, pointing to a handsome officer in the Horse Guards, who passed by them looking from the height of his lifted head over the ladies to something beyond them. "He is handsome, isn't he? They say he is to be married to that heiress. And your cousin, Drubetskoy, is very attentive to her too. They say she has millions. Oh, that's the French ambassador himself," she said in answer to the countess's inquiry as to the identity of Caulaincourt. "Just look, he's like some monarch. But yet they're nice, the French are very nice. No people more charming in society. Ah, here she is! Yes, still lovelier than any one, our Marya Antonovna! And how simply dressed! Exquisite!"

"And that stout fellow in spectacles is a universal freemason," said Madame Peronsky, indicating Bezuhov. "Set him beside his wife: he's a motley fool!"

Swinging his stout frame, Pierre slouched through the crowd, nodding to right and to left, as casually and good-naturedly as though he were walking through a crowd in a market. He made his way through the crowd unmistakably looking for some one.

Natasha looked with joy at the familiar face of Pierre, the motley fool, as Madame Peronsky called him, and knew that it was they, and she in particular, of whom Pierre was in search in the crowd. Pierre had promised her to be at the ball and to find her partners. But before reaching them, Pierre came to a standstill beside a very handsome, dark man of medium height in a white uniform, who was standing in a window talking to a tall man wearing stars and a ribbon.

Natasha at once recognised the handsome young man in the white uniform; it was Bolkonsky, who seemed to her to have grown much younger, happier, and better looking.

"There's some one else we know, Bolkonsky, do you see, mamma?" said Natasha, pointing out Prince Andrey. "Do you remember he stayed a night at home, at Otradnoe?"

"Oh, do you know him?" said Madame Peronsky. "I can't bear him. Every one is crazy over him. And his conceit! it's beyond all bounds! He takes after his worthy papa! And he's hand in glove now with Speransky, making out some sort of plans for reform. Just look how he behaves with ladies! She's speaking to him, and he has turned his back on her," she said, pointing to him. "I would soon send him about his business if he were to treat me like those ladies."

XVI

THERE was a sudden stir, the crowd began talking, rushed forward, then moved apart again, and down the space left open through it, the Tsar walked to the strains of the band, which struck up at once. Behind him walked the host and hostess. The Tsar walked in rapidly, bowing to right and to left, as though trying to hurry over the first moments of greeting. The musicians played the polonaise in vogue at the time on account of the words set to it. The words began: "Alexander, Elisaveta, our hearts ye ravish quite." The Tsar went into the drawing-room, the crowd made a dash for the door; several persons ran hurriedly to the door and back with excited faces. The crowd made another rush back, away from the drawing-room door at which the Tsar appeared in conversation with the hostess. A young man, looking distraught, pounced down on the ladies and begged them to move aside. Several, with faces that betrayed a total oblivion of all the rules of decorum, squeezed forward, to the destruction of their dresses. The men began approaching the ladies, and couples were formed for the polonaise.

There was a general movement of retreat, and the Tsar, smiling, came out of the drawing-room door, leading out the lady of the house, and not keeping time to the music. He was followed by the host with Marya Antonovna Narishkin; then came ambassadors, ministers, and various generals, whose names Madame Peronsky never tired of reciting. More than half the ladies had partners, and were taking part, or preparing to take part, in the polonaise.

Natasha felt that she would be left with her mother and Sonya in that minority of the ladies who were crowded back against the wall, and not invited to dance the polonaise. She stood, her thin arms hanging at her sides, and her scarcely outlined bosom heaving regularly. She held her breath, and gazed before her with shining, frightened eyes, with an expression of equal readiness for the utmost bliss or the utmost misery. She took no interest in the Tsar, nor in all the great people Madame Peronsky was pointing out; her mind was filled by one thought: "Is it possible no one will come up to me? Is it possible that I shall not dance among the foremost? Is it possible I shall not be noticed by all these men, who now don't even seem to see me, but if they look at me, look with an expression as though they would say: 'Ah! that's not she, so it's no use looking'?" "No, it cannot be!" she thought. "They must know how I long to dance, how well I dance, and how they would enjoy dancing with me."

The strains of the polonaise, which had already lasted some time, were beginning to sound like a melancholy reminiscence in the ears of Natasha. She wanted to cry. Madame Peronsky had left them. The count was at the other end of the ballroom, the countess, Sonya, and she stood in that crowd of strangers as lonely as in a forest, of no interest, of no use to any one. Prince Andrey with a lady passed close by them, obviously not recognising them. The handsome Anatole said something smiling to the lady on his arm, and he glanced at Natasha's face as one looks at a wall. Boris passed by them, twice, and each time turned away. Berg and his wife, who were not dancing, came towards them.

This family meeting here, in a ballroom, seemed a humiliating thing to Natasha, as though there were nowhere else for family talk but here at a ball. She did not listen, and did not look at Vera, who said something to her about her own green dress.

At last the Tsar stood still beside the last of his partners (he had danced with three), the music ceased. An anxious-looking adjutant ran up to the Rostovs, begging them to move a little further back, though they were already close to the wall, and from the orchestra came the circumspect, precise, seductively, stately rhythm of the waltz. The Tsar glanced with a smile down the ballroom. A moment passed; no one had yet begun. An adjutant, who was a steward, went up to Countess Bezuhov and asked her to dance. Smiling, she raised her hand and laid it on the adjutant's shoulder without looking at him. The adjutant-steward, a master of his art, grasped his partner firmly, and with confident deliberation and smoothness broke with her into the first gallop round the edge of the circle, then at the corner of the ballroom caught his partner's left hand, turned her; and through the quickening strains of the music nothing could be heard but the regular jingle of the spurs on the adjutant's rapid, practised feet, and at every third beat the swish of his partner's flying velvet skirt as she whirled round.

Natasha looked at them, and was ready to cry that it was not she dancing that first round of the waltz.

Prince Andrey, in his white uniform of a cavalry colonel, wearing stockings and dancing-shoes, stood looking eager and lively, in the front of the ring not far from the Rostovs. Baron Firhoff was talking to him of the proposed first sitting of the State Council to be held next day. From his intimacy with Speransky, and the part he was taking in the labours of the legislative commission, Prince Andrey was in a position to give authoritative information in regard to that sitting, about which the most diverse rumours were current. But he did not hear what Firhoff was saying to him, and looked from the Tsar to the gentlemen preparing to dance, who had not yet stepped out into the ring.

Prince Andrey was watching these gentlemen, who were timid in the presence of the Tsar, and the ladies, who were dying to be asked to dance.

Pierre went up to Prince Andrey and took him by the arm.

"You always dance. Here is my protégée, the younger Rostov girl, ask her," he said.

"Where?" asked Bolkonsky. "I beg your pardon," he said, turning to the baron, "we will finish this conversation in another place, but at a ball one must dance." He went forward in the direction indicated by

Pierre. Natasha's despairing, tremulous face broke upon Prince Andrey. He recognised her, guessed her feelings, saw that it was her début, remembered what she had said at the window, and with an expression of pleasure on his face he approached Countess Rostov.

"Permit me to introduce you to my daughter," said the countess, reddening.

"I have the pleasure of her acquaintance already, if the countess remembers me," said Prince Andrey, with a low and courteous bow, which seemed a direct contradiction to Madame Peronsky's remarks about his rudeness. He went up to Natasha, and raised his hand to put it round her waist before he had fully uttered the invitation to dance. He proposed a waltz to her. The tremulous expression of Natasha's face, ready for despair or for ecstasy, brightened at once into a happy, grateful, childlike smile.

"I have been a long while waiting for you," that alarmed and happy young girl seemed to say to him in the smile that peeped out through the starting tears as she raised her hand to Prince Andrey's shoulder. They were the second couple that walked forward into the ring.

Prince Andrey was one of the best dancers of his day. Natasha danced exquisitely. Her little feet in their satin dancing-shoes performed their task lightly and independently of her, and her face beamed with a rapture of happiness.

Her bare neck and arms were thin, and not beautiful compared with Ellen's shoulders. Her shoulders were thin, her bosom undefined, her arms were slender. But Ellen was, as it were, covered with the hard varnish of those thousands of eyes that had scanned her person, while Natasha seemed like a young girl stripped for the first time, who would have been greatly ashamed if she had not been assured by every one that it must be so.

Prince Andrey loved dancing. He was anxious to escape as quickly as he could from the political and intellectual conversations into which every one tried to draw him, and anxious too to break through that burdensome barrier of constraint arising from the presence of the Tsar; so he made haste to dance, and chose Natasha for a partner because Pierre pointed her out to him, and because she was the first pretty girl who caught his eyes. But he had no sooner put his arm round that slender, supple waist, and felt her stirring so close to him, and smiling so close to him, than the intoxication of her beauty flew to his head. He felt full of life and youth again as, drawing a deep breath, he brought her to a standstill and began to watch the other couples.

XVII

AFTER Prince Andrey, Boris came up to ask Natasha to dance, and he was followed by the dancing adjutant who had opened the ball, and many other young men. Natasha, flushed and happy, passed on her superfluous partners to Sonya, and never ceased dancing all the evening. She noticed nothing and saw nothing of what was absorbing every one else at that ball. She did not notice that the Tsar talked a long time with the French ambassador, that his manner was particularly gracious to a certain lady, that Prince So-and-So and Mr. So-and-So had said and done this and that, that Ellen's success had been brilliant, and that So-and-So had paid her marked attention. She did not even see the Tsar, and was only aware that he was gone from noticing that the ball became livelier after his departure.

In one of the most enjoyable cotillions before supper, Prince Andrey danced again with Natasha. He reminded her of how he had first seen her in the avenue at Otradnoe, and how she could not sleep on that moonlight night, and told her how he had unwittingly listened to her. Natasha blushed at these recollections, and tried as it were to excuse herself, as though there were something to be ashamed of in the emotion to which Prince Andrey had unwittingly played the eavesdropper.

Like all men who have grown up in society, Prince Andrey liked meeting anything not of the conventional society stamp. And such was Natasha with her wonder, her delight, her shyness, and even her mistakes in talking French. His manner was particularly tender and circumspect as he talked to her. Sitting beside her, and talking of the simplest and most trifling subjects, Prince Andrey admired the radiant brilliance of her eyes and her smile, that had no concern with what was said but was due simply to her own happiness. When Natasha was chosen again, and she got up with a smile and was dancing, Prince Andrey particularly admired her shy grace. In the middle of the cotillion, Natasha went back to her place, breathless at the end of a figure. Another partner again chose her. She was tired and panting, and evidently she thought for an instant of refusing, but immediately she put her hand on her partner's shoulder and was off again gaily, smiling to Prince Andrey.

"I should have been glad to rest and sit by you. I'm tired; but you see how they keep asking me, and I'm glad of it, and I'm happy, and I love every one, and you and I understand all about it," and more, much more was said in that smile. When her partner left her side, Natasha flew across the room to choose two ladies for the figure.

"If she goes first to her cousin and then to another lady, she will be my wife," Prince Andrey—greatly to his own surprise—caught himself saying mentally, as he watched her. She did go first to her cousin.

"What nonsense does sometimes come into one's mind!" thought Prince Andrey, "but one thing's certain, that girl is so charming, so original, that she won't be dancing here a month before she will be married. . . . She's a rare thing here," he thought, as Natasha settled herself beside him, sticking in the rose that was falling out of her bodice.

At the end of the cotillion, the old count in his blue frock coat went up to the young people who had been dancing. He invited Prince Andrey to come and see them, and asked his daughter whether she were enjoying herself. Natasha did not at once answer, she only smiled a smile that said reproachfully: "How can you ask such a question?"

"Enjoying myself as I never have before in my life!" she said, and Prince Andrey noticed how her thin arms were swiftly raised as though to embrace her father, and dropped again at once. Natasha was happy as she had never been in her life. She was at that highest pitch of happiness, when one becomes completely good and kind, and disbelieves in the very possibility of evil, unhappiness, and sorrow.

At that ball Pierre for the first time felt humiliated by the position his wife took in the highest court circle. He was sullen and absent-minded. There was a broad furrow right across his forehead, as he stood in a window, staring over his spectacles and seeing no one. Natasha passed close by him on her way in to supper. Pierre's gloomy, unhappy face struck her. She stopped, facing him. She longed to come to his aid, to bestow on him some of her own overflowing happiness. "How delightful it is," she said; "isn't it?"

Pierre smiled an absent-minded smile, obviously not grasping what was said to him. "Yes, I'm very glad," he said.

"How can people be discontented at anything!" thought Natasha. "Especially any one as nice as Bezuhov."

In Natasha's eyes all the people at the ball were particularly kind, sweet, good people, loving one another; none were capable of wronging one another, and so all must be happy.

XVIII

NEXT day when Prince Andrey thought of the ball it did not occupy his mind for long. "Yes, it was a very successful ball. And besides . . . yes, the younger Rostov is very charming. There's something fresh in her, original, unlike Petersburg." That was all he thought about the previous day's ball, and after his morning tea he set to work.

But from fatigue and want of sleep he was not very well disposed for work, and could get nothing done. He was continually criticising his own work—a habit common with him—and was glad when he heard a visitor arrive.

The visitor was Bitsky, a man who was a member of various committees and of all the societies in Petersburg. He was a passionate adherent of the new ideas and of Speransky, and the busiest purveyor of news in Petersburg, one of those men who choose their opinions like their clothes—according to the fashion—but for that very reason seem the most vehement partisans. Scarcely waiting to remove his hat, he ran fussily up to Prince Andrey, and at once began talking. He had just learned particulars of the sitting of the State Council of that morning, opened by the Tsar, and began enthusiastically upon the subject. The Tsar's speech had been, he said, an extraordinary one. It had been a speech such as are only delivered by constitutional monarchs. "The Emperor directly asserted that the Council and the Senate are the estates of the realm; he said that government should be founded, not on arbitrary authority, but on a *secure basis*. The Emperor said that the fiscal system must be reconstituted and the accounts must be public," Bitsky announced, laying stress on certain words, and opening his eyes significantly. "Yes, to-day's sitting marks an epoch, the greatest epoch in our history," he concluded.

Prince Andrey heard his account of the opening of the State Council, to which he had been looking forward with such eagerness, and to which he had attached so much consequence, and was amazed that now, when it had come to pass, this event, far from affecting him, struck him as less than insignificant. With quiet irony he listened to Bitsky's enthusiastic description. The idea in his mind was of the simplest. "What is it to me and Bitsky," he thought, "what is it to us, whatever the Emperor is pleased to say in the Council? Can all that make me any happier or better?"

And this simple reflection suddenly destroyed all Prince Andrey's former interest in the reforms that were being made. That day Prince Andrey was to dine with Speransky, "with only a few friends," as the host had said in inviting him. That dinner, in the intimate home circle of the man who had so fascinated him, had seemed very attractive to Prince Andrey, especially as he had not hitherto seen Speransky in his home surroundings. But now he had no wish to go to it.

At the hour fixed,. however, Prince Andrey was entering the small house in Tavritchesky Garden. The little house, which was Speransky's property, was distinguished by an extraordinary cleanliness, suggestive of the cleanliness of a convent. In the parqueted dining-room, Prince Andrey, who was a little late, found all that circle of Speransky's intimate friends already gathered together at five o'clock. There were no ladies present, except Speransky's little daughter (with a long face like her father's) and her governess. The guests were Gervais, Magnitsky and Stolypin. From the vestibule Prince Andrey had caught the sound of loud voices and a ringing, staccato laugh—a laugh such as one hears on the stage. Some one—it sounded like Speransky—was giving vent to a staccato "ha . . . ha . . . ha . . ." Prince Andrey had never before heard Speransky laugh, and this shrill, ringing laugh from the great statesman made a strange impression on him.

Prince Andrey went into the dining-room. The whole party were standing between the two windows at a little table laid with *hors d'œuvres*. Speransky was standing at the table with a mirthful countenance, wearing a grey frock coat with a star, and the white waistcoat and high white stock, in which he had been at the famous sitting of the State Council. His guests formed a ring round him. Turning towards him Magnitsky was relating an anecdote. Speransky listened, laughing beforehand at what Magnitsky was going to say. Just as Prince Andrey walked into the room, Magnitsky's words were again drowned in laughter. Stolypin gave vent to a bass guffaw as he munched a piece of bread and cheese. Gervais softly hissed a chuckle, and Speransky laughed his shrill, staccato laugh.

Speransky, still laughing, gave Prince Andrey his soft, white hand. "Very glad to see you, prince," he said. "One minute . . ." he turned to Magnitsky, whose tale he was interrupting. "We have made a compact to-day; this is a holiday dinner, and not one word about business." And he turned again to the story-teller, and again he laughed.

With a sense of wondering and melancholy disillusion, Prince Andrey heard his laughter and looked at Speransky laughing. It was not Speransky, but some other man, it seemed to Prince Andrey. All that had seemed mysterious and attractive in Speransky suddenly seemed to Prince Andrey obvious and unattractive.

At dinner the conversation never paused for a moment, and consisted of something like the contents of a jest-book. Magnitsky had hardly finished his anecdote when another gentleman expressed his readiness to relate something even more amusing. The anecdotes for the most part related, if not to the service itself, to persons prominent in the service. It was as though in this circle the utter insignificance of these prominent persons was so completely accepted that the only attitude possible towards them was one of good-humoured hilarity. Speransky told them how at the council that morning a deaf statesman, on being asked his opinion, replied that he was of the same opinion. Gervais described a whole episode of the revision, only remarkable for the imbecility of all concerned in it. Stolypin, stammering, took up the conversation and began talking of the abuses of the old order of things, with a warmth that threatened to give the conversation a serious turn. Magnitsky began to make fun of Stolypin's earnestness. Gervais put in his joke, and the conversation resumed its former lively tone. It was obvious that after his labours Speransky liked to rest and be amused in the circle of his friends; and all his friends understood his tastes, and were trying to amuse him and themselves. But this kind of gaiety seemed to Prince Andrey tiresome and anything but gay. Speransky's high voice struck him unpleasantly, and his continual laugh in its high-pitched, falsetto note was for some reason an offence to Prince Andrey's feelings. Prince Andrey did not laugh, and was afraid he would be felt uncongenial by this party. But no one noticed his lack of sympathy with the general merriment. All of them appeared to be greatly enjoying themselves.

Several times he tried to enter into the conversation, but every time the word was snatched out of his mouth, like a cork out of water, and he could not bandy jokes with them. There was nothing wrong or unseemly in what they said; it was all witty, and might have been amusing, but something—that very something that makes the zest of gaiety —was wanting, and they did not even know of its existence.

After dinner Speransky's daughter and her governess rose from the table. Speransky patted his daughter with his white hand, and kissed her. And that gesture, too, seemed to Prince Andrey unnatural.

The men sat on over their port, after the English fashion. A conversation sprang up about Napoleon's doings in Spain, of which all were united in approving, while Prince Andrey attacked them. But in the

middle of this discussion Speransky, obviously wishing to change the
subject, began with a smile telling an anecdote, which had no connection
with it. For several instants every one was silent.

As they sat at table, Speransky, corking up a bottle of wine and saying, "Nowadays good wine doesn't go a-begging!" gave it to the servant
and got up. All rose, and talking just as noisily, went into the drawing-
room. Speransky was handed two envelopes brought by a special courier.
He took them and went into his study. As soon as he had gone, there
was a lull in the general gaiety, and the guests began conversing sensibly
in low tones together.

"Well, now for the recitation!" said Speransky, coming out of his
study. "A marvellous talent!" he said to Prince Andrey. Magnitsky at
once threw himself into an attitude, and began to recite comic French
verses, a skit he had composed on various well-known persons. Several
times he was interrupted by applause. At the conclusion of the recitation
Prince Andrey went up to Speransky to say good-bye.

"Why so early?" said Speransky.

"I promised to be at a *soirée*. . . ."

They said no more. Prince Andrey looked at those mirror-like, impenetrable eyes, so close to his, and he felt it ludicrous that he should
have expected anything from Speransky, and from all his own work
connected with him, and marvelled how he could have ascribed any
value to what Speransky was doing. That punctual, mirthless laugh was
ringing in Prince Andrey's ears long after he had left Speransky's.

On reaching home Prince Andrey began looking at his life in Petersburg during the last four months, as though it were something new. He
thought of the efforts he had made, and the people he had tried to see,
and the history of his project of army reform, which had been accepted
for consideration, and had been shelved because another scheme, a very
poor one, had already been worked out and presented to the Tsar. He
thought of the sittings of the committee, of which Berg was a member.
He thought of the conscientious and prolonged deliberations that took
place at those sittings on every point relating to the formalities of the
sittings themselves, and the studious brevity with which anything relating to the reality of their duties was touched on in passing. He
thought of his work on the legislative reforms, of his careful translation
of the Roman and French codes into Russian, and he felt ashamed of
himself. Then he vividly imagined Bogutcharovo, his pursuits in the
country, his expedition to Ryazan; he thought of his peasants, of Dron
the village elder; and applying the section on Personal Rights, which he
had divided into paragraphs, to them, he marvelled how he could have
so long busied himself on work so idle.

XIX

THE next day Prince Andrey paid calls on various people whom he had not visited before, and among them on the Rostovs, with whom he had renewed his acquaintance at the ball. Apart from considerations of politeness, which necessitated a call on the Rostovs, Prince Andrey wanted to see at home that original, eager girl, who had left such a pleasant recollection with him.

Natasha was one of the first to meet him. She was in a blue everyday dress, in which she struck Prince Andrey as looking prettier than in her ball-dress. She and all the family received Prince Andrey like an old friend, simply and cordially. All the family, which Prince Andrey had once criticised so severely, now seemed to him to consist of excellent, simple, kindly people. The hospitality and good-nature of the old count, particularly striking and attractive in Petersburg, was such that Prince Andrey could not refuse to stay to dinner. "Yes, these are good-natured, capital people," thought Bolkonsky. "Of course they have no conception, what a treasure they possess in Natasha; but they are good people, who make the best possible background for the strikingly poetical figure of that charming girl, so full of life!"

Prince Andrey was conscious in Natasha of a special world, utterly remote from him, brimful of joys unknown to him, that strange world, which even in the avenue at Otradnoe, and on that moonlight night at the window had tantalised him. Now that no longer tantalised him, it seemed no longer an alien world; but he himself was stepping into it, and finding new pleasures in it.

After dinner Natasha went to the clavichord, at Prince Andrey's request, and began singing. Prince Andrey stood at the window talking to the ladies, and listened to her. In the middle of a phrase, Prince Andrey ceased speaking, and felt suddenly a lump in his throat from tears, the possibility of which he had not dreamed of in himself. He looked at Natasha singing, and something new and blissful stirred in his soul. He was happy, and at the same time he was sad. He certainly had nothing to weep about, but he was ready to weep. For what? For his past love? For the little princess? For his lost illusions? . . . For his hopes for the future? . . . Yes, and no. The chief thing which made him ready to weep was a sudden, vivid sense of the fearful contrast between something infinitely great and illimitable existing in him, and something limited and material, which he himself was, and even she was. This contrast made his heart ache, and rejoiced him while she was singing.

As soon as Natasha had finished singing, she went up to him, and asked how she liked her voice. She asked this, and was abashed after saying it, conscious that she ought not to have asked such a question. He smiled, looking at her, and said he liked her singing, as he liked everything she did.

It was late in the evening when Prince Andrey left the Rostovs'. He went to bed from the habit of going to bed, but soon saw that he could not sleep. He lighted a candle and sat up in bed; then got up, then lay down again, not in the least wearied by his sleeplessness: he felt a new joy in his soul, as though he had come out of a stuffy room into the open daylight. It never even occurred to him that he was in love with this little Rostov girl. He was not thinking about her. He only pictured her to himself, and the whole of life rose before him in a new light as he did so. "Why do I struggle? Why am I troubled in this narrow, cramped routine, when life, all life, with all its joys, lies open before me?" he said to himself. And for the first time for a very long while, he began making happy plans for the future. He made up his mind that he ought to look after his son's education, to find a tutor, and entrust the child to him. Then he ought to retire from the army, and go abroad, see England, Switzerland, Italy. "I must take advantage of my liberty, while I feel so much youth and strength in me," he told himself. "Pierre was right in saying that one must believe in the possibility of happiness, in order to be happy, and now I do believe in it. Let us leave the dead to bury the dead; but while one is living, one must live and be happy," he thought.

XX

ONE morning Colonel Adolphe Berg, whom Pierre knew just as he knew every one in Moscow and Petersburg, called upon him. He was wearing a brand-new uniform, and had his powdered locks standing up over his forehead, as worn by the Tsar Alexander Pavlovitch.

"I have just been calling on the countess, your spouse, and to my misfortune, my request could not be granted. I hope I shall be more fortunate with you, count," he said, smiling.

"What is it you desire, colonel? I am at your disposal."

"I am by now, quite settled in my new quarters," Berg informed him, with perfect conviction that to hear this fact could not but be agreeable; "and so I was desirous of giving a little *soirée* for my friends and my spouse." (He smiled still more blandly.) "I meant to ask the countess and you to do me the honour to come to us for a cup of tea, and . . . to supper."

Only the Countess Elena Vassilyevna, who considered it beneath her to associate with nobodies like the Bergs, could have had the cruelty to refuse such an invitation. Berg explained so clearly why he wanted to gather together a small and select company at his new rooms; and why it would be agreeable to him to do so; and why he would grudge spending money on cards, or anything else harmful; but was ready for the sake of good society to incur expense, that Pierre could not refuse, and promised to come.

"Only not late, count, if I may venture to beg. Ten minutes to eight, I venture to beg. We will make up a party for boston. Our general is coming; he is very kind to me. We will have a little supper, count, so I shall esteem it an honour."

Contrary to his usual habit (he was almost always late) Pierre arrived at the Bergs' not at ten minutes to eight, but at a quarter to eight.

The Bergs had made all necessary preparations for their little party, and were quite ready to receive their guests.

Berg and his wife were sitting in a new, clean, light study, furnished with little busts and pictures and new furniture. Berg, with his new uniform closely buttoned up, sat beside his wife, and was explaining to her that one always could and ought to cultivate the acquaintance of people above one—for only then is there anything agreeable in acquaintances. "You pick up something, you can put in a word for something. Look at me now, how I used to manage in the lower grades" (Berg reckoned his life not by years but by promotions). "My comrades are nothing still, while I'm a lieutenant-colonel. I have the happiness of being your husband" (he got up and kissed Vera's hand, but on the way turned back the corner of the rug, which was rucked-up). "And how did I obtain all this? Chiefly by knowing how to select my acquaintances. It goes without saying, of course, that one has to be conscientious and punctual in the discharge of one's duties."

Berg smiled with a sense of his own superiority over a mere weak woman, and paused, reflecting that this charming wife of his was, after all, a weak woman, who could never attain all that constituted a man's dignity,—*ein Mann zu sein*. Vera smiled, too, at the same time with a sense of her superiority over her conscientious, excellent husband, who yet, like all men, according to Vera's ideas of them, took such a mistaken view of life. Berg, judging from his wife, considered all women weak and foolish. Vera, judging from her husband only, and generalising from her observation of him, supposed that all men ascribed common-sense to none but themselves, and at the same time had no understanding for anything, and were conceited and egoistic.

Berg got up, and cautiously embracing his wife so as not to crush the lace bertha, for which he had paid a round sum, he kissed her just on her lips.

"There's only one thing: we mustn't have children too soon," he said, by a connection of ideas of which he was himself unconscious.

"Yes," answered Vera, "I don't at all desire that. We must live for society."

"Princess Yusupov was wearing one just like that," said Berg, pointing with a happy and good-humoured smile to the bertha.

At that moment they were informed that Count Bezuhov had arrived. Both the young couple exchanged glances of self-satisfaction, each mentally claiming the credit of this visit.

"See what comes of knowing how to make acquaintances," thought Berg. "See what comes of behaving properly!"

"But, please, when I am entertaining guests," said Vera, "don't you interrupt me, because I know with what to entertain each of them, and what to say in the company of different people."

Berg, too, smiled.

"Oh, but sometimes men must have their masculine conversation," he said.

Pierre was shown into the little drawing-room, in which it was impossible to sit down without disturbing the symmetry, tidiness, and order; and consequently it was quite comprehensible, and not strange, that Berg should magnanimously offer to disturb the symmetry of the arm-chair or of the sofa for an honoured guest, and apparently finding himself in miserable indecision in the matter, should leave his guest to solve the question of selection. Pierre destroyed the symmetry, moved out a chair for himself, and Berg and Vera promptly began their *soirée*, interrupting each other in their efforts to entertain their guest.

Vera, deciding in her own mind that Pierre ought to be entertained with conversation about the French Embassy, promptly embarked upon that subject. Berg, deciding that masculine conversation was what was required, interrupted his wife's remarks by reference to the question of war with Austria, and made an unconscious jump from that general subject to personal considerations upon the proposal made him to take part in the Austrian campaign, and the reasons which had led him to decline it. Although the conversation was extremely disconnected, and Vera resented the intervention of the masculine element, both the young people felt with satisfaction that although only one guest was present, the *soirée* had begun very well, and that their *soirée* was as like every other *soirée* as two drops of water,—with the same conversation and tea and lighted candles.

The next to arrive was Boris, an old comrade of Berg's. There was a certain shade of patronage and condescension in his manner to Berg and Vera. After Boris came the colonel and his lady, then the general himself, then the Rostovs, and the *soirée* now began to be exactly, incontestably, like all other *soirées*. Berg and Vera could hardly repress their smiles of glee at the sight of all this movement in their drawing-room, at the sound of the disconnected chatter, and the rustle of skirts and of curtsies. Everything was precisely as everybody always has it; especially so was the general, who admired their rooms, clapped Berg on the shoulder, and with paternal authority insisted on arranging the table for boston. The general sat by Count Ilya Andreivitch, as the guest next in precedence to himself. The elderly guests were together, the younger people together, the hostess at the tea-table, on which there were cakes in the silver cake-basket exactly like the cakes at the Panins' *soirée*. Everything was precisely like what everybody else had.

XXI

PIERRE, as one of the most honoured guests, was obliged to sit down to boston with the old count, the general, and the colonel. As he sat at the boston-table he happened to be directly facing Natasha and he was struck by the curious change that had come over her since the day of the ball. Natasha was silent, and not only was she not so pretty as she had been at the ball, she would have been positively plain but for the look of gentle indifference to everything in her face.

"What is wrong with her?" Pierre wondered, glancing at her. She was sitting by her sister at the tea-table; she gave reluctant answers to Boris at her side and did not look at him. After playing all of one suit and taking five tricks to his partner's satisfaction, Pierre, having caught the sound of greetings and the steps of some one entering while he took his tricks glanced at her again.

"Why, what has happened to her?" he said to himself in still greater wonder.

Prince Andrey was standing before her saying something to her with an expression of guarded tenderness on his face. She, lifting her head, was looking at him, flushing crimson, and visibly trying to control her breathing, which came in panting gasps. And the vivid glow of some inner fire that had been quenched before was alight in her again. She was utterly transformed. From a plain girl she was once more the beautiful creature she had been at the ball.

Prince Andrey went up to Pierre, and Pierre noticed a new, youthful expression in his friend's face. Several times Pierre changed his seat during the play, sitting sometimes with his back to Natasha, sometimes facing her, and during all the six rubbers he was observing her and his friend.

"Something very serious is happening between them," thought Pierre, and a feeling at once of gladness and of bitterness made him agitated and forgetful of the game.

After six rubbers the general got up, saying it was of no use playing like that, and Pierre was at liberty. Natasha, at one side of the room, was talking to Sonya and Boris. Vera, with a subtle smile, was saying something to Prince Andrey. Pierre went up to his friend, and, asking whether they were talking secrets, sat down beside them. Vera, noticing Prince Andrey's attention to Natasha, felt that at a *soirée*, at a real *soirée*, it was absolutely necessary there should be delicate allusions to the tender passion, and seizing an opportunity when Prince Andrey was alone, began a conversation with him upon the emotions generally, and her sister in particular. She felt that, with a guest so intellectual as she considered Prince Andrey, she must put all her diplomatic tact into the task before her. When Pierre went up to them he noticed that Vera was in full flow of self-complacent talk, while Prince Andrey seemed embarrassed—a thing that rarely happened to him.

"What do you think?" Vera was saying with a subtle smile. "You, prince, have so much penetration and see into people's characters at once. What do you think about Natalie? Is she capable of constancy in her attachments? Is she capable, like other women" (Vera meant herself) "of loving a man once for all and remaining faithful to him for ever? That's what I regard as true love! What do you think, prince?"

"I know your sister too little," answered Prince Andrey, with a sarcastic smile, under which he tried to conceal his embarrassment, "to decide a question so delicate; and, besides, I have noticed that the less attractive a woman is, the more constant she is apt to be," he added, and he looked at Pierre, who at that moment joined them.

"Yes, that is true, prince. In these days," pursued Vera (talking of "these days," as persons of limited intellect as a rule love to do, supposing they have discovered and estimated the peculiarities of the times, and that human characteristics do change with the times), "in these days a girl has so much liberty that the pleasure of being paid attention often stifles these feelings in her. And Natalie, it must be confessed, is very susceptible on that side."

This going back to Natasha again made Prince Andrey contract his brows disagreeably. He tried to get up, but Vera persisted with a still more subtle smile.

"Nobody, I imagine, has been so much run after as she has," Vera went on; "but no one, until quite of late, has ever made a serious impression on her. Of course, you know, count," she turned to Pierre, "even our charming cousin, Boris, who, *entre nous*, was very, very far gone in the region of the tender passion . . ." She intended an allusion to the map of love then in fashion.

Prince Andrey scowled, and was mute.

"But, of course, you are a friend of Boris's?" Vera said to him.

"Yes, I know him. . . ."

"He has probably told you of his childish love for Natasha?"

"Oh, was there a childish love between them?" asked Prince Andrey, with a sudden, unexpected flush on his face.

"Yes. You know between cousins the close intimacy often leads to love. Cousinhood is a dangerous neighbourhood. Isn't it?"

"Oh, not a doubt of it," said Prince Andrey, and with sudden and unnatural liveliness, he began joking with Pierre about the necessity of his being careful with his cousins at Moscow, ladies of fifty, and in the middle of these jesting remarks he got up, and taking Pierre's arm, drew him aside.

"Well, what is it?" said Pierre, who had been watching in wonder his friend's excitement, and noticed the glance he turned upon Natasha as he got up.

"I must, I must talk to you," said Prince Andrey. "You know that pair of women's gloves" (he referred to the masonic gloves given to a newly initiated brother to be entrusted to the woman he loved). "I . . . but no, I will talk to you later on. . . ." And with a strange light in his eyes and a restlessness in his movements, Prince Andrey approached Natasha and sat down beside her. Pierre saw that Prince Andrey asked her some question, and she answered him, flushing hotly.

But at that moment Berg approached Pierre, and insisted upon his taking part in an argument between the general and the colonel on affairs in Spain.

Berg was satisfied and happy. The smile of glee never left his face. The *soirée* was a great success, and exactly like other *soirées* he had seen. Everything was precisely similar: the ladies' refined conversation, and the cards, and after the cards the general raising his voice and the samovar and the tea cakes; but one thing was still lacking, which he had always seen at *soirées,* and wished to imitate. There was still wanting the usual loud conversation between the gentlemen and discussion about some serious intellectual question. The general had started that conversation, and Berg drew Pierre into it.

XXII

Next day Prince Andrey went to dine at the Rostovs', as Count Ilya Andreitch had invited him, and spent the whole day with them.

Every one in the house perceived on whose account Prince Andrey came, and he openly tried to be all day long with Natasha.

Not only in the soul of Natasha—scared, but happy and enthusiastic —in the whole household, too, there were a feeling of awe, of something of great gravity being bound to happen. With sorrowful and sternly serious eyes the countess looked at Prince Andrey as he talked to Natasha, and shyly and self-consciously tried to begin some insignificant talk with him as soon as he looked round at her. Sonya was afraid to leave Natasha, and afraid of being in their way if she stayed with them. Natasha turned pale in a panic of expectation every time she was left for a moment alone with him. Prince Andrey's timidity impressed her. She felt that he wanted to tell her something, but could not bring himself up to the point.

When Prince Andrey had gone away in the evening, the countess went up to Natasha and whispered:

"Well?"

"Mamma, for God's sake, don't ask me anything just now. This one can't talk of," said Natasha.

But in spite of this answer, Natasha lay a long while in her mother's bed that night, her eyes fixed before her, excited and scared by turns. She told her how he had praised her, how he had said he was going abroad, how he had asked where they were going to spend the summer, and how he had asked her about Boris.

"But anything like this, like this . . . I have never felt before!" she said. "Only I'm afraid with him, I'm always afraid with him. What does that mean? Does it mean that it's the real thing? Mamma, are you asleep?"

"No, my darling. I'm afraid of him myself," answered her mother. "Go to bed."

"Anyhow, I shouldn't go to sleep. How stupid sleep is! Mamma, mamma, nothing like this have I ever felt before," she said, with wonder and terror at the feeling she recognised in herself. "And could we ever have dreamed! . . ."

It seemed to Natasha that she had fallen in love with Prince Andrey the first time she saw him at Otradnoe. She was as it were terrified at

this strange, unexpected happiness that the man she had chosen even
then (she was firmly convinced that she had done so)—that very man
should meet them again now and be apparently not indifferent to her.

"And it seems as though it all happened on purpose—his coming to
Petersburg just while we are here. And our meeting at that ball. It was
all fate. It's clear that it is fate, that it has all led up to this. Even then,
as soon as I saw him, I felt something quite different."

"What has he said to you? What are those verses? Read them . . ."
said the mother thoughtfully, referring to the verses Prince Andrey had
written in Natasha's album.

"Mamma, does it matter his being a widower?"

"Hush, Natasha. Pray to God. Marriages are made in heaven," she
said, quoting the French proverb.

"Mamma, darling, how I love you! how happy I am!" cried Natasha,
shedding tears of excitement and happiness and hugging her mother.

At that very time Prince Andrey was telling Pierre of his love for Natasha and of his fixed determination to marry her.

That evening the Countess Elena Vassilyevna gave a reception; the
French ambassador was there, and a royal prince who had become a
very frequent visitor at the countess's of late and many brilliant ladies
and gentlemen. Pierre came down to it, wandered through the rooms and
impressed all the guests by his look of concentrated preoccupation and
gloom.

Pierre had been feeling one of his attacks of nervous depression
coming upon him ever since the day of the ball and had been making
desperate efforts to struggle against it. Since his wife's intrigue with the
royal prince, Pierre had been to his surprise appointed a kammerherr,
and ever since he had felt a sense of weariness and shame in court society, and his old ideas of the vanity of all things human began to come
back oftener and oftener. The feeling he had lately noticed between his
protégée Natasha and Prince Andrey had aggravated his gloom by the
contrast between his own position and his friend's. He tried equally to
avoid thinking of his wife and also of Natasha and Prince Andrey. Again
everything seemed to him insignificant in comparison with eternity;
again the question rose before him: "What for?" And for days and
nights together he forced himself to work at masonic labours, hoping to
keep off the evil spirit. Pierre had come out of the countess's apartments
at midnight, and was sitting in a shabby dressing-gown at the table in
his own low-pitched, smoke-blackened room upstairs, copying out long
transactions of the Scottish freemasons, when some one came into his
room. It was Prince Andrey.

"Oh, it's you," said Pierre, with a preoccupied and dissatisfied air.
"I'm at work, you see," he added, pointing to the manuscript book with
that look of escaping from the ills of life with which unhappy people
look at their work.

Prince Andrey stood before Pierre with a radiant, ecstatic face, full of new life, and with the egoism of happiness smiled at him without noticing his gloomy face.

"Well, my dear boy," he said, "I wanted to tell you yesterday, and I have come to do so to-day. I have never felt anything like it. I am in love."

Pierre suddenly heaved a heavy sigh, and dumped down his heavy person on the sofa beside Prince Andrey.

"With Natasha Rostov, yes?" he said.

"Yes, yes, who else could it be? I would never have believed it, but the feeling is too strong for me. Yesterday I was in torment, in agony, but I would not exchange that agony even for anything in the world. I have never lived till now, but I cannot live without her. But can she love me? . . . I'm too old for her. . . . Why don't you speak? . . ."

"I? I? What did I tell you?" said Pierre, suddenly getting up and walking about the room. "I always thought so. . . . That girl is a treasure. . . . She's a very rare sort of girl. . . . My dear fellow, don't, I entreat you, be too wise, don't doubt, marry, marry, marry! . . . And I am sure no man was ever happier than you will be."

"But she?"

"She loves you."

"Don't talk nonsense . . ." said Prince Andrey, smiling and looking into Pierre's face.

"She loves you, I know it," Pierre cried angrily.

"No; do listen," said Prince Andrey, taking hold of him by the arm and stopping him. "Do you know the state I am in? I must talk about it to some one."

"Well, well, talk away, I'm very glad," said Pierre, and his face did really change, the line of care in his brow was smoothed away, and he listened gladly to Prince Andrey. His friend seemed, and was indeed, an utterly different, new man. What had become of his ennui, his contempt of life, his disillusionment? Pierre was the only person to whom he could have brought himself to speak quite openly; but to him he did reveal all that was in his heart. Readily and boldly he made plans reaching far into the future; said he could not sacrifice his own happiness to the caprices of his father; declared that he would force his father to agree to the marriage and like her, or dispense with his consent altogether; then he marvelled at the feeling which had taken possession of him, as something strange, and apart, independent of himself.

"I should never have believed it, if any one had told me I could love like this," said Prince Andrey. "It is utterly different from the feeling I once had. The whole world is split into two halves for me: one—she, and there all is happiness, hope, and light; the other half—all where she is not, there all is dejection and darkness. . . ."

"Darkness and gloom," repeated Pierre; "yes, yes, I understand that."

"I can't help loving the light; that's not my fault; and I am very happy. Do you understand me? I know you are glad for me."

"Yes, yes," Pierre assented, looking at his friend with eyes full of tenderness and sadness. The brighter the picture of Prince Andrey's fate before his mind, the darker seemed his own.

XXIII

To get married his father's consent was wanted, and to obtain this Prince Andrey set off to see his father.

The father received his son's communication with external composure, but with inward wrath. He could not comprehend how any one could want to alter his life, to introduce any new element into it, when life was for him so near its end. "If they would only let me live my life out as I want to, and then do as they like," the old man said to himself. With his son, however, he made use of that diplomacy to which he always had resort in case of gravity. Assuming a calm tone, he went into the whole question judicially.

In the first place, the marriage was not a brilliant one from the point of view of birth, fortune, or distinction. Secondly, Prince Andrey was not in his first youth, and was delicate in health (the old man laid special stress on this), and the girl was very young. Thirdly, there was his son, whom it would be a pity to entrust to a mere girl. "Fourthly, and finally," said the father, looking ironically at his son, "I beg you to defer the matter for a year; go abroad, and get well; find a German, as you want to do so, for Prince Nikolay, and then, if your love, your passion, your obstinacy—what you choose—are so great, then get married. And that's my last word on the subject; you know, the last . . ." the old prince concluded, in a tone that showed that nothing would compel him to alter his decision.

Prince Andrey saw clearly that the old man hoped that either his feeling or that of his betrothed would not stand the test of a year or that he, the old prince, would die himself in the course of it, and he decided to act in accordance with his father's wish; to make an offer and to defer the marriage for a year.

Three weeks after his last visit to the Rostovs, Prince Andrey returned to Petersburg.

The day after her conversation with her mother, Natasha spent the whole day expecting Bolkonsky but he did not come. The next day, and the third, it was just the same. Pierre too stayed away, and Natasha, not knowing Prince Andrey had gone away to see his father, did not know how to interpret his absence.

So passed the three weeks. Natasha would not go out anywhere, and wandered like a shadow about the house, idle and listless, wept at night in secret, and did not go in to her mother in the evenings. She was continually flushing and very irritable. It seemed to her that every one knew of her disappointment, was laughing at her, and pitying her. In spite of all the intensity of her inward grief, the wound to her vanity aggravated her misery.

She came in to the countess one day, tried to say something, and all at once burst into tears. Her tears were the tears of an offended child, who does not know why it is being punished. The countess tried to comfort Natasha. At first she listened to her mother's words, but suddenly she interrupted her:

"Stop, mamma, I don't think of him or want to think of him! Why, he kept coming, and he has left off, and he has left off . . ." Her voice quivered, she almost began to cry, but recovered herself, and went on calmly:

"And I don't want to be married at all. And I'm afraid of him; I have quite, quite got over it now . . ."

The day after this conversation, Natasha put on the old dress she specially associated with the fun she had often had when wearing it in the mornings, and began from early morning to take up her old manner of life, which she had given up ever since the ball. After morning tea, she went into the big hall, which she particularly liked on account of the loud resonance in it, and began singing her sol-fa exercises. When she had finished the first exercise she stood still in the middle of the room and repeated a single musical phrase which particularly pleased her. She listened with delight, as though it were new to her, to the charm of these notes ringing out, filling the empty space of the great room and dying slowly away, and she felt all at once cheerful. "Why think so much about it; things are nice even as it is," she said to herself; and she began walking up and down the room, not putting her feet simply down on the resounding parquet, but at each step bending her foot from the heel to the toe (she had on some new shoes she particularly liked), and listening to the regular tap of the heel and creak of the toe with the same pleasure with which she had listened to the sound of her own voice. Passing by the looking-glass, she glanced into it. "Yes, that's me!" the expression of her face seemed to say at the sight of herself. "Well, and very nice too. And I need nobody."

A footman would have come in to clear away something in the room, but she would not let him come in. She shut the door after him, and continued her promenade about the room. She had come back that morning to her favourite mood of loving herself and being ecstatic over herself. "What a charming creature that Natasha is!" she said again of herself, speaking as some third person, a generic, masculine person.

"Pretty, a voice, young, and she's in nobody's way, only leave her in peace." But, however much she might be left in peace, she could not now be at peace, and she felt that immediately.

In the vestibule the hall-door opened; someone was asking, "At home?" and steps were audible. Natasha was looking at herself in the glass, but she did not see herself. She heard sounds in the vestibule. When she saw herself, her face was pale. It was *he*. She knew it for certain, though she herself caught the sound of his voice at the opened door.

Natasha, pale and panic-stricken, flew into the drawing-room

"Mamma, Bolkonsky has come," she said. "Mamma, this is awful, unbearable! . . . I don't want . . . to be tortured! What am I to do?"

The countess had not time to answer her before Prince Andrey with a troubled and serious face walked into the drawing-room. As soon as he saw Natasha his face beamed with delight. He kissed the countess's hand and Natasha's, and sat down beside the sofa.

"It's a long while since we have had the pleasure . . ." the countess was beginning, but Prince Andrey cut her short, answering her implied question, and obviously in haste to say what he had to say.

"I have not been to see you all this time because I have been to see my father; I had to talk over a very important matter with him. I only returned last night," he said, glancing at Natasha. "I want to have a talk with you, countess," he added after a moment's silence.

The countess dropped her eyes, sighing heavily.

"I am at your disposal," she brought out.

Natasha knew she ought to go, but she was unable to do so: something seemed gripping her throat, and, regardless of civility, she stared straight at Prince Andrey with wide-open eyes.

"At once? . . . This minute? . . . No, it cannot be!" she was thinking.

He glanced at her again, and that glance convinced her that she was not mistaken. Yes, at once, this very minute her fate was to be decided.

"Run away, Natasha; I will call you," the countess whispered.

With frightened and imploring eyes Natasha glanced at Prince Andrey and at her mother, and went out.

"I have come, countess, to ask for your daughter's hand," said Prince Andrey.

The countess's face flushed hotly, but she said nothing.

"Your offer . . ." the countess began at last, sedately. He sat silent, looking into her face. "Your offer" . . . (she hesitated in confusion) "is agreeable to us, and . . . I accept your offer. I am glad of it. And my husband . . . I hope . . . but it must rest with herself . . ."

"I will speak to her, when I have received your consent. . . . Do you give it me?" said Prince Andrey.

"Yes," said the countess, and she held out her hand to him, and with mingled feelings of aversion and tenderness she pressed her lips to his forehead as he bent to kiss her hand. Her wish was to love him as a son; but she felt that he was a man alien to her, and that she was afraid of him.

"I am sure my husband will consent," said the countess; "but your father . . ."

"My father, whom I have informed of my plans, has made it an express condition that the marriage should not take place for a year. That too, I meant to speak of to you," said Prince Andrey.

"It is true that Natasha is very young, but—so long as that?"

"It could not be helped," said Prince Andrey with a sigh.

"I will send her to you," said the countess, and she went out of the room.

"Lord, have mercy upon us!" she kept repeating as she looked for her daughter.

Sonya told her that Natasha was in her bedroom. She was sitting on her bed, with a pale face and dry eyes; she was gazing at the holy picture, and murmuring something to herself as she rapidly crossed herself. Seeing her mother she leaped up and flew towards her.

"Well, mamma, . . . well?"

"Go, go to him. He asks your hand," said the countess, coldly it seemed to Natasha. . . . "Yes . . . go . . ." the mother murmured mournfully and reproachfully with a deep sigh as her daughter ran off.

Natasha could not have said how she reached the drawing-room. As she entered the door and caught sight of him, she stopped short: "Is it possible that this stranger has now become *everything* to me?" she asked herself, and instantly answered: "Yes, everything: he alone is dearer to me now than everything in the world." Prince Andrey approached her with downcast eyes.

"I have loved you from the first minute I saw you. Can I hope?"

He glanced at her and was struck by the serious, impassioned look in her face. Her face seemed to say: "Why ask? Why doubt of what you cannot but know? Why talk when no words can express what one feels?"

She came nearer to him and stopped. He took her hand and kissed it.

"Do you love me?"

"Yes, yes," said Natasha, almost angrily it seemed. She drew a deep sigh, and another, her breathing came more and more quickly, and she burst into sobs.

"What is it? What's the matter?"

"Oh, I am so happy," she answered, smiling through her tears. She bent over closer to him, thought a second, as though wondering whether it were possible, and then kissed him.

Prince Andrey held her hands, looked into her eyes and could find no trace of his former love for her in his heart. Some sudden reaction seemed to have taken place in his soul; there was none of the poetic and mysterious charm of desire left in it; instead of that there was pity for her feminine and childish weakness, terror at her devotion and trustfulness, an irksome, yet sweet, sense of duty, binding him to her for ever. The actual feeling, though not so joyous and poetical as the former feeling, was more serious and deeper.

"Did your mamma tell you that it cannot be for a year?" said Prince Andrey, still gazing into her eyes.

"Can this be I, the baby-girl (as every one used to call me)?" Natasha was thinking. "Can I really be from this minute a *wife*, on a level with this unknown, charming, intellectual man, who is looked up to even by my father? Can it be true? Can it be true that now there can be no more playing with life, that now I am grown up, that now a responsibility is laid upon me for every word and action? Oh, what did he ask me?"

"No," she answered, but she had not understood his question.

"Forgive me," said Prince Andrey, "but you are so young, and I have had so much experience of life. I am afraid for you. You don't know yourself."

Natasha listened with concentrated attention, trying to take in the meaning of his words; but she did not understand them.

"Hard as that year will be to me, delaying my happiness," continued Prince Andrey, "in that time you will be sure of yourself. I beg you to make me happy in a year, but you are free; our engagement shall be kept a secret, and if you should find out that you do not love me, or if you should come to love . . ." said Prince Andrey with a forced smile.

"Why do you say that?" Natasha interrupted. "You know that from the very day when you first came to Otradnoe, I have loved you," she said, firmly persuaded that she was speaking the truth.

"In a year you will learn to know yourself. . . ."

"A who-ole year!" cried Natasha suddenly, only now grasping that their marriage was to be deferred for a year. "But why a year? . . . Why a year? . . ."

Prince Andrey began to explain to her the reasons for this delay. Natasha did not hear him.

"And can't it be helped?" she asked. Prince Andrey made no reply, but his face expressed the impossibility of altering this decision.

"That's awful! Oh, it's awful, awful!" Natasha cried suddenly, and she broke into sobs again. "I shall die if I have to wait a year; it's impossible, it's awful." She glanced at her lover's face and saw the look of sympathetic pain and perplexity on it.

"No, no, I'll do anything," she said, suddenly checking her tears; "I'm so happy!"

Her father and mother came into the room and gave the betrothed couple their blessing. From that day Prince Andrey began to visit the Rostovs as Natasha's affianced lover.

XXIV

THERE was no formal betrothal and no announcement was made of the engagement of Bolkonsky and Natasha; Prince Andrey insisted upon that. He said that since he was responsible for the delay of their marriage, he ought to bear the whole burden of it. He said that he was bound for ever by his word, but he did not want to bind Natasha and would leave her perfect freedom. If in another six months she were to feel that she did not love him, she would have a perfect right to refuse him. It need hardly be said that neither Natasha nor her parents would hear of this possibility; but Prince Andrey insisted on having his own way. Prince Andrey came every day to the Rostovs', but he did not behave with Natasha as though he were engaged to her; he addressed her formally and kissed only her hand. From the day cf his proposal Prince Andrey's relations with Natasha had become quite different from what had existed between them before: their relations were simple and intimate. It seemed as though till then they had not known each other.

Both loved to recall how they had regarded one another when they were *nothing* to each other. Now they both felt utterly different creatures— then affected, now simple and sincere. At first there had been a feeling of awkwardness in the family in regard to Prince Andrey. He seemed a man from another world, and Natasha used for a long while to try and make her people understand Prince Andrey, and declared to every one with pride that he only seemed to be so different, that he was really like every one else, and that she was not afraid of him and no one need be. After a few days, the rest of the family got accustomed to seeing him, and went on without constraint with their usual manner of life, in which he took part. He knew how to talk to the count about the management of his estates, to the countess and Natasha about dress, and to Sonya about her album and embroidery. Sometimes the Rostovs among themselves, and in Prince Andrey's presence, expressed their wonder at the way it had all happened, and at the events that obviously betokened that it was to be: Prince Andrey's coming to Otradnoe, and their coming to Petersburg, and the resemblance between Natasha and Prince Andrey, which the old nurse had remarked on Prince Andrey's first visit, and the meeting in 1805 between Andrey and Nikolay, and many other incidents betokening that it was to be, were observed by the family.

The house was full of that poetic atmosphere of dullness and silence, which always accompanies the presence of an engaged couple. Often as they all sat together every one was silent. Sometimes the others got up and went away, and the engaged pair were still as mute when they were left alone. Rarely they spoke of their future life together. Prince Andrey felt frightened and ashamed to speak of it. Natasha shared the feeling, as she did all his feelings, which she never failed to divine. Once Natasha began questioning him about his son.

Prince Andrey blushed—a thing frequent with him at that time, which Natasha particularly liked to see—and said that his son would not live with them.

"Why not?" said Natasha, taking fright.

"I cannot take him from his grandfather and then . . ."

"How I should have loved him!" said Natasha, at once divining his thought; "but I know you want to avoid any pretext for our being blamed."

The old count sometimes came up to Prince Andrey, kissed him and asked his advice about some question relating to Petya's education or Nikolay's position. The old countess sighed as she looked at them. Sonya was afraid every instant of being in their way, and was always trying to find excuses for leaving them alone, even when they had no wish to be alone. When Prince Andrey talked—he described things very well— Natasha listened to him with pride. When she talked, she noticed with joy and dread that he watched her with an intent and scrutinising look. She asked herself in perplexity: "What is it he seeks in me? What is it he is probing for with that look? What if I haven't in me what he is searching for in that look?" Sometimes she fell into the mood of wild gaiety characteristic of her, and then she particularly loved to see and hear how Prince Andrey laughed. He rarely laughed, but when he did laugh he abandoned himself utterly to his mirth, and she always felt herself drawn closer to him by this laughter. Natasha would have been perfectly happy if the thought of the separation before her, coming closer and closer, had not terrified her. He too turned pale and cold at the mere thought of it.

On the day before he was to leave Petersburg, Prince Andrey brought with him Pierre, who had not been at the Rostovs' since the day of the ball. Pierre seemed absent-minded and embarrassed. He talked chiefly to the countess. Natasha was sitting at the chess-board with Sonya, and invited Prince Andrey to join them. He went to them.

"You have known Bezuhov a long while, haven't you?" he asked. "Do you like him?"

"Yes; he's very nice, but very absurd."

And she began, as people always did when speaking of Pierre, to tell anecdotes of his absent-mindedness, anecdotes which were made up, indeed, about him.

"You know, I have confided our secret to him," said Prince Andrey. "I have known him from childhood. He has a heart of gold. I beg you, Natalie," he said, with sudden seriousness, "I am going away; God knows what may happen. You may change . . . Oh, I know I ought not to speak of that. Only one thing—if anything were to happen to you, while I am away . . ."

"What could happen?"

"If any trouble were to come," pursued Prince Andrey. "I beg you, Mademoiselle Sophie, if anything were to happen, to go to him and no one else for advice and help. He is a most absent-minded and eccentric person, but he has the truest heart."

Neither her father nor her mother, neither Sonya nor Prince Andrey could have foreseen the effect of the parting on Natasha. She wandered about the house all that day, flushed, excited, and tearless, busying herself about the most trivial matters as though she had no notion of what was before her. She did not weep even at the moment when he kissed her hand for the last time.

"Don't go away!" was all she said, in a voice that made him wonder whether he ought not really to remain, and that he remembered long after. When he had gone, she still did not weep; but for several days she sat in her room, not crying, but taking no interest in anything, and only saying from time to time: "Oh, why did he go?" But a fortnight after his departure, she surprised those around her equally by recovering from her state of spiritual sickness, and became herself again, only with a change in her moral physiognomy, such as one sees in the faces of children after a long illness.

XXV

THE health and character of Prince Nikolay Andreitch Bolkonsky had, during that year, after his son had left him, grown considerably feebler. He became more irritable than ever, and it was Princess Marya who as a rule bore the brunt of his outbursts of causeless fury. He seemed studiously to seek out all the tender spots in her consciousness so as to inflict on her the cruellest wounds possible. Princess Marya had two passions and consequently two joys: her nephew, Nikolushka, and religion; and both were favourite subjects for the old prince's attacks and jeers. Whatever was being spoken of, he would bring the conversation round to the superstitiousness of old maids, or the petting and spoiling of children. "You want to make him" (Nikolushka) "just such another old maid as you are yourself. Prince Andrey wants a son and not an old maid," he would say. Or addressing Mademoiselle Bourienne he would ask her, before Princess Marya, how she liked our village priests and holy pictures, and make jests about them. . . .

He was constantly wounding Princess Marya's feelings, but his daughter needed no effort to forgive him. Could he be to blame in anything he did to her, could her father, who as she knew in spite of it all, loved her, be unjust? And indeed what is justice? Princess Marya never gave a thought to that proud word, "justice." All the complex laws of humanity were summed up for her in one clear and simple law—the law of love and self-sacrifice, laid down by Him who had in His love suffered for humanity, though He was God Himself. What had she to do with the justice or injustice of other people? All she had to do was to suffer and to love; and that she did.

In the winter Prince Andrey had come to Bleak Hills, had been gay, gentle, and affectionate, as Princess Marya had not seen him for years. She felt that something had happened to him, but he said nothing to his sister of his love. Before his departure, Prince Andrey had a long conversation with his father, and Princess Marya noticed that they were ill pleased with each other at parting.

Soon after Prince Andrey had gone, Princess Marya wrote from Bleak Hills to her friend in Petersburg, Julie Karagin, whom Princess Marya had dreamed—as girls always do dream—of marrying to her brother. She was at this time in mourning for the death of a brother, who had been killed in Turkey.

"Sorrow, it seems, is our common lot, my sweet and tender friend Julie.

"Your loss is so terrible that I can only explain it to myself, as a special sign of the grace of God, who in His love for you would chasten you and your incomparable mother.

"Ah, my dear, religion, and religion alone can—I don't say comfort us—but save us from despair. Religion alone can interpret to us what, without its aid, man cannot comprehend: to what end, for what cause, good, elevated beings who are able to find happiness in life, not injuring others, but indispensable to their happiness, are called away to God, while the wicked, the useless, injuring others and a burden to themselves and others, are left living. The first death which I have seen, and which I shall never forget—the death of my dear little sister-in-law—made on me just the same impression. Just as you question destiny, and ask why your noble brother had to die, so did I wonder what reason there was for that angel Liza to die—who had never done the slightest harm to any one, never even had a thought in her heart that was not kind. And yet— do you know, dear friend—five years have passed since then, and even I, with my poor intelligence, begin now to understand clearly why it was needful she should die, and in what way that death was but an expression of the boundless grace of the Creator, all of whose acts, though for the most part we comprehend them not, are but manifestations of His infinite love for His creatures. Perhaps, I often think, she was of too angelic an innocence to have the force to perform all a mother's duties. As a young wife, she was irreproachable; possibly she could not have been equally so as a mother. As it is, not only has she left us, and particularly Prince Andrey, the purest memories and regrets, but there she is in all likelihood receiving a place for which I dare not hope for myself. But not to speak of her alone, that early and terrible death has had the most blessed influence on me and on my brother, in spite of all our grief. At the time, at the moment of our loss, I could not have entertained such thoughts; at that time I should have dismissed them in horror, but now it seems clear and incontestable. I write all this to you, dear friend, simply to convince you of the Gospel truth, which has become a principle of life for me: not one hair of our head falls without His will. And the guiding principle of His will is only His infinite love for us, and so whatever may befall us, all is for our good.

"You ask whether we shall spend next winter in Moscow. In spite of all my desire to see you, I do not expect and do not wish to do so. And you will be surprised to hear that Bonaparte is responsible for this! I will tell you why: my father's health is noticeably weaker; he cannot endure contradiction and is easily irritated. This irritability is, as you are aware, most readily aroused on political subjects. He cannot endure the idea that Bonaparte is treating on equal terms with all the sovereigns of Europe, especially our own, the grandson of the great Catherine! As you know, I take absolutely no interest in politics, but from my father and his conversations with Mihail Ivanovitch, I know all that goes on in the world, and have heard of all the honours conferred on Bonaparte. It seems that Bleak Hills is now the only spot on the terrestrial globe where he is not recognised as a great man—still less as Emperor of France. And my father cannot tolerate this state of things. It seems to me that my father shows a disinclination for the visit to Moscow, chiefly owing to his political views and his foreseeing the difficulties likely to arise from his habit of expressing his opinions freely, with no regard for any one. All that he would gain from medical treatment in Moscow, he would lose from the inevitable discussions upon Bonaparte. In any case the matter will very soon be settled.

"Our home life goes on in its old way, except for the absence of my brother Andrey. As I wrote to you before, he has greatly changed of late, It is only of late, during this year that he seems to have quite recovered from the shock of his loss. He has become again just as I knew him as a child, good-natured, affectionate, with a heart such as I know in no one else. He feels now, it seems to me, that life is not over for him. But, together with this moral change, he has become very weak physically. He is thinner than ever and more nervous. I feel anxious about him and glad that he is taking this tour abroad, which the doctors prescribed long ago. I hope that it will cure him. You write to me that he is spoken of in Petersburg as one of the most capable, cultivated, and intellectual young men. Forgive me for the pride of family—I never doubted it. The good he did here to every one—from his peasants to the local nobility— is incalculable. When he went to Petersburg he was received as he deserved. I wonder at the way reports fly from Petersburg to Moscow, and especially such groundless ones as the rumour you wrote to me about, of my brother's supposed engagement to the little Rostov girl. I don't imagine that Andrey will ever marry any one at all, and certainly not her. And I will tell you why. In the first place, I know that though he rarely speaks of his late wife, the grief of his loss has penetrated too deeply into his heart for him ever to be ready to give her a successor, and our little angel a stepmother. Secondly, because, as far as I can ascertain, that girl is not one of the kind of women who could attract my brother Andrey. I do not believe that Andrey has chosen her for his wife; and I will frankly confess, I should not wish for such a thing. But how I have been running on; I am finishing my second sheet. Farewell, my sweet friend; and may God keep you in His holy and mighty care. My dear companion, Mademoiselle Bourienne, sends you kisses.

MARIE."

XXVI

IN the middle of the summer Princess Marya, to her surprise, received a letter from Prince Andrey, who was in Switzerland. In it he told her strange and surprising news. He informed his sister of his engagement to the younger Rostov. His whole letter was full of loving enthusiasm for his betrothed, and tender and confiding affection for his sister. He wrote that he had never loved as he loved now, and that it was only now that he saw all the value and meaning of life. He begged his sister to forgive him for having said nothing of his plans to her on his last visit to Bleak Hills, though he had spoken of it to his father. He had said nothing to her for fear Princess Marya would beg her father to give his consent, and, without attaining her object, would irritate her father and draw all the weight of his displeasure upon herself. The matter was not, however, then, he wrote to her, so completely settled as now. "At that time our father insisted on a delay of a year, and now *six months,* half of the period specified, is over, and I remain firmer than ever in my resolution. If it were not for the doctors keeping me here at the waters I should be back in Russia myself; but, as it is, I must put off my return for another three months. You know me and my relations with our father. I want nothing from him. I have been, and always shall be, independent; but to act in opposition to his will, to incur his anger when he has perhaps not long left to be with us, would destroy half my happiness. I am writing a letter to him now, and I beg you to choose a favourable moment to give him the letter, and to let me know how he looks at the whole matter, and if there is any hope of his agreeing to shorten the year by three months."

After long hesitations, doubts, and prayers, Princess Marya gave the letter to her father. The next day the old prince said to her calmly: "Write to your brother to wait till I'm dead. . . . He won't have long to wait. I shall soon set him free."

The princess tried to make some reply, but her father would not let her speak, and went on, getting louder and louder. "Let him marry, let him marry, the dear fellow. . . . A nice connection! . . . Clever people, eh? Rich, eh? Oh yes, a fine stepmother for Nikolushka she'll make! You write to him he can marry her to-morrow. Nikolushka shall have her for a stepmother, and I'll marry little Bourienne! . . . Ha, ha, ha, and so he shall have a stepmother too! Only there's one thing, I won't have any more women-folk about my nouse; he may marry and go and live by himself. Perhaps you'll go and live with him too?" He turned to Princess Marya: "You're welcome to, and good luck to you!"

After this outburst the prince did not once allude to the subject again. But his repressed anger at his son's poor-spirited behaviour found a vent in his treatment of his daughter. He now added to his former subjects for jeering and annoying her a new one—allusions to a stepmother and gallantries to Mademoiselle Bourienne.

"Why shouldn't I marry her?" he would say to his daughter. "A capital princess she will make!" And latterly, to her perplexity and amazement, Princess Marya began to notice that her father was really beginning to attach himself more and more closely to the Frenchwoman. Princess Marya wrote to Prince Andrey and told him how their father had taken the letter, but comforted her brother with hopes that he would become reconciled to the idea.

Nikolushka and his education, her brother Andrey and religion, were Princess Marya's joys and consolations. But apart from those, since every one must have personal hopes, Princess Marya cherished, in the deepest secrecy of her heart, a hidden dream and hope that was the source of the chief comfort in her life. This comforting dream and hope was given her by "God's folk"—the crazy prophets and the pilgrims, who visited her without the prince's knowledge. The longer Princess Marya lived, the more experience and observation she had of life the more she wondered at the shortsightedness of men, who seek here on earth for enjoyment, toil, suffer, strive and do each other harm to attain that impossible, visionary, and sinful happiness. Prince Andrey had loved a wife; she died; that was not enough for him, he wanted to bind his happiness to another woman. Her father did not want that, because he coveted a more distinguished or a wealthier match for Andrey. And they were all striving, and suffering, and in torment, and sullying their souls, their eternal souls, to attain a bliss the duration of which was but a moment. Not only do we know that for ourselves. Christ, the Son of God, came down upon earth and told us that this life is but for a moment, is but a probation; yet we still cling to it and think to find happiness in it. "How is it no one has realised that?" Princess Marya wondered. "No one but these despised people of God who, with wallets over their shoulders, come to me by the back stairs, afraid of the prince catching sight of them, and not from fear of ill-usage, but from fear of tempting him to sin. To leave home and country, give up all thoughts of worldly blessings, and clinging to nothing, to wander from place to place in a home-spun smock under a different name, doing people no harm, but praying for them, praying equally for those who drive them away and those who succour them: higher than that truth and that life there is no truth and no life!"

There was one Pilgrim-woman, Fedosyushka, a quiet, little woman of about fifty, marked by smallpox, who had been wandering for over thirty years barefooted and wearing chains. Princess Marya was particularly fond of her. One day when sitting in a dark room, by the light only of the lamp before the holy picture, Fedosyushka told her about her life. Princess Marya felt all at once so strongly that Fedosyushka was the one person who had found the right way of life, that she resolved to go on a pilgrimage herself. When Fedosyushka had gone to bed Princess Marya pondered a long while over it, and at last made up her mind that—however strange it might be—she must go on a pilgrimage. She confided her intention to no one but a monk, Father Akinfy, and this priest approved of her project. On the pretence of getting presents for pilgrim women, Princess Marya had prepared for herself the complete outfit of a pilgrim—a smock, plaited shoes, a full-skirted coat, and a black kerchief. Often she went to her secret wardrobe, where she kept them, and stood in uncertainty whether the time to carry out her plan had come or not.

Often as she listened to the pilgrims' tales, their simple phrases—that had become mechanical to them, but were to her ears full of the deepest significance—worked upon her till she was several times ready to throw up everything and run away from home. In imagination she already saw herself with Fedosyushka in a coarse smock, trudging along the dusty road with her wallet and her staff, going on her pilgrimage, free from envy, free from earthly love, free from all desires, from one saint to another; and at last thither where there is neither sorrow nor sighing, but everlasting joy and blessedness.

"I shall come to one place. I shall pray there, and before I have time to grow used to it, to love it, I shall go on further. And I shall go on till my legs give way under me and I lie down and die somewhere, and reach

at last that quiet, eternal haven, where is neither sorrow nor sighing!
. . ." thought Princess Marya.

But then at the sight of her father, and still more of little Nikolushka,
she wavered in her resolution, wept in secret, and felt that she was a
sinner, that she loved her father and her nephew more than God.

PART SEVEN

I

THE BIBLICAL tradition tells us that the absence of work—idleness—was a condition of the first man's blessedness before the Fall. The love of idleness has remained the same in fallen man; but the curse still lies heavy upon man, and not only because in the sweat of our brow we must eat bread, but because from our moral qualities we are unable to be idle and at peace. A secret voice tells us that we must be to blame for being idle. If a man could find a state in which while being idle he could feel himself to be of use and to be doing his duty, he would have attained to one side of primitive blessedness. And such a state of obligatory and irreproachable idleness is enjoyed by a whole class—the military class. It is in that obligatory and irreproachable idleness that the chief attraction of military service has always consisted, and will always consist.

Nikolay Rostov was enjoying this blessed privilege to the full, as after the year 1807 he remained in the Pavlograd regiment, in command of the squadron that had been Denisov's.

Rostov had become a bluff, good-natured fellow, who would have been thought rather bad form by his old acquaintances in Moscow, though he was loved and respected by his comrades, his subordinates, and his superior officers, and was well content with his life. Of late—in the year 1809—he had found more and more frequently in letters from home complaints on the part of his mother that their pecuniary position was going from bad to worse, and that it was high time for him to come home, to gladden and comfort the hearts of his old parents.

As he read those letters, Nikolay felt a pang of dread at their wanting to drag him out of the surroundings in which, by fencing himself off from all the complexities of existence, he was living so quietly and peacefully. He felt that sooner or later he would have to plunge again into that whirlpool of life, with many difficulties and business to attend to, with the steward's accounts, with quarrels and intrigues, and ties, with society, with Sonya's love and his promise to her. All that was terribly difficult and complicated; and he answered his mother's letters with cold letters in French on the classic model, beginning *"Ma chère maman,"* and ending: *"Votre obéissant fils,"* saying nothing of any intention of coming home. In 1810 he received letters from home in which he was told of Natasha's engagement to Bolkonsky, and of the marriage being deferred for a year, because the old prince would not consent to it. This letter chagrined and mortified Nikolay. In the first place, he was sorry to be losing from home Natasha, whom he cared more for

453

than all the rest of the family. Secondly, from his hussar point of view, he regretted not having been at home at the time, as he would have shown this Bolkonsky that it was by no means such an honour to be connected with him, and that if he cared for Natasha he could get on just as well without his crazy old father's consent. For a moment he hesitated whether to ask for leave, so as to see Natasha engaged, but then the manœuvres were just coming on, and thoughts of Sonya, of complications, recurred to him, and again he put it off. But in the spring of the same year he got a letter from his mother, written without his father's knowledge, and that letter decided him. She wrote that if Nikolay did not come and look after things, their whole estate would have to be sold by auction, and they would all be beggars. The count was so weak, put such entire confidence in Mitenka, and was so good-natured, and every one took advantage of him, so that things were going from bad to worse. "I beseech you, for God's sake, to come at once, if you don't want to make me and all your family miserable," wrote the countess.

That letter produced an effect on Nikolay. He had that common sense of mediocrity which showed him what was his duty.

His duty now was, if not to retire from the army, at least to go home on leave. Why he had to go, he could not have said; but, after his after-dinner nap, he ordered his grey mare to be saddled, a terribly vicious beast that he had not ridden for a long while.

He returned home with his horse in a lather, and told Lavrushka—he had kept on Denisov's old valet—and the comrades who dropped in that evening, that he had applied for leave and was going home. It was strange and difficult for him to believe that he was going away without hearing from the staff whether he had been promoted to be a captain or had received the St. Anne for the last manœuvres (a matter of the greatest interest to him). It was strange to him to think of going away like this without having sold Count Goluhovsky his three roan horses, over which the Polish count was haggling with him. Rostov had taken a bet that he would get two thousand for them. It seemed inconceivable that without him the ball could take place which the hussars were to give in honour of their favourite Polish belle, Madame Pshazdetsky, to outdo the Uhlans, who had given a ball to their favourite belle, Madame Borzhozovsky. Yet he knew he must leave this world, where all was well and all was clear, to go where all was nonsensical and complicated. A week later his leave came. His comrades—not only in the regiment, but throughout the whole brigade—gave Rostov a dinner that cost a subscription of fifteen roubles a head. Two bands of musicians played, two choruses sang; Rostov danced the *trepak* with Major Bazov; the drunken officers tossed him in the air, hugged him, dropped him; the soldiers of the third squadron tossed him once more and shouted hurrah! Then they put Rostov in a sledge and escorted him as far as the first posting-station on his way.

For the first half of the journey, from Krementchug to Kiev, all Rostov's thoughts—as is apt to be the case with travellers—turned to what he had left behind—to his squadron. But after being jolted over the first half of the journey, he had begun to forget his three roans and his quartermaster, Dozhoyveyky, and was beginning to wonder uneasily what he should find on reaching Otradnoe. The nearer he got, the more intense, far more intense, were his thoughts of home (as though moral feeling were subject to the law of acceleration in inverse ratio with the square of the distance). At the station nearest to Otradnoe he gave the sledge-driver a tip of three roubles, and ran breathless up the steps of his home, like a boy.

After the excitement of the first meeting, and the strange feeling of disappointment after his expectations—the feeling that "it's just the same; why was I in such a hurry?"—Nikolay began to settle down in his old world of home. His father and mother were just the same, only a little older. All that was new in them was a certain uneasiness and at times a difference of opinion, which he had never seen between them before, and soon learned to be due to the difficulties of their position.

Sonya was now nearly twenty. She would grow no prettier now; there was no promise in her of more to come; but what she had was enough. She was brimming over with love and happiness as soon as Nikolay came home, and this girl's faithful, steadfast love for him gladdened his heart. Petya and Natasha surprised Nikolay more than all the rest. Petya was a big, handsome lad of thirteen, whose voice was already cracking; he was full of gaiety and clever pranks. Nikolay did not get over his wonder at Natasha for a long while, and laughed as he looked at her.

"You're utterly different," he told her.

"How? Uglier?"

"No, quite the contrary; but what dignity! A real princess!" he whispered to her.

"Yes, yes, yes," cried Natasha gleefully.

Natasha told him all the story of Prince Andrey's lovemaking, of his visit to Otradnoe, and showed him his last letter.

"Well, are you glad?" asked Natasha. "I'm so at peace and happy now."

"Very glad," answered Nikolay. "He's a splendid fellow. Are you very much in love, then?"

"How shall I say?" answered Natasha. "I was in love with Boris, with our teacher, with Denisov; but this is utterly different. I feel calm, settled. I know there is no one better than he in the world, and so I am calm now and content. It's utterly different from anything before . . ."

Nikolay expressed his dissatisfaction at the marriage being put off for a year. But Natasha fell on him with exasperation, proving to him that no other course was possible, that it would be a horrid thing to enter a family against the father's will, and that she would not consent to it herself.

"You don't understand at all, at all," she kept saying.

Nikolay paused a moment, and then said he agreed with her.

Her brother often wondered as he looked at her. It seemed quite incredible that she was a girl in love and parted from her betrothed lover.

She was even-tempered, serene, and quite as light-hearted as ever. This made Nikolay wonder, and look on the engagement to Bolkonsky rather sceptically. He could not believe that her fate was by now sealed, especially as he had never seen her with Prince Andrey. It still seemed to him that there was something not real in this proposed marriage.

"Why this delay? Why were they not formally betrothed?" he thought.

Once in talking to his mother about his sister, he found to his surprise, and partly to his satisfaction, that at the bottom of her heart his mother sometimes regarded the marriage as sceptically as he did.

"Here, you see, he writes," she said, showing her son a letter from Prince Andrey with that latent feeling of grudge which mothers always have in regard to their daughter's happiness in marriage, "he writes that he won't be coming before December. What can it be that keeps him? Illness, no doubt! His health is very weak. Don't tell Natasha. Don't make a mistake, because she seems in good spirits; it's the last she has of her girlhood, and I know how she is when she gets his letters. Still, God grant, all may be well yet," she always concluded: "he's a splendid fellow."

II

IN the early part of his time at home Nikolay was serious and even dull. He was worried by the necessity of meddling in the stupid business matters which his mother had sent for him to look after. To be rid of this burden as soon as possible, on the third day after his return, he marched angrily off, making no reply to inquiries where he was going, with scowling brows entered Mitenka's lodge, and demanded from him an *account* in full. What he meant by an account in full, Nikolay knew even less than the panic-stricken and bewildered Mitenka. The conversation and Mitenka's accounts did not last long. The village elder, the deputy, and the village clerk, waiting in the entry of the lodge, heard with awe and delight at first the booming and snapping of the young count's voice in a constantly ascending scale, then terrible words of abuse, flung one after another.

"Robber! Ungrateful brute! . . . I'll thrash the dog! . . . not papa to deal with . . . plundering us . . ." and so on.

Then, with no less awe and delight, these persons saw the young count, with a red face and bloodshot eyes, dragging Mitenka out by the collar, kicking him with great dexterity at every appropriate moment between his words, and shouting:

"Away with you! Never let me set eyes on you, blackguard!"

Mitenka flew head first down six steps and ran to the shrubbery. This shrubbery was well known as a haven of refuge for delinquents at Otradnoe. Mitenka had, on coming home drunk from the town, himself hidden in the shrubbery, and many of the residents of Otradnoe had been indebted to the saving power of the shrubbery when anxious to conceal themselves from Mitenka.

Mitenka's wife and sister-in-law, with frightened faces, peeped into the passage from the door of their room, where was a bright samovar boiling, and the bailiff's high bedstead stood under a quilted patchwork coverlet.

The young count walked by, treading resolutely and breathing hard, taking no notice of them, and went into the house.

The countess heard at once through her maids of what had been happening in the lodge, and on one side was comforted by the reflection that now their position would be sure to improve, though on the other hand she was uneasy as to the effect of the scene on her son. She went several times on tiptoe to his door, and listened as he lighted one pipe after another.

The next day the old count drew his son on one side, and, with a timid smile, said to him, "But you know, my dear boy, you had no reason to be so angry. Mitenka has told me all about it."

"I knew," thought Nikolay, "that I should never make head or tail of anything in this crazy world."

"You were angry at his not having put down these seven hundred and eight roubles. But you see they were carried forward by double entry, and you didn't look at the next page."

"Papa, he's a blackguard and a thief, I am certain. And what I have done, I have done. But if you don't wish it, I will say nothing to him."

"No, my dear boy!" (The old count was confused. He was conscious that he had mismanaged his wife's estate and had wronged his children, but he had no notion how to rectify the position.) "No, I beg you to go into things. I am old. I . . ."

"No, papa, forgive me if I have done what you dislike. I know less about it than you do."

"Damn them all, these peasants, and money matters and double entries," he thought. "I used once to understand scoring at cards, but bookkeeping by the double entry is quite beyond me," he said to himself, and from that time he did not meddle further with the management of the family affairs. But one day the countess called her son into her room, told him that she had a promissory note from Anna Mihalovna for two thousand roubles, and asked Nikolay what he thought it best to do about it.

"Well," answered Nikolay, "you say that it rests with me. I don't like Anna Mihalovna, and I don't like Boris, but they were our friends, and they were poor. So that's what I would do!" and he tore up the note, and by so doing made the countess sob with tears of joy. After this young Rostov took no further part in business of any sort, but devoted himself with passionate interest to everything to do with the chase, which was kept up on a great scale on the old count's estate.

III

Wɪɴᴛʀʏ weather was already setting in, the morning frosts hardened the earth drenched by the autumn rains. Already the grass was full of tufts, and stood out bright green against the patches of brown winter cornland trodden by the cattle, and the pale yellow stubble of the summer corn-fields, and the reddish strips of buckwheat. The uplands and copses, which at the end of August had still been green islands among the black fields ploughed ready for winter corn, and the stubble had become golden and lurid red islands in a sea of bright green autumn crops. The grey hare had already half-changed its coat, the foxes' cubs were begin-ning to leave their parents, and the young wolves were bigger than dogs. It was the best time of the year for the chase. The dogs of an ardent young sportsman like Rostov were only just coming into fit state for hunting, so that at a common council of the huntsmen it was decided to give the dogs three days' rest, and on the 16th of September to go off on a hunting expedition, beginning with Dubravy, where there was a litter of wolves that had never been hunted.

Such was the position of affairs on the 14th of September.

All that day the dogs were kept at home. It was keen and frosty weather, but towards evening the sky clouded over and it began to thaw. On the morning of the 15th of September when young Rostov in his dressing-gown looked out of window he saw a morning which was all the heart could desire for hunting. It looked as though the sky were melting, and without the slightest wind, sinking down upon the earth. The only movement in the air was the soft downward motion of micro-scopic drops of moisture or mist. The bare twigs in the garden were hung with transparent drops which dripped on to the freshly fallen leaves. The earth in the kitchen-garden had a gleaming, wet, black look like the centre of a poppy, and at a short distance away it melted off into the damp, dim veil of fog.

Nikolay went out on to the wet and muddy steps. There was a smell of decaying leaves and dogs. The broad-backed, black and tan bitch Milka, with her big, prominent, black eyes, caught sight of her master, got up, stretched out her hindlegs, lay down like a hare, then suddenly jumped up and licked him right on his nose and moustache. Another harrier, catching sight of his master from the bright coloured path, arched its back, darted headlong to the steps, and, lifting its tail, rubbed itself against Nikolay's legs.

"O, hoy!" He heard at that moment the inimitable hunting halloo which unites the deepest bass and the shrillest tenor notes. And round the corner came the huntsman and whipper-in, Danilo, a grey, wrinkled man, with his hair cropped round in the Ukrainian fashion. He held a bent whip in his hand, and his face had that expression of independence and scorn for everything in the world, which is only to be seen in hunts-men. He took off his Circassian cap to his master and looked scornfully at him. That scorn was not offensive to his master. Nikolay knew that this Danilo, disdainful of all, and superior to everything, was still his man and his huntsman.

"Danilo," said Nikolay, at the sight of this hunting weather, those dogs, and the huntsman, feeling shyly that he was being carried away by that irresistible sporting passion in which a man forgets all his previous intentions, like a man in love at the sight of his mistress.

"What is your bidding, your excellency?" asked a bass voice, fit for a head deacon, and hoarse from hallooing, and a pair of flashing black eyes glanced up from under their brows at the silent young master. "Surely you can't resist it?" those two eyes seemed to be asking.

"It's a good day, eh? Just right for riding and hunting, eh?" said Nikolay, scratching Milka behind the ears.

Danilo winked and made no reply.

"I sent Uvarka out to listen at daybreak," his bass boomed out after a moment's silence. "He brought word *she's moved* into the Otradnoe enclosure; there was howling there." ("She's moved" meant that the mother wolf, of whom both knew, had moved with her cubs into the Otradnoe copse, which was a small hunting preserve about two versts away.)

"Shouldn't we go, eh?" said Nikolay. "Come to me with Uvarka."

"As you desire."

"Then put off feeding them."

"Yes, sir!"

Five minutes later Danilo and Uvarka were standing in Nikolay's big study. Although Danilo was not tall, to see him in a room gave one an impression such as one has on seeing a horse or bear standing on the floor among the furniture and surroundings of human life. Danilo felt this himself, and as usual he kept close to the door and tried to speak more softly, and not to move for fear of causing some breakage in the master's apartments. He did his utmost to get everything said quickly so as to get as soon as might be out into the open again, from under a ceiling out under the sky.

After making inquiries and extracting from Danilo an admission that the dogs were fit (Danilo himself was longing to go), Nikolay told them to have the horses saddled. But just as Danilo was about to go, Natasha, wrapped in a big shawl of her old nurse's, ran into the room, not yet dressed, and her hair in disorder. Petya ran in with her.

"Are you going?" said Natasha. "I knew you would! Sonya said you weren't going. I knew that on such a day you couldn't help going!"

"Yes, we're going," Nikolay answered reluctantly. As he meant to attempt serious hunting he did not want to take Natasha and Petya. "We are going, but only wolf-hunting; it will be dull for you."

"You know that it's the greatest of my pleasures," said Natasha. "It's too bad—he's going himself, has ordered the horses out and not a word to us."

"No hindrance bars a Russian's path!" declaimed Petya; "let's go!"

"But you mustn't, you know; mamma said you were not to," said Nikolay to Natasha.

"No, I'm going, I must go," said Natasha stoutly. "Danilo, bid them saddle my horse, and tell Mihailo to come with my leash," she said to the huntsman.

Simply to be in a room seemed irksome and unfitting to Danilo, but to have anything to do with a young lady he felt to be utterly impossible. He cast down his eyes and made haste to get away, making as though it were no affair of his, and trying to avoid accidentally doing some hurt to the young lady.

IV

THE old count, whose hunting establishment had always been kept up on a large scale, had now handed it all over to his son's care, but on that day, the 15th of September, being in excellent spirits he prepared to join the expedition. Within an hour the whole party was before the porch. When Natasha and Petya said something to Nikolay he walked by them with a stern and serious air, betokening that he had no time to waste on trifles. He looked over everything to do with the hunt, sent a pack of hounds and huntsmen on ahead to cut off the wolf from behind, got on his chestnut Don horse, and whistling to the dogs of his leash, he set off across the threshing-floor to the field leading to the Otradnoe preserve. The old count's horse, a sorrel gelding, with a white mane and tail, called Viflyanka, was led by the count's groom; he was himself to drive straight in a light gig to the spot fixed for him to stand.

Fifty-four hounds were led out under the charge of six whippers-in and grooms. Of huntsmen, properly speaking, there were taking part in the hunt eight men besides the members of the family, and more than forty greyhounds ran behind them, so that with the hounds in leashes there were about a hundred and thirty dogs and twenty persons on horseback.

Every dog knew its master and its call. Every man in the hunt knew his task, his place, and the part assigned him. As soon as they had passed beyond the fence, they all moved without noise or talk, lengthening out along the road and the field to the Otradnoe forest.

The horses stepped over the field as over a soft carpet, splashing now and then into pools as they crossed the road. The foggy sky still seemed falling imperceptibly and regularly down on the earth; the air was still and warm, and there was no sound but now and then the whistle of a huntsman, the snort of a horse, the clack of a whip, or the whine of a dog who had dropped out of his place. When they had gone a verst, five more horsemen accompanied by dogs appeared out of the mist to meet the Rostovs. The foremost of them was a fresh, handsome old man with large, grey moustaches.

"Good-day, uncle," said Nikolay as the old man rode up to him.

"All's well and march! . . . I was sure of it," began the man addressed as uncle. He was not really the Rostovs' uncle, but a distant relative, who had a small property in their neighbourhood.

"I was sure you couldn't resist it, and a good thing you have come out. All's well and quick march." (This was the uncle's favourite saying.) "You had better attack the preserve at once, for my Girtchik brought me word that the Ilagins are out with their hounds at Korniky; they'll snatch the litter right under your noses."

"That's where I'm going. Shall we join the packs?" asked Nikolay.

The hounds were joined into one pack, and the uncle and Nikolay rode on side by side.

Natasha, muffled up in a shawl which did not hide her eager face and shining eyes, galloped up to them, accompanied by Petya, who kept beside her, and Mihailo, the huntsman and groom, who had been told to look after her. Petya was laughing and switching and pulling his horse. Natasha sat her raven Arabtchick with grace and confidence and controlled him with an easy and steady hand.

The uncle looked with disapproval at Petya and Natasha. He did not like a mixture of frivolity with the serious business of the hunt.

"Good-day, uncle; we're coming to the hunt too!" shouted Petya.

"Good-day, good-day, and mind you don't ride down the dogs," said the uncle sternly.

"Nikolenka, what a delightful dog Trunila is! he knew me," said Natasha of her favourite dog.

"In the first place, Trunila's not a dog, but a wolf-hound," thought Nikolay. He glanced at his sister trying to make her feel the distance that lay between them at that moment. Natasha understood it.

"Don't imagine we shall get in anybody's way, uncle," said Natasha. "We'll stay in our right place and not stir from it."

"And you'll do well, little countess," said the uncle. "Only don't fall off your horse," he added, "or you'd never get on again—all's well, quick march!"

The Otradnoe preserve came into sight, an oasis of greenness, two hundred and fifty yards away. Rostov, settling finally with the uncle from what point to set the dogs on, pointed out to Natasha the place where she was to stand, a place where there was no chance of anything running out, and went round to close in from behind above the ravine.

"Now, nephew, you're on the track of an old wolf," said the uncle; "mind he doesn't give you the slip."

"That's as it happens," answered Rostov. "Karay, hey!" he shouted, replying to the uncle's warning by this call to his dog. Karay was an old, misshapen, muddy-coloured hound, famous for attacking an old wolf unaided. All took their places.

The old count, who knew his son's ardour in the hunt, hurried to avoid being late, and the whippers-in had hardly reached the place when Count Ilya Andreitch, with a cheerful face, and flushed and quivering cheeks, drove up with his pair of raven horses, over the green field to the place left for him. Straightening his fur coat and putting on his hunting appurtenances, he mounted his sleek, well-fed, quiet, good-humoured Viflyanka, who was turning grey like himself. The horses with the gig were sent back. Count Ilya Andreitch, though he was at heart no sportsman, knew well all the rules of sport. He rode into the edge of the thicket of bushes, behind which he was standing, picked up the reins, settled himself at his ease in the saddle, and, feeling that he was ready, looked about him smiling.

Near him stood his valet, Semyon Tchekmar, a veteran horseman, though now heavy in the saddle. Tchekmar held on a leash three wolf-hounds of a special breed, spirited hounds, though they too had grown fat like their master and his horse. Two other keen old dogs were lying beside them not in a leash. A hundred paces further in the edge of the copse stood another groom of the count's, Mitka, a reckless rider and passionate sportsman. The count had followed the old custom of drink-ing before hunting a silver goblet of spiced brandy; he had had a slight lunch and after that half a bottle of his favourite bordeaux.

Count Ilya Andreitch was rather flushed from the wine and the drive; his eyes, covered by moisture, were particularly bright, and sitting in the saddle wrapped up in his fur coat, he looked like a baby taken out for a drive.

After seeing after his duties, Tchekmar, with his thin face and sunken cheeks, looked towards his master, with whom he had lived on the best of terms for thirty years. Perceiving that he was in a genial humour, he anticipated a pleasant chat. A third person rode circumspectly—he had no doubt been cautioned—out of the wood, and stood still behind the count. This personage was a grey-bearded old man, wearing a woman's gown and a high, peaked cap. It was the buffoon, Nastasya Ivanovna.

"Well, Nastasya Ivanovna," whispered the count, winking at him, "you only scare off the game, and Danilo will give it you."

"I wasn't born yesterday," said Nastasya Ivanovna.

"Sh!" hissed the count, and he turned to Semyon. "Have you seen Natalya Ilyinitchna?" he asked Semyon. "Where is she?"

"Her honour's with Pyotr Ilyitch, behind the high grass at Zharvry," answered Semyon, smiling. "Though she is a lady, she has a great love for the chase."

"And you wonder at her riding, Semyon, . . . eh?" said the count, "for a man even it wouldn't be amiss!"

"Who wouldn't wonder! So daring, so smart!"

"And where's Nikolasha? Above the Lyadovsky upland, eh?" the count asked still in a whisper.

"Yes, sir. His honour knows where he had best stand. He knows the ins and outs of hunting, so that Danilo and I are sometimes quite as-tonished at him," said Semyon, who knew how to please his master.

"He's a good, clever sportsman, eh? And what do you say to his riding, eh?"

"A perfect picture he is! How he drove the fox out of the Zavarzinsky thicket the other day. He galloped down from the ravine, it was a sight —the horse worth a thousand roubles, and the rider beyond all price. Yes, you would have to look a long while to find his match!"

"To look a long while . . ." repeated the count, obviously regretting that Semyon's praises had come to so speedy a termination. "A long while," he repeated, turning back the skirt of his coat and looking for his snuff-box.

"The other day they were coming out from Mass in all their glory, Mihail Sidoritch . . ." Semyon stopped short, hearing distinctly in the still air the rush of the hounds, with no more than two or three dogs giving tongue. With his head on one side, he listened, shaking a warning finger at his master. "They're on the scent of the litter . . ." he whispered; "they have gone straight toward Lyadovsky upland."

The count, with a smile still lingering on his face, looked straight before him along the path, and did not take a pinch from the snuff-box he held in his hand. The hounds' cry was followed by the bass note of the hunting cry for a wolf sounded on Danilo's horn. The pack joined the first three dogs, and the voices of the hounds could be heard in full cry with the peculiar note which serves to betoken that they are after a wolf. The whippers-in were not now hallooing, but urging on the hounds with cries of "Loo! loo! loo!" and above all the voices rose the voice of Danilo, passing from a deep note to piercing shrillness. Danilo's voice seemed to fill the whole forest, to pierce beyond it, and echo far away in the open country.

After listening for a few seconds in silence, the count and his groom felt certain that the hounds had divided into two packs: one, the larger, was going off into the distance, in particularly hot cry; the other part of the pack was moving along the forest past the count, and it was with this pack that Danilo's voice was heard urging the dogs on. The sounds from both packs melted into unison and broke apart again, but both were getting further away. Semyon sighed and stooped down to straighten the leash, in which a young dog had caught his leg. The count too sighed, and noticing the snuff-box in his hand, he opened it and took a pinch.

"Back!" cried Semyon to the dog, which had poked out beyond the bushes. The count started, and dropped the snuff-box. Nastasya Ivanovna got off his horse and began picking it up.

The count and Semyon watched him. All of a sudden, as so often happens, the sound of the hunt was in an instant close at hand, as though the baying dogs and Danilo's cries were just upon them.

The count looked round, and on the right he saw Mitka, who was staring at the count with eyes starting out of his head. Lifting his cap, he pointed in front to the other side.

"Look out!" he shouted in a voice that showed the words had long been fretting him to be uttered. And letting go the dogs, he galloped towards the count.

The count and Semyon galloped out of the bushes, and on their left they saw a wolf. With a soft, rolling gait it moved at a slow amble further to their left into the very thicket in which they had been standing. The angry dogs whined, and pulling themselves free from the leash, flew by the horses' hoofs after the wolf.

The wolf paused in his flight; awkwardly, like a man with a quinsy, he turned his heavy-browed head towards the dogs, and still with the same soft, rolling gait gave one bound and a second, and, waving its tail, disappeared into the bushes. At the same instant, with a cry like a wail, there sprang desperately out of the thicket opposite one hound, then a second and a third, and all the pack flew across the open ground towards the very spot where the wolf had vanished. The bushes were parted behind the dogs, and Danilo's brown horse, dark with sweat, emerged from them. On its long back Danilo sat perched up and swaying forward. He had no cap on his grey hair, that fluttered in disorder above his red, perspiring face.

"Loo! loo! loo! . . ." he was shouting. When he caught sight of the count, there was a flash like lightning in his eyes.

"B——!" he shouted, using a brutally coarse term of abuse and menacing the count with his lifted whip. "Let the wolf slip! . . . sportsmen indeed!" And as though scorning to waste more words on the confused and frightened count, he lashed the moist and heavy sides of his brown gelding with all the fury that had been ready for the count, and flew off after the dogs. The count stood like a man who has been thrashed, looking about him and trying to smile and call for Semyon to sympathise with his plight. But Semyon was not there; he had galloped round to cut the wolf off from the forest. The greyhounds, too, were running to and fro on both sides. But the wolf got off into the bushes, and not one of the party succeeded in coming across him.

V

NIKOLAY ROSTOV was standing meanwhile at his post waiting for the wolf. He was aware of what must be taking place within the copse from the rush of the pack coming closer and going further away, from the cries of the dogs, whose notes were familiar to him, from the nearness, and then greater remoteness, and sudden raising of the voices of the huntsmen. He knew that there were both young and also old wolves in the enclosure. He knew the hounds had divided into two packs, that in one place they were close on the wolf, and that something had gone wrong. Every second he expected the wolf on his side. He made a thousand different suppositions of how and at what spot the wolf would run out, and how he would set upon it. Hope was succeeded by despair. Several times he prayed to God that the wolf would rush out upon him. He prayed with that feeling of passion and compunction with which men pray in moments of intense emotion due to trivial causes. "Why, what is it to Thee," he said to God, "to do this for me? I know Thou art great and that it's a sin to pray to Thee about this, but for God's sake do make the old wolf come out upon me, and make Karay fix his teeth in his throat and finish him before the eyes of 'uncle,' who is looking this way." A thousand times over in that half-hour, with intent, strained, and uneasy eyes Rostov scanned the thickets at the edge of the copse, with two scraggy oaks standing up above the undergrowth of aspen, and the ravine with its overhanging bank, and "uncle's" cap peering out from behind a bush on the right. "No, that happiness is not to be," thought Rostov, "yet what would it cost Him! It's not to be! I'm always unlucky, at cards, in war, and everything." Austerlitz and Dolohov flashed in distinct but rapid succession through his imagination. "Only once in my life to kill an old wolf; I ask for nothing beyond!" he thought, straining eyes and ears, looking from left to right, and back again, and listening to the slightest fluctuations in the sounds of the dogs. He looked again to the right and saw something running across the open ground towards him. "No, it can't be!" thought Rostov, taking a deep breath, as a man does at the coming of what he has long been hoping for. The greatest piece of luck had come to him, and so simply, without noise, or flourish, or display to signalise it. Rostov could not believe his eyes, and this uncertainty lasted more than a second. The wolf was running forward; he leaped clumsily over a rut that lay across his path.

It was an old wolf with a grey back and full, reddish belly. He was running without haste, plainly feeling secure of being unseen. Rostov held his breath and looked round at the dogs. They were lying and standing about, not seeing the wolf and quite unaware of him. Old Karay had his head turned round, and was angrily searching for a flea, snapping his yellow teeth on his haunches. "Loo! loo! loo!" Rostov whispered, pouting out his lips. The dogs leaped up, jingling the iron rings of the leashes, and pricked up their ears. Karay scratched his hindleg and got up, pricking up his ears and wagging his tail, on which there were hanging matted locks of his coat.

"Loose them? or not loose them?" Nikolay said to himself as the wolf moved away from the copse towards him. All at once the whole physiognomy of the wolf was transformed. He started, seeing—probably for the first time—human eyes fixed upon him; and, turning his head a little towards Rostov, stood still, in doubt whether to go back or forward. "Ay! Never mind, forward! . . ." the wolf seemed to be saying to himself, and he pushed on ahead, without looking round, softly and not rapidly, with an easy but resolute movement. "Loo! loo! . . ." Nikolay cried in a voice not his own, and of its own accord his gallant horse galloped at break-neck pace downhill, and leaped over the watercourse to cut off the wolf's retreat; the hounds dashed on even more swiftly, overtaking it.

Nikolay did not hear his own cry; he had no consciousness of galloping; he saw neither the dogs nor the ground over which he galloped. He saw nothing but the wolf, which, quickening its pace, was bounding in the same direction across the glade. Foremost of the hounds was the black and tan, broad-backed bitch, Milka, and she was getting close upon him. But the wolf turned a sidelong glance upon her, and instead of flying at him, as she always had done, Milka suddenly stopped short, her fore-legs held stiffly before her and her tail in the air.

"Loo! loo! loo!" shouted Nikolay.

The red hound, Lyubima, darted forward from behind Milka, dashed headlong at the wolf, and got hold of him by the hind-leg, but in the same second bounded away on the other side in terror. The wolf crouched, gnashed its teeth, rose again, and bounded forward, followed at a couple of yards' distance by all the dogs: they did not try to get closer.

"He'll get away! No, it's impossible!" thought Nikolay, still shouting in a husky voice.

"Karay! Loo! loo! . . ." he kept shouting, looking for the old hound, who was his one hope now.

Karay, straining his old muscles to the utmost, and watching the wolf intently, was bounding clumsily away from the beast, to cut across his path in front of him. But it was plain from the swiftness of the wolf's course and the slowness of the hounds that Karay was out in his reckoning. Nikolay saw the copse not far now ahead of him. If once the wolf reached it, he would escape to a certainty. But in front dogs and men came into sight, dashing almost straight towards the wolf. There was still hope. A long, young hound, not one of the Rostovs'—Nikolay did not recognise him—flew from in front straight at the wolf, and almost knocked him over. The wolf got up again with a surprising rapidity and flew at the young hound; his teeth clacked, and the hound, covered with blood from a gash in its side, thrust its head in the earth, squealing shrilly.

"Karay! old man!" Nikolay wailed.

The old dog, with the tufts of matted hair, quivering on his haunches, had succeeded, thanks to the delay, in cutting across the wolf's line of advance, and was now five paces in front of him. The wolf stole a glance at Karay, as though aware of his danger, and tucking his tail further between his legs, he quickened his pace. But then—Nikolay could only see that something was happening with Karay—the hound had dashed instantly at the wolf and had rolled in a struggling heap with him into the watercourse before them.

The moment when Nikolay saw the dogs struggling with the wolf in the watercourse, saw the wolf's grey coat under them, his outstretched hind-leg, his head gasping in terror, and his ears turned back (Karay had him by the throat)—the moment when Nikolay saw all this was the happiest moment of his life. He had already grasped the pommel of his saddle to dismount and stab the wolf, when suddenly the beast's head was thrust up above the mass of dogs, then his fore-legs were on the bank of the watercourse. The wolf clacked his teeth (Karay had not hold of his throat now), leaped with his hind-legs out of the hollow, and with his tail between his legs, pushed forward, getting away from the dogs again. Karay, his hair starting up, had difficulty in getting out of the watercourse; he seemed to be bruised or wounded. "My God, why is this!" Nikolay shouted in despair. The uncle's huntsman galloped across the line of the wolf's advance from the other side, and again his hounds stopped the wolf, again he was hemmed in.

Nikolay, his groom, the uncle, and his huntsman pranced about the beast with shouts and cries of "loo," every minute on the point of dismounting when the wolf crouched back, and dashing forward again every time the wolf shook himself free and moved towards the copse, where his safety lay.

At the beginning of this onset Danilo, hearing the hunters' cries, had darted out of the copse. He saw that Karay had hold of the wolf and checked his horse, supposing the deed was done. But seeing that the hunters did not dismount from their horses, and that the wolf was shaking himself free, and again making his escape, Danilo galloped his own horse, not towards the wolf, but in a straight line towards the copse, to cut him off, as Karay had done. Thanks to this manœuvre, he bore straight down on the wolf when the uncle's dogs had a second time fallen behind him.

Danilo galloped up in silence, holding a drawn dagger in his left hand, and thrashing the heaving sides of his chestnut horse with his riding whip, as though it were a flail.

Nikolay neither saw nor heard Danilo till his panting chestnut darted close by him, and he heard the sound of a falling body and saw Danilo lying in the midst of the dogs on the wolf's back, trying to get him by the ears. It was obvious to the dogs, to the hunters, and to the wolf that all was over now. The beast, its ears drawn back in terror, tried to get up, but the dogs clung to him. Danilo, as he got up, stumbled, and as though sinking down to rest, rolled with all his weight on the wolf, and snatched him by the ears. Nikolay would have stabbed him, but Danilo whispered: "Don't; we will string him up!" and shifting his position he put his foot on the wolf's neck. They put a stick in the wolf's jaws, fastened it, as it were bridling him with a leash, and tied his legs. Danilo swung the wolf twice from side to side. With happy, exhausted faces they tied the great wolf alive on a horse, that started and snorted in alarm at it; and with all the dogs trooping after and whining at the wolf, they brought it to the place where all were to meet. The wolf hounds had captured two cubs, and the greyhounds three. The party met together to show their booty and tell their stories, and every one went to look at the big wolf, which with its heavy-browed head hanging downward and the stick in its teeth, gazed with its great, glassy eyes at the crowd of dogs and men around it. When they touched him, his fastened legs quivered and he looked wildly and yet simply at all of them. Count Ilya Andreitch too went up and touched the wolf.

"Oh, what a great beast!" he said. "He's an old one, eh?" he asked Danilo, who was standing near him.

"That he is, your excellency," answered Danilo, hurriedly taking off his cap.

The count remembered the wolf he had let slip and Danilo's outburst. "You have a hot temper though, my man," said the count.

Danilo said nothing, but he shyly smiled a smile of childlike sweetness and amiability.

VI

THE old count went home. Natasha and Petya promised to follow immediately. The hunting party went on further as it was still early. In the middle of the day they set the hounds into a ravine covered with thickly growing young copse. Nikolay, standing on the stubble land above, could see all his party.

Facing Nikolay on the opposite side was a field of green corn, and there stood his huntsman, alone in a hollow behind a nut bush. As soon as they loosed the hounds, Nikolay heard a hound he knew—Voltorn—give tongue at intervals; other hounds joined him, pausing now and then, and taking up the cry again. A moment later he heard from the ravine the cry that they were on the scent of a fox, and all the pack joining together made for the opening towards the green corn away from Nikolay.

He saw the whippers-in in their red caps galloping along the edge of the overgrown ravine; he could see the dogs even, and was every instant expecting the fox to come into sight on the further side among the green corn.

The huntsman standing in the hollow started off and let his dogs go, and Nikolay saw the red, uncouth-looking fox hurrying along close to the ground, with its bushy tail, through the green corn. The dogs bore down on it. And now they were getting close, and now the fox was beginning to wind in circles between them, making the circles more and more rapidly, and sweeping its bushy brush around it, when all of a sudden a strange white dog flew down upon it, and was followed by a black one, and everything was confusion, and the dogs formed a star-shaped figure round it, scarcely moving, with their heads together, and their tails out. Two huntsmen galloped down to the dogs; one in a red cap, the other, a stranger, in a green coat.

"What's the meaning of it?" wondered Nikolay. "Where did that huntsman spring from? That's not uncle's man."

The huntsmen got the fox, and remained a long while standing on foot there, without hanging the fox on the saddle.

He could see the horses with their snaffles jutting up standing close by the huntsmen, and the dogs lying down. The huntsmen were waving their arms and doing something with the fox. A horn was sounded—the signal agreed upon in case of a dispute.

"That's Ilagin's huntsman getting up a row of some sort with our Ivan," said Nikolay's groom.

Nikolay sent the groom to call his sister and Petya to come to him, and rode at a walking pace towards the spot where the whippers-in were getting the hounds together. Several of the party galloped to the scene of the squabble.

Nikolay dismounted, and, with Natasha and Petya, who had ridden up, he stood by the hounds waiting to hear how the difficulty was settled. The huntsman who had been quarrelling came riding out of the bushes with the fox on the crupper, and rode towards his young master. He took off his cap a long way off and tried as he came up to speak respectfully. But he was pale and gasping for breath, and his face was wrathful. One of his eyes was blackened, but he was probably not aware of it.

"What was the matter over there?" asked Nikolay.

"Why, he was going to kill the fox right under our hounds' noses! And my bitch it was—the mouse-coloured one—that had got hold of it. You can go and have me up for it! Snatching hold of the fox! I gave him one with the fox. Here it is on my saddle. Is it a taste of this you want?" said the huntsman, pointing to his hunting-knife and apparently imagining that he was still talking to his enemy.

Nikolay did not waste words on the man, but asking his sister and Petya to wait for him, rode over to where the hounds and the men of the enemy, Ilagin, were gathered together.

The victorious huntsman rode off to join his fellows, and there, the centre of a sympathetic and inquisitive crowd, he recounted his exploit.

The point was that Ilagin, with whom the Rostovs had some quarrel and were engaged in a lawsuit, was hunting over places that by old custom belonged to the Rostovs, and now, as though of design, had sent his men to the ravine where the Rostovs were, and had allowed his man to snatch a fox under a stranger's dogs.

Nikolay had never seen Ilagin, but he had heard of the quarrelsomeness and obstinacy of their neighbour; and rushing, as he always did, to an extreme in his judgments and feelings, he cordially detested him, and looked upon him as his bitterest foe. Excited and angry, he rode up to him now, grasping his whip in his hand, fully prepared to take the most energetic and desperate measures in dealing with the enemy.

He had scarcely ridden beyond the ridge of the copse when he saw a stout gentleman in a beaver cap riding towards him on a handsome raven horse, accompanied by two grooms.

Instead of an enemy Nikolay found in Ilagin a courteous gentleman of imposing appearance, who was particularly anxious to make the young count's acquaintance. Ilagin took off his beaver cap as he approached Rostov, and said that he greatly regretted what had occurred, that he would have the man punished, that he begged the count to let them be better acquainted, and offered him the use of his preserves for hunting.

Natasha had ridden up not far behind her brother, in some excitement, fearing he might do something awful. Seeing that the opponents were exchanging affable greetings, she rode up to them. Ilagin lifted his beaver cap higher than ever to Natasha, and, smiling agreeably, said that the countess was indeed a Diana both in her passion for the chase and her beauty, of which he had heard so much.

Ilagin, to efface the impression of his huntsman's crime, insisted on Rostov coming to his upland a verst away, which he preserved for his own shooting, and described as teeming with hares. Nikolay agreed, and the whole party, its numbers now doubled, moved on. They had to ride through the fields to get there. The huntsmen moved in a line, and the gentry rode together. The uncle, Rostov, and Ilagin glanced stealthily at each other's dogs, trying not to be observed by the others, and looking uneasily for rivals likely to excel their own dogs.

Rostov was particularly struck by the beauty of a small thoroughbred, slender, black and tan bitch of Ilagin's, with muscles like steel, a delicate nose, and prominent black eyes. He had heard of the sporting qualities of Ilagin's dogs, and in that handsome bitch he saw a rival of his Milka.

In the middle of a sedate conversation about the crops of the year, started by Ilagin, Nikolay pointed out the black and tan bitch.

"You have a fine bitch there!" he said, in a careless tone. "Is she clever?"

"That one? Yes, she's a good beast—she can catch a hare," Ilagin said indifferently of his black and tan Yerza, a bitch for whom he had a year before given a neighbour three families of house-serfs. "So they don't brag of their thrashing, count," he went on, taking up their previous conversation. And feeling it only polite to repay the young count's compliment, Ilagin scanned his dogs, and pitched on Milka, whose broad back caught his eye.

"That's a good black and tan you have there—a fine one!" he said.

"Yes, she's all right, she can run," answered Nikolay. "Oh, if only a good big hare would run into the field, I would show you what she's like!" he thought, and turning to his groom, he said he would give a rouble to any one who would unearth a hare.

"I can't understand," Ilagin went on, "how it is other sportsmen are so envious over game and dogs. I will tell you for myself, count. I enjoy hunting, as you know; the chase in such company . . . what could be more delightful" (he doffed his beaver cap again to Natasha); "but this reckoning up of the skins one has carried off—I don't care about that."

"Oh no!"

"Nor could I be chagrined at my dog's being outdone by another man's—all I care about is the chase itself, eh, count? And so I consider . . ."

"Oh, . . . ho . . . ho," sounded at that moment in a prolonged call from one of the grooms. He was standing on a knoll in the stubble with his whip held up, and he called once more, "O . . . ho . . . aho!" (This call, and the lifted whip, meant that he saw a hare squatting before him.)

"Ah, he has started a hare, I fancy," said Ilagin carelessly. "Well, let us course it, count!"

"Yes, we must . . . but what do you say, together?" answered Nikolay, looking intently at Yerza and the uncle's red Rugay, the two rivals against whom he had never before had a chance of putting his dogs. "What if they outdo my Milka from the first?" he thought, riding by the uncle and Ilagin towards the hare.

"Is it full-grown?" asked Ilagin, going up to the groom who had started it, and looking about him with some excitement, as he whistled to his Yerza. . . . "And you, Mihail Nikanoritch?" he said to the uncle.

The uncle rode on, looking sullen.

"What's the use of my competing with you? Why, your dogs—you have paid a village for each of them; they're worth thousands. You try yours against each other, and I'll look on!"

"Rugay! Hey, hey," he shouted. "Rugayushka!" he added, involuntarily expressing his tenderness, and the hope he put in the red dog by this affectionate diminutive. Natasha saw and felt the emotion concealed by the two elderly men and by her brother, and was herself excited by it. The groom on the knoll was standing with his whip lifted; the gentlemen rode up to him at a walking pace; the pack were on the rim of the horizon, moving away from the hare; the rest of the hunting party too were riding away. Everything was done slowly and deliberately.

"Which way is its head?" asked Nikolay, after riding a hundred paces towards the groom. But before the groom had time to answer, the hare, who had been sniffing in the ground the frost coming next morning, leapt up from its squatting posture. The pack of hounds on leashes flew baying downhill after the hare; the harriers, who were not on leash, rushed from all sides towards the hounds or after the hare. The whippers-in, who had been moving so deliberately, galloped over the country getting the dogs together, with shouts of "stop!" while the huntsmen directed their course with shouts of "o . . . o . . . ahoy!" Nikolay, Natasha, and the uncle and Ilagin, who had been hitherto so composed, flew ahead, reckless of how or where they went, seeing nothing but the dogs and the hare, and afraid of nothing but losing sight for an instant of the course. The hare turned out to be a fleet and strong one. When he jumped up he did not at once race off, but cocked up his ears, listening to the shouts and tramp of hoofs, that came from all sides at once. He took a dozen bounds not very swiftly, letting the dogs gain on him, but at last choosing his direction, and grasping his danger, he put his ears back, and dashed off at full speed. He had been crouching in the stubble, but the green field was in front of him, and there it was marshy ground. The two dogs of the groom who had started him were the nearest and the first to be on the scent after him. But they had not got near him, when Ilagin's black and tan Yerza flew ahead of them, got within a yard, pounced on him with fearful swiftness, aiming at the hare's tail, and rolled over, thinking she had hold of him. The hare arched his back, and bounded off more nimbly than ever. The broad-backed, black and tan Milka flew ahead of Yerza, and began rapidly gaining on the hare.

"Milashka! little mother!" Nikolay shouted triumphantly. Milka seemed on the point of pouncing on the hare, but she overtook him and flew beyond. The hare doubled back. Again the graceful Yerza dashed at him, and kept close to the hare's tail, as though measuring the distance, so as not to miss getting hold of the hare, by the haunch this time.

"Yerzinka, little sister!" wailed Ilagin, in a voice unlike his own. Yerza did not heed his appeals. At the very moment when she seemed

about to seize the hare, he doubled and darted away to the ditch between the stubble and the green field. Again Yerza and Milka, running
side by side, like a pair of horses, flew after the hare; the hare was
better off in the ditch, the dogs could not gain on him so quickly.

"Rugay! Rugayushka! Forward—quick march," another voice
shouted this time. And Rugay, the uncle's red, broad-shouldered dog,
stretching out and curving his back, caught up the two foremost dogs,
pushed ahead of them, flung himself with complete self-abandonment
right on the hare, turned him out of the ditch into the green field, flung
himself still more viciously on him once more, sinking up to his knees in
the swampy ground, and all that could be seen was the dog rolling over
with the hare, covering his back with mud. The dogs formed a star-
shaped figure round him. A moment later all the party pulled their
horses up round the crowding dogs. The uncle alone dismounted in a
rapture of delight, and cutting off the feet, shaking the hare for the
blood to drip off, he looked about him, his eyes restless with excitement,
and his hands and legs moving nervously. He went on talking, regardless
of what or to whom he spoke. "That's something like, quick march . . .
there's a dog for you . . . he outstripped them all . . . if they cost a
thousand or they cost a rouble . . . forward, quick march, and no mistake!" he kept saying, panting and looking wrathfully about him, as
though he were abusing some one, as though they had all been his
enemies, had insulted him, and he had only now at last succeeded in
paying them out. "So much for your thousand rouble dogs—forward,
quick march! Rugay, here's the foot," he said, dropping the dog the
hare's muddy foot, which he had just cut off; "you've deserved it—
forward, quick march!"

"She wore herself out—ran it down three times all alone," Nikolay
was saying, listening to no one, and heedless whether he were heard or
not.

"To be sure, cutting in sideways like that!" Ilagin's groom was saying.

"Why, when it had been missed like that, and once down, any yard-
dog could catch it of course," said Ilagin, at the same moment, red and
breathless from the gallop and the excitement. At the same time Natasha, without taking breath, gave vent to her delight and excitement
in a shriek so shrill that it set every one's ears tingling. In that shriek
she expressed just what the others were expressing by talking all at once.
And her shriek was so strange that she must have been ashamed of that
wild scream, and the others must have been surprised at it at any other
time. The uncle himself twisted up the hare, flung him neatly and
smartly across his horse's back, seeming to reproach them all by this
gesture, and with an air of not caring to speak to anyone, he mounted
his bay and rode away. All but he, dispirited and disappointed, rode on,
and it was some time before they could recover their previous affectation
of indifference. For a long time after they stared at the red dog, Rugay,
who with his round back spattered with mud, and clinking the rings of
his leash, walked with the serene air of a conqueror behind the uncle's
horse.

"I'm like all the rest till it's a question of coursing a hare; but then you had better look out!" was what Nikolay fancied the dog's air expressed.

When the uncle rode up to Nikolay a good deal later, and addressed a remark to him, he felt flattered at the uncle's deigning to speak to him after what had happened.

VII

WHEN Ilagin took leave of them in the evening, Nikolay found himself so great a distance from home that he accepted the uncle's invitation to stop hunting and to stay the night at the uncle's little place, Mihailovka. "And if you all come to me—forward, quick march!" said the uncle, "it would be even better; you see, the weather's damp, you could rest, and the little countess could be driven back in a trap." The invitation was accepted; a huntsman was sent to Otradnoe for a trap, and Nikolay, Natasha, and Petya rode to the uncle's house.

Five men servants—little and big—ran out on to the front steps to meet their master. Dozens of women, old and big and little, popped out at the back entrance to have a look at the huntsmen as they arrived. The presence of Natasha—a woman, a lady, on horseback—excited the curiosity of the uncle's house-serfs to such a pitch that many of them went up to her, stared her in the face, and, unrestrained by her presence, made remarks about her, as though she were some prodigy on show, not a human being, and not capable of hearing and understanding what was said about her.

"Arinka, look-ée, she sits sideways! Sits on so, while her skirt flies about. . . . And look at the little horn!"

"Sakes alive! and the knife too. . . ."

"A regular Tatar woman!"

"How do you manage not to tumble off?" said the forwardest of them, addressing Natasha boldly.

The uncle got off his horse at the steps of his little wooden house, which was shut in by an overgrown garden. Looking from one to another of his household, he shouted peremptorily to those who were not wanted to retire, and for the others to do all that was needed for the reception of his guests.

They all ran off in different directions. The uncle helped Natasha to dismount, and gave her his arm up the shaky, plank steps.

Inside, the house, with boarded, unplastered walls, was not very clean; there was nothing to show that the chief aim of the persons living in it was the removal of every spot, yet there were not signs of neglect. There was a smell of fresh apples in the entry, and the walls were hung with foxskins and wolfskins.

The uncle led his guests through the vestibule into a little hall with a folding-table and red chairs, then into a drawing-room with a round birchwood table and a sofa, and then into his study, with a ragged sofa, a threadbare carpet, and portraits of Suvorov, of his father and mother, and of himself in military uniform. The study smelt strongly of tobacco and dogs. In the study the uncle asked his guests to sit down and make themselves at home, and he left them. Rugay came in, his back still covered with mud, and lay on the sofa, cleaning himself with his tongue and his teeth. There was a corridor leading from the study, and in it they could see a screen with ragged curtains. Behind the screen they heard feminine laughter and whispering. Natasha, Nikolay, and Petya took off their wraps and sat down on the sofa. Petya leaned on his arm and fell asleep at once; Natasha and Nikolay sat without speaking. Their faces were burning; they were very hungry and very cheerful. They looked at one another—now that the hunt was over and they were indoors, Nikolay did not feel called upon to show his masculine superiority over his sister. Natasha winked at her brother; and they could neither of them restrain themselves long, and broke into a ringing laugh before they had time to invent a pretext for their mirth.

After a brief interval, the uncle came in wearing a Cossack coat, blue breeches, and little top-boots. And this very costume, at which Natasha had looked with surprise and amusement when the uncle wore it at Otradnoe, seemed to her now the right costume here, and in no way inferior to frock coats or ordinary jackets. The uncle, too, was in good spirits; far from feeling mortified at the laughter of the brother and sister (he was incapable of imagining that they could be laughing at his mode of life), he joined in their causeless mirth himself.

"Well, this young countess here—forward, quick march!—I have never seen her like!" he said, giving a long pipe to Rostov, while with a practised motion of three fingers he filled another—a short broken one— for himself.

"She's been in the saddle all day—something for a man to boast of— and she's just as fresh as if nothing had happened!"

Soon the door was opened obviously, from the sound, by a barefoot servant-girl, and a stout, red-cheeked, handsome woman of about forty, with a double chin and full red lips, walked in, with a big tray in her hands. With hospitable dignity and cordiality in her eyes and in every gesture, she looked round at the guests, and with a genial smile bowed to them respectfully.

In spite of her exceptional stoutness, which made her hold her head flung back, while her bosom and all her portly person was thrust forward, this woman (the uncle's housekeeper) stepped with extreme lightness. She went to the table, put the tray down, and deftly with her plump, white hands set the bottles and dishes on the table. When she had finished this task she went away, standing for a moment in the doorway with a smile on her face. "Here I am—I am she! Now do you understand the uncle?" her appearance had said to Rostov. Who could fail to understand? Not Nikolay only, but even Natasha understood the uncle now and the significance of his knitted brows, and the happy, complacent smile, which puckered his lips as Anisya Fyodorovna came in. On the tray there were liqueurs, herb-brandy, mushrooms, biscuits of rye flour made with buttermilk, honey in the comb, foaming mead made from honey, apples, nuts raw and nuts baked, and nuts preserved in honey. Then Anisya Fyodorovna brought in preserves made with honey and with sugar, and ham and a chicken that had just been roasted.

All these delicacies were of Anisya Fyodorovna's preparing, cooking or preserving. All seemed to smell and taste, as it were, of Anisya Fyodorovna. All seemed to recall her buxomness, cleanliness, whiteness, and cordial smile.

"A little of this, please, little countess," she kept saying, as she handed Natasha first one thing, then another. Natasha ate of everything, and it seemed to her that such buttermilk biscuits, such delicious preserves, such nuts in honey, such a chicken, she had never seen nor tasted anywhere. Anisya Fyodorovna withdrew. Rostov and the uncle, as they sipped cherry brandy after supper, talked of hunts past and to come, of Rugay and Ilagin's dogs. Natasha sat upright on the sofa, listening with sparkling eyes. She tried several times to waken Petya, and make him eat something, but he made incoherent replies, evidently in his sleep. Natasha felt so gay, so well content in these new surroundings, that her only fear was that the trap would come too soon for her. After a silence had chanced to fall upon them, as almost always happens when any one receives friends for the first time in his own house, the uncle said, in response to the thought in his guests' minds:

"Yes, so you see how I am finishing my days. . . . One dies—forward, quick march!—nothing is left. So why sin!"

The uncle's face was full of significance and even beauty as he said this. Rostov could not help recalling as he spoke all the good things he had heard said by his father and the neighbours about him. Through the whole district the uncle had the reputation of being a most generous and disinterested eccentric. He was asked to arbitrate in family quarrels; he was chosen executor; secrets were entrusted to him; he was elected a justice, and asked to fill other similar posts; but he had always persisted in refusing all public appointments, spending the autumn and spring in the fields on his bay horse, the winter sitting at home, and the summer lying in his overgrown garden.

"Why don't you enter the service, uncle?"

"I have been in the service, but I flung it up. I'm not fit for it. I can't make anything of it. That's your affair. I haven't the wit for it. The chase, now, is a very different matter; there it's all forward and quick march! Open the door there!" he shouted. "Why have you shut it?" A door at the end of the corridor (which word the uncle always pronounced *collidor*, like a peasant) led to the huntsmen's room, as the sitting-room for the huntsmen was called. There was a rapid patter of bare feet, and an unseen hand opened the door into the huntsmen's room. They could then hear distinctly from the corridor the sounds of the balalaïka, unmistakably played by a master hand. Natasha had been for some time listening, and now she went out into the corridor to hear the music more clearly.

"That's Mitka, my coachman . . . I bought him a good balalaïka;

I'm fond of it," said the uncle. It was his custom to get Mitka to play the balalaika in the men's room when he came home from the chase. He was fond of hearing that instrument.

"How well he plays! It's really very nice," said Nikolay, with a certain unconscious superciliousness in his tone, as though he were ashamed to admit he liked this music.

"Very nice?" Natasha said reproachfully, feeling the tone in which her brother had spoken. "It's not nice, but splendid, really!" Just as the uncle's mushrooms and honey and liqueurs had seemed to her the most delicious in the world, this playing struck her at that moment as the very acme of musical expression.

"More, more, please," said Natasha in the doorway, as soon as the balalaika ceased. Mitka tuned up and began again gallantly twanging away at "My Lady," with shakes and flourishes. The uncle sat listening with his head on one side, and a slight smile. The air of "My Lady" was repeated a hundred times over. Several times the balalaika was tuned up and the same notes were thrummed again, but the audience did not weary of it, and still longed to hear it again and again. Anisya Fyodorovna came in and stood with her portly person leaning against the doorpost.

"You are pleased to listen!" she said to Natasha, with a smile extraordinarily like the uncle's smile. "He does play nicely," she said.

"That part he never plays right," the uncle said suddenly with a vigorous gesture. "It ought to be taken more at a run—forward, quick march! . . . to be played lightly."

"Why, can you do it?" asked Natasha.

The uncle smiled, and did not answer.

"Just you look, Anisyushka, whether the strings are all right on the guitar, eh? It's a long while since I have handled it. I had quite given it up!"

Anisya Fyodorovna went very readily with her light step to do her master's bidding, and brought him his guitar. Without looking at any one the uncle blew the dust off it, tapped on the case with his bony fingers, tuned it, and settled himself in a low chair. Arching his left elbow with a rather theatrical gesture, he held the guitar above the finger-board, and winking at Anisya Fyodorovna, he played, not the first notes of "My Lady," but a single pure musical chord, and then smoothly, quietly, but confidently began playing in very slow time the well-known song, "As along the high road." The air of the song thrilled in Nikolay's and Natasha's hearts in time, in tune with it, with the same sober gaiety—the same gaiety as was manifest in the whole personality of Anisya Fyodorovna. Anisya Fyodorovna flushed, and hiding her face in her kerchief, went laughing out of the room. The uncle still went on playing the song carefully, correctly, and vigorously, gazing with a transformed, inspired face at the spot where Anisya Fyodorovna had stood. Laughter came gradually into his face on one side under his grey moustache, and it grew stronger as the song went on, as the time quickened, and breaks came after a flourish.

"Splendid, splendid, uncle! Again, again!" cried Natasha, as soon as he had finished. She jumped up from her place and kissed and hugged the uncle. "Nikolenka, Nikolenka!" she said, looking round at her brother as though to ask, "What do you say to it?"

Nikolay, too, was much pleased by the uncle's playing. He played the song a second time. The smiling face of Anisya Fyodorovna appeared again in the doorway and other faces behind her. . . . "For the water from the well, a maiden calls to him to stay!" played the uncle. He made another dexterous flourish and broke off, twitching his shoulders.

"Oh, oh, uncle darling!" wailed Natasha, in a voice as imploring as though her life depended on it. The uncle got up, and there seemed to be two men in him at that moment—one smiled seriously at the antics of the merry player, while the merry player naïvely and carefully exe-cuted the steps preliminary to the dance.

"Come, little niece!" cried the uncle, waving to Natasha the hand that had struck the last chord.

Natasha flung off the shawl that had been wrapped round her, ran forward facing the uncle, and setting her arms akimbo, made the move-ments of her shoulder and waist.

Where, how, when had this young countess, educated by a French *émigrée*, sucked in with the Russian air she breathed the spirit of that dance? Where had she picked up these movements which the *pas de châle* would, one might have thought, long ago have eradicated? But the spirit, the motions were those inimitable, unteachable, Russian gestures the uncle had hoped for from her. As soon as she stood up, and smiled that triumphant, proud smile of sly gaiety, the dread that had come on Nikolay and all the spectators at the first moment, the dread that she would not dance it well, was at an end and they were already admiring her.

She danced the dance well, so well indeed, so perfectly, that Anisya Fyodorovna, who handed her at once the kerchief she needed in the dance, had tears in her eyes, though she laughed as she watched that slender, graceful little countess, reared in silk and velvet, belonging to another world than hers, who was yet able to understand all that was in Anisya and her father and her mother and her aunt and every Russian soul.

"Well done, little countess—forward, quick march!" cried the uncle, laughing gleefully as he finished the dance. "Ah, that's a niece to be proud of! She only wants a fine fellow picked out now for her husband, —and then, forward, quick march!"

"One has been picked out already," said Nikolay, smiling.

"Oh!" said the uncle in surprise, looking inquiringly at Natasha. Natasha nodded her head with a happy smile.

"And such an one!" she said. But as soon as she said it a different, new series of ideas and feelings rose up within her. "What was the mean-ing of Nikolay's smile when he said: 'One has been picked out already'? Was he glad of it, or not glad? He seemed to think my Bolkonsky would not approve, would not understand our gaiety now. No, he would quite

understand it. Where is he now?" Natasha wondered, and her face became serious at once. But that lasted only one second. "I mustn't think,
I mustn't dare to think about that," she said to herself; and smiling, she
sat down again near the uncle, begging him to play them something
more.

The uncle played another song and waltz. Then, after a pause, he
cleared his throat and began to sing his favourite hunting song:—

> "When there fall at evening glow
> The first flakes of winter snow." . . .

The uncle sang, as peasants sing, in full and naïve conviction that in a
song the whole value rests in the words, that the tune comes of itself,
and that a tune apart is nothing, that the tune is only for the sake of the
verse. And this gave the uncle's unself-conscious singing a peculiar
charm, like the song of birds. Natasha was in ecstasies over the uncle's
singing. She made up her mind not to learn the harp any longer, but
to play only on the guitar. She asked the uncle for the guitar and at
once struck the chords of the song.

At ten o'clock there arrived the wagonette, a trap, and three men on
horseback, who had been sent to look for Natasha and Petya. The
count and countess did not know where they were and were very
anxious, so said one of the men.

Petya was carried out and laid in the wagonette as though he had
been a corpse. Natasha and Nikolay got into the trap. The uncle
wrapped Natasha up, and said good-bye to her with quite a new tenderness. He accompanied them on foot as far as the bridge which they had
to ride round, fording the stream, and bade his huntsmen ride in front
with lanterns.

"Farewell, dear little niece!" they heard called in the darkness by his
voice, not the one Natasha had been familiar with before, but the voice
that had sung "When fall at evening glow."

There were red lights in the village they drove through and a cheerful
smell of smoke.

"What a darling that uncle is!" said Natasha as they drove out into
the highroad.

"Yes," said Nikolay. "You're not cold?"

"No, I'm very comfortable; very. I am so happy," said Natasha, positively perplexed at her own well-being. They were silent for a long
while.

The night was dark and damp. They could not see the horses, but
could only hear them splashing through the unseen mud.

What was passing in that childlike, responsive soul, that so eagerly
caught and made its own all the varied impressions of life? How were
they all stored away in her heart? But she was very happy. They were
getting near home when she suddenly hummed the air of "When fall at
evening glow," which she had been trying to get all the way, and had
only just succeeded in catching.

"Have you caught it?" said Nikolay.

"What are you thinking of just now, Nikolay?" asked Natasha. They were fond of asking each other that question.

"I?" said Nikolay, trying to recall. "Well, you see, at first I was thinking that Rugay, the red dog, is like the uncle, and that if he were a man he would keep uncle always in the house with him, if not for racing, for music he'd keep him anyway. How jolly uncle is! Isn't he? Well, and you?"

"I? Wait a minute; wait a minute! Oh, I was thinking at first that here we are driving and supposing that we are going home, but God knows where we are going in this darkness, and all of a sudden we shall arrive and see we are not at Otradnoe but in fairyland. And then I thought, too . . . no; nothing more."

"I know, of course, you thought of *him*," said Nikolay, smiling, as Natasha could tell by his voice.

"No," Natasha answered, though she really had been thinking at the same time of Prince Andrey and how he would like the uncle. "And I keep repeating, too, all the way I keep repeating: how nicely Anisyushka walked; how nicely . . ." said Natasha. And Nikolay heard her musical, causeless, happy laugh.

"And do you know?" she said suddenly. "I know I shall never be as happy, as peaceful as I am now . . ."

"What nonsense, idiocy, rubbish!" said Nikolay, and he thought: "What a darling this Natasha of mine is! I have never had, and never shall have, another friend like her. Why should she be married? I could drive like this with her for ever!"

"What a darling this Nikolay of mine is!" Natasha was thinking.

"Ah! Still a light in the drawing-room," she said, pointing to the windows of their house gleaming attractively in the wet, velvety darkness of the night.

VIII

COUNT ILYA ANDREITCH had given up being a marshal of nobility, because that position involved too heavy an expenditure. But his difficulties were not removed by that. Often Natasha and Nikolay knew of uneasy, private consultations between their parents, and heard talk of selling the sumptuous ancestral house of the Rostovs and the estate near Moscow. When the count was no longer marshal it was not necessary to entertain on such a large scale, and they led a quieter life at Otradnoe than in former years. But the immense house and the lodges were still full of people; more than twenty persons still sat down to table with them. These were all their own people, time-honoured inmates of their household, almost members of the family, or persons who must, it seemed, inevitably live in the count's house. Such were Dimmler, the music-master, and his wife; Vogel the dancing-master, with his family; an old Madame Byelov, and many others besides; Petya's tutors, the girls' old governess, and persons who simply found it better or more profitable to live at the count's than in a house of their own. They did not entertain so many guests as before, but they still lived in that manner, apart from which the count and countess could not have conceived of life at all. There was still the same hunting establishment, increased indeed by Nikolay. There were still the same fifty horses and fifteen grooms in the stables; the same costly presents on name-days, and ceremonial dinners to the whole neighbourhood. There were still the count's games of whist and boston, at which, letting every one see his cards, he allowed himself to be plundered every day of hundreds by his neighbours, who looked upon the privilege of making up a rubber with Count Ilya Andreitch as a profitable investment.

The count went into his affairs as though walking into a huge net, trying not to believe that he was entangled, and at every step getting more and more entangled, and feeling too feeble either to tear the nets that held him fast, or with care and patience to set about disentangling them. The countess with her loving heart felt that her children were being ruined, that the count was not to blame, that he could not help being what he was, that he was distressed himself (though he tried to conceal it) at the consciousness of his own and his children's ruin, and was seeking means to improve their position. To her feminine mind only one way of doing so occurred—that was, to marry Nikolay to a wealthy heiress. She felt that this was their last hope, and that if Nikolay were to refuse the match she had found for him she must bid farewell for ever to all chance of improving their position. This match was Julie Karagin, the daughter of excellent and virtuous parents, known to the Rostovs from childhood, and now left a wealthy heiress by the death of her last surviving brother.

The countess wrote directly to Madame Karagin in Moscow, suggesting to her the marriage of her daughter to her own son, and received a favourable reply from her. Madame Karagin replied that she was quite ready for her part to consent to the match, but everything must depend on her daughter's inclinations. Madame Karagin invited Nikolay to come to Moscow. Several times the countess, with tears in her eyes, had told her son that now that both her daughters were settled, her only wish was to see him married. She said that she could rest quietly in her grave if this were settled. Then she would say that she had an excellent, girl in her eye, and would try and get from him his views on matrimony.

On other occasions she praised Julie and advised Nikolay to go to Moscow for the holidays to amuse himself a little. Nikolay guessed what his mother's hints were aiming at, and on one such occasion he forced her to complete frankness. She told him plainly that all hope of improving their position rested now on his marrying Julie Karagin.

"What, if I loved a girl with no fortune would you really desire me, mamma, to sacrifice my feeling and my honour for the sake of money?" he asked his mother, with no notion of the cruelty of his question, but simply wishing to show his noble sentiments.

"No; you misunderstand me," said his mother, not knowing how to retrieve her mistake. "You misunderstand me, Nikolenka. It is your happiness I wish for," she added, and she felt she was speaking falsely, that she was blundering. She burst into tears.

"Mamma, don't cry, and only tell me that you wish it, and you know that I would give my whole life, everything for your peace of mind," said Nikolay; "I will sacrifice everything for you, even my feelings."

But the countess did not want the question put like that; she did not want to receive sacrifices from her son, she would have liked to sacrifice herself to him.

"No; you don't understand me, don't let us talk of it," she said, wiping away her tears.

"Yes, perhaps I really do love a poor girl," Nikolay said to himself; "what, am I to sacrifice my feeling and my honour for fortune? I wonder how mamma could say such a thing. Because Sonya is poor I must not love her," he thought; "I must not respond to her faithful, devoted love. And it is certain I should be happier with her than with any doll of a Julie. To sacrifice my feelings for the welfare of my family I can always do," he said to himself, "but I can't control my feelings. If I love Sonya, that feeling is more than anything and above anything for me."

Nikolay did not go to Moscow, the countess did not renew her conversations with him about matrimony, and with grief, and sometimes with exasperation, saw symptoms of a growing attachment between her son and the portionless Sonya. She blamed herself for it, yet could not refrain from scolding and upbraiding Sonya, often reproving her without cause and addressing her as "my good girl." What irritated the kind-hearted countess more than anything was that this poor, dark-eyed niece was so meek, so good, so devoutly grateful to her benefactors, and so truly, so constantly, and so unselfishly in love with Nikolay that it was impossible to find any fault with her.

Nikolay went on spending his term of leave with his parents. From Prince Andrey a fourth letter had been received from Rome. In it he wrote that he would long ago have been on his way back to Russia, but that in the warm climate his wound had suddenly re-opened, which would compel him to defer his return till the beginning of the new year. Natasha was as much in love with her betrothed, as untroubled in her love, and as ready to throw herself into all the pleasures of life as ever. But towards the end of the fourth month of their separation she began to suffer from fits of depression, against which she was unable to contend. She felt sorry for herself, sorry that all this time should be wasted and be of no use to any one, while she felt such capacity for loving and being loved.

Life was not gay in the Rostovs' household.

IX

CHRISTMAS came and except for the High Mass, the solemn and wearisome congratulations to neighbours and house-serfs, and the new gowns donned by every one, nothing special happened to mark the holidays, though the still weather with twenty degrees of frost, the dazzling sunshine by day and the bright, starlit sky at night seemed to call for some special celebration of the season.

On the third day of Christmas week, after dinner, all the members of the household had separated and gone to their respective rooms. It was the dullest time of the day. Nikolay, who had been calling on neighbours in the morning, was asleep in the divan-room. The old count was resting in his own room. In the drawing-room Sonya was sitting at a round table copying a design for embroidery. The countess was playing patience. Nastasya Ivanovna, the buffoon, with a dejected countenance, was sitting in the window with two old ladies. Natasha came into the room, went up to Sonya, looked at what she was doing, then went up to her mother and stood there mutely.

"Why are you wandering about like an unquiet spirit?" said her mother. "What do you want?"

"I want *him* . . . I want *him* at once, this minute," said Natasha, with a gleam in her eyes and no smile on her lips. The countess raised her head and looked intently at her daughter.

"Don't look at me, mamma; don't look at me like that; I shall cry in a minute."

"Sit down; come and sit by me," said the countess.

"Mamma, I want *him*. Why should I be wasting time like this, mamma?" . . . Her voice broke, tears gushed into her eyes, and to hide them, she turned quickly and went out of the room. She went into the divan-room, stood there, thought a moment and went to the maids' room. There an old maid-servant was scolding a young girl who had run in breathless from the cold outside.

"Give over playing," said the old woman; "there is a time for everything."

"Let her off, Kondratyevna," said Natasha. "Run along, Mavrusha, run along."

And after releasing Mavrusha, Natasha crossed the big hall and went to the vestibule. An old footman and two young ones were playing cards. They broke off and rose at the entrance of their young mistress. "What am I to do with them?" Natasha wondered.

"Yes, Nikita, go out, please . . . Where am I to send him? . . . Yes, go to the yard and bring me a cock, please; and you, Misha, bring me some oats."

"Just a few oats, if you please?" said Misha, with cheerful readiness.

"Run along; make haste," the old man urged him.

"Fyodor, you get me some chalk."

As she passed the buffet she ordered the samovar, though it was not the right time for it.

The buffet-waiter, Foka, was the most ill-tempered person in the house. Natasha liked to try her power over him. He did not believe in her order, and went to inquire if it were really wanted.

"Ah, you're a nice young lady!" said Foka, pretending to frown at Natasha.

No one in the house sent people on errands and gave the servants so much work as Natasha. She could not see people without wanting to send them for something. She seemed to be trying to see whether one of them would not be cross or sulky with her; but no one's orders were so readily obeyed by the servants as Natasha's. "What am I to do? Where am I to go?" Natasha wondered, strolling slowly along the corridor.

"Nastasya Ivanovna, what will my children be?" she asked the buffoon, who came towards her in his woman's jacket.

"Fleas, and dragon-flies, and grasshoppers," answered the buffoon.

"My God! my God! always the same. Oh, where am I to go? What am I to do with myself?" And she ran rapidly upstairs, tapping with her shoes, to see Vogel and his wife, who had rooms on the top floor. The two governesses were sitting with the Vogels and on the table were plates of raisins, walnuts, and almonds. The governesses were discussing the question which was the cheaper town to live in, Moscow or Odessa. Natasha sat down, listened to their talk with a serious and dreamy face, and got up. "The island Madagascar," she said. "Māda-ga-scar," she repeated, articulating each syllable distinctly; and making no reply to Madame Schoss's inquiry into her meaning, she went out of the room.

Petya, her brother, was upstairs too. He was engaged with his tutor making fireworks to let off that night.

"Petya! Petya!" she shouted to him, "carry me downstairs." Petya ran to her and offered her his back, and he pranced along with her. "No, enough. The island Madagascar," she repeated, and jumping off his back she went downstairs.

Having as it were reviewed her kingdom, tried her power, and made sure that all were submissive, but yet that she was dull, Natasha went into the big hall, took up the guitar, and sat down with it in a dark corner behind a bookcase. She began fingering the strings in the bass, picking out a phrase she recalled from an opera she had heard in Petersburg with Prince Andrey. For other listeners the sounds that came from her guitar would have had no sort of meaning, but these sounds called up in her imagination a whole series of reminiscences. She sat behind the bookcase with her eyes fixed on a streak of light that fell from the crack in the pantry door, and listened to herself and recalled the past. She was in the mood for brooding over memories.

Sonya crossed the hall, and went into the pantry with a glass in her hand. Natasha glanced at her through the crack in the pantry door, and it seemed to her that she remembered the light falling through the crack in the pantry door, and Sonya passing with the glass in just the same way. "Yes, and it was exactly the same in every detail," thought Natasha.

"Sonya, what is this?" called Natasha, twanging the thick cord with her fingers.

"Oh, are you there?" said Sonya starting, and she came up and listened. "I don't know. A storm?" she said timidly, afraid of being wrong.

"Why, she started in just the same way, and came up and smiled the same timid smile when it all happened before," thought Natasha; "and just in the same way, too. . . . I thought there was something wanting in her."

"No, it's the chorus from the 'Water Carrier,' listen." And Natasha hummed the air of the chorus, so that Sonya might catch it. "Where were you going?" asked Natasha.

"To change the water in my glass. I am just finishing colouring the design."

"You always find something to do, but I can't, you know," said Natasha. "And where's Nikolenka?"

"I think he's asleep."

"Sonya, do go and wake him," said Natasha. "Tell him I want him to sing with me."

She sat a little longer, pondering on what was the meaning of its all having happened before, and not solving that question, and not in the least chagrined at being unable to do so, she passed again in her imagination to the time when she was with him, and he gazed at her with eyes of love.

"Oh, if he would come quickly! I'm so afraid it will never come! And worst of all, I'm getting older, that's the thing. There won't be in me what there is in me now. Perhaps he is coming to-day, will be here immediately. Perhaps he has come, and is sitting there in the drawing-room. Perhaps he did come yesterday, and I have forgotten." She got up, put down her guitar, and went into the parlour. All their domestic circle, tutors, governesses, and guests were sitting at the tea-table. The servants were standing round the table. But Prince Andrey was not there, and the same old life was still going on.

"Here she is," said the count, seeing Natasha coming in. "Come, sit by me." But Natasha stayed by her mother, looking about her as though seeking for something.

"Mamma!" she said. "Give me *him*, give me him, mamma, quickly, quickly," and again she could hardly suppress her sobs. She sat down to the table and listened to the talk of the elders and Nikolay, who had come in to tea. "My God, my God, the same people, the same talk, papa holding his cup, and blowing it just the same as always," thought Natasha, feeling with horror an aversion rising up in her for all her family, because they were always the same.

After tea Nikolay, Sonya, and Natasha went into the divan-room to their favourite corner, where their most intimate talks always began.

X

"Does it happen to you," said Natasha to her brother, when they were settled in the divan-room, "to feel that nothing will ever happen—nothing; that all that is good is past? And it's not exactly a bored feeling, but melancholy?"

"I should think so!" said he. "It has sometimes happened to me that when everything's all right, and every one's cheerful, it suddenly strikes one that one's sick of it all, and all must die. Once in the regiment when I did not go to some merrymaking, and there the music was playing . . . and I felt all at once so dreary . . ."

"Oh, I know that feeling; I know it, I know it," Natasha assented; "even when I was quite little, I used to have that feeling. Do you remember, once I was punished for eating some plums, and you were all dancing, and I sat in the schoolroom sobbing. I shall never forget it; I felt sad and sorry for every one, sorry for myself, and for every—every one. And what was the chief point, I wasn't to blame," said Natasha; "do you remember?"

"I remember," said Nikolay. "I remember that I came to you afterwards, and I longed to comfort you, but you know, I felt ashamed to. Awfully funny we used to be. I had a wooden doll then, and I wanted to give it you. Do you remember?"

"And do you remember," said Natasha, with a pensive smile, "how long, long ago, when we were quite little, uncle called us into the study' in the old house, and it was dark; we went in, and all at once there stood . . ."

"A Negro," Nikolay finished her sentence with a smile of delight; "of course, I remember. To this day I don't know whether there really was a Negro, or whether we dreamed it, or were told about it."

"He was grey-headed, do you remember, and had white teeth; he stood and looked at us . . ."

"Do you remember, Sonya?" asked Nikolay.

"Yes, yes, I do remember something too," Sonya answered timidly.

"You know I have often asked both papa and mamma about that Negro," said Natasha. "They say there never was a Negro at all. But you remember him!"

"Of course, I do. I remember his teeth, as if it were to-day."

"How strange it is, as though it were a dream. I like that."

"And do you remember how we were rolling eggs in the big hall, and all of a sudden two old women came in, and began whirling round on the carpet. Did that happen or not? Do you remember what fun it was?"

"Yes. And do you remember how papa, in a blue coat, fired a gun off on the steps?"

Smiling with enjoyment, they went through their reminiscences; not the melancholy memories of old age, but the romantic memories of youth, those impressions of the remotest past in which dreamland melts into reality. They laughed with quiet pleasure.

Sonya was, as always, left behind by them, though their past had been spent together.

Sonya did not remember much of what they recalled, and what she did remember, did not rouse the same romantic feeling in her. She was simply enjoying their pleasure, and trying to share it.

She could only enter into it fully when they recalled Sonya's first arrival. Sonya described how she had been afraid of Nikolay, because he had cording on his jacket, and the nurse had told her that they would tie her up in cording too.

"And I remember, I was told you were found under a cabbage," said Natasha; "and I remember I didn't dare to disbelieve it then, though I knew it was untrue, and I felt so uncomfortable."

During this conversation a maid popped her head in at a door leading into the divan-room.

"Miss, they've brought you a cock," she said in a whisper.

"I don't want it, Polya; tell them to take it away," said Natasha.

In the middle of their talk in the divan-room, Dimmler came into the room, and went up to the harp that stood in the corner. He took off the cloth-case, and the harp gave a jarring sound. "Edward Karlitch, do, please, play my favourite nocturne of M. Field," said the voice of the old countess from the drawing-room.

Dimmler struck a chord, and turning to Natasha, Nikolay, and Sonya, he said.

"How quiet you young people are!"

"Yes, we're talking philosophy," said Natasha, looking round for a minute, and going on with the conversation. They were talking now about dreams.

Dimmler began to play. Natasha went noiselessly on tiptoe to the table, took the candle, carried it away, and going back, sat quietly in her place. It was dark in the room, especially where they were sitting on the sofa, but the silver light of the full moon shone in at the big windows and lay on the floor.

"Do you know, I think," said Natasha, in a whisper, moving up to Nikolay and Sonya, when Dimmler had finished, and still sat, faintly twanging the strings, in evident uncertainty whether to leave off playing or begin something new, "that one goes on remembering, and remembering; one remembers till one recalls what happened before one was in this world. . . ."

"That's metempsychosis," said Sonya, who had been good at lessons, and remembered all she had learned. "The Egyptians used to believe that our souls had been in animals, and would go into animals again."

"No, do you know, I don't believe that we were once in animals," said Natasha, still in the same whisper, though the music was over; "but I know for certain that we were once angels somewhere beyond, and we have been here, and that's why we remember everything. . . ."

"May I join you?" said Dimmler, coming up quietly, and he sat down by them.

"If we had been angels, why should we have fallen lower?" said Nikolay. "No, that can't be!"

"Not lower . . . who told you we were lower? . . . This is how I know I have existed before," Natasha replied, with conviction: "The soul is immortal, you know . . . so, if I am to live for ever, I have lived before too, I have lived for all eternity."

"Yes, but it's hard for us to conceive of eternity," said Dimmler, who had joined the young people, with a mildly condescending smile, but now talked as quietly and seriously as they did.

"Why is it hard to conceive of eternity?" said Natasha. "There will be to-day, and there will be to-morrow, and there will be for ever, and yesterday has been, and the day before. . . ."

"Natasha! now it's your turn. Sing me something," called the voice of the countess. "Why are you sitting there so quietly, like conspirators?"

"Mamma, I don't want to a bit!" said Natasha, but she got up as she said it.

None of them, not even Dimmler, who was not young, wanted to break off the conversation, and come out of the corner of the divan-room; but Natasha stood up, and Nikolay sat down to the clavichord. Standing, as she always did, in the middle of the room, and choosing the place where the resonance was greatest, Natasha began singing her mother's favourite song.

She had said she did not want to sing, but it was long since she had sung, and long before she sang again as she sang that evening. Count Ilya Andreitch listened to her singing from his study, where he was talking to Mitenka, and like a schoolboy in haste to finish his lesson and run out to play, he blundered in his orders to the steward, and at last paused, and Mitenka stood silent and smiling before him, listening too. Nikolay never took his eyes off his sister, and drew his breath when she did, Sonya, as she listened, thought of the vast difference between her and her friend, and how impossible it was for her to be in ever so slight a degree fascinating like her cousin. The old countess sat with a blissful, but mournful smile, and tears in her eyes, and now and then she shook her head. She, too, was thinking of Natasha and of her own youth, and of how there was something terrible and unnatural in Natasha's marrying Prince Andrey.

Dimmler, sitting by the countess, listened with closed eyes. "No, countess," he said, at last, "that's a European talent; she has no need of teaching: that softness, tenderness, strength . . ."

"Ah, I'm afraid for her, I'm afraid," said the countess, not remembering with whom she was speaking. Her motherly instinct told her that there was too much of something in Natasha, and that it would prevent her being happy.

Natasha had not finished singing when fourteen-year-old Petya ran in great excitement into the room to announce the arrival of the mummers, Natasha stopped abruptly.

"Idiot!" she screamed at her brother. She ran to a chair, sank into it, and broke into such violent sobbing that it was a long while before she could stop.

"It's nothing, mamma, it's nothing really, it's all right; Petya startled me," she said, trying to smile; but the tears still flowed, and the sobs still choked her.

The mummers—house-serfs dressed up as bears, Turks, tavern-keepers, and ladies—awe-inspiring or comic figures, at first huddled shyly together in the vestibule, bringing in with them the freshness of the cold outside, and a feeling of gaiety. Then, hiding behind one another, they crowded together in the big hall; and at first with constraint, but afterwards with more liveliness and unanimity, they started singing songs, and performing dances, and songs with dancing, and playing Christmas games. The countess after identifying them, and laughing at their costumes, went away to the drawing-room. Count Ilya Andreitch sat with a beaming smile in the big hall, praising their performances. The young people had disappeared.

Half an hour later there appeared in the hall among the other mummers an old lady in a crinoline—this was Nikolay. Petya was a Turkish lady, Dimmler was a clown, Natasha a hussar, and Sonya a Circassian with eyebrows and moustaches smudged with burnt cork.

After those of the household who were not dressed up had expressed condescending wonder and approval, and had failed to recognise them, the young people began to think their costumes so good that they must display them to some one else.

Nikolay, who wanted to drive them all in his sledge, as the road was in capital condition, proposed to drive to their so-called uncle's, taking about a dozen of the house-serfs in their mummer-dress with them.

"No; why should you disturb the old fellow?" said the countess. "Besides you wouldn't have room to turn round there. If you must go, let it be to the Melyukovs'."

Madame Melyukov was a widow with a family of children of various ages, and a number of tutors and governesses living in her house, four versts from the Rostovs'.

"That's a good idea, my love," the old count assented, beginning to be aroused. "Only let me dress up and I'll go with you. I'll make Pashette open her eyes."

But the countess would not agree to the count's going; for several days he had had a bad leg. It was decided that the count must not go, but that if Luisa Ivanovna (Madame Schoss) would go with them, the young ladies might go to Madame Melyukov's. Sonya, usually so shy and reticent, was more urgent than any in persuading Luisa Ivanovna not to refuse.

Sonya's disguise was the best of all. Her moustaches and eyebrows were extraordinarily becoming to her. Every one told her she looked very pretty, and she was in a mood of eager energy unlike her. Some inner voice told her that now or never her fate would be sealed, and in her masculine attire she seemed quite another person. Luisa Ivanovna consented to go; and half an hour later four sledges with bells drove up to the steps, their runners crunching, with a clanging sound, over the frozen snow.

Natasha was foremost in setting the note tone of holiday gaiety; and that gaiety, reflected from one to another, grew wilder and wilder, and reached its climax when they all went out into the frost, and talking, and calling to one another, laughing and shouting, got into the sledges.

Two of the sledges were the common household sledges; the third was the old count's, with a trotting horse from Orlov's famous stud; the fourth, Nikolay's own, with his own short, shaggy, raven horse in the shafts. Nikolay, in his old lady's crinoline and a hussar's cloak belted over it, stood up in the middle of the sledge picking up the reins. It was so light that he could see the metal discs of the harness shining in the moonlight, and the eyes of the horses looking round in alarm at the noise made by the party under the portico of the approach.

Sonya, Natasha, Madame Schoss, and two maids got into Nikolay's sledge. In the count's sledge were Dimmler with his wife and Petya; the other mummers were seated in the other two sledges.

"You go ahead, Zahar!" shouted Nikolay to his father's coachman, so as to have a chance of overtaking him on the road.

The count's sledge with Dimmler and the others of his party started forward, its runners creaking as though they were frozen to the snow, and the deep-toned bell clanging. The trace-horses pressed close to the shafts and sticking in the snow kicked it up, hard and glittering as sugar.

Nikolay followed the first sledge: behind him he heard the noise and crunch of the other two. At first they drove at a slow trot along the narrow road. As they drove by the garden, the shadows of the leafless trees often lay right across the road and hid the bright moonlight. But as soon as they were out of their grounds, the snowy plain, glittering like a diamond with bluish lights in it, lay stretched out on all sides, all motionless and bathed in moonlight. Now and again a hole gave the first sledge a jolt; the next was jolted in just the same way, and the next, and the sledges followed one another, rudely breaking the iron-bound stillness.

"A hare's track, a lot of tracks!" Natasha's voice rang out in the frostbound air.

"How light it is, Nikolenka," said the voice of Sonya.

Nikolay looked round at Sonya, and bent down to look at her face closer. It was a quite new, charming face with black moustaches, and eyebrows that peeped up at him from the sable fur—so close yet so distant—in the moonlight.

"That used to be Sonya," thought Nikolay. He looked closer at her and smiled.

"What is it, Nikolenka?"

"Nothing," he said, and turned to his horses again.

As they came out on the trodden highroad, polished by sledge runners, and all cut up by the tracks of spiked horseshoes—visible in the snow in the moonlight—the horses of their own accord tugged at the reins and quickened their pace. The left trace-horse, arching his head, pulled in jerks at his traces. The shaft-horse swayed to and fro, pricking up his ears as though to ask: "Are we to begin or is it too soon?" Zahar's sledge could be distinctly seen, black against the white snow, a long way ahead now, and its deep-toned bell seemed to be getting further away. They could hear shouts and laughter and talk from his sledge.

"Now then, my darlings!" shouted Nikolay, pulling a rein on one

side, and moving his whip hand. It was only from the wind seeming to
blow more freely in their faces, and from the tugging of the pulling
trace-horses, quickening their trot, that they saw how fast the sledge
was flying along. Nikolay looked behind. The other sledges, with crunching runners, with shouts, and cracking of whips, were hurrying after
them. Their shaft-horse was moving vigorously under the yoke, with no
sign of slackening, and every token of being ready to go faster and
faster if required.

Nikolay overtook the first sledge. They drove down a hill and into a
wide, trodden road by a meadow near a river.

"Where are we?" Nikolay wondered. "Possibly Kosoy Meadow, I
suppose. But no; this is something new I never saw before. This is not
the Kosoy Meadow nor Demkin hill. It's something—there's no knowing what. It's something new and fairy-like. Well, come what may!" And
shouting to his horses, he began to drive by the first sledge. Zahar pulled
up his horses and turned his face, which was white with hoar-frost to
the eyebrows.

Nikolay let his horses go; Zahar, stretching his hands forward, urged
his on. "Come, hold on, master," said he.

The sledges dashed along side by side, even more swiftly, and the
horses' hoofs flew up and down more and more quickly. Nikolay began
to get ahead. Zahar, still keeping his hands stretched forward, raised
one hand with the reins.

"Nonsense, master," he shouted. Nikolay put his three horses into a
gallop and outstripped Zahar. The horses scattered the fine dry snow
in their faces; close by they heard the ringing of the bells and the
horses' legs moving rapidly out of step, and they saw the shadows of
the sledge behind. From different sides came the crunch of runners over
the snow, and the shrieks of girls. Stopping his horses again, Nikolay
looked round him. All around him lay still the same enchanted plain,
bathed in moonlight, with stars scattered over its surface.

"Zahar's shouting that I'm to turn to the left, but why to the left?"
thought Nikolay. "Are we really going to the Melyukovs'; is this really
Melyukovka? God knows where we are going, and God knows what is
going to become of us—and very strange and nice it is what is happening to us." He looked round in the sledge.

"Look, his moustache and his eyelashes are all white," said one of the
strange, pretty, unfamiliar figures sitting by him, with fine moustaches
and eyebrows.

"I believe that was Natasha," thought Nikolay; "and that was Madame Schoss; but perhaps it's not so; and that Circassian with the moustaches I don't know, but I love her."

"Aren't you cold?" he asked them. They laughed and did not answer.
Dimmler from the sledge behind shouted, probably something funny,
but they could not make out what he said.

"Yes, yes," voices answered, laughing.

But now came a sort of enchanted forest with shifting, black shadows,
and the glitter of diamonds, and a flight of marble steps, and silver roofs

of enchanted buildings, and the shrill whine of some beasts. "And if it really is Melyukovka, then it's stranger than ever that after driving, God knows where, we should come to Melyukovka," thought Nikolay.

It certainly was Melyukovka, and footmen and maid-servants were running out with lights and beaming faces.

"Who is it?" was asked from the entrance.

"The mummers from the count's; I can see by the horses," answered voices.

XI

PELAGEA DANILOVNA MELYUKOV, a broad-shouldered, energetic woman in spectacles and a loose house dress, was sitting in her drawing-room, surrounded by her daughters, and doing her utmost to keep them amused. They were quietly occupied in dropping melted wax into water and watching the shadows of the shapes it assumed, when they heard the noise of steps in the vestibule, and the voices of people arriving.

The hussars, fine ladies, witches, clowns, and bears, coughing and rubbing the hoar-frost off their faces, came into the hall, where they were hurriedly lighting candles. The clown—Dimmler—and the old lady —Nikolay—opened the dance. Surrounded by the shrieking children, the mummers hid their faces, and disguising their voices, bowed to their hostess and dispersed about the room.

"Oh, there's no recognising them. And Natasha! See what she looks like! Really, she reminds me of some one. How good Edward Karlitch is! I didn't know him. And how he dances! Oh, my goodness, and here's a Circassian too, upon my word; how it suits Sonyushka! And who's this? Well, you have brought us some fun! Take away the tables, Nikita Vanya. And we were sitting so quiet and dull!"

"Ha—ha—he! . . . The hussar, the hussar! Just like a boy; and the legs! . . . I can't look at him, . . ." voices cried.

Natasha, the favourite of the young Melyukovs, disappeared with them into rooms at the back of the house, and burnt cork and various dressing-gowns and masculine garments were sent for and taken from the footman by bare, girlish arms through the crack of the half-open door. In ten minutes all the younger members of the Melyukov family reappeared in fancy dresses too.

Pelagea Danilovna, busily giving orders for clearing the room for the guests and preparing for their entertainment, walked about among the mummers in her spectacles, with a suppressed smile, looking close at them and not recognising any one. She not only failed to recognise the Rostovs and Dimmler, but did not even know her own daughters, or identify the masculine dressing-gowns and uniforms in which they were disguised.

"And who is this?" she kept saying, addressing her governess and gazing into the face of her own daughter disguised as a Tatar of Kazan. "One of the Rostovs, I fancy. And you, my hussar, what regiment are you in, pray?" she asked Natasha. "Give the Turk a preserved fruit," she said to the footman carrying round refreshments; "that's not forbidden by his law."

Sometimes, looking at the strange and ludicrous capers cut by the dancers, who, having made up their minds once for all that no one recognised them, were quite free from shyness, Pelagea Danilovna hid her face in her handkerchief, and all her portly person shook with irrepressible, good-natured, elderly laughter.

"My Sashinette, my Sashinette!" she said.

After Russian dances and songs in chorus, Pelagea Danilovna made all the party, servants and gentry alike, join in one large circle. They brought in a string, a ring, and a silver rouble, and began playing games.

An hour later all the fancy dresses were crumpled and untidy. The corked moustaches and eyebrows were wearing off the heated, perspiring, and merry faces. Pelagea Danilovna began to recognise the mummers. She was enthusiastic over the cleverness of the dresses and the way they suited them, especially the young ladies, and thanked them all for giving them such good fun. The guests were invited into the drawing-room for supper, while the servants were regaled in the hall.

"Oh, trying one's fate in the bath-house, that's awful!" was said at the supper-table by an old maiden lady who lived with the Melyukovs.

"Why so?" asked the eldest daughter of the Melyukovs.

"Well, you won't go and try. It needs courage . . ."

"I'll go," said Sonya.

"Tell us what happened to the young lady," said the second girl.

"Well, it was like this," said the old maid. "The young lady went out; she took a cock, two knives and forks, and everything proper, and sat down. She sat a little while, and all of a sudden she hears some one coming—a sledge with bells driving up. She hears him coming. He walks in, precisely in the shape of a man, like an officer, and sat down beside her at the place laid for him."

"Ah! ah! . . ." screamed Natasha, rolling her eyes with horror.

"But what did he do? Did he talk like a man?"

"Yes, like a man. Everything as it should be, and began to try and win her over, and she should have kept him in talk till the cock crew; but she got frightened,—simply took fright, and hid her face in her hands. And he caught her up. Luckily the maids ran in that minute . . ."

"Come, why are you scaring them?" said Pelagea Danilovna.

"Why, mamma, you tried your fate yourself . . ." said her daughter.

"And how do they try fate in a granary?" asked Sonya.

"Why, at a time like this they go to the granary and listen. And according to what you hear,—if there's a knocking and a tapping, it's bad; but if there's a sound of sifting corn, it is good. But sometimes it happens . . ."

"Mamma, tell us what happened to you in the granary?"

Pelagea Danilovna smiled.

"Why, I have forgotten . . ." she said. "I know none of you will go."

"No, I'll go. Pelagea Danilovna, do let me, and I'll go," said Sonya.

"Oh, well, if you're not afraid."

"Luisa Ivanovna, may I?" asked Sonya.

Whether they were playing at the ring and string game, or the rouble game, or talking as now, Nikolay did not leave Sonya's side, and looked at her with quite new eyes. It seemed to him as though to-day, for the first time, he had, thanks to that corked moustache, seen her fully as she was. Sonya certainly was that evening gay, lively, and pretty, as Natasha had never seen her before.

"So, this is what she is, and what a fool I have been!" he kept think-ing, looking at her sparkling eyes, at the happy, ecstatic smile dimpling her cheeks under the moustache. He had never seen that smile before.

"I'm not afraid of anything," said Sonya. "May I go at once?" She got up. They told Sonya where the granary was; how she was to stand quite silent and listen, and they gave her a cloak. She threw it over her head and glanced at Nikolay.

"How exquisite that girl is!" he thought. "And what have I been thinking about all this time?"

Sonya went out into the corridor to go to the granary. Nikolay hastily went out to the front porch, saying he was too hot. It certainly was stuffy indoors from the crowd of people.

Outside there was the same still frost, the same moonlight, only even brighter than before. The light was so bright, and there were so many stars sparkling in the snow, that the sky did not attract the eye, and the real stars were hardly noticeable. The sky was all blackness and dreariness, the earth all brightness.

"I'm a fool; a fool! What have I been waiting for all this time?" thought Nikolay; and running out into the porch he went round the corner of the house along the path leading to the back door. He knew Sonya would come that way. Half-way there was a pile of logs of wood, seven feet long. It was covered with snow and cast a shadow. Across it and on one side of it there fell on the snow and the path a network of shadows from the bare old lime-trees. The wall and roof of the granary glittered in the moonlight, as though hewn out of some precious stone. There was the sound of the snapping of wood in the garden, and all was perfect stillness again. The lungs seemed breathing in, not air, but a sort of ever-youthful power and joy.

From the maid-servants' entrance came the tap of feet on the steps; there was a ringing crunch on the last step where the snow was heaped, and the voice of the old maid said:

"Straight on, along this path, miss. Only don't look round!"

"I'm not afraid," answered Sonya's voice, and Sonya's little feet in their dancing-shoes came with a ringing, crunching sound along the path towards Nikolay.

Sonya was muffled up in the cloak. She was two paces away when she saw him. She saw him, too, not as she knew him, and as she was always a little afraid of him. He was in a woman's dress, with towzled hair, and a blissful smile that was new to Sonya. She ran quickly to him.

"Quite different, and still the same," thought Nikolay, looking at her face, all lighted up by the moon. He slipped his hands under the cloak that covered her head, embraced her, drew her to him, and kissed the lips that wore a moustache and smelt of burnt cork. Sonya kissed him full on the lips, and putting out her little hands held them against his cheeks on both sides.

"Sonya! . . . Nikolenka! . . ." was all they said. They ran to the granary and went back to the house, each at their separate door.

XII

WHEN they were all driving back from Pelagea Danilovna's, Natasha, who always saw and noticed everything, managed a change of places, so that Luisa Ivanovna and she got into the sledge with Dimmler, while Sonya was with Nikolay and the maids.

Nikolay drove smoothly along the way back, making no effort now to get in front. He kept gazing in the fantastic moonlight at Sonya, and seeking, in the continually shifting light behind those eyebrows and moustaches, his own Sonya, the old Sonya, and the Sonya of to-day, from whom he had resolved now never to be parted. He watched her intently, and when he recognised the old Sonya and the new Sonya, and recalled, as he smelt it, that smell of burnt cork that mingled with the thrill of the kiss, he drew in a deep breath of the frosty air, and as he saw the earth flying by them, and the sky shining above, he felt himself again in fairyland.

"Sonya, is it well with *thee*?" he asked her now and then.

"Yes," answered Sonya. "And *thee*?"

Half-way home, Nikolay let the coachman hold the horses, ran for a moment to Natasha's sledge, and stood on the edge of it.

"Natasha," he whispered in French, "do you know I have made up my mind about Sonya?"

"Have you told her?" asked Natasha, beaming all over at once with pleasure.

"Ah, how strange you look with that moustache and those eyebrows, Natasha! Are you glad?"

"I'm so glad; so glad! I was beginning to get cross with you. I never told you so, but you have not been treating her nicely. Such a heart as she has, Nikolenka. I am so glad! I'm horrid sometimes; but I felt ashamed of being happy without Sonya," Natasha went on. "Now, I'm so glad; there, run back to her."

"No; wait a moment. Oh, how funny you look!" said Nikolay, still gazing intently at her; and in his sister, too, finding something new, extraordinary, and tenderly bewitching that he had never seen in her before. "Natasha, isn't it fairylike? Eh?"

"Yes," she answered, "you have done quite rightly."

"If I had seen her before as she is now," Nikolay was thinking. "I should have asked her long ago what to do, and should have done any-thing she told me, and it would have been all right."

"So you're glad," he said, "and I have done right?"

"Oh, quite right! I had a quarrel with mamma about it a little while ago. Mamma said she was trying to catch you. How could she say such a thing! I almost stormed at mamma. I will never let any one say or think any harm of her, for there's nothing but good in her."

"So it's all right?" said Nikolay, once more gazing intently at his sister's expression to find out whether that were the truth. Then he jumped off the sledge and ran, his boots crunching over the snow, to his sledge. The same happy, smiling Circassian, with a moustache and sparkling eyes, peeping from under the sable hood, was still sitting there, and that Circassian was Sonya, and that Sonya was for certain now his happy and loving future wife.

On reaching home, the young ladies told the countess how they had spent the time at the Melyukovs', and then went to their room. They changed their dresses, but without washing off their moustaches, sat for a long while talking of their happiness. They talked of how they would live when they were married, how their husbands would be friends, and they would be happy. Looking-glasses were standing on Natasha's table, set there earlier in the evening by Dunyasha, and arranged in the tradi-tional way for looking into the future.

"Only when will that be? I'm so afraid it never will be. . . . It would be too happy!" said Natasha, getting up and going to the looking-glasses.

"Sit down, Natasha, perhaps you will see him," said Sonya.

Natasha lighted the candles and sat down. "I do see some one with a moustache," said Natasha, seeing her own face.

"You mustn't laugh, miss," said Dunyasha.

With the assistance of Sonya and the maid, Natasha got the mirrors into the correct position. Her face took a serious expression, and she was silent. For a long while she went on sitting, watching the series of re-treating candles reflected in the looking-glasses, and expecting (in ac-cordance with the tales she had heard) at one minute to see a coffin, at the next to see *him*, Prince Andrey, in the furthest, dimmest, indistinct square. But ready as she was to accept the slightest blur as the form of a man or of a coffin, she saw nothing. She began to blink, and moved away from the looking-glass.

"Why is it other people see things and I never see anything?" she said. "Come, you sit down, Sonya; to-day you really must. Only look for me . . . I feel so full of dread to-day!"

Sonya sat down to the looking-glass, got the correct position, and began looking.

"You will see, Sonya Alexandrovna will be sure to see something," whispered Dunyasha, "you always laugh."

Sonya heard these words, and heard Natasha say in a whisper: "Yes, I know she'll see something; she saw something last year too." For three minutes all were mute.

"Sure to!" whispered Natasha, and did not finish. . . . All at once Sonya drew back from the glass she was holding and put her hand over her eyes. "O Natasha!" she said. "Seen something? Seen something? What did you see?" cried Natasha, supporting the looking-glass. Sonya had seen nothing. She was just meaning to blink and to get up, when she heard Natasha's voice say: "Sure to!" . . . She did not want to deceive either Dunyasha or Natasha, and was weary of sitting there. She did not know herself how and why that exclamation had broken from her as she covered her eyes.

"Did you see him?" asked Natasha, clutching her by the hand.

"Yes. Wait a bit. . . . I . . . did see him," Sonya could not help saying, not yet sure whether by *him* Natasha meant Nikolay or Andrey. "Why not say I saw something? Other people see things! And who can tell whether I have or have not?" flashed through Sonya's mind.

"Yes, I saw him," she said.

"How was it? How? Standing or lying down?"

"No, I saw . . . At first there was nothing; then I saw him lying down."

"Andrey lying down? Is he ill?" Natasha asked, fixing eyes of terror on her friend.

"No, on the contrary—on the contrary, his face was cheerful, and he turned to me"; and at the moment she was saying this, it seemed to herself that she really had seen what she described.

"Well, and then, Sonya? . . ."

"Then I could make out more; something blue and red. . . ."

"Sonya, when will he come back? When shall I see him? My God! I feel so frightened for him, and for me, and frightened for everything . . ." cried Natasha; and answering not a word to Sonya's attempts to comfort her, she got into bed, and long after the candle had been put out she lay with wide-open eyes motionless on the bed, staring into the frosty moonlight through the frozen window-panes.

XIII

Soon after the Christmas fêtes were over, Nikolay spoke to his mother of his love for Sonya, and his immovable resolution to marry her. The countess had long before observed what was passing between Sonya and Nikolay, and was expecting this announcement. She listened to his words without comment, and then told her son that he could marry whom he chose, but that neither she nor his father would give their blessing to such a marriage. For the first time in his life Nikolay felt that his mother was displeased with him, that in spite of all her love for him she would not give way to him. Coldly, without looking at her son, she sent for her husband; and when he came in, the countess would have briefly and coldly, in Nikolay's presence, told him her son's intention, but she could not control herself, burst into tears of anger, and went out of the room. The old count began irresolutely persuading and entreating Nikolay to give up his intention. Nikolay replied he could not be false to his word, and his father, sighing and visibly embarrassed, quickly cut short the conversation and went in to the countess. In all difficulties with his son, the old count could never lose his sense of guiltiness to him for having wasted their fortunes, and so he could not feel angry with his son for refusing to marry an heiress and choosing the portionless Sonya. He only felt more keenly that if their fortune had not been squandered, no better wife could have been desired for Nikolay than Sonya; and that he, with his Mitenka and his invincible bad habits, was alone to blame for their fortune having been squandered. The father and mother did not speak of the subject again with their son; but a few days later the countess sent for Sonya to her room, and with a cruelty that surprised them both, the countess upbraided her niece for alluring her son and for ingratitude. Sonya, with downcast eyes, listened in silence to the countess's cruel words, and did not understand what was expected of her. She was ready to sacrifice everything for her benefactors. The idea of self-sacrifice was her favourite idea. But in this case she could not see whom and what she ought to sacrifice. She could not help loving the countess and all the Rostov family, but neither could she help loving Nikolay and knowing that his happiness depended on that love. She was silent and dejected; she made no reply. Nikolay could not, so he fancied, endure this position any longer, and he went in to his mother to have it out with her. Nikolay first besought his mother to forgive him and Sonya and to agree to their marriage; then threatened his mother that if Sonya were persecuted he would at once marry her in secret. The countess, with a coldness her son had never seen before, replied that he was of full age, that Prince Andrey was marrying without his father's consent, and that he could do the same, but that she would never receive that *intriguing creature* as her daughter.

Stung to fury by the words *"intriguing creature,"* Nikolay, raising his voice, told his mother that he had never expected her to try and force him to tell his feelings, and that since it was so, then for the last time he . . . But he had not time to utter the fatal word, which his mother seemed, from her expression, to be awaiting in terror, and which would, perhaps, have remained a cruel memory between them for ever. He had not time to finish, because Natasha, who had been listening at the door, ran into the room with a pale and set face.

"Nikolenka, you are talking nonsense; hush, hush, hush! I tell you hush!" . . . she almost screamed to overpower his voice.

"Mamma, darling, it's not at all so . . . my sweet, poor darling," she said, turning to her mother, who gazed in terror at her son, feeling herself on the edge of an abyss; but in the obstinacy and heat of the conflict unwilling and unable to give in. "Nikolenka, I'll explain to you; you go away—listen, mamma, darling." she said to her mother.

Her words were incoherent, but they attained the effect at which she was aiming.

The countess, with a deep sob, hid her face on her daughter's bosom, while Nikolay got up, clutched at his head, and went out of the room.

Natasha set to work to bring about a reconciliation, and succeeded so far that Nikolay received a promise from his mother that Sonya should not be worried, and himself made a promise that he would take no step without his parents' knowledge.

Firmly resolved to settle things in his regiment, to retire, come home, and marry Sonya, Nikolay at the beginning of January went back to his regiment, sad and serious at being on bad terms with his parents, but, as it seemed to him, passionately in love.

After Nikolay's departure, it was more depressing than ever in the Rostovs' house. The countess fell ill from the emotional strains she had passed through.

Sonya was depressed at parting from Nikolay, and still more at the hostile tone the countess could not help adopting towards her. The count was more worried than ever by the difficulties of his position, which called for some decisive action. It was necessary to sell the Moscow house and the estate near Moscow, and to do so it was necessary to go to Moscow. But the countess's illness forced them to put off going from day to day. Natasha, who had at first borne the separation from her betrothed so easily and even cheerfully, grew now more impatient and overstrung every day. The thought that her best time, that might have been spent in loving him, was being wasted like this for no object, continually fretted her. Prince Andrey's letters generally angered her. It mortified her to think that while she was simply living in the thought of him, he was living a real life, seeing new places and new people who were interesting to him. The more interesting his letters were, the more they vexed her. Her letters to him, far from giving her comfort, were looked upon by her as a wearisome and artificial duty. She could not write, because she could not attain to expressing truly in a letter a thousandth part of what she habitually expressed in voice and smile and eyes. She wrote him formal letters, all on one pattern. She did not attach the smallest importance to them herself, and the countess corrected the mistakes in spelling in the rough copy of them. The countess's health still did not mend, but the visit to Moscow could be deferred no longer. The trousseau had to be got, the house had to be sold, and Prince Andrey was to arrive first in Moscow, where his father was spending the winter, and Natasha believed that he had already arrived there. The countess was left in the country, and towards the end of January the count took Sonya and Natasha with him to Moscow.

PART EIGHT

I

AFTER PRINCE ANDREY's engagement to Natasha, Pierre suddenly, for no apparent reason, felt it impossible to go on living in the same way as before. Firm as his belief was in the truths revealed to him by his benefactor, the old freemason, and happy as he had been at first in the task of perfecting his inner spiritual self, to which he had devoted himself with such ardour, yet after Prince Andrey's engagement to Natasha, and the death of Osip Alexyevitch, the news of which reached him almost simultaneously, the whole zest of his religious life seemed to have suddenly vanished. Nothing but the skeleton of life remained: his house with his brilliant wife, now basking in the favours of a very grand personage indeed, the society of all Petersburg, and his service at court with its tedious formalities. And that life suddenly filled Pierre with unexpected loathing. He gave up keeping his diary, avoided the society of brother-masons, took to visiting the club again and to drinking a great deal; associated once more with gay bachelor companions, and began to lead a life so dissipated that Countess Elena Vassilyevna thought it necessary to make severe observations to him on the subject. Pierre felt that she was right; and to avoid compromising his wife, he went away to Moscow.

In Moscow, as soon as he entered his huge house with the faded and fading princesses, his cousins, and the immense retinue of servants, as soon as, driving through the town, he saw the Iversky chapel with the lights of innumerable candles before the golden setting of the Madonna, the square of the Kremlin with its untrodden snow, the sledge-drivers, and the hovels of Sivtsev Vrazhok; saw the old Moscow gentlemen quietly going on with their daily round, without hurry or desire of change; saw the old Moscow ladies, the Moscow balls, and the English Club—he felt himself at home, in a quiet haven of rest. In Moscow he felt comfortable, warm, at home, and snugly dirty, as in an old dressing-gown.

All Moscow society, from the old ladies to the children, welcomed Pierre back like a long-expected guest, whose place was always ready for him, and had never been filled up. For the Moscow world, Pierre was the most delightful, kind-hearted, intellectual, good-humoured, and generous eccentric, and a heedless and genial Russian gentleman of the good old school. His purse was always empty, because it was always open to every one.

Benefit-entertainments, poor pictures and statues, benevolent societies, gypsy choruses, schools, subscription dinners, drinking parties, the masons, churches, and books—no one and nothing ever met with a refusal, and had it not been for two friends, who had borrowed large sums of money from Pierre and constituted themselves guardians of a sort over him, he would have parted with everything. Not a dinner, not a *soirée* took place at the club without him.

As soon as he was lolling in his place on the sofa, after a couple of bottles of margot, he was surrounded by a circle of friends, and arguments, disputes, and jokes sprang up round him. Where there were quarrels, his kindly smile and casually uttered jokes were enough to reconcile the antagonists. The masonic dining lodges were dull and dreary when he was absent.

When after a bachelor supper, with a weak and good-natured smile, he yielded to the entreaties of the festive party that he would drive off with them to share their revels, there were shouts of delight and triumph. At balls he danced if there were a lack of partners. Girls and young married ladies liked him, because he paid no special attention to any one, but was equally amiable to all, especially after supper. "He is charming; he is of no sex," they used to say of him.

Pierre was just a kammerherr, retired to end his days in Moscow, like hundreds of others. How horrified he would have been if, seven years before, when he had just come home from abroad, any one had told him that there was no need for him to look about him and rack his brains, that the track had long ago been trodden, marked out from all eternity for him, and that, struggle as he would, he would be just such another as all men in his position. He could not have believed it then! Had he not longed with his whole heart to establish a republic in Russia; then to be himself a Napoleon; then to be a philosopher; and then a great strategist and the conqueror of Napoleon? Had he not passionately desired and believed in the regeneration of the sinful race of man and the schooling of himself to the highest point of perfect virtue? Had he not founded schools and hospitals and liberated his serfs?

But instead of all that, here he was the wealthy husband of a faithless wife, a retired kammerherr, fond of dining and drinking, fond, too, as he unbuttoned his waistcoat after dinner, of indulging in a little abuse of the government, a member of the Moscow English Club, and a universal favourite in Moscow society. For a long while he could not reconcile himself to the idea that he was precisely the retired Moscow kammerherr, the very type he had so profoundly scorned seven years before.

Sometimes he consoled himself by the reflection that it did not count, that he was only temporarily leading this life. But later on he was horrified by another reflection, that numbers of other men, with the same idea of its being temporary, had entered that life and that club with all their teeth and a thick head of hair, only to leave it when they were toothless and bald.

In moments of pride, when he was reviewing his position, it seemed to him that he was quite different, distinguished in some way from the retired kammerherrs he had looked upon with contempt in the past;

that they were vulgar and stupid, at ease and satisfied with their position, "while I am even now still dissatisfied; I still long to do something for humanity," he would assure himself in moments of pride. "But possibly all of them too, my fellows, struggled just as I do, tried after something new, sought a path in life for themselves, and have been brought to the same point as I have by the force of surroundings, of society, of family, that elemental force against which man is powerless," he said to himself in moments of modesty. And after spending some time in Moscow he no longer scorned his companions in destiny, but began even to love them, respect them, and pity them like himself.

Pierre no longer suffered from moments of despair, melancholy, and loathing for life as he had done. But the same malady that had manifested itself in acute attacks in former days was driven inwards and never now left him for an instant. "What for? What's the use? What is it is going on in the world?" he asked himself in perplexity several times a day, instinctively beginning to sound the hidden significance in the phenomena of life. But knowing by experience that there was no answer to these questions, he made haste to try and turn away from them, took up a book, or hurried off to the club, or to Apollon Nikolaevitch's to chat over the scandals of the town.

"Elena Vassilyevna, who has never cared for anything but her own body, and is one of the stupidest women in the world," Pierre thought, "is regarded by people as the acme of wit and refinement, and is the object of their homage. Napoleon Bonaparte was despised by every one while he was really great, and since he became a pitiful buffoon the Emperor Francis seeks to offer him his daughter in an illegal marriage. The Spaniards, through their Catholic Church, return thanks to God for their victory over the French on the 14th of June, and the French, through the same Catholic Church, return thanks to God for their victory over the Spaniards on the same 14th of June. My masonic brothers swear in blood that they are ready to sacrifice all for their neighbour, but they don't give as much as one rouble to the collections for the poor, and they intrigue between Astraea and the manna-seekers, and are in a ferment about the authentic Scottish rug, and an act, of which the man who wrote it did not know the meaning and no one has any need. We all profess the Christian law of forgiveness of sins and love for one's neighbour—the law, in honour of which we have raised forty times forty churches in Moscow—but yesterday we knouted to death a deserter; and the minister of that same law of love and forgiveness, the priest, gave the soldier the cross to kiss before his punishment."

Such were Pierre's reflections, and all this universal deception recognised by all, used as he was to seeing it, was always astounding him, as though it were something new. "I understand this deceit and tangle of cross-purposes," he thought, "but how am I to tell them all I understand? I have tried and always found that they understood it as I did, at the bottom of their hearts, but were only trying not to see it. So I suppose it must be so! But me—what refuge is there for me?" thought Pierre.

He suffered from an unlucky faculty—common to many men, especially Russians—the faculty of seeing and believing in the possibility of good and truth, and at the same time seeing too clearly the evil and falsity of life to be capable of taking a serious part in it. Every sphere of activity was in his eyes connected with evil and deception. Whatever he tried to be, whatever he took up, evil and falsity drove him back again and cut him off from every field of energy. And meanwhile he had to live, he had to be occupied. It was too awful to lie under the burden of those insoluble problems of life, and he abandoned himself to the first distraction that offered, simply to forget them. He visited every possible society, drank a great deal, went in for buying pictures, building, and above all reading.

He read and re-read everything he came across. On getting home he would take up a book, even while his valets were undressing him, and read himself to sleep; and from sleep turned at once to gossip in the drawing-rooms and the club; from gossip to carousals and women; from dissipation back again to gossip, reading, and wine. Wine was more and more becoming a physical necessity to him, and at the same time a moral necessity. Although the doctors told him that in view of his corpulence wine was injurious to him, he drank a very great deal. He never felt quite content except when he had, almost unconsciously, lifted several glasses of wine to his big mouth. Then he felt agreeably warm all over his body, amiably disposed towards all his fellows, and mentally ready to respond superficially to every idea, without going too deeply into it. It was only after drinking a bottle or two of wine that he felt vaguely that the terrible tangled skein of life which had terrified him so before was not so terrible as he had fancied. With a buzzing in his head, chatting, listening to talk or reading after dinner and supper, he invariably saw that tangled skein on some one of its sides. It was only under the influence of wine that he said to himself: "Never mind. I'll disentangle it all; here I have a solution all ready. But now's not the time. I'll go into all that later on!" But that *later on* never came.

In the morning, before breakfast, all the old questions looked as insoluble and fearful as ever, and Pierre hurriedly snatched up a book and rejoiced when any one came in to see him.

Sometimes Pierre remembered what he had been told of soldiers under fire in ambuscade when they have nothing to do, how they try hard to find occupation so as to bear their danger more easily. And Pierre pictured all men as such soldiers trying to find a refuge from life: some in ambition, some in cards, some in framing laws, some in women, some in playthings, some in horses, some in politics, some in sport, some in wine, some in the government service. "Nothing is trivial, nothing is important, everything is the same; only to escape from it as best one can," thought Pierre. "Only not to see *it*, that terrible *it*."

II

AT the beginning of the winter Prince Nikolay Andreïtch Bolkonsky and his daughter moved to Moscow. His past, his intellect and originality, and still more the falling off at about that time of the popular enthusiasm for the rule of the Tsar Alexander and the anti-French and patriotic sentiments then prevailing at Moscow, all contributed to make Prince Nikolay Andreïtch at once an object of peculiar veneration and the centre of the Moscow opposition to the government.

The prince had greatly aged during that year. He had begun to show unmistakable signs of failing powers, sudden attacks of drowsiness, and forgetfulness of events nearest in time, and exact memory of remote incidents, and a childlike vanity in playing the part of leader of the Moscow opposition. But in spite of that, when the old man came into the drawing-room in the evenings to tea, in his wig and fur coat, and on being incited to do so by some one, began uttering abrupt observations on the past, or still more abrupt and harsh criticisms on the present—he aroused the same feeling of esteem and reverence in all his guests. For visitors, that old-fashioned house, with its huge mirrors, pre-revolutionary furniture, and powdered lackeys, and the stern and shrewd old man, himself a relic of a past age, with the gentle daughter and the pretty Frenchwoman, both so reverently devoted to him, made a stately and agreeable spectacle. But those visitors did not reflect that, apart from the couple of hours during which they saw the household, there were twenty-two hours of the day and night during which the secret, private life of the house went on its accustomed way.

That inner life had become very hard for Princess Marya of late in Moscow. She was deprived in Moscow of her two greatest pleasures— talks with God's folk and the solitude which had refreshed her spirit at Bleak Hills, and she had none of the advantages and pleasures of town life. She did not go into society; every one knew that her father would not allow her to go anywhere without him, and owing to his failing health he could go nowhere himself. She was not even invited now to dinner-parties or balls. Princess Marya had laid aside all hopes of marriage. She saw the coldness and hostility with which the old prince received and dismissed the young men, possible suitors, who sometimes appeared at the house. Friends, Princess Marya now had none; during this stay in Moscow she had lost all faith in the two friends who had been nearest to her. Mademoiselle Bourienne, with whom she had never been able to be perfectly open, she now regarded with dislike, and for certain reasons kept at a distance. Julie, with whom Princess Marya had kept up an unbroken correspondence for five years, was in Moscow. When Princess Marya renewed her personal relations with her, she felt her former friend to be utterly alien to her. Julie, who had become, by the death of her brothers, one of the wealthiest heiresses in Moscow, was at that time engrossed in a giddy whirl of fashionable amusements. She was surrounded by young men, whom she believed to have become sud-

denly appreciative of her qualities. Julie was at that stage when a young
lady is somewhat past her first youth in society and feels that her last
chance of marrying has come, and that now or never her fate must be
decided. With a mournful smile Princess Marya reflected every Thursday that she had now no one to write to, seeing that Julie was here and
saw her every week, though her friend's actual presence gave her no
sort of pleasure. Like the old French *émigré*, who declined to marry the
lady with whom he had for so many years spent his evenings, she
regretted that Julie was here and she had no one to write to. In Moscow
Princess Marya had no one to speak to, no one to confide her sorrows
to, and many fresh sorrows fell to her lot about this time. The time for
Prince Andrey's return and marriage was approaching, and his commission to her to prepare her father's mind was so far from being successfully carried out that the whole thing seemed hopeless; and any
reference to the young Countess Rostov infuriated the old prince, who
was for the most part out of humour at all times now. Another trouble
that weighed on Princess Marya of late was due to the lessons she gave
to her six-year-old nephew. In her relations with little Nikolay she recognised to her consternation symptoms of her father's irritable character
in herself. However often she told herself that she must not let herself
lose her temper, when teaching her nephew, almost every time she sat
down with a pointer showing him the French alphabet, she so longed
to hasten, to make easy the process of transferring her knowledge to
the child, who was by now always afraid his auntie would be angry the
next moment, that at the slightest inattention she was quivering in
nervous haste and vexation, she raised her voice and sometimes pulled
him by his little hand and stood him in the corner. When she had stood
him in the corner she would begin to cry herself over her evil, wicked
nature, and little Nikolay, his sobs vying with hers, would come unbidden out of the corner to pull her wet hands from her face and try
to comfort her. But the greatest, far the greatest of the princess's burdens was her father's irascibility, which was invariably directed against
his daughter, and had of late reached the point of cruelty. Had he forced
her to spend the night bowing to the ground, had he beaten her, or
made her carry in wood and water, it would never have entered her head
that her position was a hard one. But this loving despot—most cruel of
all because he loved, and for that very reason tortured himself and her
—knew not only how to mortify and humiliate her, but of set purpose,
to prove to her that she was always to blame in everything. Of late he
had taken a new departure, which caused Princess Marya more misery
than anything—that was his closer and closer intimacy with Mademoiselle Bourienne. The idea, that had occurred to him in jest at the
first moment of receiving the news of his son's intentions, that if Andrey
got married he, too, would marry Mademoiselle Bourienne, obviously
pleased him, and he had of late—simply, as Princess Marya fancied, to
annoy her—persisted in being particularly gracious to Mademoiselle
Bourienne and manifesting his dissatisfaction with his daughter by
demonstrations of love for the Frenchwoman.

One day in Princess Marya's presence (it seemed to her that her father did it on purpose because she was there) the old prince kissed Mademoiselle Bourienne's hand, and drawing her to him embraced her affectionately. Princess Marya flushed hotly and ran out of the room. A few minutes later, Mademoiselle Bourienne went into Princess Marya's room, smiling and making some cheerful remarks in her agreeable voice. Princess Marya hastily wiped away her tears, with resolute steps went, up to the Frenchwoman, and obviously unconscious of what she was doing, with wrathful haste and breaks in her voice she began screaming at her:

"It's loathsome, vile, inhuman to take advantage of feebleness . . ." She could not go on. "Go out of my room," she cried, and broke into sobs.

The next day the old prince did not say a word to his daughter, but she noticed that at dinner he gave orders for the dishes to be handed to Mademoiselle Bourienne first. When towards the end of dinner, the footman from habit handed the coffee, beginning with the princess, the old prince flew into a sudden frenzy of rage, flung his cane at Filipp, and immediately gave orders for him to be sent for a soldier.

"He won't obey . . . twice I told him! . . . and he didn't obey. She's the first person in this house, she's my best friend," screamed the old prince. "And if you allow yourself," he shouted in a fury, for the first time addressing Princess Marya, "ever again, as you dared yesterday . . . to forget yourself in her presence, I'll show you who is master in this house. Away! don't let me set eyes on you! Beg her pardon!"

Princess Marya begged Amalia Yevgenyevna's pardon and also her father's, both for herself and the footman Filipp, who implored her intervention.

At such moments the feeling that prevailed in Princess Marya's soul was akin to the pride of sacrifice. And all of a sudden at such moments, that father whom she was judging would look for his spectacles, fumbling by them and not seeing them, or would forget what had just happened, or would take a tottering step with his weak legs, and look round to see whether any one had noticed his feebleness, or what was worst of all, at dinner when there were no guests to excite him, he would suddenly fall asleep, letting his napkin drop and his shaking head sink over his plate. "He is old and feeble, and I dare to judge him!" she thought, revolted by herself.

III

In the year 1811 there was living in Moscow a French doctor called Metivier, who was rapidly coming into fashion. He was a very tall, handsome man, polite as only a Frenchman is, and was said by every one in Moscow to be an extraordinarily clever doctor. He was received in the very best houses, not merely as a doctor, but as an equal.

Prince Nikolay Andreitch had always ridiculed medicine, but of late he had by Mademoiselle Bourienne's advice allowed this doctor to see him, and had become accustomed to his visits. Metivier used to see the old prince twice a week.

On St. Nikolay's day, the name-day of the old prince, all Moscow was driving up to the approach of his house, but he gave orders for no one to be admitted to see him. Only a few guests, of whom he gave a list to Princess Marya, were to be invited to dinner.

Metivier, who arrived in the morning with his felicitations, thought himself as the old prince's doctor entitled to *forcer la consigne*, as he told Princess Marya, and went in to the prince. It so happened that on that morning of his name-day the old prince was in one of his very worst tempers. He had spent the whole morning wandering about the house, finding fault with every one, and affecting not to understand what was said to him and to be misunderstood by everybody. Princess Marya knew that mood well from subdued and fretful grumbling, which usually found vent in a violent outburst of fury, and as though facing a cocked and loaded gun, she went all the morning in expectation of an explosion. The morning passed off fairly well, till the doctor's arrival. After admitting the doctor, Princess Marya sat down with a book in the drawing-room near the door, where she could hear all that passed in the prince's study.

At first she heard Metivier's voice alone, then her father's voice, then both voices began talking at once. The door flew open, and in the doorway she saw the handsome, terrified figure of Metivier with his shock of black hair, and the old prince in a skull-cap and dressing-gown, his face hideous with rage and his eyes lowered.

"You don't understand," screamed the old prince, "but I do! French spy, slave of Bonaparte, spy, out of my house—away, I tell you!" And he slammed the door. Metivier, shrugging his shoulders, went up to Mademoiselle Bourienne, who ran out of the next room at the noise.

"The prince is not quite well, bile and rush of blood to the head. Calm yourself, I will look in to-morrow," said Metivier; and putting his fingers to his lips he hurried off.

Through the door could be heard steps shuffling in slippers and shouts: "Spies, traitors, traitors everywhere! Not a minute of peace in my own house!"

After Metivier's departure the old prince sent for his daughter, and the whole fury of his passion spent itself on her. She was to blame for the spy's having been admitted to see him. Had not he told her, told her to make a list, and that those not on the list were on no account to be admitted? Why then had that scoundrel been shown up? She was to blame for everything. With her he could not have a minute of peace, could not die in peace, he told her.

"No, madame, we must part, we must part, I tell you! I can put up with no more," he said, and went out of the room. And as though afraid she might find some comfort, he turned back and trying to assume an air of calmness, he added: "And don't imagine that I have said this in a moment of temper; no, I'm quite calm and I have thought it well over, and it shall be so—you shall go away, and find some place for yourself! . . ." But he could not restrain himself, and with the vindic- tive fury which can only exist where a man loves, obviously in anguish, he shook his fists and screamed at her: "Ah! if some fool would marry her!" He slammed the door, sent for Mademoiselle Bourienne, and sub-· sided into his study.

At two o'clock the six persons he had selected arrived to dinner. Those guests—the celebrated Count Rastoptchin, Prince Lopuhin and his nephew, General Tchatrov, an old comrade of the prince's in the field, and of the younger generation Pierre and Boris Drubetskoy were await- ing him in the drawing-room. Boris, who had come on leave to Moscow shortly before, had been anxious to be presented to Prince Nikolay Andreitch, and had succeeded in so far ingratiating himself in his favour, that the old prince made in his case an exception from his usual rule of excluding all young unmarried men from his house.

The prince did not receive what is called "society," but his house was the centre of a little circle into which—though it was not talked of much in the town—it was more flattering to be admitted than any- where else. Boris had grasped that fact a week previously, when he heard Rastoptchin tell the commander-in-chief of Moscow, who had invited him to dine on St. Nikolay's day, that he could not accept his invitation.

"On that day I always go to pay my devotions to the relics of Prince Nikolay Andreitch."

"Oh yes, yes . . ." assented the commander-in-chief. "How is he? . . ."

The little party assembled before dinner in the old-fashioned, lofty drawing-room, with its old furniture, was like the solemn meeting of some legal council board.

All sat silent, or if they spoke, spoke in subdued tones. Prince Nikolay Andreitch came in, serious and taciturn. Princess Marya seemed meeker and more timid than usual. The guests showed no inclination to address their conversation to her, for they saw that she had no thought for what they were saying. Count Rastoptchin maintained the conversation alone, relating the latest news of the town and the political world. Lopuhin and the old general took part in the conversation at rare in- tervals. Prince Nikolay Andreitch listened like a presiding judge receiv- ing a report submitted to him, only testifying by his silence, or from time to time by a brief word, that he was taking cognizance of the facts laid before him.

The tone of the conversation was based on the assumption that no one approved of what was being done in the political world. Incidents were related obviously confirming the view that everything was going from bad to worse. But in every story that was told, and in every criticism that was offered, what was striking was the way that the speaker checked himself, or was checked, every time the line was reached where a criticism might have reference to the person of the Tsar him- self.

At dinner the conversation turned on the last political news, Napoleon's seizure of the possessions of the Duke of Oldenburg, and the Russian note, hostile to Napoleon, which had been despatched to all the European courts.

"Bonaparte treats all Europe as a pirate does a captured vessel," said Rastoptchin, repeating a phrase he had uttered several times before. "One only marvels at the long-suffering or the blindness of the ruling sovereigns. Now it's the Pope's turn, and Bonaparte doesn't scruple to try and depose the head of the Catholic Church, and no one says a word. Our Emperor alone has protested against the seizure of the possessions of the Duke of Oldenburg. And even . . ." Count Rastoptchin broke off, feeling that he was on the very border line beyond which criticism was impossible.

"Other domains have been offered him instead of the duchy of Oldenburg," said the old prince. "He shifts the dukes about, as I might move my serfs from Bleak Hills to Bogutcharovo and the Ryazan estates."

"The Duke of Oldenburg supports his misfortune with admirable force of character and resignation," said Boris putting in his word respectfully. He said this because on his journey from Petersburg he had had the honour of being presented to the duke. The old prince looked at the young man as though he would have liked to say something in reply, but changed his mind, considering him too young.

"I have read our protest about the Oldenburg affair, and I was surprised at how badly composed the note was," said Count Rastoptchin in the casual tone of a man criticising something with which he is very familiar.

Pierre looked at Rastoptchin in naïve wonder, unable to understand why he should be troubled by the defective composition of the note.

"Does it matter how the note is worded, count," he said, "if the meaning is forcible?"

"My dear fellow, with our five hundred thousand troops, it should be easy to have a good style," said Count Rastoptchin.

Pierre perceived the point of Count Rastoptchin's dissatisfaction with the wording of the note.

"I should have thought there were scribblers enough to write it," said the old prince. "Up in Petersburg they do nothing but write—not notes only, but new laws they keep writing. My Andryusha up there has written a whole volume of new laws for Russia. Nowadays they're always at it!" And he laughed an unnatural laugh.

The conversation paused for a moment; the old general cleared his throat to draw attention.

"Did you hear of the last incident at the review in Petersburg? Didn't the new French ambassadors expose themselves!"

"Eh? Yes, I did hear something; he said something awkward in the presence of his majesty."

"His majesty drew his attention to the grenadier division and the parade march," pursued the general; "and it seems the ambassador took no notice and had the insolence to say 'We in France,' says he, 'don't pay attention to such trivial matters.' The emperor did not vouchsafe him a reply. At the review that followed the emperor, they say, did not once deign to address him."

Every one was silent; upon this fact which related to the Tsar personally, no criticism could be offered.

"Impudent rogues!" said the old prince. "Do you know Metivier? I turned him out of the house to-day. He was here, he was allowed to come in, in spite of my begging no one should be admitted," said the old prince, glancing angrily at his daughter. And he told them his whole conversation with the French doctor and his reasons for believing Metivier to be a spy. Though his reasons were very insufficient and obscure, no one raised an objection.

After the meat, champagne was handed round. The guests rose from their places to congratulate the old prince. Princess Marya too went up to him. He glanced at her with a cold, spiteful glance, and offered her his shaven, wrinkled cheek. The whole expression of his face told her that their morning's conversation was not forgotten, that his resolution still held good, and that it was only owing to the presence of their visitors that he did not tell her so now.

When they went into the drawing-room to coffee, the old men sat together.

Prince Nikolay Andreitch grew more animated, and began to express his views on the impending war. He said that our wars with Bonaparte would be unsuccessful so long as we sought alliances with the Germans and went meddling in European affairs, into which we had been drawn by the Peace of Tilsit. We had no business to fight for Austria or against Austria. Our political interests all lay in the East, and as regards Bonaparte, the one thing was an armed force on the frontier, and a firm policy, and he would never again dare to cross the Russian frontier, as he had done in 1807.

"And how should we, prince, fight against the French!" said Count Rastoptchin. "Can we arm ourselves against our teachers and divinities? Look at our young men, look at our ladies. Our gods are the French, and Paris—our Paradise."

He began talking more loudly, obviously with the intention of being heard by every one.

"Our fashions are French, our ideas are French, our feelings are French! You have sent Metivier about his business because he's a Frenchman and a scoundrel, but our ladies are crawling on their hands and knees after him. Yesterday I was at an evening party, and out of five ladies three were Catholics and had a papal indulgence for embroidering on Sundays. And they sitting all but naked, like the signboards of some public bath-house, if you'll excuse my saying so. Ah, when one looks at our young people, prince, one would like to take Peter the Great's old cudgel out of the museum and break a few ribs in the good old Russian style, to knock the nonsense out of them!"

All were silent. The old prince looked at Rastoptchin with a smile on his face and shook his head approvingly.

"Well, good-bye, your excellency; don't you be ill," said Rastoptchin, getting up with the brisk movements characteristic of him, and holding out his hand to the old prince.

"Good-bye, my dear fellow. Your talk is a music I'm always glad to listen to!" said the old prince, keeping hold of his hand and offering him his cheek for a kiss. The others, too, got up when Rastoptchin did.

IV

PRINCESS MARYA, sitting in the drawing-room, and hearing the old men's talk and criticisms, did not understand a word of what she was hearing. She thought of nothing but whether all their guests were noticing her father's hostile attitude to her. She did not even notice the marked attention and amiability shown her during the whole of dinner by Drubetskoy, who was that day paying them his third visit.

Princess Marya turned with an absent-minded, questioning glance to Pierre, who, with a smile on his face, came up to her, hat in hand, the last of the guests, after the prince had gone out, and they were left alone together in the drawing-room.

"Can I stay a little longer?" he said, dropping his bulky person into a low chair beside Princess Marya.

"Oh, yes," she said. "You noticed nothing?" her eyes asked.

Pierre was in an agreeable, after-dinner mood. He looked straight before him and smiled softly. "Have you known that young man long, princess?" he said.

"Which one?"

"Drubetskoy."

"No, not long. . . ."

"Well, do you like him?"

"Yes; he's a very agreeable young man. Why do you ask me?" said Princess Marya, still thinking of her conversation in the morning with her father.

"Because I have observed, that when a young man comes from Petersburg to Moscow on leave, it is invariably with the object of marrying an heiress."

"Have you observed that?" said Princess Marya.

"Yes," Pierre went on with a smile, "and that young man now manages matters so that wherever there are wealthy heiresses—there he is to be found. I can read him like a book. He is hesitating now which to attack, you or Mademoiselle Julie Karagin. He is very attentive to her."

"Does he visit them?"

"Yes, very often. And do you know the new-fashioned method of courting?" said Pierre, smiling good-humouredly, and obviously feeling in that light-hearted mood of good-natured irony, for which he had so often reproached himself in his diary.

"No," said Princess Marya.

"To please the Moscow girls nowadays one has to be melancholy. He is very melancholy with Mademoiselle Karagin," said Pierre.

"Really!" said Princess Marya, looking at the kindly face of Pierre, and thinking all the time of her own trouble. "It would ease my heart," she was thinking, "if I could make up my mind to confide all I am feeling to some one. And it is just Pierre I should like to tell it all to. He is so kind and generous. It would ease my heart. He would give me advice."

"Would you marry him?" asked Pierre.

"O my God, count! there are moments when I would marry any one" —to her own surprise Princess Marya said, with tears in her voice. "Ah! how bitter it is to love some one near to one and to feel," she went on in a shaking voice, "that you can do nothing for him, but cause him sorrow, and when you know you cannot alter it. There's only one thing —to go away, and where am I to go?"

"What is wrong? what is the matter with you, princess?"

But Princess Marya, without explaining further, burst into tears.

"I don't know what is the matter with me to-day. Don't take any notice of me, forget what I said to you."

All Pierre's gaiety had vanished. He questioned the princess anxiously, begged her to speak out, to confide her trouble to him. But she would only repeat that she begged him to forget what she had said, that she did not remember what she had said, and that she had no trouble except the one he knew—her anxiety lest Prince Andrey's marriage should cause a breach between him and his father.

"Have you heard anything of the Rostovs?" she asked to change the subject. "I was told they would soon be here. I expect Andrey, too, every day. I should have liked them to see each other here."

"And how does he look at the matter now?" said Pierre, meaning by *he* the old prince. Princess Marya shook her head.

"But it can't be helped. There are only a few months left now before the year is over. And it can't go on like this. I should only have liked to spare my brother the first minutes. I could have wished they were coming sooner. I hope to get to know her well. . . . You have known them a long while," said Princess Marya. "Tell me the whole truth, speaking quite seriously. What sort of a girl is she, and how do you like her? But the whole truth, because, you see, Andrey is risking so much in doing this against our father's will, that I should like to know . . ."

A vague instinct told Pierre that these pleas and repeated requests to him to tell her the *whole truth* betrayed Princess Marya's ill-will towards her future sister-in-law, that she wanted Pierre not to approve of Prince Andrey's choice; but Pierre said what he felt rather than what he thought. "I don't know how to answer your question," said he, blushing though he could not have said why himself. "I really don't know what kind of girl she is. I can't analyse her. She's fascinating; and why she is, I don't know; that's all that one can say about her."

Princess Marya sighed, and her face expressed: "Yes; that's what I expected and feared."

"Is she clever?" asked Princess Marya. Pierre thought a moment.

"I suppose not," he said. "Yes, though. She does not think it worth while to be clever. . . . Yes, no; she is fascinating, and nothing more."

Princess Marya again shook her head disapprovingly.

"Ah, I do so want to like her! You tell her so if you see her before I do."

"I have heard that they will be here in a few days," said Pierre.

Princess Marya told Pierre her plan of getting to know her future sister-in-law as soon as the Rostovs arrived, and trying to get the old prince accustomed to her.

V

BORIS had not succeeded in marrying a wealthy heiress in Petersburg, and it was with that object that he had come to Moscow. In Moscow Boris found himself hesitating between two of the wealthiest heiresses,— Julie and Princess Marya. Though Princess Marya, in spite of her plainness, seemed to him anyway more attractive than Julie, he felt vaguely awkward in paying court to the former. In his last conversation with her, on the old prince's name-day, she had met all his attempts to talk of the emotions with irrelevant replies, and had obviously not heard what he was saying.

Julie, on the contrary, received his attentions eagerly, though she showed it in a peculiar fashion of her own.

Julie was seven-and-twenty. By the death of her two brothers she had become extremely wealthy. She had by now become decidedly plain. But she believed herself to be not merely as pretty as ever, but actually far more attractive than she had ever been. She was confirmed in this delusion by having become a very wealthy heiress, and also by the fact that as she grew older her society involved less risk for men, and they could behave with more freedom in their intercourse with her, and could profit by her suppers, her *soirées,* and the lively society that gathered about her, without incurring any obligations to her. A man who would have been afraid of going ten years before to a house where there was a young girl of seventeen, for fear of compromising her and binding himself, would now boldly visit her every day, and treat her not as a marriageable girl, but as an acquaintance of no sex.

The Karagins' house was that winter one of the most agreeable and hospitable houses in Moscow. In addition to the dinner-parties and *soirées,* to which guests came by invitation, there were every day large informal gatherings at the Karagins', principally of men, who had supper there at midnight and stayed on till three o'clock in the morning. Julie did not miss a single ball, entertainment, or theatre. Her dresses were always of the most fashionable. But in spite of that, Julie appeared to have lost all illusions, told every one that she had no faith in love or friendship, or any of the joys of life, and looked for consolation only to the *realm beyond.* She had adopted the tone of a girl who has suffered a

great disappointment, a girl who has lost her lover or been cruelly deceived by him. Though nothing of the kind had ever happened to her,
she was looked upon as having been disappointed in that way, and she
did in fact believe herself that she had suffered a great deal in her life.
This melancholy neither hindered her from enjoying herself nor hindered
young men from spending their time very agreeably in her society.
Every guest who visited at the house paid his tribute to the melancholy
temper of the hostess, and then proceeded to enjoy himself in society
gossip, dancing, intellectual games, or *bouts rimés* which were in fashion
at the Karagins'. A few young men only, among them Boris, entered
more deeply into Julie's melancholy, and with these young men she had
more prolonged and secluded conversations on the nothingness of all
things earthly, and to them she opened her albums, full of mournful
sketches, sentences, and verses.

Julie was particularly gracious to Boris. She deplored his early disillusionment with life, offered him those consolations of friendship she
was so well able to offer, having herself suffered so cruelly in life, and
opened her album to him. Boris sketched two trees in her album, and
wrote under them: "Rustic trees, your gloomy branches shed darkness
and melancholy upon me."

In another place he sketched a tomb and inscribed below it:—

> "Death is helpful, and death is tranquil,
> Ah, there is no other refuge from sorrow!"

Julie said that couplet was exquisite.

"There is something so ravishing in the smile of melancholy," she
said to Boris, repeating word for word a passage copied from a book. "It
is a ray of light in the shadow, a blend between grief and despair, which
shows consolation possible."

Upon that Boris wrote her the following verses in French:—

> "Poisonous nourishment of a soul too sensitive,
> Thou, without whom happiness would be impossible to me,
> Tender melancholy, ah, come and console me,
> Come, calm the torments of my gloomy retreat,
> And mingle a secret sweetness with the tears I feel flowing.'

Julie played to Boris the most mournful nocturnes on the harp. Boris
read aloud to her the romance of *Poor Liza,* and more than once broke
down in reading it from the emotion that choked his utterance. When
they met in general society Julie and Boris gazed at one another as
though they were the only people existing in the world, disillusioned and
comprehending each other.

Anna Mihalovna, who often visited the Karagins, took a hand at cards
with the mother, and meanwhile collected trustworthy information as
to the portion that Julie would receive on her marriage (her dowry was
to consist of two estates in the Penza province and forests in the Nizhnigorod province). With tender emotion and deep resignation to the will

of Providence, Anna Mihalovna looked on at the refined sadness that united her son to the wealthy Julie.

"Still as charming and as melancholy as ever, my sweet Julie," she would say to the daughter. "Boris says he finds spiritual refreshment in your house. He has suffered such cruel disillusionment, and he is so sensitive," she would say to the mother.

"Ah, my dear, how attached I have grown to Julie lately," she would say to her son, "I can't tell you. But, indeed, who could help loving her! A creature not of this earth! Ah, Boris! Boris!" She paused for a moment. "And how I feel for her mother," she would go on. "She showed me to-day the letters and accounts from Penza (they have an immense estate there), and she, poor thing, with no one to help her. They do take such advantage of her!"

Boris heard his mother with a faintly perceptible smile. He laughed blandly at her simple-hearted wiles, but he listened to her and sometimes questioned her carefully about the Penza and Nizhnigorod estates.

Julie had long been expecting an offer from her melancholy adorer, and was fully prepared to accept it. But a sort of secret feeling of repulsion for her, for her passionate desire to be married, for her affectation, and a feeling of horror at renouncing all possibility of real love made Boris still delay. The term of his leave was drawing to a close. Whole days at a time, and every day he spent at the Karagins'; and each day Boris resolved, as he thought things over, that he would make an offer on the morrow. But in Julie's presence, as he watched her red face and her chin, almost always sprinkled with powder, her moist eyes, and the expression of her countenance, which betokened a continual readiness to pass at once from melancholy to the unnatural ecstasies of conjugal love, Boris could not utter the decisive word, although in imagination he had long regarded himself as the owner of the Penza and Nizhnigorod estates, and had disposed of the expenditure of their several revenues. Julie saw the hesitation of Boris, and the idea did sometimes occur to her that she was distasteful to him. But feminine self-flattery promptly afforded her comfort, and she assured herself that it was love that made him retiring. Her melancholy was, however, beginning to pass into irritability, and not long before the end of Boris's leave she adopted a decisive plan of action. Just before the expiration of Boris's leave there appeared in Moscow, and—it need hardly be said—also in the drawing-room of the Karagins', no less a person than Anatole Kuragin, and Julie, abruptly abandoning her melancholy, became exceedingly lively and cordial to Kuragin.

"My dear," said Anna Mihalovna to her son, "I know from a trust-worthy source that Prince Vassily is sending his son to Moscow to marry him to Julie. I am so fond of Julie that I should be most sorry for her. What do you think about it, my dear?" said Anna Mihalovna.

Boris was mortified at the idea of being unsuccessful, of having wasted all that month of tedious, melancholy courtship of Julie, and of seeing all the revenues of those Penza estates—which he had mentally assigned to the various purposes for which he needed them—pass into other hands, especially into the hands of that fool Anatole. He drove off to the Karagins' with the firm determination to make an offer. Julie met him with a gay and careless face, casually mentioned how much she had enjoyed the ball of the evening, and asked him when he was leaving. Although Boris had come with the intention of speaking of his love, and was therefore resolved to take a tender tone, he began to speak irritably of the fickleness of woman; saying that women could so easily pass from sadness to joy, and their state of mind depended entirely on what sort of man happened to be paying them attention. Julie was offended, and said that that was quite true, indeed, that a woman wanted variety, and that always the same thing would bore any one.

"Then I would advise you . . ." Boris was beginning, meaning to say something cutting; but at that instant the mortifying reflection occurred to him that he might leave Moscow without having attained his object, and having wasted his efforts in vain (an experience he had never had yet). He stopped short in the middle of a sentence, dropped his eyes, to avoid seeing her disagreeably exasperated and irresolute face, and said, "But it was not to quarrel with you that I have come here. On the contrary . . ." He glanced at her to make sure whether he could go on. All irritation had instantly vanished from her face, and her uneasy and imploring eyes were fastened upon him in greedy expectation.

"I can always manage so as to see very little of her," thought Boris. "And the thing's been begun and must be finished!" He flushed crimson, raised his eyes to her face, and said to her, "You know my feeling for you!" There was no need to say more. Julie's countenance beamed with triumph and self-satisfaction; but she forced Boris to say everything that is usually said on such occasions, to say that he loved her, and had never loved any woman more than her. She knew that for her Penza estates and her Nizhnigorod forests she could demand that, and she got all she demanded.

The young engaged couple, with no further allusions to trees that enfolded them in gloom and melancholy, made plans for a brilliant establishment in Petersburg, paid visits, and made every preparation for a splendid wedding.

VI

Count Ilya Andreitch Rostov arrived in Moscow towards the end of January with Natasha and Sonya. The countess was still unwell, and unable to travel, but they could not put off coming till she recovered, for Prince Andrey was expected in Moscow every day. They had, besides, to order the trousseau, to sell the estate in the suburbs of Moscow, and to take advantage of old Prince Bolkonsky's presence in Moscow to present his future daughter-in-law to him. The Rostovs' house in Moscow had not been heated all the winter; and as they were coming only for a short time, and the countess was not with them, Count Ilya Andreitch made up his mind to stay with Marya Dmitryevna Ahrostimov, who had long been pressing her hospitality upon the count.

Late in the evening the four loaded sledges of the Rostovs drove into the courtyard of Marya Dmitryevna in Old Equerrys' Place. Marya Dmitryevna lived alone. She had by now married off her daughter. Her sons were all in the service.

She still held herself as erect; still gave every one her opinions in the same loud, outspoken, decided fashion; and her whole bearing seemed a reproof to other people for every sort of weakness, passion, and temptation, of which she would not admit the bare possibility. In the early morning, in a house-jacket, she looked after the management of her household. Then she drove on saints' days to Mass, and from Mass to the gaols and prisons; and of what she did there, she never spoke to any one.

On ordinary days she dressed and received petitioners of various classes, of whom some sought her aid every day. Then she had dinner, an abundant and appetising meal, at which some three or four guests were always present. After dinner she played a game of boston; and at night had the newspapers and new books read aloud to her while she knitted. It was only as a rare exception that she went out in the evening; if she did so, it was only to visit the most important people in the town.

She had not gone to bed when the Rostovs arrived, and the door in the vestibule squeaked on the block, as the Rostovs and their servants came in from the cold outside. Marya Dmitryevna stood in the doorway of the hall, with her spectacles slipping down on her nose, and her head flung back, looking with a stern and irate face at the new-comers. It might have been supposed that she was irritated at their arrival, and would pack them off again at once, had she not at the very time been giving careful instructions to her servants where to install her guests and their belongings.

"The count's things? Bring them here," she said, pointing to the trunks, and not bestowing a greeting on any one. "The young ladies', this way to the left. Well, what are we pottering about for?" she called to her maids. "Warm the samovar! She's plumper, prettier," she pronounced of Natasha, flushed from the frosty air, as she drew her closer by her hood. "Foo! she is cold! You make haste and get your wraps off," she shouted to the count, who would have kissed her hand. "You're frozen, I warrant. Rum for the tea! Sonyushka, *bonjour*," she said to Sonya, indicating by this French phrase the slightly contemptuous affectionateness of her attitude to Sonya.

When they had all taken off their outdoor things, set themselves straight after the journey, and come in to tea, Marya Dmitryevna kissed them all in due course.

"Heartily glad you have come, and are staying with me," she said. "It's long been time you were here," she said, with a significant glance at Natasha. . . . "The old fellow's here, and his son's expected from day to day. You must, you must make their acquaintance. Oh, well, we shall talk of that later on," she added, with a glance at Sonya, showing that she did not care to talk of it before her. "Now, listen," she turned to the count, "what do you want to do to-morrow? Whom will you send for? Shinshin?"—she crooked one finger. "The tearful Anna Mihalovna —two. She's here with her son. The son's to be married too! Then Bezuhov. He's here, too, with his wife. He ran away from her, and she has come trotting after him. He dined with me last Wednesday. Well, and I'll take them"—she indicated the young ladies—"to-morrow to Iversky chapel, and then we shall go to Aubert-Chalmey. You'll be getting everything now, I expect! Don't judge by me—the sleeves nowadays are like this! The other day the young princess, Irina Vassilyevna, came to see me, just as though she had put two barrels on her arms, a dreadful fright. Every day there's a new fashion. And what sort of business is it you have come for yourself?" she said severely, addressing the count.

"Everything has come together," answered the count. "There's the girl's rags to buy; and now there's a purchaser turned up for the Moscow estate and the house. If you'll graciously permit it, I'll choose an opportunity and drive over to Maryinskoe for a day, leaving my girls on your hands."

"Very good, very good, they'll be safe enough with me. I'm as safe as the Mortgage Bank. I'll take them where they must go, and scold them and pet them too," said Marya Dmitryevna, putting her big hand on the cheek of her favourite and god-daughter Natasha.

Next morning Marya Dmitryevna bore the young ladies off to Iversky chapel and to Madame Aubert-Chalmey, who was so frightened of Marya Dmitryevna that she always sold her dresses at a loss simply to get rid of her as soon as possible. Marya Dmitryevna ordered almost the whole trousseau. On their return, she sent every one out of the room but Natasha, and called her favourite to sit beside her arm-chair.

"Well, now we can have a chat. I congratulate you on your betrothed. A fine fellow you have hooked! I'm glad of it for your sake, and I have known him since he was that high"—she held her hand a yard from the floor. Natasha flushed joyfully. "I like him and all his family. Now, listen! You know, of course, that old Prince Nikolay was very much against his son's marrying. He's a whimsical old fellow! Of course, Prince Andrey is not a child, he can get on without him, but to enter a family against the father's will is not a nice thing to do. One wants peace and love in a family. You're a clever girl, you'll know how to manage things. You must use your wits and your kind heart. And every thing will come right."

Natasha was silent, not as Marya Dmitryevna supposed from shyness. In reality Natasha disliked any one's interfering in what touched her love for Prince Andrey, which seemed to her something so apart from all human affairs, that no one, as she imagined, could understand it. She loved Prince Andrey, and only him, and knew only him; he loved her, and was to arrive in a day or two and carry her off. She did not care about anything else.

"I have known him a long while, do you see; and Masha, your sister-in-law, I love. Sisters-in-law are said to be mischief-makers, but she—well, she wouldn't hurt a fly. She has begged me to bring you two together. You must go to see her to-morrow with your father, and be as

nice as possible; you are younger than she is. By the time your young
man comes back, you'll be friends with his sister and his father, and they
will have learned to love you. Yes or no? It will be better so, eh?"

"Oh yes!" Natasha responded reluctantly.

VII

NEXT day, by the advice of Marya Dmitryevna, Count Ilya Andreitch
went with Natasha to call on Prince Nikolay Andreitch. The count prepared for the visit by no means in a cheerful spirit: in his heart he was
afraid. Count Ilya Andreitch had a vivid recollection of his last interview with the old prince at the time of the levying of the militia, when,
in reply to his invitation to dinner, he had had to listen to a heated reprimand for furnishing less than the required number of men. Natasha in
her best dress was, on the contrary, in the most cheerful frame of mind.
"They can't help liking me," she thought; "every one always does like
me. And I'm so ready to do anything they please for them, so readily to
love them—him for being his father, and her for being his sister—they
can have no reason for not loving me!"

They drove to the gloomy old house in Vosdvizhenka, and went into
the vestibule.

"Well now, with God's blessing," said the count, half in jest, half in
earnest. But Natasha noticed that her father was in a nervous fidget as
he went into the entry, and asked timidly and softly whether the prince
and the princess were at home. After their arrival had been announced,
there was some perturbation visible among the prince's servants. The
footman, who was running to announce them, was stopped by another
footman in the big hall, and they whispered together. A maid-servant
ran into the hall, and hurriedly said something, mentioning the princess.
At last one old footman came out with a wrathful air, and announced to
the Rostovs that the prince was not receiving, but the princess begged
them to walk up. The first person to meet the visitors was Mademoiselle
Bourienne. She greeted the father and daughter with marked courtesy,
and conducted them to the princess's apartment. The princess, with a
frightened and agitated face, flushed in patches, ran in, treading heavily,
to meet her visitors, doing her best to seem cordial and at ease. From the
first glance Princess Marya disliked Natasha. She thought her too fash-
ionably dressed, too frivolously gay and vain. Princess Marya had no
idea that before she had seen her future sister-in-law she had been unfavourably disposed to her, through unconscious envy of her beauty, her
youth, and her happiness, and through jealousy of her brother's love for
her. Apart from this insuperable feeling of antipathy to her, Princess
Marya was at that moment agitated by the fact that on the Rostovs
having been announced the old prince had shouted that he didn't want
to see them, that Princess Marya could see them if she chose, but they
were not to be allowed in to see him. Princess Marya resolved to see the
Rostovs, but she was every instant in dread of some freak on the part of

the old prince, as he had appeared greatly excited by the arrival of the Rostovs.

"Well, here I have brought you my songstress, princess," said the count, bowing and scraping, while he looked round uneasily as though he were afraid the old prince might come in. "How glad I am that you should make friends. . . . Sorry, very sorry, the prince is still unwell"; and uttering a few more stock phrases, he got up. "If you'll allow me, princess, to leave you my Natasha for a quarter of an hour, I will drive round—only a few steps from here—to Dogs' Square to see Anna Semyonovna, and then come back for her."

Count Ilya Andreitch bethought himself of this diplomatic stratagem to give the future sisters-in-law greater freedom to express their feelings to one another (so he told his daughter afterwards), but also to avoid the possibility of meeting the prince, of whom he was afraid. He did not tell his daughter this; but Natasha perceived this dread and uneasiness of her father's, and felt mortified by it. She blushed for her father, felt still angrier at having blushed, and glanced at the princess with a bold, challenging air, meant to express that she was not afraid of any one. The princess told the count that she would be delighted, and only begged him to stay a little longer at Anna Semyonovna's, and Ilya Andreitch departed.

In spite of the uneasy glances flung at her by Princess Marya, who wanted to talk to Natasha by herself, Mademoiselle Bourienne would not leave the room, and persisted in keeping up a conversation about Moscow entertainments and theatres. Natasha felt offended by the delay in the entry, by her father's nervousness, and by the constrained manner of the princess, who seemed to her to be making a favour of receiving her. And then everything displeased her. She did not like Princess Marya. She seemed to her very ugly, affected, and frigid. Natasha suddenly, as it were, shrank into herself, and unconsciously assumed a nonchalant air, which repelled Princess Marya more and more. After five minutes of irksome and constrained conversation, they heard the sound of slippered feet approaching rapidly. Princess Marya's face expressed terror: the door of the room opened, and the prince came in, in a white night-cap and dressing-gown.

"Ah, madam," he began, "madam, countess. . . . Countess Rostov . . . if I'm not mistaken . . . I beg you to excuse me, to excuse me . . . I didn't know, madam. As God's above, I didn't know that you were deigning to visit us, and came in to my daughter in this costume. I beg you to excuse me . . . as God's above, I didn't know," he repeated so unnaturally, with emphasis on the word "God," and so unpleasantly, that Princess Marya rose to her feet with her eyes on the ground, not daring to look either at her father or at Natasha. Natasha, getting up and curtseying, did not know either what she was to do. Only Mademoiselle Bourienne smiled agreeably.

"I beg you to excuse me, I beg you to excuse me! As God's above, I didn't know," muttered the old man, and looking Natasha over from head to foot, he went out.

Mademoiselle Bourienne was the first to recover herself after this apparition, and began talking about the prince's ill-health. Natasha and Princess Marya gazed dumbly at one another, and the longer they gazed dumbly at one another without saying what they wanted to say, the more unfavourably each felt disposed to the other.

When the count returned, Natasha showed a discourteous relief at seeing him, and made haste to get away. At that moment she almost hated that stiff, oldish princess, who could put her in such an awkward position, and spend half an hour with her without saying a word about Prince Andrey. "I couldn't be the first to speak of him before that Frenchwoman," thought Natasha. Princess Marya meanwhile was tortured by the very same feeling. She knew what she had to say to Natasha, but she could not do it, both because Mademoiselle Bourienne prevented her, and because—she did not know herself why—it was difficult for her to begin to speak of the marriage. The count was already going out of the room when Princess Marya moved rapidly up to Natasha, took her hand, and, with a heavy sigh, said: "Wait a moment, I want . . ." Natasha's expression as she looked at Princess Marya was ironical, though she did not know why.

"Dear Natalie," said Princess Marya, "do believe how glad I am that my brother has found such happiness . . ." She paused, feeling she was telling a lie. Natasha noticed the pause, and guessed the reason of it.

"I imagine, princess, that it is not now suitable to speak of that," said Natasha, with external dignity and coldness, though she felt the tears rising in her throat.

"What have I said, what have I done?" she thought as soon as she had gone out of the room.

They had to wait a long while for Natasha to come to dinner that day. She was sitting in her room, crying like a child, choking, and sobbing. Sonya stood over her, and kept kissing her on the head.

"Natasha, what is it?" she kept saying. "Why need you mind about them? It will pass, Natasha."

"No, if only you knew how insulting it was . . . as though I . . ."

"Don't talk of it, Natasha; it's not your fault, you see, so what does it matter to you! Kiss me," said Sonya.

Natasha raised her head, and kissing her friend on the lips, pressed her wet face against her.

"I can't say; I don't know. It's no one's fault," said Natasha; "it's my fault. But it's all awfully painful. Oh, why doesn't he come? . . ."

She went down to dinner with red eyes. Marya Dmitryevna, who had heard how the old prince had received the Rostovs, pretended not to notice Natasha's troubled face, and kept up a loud, jesting conversation at table with the count and the other guests.

VIII

THAT evening the Rostovs went to the opera, for which Marya Dmitryevna had obtained them a box.

Natasha had no wish to go, but it was impossible to refuse after Marya Dmitryevna's kindness, especially as it had been arranged expressly for her. When she was dressed and waiting for her father in the big hall, she looked at herself in the big looking-glass, and saw that she was looking pretty, very pretty. She felt even sadder, but it was a sweet and tender sadness.

"My God, if he were only here, I wouldn't have any stupid shyness of something as I used to, but in quite a new way, simply, I would embrace him, press close to him, force him to look at me with those scrutinising, inquisitive eyes, with which he used so often to look at me, and then I would make him laugh, as he used to laugh then; and his eyes—how I see those eyes!" thought Natasha. "And what does it matter to me about his father and sister; I love no one but him, him, him, with that face and those eyes, with his smile, manly, and yet childlike. . . . No, better not think of him, not think, forget, utterly forget him for the time. I can't bear this suspense; I shall sob in a minute," and she turned away from the looking-glass, making an effort not to weep. "And how can Sonya love Nikolenka so quietly, so calmly, and wait so long and so patiently!" she wondered, looking at Sonya, who came in, dressed for the theatre with a fan in her hand. "No, she's utterly different. I can't."

Natasha at that moment felt so softened and moved that to love and know that she was loved was not enough for her: she wanted now, now at once to embrace the man she loved, and to speak and hear from him the words of love, of which her heart was full. When she was in the carriage sitting beside her father and pensively watching the lights of the street lamps flitting by the frozen window, she felt even sadder and more in love, and forgot with whom and where she was going. The Rostovs' carriage fell into the line of carriages, and drove up to the theatre, its wheels crunching slowly over the snow. Natasha and Sonya skipped hurriedly out holding up their dresses; the count stepped out supported by the footmen, and all three walked to the corridor for the boxes in the stream of ladies and gentlemen going in and people selling programmes. They could hear the music already through the closed doors.

"Natasha, your hair . . ." whispered Sonya. The box-opener deferentially and hurriedly slipped before the ladies and opened the door of the box. The music became more distinctly audible at the door, and they saw the brightly lighted rows of boxes, with the bare arms and shoulders of the ladies, and the stalls below, noisy, and gay with uniforms. A lady entering the next box looked round at Natasha with an envious, feminine glance. The curtain had not yet risen and they were playing the overture. Natasha smoothing down her skirt went in with Sonya, and sat down looking round at the brightly lighted tiers of boxes facing them. The sensation she had not experienced for a long while—that hundreds of eyes were looking at her bare arms and neck—suddenly came upon her both pleasantly and unpleasantly, calling up a whole swarm of memories, desires, and emotions connected with that sensation.

The two strikingly pretty girls, Natasha and Sonya, with Count Ilya Andreitch, who had not been seen for a long while in Moscow, attracted general attention. Moreover, every one had heard vaguely of Natasha's engagement to Prince Andrey, knew that the Rostovs had been living in the country ever since, and looked with curiosity at the girl who was to make one of the best matches in Russia.

Natasha had, so every one told her, grown prettier in the country; and that evening, owing to her excited condition, she was particularly pretty. She made a striking impression of fulness of life and beauty, together with indifference to everything around her. Her black eyes gazed at the crowd, seeking out no one, while her slender arm, bare to above the elbow, leaned on the velvet edge of the box, and her hand, holding the programme, clasped and unclasped in time to the music with obvious unconsciousness.

"Look, there's Alenina," said Sonya, "with her mother, isn't it?"

"Heavens, Mihail Kirillitch is really stouter than ever," said the old count.

"Look! our Anna Mihalovna in such a cap!"

"The Karagins, Julie, and Boris with them. One can see at once they are engaged."

"Drubetskoy has made his offer! To be sure, I heard so to-day," said Shinshin, coming into the Rostovs' box.

Natasha looked in the direction her father was looking in and saw Julie with diamonds on her thick, red neck (Natasha knew it was powdered), sitting with a blissful face beside her mother.

Behind them could be seen the handsome, well-brushed head of Boris, with a smile inclining his ear towards Julie's mouth. He looked from under his brows at the Rostovs, and said something, smiling, to his betrothed.

"They are talking about us, about me and himself!" thought Natasha. "And he is, most likely, soothing his fiancée's jealousy of me; they needn't worry themselves! If only they knew how little they matter to me, any one of them."

Behind the engaged couple sat Anna Mihalovna in a green cap, with a face happy, in honour of the festive occasion, and devoutly resigned to the will of God. Their box was full of that atmosphere of an engaged couple—which Natasha knew so well and liked so much. She turned away; and suddenly all that had been humiliating in her morning visit came back to her mind.

"What right has he not to want to receive me into his family? Ah, better not think about it, not think till he comes back!" she said to herself, and began to look about at the faces, known and unknown, in the stalls.

In the front of the stalls, in the very centre, leaning back against the rail stood Dolohov, in a Persian dress, with his huge shock of curly hair combed upwards. He stood in the most conspicuous place in the theatre, well aware that he was attracting the attention of the whole audience, and as much at his ease as though he had been alone in his room. The most brilliant young men in Moscow were all thronging about him, and he was obviously the leading figure among them.

Count Ilya Andreitch, laughing, nudged the blushing Sonya, pointing out her former admirer.

"Did you recognise him?" he asked. "And where has he dropped from?" said he, turning to Shinshin. "I thought he had disappeared somewhere?"

"He did disappear," answered Shinshin. "He was in the Caucasus, and he ran away from there, and they say he has been acting as minister to some reigning prince in Persia, and there killed the Shah's brother. Well, all the Moscow ladies are wild about him! 'Dolohov the Persian,' that's what does it! Nowadays there's nothing can be done without Dolohov; they do homage to him, invite you to meet him, as if he were a sturgeon," said Shinshin. "Dolohov and Anatole Kuragin have taken all the ladies' hearts by storm."

A tall, handsome woman with a mass of hair and very naked, plump, white arms and shoulders, and a double row of big pearls round her throat, walked into the next box, and was a long while settling into her place and rustling her thick silk gown.

Natasha unconsciously examined that neck and the shoulders, the pearls, the coiffure of this lady, and admired the beauty of the shoulders and the pearls. While Natasha was scrutinising her a second time, the lady looked round, and meeting the eyes of Count Ilya Andreitch, she nodded and smiled to him. It was the Countess Bezuhov, Pierre's wife. The count, who knew every one in society, bent over and entered into conversation with her.

"Have you been here long?" he began. "I'm coming; I'm coming to kiss your hand. I have come to town on business and brought my girls with me. They say Semyonovna's acting is superb," the count went on. "Count Pyotr Kirillovitch never forgot us. Is he here?"

"Yes, he meant to come," said Ellen, looking intently at Natasha.

Count Ilya Andreitch sat down again in his place.

"Handsome, isn't she?" he whispered to Natasha.

"Exquisite!" said Natasha. "One might well fall in love with her!"

At that moment they heard the last chords of the overture, and the tapping of the conductor's stick. Late comers hurried to their seats in the stalls, and the curtain rose.

As soon as the curtain rose, a hush fell on the boxes and stalls, and all the men, old and young, in their frock coats or uniforms, all the women with precious stones on their bare flesh concentrated all their attention with eager curiosity on the stage. Natasha too began to look at it.

IX

THE stage consisted of a boarded floor in the middle, with painted cardboard representing trees at the sides, and linen stretched over the boards at the back. In the middle of the stage there were sitting maidens in red bodices and white skirts. An excessively stout woman in a white silk dress was sitting apart on a low bench with green cardboard fixed on the back of it. They were all singing something. When they had finished their song, the woman in white moved towards the prompter's box, and a man, with his stout legs encased in silk tights, with a plume and a dagger, went up to her and began singing and waving his arms.

The man in the tights sang alone, then she sang alone. Then both paused, while the music played, and the man fumbled with the hand of the woman in white, obviously waiting for the bar at which he was to begin singing with her. They sang a duet, and every one in the theatre began clapping and shouting, while the man and woman on the stage, supposed to represent lovers, began bowing with smiles and gesticulations.

After the country, and in her serious mood, Natasha felt it all grotesque and extraordinary. She could not follow the opera; she could not even listen to the music: she saw nothing but painted cardboard and strangely dressed-up men and women, talking, singing, and moving strangely about in the bright light. She knew what it all was meant to represent; but it was all so grotesquely false and unnatural that she felt alternately ashamed and amused at the actors. She looked about her at the faces of the spectators, seeking in them signs of the same irony and bewilderment that she was feeling herself. But all the faces were watching what was passing on the stage, and expressed nothing but an affected—so Natasha thought—rapture. "I suppose it is meant to be like this!" thought Natasha. She looked alternately at the rows of pomaded masculine heads in the stalls, and at the naked women in the boxes, especially at her next neighbour Ellen, who, quite undressed, sat gazing intently, with a quiet and serene smile, at the stage, and basking in the bright light that flooded the theatre, and the warm air, heated by the crowd. Natasha began gradually to pass into a state of intoxication she had not experienced for a long while. She lost all sense of what she was and where she was and what was going on before her eyes. She gazed and dreamed, and the strangest ideas flashed unexpectedly and disconnectedly into her mind. At one moment the idea occurred to her to leap over the footlights and sing that air the actress was singing; then she felt inclined to hook her fan into an old gentleman sitting near her, or to bend over to Ellen and tickle her.

At a moment when there was a lull on the stage before the beginning of a song, the door opening to the stalls creaked on the side nearest the Rostovs' box, and there was the sound of a man's footsteps. "Here he is, Kuragin!" whispered Shinshin. Countess Bezuhov turned smiling to the new-comer. Natasha looked in the direction of the Countess Bezu-

hov's eyes, and saw an exceedingly handsome adjutant coming towards
their box with a confident, but yet courteous, bearing. It was Anatole
Kuragin, whom she had seen long before, and noticed at the Petersburg
ball. He was now wearing an adjutant's uniform, with one epaulette and
a shoulder knot. He walked with a jaunty strut, which would have been
ridiculous if he had not been so handsome, and if his good-looking face
had not expressed such simple-hearted satisfaction and good spirits.
Although the performance was going on he walked lightly, without haste,
along the carpeted corridor, holding his scented, handsome head high,
and accompanied by a slight clank of spurs and sword. Glancing at Natasha, he went up to his sister, laid his hand in a close-fitting glove on
the edge of her box, nodded his head at her, and, bending down, asked
her a question, with a motion towards Natasha.

"Very, very charming!" he said, obviously speaking of Natasha. She
did not exactly hear the words, but divined them from the movement
of his lips. Then he went on to the front row and sat down beside Dolohov, giving a friendly and careless nudge with his elbow to the man
whom other people treated with such punctilio. With a merry wink, he
smiled at him, and leaned with his foot against the footlights.

"How like the brother is to his sister!" said the count. "And how
handsome they both are!"

Shinshin began telling the count in an undertone some story of an
intrigue of Kuragin's in Moscow, to which Natasha listened, simply
because he had said of her "very charming."

The first act was over; every one stood up in the stalls, changed
places, and began going out and coming in.

Boris came to the Rostovs' box, received their congratulations very
simply, and lifting his eyebrows with an absent-minded smile, gave
Natasha and Sonya his fiancée's message, begging them to come to her
wedding, and went away. Natasha, with a gay and coquettish smile,
talked to him and congratulated him on his approaching marriage—the
very Boris she had once been in love with. In the condition of emotional
intoxication in which she found herself everything seemed simple and
natural.

Ellen sat in her nakedness close by her, and smiled on all alike, and
just such a smile Natasha bestowed on Boris.

Ellen's box was filled and surrounded on the side of the stalls by the
most distinguished and intellectual men, who seemed vying with one
another in their desire to show every one that they knew her.

All throughout that entr'acte Kuragin stood with Dolohov in front of
the footlights staring at the Rostovs' box. Natasha knew he was talking
about her, and that afforded her satisfaction. She even turned so that
he could see her profile from what she believed to be the most becoming
angle. Before the beginning of the second act she observed in the stalls
the figure of Pierre, whom the Rostovs had not seen since their arrival.
His face looked sad, and he had grown stouter since Natasha had seen
him last. He walked up to the front rows, not noticing any one. Anatole
went up to him, and began saying something to him, with a look and

a gesture towards the Rostovs' box. Pierre looked pleased at seeing
Natasha, and walked hurriedly along the rows of stalls towards their
box. Leaning on his elbow, he talked smiling to Natasha for a long while.
While she was talking to Pierre, Natasha heard a man's voice speaking
in Countess Bezuhov's box, and something told her it was Kuragin. She
looked round and met his eyes. He looked her straight in the eyes,
almost smiling, with a look of such warmth and admiration that it
seemed strange to be so near him, to look at him like that, to be so certain that he admired her, and not to be acquainted with him.

In the second act there was scenery representing monuments, and a
hole in the drop at the back that represented the moon, and shades were
put over the footlights, and trumpets and bassoons began playing, and
a number of people came in on the right and on the left wearing black
cloaks. These people began waving their arms, and in their hands they
had something of the nature of a dagger. Then some more people ran
in and began dragging away the woman who had been in white but who
was now in a blue dress. They did not drag her away at once; they spent
a long while singing with her; but finally they did drag her away, and
behind the scenes they struck something metallic three times, and then
all knelt down and began singing a prayer. All these performances were
interrupted several times by the enthusiastic shouts of the spectators.

During that act, every time Natasha glanced towards the stalls, she
saw Anatole Kuragin, with one arm flung across the back of his chair,
staring at her. It pleased her to see that he was so captivated by her,
and it never entered her head that there could be anything amiss in it.

When the second act was over, Countess Bezuhov got up, turned towards the Rostovs' box (the whole of her bosom was completely exposed), with her gloved little finger beckoned the old count to her, and
taking no notice of the men who were thronging about her box, began
with an amiable smile talking to him.

"Oh, do make me acquainted with your charming daughters," she said.
"All the town is singing their praises, and I don't know them."

Natasha got up and curtseyed to the magnificent countess. Natasha
was so delighted at the praise from this brilliant beauty that she blushed
with pleasure.

"I quite want to become a Moscow resident myself," said Ellen.
"What a shame of you to bury such pearls in the country!"

Countess Bezuhov had some right to her reputation of being a fascinating woman. She could say what she did not think, especially what was
flattering, with perfect simplicity and naturalness.

"No, dear count, you must let me help to entertain your daughters,
though I'm not here now for very long, nor you either. But I'll do my
best to amuse them. I have heard a great deal about you in Petersburg,
and wanted to know you," she said to Natasha, with her unvarying
beautiful smile. "I have heard of you, too, from my page, Drubetskoy—
you have heard he is to be married—and from my husband's friend,
Bolkonsky, Prince Andrey Bolkonsky," she said, with peculiar emphasis,
by which she meant to signify that she knew in what relation he stood

to Natasha. She asked that one of the young ladies might be allowed to sit through the rest of the performance in her box that they might become better acquainted, and Natasha moved into it.

In the third act the scene was a palace in which a great many candles were burning, and pictures were hanging on the walls, representing knights with beards. In the middle stood a man and a woman, probably meant for a king and a queen. The king waved his right hand, and, obviously nervous, sang something very badly, and sat down on a crimson throne. The actress, who had been in white at first and then in blue, was now in nothing but a smock, and had let her hair down. She was standing near the throne, singing something very mournful, addressed to the queen. But the king waved his hand sternly, and from the sides there came in men and women with bare legs who began dancing all together. Then the violins played very shrilly and merrily: one of the actresses, with thick, bare legs and thin arms, leaving the rest, went to the side to set straight her bodice, then walked into the middle of the stage and began skipping into the air and kicking one leg very rapidly with the other. Every one in the stalls clapped their hands and roared "bravo!" Then one man stood alone at one corner of the stage. The cymbals and trumpets struck up more loudly in the orchestra, and this man began leaping very high in the air and rapidly waving his legs. (This was Duport, who earned sixty thousand a year by this accomplishment.) Every one in the boxes and in the stalls began clapping and shouting with all their might, and the man stood still and began smiling and bowing in all directions. Then other men and women with bare legs danced; then again the king shouted something to music, and they all began singing. But suddenly a storm came on, chromatic scales and chords with the diminishing sevenths could be heard in the orchestra, and they all ran off, dragging one of the performers again behind the scenes, and the curtain dropped. Again a fearful uproar of applause arose among the spectators, and all began screaming with rapturous faces:

"Duport! Duport! Duport!"

Natasha did not now feel this strange. She looked about her with pleasure, smiling joyfully.

"Isn't Duport admirable?" said Ellen, turning to her.

"Oh yes," answered Natasha.

X

IN THE entr'acte there was a current of chill air in Ellen's box, the door was opened, and Anatole walked in, bending and trying not to brush against any one.

"Allow me to introduce my brother," said Ellen, her eyes shifting uneasily from Natasha to Anatole. Natasha turned her pretty little head towards the handsome adjutant and smiled over her bare shoulder. Anatole, who was as handsome on a closer view as he was from a distance, sat down beside her, and said he had long wished to have this pleasure.

ever since the Narishkins' ball, at which he had had the pleasure he had not forgotten of seeing her. Kuragin was far more sensible and straightforward with women than he was in men's society. He talked boldly and simply, and Natasha was strangely and agreeably impressed by finding nothing so formidable in this man, of whom such stories were told, but, on the contrary, seeing on his face the most innocent, merry, and simple-hearted smile.

Kuragin asked her what she thought of the performance, and told her that at the last performance Semyonovna had fallen down while she was acting.

"And do you know, countess," said he, suddenly addressing her as though she were an old friend, "we are getting up a costume ball; you ought to take part in it; it will be great fun. They are all assembling at the Karagins'. Please, do come, really now, eh?" he said. As he said this he never took his smiling eyes off the face, the neck, the bare arms of Natasha. Natasha knew beyond all doubt that he was fascinated by her. That pleased her, yet she felt for some reason constrained and oppressed in his presence. When she was not looking at him she felt that he was looking at her shoulders, and she could not help trying to catch his eyes that he might rather look in her face. But as she looked into his eyes, she felt with horror that, between him and her, there was not that barrier of modest reserve she had always been conscious of between herself and other men. In five minutes she felt—she did not know how—that she had come fearfully close to this man. When she turned away, she felt afraid he might take her from behind by her bare arm and kiss her on the neck. They talked of the simplest things, and she felt that they were close as she had never been with any man. Natasha looked round at Ellen and at her father, as though to ask them what was the meaning of it. But Ellen was absorbed in talking to a general and did not respond to her glance, and her father's eyes said nothing to her but what they always said: "Enjoying yourself? Well, I'm glad then."

In one of the moments of awkward silence, during which Anatole gazed calmly and persistently at her, Natasha, to break the silence, asked him how he liked Moscow. Natasha asked this question and blushed as she did so; she was feeling all the while that there she was doing something improper in talking to him. Anatole smiled as though to encourage her.

"At first I didn't like it much, for what is it makes one like a town? It's the pretty women, isn't it? Well, but now I like it awfully," he said, with a meaning look at her. "You'll come to the fancy dress ball, countess? Do come," he said, and putting his hand out to her bouquet he said, dropping his voice, "You will be the prettiest. Come, dear countess, and as a pledge give me this flower."

Natasha did not understand what he was saying, nor did he himself; but she felt that in his uncomprehended words there was some improper intention. She did not know what to say, and turned away as though she had not heard what he said. But as soon as she turned away she felt that he was here behind her, so close to her.

"What is he feeling now? Is he confused? Is he angry? Must I set it right?" she wondered. She could not refrain from looking round. She glanced straight into his eyes, and his nearness and confidence, and the simple-hearted warmth of his smile vanquished her. She smiled exactly as he did, looking straight into his eyes. And again, she felt with horror that no barrier lay between him and her.

The curtain rose again. Anatole walked out of the box, serene and good-humoured. Natasha went back to her father's box, completely under the spell of the world in which she found herself. All that passed before her eyes now seemed to her perfectly natural. But on the other hand all previous thoughts of her betrothed, of Princess Marya, of her life in the country, did not once recur to her mind, as though all that belonged to the remote past.

In the fourth act there was some sort of devil who sang, waving his arms till the boards were moved away under him and he sank into the opening. That was all Natasha saw of the fourth act; she felt harassed and excited; and the cause of that excitement was Kuragin, whom she could not help watching. As they came out of the theatre Anatole came up to them, called their carriage and helped them into it. As he assisted Natasha he pressed her arm above the elbow. Natasha, flushed and excited, looked round at him. He gazed at her with flashing eyes and a tender smile.

It was only on getting home that Natasha could form any clear idea of what had happened. All at once, remembering Prince Andrey, she was horrified, and at tea, to which they all sat down after the theatre, she groaned aloud, and flushing crimson ran out of the room. "My God! I am ruined!" she said to herself. "How could I sink to such a depth?" she thought. For a long while she sat, with her flushed face hidden in her hands, trying to get a clear idea of what had happened and unable to grasp either what had happened or what she was feeling. Everything seemed to her dark, obscure, and dreadful. In that immense, lighted hall, where Duport had jumped about to music with his bare legs on the damp boards in his short jacket with tinsel, and young girls and old men, and that Ellen, proudly and serenely smiling in her nakedness, had enthusiastically roared "bravo"; there, in the wake of that Ellen, all had been clear and simple. But now, alone by herself, it was past comprehending. "What does it mean? What is that terror I felt with him? What is the meaning of those gnawings of conscience I am feeling now?" she thought.

To no one but to her mother at night in bed Natasha could have talked of what she was feeling. Sonya she knew, with her strict and single-minded view of things, would either have failed to understand at all, or would have been horrified at the avowal. Natasha all by herself had to try and solve the riddle that tormented her.

"Am I spoilt for Prince Andrey's love or not?" she asked herself, and with reassuring mockery she answered herself: "What a fool I am to ask such a thing! What has happened to me? Nothing. I have done nothing; I did nothing to lead him on. No one will ever know, and I shall never see him again," she told herself. "So it's plain that nothing has happened, that there's nothing to regret, that Prince Andrey can love me *still*. But why *still*? O my God, my God, why isn't he here!" Natasha felt comforted for a moment; but again some instinct told her that though that was all true, and though nothing had happened, yet some instinct told her that all the old purity of her love for Prince Andrey was lost. And again, in her imagination, she went over all her conversation with Kuragin, and saw again the face, the gestures, and the tender smile of that handsome, daring man at the moment when he had pressed her arm.

XI

ANATOLE KURAGIN was staying in Moscow because his father had sent him away from Petersburg, where he had been spending twenty thousand a year in hard cash and running up bills for as much more, and his creditors had been dunning his father. The father informed his son that for the last time he would pay half his debts; but only on condition that he would go away to Moscow, where his father had, by much exertion, secured a post for him as adjutant to the commander-in-chief, and would try finally to make a good match there. He suggested to him either Princess Marya or Julie Karagin.

Anatole consented, and went away to Moscow, where he stayed with Pierre. Pierre at first was by no means pleased to receive Anatole, but after a while he got used to his presence; sometimes accompanied him on his carousals, and by way of loans gave him money.

As Shinshin had with truth said of him, Anatole had won the hearts of all the Moscow ladies, especially by the nonchalance with which he treated them and the preference he openly showed for gypsy girls and actresses, with the most prominent of whom, Mademoiselle George, he was said to have an intrigue. He never missed a single drinking party at Danilov's, or any other Moscow festivity, spent whole nights drinking, outdoing all the rest, and was at every *soirée* and ball in the best society. There were rumours of several intrigues of his with Moscow ladies, and at balls he flirted with a few of them. But he fought shy of unmarried ladies, especially the wealthy heiresses, who were most of them plain. He had a good reason for this, of which no one knew but his most intimate friends: he had been for the last two years married. Two years previously, while his regiment had been stationed in Poland, a Polish landowner, by no means well-to-do, had forced Anatole to marry his daughter.

Anatole had very shortly afterwards abandoned his wife, and in consideration of a sum of money, which he agreed to send his father-in-law, he was allowed by the latter to pass as a bachelor unmolested.

Anatole was very well satisfied with his position, with himself, and with other people. He was instinctively and thoroughly convinced that he could not possibly live except just in the way he did live, and that he had never in his life done anything base. He was incapable of considering either how his actions might be judged by others, or what might be the result of this or that action on his part. He was convinced that just as the duck is created so that it must always live in the water, so he was created by God such that he must spend thirty thousand a year, and always take a good position in society. He had such perfect faith in this that, looking at him, others too were persuaded of it, and refused him neither the exalted position in society nor the money, which he borrowed right and left, obviously with no notion of repaying it.

He was not a gambler, at least he never greatly cared about winning money at cards. He was not vain. He did not care a straw what people thought of him. Still less could he have been reproached with ambition. Several times he had, to his father's irritation, spoiled his best chances of a career, and he laughed at distinctions of all kinds. He was not stingy, and never refused any one who asked him for anything. What he loved was dissipation and women; and as, according to his ideas, there was nothing dishonourable in these tastes, and as he was incapable of considering the effect on others of the gratification of his tastes, he believed himself in his heart to be an irreproachable man, felt a genuine contempt for scoundrels and mean persons, and with an untroubled conscience held his head high. Rakes, those masculine Magdalens, have a secret feeling of their own guiltlessness, just as have women Magdalens, founded on the same hope of forgiveness. "All will be forgiven her, because she loved much; and all will be forgiven him, because he has enjoyed himself much."

Dolohov had that year reappeared in Moscow after his exile and his Persian adventures. He spent his time in luxury, gambling, and dissipation; renewed his friendship with his old Petersburg comrade Kuragin, and made use of him for his own objects.

Anatole sincerely liked Dolohov for his cleverness and daring. Dolohov, for whom Anatole's name and rank and connections were of use in ensnaring wealthy young men into his society for gambling purposes, made use of Kuragin without letting him feel it, and was amused by him too. Apart from interested motives, for which he needed Anatole, the process itself of controlling another man's will was an enjoyment, a habit, and a necessity for Dolohov.

Natasha had made a great impression on Kuragin. At supper, after the theatre, he analysed to Dolohov, with the manner of a connoisseur, the points of her arms, her shoulders, her foot, and her hair, and announced his intention of getting up a flirtation with her. What might come of such a flirtation—Anatole was incapable of considering, and had no notion, as he never had a notion of what would come of any of his actions.

"She's pretty, my lad, but she's not for us," Dolohov said to him.

"I'll tell my sister to ask her to dinner," said Anatole. "Eh?"

"You'd better wait till she's married. . . ."

"You know I adore little girls," said Anatole; "they're all confusion in a minute."

"You've come to grief once already over a 'little girl,'" said Dolohov, who knew of Anatole's marriage. "Beware!"

"Well, one can't do it twice! Eh?" said Anatole, laughing good-humouredly.

XII

THE next day the Rostovs did not go anywhere, and no one came to see them. Marya Dmitryevna had a discussion with Natasha's father, which she kept secret from her. Natasha guessed they were talking of the old prince and making some plan, and she felt worried and humiliated by it. Every minute she expected Prince Andrey, and twice that day she sent a man to Vosdvizhenka to inquire whether he had not arrived. He had not arrived. She felt more dreary now than during the first days in Moscow. To her impatience and pining for him there were now added the unpleasant recollections of her interview with Princess Marya and the old prince, and a vague dread and restlessness, of which she did not know the cause. She was continually fancying either that he would never come or that something would happen to her before he came. She could not brood calmly for long hours over his image by herself as she had done before. As soon as she began to think of him, her memory of him was mingled with the recollection of the old prince and Princess Marya, and of the theatre and of Kuragin. Again the question presented itself whether she had not been to blame, whether she had not broken her faith to Prince Andrey, and again she found herself going over in the minutest detail every word, every gesture, every shade in the play of expression on the face of that man, who had known how to awaken in her a terrible feeling that was beyond her comprehension. In the eyes of those about her, Natasha seemed livelier than usual, but she was far from being as serene and happy as before.

On Sunday morning Marya Dmitryevna invited her guests to go to Mass to her parish church of Uspenya on Mogiltse.

"I don't like those fashionable churches," she said, obviously priding herself on her independence of thought. "God is the same everywhere. Our parish priest is an excellent man, and conducts the service in a suitable way, so that is all as it should be, and his deacon too. Is there something holier about it when there are concerts in the choir? I don't like it; it's simply self-indulgence!"

Marya Dmitryevna liked Sundays, and knew how to keep them as holidays. Her house was always all scrubbed out and cleaned on Saturday; neither she nor her servants did any work, and every one wore holiday-dress and went to service. There were additional dishes at the mistress's dinner, and the servants had vodka and roast goose or a suckling-pig at theirs. But in nothing in the whole house was the holiday so marked as in the broad, severe face of Marya Dmitryevna, which on that day wore a never-varying expression of solemnity.

When after service they were drinking coffee in the drawing-room, where the covers had been removed from the furniture, the servant announced that the carriage was ready, and Marya Dmitryevna, dressed in her best shawl in which she paid calls, rose with a stern air, and announced that she was going to call on Prince Nikolay Andreitch Bolkonsky to ask for an explanation of his conduct about Natasha. After Marya Dmitryevna had gone, a dressmaker waited upon the Rostovs from Madame Chalmey, and Natasha, very glad of a diversion, went into a room adjoining the drawing-room, and shutting the door between, began trying on her new dresses. Just as she had put on a bodice basted together, with the sleeves not yet tacked in, and was turning her head to look at the fit of the back in the looking-glass, she caught the sound of her father's voice in the drawing-room in eager conversation with another voice, a woman's voice, which made her flush red. It was the voice of Ellen. Before Natasha had time to take off the bodice she was trying on, the door opened, and Countess Bezuhov walked into the room, wearing a dark heliotrope velvet gown with a high collar, and beaming with a good-natured and friendly smile.

"O my enchantress!" she said to the blushing Natasha. "Charming! No, this is really beyond anything, count," she said to Count Ilya Andreitch, who had followed her in. "How can you be in Moscow, and go nowhere? No, I won't let you off! This evening we have Mademoiselle George giving a recitation, and a few people are coming; and if you don't bring your lovely girls, who are much prettier than Mademoiselle George, I give up knowing you! My husband's not here, he has gone away to Tver, or I should have sent him for you. You must come, you positively must, before nine o'clock."

She nodded to the dressmaker, who knew her, and was curtseying respectfully, and seated herself in a low chair beside the looking-glass, draping the folds of her velvet gown picturesquely about her. She kept up a flow of good-humoured and light-hearted chatter, and repeatedly expressed her enthusiastic admiration of Natasha's beauty. She looked through her dresses and admired them, spoke with admiration, too, of a new dress of her own "of metallic gas," which she had received from Paris, and advised Natasha to have one like it.

"But anything suits you, my charmer!" she declared. The smile of pleasure never left Natasha's face. She felt happy, and as it were blossoming out under the praises of this charming Countess Bezuhov, who had seemed to her before a lady so unapproachable and dignified, and was now being so kind to her. Natasha's spirits rose, and she felt almost in love with this handsome and good-natured woman. Ellen, for her part, was genuine in her admiration of Natasha, and in her desire to make her enjoy herself. Anatole had begged her to throw him with Natasha, and it was with that object she had come to the Rostovs'. The idea of throwing her brother and Natasha together amused her.

Although Ellen had once owed Natasha a grudge for carrying off Boris from her in Petersburg, she thought no more of that now, and with all her heart wished Natasha nothing but good. As she was leaving the Rostovs', she drew her protégée aside.

"My brother was dining with me yesterday—we half died with laughing at him—he won't eat, and does nothing but sigh for you, my charmer! He is madly, madly in love with you, my dear."

Natasha flushed crimson on hearing those words.

"How she blushes, how she blushes, my pretty!" Ellen went on. "You must be sure to come. If you do love some one, it is not a reason to cloister yourself. Even if you are betrothed, I am sure your betrothed would have preferred you to go into society rather than to languish in ennui."

"So then she knows I am engaged. So then they with her husband, with Pierre, with that good Pierre, talked and laughed about it. So that it means nothing."

And again under Ellen's influence what had struck her before as terrible seemed to her simple and natural. "And she, such a *grande dame,* is so kind, and obviously she likes me with all her heart," thought Natasha. "And why not enjoy myself," thought Natasha, gazing at Ellen with wide-open, wondering eyes.

Marya Dmitryevna came back to dinner silent and serious, having evidently been defeated by the old prince. She was too much agitated by the conflict she had been through to be able to describe the interview. To the count's inquiries, she replied that everything had been all right and she would tell him about it next day. On hearing of the visit of Countess Bezuhov and the invitation for the evening, Marya Dmitryevna said:

"I don't care to associate with Countess Bezuhov and I don't advise you to, but still, since you have promised, better go. It will divert your mind," she added, addressing Natasha.

XIII

COUNT ILYA ANDREITCH took his two girls to the Countess Bezuhov's. There were a good many people assembled there. But Natasha hardly knew any of the persons present. Count Ilya Andreitch observed with dissatisfaction that almost all the company consisted of men or of ladies notorious for the freedom of their behaviour. Mademoiselle George was standing in one corner of the room, surrounded by young men. There were several Frenchmen present, and among them Metivier, who had been a constant visitor at Countess Bezuhov's ever since her arrival in Moscow. Count Ilya Andreitch made up his mind not to take a hand at cards, not to leave his daughter's side, and to get away as soon as Mademoiselle George's performance was over.

Anatole was at the door, unmistakably on the look-out for the Rostovs. At once greeting the count, he went up to Natasha and followed her in. As soon as Natasha saw him, the same feeling came upon her as at the theatre—the feeling of gratified vanity at his admiration of her, and terror at the absence of any moral barrier between them.

Ellen gave Natasha a delighted welcome, and was loud in her admiration of her loveliness and her dress. Soon after their arrival, Mademoiselle George went out of the room to change her dress. In the drawing-room chairs were being set in rows and people began to sit down. Anatole moved a chair for Natasha, and would have sat down by her, but the count, who was keeping his eye on Natasha, took the seat beside her. Anatole sat down behind.

Mademoiselle George, with bare, fat, dimpled arms, and a red scarf flung over one shoulder, came into the empty space left for her between the chairs and threw herself into an unnatural pose. An enthusiastic whisper was audible.

Mademoiselle George scanned her audience with stern and gloomy eyes, and began reciting French verses, describing her guilty love for her son. In places she raised her voice, in places she dropped to a whisper solemnly lifting her head; in places she broke off and hissed with rolling eyes.

"Exquisite, divine, marvellous!" was heard on all sides. Natasha gazed at the fat actress; but she heard nothing, saw nothing and understood nothing of what was passing before her. She felt nothing, but that she was borne away again irrevocably into that strange and senseless world so remote from her old world, a world in which there was no knowing what was good and what was bad, what was sensible and what was senseless. Behind her was sitting Anatole; and conscious of his nearness, she was in frightened expectation of something.

After the first monologue all the company rose and surrounded Mademoiselle George, expressing their admiration.

"How handsome she is!" said Natasha to her father, as he got up with the rest and moved through the crowd to the actress.

"I don't think so, looking at you," said Anatole, following Natasha. He said this at a moment when no one but she could hear him. "You are charming . . . from the moment I first saw you, I have not ceased . . ."

"Come along, come along, Natasha!" said the count, turning back for his daughter. "How pretty she is!"

Natasha saying nothing went up to her father, and gazed at him with eyes of inquiring wonder.

After several recitations in different styles, Mademoiselle George went away, and Countess Bezuhov invited all the company to the great hall.

The count would have taken leave, but Ellen besought him not to spoil her improvised ball. The Rostovs stayed on. Anatole asked Natasha for a waltz, and during the waltz, squeezing her waist and her hand, he told her she was bewitching and that he loved her. During the écossaise, which she danced again with Kuragin, when they were left alone Anatole said nothing to her, he simply looked at her. Natasha was in doubt whether she had not dreamed what he said to her during the waltz. At the end of the first figure he pressed her hand again. Natasha lifted her frightened eyes to his face, but there was an expression of such assurance and warmth in his fond look and smile that she could not as she looked at him say what she had to say to him. She dropped her eyes.

"Don't say such things to me. I am betrothed, and I love another man . . ." she articulated rapidly. She glanced at him. Anatole was neither disconcerted nor mortified at what she had said.

"Don't talk to me of that. What is that to me," he said; "I tell you I am mad, mad with love of you. Is it my fault that you are fascinating? . . . It's for us to begin."

Natasha, eager and agitated, looked about her with wide-open, fright-ened eyes, and seemed to be enjoying herself more than usual. She scarcely grasped anything that happened that evening. They danced the écossaise and "Grandfather." Her father suggested their going, and she begged to stay longer. Wherever she was, and with whomsoever she was speaking, she felt his eyes upon her. Then she remembered that she had asked her father's permission to go into a dressing-room to rearrange her dress, that Ellen had followed her, had talked to her, laughing, of her brother's passion, and that in the little divan-room she had been met again by Anatole; that Ellen had somehow vanished, they were left alone, and Anatole taking her by the hand, had said in a tender voice:

"I can't come to see you, but is it possible that I shall never see you? I love you madly. Can I never . . . ?" and barring her way he brought his face close to hers.

His large, shining, masculine eyes were so close to her eyes, that she could see nothing but those eyes.

"Natalie?" his voice whispered interrogatively, and her hands were squeezed till it hurt. "Natalie?"

"I don't understand; I have nothing to say," was the answer in her eyes.

Burning lips were pressed to her lips, and at the same instant she felt herself set free again, and caught the sound of Ellen's steps and rustling gown in the room again. Natasha looked round towards Ellen; then, red and trembling, she glanced at him with alarmed inquiry, and moved towards the door.

"One word, just one word, for God's sake," Anatole was saying. She stopped. She so wanted him to say that word, that would have explained to her what had happened and to which she could have found an answer.

"Natalie, one word . . . one . . ." he kept repeating, plainly not knowing what to say, and he repeated it till Ellen reached them.

Ellen went back with Natasha to the drawing-room. The Rostovs went away without staying to supper.

When she got home, Natasha did not sleep all night. She was tortured by the insoluble question, Which did she love, Anatole or Prince Andrey? Prince Andrey, she did love—she remembered clearly how great her love was for him. But she loved Anatole too, of that there was no doubt. "Else could all that have happened?" she thought. "If after that I could answer with a smile to his smile at parting, if I could sink to that, it means that I fell in love with him from the first minute. So he must be kind, noble, and good, and I could not help loving him. What am I to do, if I love him and the other too?" she said to herself, and was unable to find an answer to those terrible questions.

XIV

THE morning came with daily cares and bustle. Every one got up and began to move about and to talk; dressmakers came again; again Marya Dmitryevna went out and they were summoned to tea. Natasha kept uneasily looking round at every one with wide-open eyes, as though she wanted to intercept every glance turned upon her. She did her utmost to seem exactly as usual.

After luncheon—it was always her best time—Marya Dmitryevna seated herself in her own arm-chair and drew Natasha and the old count to her.

"Well, my friends, I have thought the whole matter over now, and I'll tell you my advice," she began. "Yesterday, as you know, I was at Prince Bolkonsky's; well, I had a talk with him . . . He thought fit to scream at me. But there's no screaming me down! I had it all out with him."

"Well, but what does he mean?" asked the count.

"He's crazy . . . he won't hear of it, and there's no more to be said. As it is we have given this poor girl worry enough," said Marya Dmitryevna. "And my advice to you is, to make an end of it and go home to Otradnoe . . . and there to wait."

"Oh no!" cried Natasha.

"Yes, to go home," said Marya Dmitryevna, "and to wait there. If your betrothed comes here now, there'll be no escaping a quarrel; but alone here he'll have it all out with the old man, and then come on to you."

Count Ilya Andreitch approved of this suggestion, and at once saw all the sound sense of it. If the old man were to come round, then it would be better to visit him at Moscow or Bleak Hills, later on; if not, then the wedding, against his will, could only take place at Otradnoe.

"And that's perfectly true," said he. "I regret indeed that I ever went to see him and took her too," said the count.

"No, why regret it? Being here, you could do no less than show him respect. If he wouldn't receive it, that's his affair," said Marya Dmitryevna, searching for something in her reticule. "And now the trousseau's ready, what have you to wait for? What is not ready, I'll send after you. Though I'm sorry to lose you, still the best thing is for you to go, and God be with you." Finding what she was looking for in her reticule, she handed it to Natasha. It was a letter from Princess Marya. "She writes to you. How worried she is, poor thing! She is afraid you might think she does not like you."

"Well, she doesn't like me," said Natasha.

"Nonsense, don't say so," cried Marya Dmitryevna.

"I won't take any one's word for that, I know she doesn't like me."

said Natasha boldly as she took the letter, and there was a look of cold
and angry resolution in her face, that made Marya Dmitryevna look at
her more closely and frown.

"Don't you answer me like that, my good girl," she said. "If I say so,
it's the truth. Write an answer to her."

Natasha made no reply, and went to her own room to read Princess
Marya's letter.

Princess Marya wrote that she was in despair at the misunderstanding
that had arisen between them. Whatever her father's feelings might be,
wrote Princess Marya, she begged Natasha to believe that she could
not fail to love her, as the girl chosen by her brother, for whose happiness she was ready to make any sacrifice.

"Do not believe, though," she wrote, "that my father is ill-disposed to
you. He is an old man and an invalid, for whom one must make excuses.
But he is good-hearted and generous, and will come to love the woman
who makes his son happy." Princess Marya begged Natasha, too, to fix a
time when she might see her again.

After reading the letter, Natasha sat down to the writing-table to
answer it. "Dear princess," she began, writing rapidly and mechanically
in French, and there she stopped. What more could she write after what
had happened the day before? "Yes, yes, all that had happened, and
now everything was different," she thought, sitting before the letter she
had begun. "Must I refuse him? Must I really? That's awful! . . ."
And to avoid these horrible thoughts, she went in to Sonya, and began
looking through embroidery designs with her.

After dinner Natasha went to her own room and took up Princess
Marya's letter again. "Can everything be over?" she thought. "Can all
this have happened so quickly and have destroyed all that went before?"
She recalled in all its past strength her love for Prince Andrey, and at
the same time she felt that she loved Kuragin. She vividly pictured herself the wife of Prince Andrey, of her happiness with him, called up the
picture she had so often dwelt on in her imagination, and at the same
time, all aglow with emotion, she recalled every detail of her interview
the previous evening with Anatole.

"Why could not that be as well?" she wondered sometimes in complete bewilderment. "It's only so that I could be perfectly happy: as it
is, I have to choose, and without either of them I can't be happy. There's
one thing," she thought, "to tell Prince Andrey what has happened; to
hide it from him—are equally impossible. But with *him* nothing is
spoilt. But can I part for ever from the happiness of Prince Andrey's
love, which I have been living on for so long?"

"Madame," whispered a maid, coming into the room with a mysterious
air, "a man told me to give you this." The girl gave her a letter. "Only
for Christ's sake . . ." said the girl, as Natasha, without thinking, mechanically broke the seal and began reading a love-letter from Anatole,
of which she did not understand a word, but understood only that it was
a letter from him, from the man whom she loved. "Yes, she loved him;

otherwise, how could what had happened have happened? How could a love-letter from him be in her hand?"

With trembling hands Natasha held that passionate love-letter, com- posed for Anatole by Dolohov, and as she read it, she found in it echoes of all that it seemed to her she was feeling herself.

"Since yesterday evening my fate is sealed: to be loved by you or to die. There is nothing else left for me," the letter began. Then he wrote that he knew her relations would never give her to him, to Anatole; that there were secret reasons for that which he could only reveal to her alone; but that if she loved him, she had but to utter the word *Yes*, and no human force could hinder their happiness. Love would conquer all. He could capture her and bear her away to the ends of the earth.

"Yes, yes, I love him!" thought Natasha, reading the letter over for the twentieth time, and finding some special deep meaning in every word.

That evening Marya Dmitryevna was going to the Arharovs', and pro- posed taking the young ladies with her. Natasha pleaded a headache and stayed at home.

XV

ON returning late in the evening, Sonya went into Natasha's room, and to her surprise found her not undressed asleep on the sofa. On the table near her Anatole's letter lay open. Sonya picked up the letter and began to read it.

She read it, and looked at Natasha asleep, seeking in her face some explanation of what she had read and not finding it. Her face was quiet, gentle, and happy. Clutching at her own chest to keep herself from choking, Sonya, pale and shaking with horror and emotion, sat down in a low chair and burst into tears.

"How was it I saw nothing? How can it have gone so far? Can she have ceased loving Prince Andrey? And how could she have let this Kuragin go as far as this? He's a deceiver and a villain, that's clear. What will Nikolenka—dear, noble Nikolenka—do when he hears of it? So that was the meaning of her excited, determined, unnatural face the day before yesterday, and yesterday and to-day," thought Sonya. "But it's impossible that she can care for him! Most likely she opened the letter not knowing from whom it was. Most likely she feels insulted by it. She's not capable of doing such a thing!"

Sonya dried her tears and went up to Natasha, carefully scrutinising her face again.

"Natasha!" she said, hardly audibly.

Natasha waked up and saw Sonya.

"Ah, you have come back?"

And with the decision and tenderness common at the moment of awakening she embraced her friend. But noticing embarrassment in Sonya's face, her face too expressed embarrassment and suspicion.

"Sonya, you have read the letter?" she said.

"Yes," said Sonya softly.

Natasha smiled ecstatically.

"No, Sonya, I can't help it!" she said. "I can't keep it secret from you any longer. You know we love each other! . . . Sonya, darling, he writes . . . Sonya . . ."

Sonya gazed with wide-open eyes at Natasha, as though unable to believe her ears.

"But Bolkonsky?" she said.

"O Sonya, oh, if you could only know how happy I am!" said Natasha. "You don't know what love . . ."

"But, Natasha, you can't mean that all *that* is over?"

Natasha looked with her big, wide eyes at Sonya as though not understanding her question.

"Are you breaking it off with Prince Andrey then?" said Sonya.

"Oh, you don't understand; don't talk nonsense; listen," said Natasha, with momentary annoyance.

"No, I can't believe it," repeated Sonya. "I don't understand it. What, for a whole year you have been loving one man, and all at once . . . Why, you have only seen him three times. Natasha, I can't believe you, you're joking. In three days to forget everything, and like this . . ."

"Three days," Natasha. "It seems to me as though I had loved him for a hundred years. It seems to me that I have never loved any one before him. You can't understand that. Sonya, stay, sit here." Natasha hugged and kissed her. "I have been told of its happening, and no doubt you have heard of it too, but it's only now that I have felt such love. It's not what I have felt before. As soon as I saw him, I felt that he was my sovereign and I was his slave, and that I could not help loving him. Yes, his slave! Whatever he bids me, I shall do. You don't understand that. What am I to do? What am I to do, Sonya?" said Natasha, with a blissful and frightened face.

"But only think what you are doing," said Sonya. "I can't leave it like this. These secret letters . . . How could you let him go so far as that?" she said, with a horror and aversion she could with difficulty conceal.

"I have told you," answered Natasha, "that I have no will. How is it you don't understand that? I love him!"

"Then I can't let it go on like this. I shall tell about it," cried Sonya, with a burst of tears.

"What . . . for God's sake . . . If you tell, you are my enemy," said Natasha. "You want to make me miserable, and you want us to be separated . . ."

On seeing Natasha's alarm, Sonya wept tears of shame and pity for her friend.

"But what has passed between you?" she asked. "What has he said to you? Why doesn't he come to the house?"

Natasha made no answer to her question.

"For God's sake, Sonya, don't tell any one; don't torture me," Natasha implored her. "Remember that it doesn't do to meddle in such matters. I have told you . . ."

"But why this secrecy? Why doesn't he come to the house?" Sonya persisted. "Why doesn't he ask for your hand straight out? Prince Andrey, you know, gave you complete liberty, if it really is so; but I can't believe in it. Natasha, have you thought what the *secret reasons* can be?"

Natasha looked with wondering eyes at Sonya. Evidently it was the first time that question had presented itself to her, and she did not know how to answer it.

"What the reasons are, I don't know. But there must be reasons!" Sonya sighed and shook her head distrustfully.

"If there were reasons . . ." she was beginning. But Natasha, divining her doubts, interrupted her in dismay.

"Sonya, you mustn't doubt of him; you mustn't, you mustn't! Do you understand?" she cried.

"Does he love you?"

"Does he love me?" repeated Natasha, with a smile of compassion for her friend's dullness of comprehension. "Why, you have read his letter, haven't you? You've seen him."

"But if he is a dishonourable man?"

"*He!* . . . a dishonourable man? If only you knew!" said Natasha.

"If he is an honourable man, he ought either to explain his intentions, or to give up seeing you; and if you won't do that, I will do it. I'll write to him. I'll tell papa," said Sonya resolutely.

"But I can't live without him!" cried Natasha.

"Natasha, I don't understand you. And what are you saying? Think of your father, of Nikolenka."

"I don't care for any one, I don't love any one but him. How dare you say he's dishonourable! Don't you know that I love him?" cried Natasha. "Sonya, go away; I don't want to quarrel with you; go away, for God's sake, go away; you see how wretched I am," cried Natasha angrily, in a voice of repressed irritation and despair. Sonya burst into sobs and ran out of the room.

Natasha went to the table, and without a moment's reflection wrote that answer to Princess Marya, which she had been unable to write all the morning. In her letter she told Princess Marya briefly that all misunderstandings between them were at an end, as taking advantage of the generosity of Prince Andrey, who had at parting given her full liberty, she begged her to forget everything and forgive her if she had been in fault in any way, but she could not be his wife. It all seemed to her so easy, so simple, and so clear at that moment.

The Rostovs were to return to the country on Friday, but on Wednesday the count went with the intending purchaser to his estate near Moscow.

On the day the count left, Sonya and Natasha were invited to a big dinner-party at Julie Karagin's, and Marya Dmitryevna took them. At that dinner Natasha met Anatole again, and Sonya noticed that Natasha said something to him, trying not to be overheard, and was all through the dinner more excited than before. When they got home, Natasha was the first to enter upon the conversation with Sonya that her friend was expecting.

"Well, Sonya, you said all sorts of silly things about him," Natasha began in a meek voice, the voice in which children speak when they want to be praised for being good. "I have had it all out with him to-day."

"Well, what did he say? Well? Come, what did he say? Natasha, I'm so glad you're not angry with me. Tell me everything, all the truth. What did he say?"

Natasha sank into thought.

"O Sonya, if you knew him as I do! He said . . . He asked me what promise I had given Bolkonsky. He was so glad that I was free to refuse him."

Sonya sighed dejectedly.

"But you haven't refused Bolkonsky, have you?" she said.

"Oh, perhaps I have refused him! Perhaps it's all at an end with Bolkonsky. Why do you think so ill of me?"

"I don't think anything, only I don't understand this. . . ."

"Wait a little, Sonya, you will understand it all. You will see the sort of man he is. Don't think ill of me, or of him."

"I don't think ill of any one; I like every one and am sorry for every one. But what am I to do?"

Sonya would not let herself be won over by the affectionate tone Natasha took with her. The softer and the more ingratiating Natasha's face became, the more serious and stern became the face of Sonya.

"Natasha," she said, "you asked me not to speak to you, and I haven't spoken; now you have begun yourself. Natasha, I don't trust him. Why this secrecy?"

"Again, again!" interrupted Natasha.

"Natasha, I am afraid for you."

"What is there to be afraid of?"

"I am afraid you will be ruined," said Sonya resolutely, herself horrified at what she was saying.

Natasha's face expressed anger again.

"Then I will be ruined, I will; I'll hasten to my ruin. It's not your business. It's not you, but I, will suffer for it. Leave me alone, leave me alone. I hate you!"

"Natasha!" Sonya appealed to her in dismay.

"I hate you, I hate you! And you're my enemy for ever!"

Natasha ran out of the room.

Natasha avoided Sonya and did not speak to her again. With the same expression of agitated wonder and guilt she wandered about the rooms, taking up first one occupation and then another, and throwing them aside again at once.

Hard as it was for Sonya, she kept watch over her friend and never let her out of her sight.

On the day before that fixed for the count's return, Sonya noticed that Natasha sat all the morning at the drawing-room window, as though expecting something, and that she made a sign to an officer who passed by, whom Sonya took to be Anatole.

Sonya began watching her friend even more attentively, and she noticed that all dinner-time and in the evening Natasha was in a strange and unnatural state, unlike herself. She made irrelevant replies to questions asked her, began sentences and did not finish them, and laughed at everything.

After tea Sonya saw the maid timidly waiting for her to pass at Natasha's door. She let her go in, and listening at the door, found out that another letter had been given her. And all at once it was clear to Sonya that Natasha had some dreadful plan for that evening. Sonya knocked at her door. Natasha would not let her in.

"She is going to run away with him!" thought Sonya. "She is capable of anything. There was something particularly piteous and determined in her face to-day. She cried as she said good-bye to uncle," Sonya remembered. "Yes, it's certain, she's going to run away with him; but what am I to do?" wondered Sonya, recalling now all the signs that so clearly betokened some dreadful resolution on Natasha's part. "The count is not here. What am I to do? Write to Kuragin, demanding an explanation from him? But who is to make him answer? Write to Pierre, as Prince Andrey asked me to do in case of trouble? . . . But perhaps she really has refused Bolkonsky (she sent off a letter to Princess Marya yesterday). Uncle is not here."

To tell Marya Dmitryevna, who had such faith in Natasha, seemed to Sonya a fearful step to take.

"But one way or another," thought Sonya, standing in the dark corridor, "now or never the time has come for me to show that I am mindful of all the benefits I have received from their family and that I love Nikolay. No, if I have to go three nights together without sleep; I won't leave this corridor, and I will prevent her passing by force, and not let disgrace come upon their family," she thought.

XVI

ANATOLE had lately moved into Dolohov's quarters. The plan for the abduction of Natasha Rostov had been all planned out and prepared several days before by Dolohov, and on the day when Sonya had listened at Natasha's door and resolved to protect her, that plan was to be put into execution. Natasha had promised to come out to Kuragin at the back entrance at ten o'clock in the evening. Kuragin was to get her into a sledge that was to be all ready with three horses in it, and to drive her off sixty versts from Moscow to the village of Kamenka, where an unfrocked priest was in readiness to perform a marriage ceremony over them. At Kamenka a relay of horses was to be in readiness, which was to take them as far as the Warsaw road, and thence they were to hasten abroad by means of post-horses.

Anatole had a passport and an order for post-horses and ten thousand roubles borrowed from his sister, and ten thousand more raised by the assistance of Dolohov.

The two witnesses of the mock marriage ceremony—Hvostikov, once a petty official, a man of whom Dolohov made use at cards, and Makarin, a retired hussar, a weak and good-natured man, whose devotion to Kuragin was unbounded—were sitting over their tea in the outer room.

In Dolohov's big study, decorated from the walls to the ceiling with Persian rugs, bearskins, and weapons, Dolohov was sitting in a travelling tunic and high boots in front of an open bureau on which lay accounts and bundles of bank notes. Anatole, in an unbuttoned uniform, was walking to and fro from the room where the witnesses were sitting through the study into a room behind, where his French valet with some other servants was packing up the last of his belongings. Dolohov was reckoning up money and noting down sums.

"Well," he said, "you will have to give Hvostikov two thousand."

"Well, give it him then," said Anatole.

"Makarka now" (their name for Makarin), "he would go through fire and water for you with nothing to gain by it. Well, here then, our accounts are finished," said Dolohov, showing him the paper. "That's all right?"

"Yes, of course, it's all right," said Anatole, evidently not attending to Dolohov, and looking straight before him with a smile that never left his face.

Dolohov shut the bureau with a slam, and turned to Anatole with an ironical smile.

"But I say, you drop it all; there's still time!" he said.

"Idiot!" said Anatole. "Leave off talking rubbish. If only you knew. . . . Devil only knows what this means to me!"

"You'd really better drop it," said Dolohov. "I'm speaking in earnest. It's no joking matter this scheme of yours."

"Why, teasing again, again? Go to the devil! Eh. . . ." said Anatole, frowning. "Really, I'm in no humour for your stupid jokes." And he went out of the room.

Dolohov smiled a contemptuous and supercilious smile when Anatole had gone.

"Wait a bit," he called after Anatole. "I'm not joking. I'm in earnest. Come here, come here!"

Anatole came back into the room, and trying to concentrate his attention, looked at Dolohov, obviously obeying him unwillingly.

"Listen to me. I'm speaking to you for the last time. What should I want to joke with you for? Have I ever thwarted you? Who was it arranged it all for you? Who found your priest? Who took your passport? Who got you your money? It has all been my doing."

"Well, and thank you for it. Do you suppose I'm not grateful?" Anatole sighed and embraced Dolohov.

"I have helped you; but still I ought to tell you the truth: it's a dangerous business, and if you come to think of it, it's stupid. Come, you carry her off, well and good. Do you suppose they'll let it rest? It will come out that you are married. Why, they will have you up on a criminal charge, you know . . ."

"Oh, nonsense, nonsense!" said Anatole, frowning again. "Why, didn't I explain to you? Eh?" and Anatole, with that peculiar partiality (common in persons of dull brain), for any conclusion to which they have been led by their own mental processes, repeated the argument he had repeated a hundred times over to Dolohov already. "Why, I explained it; I settled that. If this marriage is invalid," he said, crooking his finger, "then it follows I'm not answerable for it. Well, and if it is valid, it won't matter. No one will ever know of it abroad, so, you see, it's all right, isn't it? And don't talk to me; don't talk to me; don't talk to me!"

"Really, you drop it. You'll get yourself into a mess . . ."

"You go to the devil!" said Anatole, and clutching at his hair he went off into the next room, but at once returning he sat with his legs up on an arm-chair close to Dolohov and facing him. "Devil only knows what's the matter with me! Eh? See how it beats." He took Dolohov's hand and put it on his heart. "Ah, what a foot, my dear boy, what a glance! A goddess!" he said in French. "Eh?"

Dolohov, with a cold smile and a gleam in his handsome impudent eyes, looked at him, obviously disposed to get a little more amusement out of him.

"Well, your money will be gone, what then?"

"What then? Eh?" repeated Anatole, with genuine perplexity at the thought of the future. "What then? I don't know what then . . . Come, why talk nonsense?" He looked at his watch. "It's time!"

Anatole went into the back room.

"Well, will you soon have done? You're dawdling there," he shouted at the servants.

Dolohov put away the money; and calling a servant to give him orders about getting something to eat and drink before the journey, he went into the room where Hvostikov and Makarin were sitting.

Anatole lay down on the sofa in the study, and, propped on his elbows, smiled pensively and murmured something fervently to himself.

"Come and have something to eat. Here, have a drink!" Dolohov shouted to him from the other room.

"I don't want to," answered Anatole, still smiling.

"Come, Balaga is here."

Anatole got up, and went into the dining-room. Balaga was a well-known driver, who had known Dolohov and Anatole for the last six years, and driven them in his three-horse sledges. More than once, when Anatole's regiment had been stationed at Tver, he had driven him out of Tver in the evening, reached Moscow by dawn, and driven him back the next night. More than once he had driven Dolohov safe away when he was being pursued. Many a time he had driven them about the town with gypsies and "gay ladies," as he called them. More than one horse had he ruined in driving them. More than once he had driven over people and upset vehicles in Moscow, and always his "gentlemen," as he called them, had got him out of trouble. Many a time had they beaten him, many a time made him drunk with champagne and madeira, a wine he loved, and more than one exploit he knew of each of them, which would long ago have sent any ordinary man to Siberia. They often called Balaga in to their carousals, made him drink and dance with the gypsies, and many a thousand roubles of their money had passed through his hands. In their service, twenty times a year, he risked his life and his skin, and wore out more horses than they repaid him for in money. But he liked them, liked their furious driving, eighteen versts an hour, liked upsetting coachmen, and running down people on foot in Moscow, and always flew full gallop along the Moscow streets. He liked to hear behind him the wild shout of drunken voices, "Get on; get on!" when it was impossible to drive faster; liked to give a lash on the neck to a passing peasant who was already hastening out of his way more dead than alive. "Real gentlemen!" he thought.

Anatole and Dolohov liked Balaga, too, for his spirited driving, and because he liked the same things that they liked. With other people Balaga drove hard bargains; he would take as much as twenty-five roubles for a two hours' drive, and rarely drove himself, generally sending one of his young men. But with his own gentlemen, as he called them, he always drove himself, and never asked for anything for the job.

Only after learning through their valets when money was plentiful, he would turn up once every few months in the morning; and sober, and bowing low, would ask them to help him out of his difficulties. The gentlemen always made him sit down.

"Please, help me out of a scrape, Fyodor Ivanovitch, or your excellency," he would say. "I'm quite run out of horses; lend me what you can to go to the fair."

And whenever they were flush of money Anatole and Dolohov would give him a thousand or two.

Balaga was a flaxen-headed, squat, snub-nosed peasant of seven and twenty, with a red face and a particularly red, thick neck, little sparkling eyes, and a little beard. He wore a fine blue silk-lined full coat, put on over a fur pelisse.

He crossed himself, facing the opposite corner, and went up to Dolohov, holding out his black, little hand.

"Respects to Fyodor Ivanovitch!" said he, bowing.

"Good-day to you, brother. Well, here he comes!"

"Good-morning, your excellency!" he said to Anatole as he came in, and to him, too, he held out his hand.

"I say, Balaga," said Anatole, laying his hands on his shoulders, "do you care for me or not? Eh? Now's the time to do me good service. . . . What sort of horses have you come with? Eh?"

"As the messenger bade me; your favourite beasts," said Balaga.

"Come, Balaga, do you hear? You may kill all three of them; only get there in three hours. Eh?"

"If I kill them, how are we to get there?" said Balaga, winking.

"None of your jokes now. I'll smash your face in!" cried Anatole suddenly, rolling his eyes.

"Jokes!" said the driver, laughing. "Do I grudge anything for my gentlemen? As fast as ever the horses can gallop we shall get there."

"Ah!" said Anatole. "Well, sit down."

"Come, sit down," said Dolohov.

"Oh, I'll stand, Fyodor Ivanovitch."

"Sit down; nonsense! have a drink," said Anatole, and he poured him out a big glass of madeira. The driver's eyes sparkled at the sight of the wine. Refusing it at first for manners' sake, he tossed it off, and wiped his mouth with a red silk handkerchief that lay in his cap.

"Well, and when are we to start, your excellency?"

"Oh . . ." Anatole looked at his watch. "We must set off at once. Now mind, Balaga. Eh? You'll get there in time?"

"To be sure, if we've luck in getting off. Why shouldn't we do it in the time?" said Balaga. "We got you to Tver, and got there in seven hours. You remember, I bet, your excellency!"

"Do you know, I once drove from Tver at Christmas time," said Anatole, with a smile at the recollection, addressing Makarin, who was gazing admiringly at him. "Would you believe it, Makarka, one could hardly breathe we flew so fast. We drove into a train of wagons and rode right over two of them! Eh?"

"They were horses, too," Balaga went on. "I'd put two young horses in the traces with the bay in the shafts"—he turned to Dolohov—"and, would you believe me, Fyodor Ivanovitch, sixty versts those beasts galloped. There was no holding them, for my hands were numb; it was a frost. I flung down the reins. "You hold them yourself, your excellency," said I, and I rolled up inside the sledge. No need of driving them. Why, we couldn't hold them in when we got there. In three hours the devils brought us. Only the left one died of it."

XVII

ANATOLE went out of the room, and a few minutes later he came back wearing a fur pelisse, girt with a silver belt, and a sable cap, jauntily stuck on one side, and very becoming to his handsome face. Looking at himself in the looking-glass, and then standing before Dolohov in the same attitude he had taken before the looking-glass, he took a glass of wine.

"Well, Fedya, farewell; thanks for everything, and farewell," said Anatole. "Come, comrades, friends . . ."—he grew pensive—"of my youth . . . farewell," he turned to Makarin and the others.

Although they were all going with him, Anatole evidently wanted to make a touching and solemn ceremony of this address to his comrades. He spoke in a loud, deliberate voice, squaring his chest and swinging one leg.

"All take glasses; you too, Balaga. Well, lads, friends of my youth, we have had jolly sprees together. Eh? Now, when shall we meet again? I'm going abroad! We've had a good time, and farewell, lads. Here's to our health! Hurrah! . . ." he said, tossing off his glass, and flinging it on the floor.

"To your health!" said Balaga. He, too, emptied his glass and wiped his lips with his handkerchief.

Makarin embraced Anatole with tears in his eyes.

"Ah, prince, how it grieves my heart to part from you," he said.

"Start! start!" shouted Anatole.

Balaga was going out of the room.

"No; stay," said Anatole. "Shut the door; we must sit down. Like this." They shut the door and all sat down.

"Well, now, quick, march, lads!" said Anatole, getting up.

The valet, Joseph, gave Anatole his knapsack and sword, and they all went out into the vestibule.

"But where's a fur cloak?" said Dolohov. "Hey, Ignatka! Run in to Matryona Matveyevna, and ask her for the sable cloak. I've heard what elopements are like," said Dolohov, winking. "She'll come skipping out more dead than alive just in the things she had on indoors; the slightest delay and then there are tears, and dear papa and dear mamma, and she's frozen in a minute and for going back again—you wrap her up in a cloak at once and carry her to the sledge."

The valet brought a woman's fox-lined pelisse.

"Fool, I told you the sable. Hey, Matryoshka, the sable," he shouted, so that his voice rang out through the rooms.

A handsome, thin, and pale gypsy woman, with shining black eyes and curly black hair, with a bluish shade in it, ran out, wearing a red shawl and holding a sable cloak on her arm.

"Here, I don't grudge it; take it," she said, in visible fear of her lord, and regretful at losing the cloak.

Dolohov, making her no answer, took the cloak, flung it about Matryosha, and wrapped her up in it.

"That's the way," said Dolohov. "And then this is the way," he said, and he turned the collar up round her head, leaving it only a little open before the face. "And then this is the way, do you see?" and he moved Anatole's head forward to meet the open space left by the collar, from which Matryosha's flashing smile peeped out.

"Well, good-bye, Matryosha," said Anatole, kissing her. "Ah, all my fun here is over! Give my love to Styoshka. There, good-bye! Good-bye, Matryosha; wish me happiness."

"God grant you great happiness, prince," said Matryosha, with her gypsy accent.

At the steps stood two three-horse sledges; two stalwart young drivers were holding them. Balaga took his seat in the foremost, and holding his elbows high, began deliberately arranging the reins in his hands. Anatole and Dolohov got in with him. Makarin, Hvostikov, and the valet got into the other sledge.

"Ready, eh?" queried Balaga. "Off!" he shouted, twisting the reins round his hands, and the sledge flew at break-neck pace along the Nikitsky Boulevard.

"Tprroo! Hi! . . . Tproo!!" Balaga and the young driver on the box were continually shouting.

In Arbatsky Square the sledge came into collision with a carriage; there was a crash and shouts, and the sledge flew off along Arbaty. Turning twice along Podnovinsky, Balaga began to pull up, and turning back, stopped the horses at the Old Equerrys' crossing.

A smart young driver jumped down to hold the horses by the bridle; Anatole and Dolohov walked along the pavement. On reaching the gates, Dolohov whistled. The whistle was answered, and a maid-servant ran out.

"Come into the courtyard, or you'll be seen; she is coming in a minute," she said.

Dolohov stayed at the gate. Anatole followed the maid into the courtyard, turned a corner, and ran up the steps.

He was met by Gavrilo, Marya Dmitryevna's huge groom.

"Walk this way to the mistress," said the groom in his bass, blocking up the doorway.

"What mistress? And who are you?" Anatole asked in a breathless whisper.

"Walk in; my orders are to show you in."

"Kuragin! back!" shouted Dolohov. "Treachery, back!"

Dolohov, at the little back gate where he had stopped, was struggling with the porter, who was trying to shut the gate after Anatole as he ran in. With a desperate effort Dolohov shoved away the porter, and clutching at Anatole, pulled him through the gate, and ran back with him to the sledge.

XVIII

MARYA DMITRYEVNA coming upon Sonya weeping in the corridor had forced her to confess everything. Snatching up Natasha's letter and reading it, Marya Dmitryevna went in to Natasha, with the letter in her hand.

"Vile girl, shameless hussy!" she said to her. "I won't hear a word!" Pushing aside Natasha, who gazed at her with amazed but tearless eyes, she locked her into the room, and giving orders to her gate porter to admit the persons who would be coming that evening, but not to allow them to pass out again, and giving her grooms orders to show those persons up to her, she seated herself in the drawing-room awaiting the abductors.

When Gavrilo came to announce to Marya Dmitryevna that the persons who had come had run away, she got up frowning, and clasping her hands behind her, walked a long while up and down through her rooms, pondering what she was to do. At midnight she walked towards Natasha's room, feeling the key in her pocket. Sonya was sitting sobbing in the corridor, "Marya Dmitryevna, do, for God's sake, let me go in to her!" she said.

Marya Dmitryevna, making her no reply, opened the door and went in. "Hateful, disgusting, in my house, the nasty hussy, only I'm sorry for her father!" Marya Dmitryevna was thinking, trying to allay her wrath. "Hard as it may be, I will forbid any one to speak of it, and will conceal it from the count." Marya Dmitryevna walked with resolute steps into the room.

Natasha was lying on the sofa; she had her head hidden in her hands and did not stir. She was lying in exactly the same position in which Marya Dmitryevna had left her.

"You're a nice girl, a very nice girl!" said Marya Dmitryevna. "Encouraging meetings with lovers in my house! There's no use in humbugging. You listen when I speak to you." Marya Dmitryevna touched her on the arm. "You listen when I speak. You've disgraced yourself like the lowest wench. I don't know what I couldn't do to you, but I feel for your father. I will hide it from him."

Natasha did not change her position, only her whole body began to writhe with noiseless, convulsive sobs, which choked her. Marya Dmitryevna looked round at Sonya, and sat down on the edge of the sofa beside Natasha.

"It's lucky for him that he escaped me; but I'll get hold of him," she said in her coarse voice. "Do you hear what I say, eh?" She put her big hand under Natasha's face, and turned it towards her. Both Marya Dmitryevna and Sonya were surprised when they saw Natasha's face. Her eyes were glittering and dry; her lips tightly compressed; her cheeks looked sunken.

"Let me be . . . what do I . . . I shall die. . . ." she articulated, with angry effort, tore herself away from Marya Dmitryevna, and fell back into the same attitude again.

"Natalya! . . ." said Marya Dmitryevna. "I wish for your good. Lie still; come, lie still like that then, I won't touch you, and listen. . . . I'm not going to tell you how wrongly you have acted. You know that yourself. But now your father's coming back to-morrow. What am I to tell him? Eh?"

Again Natasha's body heaved with sobs.

"Well, he will hear of it, your brother, your betrothed!"

"I have no betrothed; I have refused him," cried Natasha.

"That makes no difference," pursued Marya Dmitryevna. "Well, they hear of it. Do you suppose they will let the matter rest? Suppose he—your father, I know him—if he challenges him to a duel, will that be all right? Eh?"

"Oh, let me be; why did you hinder everything! Why? why? who asked you to?" cried Natasha, getting up from the sofa, and looking vindictively at Marya Dmitryevna.

"But what was it you wanted?" screamed Marya Dmitryevna, getting hot again. "Why, you weren't shut up, were you? Who hindered his coming to the house? Why carry you off, like some gypsy wench? . . .

If he had carried you off, do you suppose they wouldn't have caught him? Your father, or brother, or betrothed? He's a wretch, a scoundrel, that's what he is!"

"He's better than any of you," cried Natasha, getting up. "If you hadn't meddled . . . O my God, what does it mean? Sonya, why did you? Go away! . . ." And she sobbed with a despair with which people only bewail a trouble they feel they have brought on themselves.

Marya Dmitryevna was beginning to speak again; but Natasha cried, "Go away, go away, you all hate me and despise me!" And she flung herself again on the sofa.

Marya Dmitryevna went on for some time longer lecturing Natasha, and urging on her that it must all be kept from the count, that no one would know anything of it if Natasha would only undertake to forget it all, and not to show a sign to any one of anything having happened. Natasha made no answer. She did not sob any more, but she was taken with shivering fits and trembling. Marya Dmitryevna put a pillow under her head, laid two quilts over her, and brought her some lime-flower water with her own hands; but Natasha made no response when she spoke to her.

"Well, let her sleep," said Marya Dmitryevna, as she went out of the room, supposing her to be asleep. But Natasha was not asleep, her wide-open eyes gazed straight before her out of her pale face. All that night Natasha did not sleep, and did not weep, and said not a word to Sonya, who got up several times and went in to her.

Next day, at lunch time, as he had promised, Count Ilya Andreitch arrived from his estate in the environs. He was in very good spirits: he had come to terms with the purchaser, and there was nothing now to detain him in Moscow away from his countess, for whom he was pining. Marya Dmitryevna met him, and told him that Natasha had been very unwell on the previous day, that they had sent for a doctor, and that now she was better. Natasha did not leave her room that morning. With tightly shut, parched lips, and dry, staring eyes, she sat at the window, uneasily watching the passers-by along the street, and hurriedly looking round at any one who entered her room. She was obviously expecting news of him, expecting that he would come himself or would write to her.

When the count went in to her, she turned uneasily at the sound of his manly tread, and her face resumed its previous cold and even vindictive expression. She did not even get up to meet him.

"What is it, my angel; are you ill?" asked the count.

Natasha was silent a moment.

"Yes, I am ill," she answered.

In answer to the count's inquiries why she was depressed and whether anything had happened with her betrothed, she assured him that nothing had, and begged him not to be uneasy. Marya Dmitryevna confirmed Natasha's assurances that nothing had happened. From the pretence of illness, from his daughter's agitated state, and the troubled faces of Sonya and Marya Dmitryevna, the count saw clearly that something had happened in his absence. But it was so terrible to him to believe that anything disgraceful had happened to his beloved daughter, and he so prized his own cheerful serenity, that he avoided inquiries and tried to assure himself that it was nothing very out of the way, and only grieved that her indisposition would delay their return to the country.

XIX

From the day of his wife's arrival in Moscow, Pierre had been intending to go away somewhere else, simply not to be with her. Soon after the Rostovs' arrival in Moscow, the impression made upon him by Natasha had impelled him to hasten in carrying out his intention. He went to Tver to see the widow of Osip Alexyevitch, who had long before promised to give him papers of the deceased's.

When Pierre came back to Moscow, he was handed a letter from Marya Dmitryevna, who summoned him to her on a matter of great importance, concerning Andrey Bolkonsky and his betrothed. Pierre had been avoiding Natasha. It seemed to him that he had for her a feeling stronger than a married man should have for a girl betrothed to his friend. And some fate was continually throwing him into her company.

"What has happened? And what do they want with me?" he thought as he dressed to go to Marya Dmitryevna's. "If only Prince Andrey would make haste home and marry her," thought Pierre on the way to the house.

In the Tverskoy Boulevard some one shouted his name.

"Pierre! Been back long?" a familiar voice called to him. Pierre raised his head. Anatole, with his everlasting companion Makarin, dashed by in a sledge with a pair of grey trotting-horses, who were kicking up the snow on to the forepart of the sledge. Anatole was sitting in the classic pose of military dandies, the lower part of his face muffled in his beaver collar, and his head bent a little forward. His face was fresh and rosy; his hat, with its white plume, was stuck on one side, showing his curled, pomaded hair, sprinkled with fine snow.

"Indeed, he is the real philosopher!" thought Pierre. "He sees nothing beyond the present moment of pleasure; nothing worries him, and so he is always cheerful, satisfied, and serene. What would I not give to be just like him!" Pierre mused with envy.

In Marya Dmitryevna's entrance-hall the footman, as he took off Pierre's fur coat, told him that his mistress begged him to come to her in her bedroom.

As he opened the door into the reception-room, Pierre caught sight of Natasha, sitting at the window with a thin, pale, and ill-tempered face. She looked round at him, frowned, and with an expression of frigid dignity walked out of the room.

"What has happened?" asked Pierre, going in to Marya Dmitryevna.

"Fine doings," answered Marya Dmitryevna. "Fifty-eight years I have lived in the world—never have I seen anything so disgraceful." And exacting from Pierre his word of honour not to say a word about all he was to hear. Marya Dmitryevna informed him that Natasha had broken off her engagement without the knowledge of her parents; that the cause of her doing so was Anatole Kuragin, with whom Pierre's wife had thrown her, and with whom Natasha had attempted to elope in her father's absence in order to be secretly married to him.

Pierre, with hunched shoulders and open mouth, listened to what Marya Dmitryevna was saying, hardly able to believe his ears. That Prince Andrey's fiancée, so passionately loved by him, Natasha Rostov, hitherto so charming, should give up Bolkonsky for that fool Anatole, who was married already (Pierre knew the secret of his marriage), and be so much in love with him as to consent to elope with him—that Pierre could not conceive and could not comprehend. He could not reconcile the sweet impression he had in his soul of Natasha, whom he had known from childhood, with this new conception of her baseness, folly, and cruelty. He thought of his wife. "They are all alike," he said to himself, reflecting he was not the only man whose unhappy fate it was to be bound to a low woman. But still he felt ready to weep with sorrow for Prince Andrey, with sorrow for his pride. And the more he felt for his friend, the greater was the contempt and even aversion with which he thought of Natasha, who had just passed him with such an expression of rigid dignity. He could not know that Natasha's heart was filled with despair, shame, and humiliation, and that it was not her fault that her face accidentally expressed dignity and severity.

"What! get married?" cried Pierre at Marya Dmitryevna's words. "He can't get married; he is married."

"Worse and worse," said Marya Dmitryevna. "He's a nice youth. A perfect scoundrel. And she's expecting him; she's been expecting him these two days. We must tell her; at least she will leave off expecting him."

After learning from Pierre the details of Anatole's marriage, and pouring out her wrath against him in abusive epithets, Marya Dmitryevna informed Pierre of her object in sending for him. Marya Dmitryevna was afraid that the count or Bolkonsky, who might arrive any moment, might hear of the affair, though she intended to conceal it from them, and might challenge Kuragin, and she therefore begged Pierre to bid his brother-in-law from her to leave Moscow and not to dare to show himself in her presence. Pierre promised to do as she desired him, only then grasping the danger menacing the old count, and Nikolay, and Prince Andrey. After briefly and precisely explaining to him her wishes, she let him go to the drawing-room.

"Mind, the count knows nothing of it. You behave as though you know nothing," she said to him. "And I'll go and tell her it's no use for her to expect him! And stay to dinner, if you care to," Marya Dmitryevna called after Pierre.

Pierre met the old count. He seemed upset and anxious. That morning Natasha had told him that she had broken off her engagement to Bolkonsky.

"I'm in trouble, in trouble, my dear fellow," he said to Pierre, "with those girls without the mother. I do regret now that I came. I will be open with you. Have you heard she has broken off her engagement without a word to any one? I never did, I'll admit, feel very much pleased at the marriage. He's an excellent man, of course, but still there could be no happiness against a father's will, and Natasha will never want for suitors. Still it had been going on so long, and then such a step, without her father's or her mother's knowledge! And now she's ill, and God knows what it is. It's a bad thing, count, a bad thing to have a daughter away from her mother. . . ." Pierre saw the count was greatly troubled, and tried to change the conversation to some other subject, but the count went back again to his troubles.

Sonya came into the drawing-room with an agitated face.

"Natasha is not very well; she is in her room and would like to see you. Marya Dmitryevna is with her and she asks you to come too."

"Why, yes, you're such a great friend of Bolkonsky's; no doubt she wants to send him some message," said the count. "Ah, my God, my God! How happy it all was!" And clutching at his sparse locks, the count went out of the room.

Marya Dmitryevna had told Natasha that Anatole was married. Natasha would not believe her, and insisted on the statement being confirmed by Pierre himself. Sonya told Pierre this as she led him across the corridor to Natasha's room.

Natasha, pale and stern, was sitting beside Marya Dmitryevna, and she met Pierre at the door with eyes of feverish brilliance and inquiry. She did not smile nor nod to him. She simply looked hard at him, and that look asked him simply: was he a friend or an enemy like the rest, as regards Anatole? Pierre in himself had evidently no existence for her.

"He knows everything," said Marya Dmitryevna, addressing Natasha. "Let him tell you whether I have spoken the truth."

As a hunted, wounded beast looks at the approaching dogs and hunters, Natasha looked from one to the other.

"Natalya Ilyinitchna," Pierre began, dropping his eyes and conscious of a feeling of pity for her and loathing for the operation he had to perform, "whether it is true or not cannot affect you since . . ."

"Then it is not true that he is married?"

"No; it is true."

"Has he been married long?" she asked. "On your word of honour?"

Pierre told her so on his word of honour.

"Is he still here?" she asked rapidly.

"Yes, I have just seen him."

She was obviously incapable of speaking; she made a sign with her hands for them to leave her alone.

XX

PIERRE did not stay to dinner but went away at once on leaving Natasha's room. He drove about the town looking for Anatole Kuragin, at the very thought of whom the blood rushed to his heart, and he felt a difficulty in breathing. On the ice-hills, at the gypsies', at Somoneno he was not to be found. Pierre drove to the club. In the club everything was going on just as usual: the members who had come in to dinner were sitting in groups; they greeted Pierre, and talked of the news of the town. The footman, after greeting him, told him, as he knew his friends and his habits, that there was a place left for him in the little dining-room, that Prince Mihail Zaharitch was in the library, and that Pavel Timofeitch had not come in yet. One of Pierre's acquaintances asked him in the middle of a conversation about the weather, whether he had heard of Kuragin's elopement with Natalie Rostov, of which every one was talking in the town; was it true? Pierre said, laughing, that it was all nonsense, for he had just come from the Rostovs'. He asked every one about Anatole; one man told him he had not come in yet; another said he was to dine there that day. It was strange to Pierre to look at that calm, indifferent crowd of people, who knew nothing of what was passing in his soul. He walked about the hall, waited till every one had come in, and still seeing nothing of Anatole, he did not dine, but drove home.

Anatole was dining that day with Dolohov, and consulting with him how to achieve the exploit that had miscarried. It seemed to him essential to see Natasha. In the evening he went to his sister's, to discuss with her means for arranging their meeting. When Pierre, after vainly driving about all Moscow, returned home, his valet told him that Prince Anatole Vassilyevitch was with the countess. The drawing-room of the countess was full of guests.

Pierre did not bestow a greeting on his wife, whom he had not seen since his return (she was more hateful to him than ever at that moment); he walked into the drawing-room, and seeing Anatole, went straight up to him.

"Ah, Pierre," said the countess, going up to her husband, "you don't know what a plight our poor Anatole is in . . ." She stopped short, seeing in her husband's bowed head, in his glittering eyes, in his resolute tread, that terrible look of rage and power, which she knew and had experienced in her own case after the duel with Dolohov.

"Wherever you are, there is vice and wickedness," said Pierre to his wife. "Anatole, come along, I want a word with you," he said in French. Anatole looked round at his sister, and got up obediently, prepared to follow Pierre.

Pierre took him by the arm, drew him to him, and walked out of the room.

"If you allow yourself in my drawing-room . . ." Ellen whispered; but Pierre walked out of the room, without answering her.

Anatole followed him, with his usual jaunty swagger. But his face betrayed uneasiness. Going into his own room, Pierre shut the door, and addressed Anatole without looking at him. "Did you promise Countess Rostov to marry her? Did you try to elope with her?"

"My dear fellow," answered Anatole, in French (as was the whole conversation), "I don't consider myself bound to answer questions put to me in that tone."

Pierre's face, which had been pale before, was distorted by fury. With his big hand he clutched Anatole by the collar of his uniform, and proceeded to shake him from side to side, till Anatole's face showed a sufficient degree of terror.

"When I say I *want* a word with you . . ." Pierre repeated.

"Well, what? this is stupid. Eh?" said Anatole, feeling a button of his collar that had been torn off with the cloth.

"You're a scoundrel and a blackguard; and I don't know what prevents me from permitting myself the pleasure of braining you with this, see," said Pierre, expressing himself so artificially, because he was speaking French. He took up a heavy paper-weight, and lifted it in a menacing way, but at once hurriedly put it down in its place.

"Did you promise to marry her?"

"I, I, . . . I . . . didn't think . . . I never promised, though, because . . ."

Pierre interrupted him.

"Have you any of her letters? Have you any letters?" Pierre repeated, advancing upon Anatole. Anatole glanced at him, and at once thrust his hand in his pocket, and took out a pocket-book.

Pierre took the letter he gave him, and pushing away a table that stood in the way, he plumped down on the sofa.

"I won't be violent, don't be afraid," said Pierre, in response to a gesture of alarm from Anatole. "Letters—one," said Pierre, as though repeating a lesson to himself. "Two"—after a moment's silence he went on, getting up again and beginning to walk about—"to-morrow you are to leave Moscow."

"But how can I . . . ?"

"Three"—Pierre went on, not heeding him—"you are never to say a word of what has passed between you and the young countess. That I know I can't prevent your doing; but if you have a spark of conscience . . ." Pierre walked several times up and down the room. Anatole sat at the table, scowling and biting his lips.

"You surely must understand that, apart from your own pleasure, there's the happiness, the peace of other people; that you are ruining a whole life, simply because you want to amuse yourself. Amuse yourself with women like my wife—with them you're within your rights, they know what it is you want of them. They are armed against you by the same experience of vice; but to promise a girl to marry her . . . to deceive, to steal . . . Surely you must see that it's as base as attacking an old man or a child! . . ."

Pierre paused and glanced at Anatole, more with inquiry now than with wrath.

"I don't know about that. Eh?" said Anatole, growing bolder as Pierre gained control over his rage. "I don't know about that, and I

don't want to," he said, looking away from Pierre, and speaking with a
slight quiver of his lower jaw, "but you have said words to me, base and
all that sort of thing, which as a man of honour I can't allow any one to
do."

Pierre looked at him in amazement, not able to understand what it
was he wanted.

"Though it has been only *tête-à-tête*," Anatole went on, "still I
can't . . ."

"What, do you want satisfaction?" said Pierre sarcastically.

"At any rate you might take back your words. Eh? If you want me to
do as you wish. Eh!"

"I'll take them back, I'll take them back," said Pierre, "and beg you
to forgive me." Pierre could not help glancing at the loose button. "And
here's money too, if you want some for your journey."

Anatole smiled.

The expression of that base and cringing smile, that he knew so well
in his wife, infuriated Pierre. "Oh, you vile, heartless tribe!" he cried,
and walked out of the room.

Next day Anatole left for Petersburg.

XXI

PIERRE drove to Marya Dmitreyevna's to report to her the execution of
her commands, as to Kuragin's banishment from Moscow. The whole
house was in excitement and alarm. Natasha was very ill; and as Marya
Dmitryevna told him in secret, she had on the night after she had been
told Anatole was married, taken arsenic, which she had procured by
stealth. After swallowing a little, she had been so frightened that she
waked Sonya, and told her what she had done. Antidotes had been given
in time, and now she was out of danger; but she was still so weak, that
they could not dream of moving her to the country, and the countess
had been sent for. Pierre saw the count in great trouble, and Sonya in
tears, but he could not see Natasha.

That day Pierre dined at the club, and heard on every side gossip
about the attempted abduction of the young Countess Rostov, and persistently denied the story, assuring every one that the only foundation
for it was that his brother-in-law had made the young lady an offer and
had been refused. It seemed to Pierre that it was part of his duty to
conceal the whole affair, and to save the young countess's reputation.

He was looking forward with terror to Prince Andrey's return, and
drove round every day to ask for news of him from the old prince.

Prince Nikolay Andreitch heard all the rumours current in the town
through Mademoiselle Bourienne; and he had read the note to Princess
Marya, in which Natasha had broken off her engagement. He seemed
in better spirits than usual, and looked forward with impatience to see
ing his son.

A few days after Anatole's departure, Pierre received a note from Prince Andrey to inform him that he had arrived, and to beg him to go and see him.

The first minute of Prince Andrey's arrival in Moscow, he was handed by his father Natasha's note to Princess Marya, in which she broke off her engagement (the note had been stolen from Princess Marya, and given to the old prince by Mademoiselle Bourienne). He heard from his father's lips the story of Natasha's elopement, with additions.

Prince Andrey had arrived in the evening; Pierre came to see him the following morning. Pierre had expected to find Prince Andrey almost in the same state as Natasha, and he was therefore surprised when as he entered the drawing-room he heard the sound of Prince Andrey's voice in the study, loudly and eagerly discussing some Petersburg intrigue. The old prince and some other voice interrupted him from time to time. Princess Marya came out to meet Pierre. She sighed, turning her eyes towards the door of the room, where Prince Andrey was, plainly intending to express her sympathy with his sorrow; but Pierre saw by Princess Marya's face that she was glad both at what had happened and at the way her brother had taken the news of his fiancée's treachery.

"He said he had expected it," she said. "I know his pride will not allow him to express his feelings; but anyway, he has borne it better, far better, than I had expected. It seems it was to be so . . ."

"But is it all really at an end?" said Pierre.

Princess Marya looked at him with surprise. She could not understand how one could ask such a question. Pierre went into the study. Prince Andrey was very much changed, and visibly much more robust, but there was a new horizontal line between his brows. He was in civilian dress, and standing facing his father and Prince Meshtchersky, he was hotly arguing, making vigorous gesticulations.

The subject was Speransky, of whose sudden dismissal and supposed treason news had just reached Moscow.

"Now he" (Speransky) "will be criticised and condemned by all who were enthusiastic about him a month ago," Prince Andrey was saying, "and were incapable of understanding his aims. It's very easy to condemn a man when he's out of favour, and to throw upon him the blame of all the mistakes of other people. But I maintain that if anything of value has been done in the present reign, it has been done by him—by him alone . . ." He stopped, seeing Pierre. His face quivered, and at once assumed a vindictive expression. "And posterity will do him justice," he finished, and at once turned to Pierre. "Well, how are you, still getting stouter?" he said eagerly, but the new line was still more deeply furrowed on his forehead. "Yes, I'm very well," he answered to Pierre's question, and he smiled. It was clear to Pierre that his smile meant, "I am well, but my health is of no use to any one now."

After saying a few words to Pierre of the awful road from the frontiers of Poland, of people he had met in Switzerland who knew Pierre, and of M. Dessalle, whom he had brought back from Switzerland as a tutor for his son, Prince Andrey warmly took part again in the conversation about Speransky, which had been kept up between the two old gentlemen.

"If there had been treason, and there were proofs of his secret relations with Napoleon, they would have made them public," he said, with heat and haste. "I don't and I didn't like Speransky personally, but I do like justice."

Pierre recognized now in his friend that desire he knew only too well, for excitement and discussion of something apart from himself, simply in order to stifle thoughts that were too painful and too near his heart.

When Prince Meshtchersky had gone, Prince Andrey took Pierre's arm, and asked him to come to the room that had been assigned him. In that room there was a folding bedstead and open trunks and boxes. Prince Andrey went up to one of them and took out a case. Out of the case he took a packet of letters. He did all this in silence, and very rapidly. He stood up again and cleared his throat. His face was frowning, and his lips set.

"Forgive me, if I'm troubling you . . ." Pierre saw that Prince Andrey was going to speak of Natasha, and his broad face showed sympathy and pity. That expression in Pierre's face exasperated Prince Andrey. He went on resolutely, clearly, and disagreeably: "I have received a refusal from Countess Rostov, and rumours have reached me of your brother-in-law's seeking her hand, or something of the kind. Is that true?"

"Both true and untrue," began Pierre; but Prince Andrey cut him short.

"Here are her letters and her portrait," he said. He took the packet from the table and gave it to Pierre.

"Give that to the countess . . . if you will see her."

"She is very ill," said Pierre.

"So she's still here?" said Prince Andrey. "And Prince Kuragin?" he asked quickly.

"He has been gone a long while. She has been at death's door."

"I am very sorry to hear of her illness," said Prince Andrey. He laughed a cold, malignant, unpleasant laugh like his father's.

"But M. Kuragin, then, did not deign to bestow his hand on Countess Rostov?" said Prince Andrey. He snorted several times.

"He could not have married her, because he is married," said Pierre. Prince Andrey laughed unpleasantly, again recalling his father.

"And where is he now, your brother-in-law, may I ask?" he said.

"He went to Peter . . . but, really, I don't know," said Pierre.

"Well, that's no matter," said Prince Andrey. "Tell Countess Rostov from me that she was and is perfectly free, and that I wish her all prosperity."

Pierre took the packet. Prince Andrey, as though reflecting whether he had not something more to say, or waiting for Pierre to say something, looked at him with a fixed gaze.

"Listen. Do you remember our discussion in Petersburg?" said Pierre. "Do you remember about———?"

"I remember," Prince Andrey answered hurriedly. "I said that a fallen woman should be forgiven, but I did not say I could forgive one. I can't."

"How can you compare it? . . ." said Pierre.

Prince Andrey cut him short. He cried harshly: "Yes, ask her hand again, be magnanimous, and all that sort of thing? . . . Oh, that's all very noble, but I'm not equal to following in that gentleman's tracks. If you care to remain my friend, never speak to me of that . . . of all this business. Well, good-bye. So you'll give that? . . ."

Pierre left him, and went in to the old prince and Princess Marya.

The old man seemed livelier than usual. Princess Marya was the same as usual, but behind her sympathy for her brother, Pierre detected her relief that her brother's marriage was broken off. Looking at them, Pierre felt what a contempt and dislike they all had for the Rostovs; felt that it would be impossible in their presence even to mention the name of the girl who could give up Prince Andrey for any one in the world.

At dinner they talked of the coming war, of which there could now be no doubt in the near future. Prince Andrey talked incessantly, and argued first with his father, and then with Dessalle, the Swiss tutor. He seemed more eager than usual, with that eagerness of which Pierre knew so well the inner cause.

XXII

That evening Pierre went to the Rostovs' to fulfil Prince Andrey's commission. Natasha was in bed, the count was at the club, and Pierre, after giving the letters to Sonya, went in to see Marya Dmitryevna, who was interested to know how Prince Andrey had taken the news. Ten minutes later, Sonya came in to Marya Dmitryevna.

"Natasha insists on seeing Count Pyotr Kirillitch," she said.

"Why, are we to take him up to her, eh? Why, you are all in a muddle there," said Marya Dmitryevna.

"No, she has dressed and gone into the drawing-room," said Sonya.

Marya Dmitryevna could only shrug her shoulders. "When will the countess come? She has quite worn me out! You mind now, don't tell her everything," she said to Pierre. "One hasn't the heart to scold her, she's so piteous, poor thing."

Natasha was standing in the middle of the drawing-room, looking thinner, and with a pale, set face (not at all overcome with shame, as Pierre had expected to see her). When Pierre appeared in the doorway, she made a hurried movement, evidently in uncertainty whether to go to meet him, or to wait for him to come to her.

Pierre went hurriedly towards her. He thought she would give him her hand as usual. But coming near him she stopped, breathing hard, and letting her hands hang lifelessly, exactly in the same pose in which she ased to stand in the middle of the room to sing, but with an utterly different expression.

"Pyotr Kirillitch," she began, speaking quickly, "Prince Bolkonsky was your friend—he is your friend," she corrected herself. (It seemed to her that everything was in the past, and now all was changed.) "He told me to apply to you . . ."

Pierre choked dumbly as he looked at her. Till then he had in his heart blamed her, and tried to despise her; but now he felt so sorry for her, that there was no room in his heart for blame.

"He is here now, tell him . . . to for . . . to forgive me." She stopped short and breathed even more quickly, but she did not weep.

"Yes . . . I will tell him," said Pierre; "but . . ." He did not know what to say.

Natasha was evidently dismayed at the idea that might have occurred to Pierre.

"No, I know that everything is over," she said hurriedly. "No, that can never be. I'm only wretched at the wrong I have done him. Only tell him that I beg him to forgive, to forgive, forgive me for everything . . ." Her whole body was heaving; she sat down on a chair.

A feeling of pity he had never known before flooded Pierre's heart.

"I will tell him, I will tell him everything once more," said Pierre; "but . . . I should like to know one thing . . ."

"To know what?" Natasha's eyes asked.

"I should like to know, did you love . . ." Pierre did not know what to call Anatole, and flushed at the thought of him—"did you love that bad man?"

"Don't call him bad," said Natasha. "But I don't . . . know, I don't know . . ." She began crying again, and Pierre was more than ever overwhelmed with pity, tenderness, and love. He felt the tears trickling under his spectacles, and hoped they would not be noticed.

"We won't talk any more of it, my dear," he said. It seemed suddenly so strange to Natasha to hear the gentle, tender, sympathetic voice in which he spoke. "We won't talk of it, my dear, I'll tell him everything. But one thing I beg you, look on me as your friend; and if you want help, advice, or simply want to open your heart to some one—not now, but when things are clearer in your heart—think of me." He took her hand and kissed it. "I shall be happy, if I am able . . ." Pierre was confused.

"Don't speak to me like that; I'm not worth it!" cried Natasha, and she would have left the room, but Pierre held her hand. He knew there was something more he must say to her. But when he said it, he was surprised at his own words.

"Hush, hush, your whole life lies before you," he said to her.

"Before me! No! All is over for me," she said, with shame and self-humiliation.

"All over?" he repeated. "If I were not myself, but the handsomest, cleverest, best man in the world, and if I were free I would be on my knees this minute to beg for your hand and your love."

For the first time for many days Natasha wept with tears of gratitude and softened feeling, and glancing at Pierre, she went out of the room.

Pierre followed her, almost running into the vestibule, and restraining the tears of tenderness and happiness that made a lump in his throat. He flung on his fur coat, unable to find the armholes, and got into his sledge.

"Now where, your excellency?" asked the coachman.

"Where?" Pierre asked himself. "Where can I go now? Not to the club or to pay calls." All men seemed to him so pitiful, so poor in comparison with the feeling of tenderness and love in his heart, in comparison with that softened, grateful glance she had turned upon him that last minute through her tears.

"Home," said Pierre, throwing open the bearskin coat over his broad, joyously breathing chest in spite of ten degrees of frost.

It was clear and frosty. Over the dirty, half-dark streets, over the black roofs was a dark, starlit sky. It was only looking at the sky that Pierre forgot the mortifying meanness of all things earthly in comparison with the height his soul had risen to. As he drove into Arbatsky Square, the immense expanse of dark, starlit sky lay open before Pierre's eyes. Almost in the centre of it above the Prechistensky Boulevard, surrounded on all sides by stars, but distinguished from all by its nearness to the earth, its white light and long, upturned tail, shone the huge, brilliant comet of 1812; the comet which betokened, it was said, all manner of horrors and the end of the world. But in Pierre's heart that bright comet, with its long, luminous tail, aroused no feeling of dread. On the contrary, his eyes wet with tears, Pierre looked joyously at this bright comet, which seemed as though after flying with inconceivable swiftness through infinite space in a parabola, it had suddenly, like an arrow piercing the earth, stuck fast at one chosen spot in the black sky, and stayed there, vigorously tossing up its tail, shining and playing with its white light among the countless other twinkling stars. It seemed to Pierre that it was in full harmony with what was in his softened and emboldened heart, that had gained vigour to blossom into a new life.

PART NINE

I

TOWARDS THE end of the year 1811, there began to be greater activity in levying troops and in concentrating the forces of Western Europe, and in 1812 these forces—millions of men, reckoning those engaged in the transport and feeding of the army—moved from the west eastward, towards the frontiers of Russia, where, since 1811, the Russian forces were being in like manner concentrated.

On the 12th of June the forces of Western Europe crossed the frontier, and the war began, that is, an event took place opposed to human reason and all human nature. Millions of men perpetrated against one another so great a mass of crime—fraud, swindling, robbery, forgery, issue of counterfeit money, plunder, incendiarism, and murder—that the annals of all the criminal courts of the world could not muster such a sum of wickedness in whole centuries, though the men who committed those deeds did not at that time look on them as crimes.

What led to this extraordinary event? What were its causes? Historians, with simple-hearted conviction, tell us that the causes of this event were the insult offered to the Duke of Oldenburg, the failure to maintain the continental system, the ambition of Napoleon, the firmness of Alexander, the mistakes of the diplomatists, and so on.

According to them, if only Metternich, Rumyantsev, or Talleyrand had, in the interval between a levée and a court ball, really taken pains and written a more judicious diplomatic note, or if only Napoleon had written to Alexander, "I consent to restore the duchy to the Duke of Oldenburg," there would have been no war.

We can readily understand that being the conception of the war that presented itself to contemporaries. We can understand Napoleon's supposing the cause of the war to be the intrigues of England (as he said, indeed, in St. Helena); we can understand how to the members of the English House of Commons the cause of the war seemed to be Napoleon's ambition; how to the Duke of Oldenburg the war seemed due to the outrage done him; how to the trading class the war seemed due to the continental system that was ruining Europe; to the old soldiers and generals the chief reason for it seemed their need of active service; to the regiments of the period, the necessity of re-establishing *les bons principes*; while the diplomatists of the time set it down to the alliance of Russia with Austria in 1809 not having been with sufficient care concealed from Napoleon, and the memorandum, No. 178, having been awkwardly worded. We may well understand contemporaries believing in those causes, and in a countless, endless number more, the multiplicity of which is due to the infinite variety of men's points of view. But to us of a later generation, contemplating in all its vastness the immensity of the accomplished fact, and seeking to penetrate its simple and fearful significance, those explanations must appear insufficient. To us it is inconceivable that millions of Christian men should have killed and tortured each other, because Napoleon was ambitious, Alexander firm, English policy crafty, and the Duke of Oldenburg hardly treated. We cannot grasp the connection between these circumstances and the bare fact of murder and violence, nor why the duke's wrongs should induce thousands of men from the other side of Europe to pillage and murder the inhabitants of the Smolensk and Moscow provinces and to be slaughtered by them.

For us of a later generation, who are not historians led away by the process of research, and so can look at the facts with common-sense unobscured, the causes of this war appear innumerable in their multiplicity. The more deeply we search out the causes the more of them we discover; and every cause, and even a whole class of causes taken separately, strikes us as being equally true in itself, and equally deceptive through its insignificance in comparison with the immensity of the result, and its inability to produce (without all the other causes that concurred with it) the effect that followed. Such a cause, for instance, occurs to us as Napoleon's refusal to withdraw his troops beyond the Vistula, and to restore the duchy of Oldenburg; and then again we remember the readiness or the reluctance of the first chance French corporal to serve on a second campaign; for had he been unwilling to serve, and a second and a third, and thousands of corporals and soldiers had shared that reluctance, Napoleon's army would have been short of so many men, and the war could not have taken place.

If Napoleon had not taken offence at the request to withdraw beyond the Vistula, and had not commanded his troops to advance, there would have been no war. But if all the sergeants had been unwilling to serve on another campaign, there could have been no war either.

And the war would not have been had there been no intrigues on the part of England, no Duke of Oldenburg, no resentment on the part of Alexander; nor had there been no autocracy in Russia, no French Revolution and consequent dictatorship and empire, nor all that led to the French Revolution, and so on further back: without any one of those causes, nothing could have happened. And so all those causes—myriads of causes—coincided to bring about what happened. And consequently nothing was exclusively the cause of the war, and the war was bound to happen, simply because it was bound to happen. Millions of men, repudiating their common-sense and their human feelings, were bound to move from west to east, and to slaughter their fellows, just as some centuries before hordes of men had moved from east to west to slaughter their fellows.

The acts of Napoleon and Alexander, on whose words it seemed to depend whether this should be done or not, were as little voluntary as the act of each soldier, forced to march out by the drawing of a lot or by conscription. This could not be otherwise, for in order that the will of Napoleon and Alexander (on whom the whole decision appeared to rest) should be effective, a combination of innumerable circumstances was essential, without any one of which the effect could not have followed. It was essential that the millions of men in whose hands the real power lay—the soldiers who fired guns and transported provisions and cannons—should consent to carry out the will of those feeble and isolated persons, and that they should have been brought to this acquiescence by an infinite number of varied and complicated causes.

We are forced to fall back upon fatalism in history to explain irrational events (that is those of which we cannot comprehend the reason). The more we try to explain those events in history rationally, the more irrational and incomprehensible they seem to us. Every man lives for himself, making use of his free-will for attainment of his own objects, and feels in his whole being that he can do or not do any action. But as soon as he does anything, that act, committed at a certain moment in time, becomes irrevocable and is the property of history, in which it has a significance, predestined and not subject to free choice.

There are two aspects to the life of every man: the personal life, which is free in proportion as its interests are abstract, and the elemental life of the swarm, in which a man must inevitably follow the laws laid down for him.

Consciously a man lives on his own account in freedom of will, but he serves as an unconscious instrument in bringing about the historical ends of humanity. An act he has once committed is irrevocable, and that act of his, coinciding in time with millions of acts of others, has an historical value. The higher a man's place in the social scale, the more connections he has with others, and the more power he has over them, the more conspicuous is the inevitability and predestination of every act he commits. "The hearts of kings are in the hand of God." The king is the slave of history.

History—that is the unconscious life of humanity in the swarm, in the community—makes every minute of the life of kings its own, as an instrument for attaining its ends.

Although in that year, 1812, Napoleon believed more than ever that to shed or not to shed the blood of his peoples depended entirely on his will (as Alexander said in his last letter to him), yet then, and more than at any time, he was in bondage to those laws which forced him, while to himself he seemed to be acting freely, to do what was bound to be his share in the common edifice of humanity, in history.

The people of the west moved to the east for men to kill one another. And by the law of the coincidence of causes, thousands of petty causes backed one another up and coincided with that event to bring about that movement and that war: resentment at the non-observance of the continental system, and the Duke of Oldenburg, and the massing of troops in Prussia—a measure undertaken, as Napoleon supposed, with the object of securing armed peace—and the French Emperor's love of war, to which he had grown accustomed, in conjunction with the inclinations of his people, who were carried away by the grandiose scale of the preparations, and the expenditure on those preparations, and the necessity of recouping that expenditure. Then there was the intoxicating effect of the honours paid to the French Emperor in Dresden, and the negotiations too of the diplomatists, who were supposed by contemporaries to be guided by a genuine desire to secure peace, though they only inflamed the *amour-propre* of both sides; and millions upon millions of other causes, chiming in with the fated event and coincident with it.

When the apple is ripe and falls—why does it fall? Is it because it is drawn by gravitation to the earth, because its stalk is withered, because it is dried by the sun, because it grows heavier, because the wind shakes it, or because the boy standing under the tree wants to eat it?

Not one of those is the cause. All that simply makes up the conjunction of conditions under which every living, organic, elemental event takes place. And the botanist who says that the apple has fallen because the cells are decomposing, and so on, will be just as right as the boy standing under the tree who says the apple has fallen because he wanted to eat it and prayed for it to fall. The historian, who says that Napoleon went to Moscow because he wanted to, and was ruined because Alexander desired his ruin, will be just as right and as wrong as the man who says that the mountain of millions of tons, tottering and undermined, has been felled by the last stroke of the last workingman's pickaxe. In historical events great men—so called—are but the labels that serve to give a name to an event, and like labels, they have the least possible connection with the event itself.

Every action of theirs, that seems to them an act of their own freewill, is in an historical sense not free at all, but in bondage to the whole course of previous history, and predestined from all eternity.

II

On the 29th of May Napoleon left Dresden, where he had been spending three weeks surrounded by a court that included princes, dukes, kings, and even one emperor. Before his departure, Napoleon took a gracious leave of the princes, kings, and emperor deserving of his favour, and sternly upbraided the kings and princes with whom he was displeased. He made a present of his own diamonds and pearls—those, that is, that he had taken from other kings—to the Empress of Austria. He tenderly embraced the Empress Marie Louise—who considered herself his wife, though he had another wife still living in Paris—and left her, so his historian relates, deeply distressed and hardly able to support the separation. Although diplomatists still firmly believed in the possibility of peace, and were zealously working with that object, although the Emperor Napoleon, with his own hand, wrote a letter to the Emperor Alexander calling him "*Monsieur mon frère*," and assuring him with sincerity that he had no desire of war, and would always love and honour him, he set off to join the army, and at every station gave fresh commands, hastening the progress of his army from west to east. He drove in a travelling carriage, drawn by six horses and surrounded by pages, adjutants, and an armed escort, along the route by Posen, Thorn, Danzig, and Königsberg. In each of these towns he was welcomed with enthusiasm and trepidation by thousands of people.

The army was moving from west to east, and he was driven after it by continual relays of six horses. On the 10th of June he overtook the army and spent the night in the Vilkovik forest, in quarters prepared for him on the property of a Polish count.

The following day Napoleon drove on ahead of the army, reached the Niemen, put on a Polish uniform in order to inspect the crossing of the river, and rode out on the river bank.

When he saw the Cossacks posted on the further bank and the expanse of the steppes—in the midst of which, far away, was the holy city, Moscow, capital of an empire, like the Scythian empire invaded by Alexander of Macedon—Napoleon surprised the diplomatists and contravened all rules of strategy by ordering an immediate advance, and his troops began crossing the Niemen next day.

Early on the morning of the 12th of June he came out of his tent, which had been pitched that day on the steep left bank of the Niemen, and looked through a field-glass at his troops pouring out of the Vilkovik forest, and dividing into three streams at the three bridges across the river. The troops knew of the Emperor's presence, and were on the lookout for him. When they caught sight of his figure in his greatcoat and hat standing apart from his suite in front of his tent on the hill opposite, they threw up their caps and shouted, *"Vive l'Empereur!"* And one regiment after another, in a continuous stream, flowed out of the immense forest that had concealed them, and split up to cross the river by the three bridges. "We shall make some way this time. Oh, when he takes a hand himself things begin to get warm! . . . Name of God! . . . There he is! . . . Hurrah for the Emperor! So those are the Steppes of Asia! A nasty country it is, though. Good-bye, Beauché; I'll keep the finest palace in Moscow for you. Good-bye! good-luck! . . . Have you seen the Emperor? Hurrah for the Emperor! If they make me Governor of the Indies, Gérard, I'll make you Minister of Cashmere, that's settled. Hurrah for the Emperor! Hurrah! hurrah! hurrah! The rascally Cossacks, how they are running. Hurrah for the Emperor! There he is! Do you see him? I have seen him twice as I am seeing you. The little corporal . . . I saw him give the cross to one of the veterans. . . . Hurrah for the Emperor!" Such was the talk of old men and young, of the most diverse characters and positions in society. All the faces of those men wore one common expression of joy at the commencement of a long-expected campaign, and enthusiasm and devotion to the man in the grey coat standing on the hill opposite.

On the 13th of June Napoleon mounted a small thoroughbred Arab horse and galloped towards one of the bridges over the Niemen, deafened all the while by shouts of enthusiasm, which he obviously endured simply because they could not be prevented from expressing in such shouts their love for him. But those shouts, invariably accompanying him everywhere, wearied him and hindered his attending to the military problems which beset him from the time he joined the army. He rode over a swaying bridge of boats to the other side of the river, turned sharply to the left, and galloped in the direction of Kovno, preceded by horse guards, who were breathless with delight and enthusiasm, as they cleared the way before him. On reaching the broad river Niemen, he pulled up beside a regiment of Polish Uhlans on the bank.

"*Vive l'Empereur!*" the Poles shouted with the same enthusiasm, breaking their line and squeezing against each other to get a view of him. Napoleon looked up and down the river, got off his horse, and sat down on a log that lay on the bank. At a mute sign from him, they handed him the field-glass. He propped it on the back of a page who ran up delighted. He began looking at the other side, then, with absorbed attention, scrutinised the map that was unfolded on the logs. Without raising his head he said something, and two of his adjutants galloped off to the Polish Uhlans.

"What? what did he say?" was heard in the ranks of the Polish Uhlans as an adjutant galloped up to them. They were commanded to look for a fording-place and to cross to the other side. The colonel of the Polish Uhlans, a handsome old man, flushing red and stammering from excitement, asked the adjutant whether he would be permitted to swim across the river with his men instead of seeking for a ford. In obvious dread of a refusal, like a boy asking permission to get on a horse, he asked to be allowed to swim across the river before the Emperor's eyes. The adjutant replied that probably the Emperor would not be displeased at this excess of zeal.

No sooner had the adjutant said this than the old whiskered officer, with happy face and sparkling eyes, brandished his sabre in the air shouting "*Vive l'Empereur!*" and commanding his men to follow him, he set spurs to his horse and galloped down to the river. He gave a vicious thrust to his horse, that floundered under him, and plunged into the water, making for the most rapid part of the current. Hundreds of Uhlans galloped in after him. It was cold and dangerous in the middle in the rapid current. The Uhlans clung to one another, falling off their horses. Some of the horses were drowned, some, too, of the men; the others struggled to swim across, some in the saddle, others clinging to their horse's manes. They tried to swim straight across, and although there was a ford half a verst away they were proud to be swimming and drowning in the river before the eyes of that man sitting on the log and not even looking at what they were doing. When the adjutant, on going back, chose a favourable moment and ventured to call the Emperor's attention to the devotion of the Poles to his person, the little man in the grey overcoat got up, and summoning Berthier, he began walking up and down the bank with him, giving him instructions, and casting now and then a glance of displeasure at the drowning Uhlans who had interrupted his thoughts.

It was no new conviction for him that his presence in any quarter of the earth, from Africa to the steppes of Moscow, was enough to impres**s** men and impel them to senseless acts of self-sacrifice. He sent for his horse and rode back to his bivouac.

Forty Uhlans were drowned in the river in spite of the boats sent to their assistance. The majority struggled back to the bank from which they had started. The colonel, with several of his men, swam across the river and with difficulty clambered up the other bank. But as soon as they clambered out in drenched and streaming clothes they shouted *"Vive l'Empereur!"* looking ecstatically at the place where Napoleon had stood, though he was no longer there, and at that moment thought themselves happy.

In the evening between giving two orders—one for hastening the arrival of the counterfeit rouble notes that had been prepared for circulation in Russia, and the other for shooting a Saxon who had been caught with a letter containing a report on the disposition of the French army —Napoleon gave a third order for presenting the colonel, who had quite unnecessarily flung himself in the river, the order of the Légion d'Honneur, of which he was himself the head. *Quos vult perdere, dementat.*

III

THE Russian Emperor had meanwhile been spending more than a month in Vilna, holding reviews and inspecting manœuvres. Nothing was in readiness for the war, which all were expecting, though it was to prepare for it that the Tsar had come from Petersburg. There was no general plan of action. The vacillation between all the plans that were proposed and the inability to fix on any one of them, was more marked than ever after the Tsar had been for a month at headquarters. There was a separate commander-in-chief at the head of each of the three armies; but there was no commander with authority over all of them, and the Tsar did not undertake the duties of such a commander-in-chief himself.

The longer the Tsar stayed at Vilna, the less ready was the Russian army for the war, which it had grown weary of expecting. Every effort of the men who surrounded the Tsar seemed to be devoted to making their sovereign spend his time pleasantly and forget the impending war.

Many balls and fêtes were given by the Polish magnates, by members of the court, and by the Tsar himself; and in the month of June it occurred to one of the Polish generals attached to the Tsar's staff that all the generals on the staff should give a dinner and a ball to the Tsar. The suggestion was eagerly taken up. The Tsar gave his consent. The generals on the staff subscribed the necessary funds. The lady who was most likely to please the Tsar's taste was selected as hostess for the ball. Count Bennigsen, who had land in the Vilna province, offered his house in the outskirts for this fête, and the 13th of June was the day fixed for a ball, a dinner, with a regatta and fireworks at Zakreta, Count Bennigsen's suburban house.

On the very day on which Napoleon gave the order to cross the Niemen, and the vanguard of his army crossed the Russian frontier, driving back the Cossacks, Alexander was at the ball given by the generals on his staff at Count Bennigsen's house.

It was a brilliant and festive entertainment. Connoisseurs declared that rarely had so many beauties been gathered together at one place. Countess Bezuhov, who had been among the Russian ladies who had followed the Tsar from Petersburg to Vilna, was at that ball, her heavy, Russian style of beauty—as it is called—overshadowing the more refined Polish ladies. She was much noticed, and the Tsar had deigned to bestow a dance upon her.

Boris Drubetskoy, who had left his wife at Moscow, and was living "*en garçon*," as he said, at Vilna, was also at that ball; and although he was not a general on the staff, he had subscribed a large sum to the ball. Boris was now a wealthy man who had risen to high honours. He no longer sought patronage, but was on an equal footing with the most distinguished men of his age. At Vilna he met Ellen, whom he had not seen for a long while. As Ellen was enjoying the good graces of a very important personage indeed, and Boris had so recently been married, they made no allusion to the past, but met as good-natured, old friends.

At midnight dancing was still going on. Ellen happening to have no suitable partner had herself proposed a mazurka to Boris. They were the third couple. Boris was looking coldly at Ellen's splendid bare shoulders, which rose out of her dress of dark gauze and gold, and was talking to her of old acquaintances, and yet though others and himself too were unaware of it, he never for a second ceased observing the Tsar who was in the same room. The Tsar was not dancing; he was standing in the doorway, stopping one person after the other with the gracious words he alone knew how to utter.

At the beginning of the mazurka, Boris saw that a general of the staff, Balashov, one of the persons in closest attendance on the Tsar, went up to him, and, regardless of court etiquette, stopped close to him, while he conversed with a Polish lady. After saying a few words to the lady, the Tsar glanced inquiringly at Balashov, and apparently seeing that he was behaving like this only because he had weighty reasons for doing so, he gave the lady a slight nod and turned to Balashov. The Tsar's countenance betrayed amazement, as soon as Balashov had begun to speak. He took Balashov's arm and walked across the room with him, unconsciously clearing a space of three yards on each side of him as people hastily drew back. Boris noticed the excited face of Araktcheev as the Tsar walked up the room with Balashov. Araktcheev, looking from under his brows at the Tsar, and sniffing with his red nose, moved forward out of the crowd as though expecting the Tsar to apply to him. (Boris saw that Araktcheev envied Balashov and was displeased at any important news having reached the Tsar not through him.) But the Tsar and Balashov walked out by the door into the lighted garden, without noticing Araktcheev. Araktcheev, holding his sword and looking wrathfully about him, followed twenty paces behind them.

Boris went on performing the figures of the mazurka, but he was all the while fretted by wondering what the news could be that Balashov had brought, and in what way he could find it out before other people. In the figure in which he had to choose a lady, he whispered to Ellen that he wanted to choose Countess Pototsky, who had, he thought, gone out on to the balcony, and gliding over the parquet, he flew to the door that opened into the garden, and seeing the Tsar and Balashov coming into the verandah, he stood still there. The Tsar and Balashov moved towards the door. Boris, with a show of haste, as though he had not time to move away, squeezed respectfully up to the doorpost and bowed his head. The Tsar in the tone of a man resenting a personal insult was saying:

"To enter Russia with no declaration of war! I will consent to conciliation only when not a single enemy under arms is left in my country," he said.

It seemed to Boris that the Tsar liked uttering these words: he was pleased with the form in which he had expressed his feelings, but displeased at Boris overhearing them.

"Let nobody know of it!" the Tsar added, frowning.

Boris saw that this was aimed at him, and closing his eyes, inclined his head a little. The Tsar went back to the ballroom, and remained there another half hour.

Boris was the first person to learn the news that the French troops had crossed the Niemen; and, thanks to that fact, was enabled to prove to various persons of great consequence, that much that was hidden from others was commonly known to him, and was thereby enabled to rise even higher than before in the opinion of those persons.

The astounding news of the French having crossed the Niemen seemed particularly unexpected from coming after a month's uninterrupted expectation of it, and arriving at a ball! At the first moment of amazement and resentment on getting the news, Alexander hit on the declaration that has since become famous—a declaration which pleased him and fully expressed his feelings. On returning home after the ball at two o'clock in the night, the Tsar sent for his secretary, Shishkov, and told him to write a decree to the army and a rescript to Field-Marshal Prince Saltykov; and he insisted on the words being inserted that he would never make peace as long as one Frenchman under arms remained in Russia.

The next day the following letter was written to Napoleon:

MONSIEUR MON FRÈRE,—I learnt yesterday that in spite of the loyalty with which I have kept my engagements with your Majesty, your troops have crossed the frontiers of Russia, and I have this moment received from Petersburg the note in which Count Lauriston informs me as cause of this invasion that your majesty considers us to be in hostile relations ever since Prince Kurakin asked for his passport. The causes on which the Duc de Bassano based his refusal to give these passports would never have led me to suppose that the action of my ambassador could serve as a ground for invasion. And, indeed, he received no authorisation from me in his action, as has been made known by him; and as soon as I heard of it I immediately expressed my displeasure to Prince Kurakin, commanding him to perform the duties entrusted to him as before. If your majesty is not inclined to shed the blood of your subjects for such a misunderstanding, and if you consent to withdraw your troops from Russian territory, I will pass over the whole incident unnoticed, and agreement between us will be possible. In the opposite case, I shall be forced to repel an invasion which has been in no way provoked on my side. Your Majesty has it in your power to preserve humanity from the disasters of another war.—I am, etc.,

(Signed)   ALEXANDER.

IV

At two o'clock in the night of the 13th of June, the Tsar sent for Balashov, and, reading him his letter to Napoleon, commanded him to go in person and give the letter to the French Emperor. As he dismissed Balashov, he repeated to him his declaration that he would never make peace as long as a single enemy under arms remained on Russian soil, and told him to be sure to repeat those words to Napoleon. The Tsar had not inserted them in his letter to Napoleon, because, with his characteristic tact, he felt those words would be inappropriate at the moment when the last efforts were being made for conciliation; but he expressly charged Balashov to repeat that message by word of mouth to Napoleon.

Balashov rode out on the night between the 13th and the 14th, accompanied by a trumpeter and two Cossacks; and at dawn he reached the French outposts at the village of Rykonty on the Russian side of the Niemen. He was stopped by the sentinels of the French cavalry.

A French subaltern of hussars, in a crimson uniform and a fur cap, shouted to Balashov to stop. Balashov did not immediately obey, but went on advancing along the road at a walking pace.

The subaltern, with scowls and muttered abuse, swooped down upon Balashov, drew his sword, and shouted rudely to the Russian general: "Was he deaf that he did not hear when he was spoken to?" Balashov gave him his name. The subaltern sent a soldier to his superior officer.

Paying no further attention to Balashov, the subaltern began talking with his comrades about regimental matters, without looking at the Russian general. It was an exceedingly strange sensation for Balashov, who was used at all times to the dignities of his position, was always in contact with the highest power and authority, and only three hours before had been conversing with the Tsar, to be brought here on Russian soil into collision with this hostile, and still more, disrespectful display of brute force.

The sun was only beginning to rise behind storm-clouds, the air was fresh and dewy. A herd of cattle was being driven along the road from the village. Larks sprang up trilling one after another in the fields, like bubbles rising to the surface of water.

Balashov looked about him, awaiting the arrival of the officer from the village. The Russian Cossacks and trumpeter and the French hussars looked at one another now and then in silence.

A French colonel of hussars, evidently only just out of bed, came riding out of the village on a handsome, sleek, grey horse, accompanied by two hussars. The officers, the soldiers, and the horses all looked smart and well satisfied.

In this early stage of the campaign the troops were well in a state of good discipline, in good, almost parade, order, and engaged in peaceful pursuits, with a shade of martial swagger in their dress, and a shade of gaiety and spirit of adventure in their temper that always accompanies the commencement of a war.

The French colonel had much ado to suppress his yawns, but was courteous in his manner, and evidently understood all the importance of Balashov's position. He led him past the line of outposts, and informed him that his desire to be presented to the Emperor would in all probability immediately be satisfied, as the Emperor's quarters were, he believed, not far off.

They rode through the village of Rykonty, past French picket ropes, sentinels, and soldiers, who saluted their colonel and stared with curiosity at the Russian uniform. They came out on the other side of the village, and the colonel told Balashov that they were only two kilomètres from the commander of the division, who would receive him and conduct him to his destination.

The sun had by now fully risen and was shining cheerfully on the bright green fields.

They had just passed an inn and were riding uphill when a party of horsemen came riding downhill towards them. The foremost figure was a tall man, in a hat with plumes, mounted on a raven horse, with trappings glittering in the sun. He had a scarlet cloak, and curly black hair, that floated on his shoulders, and he rode in the French fashion, with his long legs thrust out in front. This personage galloped towards Balashov, with his jewels and gold lace and feathers all fluttering and glittering in the bright June sun.

Balashov was some ten yards from this majestically theatrical figure in bracelets, feathers, necklaces, and gold, when Julner, the French colonel, whispered to him reverentially, "The King of Naples!" It was in fact Murat, who was now styled the "King of Naples." Though it was utterly incomprehensible that he should be the King of Naples, he was addressed by that title, and was himself persuaded of his royal position. and consequently behaved with an air of greater solemnity and dignity than heretofore. So firmly did he believe that he really was the King of Naples, that when, just before leaving Naples, he was greeted by some

Italians with shouts of "Long live the King!" when walking in the streets with his wife, he turned to her with a pensive smile and said, "Poor fellows, they don't know I am quitting them to-morrow."

But though he believed so implicitly that he was King of Naples, and sympathised with his subjects' grief at losing him, after he had been commanded to return to the service, and especially after his interview with Napoleon at Danzig, when his most august brother-in-law had said, "I have made you king that you may rule in my way, and not in your own," he had cheerfully resumed his familiar duties; and, like a well-fed, but not over-fed stallion feeling himself in harness, prancing in the shafts, and decked out in all possible motley magnificence, he went galloping along the roads of Poland, with no notion where or why he was going.

On seeing the Russian general he made a royal, majestic motion of his head with his floating curls, and looked inquiringly at the French colonel. The colonel deferentially informed his majesty of the mission of Balashov, whose name he could not pronounce. "De Bal-macheve!" said the King, resolutely attacking and vanquishing the colonel's difficulty. "Charmed to make your acquaintance, general," he added, with a gesture of royal condescension. As soon as the King spoke loudly and rapidly, all his royal dignity instantly deserted him, and, without himself being aware of it, he passed into the tone of good-humoured familiarity natural to him. He laid his hand on the forelock of Balashov's horse. "Well, general, everything looks like war," he said, as it were regretting a circumstance on which he could not offer an opinion. "Your majesty," answered Balashov, "the Emperor, my master, does not desire war, and as your majesty sees." Balashov declined "your majesty" in all its cases, using the title with an affectation inevitable in addressing a personage for whom such a title was a novelty.

Murat's face beamed with foolish satisfaction as he listened to "Monsieur de Balacheff." But royalty has its obligations. He felt it incumbent on him to converse with Alexander's envoy on affairs of state as a king and an ally. He dismounted, and taking Balashov's arm, and moving a little away from the suite, who remained respectfully waiting, he began walking up and down with him, trying to speak with grave significance. He mentioned that the Emperor Napoleon had been offended at the demand that his troops should evacuate Prussia, especially because that demand had been made public, and was so derogatory to the dignity of France. Balashov said that there was nothing derogatory in that demand, seeing that . . . Murat interrupted him.

"So you consider that the Emperor Alexander is not responsible for the commencement of hostilities?" he said suddenly, with a foolish and good-humoured smile.

Balashov began to explain why he did consider that Napoleon was responsible for the war.

"Ah, my dear general," Murat interrupted him again, "with all my heart I wish that the Emperors would settle the matter between themselves; and that the war, which has been begun by no desire of mine, may be concluded as quickly as possible," he said in the tone in which servants speak who are anxious to remain on friendly terms though their masters have quarrelled. And he changed the subject; inquiring after the health of the Grand Duke, and recalling the agreeable time he had spent with him in Naples. Then suddenly, as though recollecting his royal dignity, Murat drew himself up majestically, threw himself into the pose in which he had stood at his coronation, and waving his right arm, said: "I will detain you no longer, general; I wish you success in your mission." And, with a flutter of his scarlet cloak and his feathers, and a flash of his precious stones, he rejoined the suite, who were respectfully awaiting him.

Balashov rode on further, expecting from Murat's words that he would be very shortly brought before Napoleon himself. But at the next village he was detained by the sentinels of Davoust's infantry corps, just as he had been at the outposts. An adjutant of the commander of that corps was sent for to conduct him to the village to see Marshal Davoust.

V

DAVOUST was to the Emperor Napoleon what Araktcheev was to Alexander. Davoust was not like Araktcheev a coward, but he was as exacting and as cruel, and as unable to express his devotion except by cruelty.

In the mechanism of the state organism these men are as necessary as wolves in the organism of nature. And they are always to be found in every government; they always make their appearance and hold their own, incongruous as their presence and their close relations with the head of the state may appear. It is only on the theory of this necessity that one can explain the fact that a man so cruel—capable of pulling out grenadiers' moustaches with his own hand—though unable, from the weakness of his nerves, to face danger, so uncultured, so boorish as Araktcheev, was able to retain such influence with a sovereign of chivalrous tenderness and nobility of character like Alexander.

Balashov found Davoust sitting on a tub in a barn adjoining a peasant's hut. He was occupied in writing, auditing accounts. An adjutant was standing beside him. Better quarters could have been found, but Marshal Davoust was one of these people who purposely put themselves into the most dismal conditions of life in order to have a right to be dismal. For the same reason they always persist in being busy and in a hurry.

"How could one be thinking of the bright side of life when, as you see, I am sitting on a tub in a dirty barn, hard at work?" was what his face expressed.

The great desire and delight of such people on meeting others enjoying life is to throw their own gloomy, dogged activity into their faces. Davoust gave himself that satisfaction when Balashov was brought in. He appeared even more deeply engrossed in his work when the Russian

general entered, and glancing through his spectacles at the face of Balashov, who looked cheerful from the brightness of the morning and his
talk with Murat, he did not get up, did not stir even, but scowled more
than before, and grinned malignantly.

Observing the disagreeable impression made on Balashov by this reception, Davoust raised his head, and asked him frigidly what he wanted.

Assuming that such a reception could only be due to Davoust's being
unaware that he was a general on the staff of Alexander, and his representative indeed before Napoleon, Balashov hastened to inform him of
his rank and his mission. But, contrary to his expectations, Davoust became even surlier and ruder on hearing Balashov's words.

"Where is your despatch?" he said. "Give it to me. I will send it to
the Emperor."

Balashov said that he was under orders to hand the document to the
Emperor in person.

"The commands of your Emperor are obeyed in your army; but here,"
said Davoust, "you must do what you are told."

And, as though to make the Russian general still more sensible of his
dependence on brute force, Davoust sent the adjutant for the officer on
duty.

Balashov took out the packet that contained the Tsar's letter, and laid
it on the table (a table consisting of a door laid across two tubs with the
hinges still hanging on it). Davoust took the packet and read the address on it.

"You are perfectly at liberty to show me respect or not, as you
please," said Balashov. "But, permit me to observe that I have the
honour to serve as a general on the staff of his majesty . . ."

Davoust glanced at him without a word, and plainly derived satisfaction from signs of emotion and confusion on Balashov's face.

"You will be shown what is fitting," he said, and putting the envelope
in his pocket he walked out of the barn.

A minute later an adjutant of the marshal's, Monsieur de Castre, came
in and conducted Balashov to the quarters that had been assigned him.

He dined that day in the barn with the marshal, sitting down to the
door laid across the tubs.

Next day Davoust went out early in the morning, but before starting
he sent for Balashov, and told him peremptorily that he begged him to
remain there, to move on with the baggage-wagons should the command be given to do so, and to have no conversation with any one but
Monsieur de Castre.

After four days spent in solitude and boredom, with a continual sense
of dependence and insignificance, particularly galling after the position
of power which he had hitherto occupied, after several marches with the
marshal's baggage and the French troops, who were in possession of the
whole district, Balashov was brought back to Vilna, now occupied by the
French, and re-entered the town by the very gate by which he had left it
four days earlier.

Next day the Emperor's gentleman-in-waiting, Count de Turenne, came to Balashov with a message that it was the Emperor Napoleon's pleasure to grant him an audience.

Four days before sentinels of the Preobrazhensky regiment had been on guard before the very house to which Balashov was conducted. Now two French grenadiers were on duty before it, wearing fur caps and blue uniforms open over the breast, while an escort of hussars and Uhlans, and a brilliant suite of adjutants, pages, and generals were waiting for Napoleon to come out, forming a group round his saddle-horse at the steps and his Mameluke, Rustan. Napoleon received Balashov in the very house in Vilna from which Alexander had despatched him.

VI

THOUGH Balashov was accustomed to the pomp of courts, he was impressed by the splendour and luxury of Napoleon's court.

Count de Turenne led him into the great reception-room, where a number of generals, gentlemen-in-waiting, and Polish magnates were waiting to see the Emperor. Many of them Balashov had seen at the court of the Russian Emperor. Duroc told him that the Emperor Napoleon would receive the Russian general before going out for his ride.

After a delay of several moments, a gentleman-in-waiting came into the great reception-room, and bowing courteously to Balashov, invited him to follow him.

Balashov went into the little reception-room, from which one door led to the study, the room where he had received the Russian Emperor's last charges before setting off. Balashov stood for a couple of minutes waiting. Hurried steps were audible through the door. Both halves of the door were swiftly thrown open, and in the complete stillness that followed other firm and resolute steps could be heard from the study: it was Napoleon. He had only just finished dressing for his ride. He was wearing a blue uniform, open over a white waistcoat, that came low down over his round belly, riding-boots, and white doeskin breeches, fitting tightly over his fat, short legs. His short hair had evidently just been brushed, but one lock hung down in the middle of his broad forehead. His plump, white neck stood out in sharp contrast to the black collar of his uniform; he smelt of eau-de-cologne. His still young-looking, full face, with its prominent chin, wore an expression of imperial graciousness and majestically condescending welcome.

He walked out with a quivering strut, his head thrown a little back. His whole stout, short figure, with his broad, fat shoulders and his prominent stomach and chest, had that imposing air of dignity common in men of forty who live in comfort. It was evident, too, that he happened that day to be in a particularly good humour.

He nodded in acknowledgment of Balashov's low and respectful bow, and going up to him, began to talk at once like a man who values every minute of his time, and will not deign to preface what he is going to say, as he is sure of always speaking well and saying the right thing.

"Good-day, general!" said he. "I have received the Emperor Alexander's letter that you brought, and I am very glad to see you." He glanced at Balashov's face with his large eyes, and immediately looked past him. It was obvious that he took no interest in Balashov's personality. It was plain that only what was passing in *his* soul had for him any interest. All that was outside him had no significance for him, because everything in the world depended, as he fancied, on his will.

"I do not, and did not, desire war," he said, "but you have forced me to it. Even *now*" (he threw emphasis on the word) "I am ready to receive any explanations you can give me." And he began briefly and clearly explaining the grounds of his displeasure with the Russian government.

Judging from the studiously composed and amicable tone of the French Emperor, Balashov was thoroughly persuaded that he was desirous of peace, and intended to enter into negotiations.

"Sire! The Emperor, my sovereign," Balashov began, meaning to utter the speech he had prepared long before as soon as Napoleon had finished speaking, and looked inquiringly at him. But the look the Emperor turned upon him disconcerted him. "You are embarrassed; recover yourself," Napoleon seemed to say, as with a hardly perceptible smile he scanned Balashov's sword and uniform. Balashov regained his composure, and began to speak. He said that the Emperor Alexander did not regard Kurakin's asking for his passport a sufficient cause for war; that Kurakin had acted on his own initiative without the Tsar's consent; that the Tsar did not desire war, and that he had no relations with England.

"Not *as yet*," Napoleon put in, and as though afraid to abandon himself to his feelings, he frowned and nodded slightly as a sign to Balashov that he might continue.

After saying all he had been instructed to say, Balashov wound up by saying that the Emperor Alexander was desirous of peace, but that he would not enter into negotiations except upon condition that . . . At that point Balashov hesitated; he recollected words the Emperor Alexander had not written in his letter, but had insisted on inserting in the rescript to Saltykov, and had commanded Balashov to repeat to Napoleon. Balashov remembered those words: "As long as a single enemy under arms remains on Russian soil," but some complicated feeling checked his utterance of them. He could not utter those words, though he tried to do so. He stammered, and said: "On condition the French troops retreat beyond the Niemen."

Napoleon observed Balashov's embarrassment in the utterance of those last words: his face quivered, and the calf of his left leg began twitching rhythmically. Not moving from where he stood, he began speaking in a louder and more hurried voice than before. During the speech that followed Balashov could not help staring at the twitching of Napoleon's left leg, which grew more marked as his voice grew louder.

"I am no less desirous of peace than the Emperor Alexander," he began. "Haven't I been doing everything for the last eighteen months to obtain it? For eighteen months I have been waiting for an explanation, but before opening negotiations, what is it that's required of me?" he said, frowning and making a vigorous gesticulation with his fat, little white hand.

"The withdrawal of the forces beyond the Niemen, sire," said Balashov.

"Beyond the Niemen?" repeated Napoleon. "So now you want me to retreat beyond the Niemen—only beyond the Niemen?" repeated Napoleon, looking straight at Balashov.

Balashov bowed his head respectfully.

Four months before he had been asked to withdraw from Pomerania; now withdrawal beyond the Niemen was all that was required. Napoleon turned quickly away, and began walking up and down the room.

"You say that I am required to withdraw beyond the Niemen before opening negotiations; but two months ago I was required in the same way to withdraw beyond the Oder and the Vistula, and in spite of that you agree to enter into negotiations."

He strode in silence from one corner of the room to the other and stopped again, facing Balashov. Balashov noticed that his left leg was twitching more rapidly than ever, and his face looked as though petrified in its stern expression. Napoleon was aware of this twitching. "The vibration of my left calf is a great sign with me," he said in later days.

"Such demands as to retire beyond the Oder and the Vistula may be made to a prince of Baden, but not to me," Napoleon almost screamed, quite to his own surprise. "If you were to give me Petersburg and Moscow I wouldn't accept such conditions. You say: I began the war. But who was the first to join his army? The Emperor Alexander, and not I. And you offer me negotiations when I have spent millions, when you are in alliance with England, and when your position is weak—you offer me negotiations! What is the object of your alliance with England? What has it given you?" he asked hurriedly. The motive of his words was obviously now not to enlarge on the benefits of peace and to consider its possibility, but simply to prove his own rectitude, and his own power, and point out the duplicity and the errors of Alexander.

He had plainly intended in entering on this conversation to point out the advantages of his own position, and to signify that in spite of them he would entertain the proposal of negotiations. But he had begun talking, and the more he talked the less able was he to control the tenor of his words.

The whole gist of his words now was obviously to glorify himself and to insult Alexander, precisely what he had least intended doing at the beginning of the interview.

"I am told you have concluded a peace with the Turks?"

Balashov bent his head affirmatively. "Peace has been concluded . . ." he began. But Napoleon did not allow him to speak. He clearly did not wish any one to speak but himself, and he went on with the unrestrained volubility and irritability to which people spoilt by success are so prone. "Yes, I know you have made peace with the Turks without gaining Moldavia and Wallachia. I would have given your Emperor those provinces just as I gave him Finland. Yes," he went on, "I promised, and would have given the Emperor Alexander Moldavia and Wallachia, but now he will not possess those fair provinces. He might have united them to his empire, however, and he would have enlarged the frontiers of Russia from the Gulf of Bothnia to the mouth of the Danube. Catherine the Great could have done no more," Napoleon declared, growing hotter and hotter as he walked up and down the room, and repeated to Balashov almost the words he had used to Alexander himself at Tilsit. "All that he would have owed to my friendship. Ah, what a fine reign! what a fine reign *might have been* that of the Emperor Alexander. Oh, what a grand reign," he repeated several times. He stopped, took a gold snuffbox out of his pocket, and greedily put it to his nose.

He turned a commiserating glance on Balashov, and as soon as he would have made some observation, he hurriedly interrupted him again.

"What could he desire and look for that he would not have gained from my friendship? . . ." said Napoleon, shrugging his shoulders with an air of perplexity. "No, he has thought better to surround himself with my enemies. And with whom?" he went on. "He has gathered round him the Steins, the Armfeldts, the Bennigsens, the Wintzengerodes. Stein is a traitor, driven out of his own country; Armfeldt an intriguing debauchee; Wintzengerode a renegade French subject; Bennigsen is, indeed, rather more of a soldier than the rest, but still he's incompetent; he could do nothing in 1807, and I should have thought he must recall painful memories to the Emperor Alexander. . . . Even supposing he might make use of them if they were competent," Napoleon went on, his words hardly able to keep pace with the rush of ideas that proved to him his right or his might (which to his mind meant the same), "but they are not even that! They are no use for war or for peace! Barclay, I'm told, is more capable than all of them, but I shouldn't say so, judging from his first manœuvres. And what are they doing, what are all these courtiers doing? Pfuhl is making propositions, Armfeldt is quarrelling, Bennigsen is considering, while Barclay, who has been sent for to act, can come to no decision, and is wasting time and doing nothing. Bagration is the only one that is a real general. He is stupid, but he has experience, judgment, and determination. . . . And what part does your young Emperor play in this unseemly crowd? They compromise him and throw upon him the responsibility of all that happens. A sovereign ought not to be with the army except when he is a general," he said, obviously uttering these words as a direct challenge to the Tsar. Napoleon knew how greatly Alexander desired to be a great general. "It's a week now since the campaign commenced, and you haven't even succeeded in defending Vilna. You have been divided in two and driven out of the Polish provinces. Your army is discontented . . ."

"On the contrary, your majesty," said Balashov, who scarcely had time to recollect what had been said to him, and had difficulty in following these verbal fireworks, "the troops are burning with eagerness . . ."

"I know all that," Napoleon cut him short; "I know all that, and I know the number of your battalions as exactly as I know my own. You have not two hundred thousand troops, while I have three times as many. I give you my word of honour," said Napoleon, forgetting that his word of honour could carry no weight—"my word of honour that I have five hundred and thirty thousand men this side of the Vistula. The Turks will be no help to you; they are good for nothing, and have proved it by making peace with you. As for the Swedes, it's their destiny to be governed by mad kings. Their king was mad. They changed him for another, Bernadotte, who promptly went mad; for no one not a madman could, being a Swede, ally himself with Russia."

Napoleon laughed malignantly, and again put his snuff-box to his nose.

To each of Napoleon's phrases Balashov had a reply ready, and tried to utter it. He was continually making gestures indicative of a desire to speak, but Napoleon always interrupted him. To his remarks on the insanity of the Swedes, Balashov would have replied that Sweden was as good as an island with Russia to back her. But Napoleon shouted angrily to drown his voice. Napoleon was in that state of exasperation when a man wants to go on talking and talking simply to prove to himself that he is right. Balashov began to feel uncomfortable. As an envoy, he was anxious to keep up his dignity, and felt it essential to make some reply. But as a man he felt numb, repelled by the uncontrolled, irrational fury to which Napoleon abandoned himself. He knew that nothing Napoleon might say now had any significance and believed that he would himself on regaining his composure be ashamed of his words. Balashov remained standing, looking with downcast eyes at Napoleon's fat legs as they moved to and fro. He tried to avoid his eyes.

"And what are your allies to me?" said Napoleon. "I have allies too— the Poles. There are eighty thousand of them and they fight like lions. And there will be two hundred thousand."

He was probably still more exasperated at having told this obvious falsehood and at Balashov's standing mutely before him in that pose of resignation to his fate. He turned sharply round and going right up to Balashov, gesticulating rapidly and vigorously with his white hands close to his face, he almost shouted: "Let me tell you, if you stir Russia up against me, let me tell you, I'll wipe her off the map of Europe," he said, his face pale and distorted with anger, as he smote one little hand vigorously against the other. "Yes, I'll thrust you beyond the Dwina, beyond the Dnieper, and I'll restore the frontier that Europe was criminal and blind to let you overstep. Yes, that's what's in store for you, that's what you will gain by alienating me," he said, and he walked in silence several times up and down the room, his thick shoulders twitching. He put the snuff-box in his waistcoat pocket, pulled it out again, held it several times to his nose, and stood still facing Balashov. He paused, looked sarcastically straight into Balashov's face and said in a low voice: "And yet what a fine reign your master *might have had*."

Balashov, feeling it incumbent upon him to reply, said Russia did not look at things in such a gloomy light. Napoleon was silent, still looking ironically at him and obviously not listening to him. Balashov said that in Russia the best results were hoped for from the war. Napoleon nodded condescendingly, as though to say, "I know it's your duty to say that, but you don't believe in it yourself; you are convinced by me." Towards the end of Balashov's speech, Napoleon pulled out his snuff-box again, took a sniff from it and tapped twice with his foot on the ground as a signal. The door opened, a gentleman-in-waiting, threading his way in respectfully, handed the Emperor his hat and gloves, another handed him a pocket-handkerchief. Napoleon, without bestowing a glance upon them, turned to Balashov.

"Assure the Emperor Alexander from me," he said, taking his hat, "that I am devoted to him as before; I know him thoroughly, and I prize very highly his noble qualities. I detain you no longer, general; you shall receive my letter to the Emperor." And Napoleon walked rapidly to the door. There was a general stampede from the great reception-room down the staircase.

VII

AFTER all Napoleon had said to him, after those outbursts of wrath, and after the last frigidly uttered words, "I will not detain you, general; you shall receive my letter," Balashov felt certain that Napoleon would not care to see him again, would avoid indeed seeing again the envoy who had been treated by him with contumely, and had been the eyewitness of his undignified outburst of fury. But to his surprise Balashov received through Duroc an invitation to dine that day at the Emperor's table.

There were present at dinner, Bessières, Caulaincourt, and Berthier.

Napoleon met Balashov with a good-humoured and friendly air. He had not the slightest appearance of embarrassment or regret for his outbreak in the morning. On the contrary he seemed trying to encourage Balashov. It was evident that it had long been Napoleon's conviction that no possibility existed of his making mistakes. To his mind all he did was good, not because it was in harmony with any preconceived notion of good or bad, but simply because it was *he* who did it.

The Emperor was in excellent spirits after his ride about Vilna, greeted and followed with acclamations by crowds of the inhabitants. From every window in the streets through which he had passed draperies and flags with his monogram had been hanging, and Polish ladies had been waving handkerchiefs to welcome him.

At dinner he sat Balashov beside him, and addressed him affably. He addressed him indeed as though he regarded Balashov as one of his own courtiers, as one of the people, who would sympathise with his plans and be sure to rejoice at his successes. He talked, among other things, of Moscow, and began asking Balashov questions about the ancient Russian capital, not simply as a traveller of inquiring mind asks about a new place he intends to visit, but apparently with the conviction that Balashov as a Russian must be flattered at his interest in it.

"How many inhabitants are there in Moscow, how many horses? Is it true that Moscow is called the holy city? How many churches are there in Moscow?" he asked.

And when he was told there were over two hundred churches, he said: "Why is there such a great number of churches?"

"The Russians are very religious," replied Balashov.

"A great number, however, of monasteries and churches is always a sign of the backwardness of a people," said Napoleon, looking at Caulaincourt for appreciation of this remark.

Balashov ventured respectfully to differ from the opinion of the French Emperor.

"Every country has its customs," he observed.

"But there's nothing like that anywhere else in Europe," said Napoleon.

"I beg your majesty's pardon," said Balashov; "besides Russia, there is Spain, where there is also a great number of churches and monasteries."

This reply of Balashov's, which suggested a covert allusion to the recent discomfiture of the French in Spain, was highly appreciated when Balashov repeated it at the court of the Emperor Alexander, though at the time at Napoleon's dinner-table it was very little appreciated and passed indeed unnoticed.

From the indifferent and perplexed faces of the marshals present it was obvious that they were puzzled to discover wherein lay the point of the retort, suggested by Balashov's intonation. "If there were a point, we fail to catch it, or the remark was perhaps really pointless," their expression seemed to say. So little effect had this retort that Napoleon indeed certainly saw nothing in it; and he naïvely asked Balashov through what towns the direct road from Vilna to Moscow passed. Balashov, who had been all dinner-time on his guard, replied that as, according to the proverb, every road leads to Rome, every road leads to Moscow; that there were very many roads, and among them was the road to *Poltava*, the one selected by Charles XII. Balashov could not help flushing with delight at the felicity of this reply. Balashov had hardly uttered the last word "Poltava" when Caulaincourt began talking of the badness of the road from Petersburg to Moscow and his own Petersburg reminiscences.

After dinner they went to drink coffee in Napoleon's study, which had four days before been the study of the Emperor Alexander. Napoleon sat down, stirring his coffee in a Sèvres cup, and motioned Balashov to a seat beside him.

There is a well-known after-dinner mood which is more potent than any rational consideration in making a man satisfied with himself and disposed to regard every one as a friend. Napoleon was under the influence of this mood. He fancied himself surrounded by persons who adored him. He felt no doubt that Balashov too after his dinner was his friend and his worshipper. Napoleon addressed him with an amicable and rather ironical smile.

"This is the very room, I am told, in which the Emperor Alexander used to sit. Strange, isn't it, general?" he said, obviously without the slightest misgiving that this remark could be other than agreeable to the Russian, since it afforded a proof of his, Napoleon's, superiority over Alexander.

Balashov could make no reply to this, and he bowed in silence.

"Yes, four days ago, Wintzengerode and Stein were deliberating in this very room," Napoleon continued, with the same confident and ironical smile. "What I can't understand," he said, "is the Emperor Alexander's gathering round him all my personal enemies. That I do not understand. Didn't he consider that I might do the same?" he asked Balashov; and obviously the question brought him back to a reminiscence of the morning's anger, which was still fresh in him. "And let him know that I will do so," Napoleon said, getting up and pushing away his cup. "I'll drive all his kith and kin out of Germany—the Würtembergs and Badens and Weimars . . . Yes, I'll drive them out. Let him get a refuge ready for them in Russia."

Balashov bowed his head, with an air that indicated that he would be glad to withdraw, and was simply listening because he had no alternative but to listen to what was said to him. Napoleon did not notice this expression. He was addressing Balashov now, not as the envoy of his enemy, but as a man now quite devoted to him and certain to rejoice at the humiliation of his former master.

"And why has the Emperor Alexander taken the command of his troops? What's that for? War is my profession, but his work is to reign and not to command armies. What has induced him to take such a responsibility on himself?"

Napoleon again took his snuff-box, walked several times in silence up and down the room, and all at once surprised Balashov by coming close up to him. And with a faint smile, as confidently, rapidly, and swiftly, as though he were doing something that Balashov could not but regard as an honour and a pleasure, he put his hand up to the face of the Russian general of forty, and gave him a little pinch on the ear with a smile on his lips.

To have the ear pulled by the Emperor was regarded as the greatest honour and mark of favour at the French court.

"Well, you say nothing, admirer and courtier of the Emperor Alexander," he said, as though it were comic that there should be in his presence a courtier and worshipper of any man other than him, Napoleon. "Are the horses ready for the general?" he added, with a slight nod in acknowledgment of Balashov's bow. "Give him mine; he has *a long way to go.* . . ."

The letter taken back by Balashov was Napoleon's last letter to Alexander. Every detail of the conversation was transmitted to the Russian Emperor, and the war began.

VIII

AFTER his interview with Pierre in Moscow, Prince Andrey went away to Petersburg, telling his family that he had business there. In reality his object was to meet Anatole Kuragin there. He thought it necessary to meet him, but on inquiring for him when he reached Petersburg, he found he was no longer there. Pierre had let his brother-in-law know that Prince Andrey was on his track. Anatole Kuragin had promptly obtained a commission from the minister of war, and had gone to join the army in Moldavia. While in Petersburg Prince Andrey met Kutuzov, his old general, who was always friendly to him, and Kutuzov proposed that he should accompany him to Moldavia, where the old general was being sent to take command of the army. Prince Andrey received an appointment on the staff of the commander, and went to Turkey.

Prince Andrey did not think it proper to write to Kuragin to challenge him to a duel. He thought that a challenge coming from him, without any new pretext for a duel, would be compromising for the young Countess Rostov; and therefore he was seeking to encounter Kuragin in person in order to pick a quarrel with him that would serve as a pretext for a duel. But in the Turkish army too Prince Andrey failed to come across Kuragin. The latter had returned to Russia shortly after Prince Andrey reached the Turkish army. In a new country, amid new surroundings, Prince Andrey found life easier to bear. After his betrothed's betrayal of him, which he felt the more keenly, the more studiously he strove to conceal its effect on him from others, he found it hard to bear the conditions of life in which he had been happy, and felt still more irksome the freedom and independence he had once prized so highly. He could not now think the thoughts that had come to him for the first time on the field of Austerlitz, that he had loved to develop with Pierre, and that had enriched his solitude at Bogutcharovo, and later on in Switzerland and in Rome. Now he dreaded indeed those ideas that had then opened to him boundless vistas of light. Now he was occupied only with the most practical interests lying close at hand, and in no way associated with those old ideals. He clutched at these new interests the more eagerly the more the old ideals were hidden from him. It was as though the infinite, fathomless arch of heaven that had once stood over him had been suddenly transformed into a low, limited vault weighing upon him, with everything in it clear, but nothing eternal and mysterious.

Of the pursuits that presented themselves, military service was the simplest and the most familiar to him. He performed the duties of a general on duty on Kutuzov's staff with zeal and perseverance, surprising Kutuzov by his eagerness for work and his conscientiousness. When he missed Kuragin in Turkey, Prince Andrey did not feel it necessary to gallop back to Russia in search of him. Yet in spite of all his contempt for Kuragin, in spite of all the arguments by which he sought to persuade himself that Kuragin was not worth his stooping to quarrel with him, he knew that whatever length of time might elapse, when he did meet him, he would be unable to help challenging him, as a starving man cannot help rushing upon food. And the consciousness that the insult was not yet avenged, that his wrath had not been expended, but was still stored up in his heart, poisoned the artificial composure, which Prince Andrey succeeded in obtaining in Turkey in the guise of studiously busy and somewhat ambitious and vain energy.

In 1812, when the news of the war with Napoleon reached Bucharest (where Kutuzov had been fourteen months, spending days and nights together with his Wallachian mistress), Prince Andrey asked to be transferred to the western army. Kutuzov, who was by now sick of Bolkonsky's energy, and felt it a standing reproach to his sloth, was very ready to let him go, and gave him a commission for Barclay de Tolly.

Before joining the army of the west, which was in May encamped at Drissa, Prince Andrey went to Bleak Hills, which was directly in his road, only three versts from the Smolensk high-road. The last three years of Prince Andrey's life had been so full of vicissitudes, he had passed through such changes of thought and feeling, and seen such varied life (he had travelled both in the east and the west), that it struck him as strange and amazing to find at Bleak Hills life going on in precisely the same routine as ever. He rode up the avenue to the stone gates of the house, feeling as though it were the enchanted, sleeping castle. The same sedateness, the same cleanliness, the same silence reigned in the house; there was the same furniture, the same walls, the same sounds, the same smell, and the same timid faces, only a little older. Princess Marya was just the same timid, plain girl, no longer in her first youth, wasting the best years of her life in continual dread and suffering, and getting no benefit or happiness out of her existence. Mademoiselle Bourienne was just the same self-satisfied, coquettish girl, enjoying every moment of her life, and filled with the most joyous hopes for the future. She seemed only to have gained boldness, so Prince Andrey thought. The tutor he had brought back from Switzerland, Dessalle, was wearing a coat of Russian cut, and talked broken Russian to the servants, but he was just the same narrow-minded, cultivated, conscientious, pedantic preceptor. The only physical change apparent in the old prince was the loss of a tooth, that left a gap at the side of his mouth. In character he was the same as ever, only showing even more irritability and scepticism as to everything that happened in the world. Nikolushka was the only one who had changed: he had grown taller, and rosy, and had curly dark hair. When he was merry and laughing, he unconsciously lifted the upper lip of his pretty little mouth, just as his dead mother, the little princess, used to do. He was the only one not in bondage to the law of sameness that reigned in that spellbound sleeping castle. But though externally all was exactly as of old, the inner relations of all the persons concerned had changed since Prince Andrey had seen them last. The household was split up into two hostile camps, which held aloof from one another, and only now came together in his presence, abandoning their ordinary habits on his account. To one camp belonged the old prince, Mademoiselle Bourienne, and the architect; to the other—Princess Marya, Dessalle, Nikolushka, and all the nurses.

During his stay at Bleak Hills all the family dined together, but every one was ill at ease, and Prince Andrey felt that he was being treated as a guest for whom an exception was being made, and that his presence made all of them feel awkward. The first day Prince Andrey could not help being aware of this at dinner, and sat in silence. The old prince noticed his unnatural dumbness, and he, too, preserved a sullen silence, and immediately after dinner withdrew to his own room. Later in the evening when Prince Andrey went in to him, and began telling him about the campaign of the young Prince Kamensky to try and rouse him, the old prince, to his surprise, began talking about Princess Marya, grumbling at her superstitiousness, and her dislike of Mademoiselle Bourienne, who was, he said, the only person really attached to him.

The old prince declared that it was all Princess Marya's doing if he were ill; that she plagued and worried him on purpose, and that she was spoiling little Prince Nikolay by the way she petted him, and the silly tales she told him. The old prince knew very well that he tormented his daughter, and that her life was a very hard one. But he knew, too, that he could not help tormenting her, and considered that she deserved it. "Why is it Andrey, who sees it, says nothing about his sister?" the old prince wondered. "Why, does he suppose I'm a scoundrel or an old fool to be alienated from my daughter and friendly with this Frenchwoman for no good reason? He doesn't understand, and so I must explain it to him; he must hear what I have to say about it," thought the old prince, and so he began to explain the reason why he could not put up with his daughter's unreasonable character.

"If you ask me," said Prince Andrey, not looking at his father (it was the first time in his life that he had blamed his father), "I did not wish to speak of it—but, if you ask me, I'll tell you my opinion frankly in regard to the whole matter. If there is any misunderstanding and estrangement between you and Masha, I can't blame her for it—I know how she loves and respects you. If you ask me," Prince Andrey continued, losing his temper, as he very readily did in these latter days, "I can only say one thing; if there are misunderstandings, the cause of them is that worthless woman, who is not fit to be my sister's companion."

The old man stared for a moment at his son, and a forced smile revealed the loss of a tooth, to which Prince Andrey could not get accustomed, in his face.

"What companion, my dear fellow? Eh! So you've talked it over already! Eh?"

"Father, I had no wish to judge you," said Prince Andrey, in a hard and spiteful tone, "but you have provoked me, and I have said, and shall always say, that Marie is not to blame, but the people to blame—the person to blame—is that Frenchwoman . . ."

"Ah, he has passed judgment! . . . he has passed judgment!" said the old man, in a low voice, and Prince Andrey fancied, with embarrassment. But immediately after he leapt up and screamed, "Go away, go away! Let me never set eyes on you again! . . ."

Prince Andrey would have set off at once, but Princess Marya begged him to stay one day more. During that day Prince Andrey did not see his father, who never left his room, and admitted no one to see him but Mademoiselle Bourienne and Tihon, from which he inquired several times whether his son had gone. The following day before starting, Prince Andrey went to the part of the house where his son was to be found. The sturdy little boy, with curls like his mother's, sat on his knee. Prince Andrey began telling him the story of Bluebeard, but he sank into dreamy meditation before he had finished the story. He was not thinking of the pretty boy, his child, even while he held him on his knee; he was thinking of himself. He sought and was horrified not to find in himself either remorse for having provoked his father's anger, or regret at leaving home (for the first time in his life) on bad terms with him. What meant still more to him was that he could not detect in himself a trace of the tender affection he had once felt for his boy, and had hoped to revive in his heart, when he petted the child and put him on his knee.

"Come, tell me the rest," said the boy. Prince Andrey took him off his knee without answering, and went out of the room.

As soon as Prince Andrey gave up his daily pursuits, especially to return to the old surroundings in which he had been when he was happy, weariness of life seized upon him as intensely as ever, and he made haste to escape from these memories, and to find some work to do as quickly as possible.

"Are you really going, Andrey?" his sister said to him.

"Thank God that I can go," said Prince Andrey. "I am very sorry you can't too."

"What makes you say that?" said Princess Marya. "How can you say that when you are going to this awful war, and he is so old? Mademoiselle Bourienne told me he keeps asking about you. . . ." As soon as she spoke of that, her lips quivered, and tears began to fall. Prince Andrey turned away and began walking up and down the room.

"Ah, my God! my God!" he said. "And to think what and who—what scum can be the cause of misery to people!" he said with a malignance that terrified Princess Marya.

She felt that when he uttered the word "scum," he was thinking not only of Mademoiselle Bourienne, who was the cause of her misery, but also of the man who had ruined his own happiness. "Andrey, one thing I beg, I beseech of you," she said, touching his elbow and looking at him with eyes that shone through her tears. "I understand you." (Princess Marya dropped her eyes.) "Don't imagine that sorrow is the work of men. Men are His instruments." She glanced upwards a little above Prince Andrey's head with the confident, accustomed glance with which one looks towards a familiar portrait. "Sorrow is sent by Him, and not by men. Men are the instrument of His will, they are not to blame. If it seems to you that some one has wronged you—forget it, and forgive. We have no right to punish. And you will know the happiness of forgiveness."

"If I were a woman, I would, Marie. That's a woman's virtue. But a man must not, and cannot, forgive and forget," he said, and though till that minute he had not been thinking of Kuragin, all his unsatisfied revenge rose up again in his heart. "If Marie is beginning to persuade me to forgive, it means that I ought long ago to have punished him," he thought.

And making no further reply to Princess Marya, he began dreaming now of the happy moment of satisfied hate when he would meet Kuragin. He knew he was with the army.

Princess Marya besought her brother to stay another day, telling him how wretched her father would be, she knew, if Andrey went away without being reconciled to him. But Prince Andrey answered that he would probably soon be back from the army, that he would certainly write to his father, and that their quarrel would only be more embittered by his staying longer now. "Remember that misfortunes come from God, and that men are never to blame," were the last words he heard from his sister, as he said good-bye to her.

"So it must be so!" thought Prince Andrey, as he drove out of the avenue. "She, poor innocent creature, is left to be victimised by an old man, who has outlived his wits. The old man feels he is wrong, but he can't help himself. My boy is growing up and enjoying life in which he will be deceived or deceiving like every one else. I am going to the army—what for? I don't know myself; and I want to meet that man whom I despise, so as to give him a chance to kill me and sneer at me!" All the conditions of life had been the same before, but before they had all seemed to him coherent, and now they had all fallen apart. Life seemed to Prince Andrey a series of senseless phenomena following one another without any connection.

IX

PRINCE ANDREY reached the headquarters of the army at the end of June. The first army, with which the Tsar was, was stationed in a fortified camp at Drissa. The second army was retreating, striving to effect a junction with the first army, from which—so it was said—it had been cut off by immense forces of the French. Every one was dissatisfied with the general course of events in the Russian army. But no one even dreamed of any danger of the Russian provinces being invaded, no one imagined the war could extend beyond the frontiers of the western Polish provinces.

Prince Andrey found Barclay de Tolly, to whom he was sent, on the bank of the Drissa. Since there was not one large village nor dwelling-place in the neighbourhood of the camp, the immense multitude of generals and courtiers accompanying the army were distributed about the neighbourhood for ten versts round in the best houses of the villages on both sides of the river. Barclay de Tolly was staying four versts away from the Tsar. He gave Bolkonsky a dry and frigid reception, and said in his German accent that he would mention him to the Tsar so that a definite appointment might be given him, and that meanwhile he begged him to remain on his staff. Anatole Kuragin, whom Prince Andrey had expected to find in the army, was not here. He was in Petersburg, and Bolkonsky was glad to hear it. He was absorbed in the interest of being at the centre of the immense war that was in progress, and he was relieved to be free for a time from the irritability produced in him by the idea of Kuragin. The first four days, during which he was not called upon to do anything, he spent in riding round the whole of the fortified camp, and by the aid of his experiences and his conversations with persons of greater experience, he tried to form a definite idea about it. But the question whether such a camp were of use at all or not remained an open one in his mind. He had already, from his own military experience, formed the conviction that in war the most deeply meditated plans are of no avail (as he had seen at Austerlitz), that everything depends on how unexpected actions of the enemy, actions that cannot possibly be foreseen, are met; that all depends on how, and by whom, the battle is led. In order to settle this last question to his own satisfaction, Prince Andrey took advantage of his position and his acquaintances to try to get an insight into the character of the persons and parties who had a hand in the organisation of the army. This was the general idea he gained of the position of affairs.

While the Tsar had been at Vilna, the army had been divided into three. The first army was under the command of Barclay de Tolly, the second under the command of Bagration, and the third under the command of Tormasov. The Tsar was with the first army, but not in the capacity of commander-in-chief. In the proclamations, it was announced that the Tsar would be with the army, but it was not announced that he would take the command. Moreover, there was in attendance on the Tsar personally not a commander-in-chief's staff, but the staff of the imperial headquarters. The chief officer of the imperial staff was General-Quartermaster Volkonsky, and it contained generals, aides-de-camp, diplomatic officials, and an immense number of foreigners, but it was not a military staff. The Tsar had also in attendance on him in no definite capacity, Araktcheev, the late minister of war; Count Bennigsen, by seniority the first of the generals; the Tsarevitch, Konstantin Pavlovitch; Count Rumyantsev, the chancellor; Stein, the former Prussian minister; Armfeldt, the Swedish general; Pfuhl, the chief organiser of the plan of the campaign; Paulucci, a Sardinian refugee, who had been made a general-adjutant; Woltzogen; and many others. Though those personages had no definite posts in the army, yet, from their position, they had influence, and often the commander of a corps, or even one of the commanders-in-chief, did not know in what capacity Bennigsen or the Tsarevitch or Araktcheev or Prince Volkonsky addressed some advice or inquiry to him, and could not tell whether some command in the form of advice came directly from the person who got it or through him from the Tsar, and whether he ought or ought not to obey it. But all this formed simply the external aspect of the situation; the inner import of the presence of the Tsar and all these great personages was, from a courtier's point of view (and in the presence of a monarch all men become courtiers), plain to all. All grasped the fact that though the Tsar was not formally assuming the position of commander-in-chief, he did, in fact, hold the supreme control of all the armies in his hands, and the persons about him were his councillors. Araktcheev was a trusty administrator, a stern upholder of discipline, and careful of the safety of the Tsar. Bennigsen was a landholder in the neighbourhood, and seemed to feel it his function to entertain the Tsar there; while he was in reality, too, a good general, useful as an adviser, and useful to have in readiness to replace Barclay at any time. The Tsarevitch was there because he thought fit to be. The former Prussian minister, Stein, was there because his advice might be useful, and the Emperor Alexander had a high opinion of his personal qualities. Armfeldt was a bitter enemy of Napoleon, and had self-confidence, which never failed to have influence with Alexander. Paulucci was there because he was bold and decided in his utterances. The generals on the staff were there because they were always where the Emperor was; and the last and principal figure, Pfuhl, was there because he had created a plan of warfare against Napoleon, and having made Alexander believe in the consistency of this plan, was now conducting the plan of the whole campaign. Pfuhl was accompanied by Woltzogen, who put Pfuhl's ideas into a more easily comprehensible form than could be done by Pfuhl himself, who was a rigid theorist, with an implicit faith in his own views, and an absolute contempt for everything else.

The above-mentioned were the most prominent personages about the Tsar, and among them the foreigners were in the ascendant, and were every day making new and startling suggestions with the audacity characteristic of men who are acting in a sphere not their own. But, besides those, there were many more persons of secondary importance, who were with the army because their principals were there.

In this vast, brilliant, haughty, and uneasy world, among all these conflicting voices, Prince Andrey detected the following sharply opposed parties and differences of opinion.

The first party consisted of Pfuhl and his followers; military theorists, who believe in a science of war, having its invariable laws—laws of oblique movements, out-flanking, etc. Pfuhl and his adherents demanded that the army should retreat into the heart of the country in accordance with the exact principles laid down by their theory of war, and in every departure from this theory they saw nothing but barbarism, ignorance, or evil intention. To this party belonged Woltzogen, Wintzengerode, and others—principally Germans.

The second party was in direct opposition to the first. As is always the case where there is one extreme opinion, representatives had come forward of the opposite extreme. This party had urged an advance from Vilna into Poland regardless of all previous plans. This party, while advocating bold action, consisted of the representatives of nationalism, which made them even more one-sided in their views. They were Russians: Bagration, Yermolov, who was just beginning to make his mark, and some others. Yermolov's well-known joke was much quoted at the time—a supposed petition to the Tsar for promotion to be a "German." The members of this party, recalling Suvorov, maintained that what was wanted was not reasoning and sticking pins into maps, but fighting, beating the enemy, preventing the enemy from getting into Russia, and keeping up the spirits of the army.

To the third party, in which the Tsar was disposed to place most confidence, belonged the courtiers, who tried to effect a compromise between the two contending sides. The members of this party—to which Araktcheev belonged—were mostly not military men, and they spoke and reasoned as men usually do who have no convictions, but wish to pass for having them. They admitted that a war with such a genius as Bonaparte (they called him Bonaparte again now) did undoubtedly call for the profoundest tactical considerations and thorough scientific knowledge, and that on that side Pfuhl was a genius. But, at the same time, they acknowledged that it could not be denied that theorists were often one-sided, and so one should not put implicit confidence in them, but should listen too to what Pfuhl's opponents urged, and also to the views of practical men who had experience, and should take a middle course. They advocated maintaining the camp at Drissa on Pfuhl's plan, but altering his disposition of the other two armies. Though by this course of action neither aim could be attained, this seemed to the party of compromise the best line to adopt.

Of the fourth section of opinions, the most prominent representative was the Grand Duke, and heir-apparent, who could not get over his rude awakening at Austerlitz. He had ridden out at the head of his guards in helmet and cuirass as though to a review, expecting gallantly to rout the French, and finding himself unexpectedly just in the line of the enemy's fire, had with difficulty escaped in the general disorder. The members of this party had at once the merit and the defect of sincerity in their convictions. They feared Napoleon; they saw his strength and their own weakness, and frankly admitted it. They said: "Nothing but a huge disgrace and ruin can come of the war! We have abandoned Vilna, and abandoned Vitebsk, and we are abandoning the Drissa too. The only sensible thing left for us to do is to conclude peace, and as soon as possible, before we have been driven out of Petersburg!"

This view was widely diffused in the higher military circles, and found adherents, too, in Petersburg—one of them being the chancellor Rumyantsev, who advocated peace on other political considerations.

A fifth section were the adherents of Barclay de Tolly, not so much from his qualities as a man, as a minister of war and commander-in-chief. "Whatever he may be," they always began, "he is an honest, practical man, and there is nobody better. Let him have sole responsibility, since war can never be prosecuted successfully under divided authority, and he will show what he can do, as he did in Finland. We owe it simply to Barclay that our army is strong and well organised, and has retreated, to the Drissa without disaster. If Barclay is replaced by Bennigsen now, everything will be lost; for Bennigsen has proved his incapacity already in 1807." Such was the line of argument of the fifth party.

The sixth party, the partisans of Bennigsen, maintained on the contrary that there was after all no one more capable and experienced than Bennigsen, and that whatever else were done they would have to come back to him. They maintained that the whole Russian retreat to Drissa had been an uninterrupted series of shameful disasters and blunders. "Let them blunder now if they will," they said; "the more blunders the better, at least it will teach them all the sooner that we can't go on like this. And we want none of your Barclays, but a man like Bennigsen, who showed what he was in 1807, so that Napoleon himself had to do him justice, and a man, too, is needed to whom all would readily intrust authority, and Bennigsen is the only such man."

The seventh class were persons such as are always found in courts, and especially in the courts of young sovereigns, and were particularly plentiful in the suite of Alexander—generals and adjutants, who were passionately devoted to the Tsar, not merely as an emperor, but sincerely and disinterestedly adored him as a man, as Rostov had adored him in 1805, and saw in him every virtue and good quality of humanity. These persons, while they were ecstatic over the modesty of the Tsar in declining the chief command of the army, deplored that excess of modesty, and desired and urged one thing only, that their adored Tsar, conquering his excessive diffidence, would openly proclaim that he put himself at the head of the army, would gather the staff of the commander-in-chief about him, and, consulting experienced theorists and practical men where necessary, would himself lead his forces, who would be excited to the highest pitch of enthusiasm by this step.

The eighth and largest group, numbering ninety-nine to every one of the others, consisted of people who were eager neither for peace nor for war, neither for offensive operations nor defensive camps, neither at Drissa nor anywhere else; who did not take the side of Barclay, nor of the Tsar, nor of Pfuhl, nor of Bennigsen, but cared only for the one thing most essential—their own greatest gain and enjoyment. In the troubled waters of those cross-currents of intrigue, eddying about the Tsar's headquarters, success could be attained in very many ways that would have been inconceivable at other times. One courtier, with the single-hearted motive of retaining a lucrative position, would agree to-day with Pfuhl, and to-morrow with his opponents, and the day after to-morrow would declare that he had no opinion on the subject in question, simply to avoid responsibility and to gratify the Tsar. Another, in the hope of bettering his position, would seek to attract the Tsar's attention by loudly-clamouring a suggestion hinted at by the Tsar on the previous day, by quarrelling noisily at the council, striking himself on the chest and challenging opponents to a duel to prove his readiness to sacrifice himself for the common good. A third simply took advantage of the absence of enemies between two councils to beg a grant from the

Single Assistance Fund for his faithful service, knowing there would be no time now for a refusal. A fourth took care to place himself where the Tsar might quite casually find him deeply engrossed in work. A fifth tried to reach the long-desired goal of his ambition—a dinner at the Tsar's table—by violently espousing one side or another and collecting more or less true and valid arguments in support of it.

All the members of this party were on the hunt after roubles, crosses, and promotions; and in that chase they simply followed the scent given them by the fluctuations of imperial favour. As soon as they saw the imperial weather-cock shifting to one quarter the whole swarm of these drones began buzzing away in that direction, making it more difficult for the Tsar to shift his course back again. In the uncertainty of the position, with the menace of serious danger, which gave a peculiarly intense character to everything, in this whirlpool of ambitions, of conflicting vanities, and views, and feelings, and different nationalities, this eighth and largest party, absorbed only in the pursuit of personal interests, greatly increased the complexity and confusion. Whatever question arose, the swarm of drones, still humming over the last subject, flew to the new one, and by their buzzing drowned and confused the voices of sincere disputants.

At the time when Prince Andrey reached the army yet another—a ninth party—was being formed out of all the rest, and was just making its voice heard. It consisted of sensible men of age and political experience, sharing none of the conflicting opinions, and able to take a general view of all that was being done at headquarters, and to consider means for escaping from the vagueness, uncertainty, confusion, and feebleness.

The members of this party thought and said that the whole evil was primarily due to the presence of the Tsar with his military court in the army; that it brought into the army that indefinite, conditional, and fluctuating uncertainty of relations which is in place in a court, but mischievous in an army; that it was for the Tsar to govern and not to lead his troops; that the only escape from the position was the departure of the Tsar and his court from the army; that the simple presence of the Tsar paralysed fifty thousand troops, which must be retained to secure his personal safety; that the worst commander-in-chief, acting independently, would be better than the best commander-in-chief with his hands tied by the presence and authority of the Tsar.

While Prince Andrey was staying, with nothing to do, at Drissa, Sishkov, the secretary of state, one of the leading representatives of this last group, wrote to the Tsar a letter to which Balashov and Araktcheev agreed to add their signatures. In this letter he took advantage of the Tsar's permitting him to offer his opinion on the general question, and respectfully suggested the sovereign's leaving the army, urging as a pretext for his doing so the absolute necessity of his presence to rouse public feeling in the capital.

To appeal to the people, and to rouse them in defence of their fatherland, was represented as urgently necessary to the Tsar, and was accepted by him as a sufficient reason for leaving. The outburst of patriot-ism that followed that appeal (so far indeed as it can be said to have been produced by the Tsar's visit to Moscow) was the principal cause of the subsequent triumph of Russia.

X

THIS letter had not yet been given to the Tsar, when Barclay, at dinner one day, informed Bolkonsky that his majesty would be graciously pleased to see Prince Andrey in person, to ask him some questions about Turkey, and that Prince Andrey was to present himself at Bennigsen's quarters at six o'clock in the evening.

That day news had reached the Tsar's quarters of a fresh advance on Napoleon's part that might be regarded as menacing the army—news that turned out in the sequel to be false. And that morning Colonel Michaud had accompanied the Tsar on a tour of inspection about the Drissa fortifications; and had tried to convince the Tsar that the forti-fied camp, constructed on Pfuhl's theory, and hitherto regarded as the *chef d'œuvre* of tactical science, destined to overthrow Napoleon—that that camp was a senseless absurdity that would lead to the destruction of the Russian army.

Prince Andrey arrived at Bennigsen's quarters, a small manor-house on the very bank of the river. Neither Bennigsen nor the Tsar was there; but Tchernishev, the Tsar's aid-de-camp, received Bolkonsky, and in-formed him that the Tsar had set off with General Bennigsen and Marchese Paulucci to make his second inspection that day of the forti-fications of the Drissa camp, of the utility of which they were beginning to entertain grave doubts.

Tchernishev sat in the window of the outer room with a French novel. This room had once probably been the main hall; there was still an organ in it, on which were piled rugs of some sort, and in the corner of the room was a folding bedstead belonging to Bennigsen's adjutant. The owner of the bedstead, too, was there. Apparently exhausted by work or festivities, he sat dozing on the folded bed. Two doors led from the room: one straight in front opening into the drawing-room, another on the right opening into the study. From the first door came the sound of voices speaking German and occasionally French. In the drawing-room there was being held, by the Tsar's desire, not a military council—the Tsar loved to have things vague—but a meeting of a few persons, whose opinions he wished to hear in the present difficult position. It was not a military council, but a sort of council for the elucidation of certain questions for the benefit of the Tsar personally. To this sort of semi-council had been bidden the Swedish general, Armfeldt, the general on the staff Woltzogen, Wintzengerode (whom Napoleon had called a rene-gade French subject), Michaud, Toll, Count Stein—by no means a military man—and finally Pfuhl, who was, so Prince Andrey had heard, *la cheville ouvrière* of everything. Prince Andrey had the opportunity of getting a good view of him, as Pfuhl came in shortly after nis arrival and stopped for a minute to say a few words to Tchernishev before going on into the drawing-room.

At the first glance Pfuhl, in his badly cut uniform of a Russian general, which looked out of keeping, like some fancy dress costume on him, seemed to Prince Andrey like a familiar figure, though he had never seen him before. He was of the same order as Weierother, and Mack, and Schmidt, and many other German generals, men of theory, whom Prince Andrey had seen in the war of 1808; but he was a more perfect type of the class than any of them. Such a typical German theorist, combining in himself all the characteristics of those other Germans, Prince Andrey had never seen before.

Pfuhl was short and very thin, but broad-boned, of a coarsely robust build, with broad hips and projecting shoulder-blades. His face was wrinkled; he had deep-set eyes; his hair had obviously been hastily brushed smooth in front, but stuck out behind in quaint wisps. Looking nervously and irritably about him, he walked in as though he were afraid of everything in the great room he had entered. With a clumsy gesture, holding his sword, he turned to Tchernishev, asking him where the Tsar was. He was unmistakably eager to get through the rooms, to get the bows and greetings over as quickly as possible, and to sit down to work at a map, where he would feel at home. He gave a hurried nod in response to Tchernishev's words, and smiled ironically on hearing that the Tsar was inspecting the fortifications that he, Pfuhl, had planned in accordance with his theory. He muttered something in the jerky bass, in which conceited Germans often speak, "silly fool . . ." or "damn the whole business . . ." or "some idiocy's sure to come of that." Prince Andrey did not catch his words, and would have passed on, but Tchernishev introduced him to Pfuhl, observing that he had just come from Turkey, where the war had been so successfully concluded. Pfuhl barely glanced, not at, but across Prince Andrey, and commented, laughing: "A model that war must have been of every principle of tactics!" And, laughing contemptuously, he went on into the room, from which the sound of voices came.

It was evident that Pfuhl—disposed at all times to be irritable and sarcastic—was that day particularly irritated at their having dared to inspect his camp and to criticise it without him. Thanks to his Austerlitz experiences, Prince Andrey could from this one brief interview form a clear idea of the man's character. Pfuhl was one of those hopelessly, immutably conceited men, ready to face martyrdom for their own ideas, conceited as only Germans can be, just because it is only a German's conceit that is based on an abstract idea—science, that is, the supposed possession of absolute truth. The Frenchman is conceited from supposing himself mentally and physically to be inordinately fascinating both to men and to women. An Englishman is conceited on the ground of being a citizen of the best-constituted state in the world, and also because he as an Englishman always knows what is the correct thing to do, and knows that everything that he, as an Englishman, does do is indisputably the correct thing. An Italian is conceited from being excitable and easily forgetting himself and other people. A Russian is conceited precisely because he knows nothing and cares to know nothing, since he does not believe it possible to know anything fully. A conceited German is the worst of them all, and the most hardened of all, and the most repulsive of all; for he imagines that he possesses the truth in a science of his own invention, which is to him absolute truth.

Pfuhl was evidently one of these men. He had a science—the theory of the oblique attack—which he had deduced from the wars of Frederick the Great; and everything he came across in more recent military history seemed to him imbecility, barbarism, crude struggles in which so many blunders were committed on both sides that those wars could not be called war at all. They had no place in his theory and could not be made a subject for science at all.

In 1806 Pfuhl had been one of those responsible for the plan of campaign that ended in Jena and Auerstadt. But in the failure of that war he did not see the slightest evidence of the weakness of his theory. On the contrary, the whole failure was to his thinking entirely due to the departures that had been made from his theory, and he used to say with his characteristic gleeful sarcasm: "Didn't I always say the whole thing was going to the devil?" Pfuhl was one of those theorists who so love their theory that they lose sight of the object of the theory—its application to practice. His love for his theory led him to hate all practical considerations, and he would not hear of them. He positively rejoiced in failure, for failure, being due to some departure in practice from the purity of the abstract theory, only convinced him of the correctness of his theory.

He said a few words about the present war to Prince Andrey and Tchernishev with the expression of a man who knows beforehand that everything will go wrong, and is not, indeed, displeased at this being so. The uncombed wisps of hairs sticking out straight from his head behind, and the hurriedly brushed locks in front, seemed to suggest this with a peculiar eloquence.

He went on into the next room, and the querulous bass notes of his voice were at once audible there.

XI

PRINCE ANDREY had hardly seen the last of Pfuhl when Count Bennigsen came hurrying into the room, and bestowing a nod on Bolkonsky, went straight through to the study, giving some instruction to his adjutant. The Tsar was following him, and Bennigsen had hurried on to prepare something, and to be in readiness to meet him. Tchernishev and Prince Andrey went out into the porch. The Tsar, looking tired out, was dismounting from his horse. Marchese Paulucci was saying something to him. Turning his head to the left, the Tsar was listening with a look of displeasure to Paulucci, who was speaking with peculiar warmth. The

Tsar moved, evidently anxious to end the conversation; but the Italian, flushed and excited, followed him, still talking, and oblivious of etiquette.

"As for the man who has counselled the camp at Drissa," Paulucci was saying just as the Tsar, mounting the steps and noticing Prince Andrey, was looking more intently at his unfamiliar face. "As for him, sire," Paulucci persisted desperately, as though unable to restrain himself, "I see no alternative but the madhouse or the gallows."

Not attending, and appearing not to hear the Italian, the Tsar recognised Bolkonsky and addressed him graciously:

"I am very glad to see you. Go in where they are meeting and wait for me."

The Tsar passed on into the study. He was followed by Prince Pyotr Mihalovitch Volkonsky and Baron Stein, and the study door was closed after them. Prince Andrey, taking advantage of the Tsar's permission to do so, accompanied Paulucci, whom he had met in Turkey, into the drawing-room where the council had assembled.

Prince Pyotr Mihalovitch Volkonsky was performing the duties of a sort of informed head of the Tsar's staff. Volkonsky came out of the study and bringing out maps laid them on the table, and mentioned the questions on which he wished to hear the opinion of the gentlemen present. The important fact was that news (which afterwards proved to be false) had been received in the night of movements of the French with the object of making a circuit round the camp at Drissa.

The first to begin speaking was General Armfeldt, who unexpectedly proposed, as a means of avoiding the present difficulty, a quite new project, inexplicable except as a proof of his desire to show that he, too, had a suggestion of his own. His idea was that the army should move into a position away from the Petersburg and Moscow roads, and, united there, await the enemy. It was evident that this project had been formed by Armfeldt long before, and that he brought it forward now not so much with the object of meeting the present problem, to which it presented no solution, as of seizing the opportunity of explaining its merits. It was one of the millions of suggestions which might be made, one as reasonable as another, so long as no one had any idea what form the war would take. Some of those present attacked his idea, others supported it. The young Colonel Toll criticised the Swedish general's project with more heat than any one; and in the course of his remarks upon it drew out of a side pocket a manuscript, which he asked leave to read aloud. In this somewhat diffuse note, Toll proposed another plan of campaign— entirely opposed to Armfeldt's, and also to Pfuhl's plan. Paulucci, in raising objections to Toll's scheme, proposed a plan of direct advance and attack, which he declared to be the only means of extricating us from our present precarious position, and from the trap (so he called the Drissa camp) in which we were placed. During all this discussion, Pfuhl and his interpreter Woltzogen (who was his mouthpiece in the court world) were silent. Pfuhl merely snorted contemptuously and turned his back to indicate that he would never stoop to reply to the rubbish he was hearing. But when Prince Volkonsky, who presided over the debate, called upon him to give his opinion, he simply said: "Why ask me? General Armfeldt has proposed an excellent position with the rear exposed to the enemy. Or why not the attack suggested by this Italian gentleman? A fine idea! Or a retreat? Excellent, too. Why ask me?" said he. "You all know better than I do, it appears."

But when Volkonsky, frowning, said that it was in the Tsar's name that he asked his opinion, Pfuhl rose, and growing suddenly excited, began to speak:

"You have muddled and spoilt it all. You would all know better than I, and now you come to me to ask how to set things right. There is nothing that needs setting right. The only thing is to carry out in exact detail the plan laid down by me," he said, rapping his bony fingers on the table. "Where's the difficulty? It's nonsense; child's play!" He went up to the map, and began talking rapidly, pointing with his wrinkled finger about the map, and proving that no sort of contingency could affect the adaptability of the Drissa camp to every emergency, that every chance had been foreseen, and that if the enemy actually did make a circuit round it, then the enemy would infallibly be annihilated.

Paulucci, who did not know German, began to ask him questions in French. Woltzogen came to the assistance of his leader, who spoke French very badly, and began translating his utterances, hardly able to keep pace with Pfuhl, who was proceeding at a great rate to prove that everything, everything, not only what was happening, but everything that possibly could happen, had been provided for in his plan, and that if difficulties had arisen now, they were due simply to the failure to carry out that plan with perfect exactitude. He was continually giving vent to a sarcastic laugh as he went on proving, and at last scornfully abandoned all attempt to prove, his position, as a mathematician will refuse to establish by various different methods a problem he has once for all proved to be correctly solved. Woltzogen took his place, continuing to explain his views in French, and occasionally referring to Pfuhl himself: "Is that not true, your excellency?" But Pfuhl, as a man in the heat of the fray will belabour those of his own side, shouted angrily at his own follower—at Woltzogen, too.

"To be sure, what is there to explain in that?"

Paulucci and Michaud fell simultaneously on Woltzogen in French. Armfeldt addressed Pfuhl himself in German. Toll was interpreting to Prince Volkonsky in Russian. Prince Andrey listened and watched them in silence.

Of all these men the one for whom Prince Andrey felt most sympathy was the exasperated, determined, insanely conceited Pfuhl. He was the only one of all the persons present who was unmistakably seeking nothing for himself, and harbouring no personal grudge against anybody else. He desired one thing only—the adoption of his plan, in accordance with the theory that was the fruit of years of toil. He was ludicrous; he was disagreeable with his sarcasm, but yet he roused an involuntary feeling of respect from his boundless devotion to an idea.

Apart from this, with the single exception of Pfuhl, every speech of every person present had one common feature, which Prince Andrey had not seen at the council of war in 1805—that was, a panic dread of the genius of Napoleon, a dread which was involuntarily betrayed in every utterance now, in spite of all efforts to conceal it. Anything was assumed possible for Napoleon; he was expected from every quarter at once, and to invoke his terrible name was enough for them to condemn each other's suggestions. Pfuhl alone seemed to look on him too, even Napoleon, as a barbarian, like every other opponent of his theory; and Pfuhl roused a feeling of pity, too, as well as respect, in Prince Andrey. From the tone with which the courtiers addressed him, from what Paulucci had ventured to say to the Tsar, and above all from a certain despairing expression in Pfuhl himself, it was clear that others knew, and he himself felt, that his downfall was at hand. And for all his conceit and his German grumpy irony, he was pitiful with his flattened locks on his forehead and his wisps of uncombed hair sticking out behind. Though he tried to conceal it under a semblance of anger and contempt, he was visibly in despair that the sole chance left him of testing his theory on a vast scale and proving its infallibility to the whole world was slipping away from him.

The debate lasted a long while, and the longer it continued the hotter it became, passing into clamour and personalities, and the less possible it was to draw any sort of general conclusion from what was uttered. Prince Andrey simply wondered at what they were all saying as he listened to the confusion of different tongues, and the propositions, the plans, the shouts, and the objections. The idea which had long ago and often occurred to him during the period of his active service, that there was and could be no sort of military science, and that therefore there could not be such a thing as military genius, seemed to him now to be an absolutely obvious truth. "What theory and science can there be of a subject of which the conditions and circumstances are uncertain and can never be definitely known, in which the strength of the active forces engaged can be even less definitely measured? No one can, or possibly could, know the relative positions of our army and the enemy's in another twenty-four hours, and no one can gauge the force of this or the other detachment. Sometimes when there is no coward in front to cry, 'We are cut off!' and to run, but a brave, spirited fellow leads the way, shouting 'Hurrah!' a detachment of five thousand is as good as thirty thousand, as it was at Schöngraben, while at times fifty thousand will run from eight thousand, as they did at Austerlitz. How can there be a science of war in which, as in every practical matter, nothing can be definite and everything depends on countless conditions, the influence of which becomes manifest all in a moment, and no one can know when that moment is coming. Armfeldt declares that our army is cut off, while Paulucci maintains that we have caught the French army between two fires; Michaud asserts that the defect of the Drissa camp is having the river in its rear, while Pfuhl protests that that is what constitutes its strength; Toll proposes one plan, Armfeldt suggests another; and all are good and all are bad, and the suitability of any proposition can only be seen at the moment of trial. And why do they all talk of military genius? Is a man to be called a genius because he knows when to order biscuits to be given out, and when to march his troops to the right and when to the left? He is only called a genius because of the glamour and authority with which the military are invested, and because masses of sycophants are always ready to flatter power, and to ascribe to it qualities quite alien to it. The best generals I have known are, on the contrary, stupid or absent-minded men. The best of them is Bagration—Napoleon himself admitted it. And Bonaparte himself! I remember his fatuous and limited face on the field of Austerlitz. A good general has no need of genius, nor of any great qualities; on the contrary, he is the better for the absence of the finest and highest of human qualities—love, poetry, tenderness, philosophic and inquiring doubt. He should be limited, firmly convinced that what he is doing is of great importance (or he would never have patience to go through with it), and only then will he be a gallant general. God forbid he should be humane, should feel love and compassion, should pause to think what is right and wrong. It is perfectly comprehensible that the theory of their genius should have been elaborated long, long ago, for the simple reason that they are the representatives of power. The credit of success in battle is not by right theirs; for victory or defeat depends in reality on the soldier in the ranks who first shouts 'Hurrah!' or 'We are lost!' And it is only in the ranks that one can serve with perfect conviction, that one is of use!"

Such were Prince Andrey's reflections as he heard the discussion going on around him, and he was only roused from his musing when Paulucci called to him and the meeting was breaking up.

Next day at the review the Tsar asked Prince Andrey where he desired to serve; and Bolkonsky ruined his chances for ever in the court world by asking to be sent to the front, instead of begging for a post in attendance on the Tsar's person.

XII

BEFORE the beginning of the campaign Rostov had received a letter from his parents, in which they informed him briefly of Natasha's illness and the breaking off of her engagement, and again begged him to retire from the army and come home to them. Natasha had, they explained, broken off the engagement by her own wish. On receiving this letter Nikolay did not even attempt to retire from the army or to obtain leave, but wrote to his parents that he was very sorry to hear of Natasha's illness and her rupture with her betrothed, and that he would do everything in his power to follow their wishes. To Sonya he wrote separately.

"Adored friend of my heart," he wrote; "nothing but honour could avail to keep me from returning to the country. But now, at the beginning of a campaign, I should feel myself dishonoured in my comrades' eyes, as well as my own, if I put my own happiness before my duty and my love for my country. But this shall be our last separation. Believe me, immediately after the war, if I be living and still loved by thee, I shall throw up everything and fly to thee to press thee for ever to my ardent breast."

It was, in fact, only the outbreak of the war that detained Rostov and hindered him from returning home, as he had promised, and marrying Sonya. The autumn at Otradnoe with the hunting, and the winter with the Christmas festivities and Sonya's love had opened before his imagination a vista of peace and quiet country delights unknown to him before, and this prospect now lured him back. "A charming wife, children, a good pack of hounds, ten to twelve leashes of swift harriers, the estate to look after, the neighbours, election to offices, perhaps, by the provincial nobility," he mused. But now war was breaking out, and he had to remain with his regiment. And since this had to be, Nikolay Rostov was characteristically able to be content too with the life he led in the regiment, and to make that life a pleasant one.

On his return from his leave, Nikolay had been joyfully welcomed by his comrades and sent off for remounts. He succeeded in bringing back from Little Russia some first-rate horses that gave him great satisfaction, and won him the commendation of his superior officers. In his absence he had been promoted to be captain, and when the regiment was being made ready with reinforcements for active service, he was again put in command of his old squadron.

The campaign was beginning, pay was doubled, the regiment was reinforced with new officers, new men, and fresh horses, and had moved into Poland. The temper of eager cheerfulness, always common at the beginning of a war, was general in the army, and Rostov, fully conscious of his improved position in the regiment, gave himself up heart and soul to the pleasures and interests of the army, though he knew that sooner or later he would have to leave it.

The army had been compelled to retreat from Vilna owing to various complex considerations of state, of policy, and tactics. Every step of that retreat had been accompanied by a complicated play of interests, arguments, and passions at headquarters. For the hussars of the Pavlograd regiment, however, this whole march in the finest part of the summer, with ample supplies of provisions, was a most simple and agreeable business. Depression, uneasiness, and intrigue were possible only at headquarters; the rank and file of the army never even wondered where and why they were going. If the retreat was a subject of regret, it was simply owing to the necessity of leaving quarters one had grown used to or a pretty Polish hostess. If the idea did occur to any one that things were amiss, he tried, as a good soldier should, to put a cheerful face on it; and to keep his thoughts fixed on the duty that lay nearest, and not on the general progress of the war. At first they had been very pleasantly stationed near Vilna, where they made acquaintance with the Polish gentry of the neighbourhood, prepared for reviews, and were reviewed by the Tsar and various commanders of high authority. Then came the command to retreat to Sventsyany, and to destroy all the stores that could not be carried away. Sventsyany was memorable to the hussars simply as the *drunken camp*, the name given to the encampment there by the whole army, and as the scene of many complaints against the troops, who had taken advantage of orders to collect stores, and under the head of stores had carried off horses and carriages and carpets from the Polish landowners. Rostov remembered Sventsyany, because on the very day of his arrival there he had dismissed his quartermaster and did not know how to manage the men of his squadron, who had, without his knowledge, carried off five barrels of strong old ale and were all drunk. From Sventsyany they had fallen further back, and then further again, till they reached Drissa; and from Drissa they retreated again, till they were getting near the frontiers of Russia proper.

On the 13th of July the Pavlograd hussars took part in their first serious action.

On the previous evening there had been a violent storm of rain and hail. The summer of 1812 was remarkably stormy throughout.

The two Pavlograd squadrons were bivouacking in the middle of a field of rye, which was already in ear, but had been completely trodden down by the cattle and horses. The rain was falling in torrents, and Rostov was sitting with a young officer, Ilyin, a protégé of his, under a shanty, that had been hastily rigged up for them. An officer of their regiment, adorned with long moustaches, that hung down from his cheeks, was caught in the rain on his way back from visiting the staff, and he went into Rostov's shanty for shelter.

"I'm on my way from the staff, count. Have you heard of Raevsky' exploit?" And the officer proceeded to relate to them details of the Saltanov battle that had been told him at the staff.

Rostov smoked his pipe, and wriggled his neck, down which the water was trickling. He listened with little interest, looking from time to time at the young officer Ilyin, who was squatting beside him. Ilyin, a lad of sixteen, who had lately joined the regiment, took now with Nikolay the place Nikolay had taken seven years before with Denisov. Ilyin tried to imitate Rostov in everything and adored him, as a girl might have done.

The officer with the double moustaches, Zdrzhinsky, in a very high-flown manner, described the dike at Saltanov as the Russian Thermopylae, and the heroic deed of General Raevsky on that dike as worthy of antiquity. Zdrzhinsky told then how Raevsky had thrust his two sons forward on the dike under a terrific fire, and had charged at their side. Rostov listened to the tale, and said nothing betokening sympathy with Zdrzhinsky's enthusiasm. He looked, indeed, as though ashamed of what he was told, but not intending to gainsay it. After Austerlitz and the campaign of 1807, Rostov knew from his own experience that men always lie when they describe deeds of battle, as he did himself indeed. He had had too sufficient experience to know that everything in battle happens utterly differently from our imagination and description of it. And so he did not like Zdrzhinsky's story, and did not, indeed, like

Zdrzhinsky himself, who had, besides his unprepossessing moustaches, a habit of bending right over into the face of the person he was speaking to. He was in their way in the cramped little shanty. Rostov looked at him without speaking. "In the first place, on the dike they were charging there must have been such a crowd and confusion that, if Raevsky really thrust his sons forward, it would have had no effect except on the dozen men closest to him," thought Rostov; "the rest could not have even seen who were with Raevsky on the dike. And those who did see it were not likely to be greatly affected by it, for what thought had they to spare for Raevsky's tender, parental feelings, when they had their own skins to think of saving? And besides the fate of the country did not depend on whether that dike was taken or not, as we are told the fate of Greece did depend on Thermopylae. And then what was the object of such a sacrifice? Why do your own children a mischief in war? I wouldn't put Petya, my brother, in a place of danger; no, even Ilyin here, who's nothing to me but a good-natured lad, I would do my best to keep safe and sheltered," Rostov mused, as he listened to Zdrzhinsky. But he did not give utterance to his thoughts, he had experience of that too He knew that this tale redounded to the glory of our arms, and therefore one must appear not to doubt its truth: and he acted accordingly.

"I can't stand this, though," said Ilyin, noticing that Rostov did not care for Zdrhinsky's story; "stockings and shirt, and all—I'm wet through. I'm going to look for shelter. I fancy the rain's not so heavy." Ilyin ran out and Zdrzhinsky rode away.

Five minutes later Ilyin came splashing through the mud to the shanty.

"Hurrah! Rostov, make haste and come along. I have found an inn, two hundred paces or so from here; a lot of our fellows are there already. We can get dry anyway, and Marya Hendrihovna's there."

Marya Hendrihovna was the wife of the regimental doctor; a pretty young German woman, whom he had married in Poland. Either from lack of means or disinclination to part from his young wife in the early days of their marriage, the doctor had brought her with him in the regiment, and his jealousy was a favourite subject for the jibes of the hussars.

Rostov flung on a cape, shouted to Lavrushka to follow them with their things, and went off with Ilyin, slipping in the mud, and splashing through the pools in the drizzling rain and the darkness, which was rent at intervals by distant lightning.

"Rostov, where are you?"

"Here. What a flash!" they called to one another as they went.

XIII

IN the inn, before which was standing the doctor's covered cart, there were already some half-dozen officers. Marya Hendrihovna, a plump, flaxen-headed little German in a dressing-jacket and nightcap, was sitting on a board bench in the foremost corner. Her husband, the doctor, lay asleep behind her. Rostov and Ilyin entered the room, welcomed with merry shouts and laughter.

"I say! You are having a jolly time here!" said Rostov, laughing.

"And what are you yawning over?"

"Pretty figures you look! There's a perfect waterfall from them! Don't swamp our drawing-room."

"Mind you don't spatter Marya Hendrihovna's dress," chimed in voices.

Rostov and Ilyin made haste to look for a retreat where, without offence to the modesty of Marya Hendrihovna, they might change their wet clothes. They went behind a partition wall to change; but in the little recess were three officers, who completely filled it up. They were sitting playing cards by the light of a single candle on an empty box, and nothing would induce them to budge from their places. Marya Hendrihovna lent them her petticoat to be hung by way of a curtain; and screened by it, Rostov and Ilyin took off their wet things and put on dry clothes, with the aid of Lavrushka, who had brought their packages.

They made up a fire in the broken-down stove. They got hold of a board, propped it on two saddles, and covered it with a horse-cloth; then brought out a little samovar, a case of wine, and half a bottle of rum. All crowded round Marya Hendrihovna, begging her to preside. One offered her a clean handkerchief, to wipe her charming hands; another put his tunic under her little feet, to keep them from the damp floor; a third hung a cape over the window, to screen her from the draught; while a fourth brushed the flies off her husband's face, to prevent their waking him.

"Let him alone," said Marya Hendrihovna, with a timid, and happy smile; "he will sleep well anyhow after being up all night."

"Oh no, Marya Hendrihovna," answered the officer, "one must look after the doctor well! Anything may happen; and he will be kind to me, I dare say, when he has to cut off my leg or my arm."

There were only three glasses; the water was so dirty that there was no telling whether the tea were strong or weak, and the samovar would only hold water enough for six glasses. But that made it all the more fun to take turns in order of seniority to receive a glass from the plump, short-nailed, and not over clean fingers of Marya Hendrihovna. All the officers seemed indeed to be genuinely in love for that evening with Marya Hendrihovna. Even the officers who had been playing cards behind the screen soon threw up their game, and gathered round the samovar, catching the general mood, and joining in the homage paid to Marya Hendrihovna. The latter, seeing herself surrounded by these splendid and devoted young men, beamed with delight, which she sought in vain to conceal, though she was unmistakably alarmed at every movement made by her husband, who was slumbering behind her. There was only one spoon; sugar there was in plenty. but it took so long for all to stir their glasses, that it was settled that Marya Hendrihovna must stir the sugar for each in turn. Rostov took his glass of tea, and adding rum to it, begged Marya Hendrihovna to stir it for him.

"But you take it without sugar?" she said, smiling all the while, as though whatever she said or the others said had a quite different and very amusing meaning.

"I don't care about sugar, all I want is for you to stir it with your little hand."

Marya Hendrihovna began looking for the spoon, which some one had pounced upon.

"Use your little finger, Marya Hendrihovna," said Rostov; "it will be all the sweeter."

"It's hot," said Marya Hendrihovna, blushing with pleasure.

Ilyin took the bucket of water, and pouring a few drops of rum in it, went up to Marya Hendrihovna, begging her to stir it with her finger.

"This is my cup," he said. "Only dip your finger in and I'll drink it all up."

When the samovar was empty, Rostov took up the cards and proposed a game of "Kings" with Marya Hendrihovna. They tossed to decide which was to have the lady for a partner. Rostov proposed as a rule of the game that the one who was "king" should have the right to kiss Marya Hendrihovna's hand, and the one who was left knave should have to fetch another samovar for the doctor, when he waked.

"Well, but what if Marya Hendrihovna is king?" asked Ilyin.

"She is our queen already! And her commands are law."

The game was just beginning when the doctor's dishevelled head popped up behind his wife. He had been awake for some time and listening to the conversation, and apparently he saw nothing agreeable, funny, or amusing in what was being said and done. His face looked depressed and weary. He did not greet the officers, but scratching himself, he asked them to move to let him pass. As soon as he had left the room, all the officers broke into loud peals of laughter, and Marya Hendrihovna blushed till the tears came, making her even more charming in the eyes of the officers. Coming in again from the yard, the doctor told his wife (who had lost her radiant smile, and looked at him in dismay in expectation of the sentence in store for her) that the rain was over and they must spend the night in their covered cart, or they would have all their things stolen.

"But I'll put an orderly on guard . . . two, indeed!" said Rostov. "That's nonsense, doctor."

"I'll be sentinel myself!" said Ilyin.

"No, gentlemen, you have had plenty of sleep, but I have been up these two nights," said the doctor, and he sat gloomily by his wife's side, waiting for the end of the game.

Looking at the doctor's gloomy face and sidelong glances at his wife, the officers grew even more lively, and many of them could not suppress their laughter, for which they hastily sought presentable pretexts. When the doctor had led his wife away, and settled himself with her in their cart, the officers lay down in the inn, covering themselves with their wet overcoats. But for a long while they stayed awake, chatting, recalling the dismay of the doctor, and the delight of the doctor's wife, or running out on to the steps to report on what was going on in the cart. Several times Rostov muffled his head up and tried to go to sleep. But again some remark roused him, again a conversation sprang up, and again there were peals of causeless, merry, childish laughter.

XIV

IT was past two o'clock, no one was yet asleep, when the quartermaster appeared, bringing a command to advance upon a little place called Ostrovna. Still with the same chatter and laughter the officers began hurriedly getting ready; again the samovar was filled up with dirty water. But Rostov, without waiting for tea, went off to his squadron. It was already light; the rain had ceased, and the clouds were parting. It was chill and damp, especially in their still wet clothes. As they came out of the inn, in the twilight of the dawn, Rostov and Ilyin both glanced at the leather cover of the doctor's cart, still glistening from the rain. The doctor's feet were sticking out from under the cover, and in the middle of the cart they caught a glimpse of his wife's nightcap, and heard sleepy breathing.

"She's really very charming," said Rostov to Ilyin.

"An exquisite woman!" responded Ilyin, with all the gravity of a boy of sixteen.

Half an hour later the squadron stood drawn up on the road. The word of command was heard, "Mount!" and the soldiers crossed themselves and got on their horses. Rostov, riding ahead of them, gave the word: "Forward!" and drawing out four abreast, the hussars started with a sound of subdued talk, splashing hoofs, and jingling sabres. They trotted along the broad high-road, with birch-trees on each side of it, following the infantry and artillery, who had gone on before.

The broken, purplish-blue clouds, flushed red by the sunrise, were scudding before the wind. It grew lighter and lighter. They could see distinctly, still glistening from the rain, the feathery grass which always grows beside by-roads. The drooping branches of the birch-trees swayed in the wind, and dripped bright drops aslant across the road. The faces of the soldiers showed more and more distinctly. Rostov, with Ilyin, who would not drop behind, rode on one side of the road between the two rows of birch-trees.

On active service Rostov allowed himself the indulgence of riding a Cossack horse instead of the regimental horse, broken in for parade. He was a connoisseur and lover of horses, and had lately obtained a big sorrel horse with white tail and mane, a fine spirited beast of the Don breed, on whom he could out-gallop every one. It was an enjoyment to Rostov to ride this horse. He rode on, thinking of the horse, of the morning, of the doctor's wife, and never once giving a thought to the danger awaiting him.

In former days Rostov had felt fear when he was going into an engagement; now he had not the slightest feeling of fear. He had not lost his fears from growing used to being under fire (one can never get accustomed to danger) but from gaining control of his feelings in face of danger. He had schooled himself when going into action to think of anything except what one would have supposed to be more interesting than anything else—the danger in store for him. Earnestly as he strove to do this, and bitterly as he reproached himself for cowardice, he could not at first succeed in this. But with years it had come of itself. He rode now beside Ilyin, between the birch-trees, stripping leaves off the twigs that met his hand, sometimes touching his horse's side with his foot, handing the pipe he had finished to an hussar behind, without turning his head, all with as calm and careless an air as though he were out for a ride. He felt sorry to see the excited face of Ilyin, who talked a great deal nervously. He knew by experience the agonising state of anticipation of terror and of death, in which the cornet was plunged, and he knew that nothing but time could help him out of it.

As soon as the sun appeared in the clear strip of sky under the storm-clouds, the wind sank, as though not daring to spoil the beauty of the summer morning after the storm; the trees still dripped, but the drops fell vertically now—and all was hushed. The sun rose completely above the horizon, and vanished in a long, narrow cloud that hung over it. A few minutes later the sun showed even more brightly on the upper side of the cloud, tearing its edge. Everything grew bright and shining. And with the bright light, as though in response to it, rang out shots in front of them.

Rostov had not time to collect his thoughts and decide how far off these shots were, when an adjutant of Count Osterman-Tolstoy galloped up from Vitebsk, bringing the order to advance at full speed along the road.

The squadron overtook and passed the infantry and the battery, who were also quickening their pace. Then the hussars raced downhill, passed through an empty and deserted village, and trotted uphill again. The horses were beginning to get in a lather and the men looked flushed.

"Halt! in line!" said the officer in command of the division. "Left about face, walking pace!" sounded the command in advance.

And the hussars passed along the lines of the other troops to the left flank of the position, and halted behind our Uhlans, who formed the front line. On the right was a dense column of our infantry—they formed the reserves; on the hill above them, in the pure, clear air, in the brilliant, slanting, morning sunshine, could be seen our cannons on the very horizon line. In front, beyond a hollow dale, could be seen the enemy's columns and cannons. In the dale could be heard our advance pickets, already keeping up a lively interchange of shots with the enemy.

Rostov felt his spirits rise at those sounds, so long unheard, as though they had been the liveliest music. Trap-ta-ta-tap! rang out several shots, first together, then in rapid succession. All sank into silence again, and again there was a sound as of popping squibs.

The hussars remained for about an hour in the same spot. The cannons began firing. Count Osterman, with his suite behind the squadron, rode up; he stopped to say a word to the colonel of the regiment, and rode off to the cannons on the hill.

After Osterman had ridden away, the command rang out among the Uhlans, "Form in column; make ready to charge!" The infantry in front parted in two to let the cavalry pass through. The Uhlans galloped off, the streamers on their lances waving, and trotted downhill towards the French cavalry, who came into sight below on the left.

As soon as the Uhlans had started downhill, the hussars received the order to ride off uphill to cover the battery. Just as the hussars were moving into the place of the Uhlans, there came flying from the outposts some cannon-balls, hissing and whistling out of the distance, and hitting nothing.

This sound, which he had not heard for so long, had an even more inspiriting and cheering effect on Rostov than the report of the muskets. Drawing himself up, he surveyed the field of battle, as it opened out before him riding uphill, and his whole heart went with the movements of the Uhlans. They were swooping down close upon the French dragoons; there was some confusion yonder in the smoke, and five minutes later the Uhlans were dashing back, not towards the spot where they had been posted, but more to the left. Between the ranks of Uhlans on the chestnut horses, and in a great mass behind them, could be seen blue French dragoons on grey horses.

XV

ROSTOV, with his keen sportsman's eye, was one of the first to descry these blue dragoons pursuing our Uhlans. Nearer and nearer flew the disordered crowds of the Uhlans and the French dragoons in pursuit of them. He could see now separate figures, looking small at the bottom of the hill, fighting, overtaking one another, and waving their arms and their swords.

Rostov gazed at what was passing before him as at a hunt. He felt instinctively that if he were to charge with his hussars on the French dragoons now, they could not stand their ground; but if he were to charge it must be that very minute or it would be too late. He looked round. The captain standing beside him had his eyes too fixed on the cavalry below.

"Andrey Sevastianitch," said Rostov, "we could close them in, surely . . ."

"And a smart job, too," said the captain, "and indeed . . ."

Rostov, without waiting for his answer, set spurs to his horse and galloped off in front of his squadron. Before he had time to give the command, the whole squadron, sharing his feeling, flew after him. Rostov himself could not have said how or why he did it. He did it all, as he did everything in a wolf hunt, without thinking or considering. He saw that the dragoons were near, that they were galloping in no order, he knew they could not stand their ground; he knew there was only one minute to act in, which would not return if he let it slip. The cannon balls were hissing and whistling so inspiritingly about him, his horse pulled so eagerly forward that he could not resist it. He spurred his horse, shouted the command, and the same instant flew full trot downhill towards the dragoons, hearing the tramp of his squadron behind him. As they dashed downhill, the trot insensibly passed into a gallop that became swifter and swifter, as they drew nearer their Uhlans and the French dragoons pursuing them. The dragoons were close now. The foremost, seeing the hussars, began turning back; the hindmost halted. With the same feeling with which he had dashed off to cut off the wolf's escape, Rostov, letting his Don horse go at his utmost speed, galloped to cut off the broken ranks of the dragoons. One Uhlan halted; another, on foot, flung himself to the ground to avoid being knocked down; a riderless horse was carried along with the hussars. Almost all the dragoons were galloping back. Rostov picked out one of them on a grey horse and flew after him. On the way he rode straight at a bush; his gallant horse cleared it; and Nikolay was hardly straight in the saddle again when he saw in a few seconds he would overtake the enemy he had pitched upon as his aim. The Frenchman, probably an officer from his uniform, sat crouched upon his grey horse, and urging it on with his sword. In another instant Rostov's horse dashed up against the grey horse's hindquarters, almost knocking it over, and at the same second Rostov, not knowing why he did so, raised his sword, and aimed a blow at the Frenchman.

The instant he did this all Rostov's eagerness suddenly vanished. The officer fell to the ground, not so much from the sword cut, for it had only just grazed his arm above the elbow, as from fright and the shock to his horse. As Rostov pulled his horse in, his eyes sought his foe to see what sort of man he had vanquished. The French officer was hopping along on the ground, with one foot caught in the stirrup. Screwing up his eyes, as though expecting another blow every instant, he glanced up at Rostov frowning with an expression of terror. His pale, mud-stained face—fair and young, with a dimple on the chin and clear blue eyes—was the most unwarlike, most good-natured face, more in place by a quiet fireside than on the field of battle. Before Rostov could make up his mind what to do with him, the officer shouted, "I surrender." He tried hurriedly and failed to extricate his foot from the stirrup, and still gazed with his frightened blue eyes at Rostov. The hussars, galloping up, freed his foot, and got him into his saddle. The hussars were busily engaged on all sides with the dragoons; one was wounded, but though his face was streaming with blood he would not let go of his horse; another put his arms round an hussar as he sat perched up behind on his horse; a third was clambering on to his horse, supported by an hussar. The French infantry were in front, firing as they ran. The hussars galloped hastily back with their prisoners. Rostov galloped back with the rest, conscious of some disagreeable sensation, a kind of ache at his heart. A glimpse of something vague and confused, of which he could not get a clear view, seemed to have come to him with the capture of that French officer and the blow he had dealt him.

Count Osterman-Tolstoy met the hussars on their return, summoned Rostov, thanked him and told him he would report his gallant action to the Tsar and would recommend him for the cross of St. George. When Rostov was called up to Count Osterman, bethinking himself that he had received no command to charge, he had no doubt that his commanding officer sent for him to reprimand him for his breach of discipline. Osterman's flattering words and promise of a reward should, therefore, have been a pleasant surprise to Rostov; but he still suffered from that unpleasant vague feeling of moral nausea. "Why, what on earth is it that's worrying me?" he wondered, as he rode away from the general. "Ilyin? No, he's all right. Did I do anything disgraceful? No, that's not it either!" Something else fretted him like a remorse. "Yes, yes, that officer with the dimple. And I remember clearly how my hand paused when I had lifted it."

Rostov saw the prisoners being led away, and galloped after them to look at his Frenchman with the dimple in his chin. He was sitting in his strange uniform on one of the spare horses, looking uneasily about him. The sword-cut in his arm could hardly be called a wound. He looked at Rostov with a constrained smile, and waved his hand by way of a greeting. Rostov still felt the same discomfort and vague remorse.

All that day and the next Rostov's friends and comrades noticed that, without being exactly depressed or irritable, he was silent, dreamy, and preoccupied. He did not care to drink, tried to be alone, and seemed absorbed in thought. Rostov was still pondering on his brilliant exploit, which, to his amazement, had won him the St. George's Cross and made his reputation indeed for fearless gallantry. There was something he could not fathom in it. "So they are even more frightened than we are," he thought. "Why, is this all that's meant by heroism? And did I do it for the sake of my country? And was he to blame with his dimple and his blue eyes? How frightened he was! He thought I was going to kill him. Why should I kill him? My hand trembled. And they have given me the St. George's Cross. I can't make it out, I can't make it out!"

But while Nikolay was worrying over these questions in his heart and unable to find any clear solution of the doubts that troubled him, the wheel of fortune was turning in his favour, as so often happens in the service. He was brought forward after the affair at Ostrovna, received the command of a battalion of hussars, and when an officer of dauntless courage was wanted he was picked out.

XVI

Countess Rostov had not recovered her strength when she received the news of Natasha's illness. Weak as she still was, she set out at once for Moscow with Petya and the whole household, and the Rostovs moved from Marya Dmitryevna's into their own house, where the whole family were installed.

Natasha's illness was so serious that, luckily for herself and her parents, all thought of what had caused it, of her conduct and of the breaking off of her engagement, fell into the background. She was so ill that no one could consider how far she was to blame for all that had happened, while she could not eat nor sleep, was growing visibly thinner, coughed, and was, as the doctors gave them to understand, in actual danger. Nothing could be thought of but how to make her well again. Doctors came to see Natasha, both separately and in consultation. They said a great deal in French, in German, and in Latin. They criticised one another, and prescribed the most diverse remedies for all the diseases they were familiar with. But it never occurred to one of them to make the simple reflection that they could not understand the disease from which Natasha was suffering, as no single disease can be fully understood in a living person; for every living person has his individual peculiarities and always has his own peculiar, new, complex complaints unknown to medicine—not a disease of the lungs, of the kidneys, of the skin, of the heart, and so on, as described in medical books, but a disease that consists of one out of the innumerable combinations of ailments of those organs. This simple reflection can never occur to doctors (just as a sorcerer cannot entertain the idea that he is unable to work magic spells) because it is the work of their life to undertake the cure of disease, because it is for that that they are paid, and on that they have wasted the best years of their life. And what is more, that reflection could not occur to the doctors because they saw that they unquestionably were of use; and they certainly were of use to all the Rostov household. They were of use, not because they made the patient swallow drugs, mostly injurious (the injury done by them was hardly perceptible because they were given in such small doses). They were of use, were indispensable in fact (for the same reason that there have always been, and always will be, reputed healers, witches, homœopaths, and allopaths), because they satisfied the moral cravings of the patient and those who loved her. They satisfied that eternal human need of hope for relief, that need for sympathetic action that is felt in the presence of suffering, that need that is shown in its simplest form in the little child, who must have the place rubbed when it has hurt itself. The child is hurt, and runs at once to the arms of its mother or nurse for them to kiss or rub the tender spot, and it feels better for the kissing and rubbing. The child cannot believe that these stronger, cleverer creatures have not the power to relieve its pain. And the hope of relief and the expressions of sympathy as the mother rubs it comfort it. To Natasha the doctors took the place of the mother, kissing and rubbing her "bobo," when they declared that all the trouble would soon be over, if the coachman were to drive to the chemist's shop, in Arbatsky Place, and buy—for a rouble and seventy copecks—those powders and pills in a pretty little box, and if those powders were given to the patient in boiled water precisely every two hours, neither more nor less.

What would Sonya, and the count, and the countess have done, how would they have felt if they had taken no steps, if they had not had those pills at certain hours, and the warm beverage, and the chicken cutlets, and all the detailed régime laid down by the doctors, which gave occupation and consolation to all of them. How could the count have borne his dearly loved daughter's illness if he had not known that it was costing him a thousand roubles, and that he would not grudge thousands more, if that would do her any good; if he had not known that, in case she did not get better, he would spend thousands more on taking her abroad and consulting doctors there; if he had not been able to tell people how Metivier and Feller had failed to diagnose the complaint, but Friez had fathomed it, and Mudrov had succeeded even better in defining it? What would the countess have done if she had not sometimes been able to scold her sick Natasha for not following the doctors' orders quite faithfully?

"You can never get well like this," she would say, finding a refuge from her grief in anger, "if you won't listen to the doctors and take your medicine properly! We can't have any nonsense, when it may turn to pneumonia," said the countess, and in pronouncing that—not to her only —mysterious word, she found great comfort. What would Sonya have done, had she not had the glad consciousness that at first she had not had her clothes off for three nights running, so as to be in readiness to carry out the doctors' orders, and that now she did not sleep at night for fear of missing the exact hour at which the innocuous pills were to be given out of the gilt pill-box? Even Natasha herself, though she did declare that no medicines could do her any good, and that it was all nonsense, was glad to see so many sacrifices being made for her, and glad to have to take medicines at certain hours. And she was even glad, indeed, to be able by her disregard of the doctors' prescription to show how little faith she put in them, and how little she cared for life.

The doctor came every day, felt her pulse, looked at her tongue, and made jokes, regardless of her dejected face. But then when he had gone into the next room, and the countess had hastily followed him, he assumed a serious face, and shaking his head gravely, said that though there was indeed danger, he had hopes from the effect of the most recent medicine, and that they could only wait and see; that the illness was more due to moral than physical causes, but . . . The countess slipped some gold into his hand, trying to conceal the action from herself and from him, and always went back to the sick-room with a lighter heart.

The symptoms of Natasha's illness were loss of appetite, sleeplessness, a cough, and continual depression. The doctors declared that she must have medical treatment, and therefore kept her in the stifling atmosphere of the town. And all the summer of 1812 the Rostovs did not visit the country.

In spite of the numerous little bottles and boxes of pills, drops, and powders, of which Madame Schoss, who had a passion for them, made a complete collection, in spite of the loss of the country life to which she was accustomed, youth gained the upper hand; Natasha's grief began to be covered up by the impressions of daily life; it ceased to lie like an aching load on her heart; it began to fade into the past; and Natasha began to return to physical health again.

XVII

NATASHA was calmer, but no happier. She did not merely shun every external form of amusement—balls, skating, concerts, and theatres—but she never even laughed without the sound of tears behind her laughter. She could not sing. As soon as she began to laugh or attempted to sing all by herself, tears choked her: tears of remorse; tears of regret for that time of pure happiness that could never return; tears of vexation that she should so wantonly have ruined her young life, that might have been so happy. Laughter and singing especially seemed to her like scoffing at her grief. She never even thought of desiring admiration; she had no impulse of vanity to restrain. She said and felt at that time that all men were no more to her than Nastasya Ivanovna, the buffoon. An inner sentinel seemed to guard against every sort of pleasure. And, indeed, she seemed to have lost all the old interests of her girlish, careless life, that had been so full of hope. Most often, and with most pining, she brooded over the memory of those autumn months, the hunting, the old uncle, and the Christmas holidays spent with Nikolay at Otradnoe. What would she not have given to bring back one single day of that time! But it was all over for her. Her presentiment at the time had not deceived her, that such a time of freedom and readiness for every enjoyment would never come again. But yet she had to live.

It comforted her to think, not that she was better, as she had once fancied, but worse, far worse than any one, than any one in the whole world. But that meant little to her. She believed it; but then she asked: "And what next?" And there was nothing to come. There was no gladness in life, but life was passing. All Natasha tried after was plainly to be no burden to others, and not to hinder other people's enjoyment; but for herself she wanted nothing. She held aloof from all the household. It was only with her brother, Petya, that she felt at ease. She liked being with him better than being with the rest, and sometimes even laughed when she was alone with him. She hardly left the house to go anywhere; and of the guests who came to the house she was only glad to see one person—Pierre. No one could have been more tender, circumspect, and at the same time serious, than Count Bezuhov in his manner to her. Natasha was unconsciously aware of this tenderness, and it was owing to it that she found more pleasure in his society. But she was not even grateful to him for it. Nothing good in him seemed to her due to an effort on Pierre's part. It seemed so natural to Pierre to be kind that there was no merit in his kindness. Sometimes Natasha noticed some confusion or awkwardness in Pierre in her presence, especially when he was trying to do something for her pleasure or afraid something in the conversation might suggest to her painful reminiscences. She observed this, and put it down to his general kindliness and shyness, which she supposed would be the same with every one else. Ever since those unforeseen words—that if he had been free, he would have asked on his knees for her hand and her love—uttered in a moment full of violent emotion for her, Pierre had said nothing of his feelings to Natasha; and it seemed to her clear that those words, which had so comforted her, had been uttered, just as one says any meaningless nonsense to console a weeping child. It was not because Pierre was a married man, but because Natasha felt between herself and him the force of that moral barrier— of the absence of which she had been so conscious with Kuragin—that the idea never occurred to her that her relations with Pierre might develop into love on her side, and still less on his, or even into that tender, self-conscious, romantic friendship between a man and a woman, of which she had known several instances.

Towards the end of St. Peter's fast, Agrafena Ivanovna Byelov, a country neighbour of the Rostovs, came to Moscow to pay her devotions to the saints there. She suggested to Natasha that she should prepare herself for the Sacrament, and Natasha caught eagerly at the suggestion. Although the doctors forbade her going out early in the morning, Natasha insisted on keeping the fast, and not simply as it was kept in the Rostovs' household, by taking part in three services in the house, but keeping it as Agrafena Ivanova was doing, that is to say, for a whole week, not missing a single early morning service, or litany, or vesper.

The countess was pleased at these signs of religious fervour in Natasha. After the poor results of medical treatment, at the bottom of her heart she hoped that prayer would do more for her than medicine; and though she concealed it from the doctors and had some inward misgivings, she fell in with Natasha's wishes, and intrusted her to Madame Byelov.

Agrafena Ivanovna went in to wake Natasha at three o'clock in the night, and frequently found her not asleep. Natasha was afraid of sleeping too late for the early morning service. Hurriedly washing, and in all humility putting on her shabbiest dress and old mantle, Natasha, shuddering at the chill air, went out into the deserted streets, in the limpid light of the early dawn. By the advice of Agrafena Ivanovna, Natasha did not attend the services of her own parish church, but went to a church where the priest was esteemed by the devout Madame Byelov as being of a particularly severe and exemplary life. There were few people in the church. Natasha and Madame Byelov always took the same seat before an image of the Mother of God, carved at the back of the left choir; and a new feeling of humility before the great mystery came over Natasha, as at that unusual hour in the morning she gazed at the black outline of the Mother of God, with the light of the candles burning in front of it, and the morning light falling on it from the window. She listened to the words of the service, and tried to follow and understand them. When she did understand them, all the shades of her personal feeling blended with her prayer; when she did not understand, it was still sweeter for her to think that the desire to understand all was pride, that she could not comprehend all; that she had but to believe and give herself up to God, Who was, she felt, at those moments guiding her soul. She crossed herself, bowed to the ground, and when she did not follow, simply prayed to God to forgive her everything, everything, and to have mercy on her, in horror at her own vileness. The prayer into which she threw herself heart and soul was the prayer of repentance. On the way home in the early morning, when they met no one but masons going to their work, or porters cleaning the streets, and every one was asleep in the houses, Natasha had a new sense of the possibility of correcting herself of her sins and leading a new life of purity and happiness.

During the week she spent in this way, that feeling grew stronger with every day. And the joy of "communication," as Agrafena Ivanovna liked to call taking the Communion, seemed to her so great that she fancied she could not live till that blissful Sunday.

But the happy day did come. And when on that memorable Sunday Natasha returned from the Sacrament wearing a white muslin dress, for the first time for many months she felt at peace, and not oppressed by the life that lay before her.

The doctor came that day to see Natasha, and gave directions for the powders to be continued that he had begun prescribing a fortnight ago. "She must certainly go on taking them morning and evening," he said, with visible and simple-hearted satisfaction at the success of his treatment. "Please, don't forget them. You may set your mind at rest, countess," the doctor said playfully, as he deftly received the gold in the hollow of his palm. "She will soon be singing and dancing again. The last medicine has done her great, great good. She is very much better."

The countess looked at her finger-nails and spat, to avert the ill-omen of such words, as with a cheerful face she went back to the drawing-room.

XVIII

At the beginning of July the rumours as to the progress of the war current in Moscow became more and more alarming; and there was talk of the Tsar's appeal to the people, and the Tsar himself was said to be coming from the army to Moscow. And as up to the 11th of July the manifesto and appeal to the people had not been received, the most exaggerated reports about them and the position of Russia were common. It was said that the Tsar was coming away because the army was in danger; it was said that Smolensk had surrendered; that Napoleon had millions of troops, and that nothing short of a miracle could save Russia.

On Saturday, the 11th of July, the manifesto was received, but was not yet in print; and Pierre, who happened to be at the Rostovs', promised to come next day, Sunday, to dinner, and to bring the manifesto, which he could obtain from Count Rastoptchin.

That Sunday the Rostovs attended service as usual in the private chapel of the Razumovskys. It was a hot July day. Even by ten o'clock, when the Rostovs got out of their carriage before the chapel, the sultry air, the shouts of the street hawkers, the gay, light summer dresses of the crowd, the dusty leaves of the trees on the boulevard, the martial music and white trousers of the battalion marching by to parade, the rattle of the pavements, and the brilliant, hot sunshine, were all full of that summer languor, that content and discontent with the present, which is felt particularly vividly on a bright, hot day in town. All the fashionable world of Moscow, all the Rostovs' acquaintances were in the chapel. A great number of wealthy families, who usually spent the summer in the country, were staying on in Moscow that year, as though in vague anticipation of something.

As Natasha walked beside her mother, behind a footman in livery, who made way for them through the crowd, she heard the voice of some young man speaking in too loud a whisper about her:

"That's the young Countess Rostov, the very girl!"

"She's ever so much thinner, but still pretty!" she caught, and fancied that the names of Kuragin and Bolkonsky were mentioned. But that was always happening. She was always fancying that any one who looked at her could be thinking of nothing but what happened to her. With a sinking heart, wretched as she always was now in a crowd, Natasha, in her lilac silk dress, trimmed with black lace, walked on, as only women know how to do, with an air of ease and dignity all the greater for the pain and shame in her heart. She knew for a fact that she was pretty, but that did not give her pleasure now, as once it had. On the contrary, it had been a source of more misery than anything of late, and especially so on this bright, hot summer day in town. "Another Sunday, another week," she said to herself, recalling how she had been here on that memorable Sunday; "and still the same life that is no life, and still the same circumstances in which life used to seem so easy once. Young and pretty, and I know that now I am good, and before I was wicked! But now I am good," she mused, "but yet the best years, the best of my life, are all being wasted, and no good to any one." She stood by her mother's side, and nodded to the acquaintances who were standing near. From force of habit Natasha scrutinised the dresses of the ladies, and criticised the *tenue* of a lady standing near her, and the awkward and cramped way in which she was crossing herself. Then she thought with vexation that she was herself being criticised again, and was criticising others; and at the first sounds of the service she was horrified at her sinfulness, horrified that her purity of heart should be lost again.

A handsome, clean-looking old priest read the service with the mild solemnity that has such an elevating and soothing effect on the souls of those who pray. The sanctuary doors were closed, the curtain was slowly drawn, and a voice, mysteriously subdued, uttered some word from it. Tears, that she could not herself have explained, rose to Natasha's eyes, and a feeling of joyful agitation came upon her.

"Teach me what to do, how to live my life, how to conquer my sins for ever, for ever!" . . . she prayed. The deacon came out to the steps before the altar screen; with his thumb held out apart from the rest, he pulled his long hair out from under his surplice, and laying the cross on his breast, he began in a loud voice solemnly reading the prayer:

"As one community let us pray to the Lord."

"As one community, all together without distinction of class, free from enmity, all united in brotherly love, let us pray," thought Natasha.

"For the world above and the salvation of our souls!"

"For the world of angels and the souls of all spiritual beings who live above us," prayed Natasha.

When they prayed for the army, she thought of her brother and Denisov. When they prayed for all travelling by sea and by land, she thought of Prince Andrey, and prayed for him, and prayed that God would forgive her the wrong she had done him. When they prayed for all who love us, she prayed for all her family, her father and mother, and Sonya—for the first time feeling all the shortcomings in her behaviour to them, and all the strength of her own love for them. When they prayed for those who hate us, she tried to think of enemies, to pray for them. She reckoned as enemies all her father's creditors, and every one who had business relations with him; and always at the thought of enemies who hated her she thought of Anatole, who had done her so cruel an injury, and though he had not hated her, she prayed gladly for him, as an enemy. It was only at her prayers that she felt able to think calmly and clearly either of Prince Andrey or of Anatole, with a sense that her feelings for them were as nothing compared with her feeling of worship and awe of God. When they prayed for the Imperial family and the Synod, she bowed and crossed herself more devoutly than ever, telling herself that if she did not comprehend, she could not doubt, and anyway loved the Holy Synod and prayed for it.

When the litany was over, the deacon crossed his stole over his breast and pronounced:

"Ourselves and our life we offer up to Christ the Lord!"

"Ourselves we offer up to God," Natasha repeated in her heart. "My God, I give myself unto Thy keeping!" she thought. "I ask for nothing, I desire nothing; teach me how to act, how to do Thy will! Yes, take me; take me to Thee!" Natasha said, with devout impatience in her heart. She did not cross herself, but stood with her thin arms hanging down, as though in expectation every moment that an unseen force would come and carry her off and rescue her from herself, from her regrets and desires and remorse and hopes and sins.

Several times during the service the countess looked round at her daughter's devout face and shining eyes, and prayed to God to help her.

To the general surprise, in the middle of the service, which Natasha knew so well, the deacon brought forward the little bench, from which they repeated the prayers, kneeling, on Trinity Day, and set it before the sanctuary doors. The priest advanced in his lilac velvet calotte, threw back his hair, and, with an effort, dropped on his knees. All the congregation did the same, looking at one another in surprise. There followed the prayer, which had just been received from the Synod, the prayer for the delivery of Russia out of the hands of the enemy.

"Lord God of our might, God of our salvation," began the priest in that clear, mild, unemphatic voice, that is only used by the Slavonic priesthood, and has such an indescribable effect on the Russian heart.

"Lord God of might, God of our salvation! Look in grace and blessing on Thy humble people, and hear with loving-kindness, and spare and have mercy on us. The foe is confounding Thy land, and is fain to rise up against all the earth and lay it waste. These lawless men are gathered together to overwhelm Thy kingdom, to destroy Thy holy Jerusalem, Thy beloved Russia: to defile Thy temples, to overturn the altars and violate our holy shrines. How long, O Lord, how long shall the wicked prevail? How long shall they wreak their sinful will?

"Almighty God! Hear us when we pray to Thee, strengthen with Thy might our most gracious and supreme sovereign, Emperor Alexander Pavlovitch. Be mindful of his truth and mercy, recompense him according to his good deeds, and let them preserve Thy chosen Israel. Bless his counsels, his undertakings, and his deeds; fortify his kingdom with Thy Almighty hand, and vouchsafe him victory over the enemy, even as Thou gavest Moses victory over Amalek, and Gideon over Midian, and David over Goliath. Preserve his army; put weapons of brass in the hands that wage war in Thy name, and gird them about with strength for the battle. Take Thou the lance and shield, and rise up to succour us, and put to shame and to confusion them that devise evil against us, and let them be scattered before the face of Thy faithful armament like dust before the wind; and may Thy mighty angel put them to flight and to confusion. And let the net ensnare them when they wot not of it, and their plots that they have hatched in secret be turned against them. And let them be laid low before the feet of Thy servants and vanquished by our hosts. Lord! it is nought for Thee to save both great and small. Thou art God, and man can do nought against Thee!

"God of our Fathers! Remember Thy mercy and loving-kindness, that are everlasting. Turn not Thy face away from us; be gracious to our unworthiness; but in the greatness of Thy mercy and the infinity of Thy goodness, overlook our transgressions and our iniquities. Purify our hearts, and renew the true spirit within us; strengthen us all by faith in Thee; fortify us with hope; breathe into us true love for one another; arm us with unity of spirit in the righteous defence of the heritage Thou hast given us and our fathers; and let not the sceptre of the unrighteous be exalted above the destinies of Thy holy people.

"O Lord our God, in Whom we believe, and in Whom we put our trust, let us not be confounded in our faith in Thy mercy, and give us a sign for our blessing that they that hate us and our holy faith may see it and be put to shame and confusion, and that all lands may know that the Lord is Thy Name, and we are Thy people. Show Thy mercy upon us this day, O Lord, and grant us Thy salvation. Rejoice the hearts of Thy servants with Thy mercy; strike down our enemies and trample them swiftly under the feet of Thy faithful. Thou art the defence, the succour, and the victory of them that put their trust in Thee; and to Thee be the glory, to Father, and to Son, and to Holy Ghost, now and ever has been, for ever and ever. Amen!''

In Natasha's religiously impressionable state, this prayer affected her strongly. She heard every word about Moses's victory over Amalek, and Gideon's over Midian, and David's over Goliath, and about the destruction of Thy Jerusalem; and she prayed to God with all the tenderness and fervour with which her heart was overflowing, but she had no distinct idea what she was asking for in this prayer. With all her soul she joined in the petition for the true spirit, for the strengthening of hearts with faith and hope, and the breathing into them of love. But she could not pray for the trampling of her enemies underfoot, when she had only a few minutes before been wishing she had more of them to forgive and pray for. But yet she could have no doubts of the righteousness of this prayer that had been read by the priest on his knees. She felt in her heart a thrill of awe and horror at the punishment in store for men's sins, and especially for her sins, and prayed to God to forgive them all, and her too, and give them all and her peace and happiness. And it seemed to her that God heard her prayer.

XIX

EVER since the day when Pierre had looked up at the comet in the sky, on his way home from the Rostovs', and recalling Natasha's grateful look, had felt as though some new vista was opening before him, the haunting problem of the vanity and senselessness of all things earthly had ceased to torment him. That terrible question: Why? what for? which had till then haunted him in the midst of every occupation, was not now replaced by any other question, nor by an answer to the old question; its place was filled by the image of *her*. If he heard or talked of trivialities, or read or was told of some instance of human baseness or folly, he was not cast down as of old; he did not ask himself why people troubled, when all was so brief and uncertain. But he thought of her as he had seen her last, and all his doubts vanished; not because she had answered the questions that haunted him, but because her image lifted him instantly into another bright realm of spiritual activity, in which there could be neither right nor wrong, into a region of beauty and love, which was worth living for. Whatever infamy he thought of, he said to himself, "Well, let so and so rob the state and the Tsar, while the state and the Tsar heap honours on him; but she smiled at me yesterday, and begged me to come, and I love her, and nobody will ever know it," he thought.

Pierre still went into society, drank as much, and led the same idle and aimless life, because, apart from the hours he spent at the Rostovs', he had to get through the rest of his time somehow, and the habits and the acquaintances he had made in Moscow drew him irresistibly into the same life. But of late, since the reports from the seat of war had become more and more disquieting, and Natasha's health had improved, and she had ceased to call for the same tender pity, he had begun to be more and more possessed by a restlessness that he could not explain. He felt that the position he was in could not go on for long, that a catas- 'trophe was coming that would change the whole course of his life, and he sought impatiently for signs of this impending catastrophe. One of his brother masons had revealed to Pierre the following prophecy relating to Napoleon, and taken from the Apocalypse of St. John.

In the Apocalypse, chapter thirteen, verse seventeen, it is written: "Here is wisdom; let him that hath understanding, count the number of the beast; for it is the number of a man, and his number is six hundred three-score and six."

And in the fifth verse of the same chapter: "And there was given unto him a mouth speaking great things and blasphemies, and power was given unto him to continue forty and two months."

If the French alphabet is treated like the Hebrew system of enumera- tion, by which the first ten letters represent the units, and the next the tens, and so on, the letters have the following value:—

a b c d e f g h i k l m n o p q r s t   u   v   w   x   y   z
1 2 3 4 5 6 7 8 9 10 20 30 40 50 60 70 80 90 100 110 120 130 140 150 160

Turning out the words *l'empereur Napoléon* into ciphers on this sys- tem, it happens that the sum of these numbers equals 666, and Napoleon is thereby seen to be the beast prophesied in the Apocalypse. Moreover, working out in the same way the words *quarante-deux*, that is, the term for which the beast was permitted to continue, the sum of these numbers again equals 666, from which it is deduced that the terms of Napoleon's power had come in 1812, when the French Emperor reached his forty- second year. This prophecy made a great impression on Pierre. He fre- quently asked himself what would put an end to the power of the beast, that is, of Napoleon; and he tried by the same system of turning letters into figures, and reckoning them up to find an answer to this question. He wrote down as an answer, *l'empereur Alexandre? La nation russe?* He reckoned out the figures, but their sum was far more or less than 666. Once he wrote down his own name "Comte Pierre Bezuhov," but the sum of the figure was far from being right. He changed the spelling, put- ing s for z, added "de," added the article "le," and still could not obtain the desired result. Then it occurred to him that if the answer sought for were to be found in his name, his nationality ought surely to find a place 'in it too. He tried *Le russe Besuhof*, and adding up the figure made the sum 671. This was only five too much; the 5 was denoted by the letter "e," the letter dropped in the article in the expression *l'empereur Na- poléon*. Dropping the "e" in a similar way, though of course incorrectly, Pierre obtained the answer he sought in *L'russe Besuhof*, the letters of which on that system added up to 666. This discovery greatly excited him. How, by what connection, he was associated with the great event foretold in the Apocalypse, he could not tell. But he did not for a moment doubt of that connection. His love for Natasha, Antichrist, Napoleon's invasion, the comet, the number 666, *l'empereur Napoléon*, and *l'russe Besuhof*—all he thought were to develop, and come to some crisis together to extricate him from that spellbound, trivial round of Moscow habits, to which he felt himself in bondage, and to lead him to some great achievement and great happiness.

The day before that Sunday on which the new prayer had been read in the churches, Pierre had promised the Rostovs to call on Count Rastoptchin, whom he knew well, and to get from him the Tsar's appeal to the country, and the last news from the army. On going to Count Rastoptchin's in the morning, Pierre found there a special courier, who had only just arrived from the army. The courier was a man whom Pierre knew, and often saw at the Moscow balls.

"For mercy's sake, couldn't you relieve me of some of my burden," said the courier; "I have a sack full of letters to parents."

Among these letters was a letter from Nikolay Rostov to his father. Pierre took that; and Count Rastoptchin gave him a copy of the Tsar's appeal to Moscow, which had just been printed, the last announcements in the army, and his own last placard. Looking through the army announcements, Pierre found in one of them, among lists of wounded, killed and promoted, the name of Nikolay Rostov, rewarded with the order of St. George, of the fourth degree, for distinguished bravery in the Ostrovna affair, and in the same announcement the appointment of Prince Andrey Bolkonsky to the command of a regiment of light cavalry. Though he did not want to remind the Rostovs of Bolkonsky's existence, Pierre could not resist the inclination to rejoice their hearts with the news of their son's decoration. Keeping the Tsar's appeal, Rastoptchin's placard, and the other announcement to bring with him at dinner-time, Pierre sent the printed announcement and Nikolay's letter to the Rostovs.

The conversation with Rastoptchin, and his tone of anxiety and hurry, the meeting with the courier, who had casually alluded to the disastrous state of affairs in the army, the rumours of spies being caught in Moscow, of a sheet circulating in the town stating that Napoleon had sworn to be in both capitals before autumn, of the Tsar's expected arrival next day—all combined to revive in Pierre with fresh intensity that feeling of excitement and expectation, that he had been conscious of ever since the appearance of the comet, and with even greater force since the beginning of the war.

The idea of entering the army had long before occurred to Pierre, and he would have acted upon it, but that, in the first place, he was pledged by his vow to the Masonic brotherhood, which preached universal peace and the abolition of war; and secondly, when he looked at the great mass of Moscow gentlemen, who put on uniforms, and professed themselves patriots, he felt somehow ashamed to take the same step. A cause that weighed with him even more in not entering the army was the obscure conception that he, *l'russe Besuhof*, had somehow the mystic value of the number of the beast, 666, that his share in putting a limit to the power of the beast, "speaking great things and blasphemies," had been ordained from all eternity, and that therefore it was not for him to take any step whatever; it was for him to wait for what was bound to come to pass.

XX

A few intimate friends were, as usual on Sundays, dining with the Rostovs.

Pierre came early, hoping to find them alone.

Pierre had that year grown so stout, that he would have been grotesque, had not he been so tall, so broad-shouldered, and so powerfully built that he carried off his bulky proportions with evident ease.

Puffing, and muttering something to himself, he went up the stairs. His coachman did not even ask whether he should wait. He knew that when the count was at the Rostovs', it was till midnight. The Rostovs' footmen ran with eager welcome to take off his cloak, and take his stick and hat. From the habit of the club, Pierre always left his stick and hat in the vestibule.

The first person he saw at the Rostovs' was Natasha. Before he saw her, while taking off his cloak, he heard her. She was practising her sol-fa exercises in the hall. He knew she had given up singing since her illness, and so he was surprised and delighted at the sound of her voice. He opened the door softly, and saw Natasha, in the lilac dress she had worn at the service, walking up and down the room singing. She had her back turned to him as he opened the door; but when she turned sharply round and saw his broad, surprised face, she flushed and ran quickly up to him.

"I want to try and sing again," she said. "It's something to do, any way," she added as though in excuse.

"Quite right too!"

"How glad I am you have come! I'm so happy to-day," she said with the old eagerness that Pierre had not seen for so long. "You know, Nikolenka has got the St. George's Cross. I'm so proud of him."

"Of course, I sent you the announcement. Well, I won't interrupt you," he added, and would have gone on to the drawing-room.

Natasha stopped him.

"Count, is it wrong of me to sing?" she said, blushing, but still keeping her eyes fixed inquiringly on Pierre.

"No. . . . Why should it be? On the contrary. . . . But why do you ask me?"

"I don't know myself," Natasha answered quickly; "but I shouldn't like to do anything you wouldn't like. I trust you in everything. You don't know how much you are to me, and what a great deal you have done for me!" . . . She spoke quickly, and did not notice how Pierre flushed at these words. "I saw in that announcement, *he*, Bolkonsky" (she uttered the word in a rapid whisper), "he is in Russia, and in the army again. What do you think," she said hurriedly, evidently in haste to speak because she was afraid her strength would fail her, "will he ever forgive me? Will he not always have an evil feeling for me? What do you think? What do you think?"

"I think . . ." said Pierre. "He has nothing to forgive . . . If I were in his place . . ." From association of ideas, Pierre was instantly carried back in imagination to the time when he had comforted her by saying that if he were not himself, but the best man in the world and free, he would beg on his knees for her hand, and the same feeling of pity, tenderness, and love took possession of him, and the same words rose to his lips. But she did not give him time to utter them.

"Yes, you—you," she said, uttering that word *you* with enthusiasm, "that's a different matter. Any one kinder, more generous than you, I have never known—no one could be. If it had not been for you then, and now too . . . I don't know what would have become of me, because . . ." Tears suddenly came into her eyes: she turned away, held her music before her eyes, and began again singing and walking up and down the room.

At that moment Petya ran in from the drawing-room.

Petya was by now a handsome, rosy lad of fifteen, with full red lips, very like Natasha. He was being prepared for the university, but had lately resolved in secret with his comrade, Obolensky, to go into the hussars.

Petya rushed up to his namesake, Pierre, to talk to him of this scheme. He had begged him to find out whether he would be accepted in the hussars.

Pierre walked about the drawing-room, not heeding Petya.

The boy pulled him by the arm to attract his attention.

"Come, tell me about my plan, Pyotr Kirillitch, for mercy's sake! You're my only hope," said Petya.

"Oh yes, your plan. To be an hussar? I'll speak about it; to-day I'll tell them all about it."

"Well, my dear fellow, have you got the manifesto?" asked the old count. "My little countess was at the service in the Razumovsky's chapel; she heard the new prayer there. Very fine it was, she tells me."

"Yes, I have got it," answered Pierre. "The Tsar will be here to-morrow. . . . There's to be an extraordinary meeting of the nobility and a levy they say of ten per thousand. Oh, I congratulate you."

"Yes, yes, thank God. Well, and what news from the army?"

"Our soldiers have retreated again. They are before Smolensk, they say," answered Pierre.

"Mercy on us, mercy on us!" said the count. "Where's the manifesto?"

"The Tsar's appeal? Ah, yes!" Pierre began looking for the papers in his pockets, and could not find them. Still slapping his pockets, he kissed the countess's hand as she came in, and looked round uneasily, evidently expecting Natasha, who had left off singing now, but had not come into the drawing-room. "Good Heavens, I don't know where I have put it," he said.

"To be sure, he always mislays everything," said the countess.

Natasha came in with a softened and agitated face and sat down, looking mutely at Pierre. As soon as she came into the room, Pierre's face, which had been overcast, brightened, and while still seeking for the paper, he looked several times intently at her.

"By God, I'll drive round, I must have forgotten them at home. Of course . . ."

"Why, you will be late for dinner."

"Oh! and the coachman has not waited."

But Sonya had gone into the vestibule to look for the papers, and there found them in Pierre's hat, where he had carefully put them under the lining. Pierre would have read them.

"No, after dinner," said the old count, who was obviously looking forward to the reading of them as a great treat.

At dinner they drank champagne to the health of the new cavalier of St. George, and Shinshin told them of the news of the town, of the illness of the old Georgian princess, and of the disappearance of Metivier from Moscow, and described how a German had been brought before Rastoptchin by the people, who declared (so Count Rastoptchin told the story) that he was a *champignon,* and how Count Rastoptchin had bade them let the *champignon* go, as he was really nothing but an old German mushroom.

"They keep on seizing people," said the count. "I tell the countess she ought not to speak French so much. Now's not the time to do it."

"And did you hear," said Shinshin, "Prince Galitzin has engaged a Russian teacher—he's learning Russian. It begins to be dangerous to speak French in the streets."

"Well, Count Pyotr Kirillitch, now if they raise a general militia, you will have to mount a horse too, ah?" said the old count addressing Pierre.

Pierre was dreamy and silent all dinner-time. He looked at the count as though not understanding.

"Yes, yes, for the war," he said. "No! A fine soldier I should make! And yet everything's so strange; so strange! Why, I don't understand it myself. I don't know, I am far from being military in my taste, but in these days no one can answer for himself."

After dinner the count settled himself comfortably in a low chair, and with a serious face asked Sonya, who enjoyed the reputation of a good reader, to read the Tsar's appeal.

"To our metropolitan capital Moscow. The enemy has entered our border with an immense host and comes to lay waste our beloved country," Sonya read conscientiously in her thin voice. The count listened with closed eyes, heaving abrupt sighs at certain passages.

Natasha sat erect, looking inquisitively and directly from her father to Pierre.

Pierre felt her eyes on him and tried not to look round. The countess shook her head disapprovingly and wrathfully at every solemn expression in the manifesto. In all these words she saw nothing but that the danger menacing her son would not soon be over. Shinshin, pursing his lips up into a sarcastic smile, was clearly preparing to make a joke at the first subject that presented itself: at Sonya's reading, the count's next remark, or even the manifesto itself, if no better pretext should be found.

After reading of the dangers threatening Russia, the hopes the Tsar rested upon Moscow, and particularly on its illustrious nobility, Sonya, with a quiver in her voice, due principally to the attention with which they were listening to her, read the last words: "We shall without delay be in the midst of our people in the capital, and in other parts of our empire, for deliberation, and for the guidance of all our militia levies both those which are already barring the progress of the foe, and those to be formed for conflict with him, wherever he may appear. And may the ruin with which he threatens us recoil on his own head, and may Europe, delivered from bondage, glorify the name of Russia!"

"That's right!" cried the count, opening his wet eyes, and several times interrupted by a sniff, as though he had put a bottle of strong smelling-salts to his nose. He went on, "Only let our sovereign say the word, we will sacrifice everything without grudging."

Before Shinshin had time to utter the joke he was ready to make on the count's patriotism, Natasha had jumped up from her seat and run to her father.

"What a darling this papa is!" she cried, kissing him, and she glanced again at Pierre with the unconscious coquetry that had come back with her fresh interest in life.

"Oh, what a patriot she is!" said Shinshin.

"Not a patriot at all, but simply . . ." Natasha began, nettled. "You think everything funny, but this isn't at all a joke . . ."

"A joke," repeated the count. "Only let him say the word, we will all go . . . We're not a set of Germans!"

"Did you notice," said Pierre, "the words, 'for deliberation . . .'"

"Yes, to be sure, for whatever might come . . ."

Meanwhile Petya, to whom no one was paying attention, went up to his father, and very red, said in a voice that passed abruptly from gruffness to shrillness, "Well, now, papa, I tell you positively—and mamma too, say what you will—I tell you you must let me go into the army, because I cannot . . . and that's all about it."

The countess in dismay turned her eyes up to heaven, clasped her hands, and said angrily to her husband:

"See, what your talk has brought us to!"

But the count recovered the same instant from the excitement.

"Come, come," he said. "A fine warrior you'd make! Don't talk nonsense; you have your studies to attend to."

"It's not nonsense, papa. Fedya Obolensky's younger than I am, and he's going too; and what's more, I can't anyhow study now, when . . ." Petya stopped, flushed till his face was perspiring, yet stoutly went on . . . "when the country's in danger."

"Hush, hush, nonsense! . . ."

"Why, but you said yourself you would sacrifice everything."

"Petya! I tell you be quiet," cried the count, looking at his wife, who was gazing with a white face and fixed eyes at her younger son.

"Let me say . . . Pyotr Kirillovitch here will tell you . . ."

"I tell you, it's nonsense; the milk's hardly dry on his lips, and he wants to go into the army! Come, come, I tell you," and the count, taking the papers with him, was going out of the room, probably to read them once more in his study before his nap.

"Pyotr Kirillovitch, let us have a smoke. . . ."

Pierre felt embarrassed and hesitating. Natasha's unusually brilliant and eager eyes, continually turned upon him with more than cordiality in them, had reduced him to this condition.

"No; I think I'll go home. . . ."

"Go home? But you meant to spend the evening with us. . . . You come rarely enough, as it is. And this girl of mine," said the count good-humouredly, looking towards Natasha, "is never in spirits but when you are here. . . ."

"But I have forgotten something. I really must go home. . . . Business. . . ." Pierre said hurriedly.

"Well, good-bye then," said the count as he went out of the room.

"Why are you going away? Why are you so upset? What for?" Natasha asked Pierre, looking with challenging eyes into his face.

"Because I love you!" he wanted to say, but he did not say it. He crimsoned till the tears came, and dropped his eyes.

"Because it is better for me not to be so often with you. . . . Because . . . no, simply I have business. . . ."

"What for? No, do tell me," Natasha was beginning resolutely, and she suddenly stopped. Both in dismay and embarrassment looked at one another. He tried to laugh, but could not; his smile expressed suffering, and he kissed her hand and went out without a word.

Pierre made up his mind not to visit the Rostovs again.

XXI

AFTER the uncompromising refusal he had received, Petya went to his own room, and there locking himself in, he wept bitterly. All his family behaved as though they noticed nothing when he came in to tea, silent and depressed with tear-stained eyes.

Next day, the Tsar arrived in Moscow. Several of the Rostovs' servants asked permission to go out to see the Tsar. That morning Petya spent a long time dressing. He combed his hair and arranged his collar like a grown-up man. He screwed up his eyes before the looking-glass, gesticulated, shrugged his shoulders, and finally, without saying anything to any one, he put on his cap and went out of the house by the back way, trying to escape observation. Petya had resolved to go straight to where the Tsar was, and to explain frankly to some gentleman-in-waiting (Petya fancied that the Tsar was always surrounded by gentlemen-in-waiting) that he, Count Rostov, wished, in spite of his youth, to serve his country, that youth could be no hindrance to devotion, and that he was ready . . . Petya had, while he was dressing, prepared a great many fine speeches to make to the gentleman-in-waiting.

Petya reckoned on the success of his presentation to the Tsar simply because he was a child (Petya dreamed, indeed, of how they would wonder at his youth), and yet in his arrangement of his collar, and his hair, and in the sedate, deliberate walk he adopted, he tried to act the part of an elderly man. But the further he went, the more interested he became in the growing crowds about the Kremlin, and he forgot to keep up the sedateness and deliberation characteristic of grown-up people. As he got closer to the Kremlin, he began to try to avoid being crushed, and with a resolute and threatening mien, stuck elbows out on each side of him. But in spite of his determined air, in the Toistsky Gate the crowd, probably unaware of his patriotic object in going to the Kremlin, so pushed him against the wall, that he was obliged to submit and stand still, while carriages drove in with a rumbling sound under the archway. Near Petya stood a peasant woman, a footman, two merchants, and a discharged soldier. After standing for some time in the gateway, Petya, not caring to wait for all the carriages to pass, tried to push on before the rest, and began resolutely working away with his elbows, but the peasant woman standing next him, who was the first person he poked, shouted angrily to him:

"Why are you shoving away, little master? You see everybody's standing still. What do you want to push for?"

"What, if every one were to push then!" said the footman; and he too setting to work with his elbows shoved Petya into the stinking corner of the gateway.

Petya rubbed the sweat off his face with his hands, and set straight the soaking collar, that he had so carefully arranged at home like a grown-up person's.

Petya felt that he looked unpresentable, and was afraid that if he showed himself in this guise to the gentlemen-in-waiting, they would not admit him to the Tsar's presence. But the crush gave him no possibility of setting himself straight or getting into another place. One of the generals who rode by was an acquaintance of the Rostovs. Petya wanted to ask him for help, but considered this would be below his manly dignity. When all the carriages had driven by, the crowd made a rush, and swept Petya along with it into the square, which was already full of people. Not only in the square, but on the slopes, and the roofs, and everywhere there were crowds of people. As soon as Petya got into the square, he heard the ringing of bells and the joyous hum of the crowd filling the whole Kremlin.

For a while the crush was less in the square, but all at once all heads were bared, and there was another rush forward. Petya was so crushed that he could hardly breathe, and there was a continual shouting: "Hurrah! hurrah! hurrah!"

Petya tip-toed, pushed, and pinched, but he could see nothing but the crowd around him.

All the faces wore the same expression of excitement and enthusiasm. A shopkeeper's wife standing near Petya sobbed, and tears flowed down her cheeks.

"Father, angel!" she kept saying, wiping her tears with her fingers.

"Hurrah!" shouted the crowd on all sides.

For a minute the crowd remained stationary; then there was another rush forward.

Petya, beside himself with excitement, clenched his teeth, and rolling his eyes savagely, rushed forward, elbowing his way and shouting "Hurrah!" as though he were prepared to kill himself and every one else at that moment, but just as savage faces pushed on each side of him with the same shouts of "hurrah!"

"So this is the Tsar!" thought Petya. "No, I could never give him the petition myself, it would be too bold!"

In spite of that, he still forced his way forward as desperately, and over the backs of those in front of him caught a glimpse of open space with a passage covered with red cloth in the midst of it. But at that moment the crowd began heaving back; the police in front were forcing back those who had pressed too close to the procession. The Tsar was passing from the palace to the Uspensky Sobor. Petya received such a sudden blow in the ribs, and was so squeezed, that all at once a mist passed before his eyes, and he lost consciousness. When he came to himself, a clerical personage, with a mane of grey hair on his shoulders, in a shabby blue cassock—probably a deacon—was holding him up with one arm, while with the other he kept off the crowd.

"A young gentleman's been crushed!" the deacon was saying, "Mind what you're about! . . . easy there! . . . you're crushing him, you're crushing him!"

The Tsar had entered the Uspensky Sobor. The crowd spread out again, and the deacon got Petya pale and breathless on to the big cannon. Several persons pitied Petya; and suddenly quite a crowd noticed his plight, and began to press round him. Those who were standing near him looked after him, unbuttoned his coat, sat him on the highest part of the cannon, and scolded those who were squeezing too close to him.

"Any one may be crushed to death like that. What next! Killing people! Why, the poor dear's as white as a sheet," said voices.

Petya soon recovered, and the colour came back into his face; the pain was over, and by this temporary inconvenience he had gained a seat on the cannon, from which he hoped to see the Tsar, who was to walk back. Petya thought no more now of presenting his petition. If only he could see him, he would think himself lucky! During the service in the Uspensky Sobor, in celebration of the Tsar's arrival, and also in thanksgiving for the peace with the Turks, the crowd dispersed about the square, and hawkers appeared crying kvass, gingerbread, and poppyseed sweets—of which Petya was particularly fond—and he could hear the usual talk among the people. One shopkeeper's wife was showing her torn shawl, and saying how much she had paid for it; while another observed that all silk things were very dear nowadays. The deacon who had rescued Petya was talking to a clerk of the different priests who were taking part in the service to-day with the most reverend bishop. The deacon several times repeated the word "*soborne*," which Petya did not understand. Two young artisans were joking with some servant-girls, cracking nuts. All these conversations, especially the jokes with the servant-girls—which would have seemed particularly attractive at his age to Petya—did not interest him now. He sat on his high perch on the cannon, still in the same excitement at the thought of the Tsar and his love for him. The blending of the feeling of pain and fright when he was crushed with the feeling of enthusiasm intensified his sense of the gravity of the occasion.

Suddenly cannon shots were heard from the embankment—the firing was in celebration of the peace with the Turks—and the crowd made a dash for the embankment to see the firing. Petya, too, would have liked to run there, but the deacon, who had taken the young gentleman under his protection, would not let him. The firing still continued, when officers, generals, and gentlemen-in-waiting came running out of the Uspensky Sobor. Then others came out with less haste, and again caps were lifted, and those who had run to look at the cannons ran back. At last four men in uniforms and decorations came out from the doors of the Sobor. "Hurrah! hurrah!" the crowd shouted again.

"Which? which one?" Petya asked in a weeping voice of those around him, but no one answered him. Every one was too much excited, and Petya, picking out one of the four, and hardly able to see him for the tears that started into his eyes, concentrated all his enthusiasm on him, though it happened not to be the Tsar. He shouted "Hurrah!" in a voice of frenzy, and resolved that to-morrow, come what might of it, he would join the army. The crowd ran after the Tsar, accompanied him to the palace, and began to disperse. It was late, and Petya had had nothing to eat, and the sweat was dripping from his face. But he did not go home. He remained with a smaller, though still considerable, crowd before the palace during the Tsar's dinner-time. He gazed up at the palace windows, expecting something to happen, and envying equally the grand personages who drove up to the entrance to dine with the Tsar, and the footmen waiting at table, of whom he caught glimpses at the window.

At the Tsar's dinner, Valuev said, looking out of the window:

"The people are still hoping to get a sight of your majesty."

The dinner was almost over, the Tsar got up, and still munching a biscuit, came out on the balcony. The crowd, with Petya in the midst, rushed towards the balcony.

"Angel, father! Hurrah!" . . . shouted the crowd, and with it Petya. And again women, and, in a less degree some men—among them Petya—shed tears of happiness.

A good sized piece of the biscuit in the Tsar's hand broke off, fell on the balcony railing, and from the railing to the ground. A coachman in a jerkin, who stood nearest, pounced on the piece of biscuit and snatched it up. Several persons rushed at the coachman. Noticing this the Tsar asked for a plate of biscuits, and began dropping them from the balcony. Petya's eyes almost started out of his head; the danger of being crushed excited him more than ever, and he rushed at the biscuits. He did not know why, but he felt he must have a biscuit from the Tsar's hands, and he must not give in. He made a dash and upset an old woman, who was just about to seize a biscuit. But the old woman refused to con-sider herself beaten, though she was on the ground; she snatched at the biscuits on her hands and knees. Petya pushed her hand away with his knee, snatched up a biscuit, and as though afraid of being late, hastily shouted again, "Hurrah!" in a hoarse voice.

The Tsar went in, and after that the greater part of the crowd dis-persed.

"There, I said if only we waited—and so it was," was the delighted comment on various sides in the crowd.

Happy as Petya was, he felt sad to go home, and to feel that all the enjoyment of that day was over. From the Kremlin, Petya went not home, but to his comrade Obolensky's. He was fifteen, and he, too, was going into the army. On getting home, Petya announced with decision and firmness that if they would not let him do so too, he would run away. And next day, though Count Ilya Andreitch had not quite yielded, he went to inquire if a commission could be obtained for Petya somewhere where there would be little danger.

XXII

On the morning of the 15th, the next day but one, a great number of carriages stood outside the Slobodsky palace.

The great halls were full. In the first were the noblemen in their uni-forms; in the second there were merchants with medals and long beards, wearing blue, full-skirted coats. The first room was full of noise and movement. The more important personages were sitting on high-backed chairs at a big table under the Tsar's portrait; but the greater number of the noblemen were walking about the hall.

The noblemen, whom Pierre saw every day either at the club or at their houses, were all in uniforms; some in those of Catherine's court, some in those of the Emperor Pavel, and some in the new uniforms of Alexander's reign, others in the common uniforms of the nobility, and the general character of their dress gave a strange and fantastic look to these old and young, most diverse and familiar faces. Particularly striking were the older men, dim-eyed, toothless, bald, and thin, with faces wrinkled or lost in yellow fat. They sat still for the most part and were silent, or if they walked and talked, attached themselves to some one younger. Just like the faces Petya had seen in the crowd, all these faces, in their universal expectation of something solemn, presented a striking contrast with their everyday, yesterday's aspect, when talking over their game of boston, Petrushka the cook, the health of Zinaida Dmitryevna, etc., etc.

Pierre, who had been since early morning in an uncomfortable uni-form, that had become too tight for him, was in the room. He was in a state of excitement; this extraordinary assembly, not only of the no-bility, but of the merchant class too—the estates, *états généraux*—called up in him a whole series of ideas of the *Contrat Social* and the French Revolution, ideas imprinted deeply on his soul, though they had long been laid aside. The words he had noticed in the manifesto, that the Tsar was coming to the capital *for deliberation* with his people, confirmed him in this chain of thought. And supposing that something of importance in that direction was near at hand, that what he had long been looking for was coming, he looked and listened attentively, but he saw nowhere any expression of the ideas that engrossed him.

The Tsar's manifesto was read, and evoked enthusiasm; and then all moved about, talking. Apart from their everyday interests, Pierre heard discussion as to where the marshals were to stand when the Tsar should come in, when the ball was to be given for the Tsar, whether they were to be divided according to districts or the whole province together . . . and so on. But as soon as the war and the whole object of their meeting together was touched upon, the talk was uncertain and hesitating. Every one seemed to prefer listening to speaking.

A manly looking, handsome, middle-aged man, wearing the uniform of a retired naval officer, was speaking, and a little crowd was gathered about him in one of the rooms. Pierre went up to the circle that had formed round him, and began to listen. Count Ilya Andreitch, in his uniform of Catherine's time, was walking about with a pleasant smile among the crowd, with all of whom he was acquainted. He too approached this group, and began to listen with a good-humoured smile, as he always did listen, nodding his head approvingly in token of his agreeing with the speaker. The retired naval officer was speaking very boldly (that could be seen from the expression on the faces of the listeners and from the fact that some persons, known to Pierre as particularly submissive and timid, drew back from him in disapprobation or expressed dissent). Pierre pushed his way into the middle of the circle, listened, and gained the conviction that the speaker certainly was a liberal, but in quite a different sense from what Pierre was looking for. The naval officer spoke in the peculiarly mellow, sing-song baritone of a Russian nobleman, with peculiar burring of the r's and suppression of the consonants, in the voice in which men shout: "Waiter, pipe!" and such phrases. He talked with the habit of riotous living and of authority in his voice.

"What if the Smolensk people have offered the Emperor a levy of militia. Are the Smolensk people any rule for us? If the nobility of the Moscow province thinks fit, it can show its devotion to our sovereign the Emperor by other means. Have we forgotten the militia in the year 1807? It was only the beggarly priests' sons and thieves made a good thing of it. . . ."

Count Ilya Andreitch, smiling blandly, nodded his head in approval.

"And were our militiamen of any service to the state? Not the slightest! They only ruined our agriculture. Even conscription is better. . . . As it is, a man comes back to you neither soldier nor peasant, nothing, but only demoralised. The nobility don't grudge their lives. We will go ourselves to a man; take recruits, too; and the Tsar has but to say the word, and we will all die for him," added the orator, warming up.

Ilya Andreitch's mouth was watering with satisfaction, and he nudged Pierre, but Pierre wanted to speak too. He moved forward, feeling stirred, though he did not yet know why nor what he would say. He was just opening his mouth to speak when he was interrupted by a perfectly toothless senator with a shrewd and wrathful face, who was standing close by the last orator. Evidently accustomed to lead debates and bring forward motions, he began speaking in a low but audible voice:

"I imagine, my dear sir," said the senator, mumbling with his toothless mouth, "that we are summoned here not to discuss which is more suitable for the country at the present moment—conscription or the militia. We are summoned to reply to the appeal which our sovereign the Emperor graciously deigns to make to us. And to judge which is the fitter means —recruiting or a levy for militia—we leave to a higher power. . . ."

Pierre suddenly found the right outlet for his excitement. He felt exasperated with the senator, who introduced this conventional and narrow view of the duties that lay before the nobility. Pierre stepped forward and cut him short. He did not know himself what he was going to say, but he began eagerly, using bookish Russian, and occasionally relapsing into French.

"Excuse me, your excellency," he began (Pierre was well acquainted with this senator, but he felt it necessary on this occasion to address him formally), "though I differ from the gentleman . . ." (Pierre hesitated; he would have liked to say *Mon trè honorable préopinante*) "with the gentleman . . . whom I have not the honour of knowing; but I imagine the estate of the nobility, apart from the expression of its sympathy and enthusiasm, has been convoked also to deliberate upon the measures by which we can assist our country. I imagine," said Pierre, growing warmer, "that the Tsar would himself be displeased if he should find in us only the owners of peasants, whom we give up to him, and *chair à canon*, which we offer in ourselves—and should not find in us co . . co . . . counsel. . . ."

Many persons moved a little away from the circle, noticing the disdainful smile of the senator and the freedom of Pierre's words. Ilya Andreitch was the only person pleased at what Pierre said, just as he had been pleased with the naval officer's speech and the senator's, as he always was with the last speech he had heard.

"I consider that before discussing these questions," Pierre continued, "we ought to ask the Emperor, most respectfully to ask his majesty, to communicate to us what forces we have, what is the position of our men and our army, and then . . ."

Pierre had hardly uttered these words when he was promptly attacked on three sides at once. The most violent onslaught was made upon him by an old acquaintance and partner at boston, who had always been on the friendliest terms with him, Stepan Stepanovitch Adraksin. Stepan Stepanovitch was, of course, in uniform, and whether it was due to the uniform or to other causes, Pierre saw before him quite a changed man.

Stepan Stepanovitch, with an old man's anger in his face, screamed at Pierre:

"In the first place, let me tell you that we have no right to ask such questions of the Emperor; and secondly, if the nobility had any such right, the Emperor could not answer such questions. The movements of the troops depend on the movements of the enemy; the troops are augmented and decreased . . ."

Another voice interrupted Adraksin. The speaker was a man of forty, of medium height, whom Pierre had seen in former days at the gypsies' entertainments, and knew as a bad card-player. But now he, too, was quite transformed by his uniform, as he moved up to Pierre.

"Yes, and it's not the time for deliberation," said this nobleman. "What's needed is action; there is war in Russia. Our foe comes to ruin Russia, to desecrate the tombs of our fathers, to carry away our wives and children." The gentleman struck himself a blow on the chest. "We will all rise up; we will all go to a man, we will follow our father the Tsar!" he cried, rolling his bloodshot eyes. Several approving voices could be heard in the crowd. "We are Russians and we do not grudge our blood for the defence of our faith, our throne, and our country. But we must put a stop to idle talk, if we are true sons of our fatherland. We will show Europe how Russia can defend Russia!" shouted this gentleman.

Pierre tried to reply, but he could not get in a word. He felt that the sound of his words, apart from any meaning they conveyed, was less audible than the sound of his excited adversary's voice.

In the rear of the group, Ilya Andreitch was nodding approval; several of the audience turned their shoulders briskly to the orator at the conclusion of a phrase and said:

"That's so, that's so, indeed!"

Pierre wanted to say that he was by no means averse to the sacrifice of his money, or his peasants, or himself, but that one ought to know the true position of affairs, in order to be able to assist, but he could not speak.

A number of voices were speaking and shouting together, so much so that Ilya Andreitch had not time to nod approval to all of them. And the group grew larger and broke up into knots, re-formed again, and moved all together with a hum of talk to the big table in the big room. Pierre was not allowed to speak; they rudely interrupted him, indeed hustled him and turned their backs on him as though he were the common foe. This was not really due to their dislike of the tenor of his speech, which they had forgotten, indeed, after the great number of speeches that followed it. But a crowd is always pleased to have a concrete object for its love or its hatred. Pierre furnished it with the latter.

Many orators spoke after the eager nobleman, but all spoke in the same tone. Some spoke eloquently and originally.

The editor of the *Russian Messenger*, Glinka, who was recognised and greeted with shouts of "the author, the author!" said that hell must be driven back by hell, that he had seen a child smiling at the lightning flash and the thunder clap, but we would not be like that child.

"Yes, yes, at the thunder clap!" was repeated with approval at the back of the crowd.

"The crowd approached the great table, where grey or bald old noble-men of seventy were sitting, wearing uniforms and decorations. Almost all of them Pierre had seen with their buffoons in their own homes or playing boston at the club. The crowd drew near the table, still with the same buzz of talk. The orators, squeezed in behind the high chair backs by the surging crowd, spoke one after another and sometimes two at once. Those who stood further back noticed what the speaker had left unsaid and hastened to supply the gap. Others were busy in the heat and crush, ransacking their brains to find some idea and hurriedly uttering it. The old grandees at the table sat looking from one to another, and their expression for the most part betrayed nothing but that they were very hot. Pierre however felt excited, and the general feeling of desire to show that they were ready for anything, expressed for the most part more in tones and looks than in the tenor of the speeches, infected him too. He did not disavow his ideas, but felt somehow in fault and tried to defend himself.

"I only said that we could make sacrifices to better purpose when we know what is needed," he cried, trying to shout down the other voices.

One old man close by him looked round, but his attention was imme-diately called off by a shout at the other end of the table.

"Yes, Moscow will be surrendered! She will be the expiation!" one man was shouting.

"He is the enemy of mankind!" another shouted.

"Allow me to say . . ."

"Gentlemen, you are crushing me! . . ."

XXIII

At that moment Count Rastoptchin, with his prominent chin and alert eyes, strode in rapidly through the parting crowd, wearing the uniform of a general and a ribbon over his shoulder.

"Our sovereign the Emperor will be here immediately," said Rastop-tchin. "I have just come from him. I presume that in the position in which we are placed, there is no need of much discussion. The Emperor has graciously seen fit to summon us and the merchants," said Count Rastoptchin. "They will pour out their millions" (he pointed to the mer-chants' hall); "it is our duty to raise men and not to spare ourselves. . . . It is the least we can do."

A consultation took place between the great noblemen at the table only. The whole consultation was more than subdued, it seemed even mournful, when, after all the hubbub that had gone before, the old voices could be heard, one at a time, saying "agreed," or for the sake of variety, "I am of the same opinion."

The secretary was told to write down the resolution of the Moscow

nobility: that the nobles of Moscow, like those of Smolensk, would furnish a levy of ten men in every thousand, with their complete equipment.

The gentlemen, who had been sitting, got up with an air of relief;
there was a scraping of chairs and the great noblemen walked about to
stretch their legs, taking their friends' arms and chatting together.

"The Tsar! the Tsar!" was suddenly heard all through the rooms, and
the whole crowd rushed towards the entrance.

The Tsar walked in along the wide, free space left for him, between
walls of noblemen close packed on each side. Every face expressed reverent and awe-stricken curiosity. Pierre was at some distance, and could
not quite catch all the Tsar said. He knew from what he did hear that
the Tsar was speaking of the danger in which the empire was placed,
and the hopes he rested on the Moscow nobility. The Tsar was answered
by a voice informing him of the resolution just passed by the nobility.

"Gentlemen!" said the trembling voice of the Tsar. A stir passed
through the crowd, and then a hush fell on it again, and Pierre distinctly
heard the voice of the Tsar, warmly humane and deeply touched: "I
have never doubted of the devotion of the Russian nobility. But this day
it has surpassed my expectations. I thank you in the name of the fatherland. Gentlemen, let us act—time is more precious than anything. . . ."

The Tsar ceased speaking; the crowd began pressing round him, and
cries of enthusiasm were heard on all sides.

"Yes, more precious than anything . . . a royal saying," said the
voice of Ilya Andreitch with a sob. He had heard nothing, but understood everything in his own way.

From the nobility's room the Tsar went into the merchants' room. He
was there for about ten minutes. Pierre amongst the rest saw the Tsar
coming back from the merchants' room with tears of emotion in his eyes.
They learned afterwards that the Tsar had hardly begun to speak to the
mechants when the tears gushed from his eyes and he continued in a
trembling voice. When Pierre saw the Tsar come out, he was accompanied by two merchants. One of them Pierre knew, a stout contractor;
the other was the mayor, with a thin, yellow face and narrow beard.
Both were weeping. The tears stood in the thin man's eyes, but the stout
contractor was sobbing like a child and continually repeating:

"Take life and property too, your majesty!"

Pierre felt nothing at that moment but the desire to show that nothing was too much for him and that he was ready to sacrifice everything.
The constitutional tenor of his speech weighed on him like a sin; he
sought an opportunity of glossing it over. On hearing that Count Mamonov was furnishing a regiment, Bezuhov at once told Count Rastoptchin that he would furnish one thousand men and their equipment.

Old Rostov could not tell his wife what had passed without tears, and
he agreed at once to Petya's wishes, and went himself to enter his name.

Next day the Tsar went away. All the assembled noblemen went back
to their homes and their clubs, took off their uniforms, and with some
groans gave orders to their stewards to raise the levy, wondering themselves at what they had done.

PART TEN

I

NAPOLEON BEGAN the war with Russia because he could not help going to Dresden, being dazzled by the homage paid him there, putting on the Polish uniform, yielding to the stimulating influence of a June morning, and giving way to an outburst of fury in the presence of Kurakin and afterwards of Balashev.

Alexander refused all negotiations because he felt himself personally insulted. Barclay de Tolly did his utmost to command the army in the best way possible, so as to do his duty and gain the reputation of a great general. Rostov charged the French because he could not resist the temptation to gallop across the level plain. And all the innumerable persons who took part in the war acted similarly, in accordance with their personal peculiarities, habits, circumstances, and aims. They were all impelled by fear or vanity, enjoyment, indignation, or national consideration, supposing that they knew what they were about and that they were acting independently, while they were all the involuntary tools of history and were working out a result concealed from themselves but comprehensible to us. Such is the invariable fate of all practical leaders, and the higher their place in the social hierarchy, the less free they are.

Now the leading men of 1812 have long left their places; their personal interests have vanished, leaving no trace, and nothing remains before us but the historical results of the time.

But once let us admit that the people of Europe under Napoleon's leadership *had* to make their way into the heart of Russia and there to perish, and all the self-contradictory, meaningless, cruel actions of the men who took part in this war become intelligible to us.

Providence compelled all those men in striving for the attainment of their personal aims to combine in accomplishing one immense result, of which no one individual man (not Napoleon, not Alexander, still less any one taking practical part in the campaign) had the slightest inkling.

Now it is clear to us what was the cause of the destruction of the French army in 1812. No one disputes that the cause of the loss of Napoleon's French forces was, on one hand, their entering at too late a season upon a winter march in the heart of Russia without sufficient preparation; and on the other, the character the war had assumed from the burning of Russian towns and the hatred the enemy aroused in the peasantry. But obvious as it seems now, no one at the time foresaw that this was the only means by which the best army in the world, eight hundred thousand strong, led by the best of generals, could be defeated in a conflict with the inexperienced Russian army of half the strength, led by inexperienced generals. Not only was this utterly unforeseen, but every effort indeed was being continually made *on the Russian side* to hinder the one means that could save Russia; and in spite of the experience and so-called military genius of Napoleon, every effort was made *on the French side* to push on to Moscow at the end of the summer, that is to do the very thing bound to bring about their ruin.

In historical works on the year 1812, the French writers are very fond of saying that Napoleon was aware of the danger of lengthening out his line, that he sought a decisive engagement, that his marshals advised him to stay at Smolensk, and similar statements to show that even at the time the real danger of the campaign was seen. The Russian historians are still fonder of declaring that from the beginning of the campaign there existed a plan of Scythian warfare by leading Napoleon on into the heart of Russia. And this plan is ascribed by some writers to Pfuhl, by others to some Frenchman, and by others to Barclay de Tolly; while other writers give the credit of this supposed scheme to the Emperor Alexander himself, supporting their view by documents, proclamations, and letters, in which such a course of action certainly is hinted at. But all these hints at foreseeing what actually did happen on the French as well as on the Russian side are only conspicuous now because the event justified them. If the event had not come to pass, these hints would have been forgotten, as thousands and millions of suggestions and suppositions are now forgotten that were current at the period, but have been shown by time to be unfounded and so have been consigned to oblivion. There are always so many presuppositions as to the cause of every event that, however the matter ends, there are always people who will say: "I said at the time that it would be so": quite oblivious of the fact that among the numerous suppositions they made there were others too suggesting just the opposite course of events.

The notion that Napoleon was aware of the danger of extending his line, and that the Russians had a scheme for drawing the enemy into the heart of Russia, obviously belong to the same category; and only historians with a great bias can ascribe such reflections to Napoleon and his marshals, or such plans to the Russian generals. All the facts are directly opposed to such a view. Far from desiring to lure the French into the heart of Russia, the Russians did their utmost to arrest their progress throughout the war from the time they crossed the frontier. And far from dreading the extension of his line of communications, Napoleon rejoiced at every step forward as a triumph, and did not seek pitched battles as eagerly as he had done in his previous campaigns.

At the very beginning of the campaign, our armies were divided up, and the sole aim for which we strove was to unite them; though there was no benefit to be derived from uniting them, if our object was to retreat and draw the enemy into the heart of the country. The Emperor was with the army to inspire it not to yield an inch of Russian soil and on no account to retreat. An immense camp was fortified at Drissa in accordance with Pfuhl's plan, and it was not proposed to retreat further. The Tsar reprimanded the commander-in-chief for every retreat. The

Tsar can never have anticipated the burning of Moscow, or even the ene-my's presence at Smolensk, and when the armies had been reunited, the Tsar was indignant at the taking and burning of Smolensk without a general engagement having been fought before its walls. Such was the Tsar's feeling, but the Russian generals, and the whole Russian people, were even more indignant at the idea of our men retreating.

Napoleon, after dividing up the army, moved on into the heart of the country, letting slip several opportunities of an engagement. In August he was in Smolensk and thinking of nothing but advancing further, though, as we see now, that advance meant inevitable ruin.

The fact shows perfectly clearly that Napoleon foresaw no danger in the advance on Moscow, and that Alexander and the Russian generals did not dream at the time of luring Napoleon on, but aimed at the very opposite. Napoleon was drawn on into Russia, not through any plans— no one dreamed of the possibility of it—but simply through the complex play of intrigues and desires and motives of the actors in the war, who had no conception of what was to come and of what was the sole means of saving Russia. Everything came to pass by chance. The army was split up early in the campaign. We tried to effect a junction between the parts with the obvious intention of fighting a battle and checking the enemy's advance; and in this effort to effect a junction, avoiding a battle with a far stronger enemy, we were forced to retreat at an acute angle, and so drew the French after us to Smolensk. But it is not enough to say that both parts of the army retreated on lines inclined at an acute angle, because the French were advancing between the two armies. The angle was made the more acute and we retreated further because Barclay de Tolly, an unpopular German, was detested by Bagration, and the latter, in command of the second half of the army, did his utmost to delay a junction with Barclay de Tolly in order to avoid being under his command. Bagration delayed the junction of the armies, though this was the chief aim of all the authorities, because he believed that he would expose his army to danger on the march, and that it would be more advantage-ous for him to retreat more to the left and the south, annoying the enemy on the flank and rear, and reinforcing his army in Ukraine. And he be-lieved this, because he did not want to put himself under the command of the German Barclay, who was his junior in the service, and personally disliked by him.

The Emperor accompanied the army in order to excite its patriotic ardour; but his presence and inability to decide on any course of action and the immense number of counsellors and plans that swarmed about him, nullified all action on the part of the first army, and that army too had to retreat.

At the camp at Drissa it was proposed to take a stand. But the energy of Paulucci, scheming to become a leading general, affected Alexander; and Pfuhl's whole plan was abandoned, and the scheme of campaign in-trusted to Barclay. But as the latter did not inspire complete confidence, his power too was limited. The armies were split up, there was no unity, no supreme command: Barclay was unpopular. But on one side the con-

fusion and division and unpopularity of the German commander-in-chief
led to vacillation and to avoiding a battle, which would have been inevitable had the armies been united and any one but Barclay in command
of them. And on the other hand, it all led to a growing indignation with
the Germans and a growing fervour of patriotism.

At last the Tsar left the army, and, as the only suitable excuse to get
rid of him, the happy suggestion was made that he must rouse up the
people in the capitals to wage the war on a truly national scale. And the
Tsar's visit to Moscow did in fact treble the forces of the Russian army.
The Tsar left the army in the hope that the commander-in-chief would
be able to act alone, and that more decisive measures would be taken.
But the commander's position became weaker and even more difficult.
Bennigsen, the Grand Duke, and a swarm of adjutant generals, remained
with the army to watch over the actions of the commander-in-chief, and
to urge him to greater activity; and Barclay, feeling less than ever free
to act under the watchful gaze of all these "eyes of the Tsar," became
still more cautious and anxious to avoid a pitched battle, and clung to
a prudent inaction. The Grand Duke hinted at treachery, and demanded
a general engagement. Lubomirsky, Bronnitsky, Vlotsky, and others of
the same sort, helped to swell the clamour to such a point that Barclay,
on the pretext of sending papers to the Tsar in Petersburg, got rid of the
Polish generals, and entered into open conflict with Bennigsen and the
Grand Duke.

In Smolensk, in spite of Bagration's wishes to the contrary, the armies
were at last united.

Bagration drove up in his carriage to the house occupied by Barclay.
Barclay put on his official scarf, and came out to greet and to present
his report to his senior officer, Bagration. Bagration, to rival his magnanimity, acknowledged Barclay as his superior officer, in spite of his own
seniority; but he was less in accord with him than ever. At the Tsar's
command, he sent reports personally to him, and wrote to Araktcheev:
"My sovereign's will is law, but I can do nothing acting with the *minister*" (so he called Barclay). "For God's sake, send me somewhere else,
if only in command of a regiment, for here I can do nothing. The headquarters are crammed full of Germans, there's no living here for
a Russian, and no making head or tail of anything. I supposed I was
serving my sovereign and my country, but in practice it comes to serving
Barclay. I must own I do not care to."

The swarm of Bronnitskys, Wintzengerodes, and others like them,
embittered the feud between the commanders still further, and there was
less unity than ever. Preparations were made to attack the French before Smolensk. A general was sent to review the position. This general,
detesting Barclay, visits a friend of his own, a commander of a corps,
and after spending the day with him, returns and condemns on every
point the proposed field of battle without having seen it.

While disputes and intrigues were going on as to the suitable spot for
a battle, and while we were looking for the French and mistaking their

line of advance, the French fell upon Nevyerovsky's division, and advanced upon the walls of Smolensk itself.

We were surprised into having to fight at Smolensk to save our communications. A battle was fought. Thousands were slain on both sides.

Smolensk was abandoned against the will of the Tsar and the whole people. But Smolensk was burnt by its own inhabitants, who had been deceived by their governor. And those ruined inhabitants, after setting an example to the rest of Russia, full of their losses, and burning with hatred of the enemy, moved on to Moscow. Napoleon advances; we retreat; and so the very result is attained that is destined to overthrow Napoleon.

II

The day after his son's departure, Prince Nikolay Andreitch sent for Princess Marya.

"Well, now are you satisfied?" he said to her. "You have made me quarrel with my son! Are you satisfied? That was all you wanted! Satisfied? . . . It's a grief to me, a grief. I'm old and weak, and it was your wish. Well, now, rejoice over it. . . ." And after that, Princess Marya did not see her father again for a week. He was ill and did not leave his study.

Princess Marya noticed to her surprise that during this illness the old prince excluded Mademoiselle Bourienne too from his room. Tihon was the only person who looked after him.

A week later the prince reappeared, and began to lead the same life as before, showing marked energy in the laying out of farm buildings and gardens, and completely breaking off all relations with Mademoiselle Bourienne. His frigid tone and air with Princess Marya seemed to say: "You see, you plotted against me, told lies to Prince Andrey of my relations with that Frenchwoman, and made me quarrel with him, but you see I can do without you, and without the Frenchwoman too."

One half of the day Princess Marya spent with Nikolushka, giving him his Russian lessons, following his other lessons, and talking to Dessalle. The rest of the day she spent in reading, or with her old nurse and "God's folk," who came by the back stairs sometimes to visit her. The war Princess Marya looked on as women do look on war. She was apprehensive for her brother who was at the front, and was horrified, without understanding it, at the cruelty of men, that led them to kill one another. But she had no notion of the significance of this war, which seemed to her exactly like all the preceding wars. She had no notion of the meaning of this war, although Dessalle, who was her constant companion, was passionately interested in the course of the war, and tried to explain his views on the subject to her, and although "God's folk" all, with terror, told her in their own way of the rumours among the peasantry of the coming of Antichrist, and although Julie, now Princess Drubetskoy, who had renewed her correspondence with her, was continually writing her patriotic letters from Moscow.

"I write to you in Russian, my sweet friend," Julie wrote, "because I feel a hatred for all the French and for their language too; I can't bear to hear it spoken. . . . In Moscow we are all wild with enthusiasm for our adored Emperor.

"My poor husband is enduring hardships and hunger in wretched Jewish taverns, but the news I get from him only increases my ardour.

"You have doubtless heard of the heroic action of Raevsky, who embraced his two sons and said, 'We will die together, but we will not flinch!' And though the enemy were twice as strong, we did not in fact flinch. We kill time here as best we can; but in war, as in war. Princess Alina and Sophie spend whole days with me, and we, unhappy widows of living husbands, have delightful talks over scraping lint. We only want you, my darling, to make us complete," etc., etc.

The principal reason why Princess Marya failed to grasp the significance of the war was that the old prince never spoke of it, refused to recognize its existence, and laughed at Dessalle when he mentioned the war at dinner-time. The prince's tone was so calm and confident that Princess Marya put implicit faith in him.

During the whole of July the old prince was excessively active and even lively. He laid out another new garden and a new wing for the servants. The only thing that made Princess Marya anxious about him was that he slept badly, and gave up his old habit of sleeping in his study, and had a bed made up for him in a new place every day. One night he would have his travelling bedstead set up in the gallery, the next night he would spend dozing dressed on the sofa or in the lounge-chair in the drawing-room, while the lad Petrushka, who had replaced Mademoiselle Bourienne in attendance on him, read aloud to him; then he would try spending a night in the dining-room.

On the first of August a second letter came from Prince Andrey. In his first letter, which had been received shortly after he left home, Prince Andrey had humbly asked his father's forgiveness for what he had permitted himself to say to him, and had begged to be restored to his favour. To this letter, the old prince had sent an affectionate answer, and from that time he had kept the Frenchwoman at a distance. Prince Andrey's second letter was written under Vitebsk, after the French had taken it. It consisted of a brief account of the whole campaign, with a plan sketched to illustrate it, and of reflections on the probable course it would take in the future. In this letter Prince Andrey pointed out to his father the inconvenience of his position close to the theatre of war, and in the direct line of the enemy's advance, and advised him to move to Moscow.

At dinner that day, on Dessalle's observing that he had heard that the French had already entered Vitebsk, the old prince recollected Prince Andrey's letter.

"I have heard from Prince Andrey to-day," he said to Princess Marya; "have you read the letter?"

"No, *mon père*," the princess answered timidly. She could not possibly have read the letter, of which indeed she had not heard till that instant.

"He writes about this war," said the prince, with the contemptuous smile that had become habitual with him in speaking of the present war.

"It must be very interesting," said Dessalle. "Prince Andrey is in a position to know. . . ."

"Ah, very interesting!" said Mademoiselle Bourienne.

"Go and get it for me," said the old prince to Mademoiselle Bourienne. "You know, on the little table under the paper-weight."

Mademoiselle Bourienne jumped up eagerly.

"Ah, no," he shouted, frowning. "You run, Mihail Ivanitch!" Mihail Ivanitch got up and went to the study. But he had hardly left the room when the old prince, looking about him nervously, threw down his dinner napkin and went himself.

"They never can do anything, always make a muddle."

As he went out, Princess Marya, Dessalle, Mademoiselle Bourienne, and even little Nikolushka, looked at one another without speaking. The old prince accompanied by Mihail Ivanitch came back with a hurried step, bringing the letter and a plan, which he laid beside him, and did not give to any one to read during dinner.

When they went into the drawing-room, he handed the letter to Princess Marya, and spreading out before him the plan of his new buildings, he fixed his eyes upon it, and told her to read the letter aloud.

After reading the letter, Princess Marya looked inquiringly at her father. He was gazing at the plan, evidently engrossed in his own ideas.

"What do you think about it, prince?" Dessalle ventured to inquire.

"I? eh? . . ." said the old prince, seeming to rouse himself with a painful effort, and not taking his eyes from the plan of the building. "It is very possible that the field of operations may be brought so close to us . . ."

"Ha-ha-ha! The field of operations indeed!" said the old prince. "I have always said, and I say still, that the field of operations is bound to be Poland, and the enemy will never advance beyond the Niemen." Dessalle looked in amazement at the prince, who was talking of the Niemen, when the enemy was already at the Dnieper. But Princess Marya, forgetting the geographical position of the Niemen, supposed that what her father said was true.

"When the snows thaw they'll drown in the marshes of Poland. It's only that they can't see it," said the old prince, obviously thinking of the campaign of 1807, which seemed to him so recent. "Bennigsen ought to have entered Prussia earlier, and things would have taken quite another turn. . . ."

"But, prince!" said Dessalle timidly, "the letter speaks of Vitebsk. . . ."

"Ah, the letter? Yes, . . ." said the prince, with displeasure. "Yes . . . yes . . ." His face suddenly assumed a gloomy expression. He paused. "Yes, he writes, the French have been beaten. On what river was it?"

Dessalle dropped his eyes. "The prince says nothing about that," he said gently.

"What, doesn't he? Why, you don't suppose I imagined it."

Every one was for a long time silent.

"Yes . . . yes . . . Well, Mihail Ivanitch," he said suddenly, raising his head and pointing to the plan of the building, "tell me how you propose to make that alteration. . . ."

Mihail Ivanitch went up to the plan, and the old prince, talking to him about it, went off to his own room, casting a wrathful glance at Princess Marya and Dessalle.

Princess Marya saw Dessalle's embarrassed and amazed expression as he looked at her father. She noticed his silence and was struck by the fact that her father had left his son's letter forgotten on the drawing-room table. But she was afraid to speak of it, to ask Dessalle the reason of his embarrassed silence, afraid even to think about it.

In the evening Mihail Ivanitch was sent by the prince to Princess Marya to ask for the letter that had been forgotten on the table. Princess Marya gave him the letter, and much as she disliked doing so, she ventured to ask what her father was doing.

"Still very busy," said Mihail Ivanitch, in a tone of deferential irony, that made her turn pale. "Worrying very much over the new wing. Been reading a little: but now"—Mihail Ivanitch dropped his voice—"he's at his bureau looking after his will, I expect." One of the old prince's favourite occupations of late had been going over the papers which he meant to leave at his death, and called his "will."

"And is Alpatitch being sent to Smolensk?" asked Princess Marya.

"To be sure; he's been waiting a long while for his orders."

III

WHEN Mihail Ivanitch went back to the study with the letter, the old prince was sitting in his spectacles with a shade over his eyes and shades on the candles, at his open bureau, surrounded by papers, held a long distance off. He was in a rather solemn attitude, reading the papers (the "remarks," as he called them) which were to be given to the Tsar after his death.

When Mihail Ivanitch went in, there were tears in his eyes, called up by the memory of the time when he had written what he was now reading. He took the letter out of Mihail Ivanitch's hand, put it in his pocket, folded up his papers and called in Alpatitch, who had been waiting a long while to see him.

He had noted down on a sheet of paper what he wanted in Smolensk, and he began walking up and down the room, as he gave his instructions to Alpatitch, standing at the door.

"First, letter paper, do you hear, eight quires, like this pattern, you see; gilt edged . . . take the pattern, so as to be sure to match it; varnish, sealing-wax—according to Mihail Ivanitch's list."

He walked up and down the room and glanced at the memorandum.

"Then deliver the letter about the enrolment to the governor in person."

Then bolts for the doors of the new building were wanted, and must be of a new pattern, which the old prince had himself designed. Then an iron-bound box was to be ordered for keeping his will in.

Giving Alpatitch his instructions occupied over two hours. The prince still would not let him go. He sat down, sank into thought, and closing his eyes, dropped into a doze. Alpatitch made a slight movement.

"Well, go along, go along," said the old prince; "if anything is wanted I'll send."

Alpatitch went away. The prince went back to the bureau; glancing into it, he passed his hand over his papers, closed it again, and sat down to the table to write to the governor.

It was late when he sealed the letter and got up. He was sleepy, but he knew he would not sleep, and that he would be haunted by most miserable thoughts in bed. He called Tihon, and went through the rooms with him, to tell him where to make up his bed for that night. He walked about, measuring every corner.

There was no place that pleased him, but worst of all was the couch in the study that he had been used to. That couch had become an object of dread to him, probably from the painful thoughts he had thought lying on it. No place was quite right, but best of them all was the corner in the divan-room, behind the piano; he had never slept there yet.

Tihon brought the bedstead in with the footmen, and began putting it up.

"That's not right, that's not right!" cried the old prince. With his own hands he moved the bed an inch further from the corner, and then closer to it again.

"Well, at last, I have done everything; now I shall rest," thought the prince, and he left it to Tihon to undress him.

Frowning with vexation at the effort he had to make to take off his coat and trousers, the prince undressed, dropped heavily down on his bed, and seemed to sink into thought, staring contemptuously at his yellow, withered legs. He was not really thinking, but simply pausing before the effort to lift his legs up and lay them in the bed. "Ugh, how hard it is! Ugh, if these toils could soon be over, and if *you* would let me go!" he mused. Pinching his lips tightly, he made that effort for the twenty thousandth time, and lay down. But he had hardly lain down, when all at once the bed seemed to rock regularly to and fro under him, as though it were heaving and jolting. He had this sensation almost every night. He opened his eyes that were closing themselves.

"No peace, damn them!" he grumbled, with inward rage at some persons unknown. "Yes, yes, there was something else of importance—something of great importance I was saving up to think of in bed. The bolts? No, I did speak about them. No, there was something, something in the drawing-room. Princess Marya talked some nonsense. Dessalle—he's a fool—said something, something in my pocket—I don't remember."

"Tishka! what were we talking about at dinner?"

"About Prince Mihail . . ."

"Stay, stay"—the prince slapped his hand down on the table. "Yes, I know, Prince Andrey's letter. Princess Marya read it. Dessalle said something about Vitebsk. I'll read it now."

He told Tihon to get the letter out of his pocket, and to move up the little table with the lemonade and the spiral wax candle on it, and putting on his spectacles he began reading. Only then in the stillness of the night, as he read the letter, in the faint light under the green shade, for the first time he grasped for an instant its meaning. "The French are at Vitebsk, in four days' march they may be at Smolensk; perhaps they are there by now. Tishka!" Tihon jumped up. "No, nothing, nothing!" he cried.

He put the letter under the candlestick and closed his eyes. And there rose before his mind the Danube, bright midday, the reeds, the Russian camp, and he, a young general, without one wrinkle on his brow, bold, gay, ruddy, entering Potyomkin's gay-coloured tent, and the burning sensation of envy of the favourite stirs within him as keenly as at the time. And he recalls every word uttered at that first interview with Potyomkin. And then he sees a plump, short woman with a sallow, fat face, the mother empress, her smiles and words at her first gracious reception for him; and then her face as she lay on the bier, and the quarrel with Zubov over her coffin for the right to kiss her hand.

"Oh, to make haste, to make haste back to that time, and oh, that the present might soon be over and they might leave me in peace!"

IV

BLEAK HILLS, the estate of Prince Nikolay Andreitch Bolkonsky, was sixty versts from Smolensk, a little to the rear of it, and three versts from the main road to Moscow.

The same evening on which the old prince gave Alpatitch his instructions, Dessalle asked for a few words with Princess Marya, and told her that since the prince was not quite well and was taking no steps to secure his own safety, though from Prince Andrey's letter it was plain that to stay on at Bleak Hills was not free from danger, he respectfully advised her to write herself, and send by Alpatitch a letter to the governor at Smolensk, and to ask him to let her know the position of affairs and the degree of danger they were running at Bleak Hills. Dessalle wrote the letter to the governor for Princess Marya and she signed it, and the letter was given to Alpatitch with instructions to give it to the governor, and in case there was danger, to come back as quickly as possible.

When he had received all his orders, Alpatitch put on his white beaver hat—a gift from the prince—and carrying a stick in his hand, like the prince, went out, accompanied by all his household, to get into the leather gig harnessed to three sleek, roan horses.

The bells were tied up and stuffed with paper. The prince allowed no one at Bleak Hills to drive with bells. But Alpatitch loved to have bells ringing when he went a long journey. All Alpatitch's satellites, the counting-house clerk, the servants' cook and the head cook, two old women, a foot-boy, a coachman, and various other servants saw him off.

His daughter put chintz-covered, down pillows under him and behind his back. His old sister-in-law slyly popped in a kerchief full of things. One of the coachmen helped him to get in.

"There, there, women's fuss! Women folk, women folk!" said Alpatitch, puffing and talking rapidly, just as the old prince used to talk. He sat down in the gig, giving the counting-house clerk his last directions about the work to be done in the fields; and then dropping his imitation of the prince, Alpatitch took his hat off his bald head and crossed himself three times.

"If there's anything . . . you turn back, Yakov Alpatitch; for Christ's sake, think of us," his wife called to him, alluding to the rumours of war and of the enemy near.

"Ah, these women and their fuss!" Alpatitch muttered to himself as he drove off, looking about him at the fields. He saw rye turning yellow, thick oats still green, and here and there patches still black, where they were only just beginning the second ploughing. Alpatitch drove on, admiring the crop of corn, singularly fine that season, staring at the rye fields, in some of which reaping was already beginning, meditating like a true husbandman on the sowing and the harvest, and wondering whether he had forgotten any of the prince's instructions. He stopped twice to feed his horses on the way, and towards the evening of the 4th of August reached the town.

All the way Alpatitch had met and overtaken waggons and troops, and as he drove into Smolensk he heard firing in the distance, but he scarcely heeded the sound. What struck him more than anything was that close to Smolensk he saw a splendid field of oats being mown down by some soldiers evidently for forage; there was a camp, too, pitched in the middle of it. This did make an impression upon Alpatitch, but he soon forgot it in thinking over his own affairs.

All the interests of Alpatitch's life had been for over thirty years bounded by the will of the prince, and he never stepped outside that limit. Anything that had nothing to do with carrying out the prince's orders had no interest, had in fact no existence for Alpatitch.

On reaching Smolensk on the evening of the 4th of August, Alpatitch put up where he had been in the habit of putting up for the last thirty years, at a tavern kept by a former house-porter, Ferapontov, beyond the Dnieper in the Gatchensky quarter. Twelve years before, Ferapontov had profited by Alpatitch's good offices to buy timber from the old prince, and had begun going into trade; and by now he had a house, an inn and a corn-dealer's shop in the town. Ferapontov was a stout, dark, ruddy peasant of forty, with thick lips, a thick, knobby nose, similar knobby bumps over his black, knitted brows, and a round belly.

He was standing in his print shirt and his waistcoat in front of his shop, which looked into the street. He saw Alpatitch, and went up to him.

"You're kindly welcome, Yakov Alpatitch. Folk are going out of the town, while you come into it," said he.

"How's that? Out of town?" said Alpatitch.

"To be sure, I always say folks are fools. Always frightened of the French."

"Women's nonsense, women's nonsense!" replied Alpatitch.

"That's just what I think, Yakov Alpatitch. I say there's a notice put up that they won't let them come in, so to be sure that's right. But the peasants are asking as much as three roubles for a cart and horse— they've no conscience!"

Yakov Alpatitch heard without heeding. He asked for a samovar, and for hay for his horses; and after drinking tea lay down to sleep.

All night long the troops were moving along the street by the tavern. Next day Alpatitch put on a tunic, which he kept for wearing in town, and went out to execute his commissions. It was a sunny morning, and by eight o'clock it was hot. "A precious day for the harvest," as Alpatitch thought. From early morning firing could be heard from beyond the town.

At eight o'clock the boom of cannon mingled with the rattle of musketry. The streets were thronged with people, hurrying about, and also with soldiers, but drivers plied for hire, the shopkeepers stood at their shops, and services were being held in the churches just as usual. Alpatitch went to the shops, to the government offices, to the post and to the governor's. Everywhere that he went every one was talking of the war, and of the enemy who was attacking the town. All were asking one another what was to be done, and trying to calm each other's fears.

At the governor's house, Alpatitch found a great number of people, and saw Cossacks, and a travelling carriage belonging to the governor at the entrance. On the steps Yakov Alpatitch met two gentlemen, one of whom he knew. This gentleman, a former police-captain, was speaking with great heat.

"Well, this is no jesting matter," he said. "Good luck for him who has only himself to think of. It's bad enough for one alone, but when one has a family of thirteen and a whole property. . . . Things have come to such a pass that we shall all be ruined; what's one to say of the government after that? . . . Ugh, I'd hang the brigands. . . ."

"Come, come, hush!" said the other.

"What do I care! let him hear! Why, we're not dogs!" said the former police-captain, and looking round. he caught sight of Alpatitch.

"Ah, Yakov Alpatitch, how do you come here?"

"By command of his excellency to his honour the governor," answered Alpatitch, lifting his head proudly and putting his hand into his bosom, as he always did when he mentioned the old prince. . . . "His honour was pleased to bid me inquire into the position of affairs," he said.

"Well, you may as well know then," cried the gentleman: "they have

brought matters to such a pass that there are no carts to be got, nothing!
. . . That's it again, do you hear?" he said, pointing in the direction
from which the sounds of firing came.

"They have brought us all to ruin . . . the brigands!" he declared
again, and he went down the steps.

Alpatitch shook his head and went up. The waiting-room was full of
merchants, women, and clerks, looking dumbly at one another. The door
of the governor's room opened, all of them got up and made a forward
movement. A clerk ran out of the room, said something to a merchant,
called a stout official with a cross on his neck to follow him, and vanished
again, obviously trying to avoid all the looks and the questions addressed
to him. Alpatitch moved forward, and the next time the same clerk
emerged, he put his hand into his buttoned coat, and addressed him,
handing him the two letters.

"To his honour the Baron Ash from the general-in-chief Prince Bolkonsky," he boomed out with so much pomposity and significance that
the clerk turned to him and took the letters. A few minutes afterwards
Alpatitch was shown into the presence of the governor, who said to him
hurriedly, "Inform the prince and the princess that I knew nothing
about it. I acted on the highest instructions—here. . . ."

He gave Alpatitch a document.

"Still, as the prince is not well my advice to him is to go to Moscow.
I'm setting off myself immediately. Tell them . . ." But the governor
did not finish; a dusty and perspiring officer ran into the room and began
saying something in French. A look of horror came into the governor's
face.

"You can go," he said, nodding to Alpatitch, and he put some questions to the officer. Eager, panic-stricken, helpless glances were turned
upon Alpatitch when he came out of the governor's room. Alpatitch
could not help listening now to firing, which seemed to come closer and
to be getting hotter, as he hurried back to the inn. The document the
governor had given to Alpatitch ran as follows:

"I guarantee that the town of Smolensk is not in the slightest danger,
and it is improbable that it should be threatened in any way. I myself
from one side, and Prince Bagration from the other, will effect a junction
before Smolensk on the 22nd instant, and both armies will proceed with
their joint forces to defend their compatriots of the province under your
government, till their efforts beat back the enemies of our country, or
till their gallant ranks are cut down to the last warrior. You will see
from this that you have a perfect right to reassure the inhabitants of
Smolensk, as they are defended by two such valiant armies and can be
confident of their victory.

("By order of Barclay de Tolly to the civil governor of Smolensk,
Baron Ash. 1812.")

Crowds of people were moving uneasily about the streets. Waggons,
loaded up with household crockery, chairs, and cupboards, were constantly emerging from the gates of houses, and moving along the streets.
Carts were standing at the entrance of the house next to Ferapontov's,

and women were wailing and exchanging good-byes. The yard dog was frisking about the horses, barking.

Alpatitch's step was more hurried than usual as he entered the yard, and went straight under the shed to his horses and cart. The coachman was asleep; he waked him up, told him to put the horses in, and went into the outer room of the house. In the private room of the family, he heard the wailing of children, the heartrending sobs of a woman, and the furious, husky shouting of Ferapontov. The cook came fluttering into the outer room like a frightened hen, just as Alpatitch walked in.

"He's beating her to death—beating the mistress! . . . He's beaten her so, thrashed her so! . . ."

"What for?" asked Alpatitch.

"She kept begging to go away. A woman's way! Take me away, says she; don't bring me to ruin with all my little children; folks are all gone, says she, what are we about? So he fell to beating her . . . beating and thrashing her!"

Alpatitch nodded his head, apparently in approval at those words; and not caring to hear more he went towards the door on the opposite side leading to the room in which his purchases had been left.

"Wretch, villain," screamed a thin, pale woman, bursting out at that moment with a child in her arms and her kerchief torn off her head. She ran down the steps into the yard. Ferapontov was going after her, but seeing Alpatitch, he pulled down his waistcoat, smoothed his hair yawned and followed Alpatitch into the room.

"Do you want to be getting off already?" he asked. Without answering the question or looking round at him, Alpatitch collected his purchases and asked how much he owed him.

"We'll reckon up! Been at the governor's, eh?" asked Ferapontov. "What did you hear?"

Alpatitch replied that the governor had told him nothing definite.

"How are we to pack up and go with our business?" said Ferapontov. "Seven roubles to pay for cartage to Dorogobuzh. What I say is: they have no conscience!" said he. "Selivanov, he did a good turn on Friday, sold flour to the army for nine roubles the sack. What do you say to some tea?" he added. While the horses were being harnessed, Alpatitch and Ferapontov drank tea and discussed the price of corn, the crops, and the favourable weather for the harvest.

"It's getting quieter though," said Ferapontov, getting up after drinking three cups of tea. "I suppose, our side has got the best of it. It's been said they won't let them in. So we're in force it seems. . . . The other day they were saying Matvey Ivanitch Platov drove them into the river Marina: eighteen thousand of them he drowned in one day."

Alpatitch gathered up his purchases, handed them to the coachman, and settled his accounts with Ferapontov. There was the sound of wheels and hoofs and the ringing of bells as the gig drove out of the gates.

It was by now long past midday, half the street lay in shadow, while half was in brilliant sunshine. Alpatitch glanced out of the window and went to the door. All of a sudden there came a strange sound of a far-away hiss and thump, followed by the boom of cannons, mingling into a dim roar that set the windows rattling.

Alpatitch went out into the street; two men were running along the street towards the bridge. From different sides came the hiss and thud of cannon balls and the bursting of grenades, as they fell in the town. But these sounds were almost unheard, and the inhabitants scarcely noticed them, in comparison with the boom of the cannons they heard beyond the town. It was the bombardment, which Napoleon had ordered to be opened upon the town at four o'clock from one hundred and thirty cannons. The people did not at first grasp the meaning of this bombardment.

The sounds of the dropping grenades and cannon balls at first only excited the curiosity of the people. Ferapontov's wife, who had till then been wailing in the shed, ceased, and with the baby in her arms went out to the gate, staring in silence at the people, and listening to the sounds.

The cook and shopman came out to the gate. All of them were trying with eager curiosity to get a glimpse of the projectiles as they flew over their heads. Several persons came round the corner in eager conversation.

"What force!" one was saying; "roof and ceiling were smashed up to splinters."

"Like a pig routing into the earth, it went!" said another.

"Isn't it first-rate? Wakes one up!" he said laughing.

"It's as well you skipped away or it would have flattened you out."

Others joined this group. They stopped and described how a cannon-ball had dropped on a house close to them. Meanwhile other projectiles —now a cannon ball, with rapid, ominous hiss, and now a grenade with a pleasant whistle—flew incessantly over the people's heads: but not one fell close, all of them flew over. Alpatitch got into his gig. Ferapontov was standing at the gate.

"Will you never have done gaping!" he shouted to the cook, who in her red petticoat, with her sleeves tucked up and her bare elbows swinging, had stepped to the corner to listen to what was being said.

"A wonder it is!" she was saying, but hearing her master's voice, she came back, pulling down her tucked-up skirt.

Again something hissed, but very close this time, like a bird swooping down; there was a flash of fire in the middle of the street, the sound of a shot, and the street was filled with smoke.

"Scoundrel, what are you about?" shouted Ferapontov, running up to the cook.

At the same instant there rose a piteous wailing from the women; the baby set up a terrified howling, and the people crowded with pale faces round the cook. Above them all rose out of the crowd the moans and cries of the cook.

"O-o-oy, good kind souls, blessed friends! don't let me die! Good kind souls! . . ."

Five minutes later no one was left in the street. The cook, with her leg broken by the bursting grenade, had been carried into the kitchen. Alpatitch, his coachman, Ferapontov's wife and children and the porter were sitting in the cellar listening. The thunder of the cannon, the hiss of the balls, and the piteous moaning of the cook, which rose above all the noise, never ceased for an instant. Ferapontov's wife alternately dandled and soothed her baby, and asked in a frightened whisper of every one who came into the cellar where was her husband, who had remained in the street. The shopman told her the master had gone with the crowd to the cathedral, where they were raising on high the wonder-working, holy picture of Smolensk.

Towards dusk the cannonade began to subside. Alpatitch came out of the cellar and stood in the doorway.

The clear evening sky was all overcast with smoke. And a new crescent moon looked strange, shining high up in the sky, through that smoke. After the terrible thunder of the cannons had ceased, a hush seemed to hang over the town, broken only by the footsteps, which seemed all over the town, the sound of groans and distant shouts, and the crackle of fires. The cook's moans had ceased now. On two sides black clouds of smoke from fires rose up and drifted away. Soldiers in different uniforms walked and ran about the streets in different directions, not in ranks, but like ants out of a disturbed ant heap. Several of them ran in Ferapontov's yard before Alpatitch's eyes. He went out to the gate. A regiment, crowded and hurrying, blocked up the street, going back.

"The town's surrendered; get away, get away," said an officer noticing his figure; and turning immediately to the soldiers, he shouted, "I'll teach you to run through the yards!"

Alpatitch went back to the house, and calling the coachman told him to set off. Alpatitch and the coachman were followed out by all the household of Ferapontov. When they saw the smoke and even the flames of burning houses, which began to be visible now in the dusk, the women, who had been silent till then, broke into a sudden wail. as they gazed at the fires. As though seconding them, similar wails rose up in other parts of the street. Alpatitch and the coachman with trembling hands pulled out the tangled reins and the traces of the horses under the shed.

As Alpatitch was driving out of the gate, he saw about a dozen soldiers in loud conversation in Ferapontov's open shop. They were filling their bags and knapsacks with wheaten flour and sunflower seeds. At that moment Ferapontov returned and went into the shop. On seeing the soldiers, he was about to shout at them, but all at once he stopped short, and clutching at his hair broke into a sobbing laugh.

"Carry it all away, lads! Don't leave it for the devils," he shouted, snatching up the sacks himself and pitching them into the street. Some of the soldiers ran away in a fright, others went on filling up their bags. Seeing Alpatitch, Ferapontov turned to him.

"It's all over with Russia!" he shouted. "Alpatitch! it's all over! I'll set fire to it myself. It's over . . ." Ferapontov ran into the house.

An unbroken stream of soldiers was blocking up the whole street, so that Alpatitch could not pass and was obliged to wait. Ferapontov's wife and children were sitting in a cart too, waiting till it was possible to start.

It was by now quite dark. There were stars in the sky, and from time to time the new moon shone through the veil of smoke. Alpatitch's and nis hostess's vehicles moved slowly along in the rows of soldiers and of other conveyances, and on the slope down to the Dnieper they had to halt altogether. In a lane not far from the cross-roads where the traffic had come to a full stop, there were shops and a house on fire. The fire was by now burning down. The flame died down and was lost in black smoke, then flared up suddenly, lighting up with strange distinctness the faces of the crowd at the cross-roads. Black figures were flitting about before the fire, and talk and shouts could be heard above the unceasing crackling of the flames. Alpatitch, seeing that it would be some time before his gig could move forward, got out and went back to the lane to look at the fire. Soldiers were scurrying to and fro before the fire; and Alpatitch saw two soldiers with a man in a frieze coat dragging burning beams from the fire across the street to a house near, while others carried armfuls of hay.

Alpatitch joined a great crowd of people standing before a high corn granary in full blaze. The walls were all in flames; the back wall had fallen in; the plank roof was breaking down, and the beams were glowing. The crowd were evidently watching for the moment when the roof would fall in. Alpatitch too waited to see it.

"Alpatitch!" the old man suddenly heard a familiar voice calling to him.

"Mercy on us, your excellency," answered Alpatitch, instantly recog· nising the voice of his young master.

Prince Andrey, wearing a cape, and mounted on a black horse, was in the crowd, and looking at Alpatitch.

"How did you come here?" he asked.

"Your . . . your excellency!" Alpatitch articulated, and he broke into sobs. . . . "Your, your . . . is it all over with us, really? Mas· ter . . ."

"How is it you are here?" repeated Prince Andrey. The flames flared up at that instant, and Alpatitch saw in the bright light his young master's pale and worn face. Alpatitch told him how he had been sent to the town and had difficulty in getting away.

"What do you say, your excellency, is it all over with us?" he asked again.

Prince Andrey, making no reply, took out his note-book, and raising his knee, scribbled in pencil on a leaf he had torn out. He wrote to his sister:

"Smolensk has surrendered," he wrote. "Bleak Hills will be occupied by the enemy within a week. Set off at once for Moscow. Let me know at once when you start; send a messenger to Usvyazh."

Scribbling these words, and giving Alpatitch the paper, he gave him further directions about sending off the old prince, the princess and his son with his tutor, and how and where to let him hear, as soon as they had gone. Before he had finished giving those instructions, a staff officer, followed by his suite, galloped up to him.

"You a colonel," shouted the staff officer, in a voice Prince Andrey knew, speaking with a German accent. "Houses are being set on fire in your presence and you stand still! What's the meaning of it? You will answer for it," shouted Berg, who was now assistant to the head of the staff of the assistant of the chief officer of the staff of the commander of the left flank of the infantry of the first army, a very agreeable and prominent position, so Berg said.

Prince Andrey stared at him, and without making any reply went on addressing Alpatitch.

"Tell them then that I shall wait for an answer till the 10th, and if I don't receive news by the 10th, that they have all gone away, I shall be obliged to throw up everything and go myself to Bleak Hills."

"Prince," said Berg, recognising Prince Andrey, "I only speak because it's my duty to carry out my instructions, because I always do exactly carry out . . . You must please excuse me," Berg tried to apologise.

There was a crash in the fire. The flames subsided for an instant; black clouds of smoke rolled under the roof. There was another fearful crash, and the falling of some enormous weight.

"Ooo-roo!" the crowd yelled, as the ceiling of the granary fell in, and a smell of baked cakes rose from the burning wheat. The flames flared up again, and lighted up the delighted and careworn faces of the crowd around it.

The man in the frieze coat, brandishing his arms in the air, was shouting:

"First-rate! Now she's started! First-rate, lads! . . ." "That's the owner himself," murmured voices.

"So you tell them everything I have told you," said Prince Andrey, addressing Alpatitch. And without bestowing a word on Berg, who stood mute beside him, he put spurs to his horse and rode down the lane.

V

FROM Smolensk the troops continued to retreat. The enemy followed them. On the 10th of August the regiment of which Prince Andrey was in command was marching along the high-road past the avenue that led to Bleak Hills. The heat and drought had lasted more than three weeks. Every day curly clouds passed over the sky, rarely covering the sun; but towards evening the sky cleared again and the sun set in a glowing, red mist. But a heavy dew refreshed the earth at night. The wheat left in the fields was burnt up and dropping out of the ear. The marshes were dry. The cattle lowed from hunger, finding nothing to graze on in the sun-baked meadows. Only at night in the woods, as long as the dew lasted, it was cool. But on the road, on the high-road along which the troops marched, there was no coolness even at night, not even where the road passed through the woods. The dew was imperceptible on the sandy dust of the road, more than a foot deep. As soon as it was daylight, the soldiers began to move. The transports and artillery moved noiselessly, buried up to their axles, and the infantry sank to their ankles in the soft, stifling, burning dust, that never got cool even at night. The sandy dust clung to their legs and to the wheels, rose in a cloud over their heads, and got into the eyes and hair and nostrils and lungs of the men and beasts that moved along the road. The higher the sun rose, the higher rose the cloud of dust, and through the fine, burning dust the sun in the cloudless sky looked like a purple ball, at which one could gaze with undazzled eyes. There was no wind, and the men gasped for breath in the stagnant atmosphere. They marched with handkerchiefs tied over their mouths and noses. When they reached the villages, there was a rush for the wells. They fought over the water and drank it down to the mud.

Prince Andrey was in command of a regiment; and the management of the regiment, the welfare of his men, the necessity of receiving and giving orders occupied his mind. The burning and abandonment of Smolensk made an epoch in Prince Andrey's life. A new feeling of intense hatred of the enemy made him forget his own sorrow. He was devoted heart and soul to the interests of his regiment; he was careful of the welfare of his men and his officers, and cordial in his manner with them. They called him in the regiment "our prince," were proud of him, and loved him. But he was kind and gentle only with his own men, with Timohin, and others like him, people quite new to him, belonging to a different world, people who could have no notion of his past. As soon as he was brought into contact with any of his old acquaintances, any of the staff officers, he bristled up again at once, and was vindictive, ironical, and contemptuous. Everything associated by memories with the past was repulsive to him, and so, in his relations with that old world, he confined himself to trying to do his duty, and not to be unfair.

Prince Andrey, in fact, saw everything in the darkest, gloomiest light, especially after Smolensk, which he considered could and should have been defended, had been abandoned, on the 6th of August, and his invalid father had been forced, as he supposed, to flee to Moscow, leaving Bleak Hills, the house that he had so loved, that he had designed and settled with his peasants, to be plundered. But in spite of that, thanks to his position, Prince Andrey had another subject to think of, quite apart from all general questions, his regiment. On the 10th of August, the column of which his regiment formed part reached the turning leading off to Bleak Hills. Two days before Prince Andrey had received the news that his father, his son, and his sister had gone away to Moscow. Though there was nothing for Prince Andrey to do at Bleak Hills, he decided, with characteristic desire to aggravate his own sufferings, that he must ride over there.

He ordered his horse to be saddled, and turned off from the main line of march towards his father's house, where he had been born and had spent his childhood. As he rode by the pond, where there always used to be dozens of peasant women gossiping, rinsing their linen, or beating it with washing bats, Prince Andrey noticed that there was no one by the pond, and that the platform where they used to stand had been torn away, and was floating sideways in the middle of the pond, half under water. Prince Andrey rode up to the keeper's lodge. There was no one to be seen at the stone gates and the door was open. The paths of the garden were already overgrown with weeds, and cattle and horses were straying about the English park. Prince Andrey rode up to the conservatory: the panes were smashed, and some of the trees in tubs were broken, others quite dried up. He called Taras, the gardener. No one answered. Going round the conservatory on the terrace, he saw that the paling-fence was all broken down, and branches of the plum-trees had been pulled off with the fruit. An old peasant, whom Prince Andrey used to see in his childhood at the gate, was sitting on the green garden seat plaiting bast shoes.

He was deaf, and did not hear Prince Andrey's approach. He was sitting on the seat on which the old prince liked to sit, and near him the bast was hanging on the branches of a broken and dried-up magnolia.

Prince Andrey rode up to the house. Several lime-trees in the old garden had been cut down; a piebald mare and a colt were among the rose-trees just before the house. The shutters were all up in the house, except on one open window downstairs. A servant lad caught sight of Prince Andrey and ran into the house.

Alpatitch had sent his family away, and was staying on alone at Bleak Hills. He was sitting indoors, reading the *Lives of the Saints*. On hearing that Prince Andrey had come, he ran out, spectacles on nose, buttoning himself up, hurried up to the prince, and without uttering a word, burst into tears, kissing his knee.

Then he turned away in anger at his own weakness, and began giving him an account of the position of affairs. Everything precious and valuable had been moved to Bogutcharovo. Corn to the amount of a hundred measures had been carried away, but the hay, and the wheat—an extraordinary crop that season, so Alpatitch said—had been cut green and carried off by the troops. The peasants were ruined: some of them, too, had gone to Bogutcharovo; a small number remained. Prince Andrey, not heeding his words, asked, "When did my father and sister go?" meaning when had they set off for Moscow. Alpatitch, assuming he was asking about the removal to Bogutcharovo, answered that they had set off on the 7th, and began going off again into details about the crops, asking for instructions.

"Is it your honour's orders that I let the oats go on getting a receipt from the officers?" asked Alpatitch. "We have still six hundred measures left."

"What am I to say to him?" Prince Andrey wondered, looking at the old man's bald head shining in the sun, and reading in his face the consciousness that he knew himself the untimeliness of those questions, and asked them only to stifle his own grief.

"Yes, let it go," he said.

"If your excellency noticed any disorder in the garden," said Alpatitch, "it could not be prevented; three regiments have been here and spent the night. The dragoons were the worst; I noted down the name and rank of the commanding officer to lodge a complaint."

"Well, and what are you going to do? Shall you stay, if the enemy occupies the place?" Prince Andrey asked him.

Alpatitch turned his face towards Prince Andrey and looked at him; then all at once, with a solemn gesture, he lifted his hand upwards: "He is my protector, and His will be done!" he said. A group of peasants and house-serfs were coming across the meadow, uncovering their heads as they drew near Prince Andrey.

"Well, good-bye!" said Prince Andrey, bending over to Alpatitch. "Go away yourself; take what you can; and tell the peasants to set off for the Ryazan estate or the property near Moscow."

Alpatitch hugged his leg and broke into sobs. Prince Andrey gently moved him away, and spurring his horse galloped down the garden walk.

On the terrace the old man was still sitting as before, as uninterested as a fly on some beloved dead face, knocking on the sole of the bast shoe. And two little girls came running from the plum-trees in the conservatories with their skirts full of plums. They ran almost against Prince Andrey, and seeing their young master, the elder one clutched her younger companion by the hand, with a panic-stricken face, and hid with her behind a birch-tree not stopping to pick up the green plums they had dropped.

Prince Andrey turned away from them in nervous haste, afraid of letting them notice that he had seen them. He was sorry to have frightened the pretty child. He was afraid to glance at her, but yet he felt an irresistible inclination to do so. A new soothing and consolatory feeling came upon him, as gazing at the little girls, he became aware of the existence of other human interests, utterly remote from him, and as legitimate as his own. Those little girls were evidently possessed by one passionate desire to carry off and devour those green plums without being caught, and Prince Andrey wished them success in their enterprise. He could not resist glancing at them once more. Fancying themselves already secure, they had darted out of their hiding-place, and piping something in their shrill, little voices, and holding up their skirts, they ran gaily and swiftly through the grass with their bare, sunburnt little feet.

Prince Andrey was somewhat refreshed by his ride outside the region of the dust of the high-road along which the troops were marching. But he rode back into the road not far from Bleak Hills, and overtook his regiment at the halting-place near the dike of a small pond. It was about two o'clock in the afternoon. The sun, a red ball through the dust, baked and scorched his back intolerably in his black coat. The dust stood as immovable as ever over the buzzing, halting troops. There was not a breath of wind. As he rode towards the dike, Prince Andrey smelled the fresh, muddy smell of the pond. He longed to be in the water, however muddy it might be. He looked round at the pond, from which he heard shrieks and laughter. The small pond, thickly covered with green slime, was visibly half a yard higher and overflowing the dam, because it was full of white, naked human bodies, with brick-red hands and heads and necks, all plunging about in it. All that bare, white human flesh was splashing about with shrieks and laughter, in the muddy pool, like carp floundering in a net. There was a ring of merriment in that splashing, and that was what made it peculiarly sad.

One fair-haired young soldier—Prince Andrey knew him—of the third company, with a strap round the calf of his leg, stepped back, crossing himself, to get a good run, and plunge into the water. Another swarthy and very towzle-headed sergeant up to his waist in the water, bending his fine, muscular figure, was snorting with enjoyment, as he poured the water over his head with his blackened hands. There was a sound of them slapping each other, and shrieks and cries.

On the banks, on the dike, in the pond, everywhere there was white, healthy, muscular flesh. Timohin, the officer with the red nose, was rubbing himself with a towel on the dike, and was abashed at seeing Prince Andrey, but made up his mind to address him.

"It's pleasant, really, your excellency; you should try it!" he said.

"It's dirty," said Prince Andrey, grimacing.

"We will clear it out for you in a minute." And undressed as he was, Timohin ran to clear the men out. "The prince wants to come."

"What prince? Our prince?" cried voices, and all of them were in such haste to make way for him that Prince Andrey hardly had time to check them. He thought it would be better for him to have a bath in a barn. "Flesh, meat, *chair à canon*," he thought, looking too at his own naked body and shuddering, not so much from cold as from the repulsion and horror, mysterious to himself, that he had felt at the sight of that immense multitude of naked bodies floundering in the muddy water.

On the 7th of August, Prince Bagration, at his halting-place at Mihalovka on the Smolensk road, had written a letter to Araktcheev. Though the letter was addressed to Araktcheev, he knew it would be read to the Tsar, and therefore he weighed every word, so far as he was capable of doing so.

"DEAR COUNT ALEXEY ANDREEVITCH,—I presume that the minister has already reported the abandonment of Smolensk to the enemy. It is sad, it is pitiable, and the whole army is in despair at the most important place having been wantonly abandoned. I for my part begged him personally in the most urgent manner, and finally wrote to him; but nothing would persuade him. I swear to you on my honour that Napoleon was in a greater fix than he has ever been, and he might have lost half his army, but could not have taken Smolensk. Our troops have fought and are fighting as never before. With fifteen thousand men I have held the enemy in check for thirty-five hours and beaten them, but he wouldn't hold his ground for fourteen hours. It is a shame and a stain on our army, and as for himself, I consider he ought not to be alive. If he reports that our losses were great, it is false; perhaps about four thousand, not that, but that is nothing: if it had been ten thousand, what of it, that's war. But on the other hand the enemy's losses were immense.

"What would it have cost him to hold his ground for a couple of days?

In any case they must have retired of their own accord; for they had no water for their men or their horses. He gave me his word he would not retreat, but all of a sudden sent an announcement that he was withdrawing in the night. We cannot fight in this way, and we may soon bring the enemy on to Moscow. . . .

"There is a rumour afloat that you are thinking of peace. To make peace, God preserve us! After all the sacrifices that have been made and after such mad retreats—to make peace, you will set all Russia against you, and every one of us will feel it a disgrace to wear the uniform. If it has come to that, we ought to fight as long as Russia can, and as long as there are men able to stand. . . .

"There must be one man in command, not two. Your minister, may be, is very well in the ministry; but as a general, he's not simply useless, but contemptible, and the fate of all our fatherland has been put in his hands . . . I am frantic, truly, with rage; forgive me for writing abusively. It is plain that the man does not love his sovereign, and desires the ruin of us all, who advises peace to be concluded and the minister to be put in command of the army. And so I write to you plainly: get the militia ready. For the minister is leading our visitors to the capital in the most skilful manner. The object of chief suspicion to the whole army is the aide-de-camp Woltzogen. They say he's more for Napoleon than for us, and everything the minister does is by his advice. I am not merely civil to him, but obey him like a corporal, though I am his senior. It is hard: but loving my sovereign and benefactor, I obey. And I grieve for the Tsar that he intrusts his gallant army to such a man. Consider that on our retreat we have lost more than fifteen thousand men from fatigue, or left sick in the hospitals; if we had attacked, that would not have been so. Tell me for God's sake what will Russia—our mother—say at our displaying such cowardice, and why are we abandoning our good and gallant country to the rabble and rousing the hatred and shame of every Russian? Why are we in a panic? what are we afraid of? It is not my fault that the minister is vacillating, cowardly, unreasonable, dilatory, and has every vice. All the army is bewailing it and loading him with abuse. . . ."

VI

AMONG the innumerable categories into which it is possible to classify the phenomena of life, one may classify them all into such as are dominated by matter and such as are dominated by form. To the latter class one may refer the life of Petersburg, especially in its drawing-rooms, as distinguished from the life of the country, of the district, of the province, or even of Moscow. That life of the drawing-rooms is unchanging.

Between the years 1805 and 1812 we had made peace with Bonaparte and quarrelled with him again; we had made new constitutions and unmade them again, but the salons of Anna Pavlovna and of Ellen were precisely as they had been—the former seven, the latter five years—

before. Anna Pavlovna's circle were still speaking with incredulous wonder of Bonaparte's successes; and saw in his successes, and in the submissive attitude of the sovereigns of Europe, a malicious conspiracy, the sole aim of which was to give annoyance and anxiety to the court circle of which Anna Pavlovna was the representative. The set that gathered about Ellen, whom no less a person than Rumyantsev condescended to visit, and looked on as a remarkably intelligent woman, talked in 1812 with the same enthusiasm as in 1808, of the "great nation," and the "great man," and regretted the breach with France, which must, they believed, shortly end in peace.

Of late after the Tsar's return from the army, some increase of excitement was perceptible in these antagonistic salons, and they made something like demonstrations of hostility to one another, but the bias of each circle remained unaffected. Anna Pavlovna's set refused to admit any French people but the most unimpeachable legitimists; and in her drawing-room the patriotic view found expression that the French theatre ought not to be patronised, and that the maintenance of the French company there cost as much as the maintenance of a whole army corps. The progress of the war was eagerly followed, and rumours greatly to the advantage of our army were circulated. In the circle of Ellen, of Rumyantsev, the French circle, the reports of the enemy's cruelty and barbarous methods of warfare were discredited; and all sorts of conciliatory efforts on the part of Napoleon were discussed. This set discountenanced the premature counsels of those who advised preparations for the removal to Kazan of the court and the girls' schools, that were under the protection of the empress mother. The whole war was in fact regarded in Ellen's salon as a series of merely formal demonstrations, very shortly to be terminated by peace; and the view prevailed, expressed by Bilibin, who was now in Petersburg and constantly seen at Ellen's, as every man of wit was sure to be, that the war would be ended not by gunpowder but by those who had invented it. The patriotic fervour of Moscow, of which tidings reached Petersburg with the Tsar, was in Ellen's salon a subject of ironical, and very witty, though circumspect, raillery.

In Anna Pavlovna's circle, on the contrary, these patriotic demonstrations roused the greatest enthusiasm, and were spoken of as Plutarch speaks of his ancient Romans. Prince Vassily, who still filled the same important positions, constituted the connecting link between the two circles. He used to visit "my good friend Anna Pavlovna," and was also seen in the "diplomatic salon of my daughter"; and often was led into blunders from his frequent transitions from one to the other, and said in one drawing-room what should have been reserved for the other.

Soon after the Tsar's arrival, Prince Vassily, in conversation about the progress of the war at Anna Pavlovna's, severely criticised Barclay de Tolly, and expressed himself unable to decide who should be appointed commander-in-chief. One of the guests, usually spoken of as a "man of great abilities," described how he had that day seen the newly elected commander of the Petersburg militia, Kutuzov, presiding over the enrolment of militiamen in the Court of Exchequer, and ventured discreetly to suggest that Kutuzov would be the man who might satisfy all requirements.

Anna Pavlovna smiled mournfully, and observed that Kutuzov had done nothing but cause the Tsar annoyance.

"I have said so over and over again in the assembly of nobility," interposed Prince Vassily, "but they wouldn't listen to me. I said that his election to the command of the militia would not be pleasing to his majesty. They wouldn't listen to me. It's all this mania for being in the opposition," he went on. "And to what public are they playing, I should like to know. It's all because we are trying to ape the silly enthusiasm of Moscow," said Prince Vassily, forgetting for a moment that it was at Ellen's that that enthusiasm was jeered at, while at Anna Pavlovna's it was as well to admire it. But he hastened to retrieve his mistake. "Is it suitable for Kutuzov, the oldest general in Russia, to be presiding in the Court? *Et il en restera pour sa peine!* Did any one hear of such a thing as appointing a man commander-in-chief who cannot sit a horse, who drops asleep at a council—a man, too, of the lowest morals! A pretty reputation he gained for himself in Bucharest! To say nothing of his qualities as a general, can we appoint, at such a moment, a man decrepit and blind—yes, simply blind! A fine idea—a blind general! He sees nothing. Playing blind-man's buff—that's all he's fit for!"

No one opposed that view.

On the 24th of July it was accepted as perfectly correct. But on the 29th Kutuzov received the title of prince. The bestowal of this title might be taken to indicate a desire to shelve him, and therefore Prince Vassily's dictum still remained correct, though he was in no such hurry now to express it. But on the 8th of August a committee, consisting of General Field-Marshal Saltykov, Araktcheev, Vyazmitinov, Lopuhin, and Kotchubey was held to consider the progress of the war. This committee decided that the disasters were due to divided authority; and although the members of the committee were aware of the Tsar's dislike of Kutuzov, after a deliberation they advised the appointment of Kutuzov as commander-in-chief. And that same day Kutuzov was appointed commander-in-chief of the army, and intrusted with unlimited authority over the whole region occupied by the troops.

On the 9th of August Prince Vassily once more met the "man of great abilities" at Anna Pavlovna's. The latter gentleman was assiduous in his attendance at Anna Pavlovna's, in the hope of receiving, through her influence, an appointment on one of the institutions of female education. Prince Vassily strode into the room with the air of a victorious general, of a man who has succeeded in attaining the object of his desires.

"Well, you know the great news! Prince Kutuzov is marshal! All differences of opinion are at an end. I am so glad, so delighted!" said Prince Vassily. "At last here is a man!" he declared, looking sternly and significantly at all the company. In spite of his desire to secure the post he coveted, the "man of great abilities" could not refrain from reminding Prince Vassily of the view he had expressed shortly before. (This was a breach of civility to Prince Vassily in Anna Pavlovna's drawing-room, and also to Anna Pavlovna, who had received the tidings with equal enthusiasm; but he could not refrain.)

"But they say he is blind, prince," he said to recall to Prince Vassily his own words.

"*Allez donc, il y voit assez,*" said Prince Vassily, with the rapid bass voice and the cough with which he always disposed of all difficulties. "He sees quite enough," he repeated. "And what I'm particularly glad of," he went on, "is that the Emperor has given him unlimited authority over all the troops, over the whole region, an authority no commander-in-chief has ever had before. It's another autocrat," he concluded, with a victorious smile.

"God grant it may be," said Anna Pavlovna.

The "man of great abilities," a novice in court society, was anxious to flatter Anna Pavlovna by maintaining her former opinion against this new view of the position. He said: "They say the Emperor was unwilling to give Kutuzov such authority. They say he blushed like a young lady to whom Joconde is read, saying to him, 'The sovereign and the country decree you this honour.' "

"Perhaps the heart was not of the party," said Anna Pavlovna.

"Oh no, no," Prince Vassily maintained warmly. Now he would not put Kutuzov second to any one. To hear Prince Vassily now Kutuzov was not simply a good man in himself, but idolised by every one. "No that's impossible, for the sovereign has always known how to appreciate him," he added.

"God only grant that Prince Kutuzov may take the control of things into his own hands," said Anna Pavlovna, "and not permit *any one* to put a spoke in his wheel."

Prince Vassily knew at once who was meant. He whispered, "I know for a fact that Kutuzov made it an express condition that the Tsarevitch should not be with the army. *Vous savez ce qu'il a dit à l'Empereur'* And Prince Vassily repeated the words said to have been spoken by Kutuzov to the Tsar: " 'I can neither punish him if he does wrong, nor reward him if he does well.' Oh! he's a shrewd fellow, Prince Kutuzov. I have known him a long while."

"They do say," observed the "man of great abilities," who had not acquired a courtier's tact, "that his excellency even made it an express condition that the Emperor himself should not be with the army."

He had hardly uttered the words when Anna Pavlovna and Prince Vassily simultaneously turned their backs on him, and looked mournfully at one another, with a sigh at his naïveté.

VII

At the time when this was taking place in Petersburg, the French had passed through Smolensk, and were moving closer and closer to Moscow. Napoleon's historian, Thiers, like others of Napoleon's historians, tries to justify his hero by maintaining that he was drawn on to the walls of Moscow against his will. He is as right as any historians who seek the explanation of historic events in the will of a man; he is as right as the Russian historians, who assert that Napoleon was lured to Moscow by the skilful strategy of the Russian generals. In this case, apart from the law of "retrospectiveness," which makes all the past appear a preparation for the subsequent facts, the element of mutual interaction, too, comes in, confusing the whole subject. A good chess-player, who has lost a game, is genuinely convinced that his failure is due to his blunders, and he seeks the blunder at the commencement of the game, forgetting that at every move during the whole game there were similar errors, that not one piece has been played as perfectly as possible. The blunder on which he concentrates his attention attracts his notice simply because his opponent took advantage of it. How much more complex is the game of war, which must be played within certain limits of time, in which there is not one will controlling lifeless toys, in which the whole is the resultant of the innumerable *collisions* of diverse individual wills!

After Smolensk, Napoleon tried to force on a battle beyond Dorogobuzh, at Vyazma, and then at Tsarevo-Zaimishtche. But the Russians could not give battle, owing to innumerable combinations of circumstances, till Borodino, one hundred and twelve versts from Moscow. From Vyazma Napoleon gave instructions for an advance straight upon Moscow.

"Moscow, the Asiatic capital of this great empire, the holy city of the peoples of Alexander, Moscow, with its innumerable churches in the form of Chinese pagodas!"

This Moscow would not let Napoleon's imagination rest. On the march from Vyazma to Tsarevo-Zaimishtche Napoleon was riding on his cream-coloured English horse, accompanied by his guards, and sentinels, and pages, and adjutants. The commander of the staff, Berthier, had dropped behind to put questions to a Russian prisoner taken by the cavalry. Accompanied by the interpreter, Lelorme d'Ideville, he galloped after Napoleon, and pulled his horse up with an amused expression.

"Well?" said Napoleon.

"A Cossack of Platov's detachment says Platov is effecting a junction with the main army, and that Kutuzov has been appointed commander-in-chief. He is very shrewd and talkative."

Napoleon smiled, and bade them give the Cossack a horse and bring him before him. He wished to talk to him himself. Several adjutants galloped off, and within an hour Denisov's serf Lavrushka, whom his master had left with Rostov, rode up to Napoleon, sitting on a French cavalry saddle, wearing an orderly's short jacket, and looking sly, tipsy, and mirthful. Napoleon bade him ride at his side and began questioning him.

"Are you a Cossack?"

"Yes; a Cossack, your honour."

"The Cossack, ignorant in whose company he was, since Napoleon's plain appearance had nothing to suggest to the Oriental imagination the

presence of a monarch, talked with extraordinary familiarity of the incidents of the war," says Thiers, relating this episode. In reality Lavrushka, who had been drunk the previous evening, and had left his
master without dinner, had been thrashed for it, and sent to the village
in quest of fowls, where he was tempted on by plunder till he got caught
by the French. Lavrushka was one of those coarse, impudent lackeys,
who have seen a good deal of life, look on it as a duty to do nothing
without cunning and trickery, are ready to do any kind of service for
their masters, and are particularly keen in scenting out the baser impulses of their superiors, especially on the side of vanity and pettiness.
On coming into the presence of Napoleon, whom he easily and confidently recognised, Lavrushka was not in the least taken aback, and only
did his utmost to win the favour of his new master.

He was very well aware that this was Napoleon, and Napoleon's presence impressed him no more than Rostov's or the quartermaster's with
the rod in his hand, because he had nothing of which either the quartermaster or Napoleon could not deprive him.

He had repeated all the gossip that was talked among the officers'
servants. Much of it was true. But when Napoleon asked him whether
the Russians expected to conquer Bonaparte or not, Lavrushka screwed
up his eyes and thought a bit.

He saw in the question a sharp piece of cunning, as cunning fellows,
like Lavrushka, always do in everything. He frowned and paused a
minute.

"Well, if it does come to a battle," he said thoughtfully, "and pretty
soon, then yours will win. That's a sure thing. But if now, three days
and there's a battle after that, well then, I say, that same battle will
be a long job." This was translated to Napoleon. "If a battle is fought
within three days the French will win it, but if later, God knows what
will come of it," Lelorme d'Ideville put it, smiling. Napoleon did not
smile, though he was evidently in high good humour, and told him to
repeat the words.

Lavrushka noticed that, and to entertain him further, said, pretending not to know who he was:

"We know, you have got your Bonaparte; he has conquered every
one in the world, ay, but with us it will be a different story . . ." himself hardly aware how and why this bit of bragging patriotism slipped
out. The interpreter translated these words without the conclusion; and
Bonaparte smiled. "The young Cossack brought a smile on to the lips of
his august companion," says Thiers. After a few paces in silence, Napoleon turned to Berthier, and said he should like to try the effect "*sur
cet enfant du Don*" of learning that the man with whom he was speaking
was the Emperor himself, the very Emperor who had carved his im-
mortally victorious name on the Pyramids. The fact was communicated.
Lavrushka—discerning that this was done to test him, and that Napoleon expected him to be panic-stricken—tried to gratify his new masters
by promptly affecting to be astounded, struck dumb; he opened round
eyes, and made the sort of face usual with him when he was being

led off to be thrashed. "Hardly," says Thiers, "had Napoleon's interpreter spoken, than the Cossack was struck dumb with amazement; he did not utter another word, and walked with his eyes constantly fixed on the great conqueror, whose fame had reached him across the steppes of the East. All his loquacity suddenly vanished, and was replaced by a naïve and silent awe. Napoleon made the Cossack a present, and ordered him to be set at liberty like *un oiseau qu'on rend aux champs qui l'ont vu naître.*"

Napoleon rode on, dreaming of that Moscow that filled his imagination, while the bird returning to the fields that had seen him born, galloped back to the outposts, inventing the tale he would tell his comrades. What had really happened he did not care to relate, simply because it seemed to him not worth telling. He rode back to the Cossacks, inquired where was his regiment, now forming part of Platov's detachment; and towards evening found his master, Nikolay Rostov, encamped at Yankovo. Rostov was just mounting his horse to ride through the villages near with Ilyin. He gave Lavrushka another horse and took him with them.

VIII

PRINCESS MARYA was not in Moscow and out of danger as Prince Andrey supposed.

After Alpatitch's return from Smolensk, the old prince seemed as though he had suddenly waked out of a sleep. He gave orders for the militiamen to assemble out of the villages, and to be armed; and wrote a letter to the commander-in-chief, in which he informed him of his intention to remain at Bleak Hills to the last and to defend himself, leaving it to his discretion to take steps or not for the defence of Bleak Hills, where he said one of the oldest Russian generals would be taken prisoner or die. He announced to his household that he should remain at Bleak Hills.

But though resolved himself to remain, the prince made arrangements for sending the princess with Dessalle and the little prince to Bogutcharovo, and from there on to Moscow. Frightened at her father's feverish, sleepless energy, following on his previous apathy, Princess Marya could not bring herself to leave him alone, and for the first time in her life ventured not to obey him. She refused to go, and a fearful tempest of wrath burst upon her. The prince reminded her of every previous instance of injustice to her. Trying to find pretexts for reviling her, he said she had done everything to worry him, that she had estranged him from his son, that she harboured the vilest suspicions of him, that she made it the object of her life to poison his existence. He drove her out of his study, telling her that he did not care if she did not go away. He told her that he did not want to hear of her existence, but gave her fair warning not to dare show herself before him. Princess Marya was relieved that he had not, as she had dreaded, ordered her to be forcibly removed from Bleak Hills, but had simply commanded her not to show herself. She knew that this meant that in the secret recesses of his soul he was glad she was staying at home.

The day after Nikolushka had left, the old prince dressed himself in the morning in full uniform, and prepared to make a call on the commander-in-chief. The carriage was standing ready. Princess Marya saw him in his uniform, with all his orders on his breast, walk out of the house and go down the garden to inspect the armed peasants and house-serfs. Princess Marya sat at the window listening to his voice resounding from the garden. Suddenly several men came running up the avenue with panic-stricken faces.

Princess Marya ran out on to the steps, along the flower-bed path, and into the avenue. A great crowd of militiamen and servants were coming down it towards her, and in the middle of that crowd several men were holding up and dragging along a little old man in a uniform and decorations. Princess Marya ran towards him, and in the dancing, tiny rings of light that filtered through the shade of the lime-tree avenue, she could form no distinct impression of the change in his face. The only thing she could see was that the stern and determined expression of his face had changed to a look of timidity and submission. On seeing his daughter, he tried to move his powerless lips, and uttered a hoarse sound. It was impossible to understand what he meant. He was lifted up, carried into his study, and laid on the couch, which had been such an object of dread to him of late.

The doctor, who was brought over the same night, bled him, and declared that the prince had had a stroke, paralysing his right side.

To remain at Bleak Hills was becoming more and more dangerous, and the next day they moved the prince to Bogutcharovo. The doctor travelled with him.

When they reached Bogutcharovo, they found Dessalle had already set off for Moscow with the little prince.

For three weeks the old prince lay stricken with paralysis, getting neither better nor worse, in the new house Prince Andrey had planned at Bogutcharovo. The old prince was unconscious; he lay like a deformed corpse. He muttered incessantly, twitching his eyebrows and lips, and it was impossible to tell whether he understood his surroundings or not. Only one thing could be said for certain: that was, that he was suffering, and had a craving to express something. But what that was no one could tell: whether it were some sick and half-crazy whim; whether it related to public affairs or family circumstances.

The doctor said that this uneasiness meant nothing; that it was due to physical causes. But Princess Marya believed (and the fact that her presence seemed to intensify the restlessness, confirmed her supposition) that he wanted to tell her something.

He was evidently suffering both physically and mentally. There was no hope of recovery. It was impossible to move him. What if he were to die on the road? "Wouldn't it be better if it were over, if all were over?" Princess Marya thought sometimes. Day and night, almost without sleep, she watched him, and, terrible to say, she watched him, not in the hope of finding symptoms of a change for the better, but often in the hope of seeing symptoms of the approaching end.

Strange as it was for the princess to own it to herself, she had this feeling in her heart. And what was still more horrible to Princess Marya was the fact that ever since her father's illness (if not even before, when she resolved to stay with him, in vague expectation of something) all the forgotten hopes and desires slumbering within her head awakened. Ideas that had not entered her head for years—dreams of a life free from the terror of her father, even of the possibility of love and a happy married life, haunted her imagination like temptations of the devil. In vain she tried to drive away the thought; questions were continually in her mind how she would order her life now, after *this*. It was a temptation of the devil, and Princess Marya knew it. She knew that the sole weapon of avail against *him* was prayer, and she strove to pray. She threw herself into the attitude of prayer, gazed at the holy pictures, repeated the words of the prayer, but still she could not pray. She felt herself carried off into a new world of real life, of labour and free activity, utterly opposed to the moral atmosphere in which she had been kept in bondage, and in which the one consolation was prayer. She could not pray and could not weep, and practical cares absorbed her mind.

To remain at Bogutcharovo was becoming unsafe. Rumours came from all sides of the French being near, and in one village, fifteen versts from Bogutcharovo, a house had been sacked by French marauders. The doctor insisted on the necessity of moving the prince; the marshal of the province sent an official to Princess Marya to persuade her to get away as quickly as possible. The captain of the police visited Bogutcharovo to insist on the same thing, telling her that the French were only forty versts away; that French proclamations were circulating in the villages, and that if the princess did not move her father before the 15th, he could not answer for the consequences.

The princess made up her mind to leave on the 15th. The preparations and giving all the necessary instructions, for which every one applied to her, kept her busy the whole of the previous day. The night of the 14th she spent as usual, without undressing, in the room next to the one where the old prince lay. Several times she waked up, hearing his groaning and muttering, the creak of the bedstead, and the steps of Tihon and the doctor moving him. Several times she listened at the door, and it seemed to her that he was muttering more loudly than usual and turning more restlessly. She could not sleep, and several times she went to the door, listening, tempted to go in, but unable to make up her mind to do so. Although he could not speak, Princess Marya saw and knew how he disliked any expression of anxiety about him. She had noticed how he turned in displeasure away from her eyes, which were sometimes unconsciously fixed persistently on him. She knew her going in at night, at an unusual time, would irritate him.

But never had she felt so sorry for him; never had she felt it so dreadful to lose him. She went over all her life with him, and in every word, every action, she saw an expression of his love for her. Occasionally these reminiscences were interrupted by the temptation of the devil; dreams came back to her imagination of what would happen after his death, and how she would order her new independent existence. But she drove away such thoughts with horror. Towards morning he was quieter, and she fell asleep.

She waked up late. The perfect sincerity, which often accompanies the moment of waking, showed her unmistakably what it was that was of most interest to her in her father's illness. She waked up, listened to what was passing through the door, and catching the sound of his muttering, she told herself with a sigh that there was no change.

"But what should there be? What did I hope for? I hope for his death," she cried, with inward loathing of herself.

She washed, dressed, said her prayers, and went out on to the steps. At the entrance the carriages in which their luggage was packed were standing without horses.

The morning was warm and grey. Princess Marya lingered on the steps, still horrified at her own spiritual infamy, and trying to get her ideas into shape before going in to see him.

The doctor came downstairs and out to her.

"He is a little better to-day," said the doctor. "I was looking for you. One can make out a little of what he says. His head is clearer. Come in. He is asking for you . . ."

Princess Marya's heart beat so violently at this news that she turned pale and leaned against the door to keep from falling. To see him, to talk to him, to be under his eyes now, when all her soul was filled with these fearful, sinful imaginings was full of an agonising joy and terror for her.

"Let us go in," said the doctor.

Princess Marya went in to her father, and went up to his bedside. He was lying raised high on his back; his little bony hands, covered with knotted purple veins, were laid on the quilt; his left eye was gazing straight before him, while the right eye was distorted, and his lips and eyebrows were motionless. He looked so thin, so small, and pitiable. His face looked withered up or melted away; his features all seemed smaller. Princess Marya went up and kissed his hand. His left hand clasped her hand in a way that showed he had long been wanting her. He twitched her hand, and his eyebrows and lips quivered angrily.

She looked at him in dismay, trying to fathom what he wanted of her. When she changed her position so that his left eye could see her, he seemed satisfied, and for several seconds kept his eye fixed on her. Then his lips and tongue twitched; sounds came, and he tried to speak, looking with imploring timidity at her, evidently afraid she would not understand him.

Princess Marya strained every faculty of attention as she gazed at him. The comic effort with which he strove to make his tongue work made Princess Marya drop her eyes, and she had much ado to stifle the sobs that rose in her throat. He was saying something, several times repeating his words. Princess Marya could not understand them; but she tried to guess what he was saying, and repeated interrogatively the words she supposed him to be uttering.

"O . . . o . . . aye . . aye . . . !" he repeated several times. It was impossible to interpret these sounds. The doctor thought he had guessed it, and asked:

"The princess is afraid?"

He shook his head, and again repeated the same sounds.

"The soul, the soul is in pain!" Princess Marya guessed. He grunted affirmatively, took her hand, and began pressing it to different parts of his breast as though seeking the right place for it.

"Always thinking!—about you . . . thinking . . . !" he articulated, far more intelligibly than before now that he felt sure of being understood. Princess Marya pressed her head against his arm, trying to hide her sobs and tears.

He passed his hand over her hair.

"I called for you all night . . ." he articulated.

"If I had only known . . ." she said, through her tears. "I was afraid to come in."

He pressed her hand.

"Weren't you asleep?"

"No, I couldn't sleep," said Princess Marya, shaking her head.

Unconsciously imitating her father, she tried to speak more by signs, as he spoke, as though she, too, had a difficulty in articulating.

"Darling!" . . . or "dear one!" . . . Princess Marya could not distinguish the word; but from the expression of his eyes she had no doubt what was said was a word of caressing tenderness such as he had never used to her before. "Why didn't you come?"

"And I was wishing, wishing for his death!" thought Princess Marya. He paused.

"Thanks . . . to you . . . child, dear one! for all, for all . . . forgive . . . thanks! . . . forgive! . . . thanks! . . ." And tears flowed from his eyes. "Call Andryusha," he said suddenly, and a look of childish and deprecating misgiving came into his face at the question. He seemed to be himself aware that his question had no meaning. So at least it seemed to Princess Marya.

"I have had a letter from him," answered Princess Marya.

He looked at her with timid wonder.

"Where is he?"

"He is with the army, father, at Smolensk."

He was silent for a long while, closing his eyes. Then, as though to answer his doubts, and to assert that now he understood it all and remembered, he nodded his head and opened his eyes.

"Yes," he said, softly and distinctly. "Russia is lost! They have lost her!"

And again he broke into sobs, and tears flowed from his eyes. Princess Marya could restrain herself no more, and wept too as she looked at his face.

He closed his eyes again. His sobs ceased. He pointed to his eyes; and Tihon, understanding him, wiped away his tears.

Then he opened his eyes, and said something, which, for a long while, no one could understand; and at last Tihon understood and interpreted. Princess Marya looked for the drift of his words in the direction in which he had been speaking a minute before. She supposed he was speaking of Russia; then of Prince Andrey, of herself, of his grandson, then of his own death. And this was just why she could not understand his words.

"Put on your white dress. I like it," he had said.

When she understood those words Princess Marya sobbed louder than ever, and the doctor, taking her on his arm, led her out of the room on to the terrace, trying to persuade her to calm herself, and to devote herself to preparations for the journey. After Princess Marya had left the prince, he began talking again of his son, of the war, of the Tsar, twitched his eyebrows angrily, began to raise his hoarse voice, and was seized by a second and final stroke.

Princess Marya stayed on the terrace. The day had become brilliantly fine, sunny, and warm. She could grasp nothing, could think of nothing, and feel nothing but her passionate love for her father, of which it seemed to her that she had not been aware till that minute. She ran out into the garden, and ran sobbing towards the pond along the paths planted with young lime-trees by Prince Andrey.

"Yes . . . I . . . I . . . I longed for his death! Yes, I wanted it soon to be over . . . I wanted to be at peace . . . And what will become of me? What use will peace be to me when he is gone?" Princess Marya muttered aloud, walking with rapid steps through the garden, and pressing her hands to her bosom, which heaved with convulsive sobs. Going round the garden in a circle, which brought her back again to the house, she saw coming towards her Mademoiselle Bourienne (who was remaining at Bogutcharovo, preferring not to move away), and with her an unknown gentleman. It was the district marshal, who had come to call on the princess, to urge upon her the necessity of her immediate departure. Princess Marya listened and did not take in what he said. She took him into the house, offered him lunch, and sat down with him. Then asking him to excuse her, she went to the old prince's door. The doctor came out with a perturbed face and told her she could not go in.

"Go away, princess; go away!"

Princess Marya went out again into the garden, and by the pond at the bottom of the hill she sat down on the grass, in a place where no one could see her. She could not have said how long she was there. A woman's footsteps running along the path made her look round. She got up and saw Dunyasha, her maid, evidently running to look for her, stop short, as though in alarm, on seeing her mistress.

"Come, please, princess . . . the prince . . ." said Dunyasha, in a breaking voice.

"I'm coming. I'm coming!" the princess cried hurriedly, not letting

Dunyasha have time to say what she meant to; and trying to avoid see-ing her, she ran into the house.

"Princess, it is God's will! You must be prepared for the worst," said the marshal, meeting her at the door into the house.

"Let me be; it's not true!" she cried angrily at him.

The doctor tried to stop her. She pushed him away and ran to the door. "What are these people with scared faces stopping me for? I don't want any of them! What are they doing here?" she thought. She opened the door, and the bright daylight in the room, always hitherto darkened, frightened her. Her old nurse and other women were in the room. They all drew back from the bed, making way for her. He was still lying on the bed as before; but the stern look on his calm face arrested Princess Marya on the threshold.

"No, he is not dead, it cannot be!" Princess Marya said to herself. She went up to him, and struggling with the terror that came upon her, she pressed her lips to his cheek. But she started back from him at once. Instantaneously all the tenderness she had been feeling for him van-ished, and was followed by a feeling of horror for what lay before her. "No, no, he is no more! He is no more, and here in the place where he was, is something unfamiliar and sinister, some fearful, terrifying, and repulsive secret!" And hiding her face in her hands, Princess Marya sank into the arms of the doctor, who supported her.

In the presence of Tihon and the doctor, the women washed what had been the prince, bound a kerchief round the head that the mouth might not become rigidly open, and bound another kerchief round the limbs. Then the uniform with the decorations was put on, and the little dried-up body was laid on the table. There was no telling when or who took thought for all this; it all seemed to be done of itself. Towards night candles were lighted round the coffin, a pall was laid over it, juniper was strewn on the floor, a printed prayer was put under the dead with-ered head, and a deacon sat in the corner reading aloud the Psalter. Like horses crowding, snorting, and starting round a dead horse, numbers of familiar and unfamiliar figures crowded round the coffin—the marshal, and the village elder, and peasant women, and all with scared and fasci-nated eyes, crossed themselves, and bowed down and kissed the cold, stiff hand of the old prince.

IX

UNTIL Prince Andrey's stay at Bogutcharovo, the estate had never had an owner in residence, and the Bogutcharovo peasants were of quite a different character from the peasants of Bleak Hills. They differed from them in speech, in dress, and in manners. They said they came from the steppes. The old prince praised them for their industry when they came to Bleak Hills for harvesting, or digging ponds and ditches; but he did not like them because of their savage manners.

Prince Andrey's residence at Bogutcharovo, and his innovations—his hospitals and schools and the lowering of their rent—had not softened their manners, but, on the contrary, had intensified their traits of character, which the old prince called their savagery.

Obscure rumours were always current among them: at one time a belief that they were all to be carried off to be made Cossacks, then that they were to be converted to some new religion, then rumours of some supposed proclamations of the Tsar, or of the oath to the Tsar Pavel Petrovitch in 1797 (which was said to have granted freedom to the peasants, and to have been withdrawn by the gentry later); then of the expected return of the Tsar Peter Fedorovitch, who was to rise again from the dead in seven years, and to bring perfect freedom, and to make an end of the existing order of things. Rumours of the war, and Bonaparte and his invasion, were connected in their minds with vague conceptions of Antichrist, of the end of the world, and perfect freedom.

In the vicinity of Bogutcharovo were large villages inhabited by Crown serfs, or peasants who paid rent to absentee owners. There were very few resident landowners in the neighbourhood, and consequently very few house-serfs or peasants able to read and write. And among the peasants of that part of the country there could be seen more distinctly and strongly marked than among others those mysterious undercurrents in the life of the Russian peasantry, which are so baffling to contemporaries. Twenty years before, there had been a movement among the peasants of the district to emigrate to certain supposedly warm rivers. Hundreds of peasants, among them those of Bogutcharovo, had suddenly begun selling their cattle and moving away with their families towards the south-west. Like birds flying to unknown realms over the ocean, these men with their wives and children turned towards the south-west, where no one of them had been. They set off in caravans, redeemed their freedom one by one, ran and drove and walked to the unknown region of the warm springs. Many were punished; some sent to Siberia; many died of cold and hunger on the road; many came back of their own accord; and the movement died down as it had begun without obvious cause. But the undercurrents still flowed among the people, and were gathering force for some new manifestation, destined to appear as strangely, unexpectedly, and at the same time simply, naturally, and forcibly. In 1812 any one living in close relations with the peasants might have observed that there was a violent ferment working below the surface, and an outbreak of some kind was at hand.

Alpatitch, who came to Bogutcharovo a little while before the old prince's death, noticed that there was some excitement among the peasants; and noticed that, unlike Bleak Hills district, where within a radius of sixty versts all the peasants had moved away, abandoning their villages to be wasted by the Cossacks, in the Bogutcharovo steppe country the peasants had entered, it was said, into communication with the French, and were remaining in their homes, and there were some mysterious documents circulating among them. He learned through serfs who were attached to him that the peasant Karp, a man of great in-

fluence in the village, had a few days previously accompanied a government transport, and had returned with the news that the Cossacks were
destroying the deserted villages, while the French would not touch them.
He knew that another peasant had on the previous day even brought
from the hamlet of Vislouhovo, where the French were encamped, a
proclamation from the French general that no harm would be done to
the inhabitants, and that everything taken from them would be paid for,
if they would remain. In token of good faith, the peasant brought from
Vislouhovo a hundred-rouble note (he did not know it was false), paid
him in advance for hay.

And last, and most important of all, Alpatitch learned that on the
day on which he had given the village elder orders to collect carts to
move the princess's luggage from Bogutcharovo, there had been a meeting in the village at which it was resolved to wait and not to move.
Meanwhile, time was pressing. On the day of the prince's death, the 15th
of August, the marshal urged Princess Marya to move the same day,
as it was becoming dangerous. He said that he could not answer for
what might happen after the 16th. He drove away that evening, promising to return next morning for the funeral. But next day he could not
come, as he received information of an expected advance of the French,
and was only just in time to get his family and valuables moved away
from his own estate.

For nearly thirty years Bogutcharovo had been under the direction of
the village elder, Dron, called by the old prince, Dronushka.

Dron was one of those physically and morally vigorous peasants, who
grow a thick beard as soon as they are grown up, and go on almost
unchanged till sixty or seventy, without a grey hair or the loss of a tooth,
as upright and vigorous at sixty as at thirty.

Shortly after the attempted migration to the warm rivers, in which
he had taken part with the rest, Dron was made village elder and overseer of Bogutcharovo, and had filled those positions irreproachably for
twenty-three years. The peasants were more afraid of him than of their
master. The old prince and the young one and the steward respected
him, and called him in joke the minister. Dron had never once been
drunk or ill since he had been appointed elder; he had never after sleepless nights or severe labour shown the slightest signs of fatigue; and
though he could not read or write, he never forgot an account of the
pounds of flour in the huge waggon-loads he sold, and of the money paid
for them, nor missed a sheaf of wheat on an acre of the Bogutcharovo
fields.

This peasant Dron it was for whom Alpatitch sent on coming from
the plundered estate at Bleak Hills. He ordered him to get ready twelve
horses for the princess's carriages, and eighteen conveyances for the
move which was to be made from Bogutcharovo. Though the peasants
paid rent instead of working as serfs, Alpatitch expected to meet no difficulty on their part in carrying out this order, since there were two
hundred and thirty efficient families in Bogutcharovo, and the peasants

were well-to-do. But Dron, on receiving the order, dropped his eyes and made no reply. Alpatitch mentioned the names of peasants from whom he told him to take the carts.

Dron replied that the horses belonging to those peasants were away on hire. Alpatitch mentioned the names of other peasants. They too, according to Dron, had no horses available: some were employed in government transport, others had gone lame, and others had died through the shortness of forage. In Dron's opinion, there was no hope of getting horses enough for the princess's carriages, not to speak of the transport of baggage.

Alpatitch looked intently at Dron and scowled. Dron was a model village elder, but Alpatitch had not been twenty years managing the prince's estates for nothing, and he too was a model steward. He possessed in the highest degree the faculty of divining the needs and instincts of the peasants, with whom he had to deal, and was consequently an excellent steward. Glancing at Dron, he saw at once that his answers were not the expression of his own ideas, but the expression of the general drift of opinion in the Bogutcharovo village, by which the elder had already been carried away. At the same time, he knew that Dron, who had saved money and was detested by the village, must be hesitating between two camps—the master's and the peasants'. He detected the hesitation in his eyes, and so frowning he came closer to Dron.

"Now, Dronushka," he said, "you listen to me! Don't you talk nonsense to me. His excellency, Prince Andrey Nikolaevitch, himself gave me orders to move the folk away, and not leave them with the enemy, and the Tsar has issued a decree that it is to be so. Any one that stays is a traitor to the Tsar. Do you hear?"

"I hear," answered Dron, not raising his eyes.

Alpatitch was not satisfied with his reply.

"Ay, Dron, there'll be trouble!" said Alpatitch, shaking his head.

"It's for you to command!" said Dron dejectedly.

"Ay, Dron, drop it!" repeated Alpatitch, taking his hand out of the bosom of his coat, and pointing with a solemn gesture to the ground under Dron's feet. "I can see right through you; and more than that, I can see three yards into the earth under you," he said, looking at the ground under Dron's feet.

Dron was disconcerted; he looked furtively at Alpatitch, and dropped his eyes again.

"You drop this nonsense, and tell the folks to pack up to leave their homes and go to Moscow, and to get ready carts to-morrow morning for the princess's luggage; and don't you go to the meeting. Do you hear?"

All at once Dron threw himself at his feet.

"Yakov Alpatitch, discharge me! Take the keys from me; discharge me, for Christ's sake!"

"Stop that!" said Alpatitch sternly. "I can see through you three yards into the earth," he repeated, knowing that his skill in bee-keeping, his knowledge of the right day to sow the oats, and his success in pleasing the old prince for twenty years had 'ong ago gained him the

reputation of a wizard, and that the power of seeing for three yards under a man is ascribed to wizards.

Dron got up, and would have said something, but Alpatitch interrupted him.

"What's this you've all got in your head? Eh? . . . What are you
thinking about? Eh?"

"What am I to do with the people?" said Dron. "They're all in a ferment. I do tell them . . ."

"Oh, I dare say you do," said Alpatitch. "Are they drinking?" he
asked briefly.

"They're all in a ferment, Yakov Alpatitch; they have got hold of
another barrel."

"Then you listen to me. I'll go to the police-captain and you tell them
so, and tell them to drop all this and get the carts ready."

"Certainly," answered Dron.

Yakov Alpatitch did not insist further. He had much experience in
managing the peasants, and knew that the chief means for securing
obedience was not to show the slightest suspicion that they could do
anything but obey. Having wrung from Dron a submissive "certainly,"
Yakov Alpatitch rested content with it, though he had more than doubts
—he had a conviction—that the carts would not be provided without
the intervention of the military authorities.

And as a fact when evening came, the carts had not been provided.
There had been again a village meeting at the tavern, and at the meeting it had been resolved to drive the horses out into the forest and not
to provide the conveyances. Without saying a word of all this to the princess, Alpatitch ordered his own baggage to be unloaded from the waggons that had come from Bleak Hills and the horses to be taken from
them for the princess's carriage, while he rode off himself to the police
authorities.

X

AFTER her father's funeral Princess Marya locked herself in her room
and would not let any one come near her. A maid came to the door to
say that Alpatitch had come to ask for instructions in regard to the
journey. (This was before Alpatitch had talked to Dron.) Princess
Marya got up from the sofa on which she was lying, and through the
closed door replied that she was never going away, and begged to be left
in peace.

The windows of the room in which Princess Marya lay looked to the
west. She lay on the sofa facing the wall, and fingering the buttons on
the leather bolster, she saw nothing but that bolster, and her thoughts
were concentrated obscurely on one subject. She thought of the finality
of death and of her spiritual baseness, of which she had had no idea till
it showed itself during her father's illness. She longed to pray, but dared
not; dared not, in the spiritual state she was in, turn to God. For a long
while she lay in that position.

The sun was setting, and the slanting rays lighted up the room through the open window, and threw a glow on part of the morocco cushion at which Princess Marya was looking. The current of her thoughts was suddenly arrested. She unconsciously sat up, smoothed her hair, stood up, and walked to the window, involuntarily drawing a deep breath of the refreshing coolness of the clear, windy evening.

"Yes, now you can admire the sunset at your ease! He is not here, and there is no one to hinder you," she said to herself, and sinking into a chair, she let her head fall on the window-sill.

Some one spoke her name in a soft and tender voice from the garden and kissed her on the head. She looked up. It was Mademoiselle Bourienne in a black dress and *pleureuses*. She softly approached Princess Marya, kissed her with a sigh, and promptly burst into tears. Princess Marya looked round at her. All her old conflicts with her, her jealousy of her, recurred to Princess Marya's mind. She remembered too that *he* had changed of late to Mademoiselle Bourienne, could not bear the sight of her, and therefore how unjust had been the censure that she had in her heart passed upon her. "Yes, and is it for me, for me, after desiring his death, to pass judgment on any one?" she thought.

Princess Marya pictured vividly to herself Mademoiselle Bourienne's position, estranged from her of late, though dependent on her, and living among strangers. And she felt sorry for her. She looked at her in gentle inquiry and held out her hand to her. Mademoiselle Bourienne at once began kissing her hand with tears and talking of the princess's sorrow, making herself a partner in that sorrow. She said that her only consolation in her sorrow was that the princess permitted her to share it with her. She said that all their former misunderstandings must sink into nothing before their great sorrow: that she felt herself guiltless in regard to every one, and that *he* from above saw her love and gratitude. The princess heard her without heeding her words, though she looked at her now and then and listened to the sound of her voice.

"Your position is doubly dreadful, dear princess," said Mademoiselle Bourienne. "I know you could not and cannot think of yourself; but with my love for you I am bound to do so. . . . Has Alpatitch been with you? Has he spoken to you of moving?" she asked.

Princess Marya did not answer. She did not understand who was to move and where. "Was it possible to undertake anything now, to think of anything? Could anything matter?" she wondered. She made no reply.

"Do you know, *chère Marie*," said Mademoiselle Bourienne, "that we are in danger, that we are surrounded by the French; it is dangerous to move now. If we move, we are almost certain to be taken prisoner, and God knows . . ."

Princess Marya looked at her companion, with no notion what she was saying.

"Oh, if any one knew how little anything matters to me now," she said. "Of course, I would not on any account move away from *him* . . . Alpatitch said something about going away. . . . You talk to him . . . I can't do anything, and I don't want . . ."

"I have been talking to him. He hopes that we may manage to get away to-morrow; but I think it would be better now to remain here," said Mademoiselle Bourienne. "Because you will agree, *chère Marie,* that to fall into the hands of the soldiers or of rioting peasants on the road would be awful."

Mademoiselle Bourienne took out of her reticule a document, not on the usual Russian paper. It was the proclamation of General Rameau, announcing that protection would be given by the French commanders to all inhabitants who did not abandon their homes. She handed it to the princess.

"I imagine the best thing would be to appeal to this general," said Mademoiselle Bourienne. "I am convinced that all proper respect would be shown you."

Princess Marya read the document and her face worked with tearless sobs.

"Through whom did you get this?" she asked.

"They probably found out I was French from my name," said Mademoiselle Bourienne, flushing.

With the proclamation in her hand, Princess Marya got up from the window, and with a pale face walked out of the room into Prince Andrey's former study.

"Dunyasha! send Alpatitch to me, Dronushka, or somebody!" said Princess Marya. "And tell Amalya Karlovna not to come to me," she added, hearing Mademoiselle Bourienne's voice. "To set off at once! as quick as possible!" said Princess Marya, appalled at the idea that she might be left in the power of the French.

"That Prince Andrey should know that she was in the power of the French! That she, the daughter of Prince Nikolay Andreitch Bolkonsky, should stoop to ask General Rameau to grant her his protection, and should take advantage of his good offices." The idea appalled her, made her shudder and turn crimson. She felt a rush of vindictive wrath and pride of which she had had no conception. All the bitterness, and still more the humiliation of her position rose vividly to her imagination. "They, the French, would take up their quarters in the house: M. le Général Rameau would occupy Prince Andrey's study; would amuse himself by looking through and reading his letters and papers; Mademoiselle Bourienne would do the honours of Bogutcharovo; I should be given a room as a favour; the soldiers would break open my father's newly dug grave to take his crosses and decorations; they would tell me of their victories over the Russians, would affect hypocritical sympathy with my grief, . . ." thought Princess Marya, thinking not the thoughts natural to her, but feeling it a duty to think as her father and brother would have done. To her personally it did not matter where she stayed and what happened to her, but, at the same time, she felt herself the representative of her dead father and Prince Andrey. Unconsciously she thought their thoughts and felt their feelings. What they would have said, what they would have done now, she felt it incumbent upon her to do. She went into Prince Andrey's study, and trying to enter completely into his ideas, thought over her situation.

The exigencies of life, which she had regarded as of no consequence since her father's death, all at once rose up about Princess Marya with a force she had known nothing of before, and swept her away with them.

Flushed and excited she walked about the room, sending first for Alpatitch, then for Mihail Ivanitch, then for Tihon, then for Dron. Dunyasha, the old nurse, and the maids could not tell her how far Mademoiselle Bourienne's statements had been correct. Alpatitch was not in the house; he had gone to the police authorities. Mihail Ivanitch, the architect, came with sleepy eyes on being sent for, but could tell Princess Marya nothing. With the same smile of acquiescence with which he had been accustomed during the course of fifteen years to meet the old prince's remarks without committing himself, he now met the princess's questions, so that there was no getting any definite answer out of him. The old valet, Tihon, whose wan and sunken face wore the stamp of inconsolable grief, answered "Yes, princess," to all Princess Marya's questions, and could scarcely restrain his sobs as he looked at her.

Lastly, the village elder, Dron, came into the room, and bowing low to the princess, took up his position near the doorway.

Princess Marya walked up and down the room and stood still facing him.

"Dronushka," she said, seeing in him a staunch friend, the Dronushka who had every year brought back from the fair at Vyazma the same gingerbreads she connected with him, and had presented them to her with the same smile, "Dronushka, now, after our misfortune," . . . she began, and paused, unable to proceed.

"We are all in God's hands," he said, with a sigh.

They were silent.

"Dronushka, Alpatitch has gone off somewhere, I have no one to turn to. Is it true, as I'm told, that it is impossible for me to go away?"

"Why shouldn't you go away, your excellency? You can go," said Dron.

"I have been told there is danger from the enemy. My good friend, I can do nothing, I know nothing about it, I have nobody. I want to set off without fail to-night or to-morrow morning early."

Dron did not speak. He looked up from under his brows at Princess Marya.

"There are no horses," he said. "I have told Yakov Alpatitch so already."

"How is that?" said the princess.

"It's all the visitation of the Lord," said Dron. "Some horses have been carried off for the troops, and some are dead; it's a bad year, it is. If only we don't die of hunger ourselves, let alone feeding the horses! Here they've been three days without a bit of bread. There's nothing, they have been plundered to the last bit."

Princess Marya listened attentively to what he said to her.

"The peasants have been plundered? They have no bread?" she asked.

"They are dying of hunger," said Dron; "no use talking of horses and carts."

"But why didn't you say so, Dronushka? Can't they be helped? I'll do everything I can . . ." It was strange to Princess Marya to think that at such a moment, when her heart was overflowing with such a sorrow, there could be rich people and poor, and that the rich could possibly not help the poor. She vaguely knew that there was a store of "seignorial corn," and that it was sometimes given to the peasants. She knew, too, that neither her brother nor her father would refuse the peasants in their need; she was only afraid of making some mistake in the wording of the order for this distribution. She was glad that she had an excuse for doing something in which she could, without scruple, forget her own grief. She began to question Dronushka about the peasants' needs, and to ask whether there was a "seignorial store" at Bogutcharovo.

"I suppose we have a store of wheat of my brother's?" she asked.

"The wheat is all untouched," Dron declared with pride. "The prince gave me no orders about selling it."

"Give it to the peasants, give them all they need; I give you leave in my brother's name," said Princess Marya.

Dron heaved a deep sigh and made no answer.

"You distribute the corn among them, if it will be enough for them. Distribute it all. I give you the order in my brother's name; and tell them, what's ours is theirs. We would grudge nothing for them. Tell them so."

Dron watched the princess intently all the while she was speaking.

"Discharge me, ma'am, for God's sake, bid them take the keys from me," said he. "I have served twenty-three years, and done no wrong; discharge me, for God's sake."

Princess Marya had no notion what he wanted of her and why he asked her to discharge him. She answered that she had never doubted his fidelity, and that she was ready to do everything for him and for the peasants.

XI

An hour later Dunyasha came in to the princess with the news that Dron had come, and all the peasants by the princess's orders were assembled at the granary and desirous of speaking with their mistress.

"But I did not send for them," said Princess Marya. "I merely told Dronushka to give them the corn."

"Only, for God's sake, your excellency, order them to be sent away and don't go to them. It's all a plot," said Dunyasha, "and Yakov Alpatitch will come and we will start . . . and pray . . ."

"How a plot?" asked the princess in surprise.

"Why, I know all about it, only do listen to me, for God's sake. Ask old nurse too. They say they won't agree to move away at your orders."

"You are making some mistake. Why, I have never given them orders to go away . . ." said Princess Marya. "Call Dronushka."

Dron on coming in confirmed Dunyasha's words; the peasants had come by the princess's instructions.

"But I have never sent for them," said the princess. "You must have given them my message wrong. I only said that you were to give them the corn."

Dron sighed without replying.

"If so you command, they will go away," he said.

"No, no, I'll go out to them," said Princess Marya.

In spite of Dunyasha's and the old nurse's attempts to dissuade her, Princess Marya went out on to the steps. Dronushka, Dunyasha, the old nurse, and Mihail Ivanitch followed her.

"They probably imagine I am offering them the corn to keep them here while I go away myself, leaving them at the mercy of the French," thought Princess Marya. "I will promise them monthly rations and lodgings on the Moscow estate. I am sure Andrey would do more for them in my place," she thought, as she went out in the twilight towards the crowd, waiting on the pasture near the granary.

The crowd stirred, huddling closer, and rapidly took off their hats. Princess Marya came closer to them, her eyes cast down and her feet tripping over her gown. So many different eyes, old and young, were fixed upon her, there were so many different faces that Princess Marya did not see a single one of them, and feeling it necessary to address all at once, did not know how to set about it. But again the sense that she was the representative of her father and brother gave her strength, and she boldly began her speech.

"I am very glad you have come," she began, not raising her eyes and feeling the rapid and violent beating of her heart. "Dronushka has told me that the war has ruined you. That is our common trouble, and I will grudge nothing to aid you. I am going away myself because it is dangerous here . . . and the enemy is near . . . because . . . I give you everything, my friends, and I beg you to take everything, all our corn, that you may not suffer want. But if you have been told that I am giving you corn to keep you here, it is false. On the contrary, I beg you to move away with all your belongings to our Moscow estate, and there I undertake and promise you that you shall not be in want. You shall be given houses and bread." The princess stopped. Nothing was to be heard from the crowd but sighs.

"I don't do this on my own account," the princess went on; "I do it in the name of my dead father, who was a good master to you, and for my brother and his son."

She paused again. No one broke the silence.

"We have trouble in common, and we will share it all equally. All that is mine is yours," she said, looking up at the faces before her. All the eyes were gazing at her with the same expression, the meaning of which she could not fathom. Whether it were curiosity, devotion, gratitude, or apprehension, and distrust, the expression on all the faces was alike.

"Very thankful for your kindness, only it's not for us to take the master's corn," said a voice from the back.

"But why not?" said the princess. No one answered, and Princess Marya, looking up at the crowd, noticed that now all the eyes dropped at once on meeting hers.

"Why don't you want to?" she asked again.

No one replied.

Princess Marya was oppressed by the silence; she tried to catch somebody's eye.

"Why don't you speak!" she said, addressing a very old man who was standing near her, his arms propped on his stick. "Tell me if you think something more is needed. I will do anything," she said, catching his eye. But as though angered by her doing so, he bent his head, and said:

"Why should we agree? We don't want your corn."

"Why are we to give up everything? We're not willing . . . Not willing. It's not with our consent. We are sorry for you, but we are not willing. You go away by yourself, alone . . ." was protested from different parts of the crowd. And again all the faces in the crowd wore the same expression; and now it was unmistakably not an expression of curiosity and gratitude, but an expression of exasperated determination.

"But you misunderstand me," said Princess Marya, with a melancholy smile. "Why don't you want to move away? I promise to settle you, to provide for you. And here the enemy will plunder you . . ." But her voice was drowned by the voices of the crowd.

"We're not willing, let him plunder us! We won't take your corn, we won't agree!"

Princess Marya tried again to catch some one's eye in the crowd, but no one was looking at her; their eyes unmistakably avoided hers. She felt strange and awkward.

"To be sure, she would school us, . . . a good dodge, . . . follow her into slavery. Pull down your house and go into bondage. I dare say! I'll give you corn, says she!" voices were saying in the crowd.

Princess Marya moved out of the ring, and went to the house with a dejected countenance. Repeating her command to Dron that horses were to be ready next day for her to start, she went away to her own room and remained alone with her own thoughts.

XII

For a long while Princess Marya sat at the open window of her room listening to the sound of the peasants' voices floating across from the village, but she was not thinking of them. She felt that she could not understand them however long she thought of them. She thought all the while of one thing—of her sorrow, which now, after the break made by anxiety about the present, already seemed to belong to the past. Now she could remember, could weep, and could pray. With the setting of the sun the wind sank. The night was still and fresh. At midnight the voices in the village began to die down; a cock crowed; the full moon rose from behind a lime-tree; there rose a fresh, white, dewy mist, and stillness reigned over the village and the house.

One after another pictures of the immediate past—her father's illness and last moments—rose before her imagination. And with mournful gladness she let her mind now rest on those images, only shunning with horror the one last scene which she felt she had not the strength to contemplate even in fancy at that still and mysterious hour of the night. And those images rose with such clearness and in such detail before her, that they seemed to her now in the actual present, now in the past, and now in the future.

She had a vivid picture of the moment when he was first stricken down and was being dragged in from the garden at Bleak Hills, and he had muttered something, twitching his grey eyebrows, and looking timidly and uneasily at her. "Even then he wanted to tell me what he told me on the day of his death," she thought. "He always thought what he told me then."

And then she recalled with every detail the night at Bleak Hills before his stroke, when, with a presentiment of trouble, she had remained with him against his will. She had not slept; and at night she had stolen down on tip-toe, and going to the door of the conservatory room where her father was spending that night, she had listened to his voice. He was talking in a weary, harassed voice to Tihon. He was saying something about the Crimea, about the warm nights, about the Empress. Evidently he wanted to talk to some one. "And why didn't he send for me? Why didn't he let me be there in Tihon's place?" Princess Marya had thought then and thought again now. "Now he will never tell any one all that was in his heart. Now the moment will never return when he might have told me all he longed to express, and I and not Tihon might have heard and understood. Why didn't I go into his room then?" she thought. "Perhaps he would have said to me then what he said on the day of his death. Even then talking to Tihon he asked about me twice. He was longing to see me while I was standing there behind the door. He was sad and weary talking to Tihon, who did not understand him. I remember how he spoke to him of Liza as though she were living—he forgot that she was dead, and Tihon reminded him that she was no more, and he cried, 'Fool!' He was miserable. I heard from the door how he lay down groaning on the bed and cried out aloud, 'My God!' Why didn't I go in then? What could he have done to me? What could I have lost? And, perhaps, then he would have been comforted, he would have said that word to me." And Princess Marya uttered aloud that caressing word he had said to her on the day of his death. "Da-ar-ling!" Princess Marya repeated the word and broke into sobs that relieved her heart. She could see his face before her now. And not the face she had known ever since she could remember and had always seen at a distance; but the weak and timid face she had seen on the last day when, bending to his lips to catch what he said, she had, for the first time, looked at it quite close with all its wrinkles.

"Darling," she repeated.

"What was he thinking when he uttered that word? What is he thinking now?" was the question that rose suddenly to her mind; and in answer to it she saw him with the expression she had seen on the face bound up with a white handkerchief in the coffin. And the horror that had overcome her at the moment when she had touched him, and felt that it was not he but something mysterious and horrible, came over her now. She tried to think of something else, tried to pray, and could do nothing. With wide eyes she gazed at the moonlight and the shadows, every instant expecting to see his dead face, and feeling as though she were held spellbound in the stillness that reigned without and within the house.

"Dunyasha!" she whispered. "Dunyasha!" she shrieked wildly, and tearing herself out of the stillness, she ran towards the maids' room, meeting the old nurse and the maids running out to meet her.

XIII

ON the 17th of August Rostov and Ilyin, accompanied by Lavrushka, who had just come back from being taken prisoner by the French, and an hussar on orderly duty, rode out from Yankovo, fifteen versts from Bogutcharovo. They meant to try a new horse that Ilyin had bought, and to find out whether there was hay to be had in the village.

Bogutcharovo had been for the last three days between the two hostile armies, so that the Russian rearguard could reach the village as easily as the French vanguard; and therefore Rostov, like a careful officer, was anxious to anticipate the French in securing any provisions that might be left there.

Rostov and Ilyin were in the liveliest spirits. On the way to Bogutcharovo, which they knew to be an estate belonging to a prince, with a manor-house, where they hoped to find a large household, and, perhaps, pretty servant-girls, they questioned Lavrushka about Napoleon, and laughed at his stories; then raced their horses to test Ilyin's new purchase. Rostov had no notion that the village to which he was going was the property of the very Prince Bolkonsky who had been betrothed to his sister.

Rostov and Ilyin had just let their horses race till they were weary for the last time before Bogutcharovo, and Rostov, outstripping Ilyin, was the first to gallop into the village street.

"You started in front," said Ilyin, flushed.

"Yes, always in front, in the meadow and here too," answered Rostov, patting his foaming Don horse.

"And on my Frenchy, your excellency," said Lavrushka from behind, meaning the wretched cart-horse he was riding, "I could have overtaken you, only I didn't want to put you to shame."

They rode at a walking pace towards the granary, where there was a great crowd of peasants standing. Several of the peasants took off their caps, others stared at them without taking off their caps. Two old peasants, with wrinkled faces and scanty beards, came out of the tavern, reeling and singing a tuneless song, and advanced with smiles towards the officers. "They're fine fellows!" said Rostov, laughing. "Well, have you any hay?"

"And so alike, somehow . . ." said Ilyin.

"Ma . . . a . . . aking mer . . . ry in my sum . . . sum . . . mer . . ." chanted the peasant, with a blissful smile.

A peasant came out of the crowd and went up to Rostov.

"Which part will you be from?" asked the peasant.

"We're French," answered Ilyin, laughing. "And this is Napoleon himself," he said, pointing to Lavrushka.

"I suppose you are Russians then?" the peasant inquired.

"And have you many troops here?" asked another short peasant, approaching.

"A great many," answered Rostov. "But why are you all assembled here?" he added. "Is it a holiday or what?"

"The old men are met about the village business," answered the peasant, moving away from him.

At that moment there came into sight two women and a man in a white hat running from the prince's house towards the officers.

"The one in pink's mine; hands off, beware!" said Ilyin, noticing Dunyasha running resolutely towards them.

"She'll be the girl for us!" said Lavrushka, winking to Ilyin.

"What is it you want, my pretty?" said Ilyin, smiling.

"The princess sent me to ask of what regiment are you, and what is your name?"

"This is Count Rostov, the commander of the squadron, and I am your humble servant."

"Mer . . . mer . . . mer . . . arbour!" chanted the drunken peasant, smiling blissfully, and gazing at Ilyin as he talked to the girl. Alpatitch followed Dunyasha, taking off his hat to Rostov as he approached.

"I make bold to trouble your honour," he said, putting one hand in his bosom, and speaking with a respectfulness in which there was a shade of contempt for the officer's youth. "My mistress, the daughter of general-in-chief Prince Nikolay Andreitch Bolkonsky, who died on the 15th of this month, being in difficulties owing to the coarse ignorance of those people"—he pointed to the peasants—"begs you to come . . . Would you not be pleased," said Alpatitch, with a melancholy smile, "to move a little away, as it is not so convenient before . . ." Alpatitch indicated two peasants, who were hovering about him, like gadflies about a horse.

"Ay! . . . Alpatitch! . . . Ay! Yakov Alpatitch! first-rate job! Eh? . . . for Christ's sake, forgive us. First-rate! ay?" cried the peasants, smiling gleefully at him.

Rostov looked at the drunken peasants, and smiled.

"Or possibly this entertains your excellency?" said Yakov Alpatitch, with a sober air, pointing with his other hand to the old peasants.

"No, there's nothing very entertaining in that," said Rostov, and he moved away. "What is the matter?" he inquired.

"I make bold to submit to your excellency that the rude peasants here will not let their lady leave the estate, and threaten to take the horses out of her carriage, so that everything has been packed since morning, yet her excellency cannot get away."

"Impossible!" cried Rostov.

"I have the honour of submitting to you the simple truth," said Alpatitch.

Rostov got off his horse, and giving it to the orderly, walked with Alpatitch to the house, questioning him further about the state of affairs.

The princess's offer of corn, and her interview with Dron and with the peasants, had, in fact, made the position so much worse that Dron had finally given up the keys of office, joined the peasants and refused to appear when Alpatitch sent for him. In the morning when the princess ordered the horses to be put in for her to set off, the peasants had come out in a great crowd to the granary, and had sent to say that they would not let the princess go out of the village; that there was an edict that people were not to leave their houses, and that they would unharness the horses. Alpatitch went out to lecture them; in reply they told him (a certain Karp was the principal speaker, Dron kept in the background in the crowd) that the princess could not be allowed to go, that there was an edict forbidding it, but that only let her stay, and they would serve her and obey her in everything as before.

At the moment when Rostov and Ilyin were galloping along the village street, regardless of the efforts of Alpatitch, the old nurse, and the maid to dissuade her, Princess Marya had just ordered the horses to be put in, and was intending to start. But seeing the horsemen galloping up, the coachmen took them for the French, and ran away, and a great lamentation arose among the women of the household.

"Kind sir! protector! God has sent thee," cried voices, with much feeling, as Rostov crossed the vestibule. Princess Marya was sitting helpless and distraught in the hall, when Rostov was shown in to see her. She did not know who he was, or what brought him there, or what was happening to her. Seeing his Russian face, and recognising him at his first words and gait for a man of her own rank, she looked at him, with her deep, luminous gaze, and began speaking in a voice, broken and trembling with emotion. Rostov at once conceived a romance in this meeting. "A defenceless girl, crushed by sorrow, alone, abandoned to the mercy of coarse, rebellious peasants! And what strange destiny has brought me here!" thought Rostov, as he listened to her and looked at her. "And what mildness, what nobility in her features and expression!" he thought, as he listened to her timid story.

When she began to tell him that all this had happened the day after her father's funeral, her voice trembled. She turned away, and as though afraid Rostov might ascribe her words to a desire to work on his feelings.

she glanced at him with a look of apprehensive inquiry. There were tears in Rostov's eyes. Princess Marya noticed it, and looked at him with the luminous eyes that made one forget the plainness of her face.

"I cannot express how glad I am, princess, that I happened to come this way, and am able to serve you in anything," said Rostov, rising. "I trust you will start at once, and I answer for it on my honour, no person shall dare to cause you annoyance, if you will only permit me to escort you," and making a deep bow, such as are made to ladies of the royal family, he turned to the door.

By the respectfulness of his tone, Rostov tried to show that though he would consider it a happiness to be acquainted with her, he did not wish to take advantage of her misfortune to force an acquaintanceship upon her.

Princess Marya felt and appreciated this tone.

"I am very, very grateful to you," she said to him in French; "but I hope it was all only a misunderstanding, and that no one is to blame." She began all at once to cry.

"Excuse me," she said.

Rostov, knitting his brows, bowed low once more, and went out of the room.

XIV

"WELL, is she pretty? But, my boy, my pink girl's charming; her name is Dunyasha." . . . But glancing into Rostov's face, Ilyin paused. He saw his hero and superior officer was absorbed in a very different train of thought.

Rostov looked angrily at Ilyin, and without replying, strode off rapidly to the village.

"I'll teach them; I'll pay them out; the scoundrels," he muttered to himself.

Alpatitch followed Rostov at a quick trot, which he could only just keep from breaking into a run.

"What decision has your honour come to?" he said, overtaking him. Rostov stopped short, and clenching his fists moved suddenly up to Alpatitch with a menacing gesture.

"Decision? What decision, old shuffler?" he shouted. "What have you been thinking about? Eh? The peasants are unruly and you don't know how to manage them? You're a traitor yourself. I know you. I'll flog the skin off the lot of you . . ." And, as though afraid of wasting the energy of his anger, he left Alpatitch and went quickly ahead. Alpatitch, swallowing his wounded feelings, hurried with a swaying step after Rostov, still giving him the benefit of his reflections on the subject. He said that the peasants were in a very stubborn state, that at the moment it was imprudent to *oppositionise* them, without an armed force, and would it not be better first to send for armed force.

"I'll give them armed force. . . . I'll oppositionise them . . ." Nikolay muttered meaninglessly, choking with irrational animal rage and desire to vent that rage on some one. Without considering what he was going to do, unconsciously, he moved with a rapid, resolute step up to the crowd. And the nearer he approached, the more Alpatitch felt that his imprudent action might produce the happiest results. The peasants in the crowd were feeling the same thing as they watched his firm and rapid step and determined, frowning face.

After the hussars had entered the village and Rostov had gone in to see the princess, a certain hesitation and division of opinion had become apparent in the crowd. Some of the peasants began to say that the horsemen were Russians, and it might be expected they would take it amiss that they had not let their young lady go. Dron was of that opinion; but as soon as he expressed it, Karp and others fell upon him.

"How many years have you been fattening on the village?" shouted Karp. "It's all one to you! You'll dig up your pot of money and make off with it. What is it to you if our homes are ruined or not?"

"We were told everything was to be in order and no one to leave their homes, and not a thing to be moved away—and that's all about it!" shouted another.

"It was your son's turn; but you spared your fat youngster," a little old man suddenly burst out, pouncing upon Dron, "and sent my Vanka to be shaved for a soldier. Ugh, and yet we all have to die!"

"To be sure, we all have to die!"

"I'm not one to go against the mir," said Dron.

"Not one to go against it; you have grown fat off it." . . .

Two lanky peasants said their say. As soon as Rostov, accompanied by Ilyin, Lavrushka, and Alpatitch approached the crowd, Karp, thrusting his fingers into his sash, walked forward with a slight smile. Dron, on the contrary, retreated to the back, and the crowd huddled closer together.

"Hey! who is elder among you here?" shouted Rostov, walking quickly up to the crowd.

"The elder? What do you want him for? . . ." asked Karp. But he hardly had time to get the words out when his hat sent flying off his head, and he was sent reeling from a violent blow on the head.

"Caps off, traitors!" shouted Rostov's full-blooded voice. "Where is the elder?" he roared furiously.

"The elder, the elder's wanted. Dron Zaharitch, he calls you," voices were heard saying, hurriedly subservient, and caps were taken off.

"We can't be said to be unruly; we're following the orders," declared Karp. And several voices at the back began at the same instant:

"It's as the elders settle; there are too many of you giving orders . . ."

"Talking? . . . Mutiny! . . . Scoundrels! Traitors!" Rostov shouted, without thinking, in a voice unlike his own, as he seized Karp by the collar. "Bind him, bind him!" he shouted, though there was no one to bind him but Lavrushka and Alpatitch.

Lavrushka, however, ran up to Karp and seized his arms from behind.

"Shall I call our fellows from below the hill, your honour?" he shouted.

Alpatitch turned to the peasants, calling upon two of them by name to bind Karp. The peasants obediently stepped out of the crowd and began undoing their belts.

"Where's the village elder?" shouted Rostov.

Dron with a pale and frowning face, stepped out of the crowd.

"Are you the elder? Bind him, Lavrushka," shouted Rostov, as though the order could meet with no sort of opposition. And in fact two peasants did begin binding Dron, who took off his sash, and gave it them as though to assist in the operation.

"And all of you, listen to me," Rostov turned to the peasants. "March straight to your homes this minute, and don't let me hear your voices again."

"Why, we haven't done any harm. It was all, do you see, through foolishness. Only a bit of nonsense . . . I always said that it wasn't the right thing," said voices, blaming one another.

"Didn't I tell you?" said Alpatitch, resuming his rightful position. "You've done wrong, lads."

"It was our foolishness, Yakov Alpatitch," answered voices, and the crowd at once began to break up and to disperse about the village.

The two peasants who were bound they took to the manor-house. The two drunken peasants followed them.

"Ay, now look at you!" said one of them, addressing Karp.

"Do you suppose you can talk to the gentry like that? What were you thinking about? You are a fool," put in the other; "a regular fool."

Within two hours the horses and carts required were standing in the courtyard of the Bogutcharovo house. The peasants were eagerly hurrying out and packing in the carts their owners' goods; and Dron, who had at Princess Marya's desire, been released from the lumber-room, where they had shut him up, was standing in the yard, giving directions to the men.

"Don't pack it so carelessly," said one of the peasants, a tall man with a round, smiling face, taking a casket out of a housemaid's hands. "It's worth money too, you may be sure. Why, if you fling it down like that or put it under the cord, it will get scratched. I don't like to see things done so. Let everything be done honestly, according to rule, I say. There, like this, under the matting, and cover it up with hay; there, that's first-rate."

"Mercy on us, the books, the books," said another peasant, bringing out Prince Andrey's bookshelves. "Mind you don't stumble! Ay, but it's heavy, lads; the books are stout and solid!"

"Yes, they must have worked hard to write them!" said a tall, round-faced peasant pointing with a significant wink to a lexicon lying uppermost.

Rostov, not wishing to force his acquaintance on the princess, did not go back to the house, but remained at the village waiting for her to drive out. When Princess Marya's carriage drove out from the house, Rostov mounted his horse and escorted her as far as the road occupied by our troops, twelve versts from Bogutcharovo. At the inn at Yankovo he parted from her respectfully, for the first time permitting himself to kiss her hand.

"How can you speak of it!" he said, blushing in response to Princess Marya's expression of gratitude to him for saving her, as she called it. "Any police officer would have done as much. If we only had to wage war with peasants, we would not have let the enemy advance so far," he said, trying with a sort of bashfulness to change the conversation. "I am only happy to have had the opportunity of making your acquaintance. Good-bye, princess. I trust you may find happiness and consolation, and I hope I may meet you again in happier circumstances. If you don't want to make me blush, please don't thank me."

But if the princess thanked him no more in words, she thanked him with the whole expression of her face, which was radiant with gratitude and warmth. She could not believe that she had no cause to thank him. On the contrary, to her mind it was an incontestable fact that had it not been for him, she must inevitably have fallen a victim to the rebellious peasants or the French; that *he*, to save her, had exposed himself to obvious and fearful danger; and even more certain was the fact that he was a man of noble and lofty soul, able to sympathise with her position and her grief. His kindly and honest eyes, with tears starting to them at the moment when weeping herself she had spoken of her loss, haunted her imagination. When she had said good-bye to him and was left alone, Princess Marya suddenly felt tears in her eyes, and then—not for the first time—the question occurred to her: "Was she in love with him?" On the rest of the way to Moscow, though the princess's position was by no means a joyful one, Dunyasha, who was in the carriage with her, noticed that her mistress's face wore a vaguely happy and pensive smile, as she looked out of the window.

"Well, what if I have fallen in love with him?" Though she was ashamed at acknowledging to herself that she had fallen in love with a man who would perhaps never care for her, she comforted herself with the reflection that no one would ever know it, and she was not to blame, if she loved in secret for the first and last time and for her whole life long.

Sometimes she recalled his looks, his sympathy, his words, and happiness seemed to her not quite impossible. And then it was that Dunyasha noticed that she looked out of the window smiling.

"And to think that he should come to Bogutcharovo and at that very moment!" thought Princess Marya. "And that his sister should have refused Andrey!" And in all that, Princess Marya saw the hand of Providence.

The impression made on Rostov by Princess Marya was a very agreeable one. When he thought of her, he felt pleased. And when his comrades, hearing of his adventure at Bogutcharovo, rallied him on having gone to look for hay, and having picked up one of the greatest heiresses in Russia, it made him angry. He was angry just because the idea of marrying the gentle, and, to his mind, charming Princess Marya with her enormous fortune had more than once, against his own will, occurred to his mind. As far as he personally was concerned, Nikolay could have asked nothing better than to have Princess Marya for his wife. To marry her would make the countess, his mother, happy, and would repair his father's broken fortunes. And it would even—Nikolay felt it—make the happiness of the princess herself.

But Sonya? And his promise? And that was why it made Rostov angry to be rallied about the Princess Bolkonsky.

XV

ON receiving the chief command of the army, Kutuzov remembered Prince Andrey and sent him a summons to headquarters.

Prince Andrey reached Tsarevo-Zaimishtche on the very day and at the very hour when Kutuzov was making his first inspection of the troops. Prince Andrey stopped in the village at the house of the priest, where the commander-in-chief's carriage was standing, and sat down on a bench at the gate to await his highness, as every one now called Kutuzov. From the plain beyond the village came the sounds of regimental music, and the roar of a vast multitude, shouting "Hurrah!" to the new commander-in-chief. At the gate, some ten paces from Prince Andrey, stood two orderlies, a courier, and a butler, taking advantage of their master's absence to enjoy the fine weather. A swarthy, little lieutenant-colonel of hussars, his face covered with bushy moustaches and whiskers, rode up to the gate, and glancing at Prince Andrey asked whether his highness were putting up here and whether he would soon be back.

Prince Andrey told him that he did not belong to his highness's staff, but had only just arrived. The lieutenant-colonel of hussars turned to the smart orderly, and the orderly told him with the peculiar scornfulness with which a commander-in-chief's orderlies do speak to officers:

"His highness? We expect him back immediately. What is your business?"

The officer grinned in his moustaches at the orderly's tone, dismounted, gave his horse to a servant, and went up to Bolkonsky with a slight bow.

Bolkonsky made room for him on the bench. The hussar sat down beside him.

"You, too, waiting for the commander-in-chief?" he began. "They say he is willing to see any one, thank God! It was a very different matter with the sausage-makers! Yermolov might well ask to be promoted a German. Now, I dare say, Russians may dare to speak again. And devil knows what they have been about. Nothing but retreating and retreating. Have you been in the field?" he asked.

"I have had the pleasure," said Prince Andrey, "not only of taking part in the retreat, but also of losing everything I valued in the retreat —not to speak of my property and the home of my birth . . . my father, who died of grief. I am a Smolensk man."

"Ah! . . . Are you Prince Bolkonsky? Very glad to make your acquaintance. Lieutenant-colonel Denisov, better known by the name of Vaska," said Denisov, pressing Prince Andrey's hand and looking into his face with a particularly kindly expression. "Yes, I had heard about it," he said sympathetically, and after a brief pause he added: "Yes, this is Scythian warfare. It's all right, but not for those who have to pay the piper. So you are Prince Andrey Bolkonsky?" He shook his head. "I am very glad, prince; very glad to make your acquaintance," he added, pressing his hand again with a melancholy smile.

Prince Andrey knew of Denisov from Natasha's stories of her first suitor. The recollection of them—both sweet and bitter—carried him back to the heart-sickness of which he had of late never thought, though it still lay buried within him. Of late so many different and grave matters, such as the abandonment of Smolensk, his visit to Bleak Hills, the recent news of his father's death—so many emotions had filled his heart that those memories had long been absent, and when they returned did not affect him nearly so violently. And for Denisov, the associations awakened by the name of Bolkonsky belonged to a far-away, romantic past, when, after supper and Natasha's singing, hardly knowing what he was doing, he had made an offer to the girl of fifteen. He smiled at the recollection of that time and his love for Natasha, and passed at once to what he was just now intensely and exclusively interested in. This was a plan of campaign he had formed while on duty at the outposts during the retreat. He had laid the plan before Barclay de Tolly, and now intended to lay it before Kutuzov. The plan was based on the fact that the line of the French operations was too extended, and on the suggestion that, instead of or along with a frontal attack, barring the advance of the French, attacks should be made on their communications. He began explaining his plan to Prince Andrey.

"They are not able to defend all that line; it's impossible. I'll undertake to break through them. Give me five hundred men and I would cut their communications, that's certain! The one system to adopt is partisan warfare."

Denisov got up and began with gesticulations to explain his plans to Bolkonsky. In the middle of his exposition they heard the shouts of the army, mingling with music, and song, and apparently coming from detached groups scattered over a distance. From the village came cheers and the tramp of horses' hoofs.

"Himself is coming," shouted the Cossack, who stood at the gate; "he's coming!"

Bolkonsky and Denisov moved up to the gate, where there stood a knot of soldiers (a guard of honour), and they saw Kutuzov coming down the street mounted on a low bay horse. An immense suite of generals followed him. Barclay rode almost beside him; a crowd of officers was running behind and around them shouting "hurrah!"

His adjutants galloped into the yard before him. Kutuzov impatiently kicked his horse, which ambled along slowly under his weight, and continually nodded his head and put his hand up to his white horse-guard's cap, with a red band and no peak. When he reached the guard of honour, a set of stalwart grenadiers, mostly cavalry men, saluting him, he looked at them for a minute in silence, with the intent, unflinching gaze of a man used to command; then he turned to the group of generals and officers standing round him. His face suddenly wore a subtle expression; he shrugged his shoulders with an air of perplexity. "And with fellows like that retreat and retreat!" he said. "Well, good-bye, general," he added, and spurred his horse into the gateway by Prince Andrey and Denisov.

"Hurrah! hurrah! hurrah!" rang out shouts behind him.

Since Prince Andrey had seen him last Kutuzov had grown stouter and more corpulent than ever; he seemed swimming in fat. But the familiar scar, and the white eye, and the expression of weariness in his face and figure were unchanged. He was wearing a white horse-guard's cap and a military coat, and a whip on a narrow strap was slung over his shoulder. He sat heavily swaying on his sturdy horse.

"Fugh! . . . fugh! . . . fugh! . . ." he whistled, hardly audibly, as he rode into the courtyard. His face expressed the relief of a man who looks forward to resting after a performance. He drew his left foot out of the stirrup, and with a lurch of his whole person, frowning with the effort, brought it up to the saddle, leaned on his knee, and with a groan let himself drop into the arms of the Cossacks and adjutants, who stood ready to support him.

He pulled himself together, looked round with half-shut eyes, glanced at Prince Andrey, and evidently not recognising him, moved with his shambling gait towards the steps.

"Fugh! . . . fugh! . . . fugh!" he whistled, and again looked round at Prince Andrey. As is often the case with the aged, the impression of Prince Andrey's face did not at once call up the memory of his personality. "Ah, how are you, how are you, my dear boy, come along . . ." he said wearily, and walked heavily up the steps that creaked under his weight. He unbuttoned his coat and sat down on the seat in the porch.

"Well, how's your father?"

"The news of his death reached me yesterday," said Prince Andrey briefly.

Kutuzov looked at him with his eye opened wide with dismay, then he took off his cap, and crossed himself. "The peace of heaven be with him! And may God's will be done with all of us!" He heaved a heavy sigh and paused. "I loved him deeply and respected him, and I feel for you with all my heart." He embraced Prince Andrey, pressed him to his fat breast, and for some time did not let him go. When he released him, Prince Andrey saw that Kutuzov's thick lips were quivering and there were tears in his eye. He sighed and pressed his hands on the seat to help himself in rising from it.

"Come in, come in, we'll have a chat," he said; but at that moment Denisov, who stood as little in dread of the authorities as he did of the enemy, walked boldly up, his spurs clanking on the steps, regardless of the indignant whispers of the adjutants, who tried to prevent him. Kutuzov, his hands still pressed on the seat to help him up, looked ruefully at Denisov. Denisov, mentioning his name, announced that he had to communicate to his highness a matter of great importance for the welfare of Russia. Kutuzov bent his weary eyes on Denisov, and, lifting his hands with a gesture of annoyance, folded them across his stomach, and repeated, "For the welfare of Russia? Well, what is it? Speak." Denisov blushed like a girl (it was strange to see the colour come on that hirsute, time-worn, hard-drinking face), and began boldly explaining his plan for cutting the enemy's line between Smolensk and Vyazma. Denisov's home was in that region, and he knew the country well. His plan seemed unquestionably a good one, especially with the energy of conviction that was in his words. Kutuzov stared at his own feet, and occasionally looked round towards the yard of the next cottage, as though he were expecting something unpleasant to come from it. From the cottage there did in fact emerge, during Denisov's speech, a general with a portfolio under his arm.

"Eh?" Kutuzov inquired in the middle of Denisov's exposition, "are you ready now?"

"Yes, your highness," said the general. Kutuzov shook his head with an air that seemed to say, "How is one man to get through it all?" and gave his attention again to Denisov.

"I give you my word of honour as a Russian officer," Denisov was saying, "that I will cut Napoleon's communications."

"Is Kirill Andreevitch Denisov, the ober-intendant, any relation of yours?" Kutuzov interposed.

"My uncle, your highness."

"Oh! we used to be friends," said Kutuzov, more cheerily. "Very good, very good, my dear boy; you stay here on the staff; we'll have a talk to-morrow." Nodding to Denisov, he turned away and put out his hand for the papers Konovnitsyn had brought him.

"Will not your highness be pleased to walk into the house?" said the general on duty in a discontented voice; "it's necessary to look through the plans and to sign some papers." An adjutant appeared at the door to announce that everything was in readiness within. But apparently Kutuzov preferred to be rid of business before going indoors. He paused . . .

"No; have a table placed here, my dear boy; I'll look through them here," he said. "Don't you go away," he added, addressing Prince Andrey. Prince Andrey remained in the porch listening to the general on duty.

While the latter was presenting his report Prince Andrey heard the whisper of a woman's voice and the rustle of a woman's silk dress at the door. Several times glancing in that direction he noticed behind the door a plump, rosy-faced, good-looking woman in a pink dress with a lilac silk kerchief on her head. She had a dish in her hand and was apparently waiting for the commander-in-chief to enter. Kutuzov's adjutant explained to Prince Andrey in a whisper that this was the priest's wife, the mistress of the house, who intended to offer his highness bread

and salt, the emblems of welcome, on his entrance. Her husband had
met his highness with the cross in church, and she intended to welcome
him to the house. . . . "She's very pretty," added the adjutant with a
smile. Kutuzov looked round at the words. He heard the general's report, the subject of which was chiefly a criticism of the position of the
troops before Tsarevo-Zaimishtche, just as he had heard Denisov, and
just as, seven years before, he had heard the discussions of the military
council before Austerlitz. He was obviously hearing it simply because he
had ears, and although one of them was stuffed up with cotton-wool
they could not help hearing. But it was obvious that nothing that general could possibly say could surprise or interest him, that he knew
beforehand all he would be told, and listened only because he had to
listen to it, just as one has to listen to the litany being sung. All Denisov
had said was practical and sensible. What the general was saying was
even more practical and sensible, but apparently Kutuzov despised both
knowledge and intellect, and knew of something else that would settle
things—something different, quite apart from intellect and knowledge.
Prince Andrey watched the commander-in-chief's face attentively, and
the only expression he could detect in it was an expression of boredom,
of curiosity to know the meaning of the feminine whispering at the door,
and of a desire to observe the proprieties. It was obvious that Kutuzov
despised intellect and learning, and even the patriotic feeling Denisov
had shown; but he did not despise them through intellect, nor through
sentiment, nor through learning (for he made no effort to display anything of the kind), he despised them through something else—through
his old age, through his experience of life. The only instruction of his
own that Kutuzov inserted in the report related to acts of marauding by
Russian troops. The general, at the end of the report, presented his highness a document for signature relating to a petition for damages from a
landowner for the cutting of his oats by certain officers.

Kutuzov smacked his lips together and shook his head, as he listened
to the matter.

"Into the stove . . . into the fire with it! And I tell you once for all,
my dear fellow," he said, "all such things put into the fire. Let them cut
the corn and burn the wood to their heart's content. It's not by my
orders and it's not with my permission, but I can't pursue the matter. It
can't be helped. You can't hew down trees without the chips flying." He
glanced once more at the paper. "Oh, this German preciseness," he commented, shaking his head.

XVI

"WELL, now, that's all," said Kutuzov, as he signed the last paper, and
rising clumsily, and straightening his fat, white neck, he went to the
door with a more cheerful countenance.

The priest's wife, with the colour rushing to her face, snatched up
the dish, and though she had been so long preparing, she did not succeed

in presenting it at the right moment. With a low bow she offered it to Kutuzov. Kutuzov screwed up his eyes. He smiled, chucked her under the chin, and said:

"And what a pretty face! Thank you, my dear!"

He took some gold coins out of his trouser pocket, and put them on the dish. "Well, and how are we getting on?" he said, going towards the room that had been assigned him. The priest's wife, with smiling dimples on her rosy face, followed to show him the room. The adjutant came out to Prince Andrey in the porch, and invited him to lunch. Half an hour later Kutuzov sent for Prince Andrey. He was reclining in a low chair, still in the same unbuttoned military coat. He had a French novel in his hand, and at Prince Andrey's entrance laid a paper-knife in it and put it aside. It was *Les Chevaliers du Cygne*, a work by Madame de Genlis, as Prince Andrey saw by the cover.

"Well, sit down; sit down here. Let us have a little talk," said Kutuzov. "It's sad; very sad. But remember, my dear, think of me as a father, another father, to you . . . !"

Prince Andrey told Kutuzov all he knew about his father's end, and what he had seen at Bleak Hills.

"To think what we have been brought to!" Kutuzov cried suddenly, in a voice full of feeling, Prince Andrey's story evidently bringing vividly before him the position of Russia.

"Wait a bit; wait a bit!" he added, with a vindictive look in his face, and apparently unwilling to continue a conversation that stirred him too deeply, he said:

"I sent for you to keep you with me."

"I thank your highness!" answered Prince Andrey, "but I am afraid I am no more good for staff work," he said, with a smile, which Kutuzov noticed. He looked at him inquiringly. "And the great thing is," added Prince Andrey, "I am used to my regiment. I like the officers; and I think the men have come to like me. I should be sorry to leave the regiment. If I decline the honour of being in attendance on you, believe me . . ."

Kutuzov's podgy face beamed with a shrewd, good-natured, and yet subtly ironical expression. He cut Bolkonsky short.

"I'm sure you would have been of use to me. But you're right; you're right. It's not here that we want men. There are always a multitude of counsellors; but men are scarce. The regiments wouldn't be what they are if all the would-be counsellors would serve in them like you. I remember you at Austerlitz. I remember, I remember you with the flag!" said Kutuzov, and a flush of pleasure came into Prince Andrey's face at this reminiscence. Kutuzov held out his hand to him, offering him his cheek to kiss, and again Prince Andrey saw tears in the old man's eye. Though Prince Andrey knew Kutuzov's tears were apt to come easily, and that he was particularly affectionate and tender with him from the desire to show sympathy with his loss, yet he felt this reminder of Austerlitz agreeable and flattering.

"Go your own way, and God bless you in it. . . . I know your path is the path of honour!" He paused. "I missed you at Bucharest. I wanted some one to send . . ." And changing the subject, Kutuzov began talking of the Turkish war, and of the peace that had been concluded. "Yes, I have been roundly abused," he said, "both for the war and the peace . . . but it all happened in the nick of time." " 'Everything comes in time for him who knows how to wait,' " he said, quoting the French proverb. "And there were as many counsellors there as here, . . ." he went on, returning to the superfluity of advisers, a subject which evidently occupied his mind. "Ugh, counsellors and counsellors!" he said. "If we had listened to all of them, we should be in Turkey now. We should not have made peace, and the war would never have been over. Always in haste, and more haste, worse speed. Kamensky would have come to grief there, if he hadn't died. He went storming fortresses with thirty thousand men. It's easy enough to take fortresses, but it's hard to finish off a campaign successfully. Storms and attacks are not what's wanted, but *time* and *patience*. Kamensky sent his soldiers to attack Rustchuk, but I trusted to them alone—time and patience—and I took more fortresses than Kamensky, and made the Turks eat horseflesh!" He shook his head. "And the French shall, too. Take my word for it," cried Kutuzov, growing warmer and slapping himself on the chest, "I'll make them eat horseflesh!" And again his eye was dim with tears.

"We shall have to give battle, though, shan't we?" said Prince Andrey.

"We must, if every one wants to; there is no help for it. . . . But, mark my words, my dear boy! The strongest of all warriors are these two—time and patience. They do it all, and our wise counsellors *n'entendent pas de cette oreille, voilà le mal*. Some say ay, and some say no. What's one to do?" he asked, evidently expecting a reply. "Come, what would you have me do?" he repeated, and his eyes twinkled with a profound, shrewd expression. "I'll tell you what to do," he said, since Prince Andrey still did not answer. "I'll tell you what to do, and what I do. *Dans le doute, mon cher*"—he paused—"*abstiens-toi*." He articulated deliberately the French saying.

"Well, good-bye, my dear. Remember, with all my heart, I feel for your sorrow, and that for you I'm not his highness, nor prince, nor commander-in-chief, but simply a father to you. If you want anything, come straight to me. Good-bye, my dear boy!" Again he embraced and kissed him.

And before Prince Andrey had closed the door, Kutuzov settled himself comfortably with a sigh, and renewed the unfinished novel of Madame Genlis, *Les Chevaliers du Cygne*.

How, and why it was, Prince Andrey could not explain, but after this interview with Kutuzov, he went back to his regiment feeling reassured as to the future course of the war, and as to the man to whom its guidance was intrusted. The more clearly he perceived the absence of everything personal in the old leader, who seemed to have nothing left of his own but habits of passions, and instead of an intellect grasping events and making plans, had only the capacity for the calm contemplation of the course of events, the more confident he felt that all would be as it should be. "He will put in nothing of himself. He will contrive nothing, will undertake nothing," thought Prince Andrey; "but he will hear everything, will think of everything, will put everything in its place, will not hinder anything that could be of use, and will not allow anything that could do harm. He knows that there is something stronger and more important than his will—that is the inevitable march of events, and he can see them, can grasp their significance, and, seeing their significance, can abstain from meddling, from following his own will, and aiming at something else. And the chief reason," thought Prince Andrey, "why one believes in him is that he's Russian, in spite of Madame Genlis's novel and the French proverbs, that his voice shook when he said, 'What we have been brought to!' and that he choked when he said 'he would make them eat horseflesh!'"

It was this feeling, more or less consciously shared by all, that determined the unanimous approval given to the appointment of Kutuzov to the chief command, in accordance with national sentiment, and in opposition to the intrigues at court.

XVII

After the Tsar had left Moscow, the life of that city flowed on in its old accustomed channel, and the current of that life ran so much as usual that it was difficult to remember the days of patriotic fervour and enthusiasm, and hard to believe that Russia actually was in danger, and that the members of the English club were also her devoted sons, ready to make any sacrifice for her sake. The one thing that recalled the general patriotic fervour of the days of the Tsar's presence in Moscow was the call for contributions of men and money, and these demands were presented at once in a legal, official form, so that they seemed inevitable. As the enemy drew nearer to Moscow the attitude taken by its inhabitants in regard to their position did not become more serious, but, on the contrary, more frivolous, as is always the case with people who see a great danger approaching. At the approach of danger there are always two voices that speak with equal force in the heart of man: one very reasonably tells the man to consider the nature of the danger and the means of avoiding it; the other even more reasonably says that it is too painful and harassing to think of the danger, since it is not in a man's power to provide for everything and escape from the general march of events; and that it is therefore better to turn aside from the painful subject till it has come, and to think of what is pleasant. In solitude a man generally yields to the first voice; in society to the second. So it was now with the inhabitants of Moscow. It was long since there had been so much gaiety in Moscow as that year.

Rastoptchin's posters, with a print at the top of a gin-shop, a potman, and the Moscow artisan, Karpushka Tchigirin, "who, having gone into the militia, heard that Bonaparte meant to come to Moscow, was mightily wroth thereat, used very bad language about all the French, came out of the gin-shop and began to address the people assembled under the eagles," were as much read and discussed as the last *bouts rimés* of Vassily Lvovitch Pushkin.

In the corner room of the club the members gathered together to read these posters; and some liked the way Karpushka was made to jeer at the French, saying that "they would be blown out with Russian cabbage, that Russian porridge would rip their guts open, and cabbage soup would finish them off; that they were all dwarfs, and a village lass could toss three of them on her pitchfork single-handed!"

Some people did not approve of this tone, and said it was vulgar and stupid. People said that Rastoptchin had sent all Frenchmen, and even foreigners, out of Moscow, and that there had been spies and agents of Napoleon among them. But they talked of this principally in order to repeat the witticisms uttered by Rastoptchin on the occasion. The foreigners had been put on a barque sailing to Nizhny, and Rastoptchin had said to them: "Keep yourselves to yourselves, get into the barque, and take care it does not become the barque of Charon to you." People talked too of all the government offices having been removed from Moscow, and added Shinshin's joke, that for that alone Moscow ought to be grateful to Napoleon. People said that Mamonov's regiment was costing him eight hundred thousand; that Bezuhov was spending even more on his; but that the noblest proof of Bezuhov's patriotism was that he was going to put on the uniform himself and ride at the head of his regiment, without any charge for seats to spectators.

"You have no mercy on any one," said Julie Drubetskoy, gathering up a pinch of scraped lint in her slender fingers covered with rings.

Julie was intending to leave Moscow next day, and was giving a farewell *soirée*.

"Bezuhov *est ridicule*, but he is so good-natured, so nice; how can you take pleasure in being so *caustique?*"

"Forfeit!" said a young man in a volunteer's uniform, whom Julie called *"mon chevalier,"* and was taking with her to Nizhny.

In Julie's circle, as in many circles in Moscow, it was a principle now to speak nothing but Russian, and those who made a mistake by speaking French had to pay a forfeit for the benefit of the committee of voluntary subscriptions.

"Another forfeit for a Gallicism," said a Russian writer who happened to be present. " 'Take pleasure!' is not Russian."

"You have no mercy on any one," Julie went on to the volunteer, paying no attention to the remark of the author.

"*Caustique*, I admit," she said, "and I'll pay for the pleasure of telling you the truth. I am ready to pay even more; but I am not responsible for Gallicisms," she said to the writer. "I have neither the time nor the money to engage a teacher and learn Russian like Prince Galitzin. Ah, here he is!" added Julie. *"Quand on* . . . No, no," she protested to the volunteer, "you're not going to catch me. When one speaks of the sun, one sees its rays. We were just talking of you," she said, smiling affably to Pierre, and adding, with the easy lying characteristic of society women, "We were saying your regiment was certain to be a finer one than Mamonov's."

"Oh, don't talk to me about my regiment," answered Pierre, kissing his hostess's hand, and sitting down beside her. "I am so heartily sick of it!"

"You will take the command of it yourself, of course?" said Julie, with a sly and sarcastic look towards the volunteer.

The latter was by no means so ready to be caustic in Pierre's presence, and his countenance betokened perplexity as to what Julie's smile could signify. In spite of his absent-mindedness and good nature, Pierre's presence never failed to cut short any attempt at ridicule at his expense.

"No," answered Pierre, laughing and looking at his huge, bulky figure; "I should make too good a target for the French, and indeed I'm afraid I could hardly scramble on to a horse's back."

Among the people picked out as subjects for gossip, Julie's friends happened to pitch on the Rostovs. "Their pecuniary position is very serious, I am told," said Julie. "And the count is so unreasonable. The Razumovskys wanted to buy his house and his estate in the environs, and the matter is still dragging on. He will ask too much."

"No, I fancy purchase will be concluded in a few days," said some one. "Though it's madness to buy anything in Moscow just now."

"Why so?" said Julie. "Surely you don't suppose that Moscow is in any danger."

"Why are you leaving it then?"

"I? That's a strange question. I am going because . . . well, because everybody's going, and I am not a Jeanne d'Arc nor an Amazon."

"Oh, oh! Give me another strip of linen to scrape."

"He ought to be able to pay off all his debts, if he sets about it properly," the volunteer observed of Count Rostov.

"He's a good-hearted old fellow, but very foolish."

"And why are they staying on here so long? They were meaning to leave for the country long ago. Natalie is quite well again now, I suppose?" Julie asked Pierre, with a sly smile.

"They are waiting for their younger son," said Pierre. "He went into Obolensky's Cossacks, and was sent off to Byela Tserkov. The regiment is being formed there. But now they have transferred him to my regiment, and he is expected every day. The count wanted to get away long ago, but nothing would induce the countess to leave Moscow till her son's return."

"I saw them the day before yesterday at the Arharovs'." Natalie has quite recovered her looks and her spirits. She sang a song. How easily some people get over everything!"

"Get over what?" Pierre asked, looking displeased.

Julie smiled.

"O count, you know, such chivalrous knights as you are only to be found in Madame Suza's novels."

"Knights! What do you mean?" Pierre asked blushing.

"Come now, my dear count. *C'est la fable de tout Moscou. Je vous admire, ma parole d'honneur.*"

"Forfeit! forfeit!" said the volunteer.

"Oh, very well. One cannot talk, what a bore it is!"

"What is the talk of all Moscow?" said Pierre angrily, rising to his feet.

"Nonsense, count, you know!"

"I know nothing about it," said Pierre.

"I know what great friends you have always been with Natalie, and so . . . But, I was always more friendly with Vera. That darling Vera."

"No, madam," Pierre persisted in a tone of annoyance. "I have by no means taken upon myself the rôle of Countess Rostov's knight; indeed, it's almost a month since I have been near them. But I cannot understand the cruelty . . ."

"*Qui s'excuse s'accuse,*" cried Julie, smiling, and waving the lint triumphantly, and that she might have the last word, she promptly changed the subject. "By the way, I have heard poor Marie Bolkonsky arrived in Moscow yesterday. Have you heard she has lost her father?"

"Really? Where is she? I should like to see her," said Pierre.

"I spent the evening with her yesterday. She is going on to-day or to-morrow morning to their estate in the province with her nephew."

"Well, how is she? Tell me," said Pierre.

"Oh, she is well, but very sad. But do you know who rescued her? It is quite a romance. Nikolay Rostov. She was surrounded; they tried to kill her and wounded her servants. He rushed in and saved her. . . ."

"Another romance," said the volunteer. "This general flight is evidently intended to marry off all the old maids. Katish is one, Princess Bolkonsky another."

"You know, I really do believe she's *un petit peu amoureuse du jeune homme.*"

"Forfeit! forfeit! forfeit!"

"But how is one to say that in Russian?"

XVIII

WHEN Pierre returned home, he was handed two new placards of Rastoptchin's that had just appeared.

The first declared that the rumour, that it was forbidden to leave Moscow by Count Rastoptchin's order, was false, and that, on the contrary, he was glad that ladies and merchants' wives were leaving the town. "There will be less panic and less false news," said the notice; "but I will stake my life on it that the miscreant will never enter Moscow."

These words first showed Pierre clearly that the French certainly would enter Moscow. In the second placard it was announced that our headquarters were at Vyazma, that Count Wittgenstein had defeated the French, but that since many of the inhabitants of Moscow were desirous of arming themselves, weapons had been provided to meet their wishes in the arsenal; swords, pistols, and guns could all be procured there at a low rate.

The tone of this notice was not as jocose as the former supposed discourses of Tchigirin. The two placards made Pierre ponder. It was evident to him that the menacing storm cloud, for the advent of which his whole soul longed, though it roused an involuntary thrill of horror, it was evident that that cloud was coming closer.

"Shall I enter the service and join the army or wait here?" Pierre thought, a question he had put to himself a hundred times already. He took up a pack of cards that lay on the table to deal them for a game of patience.

"If I succeed in this game of patience," he said to himself, shuffling the pack as he held it in his hand and looked upwards; "if I succeed, it means . . . what does it mean?" . . . He had not time to decide this question when he heard at the door of his study the voice of the eldest princess, asking whether she might come in. "Then it will mean that I must set off to join the army," Pierre told himself. "Come, come in," he said to the princess.

The eldest of his cousins, the one with the long waist and the stony face, was the only one still living in Pierre's house; the two younger sisters had both married.

"Excuse my coming to you, cousin," she said in a tone of reproach and excitement. "Some decision really must be come to, you know. What is going to happen? Every one has left Moscow, and the populace are becoming unruly. Why are we staying on?"

"On the contrary, everything seems going on satisfactorily, *ma cousine*," said Pierre in the habitually playful tone he had adopted with his cousin, to carry off the embarrassment he always felt at being in the position of a benefactor to her.

"Oh, yes, satisfactorily . . . highly satisfactory, I dare say. Varvara Ivanovna told me to-day how our troops are distinguishing themselves. It is certainly a credit to them. And the populace, too, is in complete revolt, they won't obey any one now; even my maid has begun to be insolent. If it goes on like this, they will soon begin killing us. One can't walk about the streets. And the worst of it is, in another day or two the French will be here. Why are we waiting for them? One favour I beg of you, *mon cousin*," said the princess, "give orders for me to be taken to Petersburg; whatever I may be, any way I can't live under Bonaparte's rule."

"But what nonsense, *ma cousine*! where do you get your information from? On the contrary . . ."

"I'm not going to submit to your Napoleon. Other people may do as they like. . . . If you won't do this for me . . ."

"But I will, I'll give orders for it at once."

The princess was obviously annoyed at having no one to be angry with. Muttering something, she sat down on the edge of the chair.

"But you have been incorrectly informed," said Pierre. "All's quiet in the town, and there's no sort of danger. See I have just read . . ." Pierre showed the princess the placards. "The count writes that he will stake his life on it that the enemy will never be in Moscow."

"Ah, your count," the princess began spitefully, "he's a hypocrite, a miscreant who has himself stirred the mob on to disorder. Didn't he write in his idiotic placards that they were to take anybody whoever it might be and drag by the hair to the lock-up (and how silly it is!). Honour and glory, says he, to the man who does so. And this is what he has brought us to. Varvara Ivanovna told me the mob almost killed her for speaking French."

"Oh, well, well . . . You take everything too much to heart," said Pierre, and he began dealing out the patience.

Although he did succeed in the game, Pierre did not set off to join the army, but stayed on in Moscow, now rapidly emptying, and was still in the same agitation, uncertainty and alarm, and, at the same time, joyful expectation of something awful.

Next day the princess set off in the evening, and Pierre's head-steward came to inform him that it was impossible to raise the money he required for the equipment of his regiment unless he sold one of his estates. The head-steward impressed on Pierre generally that all this regimental craze would infallibly bring him to ruin. Pierre could hardly conceal a smile as he listened to the head-steward.

, "Well, sell it then," he said. "There's no help for it, I can't draw back now!"

The worse the position of affairs, and especially of his own affairs, the better pleased Pierre felt, and the more obvious it was to him that the catastrophe he expected was near at hand. Scarcely any of Pierre's acquaintances were left in the town. Julie had gone, Princess Marya had gone. Of his more intimate acquaintances the Rostovs were the only people left; but Pierre did not go to see them.

To divert his mind that day, Pierre drove out to the village of Vorontsovo, to look at a great air balloon which was being constructed by Leppich to use against the enemy, and the test balloon which was to be sent up the following day. The balloon was not yet ready; but as Pierre learned, it was being constructed by the Tsar's desire. The Tsar had written to Count Rastoptchin about it in the following terms:

"As soon as Leppich is ready, get together a crew for his car consisting of thoroughly trustworthy and intelligent men, and send a courier to General Kutuzov to prepare him for it. I have mentioned it to him. Impress upon Leppich, please, to take careful note where he descends the first time, that he may not go astray and fall into the hands of the enemy. It is essential that he should regulate his movements in accordance with the movements of the commander-in-chief."

On his way home from Vorontsovo, Pierre drove through Bolotny Square, and seeing a crowd at Lobnoye Place, stopped and got out of his chaise. The crowd were watching the flogging of a French cook, accused of being a spy. The flogging was just over, and the man who had administered it was untying from the whipping-post a stout, red-whiskered man in blue stockings and a green tunic, who was groaning piteously. Another victim, a thin, pale man, was standing by. Both, to judge by their faces, were Frenchmen. With a face of sick dread like that of the thin Frenchman, Pierre pushed his way in among the crowd.

"What is it? Who are they? What for?" he kept asking. But the attention of the crowd—clerks, artisans, shopkeepers, peasants, women in pelisses and jackets—was so intently riveted on what was taking place on the Lobnoye Place that no one answered. The stout man got up, shrugged his shoulders frowning, and evidently trying to show fortitude, began putting on his tunic without looking about him. But all at once his lips quivered and to his own rage he began to cry, as grown-up men of sanguine temperament do cry. The crowd began talking loudly, to drown a feeling of pity in themselves, as it seemed to Pierre.

"Some prince's cook. . . ."

"Eh, monsieur, Russian sauce is a bit strong for a French stomach . . . sets the teeth on edge," said a wrinkled clerk standing near Pierre, just when the Frenchman burst into tears. The clerk looked about him for signs of appreciation of his jest. Several persons laughed, but some were still gazing in dismay at the man who was undressing the second Frenchman and about to flog him.

Pierre choked, scowled, and turning quickly, went back to his chaise, still muttering something to himself as he went, and took his seat in it. During the rest of the way he several times started, and cried out so loudly that the coachman at last asked him what he desired.

"Where are you driving?" Pierre shouted to the coachman as he drove to Lubyanka.

"You told me to drive to the governor's," aswered the coachman.

"Fool! dolt!" shouted Pierre, abusing his coachman, a thing he very rarely did. "I told you home; and make haste, blockhead! This very day I must set off," Pierre said to himself.

At the sight of the tortured Frenchman and the crowd round the Lobnoye Place, Pierre had so unhesitatingly decided that he could stay no longer in Moscow, and must that very day set off to join the army, that it seemed to him either that he had told the coachman so, or that the coachman ought to know it of himself.

On reaching home Pierre told his omniscient and omnipotent head-coachman, Yevstafitch, who was known to all Moscow, that he was going to drive that night to Mozhaisk to the army, and gave orders for his saddle horses to be sent on there. All this could not be arranged in one day, and therefore by Yevstafitch's representations Pierre was induced to defer his departure till next day to allow time for relays of horses to be sent on ahead.

The 24th was a bright day after a spell of bad weather, and after dinner on that day Pierre set out from Moscow. Changing horses in the night at Perhushkovo, Pierre learned that a great battle had been fought that evening. He was told that the earth had been vibrating there at

Perhushkovo from the cannon. No one could answer Pierre's question whether the battle was a victory or a defeat. This was the battle of the 24th at Shevardino. Towards dawn Pierre approached Mozhaisk.

Troops were quartered in all the houses in Mozhaisk, and at the inn, where Pierre was met by his coachman and postillion, there was not a room to spare; the whole place was full of officers.

From Mozhaisk onwards troops were halting or marching everywhere. Cossacks, foot soldiers, horse soldiers, waggons, gun-carriages, and cannons were everywhere.

Pierre pushed on as fast as possible, and the further he got and the more deeply he plunged into this ocean of soldiers, the stronger became the thrill of uneasiness and of a new pleasurable sensation. It was a feeling akin to what he had felt at the Slobodsky Palace on the Tsar's visit, a sense of the urgent necessity of taking some step and making some sacrifice. He was conscious now of a glad sense that all that constitutes the happiness of life, comfort, wealth, even life itself, were all dust and ashes, which it was a joy to fling away in comparison with something else. . . . What that something else was Pierre could not have said, and indeed he did not seek to get a clear idea, for whose sake and for what object he found such peculiar joy in sacrificing all. He was not interested in knowing the object of the sacrifice, but the sacrifice itself afforded him a new joyful sensation.

XIX

On the 24th was fought the battle before the redoubt of Shevardino; on the 25th not a shot was fired on either side; on the 26th was fought the battle of Borodino.

How and with what object were the battles of Shevardino and Borodino fought? Why was the battle of Borodino fought? There was not the slightest sense in it, either for the French or for the Russians. The immediate result of it was, and was bound to be, for the Russians, that we were brought nearer to the destruction of Moscow (the very thing we dreaded above everything in the world); and for the French, that they were brought nearer to the destruction of their army, (which they, too, dreaded above everything in the world). That result was at the time perfectly obvious, and yet Napoleon offered battle, and Kutuzov accepted it.

If military leaders were guided by reasonable considerations only, it would seem that it must have been clear to Napoleon that in advancing two thousand versts into the heart of the country and giving battle, with the probable contingency of losing a quarter of his men, he was going to certain destruction; and that it must have been equally clear to Kutuzov that in accepting that battle and risking the loss of a fourth of his army, he would infallibly lose Moscow. For Kutuzov this was mathematically clear, as clear as it is at chess, that if I have one piece less than my adversary and I exchange pieces, I am certain to be a loser by it, and therefore must avoid exchanging pieces. When my adversary has sixteen pieces and I have fourteen, I am only one-eighth weaker than he; but when we have exchanged thirteen pieces, he is three times as strong as I am.

Up to the battle of Borodino our forces were approximately five-sixths of the French, but after that battle they were only one-half—that is, before the battle a hundred thousand against a hundred and twenty thousand, and after the battle fifty thousand against a hundred thousand. And yet the shrewd and experienced Kutuzov fought the battle. Napoleon, a military genius, as he is called, gave battle, losing a fourth of his army and drawing his line of communications out further than ever. If we are told that he expected the taking of Moscow to complete the campaign, as the taking of Vienna had done, we may say that there are many evidences to the contrary. Napoleon's historians themselves tell us that he wanted to halt as soon as he reached Smolensk; that he knew the danger of his extended line, and that he knew that the taking of Moscow would not be the end of the campaign, because from Smolensk he had learned in what condition the towns were left when abandoned to him, and he had not received a single reply to his reiterated expressions of a desire to open negotiations.

In giving and accepting battle at Borodino, Kutuzov and Napoleon acted without design or rational plan. After the accomplished fact historians have brought forward cunningly devised evidences of the foresight and genius of the generals, who of all the involuntary instruments of the world's history were the most slavish and least independent agents.

The ancients have transmitted to us examples of epic poems in which the whole interest of history is concentrated in a few heroic figures; and under their influence we are still unable to accustom our minds to the idea that history of that kind is meaningless at our stage in the development of humanity.

In answer to the next question, how the battles of Borodino and Shevardino came to be fought, we have also a very definite, well-known, and utterly false account. All the historians describe the affair thus:

The Russian army, they say, in its retreat from Smolensk sought out the best position for a general engagement, and such a position they found in Borodino. The Russians, they say, fortified the position beforehand, to the left of the road (from Moscow to Smolensk) at right angles to it, from Borodino to Utitsa, at the very place where the battle was fought.

In front of this position, they tell us, a fortified earthwork was thrown up on the Shevardino redoubt as an outpost for observation of the enemy's movements.

On the 24th, we are told, Napoleon attacked this redoubt, and took it. On the 26th he attacked the whole Russian army, which had taken up its position on the plain of Borodino.

This is what we are told in the histories, and all that is perfectly incorrect, as any one may easily see who cares to go into the matter.

The Russians did not seek out the best position; on the contrary, on their retreat they had passed by many positions better than Borodino. They did not make a stand at one of these positions, because Kutuzov did not care to take up a position he had not himself selected, because the popular clamour for a battle had not yet been so strongly expressed, because Miloradovitch had not yet arrived with reinforcements of militia, and for countless other reasons.

The fact remains that there were stronger positions on the road the Russian army had passed along, and that the plain of Borodino, on which the battle was fought, is in no respect a more suitable position than any other spot in the Russian empire to which one might point at hazard on the map.

Far from having fortified the position on the left at right angles to the road—that is the spot on which the battle was fought—the Russians never, till the 25th of August, 1812, dreamed of a battle being possible on that spot. The proof of this is, first, that there were no fortifications there before the 25th, and that the earthworks begun on that day were not completed by the 26th; and, secondly, the Shevardino redoubt, owing to its situation in front of the position on which the battle was actually fought, was of no real value. With what object was that redoubt more strongly fortified than any of the other points? And with what object was every effort exhausted and six thousand men sacrificed to defend it till late at night on the 24th? A picket of Cossacks would have been enough to keep watch on the enemy's movements. And a third proof that the position of the battlefield was not foreseen, and that the redoubt of Shevardino was not the foremost point of that position, is to be found in the fact that Barclay de Tolly and Bagration were, till the 25th, under the impression that the Shevardino redoubt was the left flank of the position, and that Kutuzov himself, in the report written in hot haste after the battle, speaks of Shevardino as the left flank of the position. Only a good time later, when reports of the battle were written at leisure, the incorrect and strange statement was invented (probably to cover the blunders of the commander-in-chief, who had, of course, to appear infallible) that the Shevardino redoubt served as an advance post, though it was in reality simply the fortified point of the left flank, and that the battle of Borodino was fought by us on a fortified position selected beforehand for it, though it was in reality fought on a position quite unforeseen, and almost unfortified.

The affair obviously took place in this way. A position had been pitched upon on the stream Kolotcha, which intersects the high-road, not at a right angle, but at an acute angle, so that the left flank was at Shevardino, the right near the village of Novoe, and the centre at Borodino, near the confluence of the Kolotcha and the Voina. Any one looking at the plain of Borodino, and not considering how the battle actually was fought, would pick out this position, covered by the Kolotcha, as the obvious one for an army, whose object was to check the advance of an enemy marching along the Smolensk road towards Moscow.

Napoleon, riding up on the 24th to Valuev, did not (we are told in the histories) see the position of the Russians from Utitsa to Borodino (he could not have seen that position since it did not exist), and did not see the advance posts of the Russian army, but in the pursuit of the Russian rearguard stumbled upon the left flank of the Russian position at the redoubt of Shevardino, and, to the surprise of the Russians, his troops crossed the Kolotcha. And the Russians, since it was too late for a general engagement, withdrew their left wing from the position they had intended to occupy, and took up a new position, which had not been foreseen, and was not fortified. By crossing to the left bank of the Kolotcha, on the left of the road, Napoleon shifted the whole battle from right to left (looking from the Russian side), and transferred it to the plain between Utitsa, Semyonovskoye and Borodino—a plain which in itself was a no more favourable position than any other plain in Russia— and on that plain was fought the whole battle of the 26th.

Had Napoleon not reached the Kolotcha on the evening of the 24th, and had he not ordered the redoubt to be attacked at once that evening, had he begun the attack next morning, no one could have doubted that the Shevardino redoubt was the left flank of the Russian position; and the battle would have been fought as we expected. In that case we should probably have defended the Shevardino redoubt by our left flank even more obstinately; we should have attacked Napoleon in the centre or on the right, and the general engagement would have been fought on the 24th on the position prepared and fortified for it. But as the attack was made on our left flank in the evening after the retreat of our rearguard, that is, immediately after the action at Gridnevo, and as the Russian generals would not, or could not, begin the general engagement on the evening of the 24th, the first and most important action of the battle of Borodino was lost on the 24th, and that loss led inevitably to the loss of the battle fought on the 26th.

After the loss of the Shevardino redoubt, we found ourselves on the morning of the 25th with our left flank driven from its position, and were forced to draw in the left wing of our position and hurriedly fortify it where we could.

So that on the 26th of August the Russian troops were only defended by weak, unfinished earthworks, and the disadvantage of that position was aggravated by the fact that the Russian generals, not fully recognising the facts of the position (the loss of the position on the left flank, and the shifting of the whole field of the coming battle from right to left), retained their extended formation from Novoe to Utitsa, and, consequently had to transfer their troops from right to left during the battle. Consequently, we had during the whole battle to face the whole French army attacking our left wing, with our forces of half the strength.

(Poniatovsky's action facing Utitsa and Uvarov's action against the French right flank were quite independent of the general course of the battle.)

And so the battle of Borodino was fought, not at all as, in order to cover the blunders of our commanders, it is described by our historians, whose accounts, consequently, diminish the credit due to the Russian army and the Russian people. The battle of Borodino was not fought on

a carefully picked and fortified position, with forces only slightly weaker
on the Russian side. After the loss of the Shevardino redoubt, the Russians fought on an open, almost unfortified position, with forces half the
strength of the French, that is, in conditions in which it was not merely
senseless to fight for ten hours and gain a drawn battle, but incredibly
difficult to keep the army for three hours together from absolute rout
and flight.

XX

On the morning of the 25th Pierre drove out of Mozhaisk. On the slope
of an immense, steep, and winding hill, leading out of the town, Pierre
got out of the carriage, and walked by a cathedral on the right of the
hill, where a service was being performed. A cavalry regiment followed
him down the hill, the singers of the regiment in front. A train of carts
came up the hill towards them, filled with wounded from the previous
day's engagement. The peasant drivers kept running from side to side,
shouting and whipping the horses. The carts, in each of which three or
four wounded soldiers were lying or sitting, jolted up and down on the
stones that had been thrown on the steep ascent to mend the road. The
wounded men, pale and bandaged up, with compressed lips and knitted
brows, clung to the sides, as they were shaken and jolted in the carts.
Almost all of them stared with naïve and childlike curiosity at Pierre's
white hat and green coat.

Pierre's coachman shouted angrily at the train of wounded men to
keep to one side of the road. The cavalry regiment, coming down the
hill in time to their song, overtook Pierre's chaise and blocked the road.
Pierre stopped, keeping close to the edge of the road that had been hollowed out in the hill. The sun did not reach over the side of the hill to
the road, and there it felt cold and damp. But overhead it was a bright
August morning, and the chimes rang out merrily. One cart full of
wounded men came to a standstill at the edge of the road quite close to
Pierre. The driver, in bast shoes, ran panting up to his cart, thrust a
stone under the hind wheels, which were without tires, and began setting
straight the breech on his horse.

An old wounded soldier, with his arm in a sling, walking behind the
cart, caught hold of it with his uninjured arm, and looked round at
Pierre.

"Well, fellow-countryman, are we to be put down here or taken on to
Moscow?" he said.

Pierre was so lost in thought that he did not hear the question. He
looked from the cavalry regiment, which was now meeting the train of
wounded, to the cart by which he stood, with the two wounded men sitting, and one lying down in it. One of the soldiers sitting in the cart had
probably been wounded in the cheek. His whole head was done up in
bandages, and one cheek was swollen as large as a baby's head. All his
mouth and nose were on one side. This soldier was looking at the cathe-

dral and crossing himself. Another, a young fellow, a light-haired re-
cruit, as white as though there were not a drop of blood in his thin face,
gazed with a fixed, good-natured smile at Pierre. The third lay so that his
face could not be seen. The singers of the cavalry regiment passed close
by the cart.

"*Al za-pro-pa-la* . . ."

they sang the military dance tune. As though seconding them, though in
a different tone of gaiety, clanged out the metallic notes of the chimes at
the top of the hill. And the hot rays of the sun bathed the top of the
opposite slope with sunshine sparkling with another suggestion of gaiety.
But where Pierre stood under the hillside, by the cart full of wounded
soldiers, and the panting, little nag, it was damp, overcast, and dismal.

The soldier with the wounded cheek looked angrily at the singing
horse soldiers.

"Oh, the smart fellows!" he murmured reproachfully.

"It's not soldiers only, but peasants, too, I have seen to-day! Peasants,
too, they are hunting up," said the soldier standing by the cart, addressing himself to Pierre, with a melancholy smile. "They can't pick and
choose now. . . . They want to mass all the people together—it's a
matter of Moscow, you see. There is only one thing to do now." In spite
of the vagueness of the soldier's words, Pierre fully grasped his meaning,
and nodded his head approvingly.

The road was clear once more, and Pierre walked downhill, and drove
on further.

Pierre drove on, looking on both sides of the road for familiar faces,
and meeting none but unfamiliar, military faces, belonging to all sorts
of regiments, and all staring with the same surprise at his white hat and
green coat.

After driving four versts, for the first time he met an acquaintance,
and greeted him joyfully. This was a doctor, one of the heads of the
medical staff. He drove to meet Pierre in a covered gig, with a young
doctor sitting beside him; and recognising Pierre, he called to the Cossack, who sat on the driver's seat, and told him to stop.

"Count, your excellency, how do you come here?" asked the doctor.

"Oh, I wanted to have a look . . ."

"Oh well, there will be something to look at . . ." Pierre got out of
his carriage, and stopped to have a talk with the doctor, explaining to
him his plan for taking part in the battle.

The doctor advised Bezuhov to go straight to his highness.

"Why, you would be God knows where during the battle, out of
sight," he said, with a glance at his young companion; "and his highness
knows you anyway, and will give you a gracious reception. That's what
I should do, my friend," said the doctor.

The doctor seemed tired and hurried.

"So you think. . . . But one thing more I wanted to ask you, where
is the position exactly?" said Pierre.

"The position?" said the doctor; "well, that's not in my line. Drive on to Tatarinovo, there's a great deal of digging going on there. There you'll come out on a mound; from there you get a view," said the doctor.

"A view from it? . . . If you would . . ."

But the doctor interrupted, and moved toward his gig.

"I would have shown you the way, but by God, you see" (the doctor made a significant gesture), "I'm racing to the commander of the corps. We're in such a fix, you see . . . you know, count, there's to be a battle to-morrow; with a hundred thousand troops, we must reckon on twenty thousand wounded at least; and we haven't the stretchers, nor beds, nor attendants, nor doctors for six thousand. There are ten thousand carts; but we want other things; one must manage as one can."

The strange idea that of those thousands of men, alive and well, young and old, who had been staring with such light-hearted amusement at his hat, twenty thousand were inevitably doomed to wounds and death (perhaps the very men whom he had seen) made a great impression on Pierre.

"They will die, perhaps, to-morrow; how can they think of anything but death?" And suddenly, by some latent connection of ideas, he saw a vivid picture of the hillside of Mozhaisk, the carts of wounded men, the chimes, the slanting sunshine, and the singing of the cavalry regiment.

"They were going into battle, and meeting wounded soldiers, and never for a minute paused to think what was in store for them, but went by and winked at their wounded comrades. And of all those, twenty thousand are doomed to death, and they can wonder at my hat! Strange!" thought Pierre, as he went on towards Tatarinovo.

Carriages, waggons, and crowds of orderlies and sentinels were standing about a gentleman's house on the left side of the road. The commander-in-chief was putting up there. But when Pierre arrived, he found his highness and almost all the staff were out. They had all gone to the church service. Pierre pushed on ahead to Gorky; and driving uphill into a little village street, Pierre saw for the first time the peasants of the militia in white shirts, with crosses on their caps. With loud talk and laughter, eager and perspiring, they were working on the right of the road at a huge mound overgrown with grass.

Some of them were digging out the earth, others were carrying the earth away in wheelbarrows, while a third lot stood doing nothing.

There were two officers on the knoll giving them instructions. Seeing these peasants, who were unmistakably enjoying the novelty of their position as soldiers, Pierre thought again of the wounded soldiers at Mozhaisk, and he understood what the soldier had tried to express by the words "they want to mass all the people together." The sight of these bearded peasants toiling on the field of battle with their queer, clumsy boots, with their perspiring necks, and here and there with shirts unbuttoned showing their sun-burnt collar-bones, impressed Pierre more strongly than anything he had yet seen and heard with the solemnity and gravity of the moment.

XXI

PIERRE got out of his carriage, and passing by the toiling peasants, clambered up the knoll from which the doctor had told him he could get a view of the field of battle.

It was eleven o'clock in the morning. The sun was a little on the left, and behind Pierre, and in the pure, clear air, the huge panorama that stretched in an amphitheatre before him from the rising ground lay bathed in brilliant sunshine.

The Smolensk high-road ran winding through that amphitheatre, intersecting it towards the left at the top, and passing through a village with a white church, which lay some five hundred paces before and below the knoll. This was Borodino. The road passed below the village, crossed a bridge, and ran winding uphill and downhill, mounting up and up to the hamlet of Valuev, visible six versts away, where Napoleon now was. Behind Valuev the road disappeared into a copse turning yellow on the horizon. In this copse of birch- and pine-trees, on the right of the road, could be seen far away the shining cross and belfry of the Kolotsky monastery. Here and there in the blue distance, to right and to left of the copse and the road, could be seen smoking camp-fires and indistinct masses of our troops and the enemy's. On the right, along the course of the rivers Kolotcha and Moskva, the country was broken and hilly. Through the gaps between the hills could be seen the villages of Bezzubovo and Zaharino. On the left the ground was more level; there were fields of corn and a smoking village that had been set on fire—Semyonovskoye.

Everything Pierre saw was so indefinite, that in no part of the scene before him could he find anything fully corresponding to his preconceptions. There was nowhere a field of battle such as he had expected to see, nothing but fields, dells, troops, woods, camp-fires, villages, mounds, and streams. With all Pierre's efforts, he could not discover in the living landscape a military position. He could not even distinguish between our troops and the enemy's.

"I must ask some one who understands it," he thought, and he addressed the officer, who was looking with curiosity at his huge, unmilitary figure.

"Allow me to ask," Pierre said, "what village is that before us?"

"Burdino, isn't it called?" said the officer, turning inquiringly to his comrade.

"Borodino," the other corrected.

The officer, obviously pleased at an opportunity for conversation, went nearer to Pierre.

"Are these our men there?" asked Pierre.

"Yes, and away further, those are the French," said the officer. "There they are, there you can see them."

"Where? where?" asked Pierre.

"One can see them with the naked eye. Look!" The officer pointed to smoke rising on the left beyond the river, and the same stern and grave expression came into his face that Pierre had noticed in many of the faces he had met.

"Ah, that's the French! And there? . . ." Pierre pointed to a knoll on the left about which troops could be seen.

"Those are our men."

"Oh, indeed! And there? . . ." Pierre pointed to another mound in the distance, with a big tree on it, near a village that could be seen in a gap between the hills, where there was a dark patch and the smoke of camp-fires.

"Ah! that's *he* again!" said the officer. (It was the redoubt of Shevardino.) "Yesterday that was ours, but now it's *his*."

"So what is our position, then?"

"Our position?" said the officer, with a smile of satisfaction. "I can describe it very clearly, because I have had to do with the making of almost all our fortifications. There, our centre, do you see, is here at Borodino." He pointed to the village with the white church, in front of them. "There's the ford across the Kolotcha. Here, do you see, where the rows of mown hay are still lying in the low ground, there's the bridge. That's our centre. Our right flank is away yonder" (he pointed to the right, far away to the hollows among the hills), "there is the river Moskva, and there we have thrown up three very strong redoubts. The left flank . . ." there the officer paused. "It's hard to explain, you see. . . . Yesterday our left flank was over there, at Shevardino, do you see, where the oak is. But now we have drawn back our left wing, now it's over there,— you see the village and the smoke—that's Semyonovskoye, and here —look," he pointed to Raevsky's redoubt. "Only the battle won't be there, most likely. *He* has moved his troops here, but that's a blind; *he* will probably try to get round on the right. Well, but however it may be, there'll be a lot of men missing at roll-call to-morrow!" said the officer.

The old sergeant, who came up during the officer's speech, had waited in silence for his superior officer to finish speaking. But at this point he interrupted him in undisguised annoyance at his last words.

"We have to send for gabions," he said severely.

The officer seemed abashed, as though he were fully aware that though he might think how many men would be missing next day, he ought not to talk about it.

"Well, send the third company again," he said hurriedly. "And who are you, not one of the doctors?"

"No, I am nothing in particular," answered Pierre. And he went downhill again, passing the peasant militiamen.

"Ah, the damned beasts!" said the officer, pinching his nose, and hurrying by them with Pierre.

"Here they come! . . . They are bringing her, they are coming. . . . Here she is . . . they'll be here in a minute," cried voices suddenly, and officers, soldiers, and peasants ran forward along the road.

A church procession was coming up the hill from Borodino. In front of it a regiment of infantry marched smartly along the dusty road, with their shakoes off and their muskets lowered. Behind the infantry came the sounds of church singing.

Soldiers and peasants came running down bareheaded to meet it, over-taking Pierre.

"They are bringing the Holy Mother! Our defender . . . the Holy Mother of Iversky! . . ."

"The Holy Mother of Smolensk . . ." another corrected.

The militiamen who had been in the village and those who had been working at the battery, flinging down their spades, ran to meet the pro-cession. The battalion marching along the dusty road was followed by priests in church robes, a little old man in a hood with attendant deacons and choristers. Behind them came soldiers and officers bearing a huge holy picture, with tarnished face in a setting of silver. This was the holy ikon that had been brought away from Smolensk, and had accompanied the army ever since. Behind, before, and all around it, walked or ran crowds of soldiers with bared heads, bowing to the earth.

On the top of the hill the procession stopped; the men bearing the holy picture on a linen cloth were relieved by others; the deacons re-lighted their censers, and the service began. The burning rays of the sun beat vertically down on the crowds; a faint, fresh breeze played with the hair of their bare heads, and fluttered the ribbons with which the holy picture was decked; the singing sounded subdued under the open sky. An immense crowd—officers, soldiers, and militiamen—stood round, all with bare heads. In a space apart, behind the priests and deacons, stood the persons of higher rank. A bald general, with the order of St. George on his neck, stood directly behind the priest. He was unmistakably a German, for he stood, not crossing himself, patiently waiting for the end of the service, to which he thought it right to listen, probably as a means of arousing the patriotism of the Russian peasantry; another general stood in a martial pose and swung his arm before his chest, looking about him as he made the sign of the cross. Pierre, standing among the peas-ants, recognised in this group of higher rank several persons he knew. But he did not look at them; his whole attention was engrossed by the serious expression of the faces in the crowd, soldiers and peasants alike, all gazing with the same eagerness at the holy picture. As soon as the weary choristers (it was their twentieth service) began languidly sing-ing their habitual chant, "O Mother of God, save Thy servants from calamity," and priest and deacon chimed in, "For to Thee we all fly as our invincible Bulwark and Protectress," there was a gleam on every face of that sense of the solemnity of the coming moment, which he had seen on the hill at Mozhaisk and by glimpses in so many of the faces meeting him that morning. And heads were bowed lower, while locks of hair fluttered in the breeze, and there was the sound of sighing and beat-ing the breast as the soldiers crossed themselves.

The crowd suddenly parted and pressed upon Pierre. Some one, prob-ably a very great person, judging by the promptitude with which they made way for him, was approaching the holy picture.

It was Kutuzov, who had been making the round of the position. On his way back to Tatarinovo, he joined the service. Pierre at once recognised him from his peculiar figure, which marked him out at once.

In a long military coat, with his enormously stout figure and bent back, with his white head uncovered, and his blind white eye, conspicuous in his puffy face, Kutuzov walked with his waddling swaying gait into the ring and stood behind the priest. He crossed himself with an habitual gesture, bent down, with his hand touching the earth, and, sighing heavily, bowed his grey head. Kutuzov was followed by Bennigsen and his suite. In spite of the presence of the commander-in-chief, which drew the attention of all persons of higher rank, the militiamen and soldiers went on praying without looking at him.

When the service was over, Kutuzov went up to the holy picture, dropped heavily down on his knees, bowing to the earth, and for a long time he attempted to get up, and was unable from his weakness and heavy weight. His grey head twitched with the strain. At last he did get up, and putting out his lips in a naïve, childlike way kissed the holy picture, and again bowed down, with one hand touching the ground. The other generals followed his example; then the officers, and after them the soldiers and militiamen ran up with excited faces, pushing each other, and shoving breathlessly forward.

XXII

STAGGERING from the crush of the crowd that carried him along with it, Pierre looked about him.

"Count! Pyotr Kirillitch! How did you come here?" said a voice. Pierre looked round.

Boris Drubetskoy, brushing his knee with his hand (he had probably made it dusty in his devotions before the holy picture) came up to Pierre smiling. Boris was elegantly dressed, though his get-up was of a style appropriate to active service. He wore a long military coat and had a riding-whip slung across his shoulder, as Kutuzov had.

Kutuzov had meanwhile reached the village, and sat down in the shade of the nearest house, on a bench which one Cossack ran to fetch him, and another hastily covered with a rug. An immense retinue of magnificent officers surrounded him.

The procession was moving on further, accompanied by the crowd. Pierre stood still about thirty paces from Kutuzov, talking to Boris.

He explained to him his desire to take part in the battle and to inspect the position.

"I tell you what you had better do," said Boris. "I will do the honours of the camp for you. You will see everything best of all from where Count Bennigsen is to be. I am in attendance on him. I will mention it to him. And if you like to go over the position, come along with us; we are just going to the left flank. And then when we come back, I beg you will stay the night with me, and we will make up a game of cards. You

know Dmitry Sergeitch, of course. He is staying there." He pointed to
the third house in Gorky.

"But I should have liked to have seen the right flank. I'm told it is
very strong," said Pierre. "I should have liked to go from the river
Moskva through the whole position."

"Well, that you can do later, but the great thing is the left flank."

"Yes, yes. And where is Prince Bolkonsky's regiment? can you point
it out to me?" asked Pierre.

"Andrey Nikolaevitch's? We shall pass it. I will take you to him."

"What about the left flank?" asked Pierre.

"To tell you the truth, between ourselves, there's no making out how
things stand with the left flank," said Boris confidentially, dropping his
voice. "Count Bennigsen had proposed something quite different. He
proposed to fortify that knoll over there, not at all as it has . . . but
. . ." Boris shrugged his shoulders. "His highness would not have it so,
or he was talked over. You see . . ." Boris did not finish because Kaisarov, Kutuzov's adjutant, at that moment came up to Pierre. "Ah, Paisy
Sergeitch," said Boris to him, with an unembarrassed smile, "I am trying, you see, to explain the position to the count. It's amazing how his
highness can gauge the enemy's plans so accurately!"

"Do you mean about the left flank?" said Kaisarov.

"Yes, yes; just so. Our left flank is now extremely strong."

Although Kutuzov had made a clearance of the superfluous persons on
the staff, Boris had succeeded, after the change he had made, in retaining a post at headquarters. Boris was in attendance on Count Bennigsen.
Count Bennigsen, like every one on whom Boris had been in attendance,
looked on young Prince Drubetskoy as an invaluable man. Among the
chief officers of the army there were two clearly defined parties: Kutuzov's party and the party of Bennigsen, the chief of the staff. Boris belonged to the latter faction, and no one succeeded better than he did in
paying the most servile adulation to Kutuzov, while managing to in-
sinuate that the old fellow was not good for much, and that everything
was really due to the initiative of Bennigsen. Now the decisive moment
of battle had come, which must mean the downfall of Kutuzov and the
transfer of the command to Bennigsen, or if Kutuzov should gain the
battle, the credit of it must be skilfully put down to Bennigsen. In any
case many promotions were bound to be made, and many new men were
certain to be brought to the front after the morrow. And Boris was consequently in a state of nervous exhilaration all that day.

Others of Pierre's acquaintances joined him; and he had not time to
answer all the questions about Moscow that were showered upon him,
nor to listen to all they had to tell him. Every face wore a look of excitement and agitation. But it seemed to Pierre that the cause of the excitement that was betrayed by some of those faces was to be found in
questions of personal success, and he could not forget that other look of
excitement he had seen in the other faces, that suggested problems, not
of personal success, but the universal questions of life and death.

Kutuzov noticed Pierre's figure and the group gathered about him. "Call him to me," said Kutuzov.

An adjutant communicated his highness's desire, and Pierre went towards the bench. But a militiaman approached Kutuzov before him. It was Dolohov.

"How does that man come to be here?" asked Pierre.

"Oh, he's such a sly dog, he pokes himself in everywhere!" was the answer he received. "He has been degraded to the ranks, you know. Now he wants to pop up again. He has made plans of some sort and spies in the enemy's lines at night . . . but he's a plucky fellow . . ."

Pierre took off his hat and bowed respectfully to Kutuzov.

"I decided that if I were to lay the matter before your highness, you might dismiss me or say that you were aware of the facts and then I shouldn't lose anything," Dolohov was saying.

"To be sure."

"And if I were right, I should do a service for my fatherland, for which I am ready to die."

"To be sure . . . to be sure . . ."

"And if your highness has need of a man who would not spare his skin graciously remember me . . . perhaps I might be of use to your highness . . ."

"To be sure . . . to be sure . . ." repeated Kutuzov, looking with a laughing, half-closed eye at Pierre.

Meanwhile Boris, with his courtier-like tact, had moved close to the commander-in-chief with Pierre, and in the most natural manner, in a quiet voice, as though continuing his previous conversation, he said to Pierre:

"The peasant militiamen have simply put on clean, white shirts to be ready to die. What heroism, count!"

Boris said this to Pierre with the evident intention of being overheard by his excellency. He knew Kutuzov's attention would be caught by those words, and his highness did in fact address him.

"What are you saying about the militia?" he said to Boris.

"They have put on white shirts, your highness, by way of preparing for to-morrow, to be ready for death."

"Ah! . . . A marvellous, unique people," said Kutuzov, and closing his eyes he shook his head. "A unique people!" he repeated, with a sigh.

"Do you want a sniff of powder?" he said to Pierre. "Yes; a pleasant smell. I have the honour to be one of your wife's worshippers; is she quite well? My quarters are at your service." And Kutuzov began, as old people often do, gazing abstractedly about him, as though forgetting all he had to say or do. Apparently recollecting the object of his search, he beckoned to Andrey Sergeitch Kaisarov, the brother of his adjutant.

"How was it, how do they go, those verses of Marin? How do they go? What he wrote on Gerakov: 'You will be teacher in the corps . . .' Tell me, tell me," said Kutuzov, his countenance relaxing in readiness for a laugh. Kaisarov repeated the lines . . . Kutuzov, smiling, nodded his head to the rhythm of the verse.

When Pierre moved away from Kutuzov, Dolohov approached and took his hand.

"I am very glad to meet you here, count," he said, aloud, disregarding the presence of outsiders, and speaking with a marked determination and gravity. "On the eve of a day which God knows who among us will be destined to survive I am glad to have the chance of telling you that I regret the misunderstandings there have been between us in the past; and I should be glad to think you had nothing against me. I beg you to forgive me."

Pierre looked with a smile at Dolohov, not knowing what to say to him. With tears starting into his eyes, Dolohov embraced and kissed Pierre.

Boris had said a few words to his general, and Count Bennigsen addressed Pierre, proposing that he should accompany them along the line.

"You will find it interesting," he said.

"Yes, very interesting," said Pierre.

Half an hour later Kutuzov was on his way back to Tatarinovo, while Bennigsen and his suite, with Pierre among them, were inspecting the position.

XXIII

FROM Gorky Bennigsen went down the high-road to the bridge, which the officer on the knoll had pointed out to Pierre as the centre of the position, where by the riverside lay rows of sweet-scented, new-mown hay. They crossed the bridge to the village of Borodino, then turned to the left, and passing immense numbers of men and cannons, came out on to the high knoll on which militiamen were at work excavating. This was the redoubt, as yet unnamed, afterwards called Raevsky's redoubt, or the battery on the mound.

Pierre did not take special notice of this redoubt. He did not dream that that spot would be more memorable for him than any other part of the plain of Borodino. Then they crossed a hollow to Semyonovskoye, where the soldiers were dragging away the last logs of the huts and barns. Then they rode on downhill and uphill again, across a field of rye, trampled and laid as though by hail, along the track newly made by the artillery, over the ridges of the ploughed field, to the earthworks, at which the men were still at work.

Bennigsen halted at the earthworks, and looked in front at the redoubt of Shevardino, which had been ours the day before. Several horsemen could be descried upon it. The officers said that Napoleon and Murat were there. And all gazed eagerly at the little group of horsemen. Pierre too stared at them, trying to guess which of the scarcely discernible figures was Napoleon. At last the group of horsemen descended the hill and passed out of sight.

Bennigsen began explaining to a general who had ridden up to him the whole position of our troops. Pierre listened to his words, straining every faculty of his mind to grasp the essential points of the coming battle, but to his mortification he felt that his faculties were not equal to the task. He could make nothing of it. Bennigsen finished speaking, and noticing Pierre's listening face, he said, turning suddenly to him:

"It's not very interesting for you, I expect."

"Oh, on the contrary, it's very interesting," Pierre repeated, not quite truthfully.

From the earthworks they turned still more to the left of the road that ran winding through a thick, low-growing, birch wood. In the middle of the wood a brown hare with white feet popped out on the road before them, and was so frightened by the tramp of so many horses, that in its terror it hopped along the road just in front of them for a long while, rousing general laughter, and only when several voices shouted at it, dashed to one side and was lost in the thicket. After a couple of versts of woodland, they came out on a clearing, where were the troops of Tutchkov's corps, destined to protect the left flank.

At this point, at the extreme left flank, Bennigsen talked a great deal with much heat; and gave instructions, of great importance from a military point of view, as it seemed to Pierre. Just in front of the spot where Tutchkov's troops were placed there rose a knoll, which was not occupied by troops. Bennigsen was loud in his criticism of this oversight, saying that it was insane to leave a height that commanded the country round unoccupied and place troops just below it. Several generals expressed the same opinion. One in particular, with martial warmth, declared that they were doomed there to certain destruction. Bennigsen, on his own responsibility, ordered the troops to be moved on to the high-road.

This change of position on the left flank made Pierre more than ever doubtful of his capacity for comprehending military matters. As he heard Bennigsen and the other generals criticising the position of the troops at the foot of the hill, Pierre fully grasped and shared their views. But that was why he could not imagine how the man who had placed them there could have made so gross and obvious a blunder.

Pierre did not know that the troops had not been placed there to defend their position, as Bennigsen supposed, but had been stationed in that concealed spot in ambush, in order unobserved to deal a sudden blow at the enemy unawares. Bennigsen, ignorant of this project, moved the troops into a prominent position without saying anything about this change to the commander-in-chief.

XXIV

PRINCE ANDREY was on that bright August evening lying propped on his elbow in a broken-down barn in the village of Knyazkovo, at the further end of the encampment of his regiment. Through a gap in the broken wall he was looking at the line of thirty-year-old pollard birches in the hedge, at the field with sheaves of oats lying about it, and at the bushes where he saw the smoke of camp-fires, at which the soldiers were doing their cooking.

Cramped and useless and burdensome as his life seemed now to Prince Andrey, he felt nervously excited and irritable on the eve of battle, just as he had felt seven years earlier before Austerlitz.

He had received and given all orders for the next day's battle. He had nothing more to do. But thoughts—the simplest, most obvious, and therefore most awful—would not leave him in peace. He knew that the battle next day would be the most awful of all he had taken part in, and death, for the first time, presented itself to him, not in relation to his actual manner of life, or to the effect of it on others, but simply in relation to himself, to his soul, and rose before him simply and awfully with a vividness that made it like a concrete reality. And from the height of this vision everything that had once occupied him seemed suddenly illumined by a cold, white light, without shade, without perspective or outline. His whole life seemed to him like a magic lantern, at which he had been looking through the glass and by artificial light. Now he saw suddenly, without the glass, in the clear light of day, those badly daubed pictures. "Yes, yes, there are they; there are the cheating forms that excited torments and ecstasies in me," he said to himself, going over in imagination the chief pictures of the magic lantern of his life, looking at them now in the cold, white daylight of a clear view of death. "These are they, these coarsely sketched figures which seemed something splendid and mysterious. Glory, the good society, love for a woman, the fatherland—what grand pictures they used to seem to me, with what deep meaning they seemed to be filled! And it is all so simple, so colourless and coarse in the cold light of the day that I feel is dawning for me." The three chief sorrows of his life held his attention especially. His love for a woman, his father's death, and the invasion of the French—now in possession of half of Russia. "Love! . . . That little girl, who seemed to me brimming over with mysterious forces. How I loved her! I made romantic plans of love, of happiness with her! O simple-hearted youth!" he said aloud bitterly. "Why, I believed in some ideal love which was to keep her faithful to me for the whole year of my absence! Like the faithful dove in the fable, she was to pine away in my absence from her! And it was all so much simpler. . . . It is all so horribly simple and loathsome!

"My father, too, laid out Bleak Hills, and thought it was his place, his land, his air, his peasants. But Napoleon came along, and without even knowing of his existence, swept him away like a chip out of his path, and his Bleak Hills laid in the dust, and all his life with it brought to nought. Princess Marya says that it is a trial sent from above. What is the trial for, since he is not and never will be? He will never come back again! He is not! So for whom is it a trial? Fatherland, the spoiling of Moscow! But to-morrow I shall be killed; and not by a Frenchman even, maybe, but by one of our own men, like the soldier who let off his gun close to my ear yesterday; and the French will come and pick me up by my head and my heels and pitch me into a hole that I may not stink under their noses; and new conditions of life will arise, and I shall know nothing of them, and I shall not be at all."

He gazed at the row of birch-trees with their motionless yellows and greens, and the white bark shining in the sun. "To die then, let them kill me to-morrow, let me be no more . . . let it all go on, and let me be at an end." He vividly pictured his own absence from that life. And those birch-trees, with their light and shade, and the curling clouds and the smoke of the fires, everything around seemed suddenly transformed into something weird and menacing. A shiver ran down his back. Rising quickly to his feet, he went out of the barn, and began to walk about.

He heard voices behind the barn.

"Who's there?" called Prince Andrey.

The red-nosed Captain Timohin, once the officer in command of Dolohov's company, now in the lack of officers promoted to the command of a battalion, came shyly into the barn. He was followed by an adjutant and the paymaster of the regiment.

Prince Andrey got up hurriedly, listened to the matters relating to their duties that the officers had come to him about, gave a few instructions, and was about to dismiss them, when he heard a familiar, lisping voice behind the barn.

"*Que diable!*" said the voice of some one stumbling over something.

Prince Andrey, peeping out of the barn, saw Pierre, who had just hit against a post lying on the ground, and had almost fallen over. Prince Andrey always disliked seeing people from his own circle, especially Pierre, who reminded him of all the painful moments he had passed through on his last stay at Moscow.

"Well!" he cried. "What fate has brought you? I didn't expect to see you."

While he said this there was in his eyes and his whole face more than coldness, positive hostility, which Pierre noticed at once. He had approached the barn with the greatest eagerness, but now, on seeing Prince Andrey's face, he felt constrained and ill at ease.

"I have come . . . you know . . . simply . . . I have come . . . it's interesting," said Pierre, who had so many times already that day repeated that word "interesting" without meaning it. "I wanted to see the battle!"

"Yes, yes; but your mason brethren, what do they say of war? How would they avert it?" said Prince Andrey sarcastically. "Well, tell me about Moscow. And my people? Have they reached Moscow at last?" he asked seriously.

"Yes. Julie Drubetskoy told me so. I went to call, but missed them. They had started for your Moscow estate."

XXV

THE officers would have taken leave, but Prince Andrey, apparently unwilling to be left alone with his friend, pressed them to stay and have some tea. Benches were set, and tea was brought. With some astonish-

ment the officers stared at Pierre's huge, bulky figure, and heard his talk
of Moscow, and of the position of our troops, which he had succeeded in
getting a view of. Prince Andrey did not speak, and his face was so forbidding that Pierre addressed his remarks more to the simple-hearted
Timohin than to Bolkonsky.

"So you understand the whole disposition of the troops?" Prince Andrey put in.

"Yes. At least, how do you mean?" said Pierre. "As I am not a military man, I can't say I do fully; but still I understand the general arrangement."

"Well, then, you know more than anybody else," said Prince Andrey.

"Oh!" said Pierre incredulously, looking over his spectacles at Prince
Andrey. "Well, and what do you say of the appointment of Kutuzov?"
he asked.

"I was very glad of his appointment; that's all I know," said Prince
Andrey.

"Well, tell me your opinion of Barclay de Tolly. In Moscow they are
saying all kinds of things about him. What do you think of him?"

"Ask them," said Prince Andrey, indicating the officers.

With the condescendingly doubtful smile with which every one addressed him, Pierre looked at Timohin.

"It was a gleam of light in the dark, your excellency, when his highness took the command," said Timohin, stealing shy glances continually
at his colonel.

"Why so?" asked Pierre.

"Well, as regards firewood and food, let me tell you. Why, all the way
we retreated from Sventsyan not a twig, nor a wisp of hay, nor anything, dare we touch. We were retreating, you see, so *he* would get it,
wouldn't he, your excellency?" he said, turning to his prince, "but we
mustn't dare to. In our regiment two officers were court-martialled for
such things. Well, since his highness is in command, it's all straightforward as regards that. We see daylight . . ."

"Then why did he forbid it?"

Timohin looked round in confusion, at a loss how to answer such a
question. Pierre turned to Prince Andrey with the same inquiry.

"Why, so as not to waste the country we were leaving for the
enemy," said Prince Andrey, with angry sarcasm. "That's a first principle: never to allow pillage and accustom your men to marauding. And
at Smolensk too he very correctly judged that the French were the
stronger and might overcome us. But he could not understand," cried
Prince Andrey in a voice suddenly shrill, "he could not understand that
for the first time we were fighting on Russian soil, that there was a
spirit in the men such as I had never seen before, that we had twice in
succession beaten back the French, and that success had multiplied our
strength tenfold. He ordered a retreat, and all our efforts and our curses
were in vain. He had no thought of treachery; he tried to do everything
for the best and thought over everything well. But for that very reason
he was no good. He is no good now just because he considers everything

soundly and accurately as every German must. How can I explain to you. . . . Well, your father has a German valet, say, and he's an excellent valet and satisfies all his requirements better than you can do, and all's well and good; but if your father is sick unto death, you'll send away the valet and wait on your father yourself with your awkward, unpractised hands, and be more comfort to him than a skilful man who's a stranger. That's how we have done with Barclay. While Russia was well, she might be served by a stranger, and an excellent minister he was, but as soon as she's in danger, she wants a man of her own kith and kin. So you in your club have been making him out to be a traitor! They slander him now as a traitor; and afterwards, ashamed of their false accusations, they will suddenly glorify him as a hero or a genius, which would be even more unfair to him. He's an honest and conscientious German . . ."

"They say he's an able general, though," said Pierre.

"I don't know what's meant by an able general," Prince Andrey said ironically.

"An able general," said Pierre; "well, it's one who foresees all contingencies . . . well, divines the enemy's projects."

"But that's impossible," said Prince Andrey, as though of a matter long ago settled.

Pierre looked at him in surprise.

"But you know they say," he said, "that war is like a game of chess."

"Yes," said Prince Andrey, "only with this little difference, that in chess you may think over each move as long as you please, that you are not limited as to time, and with this further difference that a knight is always stronger than a pawn and two pawns are always stronger than one, while in war a battalion is sometimes stronger than a division, and sometimes weaker than a company. No one can ever be certain of the relative strength of armies. Believe me," he said, "if anything did depend on the arrangements made by the staff, I would be there, and helping to make them, but instead of that I have the honour of serving here in the regiment with these gentlemen here, and I consider that the day really depends upon us to-morrow and not on them. . . . Success never has depended and never will depend on position, on arms, nor even on numbers; and, least of all, on position."

"On what then?"

"On the feeling that is in me and him," he indicated Timohin, "and every soldier."

Prince Andrey glanced at Timohin, who was staring in alarm and bewilderment at his colonel. In contrast to his usual reserved taciturnity, Prince Andrey seemed excited now. Apparently he could not refrain from expressing the ideas that suddenly rose to his mind. "The battle is won by the side that has firmly resolved to win. Why did we lose the battle of Austerlitz? Our losses were almost equalled by the French losses; but we said to ourselves very early in the day that we were losing the battle, and we lost it. And we said so because we had nothing to fight for then; we wanted to get out of fighting as quick as we could. 'We are defeated;

so let us run!' and we did run. If we had not said that till evening, God
knows what might not have happened. But to-morrow we shan't say
that. You talk of our position, of the left flank being weak, and the right
flank too extended," he went on; "all that's nonsense; that's all nothing.
But what awaits us to-morrow? A hundred millions of the most diverse
contingencies, which will determine on the instant whether they run or
we do; whether one man is killed and then another; but all that's being
done now is all mere child's play. The fact is that these people with
whom you have been inspecting the positions do nothing towards the
progress of things; they are a positive hindrance. They are entirely
taken up with their own petty interests."

"At such a moment?" said Pierre reproachfully.

"*At such a moment*," repeated Prince Andrey. "To them this is simply
a moment on which one may score off a rival and win a cross or ribbon
the more. To my mind what is before us to-morrow is this: a hundred
thousand Russian and a hundred thousand French troops have met to
fight, and the fact is that these two hundred thousand men will fight,
and the side that fights most desperately and spares itself least will conquer. And if you like, I'll tell you that whatever happens, and whatever
mess they make up yonder, we shall win the battle to-morrow; whatever happens we shall win the victory."

"Your excellency, that's the truth of it, the holy truth," put in
Timohin; "who would spare himself now! The soldiers in my battalion,
would you believe it, wouldn't drink their vodka; this isn't an ordinary
day, they say."

All were silent.

The officers rose. Prince Andrey went with them out of the barn, giving the last instructions to the adjutant. When the officers had gone,
Pierre came nearer to Prince Andrey, and was just about to begin talking
when they heard the tramp of hoofs not far away on the road, and
glancing in that direction Prince Andrey recognised Woltzogen and
Klausewitz, accompanied by a Cossack. They rode close by them, still
talking, and Pierre and Prince Andrey could not help overhearing the
following phrases in German:

"The war ought to be carried on over a wide extent of country. I cannot sufficiently strongly express that view of the matter," one said in
German.

"Oh yes," said another voice, "since the object is to wear out the
enemy, one must not consider the losses of private persons."

"Certainly not," acquiesced the first voice.

"Carried into a wide extent of country," Prince Andrey repeated with
a wrathful snort, when they had ridden by. "In that open country I
had a father and son and sister at Bleak Hills. He doesn't care about
that. That's just what I was saying to you: these excellent Germans
won't win the battle to-morrow, they will only make a mess of it, so far
as they are able, because they have nothing in their German noddles but
calculations that are not worth a rotten egg, and they haven't in their
hearts the one thing that's wanted for to-morrow, that Timohin has.

They have given all Europe up to *him,* and now they have come to teach us—fine teachers!" he added, his voice growing shrill again.

"So you think the battle to-morrow will be a victory," said Pierre.

"Yes, yes," said Prince Andrey absently. "There's one thing I would do, if I were in power," he began again. "I wouldn't take prisoners. What sense is there in taking prisoners? That's chivalry. The French have destroyed my home and are coming to destroy Moscow; they have outraged and are outraging me at every second. They are my enemies, they are all criminals to my way of thinking. And so thinks Timohin, and all the army with him. They must be put to death. Since they are my enemies, they can't be my friends, whatever they may have said at Tilsit."

"Yes, yes," said Pierre, looking with shining eyes at Prince Andrey. "I entirely agree with you!"

The question that had been disturbing Pierre all that day, since the Mozhaisk hill, now struck him as perfectly clear and fully solved. He saw now all the import and all the gravity of the war and the impending battle. All he had seen that day, all the stern, grave faces of which he had had glimpses, appeared to him in a new light now. He saw, to borrow a term from physics, the latent heat of patriotism in all those men he had seen, and saw in it the explanation of the composure and apparent levity with which they were all preparing for death. "We ought not to take prisoners," said Prince Andrey. "That change alone would transform the whole aspect of war and would make it less cruel. But playing at war, that's what's vile; and playing at magnanimity and all the rest of it. That magnanimity and sensibility is like the magnanimity and sensibility of the lady who turns sick at the sight of a slaughtered calf— she is so kindhearted she can't see blood—but eats fricasseed veal with a very good appetite. They talk of the laws of warfare, of chivalry, of flags of truce, and humanity to the wounded, and so on. That's all rubbish. I saw enough in 1805 of chivalry and flags of truce: they duped us, and we duped them. They plunder other people's homes, issue false money, and, worse than all, kill my children, my father, and then talk of the laws of warfare, and generosity to a fallen foe. No prisoners; and go to give and to meet death! Any one who has come to think this as I have, through the same sufferings . . ."

Prince Andrey, who had thought that he did not care whether they took Moscow as they had taken Smolensk, was suddenly pulled up in his speech by a nervous catch in his throat. He walked to and fro several times in silence, but his eyes blazed with feverish brilliance and his lips quivered, as he began to speak again.

"If there were none of this playing at generosity in warfare, we should never go to war, except for something worth facing certain death for, as now. Then there would not be wars because Pavel Ivanitch had insulted Mihail Ivanitch. But if there is war as now, let it be really war. And then the intensity of warfare would be something quite different. All these Westphalians and Hessians Napoleon is leading against us would not have come to fight us in Russia, and we should not have gone to war in Austria and in Prussia without knowing what for. War is not a polite recreation, but the vilest thing in life, and we ought to understand that and not play at war. We ought to accept it sternly and solemnly as a fearful necessity. It all comes to this: have done with lying, and if it's war, then it's war and not a game, or else warfare is simply the favourite pastime of the idle and frivolous. . . . The military is the most honoured calling. And what is war, what is needed for success in war, what are the morals of the military world? The object of warfare is murder; the means employed in warfare—spying, treachery, and the encouragement of it, the ruin of a country, the plundering of its inhabitants and robbery for the maintenance of the army, trickery and lying, which are called military strategy; the morals of the military class—absence of all independence, that is, discipline, idleness, ignorance, cruelty, debauchery, and drunkenness. And in spite of all that, it is the highest class, respected by every one. All sovereigns, except the Chinese, wear a military uniform, and give the greatest rewards to the man who succeeds in killing most people. . . . They meet together to murder one another, as we shall do to-morrow; they slaughter and mutilate tens of thousands of men, and then offer up thanksgiving services for the number of men they have killed (and even add to it in the telling), and glorify the victory, supposing that the more men have been slaughtered the greater the achievement. How God can look down from above and hear them!" shrieked Prince Andrey in a shrill, piercing voice. "Ah, my dear boy, life has been a bitter thing for me of late. I see that I have come to understand too much. And it is not good for man to taste of the tree of the knowledge of good and evil. . . . Ah, well, it's not for long!" he added. "But you are getting sleepy and it's time I was in bed too. Go back to Gorky," said Prince Andrey suddenly.

"Oh no!" answered Pierre, gazing with eyes full of scared sympathy at Prince Andrey.

"You must be off; before a battle one needs to get a good sleep," repeated Prince Andrey. He went quickly up to Pierre, embraced and kissed him. "Good-bye, be off," he cried, "whether we see each other again or not . . ." and turning hurriedly, he went off into the barn.

It was already dark, and Pierre could not distinguish whether the expression of his face was exasperated or affectionate.

Pierre stood for some time in silence, hesitating whether to go after him or to return to Gorky. "No; he does not want me!" Pierre made up his mind, "and I know this is our last meeting!" He heaved a deep sigh and rode back to Gorky.

Prince Andrey lay down on a rug in the barn, but he could not sleep. He closed his eyes. One set of images followed another in his mind. On one mental picture he dwelt long and joyfully. He vividly recalled one evening in Petersburg. Natasha with an eager, excited face had been telling him how in looking for mushrooms the previous summer she had lost her way in a great forest. She described incoherently the dark depths of the forest, and her feelings, and her talk with a bee-keeper she met, and every minute she broke off in her story, saying: "No, I can't, I'm not describing it properly; no, you won't understand me," although Prince Andrey tried to assure her that he understood and did really understand all she wanted to convey to him. Natasha was dissatisfied with her own words; she felt that they did not convey the passionately poetical feeling she had known that day and tried to give expression to. "It was all so exquisite, that old man, and it was so dark in the forest . . . and such a kind look in his . . . no, I can't describe it," she had said, flushed and moved.

Prince Andrey smiled now the same happy smile he had smiled then, gazing into her eyes. "I understood her," thought Prince Andrey, "and more than understood her: that spiritual force, that sincerity, that openness of soul, the very soul of her, which seemed bound up with her body, the very soul it was I loved in her . . . loved so intensely, so passionately . . ." and all at once he thought how his love had ended. "*He* cared nothing for all that. *He* saw nothing of it, had no notion of it. He saw in her a pretty and *fresh* young girl with whom he did not deign to unite his life permanently. And I? . . . And he is still alive and happy." Prince Andrey jumped up as though suddenly scalded, and began walking to and fro before the barn again.

XXVI

ON the 25th of August, on the eve of the battle of Borodino, the prefect of the French Emperor's palace, M. de Beausset, and Colonel Fabvier, arrived, the former from Paris, and the latter from Madrid, at Napoleon's encampment at Valuev.

After changing into a court uniform M. de Beausset ordered the package he had brought for the Emperor to be carried before him, and walked into the first compartment of Napoleon's tent, where he busied himself while conversing with the aides-de-camp in unpacking the box.

Fabvier stood talking with generals of his acquaintance in the entrance of the tent.

The Emperor Napoleon had not yet left his bedroom, he was finishing his toilet. With snorts and grunts of satisfaction, he was turning first his stout back and then his plump, hirsute chest towards the flesh-brush with which a valet was rubbing him down. Another valet, holding a bottle with one finger on it, was sprinkling eau de cologne on the Emperor's pampered person with an expression which seemed to say that he alone knew where and how much eau de cologne must be sprinkled. Napoleon's short hair was wet and matted on his brow. But his face, though puffy and yellow, expressed physical satisfaction.

"Go on, hard, go on . . ." he said, shrugging and clearing his throat, to the valet brushing him. An adjutant, who had come into the bedroom to report to the Emperor the number of prisoners taken in the last engagement, was standing at the door, after giving his message, awaiting permission to withdraw. Napoleon, frowning, glanced up from under his brows at the adjutant. "No prisoners," he repeated the adjutant's words.

"They are working their own destruction. So much the worse for the Russian army," said he. "Harder, brush harder," he said, hunching his fat shoulders before the valet. "Good. Let Beausset come in and Fabvier too," he said to the adjutant, nodding.

"I obey, sire," and the adjutant disappeared.

The two valets rapidly dressed his majesty, and in the blue uniform of the guards he walked into the reception-room with firm, rapid steps.

Beausset meanwhile was in great haste setting up the present he had brought from the Empress on two chairs just before the Emperor as he entered. But the Emperor had been so unaccountably rapid over getting dressed and coming in that he had not time to have the surprise ready for him.

Napoleon at once noticed what they were about, and guessed they were not ready. He did not want to deprive them of the pleasure of preparing an agreeable surprise for him. He pretended not to see M. de Beausset, and beckoned Fabvier to him. Napoleon, frowning sternly, listened in silence to what Fabvier was saying of the gallantry and devotion of his army, fighting before Salamanca, at the other end of Europe; they had, he said, but one dream—to be worthy of their Emperor, and one fear—to displease him. The result of the battle had been disastrous. Napoleon made ironical remarks during Fabvier's account of it, as though he had not expected it to be otherwise in his absence.

"I must make up for it at Moscow," said Napoleon. "*A tantôt*," he added, and summoned Beausset, who had by this time succeeded in preparing his effect, had stood something on the chairs and thrown a cover over it.

Beausset made a courtier's low bow, such as only the old retainers of the Bourbons knew how to make, and approached him, handing him a letter.

Napoleon addressed him gaily and pinched him by the ear.

"You have been quick, delighted to see you. Well, what is Paris saying?" he said, his look of sternness suddenly changing to the most cordial expression.

"Sire, all Paris is regretting your absence," answered Beausset, as in duty bound. But though Napoleon knew Beausset was bound to say this or something like it, though at his lucid moments he knew it was all false, he was glad to hear this from him. He condescended to pinch his ear again.

"I am very sorry to have made you to travel so far," he said.

"Sire, I expected to find you at least at the gates of Moscow," said Beausset.

Napoleon smiled, and lifting his head absently looked round to the right. An adjutant approached obsequiously with a gold snuffbox and offered it. Napoleon took it.

"Yes, it's a happy chance for you," he said, putting the open snuffbox to his nose. "You are fond of travelling, and in three days you will see Moscow. You probably did not expect to see the Asiatic capital. You will have a delightful journey."

Beausset bowed with gratitude for this interest in his tastes for travel of which he had till that moment been unaware).

"Ah! what's this?" said Napoleon, observing that all the courtiers were gazing at something concealed under a covering. Beausset with courtier-like agility retired two steps with a half turn, not showing his back, and at the same moment twitched off the covering, saying: "A present to your majesty from the Empress."

It was a portrait, painted in brilliant colours by Gérard, of the child of Napoleon and the daughter of the Austrian Emperor, the little boy whom every one for some unknown reason called the King of Rome.

The very pretty, curly-headed child, with eyes like the Christ with the Sistine Madonna, had been portrayed playing cup and ball. The ball represented the terrestrial globe and the cup in the other hand was a sceptre.

Though it was not altogether clear what the painter had intended to express by representing the so-called King of Rome tossing the terrestrial globe on a sceptre, the allegory apparently seemed to Napoleon, as it had to every one who had seen it in Paris, quite clear and extremely pleasing.

"The King of Rome!" he said, pointing with a graceful gesture to the portrait. "Admirable!" With the characteristic Italian facility for changing his expression at will, he went up to the portrait and assumed an air of pensive tenderness. He felt that what he might say or do at that moment would be historical. And it struck him that the best line he could take at that moment, at the height of his grandeur—so great that his child was playing cup and ball with the earth—would be to display, in contrast with that grandeur, the simplest, fatherly tenderness. His eyes were veiled by emotion; he moved up, looked round for a chair (a chair seemed to spring up under him), and sat down, facing the portrait. At a single gesture from him all withdrew on tip-toe, leaving the great man to himself and his feelings. After sitting there a little while and passing his fingers, he could not have said why, over the rough surface of the painting, he got up and again sent for Beausset and the officer on duty. He gave orders for the portrait to be carried out in front of his tent, so that the Old Guard, standing about his tent, might not be deprived of the happiness of seeing the King of Rome, the son and heir of their adored Emperor.

While he sat at breakfast with M. de Beausset—whom he had honoured by an invitation to join him—he heard, as he had expected, enthusiastic shouts from the soldiers and officers of the Old Guard, who had run up to see the portrait.

"*Vive l'Empereur! Vive le roi de Rome! Vive l'Empereur!*" shouted enthusiastic voices.

After breakfast, in Beausset's presence, Napoleon dictated his proclamation to the army.

"*Courte et énergique!*" Napoleon pronounced it, when he had read over the proclamation that he had dictated straight off without corrections. It was as follows:

"Soldiers! This is the battle you have so greatly desired. Victory is in your hands. It is essential for us; it will give us everything we need: comfortable quarters and a speedy return to our own country. Behave as you behaved at Austerlitz, Friedland, Vitebsk, and Smolensk. May posterity recall with pride your achievement on this day! And may they say of each of you: he was at the great battle before Moscow!"

"Before Moscow," repeated Napoleon, and inviting M. de Beausset, so fond of travel, to accompany him on his ride, he went out of the tent to the saddled horses awaiting them outside.

"Your majesty is too kind," said Beausset, in response to the invitation to accompany the Emperor. He was very sleepy. He could not ride well, and was afraid of horses.

But Napoleon nodded to the traveller, and Beausset had to mount. When Napoleon came out of the tent the shouts of the Guards before his son's portrait were redoubled. Napoleon frowned.

"Take him away," he said, with a gracefully majestic gesture, pointing to the portrait. "It is too early yet for him to look upon the field of battle."

Beausset, dropping his eyelids, and bowing his head, heaved a deep sigh, to testify how well he was able to appreciate and comprehend the Emperor's words.

XXVII

THE whole of that day, the 25th of August, Napoleon spent, so his historians relate, on horseback, inspecting the locality, criticising the plans submitted to him by his marshals, and giving commands in person to his generals.

The original line of the Russian disposition, along the Kolotcha, had been broken through, and, in consequence of the taking of the Shevardino redoubt on the previous day, part of that line—the left flank—had been drawn further back. That part of the line had not been strengthened, was no longer protected by the river, and more open and level ground lay before it. It was obvious to any man, military or non-military, that it was that part of the line that the French should attack. One would have thought that no great deliberation would be necessary to reach this conclusion; that all the care and anxiety of the Emperor and his marshals were unnecessary, and that there was absolutely no need of that peculiar high degree of talent called genius, which they are so fond of ascribing to Napoleon. But the historians, who described the battle afterwards, and the men surrounding Napoleon at the time, and he himself, thought otherwise.

Napoleon rode about the field, gazing with a profound air at the country, wagging his head approvingly or dubiously to himself, and without communicating to the generals around him the profound chain of reasoning that guided him in his decisions, conveyed to them merely the final conclusions in the form of commands. Upon the suggestion being made by Davoust, now styled Duke of Eckmühl, for turning the

Russian left flank, Napoleon said there was no need to do this, without explaining why there was no need. But to the proposal of General Compans (who was to attack the advanced earthworks), to lead his division through the forest, Napoleon signified his assent, although the so-called Duke of Elchingen, that is, Ney, ventured to observe that to move troops through woodland is risky, and might break up the formation of the division.

After examining tne nature of the country opposite the Shevardino redoubt, Napoleon pondered a little while in silence and pointed to the spots where two batteries were to be placed by the morrow for action against the Russian fortifications, and the spots where, in a line with them, the field artillery was to be arranged.

After giving these and other commands, he went back to his quarters, and the disposition of the troops was written down from his dictation.

This disposition, of which the French speak with enthusiasm, and other historians with profound respect, consisted of the following instructions:

"Two new batteries, to be placed during the night on the plain occupied by the Duke of Eckmühl, will open fire at dawn on the two opposite batteries of the enemy.

"At the same time General Pernetti, in command of the artillery of the 1st corps, with thirty cannons of Compans's division, and all the howitzers of Desaix and Friant's division, will move forward, open fire, and shower shells on the enemy's battery, against which there will be at once in action:

24 cannons of the artillery of the Guards,
30 cannons of Compans's division, and
8 cannons of Friant and Desaix's division

—

In all 62 cannons.

"General Fouché, in command of the artillery of the 3rd corps, will place all the sixteen howitzers of the 3rd and 8th corps at the flanks of the battery, told off to bombard the left fortification, making forty guns in all aimed against it.

"General Sorbier is to be in readiness to advance on the word being given, with all the howitzers of the artillery of the Guards against either of the enemy's fortifications.

"During the cannonade Prince Poniatovsky is to advance to the village in the wood, and to turn the enemy's position.

"General Compans will cross the wood to gain possession of the first fortification.

"After the attack has begun on these lines, further commands will be given in accordance with the enemy's movements.

"The cannonade on the left flank will begin as soon as the cannons of the right wing are heard. The sharpshooters of Morand's division and of the viceroy's division will open a hot fire on seeing the beginning of the attack of the right wing.

"The viceroy will take possession of the village of Borodino, and cross

by its three bridges, advancing to the same height with Morand's and
Gérard's divisions, which under his leadership will advance to the redoubt and come into line with the other troops of the army.

"All this is to be done in good order (*le tout se fera avec ordre et
méthode*), preserving as far as possible troops in reserve.

"The imperial camp, near Mozhaisk, September 6, 1812."

These instructions—which strike one as exceedingly confused and obscure, if one ventures to throw off the superstitious awe for Napoleon's
genius in treating of his disposition of his troops—may be condensed
into four points—four commands. Not one of those instructions was or
could be carried out.

In the first place the instruction is given: *That the batteries placed on
the spot selected by Napoleon, with the cannons of Pernetti and
Fouché, which were to join them, in all one hundred and two cannons,
were to open fire and shell the Russian earthworks and redoubts.* This
could not be done, since from the spots fixed on by Napoleon the shells
did not carry so far as the Russian earthworks, and these one hundred
and two cannons fired in the air till such time as the nearest officer in
command ordered them to advance, in opposition to Napoleon's instructions.

The second instruction given is that *Poniatovsky, advancing to the
village in the wood, should turn the Russian left flank.* This was not,
and could not be done, as Poniatovsky, on advancing to the village in
the wood, found Tutchkov there barring his way, and did not, and could
not, turn the Russian position.

The third instruction is: *General Compans will move into the wood to
take possession of the first Russian fortification.* Compans's division did
not take the first fortification, but was beaten back, because, as it came
out of the wood, it had to form under a fire of grapeshot, of which Napoleon knew nothing.

The fourth instruction is: *That the viceroy will take possession of
the village (Borodino), and crossing by its three bridges, and following
to the same high ground as Morand's and Friant's divisions* (nothing is
said of whence and when they were to advance), *which under his leadership will advance to the redoubt and form in a line with the other troops.*
As far as one can make out, not so much from this confused paragraph,
as from the attempts made by the viceroy to carry out the orders given
him, he was to advance through Borodino from the left to the redoubt,
and the divisions of Morand and Friant were to advance simultaneously
from the front. All this, like the other instructions, was impossible to
carry out. After passing through Borodino the viceroy was beaten back
at the Kolotcha, and could advance no further. The divisions of Morand
and Friant did not take the redoubt, but were driven back, and at the
end of the day the redoubt was captured by cavalry (in an action probably unforeseen by Napoleon, and not heard of by him).

And not one of the instructions given was, or could be, carried into
effect. But in the disposition was the statement, that after the battle had

begun, further instructions would be given in accordance with the enemy's movements; and so it might be supposed that all necessary instructions had been given by Napoleon during the battle. But this was not, and could not be, the case, because, during the whole battle, Napoleon was so far from the scene of action that (as it turned out later) he knew nothing of the course of the battle, and not a single instruction given by him during the fight could possibly be executed.

XXVIII

MANY historians assert that the French failed at Borodino because Napoleon had a cold in his head; that if he had not had a cold the orders given by him before and during the battle would have been even more remarkable for their genius, and Russia would have been lost and the face of the world would have been changed. To historians, who can maintain that Russia was transformed at the will of one man—Peter the Great—and that France, from a republic, became an empire, and that the French army marched into Russia at the will of one man—Napoleon —the conclusion that Russia has remained a power because Napoleon had a bad cold on the 26th of August may seem indisputable and convincing. Had it depended on Napoleon's will to fight, or not to fight, at Borodino, or had it depended on his will whether he gave this order or that, it is evident that a cold, affecting the manifestation of his will, might be the saving of Russia, and consequently the valet, who forgot to put on Napoleon's waterproof boots on the 24th, would be the saviour of Russia. On that method of reasoning such a deduction is inevitable; as inevitable as the contention which Voltaire maintains in jest (unconscious what he was ridiculing) that the Massacre of St. Bartholomew was due to an attack of dyspepsia from which Charles IX. was suffering. But for minds that cannot admit that Russia was transformed at the will of one man—Peter the Great—and the French empire was created, and the war with Russia begun, at the will of one man—Napoleon—such a contention will seem not merely unsound and irrational, but contrary to the whole nature of humanity. The question, What constitutes the cause of historical events? will suggest to them another answer, resting on the idea that the course of earthly events is predestined from on high, depends on the combination of all the wills of the men taking part in those events, and that the predominant influence of Napoleon in those events is purely external and fictitious.

Strange at first sight as appears the proposition that the Massacre of St. Bartholomew, the order for which was given by Charles IX., was not the result of his will, and that it was only in his fancy that the command he had given was the cause of it, and that the Borodino slaughter of eighty thousand men was not due to Napoleon's will (though he gave the order for the commencement of the battle), and that it was only his fancy that it was his doing, strange as this proposition appears, yet human dignity, that tells us that every one of us is neither more nor less a man than Napoleon, bids us admit that solution of the question, and historical researches abundantly confirm the proposition.

At the battle of Borodino Napoleon did not fire at any one, nor kill any one. All that was done by his soldiers. Therefore it was not he who killed those men. The soldiers of the French army went out to slay their fellow-men at Borodino, not owing to Napoleon's commands, but through their own desire to do so. The whole army—French, Italians, Germans, Poles—hungry, ragged, and exhausted by the march, felt at the sight of an army, barring their way to Moscow: the wine is drawn, it must be drunk. Had Napoleon forbidden them at that point to fight the Russians, they would have killed him, and have proceeded to fight the Russians, because it was inevitable for them.

When they heard Napoleon's proclamation, offering them as consolation for maiming and death the reminder that posterity would say that they had been at the battle before Moscow, they shouted, *"Vive l'Empereur,"* just as they shouted *"Vive l'Empereur"* at the sight of the picture of the little boy playing cup and ball with the earth, and just as they shouted *"Vive l'Empereur"* at every absurdity that was said. There was nothing left for them to do but to shout *"Vive l'Empereur!"* and to fight so as to get food and rest as conquerors in Moscow. Therefore it was not owing to Napoleon's commands that they killed their fellow-men.

And it was not Napoleon who ordained the course of the battle, because none of his instructions were put into execution, and he knew nothing of what was passing before him. Therefore the manner in which these men slaughtered one another did not depend on Napoleon's will, but proceeded independently of him, from the wills of the hundreds of thousands of men who took part in the affair. It *only seemed* to Napoleon that all this was due to his will. And therefore the question whether Napoleon had or had not a cold in his head is of no more interest to history than the cold of the lowest soldier of the commissariat.

The contention of some writers, that Napoleon's cold was the reason of his previous instructions and commands during the battle being weaker than usual, is completely groundless.

The instructions that have been reproduced here are by no means inferior, are indeed superior, to many similar arrangements by which he had gained victories in the past. His supposed instructions during the day were also in no way inferior to the commands he had given in previous battles, but were much the same as usual. But these instructions are supposed to be inferior, simply because Borodino was the first battle in which Napoleon was not victorious. The finest and profoundest combinations seem very poor, and every military student can criticise them with a consequential air, when the battle has not been won by means of them; and the stupidest combinations will seem exceedingly ingenious, and serious writers will fill volumes in proving their excellence, when the battle that followed chances to have been a victory.

The plan composed by Weierother at Austerlitz was a model of perfection in its own line, but it has yet been condemned, and condemned for its very perfection, for its over-minuteness in detail.

At Borodino Napoleon played his part as the representative of supreme power as well, or even better, than he had done at previous battles. He did nothing likely to hinder the progress of the battle; he yielded to the most sensible advice; he was not confused, did not contradict himself, did not lose his presence of mind, nor run away from the field of battle, but with his great tact and military experience, he performed calmly and with dignity his rôle of appearing to be in supreme control of it all.

XXIX

ON returning from a second careful inspection of the lines, Napoleon said.

"The pieces are on the board, the game will begin to-morrow."

He ordered some punch, and sending for Beausset began talking of Paris with him, discussing various changes he intended to make in the Empress's household, and surprising the prefect by his memory of the minutest details of court affairs.

He showed interest in trifles, jested at Beausset's love of travel, and chatted carelessly, as some renowned, skilful and confident surgeon will often chat playfully while he tucks up his sleeves and puts on his apron, and the patient is being bound down on the operating-table. "I have the whole business at my finger-tips, and it's all clear and definite in my head. When I have to set to work, I will do it as no one else could, but now I can jest, and the more serenely I jest the more calm and confidence and admiration for my genius you ought to feel."

After emptying a second glass of punch, Napoleon went to seek repose before the grave business which, as he imagined, lay before him next day.

He was so preoccupied with what lay before him that he could not sleep, and in spite of his cold, which got worse with the damp of evening, he got up at three o'clock, went out into the principal compartment of the tent, sneezing violently. He asked whether the Russians had not retreated. He was told that the enemy's fires were still in the same places. He nodded approval.

The adjutant on duty came into the tent.

"Well, Rapp, do you think we shall do good business to-day?" he said to him.

"Without doubt, sire!" answered Rapp.

Napoleon looked at him.

"Do you remember what you did me the honour to say at Smolensk?" said Rapp: "the wine is drawn, it must be drunk."

Napoleon frowned, and sat for a long while in silence, his head in his hand.

"This poor army, it has greatly diminished since Smolensk. *La fortune est une franche courtisane,* Rapp. I have always said so, and I begin to feel it; but the Guard, Rapp, the Guard is intact?" he said inquiringly.

"Yes, sire," replied Rapp.

Napoleon took a lozenge, put it in his mouth, and looked at his watch. He was not sleepy, and morning was still far off; and there were no instructions to be drawn up to get through the time, for all had been already given, and were even now being put into execution.

"Have the biscuits and the rice been distributed to the regiments of the Guard?" Napoleon asked severely.

"Yes, sire."

"The rice, too?"

Rapp answered that he had given the Emperor's orders about the rice; but Napoleon shook his head with a dissatisfied air, as though he doubted whether his command had been carried out. A servant came in with punch. Napoleon ordered another glass for Rapp, and took a few sips from his own in silence. "I have neither taste nor smell," he said, sniffing at the glass. "I am sick of this cold. They talk about medicine. What is medicine, when they can't cure a cold? Corvisart gave me these lozenges, but they do no good. What can they cure? They can't cure anything. Our body is a machine for living. It is organised for that, it is its nature; leave life to it unhindered, let life defend itself in it; it will do more than if you paralyse it, encumbering it with remedies. Our body is a perfect watch, meant to go for a certain time; the watchmaker has not the power of opening it, he can only handle it in fumbling fashion, blindfold. Our body is a machine for living, that's all." And apparently because he had dropped into making definitions, which he had a weakness for doing, he suddenly hazarded one on a fresh subject. "Do you know, Rapp, what the military art consists in?" he asked. "It is the art of being stronger than the enemy at a given moment. That is all."

Rapp made no reply.

"To-morrow we shall have to do with Kutuzov," said Napoleon. "We shall see! Do you remember, he was in command at Braunau, and never once in three weeks mounted a horse to inspect his entrenchments. We shall see!"

He looked at his watch. It was still only four o'clock. He was not sleepy; the punch was finished, and there was still nothing to do. He got up, walked up and down, put on a warm coat and hat and went out of the tent. The night was dark and damp; a slight drizzle was falling almost inaudibly. Close by in the French Guard, the camp-fires burned dimly, and far away they were blazing brightly through the smoke along the Russian line. The air was still, and a faint stir and tramp could be distinctly heard from the French troops beginning to move to occupy the position.

Napoleon walked to and fro before the tent, looked at the fires, listened to the tramp, and passed by a tall guardsman in a fur cap, a sentinel at his tent, who drew himself up like a black post on seeing the Emperor. The latter stood still, facing him.

"Since what year have you served?" he asked, with that affectation of military bluntness and geniality with which he always addressed the soldiers. The soldier answered.

"Ah! one of the veterans! Have you all had rice in the regiment?"

"Yes, your majesty."

Napoleon nodded and walked away.

At half-past five Napoleon rode to the village of Shevardino.

It began to get light; the sky cleared, only a single storm cloud lay on the eastern horizon. The deserted camp-fires burned down in the pale light of morning.

A solitary, deep cannon shot boomed out on the right, hovered in the air, and died away in the stillness. Several minutes passed. A second, and a third shot was heard, the air was full of vibration; a fourth and a fifth boomed out majestically, closely on the right.

The first shots had not died away, when others rang out, and more and more, their notes blending and overtaking one another.

Napoleon rode with his suite to the Shevardino redoubt, and dismounted there. The game had begun.

XXX

PIERRE, on returning to Gorky from seeing Prince Andrey, gave directions to his postillion to have horses ready and to call him early next morning, and promptly fell fast asleep in the corner behind a screen which Boris had put at his disposal.

When Pierre was fully awake next morning, there was no one in the hut. The panes were rattling in the little windows. The postillion was at his side, shaking him. "Your excellency, your excellency, your excellency . . ." the groom kept saying persistently, shaking him by the shoulder, without even looking at him, apparently having lost all hope of ever waking him up.

"Eh, has it begun? Is it time?" said Pierre, waking up.

"Listen to the firing, your excellency," said the postillion, an old soldier; "all the gentlemen are gone already; his highness set off long ago."

Pierre dressed in haste, and ran out into the porch. It was a bright, fresh, dewy, cheerful morning. The sun had just broken through the cloud that had screened it, and its rays filtered through the rent clouds, and over the roofs of the street opposite on to the dew-drenched dust of the road, on to the fences and the windows of the houses, and Pierre's horses standing by the cottage. The roar of the cannon could be heard more distinctly in the open air. An adjutant galloped down the street, followed by a Cossack.

"It's time, count, it's time!" cried the adjutant. Pierre gave orders that he should be followed with a horse, and walked along the street to the knoll from which he had viewed the field of battle the day before. On this knoll was a crowd of officers, and Pierre heard the French chatter of the staff, and saw Kutuzov's grey head sunk in his shoulders, and his white cap, with red braiding on it. Kutuzov was looking through a field-glass along the high-road before him.

Mounting the steps of the approach to the mound, Pierre glanced before him, and felt a thrill of delight at the beauty of the spectacle. It was the same scene that he had admired from that mound the day before. But now the whole panorama was filled with troops and the smoke of the guns, and in the pure morning air the slanting rays of the sun, behind Pierre on the left, shed on it a brilliant light full of gold and pink tones, and broken up by long, dark shadows. The distant forests that bounded the scene lay in a crescent on the horizon, looking as though carved out of some precious yellow-green stone, and through their midst behind Valuev ran the great Smolensk road, all covered with troops. In the foreground lay golden fields and copses glittering in the sun. Everywhere, to right, to left, and in front were soldiers. The whole scene was inspiriting, impressive, and unexpected; but what struck Pierre most of all was the aspect of the field of battle itself, of Borodino, and the hollow on both sides of the Kolotcha.

About the Kolotcha, in Borodino, and both sides of it, especially to the left where the Voina runs through swampy ground into the Kolotcha, a mist still hung over the scene, melting, parting, shimmering with light in the bright sunshine, and giving fairy-like beauty to the shapes seen through it. The smoke of the guns mingled with this mist, and everywhere gleams of sunlight sparkled in it from the water, from the dew, from the bayonets of the soldiers crowding on the river banks and in Borodino. Through this mist could be seen a white church, here and there roofs of cottages in Borodino, and fitful glimpses came of compact masses of soldiers, and green ammunition-boxes and cannons. And the whole scene moved, or seemed to move, as the mist and smoke trailed over the wide plain. In this low ground about Borodino in the mist, and above it, and especially along the whole line to the left, in the copses, in the meadows below, and on the tops of the heights, clouds of smoke were incessantly springing out of nothing, now singly, now several at once, then at longer intervals, then in rapid succession. These clouds of smoke, puffing, rolling, melting into one another, and sundering apart, trailed all across the wide plain. These puffs of smoke, and the reports that followed them, were, strange to say, what gave the chief charm to the scene.

"*Poooff!*" suddenly there flew up a round, compact ball of smoke, with shades of purple, grey, and milk-white in it, and "*booom!*" followed the roar of the cannon a minute later.

"*Pooff-pooff!*" two clouds of smoke rose, meeting and mingling into one; and "*boom-boom*," the sound repeated what the eye had seen.

Pierre looked round at the first puff of smoke, which he had seen a second before a round, compact ball, and already in its place were wreaths of smoke trailing away to one side, and "*pooff*" . . . (then a pause) "*pooff-pooff*"—three more flew up, and another four at once, and at the same intervals after each other "*boom . . . boom-boom-boom*," rang out the sonorous, resolute, unfailing sounds. At one moment it seemed that those clouds of smoke were scudding across the plain, at the next, that they were stationary, and the copses, fields, and glittering bayonets were flying by them. From the left side these great clouds of smoke were incessantly flying over the fields and bushes, with the stately roar resounding after each of them. Still nearer, in the low meadows and copses, there darted up from the musket-fire tiny puffs that hardly formed into balls of smoke, and each of these, too, had its tiny report echoing after it. Tra-ta-ta-ta sounded the crack of the muskets at frequent intervals, but thin and irregular in comparison with the rhythmic roar of the cannon.

Pierre longed to be there in the midst of the smoke, the glittering bayonets, the movement, and the noise. He looked round at Kutuzov and his suite to compare his own impression with that of others. All like him were looking before them at the field, and, he fancied, with the same feeling. Every face now was lighted up by that *latent heat* of feeling that Pierre had noticed the day before, and understood perfectly after his talk with Prince Andrey.

"Go, my dear fellow, go, and Christ be with you!" said Kutuzov, never taking his eyes off the field of battle, to a general standing beside him. The general, who received this order, ran by Pierre down the descent from the mound.

"To ride across! . . ." the general said coldly and severely, in answer to a question from one of the staff.

"And I too, I too," thought Pierre, and he went in the same direction.

The general mounted a horse, led up to him by a Cossack. Pierre went up to the groom, who was holding his horses. Asking him which was the quietest, Pierre got on it, clutched at the horse's mane, pressed his heels into the beast's stomach, and feeling that his spectacles were slipping off, and that he was incapable of letting go of the mane and the reins, he galloped after the general, followed by smiles from the staff officers staring at him from the mound.

XXXI

The general after whom Pierre galloped trotted downhill, turned off sharply to the left, and Pierre, losing sight of him, galloped into the middle of a battalion of infantry marching ahead of him. He tried to get away from them, turning to left and to right; but there were soldiers everywhere, all with the same anxious faces, preoccupied with some unseen, but evidently serious, business. They all looked with the same expression of annoyed inquiry at the stout man in the white hat, who was, for some unknown reason, trampling them under his horse's feet.

"What does he want to ride into the middle of a battalion for?" one man shouted at him. Another gave his horse a shove with the butt-end of his gun; and Pierre, leaning over on the saddle-bow, and scarcely able to hold in his rearing horse, galloped out to where there was open space in front of the soldiers.

Ahead of him he saw a bridge, and at the bridge stood the soldiers firing. Pierre rode towards them. Though he did not know it, he rode up to the bridge over the Kolotcha, between Gorky and Borodino, which was attacked by the French in one of the first actions. Pierre saw there was a bridge in front of him, and that the soldiers were doing something in the smoke on both sides of the bridge, and in the meadow among the new-mown hay he had noticed the day before. But in spite of the unceasing fire going on there, he had no notion that this was the very centre of the battle. He did not notice the bullets whizzing on all sides, and the shells flying over him; he did not see the enemy on the other side of the river, and it was a long time before he saw the killed and wounded, though many fell close to him. He gazed about him with a smile still on his face.

"What's that fellow doing in front of the line?" some one shouted at him again.

"To the left," "to the right," men shouted to him. Pierre turned to the right, and unwittingly rode up to an adjutant of General Raevsky's, with whom he was acquainted. The adjutant glanced wrathfully at Pierre; and he, too, was apparently about to shout at him, but recognising him, he nodded.

"How did you come here?" he said, and galloped on. Pierre, feeling out of place and of no use, and afraid of getting in some one's way again, galloped after him.

"What is it, here? Can I go with you?" he asked.

"In a minute, in a minute," answered the adjutant, and galloping up to a stout colonel in the meadow, he gave him some message, and then addressed Pierre. "What has brought you here, count?" he said to him, with a smile. "Are you still curious?"

"Yes, yes," said Pierre. But the adjutant, turning his horse's head, rode on further.

"Here it's all right," said the adjutant; "but on the left flank, in Bagration's division, it's fearfully hot."

"Really?" said Pierre. "Where's that?"

"Why, come along with me to the mound; we can get a view from there. But it's still bearable at our battery," said the adjutant. "Are you coming?"

"Yes, yes, I'll go with you," said Pierre, looking about him, trying to see his groom. It was only then for the first time that Pierre saw wounded men, staggering along and some borne on stretchers. In the meadow with the rows of sweet-scented hay, through which he had ridden the day before, there lay motionless across the rows one soldier with his shako off, and his head thrown awkwardly back. "And why haven't they taken that one?" Pierre was beginning, but seeing the adjutant's set face looking in the same direction, he was silent.

Pierre did not succeed in finding his groom, and rode along the hollow with the adjutant towards Raevsky's redoubt. His horse dropped behind the adjutant's, and jolted him at regular intervals.

"You are not used to riding, count, I fancy?" asked the adjutant.

"Oh no, it's all right; but it does seem to be hopping along somehow," said Pierre, with a puzzled look.

"Ay! . . . but he's wounded," said the adjutant, "the right fore-leg above the knee. A bullet, it must have been. I congratulate you, count," he said, "you have had your baptism of fire now."

After passing in the smoke through the sixth corps behind the artillery, which had been moved forward and was keeping up a deafening cannonade, they rode into a small copse. There it was cool and still and full of the scents of autumn. Pierre and the adjutant got off their horses and walked on foot up the hill.

"Is the general here?" asked the adjutant on reaching the redoubt.

"He was here just now; he went this way," some one answered, pointing to the right.

The adjutant looked round at Pierre, as though he did not know what to do with him.

"Don't trouble about me," said Pierre. "I'll go up on to the mound; may I?"

"Yes, do; you can see everything from there, and it's not so dangerous, and I will come to fetch you."

Pierre went up to the battery, and the adjutant rode away. They did not see each other again, and only much later Pierre learned that that adjutant had lost an arm on that day.

The mound—afterwards known among the Russians as the battery mound, or Raevsky's battery, and among the French as "the great redoubt," "fatal redoubt," and "central redoubt"—was the celebrated spot at which tens of thousands of men were killed, and upon which the French looked as the key of the position.

The redoubt consisted of a mound, with trenches dug out on three sides of it. In the entrenchments stood ten cannons, firing through the gaps left in the earthworks.

In a line with the redoubt on both sides stood cannons, and these too kept up an incessant fire. A little behind the line of cannons were troops of infantry. When Pierre ascended this mound, he had no notion that this place, encircled by small trenches and protected by a few cannons, was the most important spot in the field.

He fancied, indeed (simply because he happened to be there), that it was a place of no importance whatever.

Pierre sat down on the end of the earthwork surrounding the battery and gazed at what was passing around him with an unconscious smile of pleasure. At intervals Pierre got up, and with the same smile on his face walked about the battery, trying not to get in the way of the soldiers, who were loading and discharging the cannons and were continually running by him with bags and ammunition. The cannons were firing continually, one after another, with deafening uproar, enveloping all the country round in clouds of smoke.

In contrast to the painful look of dread in the infantry soldiers who were guarding the battery, here in the battery itself, where a limited number of men were busily engaged in their work, and shut off from the rest of the trench, there was a general feeling of eager excitement, a sort of family feeling shared by all alike.

The appearance of Pierre's unmartial figure and his white hat at first impressed this little group unfavourably. The soldiers cast sidelong glances of surprise and even alarm at him, as they ran by. The senior artillery officer, a tall, long-legged, pock-marked man, approached Pierre, as though he wanted to examine the action of the cannon at the end, and stared inquisitively at him.

A boyish, round-faced, little officer, quite a child, evidently only just out of the cadets' school, and very conscientious in looking after the two cannons put in his charge, addressed Pierre severely.

"Permit me to ask you to move out of the way, sir," he said. "You can't stay here."

The soldiers shook their heads disapprovingly as they looked at Pierre. But as the conviction gained ground among them that the man in the white hat was doing no harm, and either sat quietly on the slope of the earthwork, or, making way with a shy and courteous smile for the soldiers to pass, walked about the battery under fire as calmly as though he were strolling on a boulevard, their feeling of suspicious ill-will began to give way to a playful and kindly cordiality akin to the feeling soldiers always have for the dogs, cocks, goats, and other animals who share the fortunes of the regiment. The soldiers soon accepted Pierre in their own minds as one of their little circle, made him one of themselves, and gave him a name: "our gentleman" they called him, and laughed good-humouredly about him among themselves.

A cannon ball tore up the earth a couple of paces from Pierre. Brushing the earth off his clothes, he looked about him with a smile.

"And how is it you're not afraid, sir, upon my word?" said a broad, red-faced soldier, showing his strong, white teeth in a grin.

"Why, are you afraid then?" asked Pierre.

"Why, to be sure!" answered the soldier. "Why, she has no mercy on you. She smashes into you, and your guts are sent flying. Nobody could help being afraid," he said laughing.

Several soldiers stood still near Pierre with amused and kindly faces. They seemed not to expect him to talk like any one else, and his doing so delighted them.

"It's our business—we're soldiers. But for a gentleman—it's surprising. It's queer in a gentleman!"

"To your places!" cried the little officer-boy to the soldiers, who had gathered round Pierre. It was evidently the first, or at most, the second time, this lad had been on duty as an officer, and so he behaved with the utmost punctiliousness and formality both to the soldiers and his superior officer.

The roar of cannon and the rattle of musketry were growing louder all over the field, especially on the left, where Bagration's earthworks were, but from where Pierre was, hardly anything could be seen for the smoke. Moreover, watching the little fraternal group of men, shut off from all the world on the battery, engrossed all Pierre's attention. His first unconscious delight in the sights and sounds of the battlefield had given way to another feeling, ever since he had seen the solitary dead soldier lying on the hayfield. Sitting now on the slope of the earthwork, he watched the figures moving about him.

By ten o'clock some twenty men had been carried away from the battery; two cannons had been disabled, and more and more frequently shells fell on the battery, and cannon balls came with a hiss and whir, flying out of the distance. But the men on the battery did not seem to notice this: merry chatter and jokes were to be heard on all sides.

"Not this way, my pretty," shouted a soldier to a grenade that came whistling towards them.

"Give the infantry a turn!" another added with a chuckle, as the grenade flew across and fell among the ranks of the infantry.

"What, see a friend coming, do you?" another soldier jeered at a peasant, who had ducked low at the sight of a flying cannon ball.

Several soldiers gathered together at the earthwork, looking at what was being done in front.

"And they've taken the outposts, see, they're retreating," they said, pointing over the earthwork.

"Mind your own business," the old sergeant shouted to them. "If they have come back, it's because they have something to do further back." And the sergeant, taking one of the soldiers by the shoulder, gave him a shove with his knee. There was the sound of laughter.

"Fifth cannon, roll away!" they were shouting on one side.

"Now then, a good pull, all together!" shouted the merry voices of the men charging the cannon.

"Ay, she almost snatched 'our gentleman's' hat off," the red-faced, jocose soldier laughed, showing his teeth. "Hey, awkward hussy!" he added reproachfully to a cannon ball that hit a wheel and a man's leg. "Now, you foxes there!" laughed another, addressing the peasant militiamen, who were creeping in and out among the guns after the wounded. "Don't you care for our porridge, hey? Ah, the crows! that pulls them up!" they shouted at the militiamen, who hesitated at the sight of the soldier whose leg had been torn off. "Oo . . . oo . . . lad," they cried, mimicking the peasants, "we don't like it at all, we don't!"

Pierre noticed that after every ball that fell in their midst, after every loss, the general elation became more and more marked.

The closer the storm cloud swooped down upon them, the more bright and frequent were the gleams of latent fire that glowed like lightning flashes on those men's faces, called up, as it were, to meet and resist their danger.

Pierre did not look in front at the field of battle; he took no more interest in what was going on there. He was entirely engrossed in the contemplation of that growing fire, which he felt was burning in his own soul too.

At ten o'clock the infantry, who had been in advance of the battery, in the bushes and about the stream Kamenka, retreated. From the battery they could see them running back past them, bearing their wounded on their guns. A general with a suite came on to the redoubt, and after talking to the colonel and looking angrily at Pierre, went away again, ordering the infantry standing behind the battery guarding it to lie down, so as to be less exposed to fire. After that a drum was heard in the ranks of the infantry, more to the right of the battery, and shouts gave the word of command, and from the battery they could see the ranks of infantry moving forward.

Pierre looked over the earthwork. One figure particularly caught his eye. It was the officer, walking backwards with a pale, boyish face. He held his sword downwards and kept looking uneasily round.

The rows of infantry soldiers vanished into the smoke, but they could hear a prolonged shout from them and a rapid musketry fire. A few minutes later crowds of wounded men and a number of stretchers came back from that direction. Shells fell more and more often in the battery. Several men lay on the ground, not picked up. The soldiers bustled more busily and briskly than ever about the cannons. No one took any notice of Pierre now. Twice he was shouted at angrily for being in the way. The senior officers strode rapidly from one cannon to another with a frowning face. The officer-boy, his cheeks even more crimson, gave the soldiers their orders more scrupulously than ever. The soldiers served out the charges, turned round, loaded, and did all their work with exaggerated smartness. They moved as though worked by springs.

The storm cloud was swooping closer; and more brightly than ever glowed in every face that fire which Pierre was watching. He was standing near the senior officer. The little officer-boy ran up, his hand to his shako, saluting his superior officer.

"I have the honour to inform you, colonel, only eight charges are left; do you command to continue firing?" he asked.

"Grapeshot!" the senior officer shouted, looking away over the earthwork.

Suddenly something happened; the boy-officer groaned, and whirling round sat down on the ground, like a bird shot on the wing. All seemed strange, indistinct, and darkened before Pierre's eyes.

One after another the cannon balls came whistling, striking the breastwork, the soldiers, the cannons. Pierre, who had scarcely heard those sounds before, now could hear nothing else. On the right side of the battery, soldiers, with shouts of "hurrah," were running, not forward, it seemed to Pierre, but back.

A cannon ball struck the very edge of the earthwork, before which Pierre was sitting, and sent the earth flying; a dark, round mass flashed just before his eyes, and at the same instant flew with a thud into something. The militiamen, who had been coming into the battery, ran back.

"All with grapeshot!" shouted the officer.

The sergeant ran up to the officer, and in a frightened whisper (just as at a dinner the butler will sometimes tell the host that there is no more of some wine asked for) said that there were no more charges.

"The scoundrels, what are they about?" shouted the officer, turning to Pierre. The senior officer's face was red and perspiring, his piercing eyes glittered. "Run to the reserves, bring the ammunition-boxes!" he shouted angrily, avoiding Pierre with his eyes, and addressing the soldier.

"I'll go," said Pierre. The officer, making no reply, strode across to the other side.

"Cease firing . . . Wait!" he shouted.

The soldier who had been commanded to go for the ammunition ran against Pierre.

"Ah, sir, it's no place for you here," he said, as he ran away.

Pierre ran after the soldier, avoiding the spot where the boy-officer was sitting.

One cannon ball, a second and a third flew over him, hitting the ground in front, on each side, behind Pierre as he ran down. "Where am I going?" he suddenly wondered, just as he ran up to the green ammunition-boxes. He stopped short in uncertainty whether to go back or forward. Suddenly a fearful shock sent him flying backwards on to the ground. At the same instant a flash of flame dazed his eyes, and a roar, a hiss, and a crash set his ears ringing.

When he recovered his senses, Pierre found himself sitting on the ground leaning on his hands. The ammunition-box, near which he had been, had gone; there were a few charred green boards and rags lying scattered about on the scorched grass. A horse was galloping away with broken fragments of the shafts clattering after it; while another horse lay, like Pierre, on the ground, uttering a prolonged, piercing scream.

XXXII

Pierre, beside himself with terror, jumped up and ran back to the battery as the one refuge from the horrors encompassing him.

Just as Pierre ran up to the redoubt, he noticed that there was no sound of firing from the battery, but that there were men there doing something or other. He had not time to make out what men they were. He caught sight of the senior officer lying with his back towards him on the earth wall, as though gazing intently at something below; and he noticed one soldier, who, tearing himself away from the men who were holding him, shouted "Mates!" and he saw something else that was strange.

But before he had time to grasp that the colonel had been killed, that the soldier shouting "Mates!" was a prisoner, another soldier was stabbed in the back by a bayonet before his eyes. He had hardly run up into the redoubt when a thin man with a yellow, perspiring face, in a blue uniform, ran up to him with a sword in his hand, shouting something. Pierre, instinctively defending himself, as they came full tilt against each other, put out his hands and clutched the man (it was a French officer) by the shoulder and the throat. The officer, dropping his sword, seized Pierre by the collar.

For several seconds both gazed with frightened eyes at each other's unfamiliar-looking faces, and both were bewildered, not knowing what they were doing or what they were to do. "Am I taken prisoner or am I taking him prisoner?" each of them was wondering. But the French officer was undoubtedly more disposed to believe he was taken prisoner, because Pierre's powerful hand, moved by instinctive terror, was tightening its grip on his throat. The Frenchman tried to speak, when suddenly a cannon ball flew with a fearful whiz close over their heads, and it seemed to Pierre that the Frenchman's head had been carried off by it, so swiftly had he ducked it.

Pierre, too, ducked and let go with his hands. Giving no more thought to the question which was taken prisoner, the Frenchman ran back to the battery, while Pierre dashed downhill, stumbling over the dead and wounded, who seemed to him to be clutching at his feet.

But before he had reached the bottom he was met by dense crowds of Russian soldiers, who, stumbling against each other and tripping up, were running in wild merriment towards the battery. (This was the attack of which Yermolov claimed the credit, declaring that it was only his valour and good luck that made this feat of arms possible; it was the attack in which he is supposed to have strewn the redoubt with the St. George's crosses that were in his pocket.)

The French, who had captured the battery, fled. Our soldiers pursued them so far beyond the battery that they were with difficulty stopped. They were bringing the prisoners down from the battery, among them a wounded French general, surrounded by officers. Crowds of wounded, both French and Russians—among them men Pierre recognised—walked, or crawled, or were borne on stretchers from the battery, their faces distorted by suffering.

Pierre went up into the battery, where he had spent over an hour; and found no one left of that little fraternal group that had accepted him as one of themselves. There were many dead there, whom he had not seen before. But several he recognised. The boy-officer was still sitting huddled up in a pool of blood at the edge of the earth wall. The red-faced, merry soldier was still twitching convulsively; but they did not carry him away.

Pierre ran down the slope.

"Oh, now they will stop it, now they will be horrified at what they have done!" thought Pierre, aimlessly following the crowds of stretchers moving off the battlefield.

But the sun still stood high behind the veil of smoke, and in front, and even more so to the left, about Semyonovskoye, there was still a turmoil seething in the smoke; and the roar of cannon and musketry, far from slackening, grew louder and more desperate, like a man putting all his force into one deafening outcry as a last despairing effort.

XXXIII

THE chief action of the battle of Borodino was fought on the space seven thousand feet in width between Borodino and Bagration's flèches. Outside that region, on one side there was the action on the part of Uvarov's cavalry in the middle of the day; on the other side, behind Utitsa, there was the skirmish between Poniatovsky and Tutchkov; but those two actions were detached and of little importance in comparison with what took place in the centre of the battlefield. The chief action of the day was fought in the simplest and the most artless fashion on the open space, visible from both sides, between Borodino and the flèches by the copse.

The battle began with a cannonade from several hundreds of guns on both sides. Then, when the whole plain was covered with smoke, on the French side the two divisions of Desaix and Compans advanced on the right upon the flèches, and on the left the viceroy's regiments advanced upon Borodino. The flèches were a verst from the Shevardino redoubt, where Napoleon was standing; but Borodino was more than two versts further, in a straight line, and therefore Napoleon could not see what was passing there, especially as the smoke, mingling with the fog, completely hid the whole of that part of the plain. The soldiers of Desaix's division, advancing upon the flèches, were in sight till they disappeared from view in the hollow that lay between them and the flèches. As soon as they dropped down into the hollow, the smoke of the cannon and muskets on the flèches became so thick that it concealed the whole slope of that side of the hollow. Through the smoke could be caught glimpses of something black, probably men, and sometimes the gleam of bayonets. But whether they were stationary or moving, whether they were French or Russian, could not be seen from Shevardino.

The sun had risen brightly, and its slanting rays shone straight in Napoleon's face as he looked from under his hand towards the flèches. The smoke hung over the flèches, and at one moment it seemed as though it were the smoke that was moving, at the next, the troops moving in the smoke. Sometimes cries could be heard through the firing; but it was impossible to tell what was being done there.

Napoleon, standing on the redoubt, was looking through a field-glass, and in the tiny circle of the glass saw smoke and men, sometimes his own, sometimes Russians. But where what he had seen was, he could not tell when he looked again with the naked eye.

He came down from the redoubt, and began walking up and down before it.

At intervals he stood still, listening to the firing and looking intently at the battlefield.

It was not simply impossible from below, where he was standing, and from the redoubt above, where several of his generals were standing, to make out what was passing at the flèches; but on the flèches themselves, occupied now together, now alternately by French and Russians, living, dead, and wounded, the frightened and frantic soldiers had no idea what they were doing. For several hours together, in the midst of incessant cannon and musket fire, Russians and French, infantry and cavalry, had captured the place in turn; they rushed upon it, fell, fired, came into collision, did not know what to do with each other, screamed, and ran back again.

From the battlefield adjutants were continually galloping up to Napoleon with reports from his marshals of the progress of the action. But all those reports were deceptive; both because in the heat of battle it is impossible to say what is happening at any given moment, and because many of the adjutants never reached the actual battlefield, but simply repeated what they heard from others, and also because, while the adjutant was galloping the two or three versts to Napoleon, circumstances had changed, and the news he brought had already become untrue. Thus an adjutant came galloping from the viceroy with the news that Borodino had been taken and the bridge on the Kolotcha was in the hands of the French. The adjutant asked Napoleon should the troops cross the bridge. Napoleon's command was to form on the further side and wait; but long before he gave that command, when the adjutant indeed only just started from Borodino, the bridge had been broken down and burnt by the Russians in the very skirmish Pierre had taken part in at the beginning of the day.

An adjutant, galloping up from the flèches with a pale and frightened face, brought Napoleon word that the attack had been repulsed, and Compans wounded and Davoust killed; while meantime the flèches had been captured by another division of the troops, and Davoust was alive and well, except for a slight bruise. Upon such inevitably misleading reports Napoleon based his instructions, which had mostly been carried out before he made them, or else were never, and could never, be carried out at all.

The marshals and generals who were closer to the scene of action, but, like Napoleon, not actually taking part in it, and only at intervals riding within bullet range, made their plans without asking Napoleon, and gave their orders from where and in what direction to fire, and where the cavalry were to gallop and the infantry to run. But even their orders, like Napoleon's, were but rarely, and to a slight extent, carried out.

For the most part what happened was the opposite of what they commanded to be done. The soldiers ordered to advance found themselves under grapeshot fire, and ran back. The soldiers commanded to stand still in one place seeing the Russians appear suddenly before them, either ran away or rushed upon them; and the cavalry unbidden galloped in after the flying Russians. In this way two cavalry regiments galloped across the Semyonovskoye hollow, and as soon as they reached the top of the hill, turned and galloped headlong back again. The infantry, in the same way, moved sometimes in the direction opposite to that in which they were commanded to move.

All decisions as to when and where to move the cannons, when to send infantry to fire, when to send cavalry to trample down the Russian infantry—all such decisions were made by the nearest officers in the ranks, without any reference to Ney, Davoust, and Murat, far less to Napoleon himself. They did not dread getting into trouble for nonfulfilment of orders, nor for assuming responsibility, because in battle what is at stake is what is most precious to every man—his own life; and at one time it

seems as though safety is to be found in flying back, sometimes in flying
forward; and these men placed in the very thick of the fray acted in
accordance with the temper of the moment.

In reality all these movements forward and back again hardly improved or affected the position of the troops. All their onslaughts on one
another did little harm; the harm, the death and disablement was the
work of the cannon balls and bullets, that were flying all about the open
space, where those men ran to and fro. As soon as they got out of that
exposed space, over which the balls and bullets were flying, their superior officer promptly formed them in good order, and restored discipline,
and under the influence of that discipline led them back under fire again;
and there again, under the influence of the terror of death, they lost all
discipline, and dashed to and fro at the chance promptings of the crowd.

XXXIV

NAPOLEON's generals, Davoust, Ney, and Murat, who were close to that
region of fire, and sometimes even rode into it, several times led immense masses of orderly troops into that region. But instead of what had
invariably happened in all their previous battles, instead of hearing that
the enemy were in flight, the disciplined masses of troops came back in
undisciplined, panic-stricken crowds. They formed them in good order
again, but their number was steadily dwindling. In the middle of the day
Murat sent his adjutant to Napoleon with a request for reinforcements.

Napoleon was sitting under the redoubt, drinking punch, when
Murat's adjutant galloped to him with the message that the Russians
would be routed if his majesty would let them have another division.

"Reinforcements?" said Napoleon, with stern astonishment, staring,
as though failing to comprehend his words, at the handsome, boyish
adjutant, who wore his black hair in floating curls, like Murat's own.
"Reinforcements!" thought Napoleon. "How can they want reinforcements when they have half the army already, concentrated against one
weak, unsupported flank of the Russians?"

"Tell the King of Naples," said Napoleon sternly, "that it is not midday, and I don't yet see clearly over my chess-board. You can go."

The handsome, boyish adjutant with the long curls heaved a deep
sigh, and still holding his hand to his hat, galloped back to the slaughter.

Napoleon got up, and summoning Caulaincourt and Berthier, began
conversing with them of matters not connected with the battle.

In the middle of the conversation, which began to interest Napoleon,
Berthier's eye was caught by a general, who was galloping on a steaming horse to the redoubt, followed by his suite. It was Beliard. Dismounting from his horse, he walked rapidly up to the Emperor, and, in
a loud voice, began boldly explaining the absolute necessity of reinforcements. He swore on his honour that the Russians would be annihilated
if the Emperor would let them have another division.

Napoleon shrugged his shoulders, and continued walking up and down, without answering. Beliard began loudly and eagerly talking with the generals of the suite standing round him.

"You are very hasty, Beliard," said Napoleon, going back again to him. "It is easy to make a mistake in the heat of the fray. Go and look again and then come to me." Before Beliard was out of sight another messenger came galloping up from another part of the battlefield.

"Well, what is it now?" said Napoleon, in the tone of a man irritated by repeated interruptions.

"Sire, the prince . . ." began the adjutant.

"Asks for reinforcements?" said Napoleon, with a wrathful gesture. The adjutant bent his head affirmatively and was proceeding to give his message, but the Emperor turned and walked a couple of steps away, stopped, turned back, and beckoned to Berthier. "We must send the reserves," he said with a slight gesticulation. "Whom shall we send there? what do you think?" he asked Berthier, that "gosling I have made an eagle," as he afterwards called him.

"Claparède's division, sire," said Berthier, who knew all the divisions, regiments, and battalions by heart.

Napoleon nodded his head in assent.

The adjutant galloped off to Claparède's division. And a few moments later the Young Guards, stationed behind the redoubt, were moving out. Napoleon gazed in that direction in silence.

"No," he said suddenly to Berthier, "I can't send Claparède. Send Friant's division."

Though there was no advantage of any kind in sending Friant's division rather than Claparède's, and there was obvious inconvenience and delay now in turning back Claparède and despatching Friant, the order was carried out. Napoleon did not see that in relation to his troops he played the part of the doctor, whose action in hindering the course of nature with his nostrums he so truly gauged and condemned.

Friant's division vanished like the rest into the smoke of the battlefield. Adjutants still kept galloping up from every side, and all, as though in collusion, said the same thing. All asked for reinforcements; all told of the Russians standing firm and keeping up a hellish fire, under which the French troops were melting away.

Napoleon sat on a camp-stool, plunged in thought. M. de Beausset, the reputed lover of travel, had been fasting since early morning, and approaching the Emperor, he ventured respectfully to suggest breakfast to his majesty.

"I hope that I can already congratulate your majesty on a victory," he said.

Napoleon shook his head. Supposing the negative to refer to the victory only and not to the breakfast, M. de Beausset permitted himself with respectful playfulness to observe that there was no reason in the world that could be allowed to interfere with breakfast when breakfast was possible.

"Go to the . . ." Napoleon jerked out gloomily, and he turned his back on him. A saintly smile of sympathy, regret, and ecstasy beamed on M. de Beausset's face as he moved with his swinging step back to the other generals.

Napoleon was experiencing the bitter feeling of a lucky gambler, who, after recklessly staking his money and always winning, suddenly finds, precisely when he has carefully reckoned up all contingencies, that the more he considers his course, the more certain he is of losing.

The soldiers were the same, the generals the same, there had been the same preparations, the same disposition, the same proclamation, *"court et énergique."* He was himself the same,—he knew that; he knew that he was more experienced and skilful indeed now than he had been of old. The enemy even was the same as at Austerlitz and Friedland. But the irresistible wave of his hand seemed robbed of its might by magic.

All the old manœuvres that had invariably been crowned with success: the concentration of the battery on one point, and the advance of the reserves to break the line, and the cavalry attack of "men of iron," all these resources had been employed; and far from victory being secure, from all sides the same tidings kept pouring in of killed or wounded generals, of reinforcements needed, of the troops being in disorder, and the Russians impossible to move.

Hitherto, after two or three orders being given, two or three phrases delivered, marshals and adjutants had galloped up with radiant faces and congratulations, announcing the capture as trophies of whole corps of prisoners, of bundles of flags and eagles, of cannons and stores, and Murat had asked leave to let the cavalry go to capture the baggage. So it had been at Lodi, Marengo, Arcole, Jena, Austerlitz, Wagram, and so on, and so on. But now something strange was coming over his men.

In spite of the news of the capture of the flèches, Napoleon saw that things were not the same, not at all the same as at previous battles. He saw that what he was feeling, all the men round him, experienced in military matters, were feeling too. All their faces were gloomy; all avoided each others' eyes. It was only a Beausset who could fail to grasp the import of what was happening. Napoleon after his long experience of war knew very well all that was meant by an unsuccessful attack after eight hours' straining every possible effort. He knew that this was almost equivalent to a defeat, and that the merest chance might now, in the critical point the battle was in, be the overthrow of himself and his troops.

When he went over in his own mind all this strange Russian campaign, in which not a single victory had been gained, in which not a flag, nor a cannon, nor a corps had been taken in two months, when he looked at the concealed gloom in the faces round him, and heard reports that the Russians still held their ground—a terrible feeling, such as is experienced in a nightmare, came over him, and all the unlucky contingencies occurred to him that might be his ruin. The Russians might fall upon his left wing, might break through his centre; a stray ball might even kill himself. All that was possible. In his former battles he had only considered the possibilities of success, now an immense number of unlucky chances presented themselves, and he expected them all. Yes, it was like a nightmare, when a man dreams that an assailant is attacking him, and in his dream he lifts up his arm and deals a blow with a force at his assailant that he knows must crush him, and feels that his arm falls limp and powerless as a rag, and the horror of inevitable death comes upon him in his helplessness.

The news that the Russians were attacking the left flank of the French army aroused that horror in Napoleon. He sat in silence on a camp-stool under the redoubt, his elbows on his knees, and his head sunk in his hands. Berthier came up to him and suggested that they should inspect the lines to ascertain the position of affairs.

"What? What do you say?" said Napoleon. "Yes, tell them to bring my horse." He mounted a horse and rode to Semyonovskoye.

In the slowly parting smoke, over the whole plain through which Napoleon rode, men and horses, singly and in heaps, were lying in pools of blood. Such a fearful spectacle, so great a mass of killed in so small a space, had never been seen by Napoleon nor any of his generals. The roar of the cannon that had not ceased for ten hours, exhausted the ear and gave a peculiar character to the spectacle (like music accompanying living pictures). Napoleon rode up to the height of Semyonovskoye, and through the smoke he saw ranks of soldiers in uniforms of unfamiliar hues. They were the Russians.

The Russians stood in serried ranks behind Semyonovskoye and the redoubt, and their guns kept up an incessant roar and smoke all along their lines. It was not a battle. It was a prolonged massacre, which could be of no avail either to French or Russians. Napoleon pulled up his horse, and sank again into the brooding reverie from which Berthier had roused him. He could not stay that thing that was being done before him and about him, and that was regarded as being led by him and as depending on him, that thing for the first time, after ill success, struck him as superfluous and horrible. One of the generals, riding up to Napoleon, ventured to suggest to him that the Old Guards should advance into action. Ney and Berthier, standing close by, exchanged glances and smiled contemptuously at the wild suggestion of this general.

Napoleon sat mute with downcast head.

"Eight hundred leagues from France, I am not going to let my Guard be destroyed," he said, and turning his horse, he rode back to Shevardino.

XXXV

Kutuzov, with his grey head hanging, and his heavy, corpulent frame sunk into a heap, was sitting on a bench covered with a rug, in the same place in which Pierre had seen him in the morning. He issued no orders, and simply gave or withheld his assent to what was proposed to him.

"Yes, yes, do so," he would say in reply to various suggestions. "Yes, yes, go across, my dear boy, and see," he would cry first to one and then to another of the adjutants near him; or, "No, better not; we'd better wait a bit," he would say. He listened to the reports brought him, and gave orders, when they were asked for. But as he heard the reports, he seemed to take little interest in the import of the words spoken; something else in the expression of his face, in the tone of the voice of the speaker, seemed to interest him more. From long years of military experience he had learned, and with the wisdom of old age he had recognised, that one man cannot guide hundreds of thousands of men struggling with death; that the fate of battles is not decided by the orders given by the commander-in-chief, nor the place in which the troops are stationed, nor the number of cannons, nor of killed, but by that intangible force called the spirit of the army, and he followed that force and led it as far as it lay in his power.

The general expression of Kutuzov's face was concentrated, quiet attention and intensity, with difficulty overcoming his weak and aged body.

At eleven o'clock they brought him the news that the French had been driven back again from the flèches they had captured, but that Bagration was wounded. Kutuzov groaned, and shook his head.

"Ride over to Prince Pyotr Ivanovitch and find out exactly about it," he said to one of the adjutants, and then he turned to the Prince of Würtemberg, who was standing behind him:

"Will your highness be pleased to take the command of the first army?"

Soon after the prince's departure—so soon that he could not yet have reached Semyonovskoye—his adjutant came back with a message from him asking Kutuzov for more troops.

Kutuzov frowned, and sent Dohturov orders to take the command of the first army, and begged the prince to come back, saying that he found he could not get on without him at such an important moment. When news was brought that Murat had been taken prisoner, and the members of the staff congratulated Kutuzov, he smiled.

"Wait a little, gentlemen," he said. "The battle is won, and Murat's being taken prisoner is nothing very extraordinary. But we had better defer our rejoicings." Still he sent an adjutant to take the news to the troops.

When Shtcherbinin galloped up from the left flank with the report of the capture of the flèche, and Semyonovskoye by the French, Kutuzov, guessing from the sounds of the battlefield and Shtcherbinin's face, that the news was bad, got up as though to stretch his legs, and taking Shtcherbinin by the arm drew him aside.

"You go, my dear boy," he said to Yermolov, "and see whether something can't be done."

Kutuzov was in Gorky, the centre of the Russian position. The attack on our left flank had been several times repulsed. In the centre the French did not advance beyond Borodino. Uvarov's cavalry had sent the French flying from the left flank.

At three o'clock the attacks of the French ceased. On the faces of all who came from the battlefield, as well as of those standing round him,

Kutuzov read an expression of effort, strained to the utmost tension. He was himself satisfied with the success of the day beyond his expectations. But the old man's physical force was failing him. Several times his head sank, as though he were falling, and he dropped asleep. Dinner was brought him.

The adjutant-general, Woltzogen, the man whom Prince Andrey had overheard saying that the war ought to be *"im Raum verlegen,"* and whom Bagration so particularly detested, rode up to Kutuzov while he was at dinner. Woltzogen had come from Barclay to report on the progress of the fight on the left flank. The sagacious Barclay de Tolly, seeing crowds of wounded men running back, and the ranks in disorder, and weighing all the circumstances of the case, made up his mind that the battle was lost, and sent his favourite adjutant to the commander-in-chief to tell him so.

Kutuzov was with difficulty chewing roast chicken, and his eyes were screwed up with a more cheerful expression as he glanced at Woltzogen.

With a half-contemptuous smile Woltzogen walked carelessly up to Kutuzov, scarcely touching the peak of his cap.

He behaved to his highness with a certain affected negligence, which aimed at showing that he, as a highly trained military man, left it to the Russians to make a prodigy of this useless old person, and was himself well aware what kind of a man he had to deal with. "The 'old gentleman' "—this was how Kutuzov was always spoken of in Woltzogen's German circle—"is making himself quite comfortable," he thought; and glancing severely at the dishes before Kutuzov, he began reporting to the old gentleman Barclay's message and his own impressions and views. "Every point of our position is in the enemy's hands, and they cannot be driven back, because there are not the troops to do it; the men run away and there's no possibility of stopping them," he submitted.

Kutuzov, stopping short in his munching, stared at Woltzogen in amazement, as though not understanding what was said to him. Woltzogen, noticing the old gentleman's excitement, said with a smile:

"I did not consider I had a right to conceal from your highness what I saw. . . . The troops are completely routed. . . ."

"You saw? You saw? . . ." cried Kutuzov, getting up quickly, and stepping up to Woltzogen. "How . . . how dare you! . . ." making a menacing gesture with his trembling hands, he cried, with a catch in his breath: "How dare you, sir, tell *me* that? You know nothing about it. Tell General Barclay from me that his information is incorrect, and that I, the commander-in-chief, know more of the course of the battle than he does."

Woltzogen would have made some protest, but Kutuzov interrupted him.

"The enemy has been repulsed on the left and defeated on the right flank. If you have seen amiss, sir, do not permit yourself to speak of what you do not understand. Kindly return to General Barclay and inform him of my unhesitating intention to attack the French to-morrow," said Kutuzov sternly.

All were silent, and nothing was to be heard but the heavy breathing of the gasping, old general. "Repulsed at all points, for which I thank God and our brave men. The enemy is defeated, and to-morrow we will drive him out of the holy land of Russia!" said Kutuzov, crossing himself; and all at once he gave a sob from the rising tears.

Woltzogen, shrugging his shoulders, and puckering his lips, walked away in silence, marvelling *"über diese Eingenommenheit des alten Herrn."*

"Ah, here he is, my hero!" said Kutuzov, as a stoutish, handsome, black-haired general came up the hillside. It was Raevsky, who had spent the whole day at the most important part of the battlefield.

Raevsky reported that the men were standing their ground firmly, and that the French were not venturing a further attack.

When he had heard him out, Kutuzov said in French: "You do not think, like some others, that we are obliged to retreat?"

"On the contrary, your highness, in indecisive actions it is always the most obstinate who remains victorious," answered Raevsky; "and my opinion . . ."

"Kaisarov," Kutuzov called to his adjutant, "sit down and write the order for to-morrow. And you," he turned to another, "ride along the line and announce that to-morrow we attack."

While he was talking to Raevsky and dictating the order, Woltzogen came back from Barclay and announced that General Barclay de Tolly would be glad to have a written confirmation of the order given by the field-marshal.

Kutuzov, without looking at Woltzogen, ordered an adjutant to make out this written order, which the former commander-in-chief very prudently wished to have to screen himself from all responsibility. And through the undefinable, mysterious link that maintains through a whole army the same temper, called the spirit of the army, and constituting the chief sinew of war, Kutuzov's words, his order for the battle next day, were transmitted instantaneously from one end of the army to the other.

The words and the phrases of the order were by no means the same when they reached the furthest links in the chain. There was, indeed, not a word in the stories men were repeating to one another from one end of the army to the other, that resembled what Kutuzov had actually said; but the drift of his words spread everywhere, because what Kutuzov had said was not the result of shrewd considerations, but the outflow of a feeling that lay deep in the heart of the commander-in-chief, and deep in the heart of every Russian.

And learning that to-morrow we were to attack the enemy, hearing from the higher spheres of the army the confirmation of what they wanted to believe, the worn-out, wavering men took comfort and courage again.

XXXVI

PRINCE ANDREY'S regiment was in the reserves, which were until two o'clock stationed behind Semyonovskoye in complete inaction, under a hot artillery fire. Before two o'clock the regiment, which had already lost over two hundred men, was moved forward into the trampled oatfield, in that space between Semyonovskoye and the battery redoubt, on which thousands of men were killed that day, and on which, about two o'clock, there was directed the concentrated fire of several hundreds of the enemy's cannons.

Not leaving that spot, nor discharging a single round of ammunition, the regiment lost here another third of its men. In front, and especially on the right side, the cannons kept booming in the smoke that never lifted, and from the mysterious region of the smoke that hid all the country in front, there came flying swiftly hissing cannon balls and slowly whizzing grenades. Sometimes, as though to give them a breathing space, for a whole quarter of an hour all the cannon balls and grenades flew over them, but at other times, in the course of a single minute, several men out of the regiment would be swept off, and they were busy the whole time dragging away the dead and carrying off the wounded.

With every fresh stroke the chances of life grew less and less for those who were not yet killed. The regiment was divided into battalions three hundred paces apart; but in spite of that, all the regiment was under the influence of the same mood. All the men of the regiment were alike gloomy and silent. At rare intervals there was the sound of talk in the ranks, but that sound was hushed every time the falling thud and the cry of "stretchers!" was heard. For the greater part of the time, by command of the officers, the men sat on the ground. One, taking off his shako, carefully loosened and then drew up the folds of it; another, crumbling the dry clay in his hands, rubbed up his bayonet with it; another shifted and fastened the buckle of his shoulder straps; while another carefully undid, and did up again, his leg bandages, and changed his boots. Some built little houses of clods of the ploughed field, or plaited straws of stubble. All of them appeared entirely engrossed in these pursuits. When men were killed or wounded, when the stretchers trailed by, when our troops retreated, when immense masses of the enemy came into view through the smoke, no one took any notice of these circumstances. When our artillery or cavalry advanced, when our infantry could be seen moving, approving observations could be heard on all sides. But quite extraneous incidents that had nothing to do with the battle were what attracted most notice; as though the attention of these morally overstrained men found a rest in the commonplace incidents of everyday life. Some batteries of artillery passed in front of their line. In one of the ammunition carriages a horse had put its legs through the traces.

"Hey! look at the trace-horse! . . . Take her leg out! She'll fall!

. . . Hey! they don't see! . . ." Shouts rose from the ranks all through the regiment.

Another time the attention of all was attracted by a little brown dog, with its tail in the air, who had come no one knew from where, and was running about fussily in front of the ranks. All at once a cannon ball fell near it, and it squealed and dashed away with its tail between its legs! Roars and shrieks of laughter rang out from the whole regiment. But distractions of this kind did not last more than a minute, and the men had been eight hours without food or occupation, with the terror of death never relaxing for an instant, and their pale and haggard faces grew paler and more haggard.

Prince Andrey, pale and haggard like every one else in the regiment, walked to and fro in the meadow next to the oat-field from one boundary-line to the other, with his hands clasped behind his back, and his eyes fixed on the ground. There was no need for him to give orders, and nothing for him to do. Everything was done of itself. The killed were dragged behind the line; the wounded were removed, and the ranks closed up. If any soldiers ran away, they made haste to return at once. At first Prince Andrey, thinking it his duty to keep up the spirits of the men, and set them an example, had walked about among the ranks. But soon he felt that there was nothing he could teach them. All his energies, like those of every soldier, were unconsciously directed to restraining himself from contemplating the horror of his position. He walked about the meadow, dragging one leg after the other, making the grass rustle, and watching the dust, which covered his boots. Then he strode along, trying to step on the traces of the footsteps of the mowers on the meadow; or counting his steps, calculated how many times he would have to walk from one boundary rut to another to make a verst; or cut off the flowers of wormwood growing in the rut, and crushing them in his hands, sniffed at the bitter-sweet, pungent odour. Of all the thoughts of the previous day not a trace remained. He thought of nothing at all. He listened wearily to the sounds that were ever the same, the whiz of the shells above the booming of the cannon, looked at the faces of the men of the first battalion, which he had gazed at to weariness already, and waited. "Here it comes . . . this one's for us again!" he thought, listening to the whiz of something flying out of the region of smoke. "One, another! More! Fallen" . . . He stopped short and looked towards the ranks. "No; it has flown over. But that one has fallen!" And he fell to pacing up and down again, trying to reach the next boundary in sixteen steps.

A whiz and a thud! Five paces from him the dry soil was thrown up, as a cannon ball sank into the earth. A chill ran down his back. He looked at the ranks. Probably a number had been struck: the men had gathered in a crowd in the second battalion.

"M. l'aide-de-camp," he shouted, "tell the men not to crowd together."

The adjutant, having obeyed this instruction, was approaching Prince Andrey. From the other side the major in command of the battalion came riding up.

"Look out!" rang out a frightened cry from a soldier, and like a bird, with swift, whirring wings alighting on the earth, a grenade dropped with a dull thud a couple of paces from Prince Andrey, near the major's horse. The horse, with no question of whether it were right or wrong to show fear, snorted, reared, almost throwing the major, and galloped away. The horse's terror infected the men.

"Lie down!" shouted the adjutant, throwing himself on the ground. Prince Andrey stood in uncertainty. The shell was smoking and rotating like a top between him and the recumbent adjutant, near a bush of wormwood in the rut between the meadow and the field.

"Can this be death?" Prince Andrey wondered, with an utterly new, wistful feeling, looking at the grass, at the wormwood and at the thread of smoke coiling from the rotating top. "I can't die, I don't want to die, I love life, I love this grass and earth and air . . ."

He thought this, and yet at the same time he did not forget that people were looking at him.

"For shame, M. l'aide-de-camp!" he said to the adjutant; "what sort of . . ." He did not finish. Simultaneously there was a tearing, crashing sound, like the smash of broken crockery, a puff of stifling fumes, and Prince Andrey was sent spinning over, and flinging up one arm, fell on his face.

Several officers ran up to him. A great stain of blood was spreading over the grass from the right side of his stomach.

The militiamen stood with the stretchers behind the officers. Prince Andrey lay on his chest, with his face sunk in the grass; he was still breathing in hard, hoarse gasps.

"Well, why are you waiting, come along!"

The peasants went up and took him by the shoulders and legs, but he moaned piteously, and they looked at one another, and laid him down again.

"Pick him up, lay him on, it's all the same!" shouted some one. They lifted him by the shoulders again and laid him on the stretcher.

"Ah, my God! my God! what is it? . . . The stomach! It's all over then! Ah, my God!" could be heard among the officers. "It almost grazed my ear," the adjutant was saying. The peasants, with the stretcher across their shoulders, hurried along the path they had trodden to the ambulance station.

"Keep step! . . . Aie! . . . these peasants!" cried an officer, seizing them by the shoulders, as they jogged along, jolting the stretcher.

"Drop into it, Fyodor, eh?" said the foremost peasant.

"That's it, first-rate," said the hindmost, falling into step.

"Your excellency? Eh, prince?" said the trembling voice of Timohin, as he ran up and peeped over the stretcher.

Prince Andrey opened his eyes, and looked at the speaker from the stretcher, through which his head had dropped, and closed his eyelids again.

The militiamen carried Prince Andrey to the copse, where there were vans and an ambulance station. The ambulance station consisted of three

tents, pitched at the edge of a birch copse. In the wood stood the ambulance waggons and horses. The horses in nose-bags were munching oats,
and the sparrows flew up to them and picked up the grains they dropped.
Some crows, scenting blood, flitted to and fro among the birches, cawing
impatiently. For more than five acres round the tents there were sitting
or lying men stained with blood, and variously attired. They were surrounded by crowds of dejected-looking and intently observant soldiers,
who had come with stretchers. Officers, trying to keep order, kept driving them away from the place; but it was of no use. The soldiers, heedless of the officers, stood leaning against the stretchers, gazing intently at
what was passing before their eyes, as though trying to solve some difficult problem in this spectacle. From the tents came the sound of loud,
angry wailing, and piteous moans. At intervals a doctor's assistant ran
out for water, or to point out those who were to be taken in next. The
wounded, awaiting their turn at the tent, uttered hoarse groans and
moans, wept, shouted, swore, or begged for vodka. Several were raving
in delirium. Prince Andrey, as a colonel, was carried through the crowd
of wounded not yet treated, and brought close up to one of the tents,
where his bearers halted awaiting instructions. Prince Andrey opened his
eyes, and for a long while could not understand what was passing around
him. The meadow, the wormwood, the black, whirling ball, and his passionate rush of love for life came back to his mind. A couple of paces
from him stood a tall, handsome, dark-haired sergeant, with a bandaged
head, leaning against a branch. He had been wounded in the head and in
the leg, and was talking loudly, attracting general attention. A crowd
of wounded men and stretcher-bearers had gathered round him, greedily
listening to his words.

"We regularly hammered him out, so he threw up everything; we
took the king himself," the soldier was shouting, looking about him with
feverishly glittering black eyes. "If only the reserves had come up in the
nick of time, my dear fellow, there wouldn't have been a sign of him
left, for I can tell you . . ."

Prince Andrey, like all the men standing round the speaker, gazed at
him with bright eyes, and felt a sense of comfort. "But isn't it all the
same now?" he thought. "What will be there, and what has been here?
why was I so sorry to part with life? There was something in this life
that I didn't understand, and don't understand."

XXXVII

ONE of the doctors came out of the tent with a blood-stained apron, and
small, blood-stained hands, in one of which he had a cigar, carefully
held between his thumb and little finger, that it might not be stained
too. This doctor threw his head up, and looked about him, but over the
level of the wounded crowd. He was evidently longing for a short respite.

After turning his head from right to left for a few minutes, he sighed and dropped his eyes again.

"All right, immediately," he said in reply to an assistant, who pointed him out Prince Andrey, and he bade the bearers carry him into the tent.

A murmur rose in the crowd of wounded men waiting.

"Even in the next world it's only the gentry who will have a good time," said one.

Prince Andrey was carried in, and laid on a table that had just been cleared, and was being rinsed over by an assistant. He could not make out distinctly what was in the tent. The pitiful groans on all sides, and the excruciating pain in his thigh, his stomach, and his back distracted his attention. Everything he saw around melted for him into a single general impression of naked, blood-stained, human flesh, which seemed to fill up the whole low-pitched tent, as, a few weeks before, on that hot August day, the bare human flesh had filled up the dirty pond along the Smolensk road. Yes, it was the same flesh, the same *chair à canon,* the sight of which had aroused in him then a horror, that seemed prophetic of what he felt now.

There were three tables in the tent. Two were occupied, on the third they laid Prince Andrey. For some time he was left alone, an involuntary witness of what was being done at the other tables. On the table nearest sat a Tatar, probably of a Cossack regiment, judging from the uniform that had been thrown down close by. Four soldiers were holding him. A doctor in spectacles was cutting something in his brown, muscular back.

"Ooh! ooh! ooh! . . ." the Tatar, as it were, grunted, and all of a sudden, throwing up his broad, swarthy, sun-burned face, and showing his white teeth, he began wriggling, twitching, and shrieking a piercingly shrill, prolonged scream. On the other table, round which a number of persons were standing, a big, stout man lay on his back, with his head flung back. The colour and curliness of the hair and the shape seemed strangely familiar to Prince Andrey. Several assistants were holding him, and weighing on his chest. One white, plump leg was incessantly moving with a rapid, spasmodic twitching. This man was sobbing and choking convulsively. Two doctors—one was pale and trembling—were mutely engaged in doing something with the other red, gory leg. Having finished with the Tatar, over whom a cloak was thrown, the doctor in spectacles came up to Prince Andrey, wiping his hands.

He glanced at his face, and hurriedly turned away. "Undress him! Why are you dawdling?" he shouted angrily to the assistant.

His earliest, remotest childhood came back to Prince Andrey, when the assistant, with tucked-up sleeves, hurriedly unbuttoned his buttons, and took off his clothes. The doctor bent close down over the wound, felt it, and sighed deeply. Then he made a sign to some one. And the excruciating pain inside his stomach made Prince Andrey lose consciousness. When he regained consciousness, the broken splinters of his thigh bone had been removed, the bits of ragged flesh had been cut off, and the wound bound up. Water was sprinkled on his face. As soon as Prince Andrey opened his eyes, the doctor bent over him, kissed him on the lips without speaking, and hurried away.

After the agony he had passed through, Prince Andrey felt a blissful peace, such as he had not known for very long. All the best and happiest moments of his life, especially his earliest childhood, when he had been undressed and put to bed, when his nurse had sung lullabies over him, when, burying his head in the pillows, he had felt happy in the mere consciousness of life, rose before his imagination, not like the past even, but as though it were the actual present.

The doctors were busily engaged with the wounded man, whose head had seemed somehow familiar to Prince Andrey: they were lifting him up and trying to soothe him.

"Show it to me . . . ooo! o! ooo!" he could hear his frightened, abjectly suffering moans, broken by sobs. Hearing his moans, Prince Andrey wanted to cry. Either because he was dying thus without glory, or because he was sorry to part with life, or from these memories of a childhood that could never return, or because he was in pain, or because others were suffering, and that man was moaning so piteously, he longed to weep childlike, good, almost happy, tears.

They showed the wounded man the leg that had been amputated, wearing a boot, and covered with dry gore. "O! oooo!" he sobbed like a woman. The doctor who had been standing near him, screening his face, moved away.

"My God! How's this? Why is he here?" Prince Andrey wondered.

In the miserable, sobbing, abject creature, whose leg had just been cut off, he recognised Anatole Kuragin. It was Anatole they were holding up in their arms and offering a glass of water, the edge of which he could not catch with his trembling, swollen lips. Anatole drew a sobbing, convulsive breath. "Yes, it is he; yes, that man is somehow closely and painfully bound up with me," thought Prince Andrey, with no clear understanding yet of what was before him. "What is the connection between that man and my childhood, my life?" he asked himself, unable to find the clue. And all at once a new, unexpected memory from that childlike world of purity and love rose up before Prince Andrey. He remembered Natasha, as he had seen her for the first time at the ball in 1810, with her slender neck and slender arms, and her frightened, happy face, ready for ecstatic enjoyment, and a love and tenderness awoke in his heart for her stronger and more loving than ever. He recalled now the bond that existed between him and this man, who was looking vaguely at him through the tears that filled his swollen eyes. Prince Andrey remembered everything, and a passionate pity and love for that suffering man filled his happy heart.

Prince Andrey could restrain himself no more and wept tears of love and tenderness over his fellow-men, over himself, and over their errors and his own. "Sympathy, love for our brothers, for those who love us, love for those who hate us, love for our enemies; yes, the love that God preached upon earth, that Marie sought to teach me, and I did not understand, that is why I am sorry to part with life, that is what was left me if I had lived. But now it is too late. I know that!"

XXXVIII

THE tearful spectacle of the battlefield, heaped with dead and wounded, in conjunction with the heaviness of his head, the news that some twenty generals he knew well were among the killed or wounded, and the sense of the impotence of his once mighty army, made an unexpected impression on Napoleon, who was usually fond of looking over the dead and wounded, proving thereby, as he imagined, his dauntless spirit. On that day, the awful spectacle of the battlefield overcame this dauntless spirit, which he looked upon as a merit and a proof of greatness. He hastened away from the field of battle and returned to Shevardino. With a yellow, puffy, heavy face, dim eyes, a red nose, and a husky voice, he sat on a camp-stool, looking down and involuntarily listening to the sounds of the firing. With sickly uneasiness he awaited the end of this action, in which he considered himself the prime mover, though he could not have stopped it. The personal, human sentiment for one brief moment gained the ascendant over the artificial phantasm of life, that he had served so long. He imagined in his own case the agonies and death he had seen on the battlefield. The heaviness of his head and chest reminded him of the possibility for him too of agony and death. At that minute he felt no longing for Moscow, for victory or for glory. (What need had he for more glory?) The one thing he desired now was repose, tranquillity, and freedom. But when he was on the height above Semyonovskoye, the officer in command of the artillery proposed to him to bring several batteries up on to that height to increase the fire on the Russian troops before Knyazkovo. Napoleon assented, and gave orders that word should be brought him of the effect produced by this battery.

An adjutant came to say that by the Emperor's orders two hundred guns had been directed upon the Russians, but that they were still holding their ground.

"Our fire is mowing them down in whole rows, but they stand firm," said the adjutant.

"They want more of it!" said Napoleon in his husky voice.

"Sire?" repeated the adjutant, who had not caught the words.

"They want even more!" Napoleon croaked hoarsely, frowning, "Well, let them have it then."

Already, without orders from him, what he did not really want was being done, and he gave the order to do it simply because he thought the order was expected of him. And he passed back again into his old artificial world, peopled by the phantoms of some unreal greatness, and again (as a horse running in a rolling wheel may imagine it is acting on its own account) he fell back into submissively performing the cruel, gloomy, irksome, and inhuman part destined for him.

And not for that hour and day only were the mind and conscience darkened in that man, on whom the burden of all that was being done lay even more heavily than on all the others who took part in it. Never, down to the end of his life, had he the least comprehension of good, of beauty, of truth, of the significance of his own acts, which were too far opposed to truth and goodness, too remote from everything human for him to be able to grasp their significance. He could not disavow his own acts, that were lauded by half the world, and so he was forced to disavow truth and goodness and everything human.

Not on that day only, as he rode about the battlefield, piled with corpses and mutilated men (the work, as he supposed, of his will) he reckoned as he gazed at them how many Russians lay there for each Frenchman, and cheated himself into finding matter for rejoicing in the belief that there were five Russians for every Frenchman. Not on that day only he wrote to Paris that *"le champ de bataille a été superbe,"* because there were fifty thousand corpses on it. Even in St. Helena, in the peaceful solitude where he said he intended to devote his leisure to an account of the great deeds he had done, he wrote:

"The Russian war ought to have been the most popular of modern times: it was the war of good sense and real interests, of the repose and security of all: it was purely pacific and conservative.

"It was for the great cause, the end of uncertainties and the beginning of security. A new horizon, new labours were unfolding, all full of welfare and prosperity for all. The European system was established; all that remained was to organise it.

"Satisfied on these great points and tranquil everywhere, I too should have had my *congress* and my *holy alliance*. These are ideas stolen from me. In this assembly of great sovereigns, we could have treated of our interests like one family and have reckoned, as clerk with master, with the peoples.

"Europe would soon in that way have made in fact but one people, and every one, travelling all over it, would always have found himself in the common fatherland. I should have required all the rivers to be open for the navigation of all; the seas to be common to all; and the great standing armies to be reduced henceforth simply to the bodyguard of the sovereigns.

"Returning to France, to the bosom of the great, strong, magnificent, tranquil, and glorious fatherland, I should have proclaimed its frontiers immutable, all future war purely *defensive*, all fresh aggrandisement *anti-national*. I should have associated my son in the empire; my *dictatorship* would have been over, and his constitutional reign would have begun . . .

"Paris would have been the capital of the world, and the French the envy of the nations! . . .

"My leisure then and my old age would have been consecrated, in company with the Empress, and during the royal apprenticeship of my son, to visiting in leisurely fashion with our own horses, like a genuine country couple, every corner of the empire, receiving complaints, re‹ dressing wrongs, scattering monuments and benefits on all sides."

He, predestined by Providence to the gloomy, slavish part of executioner of the peoples, persuaded himself that the motive of his acts had been the welfare of the peoples, and that he could control the destinies of millions, and make their prosperity by the exercise of his power.

"Of the four hundred thousand men who crossed the Vistula," he wrote later of the Russian war, "half were Austrians, Prussians, Saxons, Poles, Bavarians, Würtembergers, Mecklenburgers, Spaniards, Italians, Neapolitans. The Imperial army, properly so-called, was one third composed of Dutch, Belgians, inhabitants of the Rhineland, Piedmontese, Swiss, Genevese, Tuscans, Romans, inhabitants of the thirty-second military division, of Bremen, Hamburg, etc. It reckoned barely a hundred and forty thousand men speaking French. The Russian expedition cost France itself less than fifty thousand men. The Russian army in the retreat from Vilna to Moscow in the different battles lost four times as many men as the French army. The fire in Moscow cost the lives of one hundred thousand Russians, dead of cold and want in the woods; lastly, in its march from Moscow to the Oder, the Russian army, too, suffered from the inclemency of the season: it only reckoned fifty thousand men on reaching Vilna, and less than eighteen thousand at Kalisch."

He imagined that the war with Russia was entirely due to his will, and the horror of what was done made no impression on his soul. He boldly assumed the whole responsibility of it all; and his clouded intellect found justification in the fact that among the hundreds of thousands of men who perished, there were fewer Frenchmen than Hessians and Bavarians.

XXXIX

SOME tens of thousands of men lay sacrificed in various postures and uniforms on the fields and meadows belonging to the Davidov family and the Crown serfs, on those fields and meadows where for hundreds of years the peasants of Borodino, Gorky, Shevardino, and Semyonovskoye had harvested their crops and grazed their cattle. At the ambulance stations the grass and earth were soaked with blood for two acres round. Crowds of men, wounded and unwounded, of various arms, with panic stricken faces, dragged themselves, on one side back to Mozhaisk, on the other to Valuev. Other crowds, exhausted and hungry, were led forward by their officers. Others still held their ground, and went on firing.

Over all the plain, at first so bright and gay with its glittering bayonets and puffs of smoke in the morning sunshine, there hung now a dark cloud of damp mist and smoke, and a strange, sour smell of saltpetre and blood. Storm clouds had gathered, and a drizzling rain began to fall on the dead, on the wounded, on the panic-stricken, and exhausted, and hesitating soldiers. It seemed to say: "Enough, enough; cease. . . . Consider. What are you doing?"

To the men on both sides, alike exhausted from want of food and rest, the doubt began to come whether they should still persist in slaughtering one another; and in every face could be seen hesitation, and in every heart alike there rose the question: "For what, for whom am I to slay and be slain? Slay whom you will, do what you will, but I have had enough!" This thought took shape towards evening in every heart alike. Any minute all those men might be horror-stricken at what they were doing, might throw up everything and run anywhere.

But though towards the end of the battle the men felt all the horror of their actions, though they would have been glad to cease, some unfathomable, mysterious force still led them on, and the artillerymen—the third of them left—soaked with sweat, grimed with powder and blood, and panting with weariness, still brought the charges, loaded, aimed, and lighted the match; and the cannon balls flew as swiftly and cruelly from each side and crushed human flesh, and kept up the fearful work, which was done not at the will of men, but at the will of Him who sways men and worlds.

Any one looking at the disorder in the rear of the Russian army would have said that the French had but to make one slight effort more and the Russian army would have been annihilated; and any one seeing the rear of the French army would have said that the Russians need but make a slight effort more and the French would be overthrown. But neither French nor Russians made that effort, and the flame of the battle burnt slowly out.

The Russians did not make this effort, because they were not attacking the French. At the beginning of the battle they merely stood on the road to Moscow, barring it to the French; and they still stood at the end of the battle as they had at the beginning. But even if it had been the aim of the Russians to drive back the French, they could not have made this final effort, because all the Russian troops had been routed; there was not a single part of the army that had not suffered in the battle, and the Russians, without being driven from their position, lost ONE HALF of their army.

For the French, with the memory of fifteen years of victories, with confidence in Napoleon's all-vanquishing genius, with the consciousness of having taken a part of the battlefield, of having only lost a fourth of their men, and of having a body of twenty thousand—the Guards—intact—it would have been an easy matter to make this effort. The French, attacking the Russian army with the object of driving it from its position, ought to have made this effort, because as long as the Russians still barred the way to Moscow, as before the battle, the aim of the French had not been attained, and all losses and exertions had been in vain. But the French did not make that effort. Some historians assert that if Napoleon had only let his Old Guard advance, the battle would have been gained. To talk of what might have happened if Napoleon had let his Guard advance is much the same as to talk of what would happen if spring came in autumn. That could not have been. Napoleon did not do so, not because he did not want to, but because it was impossible to do so. All the generals, officers, and soldiers of the French army knew that it was impossible to make this final effort, because the flagging spirit of the troops did not allow of it.

It was not Napoleon alone who had that nightmare feeling that the mighty arm was stricken powerless: all the generals, all the soldiers of the French army, those who fought and those who did not, after all their experiences of previous battles (when after one-tenth of the effort the enemy had always run), showed the feeling of horror before this foe, who, after losing ONE HALF of the army, still stood its ground as dauntless at the end as at the beginning of the battle. The moral force of the French, the attacking army, was exhausted. Not the victory, signalised by the capture of rags on the end of sticks, called flags, or of the ground on which the troops were standing, but a moral victory, that which compels the enemy to recognise the moral superiority of his opponent, and his own impotence, was won by the Russians at Borodino. The French invading army, like a ravening beast that has received its death-wound in its onslaught, felt its end near. But it could not stop, no more than the Russian army—of half its strength—could help retreating. After that check, the French army could still drag on to Moscow, but there, without fresh effort on the part of the Russian army, its ruin was inevitable, as its life-blood ebbed away from the deadly wound dealt it at Borodino. The direct consequence of the battle of Borodino was Napoleon's causeless flight from Moscow, his return by the old Smolensk road, the ruin of the invading army of five hundred thousand men, and the downfall of the Napoleonic rule, on which, for the first time at Borodino, was laid the hand of a foe of stronger spirit.

PART ELEVEN

I

FOR THE human mind the absolute continuity of motion is inconceivable. The laws of motion of any kind only become comprehensible to man when he examines units of this motion, arbitrarily selected. But at the same time it is from this arbitrary division of continuous motion into discontinuous units that a great number of human errors proceeds.

We all know the so-called sophism of the ancients, proving that Achilles would never overtake the tortoise, though Achilles walked ten times as fast as the tortoise As soon as Achilles passes over the space separating him from the tortoise, the tortoise advances one-tenth of that space: Achilles passes over that tenth, but the tortoise has advanced a hundredth, and so on to infinity. This problem seemed to the ancients insoluble. The irrationality of the conclusion (that Achilles will never overtake the tortoise) arises from the arbitrary assumption of disconnected units of motion, when the motion both of Achilles and the tortoise was continuous.

By taking smaller and smaller units of motion we merely approach the solution of the problem, but we never attain it. It is only by assuming an infinitely small magnitude, and a progression rising from it up to a tenth, and taking the sum of that geometrical progression, that we can arrive at the solution of the problem. A new branch of mathematics, dealing with infinitely small quantities, gives now in other more complex problems of dynamics solutions of problems that seemed insoluble.

This new branch of mathematics, unknown to the ancients, by assuming infinitely small quantities, that is, such as secure the chief condition of motion (absolute continuity), corrects the inevitable error which the human intellect cannot but make, when it considers disconnected units of motion instead of continuous motion.

In the investigation of the laws of historical motion precisely the same mistake arises.

The progress of humanity, arising from an innumerable multitude of individual wills, is continuous in its motion.

The discovery of the laws of this motion is the aim of history. But in order to arrive at the laws of the continuous motion due to the sum of all these individual wills, the human mind assumes arbitrary, disconnected units. The first proceeding of the historian is taking an arbitrary series of continuous events to examine it apart from others, while in reality there is not, and cannot be, a beginning to any event, but one event flows without any break in continuity from another. The second proceeding is to examine the action of a single person, a sovereign, or a general, as though it were equivalent to the sum of many individual wills, though the sum of individual wills never finds expression in the action of a single historical personage.

Historical science as it advances is continually taking smaller and smaller units for analysis, and in this way strives to approximate the truth. But however small the units of which history takes cognisance, we feel that the assumption of a unit, disconnected from another, the assumption of a *beginning* of any phenomenon, and the assumption that the individual wills of all men find expression in the actions of a single historical personage, are false in themselves.

Every conclusion of history can, without the slightest effort on the part of the critic, be dissipated like dust, leaving no trace, simply through criticism selecting, as the object of its analysis, a greater or smaller disconnected unit, which it has a perfect right to do, seeing that the unit of history is always selected arbitrarily.

Only by assuming an infinitely small unit for observation—a differential of history—that is, the homogeneous tendencies of men, and arriving at the integral calculus (that is, taking the sum of those infinitesimal quantities), can we hope to arrive at the laws of history.

The first fifteen years of the nineteenth century present the spectacle of an extraordinary movement of millions of men. Men leave their habitual pursuits; rush from one side of Europe to the other; plunder, slaughter one another, triumph and despair; and the whole current of life is transformed and presents a quickened activity, first moving at a growing speed, and then slowly slackening again. What was the cause of that activity, or from what laws did it arise? asks the human intellect.

The historians, in reply to that inquiry, lay before us the sayings and doings of some dozens of men in one of the buildings of the city of Paris, summing up those doings and sayings by one word—revolution. Then they give us a detailed biography of Napoleon, and of certain persons favourably or hostilely disposed to him; talk of the influence of some of these persons upon others; and then say that this it is to which that activity is due, and these are its laws.

But the human intellect not only refuses to believe in that explanation, but flatly declares that the method of explanation is not a correct one, because in this explanation a smaller phenomenon is taken as the cause of a greater phenomenon. The sum of men's individual wills produced both the revolution and Napoleon; and only the sum of those wills endured them and then destroyed them.

"But whenever there have been wars, there have been great military leaders; whenever there have been revolutions in states, there have been great men," says history. "Whenever there have been great military leaders there have, indeed, been wars," replies the human reason; "but that does not prove that the generals were the cause of the wars, and that the factors leading to warfare can be found in the personal activity of one man."

Whenever, looking at my watch, I see the hand has reached the figure x, I hear the bells beginning to ring in the church close by. But from the fact that the watch hand points to ten whenever the bells begin to ring, I have not the right to infer that the position of the hands of my watch is the cause of the vibration of the bells.

Whenever I see a steam-engine move, I hear the whistle, I see the valve open and the wheels turn; but I have no right to conclude from that the whistle and the turning of the wheels are the causes of the steam-engine's moving.

The peasants say that in the late spring a cold wind blows because the oak-buds are opening, and, as a fact, a cold wind does blow every spring when the oak is coming out. But though the cause of a cold wind's blowing just when the oaks are coming out is unknown to me, I cannot agree with the peasants that the cause of the cold wind is the opening of the oak-buds, because the force of the wind is altogether outside the influence of the buds. I see in this simply such a ccincidence of events as is common in every phenomenon of life, and I see that however long and minutely I might examine the watch hand, the valve, and the wheel of the steam-engine and the oak-bud, I shall not discover the cause of the bells ringing, of the steam-engine moving, and of the spring wind. To do that I must completely change my point of observation and study the laws of the motion of steam, of the bells, and of the wind. History must do the same. And efforts have already been made in this direction.

For the investigation of the laws of history, we must completely change the subject of observations, must let kings and ministers and generals alone, and study the homogeneous, infinitesimal elements by which masses are led. No one can say how far it has been given to man to advance in that direction in understanding of the laws of history. But it is obvious that only in that direction lies any possibility of discovering historical laws; and that the human intellect has hitherto not devoted to that method of research one millionth part of the energy that historians have put into the description of the doings of various kings, ministers, and generals, and the exposition of their own views on those doings.

II

The armed forces of twelve different nationalities of Europe invade Russia. The Russian army and population fall back, avoiding a battle, to Smolensk, and from Smolensk to Borodino. The French army moves on to Moscow, its goal, with continually increasing impetus. The impetus of its advance is increased as it approaches its goal, just as the velocity of a falling body increases as it gets nearer the earth. Behind them thousands of versts of famine-stricken, hostile country; before them some dozens of versts between them and their goal. Every soldier of Napoleon's army feels it, and the expedition advances of itself, by the force of its own impetus.

In the Russian troops the spirit of fury, of hatred of the foe, burns more and more fiercely during their retreat; it gathers strength and concentration as they draw back. At Borodino the armies meet. Neither army is destroyed, but the Russian army, immediately after the conflict, retreats as inevitably as a ball rebounds after contact with another ball flying with greater impetus to meet it. And just as inevitably (though parting with its force in the contact) the ball of the invading army is carried for a space further by the energy, not yet fully spent, within it.

The Russians retreat one hundred and twenty versts beyond Moscow; the French reach Moscow and there halt. For five weeks after this there is not a single battle. The French do not move. Like a wild beast mortally wounded, bleeding and licking its wounds, for five weeks the French remain in Moscow, attempting nothing; and all at once, with nothing new to account for it, they flee back; they make a dash for the Kaluga road (after a victory, too, for they remained in possession of the field of battle at Maley Yaroslavets); and then, without a single serious engagement, fly more and more rapidly back to Smolensk, to Vilna, to the Berezina, and beyond it.

On the evening of the 26th of August, Kutuzov and the whole Russian army were convinced that the battle of Borodino was a victory. Kutuzov wrote to that effect to the Tsar. He ordered the troops to be in readiness for another battle, to complete the defeat of the enemy, not because he wanted to deceive any one, but because he knew that the enemy was vanquished, as every one who had taken part in the battle knew it.

But all that evening and next day news was coming in of unheard-of losses, of the loss of one-half of the army, and another battle turned out to be physically impossible.

It was impossible to give battle when information had not yet come in, the wounded had not been removed, the ammunition stores had not been filled up, the slain had not been counted, new officers had not been appointed to replace the dead, and the men had had neither food nor sleep. And meanwhile, the very next morning after the battle, the French army of itself moved down upon the Russians, carried on by the force of its own impetus, accelerated now in inverse ratio to the square of the distance from its goal. Kutuzov's wish was to attack next day, and all the army shared this desire. But to make an attack it is not sufficient to desire to do so; there must also be a possibility of doing so, and this possibility there was not. It was impossible not to retreat one day's march, and then it was as impossible not to retreat a second and a third day's march, and finally, on the 1st of September, when the army reached Moscow, despite the force of the growing feeling in the troops, the force of circumstances compelled those troops to retreat beyond Moscow. And the troops retreated one more last day's march, and abandoned Moscow to the enemy.

Persons who are accustomed to suppose that plans of campaigns and of battles are made by generals in the same way as any of us sitting over a map in our study make plans of how we would have acted in such and such a position, will be perplexed by questions why Kutuzov, if he had to retreat, did not take this or that course, why he did not take up a position before Fili, why he did not at once retreat to the Kaluga road, leaving Moscow, and so on. Persons accustomed to think in this way forget, or do not know, the inevitable conditions which always limit the action of any commander-in-chief. The action of a commander-in-chief in the field has no sort of resemblance to the action we imagine to ourselves, sitting at our ease in our study, going over some campaign on the map with a certain given number of soldiers on each side, in a certain known locality, starting our plans from a certain moment. The general is never in the position of the *beginning* of any event, from which we always contemplate the event. The general is always in the very middle of a changing series of events, so that he is never at any moment in a position to deliberate on all the bearings of the event that is taking place. Imperceptibly, moment by moment, an event takes shape in all its bearings, and at every moment in that uninterrupted, consecutive shaping of events the commander-in-chief is in the centre of a most complex play of intrigues, of cares, of dependence and of power, of projects, counsels, threats, and conceptions, with one thing depending on another, and is under the continual necessity of answering the immense number of mutually contradictory inquiries addressed to him.

We are, with perfect seriousness, told by those learned in military matters that Kutuzov ought to have marched his army towards the Kaluga road long before reaching Fili; that somebody did, indeed, suggest such a plan. But the commander of an army has before him, especially at a difficult moment, not one, but dozens of plans. And each of those plans, based on the rules of strategy and tactics, contradicts all the rest. The commander's duty would, one would suppose, be merely to select one out of those plans; but even this he cannot do. Time and events will not wait. It is suggested to him, let us suppose, on the 28th to move towards the Kaluga road, but at that moment an adjutant gallops up from Miloradovitch to inquire whether to join battle at once with the French or to retire. He must be given instructions at once, at the instant. And the order to retire hinders us from turning to the Kaluga road. And then after the adjutant comes the commissariat commissioner to inquire where the stores are to be taken, and the ambulance director to ask where the wounded are to be moved to, and a courier from Petersburg with a letter from the Tsar, not admitting the possibility of abandoning Moscow, and the commander's rival, who is trying to cut the ground from under his feet (and there are always more than one such) proposes a new project, diametrically opposed to the plan of marching upon the Kaluga road. The commander's own energies, too, require sleep and support. And a respectable general, who has been overlooked when decorations were bestowed, presents a complaint, and the inhabitants of the district implore protection, and the officer sent to inspect the locality comes back with a report utterly unlike that of the officer sent on the same commission just previously; and a spy, and a prisoner, and a general who has made a reconnaissance, all describe the position of the enemy's army quite differently. Persons who forget, or fail to comprehend, those inevitable conditions under which a commander has to act, present to us, for instance, the position of the troops at Fili, and assume that the commander-in-chief was quite free on the 1st of September to decide the question whether to abandon or to defend Moscow, though, with the position of the Russian army, only five versts from Moscow, there could no longer be any question on the subject. When was that question decided? At Drissa, and at Smolensk, and most palpably of all on August the 24th at Shevardino, and on the 26th at Borodino, and every day and hour and minute of the retreat from Borodino to Fili.

III

THE Russian army, retreating from Borodino, halted at Fili. Yermolov, who had been inspecting the position, rode up to the commander-in-chief.

"There is no possibility of fighting in this position," he said.

Kutuzov looked at him in wonder, and made him repeat the words he had just uttered. When he had done so, he put out his hand to him.

"Give me your hand," he said; and turning it so as to feel his pulse, he said: "You are not well, my dear boy. Think what you are saying."

Kutuzov could not yet take in the idea of its being possible to retreat, abandoning Moscow without a battle.

On the Poklonnaya Hill, six versts from Dorogomilovsky gate, Kutuzov got out of his carriage and sat down on a bench by the side of the road. A great crowd of generals gathered about him. Count Rastoptchin, who had come out from Moscow, joined them. All this brilliant company broke up into several circles, and talked among themselves of the advantages and disadvantages of the position, of the condition of the troops, of the plans proposed, of the situation of Moscow—in fact, of military questions generally. All felt that though they had not been summoned for the purpose, it was really, if not ostensibly, a military council. All conversation was confined to public questions. If any one did repeat or inquire any piece of personal news, it was in a whisper, and the talk passed at once back to general topics. There was not a jest, nor a laugh, not even a smile, to be seen among all these men. They were all making an obvious effort to rise to the level of the situation. And all the groups, while talking among themselves, tried to keep close to the commander-in-chief, whose bench formed the centre of the whole crowd, and tried to talk so that he might hear them. The commander-in-chief listened, and sometimes asked what had been said near him, but did not himself enter into conversation or express any opinion. For the most part, after listening to the talk of some group, he turned away with an air of disappointment, as though they were not speaking of anything he cared to hear about at all. Some were discussing the position, criticising not so much the position itself as the intellectual qualifications of those who had selected it. Others argued that a blunder had been made earlier, that a battle ought to have been fought two days before. Others talked of the battle of Salamanca, which a Frenchman, Crosart, wearing a Spanish uniform, was describing to them. (This Frenchman, who had just ar-

rived, had with one of the German princes serving in the Russian army
been criticising the siege of Saragossa, foreseeing a possibility of a similar defence of Moscow.) In the fourth group, Count Rastoptchin was
saying that he, with the Moscow city guard, was ready to die under the
walls of the city, but that still he could not but complain of the uncertainty in which he had been left, and that had he known it earlier, things
would have been different. . . . A fifth group was manifesting the profundity of their tactical insight by discussing the direction the troops
should certainly take now. A sixth group were talking arrant nonsense.

Kutuzov's face grew more and more careworn and gloomy. From all
this talk Kutuzov saw one thing only: the defence of Moscow was a
physical impossibility in the fullest sense of the words. It was so utterly
impossible that even if some insane commander were to give orders for
a battle, all that would follow would be a muddle, and no battle would
be fought. There would be no battle, because all the officers in command,
not merely recognised the position to be impossible, but were only engaged now in discussing what was to be done after the inevitable abandonment of that position. How could officers lead their men to a field of
battle which they considered it impossible to hold? The officers of lower
rank, and even the soldiers themselves (they too form their conclusions),
recognised that the position could not be held, and so they could not
advance into battle with the conviction that they would be defeated.
That Bennigsen urged the defence of this position, and others still discussed it, was a fact that had no significance in itself, but only as a pretext for dissension and intrigue. Kutuzov knew that.

Bennigsen was warmly manifesting his Russian patriotism (Kutuzov
could not listen to him without wincing), by insisting on the defence of
Moscow. To Kutuzov, his object was as clear as daylight: in case of the
defence being unsuccessful, to throw the blame on Kutuzov, who had
brought the army as far as the Sparrow Hills without a battle; in case of
its being successful, to claim the credit; in case of it not being attempted, to clear himself of the crime of abandoning Moscow.

But these questions of intrigue did not occupy the old man's mind
now. One terrible question absorbed him. And to that question he heard
no reply from any one. The question for him now was this: "Can it be
that I have let Napoleon get to Moscow, and when did I do it? When did
it happen? Was it yesterday, when I sent word to Platov to retreat, or
the evening before when I had a nap and bade Bennigsen give instructions? Or earlier still? . . . When, when was it this fearful thing happened? Moscow must be abandoned. The army must retire, and I must
give the order for it."

To give that terrible order seemed to him equivalent to resigning the
command of the army. And apart from the fact that he loved power,
and was used to it (the honours paid to Prince Prozorovsky, under
whom he had been serving in Turkey, galled him), he was convinced
that he was destined to deliver Russia, and had only for that cause been
chosen commander-in-chief contrary to the Tsar's wishes by the will of
the people. He was persuaded that in these difficult circumstances he was

the one man who could maintain his position at the head of the army,
that he was the only man in the world capable of meeting Napoleon as
an antagonist without panic. And he was in terror at the idea of having
to resign the command. But he must decide on some step, he must cut
short this chatter round him, which was beginning to assume too free a
character.

He beckoned the senior generals to him.

"*Ma tête, fût-elle bonne ou mauvaise, n'a qu'à s'aider d'elle-même,*"
he said, getting up from his bench, and he rode off to Fili, where his
carriages were waiting.

IV

IN the large best room of the peasant Andrey Savostyanov's cottage, at
two o'clock, a council met. The men and women and children of the
peasant's big family all crowded together in the room on the other side
of the passage. Only Andrey's little grandchild, Malasha, a child of six,
whom his highness had petted, giving her sugar while he drank his tea,
stayed behind by the big stove in the best room. Malasha peeped out
from on the stove with shy delight at the faces, the uniforms, and the
crosses of the generals, who kept coming into the room one after another,
and sitting in a row on the broad benches in the best corner under the
holy images. "Granddad" himself, as Malasha in her own mind called
Kutuzov, was sitting apart from the rest in the dark corner behind the
stove. He sat sunk all of a heap in a folding armchair, and was continually clearing his throat and straightening the collar of his coat,
which, though it was unbuttoned, still seemed to gall his neck. The generals, as they came in one after another, walked up to the commander-
in-chief: he shook hands with some, to others he merely nodded.

The adjutant, Kaisarov, would have drawn back a curtain from the
window facing Kutuzov, but the latter shook his hand angrily at him,
and Kaisarov saw that his highness did not care for them to see his face.

Round the peasant's deal table, on which lay maps, plans, pencils, and
papers, there was such a crowd that the orderlies brought in another
bench, and set it near the table. Yermolov, Kaisarov, and Toll seated
themselves on this bench. In the foremost place, under the holy images,
sat Barclay de Tolly, with his Order of St. George on his neck, with his
pale, sickly face and high forehead that met his bald head. He had been
in the throes of fever for the last two days, and was shivering and shaking now. Beside him sat Uvarov, speaking to him with rapid gesticulations in the same low voice in which everybody spoke. Little chubby
Dohturov was listening attentively with his eyebrows raised and his
hands clasped over his stomach. On the other side, resting his broad head
on his hand, sat Count Osterman-Tolstoy, with his bold features and brilliant eyes, apparently plunged in his own thoughts. Raevsky sat twisting
his black curls on his temples, as he always did, and looking with impatience from Kutuzov to the door. Konovnitsyn's firm, handsome, good-

humoured face was bright with a sly and kindly smile. He caught Malasha's eye, and made signs to her with his eyes, that set the little girl smiling.

They were all waiting for Bennigsen, who, on the pretext of a fresh inspection of the position, was engaged in finishing his luxurious dinner. They waited for him from four to six o'clock, and all that time did not enter on their deliberations, but talked of extraneous matters in subdued tones.

Only when Bennigsen had entered the hut, Kutuzov moved out of his corner and came up to the table, but sat there so that his face did not come within the light of the candles on it.

Bennigsen opened the council by the question: Whether to abandon the holy and ancient capital of Russia, or to defend it?

A prolonged silence followed. Every face was knitted, and in the stillness Kutuzov could be heard angrily coughing and clearing his throat. All eyes were fixed on him. Malasha too gazed at "Granddad."

She was nearest of all to him, and saw that his face was working; he seemed to be going to cry. But that did not last long.

"The holy and ancient capital of Russia!" he cried suddenly, in a wrathful voice, repeating Bennigsen's words, and thereby underlining the false note in them. "Allow me to tell your excellency that that question has no meaning to a Russian." (He lurched his unwieldy figure forward.) "Such a question cannot be put; there is no sense in such a question. The question I have asked these gentlemen to meet to discuss is the question of the war. The question is: The safety of Russia lies in her army. Is it better to risk the loss of the army and of Moscow by giving battle, or to abandon Moscow without a battle? That is the question on which I desire to learn your opinion." He lurched back into his low chair again.

A debate began. Bennigsen did not yet consider that the game was lost. Overruled by the opinion of Barclay and others in admitting the impossibility of maintaining a defensive position at Fili, he proceeded to prove his Russian patriotism and devotion to Moscow by proposing to move the army during the night from the right to the left flank of the position, and to aim a blow at the French right flank next day. Opinions were divided, and arguments were advanced for and against this project. Yermolov, Dohturov, and Raevsky sided with Bennigsen. Led by a feeling that a sacrifice was called for before abandoning the city, and by other personal considerations, these generals seemed unable to grasp that the council then sitting could not affect the inevitable course of events, and that Moscow was already in effect abandoned. The other generals understood this, and leaving the question of Moscow on one side, talked of the direction the army ought to take in retreating.

Malasha, who kept her eyes fixed on what was passing before her, saw the council in quite a different light. It seemed to her that the whole point at issue was a personal struggle between "Granddad" and "Longcoat," as she called Bennigsen to herself. She saw that they were angry when they spoke to one another, and in her heart she was on "Granddad's" side. In the middle of the conversation, she caught the swift, subtle glance that "Granddad" gave Bennigsen, and immediately after, she noted with glee that "Granddad's" words had put "Longcoat" down. Bennigsen suddenly flushed, and strode angrily across the room. The words that had thus affected Bennigsen were Kutuzov's quietly and softly uttered comment on his proposal to move the troops from the right to the left flank in the night in order to attack the French right.

"I cannot approve of the count's plan, gentlemen," said Kutuzov. "Movements of troops in close proximity to the enemy are always risky, and military history affords many examples of disasters arising from them. For instance . . ." (Kutuzov seemed to ponder, seeking an example, and then looking with a frank, naïve expression at Bennigsen) . . . "well, the battle of Friedland, which, as I have no doubt the count remembers, was not . . . completely successful owing to the change of the position of the troops in too close proximity to the enemy . . ."

A momentary silence followed that seemed lengthy to all.

The debate was renewed; but pauses often interrupted it, and it was felt that there was nothing to talk about.

In one of these pauses Kutuzov heaved a heavy sigh, as though preparing to speak. All looked round at him.

"Well, gentlemen, I see that it is I who will have to pay for the broken pots," he said. And slowly rising from his seat, he walked up to the table. "Gentlemen, I have heard your opinions. Some of you will not agree with me. But I" (he stopped), "by the authority intrusted me by my Tsar and my country, give the order to retire."

After that the generals began to disperse with the solemnity and circumspect taciturnity with which people separate after a funeral. Several of the generals made some communication to the commander-in-chief in a low voice, pitched in quite a different scale from that in which they had been talking at the council.

Malasha, who had long been expected in the other room to supper, dropped backwards down from the stove, her bare toes clinging to the projections of the stove, and slipping between the generals' legs, she darted out at the door.

After dismissing the generals, Kutuzov sat a long while with his elbows on the table, pondering that terrible question: "When, when had it become inevitable that Moscow should be abandoned? When was the thing done that made it inevitable, and who is to blame for it?"

"This I did not expect!" he said to the adjutant, Schneider, who came in to him late at night; "this I did not expect! This I never thought of!"

"You must rest, your highness," said Schneider.

"Yes; but they shall eat horse-flesh like the Turks!" Kutuzov cried, net heeding him, as he brought his podgy fist down on the table. "They too, shall eat it, if only . . . !"

V

Meanwhile, in an event of even greater importance than the retreat of the army without a battle, in the abandonment and burning of Moscow, Count Rastoptchin, whom we conceive as taking the lead in that event, was acting in a very different manner from Kutuzov.

This event—the abandonment and burning of Moscow—was, after the battle of Borodino, as inevitable as the retreat of the army without fighting.

Every Russian could have foretold what happened, not as a result of any train of intellectual deductions, but from the feeling that lies at the bottom of our hearts, and lay at the bottom of our fathers'!

In every town and village on Russian soil, from Smolensk onwards, without the assistance of Count Rastoptchin and his placards, the same thing took place as happened in Moscow. The people awaited the coming of the enemy without disturbance; did not display excitement; tore nobody to pieces, but calmly awaited their fate, feeling in themselves the power to find what they must do in the moment of difficulty.

And as soon as the enemy came near, the wealthier elements of the population went away, leaving their property behind; the poorer remained, and burnt and destroyed all that was left.

The sense that this would be so, and always would be so, lay, and lies, at the bottom of every Russian's heart. And a sense of this, and more, a foreboding that Moscow would be taken by the enemy, lay in the Russian society of Moscow in 1812. Those who had begun leaving Moscow in July and the beginning of August had shown that they expected it. Those who left the city with what they could carry away, abandoning their houses and half their property, did so in consequence of that latent patriotism, which finds expression, not in phrases, not in giving one's children to death for the sake of the fatherland, and such unnatural exploits, but expresses itself imperceptibly in the most simple, organic way, and so always produces the most powerful results.

"It's a disgrace to fly from danger; only the cowards are flying from Moscow," they were told. Rastoptchin, in his placards, urged upon them that it was base to leave Moscow. They were ashamed at hearing themselves called cowards; they were ashamed of going away; but still they went away, knowing that it must be so. Why did they go away? It cannot be supposed that Rastoptchin had scared them with tales of the atrocities perpetrated by Napoleon in the countries he conquered. The first to leave were the wealthy, educated people, who knew very well that Vienna and Berlin remained uninjured, and that the inhabitants of those cities, when Napoleon was in occupation of them, had spent their time gaily with the fascinating Frenchmen, of whom all Russians, and especially the ladies, had at that period been so fond.

They went away because to Russians the question whether they would be comfortable or not under the government of the French in Moscow could never occur. To be under the government of the French was out of the question; it was worse than anything. They were going away even before Borodino, and still more rapidly after Borodino; regardless of the calls to defend the city, regardless of the proclamations of the governor of Moscow; of his intention of going with the Iversky Virgin into battle, and of the air-balloons which were to demolish the French, and all the nonsense with which Rastoptchin filled his placards. They knew that it was for the army to fight, and if the army could not, it would be of no use to rush out with young ladies and house-serfs to fight Napoleon on the Three Hills, and so they must make haste and get away, sorry as they were to leave their possessions to destruction. They drove away without a thought of the vast consequences of this immense wealthy city being abandoned by its inhabitants, and being inevitably thereby consigned to the flames. To abstain from destroying and burning empty houses would never occur to the Russian peasantry. They drove away, each on his own account, and yet it was only in consequence of their action that the grand event came to pass that is the highest glory of the Russian people. The lady who in June set off with her Negroes and her buffoons from Moscow for her Saratov estates, with a vague feeling that she was not going to be a servant of Bonaparte's, and a vague dread that she might be hindered from going by Rastoptchin's orders, was simply and genuinely doing the great deed that saved Russia.

Count Rastoptchin at one time cried shame on those who were going, then removed all the public offices, then served out useless weapons to the drunken rabble, then brought out the holy images, and prevented Father Augustin from removing the holy relics and images, then got hold of all the private conveyances that were in Moscow, then in one hundred and thirty-six carts carried out the air-balloon made by Leppich, at one time hinted that he should set fire to Moscow, at one time described how he had burnt his own house, and wrote a proclamation to the French in which he solemnly reproached them for destroying the home of his childhood. He claimed the credit of having set fire to Moscow, then disavowed it; he commanded the people to capture all spies, and bring them to him, then blamed the people for doing so; he sent all the French residents out of Moscow, and then let Madame Aubert-Chalmey, who formed the centre of French society in Moscow, remain. For no particular reason he ordered the respected old postmaster, Klucharov, to be seized and banished. He got the people together on the Three Hills to fight the French, and then, to get rid of them, handed a man over to them to murder, and escaped himself by the back door. He vowed he would never survive the disaster of Moscow, and later on wrote French verses in albums on his share in the affair.[1]

This man had no inkling of the import of what was happening. All he wanted was to do something himself, to astonish people, to perform some heroic feat of patriotism, and, like a child, he frolicked about the grand

[1] *"Je suis né Tartare*
Je voulus être Romain
Les Français m'appelèrent barbare,
Les Russes—George Dandin."

and inevitable event of the abandonment and burning of Moscow, trying with his puny hand first to urge on, and then to hold back, the tide of the vast popular current that was bearing him along with it.

VI

ELLEN had accompanied the court on its return from Vilna to Petersburg, and there found herself in a difficult position.

In Petersburg Ellen had enjoyed the special patronage of a great personage, who occupied one of the highest positions in the government. In Vilna she had formed a liaison with a young foreign prince.

When she returned to Petersburg the prince and the great dignitary were both in that town; both claimed their rights, and Ellen was confronted with a problem that had not previously arisen in her career—the preservation of the closest relations with both, without giving offence to either.

What might have seemed to any other woman a difficult or impossible task never cost a moment's thought to Countess Bezuhov, who plainly deserved the reputation she enjoyed of being a most intelligent woman. Had she attempted concealment; had she allowed herself to get out of her awkward position by subterfuges, she would have spoilt her own case by acknowledging herself the guilty party. But like a truly great man, who can always do everything he chooses, Ellen at once assumed the rectitude of her own position, of which she was indeed genuinely convinced, and the guilty responsibility of every one else concerned.

The first time the young foreign prince ventured to reproach her, she lifted her beautiful head, and, with a haughty tone towards him, said firmly:

"This is the egoism and the cruelty of men. I expected nothing else. Woman sacrifices herself for you; she suffers, and this is her reward. What right have you, your highness, to call me to account for my friendships, my affections? He is a man who has been more than a father to me!"

The prince would have said something. Ellen interrupted him.

"Well, yes, perhaps he has sentiments for me other than those of a father, but that is not a reason I should shut my door on him. I am not a person to be ungrateful. Know, your highness, that in all that relates to my private sentiments I will account only to God and to my conscience!" she concluded, laying her hand on her beautiful, heaving bosom, and looking up to heaven.

"But listen to me, in God's name!" . . .

"Marry me, and I will be your slave!"

"But it is impossible."

"You do not deign to stoop to me, you . . ." Ellen burst into tears.

The prince attempted to console her. Ellen, as though utterly distraught, declared through her tears that there was nothing to prevent her marrying; that there were precedents (they were but few at that

time, but Ellen quoted the case of Napoleon and some other persons of
exalted rank); that she had never been a real wife to her husband; that
she had been dragged an unwilling victim into the marriage.

"But the law, religion . . ." murmured the prince, on the point of
yielding.

"Religion, laws . . . what can they have been invented for, if they
are unable to manage that?" said Ellen.

The prince was astonished that so simple a reflection had never occurred to him, and applied to the council of the brotherhood of the
Society of Jesus, with which he was in close relations.

A few days later, at one of the fascinating fêtes Ellen used to give at
her summer villa at Kamenny Ostrov, a certain fascinating M. Jobert
was presented to her; a man no longer young, with snow-white hair
and brilliant black eyes, *un Jésuite à robe courte,* who walked for a long
while with Ellen among the illuminations in the garden to the strains of
music, conversing with her of the love of God, of Christ, of the heart of
the Holy Mother, and of the consolations afforded in this life and the
next by the one true Catholic faith. Ellen was touched, and several times
tears stood both in her eyes and in M. Jobert's, and their voices
trembled. A dance, to which her partner fetched Ellen away, cut short
her conversation with the future "director of her conscience," but the
next evening M. Jobert came alone to see Ellen, and from that day he
was a frequent visitor.

One day he took the countess into a Catholic church, where she fell
on her knees before the altar, up to which she was conducted. The fascinating, middle-aged Frenchman laid his hands on her head, and as she
herself afterwards described it, she felt something like a breath of fresh
air, which seemed wafted into her soul. It was explained to her that this
was the "grace of God."

Then an abbé *à robe longue* was brought to her; he confessed her, and
absolved her from her sins. Next day a box was brought containing the
Sacred Host, and left for her to partake of at her house. Several days
later Ellen learned to her satisfaction that she had now been admitted
into the true Catholic Church, and that in a few days the Pope himself
would hear of her case, and send her a document of some sort.

All that was done with her and around her at this period, the attention
paid her by so many clever men, and expressed in such agreeable and
subtle forms, and her dovelike purity during her conversion (she wore
nothing but white dresses and white ribbons all the time)—all afforded
her gratification. But this gratification never led her for one instant to
lose sight of her object. And, as always happens in contests of cunning,
the stupid person gains more than the cleverer; Ellen, fully grasping
that the motive of all these words and all this manœuvring was by her
conversion to Catholicism to get a round sum from her for the benefit of
the Jesuit order (this was hinted at, indeed), held back the money, while
insisting steadily on the various operations that would set her free from
her conjugal bonds. To her notions, the real object of every religion was
to provide recognised forms of propriety for the satisfaction of human

desires. And with this end in view, she insisted, in one of her conversations with her spiritual adviser, on demanding an answer to the question how far her marriage was binding.

They were sitting in the drawing-room window. It was dusk. There was a scent of flowers from the window. Ellen wore a white dress, transparent over the bosom and shoulders. The sleek, well-fed abbé, with his plump, clean-shaven chin, his amiable, strong mouth, and his white hands, clasped mildly on his knees, was sitting close by Ellen. With a subtle smile on his lips, and a look of discreet admiration in his eyes, he gazed from time to time at her face, as he expounded his views on the subject. Ellen, with a restless smile, stared at his curly hair and his smooth-shaven, blackish cheeks, and seemed every minute to be expecting the conversation to take a new turn. But the abbé, though unmistakably aware of the beauty of his companion, was also interested in his own skilful handling of the question. The spiritual adviser adopted the following chain of reasoning:—

"In ignorance," said he, "of the significance of your promise, you took a vow of conjugal fidelity to a man who, on his side, was guilty of sacrilege in entering on the sacrament of matrimony with no faith in its religious significance. That marriage had not the dual binding force it should have had. But in spite of that, your vow was binding upon you. You broke it. What did you commit? Venial sin or mortal sin? A venial sin, because you committed it with no intention of acting wrongly. If now, with the object of bearing children, you should enter into a new marriage, your sin might be forgiven. But the question again falls into two divisions. First . . ."

"But, I imagine," Ellen, who was getting bored, said suddenly, with her fascinating smile, "that after being converted to the true religion, I cannot be bound by any obligations laid upon me by a false religion."

Her spiritual adviser was astounded at the simplicity of this solution, as simple as the solution of Columbus's egg. He was enchanted at the unexpected rapidity of his pupil's progress, but could not abandon the edifice of subtle argument that had cost him mental effort.

"Let us understand each other," he said, with a smile; and began to find arguments to refute his spiritual daughter's contention.

VII

ELLEN perceived that the matter was very simple and easy from the ecclesiastical point of view, but that her spiritual counsellors raised difficulties simply because they were apprehensive of the way in which it might be looked at by the temporal authorities.

And, consequently, Ellen decided in her own mind that the way must be paved for society to look at the matter in the true light. She excited the jealousy of the old dignitary, and said the same thing to him as she had to her other suitor—that is, gave him to understand that the sole means of obtaining exclusive rights over her was to marry her. The elderly dignitary was, like the young foreign prince, for the first moment

taken aback at this proposal of marriage from a wife whose husband was living. But Ellen's unfaltering confidence in asserting that it was a matter as simple and natural as the marriage of an unmarried girl had its effect on him too. Had the slightest traces of hesitation, shame, or reserve been perceptible in Ellen herself, her case would have been undoubtedly lost. But far from it; with perfect directness and simplehearted naïveté, she told her intimate friends (and that term included all Petersburg), that both the prince and the dignitary had made her proposals of marriage, and that she loved both, and was afraid of grieving either.

The rumour was immediately all over Petersburg—not that Ellen wanted a divorce from her husband (had such a rumour been discussed very many persons would have set themselves against any such illegal proceeding)—but that the unhappy, interesting Ellen was in hesitation which of her two suitors to marry. The question was no longer how far any marriage was possible, but simply which would be the more suitable match for her, and how the court would look at the question. There were, indeed, certain strait-laced people who could not rise to the high level of the subject, and saw in the project a desecration of the sanctity of marriage; but such persons were few in number, and they held their tongues; while the majority were interested in the question of Ellen's happiness, and which would be the better match for her. As to whether it were right or wrong for a wife to marry when her husband was alive, that was not discussed, as the question was evidently not a subject of doubt for persons "wiser than you and me" (as was said), and to doubt the correctness of their decision would be risking the betrayal of one's ignorance and absence of *savoir faire*.

Marya Dmitryevna Ahrosimov, who had come that summer to Petersburg to see one of her sons, was the only person who ventured on the direct expression of a contrary opinion. Meeting Ellen at a ball, Marya Dmitryevna stopped her in the middle of the room, and in the midst of a general silence said to her, in her harsh voice:

"So you are going to pass on from one husband to another, I hear! You think, I dare say, it's a new fashion you are setting. But you are not the first, madam. That's a very old idea. They do the same in all the . . ." And with these words, Marya Dmitryevna tucked up her broad sleeves with her usual menacing action, and looking severely round her, walked across the ballroom.

Though people were afraid of Marya Dmitryevna, yet in Petersburg they looked on her as a sort of buffoon, and therefore of all her words they noticed only the last coarse one, and repeated it to one another in whispers, supposing that the whole point of her utterance lay in that.

Prince Vassily had of late dropped into very frequently forgetting what he had said, and repeating the same phrase a hundred times; and every time he happened to see his daughter he used to say:

"Ellen, I have a word to say to you," he would say, drawing her aside, and pulling her arm downwards. "I have got wind of certain projects relative to . . . you know. Well, my dear child, you know how my father's heart rejoices to know you are . . . You have suffered so much. But, my dear child, consult only your heart. That's all I tell you." And concealing an emotion identical on each occasion, he pressed his cheek to his daughter's cheek and left her.

Bilibin, who had not lost his reputation as a wit, was a disinterested friend of Ellen's; one of those friends always to be seen in the train of brilliant women, men friends who can never pass into the rank of lovers. One day, in a "small and intimate circle," Bilibin gave his friend Ellen his views on the subject.

"*Écoutez*, Bilibin" (Ellen always called friends of the category to which Bilibin belonged by their surnames), and she touched his coat-sleeve with her white, beringed fingers. "Tell me, as you would a sister, what ought I to do? Which of the two?"

Bilibin wrinkled up the skin over his eyebrows, and pondered with a ‚smile on his lips.

"You do not take me unawares, you know," he said. "As a true friend, I have thought, and thought again of your affair. You see, if you marry the prince"—(the younger suitor) he crooked his finger—"you lose for ever the chance of marrying the other, and then you displease the court. (There is a sort or relationship, you know.) But if you marry the old count, you make the happiness of his last days. And then as widow of the great . . . the prince will not be making a *mésalliance* in marrying you . . ." and Bilibin let the wrinkles run out of his face.

"That's a real friend!" said Ellen beaming, and once more touching Bilibin's sleeve. "But the fact is I love them both, and I don't want to make them unhappy. I would give my life for the happiness of both," she declared.

Bilibin shrugged his shoulders to denote that for such a trouble even he could suggest no remedy.

"*Une maîtresse-femme!* That is what's called putting the question squarely. She would like to be married to all three at once," thought Bilibin.

"But do tell me what is your husband's view of the question?" he said, the security of his reputation saving him from all fear of discrediting himself by so naïve a question. "Does he consent?"

"Oh, he is so fond of me!" said Ellen, who, for some unknown reason, fancied that Pierre too adored her. "*Il fera tout pour moi.*"

Bilibin puckered up his face in preparation of the coming *mot*.

"*Même le divorce?*" he said.

Ellen laughed.

Among the persons who ventured to question the legality of the proposed marriage was Ellen's mother, Princess Kuragin. She had constantly suffered pangs of envy of her daughter, and now when the ground for such envy was the one nearest to her own heart, she could not reconcile herself to the idea of it.

She consulted a Russian priest to ascertain how far divorce and re-marriage was possible for a woman in her husband's lifetime. The priest assured her that this was impossible; and to her delight referred her to the text in the Gospel in which (as it seemed to the priest) re-marriage during the lifetime of the husband was directly forbidden.

Armed with these arguments, which seemed to her irrefutable, Princess Kuragin drove round to her daughter's early one morning in order to find her alone.

Ellen heard her mother's protests to the end, and smiled with bland sarcasm.

"You see it is plainly said: 'He who marryeth her that is divorced . . .'"

"O mamma, don't talk nonsense. You don't understand. In my position I have duties . . ." Ellen began, passing out of Russian into French, for in the former language she always felt a lack of clearness about her case.

"But, my dear . . ."

"O mamma, how is it you don't understand that the Holy Father, who has the right of granting dispensations . . ."

At that moment the lady companion, who lived in Ellen's house, came in to announce that his highness was in the drawing-room, and wished to see her.

"No, tell him I don't want to see him, that I am furious with him for not keeping his word."

"Countess, there is mercy for every sin," said a young man with fair hair and a long face and long nose.

The old princess rose respectfully and curtsied at his entrance. The young man took no notice of her. Princess Kuragin nodded to her daughter, and swam to the door.

"Yes, she is right," thought the old princess, all of whose convictions had been dissipated by the appearance of his highness on the scene. "She is right; but how was it in our youth—gone now for ever—we knew nothing of this? And it is so simple," thought Princess Kuragin, as she settled herself in her carriage.

At the beginning of August Ellen's affairs were settled, and she wrote to her husband (who, as she supposed, was deeply attached to her) a letter, in which she made known to him her intention of marrying N. N. She informed him also of her conversion to the one true faith, and begged him to go through all the necessary formalities for obtaining a divorce, of which the bearer of the letter would give him further details. "On which I pray God to have you in His holy and powerful keeping. Your friend, Ellen."

This letter was brought to Pierre's house at the time when he was on the field of Borodino.

VIII

AT the end of the day of Borodino, Pierre ran for a second time from Raevsky's battery, and with crowds of soldiers crossed the ravine on the way to Knyazkovo. There he reached an ambulance tent, and seeing blood and hearing screams and groans, he hurried on, caught up in a mob of soldiers.

The one thing Pierre desired now with his whole soul was to get away from the terrible sensations in which he had passed that day, to get back into the ordinary conditions of life, and to go to sleep quietly indoors in his own bed. He felt that only in the ordinary conditions of life would he be fit to understand himself and all he had seen and felt. But the ordinary conditions of life were nowhere to be found.

Though bullets and cannon balls were not whistling here on the road along which he was going, still he saw here on all sides the same sights as on the field of battle. There were everywhere the same suffering, exhausted, and sometimes strangely indifferent faces; everywhere the same blood and soldiers' overcoats, the same sound of firing at a distance, yet still rousing the same horror. There was heat and dust besides.

After walking about three versts along the Mozhaisk road, Pierre sat down by the roadside.

The shadows of night were beginning to fall over the earth, and the roar of cannon died down. Pierre lay leaning on his elbow, and lay so a long while, gazing at the shadows passing by him in the dusk. He was continually fancying that a cannon ball was swooping down upon him with a fearful whiz. He started and sat up. He had no idea how long he had been there. In the middle of the night, three soldiers, dragging branches after them, settled themselves near him and began making a fire.

Casting sidelong glances at Pierre, the soldiers lighted the fire, set a pot on it, broke up their biscuits into it, and put in some lard. The pleasant odour of the savoury and greasy mess blended with the smell of smoke. Pierre raised himself and sighed. The soldiers (there were three of them) were eating and talking among themselves, without taking any notice of Pierre.

"And what lot will you be one of?" one of the soldiers suddenly asked Pierre, evidently suggesting in this inquiry precisely what Pierre was thinking about. "If you are hungry we'll give you some, only tell us whether you're a true man."

"I?" . . . said Pierre, feeling the necessity of minimising his social position as far as possible, so as to be closer to the soldiers and more within their range. "I am really a militia officer, but my company's nowhere about; I came to the battle and lost sight of my comrades."

"Well! Fancy that!" said one of the soldiers.

Another soldier shook his head.

"Well, you can have some of the mash, if you like!" said the first, and licking a wooden spoon he gave it to Pierre.

Pierre squatted by the fire, and fell to eating the mess in the pot, which seemed to him the most delicious dish he had ever tasted. While he was bending over the pot, helping himself to big spoonfuls and greedily munching one after another, the soldiers stared at him in silence.

"Where do you want to go? Tell us!" the first of them asked again.

"To Mozhaisk."

"You're a gentleman, then?"

"Yes."

"And what's your name?"

"Pyotr Kirillovitch."

"Well, Pyotr Kirillovitch, come along, we'll take you there."

In the pitch dark the soldiers and Pierre walked to Mozhaisk.

The cocks were crowing when they reached Mozhaisk, and began as-cending the steep hill into the town.

Pierre walked on with the soldiers, entirely forgetting that his inn was at the bottom of the hill and he had passed it. He would not have been aware of this—so preoccupied was he—if he had not chanced halfway up the hill to stumble across his groom, who had been to look for him in the town, and was on his way back to the inn. The groom recognised Pierre by his hat, which gleamed white in the dark.

"Your excellency!" he cried, "why, we had quite given you up. How is it you are on foot? And, mercy on us, where are you going?"

"Oh, to be sure . . ." said Pierre.

The soldiers halted.

"Well, found your own folks then?" said one of them.

"Well, good-bye to you—Pyotr Kirillovitch, wasn't it?"

"Good-bye, Pyotr Kirillovitch!" said the other voices.

"Good-bye," said Pierre, and with the groom he turned in the direc-tion of the inn.

"I ought to give them something!" thought Pierre, feeling for his pocket. "No, better not," some inner voice prompted him.

There was not a room at the inn: all were full. Pierre went out into the yard, and muffling his head up, lay down in his carriage.

IX

PIERRE had hardly put his head on the pillow when he felt that he was dropping asleep. But all of a sudden he heard, almost with the distinct-ness of reality, the sound of the boom, boom, boom of the cannon, the groans and shrieks and dull thud of the falling shell, smelt the blood and powder; and the feeling of horror, of the dread of death came over him. He opened his eyes in a panic, and put his head out from the cloak. All was quiet in the yard. The only sound came from a servant of some sort talking with the porter at the gate, and splashing through the mud. Over Pierre's head, under the dark, wooden eaves, he heard pigeons fluttering, startled by the movement he had made in sitting up. The whole yard was pervaded by the strong smell of a tavern—full of peaceful suggestion and soothing relief to Pierre—the smell of hay, of dung, and of tar. Be-tween two dark sheds he caught a glimpse of the pure, starlit sky.

"Thank God, that is all over!" thought Pierre, covering his head up again. "Oh, how awful terror is, and how shamefully I gave way to it! But they . . . *they* were firm and calm all the while up to the end . . ." he thought. *They*, in Pierre's mind, meant the soldiers, those who had been on the battery, and those who had given him food, and those who had prayed to the holy picture. *They*—those strange people, of whom he had known nothing hitherto—*they* stood out clearly and sharply in his mind apart from all other people.

"To be a soldier, simply a soldier!" thought Pierre as he fell asleep. "To enter with one's whole nature into that common life, to be filled with what makes them what they are. But how is one to cast off all that is superfluous, devilish in one's self, all the burden of the outer man? At one time I might have been the same. I might have run away from my father as I wanted to. After the duel with Dolohov too I might have been sent for a soldier."

And into Pierre's imagination flashed a picture of the dinner at the club, at which he had challenged Dolohov, then the image of his bene-factor at Torzhok. And there rose before his mind a solemn meeting of the lodge. It was taking place at the English Club. And some one he knew, some one near and dear to him, was sitting at the end of the table. "Why, it is he! It is my benefactor. But surely he died?" thought Pierre. "Yes, he did die, but I didn't know he was alive. And how sorry I was when he died, and how glad I am he is alive again!" On one side of the table were sitting Anatole, Dolohov, Nesvitsky, Denisov, and others like them (in Pierre's dream these people formed as distinct a class apart as those other men whom he had called *them* to himself), and those people, Anatole and Dolohov, were loudly shouting and singing. But through their clamour the voice of his benefactor could be heard speaking all the while, and the sound of his voice was as weighty and as uninterrupted as the din of the battlefield, but it was pleasant and comforting. Pierre did not understand what his benefactor was saying, but he knew (the cate-gory of his ideas, too, was distinct in his dream) that he was talking of goodness, of the possibility of being like *them*. And *they* with their sim-ple, good, plucky faces were surrounding his benefactor on all sides. But though they were kindly, they did not look at Pierre; they did not know him. Pierre wanted to attract their notice, and to speak to them. He got up, but at the same instant became aware that his legs were bare and chill.

He felt ashamed, and put his arm over his legs, from which his cloak had in fact slipped off. For an instant Pierre opened his eyes as he pulled up the cloak, and saw the same roofs, and posts, and yard, but it was now full of bluish light, and glistening with dew or frost.

"It's getting light," thought Pierre. "But that's not the point. I want to hear and understand the benefactor's words."

He muffled himself in the cloak again, but the masonic dinner and his benefactor would not come back. All that remained were thoughts, clearly expressed in words, ideas; some voice was speaking, or Pierre was thinking.

When he recalled those thoughts later, although they had been evoked by the impressions of that day, Pierre was convinced that they were uttered by some one outside himself. It seemed to him that he had never been capable of thinking those thoughts and expressing them in that form in his waking moments.

"The most difficult thing is the subjection of man's will to the law of God," said the voice. "Simplicity is the submission to God; there is no escaping from Him. And *they* are simple. *They* do not talk, but act. A word uttered is silver, but unuttered is golden. No one can be master of anything while he fears death. And all things belong to him who fears it not. If it were not for suffering, a man would know not his limits, would know not himself. The hardest thing" (Pierre thought or heard in his dream) "is to know how to unite in one's soul the significance of the whole. To unite the whole?" Pierre said to himself. "No, not to unite. One cannot unite one's thoughts, but to *harness* together all those ideas, that's what's wanted. Yes, one *must harness* together, *harness* together," Pierre repeated to himself with a thrill of ecstasy, feeling that those words, and only those words, expressed what he wanted to express, and solved the whole problem fretting him.

"Yes, one must *harness* together; it's time to *harness* . . ."

"We want to harness the horses; it's time to harness the horses, your excellency! Your excellency," some voice was repeating, "we want to harness the horses; it's time . . ."

It was the groom waking Pierre. The sun was shining full in Pierre's face. He glanced at the dirty tavern yard; at the well in the middle of it soldiers were watering their thin horses; and waggons were moving out of the gate.

He turned away with repugnance, and shutting his eyes, made haste to huddle up again on the seat of the carriage. "No, I don't want that; I don't want to see and understand that; I want to understand what was revealed to me in my sleep. Another second and I should have understood it all. But what am I to do? To harness, but how to harness all together?" And Pierre felt with horror that the whole meaning of what he had seen and thought in his dream had slipped away.

The groom, the coachman, and the porter told Pierre that an officer had come with the news that the French were advancing on Mozhaisk and our troops were retreating.

Pierre got up, and ordering the carriage to be got out and to drive after him, crossed the town on foot.

The troops were marching out, leaving tens of thousands of wounded behind. The wounded could be seen at the windows of the houses, and were crowding the yards and streets. Screams, oaths, and blows could be heard in the streets about the carts which were to carry away the wounded. Pierre put his carriage at the service of a wounded general of his acquaintance, and drove with him to Moscow. On the way he was told of the death of his brother-in-law, Anatole, and of the death of Prince Andrey.

X

On the 30th Pierre returned to Moscow. Almost at the city gates he was met by an adjutant of Count Rastoptchin's.

"Why, we have been looking for you everywhere," said the adjutant.

"The count urgently wants to see you. He begs you to come to him at once on very important business." Instead of going home, Pierre hailed a cab-driver and drove to the governor's.

Count Rastoptchin had only that morning arrived from his summer villa at Sokolniky. The ante-room and waiting-room in the count's house were full of officials, who had been summoned by him, or had come to him for instructions. Vassiltchekov and Platov had already seen the count, and informed him that the defence of Moscow was out of the question, and the city would be surrendered. Though the news was being concealed from the citizens, the heads of various departments and officials of different kinds knew that Moscow would soon be in the hands of the enemy, just as Count Rastoptchin knew it. And all of them to escape personal responsibility had come to the governor to inquire how to act in regard to the offices in their charge.

At the moment when Pierre went into the waiting-room, a courier from the army was just coming out from an interview with the count.

The courier waved his hand with a hopeless air at the questions with which he was besieged, and walked across the room.

While he waited, Pierre watched with weary eyes the various officials —young, old, military, and civilian, important and insignificant—who were gathered together in the room. All seemed dissatisfied and uneasy. Pierre went up to one group of functionaries, among whom he recognised an acquaintance. After greeting him, they went on with their conversation.

"Well, to send out and bring back again would be no harm; but in the present position of affairs there's no answering for anything."

"But look here, what he writes," said another, pointing to a printed paper he held in his hand.

"That's a different matter. That's necessary for the common people," said the first.

"What is it?" asked Pierre.

"The new proclamation."

Pierre took it and began to read.

"His highness the prince has passed Mozhaisk, so as to unite with the troops that are going to join him, and has taken up a strong position, where the enemy cannot attack him suddenly. Forty-eight cannon with shells have been sent him from here, and his highness declares that he will defend Moscow to the last drop of blood, and is ready even to fight in the streets. Don't mind, brothers, that the courts of justice are closed; we must take our measures, and we'll deal with miscreants in our own fashion. When the time comes, I shall have need of some gallant fellows, both of town and country. I will give the word in a couple of days; but now there's no need, and I hold my peace. The axe is useful; the pike, too, is not to be despised; but best of all is the three-pronged fork: a Frenchman is no heavier than a sheaf of rye. To-morrow after dinner, I shall take the Iversky Holy Mother to St. Catherine's Hospital to the wounded. There we will consecrate the water; they will soon be well again. I, too, am well now; one of my eyes was bad, but now I look well out of both."

"Why, I was told by military men," said Pierre, "that there could be no fighting in the town itself, and the position . . ."

"To be sure, that's just what we are saying," said the first speaker.

"But what does that mean: 'One of my eyes was bad, but now I look out of both'?" asked Pierre.

"The count had a sty in his eye," said the adjutant smiling; "and he was very much put out when I told him people were coming to ask what was the matter. And oh, count," he said suddenly, addressing Pierre with a smile, "we have been hearing that you are in trouble with domestic anxieties, that the countess, your spouse . . ."

"I have heard nothing about it," said Pierre indifferently. "What is it you have heard?"

"Oh, you know, stories are so often made up. I only repeat what I hear."

"What have you heard?"

"Oh, they say," said the adjutant again with the same smile, "that the countess, your wife, is preparing to go abroad. It's most likely nonsense."

"It may be," said Pierre, looking absent-mindedly about him. "Who is that?" he asked, indicating a tall old man in a clean blue overcoat, with a big, snow-white beard and eyebrows and a ruddy face.

"That? Oh, he's a merchant; that is, he's the restaurant-keeper, Vereshtchagin. You have heard the story of the proclamation, I dare say?"

"Oh, so that's Vereshtchagin!" said Pierre, scrutinising the firm, calm face of the old merchant, and seeking in it some token of treachery.

"That's not the man himself. That's the father of the fellow who wrote the proclamation," said the adjutant. "The young man himself is in custody, and I fancy it will go hard with him."

A little old gentleman with a star, and a German official with a cross on his neck, joined the group.

"It's a complicated story, you see," the adjutant was relating. "The proclamation appeared two months ago. It was brought to the count. He ordered inquiry to be made. Well, Gavrilo Ivanitch made investigations; the proclamation had passed through some sixty-three hands. We come to one and ask, From whom did you get it? From so and so. And the next refers us on to so and so; and in that way they traced it to Vereshtchagin . . . a half-educated merchant's son, one of those pretty dears, you know," said the adjutant smiling. "He too was asked, From whom did you get it? And we knew very well from whom he had it really. He could have had it from no one but the director of the post-office. But it was clear there was an understanding between them. He says he got it from no one, but had composed it himself. And threaten him and question him as they would, he stuck to it, he had written it himself. So the matter was reported, and the count had him sent for. 'From whom did you get the proclamation?' 'I wrote it myself.' Well! you know the count," said the adjutant, with a smile of pride and delight. "He was fearfully angry; and only fancy the insolence, and lying, and stubbornness!"

"Oh! the count wanted him to say it was from Klutcharyov, I understand," said Pierre.

"Oh no, not at all," said the adjutant in dismay. "Klutcharyov had sins enough to answer for without that, and that's why he was banished. But any way, the count was very indignant. 'How could you write it?' says the count. He took up the *Hamburg Gazette* that was on the table. 'Here it is. You did not compose it, but translated it, and very badly too, because you don't even know French, you fool.' What do you think? 'No,' says he, 'I have never read any gazettes; I made it up.' 'But if so, you're a traitor, and I'll hand you over for judgment, and you will be hanged.' 'Tell us from whom you got it.' 'I have not seen any gazettes; I composed it.' So the matter rests. The count sent for the father; he sticks to the same story. And they had him tried, and he was sentenced, I believe, to hard labour. Now the father has come to petition in his favour. But he is a worthless young scamp! You know the style of spoilt merchant's son, a regular dandy and lady-killer; has attended lectures of some sort, and so fancies that he's above everybody. A regular young scamp! His father has an eating-house here on the Kamenny bridge; and in the shop, you know, there is a great picture of God the Supporter of All, represented with a sceptre in one hand and the empire in the other; well, he took that picture home for a few days, and what do you suppose he did! He got hold of some wretched painter , , ,"

XI

IN the middle of this new story Pierre was summoned to the governor.

He went into Count Rastoptchin's study. Rastoptchin, frowning, passed his hand across his forehead and eyes as Pierre entered. A short man was saying something, but as soon as Pierre walked in he stopped, and went out.

"Ah! greetings to you, valiant warrior," said Rastoptchin as soon as the other man had left the room. "We have been hearing about your *prouesses*! But that's not the point. *Mon cher, entre nous*, are you a mason?" said Count Rastoptchin in a severe tone, that suggested that it was a crime to be so, but that he intended to pardon it. Pierre did not speak. "*Mon cher, je suis bien informé;* but I know that there are masons and masons, and I hope you don't belong to those among them who, by way of regenerating the human race, are trying to ruin Russia."

"Yes, I am a mason," answered Pierre.

"Well then, look here, my dear boy. You are not unaware, I dare say, of the fact that Speransky and Magnitsky have been sent—to their proper place—and the same has been done with Klutcharyov and the others who, under the guise of building up the temple of Solomon, have been trying to destroy the temple of their fatherland. You may take it for granted there are good reasons for it, and that I could not have banished the director of the post-office here if he had not been a dangerous person. Now, it has reached my ears that you sent him your carriage to get out of the town, and that you have even taken charge of his papers. I like you, and wish you no harm, and as you are half my age, I advise you, as a father might, to break off all connection with people of that sort, and to get away from here yourself as quickly as you can."

"But what was Klutcharyov's crime?" asked Pierre.

"That's my business; and it's not yours to question me," cried Rastoptchin.

"If he is accused of having circulated Napoleon's proclamation, the charge has not been proved," said Pierre, not looking at Rastoptchin. "And Vereshtchagin . . ."

"*Nous y voilà*," Rastoptchin suddenly broke in, scowling and shouting louder than ever. "Vereshtchagin is a traitor and a deceiver, who will receive the punishment he deserves," he said, with the vindictiveness with which people speak at the recollection of an affront. "But I did not send for you to criticise my actions, but in order to give you advice or a command, if you will have it so. I beg you to break off all connection with Klutcharyov and his set, and to leave the town. And I'll knock the nonsense out of them, wherever I may find it." And, probably becoming conscious that he was taking a heated tone with Bezuhov, who was as yet guilty of no offence, he added, taking Pierre's hand cordially: "We are on the eve of a public disaster, and I haven't time to say civil things to every one who has business with me. My head is at times in a perfect whirl. Well, what are you going to do, you personally?"

"Oh, nothing," answered Pierre, with his eyes still downcast, and no change in the expression of his dreamy face.

The count frowned.

"*Un conseil d'ami, mon cher.* Decamp, and as soon as may be, that's my advice. *A bon entendeur, salut!* Good-bye, my dear boy. Oh, by the way," he called after him at the door, "is it true the countess has fallen into the clutches of the holy fathers of the Society of Jesus?"

Pierre made no answer. He walked out from Rastoptchin's room, scowling and wrathful as he had never been seen before.

By the time he reached home it was getting dark. Eight persons of different kinds were waiting on him that evening. A secretary of a committee, the colonel of his battalion of militia, his steward, his bailiff, and other persons with petitions. All of them had business matters with Pierre, which he had to settle. He had no understanding of their questions, nor interest in them, and answered them with the sole object of getting rid of these people. At last he was left alone, and he broke open and read his wife's letter.

"*They*—the soldiers on the battery, Prince Andrey killed . . . the old man. . . . Simplicity is submission to God's will. One has to suffer . . . the significance of the whole . . . one must harness all together . . .

my wife is going to be married. . . . One must forget and understand
. . ." And, without undressing, he threw himself on his bed and at once
fell asleep.

When he waked up next morning his steward came in to announce
that a police official was below, sent expressly by Count Rastoptchin to
find out whether Count Bezuhov had gone, or was going away.

A dozen different people were waiting in the drawing-room to see
Pierre on business. Pierre dressed in haste, and instead of going down to
see them, he ran down the back staircase and out by the back entry to
the gates.

From that moment till the occupation of Moscow was over, no one of
Bezuhov's household saw him again, nor could discover his whereabouts,
in spite of every effort to track him down.

XII

THE Rostovs remained in Moscow till the 1st of September, the day
before the enemy entered the city.

After Petya had joined Obolensky's regiment of Cossacks and had
gone away to Byely Tserkov, where the regiment was being enrolled, the
countess fell into a panic of terror. The idea that both her sons were at
the war, that they had both escaped from under her wing, that any day
either of them—and possibly even both at once, like the three sons of a
lady of her acquaintance—might be killed, seemed for the first time that
summer to strike her imagination with cruel vividness. She tried to get
Nikolay back, wanted to go herself after Petya, or to obtain some post
for him in Petersburg; but all these seemed equally impossible. Petya
could not be brought back except by the return of his regiment, or
through being transferred to another regiment on active service. Nikolay
was somewhere at the front, and nothing had been heard from him since
the letter in which he had given a detailed account of his meeting with
Princess Marya. The countess could not sleep at nights, and when she
did sleep, she dreamed that her sons had been killed. After much talking the matter over, and many consultations of friends, the count at last
hit on a means for soothing the countess. He got Petya transferred from
Obolensky's regiment to Bezuhov's, which was in formation near Moscow. Though, even so, Petya remained in the army, by this exchange
the countess had the consolation of seeing one son at least again under
her wing; and she hoped to manage not to let her Petya escape her again,
but to succeed in getting him always appointed to places where there
would be no risk of his being in battle. While Nikolay had been the only
one in danger, the countess had fancied (and had suffered some pricks
of conscience on the subject) that she loved her elder son better than the
other children. But now that her younger boy, the scapegrace Petya,
always idle at his lessons, always in mischief, and teasing every one, her
little Petya, with his snub-nose, his merry black eyes, his fresh colour,
and the soft down just showing on his cheeks, had slipped away into the

company of those big, dreadful, cruel men, who were fighting away somewhere about something, and finding a sort of pleasure in it—now it
seemed to the mother that she loved him more, far more, than all the
rest. The nearer the time came for the return of her longed-for Petya to
Moscow, the greater was the uneasiness of the countess. She positively
thought she would never live to see such happiness. Not only Sonya's
presence, even her favourite Natasha's, even her husband's company,
irritated the countess. "What do I want with them, I want no one but
Petya!" she thought. One day towards the end of August, the Rostovs
received a second letter from Nikolay. He wrote from the province of
Voronezh, where he had been sent to procure remounts. This letter did
not soothe the countess. Knowing that one son was out of danger, she
seemed to feel even greater alarm on Petya's account.

Although by the 20th of August almost all the Rostovs' acquaintances
had left Moscow; although everybody was trying to persuade the countess to get away as quickly as possible, she would not hear of leaving till
her treasure, her idolised Petya, had come back. On the 28th of August
Petya arrived. The morbidly passionate tenderness with which his
mother received him was by no means gratifying to the sixteen-year-old
officer. Though his mother concealed her intention of never letting him
escape from under her wing again, Petya divined her plans, and instinctively afraid of his mother's making him too soft, of her "making a
ninny" of him (as he expressed it in his own mind), he treated her rather
coolly, avoided being with her, and during his stay in Moscow devoted
himself exclusively to Natasha, for whom he had always had the warmest brotherly affection, almost approaching adoration.

The count, with his characteristic carelessness, had by the 28th made
no preparations for leaving, and the waggons that were to come from
their Moscow and Ryazan estate to remove all their property out of the
house only arrived on the 30th.

From the 28th to the 31st, Moscow was all bustle and movement.
Every day thousands of wounded from the field of Borodino were
brought in at the Dorogomilov gate and conveyed across Moscow, and
thousands of vehicles, full of residents and their belongings, were driving out at the gates on the opposite side of the city. In spite of Rastoptchin's placards—either arising independently of them, or perhaps in
consequence of them—the strangest and most contradictory rumours
were circulating about the town. Some said that every one was forbidden
to leave the city; others asserted that all the holy pictures had been
taken from the churches, and every one was to be driven out of Moscow
by force. Some said there had been another battle after Borodino, in
which the French had been utterly defeated; others declared that the
whole Russian army had been annihilated. Some talked of the Moscow
militia, which was to advance, preceded by priests, to Three Hills; others
whispered that Father Augustin had been forbidden to leave, that traitors had been caught, that the peasants were in revolt, and were plundering those who left the town, and so on. But all this was only talk: in
reality even though the council at Fili, at which it was decided to aban-

don Moscow, had not yet taken place, all—those who were leaving and those who were staying—felt that Moscow would be surrendered, though they did not say so freely, and felt that they must make all haste to escape, and to save their property. There was a feeling that there must come a general crash and change, yet till the 1st of September everything went on unchanged. Like a criminal being led to the gallows, who knows in a minute he must die, and yet stares about, and puts straight the cap awry on his head, Moscow instinctively went on with the daily routine of life, though aware that the hour of ruin was approaching, when all the customary conditions of life would be at an end.

During the three days preceding the occupation of Moscow, the whole Rostov family was busily engaged in various practical ways. The head of the family, Count Ilya Andreitch, was continually driving about the town, picking up all the rumours that were in circulation, and while at home, gave superficial and hasty directions for the preparations for departure.

The countess superintended the sorting out of things to be packed; she was out of humour with every one, and was in continual pursuit of Petya, who was as continually escaping from her, and exciting her jealousy by spending all his time with Natasha. Sonya was the only person who really undertook the practical business of getting things packed. But Sonya had been particularly silent and melancholy of late. She had been present when Nikolay's letter mentioning Princess Marya had elicited the most delighted deductions from the countess, who saw in Nikolay's meeting with Princess Marya the direct intervention of Providence.

"I was never really happy," said the countess, "when Bolkonsky was engaged to Natasha, but I had always longed for Nikolay to marry the princess, and I have always had a presentiment about it. And what a good thing it would be!"

Sonya felt that this was true; that the only possibility of retrieving the Rostovs' position was by Nikolay's marriage to an heiress, and that the princess would be an excellent match for him. But this reflection was very bitter for her. In spite, or perhaps in consequence, of her sadness, she undertook the difficult task of seeing after the sorting and packing of the household goods, and for whole days together she was busily employed. The count and countess referred to her when they had any orders to give. Petya and Natasha, on the contrary, did nothing to help their parents, but were generally in every one's way, and were only a hindrance. And all day long the house resounded with their flying footsteps and shouts and shrieks of causeless mirth. They laughed and were gay, not in the least because there was reason for laughter. But they were gay and glad at heart, and so everything that happened was reason enough for gaiety and laughter in them. Petya was in high spirits because he had left home a boy, and come back (so every one told him) a fine young man, because he was at home, because he had left Byely Tserkov, where there seemed no hope of being soon on active service, and come to Moscow where there would be fighting in a few days, and above all, because Natasha, whose lead he always followed, was in high spirits. Natasha was gay, because she had too long been sad, and now nothing reminded her of the cause of her sadness, and she was quite strong again. She was gay too, because she needed some one to adore her (the adoration of others was like the grease on the wheels, without which her mechanism never worked quite smoothly), and Petya did adore her. And above all, they were both gay, because there was war at the very gates of Moscow, because there would be fighting at the barriers, because arms were being given out, and everybody was rushing about, and altogether something extraordinary was happening, which is always inspiriting, especially for the young.

XIII

ON Saturday, the 31st of August, the whole household of the Rostovs seemed turned upside down. All the doors stood wide open, all the furniture had been moved about or carried out, looking-glasses and pictures had been taken down. The rooms were littered up with boxes, with hay and packing paper and cord. Peasants and house-serfs were tramping about the parquet floors carrying out the baggage. The courtyard was crowded with peasants' carts, some piled high with goods and corded up, others still standing empty.

The voices and steps of the immense multitude of servants and of peasants, who had come with the carts, resounded through the courtyard and the house. The count had been out since early morning. The countess had a headache from the noise and bustle, and was lying down in the new divan-room with compresses steeped in vinegar on her head. Petya was not at home; he had gone off to see a comrade, with whom he was planning to get transferred from the militia to a regiment at the front. Sonya was in the great hall, superintending the packing of the china and glass. Natasha was sitting on the floor in her dismantled room among heaps of dresses, ribbons, and scarfs. She sat gazing immovably at the floor, holding in her hands an old ball-dress, the very dress, now out of fashion, in which she had been to her first Petersburg ball.

Natasha was ashamed of doing nothing when every one in the house was so busy, and several times that morning she had tried to set to work; but her soul was not in it; and she was utterly unable to do anything unless all her heart and soul were in it. She stood over Sonya while she packed the china, and tried to help; but soon threw it up, and went to her room to pack her own things. At first she had found it amusing to give away her dresses and ribbons to the maids, but afterwards when it came to packing what was left, it seemed a wearisome task.

"Dunyasha, you'll pack it all, dear? Yes? yes?"

And when Dunyasha readily undertook to do it all for her, Natasha sat down on the floor with the old ball-dress in her hands, and fell to dreaming on subjects far removed from what should have been occupying her mind then. From the reverie she had fallen into, Natasha was aroused by the talk of the maids in the next room and their hurried foot-

steps from their room to the backstairs. Natasha got up and looked out
of the window. A huge train of carts full of wounded men had stopped
in the street.

The maids, the footmen, the housekeeper, the old nurse, the cooks,
the coachmen, the grooms, and the scullion-boys were all at the gates,
staring at the wounded men.

Natasha flung a white pocket-handkerchief over her hair, and holding
the corners in both hands, went out into the street.

The old housekeeper, Mavra Kuzminishna, had left the crowd standing at the gate, and gone up to a cart with a tilt of bast-mats thrown over
it. She was talking to a pale young officer who was lying in this cart.
Natasha took a few steps forward and stood still timidly, holding her
kerchief on and listening to what the housekeeper was saying.

"So you have no one then in Moscow?" Mavra Kuzminishna was saying. "You'd be more comfortable in some apartment. . . . In our house
even. The masters are all leaving."

"I don't know if it would be allowed," said the officer in a feeble voice.
"There's our chief officer . . . ask him," and he pointed to a stout
major who had turned back and was walking along the row of carts
down the street.

Natasha glanced with frightened eyes into the face of the wounded
officer, and at once went to meet the major.

"May the wounded men stay in our house?" she asked.

The major with a smile put his hand to his cap.

"What is your pleasure, ma'mselle?" he said, screwing up his eyes and
smiling.

Natasha quietly repeated her question, and her face and her whole
manner, though she still kept hold of the corners of the pocket-handkerchief, was so serious, that the major left off smiling, and after a moment's pondering—as though asking himself how far it were possible—
he gave her an affirmative answer.

"Oh yes, why not, they may," he said.

Natasha gave a slight nod, and went back with rapid steps to Mavra
Kuzminishna, who was still talking with commiserating sympathy to the
young officer.

"They may; he said they might!" whispered Natasha.

The officer in the covered cart turned into the Rostovs' courtyard, and
dozens of carts of wounded men began at the invitation of the inhabitants to drive up to the entries of the houses in Povarsky Street. Natasha was evidently delighted at having to do with new people in conditions quite outside the ordinary routine of life. She joined Mavra
Kuzminishna in trying to get as many as possible driven into their yard.

"We must ask your papa though," said Mavra Kuzminishna.

"Nonsense, nonsense. What does it matter? For one day, we'll move
into the drawing-room. We can give them all our half of the house."

"What an idea! what next? The lodge, may be, the men's room, and
old nurse's room; and you must ask leave for that."

"Well, I will ask."

Natasha ran indoors, and went on tiptoe to the half-open door of the divan-room, where there was a strong smell of vinegar and Hoffmann's drops.

"Are you asleep, mamma?"

"Oh, what chance is there of sleep!" said the countess, who had just dropped into a doze.

"Mamma, darling!" said Natasha, kneeling before her mother and leaning her face against her mother's. "I am sorry, forgive me, I'll never do it again, I waked you. Mavra Kuzminishna sent me; they have brought some wounded men in, officers, will you allow it? They have nowhere to go; I know you will allow it, . . ." she said rapidly, not taking breath.

"Officers? Who have been brought in? I don't understand," said the countess.

Natasha laughed, the countess too smiled faintly.

"I knew you would let me . . . so I will tell them so." And Natasha, kissing her mother, got up and went to the door.

In the hall she met her father, who had come home with bad news.

"We have lingered on too long!" said the count, with unconscious anger in his voice; "the club's shut up and the police are leaving."

"Papa, you don't mind my having invited some of the wounded into the house?" said Natasha.

"Of course not," said the count absently. "But that's not to the point. I beg you now not to let yourself be taken up with any nonsense, but to help to pack and get off—to get off to-morrow . . ."

And the count gave his butler and servants the same orders. Petya came back at dinner-time, and he too had news to tell them.

He said that the mob was taking up arms to-day in the Kremlin; that though Rastoptchin's placard said he would give the word two days later, it had really been arranged that all the people should go next day in arms to the Three Hills, and there a great battle was to be fought.

The countess looked in timid horror at her son's eager, excited face, as he told them this. She knew that if she said a word to try and dissuade Petya from going to this battle (she knew how he was enjoying the prospect of it), he would say something about the duty of a man, about honour, and the fatherland—something irrational, masculine, and perverse—which it would be useless to oppose, and all hope of preventing him would be gone. And, therefore, hoping to succeed in setting off before this battle, and in taking Petya with her, to guard and protect them on the road, she said nothing to her son, but after dinner called her husband aside, and with tears besought him to take her away as soon as could be, that night if possible. With the instinctive, feminine duplicity of love, though she had till then shown not the slightest sign of alarm, she declared she should die of terror if they did not get away that very night. She was indeed without feigning afraid now of everything.

XIV

MADAME SCHOSS, who had gone out to visit her daughter, increased the countess's terrors by describing the scenes she had witnessed at a spirit dealer's in Myasnitsky Street. She entered that street on her way home, but could not pass through it owing to the drunken mob raging round the spirit dealer's. She had taken a cab and driven home by a circuitous route, and the driver had told her that the mob had broken open the casks of spirit, that orders had been given to that effect.

After dinner all the Rostov household set to work packing and preparing for their departure with eager haste. The old count, suddenly rousing himself to the task, spent the rest of the day continually trotting from the courtyard into the house and back again, shouting confused instructions to the hurrying servants, and trying to spur them on to even greater haste. Petya looked after things in the yard. Sonya was quite bewildered by the count's contradictory orders, and did not know what to do. The servants raced about the rooms, shouting, quarrelling, and making a noise. Natasha, too, suddenly set to work with the ardour that was characteristic of her in all she did. At first her intervention was sceptically received. No one expected anything serious from her or would obey her instructions. But with heat and perseverance, she insisted on being obeyed, got angry and almost shed tears that they did not heed her, and did at last succeed in impressing them. Her first achievement, which cost her immense effort, and established her authority, was the packing of the rugs. There were a number of costly Gobelin tapestries and Persian rugs in the house. When Natasha set to work, she found two boxes standing open in the hall: one packed almost full of china, the other full of rugs. There was a great deal more china left standing on the tables and there was more still to come from the storeroom. Another third box was needed, and the men had gone to get one.

"Sonya, wait a little, and we'll pack it all without that," said Natasha.

"You cannot, miss; we have tried already," said the footman.

"No, wait a minute, please." And Natasha began taking out the plates and dishes, packed up in paper.

"The dishes would go better in here with the rugs," she said.

"Why, there are rugs enough left that we shall hardly get into three boxes," said the footman.

"But do wait a little, please." And Natasha began rapidly and deftly sorting out the things. "These we don't want," she said of the plates of Kiev ware; "this and this we can pack in the rugs," she decided, fishing out the Saxony dishes.

"Come, let it alone, Natasha; come, that's enough, we'll pack them," said Sonya reproachfully.

"What a young lady!" protested the footman.

But Natasha would not give in. She pulled everything out, and began rapidly packing them again, deciding that the commoner rugs and crockery should not be taken at all. When she had taken everything out, she began repacking what was to go; and by sorting out almost all the cheaper goods which were not worth taking, all that was of value was got into two boxes. Only the lid of the box full of rugs would not shut. A few things might have been taken out, but Natasha wanted to manage it in her own way. She unpacked, repacked, squeezed the things in, made the footman and Petya, whom she had drawn into assisting in the work, press on the lid, and herself tried desperately to do the same.

"That will do, Natasha," Sonya said to her. "I see you are quite right, but take out just the top one."

"I won't," cried Natasha, with one hand holding her disordered hair off her perspiring face, while with the other she squeezed down the rugs. "Press it, Petya, press it! Vassilitch, press hard!" she cried. The rugs yielded, and the lid closed. Natasha, clapping her hands, shrieked with delight, and tears started into her eyes. But that lasted only a second. She set to work at once on a fresh job; and now the servants put complete faith in her, and the count did not take it amiss when they told him that Natalya Ilyinitshna had given some direction superseding his orders; and the servants came to Natasha to ask whether a cart was packed full enough and whether the loads were to be tied on. The packing went on fast now, thanks to Natasha's supervision; everything useless was left behind, and the most valuable goods were packed as compactly as possible.

But with all their exertions, even late at night everything was not ready. The countess had fallen asleep, and the count put off their departure till morning and went to bed.

Sonya and Natasha slept in the divan-room, without undressing.

That night another wounded officer was driven along Povarsky Street, and Mavra Kuzminishna, who was standing at the gate, had him brought into the Rostovs' yard. The wounded officer must, Mavra Kuzminishna thought, be a man of very great consequence. He was in a coach with the hood let down and a carriage apron completely covering it. An old man, a most respectable-looking valet, was sitting on the box with the driver. A doctor and two soldiers followed the carriage in another conveyance.

"Come into our house, come in. The masters are going away, the whole house is empty," said the old woman, addressing the old servant.

"Well," answered the valet, sighing, "and indeed we have no hope of getting him home alive! We have a house of our own in Moscow, but it is a long way further, and there's no one living in it either."

"Pray come in, our masters have plenty of everything, and you are welcome," said Mavra Kuzminishna. "Is the gentleman very bad, then?" she asked.

"There's no hope! I must ask the doctor." And the valet got down and went to the vehicle behind.

"Very good," said the doctor.

The valet went up to the coach again, peeped into it, shook his head, told the coachman to turn into the yard, and stood still beside Mavra Kuzminishna.

"Lord Jesus Christ, have mercy!" she murmured.

Mavra Kuzminishna suggested the wounded man being carried into the house.

"The masters won't say anything . . ." said she.

But they had to avoid lifting him up the steps, and so they carried the wounded man to the lodge, and put him in the room that had been Madame Schoss's. This wounded officer was Prince Andrey Bolkonsky.

XV

THE last day of Moscow had come. It was a bright, clear autumn day. It was Sunday. The bells were ringing for service in all the churches, just as on all other Sundays. No one seemed yet able to grasp what was awaiting Moscow.

There were only two indications in the condition of society that betrayed the position of Moscow; those were the rabble, that is, the poorer class, and the prices of different objects. Factory hands, house-serfs, and peasants came out early that morning on to Three Hills in immense crowds, which were swelled by clerks, divinity students, and gentlemen. After staying there a while waiting for Rastoptchin, who did not come, and gaining the conviction that Moscow would be surrendered, this mob dispersed about the taverns and drinkshops of Moscow. Prices, too, on that day indicated the position of affairs. The prices of weapons, of carts and horses, and the value of gold rose higher and higher, while the value of paper-money and the prices of things useful in town were continually falling, so that by the middle of the day there were instances of cab-drivers carrying off at half-price expensive goods, like cloth; and while five hundred roubles was paid for a peasant's horse, furniture, mirrors, and bronzes were given away for nothing.

In the old-fashioned and decorous house of the Rostovs the collapse of all the usual conditions of life was very slightly perceptible. In the night three out of the immense retinue of servants, did indeed disappear; but nothing was stolen, and the Rostovs were only aware of the change in the relative value of things from finding that the thirty carts from the country were of enormous value, for which they were envied by many, and offered enormous sums. Besides these would-be purchasers, all the previous evening and early in the morning of the 1st of September order-lies and servants were being continually sent into the Rostovs' courtyard from wounded officers, and wounded men were constantly dragging themselves there from the Rostovs' and neighbouring houses, to beseech the servants to try and get them a lift out of Moscow. The butler, to whom these requests were referred, resolutely refused, though he felt for the wounded men, and declared that he would never even dare to hint at such a thing to the count. Pitiable as the position of these wounded men was, it was obvious that if one gave up one cart to them, one might as well give all—and would even have to put the carriages too at their service. Thirty waggons could not save all the wounded, and in the general catastrophe one must think of oneself and one's family first. So the butler reasoned on his master's behalf.

On waking up that morning Count Ilya Andreitch slipped quietly out of his bedroom, so as not to wake his wife, who had been awake till morning, and in his lilac silk dressing-gown he came out on to the steps. The loaded waggons were standing in the courtyard. The carriages were drawn up at the steps. The butler was standing in the entrance talking with an old orderly and a pale young officer with his arm in a sling. The butler, seeing his master, made a significant and peremptory sign to them both to retire.

"Well, is everything ready, Vassilitch?" said the count, rubbing his bald head; and looking benignly at the officer and the orderly, he nodded to them. (The count was always attracted by new faces.)

"Ready to put the horses in immediately, your excellency."

"Well, that's capital; the countess will soon be awake, and, please God, we set off! What can I do for you, sir?" he said, addressing the officer. "You are staying in my house?"

The officer came closer. His pale face suddenly flushed crimson.

"Count, do me a great favour, allow me . . . for God's sake . . . to get into one of your waggons. I have nothing here with me . . . I can go quite well with the luggage . . ."

Before the officer finished speaking, the orderly came up to make the same request for his master.

"Oh! yes, yes, yes," said the count hurriedly. "I shall be very glad indeed. Vassilitch, you see to it; you have a waggon or two cleared, well . . . well . . . what's needed . . . ?" The count murmured some vague orders. But the glowing look of gratitude on the officer's face instantly put the seal on the order. The count looked about him; every-where—in the yard, at the gates, at the windows of the lodge—he saw wounded men and orderlies. They were all gazing at him and moving up towards the steps.

"Will you please walk into the gallery, your excellency; what are your orders about the pictures there?" said the butler. And the count went into the house with him, repeating his instructions that they were not to refuse the wounded men who begged to go with them.

"You can take something out of the loads, you know," he added, in a subdued and mysterious voice, as though he were afraid of being overheard.

At nine o'clock the countess woke up, and Matrona Timofyevna, who had been her maid before her marriage, and now performed the duties of a sort of *chef de gendarmes* for the countess, came in to report to her that Madame Schoss was very much aggrieved, and that the young ladies' summer dresses could not possibly be left behind. On the countess inquiring the cause of Madame Schoss's resentment, it appeared that that lady's trunk had been taken out of the waggon, and that all the waggons were being unloaded, and that the luggage was being taken out, as the waggons were to be given up to the wounded men, whom the count, with his usual readiness to be imposed upon, had consented to take away with them. The countess sent for her husband to come to her.

"What's this, my dear? I hear the luggage is being unloaded."

"Do you know, *ma chère*, I wanted to speak to you about it . . . dear little countess . . . an officer came up to me—they are imploring us to let them have a few waggons for the wounded. It's all a question of money loss to us, of course, but to be left behind . . . think what it means to them! . . . Here they are in our very yard; we asked them in ourselves; here are officers. . . . You know, I really think, *ma chère* . . . well, let them take them. We are in no hurry."

The count spoke timidly, as he always did when the subject was in any way connected with money. The countess was used to that tone, which always ushered in some matter prejudicial to her children's interests, such as the building of a new gallery, or conservatory, or a new theatre in the house, or the training of an orchestra; and she made it a habit, and regarded it as a duty, to oppose everything that was communicated in that tone.

She assumed her air of tearful resignation, and said to her husband:

"Listen, count, you have mismanaged things so, that we are getting nothing for the house, and now you want to throw away all our—all the *children's*—property. Why, you told me yourself that we have a hundred thousand roubles' worth of valuables in the house. I protest, and protest, my love. What would you have! It's for the Government to look after the wounded. They know that. Only think, the Lopuhins opposite cleared everything to the last stick out of their house the day before yesterday. That's how other people manage. It's only we who are such fools. If you have no consideration for me, do at least think of your children."

The count waved his hands in despair, and went out of the room without a word.

"Papa! why do you do that?" said Natasha, who had followed him into her mother's room.

"Nothing! It's no business of yours!" the count said angrily.

"But I heard," said Natasha. "Why won't mamma have it?"

"It's no business of yours!" cried the count.

Natasha walked away to the window and pondered.

"Papa, here's Berg coming to see us," she said, looking out of the window.

XVI

THE Rostovs' son-in-law, Berg, was by now a colonel, with the orders of Vladimir and Anne on his neck, and was still filling the same comfortable and agreeable post of assistant to the head of the staff of the assistant of the chief officer of the staff of the commander of the left flank of the infantry of the first army.

On the 1st of September he had come into Moscow from the army.

He had absolutely nothing to do in Moscow; but he noticed that every one in the army was asking leave to go into Moscow, and was busy doing something there. He, too, thought fit to ask leave of absence on account of urgent domestic and family affairs.

Berg drove up to his father-in-law's house in his spruce chaise, with his pair of sleek roans, precisely similar to those of a certain prince. He looked carefully at the luggage in the yard, and as he ran up the steps, he took out a clean pocket-handkerchief, and tied a knot in it.

Berg ran with a swimming, impatient step from the entry into the drawing-room, embraced the count, kissed Natasha's hand and Sonya's, and then hastened to inquire after mamma's health.

"Health, at a time like this! Come, tell us what news of the army!" said the count. "Are they retreating, or will there be a battle?"

"Only Almighty God can tell what will be the fate of our Fatherland, papa," said Berg. "The army is animated by the most ardent spirit of heroism, and now its chiefs, so to speak, are sitting in council. No one knows what is coming. But I can tell you, papa, that our heroic spirit, the truly antique valour of the Russian army, which they—it, I mean," he corrected himself—"showed in the fight of the 26th . . . well, there are no words that can do justice to it." (He smote himself on the chest, just as he had seen a general do, who had used much the same phrases before him—but he was a little too late, for the blow on the chest should properly have been at the words, "the Russian army.") "I can assure you, papa, that we officers, so far from having to urge the soldiers on, or anything of the sort, had much ado to keep in check this . . . yes, these exploits recalling the valour of antiquity," he rattled off. "General Barclay de Tolly risked his life everywhere in front of his troops, I can assure you. Our corps was posted on the slope of a hill. Only fancy!" And Berg proceeded to recount all the stories he had heard repeated about the battle. Natasha stared at Berg, as though seeking the solution of some problem in his face, and her eyes disconcerted him.

"Altogether, the heroism shown by the Russian soldiers is beyond praise, and beyond description!" said Berg, looking at Natasha; and as though wishing to soften her, he smiled in response to her persistent stare . . . " 'Russia is not in Moscow, she lives in the hearts of her sons!' Eh, papa?" said Berg.

At that moment the countess came in from the divan-room with a look of weariness and annoyance on her face. Berg skipped up, kissed the countess's hand, asked after her health, and stood beside her, with a sympathetic shake of his head.

"Yes, mamma, to tell the truth, these are hard and sorrowful times for every Russian. But why should you be so anxious? You have still time to get away . . ."

"I can't make out what the servants are about," said the countess, addressing her husband. "They told me just now nothing was ready. Some one really must go and look after them. It's at such times one misses Mitenka. There will be no end to it."

The count was about to make some reply; but with a visible effort to restrain himself, got up and went to the door without a word.

Berg, meanwhile, had taken out his handkerchief as though about to blow his nose, and, seeing the knot in it, he pondered a moment, shaking his head with mournful significance.

"And, do you know, papa, I have a great favour to ask . . ." he began.

"H'm?" said the count, pausing.

"I was passing by Yusupov's house just now," said Berg, laughing. "The steward, a man I know, ran out and asked me whether I wouldn't care to buy any of their things. I went in, you know, out of curiosity, and there is a little chiffonier and dressing-table. You know, just like what Verushka wanted, and we quarrelled about." (Berg unconsciously passed into a tone expressive of his pleasure in his own excellent domestic arrangements.) "And such a charming thing!—it moves forward, you know, with a secret English lock. And it's just what Verushka wanted. So I want to make it a surprise for her. I see what a number of peasants you have in the yard. Please, spare me one of them. I'll pay him well, and . . ."

The count frowned and sniffed.

"Ask the countess; I don't give the orders."

"If it's troublesome, pray don't," said Berg. "Only I should have liked it on Vera's account."

"Ah, go to damnation all of you, damnation! damnation! damnation!" cried the old count. "My head's going round." And he went out of the room.

The countess began to cry.

"Yes, indeed, these are terrible times, mamma!" said Berg.

Natasha went out with her father, and as though unable to make up her mind on some difficult question, she followed him at first, then turned and ran downstairs.

Petya was standing at the entrance, engaged in giving out weapons to the servants, who were leaving Moscow. The loaded waggons were still standing in the yards. Two of them had been uncorded, and on to one of these the wounded officer was clambering with the assistance of his orderly.

"Do you know what it was about?" Petya asked Natasha. (Natasha knew that he meant, what their father and mother had been quarrelling about.) She did not answer.

"It was because papa wanted to give up all the waggons to the wounded," said Petya. "Vassilitch told me. And what I think . . ."

"What I think," Natasha suddenly almost screamed, turning a furious face on Petya, "what I think is, that it's so vile, so loathsome . . . I don't know. Are we a lot of low Germans? . . ." Her throat was quivering with sobs, but afraid of being weak, or wasting the force of her anger, she turned and flew headlong up the stairs.

Berg was sitting beside the countess, trying with filial respectfulness to reassure her. The count was walking about the room with a pipe in his hand, when, with a face distorted by passion, Natasha burst like a tempest into the room, and ran with rapid steps up to her mother.

"It's vile! It's loathsome!" she screamed. "It can't be true that it's your order."

Berg and the countess gazed at her in alarm and bewilderment. The count stood still in the window listening.

"Mamma, it's impossible; look what's being done in the yard!" she cried; "they are being left . . ."

"What's the matter? Who are they? What do you want?"

"The wounded! It's impossible, mamma, it's outrageous. . . . No, mamma, darling, it's all wrong; forgive me, please, darling . . . Mamma, what is it to us what we take away; you only look out into the yard. . . . Mamma! . . . It can't be done. . . ."

The count stood in the window, and listened to Natasha without turning his head. All at once he gave a sort of gulp, and put his face closer to the window.

The countess glanced at her daughter, saw her face full of shame for her mother, saw her emotion, felt why her husband would not look at her now, and looked about her with a distracted air.

"Oh, do as you please. Am I doing anything to hinder any one?" she said, not giving way all at once.

"Mamma, darling, forgive me."

But the countess pushed away her daughter, and went up to the count.

"My dear, you order what is right. . . . I don't understand about it, you know," she said, dropping her eyes with a guilty air.

"The eggs, . . . the eggs teaching the hen, . . ." the count murmured through tears of gladness, and he embraced his wife, who was glad to hide her ashamed face on his breast.

"Papa, mamma! may I give the order? May I? . . ." asked Natasha. "We'll take all that's quite necessary all the same," she added.

The count nodded; and Natasha, with the same swiftness with which she used to run at "catch-catch," flew across the hall into the vestibule, and down the steps into the yard.

The servants gathered round Natasha, and could hardly believe the strange order she gave them, till the count himself in his wife's name confirmed the order that all the waggons were to be placed at the disposal of the wounded, and the boxes were to be taken down to the storerooms. When they understood, the servants gleefully and busily set to this new task. It no longer seemed strange to the servants, it seemed to them, indeed, that no other course was possible; just as a quarter of an hour before they had not thought it strange to leave the wounded behind and take the furniture; had accepted that too, in fact, as the only course possible.

All the household set to work getting the wounded men into the waggons with the greatest zeal, as though to make up for not having espoused their cause earlier. The wounded soldiers came creeping out of their rooms, and crowded round the waggons, with pale, delighted faces. The news spread to the neighbouring houses, and wounded men began to come into the yard from other houses too. Many of the wounded soldiers begged them not to take out the boxes, but only to let them sit on the top of them. But when once the work of unloading had begun there was no stopping it; it seemed of little consequence whether all were left or half. The cases of china, of bronzes, of pictures and looking-glasses, which had been so carefully packed during the previous night lay in the yard, and still they sought and found possibilities of taking out more and more, and leaving more and more, for the wounded.

"We can take four more," said the steward. "I'll leave my luggage, or else what is to become of them?"

"Oh, let them have our wardrobe cart," said the countess; "Dunyasha will go with me in the carriage."

The waggon packed with the ladies' wardrobe was unloaded, and sent to fetch wounded men from two doors off. All the family and the servants too were eager and merry. Natasha was in a state of ecstatic happiness, such as she had not known for a very long while.

"Where are we to fasten this on?" said the servant, trying to lay a trunk on the narrow footboard behind in the carriage. "We must keep just one cart for it."

"What is it?" asked Natasha.

"The count's books."

"Leave it. Vassilitch will put it away. That's not necessary."

The covered gig was full of people; they were only in doubt where Pyotr Ilyitch was to sit.

"He'll go on the box. You'll go on the box, won't you, Petya?" cried Natasha.

Sonya, too, worked with unflagging zeal; but the aim of her exertions was the opposite of Natasha's. She saw to the storing away of all that was left behind, made a list of them at the countess's desire, and tried to get as much as possible taken with them.

XVII

By two o'clock the Rostovs' four carriages, packed and ready to start, stood in the approach. The waggon-loads of wounded were filing one after another out of the yard.

The coach in which Prince Andrey was being taken drove by the front door, and attracted the attention of Sonya, who was helping a maid to arrange the countess's seat comfortably in her huge, high carriage.

"Whose carriage is that?" asked Sonya, popping her head out of the carriage window.

"Why, haven't you heard, miss?" answered the maid. "The wounded prince; he stayed the night in the house, and is going on with us."

"Oh, who is he? what's his name?"

"Our betrothed that was . . . Prince Bolkonsky himself!" answered the maid, sighing. "They say he is dying."

Sonya jumped out of the carriage and ran in to the countess. The countess, dressed for the journey, in her hat and shawl, was walking wearily about the drawing-room, waiting for the rest of the household to come in and sit down with closed doors, for the usual silent prayer before setting out. Natasha was not in the room.

"Mamma," said Sonya. "Prince Andrey is here, wounded and dying. He is going with us."

The countess opened her eyes in dismay, and clutching Sonya's arm, looked about her.

"Natasha," she said.

Both to Sonya and the countess this news had for the first moment but one significance. They knew their Natasha, and alarm at the thought of the effect the news might have on her outweighed all sympathy for the man, though they both liked him.

"Natasha does not know yet, but he is going with us," said Sonya.

"You say he is dying?"

Sonya nodded.

The countess embraced Sonya and burst into tears. "The ways of the Lord are past our finding out!" she thought, feeling that in all that was passing now the Hand of the Almighty, hitherto unseen, was beginning to be manifest.

"Well, mamma, it's all ready. What is it? . . . ." asked Natasha, running with her eager face into the room.

"Nothing," said the countess. "If we're ready, then do let us start." And the countess bent over her reticule to hide her agitated face. Sonya embraced Natasha and kissed her.

Natasha looked inquisitively at her.

"What is it? What has happened?"

"Nothing, . . . oh, no, ..."

"Something very bad, concerning me? . . . What is it?" asked the keen-witted Natasha.

Sonya sighed, and made no reply. The count, Petya, Madame Schoss, Mavra Kuzminishna, and Vassilitch came into the drawing-room; and closing the doors, they all sat down, and sat so in silence, without looking at each other for several seconds.

The count was the first to get up. With a loud sigh he crossed himself before the holy picture. All the others did the same. Then the count proceeded to embrace Mavra Kuzminishna and Vassilitch, who were to remain in Moscow; and while they caught at his hand and kissed his shoulder, he patted them on the back with vaguely affectionate and reassuring phrases. The countess went off to the little chapel, and Sonya found her there on her knees before the holy pictures, that were still left here and there on the walls. All the holy pictures most precious through association with the traditions of the family were being taken with them.

In the porch and in the yard the servants who were going—all of whom had been armed with swords and daggers by Petya—with their trousers tucked in their boots, and their sashes or leather belts tightly braced, took leave of those who were left behind.

As is invariably the case at starting on a journey, a great many things were found to have been forgotten, or packed in the wrong place; and two grooms were kept a long while standing, one each side of the open carriage door, ready to help the countess up the carriage steps, while maids were flying with pillows and bags from the house to the carriages, the coach, and the covered gig, and back again.

"They will always forget everything as long as they live!" said the countess. "You know that I can't sit like that." And Dunyasha, with clenched teeth and an aggrieved look on her face, rushed to the carriage to arrange the cushions again without a word.

"Ah, those servants," said the count, shaking his head.

The old coachman Efim, the only one whom the countess could trust to drive her, sat perched up on the box, and did not even look round at what was passing behind him. His thirty years' experience had taught him that it would be some time yet before they would say, "Now, in God's name, start!" and that when they had said it, they would stop him at least twice again to send back for things that had been forgotten; and after that he would have to pull up once more for the countess herself to put her head out of window and beg him, for Christ's sake, to drive carefully downhill. He knew this, and therefore awaited what was to come with more patience than his horses, especially the left one, the chestnut Falcon, who was continually pawing the ground and champing at the bit. At last all were seated; the carriage steps were pulled up, and the door slammed, and the forgotten travelling-case had been sent for, and the countess had popped her head out and given the usual injunctions. Then Efim deliberately took his hat off and began crossing himself. The postillion and all the servants did the same.

"With God's blessing!" said Efim, putting his hat on. "Off!" The postillion started his horse. The right-shaft horse began to pull, the high springs creaked, and the carriage swayed. The footman jumped up on the box while it was moving. The carriage jolted as it drove out of the yard on to the uneven pavement; the other vehicles jolted in the same way as they followed in a procession up the street. All the occupants of the carriages, the coach and the covered gig, crossed themselves on seeing the church opposite. The servants, who were staying in Moscow, walked along on both sides of the carriages to see them off.

Natasha had rarely felt such a joyful sensation as she experienced at that moment sitting in the carriage by the countess and watching, as they slowly moved by her, the walls of forsaken, agitated Moscow. Now and then she put her head out of the carriage window and looked back, and then in front of the long train of waggons full of wounded soldiers preceding them. Foremost of them all she could see Prince Andrey's closed carriage. She did not know who was in it, and every time she took stock of the procession of waggons she looked out for that coach. She knew it would be the foremost. In Kudrino and from Nikitsky Street, from Pryesny, and from Podnovinsky several trains of vehicles, similar to the Rostovs', came driving out, and by the time they reached Sadovoy Street the carriages and carts were two deep all along the road.

As they turned round Suharev Tower, Natasha, who was quickly and inquisitively scrutinising the crowd driving and walking by, uttered a cry of delight and surprise:

"Good Heavens! Mamma, Sonya, look; it's he!"

"Who? who?"

"Look, do look! Bezuhov," said Natasha, putting her head out of the carriage window and staring at a tall, stout man in a coachman's long coat, obviously a gentleman disguised, from his carriage and gait. He was passing under the arch of the Suharev Tower beside a yellow-looking, beardless, little old man in a frieze cloak.

"Only fancy! Bezuhov in a coachman's coat, with a queer sort of old-looking boy," said Natasha. "Do look; do look!"

"No, it's not he. How can you be so absurd!"

"Mamma," cried Natasha. "On my word of honour, I assure you, it is he. Stop, stop," she shouted to the coachman; but the coachman could not stop, because more carts and carriages were coming out of Myeshtchansky Street, and people were shouting at the Rostovs to move on, and not to keep the rest of the traffic waiting.

All the Rostovs did, however, though now at a much greater distance, see Pierre, or a man extraordinarily like him, wearing a coachman's coat, and walking along the street with bent head and a serious face beside a little, beardless old man, who looked like a footman. This old man noticed a face poked out of the carriage window staring at them, and respectfully touching Pierre's elbow, he said something to him, pointing towards the carriage. It was some time before Pierre understood what he was saying; he was evidently deeply absorbed in his own thoughts. At last he looked in the direction indicated, and recognising Natasha, he moved instantly towards the carriage, as though yielding to the first impulse. But after taking a dozen steps towards it, he stopped short, apparently recollecting something. Natasha's head beamed out of the carriage window with friendly mockery.

"Pyotr Kirillitch, come here! We recognized you, you see! It's a wonder!" she cried, stretching out a hand to him. "How is it? Why are you like this?"

Pierre took her outstretched hand, and awkwardly kissed it as he ran beside the still moving carriage.

"What has happened, count?" the countess asked him, in a surprised and commiserating tone.

"Eh? Why? Don't ask me," said Pierre, and he looked up at Natasha, the charm of whose radiant, joyous eyes he felt upon him without looking at her.

"What are you doing, or are you staying in Moscow?" Pierre was silent.

"In Moscow?" he queried. "Yes, in Moscow. Good-bye."

"Oh, how I wish I were a man, I would stay with you. Ah, how splendid that is!" said Natasha. "Mamma, do let me stay."

Pierre looked absently at Natasha, and was about to say something, but the countess interrupted him.

"You were at the battle, we have been told."

"Yes, I was there," answered Pierre. "To-morrow there will be a battle again . . ." he was beginning, but Natasha interposed:

"But what is the matter, count? You are not like yourself . . ."

"Oh, don't ask me, don't ask me, I don't know myself. To-morrow . . . No! Good-bye; good-bye," he said; "it's an awful time!" And he left the carriage and walked away to the pavement.

For a long while Natasha's head was still thrust out of the carriage window, and she beamed at him with a kindly and rather mocking, joyous smile.

XVIII

FROM the time of his disappearance, two days before, Pierre had been living in the empty abode of his dead benefactor, Osip Bazdyev. This was how it had come to pass.

On waking up the morning after his return to Moscow and his interview with Count Rastoptchin, Pierre could not for some time make out where he was and what was expected of him. When the names of the persons waiting to see him were announced to him—among them a Frenchman, who had brought a letter from his wife, the Countess Elena Vassilyevna—he felt suddenly overcome by that sense of the hopelessness and intricacy of his position to which he was particularly liable. He suddenly felt that everything was now at an end, everything was in a muddle, everything was breaking down, that no one was right nor wrong, that there was no future before him, and that there was no possible escape from the position. Smiling unnaturally and muttering to himself, he sat on the sofa in a pose expressive of utter hopelessness, or got up, approached the door, and peeped through the crack into the reception-room, where his visitors were awaiting him, then turned back with a gesture of despair and took up a book. The butler came in for the second time with a message that the Frenchman who had brought the letter from the countess was very desirous of seeing him if only for a minute, and that they had sent from the widow of Osip Alexyevitch Bazdyev to ask him to take charge of some books, as Madame Bazdyev was going away into the country.

"Oh, yes, in a minute; wait . . . No, no; go and say, I am coming immediately," said Pierre.

As soon as the butler had left the room, Pierre had taken up his hat, which was lying on the table, and gone out by the other door. He found no one in the corridor. Pierre walked the whole length of the corridor to the staircase, and frowning and rubbing his forehead with both hands, he went down as far as the first story landing. The porter was standing at the front door. A second staircase led from the landing to the back entrance. Pierre went down the back stairs and out into the yard. No one had seen him. But as soon as he turned out at the gates into the street, the coachman, standing by the carriages, and the gate-porter saw him and took off their caps to him. Aware of their eyes fixed on him,

Pierre did, as the ostrich does, hiding its head in a bush to escape being seen; ducking his head and quickening his pace he hurried along the street.

Of all the business awaiting Pierre that morning, the task of sorting the books and papers of Osip Alexyevitch seemed to him the most urgent.

He hailed the first cab-driver he came across, and told him to drive to Patriarch's Ponds, where was the house of the widow of Bazdyev.

Continually watching the loaded vehicles moving out of Moscow from all directions, and balancing his bulky person carefully not to slip out of the rickety old chaise, Pierre had the happy sensation of a runaway schoolboy, as he chatted with his driver.

The latter told him that to-day arms were being given out in the Kremlin, and that next day every one would be driven out beyond the Three Hills Gate, and there there was to be a great battle.

On reaching the Patriarch's Ponds, Pierre looked for Bazdyev's house, where he had not been for a long while past. He went up to a little garden gate. Gerasim, the yellow, beardless old man Pierre had seen five years before at Torzhok with Osip Alexyevitch, came out on hearing him knock.

"At home?" asked Pierre.

"Owing to present circumstances, Sofya Danilovna and her children have gone away into the country, your excellency."

"I'll come in, all the same; I want to look through the books," said Pierre.

"Pray do, you are very welcome; the brother of my late master—the heavenly kingdom be his!—Makar Alexyevitch has remained, but your honour is aware he is in feeble health," said the old servant.

Makar Alexyevitch was, as Pierre knew, a brother of Osip Alexyevitch, a half-mad creature, besotted by drink.

"Yes, yes, I know. Let us go in," said Pierre, and he went into the house. A tall, bald old man in a dressing-gown, with a red nose and goloshes on his bare feet, was standing in the vestibule; seeing Pierre, he muttered something angrily, and walked away into the corridor.

"He was a great intellect, but now, as your honour can see, he has grown feeble," said Gerasim. "Will you like to go into the study?" Pierre nodded. "As it was sealed up, so it has remained. Sofya Danilovna gave orders that if you sent for the books they were to be handed over."

Pierre went into the gloomy study, which he had entered with such trepidation in the lifetime of his benefactor. Now covered with dust, and untouched since the death of Osip Alexyevitch, the room was gloomier than ever.

Gerasim opened one blind, and went out of the room on tiptoe. Pierre walked round the study, went up to the bookcase, where the manuscripts were kept, and took one of the most important, at one time a sacred relic of the order. This consisted of the long Scottish acts of the order, with Bazdyev's notes and commentaries. He sat down to the dusty writing-table and laid the manuscripts down before him, opened and closed them, and at last, pushing them away, sank into thought, with his elbow on the table and his head in his hand.

Several times Gerasim peeped cautiously into the study and saw that Pierre was sitting in the same attitude.

More than two hours passed by. Gerasim ventured to make a slight noise at the door to attract Pierre's attention. Pierre did not hear him.

"Is the driver to be dismissed, your honour?"

"Oh yes," said Pierre, waking up from his reverie, and hurriedly getting up. "Listen," he said, taking Gerasim by the button of his coat and looking down at the old man with moist, shining, eager eyes. "Listen! You know that to-morrow there is to be a battle . . ."

"They have been saying so . . ." answered Gerasim.

"I beg you not to tell any one who I am. And do what I tell you . . ."

"Certainly, sir," said Gerasim. "Would your honour like something to eat?"

"No, but I want something else. I want a peasant dress and a pistol," said Pierre, suddenly flushing red.

"Certainly, sir," said Gerasim, after a moment's thought.

All the rest of that day Pierre spent alone in his benefactor's study, pacing restlessly from one corner to the other, as Gerasim could hear, and talking to himself; and he spent the night on a bed made up for him there.

Gerasim accepted Pierre's taking up his abode there with the imperturbability of a servant, who had seen many queer things in his time, and he seemed, indeed, pleased at having some one to wait upon. Without even permitting himself to wonder with what object it was wanted, he obtained for Pierre that evening a coachman's coat and cap, and promised next day to procure the pistol he required. Makar Alexyevitch twice that evening approached the door, shuffling in his goloshes, and stood there, gazing with an ingratiating air at Pierre. But as soon as Pierre turned to him, he wrapped his dressing-gown round him with a shamefaced and wrathful look, and hastily retreated. Pierre put on the coachman's coat, procured and carefully fumigated for him by Gerasim, and went out with the latter to buy a pistol at the Suharev Tower. It was there he had met the Rostovs.

XIX

ON the night of the 1st of September Kutuzov gave the Russian troops the command to fall back across Moscow to the Ryazan road.

The first troops moved that night, marching deliberately and in steady order. But at dawn the retreating troops on reaching the Dorogomilov bridge saw before them, crowding on the other side, and hurrying over the bridge, and blocking the streets and alleys on the same side, and bearing down upon them from behind, immense masses of soldiers. And the troops were overtaken by causeless panic and haste. There was a general rush forward towards the bridge, on to the bridge, to the fords and to the boats. Kutuzov had himself driven by back streets to the other side of Moscow.

At ten o'clock in the morning of the 2nd of September the only troops left in the Dorogomilov suburbs were the regiments of the rearguard, and the crush was over. The army was already on the further side of Moscow, and out of the town altogether.

At the same time, at ten o'clock in the morning of the 2nd of September, Napoleon was standing in the midst of his troops on Poklonny Hill, gazing at the spectacle that lay before him. From the 26th of August to the 2nd of September, from the day of Borodino to the entrance into Moscow, all that agitating, that memorable week, there had been that extraordinarily beautiful autumn weather, which always comes as a surprise, when though the sun is low in the sky it shines more warmly than in spring, when everything is glistening in the pure, limpid air, so that the eyes are dazzled, while the chest is braced and refreshed inhaling the fragrant autumn air; when the nights even are warm, and when in these dark, warm nights golden stars are continually falling from the sky, to the delight or terror of all who watch them.

At ten o'clock on the 2nd of September the morning light was full of the beauty of fairyland. From Poklonny Hill Moscow lay stretching wide below with her river, her gardens, and her churches, and seemed to be living a life of her own, her cupolas twinkling like stars in the sunlight.

At the sight of the strange town, with its new forms of unfamiliar architecture, Napoleon felt something of that envious and uneasy curiosity that men feel at the sight of the aspects of a strange life, knowing nothing of them. It was clear that that town was teeming with vigorous life. By those indefinable tokens by which one can infallibly tell from a distance a live body from a dead one, Napoleon could detect from Poklonny Hill the throb of life in the town, and could feel, as it were, the breathing of that beautiful, great being. Every Russian gazing at Moscow feels she is the mother; every foreigner gazing at her, and ignorant of her significance as the mother city, must be aware of the feminine character of the town, and Napoleon felt it.

"This Asiatic city with the innumerable churches, Moscow the holy. Here it is at last, the famous city! It was high time," said Napoleon; and dismounting from his horse he bade them open the plan of Moscow before him, and sent for his interpreter, Lelorme d'Ideville.

"A city occupied by the enemy is like a girl who has lost her honour," he thought (it was the phrase he had uttered to Tutchkov at Smolensk). And from that point of view he gazed at the Oriental beauty who lay for the first time before his eyes. He felt it strange himself that the desire so long cherished, and thought so impossible, had at last come to pass. In the clear morning light he gazed at the town, and then at the plan, looking up its details, and the certainty of possessing it agitated and awed him.

"But how could it be otherwise?" he thought. "Here is this capital, she lies at my feet awaiting her fate. Where is Alexander now. and what is he thinking? A strange, beautiful, and grand city! And a strange and grand moment is this! In what light must I appear to them?" he mused, thinking of his soldiers. "Here is the city—the reward for all those of little faith," he thought, looking round at his suite and the approaching troops, forming into ranks.

"One word of mine, one wave of my arm, and the ancient capital of the Tsar is no more. But my clemency is ever prompt to stoop to the vanquished. I must be magnanimous and truly great. But no, it is not true that I am in Moscow," the idea suddenly struck him. "She lies at my feet, though, her golden domes and crosses flashing and twinkling in the sun. But I will spare her. On the ancient monuments of barbarism and despotism I will inscribe the great words of justice and mercy . . . Alexander will feel that more bitterly than anything; I know him." (It seemed to Napoleon that the chief import of what had happened lay in his personal contest with Alexander.) "From the heights of the Kremlin —yes, that's the Kremlin, yes—I will dictate to them the laws of justice, I will teach them the meaning of true civilisation, I will make the generations of boyards to enshrine their conqueror's name in love. I will tell the deputation that I have not sought, and do not seek, war; but I have been waging war only with the deceitful policy of their court; that I love and respect Alexander, and that in Moscow I will accept terms of peace worthy of myself and my peoples. I have no wish to take advantage of the fortune of war to humiliate their honoured Emperor. 'Boyards,' I will say to them, 'I do not seek war; I seek the peace and welfare of all my subjects.' But I know their presence will inspire me, and I shall speak to them as I always do, clearly, impressively, and greatly. But can it be true that I am in Moscow! Yes, there she is!"

"Let the boyards be brought to me," he said, addressing his suite. A general, with a brilliant suite of adjutants, galloped off at once to fetch the boyards.

Two hours passed. Napoleon had lunched, and was again standing on the same spot on the Poklonny Hill, waiting for the deputation. His speech to the boyards had by now taken definite shape in his mind. The speech was full of dignity and of greatness, as Napoleon understood it. Napoleon was himself carried away by the magnanimity with which he intended to act in Moscow. In imagination he had already fixed the days for a "*réunion dans le palais des Czars,*" at which the great Russian nobles were to mingle with the courtiers of the French Emperor. In thought he had appointed a governor capable of winning the hearts of the people. Having heard that Moscow was full of religious institutions, he had mentally decided that his bounty was to be showered on these institutions. He imagined that as in Africa he had had to sit in a mosque wearing a burnous, in Moscow he must be gracious and bountiful as the Tsars. And being, like every Frenchman, unable to imagine anything moving without a reference to *sa chère, sa tendre, sa pauvre mère,* he decided finally to touch the Russian heart, that he would have inscribed on all these charitable foundations in large letters, "Dedicated to my beloved mother," or simply, "*Maison de ma mère,*" he decided. "But am I really in Moscow? Yes, there she lies before me; but why is the deputation from the city so long in coming?" he wondered.

Meanwhile a whispered and agitated consultation was being held among his generals and marshals in the rear of the suite. The adjutants sent to bring the deputation had come back with the news that Moscow was empty, that every one had left or was leaving the city. The faces of all the suite were pale and perturbed. It was not that Moscow had been abandoned by its inhabitants (grave as that fact appeared) that alarmed them. They were in alarm at the idea of making the fact known to the Emperor; they could not see how, without putting his majesty into the terrible position, called by the French *ridicule*, to inform him that he had been waiting so long for the boyards in vain, that there was a drunken mob, but no one else in Moscow. Some of the suite maintained that come what may, they must anyway scrape up a deputation of some sort; others opposed this view, and asserted that the Emperor must be carefully and skilfully prepared, and then told the truth.

"We shall have to tell him all the same," said some gentleman of the suite. . . . "But, gentlemen . . ."

The position was the more difficult as the Emperor, pondering on his magnanimous plans, was walking patiently up and down before the map of the city, shading his eyes to look from time to time along the road to Moscow, with a proud and happy smile.

"But it's awkward . . ." the gentlemen-in-waiting kept repeating, shrugging their shoulders and unable to bring themselves to settle the terrible word in their minds: *"le ridicule. . . ."*

Meanwhile the Emperor, weary of waiting in vain, and with his actor's instinct feeling that the great moment, being too long deferred, was beginning to lose its grandeur, made a sign with his hand. A solitary cannon shot gave the signal, and the invading army marched into Moscow —at the Tver, the Kaluga, and the Dorogomilov gates. More and more rapidly, vying with one another, at a quick run and a trot, the troops marched in, concealed in the clouds of dust they raised, and making the air ring with their deafening shouts.

Tempted on by the advance of the army, Napoleon too rode as far as the Dorogomilov gate, but there he halted again, and dismounting walked about the Kamerkolezhsky wall for a long time, waiting for the deputation.

XX

Moscow meanwhile was empty. There were still people in the city; a fiftieth part of all the former inhabitants still remained in it, but it was empty.

It was deserted as a dying, queenless hive is deserted.

In a queenless hive there is no life left. Yet at a superficial glance it seems as much alive as other hives.

In the hot rays of the midday sun the bees soar as gaily around the queenless hive as around other living hives; from a distance it smells of honey like the rest, and bees fly into and out of it just the same. Yet one has but to watch it a little to see that there is no life in the hive. The flight of the bees is not as in living hives, the smell and the sound that meet the beekeeper are changed. When the beekeeper strikes the wall of the sick hive, instead of the instant, unanimous response, the buzzing of tens of thousands of bees menacingly arching their backs, and by the rapid stroke of their wings making that whirring, living sound, he is greeted by a disconnected, droning hum from different parts of the deserted hive. From the alighting board comes not as of old the spirituous, fragrant smell of honey and bitterness, and the whiff of heat from the multitudes within. A smell of chill emptiness and decay mingles with the scent of honey. Around the entrance there is now no throng of guards, arching their backs and trumpeting the menace, ready to die in its defence. There is heard no more the low, even hum, the buzz of toil, like the singing of boiling water, but the broken, discordant uproar of disorder comes forth. The black, long-shaped, honey-smeared workers fly timidly and furtively in and out of the hive: they do not sting, but crawl away at the sight of danger. Of old they flew in only with their bags of honey, and flew out empty: now they fly out with their burdens. The beekeeper opens the lower partition and peeps into the lower half of the hive. Instead of the clusters of black, sleek bees, clinging on each other's legs, hanging to the lower side of the partition, and with an unbroken hum of toil building at the wax, drowsy, withered bees wander listlessly about over the roof and walls of the hive. Instead of the cleanly glued-up floor, swept by the bees' wings, there are now bits of wax, excrement, dying bees feebly kicking, and dead bees lying not cleared away on the floor.

The beekeeper opens the upper door and examines the super of the hive. In place of close rows of bees, sealing up every gap left in the combs and fostering the brood, he sees only the skilful, complex, edifice of combs, and even in this the virginal purity of old days is gone. All is forsaken; and soiled, black, stranger bees scurry swiftly and stealthily about the combs in search of plunder; while the dried-up, shrunken, listless, old-looking bees of the hive wander slowly about, doing nothing to hinder them, having lost every desire and sense of life. Drones, gadflies, wasps and butterflies flutter about aimlessly, brushing their wings against the walls of the hive. Here and there, between the cells full of dead brood and honey, is heard an angry buzz; here and there a couple of bees from old habit and custom, though they know not why they do it, are cleaning the hive, painfully dragging away a dead bee or a wasp, a task beyond their strength. In another corner two other old bees are languidly fighting or cleaning themselves or feeding one another, themselves unaware whether with friendly or hostile intent. Elsewhere a crowd of bees, squeezing one another, is falling upon some victim, beating and crushing it; and the killed or enfeebled bee drops slowly, light as a feather, on to the heap of corpses. The beekeeper parts the two centre partitions to look at the nursery. Instead of the dense, black rings

of thousands of bees, sitting back to back, watching the high mysteries
of the work of generation, he sees hundreds of dejected, lifeless, and
slumbering wrecks of bees. Almost all have died, unconscious of their
coming end, sitting in the holy place, which they had watched—now no
more. They reek of death and corruption. But a few of them still stir,
rise up, fly languidly and settle on the hand of the foe, without the spirit
to die stinging him; the rest are dead and as easily brushed aside as
fishes' scales. The beekeeper closes the partition, chalks a mark on the
hive, and choosing his own time, breaks it up and burns it.

So was Moscow deserted, as Napoleon, weary, uneasy and frowning,
paced up and down at the Kamerkolezhsky wall awaiting that merely
external, but still to his mind essential observance of the properties—a
deputation.

Some few men were still astir in odd corners of Moscow, aimlessly
following their old habits, with no understanding of what they were
doing.

When, with due circumspectness, Napoleon was informed that Moscow was deserted, he looked wrathfully at his informant, and turning
his back on him, went on pacing up and down in silence.

"My carriage," he said. He sat down in his carriage beside the adjutant on duty, and drove into the suburbs.

"Moscow deserted! What an incredible event!" he said to himself.

He did not drive right into the town, but put up for the night at an
inn in the Dorogomilov suburb. The dramatic scene had not come off.

XXI

THE Russian troops were crossing Moscow from two o'clock at night to
two o'clock in the day, and took with them the last departing inhabitants
and wounded soldiers.

The greatest crush took place on the Kamenny bridge, the Moskvoryetsky bridge, and Yauzsky bridge. While the troops, parting into two
about the Kremlin, were crowding on to the Moskvoryetsky and Kamenny bridges, an immense number of soldiers availed themselves of
the stoppage and the block to turn back, and slipping stealthily and
quietly by Vassily the Blessed, and under the Borovitsky gates, they
made their way uphill to the Red Square, where some instinct told them
they could easily carry off other people's property. Every passage and
alley of the Gostinny bazaar was filled with a crowd, such as throngs
there at sales. But there were no ingratiating, alluring voices of shopmen, no hawkers, no motley, female mob of purchasers—everywhere
were the uniforms and overcoats of soldiers without guns, going out in
silence with loads of booty, and coming in empty-handed. The shopkeepers and shopmen (they were few) were walking about among the
soldiers, like men distraught, opening and shutting their shops, and
helping their assistants to carry away their wares. There were drummers

In the square before the bazaar beating the muster-call. But the roll of the drum made the pillaging soldiers not run up at the call as of old, but, on the contrary, run away from the drum. Among the soldiers in the shops and passages could be seen men in the grey coats, and with the shaven heads of convicts. Two officers, one with a scarf over his uniform, on a thin, dark grey horse, the other on foot, wearing a military overcoat, stood at the corner of Ilyinka, talking. A third officer galloped up to them.

"The general has sent orders that they positively must all be driven out. Why, this is outrageous! Half the men have run off."

"Why, are you off too? . . . Where are you fellows off to?" . . . he shouted to three infantry soldiers, who ran by him into the bazaar without guns, holding up the skirts of their overcoats. "Stop, rascals!"

"Yes, you see, how are you going to get hold of them?" answered another officer. "There's no getting them together; we must push on so that the last may not be gone, that's the only thing to do!"

"How's one to push on? There they have been standing, with a block on the bridge, and they are not moving. Shouldn't a guard be set to prevent the rest running off."

"Why, come along! Drive them out," shouted the senior officer.

The officer in the scarf dismounted, called up a drummer, and went with him into the arcade. Several soldiers in a group together made a rush away. A shopkeeper, with red bruises on his cheeks about his nose, with an expression on his sleek face of quiet persistence in the pursuit of gain, came hurriedly and briskly up to the officer gesticulating.

"Your honour," said he, "graciously protect us. We are not close-fisted—any trifle now . . . we shall be delighted! Pray, your honour, walk in, I'll bring out cloth in a moment—a couple of pieces even for a gentleman—we shall be delighted! For we feel how it is, but this is simple robbery! Pray, your honour! a guard or something should be set, to let us at least shut up . . ."

Several shopkeepers crowded round the officer.

"Eh! it's no use clacking," said one of them, a thin man, with a stern face; "when one's head's off, one doesn't weep over one's hair. Let all take what they please!" And with a vigorous sweep of his arm he turned away from the officer.

"It's all very well for you to talk, Ivan Sidoritch," the first shopkeeper began angrily. "If you please, your honour."

"What's the use of talking!" shouted the thin man; "in my three shops here I have one hundred thousand worth of goods. How's one to guard them when the army is gone? Ah, fellows, God's will is not in men's hands!"

"If you please, your honour," said the first shopkeeper, bowing.

The officer stood in uncertainty, and his face betrayed indecision. "Why, what business is it of mine!" he cried suddenly, and he strode on rapidly along the arcade. In one open shop he heard blows and high words, and just as the officer was going into it, a man in a grey coat, with a shaven head, was thrust violently out of the door.

This man doubled himself up and bounded past the shopkeepers and the officer. The officer pounced on the soldiers who were in the shop. But meanwhile fearful screams, coming from an immense crowd, were heard near the Moskvoryetsky bridge, and the officer ran out into the square.

"What is it? What is it?" he asked, but his comrade had already galloped off in the direction of the screams. The officer mounted his horse and followed him. As he drew near the bridge, he saw two cannons that had been taken off their carriages, the infantry marching over the bridge, a few broken-down carts, and some soldiers with frightened, and some with laughing faces. Near the cannons stood a waggon with a pair of horses harnessed to it. Behind the wheels huddled four greyhounds in collars. A mountain of goods was piled up in the waggon, and on the very top, beside a child's chair turned legs uppermost, sat a woman, who was uttering shrill and despairing shrieks. The officer was told by his comrades that the screams of the crowd and the woman's shrieks were due to the fact that General Yermolov had come riding down on the crowd, and learning that the soldiers were straying away in the shops, and crowds of the townspeople were blocking the bridge, had commanded them to take the cannons out of their carriages, and to make as though they would fire them at the bridge. The crowd had made a rush; upsetting waggons, trampling one another, and screaming desperately, the bridge had been cleared, and the troops had moved on.

XXII

THE town itself meanwhile was deserted. There was scarcely a creature in the streets. The gates and the shops were all closed; here and there near pot-houses could be heard solitary shouts or drunken singing. No one was driving in the streets, and footsteps were rarely heard. Povarsky Street was perfectly still and deserted. In the immense courtyard of the Rostovs' house a few wisps of straw were lying about, litter out of the waggons that had gone away, and not a man was to be seen. In the Rostovs' house—abandoned with all its wealth—there were two persons in the great drawing-room. These were the porter, Ignat, and the little page, Mishka, the grandson of Vassilitch, who had remained in Moscow with his grandfather. Mishka had opened the clavichord, and was strumming with one finger. The porter, with his arms akimbo and a gleeful smile on his face, was standing before the great looking-glass.

"That's fine, eh, Uncle Ignat?" said the boy, beginning to bang with both hands at once on the keys.

"Ay, ay!" answered Ignat, admiring the broadening grin on his visage in the glass.

"Shameless fellows! Shameless, upon my word!" they heard behind them the voice of Mavra Kuzminishna, who had softly entered. "The fat-faced fellow grinning at himself! So this is what you are at! It's not all cleared away down there, and Vassilitch fairly knocked up. You wait a bit!"

Ignat, setting his belt straight, left off smiling, and with eyes submis-sively downcast, walked out of the room.

"Auntie, I was only just touching . . ." said the boy.

"I'll teach you only just to touch. Little rascal!" cried Mavra Kuzmin-ishna, waving her hand at him. "Go and set the samovar for your granddad."

Brushing the dust off, she closed the clavichord, and sighing heavily went out of the drawing-room and closed the door. Going out into the yard Mavra Kuzminishna mused where she would go next: whether to drink tea in the lodge with Vassilitch, or to the storeroom to put away what still remained to be stored away.

There was a sound of rapid footsteps in the still street. The steps paused at the gate, the latch rattled as some hand tried to open it.

Mavra Kuzminishna went up to the little gate.

"Whom do you want?"

"The count, Count Ilya Andreitch Rostov."

"But who are you?"

"I am an officer. I want to see him," said a genial voice, the voice of a Russian gentleman.

Mavra Kuzminishna opened the gate. And there walked into the courtyard a round-faced officer, a lad of eighteen, whose type of face strikingly resembled the Rostovs'.

"They have gone away, sir. Yesterday, in the evening, their honours set off," said Mavra Kuzminishna cordially. The young officer standing in the gateway, as though hesitating whether to go in or not, gave a click with his tongue expressive of disappointment.

"Ah, how annoying!" he said. "Yesterday I ought to . . . Ah, what a pity . . ."

Meanwhile Mavra Kuzminishna was intently and sympathetically scrutinising the familiar features of the Rostov family in the young man's face, and the tattered cloak and trodden-down boots he was wear-ing. "What was it you wanted to see the count for?" she asked.

"Well . . . what am I to do now!" the officer cried, with vexation in his voice, and he took hold of the gate as though intending to go away. He stopped short again in uncertainty.

"You see," he said all at once, "I am a kinsman of the count's, and he has always been very kind to me. So do you see" (he looked with a merry and good-humoured smile at his cloak and boots) "I am in rags, and haven't a farthing; so I had meant to ask the count . . ."

Mavra Kuzminishna did not let him finish.

"Would you wait just a minute, sir? Only one minute," she said. And as soon as the officer let go of the gate, Mavra Kuzminishna turned, and with her rapid, elderly step hurried into the back court to her lodge.

While she was running to her room, the officer, with downcast head and a faint smile, was pacing up and down the yard, gazing at his tattered boots.

"What a pity I have missed uncle! What a nice old body! Where has she run off to? And how am I to find out the nearest way for me to over-take the regiment, which must be at Rogozhsky by now?" the young officer was musing meanwhile. Mavra Kuzminishna came round the corner with a frightened and, at the same time, resolute face, carrying in her hands a knotted check handkerchief. A few steps from him, she un-tied the handkerchief, took out of it a white twenty-five rouble note, and gave it hurriedly to the officer.

"Had his excellency been at home, to be sure, he would have done a kinsman's part, but as it is . . . see, may be . . ." Mavra Kuzminishna was overcome with shyness and confusion. But the officer, with no haste nor reluctance, took the note, and thanked Mavra Kuzminishna. "If only the count had been at home," murmured Mavra Kuzminishna, as it were apologetically. "Christ be with you, sir. God keep you safe," she said, bowing and showing him out. The officer, smiling and shaking his head, as though laughing at himself, ran almost at a trot along the empty streets to overtake his regiment at Yauzsky bridge.

But for some time Mavra Kuzminishna remained standing with wet eyes before the closed gate, pensively shaking her head, and feeling a sudden rush of motherly tenderness and pity for the unknown boy-officer.

XXIII

IN an unfinished house in Varvarka, the lower part of which was a pot-house, there were sounds of drunken brawling and singing. Some ten factory hands were sitting on benches at tables in a little, dirty room. Tipsy, sweating, blear-eyed, with wide-gaping mouths, bloated with drink, they were singing some sort of a song. They were singing discord-antly, with toil, with labour, not because they wanted to sing, but simply to betoken that they were drunk, and were enjoying themselves. One of them, a tall, flaxen-headed fellow, in a clean, blue long coat was stand-ing over the rest. His face, with its straight, fine nose, would have been handsome, but for the thick, compressed, continually twitching lips and the lustreless, staring, and frowning eyes. He was standing over the singers, and, obviously with some notion in his head, was making solemn and angular passes over their heads with his bare, white arm, while he tried to spread his dirty fingers out unnaturally wide apart. The sleeve of his coat was incessantly slipping down, and the young fellow kept carefully tucking it up again with his left hand, as though there was something of special significance requiring that white, sinewy, waving arm to be bare. In the middle of the song, shouts and blows were heard in the passage and the porch. The tall fellow waved his arms.

"Shut up!" he shouted peremptorily. "A fight, lads!" and still tuck-ing up his sleeves, he went out to the porch.

The factory hands followed him. They had brought the tavern-keeper some skins that morning from the factory, had had drink given them for this service, and had been drinking under the leadership of the tall

young man. The blacksmiths working in a smithy hard by heard the
sounds of revelry in the pothouse, and supposing the house had been
forcibly broken into, wanted to break in too. A conflict was going on
in the porch.

The tavern-keeper was fighting with a blacksmith in the doorway, and
at the moment when the factory hands emerged, the smith had reeled
away from the tavern-keeper, and fallen on his face on the pavement.

Another smith dashed in at the door, staggering with his chest against
the tavern-keeper.

The young man with the sleeve tucked up, as he went, dealt a blow
in the face of the smith who had dashed in at the door, and shouted
wildly:

"Lads! they are beating our mates!"

Meanwhile, the smith got up from the ground, and with blood spurt-
ing from his bruised face, cried in a wailing voice:

"Help! They have killed me . . . ! They have killed a man!
Mates! . . ."

"Oy, mercy on us, killed entirely, a man killed!" squealed a woman,
coming out of the gates next door. A crowd of people gathered round
the blood-stained smith.

"Haven't you ruined folks enough, stripping the shirts off their
backs?" said a voice, addressing the tavern-keeper; "and so now you
have murdered a man! Blackguard!"

The tall young man standing on the steps turned his bleared eyes from
the tavern-keeper to the smiths, as though considering with which to
fight.

"Cut-throat!" he cried suddenly at the tavern-keeper. "Lads, bind
him!"

"Indeed, and you try and bind a man like me!" bawled the tavern-
keeper, tearing himself away from the men who threw themselves on
him, and taking off his cap, he flung it on the ground. As though this act
had some mysterious and menacing significance, the factory hands, who
had surrounded the tavern-keeper, stood still in uncertainty.

"I know the law, mate, very well, I do. I'll go to the police. Are you
thinking I won't find them? Robbery's not the order of the day for any
one!" bawled the tavern-keeper, picking up his cap.

"And go we will, so there!" . . . "And go we will . . . so there!" the
tavern-keeper and the tall fellow repeated after one another, and both
together moved forward along the street. The blood-bespattered smith
walked on a level with them. The factory-hands and a mob of outsiders
followed them with talk and shouting.

At the corner of Maroseyka, opposite a great house with closed shutters, and the signboard of a bootmaker, stood a group of some twenty
bootmakers, thin, exhausted-looking men, with dejected faces, in loose
smocks, and torn coats.

"He ought to pay folks properly!" a thin boot hand, with a scant
beard and scowling brows, was saying. "He's sucked the life-blood out
of us, and then he's quit of us. He's been promising and promising us all

the week. And now he's driven us to the last point, and he's made off."

Seeing the mob and the blood-bespattered smith, the man paused, and the bootmakers with inquisitive eagerness joined the moving crowd.

"Where are the folks going?"

"Going to the police, to be sure."

"Is it true we are beaten?"

"Why, what did you think? Look what folks are saying!"

Questions and answers were audible. The tavern-keeper, taking advantage of the increased numbers of the rabble, dropped behind the mob, and went back to his tavern.

The tall young fellow, not remarking the disappearance of his foe, the tavern-keeper, still moved his bare arm and talked incessantly, attracting the attention of all. The mob pressed about his figure principally, expecting to get from him some solution of the questions that were absorbing all of them.

"Let them show the order, let him show the law, that's what the government's for! Isn't it the truth I am saying, good Christian folk?" said the tall young man, faintly smiling.

"Does he suppose there's no government? Could we do without government? Wouldn't there be plenty to rob us, eh?"

"Why talk nonsense!" was murmured in the crowd. "Why, will they leave Moscow like this! They told you a lot of stuff in joke, and you believed them. Haven't we troops enough? No fear, they won't let him enter! That's what the government's for. Ay, listen what folks are prating of!" they said, pointing to the tall fellow.

By the wall of the Kitay-Gorod there was another small group of people gathered about a man in a frieze coat, who held a paper in his hand.

"A decree, a decree being read! A decree is being read," was heard in the crowd, and the mob surged round the reader.

The man in the frieze coat was reading the placard of the 31st of August. When the mob crowded round, he seemed disconcerted, but at the demand of the tall fellow who pressed close up to him, he began with a faint quiver in his voice reading the notice again from the beginning.

"Early to-morrow I am going to his highness the prince," he read ("his highness!" the tall young man repeated, with a triumphant smile and knitted brows), "to consult with him, to act and to aid the troops to exterminate the wretches; we, too, will destroy them root and branch . . ." the reader went on and paused ("D'ye see?" bawled the tall fellow with an air of victory. "He'll unravel the whole evil for you . . .") "and send our visitors packing to the devil; I shall come back to dinner, and we will set to work, we will be doing till we have done, and done away with the villains."

These last words were uttered by the reader in the midst of the complete silence. The tall fellow's head sank dejectedly. It was obvious that nobody had understood these last words. The words "I shall come back to dinner" in especial seemed to offend both reader and audience. The faculties of the crowd were strained to the highest pitch, and this was too easy and unnecessarily simple; it was just what any one of them might have said, and what for that reason could not be said in a decree coming from a higher authority.

All stood in depressed silence. The tall fellow's lips moved, and he staggered.

"Ask him! . . . Isn't that himself? . . . How'd it be to ask him! Or else . . . He'll explain . . ." was suddenly heard in the back rows of the crowd, and the general attention turned to the chaise of the head of the police, which drove into the square, escorted by two mounted dragoons.

The head of the police, who had driven out that morning by Count Rastoptchin's command to set fire to the barques in the river, and had received for that commission a large sum of money, at that moment in his pocket, ordered his coachman to stop on seeing a crowd bearing down upon him.

"What are those people?" he shouted to the people, who timidly approached the chaise in detached groups. "What is this crowd, I ask you?" repeated the head of police, receiving no reply.

"Your honour," said the man in the frieze coat, "it was their wish, your honour, not sparing their substance, in accord with his excellency the count's proclamation, to serve, and not to make a riot at all, as his excellency said . . ."

"The count has not gone, he is here, and will give orders about you," said the head of police. "Go on!" he said to his coachman. The crowd stood still, pressing round those who had heard what was said by the official, and looking at the departing chaise.

The head of the police meantime looked about him in alarm, and said something to his coachman; the horses trotted faster.

"Cheated, mates! Lead us to himself!" bawled the voice of the tall fellow. "Don't let him go, lads! Let him answer for it! Keep him!" roared voices, and the crowd dashed full speed after the chaise.

The mob in noisy talk pursued the head of the police to Lubyanka.

"Why, the gentry and the tradespeople are all gone, and we are left to perish. Are we dogs, pray?" was heard more frequently in the crowd.

XXIV

On the evening of the 1st of September, Count Rastoptchin had come away from his interview with Kutuzov mortified and offended at not having been invited to the council of war, and at Kutuzov's having taken no notice of his offer to take part in the defence of the city, and astonished at the new view of things revealed to him in the camp, in which the tranquillity of the city and its patriotic fervour were treated as matters of quite secondary importance, if not altogether irrelevant and trivial. Mortified, offended, and astonished at all this, Count Rastoptchin had returned to Moscow. After supper, he lay down on a sofa without undressing, and at one o'clock was waked by a courier bringing him a letter from Kutuzov. The letter asked the count, since the troops were retreating to the Ryazan road behind Moscow, to send police officials to escort troops through the town. The letter told Rastoptchin nothing new. He had known that Moscow would be abandoned not merely since his interview the previous day with Kutuzov on the Poklonny Hill, but ever since the battle of Borodino; since when all the generals who had come to Moscow had with one voice declared that another battle was impossible, and with Rastoptchin's sanction government property had been removed every night, and half the inhabitants had left. But never-theless the fact, communicated in the form of a simple note, with a command from Kutuzov, and received at night, breaking in on his first sleep, surprised and irritated the governor.

In later days, Count Rastoptchin, by way of explaining his action during this time, wrote several times in his notes that his two great aims at that time were to maintain tranquillity in Moscow, and to make the inhabitants go out of it. If this twofold aim is admitted, every act of Rastoptchin's appears irreproachable. Why were not the holy relics, the arms, the ammunition, the powder, the stores of bread taken away? Why were thousands of the inhabitants deceived into a belief that Moscow would not be abandoned and so ruined? "To preserve the tranquillity of the city," replies Count Rastoptchin's explanation. Why were heaps of useless papers out of the government offices and Leppich's balloon and other objects carried away? "To leave the town empty," replies Count Rastoptchin's explanation. One has but to admit some menace to public tranquillity and every sort of action is justified.

All the horrors of terrorism were based only on anxiety for public tranquillity.

What foundation was there for Count Rastoptchin's dread of popular disturbance in Moscow in 1812? What reason was there for assuming a disposition to revolution in the city? The inhabitants were leaving it; the retreating troops were filling Moscow. Why were the mob likely to riot in consequence?

Not in Moscow only, but everywhere else in Russia nothing like riots took place at the approach of the enemy. On the 1st and 2nd of September more than ten thousand people were left in Moscow, and except for the mob that gathered in the commander-in-chief's courtyard, attracted there by himself, nothing happened. It is obvious that there would have been even less ground for anticipating disturbances among the populace if, after the battle of Borodino, when the surrender of Moscow became a certainty, or at least a probability, Rastoptchin had taken steps for the removal of all the holy relics, of the powder, ammunition, and treasury, and had told the people straight out that the town would be abandoned, instead of exciting the populace by posting up placards and distributing arms.

Rastoptchin, an impulsive, sanguine man, who had always moved in the highest spheres of the administration, was a patriot in feeling, but had not the faintest notion of the character of the people he supposed himself to be governing. From the time when the enemy first entered Smolensk, Rastoptchin had in his own imagination been playing the part of leader of popular feeling—of the heart of Russia. He did not merely fancy—as every governing official always does fancy—that he was controlling the external acts of the inhabitants of Moscow, but fancied that he was shaping their mental attitude by means of his appeals and placards, written in that vulgar, slangy jargon which the people despise in their own class, and simply fail to understand when they hear it from persons of higher station. The picturesque figure of leader of the popular feeling was so much to Rastoptchin's taste, and he so lived in it, that the necessity of abandoning it, the necessity of surrendering Moscow with no heroic effect of any kind, took him quite unawares; the very ground he was standing on seemed slipping from under his feet, and he was utterly at a loss what to do. Though he knew it was coming, he could not till the last minute fully believe in the abandonment of Moscow, and did nothing towards it. The inhabitants left the city against his wishes. If the courts were removed, it was only due to the insistence of the officials, to which Rastoptchin reluctantly gave way. He was himself entirely absorbed by the rôle he had assumed. As is often the case with persons of heated imagination, he had known for a long while that Moscow would be abandoned; but he had known it only with his intellect, and refused with his whole soul to believe in it, and could not mentally adapt himself to the new position of affairs.

The whole course of his painstaking and vigorous activity—how far it was beneficial or had influence on the people is another question—aimed simply at awakening in the people the feeling he was himself possessed by—hatred of the French and confidence in himself.

But when the catastrophe had begun to take its true historic proportions; when to express hatred of the French in words was plainly insufficient; when it was impossible to express that hatred even by a battle; when self-confidence was of no avail in regard to the one question before Moscow; when the whole population, as one man, abandoning their property, streamed out of Moscow, in this negative fashion giving proof of the strength of their patriotism;—then the part Rastoptchin had been playing suddenly became meaningless. He felt suddenly deserted, weak, and absurd, with no ground to stand on.

On being waked out of his sleep to read Kutuzov's cold and peremptory note, Rastoptchin felt the more irritated the more he felt himself to blame. There was still left in Moscow all that was under his charge, all the government property which it was his duty to have removed to safety. There was no possibility of getting it all away. "Who is responsible for it? who has let it come to such a pass?" he wondered. "Of course, it's not my doing. I had everything in readiness; I held Moscow in my hand—like this! And see what they have brought things to! Scoundrels, traitors!" he thought, not exactly defining who were these scoundrels and traitors, but feeling a necessity to hate these vaguely imagined traitors, who were to blame for the false and ludicrous position in which he found himself.

All that night Rastoptchin was giving instructions, for which people were continually coming to him from every part of Moscow. His subordinates had never seen the count so gloomy and irascible.

"Your excellency, they have come from the Estates Department, from the director for instructions. . . . From the Consistory, from the Senate, from the university, from the Foundling Hospital, the vicar has sent . . . he is inquiring . . . what orders are to be given about the fire brigade? The overseer of the prison . . . the superintendent of the madhouse . . ." all night long, without pause, messages were being brought to the count.

To all these inquiries he gave brief and wrathful replies, the drift of which was that his instructions were now not needed, that all his careful preparations had now been ruined by somebody, and that that somebody would have to take all responsibility for anything that might happen now.

"Oh, tell that blockhead," he replied to the inquiry from the Estates Department, "to stay and keep guard over his deeds. Well, what nonsense are you asking about the fire brigade? There are horses, let them go off to Vladimir. Don't leave them for the French."

"Your excellency, the superintendent of the madhouse has come; what are your commands?"

"My commands? Let them all go, that's all. . . . And let the madmen out into the town. When we have madmen in command of our armies, it seems it's God's will they should be free."

To the inquiry about the convicts in the prison, the count shouted angrily to the overseer:

"What, do you want me to give you two battalions for a convoy for them, when we haven't any battalions at all? Let them all go, and that settles it!"

"Your excellency, there are political prisoners—Myeshkov, Vereshtchagin . . ."

"Vereshtchagin! He is not yet hanged?" cried Rastoptchin. "Send him to me."

XXV

By nine o'clock in the morning, when the troops were moving across Moscow, people had ceased coming to Rastoptchin for instructions. All who could get away were going without asking leave; those who stayed decided for themselves what they had better do.

Count Rastoptchin ordered his horses in order to drive to Sokolniky, and with a yellow and frowning face, sat in silence with folded arms in his study.

Every governing official in quiet, untroubled times feels that the whole population under his charge is only kept going by his efforts; and it is this sense of being indispensably necessary in which every governing official finds the chief reward for his toils and cares. It is easy to under-

stand that while the ocean of history is calm, the governing official holding on from his crazy little skiff by a pole to the ship of the people, and
moving with it, must fancy that it is his efforts that move the ship on to
which he is clinging. But a storm has but to arise to set the sea heaving
and the ship tossing upon it, and such error becomes at once impossible.
The ship goes on its vast course unchecked, the pole fails to reach the
moving vessel, and the pilot, from being the master, the source of power,
finds himself a helpless, weak, and useless person.

Rastoptchin felt this, and it drove him to frenzy. The head of the
police, who had got away from the crowd, went in to see him at the same
time as an adjutant, who came to announce that his horses were ready.
Both were pale, and the head of the police, after reporting that he had
discharged the commission given to him, informed Count Rastoptchin
that there was an immense crowd of people in his courtyard wanting to
see him.

Without a word in reply, Count Rastoptchin got up and walked with
rapid steps to his light, sumptuously furnished drawing-room. He went
up to the balcony door, took hold of the door-handle, let go of it, and
moved away to the window, from which the whole crowd could be better
seen. The tall young fellow was standing in the front, and with a severe
face, waving his arms and saying something. The blood-bespattered
smith stood beside him with a gloomy air. Through the closed windows
could be heard the roar of voices.

"Is the carriage ready?" said Rastoptchin, moving back from the
window.

"Yes, your excellency," said the adjutant.

Rastoptchin went again to the balcony door.

"Why, what is it they want?" he asked the head of the police.

"Your excellency, they say they have come together to go to fight the
French, by your orders; they were shouting something about treachery.
But it is an angry crowd, your excellency. I had much ado to get away.
If I may venture to suggest, your excellency . . ."

"Kindly leave me; I know what to do without your assistance," cried
Rastoptchin angrily. He stood at the door of the balcony looking at the
crowd. "This is what they have done with Russia! This is what they
have done with me!" thought Rastoptchin, feeling a rush of irrepressible
rage against the undefined some one to whose fault what was happening
could be set down. As is often the case with excitable persons, he was
possessed by fury, while still seeking an object for it. "Here is the populace, the dregs of the people," he thought, looking at the crowd, "that
they have stirred up by their folly. They want a victim," came into his
mind, as he watched the waving arm of the tall fellow in front. And the
thought struck him precisely because he too wanted a victim, an object
for his wrath.

"Is the carriage ready?" he asked again.

"Yes, your excellency. What orders in regard to Vereshtchagin? He is
waiting at the steps," answered the adjutant.

"Ah!" cried Rastoptchin, as though struck by some sudden recollection.

And rapidly opening the door, he walked resolutely out on the balcony. The hum of talk instantly died down, caps and hats were lifted, and all eyes were raised upon the governor.

"Good-day, lads!" said the count, speaking loudly and quickly. "Thanks for coming. I'll come out to you in a moment, but we have first to deal with a criminal. We have to punish the wretch by whose doing Moscow is ruined. Wait for me!" And as rapidly he returned to the apartment, slamming the door violently.

An approving murmur of satisfaction ran through the crowd. "He'll have all the traitors cut down, of course. And you talk of the French . . . he'll show us the rights and the wrongs of it all!" said the people, as it were reproaching one another for lack of faith.

A few minutes later an officer came hurriedly out of the main entrance, and gave some order, and the dragoons drew themselves up stiffly. The crowd moved greedily up from the balcony to the front steps. Coming out there with hasty and angry steps, Rastoptchin looked about him hurriedly, as though seeking some one.

"Where is he?" he said, and at the moment he said it, he caught sight of a young man with a long, thin neck, and half of his head shaven and covered with short hair, coming round the corner of the house between two dragoons. This young man was clothed in a fox-lined blue cloth coat, that had once been foppish but was now shabby, and in filthy convict's trousers of fustian, thrust into uncleaned and battered thin boots. His uncertain gait was clogged by the heavy manacles hanging about his thin, weak legs.

"Ah!" said Rastoptchin, hurriedly turning his eyes away from the young man in the fox-lined coat and pointing to the bottom steps. "Put him here!"

With a clank of manacles the young man stepped with effort on to the step indicated to him; putting his finger into the tight collar of his coat, he turned his long neck twice, and sighing, folded his thin, unworkmanlike hands before him with a resigned gesture.

For several seconds, while the young man was taking up his position on the step, there was complete silence. Only at the back of the mass of people, all pressing in one direction, could be heard sighs and groans and sounds of pushing and the shuffling of feet.

Rastoptchin, waiting for him to be on the spot he had directed, scowled, and passed his hand over his face.

"Lads!" he said, with a metallic ring in his voice, "this man, Vereshtchagin, is the wretch by whose doing Moscow is lost."

The young man in the fox-lined coat stood in a resigned pose, clasping his hands together in front of his body, and bending a little forward. His wasted young face, with its look of hopelessness and the hideous disfigurement of the half-shaven head, was turned downwards. At the count's first words he slowly lifted his head and looked up from below at the count, as though he wanted to say something to him, or at least to catch his eye. But Rastoptchin did not look at him. The blue vein behind the young man's ear stood out like a cord on his long, thin neck, and all at once his face flushed crimson.

All eyes were fixed upon him. He gazed at the crowd, and, as though made hopeful by the expression he read on the faces there, he smiled a timid, mournful smile, and dropping his head again, shifted his feet on the step.

"He is a traitor to his Tsar and his country; he deserted to Bonaparte; he alone of all the Russians has disgraced the name of Russia, and through him Moscow is lost," said Rastoptchin in a harsh, monotonous voice; but all at once he glanced down rapidly at Vereshtchagin, who still stood in the same submissive attitude. As though that glance had driven him to frenzy, flinging up his arms, he almost yelled to the crowd:

"You shall deal with him as you think fit! I hand him over to you!"

The people were silent, and only pressed closer and closer on one another. To bear each other's weight, to breathe in that tainted foulness, to be unable to stir, and to be expecting something vague, uncomprehended and awful, was becoming unbearable. The men in the front of the crowd, who saw and heard all that was passing before them, all stood with wide-open, horror-struck eyes and gaping mouths, straining all their strength to support the pressure from behind on their backs.

"Beat him! . . . Let the traitor perish and not shame the name of Russia!" screamed Rastoptchin. "Cut him down! I give the command!" Hearing not the words, but only the wrathful tones of Rastoptchin's voice, the mob moaned and heaved forward, but stopped again.

"Count!" . . . the timid and yet theatrical voice of Vereshtchagin broke in upon the momentary stillness that followed. "Count, one God is above us . . ." said Vereshtchagin, lifting his head, and again the thick vein swelled on his thin neck and the colour swiftly came and faded again from his face. He did not finish what he was trying to say.

"Cut him down! I command it! . . ." cried Rastoptchin, suddenly turning as white as Vereshtchagin himself.

"Draw sabres!" shouted the officer to the dragoons, himself drawing his sabre.

Another still more violent wave passed over the crowd, and reaching the front rows, pushed them forward, and threw them staggering right up to the steps. The tall young man, with a stony expression of face and his lifted arm rigid in the air, stood close beside Vereshtchagin. "Strike at him! ' the officer said almost in a whisper to the dragoons; and one of the soldiers, his face suddenly convulsed by fury, struck Vereshtchagin on the head with the flat of his sword.

Vereshtchagin uttered a brief "Ah!" of surprise, looking about him in alarm, as though he did not know what this was done to him for. A similar moan of surprise and horror ran through the crowd.

"O Lord!" some one was heard to utter mournfully. After the exclamation of surprise that broke from Vereshtchagin he uttered a piteous cry of pain, and that cry was his undoing. The barrier of human feeling that still held the mob back was strained to the utmost limit, and it snapped instantaneously. The crime had been begun, its completion was inevitable. The piteous moan of reproach was drowned in the angry and menacing roar of the mob. Like the great seventh wave that shatters a ship, that last, irresistible wave surged up at the back of the crowd, passed on to the foremost ranks, carried them off their feet and engulfed all together. The dragoon who had struck the victim would have repeated his blow. Vereshtchagin, with a scream of terror, putting his hands up before him, dashed into the crowd. The tall young man, against whom he stumbled, gripped Vereshtchagin's slender neck in his hands, and with a savage shriek fell with him under the feet of the trampling, roaring mob. Some beat and tore at Vereshtchagin, others at the tall young man. And the screams of persons crushed in the crowd and of those who tried to rescue the tall young man only increased the frenzy of the mob. For a long while the dragoons were unable to get the bleeding, half-murdered factory workman away. And in spite of all the feverish haste with which the mob strove to make an end of what had once been begun, the men who beat and strangled Vereshtchagin and tore him to pieces could not kill him. The crowd pressed on them on all sides, heaved from side to side like one man with them in the middle, and would not let them kill him outright or let him go.

"Hit him with an axe, eh? . . . they have crushed him . . . Traitor, he sold Christ! . . . living . . . alive . . . serve the thief right. With a bar! . . . Is he alive? . . ."

Only when the victim ceased to struggle, and his shrieks had passed into a long-drawn, rhythmic death-rattle, the mob began hurriedly to change places about the bleeding corpse on the ground. Every one went up to it, gazed at what had been done, and pressed back horror-stricken, surprised, and reproachful.

"O Lord, the people's like a wild beast; how could he be alive!" was heard in the crowd. "And a young fellow too . . . must have been a merchant's son, to be sure, the people . . . they do say it's not the right man . . . not the right man! . . . O Lord! . . . They have nearly murdered another man; they say he's almost dead . . . Ah, the people . . . who wouldn't be afraid of sin . . ." were saying now the same people, looking with rueful pity at the dead body, with the blue face fouled with dust and blood, and the long, slender, broken neck.

A punctilious police official, feeling the presence of the body unseemly in the courtyard of his excellency, bade the dragoons drag the body away into the street. Two dragoons took hold of the mutilated legs, and drew the body away. The dead, shaven head, stained with blood and grimed with dust, was trailed along the ground, rolling from side to side on the long neck. The crowd shrank away from the corpse.

When Vereshtchagin fell, and the crowd with a savage yell closed in and heaved about him, Rastoptchin suddenly turned white, and instead of going to the back entrance, where horses were in waiting for him, he strode rapidly along the corridor leading to the rooms of the lower story, looking on the floor and not knowing where or why he was going. The count's face was white, and he could not check the feverish twitching of his lower jaw.

"Your excellency, this way . . . where are you going? . . . this way," said a trembling, frightened voice behind him. Count Rastoptchin was incapable of making any reply. Obediently turning, he went in the direction indicated. At the back entrance stood a carriage. The distant roar of the howling mob could be heard even there. Count Rastoptchin hurriedly got into the carriage, and bade them drive him to his house at Sokolniky beyond the town. As he drove out into Myasnitsky Street and lost the sound of the shouts of the mob, the count began to repent. He thought with dissatisfaction now of the excitement and terror he had betrayed before his subordinates. "The populace is terrible, it is hideous. They are like wolves that can only be appeased with flesh," he thought. "Count! there is one God over us!" Vereshtchagin's words suddenly recurred to him, and a disagreeable chill ran down his back. But that feeling was momentary, and Count Rastoptchin smiled contemptuously at himself. "I had other duties. The people had to be appeased. Many other victims have perished and are perishing for the public good," he thought; and he began to reflect on the social duties he had towards his family and towards the city intrusted to his care; and on himself—not as Fyodor Vassilyevitch Rastoptchin (he assumed that Fyodor Vassilyevitch Rastoptchin was sacrificing himself for *le bien publique*)—but as governor of Moscow, as the representative of authority intrusted with full powers by the Tsar. "If I had been simply Fyodor Vassilyevitch, my course of action might have been quite different; but I was bound to preserve both the life and the dignity of the governor."

Lightly swayed on the soft springs of the carriage, and hearing no more of the fearful sounds of the mob, Rastoptchin was physically soothed, and as is always the case simultaneously with physical relief, his intellect supplied him with grounds for moral comfort. The thought that reassured Rastoptchin was not a new one. Ever since the world has existed and men have killed one another, a man has never committed such a crime against his fellow without consoling himself with the same idea. That idea is *le bien publique*, the supposed public good of others.

To a man not swayed by passion this good never seems certain; but a man who has committed such a crime always knows positively where that public good lies. And Rastoptchin now knew this.

Far from reproaching himself in his meditations on the act he had just committed, he found grounds for self-complacency in having so successfully made use of an occasion so *à propos* for executing a criminal, and at the same time satisfying the crowd. "Vereshtchagin had been tried and condemned to the death penalty," Rastoptchin reflected (though Vereshtchagin had only been condemned by the senate to hard labour). "He was a spy and a traitor; I could not let him go unpunished, and so I hit two birds with one stone. I appeased the mob by giving them a victim, and I punished a miscreant."

Reaching his house in the suburbs, the count completely regained his composure in arranging his domestic affairs.

Within half an hour the count was driving with rapid horses across the Sokolniky plain, thinking no more now of the past, but absorbed in thought and plans for what was to come. He was approaching now the Yauzsky bridge, where he had been told that Kutuzov was. In his own mind he was preparing the biting and angry speeches he would make, upbraiding Kutuzov for his deception. He would make that old court fox feel that the responsibility for all the disasters bound to follow the abandonment of Moscow, and the ruin of Russia (as Rastoptchin considered it), lay upon his old, doting head. Going over in anticipation what he would say to him, Rastoptchin wrathfully turned from side to side in the carriage, and angrily looked about him.

The Sokolniky plain was deserted. Only at one end of it, by the almshouse and lunatic asylum, there were groups of people in white garments, and similar persons were wandering about the plain, shouting and gesticulating.

One of them was running right across in front of Count Rastoptchin's carriage. And Count Rastoptchin himself and his coachman, and the dragoons, all gazed with a vague feeling of horror and curiosity at these released lunatics, and especially at the one who was running towards them.

Tottering on his long, thin legs in his fluttering dressing-gown, this madman ran at headlong speed, with his eyes fixed on Rastoptchin, shouting something to him in a husky voice, and making signs to him to stop. The gloomy and triumphant face of the madman was thin and yellow, with irregular tufts of beard growing on it. The black, agate-like pupils of his eyes moved restlessly, showing the saffron-yellow whites above. "Stay! stop, I tell you!" he shouted shrilly, and again breathlessly fell to shouting something with emphatic gestures and intonations.

He reached the carriage and ran alongside it.

"Three times they slew me, three times I rose again from the dead. They stoned me, they crucified me . . . I shall rise again . . . I shall rise again . . . I shall rise again. My body they tore to pieces. The kingdom of heaven will be overthrown . . . Three times I will overthrow it, and three times I will set it up again," he screamed, his voice growing shriller and shriller. Count Rastoptchin suddenly turned white, as he had turned white when the crowd fell upon Vereshtchagin. He turned away. "G . . . go on, faster!" he cried in a trembling voice to his coachman.

The carriage dashed on at the horses' topmost speed. But for a long while yet Count Rastoptchin heard behind him the frantic, desperate scream getting further away, while before his eyes he saw nothing but the wondering, frightened, bleeding face of the traitor in the fur-lined coat. Fresh as that image was, Rastoptchin felt now that it was deeply for ever imprinted on his heart. He felt clearly now that the bloody print of that memory would never leave him, that the further he went the

more cruelly, the more vindictively, would that fearful memory rankle
in his heart to the end of his life. He seemed to be hearing now the sound
of his own words: "Tear him to pieces, you shall answer for it to me!—
Why did I say these words? I said it somehow without meaning to . . .
I might not have said them," he thought, "and then nothing would have
happened." He saw the terror-stricken, and then suddenly frenzied face
of the dragoon who had struck the first blow, and the glance of silent,
timid reproach cast on him by that lad in the fox-lined coat. "But I
didn't do it on my own account. I was bound to act in that way. *La
plèbe . . . le traître . . . le bien publique, . . .*" he mused.

The bridge over the Yauza was still crowded with troops. It was hot.
Kutuzov, looking careworn and weary, was sitting on a bench near the
bridge, and playing with a whip on the sand, when a carriage rattled
noisily up to him. A man in the uniform of a general, wearing a hat with
plumes, came up to Kutuzov. He began addressing him in French, his
eyes shifting uneasily, with a look between anger and terror in them. It
was Count Rastoptchin. He told Kutuzov that he had come here, for
since Moscow was no more, the army was all that was left. "It might
have been very different if your highness had not told me you would not
abandon Moscow without a battle; all this would not have been!" said
he.

Kutuzov stared at Rastoptchin, and, as though not understanding the
meaning of the words addressed to him, he strove earnestly to decipher
the special meaning betrayed at that minute on the face of the man
addressing him. Rastoptchin ceased speaking in discomfiture. Kutuzov
slightly shook his head, and, still keeping his searching eyes on Rastoptchin's face, he murmured softly:

"Yes, I won't give up Moscow without a battle."

Whether Kutuzov was thinking of something different when he uttered those words, or said them purposely, knowing them to be meaningless, Count Rastoptchin made him no reply, and hastily left him. And—
strange to tell! the governor of Moscow, the proud Count Rastoptchin,
picking up a horse whip, went to the bridge, and fell to shouting and
driving on the crowded carts.

XXVI

At four o'clock in the afternoon, Murat's troops entered Moscow. In
front rode a detachment of Würtemberg hussars, behind, with an immense suite, rode the King of Naples himself.

Near the middle of Arbaty, close to Nikola Yavlenny, Murat halted to
await information from the detachment in advance as to the condition in
which the citadel of the city, "*le Kremlin,*" had been found.

A small group of inhabitants of Moscow had gathered about Murat.
All stared with timid astonishment at the strange figure of the long-
haired commander, decked in gold and feathers.

"Why, is this their Tsar himself? Nought amiss with him," voices
were heard saying softly.

An interpreter approached the group of gazers.

"Caps . . . caps off," they muttered, turning to each other in the little crowd. The interpreter accosted one old porter, and asked him if it were far to the Kremlin. The porter, listening with surprise to the unfamiliar Polish accent, and not recognising the interpreter's words for Russian, had no notion what was being said to him, and took refuge behind the others.

Murat approached the interpreter, and told him to ask where were the Russian troops. One of the Russians understood this question, and several voices began answering the interpreter simultaneously. A French officer from the detachment in advance rode up to Murat and reported that the gates into the citadel were blocked up, and that probably there was an ambush there.

"Good," said Murat, and turning to one of the gentlemen of his suite, he commanded four light cannons to be moved forward, and the gates to be shelled upon.

The artillery came trotting out from the column following Murat, and advanced along Arbaty. When they reached the end of Vosdvizhenka the artillery halted and drew up in the square. Several French officers superintended the placing of the cannon some distance apart, and looked at the Kremlin through a field-glass. A bell was ringing in the Kremlin for evening service, and that sound troubled the French. They supposed that it was the call to arms. Several infantry soldiers ran to the Kutafyev gateway. A barricade of beams and planks lay across the gateway. Two musket shots rang out from the gates, just as an officer with some men were running up to them. The general standing by the cannons shouted some words of command to the officer, and the officer and the soldiers ran back.

Three more shots were heard from the gate. One shot grazed the leg of a French soldier, and a strange shout of several voices rose from behind the barricade. Instantaneously, as though at the word of command, the expression of good humour and serenity on the faces of the French general, officers, and men was replaced by a stubborn, concentrated expression of readiness for conflict and suffering. To all of them, from the marshal to the lowest soldier, this place was not Vosdvizhenka, Mohova, Kutaf, and the Troitsky gates; it was a new battlefield, likely to be the scene of a bloody conflict. And all were ready for that conflict. The shouts from the gates died away. The cannons were moved forward. The artillerymen quenched the burning linstocks. An officer shouted "Fire!" and two whistling sounds of clinking tin rang out one after another. The grapeshot fell rattling on the stone of the gateway, on the beams and screens of planks, and two clouds of smoke rolled over the square.

Some instants after the echoes of the shots had died away over the stone Kremlin, a strange sound was heard over the heads of the French. An immense flock of jackdaws rose above the walls and swept round in the air with loud caws, and the whir of thousands of wings. Together with this sound, there rose a solitary human cry at the gate, and the figure of a man bareheaded, in a long peasant's coat, came into sight through the smoke. Holding a gun up, he took aim at the French. "Fire!" repeated the artillery officer, and at the same instant one rifle shot and two cannon shots were heard. The gate was again hidden in smoke.

Nothing more stirred behind the barricade, and the French infantry soldiers with their officers passed in at the gate. In the gateway lay three men wounded and four dead. Two men in long peasant-coats had run away along the walls toward Znamenka.

"Clear this away," said the officer, pointing to the beams and the corpses; and the French soldiers finished off the wounded, and flung the corpses over the fence below. Who these men were nobody knew. "Clear this away!" was all that was said of them, and they were flung away that they might not stink. Thiers has indeed devoted some eloquent lines to their memories. "These wretches had invaded the sacred citadel, had taken possession of the guns of the arsenal, and fired (the wretches) on the French. Some of them were sabred, and the Kremlin was purged of their presence."

Murat was informed that the way had been cleared. The French entered the gates, and began pitching their camp on Senate-house Square. The soldiers flung the chairs out of the windows of the Senate-house into the square, and began making fires.

Other detachments marched across the Kremlin and encamped in Moroseyka, Lubyanka, and Pokrovka. Others pitched their camps in Vosdvizhenka, Znamenka, Nikolskaya, and Tverskaya. Not finding citizens to entertain them, the French everywhere bivouacked as in a camp pitched in a town, instead of quartering themselves on the houses.

Tattered, hungry, and exhausted, as they were, and dwindled to one-third their original numbers, the French soldiers yet entered Moscow in good discipline. It was a harassed and exhausted, yet still active and menacing army. But it was an army only up to the moment when the soldiers of the army dispersed all over the town. As soon as the soldiers began to disperse about the wealthy, deserted houses, the army was lost for ever, and in its place was a multitude of men, neither citizens nor soldiers, but something nondescript between, known as marauders. When five weeks later these same men set out from Moscow, they no longer made up an army. They were a mob of marauders, each of whom carried or dragged along with him a mass of objects he regarded as precious and useful. The aim of each of these men on leaving Moscow was not, as it had been, to fight as a soldier, but simply to keep the booty he had obtained. Like the ape, who slipping his hand into the narrow neck of a pitcher, and snatching up a handful of nuts inside it, will not open his fist for fear of losing his prize, even to his own ruin, the French on leaving Moscow were inevitably bound to come to ruin, because they dragged their plunder along with them, and it seemed as impossible to them to fling away their booty as it seems to the ape to let go of the nuts. Ten minutes after the several French regiments had dispersed about the various quarters of Moscow, not a soldier nor an officer was left among them. At the windows of the houses men could be seen in military coats and Hessiàn boots, laughing and strolling through the rooms. In the cellars, in the storerooms similar men were busily looking after the provisions; in the courtyards they were unlocking or breaking open the doors of sheds and stables; in the kitchens they were making up fires, and with bare arms mixing, kneading, and baking, and frightening, or trying to coax and amuse, women and children. Men there were in plenty everywhere, in all the shops and houses; but the army was no more.

That day one order after another was issued by the French commanders forbidding the troops to disperse about the town, sternly forbidding violence to the inhabitants, and pillaging, and proclaiming that a general roll-call was to take place that evening. But in spite of all such measures the men, who had made up an army, flowed about the wealthy, deserted city, so richly provided with luxuries and comforts. Like a starved herd, that keeps together crossing a barren plain, but at once on reaching rich pastures inevitably strays apart and scatters over them, the army was irresistibly lured into scattering over the wealthy town.

Moscow was without its inhabitants, and the soldiers were sucked up in her, like water into sand, as they flowed away irresistibly in all directions from the Kremlin, which they had entered first. Cavalry soldiers, who had entered a merchant's house abandoned with all its belongings, and finding stabling for their horses and to spare, yet went on to take the house next door, which seemed to them better. Many took several houses, chalking their names on them, and quarrelled and even fought with other companies for their possession. Soldiers had no sooner succeeded in securing quarters than they ran along the street to look at the town, and on hearing that everything had been abandoned, hurried off where objects of value could be carried off for nothing. The officers followed to check the soldiers, and were involuntarily lured into doing the same. In Carriage Row shops had been abandoned stocked with carriages, and the generals flocked thither to choose coaches and carriages for themselves. The few inhabitants who had stayed on invited the officers into their houses, hoping thereby to secure themselves against being robbed. Wealth there was in abundance: there seemed no end to it. Everywhere all round the parts occupied by the French there were unexplored regions unoccupied beyond, in which the French fancied there were even more riches to be found. And Moscow absorbed them further and further into herself. Just as when water flows over dry land, water and dry land alike disappear and are lost in mud, so when the hungry army entered the wealthy, deserted city, the army and the wealth of the city both perished; and fires and marauding bands sprang up where they had been.

The French ascribed the burning of Moscow *au patriotisme féroce de Rastoptchine;* the Russians to the savagery of the French. In reality, explanations of the fire of Moscow, in the sense of the conflagration being brought home to the door of any one person or group of persons, there have never been, and never could be. Moscow was burned because

she was placed in conditions in which any town built of wood was bound
to be burned, quite apart from the question whether there were or were
not one hundred and thirty inefficient fire-engines in the town. Moscow
was sure to be burned, because her inhabitants had gone away, as inevitably as a heap of straw is sure to be burned where sparks are scattered on it for several days in succession. A town of wooden houses, in
which when the police and the inhabitants owning the houses are in
possession of it, fires are of daily occurrence, cannot escape being burned
when its inhabitants are gone and it is filled with soldiers smoking pipes,
making fires in Senate-house Square of the Senate-house chairs, and
cooking themselves meals twice a day. In times of peace, whenever
troops are quartered on villages in any district, the number of fires in
the district at once increases. How greatly must the likelihood of fires be
increased in an abandoned town, built of wood, and occupied by foreign
soldiers! *Le patriotisme féroce de Rastoptchine* and the savagery of the
French do not come into the question. Moscow was burned through the
pipes, the kitchen stoves, and camp-fires, through the recklessness of the
enemy's soldiers, who lived in the houses without the care of householders. Even if there were cases of incendiarism (which is very doubtful, because no one had any reason for incendiarism, and in any case
such a crime is a troublesome and dangerous one), there is no need to
accept incendiarism as the cause, for the conflagration would have been
inevitable anyway without it.

Soothing as it was to the vanity of the French to throw the blame on
the ferocity of Rastoptchin, and to that of the Russians to throw the
blame on the miscreant Bonaparte, or later on to place the heroic torch
in the hand of its patriot peasantry, we cannot disguise from ourselves
that there could be no such direct cause of the fire, since Moscow was
as certain to be burned as any village, factory, or house forsaken by its
owners, and used as a temporary shelter and cooking-place by strangers.
Moscow was burned by her inhabitants, it is true; but not by the inhabitants who had lingered on, but by the inhabitants who had abandoned her. Moscow did not, like Berlin, Vienna, and other towns, escape
harm while in the occupation of the enemy, simply because her inhabitants did not receive the French with the keys, and the bread and salt of
welcome, but abandoned her.

XXVII

THE process of the absorption of the French into Moscow in a widening
circle in all directions did not, till the evening of the 2nd of September,
reach the quarter of the town in which Pierre was staying.

After the two last days spent in solitude and exceptional conditions,
Pierre was in a condition approaching madness. One haunting idea had
complete possession of him. He could not have told how or when it had
come to him, but that idea had now such complete possession of him that
he remembered nothing in the past, and understood nothing in the

present; and everything he saw and heard seemed passing in a dream.

Pierre had left his own house simply to escape from the complicated tangle woven about him by the demands of daily life, which in his condition at that time he was incapable of unravelling. He had gone to Osip Alexyevitch's house on the pretext of sorting out the books and papers of the deceased. Simply he was in search of a quiet home of rest from the storm of life, and his memories of Osip Alexyevitch were connected in his soul with a whole world of calm, solemn, and eternal ideals, in every way the reverse of the tangled whirl of agitation into which he felt himself being drawn. He was in search of a quiet refuge, and he certainly found it in Osip Alexyevitch's study. When, in the deathlike stillness of the study, he sat with his elbows on the dusty writing-table of his deceased friend, there passed in calm and significant succession before his mental vision the impressions of the last few days, especially of the battle of Borodino, and of that overwhelming sense of his own pettiness and falsity in comparison with the truth and simplicity and force of that class of men, who were mentally referred to by him as "they." When Gerasim roused him from his reverie, the idea occurred to Pierre that he would take part in the defence of Moscow by the people, which was, he knew, expected. And with that object he had asked Gerasim to get him a peasant's coat and a pistol, and had told him that he intended to conceal his name, and to remain in Osip Alexyevitch's house. Then during the first day of solitude and idleness (Pierre tried several times in vain to fix his attention on the masonic manuscripts) there rose several times vaguely to his mind the idea that had occurred to him in the past of the cabalistic significance of his name in connection with the name of Bonaparte. But the idea that he, *l'Russe Besuhov,* was destined to put an end to the power of the *Beast,* had as yet only come to him as one of those dreams that flit idly through the brain, leaving no trace behind. When after buying the peasant's coat, simply with the object of taking part in the defence of Moscow by the people, Pierre had met the Rostovs, and Natasha said to him, "You are staying? Ah, how splendid that is!" the idea had flashed into his mind that it really might be splendid, even if they did take Moscow, for him to remain, and to do what had been foretold for him to do.

Next day with the simple aim of not sparing himself and not doing less than *they* would do, he had gone out to the Three Hills barrier. But when he came back, convinced that Moscow would not be defended, he suddenly felt that what had only occurred to him before as a possibility, had now become something necessary and inevitable. He must remain in Moscow, concealing his name, must meet Napoleon, and kill him, so as either to perish or to put an end to the misery of all Europe, which was in Pierre's opinion entirely due to Napoleon alone.

Pierre knew all the details of the German student's attempt on Napoleon's life at Vienna in 1809, and knew that that student had been shot. And the danger to which he would be exposing his own life in carrying out his design excited him even more violently.

Two equally powerful feelings drew Pierre irresistibly to his design.

The first was the craving for sacrifice and suffering through the sense of the common calamity, the feeling that had impelled him to go to Mozhaisk on the 25th, and to place himself in the very thick of the battle, and now to run away from his own house, to give up his accustomed luxury and comfort, to sleep without undressing on a hard sofa, and to eat the same food as Gerasim. The other was that vague and exclusively Russian feeling of contempt for everything conventional, artificial, human, for everything that is regarded by the majority of men as the highest good in the world. Pierre had for the first time experienced that strange and fascinating feeling in the Slobodsky palace, when he suddenly felt that wealth and power and life, all that men build up and guard with such effort, is only worth anything through the joy with which it can all be cast away.

It was the same feeling that impels the volunteer-recruit to drink up his last farthing, the drunken man to smash looking-glasses and window-panes for no apparent cause, though he knows it will cost him his little all; the feeling through which a man in doing things, vulgarly speaking, senseless, as it were, proves his personal force and power, by manifesting the presence of a higher standard of judging life, outside mere human limitations.

Ever since the day when Pierre first experienced this feeling in the Slobodsky palace, he had been continually under the influence of it, but it was only now that it found full satisfaction. Moreover at the present moment Pierre was supported in his design, and prevented from abandoning it, by the steps he had already taken in that direction. His flight from his own house, and his disguise, and his pistol, and his statement to the Rostovs that he should remain in Moscow,—all would have been devoid of meaning, would have been indeed absurd and laughable (a point to which Pierre was sensitive) if after all that he had simply gone out of Moscow like other people.

Pierre's physical state, as is always the case, corresponded with his moral condition. The coarse fare to which he was unused, the vodka he drank during those days, the lack of wine and cigars, his dirty, unchanged linen, and two half-sleepless nights, spent on a short sofa without bedding, all reduced Pierre to a state of nervous irritability bordering on madness.

It was two o'clock in the afternoon. The French had already entered Moscow. Pierre knew this, but instead of acting, he only brooded over his enterprise, going over all the minutest details of it. In his dreams Pierre never clearly pictured the very act of striking the blow, nor the death of Napoleon, but with extraordinary vividness and mournful enjoyment dwelt on his own end and his heroic fortitude.

"Yes, one man for all, I must act or perish!" he thought. "Yes, I will approach . . . and then all at once . . . with a pistol or a dagger!" thought Pierre. "But that doesn't matter. It's not I but the Hand of Providence punishes you. . . . I shall say" (Pierre pondered over the words he would utter as he killed Napoleon). "Well, take me, executme!" Pierre would murmur to himself, bowing his head with a sad but firm expression on his face.

While Pierre was standing in the middle of the room, musing in this fashion, the door of the study opened, and Makar Alexyevitch—always hitherto so timid—appeared in the doorway, completely transformed.

His dressing-gown was hanging open. His face was red and distorted. He was unmistakably drunk. On seeing Pierre he was for the first minute disconcerted, but observing discomfiture in Pierre's face too, he was at once emboldened by it; and with his thin, tottering legs walked into the middle of the room.

"They have grown fearful," he said, in a husky and confidential voice. "I say: I will not surrender, I say . . . eh, sir?" He paused and suddenly catching sight of the pistol on the table, snatched it with surprising rapidity and ran out into the corridor.

Gerasim and the porter, who had followed Makar Alexyevitch, stopped him in the vestibule, and tried to get the pistol away from him. Pierre coming out of the study looked with repugnance and compassion at the half-insane old man. Makar Alexyevitch, frowning with effort, succeeded in keeping the pistol, and was shouting in a husky voice, evidently imagining some heroic scene.

"To arms! Board them! You shan't get it!" he was shouting.

"Give over, please, give over. Do me the favour, sir, please be quiet. There now, if you please, sir, . . ." Gerasim was saying, cautiously trying to steer Makar Alexyevitch by his elbows towards the door.

"Who are you? Bonaparte! . . ." yelled Makar Alexyevitch.

"That's not the thing, sir. You come into your room and rest a little. Let me have the pistol now."

"Away, base slave! Don't touch me! Do you see?" screamed Makar Alexyevitch, brandishing the pistol. "Run them down!"

"Take hold!" Gerasim whispered to the porter.

They seized Makar Alexyevitch by the arms and dragged him towards the door.

The vestibule was filled with the unseemly sounds of scuffling and drunken, husky gasping.

Suddenly a new sound, a shrill, feminine shriek, was heard from the porch, and the cook ran into the vestibule.

"They! Merciful heavens! . . . My goodness, here they are! Four of them, horsemen!" she screamed.

Gerasim and the porter let Makar Alexyevitch go, and in the hush that followed in the corridor they could distinctly hear several hands knocking at the front door.

XXVIII

HAVING inwardly resolved that until the execution of his design, he ought to disguise his station and his knowledge of French, Pierre stood at the half-open door into the corridor, intending to conceal himself at once as soon as the French entered. But the French entered, and Pierre did not leave the door; an irresistible curiosity kept him there.

There were two of them. One—an officer, a tall, handsome man of gallant bearing; the other, obviously a soldier or officer's servant, a squat, thin, sunburnt man, with hollow cheeks and a dull expression. The officer walked first, limping and leaning on a stick. After advancing a few steps, the officer apparently making up his mind that these would be good quarters, stopped, turned round and shouted in a loud, peremptory voice to the soldiers standing in the doorway to put up the horses. Having done this the officer, with a jaunty gesture, crooking his elbow high in the air, stroked his moustaches and put his hand to his hat.

"Bonjour, la compagnie!" he said gaily, smiling and looking about him.

No one made any reply.

"Vous êtes le bourgeois?" the officer asked, addressing Gerasim.

Gerasim looked back with scared inquiry at the officer.

"Quartire, quartire, logement," said the officer, looking down with a condescending and good-humoured smile at the little man. "The French are good lads. Don't let us be cross, old fellow," he went on in French, clapping the scared and mute Gerasim on the shoulder. "I say, does no one speak French in this establishment?" he added, looking round and meeting Pierre's eyes. Pierre withdrew from the door.

The officer turned again to Gerasim. He asked him to show him over the house.

"Master not here—no understand . . . me you . . ." said Gerasim, trying to make his words more comprehensible by saying them in reverse order.

The French officer, smiling, waved his hands in front of Gerasim's nose, to give him to understand that he too failed to understand him, and walked with a limp towards the door where Pierre was standing. Pierre was about to retreat to conceal himself from him, but at that very second he caught sight of Makar Alexyevitch peeping out of the open kitchen door with a pistol in his hand. With a madman's cunning, Makar Alexyevitch eyed the Frenchmen, and lifting the pistol, took aim. "Run them down!!!" yelled the drunkard, pressing the trigger. The French officer turned round at the scream, and at the same instant Pierre dashed at the drunken man. Just as Pierre snatched at the pistol and jerked it up, Makar Alexyevitch succeeded at last in pressing the trigger, and a deafening shot rang out, wrapping every one in a cloud of smoke. The Frenchman turned pale and rushed back to the door.

Forgetting his intention of concealing his knowledge of French, Pierre pulled away the pistol, and throwing it on the ground, ran to the officer and addressed him in French. "You are not wounded?" he said.

"I think not," answered the officer, feeling himself; "but I have had a narrow escape this time," he added, pointing to the broken plaster in the wall.

"Who is this man?" he asked, looking sternly at Pierre.

"Oh, I am really in despair at what has happened," said Pierre

quickly, quite forgetting his part. "It is a madman, an unhappy creature, who did not know what he was doing."

The officer went up to Makar Alexyevitch and took him by the collar.
Makar Alexyevitch pouting out his lips, nodded, as he leaned against
the wall, as though dropping asleep.

"Brigand, you shall pay for it," said the Frenchman, letting go of him.
"We are clement after victory, but we do not pardon traitors," he added,
with gloomy dignity in his face, and a fine, vigorous gesture.

Pierre tried in French to persuade the officer not to be severe with this
drunken imbecile. The Frenchman listened in silence, with the same
gloomy air, and then suddenly turned with a smile to Pierre. For several
seconds he gazed at him mutely. His handsome face assumed an expression of melodramatic feeling, and he held out his hand.

"You have saved my life. You are French," he said. For a Frenchman,
the deduction followed indubitably. An heroic action could only be performed by a Frenchman, and to save the life of him, M. Ramballe, captain of the 13th Light Brigade, was undoubtedly a most heroic action.

But however indubitable this logic, and well grounded the conviction
the officer based on it, Pierre thought well to disillusion him on the subject.

"I am Russian," he said quickly.

"Tell that to others," said the Frenchman, smiling and waving his finger before his nose. "You shall tell me all about it directly," he said.
"Charmed to meet a compatriot. Well, what are we to do with this
man?" he added, applying to Pierre now as though to a comrade. If
Pierre were indeed not a Frenchman, he would hardly on receiving that
appellation—the most honourable in the world—care to disavow it, was
what the expression and tone of the French officer suggested. To his last
question Pierre explained once more who Makar Alexyevitch was. He
explained that just before his arrival the drunken imbecile had carried
off a loaded pistol, which they had not succeeded in getting from him,
and he begged him to let his action go unpunished. The Frenchman
arched his chest, and made a majestic gesture with his hand.

"You have saved my life! You are a Frenchman. You ask me to
pardon him. I grant you his pardon. Let this man be released," the
French officer pronounced with rapidity and energy, and taking the arm
of Pierre—promoted to be a Frenchman for saving his life—he was
walking with him into the room.

The soldiers in the yard, hearing the shot, had come into the vestibule
to ask what had happened, and to offer their services in punishing the
offender; but the officer sternly checked them.

"You will be sent for when you are wanted," he said. The soldiers
withdrew. The orderly, who had meanwhile been in the kitchen, came in
to the officer.

"Captain, they have soup and a leg of mutton in the kitchen," he said.
"Shall I bring it up?"

"Yes, and the wine," said the captain.

XXIX

As the French officer drew Pierre with him into the room, the latter thought it his duty to assure the captain again that he was not a Frenchman, and would have withdrawn, but the French officer would not hear of it. He was so courteous, polite, good-humoured, and genuinely grateful to him for saving his life that Pierre had not the heart to refuse, and sat down with him in the dining-room, the first room they entered. To Pierre's asseveration that he was not a Frenchman, the captain, plainly unable to comprehend how any one could refuse so flattering a title, shrugged his shoulders, and said that if he insisted in passing for a Russian, so be it, but that in spite of that he should yet feel bound to him for ever by sentiments of gratitude for the defence of his life.

If this man had been endowed with even the slightest faculty of perceiving the feelings of others, and had had the faintest inkling of Pierre's sentiments, the latter would probably have left him. But his lively impenetrability to everything not himself vanquished Pierre.

"Frenchman or Russian prince incognito," said the Frenchman, looking at Pierre's fine, though dirty linen, and the ring on his finger; "I owe my life to you, and I offer you my friendship. A Frenchman never forgets an insult or a service. I offer you my friendship. That's all I say."

In the tones of the voice, the expression of the face, and the gestures of the officer, there was so much naïve good nature and good breeding (in the French sense) that Pierre unconsciously responded with a smile to his smile, as he took his outstretched hand.

"Captain Ramballe of the 13th Light Brigade, decorated for the affair of the 7th September," he introduced himself, an irrepressible smile of complacency lurking under his moustache. "Will you tell me now to whom I have the honour of speaking so agreeably, instead of remaining in the ambulance with that madman's ball in my body?"

Pierre answered that he would not tell him his name, and was beginning with a blush, while trying to invent a name, to speak of the reasons for which he was unable to do so, but the Frenchman hurriedly interrupted him.

"Enough!" he said. "I understand your reasons; you are an officer . . . a staff officer, perhaps. You have borne arms against us. That's not my business. I owe you my life. That's enough for me. I am at your disposal. You are a nobleman?" he added, with an intonation of inquiry. Pierre bowed.

"Your baptismal name, if you please? I ask nothing more. M. Pierre, you say? Perfect! That's all I want to know."

When they had brought in the mutton, an omelette, a samovar, vodka, and wine from a Russian cellar brought with them by the French, Ramballe begged Pierre to share his dinner; and at once with the haste and greediness of a healthy, hungry man, set to work on the viands himself, munching vigorously with his strong teeth, and continually smacking his lips and exclaiming, *"Excellent! exquis!"* His face became flushed and perspiring Pierre was hungry, and pleased to share the repast. Morel, the orderly, brought in a pot of hot water, and put a bottle of red wine to warm in it. He brought in too a bottle of kvass from the kitchen for them to taste. This beverage was already known to the French, and had received a nickname. They called it *limonade de cochon,* and Morel praised this "pigs' lemonade," which he had found in the kitchen. But as the captain had the wine they had picked up as they crossed Moscow, he left the kvass for Morel, and attacked the bottle of bordeaux. He wrapped a napkin round the bottle, and poured out wine for himself and Pierre. The wine, and the satisfaction of his hunger, made the captain even more lively, and he chatted away without a pause all dinner-time.

"Yes, my dear M. Pierre, I owe you a fine votive candle for saving me from that maniac. I have bullets enough in my body, you know. Here is one from Wagram" (he pointed to his side), "and two from Smolensk" (he showed the scar on his cheek). "And this leg which won't walk, as you see. It was at the great battle of la Moskowa on the 7th that I got that. *Sacré Dieu,* it was fine! You ought to have seen that; it was a deluge of fire. You cut us out a tough job; you can boast of that, my word on it! And on my word, in spite of the cough I caught, I should be ready to begin again. I pity those who did not see it."

"I was there," said Pierre.

"Really!" pursued the Frenchman. "Well, so much the better. You are fine enemies, though. The great redoubt was well held, by my pipe. And you made us pay heavily for it too. I was at it three times, as I'm sitting here. Three times we were upon the cannons, and three times we were driven back like cardboard figures. Oh, it was fine, M. Pierre. Your grenadiers were superb, God's thunder. I saw them six times in succession close the ranks and march as though on parade. Fine fellows. Our king of Naples, who knows all about it, cried, Bravo! Ah, ah, soldiers like ourselves," he said after a moment's silence. "So much the better, so much the better, M. Pierre. Terrible in war . . . gallant, with the fair" (he winked with a smile)—"there you have the French, M. Pierre, eh?"

The captain was so naïvely and good-humouredly gay and obtuse and self-satisfied that Pierre almost winked in response, as he looked good-humouredly at him. Probably the word "gallant" brought the captain to reflect on the state of things in Moscow.

"By the way, tell me, is it true that all the women have left Moscow? What a queer idea! What had they to fear?"

"Would not the French ladies quit Paris, if the Russians were to enter it?" said Pierre.

"Ha—ha—ha! . . ." The Frenchman gave vent to a gay, sanguine chuckle, slapping Pierre on the shoulder. "That's a good one, that is," he went on. "Paris . . . But Paris . . ."

"Paris is the capital of the world," said Pierre, finishing the sentence for him.

The captain looked at Pierre. He had the habit of stopping short in the middle of conversation, and staring intently with his laughing genial eyes.

"Well, if you had not told me you are a Russian, I would have wagered you were a Parisian. You have that indescribable something . . ." and uttering this compliment, he again gazed at him mutely.

"I have been in Paris. I spent years there," said Pierre.

"One can see that! Paris! A man who does not know Paris is a savage . . . A Parisian can be told two leagues off. Paris—it is Talma, la Duschénois, Potier, the Sorbonne, the boulevards." Perceiving that the conclusion of his phrase was somewhat of an anticlimax, he added hurriedly, "There is only one Paris in the world. . . . You have been in Paris, and you remain Russian. Well, I don't think the less of you for that."

After the days he had spent alone with his gloomy thoughts, Pierre, under the influence of the wine he had drunk, could not help taking pleasure in conversing with this good-humoured and naïve person.

"To return to your ladies, they are said to be beautiful. What a silly idea to go and bury themselves in the steppes, when the French army is in Moscow. What a chance they have lost. Your peasants are different; but you civilised people ought to know better than that. We have taken Vienna, Berlin, Madrid, Naples, Rome, Warsaw—all the capitals in the world. We are feared, but we are loved. We are worth knowing. And then the Emperor . . ." he was beginning, but Pierre interrupted him.

"The Emperor," repeated Pierre, and his face suddenly wore a mournful and embarrassed look. "What of the Emperor?"

"The Emperor? He is generosity, mercy, justice, order, genius—that is the Emperor. It is I, Ramballe, who tell you that. I was his enemy eight years ago. My father was an emigrant count. But he has conquered me, that man. He has taken hold of me. I could not resist the spectacle of the greatness and glory with which he was covering France. When I understood what he wanted, when I saw he was preparing a bed of laurels for us, I said to myself: 'That is a monarch.' And I gave myself up to him. Oh yes, he is the greatest man of the centuries, past and to come."

"And is he in Moscow?" Pierre asked, hesitating and looking guilty.

The Frenchman gazed at Pierre's guilty face, and grinned.

"No, he will make his entry to-morrow," he said, and went on with his talk.

Their conversation was interrupted by several voices shouting at the gates, and Morel coming in to tell the captain that some Würtemberg hussars had come and wanted to put up their horses in the yard in which the captain's had been put up. The difficulty arose chiefly from the hussars not understanding what was said to them.

The captain bade the senior sergeant be brought to him, and in a stern voice asked him to what regiment he belonged, who was his commanding officer, and on what pretext he dared attempt to occupy quarters already occupied. The German, who knew very little French, succeeded in answering the first two questions, but in reply to the last one, which he did not understand, he answered in broken French and German that he was quartermaster of the regiment, and had received orders from his superior officer to occupy all the houses in the row. Pierre, who knew German, translated the German's words to the captain, and translated the captain's answer back for the Würtemberg hussar. On understanding what was said to him, the German gave in, and took his men away.

The captain went out to the entrance and gave some loud commands. When he came back into the room, Pierre was sitting where he had been sitting before, with his head in his hands. His face expressed suffering. He really was at that moment suffering. As soon as the captain had gone out, and Pierre had been left alone, he suddenly came to himself, and recognised the position he was in. It was not that Moscow had been taken, not that these lucky conquerors were making themselves at home there and patronising him, bitterly as Pierre felt it, that tortured him at that moment. He was tortured by the consciousness of his own weakness. The few glasses of wine he had drunk, the chat with this good-natured fellow, had dissipated that mood of concentrated gloom, which he had been living in for the last few days, and which was essential for carrying out his design. The pistol and the dagger and the peasant's coat were ready, Napoleon was making his entry on the morrow. Pierre felt it as praiseworthy and as beneficial as ever to slay the miscreant; but he felt now that he would not do it. He struggled against the consciousness of his own weakness, but he vaguely felt that he could not overcome it, that his past gloomy train of ideas, of vengeance, murder, and self-sacrifice, had been blown away like dust at contact with the first human being.

The captain came into the room, limping a little, and whistling some tune.

The Frenchman's chatter that had amused Pierre struck him now as revolting. And his whistling a tune, and his gait, and his gesture in twisting his moustaches, all seemed insulting to Pierre now.

"I'll go away at once, I won't say another word to him," thought Pierre. He thought this, yet went on sitting in the same place. Some strange feeling of weakness riveted him to his place; he longed to get up and go, and could not.

The captain, on the contrary, seemed in exceedingly good spirits. He walked a couple of times up and down the room. His eyes sparkled and his moustaches slightly twitched as though he were smiling to himself at some amusing notion.

"Charming fellow the colonel of these Würtembergers," he said all at once. "He's a German, but a good fellow if ever there was one. But a German."

He sat down facing Pierre.

"By the way, you know German?"

Pierre looked at him in silence.

"How do you say *'asile'* in German?"

"Asile?" repeated Pierre. *"Asile* in German is *Unterkunft."*

"What do you say?" the captain queried quickly and doubtfully.

"*Unterkunft*," repeated Pierre.

"*Onterkoff*," said the captain, and for several seconds he looked at Pierre with his laughing eyes. "The Germans are awful fools, aren't they, M. Pierre?" he concluded.

"Well, another bottle of this Moscow claret, eh? Morel, warm us another bottle!" the captain shouted gaily.

Morel brought candles and a bottle of wine. The captain looked at Pierre in the candle-light, and was obviously struck by the troubled face of his companion. With genuine regret and sympathy in his face, Ramballe approached Pierre, and bent over him.

"Eh, we are sad!" he said, touching Pierre on the hand. "Can I have hurt you? No, really, have you anything against me?" he questioned. "Perhaps it is owing to the situation of affairs?"

Pierre made no reply, but looked cordially into the Frenchman's eyes. This expression of sympathy was pleasant to him.

"My word of honour, to say nothing of what I owe you, I have a liking for you. Can I do anything for you? Dispose of me. It is for life and death. With my hand and my heart, I say so," he said, slapping himself on the chest.

"Thank you," said Pierre. The captain gazed at Pierre as he had gazed at him when he learnt the German for "refuge," and his face suddenly brightened.

"Ah, in that case, I drink to our friendship," he cried gaily, pouring out two glasses of wine.

Pierre took the glass and emptied it. Ramballe emptied his, pressed Pierre's hand once more, and leaned his elbow on the table in a pose of pensive melancholy.

"Yes, my dear friend, such are the freaks of fortune," he began. "Who would have said I should be a soldier and captain of dragoons in the service of Bonaparte, as we used to call him. And yet here I am at Moscow with him. I must tell you, my dear fellow," he continued in the mournful and measured voice of a man who intends to tell a long story, "our name is one of the most ancient in France."

And with the easy and naïve unreserve of a Frenchman, the captain told Pierre the history of his forefathers, his childhood, boyhood, and manhood, and all his relations, his fortunes, and domestic affairs. "*Ma pauvre mère*," took, of course, a prominent part in this recital.

"But all that is only the setting of life; the real thing is love. Love! Eh, M. Pierre?" he said, warming up. "Another glass."

Pierre again emptied his glass, and filled himself a third.

"O women! women!" and the captain, gazing with moist eyes at Pierre, began talking of love and his adventures with the fair sex. They were very numerous, as might readily be believed, judging from the officer's conceited, handsome face and the eager enthusiasm with which he talked of women. Although all Ramballe's accounts of his love affairs were characterised by that peculiar nastiness in which the French find the unique charm and poetry of love, the captain told his stories with such genuine conviction that he was the only man who had tasted and known all the sweets of love, and he described the women he had known in such an alluring fashion that Pierre listened to him with curiosity.

It was evident that *l'amour* the Frenchman was so fond of was neither that low and simple kind of love Pierre had at one time felt for his wife, nor the romantic love, exaggerated by himself, that he felt for Natasha. For both those kinds of love Ramballe had an equal contempt—one was *l'amour des charretiers*, the other *l'amour des nigauds*. *L'amour* for which the Frenchman had a weakness consisted principally in an unnatural relation to the woman, and in combinations of monstrous circumstances which lent the chief charm to the feeling.

Thus the captain related the touching history of his love for a fascinating marquise of five-and-thirty, and at the same time for a charming, innocent child of seventeen, the daughter of the fascinating marquise. The conflict of generosity between mother and daughter, ending in the mother sacrificing herself and offering her daughter in marriage to her lover, even now, though it was a memory in the remote past, moved the captain deeply. Then he related an episode in which the husband played the part of the lover, and he—the lover—the part of the husband, and several comic episodes among his reminiscences of Germany, where *Unterkunft* means *asile*, where the husbands eat cabbage soup, and where the young girls are too flaxen-haired.

The last episode was one in Poland, still fresh in the captain's memory, and described by him with rapid gestures and a glowing face. The story was that he had saved the life of a Pole—the episode of saving life was continually cropping up in the captain's anecdotes—and that Pole had intrusted to his care his bewitching wife, a Parisian in heart, while he himself entered the French service. The captain had been happy, the bewitching Polish lady had wanted to elope with him; but moved by a magnanimous impulse, the captain had restored the wife to the husband with the words: "I saved your life, and I save your honour."

As he repeated these words, the captain wiped his eyes and shook himself, as though to shake off the weakness that overcame him at this touching recollection.

As men often do at a late hour at night, and under the influence of wine, Pierre listened to the captain's stories, and while he followed and understood all he told him, he was also following a train of personal reminiscences which had for some reason risen to his imagination. As he listened to those love affairs, his own love for Natasha suddenly came into his mind, and going over all the pictures of that love in his imagination, he mentally compared them with Ramballe's stories. As he heard the account of the conflict between love and duty, Pierre saw before him every detail of the meeting with the object of his love at the Suharev Tower. That meeting had not at the time made much impression on him; he had not once thought of it since. But now it seemed to him that there was something very significant and romantic in that meeting.

"Pyotr Kirillitch, come here, I recognise you"; he could hear her words now, could see her eyes, her smile, her travelling cap, and the curl peeping out below it . . . and he felt that there was something moving, touching in all that.

When he had finished his tale about the bewitching Polish lady, the captain turned to Pierre with the inquiry whether he had had any similar experience of self-sacrifice for love and envy of a lawful husband.

Pierre, roused by this question, lifted his head and felt an irresistible impulse to give expression to the ideas in his mind. He began to explain that he looked upon love for woman somewhat differently. He said he had all his life long loved one woman, and still loved her, and that that woman could never be his.

"*Tiens!*" said the captain.

Then Pierre explained that he had loved this woman from his earliest youth, but had not dared to think of her because she was too young, and he had been an illegitimate son, with no name of his own. Then when he had received a name and wealth, he had not dared think of her because he loved her too much, because he set her too high above all the world, and so even more above himself. On reaching this point, Pierre asked the captain, did he understand that.

The captain made a gesture expressing that whether he understood it or not, he begged him to proceed.

"Platonic love; moonshine . . ." he muttered. The wine he had drunk, or an impulse of frankness, or the thought that this man did not know and never would know, any of the persons concerned in his story, or all together loosened Pierre's tongue. With faltering lips and with a far-away look in his moist eye, he told all his story; his marriage and the story of Natasha's love for his dearest friend and her betrayal of him, and all his own simple relations with her. In response to questions from Ramballe, he told him, too, what he had at first concealed—his position in society—and even disclosed his name.

What impressed the captain more than anything else in Pierre's story was the fact that Pierre was very wealthy, that he had two palatial houses in Moscow, and that he had abandoned everything, and yet had not left Moscow, but was staying in the town concealing his name and station.

Late in the night they went out together into the street. The night was warm and clear. On the left there was the glow of the first fire that broke out in Moscow, in Petrovka. On the right a young crescent moon stood high in the sky, and in the opposite quarter of the heavens hung the brilliant comet which was connected in Pierre's heart with his love. At the gates of the yard stood Gerasim, the cook, and two Frenchmen. Pierre could hear their laughter and talk, incomprehensible to one another. They were looking at the glow of the fire burning in the town.

There was nothing alarming in a small remote fire in the immense city.

Gazing at the lofty, starlit sky, at the moon, at the comet and the glow of the fire, Pierre felt a thrill of joyous and tender emotion. "How fair it all is! what more does one want?" he thought. And all at once, when he recalled his design, his head seemed going round; he felt so giddy that he leaned against the fence so as not to fall.

Without taking leave of his new friend, Pierre left the gate with unsteady steps, and going back to his room lay down on the sofa and at once fell asleep.

XXX

FROM various roads, and with various feelings, the inhabitants running and driving away from Moscow, and the retreating troops, gazed at the glow of the first fire that broke out in the city on the 2nd of September.

The Rostovs' party stopped for that night at Mytishtchy, twenty versts from Moscow. They had started so late on the 1st of September, the road had been so blocked by waggons and troops, so many things had been forgotten, and servants sent back to get them, that they had decided to halt for the first night five versts from Moscow. The next morning they waked late, and there were again so many delays that they only reached Great Mytishtchy. At ten o'clock the Rostov family, and the wounded soldiers travelling with them, had all found places for the night in the yards and huts of the greater village. The servants, the Rostovs' coachmen, and the orderlies of the wounded officers, after settling their masters for the night, supped, fed their horses, and came out into the porch of a hut.

In the next hut lay Raevsky's adjutant with a broken wrist, and the terrible pain made him moan incessantly, and these moans had a gruesome sound in the autumn darkness of the night. On the first night this adjutant had spent the night in a building in the same yard as the hut in which the Rostovs slept. The countess declared that she had not closed her eyes all night from that moaning, and at Mytishtchy she had moved into a less comfortable hut simply to get further away from the wounded man. One of the servants noticed in the dark night sky, above the high carriage standing at the entry, another small glow of fire. One such glow had been seen long before, and every one knew it was Little Mytishtchy, which had been set on fire by Mamonov's Cossacks.

"I say, mates, there's another fire," said the man. All of them looked towards the glow.

"Why, they told us Mamonov's Cossacks had fired Little Mytishtchy." "Nay! that's not Mytishtchy, it's further." "Look 'ee, it's in Moscow seemingly." Two of the men left the porch, went to a carriage and squatted on the step. "It's more to the left! Why, Mytishtchy is away yonder, and that's quite the other side."

Several more men joined the first group.

"I say it is flaring," said one; "that's a fire in Moscow, my friends; either in Sushtchovsky or in Rogozhsky."

No one answered this remark. And for a good while all these men gazed in silence at the flames of this new conflagration glowing far away. An old man, the count's valet (as he was called), Danilo Terentyitch, came up to the crowd and called Mishka.

"What are you gaping at? . . . The count may ask for you and nobody to be found; go and put the clothes together."

"Oh, I only ran out for some water," said Mishka.

"And what do you say, Danilo Terentyitch? that's a fire in Moscow, isn't it?" said one of the footmen.

Danilo Terentyitch made no reply, and for a long while all were mute again. The glow spread wider, and flickered further and further away.

"God have mercy! . . . a wind and the drought . . ." said a voice again.

"Look 'ee, how it's spreading. O Lord! why, one can see the jackdaws! Lord, have mercy on us poor sinners!"

"They'll put it out, never fear."

"Who's to put it out?" cried the voice of Danilo Terentyitch, silent till that moment. His voice was quiet and deliberate. "Moscow it is, mates," he said; "it's she, our mother, the white city . . ." his voice broke, and he suddenly burst into the sobs of old age. And it seemed as though all had been only waiting for that to grasp the import for all of that glow they were watching. Sighs were heard and muttered prayers, and the sobs of the old valet.

XXXI

THE valet on going in informed the count that Moscow was on fire. The count put on his dressing-gown and went out to look. With him went Sonya, who had not yet undressed, and Madame Schoss, Natasha and the countess were left alone within. Petya was no longer with the family; he had gone on ahead with his regiment marching to Troitsa.

The countess wept on hearing that Moscow was in flames. Natasha, pale, with staring eyes, sat on the bench under the holy images, the spot where she had first thrown herself down on entering, and took no notice of her father's words. She was listening to the never-ceasing moan of the adjutant, audible three huts away.

"Oh! how awful!" cried Sonya, coming in chilled and frightened from the yard. "I do believe all Moscow is burning; there's an awful fire! Natasha, do look; you can see now from the window here," she said, obviously trying to distract her friend's mind. But Natasha stared at her, as though she did not understand what was asked of her, and fixed her eyes again on the corner of the stove. Natasha had been in this petrified condition ever since the morning, when Sonya, to the amazement and anger of the countess, had for some incomprehensible reason thought fit to inform Natasha of Prince Andrey's wound, and his presence among their train. The countess had been angry with Sonya, as she was very rarely angry. Sonya had cried and begged forgiveness, and now she waited all the while on her friend, as though trying to atone for her fault.

"Look, Natasha, how frightfully it's burning," said Sonya.

"What's burning?" asked Natasha. "Oh yes, Moscow."

And to get rid of Sonya, and not hurt her by a refusal, she moved her head towards the window, looking in such a way that it was evident she could see nothing, and sat down again in the same attitude as before.

"But you didn't see?"

"Yes, I really did see," she declared in a voice that implored to be left in peace.

Both the countess and Sonya could readily understand that Moscow, the burning of Moscow, anything whatever in fact, could be of no interest to Natasha.

The count came in again behind the partition wall and lay down. The countess went up to Natasha, put the back of her hand to her head, as she did when her daughter was ill, then touched her forehead with her lips, as though to find out whether she were feverish, and kissed her.

"You are chilled? You are all shaking. You should lie down," she said.

"Lie down? Yes, very well, I'll lie down. I'll lie down in a minute," said Natasha.

When Natasha had been told that morning that Prince Andrey was seriously wounded, and was travelling with them, she had at the first moment asked a great many questions, how and why and where was he going; whether he were dangerously wounded, and whether she could see him. But after she had been told that she could not see him, that his wound was a serious one, but that his life was not in danger, though she plainly did not believe what was told her, she saw that she would get the same answer whatever she said, and gave up asking questions and speaking at all. All the way Natasha had sat motionless in the corner of the carriage with those wide eyes, the look in which the countess knew so well and dreaded so much. And she was sitting in just the same way now on the bench in the hut. She was brooding on some plan; she was making, or already by now had made some decision, in her own mind— that the countess knew, but what that decision was she did not know, and that alarmed and worried her.

"Natasha, undress, darling, get into my bed."

For the countess only a bed had been made up on a bedstead. Madame Schoss and the two girls were to sleep on hay on the floor.

"No, mamma, I'll lie here on the floor," said Natasha irritably; she went to the window and opened it. The moans of the adjutant could be heard more distinctly from the open window. She put her head out into the damp night air, and the countess saw her slender neck shaking with sobs and heaving against the window frame. Natasha knew it was not Prince Andrey moaning. She knew that Prince Andrey was in the same block of huts as they were in, that he was in the next hut just across the porch, but that fearful never-ceasing moan made her sob. The countess exchanged glances with Sonya.

"Go to bed, darling, go to bed, my pet," said the countess, lightly touching Natasha's shoulder. "Come, go to bed."

"Oh yes . . . I'll go to bed at once, at once," said Natasha, hurriedly undressing, and breaking the strings of her petticoats. Dropping off her dress, and putting on a dressing-jacket, she sat down on the bed made up on the floor, tucking her feet under her, and flinging her short, fine hair over her shoulder, began plaiting it. Her thin, long, practised fingers rapidly and deftly divided, plaited, and tied up her hair. Natasha's head turned from side to side as usual as she did this, but her eyes, feverishly wide, looked straight before her with the same fixed stare. When her toilet for the night was over, Natasha sank softly down on to the sheet laid on the hay nearest the door.

"Natasha, you lie in the middle," said Sonya.

"I'll stay here," said Natasha. "And do go to bed," she added in a tone of annoyance. And she buried her face in the pillow.

The countess, Madame Schoss, and Sonya hurriedly undressed and went to bed. The lamp before the holy images was the only light left in the room. But out of doors the fire at Little Mytishtchy lighted the country up for two versts round, and there was a noisy clamour of peasants shouting at the tavern across the street, which Mamonov's Cossacks had broken into, and the moan of the adjutant could be heard unceasingly through everything.

For a long while Natasha listened to the sounds that reached her from within and without, and she did not stir. She heard at first her mother's prayers and sighs, the creaking of her bed under her, Madame Schoss's familiar, whistling snore, Sonya's soft breathing. Then the countess called to Natasha. Natasha did not answer.

"I think she's asleep, mamma," answered Sonya.

The countess, after a brief silence, spoke again, but this time no one answered her.

Soon after this Natasha caught the sound of her mother's even breathing. Natasha did not stir, though her little bare foot, poking out below the quilt, felt frozen against the uncovered floor.

A cricket chirped in a crack, as though celebrating a victory over all the world. A cock crowed far away, and another answered close by. The shouts had died away in the tavern, but the adjutant's moaning went on still the same. Natasha sat up.

"Sonya! Are you asleep? Mamma!" she whispered. No one answered. Slowly and cautiously Natasha got up, crossed herself, and stepped cautiously with her slender, supple, bare feet on to the dirty, cold floor. The boards creaked. With nimble feet she ran like a kitten a few steps, and took hold of the cold door-handle.

It seemed to her that something with heavy, rhythmical strokes was banging on all the walls of the hut; it was the beating of her own heart, torn with dread, with love and terror.

She opened the door, stepped over the lintel, and on to the damp, cold earth of the passage outside. The cold all about her refreshed her. Her bare foot felt a man asleep; she stepped over him, and opened the door of the hut in which Prince Andrey was lying.

In that hut it was dark. A tallow candle with a great, smouldering wick stood on a bench in the further corner, by a bed, on which something was lying.

Ever since she had been told in the morning of Prince Andrey's wound and his presence there, Natasha had resolved that she must see him. She could not have said why this must be, but she knew their meeting would be anguish to her, and that made her the more certain that it must be inevitable.

All day long she had lived in the hope that at night she would see him. But now when the moment had come, a terror came over her of what she would see. How had he been disfigured? What was left of him? Was he like that unceasing moan of the adjutant? Yes, he was all over like that. In her imagination he was that awful moan of pain personified. When she caught sight of an undefined mass in the corner, and took his raised knees under the quilt for his shoulders, she pictured some fearful body there, and stood still in terror. But an irresistible force drew her forward. She made one cautious step, another, and found herself in the middle of the small hut, cumbered up with baggage. On the bench, under the holy images, lay another man (this was Timohin), and on the floor were two more figures (the doctor and the valet).

The valet sat up and muttered something. Timohin, in pain from a wound in his leg, was not asleep, and gazed, all eyes, at the strange apparition of a girl in a white night-gown, dressing-jacket, and nightcap. The valet's sleepy and frightened words "What is it? What do you want?" only made Natasha hasten towards the figure lying in the corner. However fearfully unlike a human shape that figure might be now, she must see him. She passed by the valet, the smouldering candle flickered up, and she saw clearly Prince Andrey, lying with his arms stretched out on the quilt, looking just as she had always seen him.

He was just the same as ever; but the flush on his face, his shining eyes, gazing passionately at her, and especially the soft, childlike neck, showing above the lay-down collar of the nightshirt, gave him a peculiarly innocent, childlike look, such as she had never seen in him before. She ran up to him and with a swift, supple, youthful movement dropped on her knees.

He smiled, and held out his hand to her.

XXXII

SEVEN days had passed since Prince Andrey had found himself in the ambulance station on the field of Borodino. All that time he had been in a state of almost continual unconsciousness. The fever and inflammation of the bowels, which had been injured, were, in the opinion of the doctor accompanying the wounded, certain to carry him off. But on the seventh day he ate with relish a piece of bread with some tea, and the doctor observed that the fever was going down. Prince Andrey had regained consciousness in the morning. The first night after leaving Moscow had been fairly warm, and Prince Andrey had spent the night in his carriage. But at Mytishtchy the wounded man had himself asked to be moved and given tea. The pain caused by moving him into the hut had made Prince Andrey groan aloud and lose consciousness again. When he had been laid on his camp bedstead, he lay a long while with closed eyes without moving. Then he opened his eyes and whispered softly,

"How about the tea?" The doctor was struck by this instance of consciousness of the little details of daily life. He felt his pulse, and to his surprise and dissatisfaction found that the pulse was stronger. The doctor's dissatisfaction was due to the fact that he felt certain from his experience that Prince Andrey could not live, and that if he did not die now, he would only die a little later with even greater suffering. With Prince Andrey was the red-nosed major of his regiment, Timohin, who had joined him in Moscow with a wound in his leg received at the same battle of Borodino. The doctor, the prince's valet, and coachman, and two orderlies were in charge of them.

Tea was given to Prince Andrey. He drank it eagerly, looking with feverish eyes at the door in front of him, as though trying to understand and recall something.

"No more. Is Timohin here?" he asked.

Timohin edged along the bench towards him.

"I am here, your excellency."

"How is your wound?"

"Mine? All right. But how are you?"

Prince Andrey pondered again, as though he were recollecting something.

"Could not one get a book here?" he said.

"What book?"

"The Gospel! I haven't one."

The doctor promised to get it, and began questioning the prince about his symptoms. Prince Andrey answered all the doctor's questions rationally, though reluctantly, and then said that he wanted a support put under him, as it was uncomfortable and very painful for him as he was. The doctor and the valet took off the military cloak, with which he was covered, and puckering up their faces at the sickly smell of putrefying flesh that came from the wound, began to look into the terrible place. The doctor was very much troubled about something; he made some changes, turning the wounded man over so that he groaned again, and again lost consciousness from the pain when they turned him over. He began to be delirious, and kept asking for the book to be brought and to be put under him. "What trouble would it be to you?" he kept saying. "I haven't it, get it me, please,—put it under me just for a minute," he said in a piteous voice.

The doctor went outside to wash his hands.

"Ah, you have no conscience, you fellows really," the doctor was saying to the valet, who was pouring water over his hands. "For one minute I didn't look after you. Why, it's such suffering that I wonder how he bears it."

"I thought we did put it under him right, by the Lord Jesus Christ," said the valet.

Prince Andrey had for the first time grasped where he was and what was happening to him, and had recollected that he had been wounded and how at the moment when the carriage had stopped at Mytishtchy, and he had asked to be taken into the hut. Losing consciousness again from the pain, he came fully to himself once more in the hut while he was drinking tea. And thereupon again, going over in his memory all that had happened to him, the most vivid picture in his mind was of that moment at the ambulance station when at the sight of the sufferings of a man he had not liked, those new thoughts had come to him with such promise of happiness. And those thoughts—though vague now and shapeless—took possession of his soul again. He remembered that he had now some new happiness, and that that happiness had something to do with the Gospel. That was why he asked for the Gospel. But the position he had been laid in, without support under his wound, and the new change of position, put his thoughts to confusion again; and it was only in the complete stillness of the night that he came to himself again for the third time. Every one was asleep around him. A cricket was chirping across the passage; some one was shouting and singing in the street; cockroaches were rustling over the table, the holy images and the walls; a big fly flopped on his pillow and about the tallow candle that stood with a great, smouldering wick beside him.

His soul was not in its normal state. A man in health usually thinks, feels and remembers simultaneously an immense number of different things, but he has the power and the faculty of selecting one series of ideas or phenomena and concentrating all his attention on that series. A man in health can at the moment of the profoundest thought break off to say a civil word to any one who comes in, and then return again to his thoughts. Prince Andrey's soul was not in a normal condition in this respect. All the faculties of his soul were clearer and more active than ever, but they acted apart from his will. The most diverse ideas and images had possession of his mind at the same time. Sometimes his brain suddenly began to work, and with a force, clearness, and depth with which it had never been capable of working in health. But suddenly the train of thought broke off in the midst, to be replaced by some unexpected image, and the power to go back to it was wanting. "Yes, a new happiness was revealed to me, that could not be taken away from man," he thought, as he lay in the still, half-dark hut, gazing before him with feverishly wide, staring eyes. "Happiness beyond the reach of material forces, outside material, external influences on man, the happiness of the soul alone, the happiness of love! To feel it is in every man's power, but God alone can know it and ordain it. But how did God ordain this law? Why the Son? . . ." And all at once that train of thought broke off, and Prince Andrey heard (not knowing whether in delirium or in actual fact he heard it) a kind of soft, whispering voice, incessantly beating time: "Piti-pitt-piti," and then "i-ti-ti," and again, "ipiti-piti-piti," and again "i-ti-ti." And to the sound of this murmuring music Prince Andrey felt as though a strange, ethereal edifice of delicate needles or splinters were being raised over his face, over the very middle of it. He felt that (hard though it was for him) he must studiously preserve his balance that this rising edifice might not fall to pieces; but yet it was falling to pieces, and slowly rising up again to the rhythmic beat of the murmuring music.

"It is stretching out, stretching out, and spreading and stretching out!" Prince Andrey said to himself. While he listened to the murmur and felt that edifice of needles stretching out, and rising up, Prince Andrey saw by glimpses a red ring of light round the candle, and heard the rustling of the cockroaches and the buzzing of the fly as it flopped against his pillow and his face. And every time the fly touched his face, it gave him a stinging sensation, but yet it surprised him that though the fly struck him in the very centre of the rising edifice, it did not shatter it. But, apart from all this, there was one other thing of importance. That was the white thing at the door; that was a statue of the sphinx, which oppressed him too.

"But perhaps it is my shirt on the table," thought Prince Andrey, "and that's my legs, and that's the door, but why this straining and moving and piti-piti-piti and ti-ti and piti-piti-piti . . . Enough, cease, be still, please," Prince Andrey besought some one wearily. And all at once thought and feeling floated to the surface again with extraordinary clearness and force.

"Yes, love (he thought again with perfect distinctness), but not that love that loves for something, to gain something, or because of something, but that love that I felt for the first time, when dying, I saw my enemy and yet loved him. I knew that feeling of love which is the very essence of the soul, for which no object is needed. And I know that blissful feeling now too. To love one's neighbours; to love one's enemies. To love everything—to love God in all His manifestations. Some one dear to one can be loved with human love; but an enemy can only be loved with divine love. And that was why I felt such joy when I felt that I loved that man. What happened to him? Is he alive? . . . Loving with human love, one may pass from love to hatred; but divine love cannot change. Nothing, not even death, nothing can shatter it. It is the very nature of the soul. And how many people I have hated in my life. And of all people none I have loved and hated more than her." And he vividly pictured Natasha to himself, not as he had pictured her in the past, only with the charm that had been a joy to him; for the first time he pictured to himself her soul. And he understood her feeling, her sufferings, her shame, and her penitence. Now, for the first time, he felt all the cruelty of his abandonment, saw all the cruelty of his rupture with her. "If it were only possible for me to see her once more . . . once, looking into those eyes, to say . . ."

Piti-piti-piti iti-ti, ipiti-piti—boom, the fly flapped . . . And his attention passed all at once into another world of reality and delirium, in which something peculiar was taking place. In that place the edifice was still rising, unshattered; something was still stretching out, the candle was still burning, with a red ring round it; the same shirt-sphinx still lay by the door. But beside all this, something creaked, there was a whiff of fresh air, and a new white sphinx appeared standing before the doorway. And that sphinx had the white face and shining eyes of that very Natasha he had been dreaming of just now.

"Oh, how wearisome this everlasting delirium is!" thought Prince

Andrey, trying to dispel that face from his vision. But that face stood before him with the face of reality, and that face was coming closer. Prince Andrey tried to go back to the world of pure thought, but he could not, and he was drawn back into the realm of delirium. The soft murmuring voice kept up its rhythmic whisper, something was oppressing him, and rising up, and the strange face stood before him. Prince Andrey rallied all his forces to regain his senses; he stirred a little, and suddenly there was a ringing in his ears and a dimness before his eyes, and like a man sinking under water, he lost consciousness.

When he came to himself, Natasha, the very living Natasha, whom of all people in the world he most longed to love with that new, pure, divine love that had now been revealed to him, was on her knees before him. He knew that it was the real, living Natasha, and did not wonder, but quietly rejoiced. Natasha, on her knees, in terror, but without moving (she could not have moved), gazed at him, restraining her sobs. Her face was white and rigid. There was only a sort of quiver in the lower part of it.

Prince Andrey drew a sigh of relief, smiled, and held out his hand.

"You?" he said. "What happiness!"

With a swift but circumspect movement, Natasha came nearer, still kneeling, and carefully taking his hand she bent her face over it and began kissing it, softly touching it with her lips.

"Forgive me!" she said in a whisper, lifting her head and glancing at him. "Forgive me!"

"I love you," said Prince Andrey.

"Forgive . . ."

"Forgive what?" asked Prince Andrey.

"Forgive me for what I di . . . id," Natasha murmured in a hardly audible, broken whisper, and again and again she softly put her lips to his hand.

"I love thee more, better than before," said Prince Andrey, lifting her face with his hand so that he could look into her eyes.

Those eyes, swimming with happy tears, gazed at him with timid commiseration and joyful love. Natasha's thin, pale face, with its swollen lips, was more than ugly—it looked terrible. But Prince Andrey did not see her face, he saw the shining eyes, which were beautiful. They heard talk behind them.

Pyotr, the valet, by now wide awake, had waked up the doctor. Timohin, who had not slept all night for the pain in his leg, had been long watching all that was happening, and huddled up on his bench, carefully wrapping his bare person up in the sheet.

"Why, what's this?" said the doctor, getting up from his bed on the floor. "Kindly retire, madame."

At that moment there was a knock at the door; a maid had been sent by the countess in search of her daughter.

Like a sleep-walker awakened in the midst of her trance, Natasha walked out of the room, and getting back to her hut, sank sobbing on her bed.

From that day at all the halts and resting-places on the remainder of the Rostovs' journey, Natasha never left Bolkonsky's side, and the doctor was forced to admit that he had not expected from a young girl so much fortitude, nor skill in nursing a wounded man.

Terrible as it was to the countess to think that Prince Andrey might (and very probably, too, from what the doctor said) die on the road in her daughter's arms, she could not resist Natasha. Although with the renewal of affectionate relations between Prince Andrey and Natasha the idea did occur that in case he recovered their old engagement would be renewed, no one—least of all Natasha and Prince Andrey—spoke of this. The unsettled question of life and death hanging, not only over Prince Andrey, but over all Russia, shut off all other considerations.

XXXIII

PIERRE waked up late on the 3rd of September. His head ached, the clothes in which he had slept without undressing fretted his body, and he had a vague sense in his heart of something shameful he had done the evening before. That something shameful was his talk with Captain Ramballe.

His watch told him it was eleven, but it seemed a particularly dull day. Pierre stood up, rubbed his eyes, and seeing the pistol with its engraved stock—Gerasim had put it back on the writing-table—Pierre remembered where he was and what was in store for him that day.

"Am I not too late already?" Pierre wondered.

No, probably he would not make his entry into Moscow before twelve o'clock. Pierre did not allow himself to reflect on what lay before him, but made haste to act.

Setting his clothes to rights, Pierre took up the pistol and was about to set off. But then for the first time it occurred to him to wonder how, if not in his hand, he was to carry the weapon in the street. Even under his full coat it would be hard to conceal a big pistol. It could not be put in his sash, nor under his arm, without being noticeable. Moreover, the pistol was now unloaded, and Pierre could not succeed in reloading it in time. "The dagger will do as well," Pierre said to himself; though, in considering how he should carry out his design, he had more than once decided that the great mistake made by the student in 1809 was that he had tried to kill Napoleon with a dagger. But Pierre's chief aim seemed to be, not so much to succeed in his project, as to prove to himself that he was not renouncing his design, but was doing everything to carry it out. Pierre hurriedly took the blunt, notched dagger in a green scabbard, which he had bought, together with the pistol, at the Suharev Tower, and hid it under his waistcoat.

Tying the sash round his peasant's coat, and pulling his cap forward, Pierre walked along the corridor, trying to avoid making a noise and meeting the captain, and slipped out into the street.

The fire, at which he had gazed so indifferently the evening before, had sensibly increased during the night. Moscow was on fire at various points. There were fires at the same time in Carriage Row, Zamosk-voryetche, the Bazaar, and Povarsky, and the timber market near Dorogomilov bridge and the barges in the river Moskva were in a blaze.

Pierre's way lay across a side street to Povarsky, and from there across Arbaty to the chapel of Nikola Yavlenny, where he had long before in his fancy fixed on the spot at which the deed ought to be done. Most of the houses had their gates and shutters closed. The streets and lanes were deserted; there was a smell of burning and smoke in the air. Now and then he met Russians with uneasy and timid faces, and Frenchmen with a look of the camp about them, walking in the middle of the road. Both looked at Pierre with surprise. Apart from his great height and stoutness, and the look of gloomy concentration and suffer, ing in his face and whole figure, Russians stared at Pierre because they could not make out to what class he belonged. Frenchmen looked after him with surprise, because, while all other Russians stared timidly and inquisitively at them, Pierre walked by without noticing them. At the gates of a house, three Frenchmen, disputing about something with some Russians, who did not understand their meaning, stopped Pierre to ask whether he knew French.

Pierre shook his head and walked on. In another lane a sentinel, on guard by a green caisson, shouted at him, and it was only at the repetition of his menacing shout, and the sound of his picking up his gun, that Pierre grasped that he ought to have passed the street on the other side. He heard and saw nothing around him. With haste and horror he bore within him his intention as something strange and fearful to him, fearing—from the experience of the previous night—to lose it. But Pierre was not destined to carry his design in safety to the spot to which he was bending his steps. Moreover, if he had not been detained on the road, his design could not have been carried out, because Napoleon had four hours earlier left the Dorogomilov suburb, and crossed Arbaty to the Kremlin; and he was by then sitting in the royal study in the Kremlin palace in the gloomiest temper, giving circumstantial orders for immediately extinguishing the fires, preventing pillage, and reassuring the inhabitants. But Pierre knew nothing of that; entirely engrossed in what lay before him, he was suffering the anguish men suffer when they persist in undertaking a task impossible for them—not from its inherent difficulties, but from its incompatibility with their own nature. He was tortured by the dread that he would be weak at the decisive moment, and so would lose his respect for himself.

Though he saw and heard nothing around him, he instinctively found his way, and took the right turning to reach Povarsky.

As Pierre got nearer to Povarsky Street, the smoke grew thicker and thicker, and the air was positively warm from the heat of the conflagration. Tongues of flame shot up here and there behind the house-tops. He met more people in the streets, and these people were in great excitement. But though Pierre felt that something unusual was happening around him, he did not grasp the fact that he was getting near the fire.

As he walked along a path, across the large open space adjoining on one side Povarsky Street, and on the other side the gardens of Prince Gruzinsky, Pierre suddenly heard close by him the sound of a woman, crying desperately. He stood still, as though awakened from a dream, and raised his head.

On the dried-up, dusty grass on one side of the path lay heaps of household belongings piled up: feather-beds, a samovar, holy images, and boxes. On the ground, near the boxes, sat a thin woman, no longer young, with long, projecting front teeth, dressed in a black cloak and cap. This woman was weeping violently, swaying to and fro, and muttering something. Two little girls, from ten to twelve years old, dressed in dirty, short frocks and cloaks, were gazing at their mother, with an expression of stupefaction on their pale, frightened faces. A little boy of seven, in a coat and a huge cap, obviously not his own, was crying in an old nurse's arms. A bare-legged, dirty servant-girl was sitting on a chest; she had let down her flaxen hair, and was pulling out the singed hairs, sniffing at them. The husband, a short, stooping man, in a uniform, with little, wheel-shaped whiskers, and smooth locks of hair, peeping out from under his cap, which was stuck erect on his head, was moving the chests from under one another with an immovable face, dragging garments of some sort from under them.

The woman almost flung herself at Pierre's feet as soon as she saw him.

"Merciful heavens, good Christian folk, save me, help me, kind sir! . . . somebody, help me," she articulated through her sobs. "My little girl! . . . My daughter! . . . My youngest girl left behind! . . . She's burnt! Oo . . . er! What a fate I have nursed thee for . . . Ooo!"

"Hush, Marya Nikolaevna," the husband said in a low voice to his wife, evidently only to justify himself before an outsider.

"Sister must have taken her, nothing else can have happened to her!" he added.

"Monster, miscreant!" the woman screeched furiously, her tears suddenly ceasing. "There is no heart in you, you have no feeling for your own child. Any other man would have rescued her from the fire. But he is a monster, not a man, not a father. You are a noble man," the woman turned to Pierre sobbing and talking rapidly. "The row was on fire—they rushed in to tell us. The girl screamed: Fire! We rushed to get our things out. Just as we were, we escaped. . . . This is all we could snatch up . . . the blessed images, we look at the children, and the bed that was my dowry, and all the rest is lost. Katitchka's missing. Oooo! O Lord! . . ." and again she broke into sobs. "My darling babe! burnt! burnt!"

"But where, where was she left?" said Pierre.

From the expression of his interested face, the woman saw that this man might help her.

"Good, kind sir!" she screamed, clutching at his legs. "Benefactor, set my heart at rest anyway . . . Aniska, go, you slut, show the way," she bawled to the servant-girl, opening her mouth wide in her anger, and displaying her long teeth more than ever.

"Show the way, show me, I . . . I . . . I'll do something," Pierre gasped hurriedly.

The dirty servant-girl came out from behind the box, put up her hair, and sighing, walked on in front along the path with her coarse, bare feet.

Pierre felt as though he had suddenly come back to life after a heavy swoon. He drew his head up, his eyes began to shine with the light of life, and with rapid steps he followed the girl, overtook her, and went into Povarsky Street. The whole street was full of clouds of black smoke. Tongues of flame shot up here and there out of these clouds. A great crowd had gathered in front of the fire. In the middle of the street stood a French general, saying something to those about him. Pierre, accompanied by the servant-girl, was approaching the place where the French general stood; but the French soldiers stopped him.

"Can't pass," a voice shouted to him.

"This way, master," bawled the girl. "We'll cut across Nikoliny by the lane."

Pierre turned back, breaking into a run now and then to keep pace with her. The girl ran across the street, turned into a lane on the left, and passing three houses, turned in at a gate on the right.

"It's just here," she said, and running across a yard, she opened a little gate in a paling-fence, and stopping short, pointed out to Pierre a small wooden lodge, which was blazing away brightly. One side of it had fallen in, the other was on fire, and flames peeped out at the window-holes and under the roof.

As Pierre went in at the little gate, he felt the rush of heat, and involuntarily stopped short.

"Which, which is your house?" he asked.

"Oooh!" wailed the servant-girl, pointing to the lodge. "That's it, that same was our lodging. Sure, you're burnt to death, our treasure, Katitchka, my precious little missy, ooh!" wailed Aniska, at the sight of the fire feeling the necessity of giving expression to her feelings too.

Pierre darted up to the lodge, but the heat was so great that he could not help describing a curve round it, and found himself close to a big house, which was as yet only on fire on one side, at the roof. A group of French soldiers were swarming round it. Pierre could not at first make out what these Frenchmen were about, dragging something out of the house. But seeing a French soldier in front of him beating a peasant with a blunt cutlass, and taking from him a fur-lined coat, Pierre became vaguely aware that pillaging was going on here—but he had no time to dwell on the idea.

The sound of the rumble and crash of falling walls and ceilings; the roar and hiss of the flames, and the excited shouts of the crowd; the sight of the hovering clouds of smoke—here folding over into black masses, there drawing out and lighted up by gleaming sparks; and the flames—here like a thick red sheaf, and there creeping like golden fish-scales over the walls; the sense of the heat and smoke and rapidity of movement, all produced on Pierre the usual stimulating effect of a conflagration. That effect was particularly strong on Pierre, because all at once, at the sight of the fire, he felt himself set free from the ideas weighing upon him. He felt young, gay, ready, and resolute. He ran round the lodge on the side of the house, and was about to run into that part which was still standing, when he heard several voices shouting immediately above his head, followed by the crash and bang of something heavy falling close by.

Pierre looked round, and saw at the windows of the house some French soldiers, who had just dropped out a drawer of a chest, filled with some metallic objects. Some more French soldiers standing below went up to the drawer.

"Well, what does that fellow want?" one of the French soldiers shouted, referring to Pierre.

"A child in the house. Haven't you seen a child?" said Pierre.

"What's the fellow singing? Get along, do!" shouted voices; and one of the soldiers, evidently afraid Pierre might take it into his head to snatch the silver and bronzes from them, pounced on him in a menacing fashion.

"A child?" shouted a Frenchman from above. "I did hear something crying in the garden. Perhaps it's the fellow's brat. Must be humane, you know."

"Where is it?" asked Pierre.

"This way!" the French soldier shouted to him from the window pointing to the garden behind the house. "Wait, I'll come down."

And in a minute the Frenchman, a black-eyed fellow, with a patch on his cheek, in his shirt-sleeves, did in fact jump out of a window on the ground floor, and slapping Pierre on the shoulder, he ran with him to the garden. "Make haste, you fellows," he shouted to his comrades, "it's beginning to get hot." Running behind the house to a sanded path, the Frenchman pulled Pierre by the arm, and pointed out to him a circular space. Under a garden seat lay a girl of three years old, in a pink frock.

"Here's your brat. Ah, a little girl. So much the better," said the Frenchman. "Good-bye. Must be humane, we are all mortal, you know"; and the Frenchman, with the patch on his cheek, ran back to his comrades.

Pierre, breathless with joy, ran up to the child, and would have taken her in his arms. But seeing a stranger, the little girl—a scrofulous-looking, unattractive child very like her mother—screamed and ran away. Pierre caught her, however, and lifted her up in his arms; she squealed in desperate fury, and tried to tear herself out of Pierre's arms with her little hands, and to bite him with her dirty, dribbling mouth. Pierre had a sense of horror and disgust, such as he had felt at contact with some little beast. But he made an effort to overcome it, and not to drop the child, and ran with it back to the big house. By now, however, it was impossible to get back by the same way; the servant-girl, Aniska, was nowhere to be seen, and with a feeling of pity and loathing, Pierre held close to him, as tenderly as he could, the piteously howling, and sopping wet baby, and ran across the garden to seek some other way out.

XXXIV

WHEN Pierre, after running across courtyards and by-lanes, got back with his burden to Prince Gruzinsky's garden, at the corner of Povarsky, he did not for the first moment recognise the place from which he had set out to look for the baby: it was so packed with people and goods, dragged out of the houses. Besides the Russian families with their belongings saved from the fire, there were a good many French soldiers here too in various uniforms. Pierre took no notice of them. He was in haste to find the family, and to restore the child to its mother, so as to be able to go back and save some one else. It seemed to Pierre that he had a great deal more to do, and to do quickly. Warmed up by the heat and running, Pierre felt even more strongly at that minute the sense of youth, eagerness, and resolution, which had come upon him when he was running to save the baby.

The child was quiet now, and clinging to Pierre's coat with her little hands, she sat on his arm, and looked about her like a little wild beast. Pierre glanced at her now and then, and smiled slightly. He fancied he saw something touchingly innocent in the frightened, sickly little face.

Neither the official nor his wife were in the place where he had left them. With rapid steps, Pierre walked about among the crowd, scanning the different faces he came across. He could not help noticing a Georgian or Armenian family, consisting of a very old man, of a handsome Oriental cast of face, dressed in a new cloth-faced sheepskin and new boots; an old woman of a similar type; and a young woman. The latter—a very young woman—struck Pierre as a perfect example of Oriental beauty, with her sharply marked, arched, black eyebrows, her extraordinarily soft, bright colour and beautiful, expressionless, oval face. Among the goods flung down in the crowd in the grass space, in her rich satin mantle, and the bright lilac kerchief on her head, she suggested a tender, tropical plant, thrown down in the snow. She was sitting on the baggage a little behind the old woman, and her big, black, long-shaped eyes, with their long lashes, were fixed immovably on the ground. Evidently she was aware of her beauty, and fearful because of it. Her face struck Pierre, and in his haste he looked round at her several times as he passed along by the fence. Reaching the fence, and still failing to find the people he was looking for, Pierre stood still and looked round.

Pierre's figure was more remarkable than ever now with the baby in his arms, and several Russians, both men and women, gathered about him.

"Have you lost some one, good sir? Are you a gentleman yourself, or what? Whose baby is it?" they asked him.

Pierre answered that the baby belonged to a woman in a black mantle, who had been sitting at this spot with her children; and asked whether any one knew her, and where she had gone.

"Why, it must be the Anferovs," said an old deacon addressing a pock-marked peasant woman. "Lord, have mercy on us! Lord, have mercy on us!" he added, in his professional bass.

"The Anferovs," said the woman. "Why, the Anferovs have been gone since early this morning. It will either be Marya Nikolaevna's or Ivanova's."

"He says a woman, and Marya Nikolaevna's a lady," said a house-serf.

"You know her, then; a thin woman—long teeth," said Pierre.

"To be sure, Marya Nikolaevna. They moved off into the garden as soon as these wolves pounced down on us," said the woman, indicating the French soldiers.

"O Lord, have mercy on us!" the deacon added again.

"You go on yonder, they are there. It's she, for sure. She was quite beside herself with crying," said the woman again. "It's she. Here this way."

But Pierre was not heeding the woman. For several seconds he had been gazing intently at what was passing a few paces from him. He was looking at the Armenian family and two French soldiers, who had approached them. One of these soldiers, a nimble, little man, was dressed in a blue coat, with a cord tied round for a belt. He had a nightcap on his head, and his feet were bare. Another, whose appearance struck Pierre particularly, was a long, round-shouldered, fair-haired, thin man, with ponderous movements and an idiotic expression of face. He was dressed in a frieze tunic, blue trousers and big, torn, high boots. The little bare-footed Frenchman in the blue coat, on going up to the Armenians, said something, and at once took hold of the old man's legs, and the old man began immediately in haste pulling off his boots. The other soldier in the tunic stopped facing the beautiful Armenian girl, with his hands in his pockets, and stared at her without speaking or moving.

"Take it, take the child," said Pierre, handing the child to the peasant woman, and speaking with peremptory haste. "You give her to them, you take her," he almost shouted to the woman, setting the screaming child on the ground, and looking round again at the Frenchmen and the Armenian family. The old man was by now sitting barefoot. The little Frenchman had just taken the second boot from him, and was slapping the boots together. The old man was saying something with a sob, but all that Pierre only saw in a passing glimpse. His whole attention was absorbed by the Frenchman in the tunic, who had meanwhile, with a deliberate, swinging gait, moved up to the young woman, and taking his hands out of his pockets, caught hold of her neck.

The beautiful Armenian still sat in the same immobile pose, with her long lashes drooping, and seemed not to see and not to feel what the soldier was doing to her.

While Pierre ran the few steps that separated him from the Frenchman, the long soldier in the tunic had already torn the necklace from the Armenian beauty's neck, and the young woman, clutching at her neck with both hands, screamed shrilly.

"Let that woman alone!" Pierre roared in a voice hoarse with rage, and seizing the long, stooping soldier by the shoulders he shoved him away. The soldier fell down, got up, and ran away. His comrade, dropping the boots, pulled out his sword, and moved up to Pierre in a menacing attitude.

"*Voyons, pas de bêtises!*" he shouted.

Pierre was in that transport of frenzy in which he remembered nothing, and his strength was increased tenfold. He dashed at the barefoot Frenchman, and before he had time to draw his cutlass, he knocked him down, and was pommelling him with his fists. Shouts of approval were heard from the crowd around, and at the same time a patrol of French Uhlans came riding round the corner. The Uhlans trotted up to Pierre, and the French soldiers surrounded him. Pierre had no recollection of what followed. He remembered that he beat somebody, and was beaten, and that in the end he found that his hands were tied, that a group of French soldiers were standing round him, ransacking his clothes.

"Lieutenant, he has a dagger," were the first words Pierre grasped the meaning of.

"Ah, ₂ weapon," said the officer, and he turned to the barefoot soldier, who had been taken with Pierre. "Very good, very good; you can tell all your story at the court-martial," said the officer. And then he turned to Pierre: "Do you know French?"

Pierre looked about him with bloodshot eyes, and made no reply. Probably his face looked very terrible; for the officer said something in a whisper, and four more Uhlans left the rest, and stationed themselves both sides of Pierre.

"Do you speak French?" the officer, keeping his distance, repeated the question. "Call the interpreter." From the ranks a little man came forward, in a Russian civilian dress. Pierre, from his dress and speech, at once recognised in him a French shopman from some Moscow shop.

"He doesn't look like a common man," said the interpreter, scanning Pierre.

"Oh, oh, he looks very like an incendiary," said the officer. "Ask him who he is," he added.

"Who are you?" asked the interpreter in his Frenchified Russian. "You must answer the officer."

"I will not say who I am. I am your prisoner. Take me away." Pierre said suddenly in French.

"Ah! ah!" commented the officer, knitting his brows; "well, march then!"

A crowd had gathered around the Uhlans. Nearest of all to Pierre stood the pock-marked peasant woman with the child. When the patrol was moving, she stepped forward:

"Why, where are they taking you, my good soul?" she said. "The child! what am I to do with the child if it's not theirs?" she cried.

"What does she want, this woman?" asked the officer.

Pierre was like a drunken man. His excitement was increased at the sight of the little girl he had saved.

"What does she want?" he said. "She is carrying my daughter, whom I have just saved from the flames," he declared. "Good-bye!" and utterly at a loss to explain to himself the aimless lie he had just blurted out, he strode along with a resolute and solemn step between the Frenchmen.

The patrol of Uhlans was one of those that had been sent out by Durosnel's orders through various streets of Moscow to put a stop to pillage, and still more to capture the incendiaries, who in the general opinion of the French officers in the higher ranks on that day were causing the fires. Patrolling several streets, the Uhlans arrested five more suspicious characters, a shopkeeper, two divinity students, a peasant, and a house-serf—all Russians—besides several French soldiers engaged in pillage. But of all these suspicious characters Pierre seemed to them the most suspicious of all.

When they had all been brought for the night to a big house on Zubovsky rampart, which had been fixed upon as a guardhouse, Pierre was put apart from the rest under strict guard.

PART TWELVE

I

IN THE higher circles in Petersburg the intricate conflict between the parties of Rumyantsev, of the French, of Marya Fyodorovna, of the Tsarevitch, and the rest was going on all this time with more heat than ever, drowned, as always, by the buzzing of the court drones. But the easy, luxurious life of Petersburg, troubled only about phantasms, the reflection of life, went on its old way; and the course of that life made it a difficult task to believe in the danger and the difficult position of the Russian people. There were the same levees and balls, the same French theatre, the same court interests, the same interests and intrigues in the government service. It was only in the very highest circles that efforts were made to recollect the difficulty of the real position. There was whispered gossip of how the two Empresses had acted in opposition to one another in these difficult circumstances. The Empress Marya Fyodorovna, anxious for the welfare of the benevolent and educational institutions under her patronage, had arrangements made for the removal of all the institutes to Kazan, and all the belongings of these establishments were already packed. The Empress Elizaveta Alexyevna on being asked what commands she was graciously pleased to give, had been pleased to reply that in regard to state matters she could give no commands, since that was all in the Tsar's hands; as far as she personally was concerned, she had graciously declared, with her characteristic Russian patriotism, that she would be the last to leave Petersburg.

On the 26th of August, the very day of the battle of Borodino, there was a *soirée* at Anna Pavlovna's, the chief attraction of which was to be the reading of the Metropolitan's letter, written on the occasion of his sending to the Tsar the holy picture of Saint Sergey. This letter was looked upon as a model of patriotic ecclesiastical eloquence. It was to be read by Prince Vassily himself, who was famed for his fine elocution. (He used even to read aloud in the Empress's drawing-room.) The beauty of his elocution was supposed to lie in the loud, resonant voice, varying between a despairing howl and a tender whine, in which he rolled off the words quite independently of the sense, so that a howl fell on one word and a whine on others quite at random. This reading, as was always the case with Anna Pavlovna's entertainments, had a political significance. She was expecting at this *soirée* several important personages who were to be made to feel ashamed of patronising the French theatre, and to be roused to patriotic fervour. A good many people had already arrived, but Anna Pavlovna did not yet see those persons whose presence in her drawing-room was necessary, and she was therefore starting general topics of conversation before proceeding to the reading.

The news of the day in Petersburg was the illness of Countess Bezuhov. The countess had been taken ill a few days previously; she had missed several entertainments, of which she was usually the ornament, and it was said that she was seeing no one, and that instead of the celebrated Petersburg physicians, who usually attended her, she had put herself into the hands of some Italian doctor, who was treating her on some new and extraordinary method.

Everybody was very well aware that the charming countess's illness was due to inconveniences arising from marrying two husbands at once, and that the Italian doctor's treatment consisted in the removal of such inconvenience. But in the presence of Anna Pavlovna no one ventured to think about that view of the question, or even, as it were, to know what they did know about it.

"They say the poor countess is very ill. The doctor says it is *angina pectoris*."

"*Angine*? Oh, that's a terrible illness."

"They say the rivals are reconciled, thanks to the *angine* . . ." The word *angine* was repeated with great relish.

"I am told the old count is touching. He cried like a child when the doctor told him there was danger."

"Oh, it would be a terrible loss. She is a fascinating woman."

"You speak of the poor countess," said Anna Pavlovna, coming up. "I sent to inquire after her. I was told she was getting better. Oh, no doubt of it, she is the most charming woman in the world," said Anna Pavlovna, with a smile at her own enthusiasm. "We belong to different camps, but that does not prevent me from appreciating her as she deserves. She is very unhappy," added Anna Pavlovna.

Supposing that by these last words Anna Pavlovna had slightly lifted the veil of mystery that hung over the countess's illness, one unwary young man permitted himself to express surprise that no well-known doctor had been called in, and that the countess should be treated by a charlatan, who might make use of dangerous remedies.

"Your information may be better than mine," cried Anna Pavlovna, falling upon the inexperienced youth with sudden viciousness, "but I have it on good authority that this doctor is a very learned and skilful man. He is the private physician of the Queen of Spain."

And having thus annihilated the young man, Anna Pavlovna turned to Bilibin, who was talking in another group about the Austrians, and had his forehead puckered up in wrinkles in readiness to utter *un mot*.

"I think it is charming!" he was saying of the diplomatic note which had been sent to Vienna with the Austrian flags taken by Wittgenstein, "*le héros de Pétropol*," as he was called at Petersburg.

"What? what was it?" Anna Pavlovna inquired, creating a silence for the *mot* to be heard, though she had in fact heard it before.

And Bilibin repeated the precise words of the diplomatic despatch he had composed.

"The Emperor sends back the Austrian flags," said Bilibin; *"drapeaux amis et égarés qu'il a trouvés hors de la route,"* Bilibin concluded, letting the wrinkles run off his forehead.

"Charming, charming!" said Prince Vassily.

"The road to Warsaw, perhaps," Prince Ippolit said loudly, to the general surprise. Everybody looked at him, at a loss to guess what he meant. Prince Ippolit, too, looked about him with light-hearted wonder. He had no more notion than other people what was meant by his words. In the course of his diplomatic career he had more than once noticed that words suddenly uttered in that way were accepted as highly diverting, and on every occasion he uttered in that way the first words that chanced to come to his tongue. "May be, it will come out all right," he thought, "and if it doesn't, they will know how to give some turn to it." And the awkward silence that reigned was in fact broken by the entrance of the personage of defective patriotism whom Anna Pavlovna was waiting for to convert to a better mind; and smiling, and shaking her finger at Prince Ippolit, she summoned Prince Vassily to the table, and setting two candles and a manuscript before him, she begged him to begin. There was a general hush.

"Most high and gracious Emperor and Tsar!" Prince Vassily boomed out sternly, and he looked round at his audience as though to inquire whether any one had anything to say against that. But nobody said anything. "The chief capital city, Moscow, the New Jerusalem, receives *her* Messiah"—he threw a sudden emphasis on the *"her"*—"even as a mother in the embraces of her zealous sons, and through the gathering darkness, foreseeing the dazzling glory of thy dominion, sings aloud in triumph: 'Hosanna! Blessed be He that cometh!'"

Prince Vassily uttered these last words in a tearful voice.

Bilibin scrutinised his nails attentively, and many of the audience were visibly cowed, as though wondering what they had done wrong. Anna Pavlovna murmured the words over beforehand, as old women whisper the prayer to come at communion: "Let the base and insolent Goliath . . ." she whispered.

Prince Vassily continued:

"Let the base and insolent Goliath from the borders of France encompass the realm of Russia with the horrors of death; lowly faith, the sling of the Russian David, shall smite a swift blow at the head of his pride that thirsteth for blood. This holy image of the most venerable Saint Sergey, of old a zealous champion of our country's welfare, is borne to your imperial majesty. I grieve that my failing strength hinders me from the joy of your most gracious presence. Fervent prayers I am offering up to Heaven, and the Almighty will exalt the faithful and fulfil in His mercy the hopes of your majesty."

"Quel force! Quel style!" was murmured in applause of the reader and the author. Roused by this appeal, Anna Pavlovna's guests continued for a long while talking of the position of the country, and made various surmises as to the issue of the battle to be fought in a few days.

"You will see," said Anna Pavlovna, "that to-morrow on the Emperor's birthday we shall get news. I have a presentiment of something good."

II

ANNA PAVLOVNA'S presentiment was in fact fulfilled. Next day, during the special service at court in honour of the Tsar's birthday, Prince Volkonsky was called out of church and received a despatch from Prince Kutuzov. This was the despatch Kutuzov had sent off on the day of the battle from Tatarinovo. Kutuzov wrote that the Russians had not retreated a single step, that the French had lost far more than our troops, that he was writing off in haste from the field of battle before he had time to collect the latest intelligence. So it had been a victory, it appeared. And at once, without leaving church, the assembled court offered up thanks to the Creator for His succour, and for the victory.

Anna Pavlovna's presentiment had been fulfilled, and the whole morning a mood of joyous festivity prevailed in the town. Every one accepted the victory as a conclusive one, and some people were already beginning to talk of Napoleon's having been taken prisoner, of his disposition, and the selection of a new sovereign for France.

At a distance from the scene of action and amid the conditions of court life, it is very difficult for events to be reflected in their true force and dimensions. Public events are involuntarily grouped about some private incident. So in this case, the courtiers' rejoicing was as much due to the fact of the news of this victory having arrived precisely on the Tsar's birthday as to the fact of the victory itself. It was like a successfully arranged surprise. Kutuzov's despatches had spoken, too, of the Russian losses, and among them had mentioned the names of Tutchkov, Bagration, and Kutaissov. The melancholy side, too, of the event was unconsciously in this Petersburg world concentrated about a single incident—the death of Kutaissov. Every one knew him, the Tsar liked him, he was young and interesting. All met that day with the words:

"How wonderful it should have happened so! Just in the Te Deum. But what a loss—Kutaissov! Ah, what a pity!"

"What did I tell you about Kutuzov?" Prince Vassily said now with the pride of a prophet. "I always said he was the only man capable of conquering Napoleon."

But next day no news came from the army, and the public voice began to waver. The courtiers suffered agonies over the agonies of suspense which the Tsar was suffering.

"Think of the Emperor's position!" the courtiers said; and they no longer sang the praises of Kutuzov as two days before, but upbraided him as the cause of the Tsar's uneasiness that day. Prince Vassily no longer boasted of his protégé Kutuzov, but was mute when the commander-in-chief was the subject of conversation. Moreover, on the

evening of that day everything seemed to conspire to throw the Petersburg world into agitation and uneasiness: a terrible piece of news came
to add to their alarms. Countess Elena Bezuhov died quite suddenly
of the terrible illness which had been so amusing to talk about. At larger
gatherings every one repeated the official story that Countess Bezuhov
had died of a terrible attack of angina pectoris, but in intimate circles
people told in detail how the Queen of Spain's own medical attendant
had prescribed to Ellen small doses of a certain drug to bring about
certain desired results; but that Ellen, tortured by the old count's suspecting her, and by her husband's not having answered her letter (that
unfortunate, dissipated Pierre), had suddenly taken an enormous dose
of the drug prescribed, and had died in agonies before assistance could
be given. The story ran that Prince Vassily and the old count had been
going to take proceedings against the Italian; but the latter had produced notes in his possession from the unhappy deceased of such a
character that they had promptly let him go.

Conversation centred round three melancholy facts—the Tsar's state
of suspense, the loss of Kutaissov, and the death of Ellen.

On the third day after Kutuzov's despatch, a country gentleman
arrived in Petersburg from Moscow, and the news of the surrender of
Moscow to the French was all over the town. This was awful! Think of
the position of the Emperor! Kutuzov was a traitor, and, during the
"visits of condolence" paid to Prince Vassily on the occasion of his
daughter's death, when he spoke of Kutuzov, whose praises he had once
sung so loudly—it was pardonable in his grief to forget what he had
said before—he said that nothing else was to be expected from a blind
and dissolute old man.

"I only wonder how such a man could possibly be trusted with the
fate of Russia."

So long as the news was not official, it was still possible to doubt its
truth; but next day the following communication arrived from Count
Rastoptchin:

"Prince Kutuzov's adjutant has brought me a letter in which he asks
me to furnish police-officers to escort the army to the Ryazan road. He
says that he is regretfully abandoning Moscow. Sire! Kutuzov's action
decides the fate of that capital and of your empire. Russia will shudder
to learn of the abandonment of the city, where the greatness of Russia
is centred, where are the ashes of our forefathers. I am following the
army. I have had everything carried away; all that is left me is to weep
over the fate of my country."

On receiving this communication, the Tsar sent Prince Volkonsky
with the following rescript to Kutuzov:

"Prince Mihail Ilarionovitch! I have received no communication from
you since the 29th of August. Meanwhile I have received, by way of
Yaroslavl, from the governor of Moscow the melancholy intelligence
that you have decided with the army to abandon Moscow. You can
imagine the effect this news has had upon me, and your silence redoubles

ıny astonishment. I am sending herewith Staff-General Prince Volkon-sky, to ascertain from you the position of the army and of the causes that have led you to so melancholy a decision."

III

NINE days after the abandonment of Moscow, a courier from Kutuzov reached Petersburg with the official news of the surrender of Moscow. This courier was a Frenchman, Michaud, who did not know Russian, yet was, "though a foreigner, Russian in heart and soul," as he used to say of himself.

The Tsar at once received the messenger in his study in the palace of Kamenny island. Michaud, who had never seen Moscow before the cam-paign, and did not know a word of Russian, yet felt deeply moved when he came before *"notre très gracieux souverain"* (as he wrote) with the news of the burning of Moscow, whose flames illumined his route.

Though the source of M. Michaud's sorrow must indeed have been different from that to which the grief of Russian people was due, Michaud had such a melancholy face when he was shown into the Tsar's study that the Tsar asked him at once:

"Do you bring me sad news, colonel?"

"Very sad, sire, the surrender of Moscow," answered Michaud, cast-ing his eyes down with a sigh.

"Can they have surrendered my ancient capital without a battle?" the Tsar asked quickly, suddenly flushing.

Michaud respectfully gave the message he had been commanded to give from Kutuzov, that is, that there was no possibility of fighting be-fore Moscow, and that seeing there was no chance but either to lose the army and Moscow or to lose Moscow alone, the commander-in-chief had been obliged to choose the latter.

The Tsar listened without a word, not looking at Michaud.

"Has the enemy entered the city?" he asked.

"Yes, sire, and by now the city is in ashes. I left it all in flames," said Michaud resolutely; but glancing at the Tsar, Michaud was horrified at what he had done. The Tsar was breathing hard and rapidly, his lower lip was twitching, and his fine blue eyes were for a moment wet with tears.

But that lasted only a moment. The Tsar suddenly frowned, as though vexed with himself for his own weakness; and raising his head, he addressed Michaud in a firm voice:

"I see, colonel, from all that is happening to us that Providence re-quires great sacrifices of us. I am ready to submit to His will in every-thing; but tell m.e, Michaud, how did you leave the army, seeing my ancient capital thus abandoned without striking a blow? Did you not perceive discouragement?"

Seeing that his most gracious sovereign had regained his composure, Michaud too regained his; but to the Tsar's direct question of a matter of fact which called for a direct answer, he had not yet an answer ready.

"Sire, will you permit me to speak frankly, as a loyal soldier?" he said, to gain time.

"Colonel, I always expect it," said the Tsar. "Hide nothing from me; I want to know absolutely how it is."

"Sire!" said Michaud, with a delicate, scarcely perceptible smile on his lips, as he had now had time to prepare his answer in the form of a light and respectful play of words. "Sire! I left the whole army, from the commanders to the lowest soldier without exception, in extreme, in desperate terror."

"How so?" the Tsar interrupted, frowning sternly. "My Russians let themselves be cast down by misfortune? . . . Never . . ."

This was just what Michaud was waiting for to get in his phrases.

"Sire," he said, with a respectful playfulness of expression, "they fear only that your majesty through goodness of heart may let yourself be persuaded to make peace. They burn to fight," said the plenipotentiary of the Russian people, "and to prove to your majesty by the sacrifice of their lives how devoted they are . . ."

"Ah!" said the Tsar, reassured, slapping Michaud on the shoulder, with a friendly light in his eyes. "You tranquillise me, colonel . . ."

The Tsar looked down, and for some time he was silent. "Well, go back to the army," he said, drawing himself up to his full height and with a genial and majestic gesture addressing Michaud, "and tell our brave fellows, tell all my good subjects wherever you go, that when I have not a soldier left, I will put myself at the head of my dear nobility, of my good peasants, and so use the last resources of my empire. It offers me still more than my enemies suppose," said the Tsar, more and more stirred. "But if it should be written in the decrees of divine Providence," he said, and his fine, mild eyes, shining with emotion, were raised towards heaven, "that my dynasty should cease to reign on the throne of my ancestors, then after exhausting every means in my power, I would let my beard grow to here" (the Tsar put his hand halfway down his breast), "and go and eat potatoes with the meanest of my peasants rather than sign the shame of my country and my dear people, whose sacrifice I know how to appreciate." Uttering these words in a voice of much feeling, the Tsar turned quickly away, as though wishing to conceal from Michaud the tears that were starting into his eyes, and he walked to the further end of his study. After standing there some instants, he strode back to Michaud, and with a vigorous action squeezed his arm below the elbow. The Tsar's fine, mild face was flushed, and his eyes gleamed with energy and anger. "Colonel Michaud, do not forget what I say to you here; perhaps one day we shall recall it with pleasure. . . . Napoleon or me," he said, touching his breast, "we can no longer reign together. I have learned to know him. He will not deceive me again . . ." And the Tsar paused, frowning. Hearing these words, seeing the look of firm determination in the Tsar's eyes, Michaud, though a foreigner, Russian in heart and soul, felt (as he used to recount later) at that solemn moment moved to enthusiasm by what he had just heard; and in the following phrase he sought to give expression to his own feelings and those of the Russian people, whose representative he considered himself to be.

"Sire!" he said, "your majesty is signing at this moment the glory of the nation and the salvation of Europe!"

With a motion of his head the Tsar dismissed Michaud.

IV

WHILE half of Russia was conquered, and the inhabitants of Moscow were fleeing to remote provinces, and one levy of militia after another was being raised for the defence of the country, we, not living at the time, cannot help imagining that all the people in Russia, great and small alike, were engaged in doing nothing else but making sacrifices, saving their country, or weeping over its downfall. The tales and descriptions of that period without exception tell us of nothing but the self-sacrifice, the patriotism, the despair, the grief, and the heroism of the Russians. In reality, it was not at all like that. It seems so to us, because we see out of the past only the general historical interest of that period, and we do not see all the personal human interests of the men of that time. And yet in reality these personal interests of the immediate present are of so much greater importance than public interests, that they prevent the public interest from ever being felt—from being noticed at all, indeed. The majority of the people of that period took no heed of the general progress of public affairs, and were only influenced by their immediate personal interests. And those very people played the most useful part in the work of the time.

Those who were striving to grasp the general course of events, and trying by self-sacrifice and heroism to take a hand in it, were the most useless members of society; they saw everything upside down, and all that they did with the best intentions turned out to be useless folly, like Pierre's regiment, and Mamonov's, that spent their time pillaging the Russian villages, like the lint scraped by the ladies, that never reached the wounded, and so on. Even those who, being fond of talking on intellectual subjects and expressing their feelings, discussed the position of Russia, unconsciously imported into their talk a shade of hypocrisy or falsity or else of useless fault-finding and bitterness against persons, whom they blamed for what could be nobody's fault.

In historical events we see more plainly than ever the law that forbids us to taste of the fruit of the Tree of Knowledge. It is only unself-conscious activity that bears fruit, and the man who plays a part in an historical drama never understands its significance. If he strives to comprehend it, he is stricken with barrenness.

The significance of the drama taking place in Russia at that time was the less easy to grasp, the closer the share a man was taking in it. In Petersburg, and in the provinces remote from Moscow, ladies and gentlemen in volunteer uniforms bewailed the fate of Russia and the ancient capital, and talked of self-sacrifice, and so on. But in the army, which had retreated behind Moscow, men scarcely talked or thought at all about Moscow, and, gazing at the burning city, no one swore to be avenged on the French, but every one was thinking of the next quarter's pay due to him, of the next halting-place, of Matryoshka the canteen-woman, and so on.

Nikolay Rostov, without any idea of self-sacrifice, simply because the war had happened to break out before he left the service, took an immediate and continuous part in the defence of his country, and consequently he looked upon what was happening in Russia without despair or gloomy prognostications. If he had been asked what he thought of the present position of Russia, he would have said that it was not his business to think about it, that that was what Kutuzov and the rest of them were for, but that he had heard that the regiments were being filled up to their full complements, and that they must therefore be going to fight for a good time longer, and that under the present circumstances he might pretty easily obtain the command of a regiment within a couple of years.

Since this was his point of view, it was with no regret at taking no part in the approaching battle, but with the greatest satisfaction—which he did not conceal, and his comrades fully understood—that he received the news of his appointment to go to Voronezh to purchase remounts for his division.

A few days before the battle of Borodino, Nikolay received the sums of money and official warrants required, and, sending some hussars on before him, he drove with posting-horses to Voronezh.

Only one who has had the same experience—that is, has spent several months continuously in the atmosphere of an army in the field—can imagine the delight Nikolay felt when he got out of the region overspread by the troops with their foraging parties, trains of provisions, and hospitals; when he saw no more soldiers, army waggons, and filthy traces of the camp, but villages of peasants and peasant women, gentlemen's country houses, fields with grazing oxen, and station-houses and sleepy overseers, he rejoiced as though he were seeing it all for the first time. What in particular remained for a long while a wonder and a joy to him was the sight of women, young and healthy, without dozens of officers hanging about every one of them; and women, too, who were pleased and flattered at an officer's cracking jokes with them.

In the happiest frame of mind, Nikolay reached the hotel at Voronezh at night, ordered everything of which he had so long been deprived in the army, and next day, after shaving with special care and putting on the full-dress uniform he had not worn for so long past, he drove off to present himself to the authorities.

The commander of the militia of the district was a civilian general, an old gentleman, who evidently found amusement in his military duties and rank. He gave Nikolay a brusque reception (supposing that this was the military manner), and cross-examining him with an important air, as though he had a right to do so, he expressed his approval and disapproval, as though called upon to give his verdict on the management of the war. Nikolay was in such high spirits that this only amused him.

From the commander of militia, he went to the governor's. The governor was a brisk little man, very affable and unpretentious. He mentioned to Nikolay the stud-farms, where he might obtain horses, recommended him to a horse-dealer in the town, and a gentleman living twenty versts from the town, who had the best horses, and promised him every assistance.

"You are Count Ilya Andreitch's son? My wife was a great friend of your mamma's. We receive on Thursdays: to-day is Thursday, pray come in, quite without ceremony," said the governor, as he took leave of him.

Nikolay took a posting carriage, and making his quartermaster get in beside him, galloped straight off from the governor's to the gentleman with the stud of fine horses twenty versts away.

During the early days of his stay in Voronezh, everything seemed easy and pleasant to Nikolay, and, as is always the case, when a man is himself in a happy frame of mind, everything went well and prospered with him.

The country gentleman turned out to be an old cavalry officer, a bachelor, a great horse-fancier, a sportsman, and the owner of a smoking-room, of hundred-year-old herb-brandy, of some old Hungarian wine, and of superb horses.

In a couple of words, Nikolay had bought for six thousand roubles seventeen stallions, all perfect examples of their several breeds (as he said), as show specimens of his remounts. After dining and drinking a glass or so too much of the Hungarian wine, Rostov, exchanging kisses with the country gentleman, with whom he was already on the friendliest terms, galloped back over the most atrociously bad road in the happiest frame of mind, continually urging the driver on, so that he might be in time for the *soirée* at the governor's.

After dressing, scenting himself, and douching his head with cold water, Nikolay made his appearance at the governor's, a little late, but with the phrase, "Better late than never," ready on the tip of his tongue.

It was not a ball, and nothing had been said about dancing; but every one knew that Katerina Petrovna would play waltzes and écossaises on the clavichord, and that there would be dancing, and every one reckoning on it, had come dressed for a ball.

Provincial life in the year 1812 went on exactly the same as always, the only difference being that the provincial towns were livelier owing to the presence of many wealthy families from Moscow, that, as in everything going on at that time in Russia, there was perceptible in the gaiety a certain devil-may-care, desperate recklessness, and also that the small talk indispensable between people was now not about the weather and common acquaintances, but about Moscow and the army and Napoleon.

The gathering at the governor's consisted of the best society in Voronezh.

There were a great many ladies, among them several Moscow acquaintances of Nikolay's; but among the men there was no one who could be compared with the cavalier of St. George, the gallant hussar, and good-natured, well-bred Count Rostov. Among the men there was an Italian prisoner—an officer of the French army; and Nikolay felt that the presence of this prisoner gave an added lustre to him—the Russian hero. He was, as it were, a trophy of victory. Nikolay felt this, and it seemed to him as though every one looked at the Italian in the same light, and he treated the foreign officer with gracious dignity and reserve.

As soon as Nikolay came in in his full-dress uniform of an officer of hussars, diffusing a fragrance of scent and wine about him, and said himself, and heard several times said to him, the words, "Better late than never," people clustered round him. All eyes were turned on him, and he felt at once that he had stepped into a position that just suited him in a provincial town—a position alawys agreeable, but now after his long privation of such gratifications, intoxicatingly delightful—that of a universal favourite. Not only at the posting-stations, at the taverns, and in the smoking-room of the horse-breeding gentleman, had he found servant-girls flattered by his attention, but here, at the governor's assembly, there were (so it seemed to Nikolay) an inexhaustible multitude of young married ladies and pretty girls, who were only waiting with impatience for him to notice them. The ladies and the young girls flirted with him, and the old people began even from this first evening bestirring themselves to try and get this gallant young rake of an hussar married and settled down. Among the latter was the governor's wife herself, who received Rostov as though he were a near kinsman, and called him "Nikolay."

Katerina Petrovna did in fact proceed to play waltzes and écossaises, and dancing began, in which Nikolay fascinated the company more than ever by his elegance. He surprised every one indeed by his peculiarly free and easy style in dancing. Nikolay was a little surprised himself at his own style of dancing at that *soirée*. He had never danced in that manner at Moscow, and would indeed have regarded such an extremely free and easy manner of dancing as not correct, as bad style; but here he felt it incumbent on him to astonish them all by something extraordinary, something that they would be sure to take for the usual thing in the capital, though new to them in the provinces.

All the evening Nikolay paid the most marked attention to a blue-eyed, plump, and pleasing little blonde, the wife of one of the provincial officials. With the naïve conviction of young men who are enjoying themselves, that other men's wives are created for their special benefit, Rostov never left this lady's side, and treated her husband in a friendly way, almost as though there were a private understanding between them, as though they knew without speaking of it how capitally they, that is, how Nikolay and the wife, would get on. The husband did not, however, appear to share this conviction, and tried to take a gloomy tone with Rostov. But Nikolay's good-humoured naïveté was so limitless that at times the husband could not help being drawn into his gay humour. Towards the end of the evening, however, as the wife's face grew more flushed and animated, the husband's grew steadily more melancholy and stolid, as though they had a given allowance of liveliness between them, and as the wife's increased, the husband's dwindled.

V

WITH a smile that never left his lips, Nikolay sat bent a little forward on a low chair, and stooping close over his blonde beauty, he paid her mythological compliments.

Jauntily shifting the posture of his legs in his tight riding-breeches, diffusing a scent of perfume, and admiring his fair companion and himself and the fine lines of his legs in the tight breeches, Nikolay told the blonde lady that he wanted to elope with a lady here, in Voronezh.

"What is she like?"

"Charming, divine. Her eyes" (Nikolay gazed at his companion) "are blue, her lips are coral, her whiteness . . ." he gazed at her shoulders, "the shape of Diana . . ."

The husband came up to them and asked his wife gloomily what she was talking of.

"Ah! Nikita Ivanitch," said Nikolay, rising courteously. And as though anxious for Nikita Ivanitch to take a share in his jests, he began to tell him too of his intention of running away with a blonde lady.

The husband smiled grimly, the wife gaily.

The good-natured governor's wife came up to them with a disapproving air.

"Anna Ignatyevna wants to see you, Nikolay," she said, pronouncing the name in such a way that Rostov was at once aware that Anna Ignatyevna was a very great lady. "Come, Nikolay. You let me call you so, don't you?"

"Oh, yes, *ma tante*. Who is she?"

"Anna Ignatyevna Malvintsev. She has heard about you from her niece, how you rescued her . . . Do you guess? . . ."

"Oh, I rescued so many!" cried Nikolay.

"Her niece, Princess Bolkonsky. She is here in Voronezh with her aunt. Oho! how he blushes! Eh?"

"Not a bit of it, nonsense, *ma tante*."

"Oh, very well, very well. Oh! oh! what a boy it is!"

The governor's wife led him up to a tall and very stout lady in a blue toque, who had just finished a game of cards with the personages of greatest consequence in the town. This was Madame Malvintsev, Princess Marya's aunt on her mother's side, a wealthy, childless widow, who always lived in Voronezh. She was standing up, reckoning her losses, when Rostov came up to her.

She dropped her eyelids with a severe and dignified air, glanced at him, and went on upbraiding the general who had been winning from her.

"Delighted, my dear boy," she said, holding out her hand to him. "Pray come and see me."

After saying a few words about Princess Marya and her late father, whom Madame Malvintsev had evidently disliked, and inquiring what Nikolay knew about Prince Andrey, who was apparently also not in her good graces, the dignified old lady dismissed him, repeating her invitation to come and see her.

Nikolay promised to do so and blushed again as he took leave of Madame Malvintsev. At the mention of Princess Marya's name, Rostov experienced a sensation of shyness, even of terror, which he could not have explained to himself.

On leaving Madame Malvintsev, Rostov would have gone back to the dance, but the little governor's wife laid her plump little hand on his sleeve, and saying that she wanted to have a few words with him, led him into the divan-room; the persons in that room promptly withdrew that they might not be in her way.

"Do you know, *mon cher*," said the governor's wife with a serious expression on her good-natured, little face, "this is really the match for you; if you like, I will try and arrange it."

"Whom do you mean, *me tante?*" asked Nikolay.

"I will make a match for you with the princess. Katerina Petrovna talks of Lili, but I say, no—the princess. Do you wish it? I am sure your mamma will be grateful. Really, she is such a splendid girl, charming! And she is by no means so very plain."

"Not at all so," said Nikolay, as though offended at the idea. "As for me, *ma tante*, as a soldier should, I don't force myself on any one, nor refuse anything that turns up," said Rostov, before he had time to consider what he was saying.

"So remember then; this is no jesting matter."

"How could it be!"

"Yes, yes," said the governor's wife, as though talking to herself. "And *entre autres, mon cher*, you are too assiduous with the other—the blonde. One feels sorry for the husband, really . . ."

"Oh no, we are quite friendly," said Nikolay in the simplicity of his heart: it had never occurred to him that such an agreeable pastime for him could be other than agreeable to any one else.

"What a stupid thing I said to the governor's wife though!" suddenly came into Nikolay's mind at supper. "She really will begin to arrange a match, and Sonya? . . ."

And on taking leave of the governor's wife, as she said to him once more with a smile, "Well, remember then," he drew her aside.

"But there is something . . . To tell you the truth, *ma tante* . . ."

"What is it, what is it, my dear? Come, let us sit down here."

Nikolay had a sudden desire, an irresistible impulse to talk of all his most secret feelings (such as he would never have spoken of to his mother, to his sister, to an intimate friend) to this woman, who was almost a stranger. Whenever Nikolay thought afterwards of this uncalled-for outburst of inexplicable frankness—though it had most important consequences for him—it seemed to him (as it always seems to people in such cases) that it had happened by chance, through a sudden fit of folly. But at the same time this outburst of frankness, together with other insignificant events, had consequences of immense importance to him and to all his family.

"It's like this, *ma tante*. It has long been *maman's* wish to marry me to an heiress; but the mere idea of it—marrying for money—is revolting to me."

"Oh yes, I can understand that," said the governor's wife.

"But Princess Bolkonsky, that's a different matter. In the first place, I'll tell you the truth, I like her very much, I feel drawn to her, and then, ever since I came across her in such a position, so strangely, it has often struck me, that it was fate. Only think: mamma has long been dreaming of it, but I had never happened to meet her before—it always so happened that we didn't meet. And then when my sister, Natasha, was engaged to her brother, of course it was impossible to think of a match between us then. It seems it was to happen that I met her first just when Natasha's engagement had been broken off; and well, everything afterwards . . . So you see how it is. I have never said all this to any one, and I never shall. I only say it to you."

The governor's wife pressed his elbow gratefully.

"Do you know Sophie, my cousin? I love her; I have promised to marry her, and I am going to marry her . . . So you see it's no use talking of such a thing," Nikolay concluded lamely, flushing crimson.

"My dearest boy, how can you talk so? Why, Sophie hasn't a farthing, and you told me yourself that your papa's affairs are terribly straitened. And your *maman*? It would kill her—for one thing. Then Sophie, if she is a girl of any heart, what a life it would be for her! Your mother in despair, your position ruined . . . No, my dear, Sophie and you ought to realise that."

Nikolay did not speak. It was comforting to him to hear these arguments.

"All the same, *ma tante*, it cannot be," he said, with a sigh, after a brief silence. "And besides would the princess accept me? And again she is in mourning; can such a thing be thought of?"

"Why, do you suppose I am going to marry you out of hand on the spot? There are ways of doing everything," said the governor's wife.

"What a match-maker you are, *ma tante* . . ." said Nikolay, kissing her plump little hand.

VI

On reaching Moscow, after her meeting with Rostov at Bogutcharovo, Princess Marya had found her nephew there with his tutor, and a letter from Prince Andrey, directing her what route to take to her aunt, Madame Malvintsev's at Voronezh. The arrangements for the journey, anxiety about her brother, the organisation of her life in a new house, new people, the education of her nephew—all of this smothered in Princess Marya's heart that feeling as it were of temptation, which had tormented her during her father's illness and after his death, especially since her meeting with Rostov.

She was melancholy. Now after a month had passed in quiet, undisturbed conditions, she felt more and more deeply the loss of her father, which was connected in her heart with the downfall of Russia. She was anxious: the thought of the dangers to which her brother—the one creature near to her now left—was being exposed was a continual torture to her. She was worried too by the education of her nephew, which she was constantly feeling herself unfitted to control. But at the bottom of her heart there was an inward harmony, that arose from the sense that she had conquered in herself those dreams and hopes of personal happiness, that had sprung up in connection with Rostov.

When the governor's wife called on Madame Malvintsev the day after her *soirée*, and, talking over her plans with her, explaining that though under present circumstances a formal betrothal was of course not to be thought of, yet they might bring the young people together, and let them get to know one another, and having received the aunt's approval, began to speak of Rostov in Princess Marya's presence, singing his praises, and describing how he had blushed on hearing the princess's name, her emotion was not one of joy, but of pain. Her inner harmony was destroyed, and desires, doubts, self-reproach, and hope sprang up again.

In the course of the two days that followed before Rostov called, Princess Marya was continually considering what her behaviour ought to be in regard to Rostov. At one time, she made up her mind that she would not come down into the drawing-room when he came to see her aunt, that it was not suitable for her in her deep mourning to receive visitors. Then she thought this would be rude after what he had done for her. Then the idea struck her that her aunt and the governor's wife had views of some sort upon her and Rostov; their words and glances had seemed at times to confirm this suspicion. Then she told herself that it was only her own depravity that could make her think this of them: could they possibly fail to realise that in her position, still wearing the heaviest mourning, such match-making would be an insult both to her and to her father's memory? On the supposition that she would go down to see him, Princess Marya imagined the words he would say to her, and she would say to him; and at one moment, those words seemed to her undeservedly frigid, at the next, they struck her as carrying too much meaning. Above all she dreaded the embarrassment, which she felt would be sure to overcome her, and betray her, as soon as she saw him.

But when, on Sunday after matins, the footman came into the draw ing-room to announce that Count Rostov had called, the princess showed no sign of embarrassment, only a faint flush came into her cheeks, and her eyes shone with a new, radiant light.

"You have seen him, aunt?" said Princess Marya, in a composed voice, not knowing herself how she could be externally so calm and natural.

When Rostov came into the room, the princess dropped her head for an instant, as though to give time for their visitor to greet her aunt; and then at the very moment when Nikolay turned to her, she raised her head and met his gaze with shining eyes. With a movement full of dignity and grace, she rose with a joyous smile, held out her delicate, soft hand to him, and spoke in a voice in which for the first time there was the thrill of deep, womanly chest notes. Mademoiselle Bourienne, who was in the drawing-room, gazed at Princess Marya with bewildered surprise. The most accomplished coquette herself, she could not have manœuvred better on meeting a man whom she wanted to attract.

"Either black suits her wonderfully, or she really has grown better looking without my noticing it. And above all, such tact and grace!" thought Mademoiselle Bourienne.

Had Princess Marya been capable of reflection at that moment, she would have been even more astonished than Mademoiselle Bourienne at the change that had taken place in her. From the moment she set eyes on that sweet, loved face, some new force of life seemed to take possession of her, and to drive her to speak and act apart from her own will. From the time Rostov entered the room, her face was transformed. Just as when a light is kindled within a carved and painted lantern, the delicate, intricate, artistic tracery comes out in unexpected and impressive beauty, where all seemed coarse, dark, and meaningless before; so was Princess Marya's face transformed. For the first time all the pure, spiritual, inner travail in which she had lived till then came out in her face. All her inner searchings of spirit, her self-reproach, her sufferings, her striving for goodness, her resignation, her love, her self-sacrifice—all this was radiant now in those luminous eyes, in the delicate smile, in every feature of her tender face.

Rostov saw all this as clearly as though he had known her whole life. He felt that he was in the presence of a creature utterly different from and better than all those he had met up to that moment, and, above all, far better than he was himself.

The conversation was of the simplest and most insignificant kind. They talked of the war, unconsciously, like every one else, exaggerating their sadness on that subject; they talked of their last meeting—and Nikolay then tried to turn the subject; they talked of the kind-hearted governor's wife, of Nikolay's relations, and of Princess Marya's.

Princess Marya did not talk of her brother, but turned the conversation, as soon as her aunt mentioned Prince Andrey. It was evident that of the troubles of Russia she could speak artificially, but her brother was a subject too near her heart, and she neither would nor could speak lightly of him. Nikolay noticed this, as indeed with a keenness of ob-

servation not usual with him, he noticed every shade of Princess
Marya's character, and everything confirmed him in the conviction that
she was an altogether rare and original being.

Nikolay, like Princess Marya, had blushed and been embarrassed,
when he heard the princess spoken of, and even when he thought of her;
but in her presence he felt perfectly at ease, and he said to her not at all
what he had prepared beforehand to say to her, but what came into his
mind at the moment, and always quite appropriately.

As visitors always do where there are children, Nikolay, in a momentary silence during his brief visit, had recourse to Prince Andrey's little
son, caressing him, and asking him if he would like to be an hussar. He
took the little boy in his arms, began gaily whirling him round, and
glanced at Princess Marya. With softened, happy, shy eyes, she was
watching the child she loved in the arms of the man she loved. Nikolay
caught that look too, and as though he divined its significance, flushed
with delight, and fell to kissing the child with simple-hearted gaiety.

Princess Marya was not going into society at all on account of her
mourning, and Nikolay did not think it the proper thing to call on them
again. But the governor's wife still persisted in her match-making, and
repeating to Nikolay something flattering Princess Marya had said of
him, and *vice versa*, kept urging that Rostov should declare himself to
Princess Marya. With this object, she arranged that the young people
should meet at the reverend father's before Mass.

Though Rostov did tell the governor's wife that he should make no
sort of declaration to Princess Marya, he promised to be there.

Just as at Tilsit Rostov had not allowed himself to doubt whether
what was accepted by every one as right were really right, so now after
a brief but sincere struggle between the effort to order his life in accordance with his own sense of right, and humble submission to circumstances, he chose the latter, and yielded himself to the power, which,
he felt, was irresistibly carrying him away. He knew that to declare
his feelings to Princess Marya after his promise to Sonya would be
what he called base. And he knew that he would never do a base thing.
But he knew too (it was not what he knew, but what he felt at the bottom of his heart), that in giving way now to the force of circumstances
and of the people guiding him, he was not only doing nothing wrong,
but was doing something very, very grave, something of more gravity
than anything he had done in his life.

After seeing Princess Marya, though his manner of life remained
externally the same, all his former pleasures lost their charm for him,
and he often thought of her. But he never thought of her, as he had
thought of all the young girls he had met in society, nor as he had long,
and sometimes with enthusiasm, thought of Sonya. Like almost every
honest-hearted young man, he had thought of every young girl as of
a possible future wife, had adapted to them in his imagination all the
pictures of domestic felicity: the white morning wrapper, the wife behind the samovar, the wife's carriage, the little ones, mamma and papa,
their attitude to one another, and so on, and so on. And these pictures

of the future afforded him gratification. But when he thought of Princess Marya, to whom the match-makers were trying to betroth him, he could never form any picture of his future married life with her. Even if he tried to do so, it all seemed incoherent and false. And it only filled him with dread.

VII

The terrible news of the battle of Borodino, of our losses in killed and wounded, and the even more terrible news of the loss of Moscow reached Voronezh in the middle of September. Princess Marya, learning of her brother's wound only from the newspapers, and having no definite information about him, was preparing (so Nikolay heard, though he had not seen her) to set off to try and reach Prince Andrey.

On hearing the news of the battle of Borodino and of the abandonment of Moscow, Rostov felt, not despair, rage, revenge, nor any such feeling, but a sudden weariness and vexation with everything at Voronezh, and a sense of awkwardness and uneasy conscience. All the conversations he listened to seemed to him insincere; he did not know what to think of it all, and felt that only in the regiment would all become clear to him again. He made haste to conclude the purchase of horses, and was often without good cause ill-tempered with his servant and quartermaster.

Several days before Rostov's departure there was a thanksgiving service in the cathedral for the victory gained by the Russian troops, and Nikolay went to the service. He was a little behind the governor, and was standing through the service meditating with befitting sedateness on the most various subjects. When the service was concluding, the governor's wife beckoned him to her.

"Did you see the princess?" she said, with a motion of her hand towards a lady in black standing behind the choir.

Nikolay recognised Princess Marya at once, not so much from the profile he saw under her hat as from the feeling of watchful solicitude, awe, and pity which came over him at once. Princess Marya, obviously buried in her own thoughts, was making the last signs of the cross before leaving the church.

Nikolay gazed in wonder at her face. It was the same face he had seen before; there was the same general look of refined, inner, spiritual travail; but now there was an utterly different light in it. There was a touching expression of sadness, of prayer and of hope in it. With the same absence of hesitation as he had felt before in her presence, without waiting for the governor's wife to urge him, without asking himself whether it were right, whether it were proper for him to address her here in church, Nikolay went up to her, and said he had heard of her trouble and grieved with his whole heart to hear of it. As soon as she heard his voice, a vivid colour glowed in her face, lighting up at once her joy and her sorrow.

"One thing I wanted to tell you, princess," said Rostov, "that is, that if Prince Andrey Nikolaevitch were not living, since he is a colonel, it would be announced immediately in the gazettes."

The princess looked at him, not comprehending his words, but comforted by the expression of sympathetic suffering in his face.

"And I know from so many instances that a wound from a splinter" (the papers said it was from a grenade) "is either immediately fatal or else very slight," Nikolay went on. "We must hope for the best, and I am certain . . ."

Princess Marya interrupted him.

"Oh, it would be so aw . . ." she began, and her emotion choking her utterance, she bent her head with a graceful gesture, like everything she did in his presence, and glancing gratefully at him followed her aunt.

That evening Nikolay did not go out anywhere, but stayed at home to finish some accounts with the horse-vendors. By the time he had finished his work it was rather late to go out anywhere, but still early to go to bed, and Nikolay spent a long while walking up and down the room, thinking over his life, a thing that he rarely did.

Princess Marya had made an agreeable impression on him at Bogutcharovo. The fact of his meeting her then in such striking circumstances, and of his mother having at one time pitched precisely on her as the wealthy heiress suitable for him, had led him to look at her with special attention. During his stay at Voronezh, that impression had become, not merely a pleasing, but a very strong one. Nikolay was impressed by the peculiar, moral beauty which he discerned in her at this time. He had, however, been preparing to go away, and it had not entered his head to regret that in leaving Voronezh he was losing all chance of seeing her. But his meeting with Princess Marya that morning in church had, Nikolay felt, gone more deeply to his heart than he had anticipated and more deeply than he desired for his peace of mind. That pale, delicate, melancholy face, those luminous eyes, those soft, gracious gestures, and, above all, the deep and tender melancholy expressed in all her features, agitated him and drew his sympathy. In men Rostov could not bear an appearance of higher, spiritual life (it was why he did not like Prince Andrey), he spoke of it contemptuously as philosophy, idealism; but in Princess Marya it was just in that melancholy, showing all the depth of a spiritual world, strange and remote to Nikolay, that he found an irresistible attraction.

"She must be a marvellous girl! An angel, really!" he said to himself. "Why am I not free? Why was I in such a hurry with Sonya?" And involuntarily he compared the two: the poverty of the one and the wealth of the other in those spiritual gifts, which Nikolay was himself without and therefore prized so highly. He tried to picture what would have happened if he had been free, and in what way he would have made her an offer and she would have become his wife. No, he could not imagine that. A feeling of dread came over him and that picture would take no definite shape. With Sonya he had long ago made his picture of the future, and it was all so simple and clear, just because it was all made up and he knew all there was in Sonya. But with Princess Marya he could not picture his future life, because he did not understand her— he simply loved her.

There was something light-hearted, something of child's play in his dreams of Sonya. But to dream of Princess Marya was difficult and a little terrible.

"How she was praying!" he thought. "One could see that her whole soul was in her prayer. Yes, it was that prayer that moves mountains, and I am convinced that her prayer will be answered. Why don't I pray for what I want?" he bethought himself. "What do I want? Freedom, release from Sonya. She was right," he thought of what the governor's wife had said, "nothing but misery can come of my marrying her. Muddle, mamma's grief . . . our position . . . a muddle, a fearful muddle! Besides, I don't even love her. No, I don't love her in the right way. My God! take me out of this awful, hopeless position!" he began praying all at once. "Yes, prayer will move mountains, but one must believe, and not pray, as Natasha and I prayed as children for the snow to turn into sugar, and then ran out into the yard to try whether it had become sugar. No; but I am not praying for trifles now," he said, putting his pipe down in the corner and standing with clasped hands before the holy picture. And softened by the thought of Princess Marya, he began to pray as he had not prayed for a long while. He had tears in his eyes and a lump in his throat when Lavrushka came in at the door with papers.

"Blockhead! bursting in when you're not wanted!" said Nikolay, quickly changing his attitude.

"A courier has come," said Lavrushka in a sleepy voice, "from the governor, a letter for you."

"Oh, very well, thanks, you can go!"

Nikolay took the two letters. One was from his mother, the other from Sonya. He knew them from the handwriting, and broke open Sonya's letter first. He had hardly read a few lines when his face turned white and his eyes opened wide in dismay and joy. "No, it's not possible!" he said aloud. Unable to sit still, he began walking to and fro in the room, holding the letter in both hands as he read it. He skimmed through the letter, then read it through once and again, and shrugging his shoulders and flinging up his hands, he stood still in the middle of the room with wide-open mouth and staring eyes. What he had just been praying for with the assurance that God would answer his prayer had come to pass; but Nikolay was astounded at it as though it were something extraordinary, and as though he had not expected it, and as though the very fact of its coming to pass so quickly proved that it had not come from God, to whom he had been praying, but was some ordinary coincidence.

The knot fastening his freedom, that had seemed so impossible to disentangle, had been undone by this unexpected and, as it seemed to Nikolay, uncalled-for letter from Sonya. She wrote that their late misfortunes, the loss of almost the whole of the Rostovs' property in Moscow, and the countess's frequently expressed desire that Nikolay should marry Princess Bolkonsky, and his silence and coldness of late, all taken together led her to decide to set him free from his promise, and to give him back complete liberty.

"It would be too painful to me to think that I could be a cause of sorrow and discord in the family which has overwhelmed me with benefits," she wrote; "and the one aim of my love is the happiness of those I love, and therefore I beseech you, Nicolas, to consider yourself free, and to know that in spite of everything, no one can love you more truly than your—SONYA."

Both letters were from Troitsa. The other letter was from the countess. It described the last days in Moscow, the departure, the fire and the loss of the whole of their property. The countess wrote too that Prince Andrey had been among the train of wounded soldiers who had travelled with them. He was still in a very critical condition, but that the doctor said now that there was more hope. Sonya and Natasha were nursing him.

With this letter Nikolay went next day to call on Princess Marya. Neither Nikolay nor Princess Marya said a word as to all that was implied by the words: "Natasha is nursing him"; but thanks to this letter, Nikolay was brought suddenly into intimate relations, almost those of a kinsman, with the princess.

Next day Rostov escorted Princess Marya as far as Yaroslavl, and a few days later he set off himself to join his regiment.

VIII

SONYA's letter to Nikolay, that had come as an answer to his prayer, was written at Troitsa. It had been called forth in the following way. The idea of marrying Nikolay to a wealthy heiress had taken more and more complete possession of the old countess's mind. She knew that Sonya was the great obstacle in the way of this. And Sonya's life had of late, and especially after the letter in which Nikolay described his meeting with Princess Marya at Bogutcharovo, become more and more difficult in the countess's house. The countess never let slip an opportunity for making some cruel or humiliating allusion to Sonya. But a few days before they set out from Moscow the countess, distressed and overwrought by all that was happening, sent for Sonya, and instead of insistence and upbraiding, besought her with tears and entreaties to repay all that had been done for her by sacrificing herself, and breaking off her engagement to Nikolay. "I shall have no peace of mind till you make me this promise," she said.

Sonya sobbed hysterically, answered through her sobs that she would do anything, that she was ready for anything; but she did not give a direct promise, and in her heart she could not bring herself to what was demanded of her. She had to sacrifice herself for the happiness of the family that had brought her up and provided for her. To sacrifice herself for others was Sonya's habit. Her position in the house was such that only by way of sacrifice could she show her virtues, and she was used to sacrificing herself and liked it. But in every self-sacrificing action hitherto she had been happily conscious that by her very self-sacrifice she was heightening her value in the eyes of herself and others, and becoming worthier of Nikolay, whom she loved beyond everything in life. But now her sacrifice would consist in the renunciation of what constituted for her the whole reward of sacrifice, and the whole meaning of life. And for the first time in her life she felt bitterness against the people who had befriended her only to torment her more poignantly: she felt envy of Natasha, who had never had any experience of the kind, who had never been required to make sacrifices, and made other people sacrifice themselves for her, and was yet loved by every one. And for the first time Sonya felt that there was beginning to grow up out of her quiet, pure love for Nikolay a passionate feeling, which stood above all principles, and virtue, and religion. And under the influence of that passion, Sonya, whose life of dependence had unconsciously trained her to reserve, gave the countess vague, indefinite answers, avoided talking with her, and resolved to wait for a personal interview with Nikolay, not to set him free, but, on the contrary, to bind him to her for ever.

The fuss and the horror of the Rostovs' last days in Moscow had smothered the gloomy thoughts that were weighing on Sonya. She was glad to find an escape from them in practical work. But when she heard of Prince Andrey's presence in their house, in spite of all the genuine compassion she felt for him, and for Natasha, a joyful and superstitious feeling that it was God's will that she should not be parted from Nikolay took possession of her. She knew Natasha loved no one but Prince Andrey, and had never ceased to love him. She knew that brought together now, under such terrible circumstances, they would love one another again; and that then, owing to the relationship that would (in accordance with the laws of the Orthodox Church) exist between them, Nikolay could not be married to Princess Marya. In spite of all the awfulness of what was happening during the last day or two in Moscow and the first days of the journey, that feeling, that consciousness of the intervention of Providence in her personal affairs, was a source of joy to Sonya. At the Troitsa monastery the Rostovs made the first break in their journey.

In the hostel of the monastery three big rooms were assigned to the Rostovs, one of which was occupied by Prince Andrey. The wounded man was by this time a great deal better. Natasha was sitting with him. In the next room were the count and the countess reverently conversing with the superior, who was paying a visit to his old acquaintances and patrons. Sonya was sitting with them, fretted by curiosity as to what Prince Andrey and Natasha were saying. She heard the sounds of their voices through the door. The door of Prince Andrey's room opened, Natasha came out with an excited face, and not noticing the monk, who rose to meet her, and pulled back his wide sleeve off his right hand, she went up to Sonya and took her by the arm.

"Natasha, what are you about? Come here," said the countess.

Natasha went up to receive the blessing, and the superior counselled her to turn for aid to God and to His saint.

Immediately after the superior had gone out, Natasha took her friend by the arm, and went with her into the empty third room.

"Sonya, yes, he will live," she said. "Sonya, how happy I am, and how wretched! Sonya, darling, everything is just as it used to be. If only he were going to live. He cannot, . . . because . . . be . . . cause . . ." and Natasha burst into tears.

"Yes! I knew it would be! Thank God," said Sonya. "He will live."

Sonya was no less excited than her friend, both by the latter's grief and fears, and by her own personal reflections, of which she had spoken to no one. Sobbing, she kissed and comforted Natasha. "If only he were to live!" she thought. After weeping, talking a little, and wiping their tears, the two friends went towards Prince Andrey's door. Natasha, cautiously opening the door, glanced into the room. Sonya stood beside her at the half-open door.

Prince Andrey was lying raised high on three pillows. His pale face looked peaceful, his eyes were closed, and they could see his quiet, regular breathing.

"Ah, Natasha!" Sonya almost shrieked all of a sudden, clutching at her cousin's arm, and moving back away from the door.

"What! what is it?" asked Natasha.

"It's the same, the same, you know . . ." said Sonya, with a white face and quivering lips.

Natasha softly closed the door and walked away with Sonya to the window, not yet understanding what she was talking of.

"Do you remember," said Sonya, with a scared and solemn face, "do you remember when I looked into the mirror for you . . . at Otradnoe at Christmas time . . . Do you remember what I saw?" . . .

"Yes, yes," said Natasha, opening her eyes wide, and vaguely recalling that Sonya had said something then about seeing Prince Andrey lying down.

"Do you remember?" Sonya went on. "I saw him then, and told you all so at the time, you and Dunyasha. I saw him lying on a bed," she said, at each detail making a gesture with her lifted finger, "and that he had his eyes shut, and that he was covered with a pink quilt, and that he had his hands folded," said Sonya, convinced as she described the details she had just seen that they were the very details she had *seen* then. At the time she had seen nothing, but had said she was seeing the first thing that came into her head. But what she had invented then seemed to her now as real a memory as any other. She not only remembered that she had said at the time that he looked round at her and smiled, and was covered with something red, but was firmly convinced that she had seen and said at the time, that he was covered with a pink quilt—yes, pink—and that his eyes had been closed.

"Yes, yes, pink it was," said Natasha, who began now to fancy too that she remembered her saying it was a pink quilt, and saw in that detail the most striking and mysterious point in the prediction.

"But what does it mean?" said Natasha dreamily.

"Ah, I don't know, how extraordinary it all is!" said Sonya, clutching at her head.

A few minutes later, Prince Andrey rang his bell, and Natasha went in to him; while Sonya, in a state of excitement and emotion such as she had rarely experienced, remained in the window, pondering over all the strangeness of what was happening.

That day there was an opportunity of sending letters to the army, and the countess wrote a letter to her son.

"Sonya," said the countess, raising her head from her letter, as her niece passed by her. "Sonya, won't you write to Nikolenka?" said the countess, in a soft and trembling voice; and in the tired eyes, that looked at her over the spectacles, Sonya read all that the countess meant by those words. Those eyes expressed entreaty and dread of a refusal and shame at having to beg, and readiness for unforgiving hatred in case of refusal.

Sonya went up to the countess, and kneeling down, kissed her hand.

"I will write, mamma," she said.

Sonya was softened, excited, and moved by all that had passed that day, especially by the mysterious fulfilment of her divination, which she had just seen. Now, when she knew that in case of the renewal of Natasha's engagement to Prince Andrey, Nikolay could not be married to Princess Marya, she felt with delight a return of that self-sacrificing spirit in which she was accustomed and liked to live. And with tears in her eyes, and with a glad sense of performing a magnanimous action, she sat down, and several times interrupted by the tears that dimmed her velvety black eyes, she wrote the touching letter the reception of which had so impressed Nikolay.

IX

IN the guard-room to which Pierre had been taken, the officer and soldiers in charge treated him with hostility, but at the same time with respect. Their attitude to him betrayed both doubt who he might be—perhaps a person of great importance—and hostility, in consequence of the personal conflict they had so recently had with him.

But when on the morning of the next day the guard was relieved, Pierre felt that for his new guard—both officers and soldiers—he was no longer an object of the same interest as he had been to those who had taken him prisoner. And, indeed, in the big, stout man in a peasant's coat, the sentinels in charge next day saw nothing of the vigorous person who had fought so desperately with the pillaging soldier and the convoy, and had uttered that solemn phrase about saving a child; they saw in him only number seventeen of the Russian prisoners who were to be detained for some reason by order of the higher authorities. If there were anything peculiar about Pierre, it lay only in his undaunted air of concentrated thought, and in the excellent French in which, to the surprise of the French, he expressed himself. In spite of that, Pierre was put that day with the other suspicious characters who had been apprehended, since the room he had occupied was wanted for an officer.

All the Russians detained with Pierre were persons of the lowest class. And all of them, recognising Pierre as a gentleman, held aloof from him all the more for his speaking French. Pierre mournfully heard their jeers at his expense.

On the following evening, Pierre learned that all the prisoners (and himself probably in the number) were to be tried for incendiarism. The day after, Pierre was taken with the rest to a house where were sitting a French general with white moustaches, two colonels, and other Frenchmen with scarfs on their shoulders. With that peculiar exactitude and definiteness, which is always employed in the examination of prisoners and is supposed to preclude all human weaknesses, they put questions to Pierre and the others, asking who he was, where he had been, with what object, and so on.

These questions, leaving on one side the essence of the living fact, and excluding all possibility of that essence being discovered, like all questions, indeed, in legal examinations, aimed only at directing the channel along which the examining officials desired the prisoner's answers to flow, so as to lead him to the goal of the inquiry—that is, to conviction. So soon as he began to say anything that was not conducive to this aim, then they pulled up the channel, and the water might flow where it would. Moreover, Pierre felt, as the accused always do feel at all trials, a puzzled wonder why all these questions were asked him. He had a feeling that it was only out of condescension, out of a sort of civility, that this trick of directing the channel of their replies was made use of. He knew he was in the power of these men, that it was only by superior force that he had been brought here, that it was only superior force that gave them the right to exact answers to their questions, that the whole aim of the proceeding was to convict him. And, therefore, since they had superior force, and they had the desire to convict him, there seemed no need of the network of questions and the trial. It was obvious that all the questions were bound to lead up to his conviction. To the inquiry what he was doing when he was apprehended, Pierre replied with a certain tragic dignity that he was carrying back to its parents a child he had "rescued from the flames." Why was he fighting with the soldiers? Pierre replied that he was defending a woman, that the defence of an insulted woman was the duty of every man, and so on . . . He was pulled up; this was irrelevant. With what object had he been in the courtyard of a burning house where he had been seen by several witnesses? He answered that he was going out to see what was going on in Moscow. He was pulled up again. He had not been asked, he was told, where he was going, but with what object he was near the fire. Who was he? The first question was repeated, to which he had said he did not want to answer. Again he replied that he could not answer that.

"Write that down, that's bad. Very bad," the general with the white whiskers and the red, flushed face said to him sternly.

On the fourth day, fire broke out on the Zubovsky rampart.

Pierre was moved with thirteen of the others to a coach-house belonging to a merchant's house on the Crimean Ford. As he passed through the street, Pierre could hardly breathe for the smoke, which seemed hanging over the whole city. Fires could be seen in various directions. Pierre did not at that time grasp what was implied by the burning of Moscow, and he gazed with horror at the fires.

In a coach-house behind a house in the Crimean Ford, Pierre spent another four days, and in the course of those four days he learned, from the conversation of the French soldiers, that all the prisoners in detention here were every day awaiting the decision of their fate by a marshal. Of what marshal, Pierre could not ascertain from the soldiers. For the soldiers, this marshal was evidently the highest and somewhat mysterious symbol of power.

These first days, up to the 8th of September, when the prisoners were brought up for a second examination, were the most painful for Pierre.

X

ON the 8th of September, there came into the prisoners' coach-house an officer of very great consequence, judging by the respectfulness with which he was addressed by the soldiers on guard. This officer, probably some one on the staff, held a memorandum in his hand, and called over all the Russians' names, giving Pierre the title of "the one who will not give his name." And with an indolent and indifferent glance at all the prisoners, he gave the officer on guard orders to have them decently dressed and in good order before bringing them before the marshal. In an hour a company of soldiers arrived, and Pierre with the thirteen others was taken to the Virgin's Meadow. It was a fine day, sunny after rain, and the air was exceptionally clear. The smoke did not hang low over the town as on the day when Pierre had been taken from the guard-room of the Zubovsky rampart; the smoke rose up in columns into the pure air. Flames were nowhere to be seen; but columns of smoke were rising up on all sides, and all Moscow, all that Pierre could see, was one conflagration. On all sides he saw places laid waste, with stoves and pipes left standing in them, and now and then the charred walls of a stone house.

Pierre stared at the fires, and did not recognise parts of the town that he knew well. Here and there could be seen churches that had not been touched by the fire. The Kremlin uninjured, rose white in the distance, with towers and Ivan the Great. Close at hand, the cupola of the Monastery of the New Virgin shone brightly, and the bells for service rang out gaily from it. Those bells reminded Pierre that it was Sunday and the festival of the birth of the Virgin Mother. But there seemed to be no one to keep this holiday; on all sides they saw the ruin wrought by the fires, and the only Russians they met were a few tattered and frightened-looking people, who hid themselves on seeing the French.

It was evident that the Russian nest was in ruins and destroyed; but with this annihilation of the old Russian order of life, Pierre was unconsciously aware that the French had raised up over this ruined nest an utterly different but strong order of their own. He felt this at the sight of the regular ranks of the boldly and gaily marching soldiers who were escorting him and the other prisoners; he felt it at the sight of some important French official in a carriage and pair, driven by a soldier, whom they met on their way. He felt it at the gay sounds of regimental music, which floated across from the left of the meadow; and he had felt it and realised it particularly strongly from the memorandum the French officer had read in the morning when he called over the prisoners' names. Pierre was taken by one set of soldiers, led off to one place, and thence to another, with dozens of different people. It seemed to him that they might have forgotten him, have mixed him up with other people. But no; his answers given at the examination came back to him in the form of the designation, "the one who will not give his name." And under this designation, which filled Pierre with dread, they led him away somewhere, with unhesitating conviction written on their faces that he and the other prisoners with him were the right ones, and that they were being taken to the proper place. Pierre felt himself an insignificant chip that had fallen under the wheel of a machine that worked without a hitch, though he did not understand it.

Pierre was led with the other prisoners to the right side of the Virgin's Meadow, not far from the monastery, and taken up to a big, white house with an immense garden. It was the house of Prince Shtcherbatov, and Pierre had often been inside it in former days to see its owner. Now, as he learnt from the talk of the soldiers, it was occupied by the marshal, the Duke of Eckmühl.

They were led up to the entrance, and taken into the house, one at a time. Pierre was the sixth to be led in. Through a glass-roofed gallery, a vestibule, and a hall, all familiar to Pierre, he was led to the long, low-pitched study, at the door of which stood an adjutant.

Davoust was sitting at a table at the end of the room, his spectacles on his nose. Pierre came close up to him. Davoust, without raising his eyes, was apparently engaged in looking up something in a document that lay before him. Without raising his eyes, he asked softly: "Who are you?"

Pierre was mute because he was incapable of articulating a word. Davoust was not to Pierre simply a French general; to Pierre, Davoust was a man notorious for his cruelty. Looking at the cold face of Davoust, which, like a stern teacher, seemed to consent for a time to have patience and await a reply, Pierre felt that every second of delay might cost him his life. But he did not know what to say. To say the same as he had said at the first examination he did not dare; to disclose his name and his position would be both dangerous and shameful. Pierre stood mute. But before he had time to come to any decision, Davoust raised his head, thrust his spectacles up on his forehead, screwed up his eyes, and looked intently at Pierre.

"I know this man," he said, in a frigid, measured tone, obviously reckoning on frightening Pierre. The chill that had been running down Pierre's back seemed to clutch his head in a vice.

"General, you cannot know me, I have never seen you."

"It is a Russian spy," Davoust interrupted, addressing another general in the room, whom Pierre had not noticed. And Davoust turned away. With an unexpected thrill in his voice, Pierre began speaking with sudden rapidity.

"*Non, monseigneur,*" he said, suddenly recalling that Davoust was a duke, "you could not know me. I am a militia officer, and I have not quitted Moscow."

"Your name?" repeated Davoust.

"Bezuhov."

"What proof is there that you are not lying?"

"*Monseigneur!*" cried Pierre in a voice not of offence but of supplication.

Davoust lifted his eyes and looked intently at Pierre. For several seconds they looked at one another, and that look saved Pierre. In that glance, apart from all circumstances of warfare and of judgment, human relations arose between these two men. Both of them in that one instant were vaguely aware of an immense number of different things, and knew that they were both children of humanity, that they were brothers.

At the first glance when Davoust raised his head from his memorandum, where men's lives and doings were marked off by numbers, Pierre was only a circumstance, and Davoust could have shot him with no sense of an evil deed on his conscience; but now he saw in him a man. He pondered an instant.

"How will you prove to me the truth of what you say?" said Davoust coldly.

Pierre thought of Ramballe, and mentioned his name and regiment and the street and house where he could be found.

"You are not what you say," Davoust said again.

In a trembling, breaking voice, Pierre began to bring forward proofs of the truth of his testimony.

But at that moment an adjutant came in and said something to Davoust.

Davoust beamed at the news the adjutant brought him, and began buttoning up his uniform. Apparently he had completely forgotten about Pierre. When an adjutant reminded him of the prisoner, he nodded in Pierre's direction with a frown, and told them to take him away. But where were they to take him—Pierre did not know: whether back to the shed or the place prepared for their execution which his companions had pointed out to him as they passed through the Virgin's Meadow.

He turned his head and saw that the adjutant was repeating some question.

"Yes, of course!" said Davoust. But what that "yes" meant, Pierre could not tell.

Pierre did not remember how or where he went, and how long he was going. In a condition of complete stupefaction and bewilderment, seeing nothing around him, he moved his legs in company with the others till they all stopped, and he stopped.

There was one idea all this time in Pierre's head. It was the question: Who, who was it really that was condemning him to death? It was not the men who had questioned him at the first examination; of them not one would or obviously could do so. It was not Davoust, who had looked at him in such a human fashion. In another minute Davoust would have understood that they were doing wrong, but the adjutant who had come in at that moment had prevented it. And that adjutant had obviously had no evil intent, but he might have stayed away. Who was it, after all, who was punishing him, killing him, taking his life—his, Pierre's, with all his memories, his strivings, his hopes, and his ideas? Who was doing it? And Pierre felt that it was no one's doing. It was discipline, and the concatenation of circumstances. Some sort of discipline was killing him, Pierre, robbing him of life, of all, annihilating him.

XI

FROM Prince Shtcherbatov's house the prisoners were taken straight downhill across the Virgin's Meadow to the left of the monastery of the Virgin, and led to a kitchen garden, in which there stood a post. A big pit had been dug out near the post, and the freshly turned-up earth was heaped up by it. A great crowd of people formed a semicircle about the pit and the post. The crowd consisted of a small number of Russians and a great number of Napoleon's soldiers not on duty: there were Germans, Italians, and Frenchmen in various uniforms. To the right and left of the post stood rows of French soldiers, in blue uniforms, with red epaulettes, in Hessians and shako. The prisoners were stood in a certain order, in accordance with a written list (Pierre was sixth) and led up to the post. Several drums suddenly began beating on both sides of them, and Pierre felt as though a part of his soul was being torn away from him by that sound. He lost all power of thought and reflection. He could only see and hear. And there was only one desire left in him, the desire that the terrible thing that was to be done should be done more quickly. Pierre looked round at his companions and scrutinised them.

The two men at the end were shaven convicts; one tall and thin, the other a swarthy, hirsute, muscular fellow with a flattened nose. The third was a house-serf, a man of five-and-forty, with grey hair and a plump, well-fed figure. The fourth was a peasant, a very handsome fellow with a full, flaxen beard and black eyes. The fifth was a factory hand, a thin, sallow lad of eighteen, in a dressing-gown.

Pierre heard the Frenchmen deliberating how they were to be shot, singly, or two at a time. "Two at a time," a senior officer answered coldly. There was a stir in the ranks of the soldiers, and it was evident that every one was in haste and not making haste, not as people do when they are getting through some job every one can understand, but as men hasten to get something done that is inevitable, but is disagreeable and incomprehensible.

A French official wearing a scarf came up to the right side of the file of prisoners, and read aloud the sentence in Russian and in French.

Then two couples of French soldiers came up to the prisoners by the instruction of an officer, and took the two convicts who stood at the head. The convicts went up to the post, stopped there, and while the sacks were being brought, they looked dumbly about them, as a wild beast at bay looks at the approaching hunter. One of them kept on crossing himself, the other scratched his back and worked his lips into the semblance of a smile. The soldiers with hurrying fingers bandaged their eyes, put the sacks over their heads and bound them to the post.

A dozen sharpshooters, with muskets, stepped out of the ranks with a fine, regular tread, and halted eight paces from the post. Pierre turned away not to see what was coming. There was a sudden bang and rattle that seemed to Pierre louder than the most terrific clap of thunder, and he looked round. There was a cloud of smoke, and the French soldiers, with trembling hands and pale faces, were doing something in it by the pit. The next two were led up. Those two, too, looked at every one in the same way, with the same eyes, dumbly, and in vain, with their eyes only begging for protection, and plainly unable to understand or believe in what was coming. They could not believe in it, because they only knew what their life was to them, and so could not understand, and could not believe, that it could be taken from them.

Pierre tried not to look, and again turned away; but again a sort of awful crash smote his hearing, and with the sound he saw smoke, blood, and the pale and frightened faces of the Frenchmen, again doing something at the post, and balking each other with their trembling hands. Pierre, breathing hard, looked about him as though asking, "What does it mean?" The same question was written in all the eyes that met Pierre's eyes. On all the faces of the Russians, on the faces of the French soldiers and officers, all without exception, he read the same dismay, horror, and conflict as he felt in his own heart. "But who is it doing it there really? They are all suffering as I am! Who is it? who?" flashed for one second through Pierre's mind. "Sharpshooters of the eighty-sixth, forward!" some one shouted. The fifth prisoner standing beside Pierre was led forward—alone. Pierre did not understand that he was saved; that he and all the rest had been brought here simply to be pres-ent at the execution. With growing horror, with no sense of joy or relief, he gazed at what was being done. The fifth was the factory lad in the loose gown. As soon as they touched him, he darted away in terror and clutched at Pierre (Pierre shuddered and tore himself away from him). The factory lad could not walk. He was held up under the arms and dragged along, and he screamed something all the while. When they had brought him to the post he was suddenly quiet. He seemed suddenly to have grasped something. Whether he grasped that it was no use to scream, or that it was impossible for men to kill him, he stood at the post, waiting to be bound like the others, and like a wild beast under fire looked about him with glittering eyes.

Pierre could not make himself turn away and close his eyes. The curiosity and emotion he felt, and all the crowd with him, at this fifth murder reached its highest pitch. Like the rest, this fifth man seemed calm. He wrapped his dressing-gown round him, and scratched one bare foot with the other.

When they bound up his eyes, of himself he straightened the knot, which hurt the back of his head; then, when they propped him against the blood-stained post, he staggered back, and as he was uncomfortable in that position, he shifted his attitude, and leaned back quietly, with his feet put down symmetrically. Pierre never took his eyes off him, and did not miss the slightest movement he made.

The word of command must have sounded, and after it the shots of the eight muskets. But Pierre, however earnestly he tried to recollect it afterwards, had not heard the slightest sound from the shots. He only saw the factory lad suddenly fall back on the cords, saw blood oozing in two places, and saw the cords themselves work loose from the weight of the hanging body, and the factory lad sit down, his head falling unnaturally, and one leg bent under him. Pierre ran up to the post. No one hindered him. Men with pale and frightened faces were doing something round the factory lad. There was one old whiskered Frenchman, whose lower jaw twitched all the while as he untied the cords. The body sank down. The soldiers, with clumsy haste, dragged it from the post and shoved it into the pit.

All of them clearly knew, beyond all doubt, that they were criminals, who must make haste to hide the traces of their crime.

Pierre glanced into the pit and saw that the factory lad was lying there with his knees up close to his head, and one shoulder higher than the other. And that shoulder was convulsively, rhythmically rising and falling. But spadefuls of earth were already falling all over the body. One of the soldiers, in a voice of rage, exasperation, and pain, shouted to Pierre to stand aside. But Pierre did not understand him, and still stood at the post, and no one drove him away.

When the pit was quite filled up, the word of command was heard, Pierre was taken back to his place, and the French troops, standing in ranks on both sides of the post, faced about, and began marching with a measured step past the post. The twenty-four sharpshooters, standing in the middle of the circle, with uncharged muskets, ran back to their places as their companies marched by them.

Pierre stared now with dazed eyes at these sharpshooters, who were running two together out of the circle. All of them had joined their companies except one. A young soldier, with a face of deathly pallor, still stood facing the pit on the spot upon which he had shot, his shako falling backwards off his head, and his fuse dropping on to the ground. He staggered like a drunken man, taking a few steps forward, and then a few back, to keep himself from falling. An old under-officer ran out of the ranks, and, seizing the young soldier by the shoulder, dragged him to his company. The crowd of Frenchmen and Russians began to disperse. All walked in silence, with downcast eyes.

"That will teach them to set fire to the places," said some one among the French. Pierre looked round at the speaker, and saw that it was a soldier who was trying to console himself somehow for what had been done, but could not. Without finishing his sentence, he waved his hand and went on.

XII

AFTER the execution Pierre was separated from the other prisoners and left alone in a small, despoiled, and filthy church.

Towards evening a patrol sergeant, with two soldiers, came into the church and informed Pierre that he was pardoned, and was now going to the barracks of the prisoners of war. Without understanding a word of what was said to him, Pierre got up and went with the soldiers. He was conducted to some sheds that had been rigged up in the upper part of the meadow out of charred boards, beams, and battens, and was taken into one of them. Some twenty persons of various kinds thronged round Pierre. He stared at them, with no idea of what these men were, why they were here, and what they wanted of him. He heard the words they said to him, but his mind made no kind of deduction or interpretation of them; he had no idea of their meaning. He made some answer, too, to the questions asked him, but without any notion who was hearing him, or how they would understand his replies. He gazed at faces and figures, and all seemed to him equally meaningless.

From the moment when Pierre saw that fearful murder committed by men who did not want to do it, it seemed as though the spring in his soul, by which everything was held together and given the semblance of life, had been wrenched out, and all seemed to have collapsed into a heap of meaningless refuse. Though he had no clear apprehension of it, it had annihilated in his soul all faith in the beneficent ordering of the universe, and in the soul of men, and in his own soul, and in God. This state of mind Pierre had experienced before, but never with such intensity as now. When such doubts had come upon him in the past they had arisen from his own fault. And at the very bottom of his heart Pierre had been aware then that salvation from that despair and from these doubts lay in his own hands. But now he felt that it was not his fault that the world was collapsing before his eyes, and that nothing was left but meaningless ruins. He felt that to get back to faith in life was not in his power.

Around him in the darkness stood men. Probably they found something very entertaining in him. They were telling him something, asking him something, then leading him somewhere, and at last he found himself in a corner of the shed beside men of some sort, who were talking on all sides, and laughing.

"And so, mates . . . that same prince who" (with a special emphasis on the last word) . . . some voice was saying in the opposite corner of the shed.

Sitting in the straw against the wall, mute and motionless, Pierre opened, and then closed, his eyes. As soon as he shut his eyes he saw the fearful face of the factory lad, fearful especially from its simplicity, and the faces of the involuntary murderers, still more fearful in their uneasiness. And he opened his eyes again and stared blankly about him in the darkness.

Close by him a little man was sitting bent up, of whose presence Pierre was first aware from the strong smell of sweat that rose at every movement he made. This man was doing something with his feet in the darkness, and although Pierre did not see his face, he was aware that he was continually glancing at him. Peering intently at him in the dark, Pierre made out that the man was undoing his foot-gear. And the way he was doing it began to interest Pierre.

Undoing the strings in which one foot was tied up, he wound them neatly off, and at once set to work on the other leg, glancing at Pierre. While one hand hung up the first leg-binder, the other was already beginning to untie the other leg. In this way, deftly, with rounded, effective movements following one another without delay, the man unrolled his leg-wrappers and hung them up on pegs driven in over-head, took out a knife, cut off something, shut the knife up, put it under his bolster, and settling himself more at his ease, clasped his arms round his knees, and stared straight at Pierre. Pierre was conscious of something pleasant, soothing, and rounded off in those deft movements, in his comfortable establishment of his belongings in the corner, and even in the very smell of the man, and he did not take his eyes off him.

"And have you seen a lot of trouble, sir? Eh?" said the little man suddenly. And there was a tone of such friendliness and simplicity in the sing-song voice that Pierre wanted to answer, but his jaw quivered, and he felt the tears rising. At the same second, leaving no time for Pierre's embarrassment to appear, the little man said, in the same pleasant voice:

"Ay, darling, don't grieve," he said, in that tender, caressing sing-song in which old Russian peasant women talk. "Don't grieve, dearie; trouble lasts an hour, but life lasts for ever! Ay, ay, my dear. And we get on here finely, thank God; nothing to vex us. They're men, too, and bad and good among them," he said; and, while still speaking, got with a supple movement on his knees to his feet, and clearing his throat walked away.

"Hey, the hussy, here she is!" Pierre heard at the end of the shed the same caressing voice. "Here she is, the hussy; she remembers me! There, there, lie down!" And the soldier, pushing down a dog that was jumping up on him, came back to his place and sat down. In his hands he had something wrapped up in a cloth.

"Here, you taste this, sir," he said, returning to the respectful tone he had used at first, and untying and handing to Pierre several baked potatoes. "At dinner we had soup. But the potatoes are first rate!"

Pierre had eaten nothing the whole day, and the smell of the potatoes struck him as extraordinarily pleasant. He thanked the soldier and began eating.

"But why so, eh?" said the soldier smiling, and he took one of the potatoes. "You try them like this." He took out his clasp-knife again, cut the potato in his hand into two even halves, and sprinkled them with salt from the cloth, and offered them to Pierre.

"The potatoes are first-rate," he repeated. "You taste them like that."

It seemed to Pierre that he had never eaten anything so good.

"No, I am all right," said Pierre; "but why did they shoot those poor fellows? . . . The last was a lad of twenty."

"Tss . . . tss . . ." said the little man. "Sin, indeed, . . . sin . . ." he added quickly, just as though the words were already in his mouth and flew out of it by accident; he went on: "How was it, sir, you came to stay in Moscow like this?"

"I didn't think they would come so soon. I stayed by accident," said Pierre.

"But how did they take you, darling; from your home?"

"No, I went out to see the fire, and then they took me up and brought me to judgment as an incendiary."

"Where there's judgment, there there's falsehood," put in the little man.

"And have you been here long?" asked Pierre, as he munched the last potato.

"I? On Sunday they took me out of the hospital in Moscow."

"Who are you, a soldier?"

"We are soldiers of the Apsheron regiment. I was dying of fever. We were never told anything. There were twenty of us lying sick. And we had never a thought, never a guess of how it was."

"Well, and are you miserable here?" asked Pierre.

"Miserable, to be sure, darling. My name's Platon, surname Karataev," he added, evidently to make it easier for Pierre to address him. "In the regiment they called me 'the little hawk.' How can one help being sad, my dear? Moscow—she's the mother of cities. One must be sad to see it. Yes, the maggot gnaws the cabbage, but it dies before it's done; so the old folks used to say," he added quickly.

"What, what was that you said?" asked Pierre.

"I?" said Karataev. "I say it's not by our wit, but as God thinks fit," said he, supposing that he was repeating what he had said. And at once he went on: "Tell me, sir, and have you an estate from your fathers? And a house of your own? To be sure, your cup was overflowing! And a wife, too? And are your old parents living?" he asked, and though Pierre could not see him in the dark, he felt that the soldier's lips were puckered in a restrained smile of kindliness while he asked these questions. He was evidently disappointed that Pierre had no parents, especially that he had not a mother.

"Wife for good counsel, mother-in-law for kind welcome, but none dear as your own mother!" said he. "And have you children?" he went on to ask. Pierre's negative reply seemed to disappoint him again, and he added himself: "Oh well, you are young folks; please God, there will be. Only live in peace and concord."

"But it makes no difference now," Pierre could not help saying.

"Ah, my dear man," rejoined Platon, "the beggar's bag and the prison walls none can be sure of escaping." He settled himself more comfortably, and cleared his throat, evidently preparing himself for a long story. "So it was like this, dear friend, when I used to be living at home," he began, "we have a rich heritage, a great deal of land, the peasants were well off, and our house—something to thank God for, indeed. Father used to go out to reap with six of us. We got along finely. Something like peasants we were. It came to pass . . ." and Platon Karataev told a long story of how he had gone into another man's copse for wood, and had been caught by the keeper, how he had been flogged, tried, and sent for a soldier. "And do you know, darling," said he, his voice changing from the smile on his face, "we thought it was a misfortune, while it was all for our happiness. My brother would have had to go if it hadn't been for my fault. And my younger brother had five little ones; while I, look you, I left no one behind but my wife. I had a little girl, but God had taken her before I went for a soldier. I went home on leave, I must tell you. I find them all better off than ever. The yard full of beasts, the women folk at home, two brothers out earning wages. Only Mihailo, the youngest, at home. Father says all his children are alike; whichever finger's pricked, it hurts the same. And if they hadn't shaved Platon for a soldier, then Mihailo would have had to go. He called us all together—would you believe it—made us stand before the holy picture. 'Mihailo,' says he, 'come here, bend down to his feet; and you, women, bow down; and you, grandchildren. Do you understand?' says he. Yes, so you see, my dear. Fate acts with reason. And we are always passing judgment; that's not right, and this doesn't suit us. Our happiness, my dear, is like water in a drag-net; you drag, and it is all puffed up, but pull it out and there's nothing. Yes, that's it." And Platon moved to a fresh seat in the straw.

After a short pause, Platon got up.

"Well, I dare say, you are sleepy?" he said, and he began rapidly crossing himself, murmuring:

"Lord Jesus Christ, holy Saint Nikola, Frola and Lavra; Lord Jesus Christ, holy Saint Nikola, Frola and Lavra; Lord Jesus Christ—have mercy and save us!" he concluded, bowed down to the ground, got up, sighed, and sat down on his straw. "That's right. Let me lie down like a stone, O God, and rise up like new bread!" he murmured, and lay down, pulling his military coat over him.

"What prayer was that you recited?" asked Pierre.

"Eh?" said Platon (he was already half asleep). "Recited? I prayed to God. Don't you pray, too?"

"Yes, I do," said Pierre. "But what was it you said—Frola and Lavra?"

"Eh, to be sure," Platon answered quickly. "They're the horses' saints. One must think of the poor beasts, too," he said. "Why, the little hussy, she's curled up. You're warm, child of a bitch!" he said, feeling the dog at his feet; and, turning over again, he fell asleep at once.

Outside shouting and wailing could be heard somewhere far away, and through the cracks in the walls could be seen the glow of fire; but within the shed all was dark and hushed. For a long while Pierre did not sleep, and lay with open eyes in the darkness, listening to Platon snoring rhythmically as he lay beside him, and he felt that the world that had been shattered was rising up now in his soul, in new beauty, and on new foundations that could not be shaken.

XIII

In this shed, where Pierre spent four weeks, there were twenty-three soldiers, three officers, and two civilian functionaries, all prisoners.

They were all misty figures to Pierre afterwards, but Platon Karataev remained for ever in his mind the strongest and most precious memory, and the personification of everything Russian, kindly, and round. When next day at dawn Pierre saw his neighbour, his first impression of something round was fully confirmed; Platon's whole figure in his French military coat, girt round the waist with cord, in his forage-cap and bast shoes, was roundish, his head was perfectly round, his back, his chest, his shoulders, even his arms, which he always held as though he were about to embrace something, were round in their lines; his friendly smile and big, soft, brown eyes, too, were round.

Platon Karataev must have been over fifty to judge by his stories of the campaigns in which he had taken part. He did not himself know and could not determine how old he was. But his strong, dazzlingly white teeth showed in two unbroken semicircles whenever he laughed, as he often did, and all were good and sound: there was not a grey hair in his beard or on his head, and his whole frame had a look of suppleness and of unusual hardiness and endurance.

His face had an expression of innocence and youth in spite of the curving wrinkles on it; his voice had a pleasant sing-song note. But the great peculiarity of his talk was its spontaneity and readiness. It was evident that he never thought of what he was saying, or of what he was going to say; and that gave a peculiar, irresistible persuasiveness to his rapid and genuine intonations.

His physical powers and activity were such, during the first period of his imprisonment, that he seemed not to know what fatigue or sickness meant. Every evening as he lay down to sleep, he said: "Let me lie down, Lord, like a stone; let me rise up like new bread"; and every morning on getting up, he would shake his shoulder in the same way, saying: "Lie down and curl up, get up and shake yourself." And he had, in fact, only to lie down in order to sleep at once like a stone, and he had but to shake himself to be ready at once, on waking, without a second's delay, to set to work of some sort; just as children, on waking, begin at once playing with their toys. He knew how to do everything, not particularly well, but not badly either. He baked, and cooked, and sewed, and planed, and cobbled boots. He was always busy, and only in the evenings allowed himself to indulge in conversation, which he loved, and singing. He sang songs, not as singers do, who know they are listened to, but sang, as the birds sing, obviously, because it was necessary to him to utter those sounds, as it sometimes is to stretch or to walk about; and those sounds were always thin, tender, almost feminine, melancholy notes, and his face as he uttered them was very serious.

Being in prison, and having let his beard grow, he had apparently cast off all the soldier's ways that had been forced upon him and were not natural to him, and had unconsciously relapsed into his old peasant habits.

"A soldier discharged is the shirt outside the breeches again," he used to say. He did not care to talk of his life as a soldier, though he never complained, and often repeated that he had never once been beaten since he had been in the service. When he told stories, it was always by preference of his old and evidently precious memories of his life as a "Christian," as he pronounced the word "krestyan," or peasant. The proverbial sayings, of which his talk was full, were not the bold, and mostly indecent, sayings common among soldiers, but those peasant saws, which seem of so little meaning looked at separately, and gain all at once a significance of profound wisdom when uttered appropriately.

Often he would say something directly contrary to what he had said before, but both sayings were equally true. He liked talking, and talked well, adorning his speech with caressing epithets and proverbial sayings, which Pierre fancied he often invented himself. But the great charm of his talk was that the simplest incidents—sometimes the same that Pierre had himself seen without noticing them—in his account of them gained a character of seemliness and solemn significance. He liked to listen to the fairy tales which one soldier used to tell—always the same ones over and over again—in the evenings, but most of all he liked to listen to stories of real life. He smiled gleefully as he listened to such stories, putting in words and asking questions, all aiming at bringing out clearly the moral beauty of the action of which he was told. Attachments, friendships, love, as Pierre understood them, Karataev had none; but he loved and lived on affectionate terms with every creature with whom he was thrown in life, and especially so with man—not with any particular man, but with the men who happened to be before his eyes. He loved his dog, loved his comrades, loved the French, loved Pierre, who was his neighbour. But Pierre felt that in spite of Karataev's affectionate tenderness to him (in which he involuntarily paid tribute to Pierre's spiritual life), he would not suffer a moment's grief at parting from him. And Pierre began to have the same feeling towards Karataev.

To all the other soldiers Platon Karataev was the most ordinary soldier; they called him "little hawk," or Platosha; made good-humoured jibes at his expense, sent him to fetch things. But to Pierre, such as he appeared on that first night—an unfathomable, rounded-off, and ever-lasting personification of the spirit of simplicity and truth—so he remained to him for ever.

Platon Karataev knew nothing by heart except his prayers. When he talked, he did not know on beginning a sentence how he was going to end it.

When Pierre, struck sometimes by the force of his remarks, asked him to repeat what he had said, Platon could never recall what he had said the minute before, just as he could never repeat to Pierre the words of his favourite song. There came in, "My own little birch-tree," and "My heart is sick," but there was no meaning in the words. He did not understand, and could not grasp the significance of words taken apart from the sentence. Every word and every action of his was the expression of a force uncomprehended by him, which was his life. But his life, as he looked at it, had no meaning as a separate life. It had meaning only as a part of a whole, of which he was at all times conscious. His words and actions flowed from him as smoothly, as inevitably, and as spontaneously, as the perfume rises from the flower. He could not understand any value or significance in an act or a word taken separately.

XIV

On hearing from Nikolay that her brother was at Yaroslavl with the Rostovs, Princess Marya, in spite of her aunt's efforts to dissuade her, prepared at once to go to him and to go not alone, but with her nephew; whether this were difficult or not, whether it were possible or not, she did not inquire, and did not care to know: it was her duty not only to be herself at the side of her—perhaps dying—brother, but to do everything possible to take his son to him, and she prepared to set off. If Prince Andrey had not himself communicated with her, Princess Marya put that down either to his being too weak to write, or to his considering the long journey too difficult and dangerous for her and his son.

Within a few days Princess Marya was ready for the journey. Her equipage consisted of her immense travelling coach in which she had come to Voronezh, and a covered trap and a waggon. She was accompanied by Mademoiselle Bourienne, Nikolushka, with his tutor, the old nurse, three maids, Tihon, a young valet, and a courier, whom her aunt was sending with her.

To travel by the usual route to Moscow was not to be thought of, and the circuitous route which Princess Marya was obliged to take by Lipetsk, Ryazan, Vladimir, and Shuya was very long; from lack of posting horses difficult; and in the neighbourhood of Ryazan, where they were told the French had begun to appear, positively dangerous.

During this difficult journey, Mademoiselle Bourienne, Dessalle, and Princess Marya's servants were astonished at the tenacity of her will and her energy. She was the last to go to rest, the first to rise, and no difficulty could daunt her. Thanks to her activity and energy, which infected her companions, she was towards the end of the second week close upon Yaroslavl.

The latter part of her stay in Voronezh had been the happiest period in Princess Marya's life. Her love for Rostov was not then a source of torment or agitation to her. That love had by then filled her whole soul and become an inseparable part of herself, and she no longer struggled against it. Of late Princess Marya was convinced—though she never clearly in so many words admitted it to herself—that she loved and was beloved. She had been convinced of this by her last interview with Nikolay when he came to tell her that her brother was with the Rostovs. Nikolay did not by one word hint at the possibility now (in case of Prince Andrey's recovery) of his engagement to Natasha being renewed, but Princess Marya saw by his face that he knew and thought of it. And in spite of that, his attitude to her—solicitous, tender, and loving—was so far from being changed, that he seemed overjoyed indeed that now a sort of kinship between him and Princess Marya allowed him to give freer expression to his loving friendship, as Princess Marya sometimes thought it. Princess Marya knew that she loved for the first and last time in her life, and felt that she was loved, and she was happy and at peace in that relation.

But this happiness on one side of her spiritual nature was far from hindering her from feeling intense grief on her brother's account. On the contrary, her spiritual peace on that side enabled her to give herself more completely to her feeling for her brother. This feeling was so strong at the moment of setting out from Voronezh that all her retinue were persuaded, looking at her careworn, despairing face, that she would certainly fall ill on the journey. But the very difficulties and anxieties of the journey, which Princess Marya tackled with such energy, saved her for the time from her sorrow and gave her strength.

As is always the case on a journey, Princess Marya thought of nothing but the journey itself, forgetting what was its object. But on approaching Yaroslavl, when what might await her—and not now at the end of many days, but that very evening—became clear to her mind again, her agitation reached its utmost limits.

When the courier, whom she had sent on ahead to find out in Yaroslavl where the Rostovs were staying, and in what condition Prince Andrey was, met the great travelling coach at the city gate he was frightened at the terribly pale face that looked out at him from the window.

"I have found out everything, your excellency: the Rostovs are staying in the square, in the house of a merchant, Bronnikov. Not far off, right above the Volga," said the courier.

Princess Marya looked into his face with frightened inquiry, not understanding why he did not answer her chief question. How was her brother? Mademoiselle Bourienne put this question for the princess.

"How is the prince?" she asked.

"His excellency is staying in the same house with them."

"He is living, then," thought the princess; and she softly asked "How is he?"

"The servants say, 'No change.' "

What was meant by "no change" the princess did not inquire, and with a passing, hardly perceptible, glance at little seven-year-old Nikolushka, sitting before her, delighted at the sight of the town, she bowed her head, and did not raise it again till the heavy carriage—rumbling, jolting, and swaying from side to side—came to a standstill. The carriage-steps were let down with a crash.

The carriage-door was opened. On the left was water—a broad river; on the right, entrance steps. At the entrance were people, servants, and a rosy-faced girl with a thick coil of black hair, who smiled at her in an unpleasantly affected way, as it seemed to Princess Marya (it was Sonya). The princess ran up the steps; the girl, smiling affectedly, said, "This way! this way!" and the princess found herself in the vestibule, facing an elderly woman of an Oriental type of face, who came rapidly to meet her, looking moved. It was the countess. She embraced Princess Marya and proceeded to kiss her.

"My child," she said, "I love you, and have known you a long while."

In spite of her emotion, Princess Marya knew it was the countess, and that she must say something to her. Not knowing how she did it, she uttered some polite French phrases in the tone in which she had been addressed, and asked, "How is he?"

"The doctor says there is no danger," said the countess; but as she said it she sighed, and turned her eyes upwards, and this gesture contra-dicted her words.

"Where is he? Can I see him; can I?" asked the princess.

"In a minute; in a minute, my dear. Is this his son?" she said, turning to Nikolushka, who came in with Dessalle. "We shall find room for every one; the house is large. Oh, what a charming boy!"

The countess led the princess into the drawing-room. Sonya began to converse with Mademoiselle Bourienne. The countess caressed the child. The old count came into the room to welcome the princess. He was extraordinarily changed since Princess Marya had seen him last. Then he had been a jaunty, gay, self-confident old gentleman, now he seemed a pitiful, bewildered creature. As he talked to the princess, he was continually looking about him, as though asking every one if he were doing the right thing. After the destruction of Moscow and the loss of his property, driven out of his accustomed rut, he had visibly lost the sense of his own importance, and felt that there was no place for him in life.

In spite of her one desire to see her brother without loss of time, and her vexation that at that moment, when all she wanted was to see him, they should entertain her conventionally with praises of her nephew, the princess observed all that was passing around her, and felt it inevitable for the time to fall in with the new order of things into which she had entered. She knew that all this was inevitable, and it was hard for her, but she felt no grudge against them for it.

"This is my niece," said the countess, presenting Sonya; "you do not know her, princess?"

Princess Marya turned to her, and trying to smother the feeling of hostility that rose up within her at the sight of this girl, she kissed her. But she felt painfully how out of keeping was the mood of every one around her with what was filling her own breast.

"Where is he?" she asked once more, addressing them all.

"He is downstairs; Natasha is with him," answered Sonya, flushing. "We have sent to ask. You are tired, I expect, princess?"

Tears of vexation came into Princess Marya's eyes. She turned away and was about to ask the countess again where she could see him, when she heard at the door light, eager steps that sounded to her full of gaiety. She looked round and saw, almost running in, Natasha—that Natasha whom she had so disliked when they met long before in Moscow.

But Princess Marya had hardly glanced at Natasha's face before she understood that here was one who sincerely shared her grief, and was therefore her friend. She flew to meet her, and embracing her, burst into tears on her shoulder.

As soon as Natasha, sitting by Prince Andrey's bedside, heard of Princess Marya's arrival, she went softly out of the room with those swift steps that to Princess Marya sounded so light-hearted, and ran to see her.

As she ran into the room, her agitated face wore one expression—an expression of love, of boundless love for him, for her, for all that was near to the man she loved—an expression of pity, of suffering for others, and of passionate desire to give herself up entirely to helping them. It was clear that at that moment there was not one thought of self, of her own relation to him, in Natasha's heart.

Princess Marya with her delicate intuition saw all that in the first glance at Natasha's face, and with mournful relief wept on her shoulder.

"Come, let us go to him, Marie," said Natasha, drawing her away into the next room.

Princess Marya lifted up her head, dried her eyes, and turned to Natasha. She felt that from her she would learn all, would understand all. "How . . ." she was beginning, but stopped short. She felt that no question nor answer could be put into words. Natasha's face and eyes would be sure to tell her all more clearly and more profoundly.

Natasha looked at her, but seemed to be in dread and in doubt whether to say or not to say all she knew; she seemed to feel that before those luminous eyes, piercing to the very bottom of her heart, it was impossible not to tell the whole, whole truth as she saw it. Natasha's lip suddenly twitched, ugly creases came round her mouth, and she broke into sobs, hiding her face in her hands.

Princess Marya knew everything.

But still she could not give up hope, and asked in words, though she put no faith in them:

"But how is his wound? What is his condition altogether?"

"You . . . you will see that," was all Natasha could say.

They sat a little while below, near his room, to control their tears and go in to him with calm faces.

"How has the whole illness gone? Has he been worse for long? When did *this* happen?" Princess Marya asked.

Natasha told her that at first there had been danger from inflammation and the great pain, but that that had passed away at Troitsa, and the doctor had only been afraid of one thing—gangrene. But the risk of that, too, was almost over. When they reached Yaroslavl, the wound had begun to suppurate (Natasha knew all about suppuration and all the rest of it), and the doctor had said that the suppuration might follow the regular course. Fever had set in. The doctor had said this fever was not so serious. "But two days ago," Natasha began, "all of a sudden *this* change came . . ." She struggled with her sobs. "I don't know why, but you will see the change in him."

"He is weaker? thinner? . . ." queried the princess.

"No, not that, but worse. You will see. O Marie, he is too good, he cannot, he cannot live, because . . ."

XV

WHEN Natasha opened the door with her practised hands, letting her pass in before her, Princess Marya felt the sobs rising in her throat. However much she prepared herself, however much she tried to compose herself, she knew that she would not be able to see him without tears.

She understood what Natasha had meant by the words: *two days ago this change came.* She interpreted it as meaning that he had suddenly grown softer, and that that softening, that tenderness, was the sign of death. As she approached the door, she saw already in her imagination that face of the little Andryusha, as she had known it in childhood, tender, gentle, softened, as it was so rarely, and as it affected her so strongly. She felt sure he would say soft, tender words to her like those her father had uttered on his deathbed, and that she would not be able to bear it, and would break into sobs at them. But sooner or later, it must be, and she went into the room. Her sobs seemed rising higher and higher in her throat as with her short-sighted eyes she distinguished his figure more and more clearly, and now she saw his face and met his eyes.

He was lying on a couch, propped up with cushions, in a squirrel-lined dressing-gown. He was thin and pale. One thin, transparently white hand held a handkerchief, with the other he was softly fingering the delicate moustache that had grown long. His eyes gazed at them as they came in.

On seeing his face and meeting his eyes, Princess Marya at once slackened the rapidity of her step and felt the tears dried up and the sobs checked. As she caught the expression of his face and eyes, she felt suddenly shy and guilty.

"But how am I in fault?" she asked herself. "In being alive and

thinking of the living while I! . . ." his cold, stern eyes seemed to an·
swer.

In the profound, not outward- but inward-looking gaze there was
something almost like hostility as he deliberately scanned his sister and
Natasha. He kissed his sister's hand, while she kissed his, as their
habit was.

"How are you, Marie; how did you manage to get here?" he said, in a
voice as even and as aloof as the look in his eyes. If he had uttered a
shriek of despair, that shriek would have been to Princess Marya less
awful than the sound of his voice.

"And you have brought Nikolushka?" he said, as evenly and deliberately, with an evident effort to recollect things.

"How are you now?" said Princess Marya, wondering herself at what
she was saying.

"That, my dear, you must ask the doctor," he said, and evidently
making another effort to be affectionate, he said with his lips only (it
was obvious he was not thinking of what he was saying):

"Thank you, my dear, for coming."

Princess Marya pressed his hand. He gave a hardly perceptible frown
at the pressure of her hand. She was silent, and she did not know what
to say. She understood the change that had come over him two days ago.
In his words, in his tone, above all in his eyes—those cold, almost antagonistic eyes—could be felt that aloofness from all things earthly that
is so fearful to a living man. It was evidently with difficulty that he understood anything living; but yet it seemed that he did not understand
what was living, not because he had lost the power of understanding,
but because he understood something else that the living did not and
could not understand, and that entirely absorbed him.

"Yes, see how strangely fate has brought us together again," he said,
breaking the silence, and pointing to Natasha. "She is nursing me."

Princess Marya heard him, and could not understand what he was
saying. He, Prince Andrey, with his delicate, tender intuition, how could
he say that before the girl whom he loved, and who loved him! If he
had any thought of living, he could not have said that in that slightingly cold tone. If he had not known he was going to die, how could he
have failed to feel for her, how could he speak like that before her!
There could be but one explanation of it—that was, that it was all of
no moment to him now, and of no moment because something else, more
important, had been revealed to him.

The conversation was frigid and disconnected, and broke off at every
moment.

"Marie came by Ryazan," said Natasha.

Prince Andrey did not notice that she called his sister Marie. And
Natasha, calling her by that name before him, for the first time became
aware of it herself.

"Well?" said he.

"She was told that Moscow had been burnt to the ground, all of it,
entirely. That it looks as though . . ."

Natasha stopped. It was impossible to talk. He was obviously making an effort to listen, and yet he could not.

"Yes; it's burnt, they say," he said. "That's a great pity," and he gazed straight before him, his fingers straying heedlessly about his moustache.

"And so you met Count Nikolay, Marie?" said Prince Andrey, suddenly, evidently trying to say something to please them. "He wrote here what a great liking he took to you," he went on, simply and calmly, plainly unable to grasp all the complex significance his words had for living people. "If you liked him, too, it would be a very good thing . . . for you to get married," he added, rather more quickly, apparently pleased at finding at last the words he had been seeking. Princess Marya heard his words, but they had no significance for her except as showing how terribly far away he was now from everything living.

"Why talk of me?" she said calmly, and glanced at Natasha. Natasha, feeling her eyes on her, did not look at her. Again all of them were silent.

"Andrey, would you . . ." Princess Marya said suddenly in a shaky voice, "would you like to see Nikolushka? He is always talking of you."

For the first time Prince Andrey smiled a faintly perceptible smile, but Princess Marya, who knew his face so well, saw with horror that it was a smile not of joy, not of tenderness for his son, but of quiet, gentle irony at his sister's trying what she believed to be the last resource for rousing him to feeling.

"Yes, I shall be very glad to see Nikolushka. Is he quite well?"

When they brought in little Nikolushka, who gazed in dismay at his father, but did not cry, because nobody else was crying, Prince Andrey kissed him, and obviously did not know what to say to him.

When they had taken the child away, Princess Marya went up to her brother once more, kissed him, and unable to control herself any longer, began to weep.

He looked at her intently.

"You weep for Nikolushka?" he asked.

Princess Marya nodded through her tears.

"Marie, you know the Gos . . ." he began, but suddenly paused.

"What do you say?"

"Nothing. You mustn't weep here," he said, looking at her with the same cold eyes.

When Princess Marya wept he knew that she was weeping that Nikolushka would be left without a father. With a great effort he tried to come back again to life, and to put himself at their point of view.

"Yes, it must seem sad to them," he thought. "But how simple it is!"

" 'They sow not, neither do they reap, but your Father feedeth them,' " he said to himself, and he wanted to say it to his sister. But no, they would understand it in their own way; they would not understand! What they cannot understand is that these feelings that they set store

by—all our feelings, all these thoughts, which seem of so much importance to us—that they are all not wanted! We cannot understand each
other!" and he was silent.

Prince Andrey's little son was seven years old. He could hardly read
—he knew nothing. He passed through much after that day, gaining
knowledge, observation, experience. But if he had possessed at that time
all the mental faculties he acquired afterwards, he could not have had a
truer, a deeper comprehension of all the significance of the scene he saw
passing between his father, Princess Marya, and Natasha than he had
now. He understood it all, and without weeping, went out of the room,
in silence went up to Natasha, who had followed him out; glanced shyly
at her with his beautiful, dreamy eyes: his uplifted, rosy upper lip quivered; he leaned his head against her, and burst into tears.

From that day he avoided Dessalle, avoided the countess, who would
have petted him, and either sat alone, or shyly joined Princess Marya
and Natasha, whom he seemed to love even more than his aunt, and bestowed shy and gentle caresses upon them.

When Princess Marya left her brother's side, she fully understood all
that Natasha's face had told her. She spoke no more to Natasha of hope
of saving his life. She took turns with her by his bedside, and she shed
no more tears, but prayed without ceasing, turning in spirit to the Eternal and Unfathomable whose presence was palpable now, hovering over
the dying man.

XVI

Prince Andrey did not only know that he would die, but felt indeed
that he was dying; that he was already half-dead. He experienced a
sense of aloofness from everything earthly, and a strange and joyous
lightness in his being. Neither impatient, nor troubled, he lay awaiting
what was before him. . . . The menacing, the eternal, the unknown,
and remote, the presence of which he had never ceased to feel during
the whole course of his life, was now close to him, and—from that
strange lightness of being, that he experienced—almost comprehensible
and palpable.

In the past he had dreaded the end. Twice he had experienced that
terribly agonising feeling of the dread of death, of the end, and now he
had ceased to understand it.

The first time he had experienced that feeling when the grenade was
rotating before him, and he looked at the stubble, at the bushes, at the
sky, and knew that death was facing him. When he had come to himself
after his wound, and instantly, as though set free from the cramping
bondage of life, there had sprung up in his soul that flower of love, eternal, free, not dependent on this life, he had no more fear, and no more
thought, of death.

In those hours of solitary suffering and half-delirium that he spent afterwards, the more he passed in thought into that new element of eternal love, revealed to him, the further he unconsciously travelled from earthly life. To love everything, every one, to sacrifice self always for love, meant to love no one, meant not to live this earthly life. And the further he penetrated into that element of love, the more he renounced life, and the more completely he annihilated that fearful barrier that love sets up between life and death. Whenever, during that first period, he remembered that he had to die, he said to himself: "Well, so much the better."

But after that night at Mytishtchy, when in his half-delirium she, whom he had longed for, appeared before him, and when pressing her hand to his lips, he wept soft, happy tears, love for one woman stole unseen into his heart, and bound him again to life. And glad and disturbing thoughts began to come back to him. Recalling that moment at the ambulance station, when he had seen Kuragin, he could not now go back to his feeling then. He was fretted by the question whether he were alive. And he dared not ask.

His illness went through its regular physical course; but what Natasha had called "this change" had come upon him two days before Princess Marya's arrival. It was the last moral struggle between life and death, in which death gained the victory. It was the sudden consciousness that life, in the shape of his love for Natasha, was still precious to him, and the last and vanquished onslaught of terror before the unknown.

It happened in the evening. He was, as usually after dinner, in a slightly feverish condition, and his thoughts were particularly clear. Sonya was sitting at the table. He fell into a doze. He felt a sudden sense of happiness.

"Ah, she has come in!" he thought.

Natasha had, in fact, just come in with noiseless steps, and was sitting in Sonya's place.

Ever since she had been looking after him he had always felt this physical sense of her presence. She was in a low chair beside him, knitting a stocking, and sitting so as to screen the light of the candle from him. She had learned to knit since Prince Andrey had once said to her that no one made such a good sick-nurse as an old nurse who knitted stockings, and that there was something soothing about knitting. Her slender fingers moved the needles rapidly with a slight click, and the dreamy profile of her drooping head could be clearly seen by him. She made a slight movement; the ball rolled off her knee. She started, glanced round at him, and, screening the light with her hand, bent over with a cautious, supple, and precise movement, picked up the ball, and sat back in the same attitude as before.

He gazed at her without stirring, and saw that after her movements she wanted to draw a deep breath, but did not dare to, and breathed with careful self-restraint.

At the Troitsa monastery they had spoken of the past, and he had told her that if he were to live he should thank God for ever for his wound, which had brought them together again; but since then they had never spoken of the future.

"Could it be, or could it not?" he was wondering now as he watched her and listened to the slight steel click of the needles. "Can fate have brought us together so strangely only for me to die? . . . Can the truth of life have been revealed to me only for me to have spent my life in falsity? I love her more than anything in the world! But what am I to do if I love her?" he said, and suddenly he unconsciously moaned from the habit he had fallen into in the course of his sufferings.

Hearing the sound, Natasha laid down her stocking, and bent down closer to him, and suddenly noticing his shining eyes, went up to him with a light step and stooped down.

"You are not asleep?"

"No; I have been looking at you for a long while. I felt when you came in. No one but you gives me the same soft peace . . . the same light. I want to weep with gladness!"

Natasha moved closer to him. Her face beamed with rapturous delight.

"Natasha, I love you too much! More than everything in the world!"

"And I?" She turned away for a second. "Why too much?" she said.

"Why too much? . . . Well, what do you think, what do you feel in your heart, your whole heart, am I going to live? What do you think?"

"I am sure of it; sure of it!" Natasha almost cried out, taking both his hands with a passionate gesture.

He was silent for a while.

"How good it would be!" And taking her hand, he kissed it.

Natasha was happy and deeply stirred; and she recollected at once that this must not be, and that he must have quiet.

"But you are not asleep," she said, subduing her joy. "Try and sleep . . . please do."

He pressed her hand and let it go, and she moved back to the candle, and sat down in the same position as before. Twice she glanced round at him; his eyes were bright as she met them. She set herself a task on her stocking, and told herself she would not look round till she had finished it.

He did, in fact, soon after shut his eyes and fall asleep. He did not sleep long, and woke up suddenly in a cold sweat of alarm.

As he fell asleep he was still thinking of what he had been thinking about all the time—of life and of death. And most of death. He felt he was closer to it.

"Love? What is love?" he thought.

"Love hinders death. Love is life. All, all that I understand, I understand only because I love. All is, all exists only because I love. All is bound up in love alone. Love is God, and dying means for me a particle of love, to go back to the universal and eternal source of love." These thoughts seemed to him comforting. But they were only thoughts. Something was wanting in them; there was something one-sided and personal, something intellectual; they were not self-evident. And there was un-easiness, too, and obscurity. He fell asleep.

He dreamed that he was lying in the very room in which he was lying in reality, but that he was not ill, but quite well. Many people of various sorts, indifferent people of no importance, were present. He was talking and disputing with them about some trivial matter. They seemed to be preparing to set off somewhere. Prince Andrey had a dim feeling that all this was of no consequence, and that he had other matters of graver moment to think of, but still he went on uttering empty witticisms of some sort that surprised them. By degrees all these people began to disappear, and the one thing left was the question of closing the door. He got up and went towards the door to close it and bolt it. *Everything* depended on whether he were in time to shut it or not. He was going, he was hurrying, but his legs would not move, and he knew that he would not have time to shut the door, but still he was painfully straining every effort to do so. And an agonising terror came upon him. And that terror was the fear of death; behind the door stood *It*. But while he is helplessly and clumsily struggling towards the door, that something awful is already pressing against the other side of it, and forcing the door open. Something not human—death—is forcing the door open, and he must hold it to. He clutches at the door with a last straining effort—to shut it is impossible, at least to hold it—but his efforts are feeble and awkward; and, under the pressure of that awful thing, the door opens and shuts again.

Once more *It* was pressing on the door from without. His last, supernatural efforts are vain, and both leaves of the door are noiselessly opened. *It* comes in, and it is *death*. And Prince Andrey died.

But at the instant when in his dream he died, Prince Andrey recollected that he was asleep; and at the instant when he was dying, he made an effort and waked up.

"Yes, that was death. I died and I waked up. Yes, death is an awakening," flashed with sudden light into his soul, and the veil that had till then hidden the unknown was lifted before his spiritual vision. He felt, as it were, set free from some force that held him in bondage, and was aware of that strange lightness of being that had not left him since.

When he waked up in a cold sweat and moved on the couch, Natasha went up and asked him what was the matter. He did not answer, and looked at her with strange eyes, not understanding her.

That was the change that had come over him two days before Princess Marya's arrival. The doctor said that from that day the wasting fever had assumed a more serious aspect, but Natasha paid little heed to what the doctor said; she saw the terrible moral symptoms, that for her were far more convincing.

With his awakening from sleep that day there began for Prince Andrey an awakening from life. And in relation to the duration of life it seemed to him not more prolonged than the awakening from sleep in relation to the duration of a dream. There was nothing violent or terrible in this relatively slow awakening.

His last days and hours passed in a simple and commonplace way. Princess Marya and Natasha, who never left his side, both felt that. They did not weep nor shudder, and towards the last they both felt they were waiting not on him (he was no more; he had gone far away from them), but on the nearest memory of him—his body. The feelings of both of them were so strong that the external, horrible side of death did not affect them, and they did not find it needful to work up their grief. They did not weep either in his presence nor away from him, and they never even talked of him together. They felt that they could not express in words what they understood.

They both saw that he was slowly and quietly slipping further and further away from them, and both knew that this must be so, and that it was well. He received absolution and extreme unction; every one came to bid him good-bye. When his son was brought in to him, he pressed his lips to him and turned away, not because it was painful or sad to him (Princess Marya and Natasha saw that), but simply because he supposed he had done all that was required of him. But he was told to give him his blessing, he did what was required, and looked round as though to ask whether there was anything else he must do. When the body, deserted by the spirit, passed through its last struggles, Princess Marya and Natasha were there.

"It is over!" said Princess Marya, after the body had lain for some moments motionless, and growing cold before them. Natasha went close, glanced at the dead eyes, and made haste to shut them. She closed them, and did not kiss them, but hung over what was the nearest memory of him. "Where has he gone? Where is he now? . . ."

When the body lay, dressed and washed, in the coffin on the table, every one came to take leave of him, and every one cried. Nikolushka cried from the agonising bewilderment that was rending his heart. The countess and Sonya cried from pity for Natasha, and from grief that he was gone. The old count cried because he felt that he too must soon take the same terrible step.

Natasha and Princess Marya wept too now. But they did not weep for their personal sorrow; they wept from the emotion and awe that filled their souls before the simple and solemn mystery of death that had been accomplished before their eyes.

PART THIRTEEN

I

THE COMBINATION of causes of phenomena is beyond the grasp of the human intellect. But the impulse to seek causes is innate in the soul of man. And the human intellect, with no inkling of the immense variety and complexity of circumstances conditioning a phenomenon, any one of which may be separately conceived of as the cause of it, snatches at the first and most easily understood approximation, and says here is the cause. In historical events, where the actions of men form the subject of observation, the most primitive conception of a cause was the will of the gods, succeeded later on by the will of those men who stand in the historical foreground—the heroes of history. But one had but to look below the surface of any historical event, to look, that is, into the movement of the whole mass of men taking part in that event, to be convinced that the will of the hero of history, so far from controlling the actions of the multitude, is continually controlled by them. It may be thought that it is a matter of no importance whether historical events are interpreted in one way or in another. But between the man who says that the peoples of the West marched into the East, because Napoleon willed they should do so, and the man who says that that movement came to pass because it was bound to come to pass, there exists the same difference as between the men who maintained that the earth was stationary and the planets revolved about it, and the men who said that they did not know what holds the earth in its place, but they did know that there were laws controlling its motions and the motions of the other planets. Causes of historical events—there are not and cannot be, save the one cause of all causes. But there are laws controlling these events; laws partly unknown, partly accessible to us. The discovery of these laws is only possible when we entirely give up looking for a cause in the will of one man, just as the discovery of the laws of the motions of the planets has only become possible since men have given up the conception of the earth being stationary.

After the battle of Borodino, and the taking and burning of Moscow, historians consider the most important episode of the war of 1812 to be the movement of the Russian army from the Ryazan to the Kaluga road and to the Tarutino camp, the so-called oblique march behind Krasnaya Pahra. Historians ascribe the credit of this stroke of genius to various persons, and dispute to whom it is rightfully due. Even foreign, even French historians, admit the genius of the Russian generals when they mention this flank march. But why military writers, and others following their lead, assume this oblique movement to be a project profoundly planned by some one person for the deliverance of Russia and the over-throw of Napoleon it is very difficult to see. It is difficult in the first place to see wherein the profound wisdom and genius of this march lies; for no great intellectual effort is needed to guess that the best position for an army, when not being attacked, is where supplies are most plentiful. And every one, even a stupid boy of thirteen, could have guessed that the most advantageous position for the army in 1812, after the re-treat from Moscow, would be on the Kaluga road. And so one cannot understand, in the first place, what conclusions led the historians to see some deep wisdom in this manœuvre. Secondly, it is even more difficult to understand why the historians ascribe to this manœuvre the deliver-ance of Russia and the overthrow of the French; for, had other circum-stances preceded, accompanied, or followed it, this flank movement might as well have led to the destruction of the Russian army and the deliverance of the French. If the position of the Russian army did, in fact, begin to improve from the time of that march, it does not at all follow that the improvement was caused by it.

That oblique march might have been not simply of no use; it might have led to the destruction of the Russian army, but for the conjunction of other circumstances. What would have happened if Moscow had not been burnt? If Murat had not lost sight of the Russians? If Napoleon had not remained inactive? If, as Bennigsen and Barclay advised, the Russians had given battle near Krasnaya Pahra? What would have hap-pened if the French had attacked the Russians when they were march-ing behind Pahra? What would have happened if later on Napoleon, on reaching Tarutino, had attacked the Russians with one-tenth of the energy with which he had attacked them at Smolensk? What would have happened if the French had marched to Petersburg?. . . On any of these hypotheses, the oblique march might have led to ruin instead of to safety.

The third point, most difficult of all to understand, is that students of history seem intentionally to refuse to see that this march cannot be ascribed to any one man, that no one foresaw it at any time, that, like the retreat to Fili, the manœuvre was, in reality, never conceived of by any one in its entirety, but arose step by step, incident by incident, mo-ment by moment from a countless multitude of the most diverse cir-cumstances, and is only conceived of in its entirety, when it is an accom-plished fact, and has become the past.

At the council at Fili the accepted idea among the Russians—the course taken for granted in fact—was retreat in a direct line back, that is, along the Nizhni road. Evidence of this is that the majority of votes at the council were for adopting this course, and the commander-in-chief's famous conversation after the council with Lansky, the head of the commissariat department, is an even more striking proof of it. Lan-sky submitted to the commander-in-chief that the chief supplies for the army were stored along the Oka, in the Tula and Kazan provinces, and that if they retreated along the Nizhni road, the army would be cut off from its supplies by the broad river Oka, across which transport in the early winter was impossible. This was the first proof of the necessity of departing from the course that had at first seemed the most natural one, the retreat along the Nizhni road. The army kept more to the south along the Ryazan road, closer to its supplies. Later on the inactivity of the French, who positively lost sight of the Russian army, anxiety for the defence of the Tula arsenal, and above all, the advantage of being near their supplies led the army to turn even more to the south, to the Tula road. After crossing by a forced march behind Pahra to the Tula road, the generals of the Russian army intended to remain at Podolsk, and had no idea of the Tarutino position. But an infinite number of circumstances, among them the reappearance of French troops on the scene, and plans for giving battle, and most of all, the abundance of supplies in Kaluga, led our army to turn even more to the south, and to pass from the Tula to the Kaluga road to Tarutino, a central position between their lines of communication with their supplies. Just as it is impossible to answer the question at what date Moscow was abandoned, it is impossible too to say precisely when and by whom it was decided to move the army to Tarutino. It was only after the army, through the action of innumerable infinitesimally small forces, had been brought to Tarutino, that people began to protest to themselves that that was the course they had desired, and had long foreseen as the right one.

II

THE famous oblique movement consisted simply in this. The Russian troops, which had been retreating directly back from the French, as soon as the French attack ceased, turned off from that direction, and seeing they were not pursued, moved naturally in the direction where they were drawn by the abundance of supplies.

If we imagine, instead of generals of genius at the head of the Russian army, an army acting alone, without leadership of any kind, such an army could have done nothing else but move back again towards Moscow, describing a semicircle through the country that was best provided with necessaries, and where supplies were most plentiful.

So natural was this oblique movement from the Nizhni to the Ryazan, Tula, and Kaluga road, that that direction was the one taken by the flying bands of marauders from the Russian army, and the one which the authorities in Petersburg insisted upon Kutuzov's taking. At Tarutino Kutuzov received what was almost a reprimand from the Tsar for moving the army to the Ryazan road, and he was directed to take up the very position facing Kaluga, in which he was encamped at the time when the Tsar's letter reached him.

After recoiling in the direction of the shock received during the whole campaign, and at the battle of Borodino, the ball of the Russian army, as the force of that blow spent itself, and no new blow came, took the direction that was natural for it.

Kutuzov's merit lay in no sort of military genius, as it is called, in no strategic manœuvre, but in the fact that he alone grasped the significance of what had taken place. He alone grasped even then the significance of the inactivity of the French army; he alone persisted in maintaining that the battle of Borodino was a victory; he alone—the man who from his position as commander-in-chief might have been expected to be the first to be eager for battle—he alone did everything in his power to hold the Russian army back from useless fighting.

The wild beast wounded at Borodino lay where the fleeing hunter had left him; but whether alive and strong, or only feigning, the hunter knew not. All at once a moan was heard from the creature. The moan of that wounded creature, the French army, that betrayed its hopeless plight, was the despatch of Lauriston to the camp of Kutuzov with overtures for peace.

Napoleon, with his conviction that not what was right was right, but whatever came into his head was right, wrote to Kutuzov the first words that occurred to his mind, words that had no meaning at all.

"M. LE PRINCE KOUTOUZOFF," he wrote, "I am sending you one of my aides-de-camp to converse with you on various interesting subjects. I desire that your highness will put faith in what he says, especially when he expresses the sentiments of esteem and particular consideration that I have long entertained for your person. This letter having no other object, I pray God to have you in His holy and powerful keeping.

(Signed) NAPOLEON.

"Moscow, October 30, 1812."

"I should be cursed by posterity if I were regarded as the first instigator of any sort of settlement. *Tel est l'esprit actuel de ma nation,"* answered Kutuzov, and went on doing everything in his power to hold the army back from advance.

A month spent by the French army in pillaging Moscow, and by the Russian army quietly encamped at Tarutino, brought about a change in the relative strength of the two armies, a change both in spirit and in numbers, which was all to the advantage of the Russians. Although the position of the French army and its numbers were unknown to the Russians, as soon as their relative strength had changed, a great number of signs began to show that an attack would be inevitable. Among the causes that contributed to bring about this result were Lauriston's mission, and the abundance of provisions at Tarutino, and the reports that were continually coming in from all sides of the inactivity and lack of discipline in the French army, and the filling up of our regiments by recruits, and the fine weather, and the long rest enjoyed by the Russian soldiers, and the impatience to do the work for which they have been brought together, that always arises in troops after repose, and curiosity to know what was going on in the French army, of which they had so long seen nothing, and the daring with which the Russian outposts dashed in among the French encamped at Tarutino, and the news of the easy victories gained by bands of peasants and free-lances over the French, and the envy aroused by them, and the desire of revenge, that every man cherished at heart so long as the French were in Moscow; and—stronger than all—the vague sense growing up in every soldier's heart that the relative strength of the armies had changed, and the preponderance was now on our side. The relative strength of the armies had really changed, and advance had become inevitable. And at once, as surely as the chimes in a clock begin to beat and play when the hand has made the full round of the dial, was this change reflected in the increased activity, and bustle and stir of wheels within wheels in the higher spheres.

III

The Russian army was commanded by Kutuzov and his staff and by the Tsar from Petersburg. Before the news of the abandonment of Moscow had reached Petersburg a detailed plan of the whole campaign had been drawn up and sent to Kutuzov for his guidance. In spite of the fact that this plan had been made on the supposition that Moscow was still in our hands, it was approved by the staff, and accepted as the plan to be carried out. Kutuzov simply wrote that directions from a distance were always difficult to carry out. And to solve any difficulties that might arise, fresh instructions were sent, together with newer persons, whose duty it was to be to keep a watch on his movements, and to report upon them.

Apart from these new authorities, the whole staff of generals in the Russian army was now transferred. The places of Bagration, who had been killed, and Barclay, who had taken offence and retired, had to be filled. The question was deliberated with the greatest seriousness: whether A should be put in B's place, and B in the place of D, or whether, on the other hand, D in A's place, and so on, as though the matter affected anything whatever except the satisfaction of A and B and D.

In consequence of Kutuzov's hostility to the head officer of his staff, Bennigsen, and the presence of confidential advisers of the Tsar, and these various new appointments, the struggle of parties at headquarters was even more complicated than usual. A was trying to undermine B's position, D to undermine C's position, and so on, in all the possible combinations and permutations. In all these conflicting currents the object of intrigue was for the most part the management of the war, which all these men supposed they were controlling, though it did, in fact, follow its inevitable course quite apart from their action, a course that never corresponded with their schemes, but was the outcome of the forces interacting in the masses. All these schemes, thwarting and stultifying one another, were simply accepted in the higher spheres as the correct reflection of what was bound to come to pass.

"Prince Mihail Ilarionovitch!" the Tsar wrote on the 2nd of October, a letter received by Kutuzov after the battle of Tarutino. "From the 2nd of September Moscow has been in the hands of the enemy. Your last reports were dated the 20th; and in the course of all this time since, no attempt has been made to act against the enemy, and to relieve the ancient capital, and you have even, from your last reports, retreated further. Serpuhov is by now occupied by a detachment of the enemy, and Tula, with its famous arsenal, of such importance to the army, is in danger. From the reports received from General Wintzengerode, I see that a corps of the enemy, ten thousand strong, is marching along the Petersburg road. Another, numbering some thousands, is already close upon Dmitrov. A third is advancing along the Vladimir road. A fourth force of considerable strength is stationed between Ruza and Mozhaisk. Napoleon himself was in Moscow on the 25th. In face of these facts, with the enemy's forces split up into these detached bodies, and Napoleon himself with his guards in Moscow, is it possible that the enemy's forces confronting you are too strong to permit of your acting on the offensive? One may, with far more probability, assume that you are being pursued by detachments, or at most a corps by far inferior to the army under your command. It would seem that taking advantage of these circumstances, you might with advantage have attacked forces inferior in strength to your army, and have destroyed them, or at least have forced them to retreat, and have kept in our hands a considerable part of the province now occupied by the enemy, and thereby have averted all danger from Tula and the other towns of the interior. You will be responsible, if the enemy is able to send a considerable body of men to Petersburg, to menace that capital, in which it has been impossible to keep any great number of troops; for with the army under your command, acting with energy and decision, you have ample means at your disposal for averting such a calamity. Recollect that you have still to answer to your humiliated country for the loss of Moscow. You have had experience of my readiness to reward you. That readiness is no less now, but Russia and I have the right to expect from you all the energy, decision, and success, which your intellect, your military talents, and the valour of the troops under your command should guarantee us."

But while this letter, proving that the change in the relative strength of the armies was by now reflected in opinion at Petersburg, was on its road, Kutuzov had been unable to hold the army back, and a battle had already been fought.

On the 2nd of October, a Cossack Shapovalov, out scouting, shot one hare and wounded a second. Shapovalov was led on in pursuit of the game far into the forest, and came across the left flank of Murat's army, which was encamped and quite off guard. The Cossack told his comrades with laughter the tale of how he had all but fallen into the hands of the French. The ensign, who heard the story, repeated it to his superior officer. The Cossack was sent for and questioned. The officers of the Cossacks wanted to take advantage of this to carry off some horses from the French, but one of them, who was intimate with some of the higher authorities in the army, mentioned the incident to a general on the staff. On the staff the position of late had been strained to the utmost. A few days previously, Yermolov had gone to Bennigsen and besought him to use his influence with the commander-in-chief to bring about an attack.

"If I did not know you, I should suppose you did not desire that result. I have only to advise one course for his highness to be sure to adopt the opposite one," answered Bennigsen.

The news brought by the Cossack, confirmed by scouts, proved conclusively that the time was ripe. The strained string broke, and the wheels of the clock whirred, and the chimes began to strike. In spite of all his supposed power, his intellect, his experience, and his knowledge of men, Kutuzov, taking into consideration the note from Bennigsen, who was sending a personal report on the subject to the Tsar, the desire expressed by all the generals alike, the desire assumed by them to be the Tsar's wish, and the news brought by the Cossack, could hold back the inevitable movement no longer, and gave orders for what he regarded as useless and mischievous—gave his assent, in fact, to the accomplished fact.

IV

THE note submitted by Bennigsen, and the report sent in by the Cossacks of the enemy's left flank being unguarded, were simply the last straws that showed the inevitability of giving the signal for advance, and it was arranged to advance to attack on the 5th of October.

On the morning of the 4th, Kutuzov signed the disposition of the forces. Toll read it to Yermolov, proposing that he should superintend the further instructions for carrying it out.

"Very good, very good, I haven't time just now," said Yermolov, and he hurried out of the cottage. The arrangement of the troops as drawn up by Toll was an excellent one. The disposition had been written out, as at Austerlitz, though not in German:

"The First Column marches here and there, the Second Column occupies this place," and so on.

On paper all these columns were in their proper place at a fixed time and annihilated the enemy. Everything had been, as in all such cases, carefully thought of, and as in all such cases not a single column did reach its right place at the right time. When a sufficient number of copies of the disposition were ready, an officer was summoned and sent off to give them to Yermolov, that he might see that instructions were given in accordance with them. A young officer of the horseguards, in waiting on Kutuzov, set off for Yermolov's quarters, delighted at the importance of the commission with which he was intrusted.

"Not at home," Yermolov's servant told him. The officer of the horseguards set off to the quarters of the general, with whom Yermolov was often to be found.

"Not here, nor the general either," he was told.

The officer mounted his horse again and rode off to another general's.

"No, not at home."

"If only I don't get into trouble for the delay! How annoying!" thought the officer.

He rode all over the camp. One man told him he had seen Yermolov riding away in company with some other generals; another said he was sure to be at home again by now. The officer was hunting him till six o'clock in the evening without stopping for dinner. Yermolov was nowhere to be found, and no one knew where he was. The officer took a hasty meal at a comrade's, and trotted back to the advance guard to see Miloradovitch. Miloradovitch, too, was not at home. but there he was told that he was at a ball at General Kikin's and that, most likely, Yermolov was there too.

"But where is that?"

"At Etchkino, that way," said an officer of the Cossacks, pointing out to him a country house in the far distance.

"Out there! beyond our lines!"

"Two regiments of our fellows have been sent out to the outposts, and there is a spree going on there now, fine doings! Two bands, three choruses of singers."

The officer rode out beyond our lines to Etchkino. While yet a long way off, he heard the gay sounds of a soldier's dance tune sung in chorus.

"In the meadows . . . in the meadows," he heard with a whistle and string music, drowned from time to time in a roar of voices. The officer's spirits, too, rose at these sounds, but at the same time he was in terror lest he should be held responsible for having so long delayed giving the important message intrusted to him. It was by now nearly nine o'clock. He dismounted and walked up to the entrance of a big manor-house that had been left uninjured between the French and the Russian lines. Footmen were bustling about with wines and edibles in the vestibule and the buffet. Choruses were standing under the windows. The officer was led up to a door, and he saw all at once all the most important generals in the army, among them the big, impressive figure of Yermolov. All the generals were standing in a semicircle, laughing loudly, their uniforms unbuttoned, and their faces flushed and animated. In the middle of the room a handsome, short general with a red face, was smartly and jauntily executing the steps of the *trepak*.

"Ha, ha, ha! Bravo, Nikolay Ivanovitch! ha, ha! . . ."

The officer felt doubly guilty in breaking in at such a moment with important business, and he would have waited; but one of the generals caught sight of him, and hearing what he had come for, told Yermolov. The latter, with a frowning face, came out to the officer, and hearing his story, took the papers from him without a word.

"Do you suppose it was by chance that he was not at home?" said a comrade of the officer's who was on the staff, speaking of Yermolov that evening. "That's all stuff and nonsense; it was all done on purpose. To play a trick on Konovnitsyn. You see, there'll be a pretty kettle of fish to-morrow!"

V

THE decrepit old man, Kutuzov, had bade them wake him early next day, and in the early morning he said his prayers, dressed, and with a disagreeable consciousness that he had to command in a battle of which he did not approve, he got into his carriage and drove from Letashevka, five versts behind Tarutino, to the place where the attacking columns were to be gathered together. Kutuzov drove along, dropping asleep and waking up again, and listening to hear whether that were the sound of shots on the right, whether the action had not begun. But everything was still quiet. A damp and cloudy autumn day was dawning. As he approached Tarutino, Kutuzov noticed cavalry soldiers leading their horses to a watercourse across the road along which he was riding. Kutuzov looked at them, stopped his carriage, and asked what regiment did they belong to. They belonged to a column which was to have been far away in front in ambush.

"A mistake, perhaps," thought the old commander-in-chief. But as he drove on further, Kutuzov saw infantry regiments with their arms stacked, and the soldiers in their drawers busy cooking porridge and fetching wood. He sent for their officer. The officer submitted that no command to advance had been given.

"No command . . ." Kutuzov began, but he checked himself at once, and ordered the senior officer to be summoned to him. Getting out of the carriage, with drooping head he walked to and fro in silence, breathing heavily. When the general staff officer, Eichen, for whom he had sent, arrived, Kutuzov turned purple with rage, not because that officer was to blame for the mistake, but because he was an object of sufficient importance for him to vent his wrath on. And staggering and gasping, the old man fell into that state of fury in which he would sometimes roll on the ground in frenzy, and flew at Eichen, shaking his fists, and shouting abuse in the language of the gutter. Another officer, Captain Brozin, who was in no way to blame, happening to appear, suffered the same fate.

"What will the blackguards do next? Shoot them! The scoundrels!" he shouted hoarsely, shaking his fist and staggering. He was in a state of actual physical suffering. He, his highness the commander-in-chief, who was assured by every one that no one in Russia had ever had such power as he, he put into this position—made a laughing-stock to the whole army. "Worrying myself, praying over to-day, not sleeping all night, and thinking about everything—all for nothing!" he thought about himself. "When I was a mere boy of an officer no one would have dared to make a laughing-stock of me like this . . . And now!" He was in a state of physical suffering, as though from corporal punishment, and could not help expressing it in wrathful and agonised outcries. But soon his strength was exhausted, and looking about him, feeling that he had said a great deal that was unjust, he got into his carriage and drove back in silence.

His wrath once spent did not return again, and Kutuzov, blinking feebly, listened to explanations and self-justifications (Yermolov himself did not put in an appearance till next day), and to the earnest representation of Bennigsen, Konovnitsyn, and Toll that the battle that had not come off should take place on the following day. And again Kutuzov had to acquiesce.

VI

NEXT day the troops were massed in their appointed places by the evening, and were moving forward in the night. It was an autumn night with a sky overcast by purplish-black clouds, but free from rain. The earth was damp, but not muddy, and the troops advanced noiselessly, except for a hardly audible jingling now and then from the artillery. They were forbidden to talk aloud, to smoke or to strike a light; the horses were kept from neighing. The secrecy of the enterprise increased its attractiveness. The men marched on gaily. Several columns halted, stacked their guns in piles, and lay down on the chilly ground, supposing they had reached their destination. Other columns (the majority) marched all night long, and arrived somewhere, unmistakably not where they were meant to be.

Count Orlov-Denisov with his Cossacks (the detachment of least importance of the lot) was the only one that reached the right place at the right time. This detachment halted at the extreme edge of a forest, on a path from the village of Stromilovo to Dmitrovskoe.

Before dawn Count Orlov, who had fallen asleep, was waked up. A deserter from the French camp was brought to him. It was a Polish under-officer of Poniatovsky's corps. This under-officer explained in Polish that he had deserted because he had been insulted in the service; because he ought long ago to have been an officer, and was braver than any of them, and so he had thrown them up and wanted to punish them. He said that Murat was camping for the night a verst from them, and that if they would give him a convoy of a hundred men he would take him alive. Count Orlov-Denisov took council with his comrades. The proposition was too alluring to be refused. Every one clamoured to go, everyone advised making the attempt. After many disputes and confabulations, it was settled that Major-General Grekov, with two regiments of Cossacks, should go with the Polish deserter.

"Now, remember," said Count Orlov-Denisov to the Polish deserter, as he dismissed him, "if you have been lying, I will have you shot like a dog, but if it's true, a hundred crowns."

The deserter made no reply to these words, and with a resolute air mounted his horse and rode off with Grekov's men, who were hurriedly gathered together. They disappeared into the wood. Count Orlov, shivering from the freshness of the dawning morning, and excited by the enterprise he had undertaken on his own responsibility, came out of the wood, accompanying Grekov, and began scrutinising the enemy's camp, faintly visible now in the deceptive light of the approaching dawn and the smouldering camp-fires. On the open copse on Count Orlov-Denisov's right our columns ought to have been visible. Count Orlov-Denisov looked in that direction; but although they could have been seen even if a long distance away, these columns were not in sight. Count Orlov-Denisov fancied, and his adjutant, who was extremely long-sighted, confirmed the idea, that they were beginning to move in the French camp.

"Oh, of course it's too late," said Count Orlov, staring at the camp. As so often happens when the man in whom we are putting faith is no longer before our eyes, it all seemed at once perfectly clear and obvious to him that the deserter had been playing them false, that he had been telling them lies, and was only spoiling the whole attack by removing these two regiments, which he was leading away—God only knew where! As if it were possible to capture the general out of such a mass of troops.

"No doubt he was lying, the scoundrel," said the Count.

"We can turn them back," said one of the suite, who was feeling just the same mistrust in the undertaking as he gazed at the camp.

"Ah! Yes . . . what do you think, or shall we leave them? Or not?"

"Do you command them to return?"

"To return, yes, to return!" Count Orlov said, with sudden decision, looking at his watch; "it will be too late; it's quite light."

And an adjutant galloped into the wood after Grekov. When Grekov came back, Count Orlov-Denisov, excited by giving up this enterprise, and by vainly waiting for the infantry columns, which still did not appear, and by the enemy's being so near (every man in his detachment was feeling the same), resolved to attack.

In a whisper he gave the command: "Mount!"

The men got into their places, crossed themselves . . . "In God's name, off!"

"Hurrah!" rang out in the wood, and the Cossacks, with spears lowered, flew gaily, one hundred after another, across the stream into the camp, as though they were being shot out of a sack.

One desperate, frightened scream from the first Frenchman who caught sight of the Cossacks, and every creature in the camp, undressed and half-asleep, was running away, abandoning cannons, muskets, and horses.

If the Cossacks had pursued the French without regard to what they left all around and behind them, they could have captured Murat and all there was there. Their commanding officers tried to make them do so. But there was no making the Cossacks budge when they had got booty and prisoners. No one heeded the word of command. They had taken fifteen hundred prisoners, thirty-eight cannons, flags, and, what was of most consequence in the eyes of the Cossacks, horses, saddles, coverings, and various other objects. All of this they wanted to see after, to secure the prisoners and the cannons, to divide the booty, to shout at and even fight with one another over the spoils; and all this absorbed the Cossacks' attention. The Frenchmen, finding themselves not pursued fur-

ther, began to rally; they formed into companies and began firing.
Orlov-Denisov still expected the other columns to arrive, and did not
advance further.

Meanwhile, in accordance with the disposition—"*die erste Colonne
marschirt,*" and so on—the infantry regiments of the belated columns,
under the command of Bennigsen and the direction of Toll, had started
off in due course, and had, in the usual way, arrived somewhere, but not
where they were intended to arrive. In the usual way too, the soldiers
who had set off gaily, began to halt; there were murmurs of dissatisfaction and a sense of muddle, and they were marched back to some
point. Adjutants and generals galloped to and fro, shouting angrily,
quarrelling, declaring they had come utterly wrong and were too late,
upbraiding some one, and so on; and finally, all washed their hands of
the business in despair, and marched on simply in order to get somewhere. "We must arrive somewhere sooner or later!" And so they did,
in fact, arrive somewhere, but not where they were wanted. And some
did even reach their destination, but reached it so late that their doing
so was of no use at all, and only resulted in their being fired at for nothing. Toll, who in this battle played the part of Weierother in the battle
of Austerlitz, galloped with unflagging energy from one part of the field
to another, and found everything at sixes and sevens everywhere. So, for
instance, he found Bagovut's corps in the wood, when it was broad daylight, though the corps ought to have been there long before, and to have
gone to support Orlov-Denisov. Disappointed and excited at the failure,
and supposing some one must be to blame for it, Toll galloped up to the
general in command of the corps, and began sternly reprimanding him,
declaring that he deserved to be shot. Bagovut, a sturdy old general of
placid disposition, had been worried too by all the delays, the muddles,
and the contradictory orders, and, to the amazement of everybody, he
flew into a violent rage, quite out of keeping with his character, and said
some very nasty things to Toll.

"I am not going to be taught my duty by anybody, but I can face
death with my men as well as any one," he said, and he marched forward with one division. The valiant Bagovut, not considering in his excitement whether his advance into action now with a single division was
likely to be of use or not, marched his men straight forward into the
enemy's fire. Danger, shells, and bullets were just what he wanted in his
fury. One of the first bullets killed him, the other bullets killed many of
his men. And his division remained for some time under fire for no object whatever.

VII

MEANWHILE another column was to have fallen upon the French in the
centre, but of this column Kutuzov was in command. He knew very
well that nothing but muddle would come of this battle, begun against
his will, and, as far as it was in his power, he held his forces back. He
did not move.

Kutuzov rode mutely about on his grey horse, making languid replies to the suggestions for an attack.

"You can all talk about attacking, but you don't see that we don't know how to execute complicated manœuvres," he said to Miloradovitch, who was begging to be allowed to advance.

"We couldn't take Murat alive in the morning, nor be in our places in time; now there's nothing to be done!" he said to another.

When it was reported to Kutuzov that there were now two battalions of Poles in the rear of the French, where according to the earlier reports of the Cossacks there had been none, he took a sidelong glance behind him at Yermolov, to whom he had not spoken since the previous day.

"Here they are begging to advance, proposing projects of all sorts, and as soon as you get to work, there's nothing ready, and the enemy, forewarned, takes his measures."

Yermolov half closed his eyelids, and faintly smiled, as he heard those words. He knew that the storm had blown over him, and that Kutuzov would not go beyond that hint.

"That's his little joke at my expense," said Yermolov softly, poking Raevsky, near him, with his knee.

Soon after that, Yermolov moved forward to Kutuzov and respectfully submitted:

"The time has not passed, your highness; the enemy has not gone away. If you were to command an advance? Or else the guards won't have a sight of smoke."

Kutuzov said nothing, but when news was brought him that Murat's troops were in retreat, he gave orders for an advance; but every hundred paces he halted for three-quarters of an hour.

The whole battle was confined to what had been done by the Cossacks of Orlov-Denisov; the rest of the troops simply lost a few hundreds of men for nothing.

In consequence of this battle, Kutuzov received a diamond decoration; Bennigsen, too, was rewarded with diamonds and a hundred thousand roubles; and the other generals, too, received agreeable recognition according to their rank, and more changes were made on the staff.

"That's how things are always done among us, everything topsy-turvy!" the Russian officers and generals said after the battle of Tarutino; just as they say it nowadays, with an assumption that some stupid person had muddled everything, while we would have managed quite differently. But the men who speak like this either do not understand what they are talking of, or intentionally deceive themselves. Every battle—Tarutino, Borodino, Austerlitz—fails to come off as those who planned it expected it to do. That is inevitable.

An innumerable collection of freely acting forces (and nowhere is a man freer than on the field of battle, where it is a question of life and death) influence the direction taken by a battle, and that can never be known beforehand and never corresponds with the direction of any one force.

If many forces are acting simultaneously in different directions on any body, the direction of its motion will not correspond with any one of the forces, but will always follow a middle course, the summary of them, what is expressed in mechanics by the diagonal of the parallelogram of forces.

If in the accounts given us by historians, especially by French ones, we find that wars and battles appear to follow a definite plan laid down beforehand, the only deduction we can make from that is that these accounts are not true.

The battle of Tarutino obviously failed to attain the aim which Toll had in view: to lead the army into action in accordance with his disposition of the troops, or the aim which Count Orlov-Denisov may have had; to take Murat prisoner; or the aim of destroying at one blow the whole corps, which Bennigsen and others may have entertained; or the aim of the officer who desired to distinguish himself under fire; or the Cossack, who wanted to obtain more booty than he did attain, and so on. But if we regard the object of the battle as what was actually accomplished by it, and what was the universal desire of all Russians (the expulsion of the French from Russia and the destruction of their army), it will be perfectly evident that the battle of Tarutino, precisely in consequence of its incongruities, was exactly what was wanted at that period of the campaign. It is difficult or impossible to imagine any issue of that battle more in accordance with that object than its actual result. With the very smallest effort, in spite of the greatest muddle, and with the most trifling loss, the most important results in the whole campaign were obtained—the transition was made from retreat to attack, the weakness of the French was revealed, and the shock was given which was all that was needed to put Napoleon's army to flight.

VIII

NAPOLEON enters Moscow after the brilliant victory *de la Moskowa:* there can be no doubt of the victory, since the French are left in possession of the field of battle. The Russians retreat and leave Moscow— well stocked with provisions, arms, implements, and countless riches— in the hands of Napoleon. The Russian army, of one-half the strength of the French, during the course of a whole month makes no effort to attack. Napoleon's position is most brilliant. One would have supposed that no great genius was needed with an army of double the strength to fall upon the Russian forces and destroy them, to negotiate an advantageous peace; or, in case of negotiations being refused, to make a menacing march upon Petersburg, or even, in case of failure in this, to return to Smolensk or to Vilna, or to remain in Moscow, to retain, in short, the brilliant position in which the French army now found themselves. To do all this it was only necessary to take the simplest and easiest measures: to keep the soldiers from pillage, to prepare winter clothes (of which there was a supply in Moscow amply sufficient for the whole army), and regularly to collect the provisions, of which the supply in Moscow was, on the showing of the French historians, sufficient to feed the whole army for six months. Napoleon, the greatest of all military geniuses, with absolute power, as historians assert, over the army, did nothing of all this.

Far from doing anything of the sort, he used his power to select out of all the various courses open to him the stupidest and most pernicious of all. Of all the different things Napoleon might have done—spending the winter in Moscow, going to Petersburg, going to Nizhni-Novgorod, going back a little more to the north or to the south, by the road Kutuzov afterwards took—no course one can imagine could have been more ruinous for his army (as the sequel proved) than the one Napoleon actually did adopt; that is, the course of staying in Moscow till October, letting the troops plunder the town, then in hesitation leaving a garrison behind, marching out of Moscow, going to meet Kutuzov and not giving battle, turning to the right and going as far as Maley Yaroslavets, again refusing to risk a battle, and finally retreating, not by the road Kutuzov had taken, but by Mozhaisk and the Smolensk route through devastated country. Let the most skilful tacticians, supposing that Napoleon's object was the destruction of his army, try and devise a series of actions which could, apart from any measures that might be taken by the Russian forces, have ensured with such certainty the complete destruction of the whole French army as the course taken by Napoleon.

This the genius Napoleon did. But to say that Napoleon ruined his army because he wanted to do so, or because he was very stupid, would be just as unjust as to say that Napoleon got his troops to Moscow because he wanted to, and because he was very clever and a great genius.

In both cases his personal activity, having no more force than the personal activity of every soldier, was merely coincidental with the laws by which the event was determined.

Quite falsely (and simply because the sequel did not justify Napoleon's actions) do historians represent Napoleon's faculties as flagging at Moscow. Just as before, and afterwards in the year 1813, he used all his powers and faculties to do the best for himself and his army, Napoleon's activity at this time was no less marvellous than in Egypt, in Italy, in Austria, and in Prussia. We do not know with any certainty how real was the genius of Napoleon in Egypt, where forty centuries looked down upon his greatness, because all his great exploits there are recounted to us by none but Frenchmen. We cannot judge with certainty of his genius in Austria and Prussia, as the accounts of his doings there must be drawn from French and German sources. And the unaccountable surrender of corps of soldiers without a battle, and of fortresses without a siege, must dispose Germans to postulate Napoleon's genius as the unique explanation of the war as it was waged in Germany. But we have, thank God, no need to plead his genius to cloak our shame. We have paid for the right to look facts simply and squarely in the face, and that right we will not give up.

His activity in Moscow was as marvellous and as full of genius as anywhere else. Command upon command and plan upon plan was continually being issued by him from the time he entered Moscow to the time he left it. The absence of the citizens and of a deputation, and even the burning of Moscow, did not daunt him. He did not lose sight of the welfare of his army, nor of the doings of the enemy, nor of the welfare of the people of Russia, nor the conduct of affairs at Paris, nor of diplomatic negotiations as to the terms of peace.

IX

On the military side, immediately on entering Moscow, Napoleon gives General Sebastiani strict orders to keep a watch on the movements of the Russian army, sends detachments along the various roads, and charges Murat to find Kutuzov. Then he gives careful instructions for the fortification of the Kremlin; then he makes a plan of the coming campaign over the whole map of Russia; that was a work of genius, indeed. On the diplomatic side, Napoleon summons to his presence Captain Yakovlev, who had been robbed and reduced to rags and did not know how to get out of Moscow, expounds to him minutely his whole policy and his magnanimity; and after writing a letter to the Emperor Alexander, in which he considers it his duty to inform his friend and brother that Rastoptchin had performed his duties very badly in Moscow, he despatches Yakovlev with it to Petersburg.

Expounding his views and his magnanimity with equal minuteness to Tutolmin, he despatches that old man too to Petersburg to open negotiations.

On the judicial side, orders were issued, immediately after the fires broke out, for the guilty persons to be found and executed. And the miscreant Rastoptchin was punished by the order to set fire to his houses.

On the administrative side, Moscow was presented with a constitution. A municipal council was instituted, and the following proclamation was issued:—

"Citizens of Moscow!

"Your misfortunes have been cruel, but his majesty the Emperor and King wishes to put an end to them. Terrible examples have shown you how he punishes crime and breach of discipline. Stern measures have been taken to put an end to disorder and to restore public security. A paternal council, chosen from among yourselves, will compose your municipality or town council. It will care for you, for your needs and your interests. The members of it will be distinguished by a red ribbon, which they will wear across the shoulder, and the mayor will wear a white sash over it. But except when discharging their duties, they will wear only a red ribbon round the left arm.

"The city police are established on their former footing, and they are already restoring order. The government has appointed two general commissioners, or superintendents of police, and twenty commissioners, or police inspectors, stationed in the different quarters of the town. You will recognise them by the white ribbon they will wear round the left arm. Several churches of various denominations have been opened, and divine service is performed in them without hindrance. Your fellow-citizens are returning every day to their dwellings, and orders have been given that they should find in them the aid and protection due to misfortune. These are the measures which the government has adopted to restore order and alleviate your position; but to attain that end, it is necessary that you should unite your efforts with them; should forget, if possible, the misfortunes you have suffered; should look hopefully at a fate that is not so cruel; should believe that a shameful death inevitably awaits those guilty of violence against your persons or your deserted property, and consequently leaves no doubt that they will be preserved, since such is the will of the greatest and most just of monarchs. Soldiers and citizens of whatever nation you may be! Restore public confidence, the source of the prosperity of a state; live like brothers, give mutual aid and protection to one another; unite in confounding the projects of the evil-minded; obey the civil and military authorities, and your tears will soon cease to flow."

On the commissariat side, Napoleon issued orders for all the troops to enter Moscow in turn, *à la maraude*, to gather supplies for themselves; so that in that way the army was provided with supplies for the future.

On the religious side, Napoleon ordered the priests to be brought back, and services to be performed again in the churches.

With a view to encouraging commerce and providing supplies for the troops, the following notice was placarded everywhere:—

"PROCLAMATION.

"You, peaceable inhabitants of Moscow, artisans, and working men, who have been driven out of the city by the disturbance, and you, scattered tillers of the soil, who are still kept in the fields by groundless terror, hear! Tranquillity is returning to this capital, and order is being restored in it. Your fellow-countrymen are coming boldly out of their hiding-places, seeing that they are treated with respect. Every act of violence against them or their property is promptly punished. His Majesty the Emperor and King protects them, and he reckons none among you his enemies but such as disobey his commands. He wishes to put an end to your trouble, and to bring you back to your homes and your families. Co-operate with his beneficent designs and come to us without apprehension. Citizens! Return with confidence to your habitations; you will soon find the means of satisfying your needs! Artisans and industrious handicraftsmen! Return to your employment; houses, shops, and guards to protect them are awaiting you, and you will receive the payment due to you for your toil! And you, too, peasants, come out of the forests where you have been hiding in terror, return without fear to your huts in secure reliance on finding protection. Markets have been established in the city, where peasants can bring their spare stores and country produce. The government has taken the following measures to secure freedom of sale for them: (1) From this day forward, peasants, husbandmen, and inhabitants of the environs of Moscow can, without any danger, bring their goods of any kind to two appointed markets— namely, the Mohovaya and the Ohotny Ryad. (2) Goods shall be bought from them at such a price as seller and buyer shall agree upon together; but if the seller cannot get what he asks for as a fair price, he will be at liberty to take his goods back to his village, and no one can hinder his doing so on any pretext whatever. (3) Every Sunday and Wednesday are fixed for weekly market days: to that end a sufficient number of troops will be stationed on Tuesdays and Saturdays along all the high roads at such a distance from the town as to protect the carts coming in. (4) Similar measures will be taken that the peasants with their carts and horses may meet with no hindrance on their home- ward way. (5) Steps will be immediately taken to re-establish the or- dinary shops.

"Inhabitants of the city and of the country, and you workmen and handicraftsmen of whatever nationality you may be! You are called upon to carry out the paternal designs of his majesty the Emperor and King, and to co-operate with him for the public welfare. Lay your respect and confidence at his feet, and do not delay to unite with us!"

With a view to keeping up the spirits of the troops and the people, reviews were continually being held, and rewards were distributed.

The Emperor rode about the streets and entertained the inhabitants; and in spite of his preoccupation with affairs of state, visited in person the theatre set up by his orders.

As regards philanthropy, too—the fairest jewel in the conqueror's crown—Napoleon did everything that lay within him. On the benevolent institutions he ordered the inscription to be put up, *"Maison de ma mère,"* thereby combining a touching filial sentiment with a monarch's grandeur of virtue. He visited the Foundling Home; and as he gave the orphans he had saved his white hands to kiss, he conversed graciously with Tutolmin. Then, as Thiers eloquently recounts, he ordered his soldiers' pay to be distributed among them in the false Russian notes he had counterfeited:—

"Reinforcing the use of these methods by an act worthy of him and of the French army, he had assistance distributed to those who had suf- fered loss from the fire. But as provisions were too precious to be given to strangers, mostly enemies, Napoleon preferred to furnish them with money for them to provide themselves from without, and ordered paper roubles to be distributed among them."

With a view to maintaining discipline in the army, orders were con- tinually being issued for severely punishing nonfulfilment of military duty and for putting an end to pillaging.

X

BUT, strange to say, all these arrangements, these efforts and plans, which were no whit inferior to those that had been made on similar occasions before, never touched the root of the matter; like the hands on the face of a clock, when detached from the mechanism, they turned aimlessly and arbitrarily, without catching the wheels.

The plan of campaign, that work of genius, of which Thiers says, that his genius never imagined anything more profound, more skilful, and more admirable, and entering into a polemical discussion with M. Fenn, proves that the composition of this work of genius is to be referred, not to the 4th, but to the 15th of October—that plan never was and never could be put into execution, because it had nothing in common with the actual facts of the position. The fortification of the Kremlin, for which it was necessary to pull down la Mosquée (as Napoleon called the church of Vassily the Blessed) turned out to be perfectly useless. The mining of the Kremlin was only of use for carrying out the desire the Emperor expressed on leaving Moscow, to blow up the Kremlin, like a child that beats the floor against which it has hurt itself. The pursuit of the Russian army, on which Napoleon laid so much stress, led to an unheard-of result. The French generals lost sight of the sixty thousand men of the Russian army, and it was only, in the words of Thiers, thanks to the skill, and apparently also the genius, of Murat that they succeeded at last in finding, like a lost pin, this army of sixty thousand men.

On the diplomatic side, all Napoleon's expositions of his magnanimity and justice, both to Tutolmin and to Yakovlev (the latter was principally interested in finding himself a great-coat and a conveyance for travelling) turned out to be fruitless. Alexander would not receive these envoys, and made no reply to the message they brought.

On the side of law, of order, after the execution of the supposed incendiaries, the other half of Moscow was burnt down.

The establishment of a municipal council did not check pillage, and was no benefit to any one but the few persons, who were members of it, and were able on the pretext of preserving order to plunder Moscow on their own account, or to save their own property from being plundered.

On the religious side, the difficulty had so easily been settled by Napoleon's visit to a mosque in Egypt, but here similar measures led to no results whatever. Two or three priests, picked up in Moscow, did attempt to carry out Napoleon's desire; but one of them was slapped in the face by a French soldier during the service, and in regard to the other, the following report was made by a French official: "The priest, whom I had discovered and invited to resume saying the Mass, cleaned and closed the church. In the night they came again to break in the doors, break the padlocks, tear the books, and commit other disorders."

As for the encouragement of commerce, the proclamation to "industrious artisans and peasants," met with no response at all. Industrious artisans there were none in Moscow, and the peasants set upon the messengers who ventured too far from the town with this proclamation and killed them.

The attempts to entertain the people and the troops with theatres were equally unsuccessful. The theatres set up in the Kremlin and Poznyakov's house were closed again immediately, because the actors and actresses were stripped of their belongings by the soldiers.

Even philanthropy did not bring the desired results. Moscow was full of paper money, genuine and counterfeit, and the notes had no value. The French, accumulating booty, cared for nothing but gold. The counterfeit notes, which Napoleon so generously bestowed on the unfortunate, were of no value, and even silver fell below its standard value in relation to gold.

But the most striking example of the ineffectiveness of all efforts made by the authorities was Napoleon's vain endeavour to check plunder, and to maintain discipline.

Here are reports sent in by the military authorities:

"Pillage continues in the city, in spite of the orders to stop it. Order is not yet restored, and there is not a single merchant carrying on trade in a lawful fashion. But the canteen-keepers permit themselves to sell the fruits of pillage.

"Part of my district continues to be a prey to the pillaging of the soldiers of the 3rd corps who, not satisfied with tearing from the poor wretches, who have taken refuge in the underground cellars, the little they have left, have even the ferocity to wound them with sword-cuts, as I have seen in several instances.

"Nothing new, but that the soldiers give themselves up to robbery and plunder. October 9th.

"Robbery and pillage continue. There is a band of robbers in our district, which would need strong guards to arrest it. October 11th.

"The Emperor is exceedingly displeased that, in spite of the strict orders to stop pillage, bands of marauders from the guards are continually returning to the Kremlin. In the Old Guards, the disorder and pillaging have been more violent than ever last night and to-day. The Emperor sees, with regret, that the picked soldiers, appointed to guard his person, who should set an example to the rest, are losing discipline to such a degree as to break into the cellars and stores prepared for the army. Others are so degraded that they refuse to obey sentinels and officers on guard, abuse them, and strike them.

"The chief marshal of the palace complains bitterly that, in spite of repeated prohibitions, the soldiers continue to commit nuisances in all the courtyards, and even before the Emperor's own windows."

The army, like a herd of cattle run wild, and trampling underfoot the fodder that might have saved them from starvation, was falling to pieces, and getting nearer to its ruin with every day it remained in Moscow.

But it did not move.

It only started running when it was seized by panic fear at the cap-

ture of a transport on the Smolensk road and the battle of Tarutino.
The news of the battle of Tarutino reached Napoleon unexpectedly in
the middle of a review, and aroused in him—so Thiers tells us—a desire
to punish the Russians, and he gave the order for departure that all the
army was clamouring for.

In their flight from Moscow, the soldiers carried with them all the
plunder they had collected. Napoleon, too, carried off his own private
trésor. Seeing the great train of waggons, loaded with the booty of the
army, Napoleon was alarmed (as Thiers tells us). But with his military
experience, he did not order all unnecessary waggons of goods to be
burnt, as he had done with a marshal's baggage on the way to Moscow.
He gazed at those carts and carriages, filled with soldiers, and said that
it was very well, that those conveyances would come in useful for provisions, the sick, and the wounded.

The plight of the army was like the plight of a wounded beast, that
feels its death at hand, and knows not what it is doing. Studying the
intricate manœuvres and schemes of Napoleon and his army from the
time of entering Moscow up to the time of the destruction of that army
is much like watching the death struggles and convulsions of a beast
mortally wounded. Very often the wounded creature, hearing a stir,
rushes to meet the hunter's shot, runs forward and back again, and itself hastens its end. Napoleon under the pressure of his army did like-
wise. Panic-stricken at the rumour of the battle of Tarutino, like a wild
beast, the army made a rush towards the shot, reached the hunter, and
ran back again; and at last, like every wild creature took the old familiar track, that was the worst and most disastrous way for it.

Napoleon is represented to us as the leader in all this movement, just
as the figurehead in the prow of a ship to the savage seems the force that
guides the ship on its course. Napoleon in his activity all this time was
like a child, sitting in a carriage, pulling the straps within it, and fancying he is moving it along.

XI

EARLY in the morning of the 6th of October, Pierre came out of the
shed, and when he went back, he stood in the doorway, playing with the
long bandy-legged, purplish-grey dog, that jumped about him. This dog
lived in their shed, sleeping with Karataev, though it sometimes went
off on its own account into the town, and came back again. It had probably never belonged to any one, and now it had no master, and no
name. The French called it Azor; the soldier who told stories called it
Femgalka; Karataev called it "Grey-coat," and sometimes "Floppy."
The lack of a master, of a name, of any particular breed, and even of a
definite colour, by no means troubled the purplish-grey dog. Its fluffy
tail stood up firm and round like a plume; its bandy legs served it so
well that often, as though disdaining to use all four, it would hold one
hind-leg gracefully up, and run very quickly and smartly on three paws.
Everything was a source of satisfaction to it. At one moment, it was

barking with joy, then it would bask in the sun, with a dreamy and thoughtful air, then it would frolic about, playing with a chip or a straw.

Pierre's attire now consisted of a dirty, tattered shirt, the sole relic left of his previous wardrobe, a pair of soldier's drawers, tied with string round the ankles by Karataev's advice, for the sake of warmth, a full peasant's coat and a peasant's cap. Physically Pierre had changed greatly during this period. He no longer seemed stout, though he still had that look of solidity and strength that was characteristic of the Bezuhov family. The lower part of his face was overgrown with beard and moustaches; his long, tangled hair, swarming with lice, formed a mat of curls on his head. His eyes had a look of firmness, calm, and alert readiness, such as had never been seen in Pierre's face before. All his old slackness, which had shown even in his eyes, was replaced now by a vigorous, alert look of readiness for action and for resistance. His feet were bare.

Pierre looked over the meadow, across which waggons and men on horseback were moving that morning, then far away beyond the river, then at the dog, who was pretending to be meaning to bite him in earnest, then at his bare feet, which he shifted with pleasure from one position to another, moving the dirty, thick, big toes. And every time he looked at his bare feet, a smile of eager self-satisfaction flitted across his face. The sight of those bare feet reminded him of all he had passed through and learned during this time; and the thought of that was sweet to him.

The weather had for several days been still and clear, with light frosts in the mornings—the so-called "old granny's summer."

It was warm out of doors in the sunshine, and that warmth was particularly pleasant, with the bracing freshness of the morning frost still in the air.

Over everything, over all objects near and far, lay that magical, crystal-clear brightness, which is only seen at that time in the autumn. In the distance could be seen the Sparrow Hills, with the village, the church, and the great white house. And the leafless trees, and the sand and the stones and roofs of the houses, the green spire of the church, and the angles of the white house in the distance, all stood out in the most delicate outlines with unnatural distinctness in the limpid air. Close at hand stood the familiar ruins of a half-burnt mansion, occupied by French soldiers, with lilac bushes still dark-green by the fence. And even this charred and ruined house, which looked revoltingly hideous in bad weather, had a sort of soothing comeliness in the clear, still brightness.

A French corporal, in a smoking-cap, with his coat comfortably unbuttoned, came round the corner of the shed, with a short pipe between his teeth, and with a friendly wink, approached Pierre.

"What sunshine, *hein*, M. Kiril?" (This was what all the French soldiers called Pierre.) "One would say it was spring." And the corporal leaned against the door, and offered Pierre his pipe, though he was always offering it, and Pierre always declined it.

"If one were marching in weather like this," he began.

Pierre questioned him what he had heard of the departure of the French, and the corporal told him that almost all the troops were setting out, and that to-day instructions were expected in regard to the prisoners. In the shed in which Pierre was, one of the Russian soldiers, Sokolov, was dangerously ill, and Pierre told the corporal that something ought to be done about this soldier. The corporal said that Pierre might set his mind at rest, that they had both travelling and stationary hospitals for such cases, that instructions would be given in regard to the sick, and that in fact every possible contingency was provided for by the authorities.

"And then, M. Kiril, you have only to say a word to the captain, you know. Oh, he is a man who never forgets anything. Speak to the captain when he makes his round; he will do anything for you."

The captain of whom the corporal spoke used often to have long conversations with Pierre, and did him all kinds of favours.

" 'You see, St. Thomas,' he said to me the other day, 'Kiril is a man of education, who speaks French; he is a Russian lord who has had troubles, but he is a man. And he understands . . . If he wants anything, let him tell me, he shall not meet with a refusal. When one has studied, one likes education, you see, and well-bred people.' It's for your own sake I tell you that, M. Kiril. In the affair that happened the other day, if it hadn't been for you, things would have ended badly."

(The corporal was alluding to a fight a few days before between the prisoners and the French soldiers, in which Pierre had succeeded in pacifying his companions.) After chatting a little time longer the corporal went away.

Several of the prisoners had heard Pierre talking to the corporal, and they came up immediately to ask what the latter had said. While Pierre was telling his companions what the corporal had said about setting off from Moscow, a thin, sallow, ragged French soldier came up to the door of the shed. With a shy and rapid gesture he put his fingers to his forehead by way of a salute, and addressing Pierre, asked him if the soldier, Platoche, who was making a shirt for him, were in this shed.

The French soldiers had been provided with linen and leather a week previously, and had given out the materials to the Russian prisoners to make them boots and shirts.

"It's ready, darling, it's ready!" said Karataev, coming out with a carefully folded shirt. On account of the heat and for greater convenience in working, Karataev was wearing nothing but a pair of drawers and a tattered shirt, as black as the earth. He had tied a wisp of bast round his hair, as workmen do, and his round face looked rounder and more pleasing than ever.

"Punctuality is own brother to good business. I said Friday, and so I have done it," said Platon, smiling and displaying the shirt he had made.

The Frenchman looked about him uneasily, and as though overcoming some hesitation, rapidly slipped off his uniform and put on the shirt. Under his uniform he had no shirt, but a long, greasy, flowered silk

waistcoat next his bare, yellow, thin body. The Frenchman was evi‹
dently afraid that the prisoners, who were looking at him, would laugh
at him, and he made haste to put his head through the shirt. None of
the prisoners said a word. "To be sure, it fits well," Platon observed,
pulling the shirt down. The Frenchman, after putting his head and arms
through, looked down at the shirt, and examined the stitching without
lifting his eyes.

"Well, darling, this isn't a tailor's, you know, and I had no proper
sewing materials, and there's a saying without the right tool you can't
even kill a louse properly," said Karataev, still admiring his own handi‹
work.

"Very good, thanks; but you must have some stuff left . . ." said
the Frenchman.

"It will be more comfortable as it wears to your body," said Karataev,
still admiring his work. "There, you'll be nice and comfortable."

"Thanks, thanks, old fellow; but what is left . . . ?" repeated the
Frenchman, giving Karataev a paper note. "Give me the pieces that
are over."

Pierre saw that Platon did not want to understand what the Frenchman said, and he looked on without interfering. Karataev thanked him
for the rouble and went on admiring his own work. The Frenchman persisted in asking for what was left, and asked Pierre to translate what he
said.

"What does he want with the pieces?" said Karataev. "They would
have made me capital leg wrappers. Oh well, God bless the man."

And, looking suddenly crestfallen and melancholy, Karataev took a
bundle of remnants out of his bosom and gave it to the Frenchman without looking at him. "Ach-ma!" he cried, and walked away. The Frenchman looked at the linen, he hesitated, glanced inquiringly at Pierre, and
as though Pierre's eyes had told him something:

"Here, Platoche!" he cried in a shrill voice, suddenly blushing. "Keep
them yourself," he said, and giving him the remnants, he turned and
went out.

"There, look'ee now," said Karataev, shaking his head. "They say
they're not Christians, but they have souls too. It's true what the old
folks used to say: a sweating hand is an open hand, but a dry hand is
closefisted. His own back's bare, and yet he has given me this." Karataev paused for a while, smiling dreamily and gazing at the cuttings of
linen. "But first-rate leg binders they'll make me, my dear," he added,
as he went back into the shed.

XII

Four weeks had passed since Pierre had been taken prisoner. Although
the French had offered to transfer him from the common prisoners' shed
to the officers', he had remained in the same shed as at first.

In Moscow, wasted by fire and pillage, Pierre passed through hard‹

ships almost up to the extreme limit of privation that a man can endure. But, owing to his vigorous health and constitution, of which he had hardly been aware till then; and still more, owing to the fact that these privations came upon him so gradually that it was impossible to say when they began, he was able to support his position, not only with ease, but with positive gladness. And it was just at this time that he attained that peace and content with himself, for which he had always striven in vain before. For long years of his life he had been seeking in various directions for that peace, that harmony with himself, which had struck him so much in the soldiers at Borodino. He had sought for it in philanthropy, in freemasonry, in the dissipations of society, in wine, in heroic feats of self-sacrifice, in his romantic love for Natasha; he had sought it by the path of thought; and all his researches and all his efforts had failed him. And now without any thought of his own, he had gained that peace and that harmony with himself simply through the horror of death, through hardships, through what he had seen in Karataev. Those fearful moments that he had lived through during the execution had, as it were, washed for ever from his imagination and his memory the disturbing ideas and feelings that had once seemed to him so important. No thought came to him of Russia, of the war, of politics, or of Napoleon. It seemed obvious to him that all that did not concern him, that he was not called upon and so was not able to judge of all that. "Russia and summer never do well together," he repeated Karataev's words, and those words soothed him strangely. His project of killing Napoleon, and his calculations of the cabalistic numbers, and of the beast of the Apocalypse struck him now as incomprehensible and positively ludicrous. His anger with his wife, and his dread of his name being disgraced by her, seemed to him trivial and amusing. What business of his was it, if that woman chose to lead somewhere away from him the life that suited her tastes? What did it matter to any one—least of all to him—whether they found out or not that their prisoner's name was Count Bezuhov?

He often thought now of his conversation with Prince Andrey, and agreed fully with his friend, though he put a somewhat different construction on his meaning. Prince Andrey had said and thought that happiness is only negative, but he had said this with a shade of bitterness and irony. It was as though in saying this he had expressed another thought—that all the strivings towards positive happiness, that are innate in us, were only given us for our torment. But Pierre recognised the truth of the main idea with no such undercurrent of feeling. The absence of suffering, the satisfaction of needs, and following upon that, freedom in the choice of occupation, that is, of one's manner of life, seemed to Pierre the highest and most certain happiness of man. Only here and now for the first time in his life Pierre fully appreciated the enjoyment of eating when he was hungry, of drinking when he was thirsty, of sleep when he was sleepy, of warmth when he was cold, of talking to a fellow creature when he wanted to talk and to hear men's voices. The satisfaction of his needs—good food, cleanliness, freedom— seemed to Pierre now that he was deprived of them to be perfect happiness; and the choice of his occupation, that is, of his manner of life now that that choice was so limited, seemed to him such an easy matter that he forgot that a superfluity of the conveniences of life destroys all happiness in satisfying the physical needs, while a great freedom in the choice of occupation, that freedom which education, wealth, and position in society had given him, makes the choice of occupations exceedingly difficult, and destroys the very desire and possibility of occupation.

All Pierre's dreams now turned to the time when he would be free. And yet, in all his later life, Pierre thought and spoke with enthusiasm of that month of imprisonment, of those intense and joyful sensations that could never be recalled, and above all of that full, spiritual peace, of that perfect, inward freedom, of which he had only experience at that period.

On the first day, when, getting up early in the morning, he came out of the shed into the dawn, and saw the cupolas and the crosses of the New Monastery of the Virgin, all still in darkness, saw the hoar frost on the long grass, saw the slopes of the Sparrow Hills and the wood-clad banks of the encircling river vanishing into the purple distance, when he felt the contact of the fresh air and heard the sounds of the rooks flying out of Moscow across the fields, and when flashes of light suddenly gleamed out of the east and the sun's rim floated triumphantly up from behind a cloud, and cupolas and crosses and hoar frost and the horizon and the river were all sparkling in the glad light, Pierre felt a new feeling of joy and vigour in life such as he had never experienced before.

And that feeling had not left him during the whole period of his imprisonment, but on the contrary had gone on growing in him as the hardships of his position increased.

That feeling—of being ready for anything, of moral alertness—was strengthened in Pierre by the high opinion in which he began to be held by his companions very soon after he entered the shed. His knowledge of languages, the respect shown him by the French, the good-nature with which he gave away anything he was asked for (he received the allowance of three roubles a week, given to officers among the prisoners), the strength he showed in driving nails into the wall, the gentleness of his behaviour to his companions, and his capacity—which seemed to him mysterious—of sitting stockstill doing nothing and plunged in thought, all made him seem to the soldiers a rather mysterious creature of a higher order. The very peculiarities that in the society he had previously lived in had been a source of embarrassment, if not of annoyance—his strength, his disdain for the comforts of life, his absent-mindedness, his good-nature—here among these men gave him the prestige almost of a hero. And Pierre felt that their view of him brought its duties.

XIII

ON the night of the 6th of October, the march of the retreating French army began: kitchens and shanties were broken up, waggons were packed, and troops and trains of baggage began moving.

At seven o'clock in the morning an escort of French soldiers in marching order, in shakoes, with guns, knapsacks, and huge sacks, stood before the sheds and a running fire of eager French talk, interspersed with oaths, was kept up all along the line.

In the shed they were ready, dressed and belted and shod, only waiting for the word of command to come out. The sick soldier, Sokolov, pale and thin, with blue rings round his eyes, sat alone in his place, without boots or out-of-door clothes on. His eyes, that looked prominent from the thinness of his face, gazed inquiringly at his companions, who took no notice of him, and he uttered low groans at regular intervals. It was evidently not so much his sufferings—he was ill with dysentery—as the dread and grief of being left alone that made him groan.

Pierre was shod with a pair of slippers that Karataev had made for him out of the leather cover of a tea-chest, brought him by a Frenchman for soling his boots. With a cord tied round for a belt, he went up to the sick man, and squatted on his heels beside him.

"Come, Sokolov, they are not going away altogether, you know. They have a hospital here. Very likely you will be better off than we others," said Pierre.

"O Lord! it will be the death of me! O Lord!" the soldier groaned more loudly.

"Well, I will ask them again in a minute," said Pierre, and getting up, he went to the door of the shed. While Pierre was going to the door, the same corporal, who had on the previous day offered Pierre a pipe, came in from outside, accompanied by two soldiers. Both the corporal and the soldiers were in marching order, with knapsacks on and shakoes, with straps buttoned, that changed their familiar faces.

The corporal had come to the door so as to shut it in accordance with the orders given him. Before getting them out, he had to count over the prisoners.

"Corporal, what is to be done with the sick man?" Pierre was beginning, but at the very moment that he spoke the words he doubted whether it were the corporal he knew or some stranger—the corporal was so unlike himself at that moment. Moreover, at the moment Pierre was speaking, the roll of drums was suddenly heard on both sides. The corporal scowled at Pierre's words, and uttering a meaningless oath, he slammed the door. It was half-dark now in the shed; the drums beat a sharp tattoo on both sides, drowning the sick man's groans.

"Here it is! . . . Here it is again!" Pierre said to himself, and an involuntary shudder ran down his back. In the changed face of the corporal, in the sound of his voice, in the stimulating and deafening din of the drums, Pierre recognised that mysterious, unsympathetic force which drove men, against their will, to do their fellow-creatures to death; that force, the effect of which he had seen at the execution. To be afraid, to try and avoid that force, to appeal with entreaties or with exhortations to the men who were serving as its instruments, was useless. That Pierre knew now. One could but wait and be patient. Pierre did not go near the sick man again, and did not look round at him. He stood at the door of the shed in silence, scowling.

When the doors of the shed were opened, and the prisoners, huddling against one another like a flock of sheep, crowded in the entry, Pierre pushed in front of them, and went up to the very captain who was, so the corporal had declared, ready to do anything for him. The captain was in marching trim, and from his face, too, there looked out the same "it" Pierre had recognised in the corporal's words and in the roll of the drums.

"Filez, filez!" the captain was saying, frowning sternly, and looking at the prisoners crowding by him.

Pierre knew his effort would be in vain, yet he went up to him.

"Well, what is it?" said the officer, scanning him coldly, as though he did not recognise him. Pierre spoke of the sick prisoner.

"He can walk, damn him!" said the captain.

"Filez, filez!" he went on, without looking at Pierre.

"Well, no, he is in agony . . .!" Pierre was beginning.

"Voulez-vous bien?" . . . shouted the captain, scowling malignantly.

"Dram-da-da-dam, dam-dam," rattled the drums, and Pierre knew that the mysterious force had already complete possession of those men, and that to say anything more now was useless.

The officers among the prisoners were separated from the soldiers and ordered to march in front.

The officers, among whom was Pierre, were thirty in number; the soldiers three hundred.

These officers, who had come out of other sheds, were all strangers to Pierre, and much better dressed than he was. They looked at him in his queer foot-gear with aloof and mistrustful eyes. Not far from Pierre walked a stout major, with a fat, sallow, irascible countenance. He was dressed in a Kazan gown, girt with a linen band, and obviously enjoyed the general respect of his companion prisoners. He held his tobacco-pouch in one hand thrust into his bosom; with the other he pressed the stem of his pipe. This major, panting and puffing, grumbled angrily at every one for pushing against him, as he fancied, and for hurrying when there was no need of hurry, and for wondering when there was nothing to wonder at. Another, a thin, little officer, addressed remarks to every one, making conjectures where they were being taken now, and how far they would go that day. An official, in felt high boots and a commissariat uniform, ran from side to side to get a good view of the results of the fire in Moscow, making loud observations on what was burnt, and saying what this or that district of the town was as it came into view. A third

officer, of Polish extraction by his accent, was arguing with the commissariat official, trying to prove to him that he was mistaken in his
identification of the various quarters of Moscow.

"Why dispute?" said the major angrily. "Whether it's St. Nikola or
St. Vlas, it's no matter. You see that it's all burnt, and that's all about
it. . . . Why are you pushing, isn't the road wide enough?" he said,
angrily addressing a man who had passed behind him and had not
pushed against him at all.

"Aie, aie, aie, what have they been doing?" the voices of the prisoners
could be heard crying on one side and on another as they looked at the
burnt districts. "Zamoskvoryetche, too, and Zubovo, and in the Kremlin. . . . Look, there's not half left. Why, didn't I tell you all Zamosk-
voryetche was gone, and so it is."

"Well, you know it is burnt, well, why argue about it?" said the
major.

Passing through Hamovniky (one of the few quarters of Moscow
that had not been burnt) by the church, the whole crowd of prisoners
huddled suddenly on one side, and exclamations of horror and aversion
were heard.

"The wretches! The heathens! Yes; a dead man; a dead man; it is
. . . They have smeared it with something."

Pierre, too, drew near the church, where was the object that had
called forth these exclamations, and he dimly discerned something leaning against the fence of the church enclosure. From the words of his
companions, who saw better than he did, he learnt that it was the dead
body of a man, propped up in a standing posture by the fence, with the
face smeared with soot.

"Move on, damn you! Go on, thirty thousand devils!" . . . They
heard the escort swearing, and the French soldiers, with fresh vindictiveness, used the flat sides of their swords to drive on the prisoners, who
had lingered to look at the dead man.

XIV

THROUGH the lanes of Hamovniky, the prisoners marched alone with
their escort, a train of carts and waggons, belonging to the soldiers of
the escort, following behind them. But as they came out to the provision
shops they found themselves in the middle of a huge train of artillery,
moving with difficulty, and mixed up with private baggage-waggons.

At the bridge itself the whole mass halted, waiting for the foremost
to get across. From the bridge the prisoners got a view of endless trains
of baggage-waggons in front and behind. On the right, where the Kaluga
road turns by Neskutchny Gardens, endless files of troops and waggons
stretched away into the distance. These were the troops of Beauharnais's
corps, which had set off before all the rest. Behind, along the riverside,

and across Kamenny bridge, stretched the troops and transport of Ney's corps.

Davoust's troops, to which the prisoners belonged, were crossing by the Crimean Ford, and part had already entered Kaluga Street. But the baggage-trains were so long that the last waggons of Beauharnais's corps had not yet got out of Moscow into Kaluga Street, while the vanguard of Ney's troops had already emerged from Bolshaya Ordynka.

After crossing the Crimean Ford, the prisoners moved a few steps at a time and then halted, and again moved forward, and the crowd of vehicles and people grew greater and greater on all sides. After taking over an hour in crossing the few hundred steps which separates the bridge from Kaluga Street and getting as far as the square where the Zamoskvoryetche streets run into Kaluga Street, the prisoners were jammed in a close block and kept standing for several hours at the cross-roads. On all sides there was an unceasing sound, like the roar of the sea, of rumbling wheels, and tramping troops, and incessant shouts of anger and loud abuse. Pierre stood squeezed against the wall of a charred house, listening to that sound, which in his imagination melted off into the roll of drums.

Several of the Russian officers clambered up on to the wall of the burnt house by which Pierre stood so as to get a better view.

"The crowds! What crowds! . . . They have even loaded goods on the cannons! Look at the furs! . . ." they kept saying. "I say, the vermin, they have been pillaging. . . . Look at what that one has got behind, on the cart. . . . Why, they are holy pictures, by God! . . . Those must be Germans. And a Russian peasant; by God! . . . Ah; the wretches! . . . See, how he's loaded; he can hardly move! Look, I say, chaises; they have got hold of them, too! . . . See, he has perched on the boxes. Heavens! . . . They have started fighting! . . . That's right; hit him in the face! We shan't get by before evening like this. Look, look! . . . Why, that must surely be Napoleon himself. Do you see the horses! with the monograms and a crown! That's a portable house. He has dropped his sack, and doesn't see it. Fighting again. . . . A woman with a baby, and good-looking, too! Yes, I dare say; that's the way they will let you pass. . . . Look; why, there's no end to it. Russian wenches, I do declare they are. See how comfortable they are in the carriages!"

Again a wave of general curiosity, as at the church in Hamovniky, carried all the prisoners forward towards the road, and Pierre, thanks to his height, saw over the heads of the others what attracted the prisoners' curiosity. Three carriages were blocked between caissons, and in them a number of women with rouged faces, decked out in flaring colours, were sitting closely packed together, shouting something in shrill voices.

From the moment when Pierre had recognised the manifestation of that mysterious force, nothing seemed to him strange or terrible; not the corpse with its face blacked for a jest, nor these women hurrying away, ior the burnt ruins of Moscow. All that Pierre saw now made hardly any impression on him—as though his soul, in preparation for a hard struggle, refused to receive any impression that might weaken it.

The carriages of women drove by. They were followed again by carts, soldiers, waggons, soldiers, carriages, soldiers, caissons, and again soldiers, and at rare intervals women.

Pierre did not see the people separately; he saw only their movement. All these men and horses seemed, as it were, driven along by some unseen force. During the hour in which Pierre watched them they all were swept out of the different streets with the same one desire to get on as quickly as possible. All of them, alike hindered by the rest, began to get angry and to fight. The same oaths were bandied to and fro, and white teeth flashed, and every frowning face wore the same look of reckless determination and cold cruelty, which had struck Pierre in the morning in the corporal's face, while the drums were beating.

It was almost evening when the officer in command of their escort rallied his men, and with shouts and oaths forced his way in among the baggage-trains; and the prisoners, surrounded on all sides, came out on the Kaluga road.

They marched very quickly without pausing, and only halted when the sun was setting. The baggage-carts were moved up close to one another, and the men began to prepare for the night. Every one seemed ill-humoured and dissatisfied. Oaths, angry shouts, and fighting could be heard on all sides till a late hour. A carriage, which had been following the escort, had driven into one of their carts and run a shaft into it. Several soldiers ran up to the cart from different sides; some hit the carriage horses on the head as they turned them round, others were fighting among themselves, and Pierre saw one German seriously wounded by a blow from the flat side of a sword on his head.

It seemed as though now when they had come to a standstill in the midst of the open country, in the cold twilight of the autumn evening, all these men were experiencing the same feeling of unpleasant awakening from the hurry and eager impulse forward that had carried them all away at setting off. Now standing still, all as it were grasped that they knew not where they were going, and that there was much pain and hardship in store for them on the journey.

At this halting-place, the prisoners were even more roughly treated by their escort than at starting. They were for the first time given horseflesh to eat.

In every one of the escort, from the officers to the lowest soldier, could be seen a sort of personal spite against every one of the prisoners, in surprising contrast with the friendly relations that had existed between them before.

This spite was increased when, on counting over the prisoners, it was discovered that in the bustle of getting out of Moscow one Russian soldier had managed to run away by pretending to be seized with colic. Pierre had seen a Frenchman beat a Russian soldier unmercifully for moving too far from the road, and heard the captain. who had been his friend, reprimanding an under-officer for the escape of the prisoner, and threatening him with court-martial. On the under-officer's urging that the prisoner was ill and could not walk, the officer said that their orders were to shoot those who should lag behind. Pierre felt that that fatal force which had crushed him at the execution, and had been imperceptible during his imprisonment, had now again the mastery of his existence. He was afraid; but he felt, too, that as that fatal force strove to crush him, there was growing up in his soul and gathering strength a force of life that was independent of it. Pierre supped on soup made of rye flour and horseflesh, and talked a little with his companions.

Neither Pierre nor any of his companions talked of what they had seen in Moscow, nor of the harsh treatment they received from the French, nor of the orders to shoot them, which had been announced to them. As though in reaction against their more depressing position, all were particularly gay and lively. They talked of personal reminiscences, of amusing incidents they had seen as they marched, and avoided touching on their present position.

The sun had long ago set. Stars were shining brightly here and there in the sky; there was a red flush, as of a conflagration on the horizon, where the full moon was rising, and the vast, red ball seemed trembling strangely in the grey darkness. It became quite light. The evening was over, but the night had not yet begun. Pierre left his new companions and walked between the camp-fires to the other side of the road, where he had been told that the common prisoners were camping. He wanted to talk to them. On the road a French sentinel stopped him and bade him go back.

Pierre did go back, but not to the camp-fire where his companions were, but to an unharnessed waggon where there was nobody. Tucking his legs up under him, and dropping his head, he sat down on the cold ground against the waggon wheel, and sat there a long while motionless, thinking. More than an hour passed by. No one disturbed Pierre. Suddenly he burst into such a loud roar of his fat, good-humoured laughter, that men looked round on every side in astonishment at this strange and obviously solitary laughter. "Ha, ha, ha!" laughed Pierre. And he talked aloud to himself. "The soldier did not let me pass. They have taken me—shut me up. They keep me prisoner. Who is 'me'? Me? Me—my immortal soul! ha, ha, ha! . . . Ha, ha, ha! . . ." he laughed, with the tears starting into his eyes.

A man got up and came to see what this strange big man was laughing at all by himself. Pierre left off laughing, got up, walked away from the inquisitive intruder, and looked about him.

The immense, endless bivouac, which had been full of the sound of crackling fires and men talking, had sunk to rest; the red camp-fires burnt low and dim. High overhead in the lucid sky stood the full moon. Forests and fields, that before could not be seen beyond the camp, came into view now in the distance. And beyond those fields and forests could be seen the bright, shifting, alluring, boundless distance. Pierre glanced at the sky, at the far-away, twinkling stars. "And all that is mine, and all that is in me, and all that is I!" thought Pierre. "And all this they caught and shut up in a shed closed in with boards!" He smiled and went to lie down to sleep beside his companions.

XV

EARLY in October another messenger came to Kutuzov from Napoleon with overtures for peace and a letter, falsely professing to come from Moscow, though Napoleon was in fact not far ahead of Kutuzov on the old Kaluga road. Kutuzov answered this letter as he had done the first one, brought him by Lauriston; he said that there could be no question of peace.

Soon after this Dorohov's irregulars, which were moving on the left of Tarutino, sent a report that French troops had appeared at Fominskoe, that these troops were of Broussier's division, and that that division, being separate from the rest of the army, might easily be cut to pieces. The soldiers and officers again clamoured for action. The staff generals, elated by the easy victory of Tarutino, urged on Kutuzov that Dorohov's suggestion should be acted upon.

Kutuzov did not consider any action necessary. A middle course, as was inevitable, was adopted; a small detachment was sent to Fominskoe to attack Broussier.

By strange chance this appointment, a most difficult and most important one, as it turned out to be later, was given to Dohturov, that modest little general, whom no one has depicted to us making plans of campaign, dashing at the head of regiments, dropping crosses about batteries, or doing anything of the kind; whom people looked on and spoke of as lacking decision and penetration, though all through the Russian wars with the French, from Austerlitz to the year 1813, we always find him in command where the position is particularly difficult. At Austerlitz he was the last to remain at the ford of Augest, rallying the regiments, saving what he could, when all was flight and ruin, and not a single other general was to be found in the rearguard. When ill with fever, he marched with twenty thousand men to Smolensk to defend the town against the whole of Napoleon's army. In Smolensk he had only just fallen asleep at the Malahovsky gates in a paroxysm of fever when he was waked by the cannonade of Smolensk, and Smolensk held out a whole day. At Borodino when Bagration was killed, and nine-tenths of the men of our left flank had been slain, and the fire of all the French artillery was turned upon it, Kutuzov made haste to recall another general he had sent by mistake, and sent there no other than Dohturov, who was said to be lacking in decision and penetration. And unpretentious little Dohturov went there, and Borodino became the greatest glory of the Russian arms. And many of its heroes have been celebrated in prose and verse, but of Dohturov hardly a word. Again Dohturov was sent to Fominskoe, and from there to Maley Yaroslavets, the place where the last battle was fought with the French, and where it is plain the final destruction of the French army really begun. And again many heroes and men of genius are described to us in accounts of this period of the campaign, but of Dohturov nothing is said, or but few words of dubious praise. This silence in regard to Dohturov is the plainest testimony to his merits.

It is natural that a man who does not understand the working of a machine should suppose, when he sees it in action, that a shaving that has fallen into it by chance, and flaps about in it, hindering its progress, is the most important part of the mechanism. Any one who does not understand the construction of the machine cannot conceive that this shaving is only clogging and spoiling it, while the little cog-wheel, which turns noiselessly, is one of the most essential parts of the machine.

On the 10th of October Dohturov had marched halfway to Fominskoe, and halted at the village of Aristovo, making every preparation for exactly carrying out the orders given him. On the same day the whole French army, after reaching in its spasmodic rush as far as Murat's position, seemingly with the object of giving battle, suddenly, with no apparent cause, turned off to the left to the new Kaluga road, and began marching into Fominskoe, where Broussier had before been alone. Dohturov had under his command at the time only Dorohov's troops and the two small detachments of Figner and Seslavin.

On the evening of the 11th of October, Seslavin came to the general at Aristovo with a French prisoner of the Guards. The prisoner said that the troops that had reached Fominskoe that day were the advance guard of the whole army; that Napoleon was with them; that the whole army had marched out of Moscow five days before. The same evening a house-serf coming from Borovsk brought word that he had seen an immense army entering that town. Dorohov's Cossacks reported that they had seen the French guards marching along the road to Borovsk. From all this it was evident that where they had expected to find one division there was now the whole army of the French, marching from Moscow in an unexpected direction—along the old Kaluga road. Dohturov was unwilling to take any action, as it was not clear to him now where his duty lay. He had received instructions to attack Fominskoe. But there had then been only Broussier at Fominskoe, and now the whole French army was there. Yermolov wanted to act on his own judgment, but Dohturov insisted that he must have instructions from his highness the commander-in-chief. It was resolved to send a report to the staff.

For this purpose they chose a capable officer, Bolhovitinov, who was to take a written report, and to explain the whole matter verbally. At midnight Bolhovitinov received his despatch and his verbal instructions, and galloped off to headquarters, accompanied by a Cossack with spare horses.

XVI

It was a dark, warm autumn night. Rain had been falling for the last four days. Changing horses twice, Bolhovitinov galloped in an hour and a half thirty versts over a muddy, slippery road. He reached Letashevko after one o'clock in the night. Dismounting at a hut, on the hurdle fence of which was the inscription "Headquarters of the Staff," and letting his horse go, he walked into the dark entry.

"The general on duty at once! Very important!" he cried to some one, who jumped up, wheezing in the darkness.

"His honour has been very unwell since the evening; he has not slept for three nights," an orderly's voice whispered, interposing. "You must wake the captain first."

"Very important from General Dohturov," said Bolhovitinov, feeling for the opened door and going in.

The orderly went in before him, and began waking some one up. "Your honour, your honour, a courier."

"What? what? from whom?" said a sleepy voice.

"From Dohturov and from Alexey Petrovitch. Napoleon is at Fominskoe," said Bolhovitinov, not seeing the speaker in the darkness, but assuming from the voice that it was not Konovnitsyn.

The man who had been waked yawned and stretched. "I don't want to wake him," he said, fumbling for something. "He's ill! Perhaps it's only a rumour."

"Here is the report," said Bolhovitinov. "My instructions are to give it at once to the general on duty."

"Wait a minute, I'll strike a light. What do you do with things, damn you!" said the sleepy voice addressing the orderly. The speaker was Shtcherbinin, Konovnitsyn's adjutant. "I have found it, I have found it," he added.

The orderly struck a light, Shtcherbinin felt for a candlestick.

"Ah, the nasty beasts!" he said with disgust.

By the light of the sparks in the tinderbox Bolhovitinov had a glimpse of Shtcherbinin's youthful face, and in a corner another man asleep. This was Konovnitsyn.

When the tinder broke first into a blue and then into a red flame, Shtcherbinin lighted a tallow candle—the cockroaches that had been gnawing it ran away in all directions—and looked at the messenger. Bolhovitinov was bespattered all over, and on rubbing his face with his sleeve, had smudged that too with mud.

"But who sends the report?" said Shtcherbinin, taking the packet.

"The news is certain," said Bolhovitinov. "Prisoners and Cossacks and spies, all tell the same story."

"Well there's no help for it, we must wake him," said Shtcherbinin, getting up and going to the sleeping man who wore a nightcap and was covered up with a military cloak. "Pyotr Petrovich!" he said. Konovnitsyn did not stir. "Wanted at headquarters!" he said with a smile, knowing these words would be sure to wake him. And the head in the nightcap was in fact lifted at once. Konovnitsyn's strong, handsome face, with feverishly swollen cheeks, still wore for an instant a far-away, dreamy look, but he gave a sudden start and his face resumed its customary expression of calmness and strength.

"Well, what is it? From whom?" he asked at once, but with no haste, blinking at the light. Hearing what the officer had to tell him, Konovnitsyn broke open the packet and read it. He had hardly read it before he dropped his feet in worsted stockings on to the earth floor and began putting on his boots. Then he took off the nightcap, and combing his hair, put on a forage cap.

"Did you get here quickly? Let us go to his highness."

Konovnitsyn understood at once that the news was of great importance, and that they must lose no time. As to whether it were good news or bad, he had no opinion and did not even put the question to himself. That did not interest him. He looked at the whole subject of the war, not with his intellect, not with his reason, but with something different. In his heart he had a deep, unaltered conviction that all would be well, yet that he ought not to believe in this, and still more ought not to say so, but ought simply to do his duty. And that he did do, giving all his energies to it.

Pyotr Petrovich Konovnitsyn, like Dohturov, is simply as a formality included in the list of the so-called heroes of 1812 with the Barclays, Raevskys, Yermolovs, Platovs and Miloradovitchs. Like Dohturov, he had the reputation of being a man of very limited capacities and information; and, like Dohturov, he never proposed plans of campaign, but was always to be found in the most difficult position. Ever since he had been appointed the general on duty, he had slept with his door open, and given orders to be waked on the arrival of any messenger. In battle he was always under fire, so that Kutuzov even reproached him for it, and was afraid to send him to the front. Like Dohturov, he was one of those inconspicuous cogwheels, which, moving without creaking or rattling, make up the most essential part of the machine.

Coming out of the hut into the damp, dark night, Konovnitsyn frowned, partly from his headache getting worse, and partly from the disagreeable thought that occurred to him of the stir this would make in all the nest of influential persons on the staff; of its effect on Bennigsen in particular, who since the battle of Tarutino had been at daggers drawn with Kutuzov; of the suppositions and discussions and orders and counter-orders. And the presentiment of all that was disagreeable to him, though he knew it to be inevitable.

Toll, to whom he went to communicate the news, did in fact begin at once expounding his views on the situation to the general who shared his abode; and Konovnitsyn, after listening in weary silence, reminded him that they must go to his highness.

XVII

LIKE all old people, Kutuzov slept little at night. He often dropped into sudden naps during the daytime, but at night he lay on his bed without undressing, and generally not asleep but thinking.

He was lying like that now on his bedstead, his huge, heavy, misshapen head leaning on his fat hand. He was thinking with his one eye wide open, gazing into the darkness.

Since Bennigsen, who was in correspondence with the Tsar and had more weight than all the rest of the staff, had avoided him, Kutuzov was more at ease so far as not being compelled to lead his soldiers into useless offensive operations. The lesson of Tarutino and the day before the battle, a memory that rankled in Kutuzov's mind, must, he thought, have its effect on them too.

"They ought to understand that we can but lose by taking the offensive. Time and patience, these are my champions!" thought Kutuzov. He knew the apple must not be picked while it was green. It will fall of itself when ripe, but if you pick it green, you spoil the apple and the tree and set your teeth on edge. Like an experienced hunter, he knew the beast was wounded, wounded as only the whole force of Russia could wound it; but whether to death or not, was a question not yet solved. Now from the sending of Lauriston and Bertemy, and from the reports brought by the irregulars, Kutuzov was almost sure that the wound was a deadly one. But more proof was wanted; he must wait.

"They want to run and look how they have wounded him. Wait a bit, you will see. Always manœuvres, attacks," he thought. "What for? Anything to distinguish themselves. As though there were any fun in fighting. They are like children from whom you can never get a sensible view of things because they all want to show how well they can fight. But that's not the point now. And what skilful manœuvres all these fellows propose! They think that when they have thought of two or three contingencies (he recalled the general plan from Petersburg) that they have thought of all of them. And there is no limit to them!"

The unanswered question, whether the wound dealt at Borodino were mortal or not, had been for a whole month hanging over Kutuzov's head. On one side, the French had taken possession of Moscow. On the other side, in all his being, Kutuzov felt beyond all doubt that the terrible blow for which, together with all the Russians, he had strained all his strength must have been mortal. But in any case proofs were wanted, and he had been waiting for them now a month, and as time went on he grew more impatient. As he lay on his bed through sleepless nights, he did the very thing these younger generals did, the very thing he found fault with in them. He imagined all possible contingencies, just like the younger generation, but with this difference that he based no conclusion on the suppositions, and that he saw these contingencies not as two or three, but as thousands. The more he pondered, the more of them he saw. He imagined all sorts of movements of Napoleon's army, acting as a whole or in part, on Petersburg, against him, to out-flank him (that was what he was most afraid of), and also the possibility that Napoleon would fight against him with his own weapon, that he would stay on in Moscow waiting for him to move. Kutuzov even imagined Napoleon's army marching back to Medyn and Yuhnov. But the one thing he could not foresee was what happened—the mad, convulsive stampede of Napoleon's army during the first eleven days of its march from Moscow— the stampede that made possible what Kutuzov did not yet dare to think about, the complete annihilation of the French. Dorohov's report of Broussier's division, the news brought by the irregulars of the miseries of Napoleon's army, rumours of preparations for leaving Moscow, all confirmed the supposition that the French army was beaten and preparing to take flight. But all this was merely supposition, that seemed of weight to the younger men, but not to Kutuzov. With his sixty years' experience he knew how much weight to attach to rumours; he knew how ready men are when they desire anything to manipulate all evidence so as to confirm what they desire; and he knew how readily in that case they let everything of an opposite significance pass unheeded. And the more Kutuzov desired this supposition to be correct, the less he permitted himself to believe it. This question absorbed all his spiritual energies. All the rest was for him the mere customary performance of the routine of life. Such a customary performance and observance of routine were his conversations with the staff-officers, his letters to Madame de Staël that he wrote from Tarutino, his French novels, distribution of rewards, correspondence with Petersburg, and so on. But the destruction of the French, which he alone foresaw, was the one absorbing desire of his heart.

On the night of the 11th of October he lay leaning on his arm and thinking of that.

There was a stir in the next room, and he heard the steps of Toll, Konovnitsyn and Bolhovitinov.

"Hey, who is there? Come in, come in! Anything new?" the commander-in-chief called to them.

While a footman lighted a candle, Toll told the drift of the news.

"Who brought it?" asked Kutuzov, with a face that impressed Toll when the candle was lighted by its frigid sternness.

"There can be no doubt of it, your highness."

"Call him, call him here!"

Kutuzov sat with one leg out of bed and his unwieldy, corpulent body propped on the other leg bent under him. He screwed up his one seeing eye to get a better view of the messenger, as though he hoped in his face to read what he cared to know.

"Tell me, tell me, my dear fellow," he said to Bolhovitinov, in his low, aged voice, pulling the shirt together that had come open over his chest. "Come here, come closer. What news is this you have brought me? Eh? Napoleon has marched out of Moscow? Is it truly so? Eh?"

Bolhovitinov began repeating in detail the message that had been given him.

"Tell me, make haste, don't torture me," Kutuzov interrupted him.

Bolhovitinov told him all and paused, awaiting instructions. Toll was beginning to speak, but Kutuzov checked him. He tried to say something, but all at once his face began to work, to pucker; waving his hand at Toll, he turned the other way to the corner of the hut, which looked black with the holy pictures. "Lord, my Creator! Thou hast heard our prayer . . ." he said in a trembling voice, clasping his hands. "Russia is saved. I thank Thee, O Lord." And he burst into tears.

XVIII

FROM that time up to the end of the campaign, all Kutuzov's activity was limited to trying by the exercise of authority, by guile and by entreaties, to hold his army back from useless attacks, manœuvres, and skirmishes with the perishing enemy. Dohturov marched to Maley Yaroslavets, but Kutuzov lingered with the main army, and gave orders for the clearing of the Kaluga, retreat beyond which seemed to Kutuzov quite possible.

Everywhere Kutuzov retreated, but the enemy, without waiting for him to retire, fled back in the opposite direction.

Napoleon's historians describe to us his skilful manœuvres at Tarutino, and at Maley Yaroslavets, and discuss what would have happened if Napoleon had succeeded in making his way to the wealthy provinces of the south.

But to say nothing of the fact that nothing hindered Napoleon from marching into these southern provinces (since the Russian army left the road open), the historians forget that nothing could have saved Napoleon's army, because it carried within itself at that time the inevitable germs of ruin. Why should that army, which found abundant provisions in Moscow and could not keep them, but trampled them underfoot, that army which could not store supplies on entering Smolensk, but plundered at random, why should that army have mended its ways in the Kaluga province, where the inhabitants were of the same Russian race as in Moscow, and where fire had the same aptitude for destroying whatever they set fire to.

The army could not have recovered itself any way. From the battle of Borodino and the sacking of Moscow it bore within itself, as it were, the chemical elements of dissolution.

The men of what had been an army fled with their leaders, not knowing whither they went, Napoleon and every soldier with him filled with one desire: to make his own escape as quickly as might be from the hopeless position of which all were dimly aware.

At the council in Maley Yaroslavets, when the French generals, affecting to be deliberating, gave various opinions as to what was to be done, the opinion of the blunt soldier, Mouton, who said what all were thinking, that the only thing to do was to get away as quickly as possible, closed every one's mouth; and no one, not even Napoleon, could say anything in opposition to this truth that all recognised.

But though everybody knew that they must go, there was still a feeling of shame left at acknowledging they must fly. And some external shock was necessary to overcome that shame. And that shock came when it was needed. It was *le Hourra de l'Empereur*, as the French called it.

On the day after the council, Napoleon, on the pretext of inspecting the troops and the field of a past and of a future battle, rode out early in the morning in the midst of the lines of his army with a suite of marshals and an escort. The Cossacks, who were in search of booty, swept down on the Emperor, and all but took him prisoner. What saved Napoleon from the Cossacks that day was just what was the ruin of the French army, the booty, which here as well as at Tarutino tempted the Cossacks to let their prey slip. Without taking any notice of Napoleon, they dashed at the booty, and Napoleon succeeded in getting away.

When *les enfants du Don* might positively capture the Emperor himself in the middle of his army, it was evident that there was nothing else to do but to fly with all possible haste by the nearest and the familiar road. Napoleon, with his forty years and his corpulence, had not all his old resourcefulness and courage, and he quite took the hint; and under the influence of the fright the Cossacks had given him, he agreed at once with Mouton, and gave, as the historians tell us, the order to retreat along the Smolensk road.

The fact that Napoleon agreed with Mouton, and that the army did not retreat in that direction, does not prove that his command decided that retreat, but that the forces acting on the whole army and driving it along the Mozhaisk road were simultaneously acting upon Napoleon too.

XIX

WHEN a man finds himself in movement, he always invents a goal of that movement. In order to walk a thousand versts, a man must believe that there is some good beyond those thousand versts. He needs a vision of a promised land to have the strength to go on moving. The promised land for the French on their march into Russia was Moscow; on their retreat it was their own country. But their country was too far; and a man walking a thousand versts must inevitably put aside his final goal and say to himself every day that he is going to walk forty versts to a resting-place where he can sleep; and before the first halt that resting-place has eclipsed the image of the final goal, and all his hopes and desires are concentrated on it. All impulses manifest in the individual are always greatly exaggerated in a crowd.

For the French, marching back along the old Smolensk road, the final goal, their own country, was too remote, and the nearer goal on which all hopes and desires, enormously intensified by the influence of the crowd, were concentrated, was Smolensk.

It was not because the soldiers knew that there were plentiful supplies in Smolensk and reinforcements, nor because they were told so (on the contrary, the generals and Napoleon himself knew that the supplies there were scanty), but because this was the only thing that could give them the strength to move and to bear their present hardships, that they —those that knew better and those that did not alike—deceived themselves, and rushed to Smolensk as to a land of promise.

When they got out on the high road, the French fled to their imagined goal with extraordinary energy and unheard-of rapidity. Apart from the common impulse that bound the crowds of Frenchmen together into one whole and gave them a certain momentum, there was another cause that held them together, that cause was their immense number. As in the physical law of gravitation, the immense mass of them drew the separate atoms to itself. They moved in their mass of hundreds of thousands like a whole state.

Every man among them longed for one thing only—to surrender and be taken prisoner, to escape from all the horrors and miseries of his actual position. But on one hand the momentum of the common impulse toward Smolensk drew each individual in the same direction. On the other hand, it was out of the question for a corps to surrender to a squadron; and although the French took advantage of every convenient opportunity to straggle away from one another, and on the smallest decent pretext to be taken prisoners, those opportunities did not always occur. Their very number, and their rapid movement in such a closely-packed mass, deprived them of such possibilities, and made it not only difficult but impossible for the Russians to stop that movement into which the whole energy of that great mass was thrown. No mechanical splitting up of the body could accelerate beyond certain limits the process of dissolution that was going on within it.

A snowball cannot be melted instantaneously. There is a certain limit of time within which no application of heat can thaw the snow. On the contrary, the greater the heat, the harder the snow that is left.

Of the Russian generals no one but Kutuzov understood this. When the flight of the French army took its final direction along the Smolensk road, then what Kutuzov had foreseen on the night of the 11th of October began to come to pass. All the generals and officers of the Russian army were eager to distinguish themselves, to cut off the enemy's retreat, to overtake, to capture, to fall upon the French, and all clamoured for action.

Kutuzov alone used all his powers (and the powers of any commander-in-chief are far from great) to resist this clamour for attack.

He could not tell them what we can say now: he could not ask them what was the object of fighting and obstructing the road and losing our men, and inhumanly persecuting the poor wretches, when one-third of that army melted away of itself without a battle between Moscow and Vyazma. But drawing from the stores of his aged wisdom what they could understand, he told them of the golden bridge, and they laughed at him, slandered him, pushed on and dashed forward, exulting over the wounded beast.

Near Vyazma, Yermolov, Miloradovitch, Platov, and others, finding themselves in the neighbourhood of the French, could not resist the desire to cut them off and to fall upon two French corps. In sending to inform Kutuzov of their project, they slipped a blank sheet of paper into the envelope instead of the despatch.

And in spite of Kutuzov's efforts to restrain the army, our soldiers attacked the French and tried to bar their way. The infantry regiments, we are told, marched to attack them with music and beating of drums and slew and were slain by thousands.

But as for cutting off their retreat—none were cut off nor turned aside. And the French army, brought into closer cohesion by danger, and slowly melting as it went, kept still on its fatal way to Smolensk.

PART FOURTEEN

I

THE BATTLE of Borodino with the occupation of Moscow and the flight of the French, that followed without any more battles, is one of the most instructive phenomena in history.

All historians are agreed that the external activity of states and peoples in their conflicts finds expression in wars; that the political power of states and peoples is increased or diminished as the immediate result of success or defeat in war.

Strange are the historical accounts that tell us how some king or emperor, quarrelling with another king or emperor, levies an army, fights a battle with the army of his foe, gains a victory, kills three, five, or ten thousand men, and consequently subdues a state and a whole people consisting of several millions; and incomprehensible it seems that the defeat of any army, one hundredth of the whole strength of a people, should force that people to submit. Yet all the facts of history (so far as we know it) confirm the truth of the statement, that the successes or defeats of a nation's army are the causes or, at least, the invariable symptoms of the increase or diminution of the power of a nation. An army gains a victory, and immediately the claims of the conquering people are increased to the detriment of the conquered. An army is defeated, and at once the people loses its rights in proportion to the magnitude of the defeat; and if its army is utterly defeated, the people is completely conquered. So (according to history) it has been from the most ancient times up to the present. All Napoleon's earlier wars serve as illustrations of the rule. As the Austrian armies were defeated, Austria was deprived of her rights, and the rights and power of France were increased. The victories of the French at Jena and at Auerstadt destroyed the independent existence of Prussia.

But suddenly, in 1812, the French gained a victory before Moscow. Moscow was taken, and in consequence of that, with no subsequent battles, not Russia, but the French army of six hundred thousand, and then Napoleonic France itself ceased to exist. To strain the facts to fit the rules of history, to maintain that the field of Borodino was left in the hands of the Russians, or that after the evacuation of Moscow, there were battles that destroyed Napoleon's army—is impossible.

After the victory of the French at Borodino, there was no general engagement, nor even a skirmish of any great importance, yet the French army ceased to exist. What is the meaning of it? If it had been an example from the history of China, we could have said it was not an historical fact (the resource of historians, when anything will not fit in with their rules). If it had occurred in a conflict on a small scale, in which only small numbers of soldiers had taken part, we might have looked upon it as an exception. But all this took place before the eyes of our fathers, for whom it was a question of life and death for their country; and the war was on a larger scale than any wars we know of.

The sequel of the campaign of 1812—from Borodino to the final expulsion of the French—has proved that victories are not always a cause nor even an invariable sign of conquest; it has proved that the force that decides the fate of peoples does not lie in military leaders, nor even in armies and battles, but in something else.

The French historians, who describe the position of the French troops before they marched out of Moscow, assert that everything was in good order in the Grande Armée, except the cavalry, the artillery, and the transport, and that there was no forage for the horses and cattle. There was no remedy for this defect, because the peasants of the surrounding country burned their hay rather than let the French have it.

Victory did not bring forth its usual results, because the peasants, Karp and Vlas, by no means persons of heroic feelings (after the French evacuation, they hurried with their carts to pillage Moscow), and the immense multitude of others like them burnt their hay rather than bring it to Moscow, however high the prices offered them.

Let us imagine two men, who have come out to fight a duel with swords in accordance with all the rules of the art of swordsmanship. The fencing has lasted for some time. All at once one of the combatants, feeling that he is wounded, grasping that it is no joking matter, but a question of life and death, flings away his sword, and snatching up the first cudgel that comes handy, begins to brandish that. But let us imagine that the combatant, who has so sensibly made use of the best and simplest means for the attainment of his object, should be inspired by the traditions of chivalry to try and disguise the real cause of the conflict and should persist in declaring that he had been victor in the duel in accordance with all the rules of swordsmanship. One can imagine what confusion and obscurity would arise from his description of the duel!

The duellist, who insisted on the conflict being fought in accordance with the principles of the fencer's art, stands for the French; his opponent, who flung away his sword and snatched up a cudgel, did like the Russians; and the attempted description of the duel in accordance with the rules of swordsmanship has been given us by the historians of the war.

From the time of the burning of Smolensk a war began which did not follow any of the old traditions of warfare. The burning of towns and villages, the retreat after every battle, the blow dealt at Borodino and followed by retreat, the burning of Moscow, the capture of marauders, the seizing of transports,—the whole of the irregular warfare was a departure from the rules.

Napoleon was aware of it, and from the time when he stood waiting in Moscow in the correct pose of the victorious fencer, and instead of his opponent's sword, saw the bludgeon raised against him, he never ceased complaining to Kutuzov and to the Emperor Alexander that the war was being conducted contrary to all the rules of war. (As though any rules existed for the slaughter of men!)

In spite of the complaints of the French that they did not keep to the rules, in spite of the fact that the Russians in the highest positions felt it somehow shameful to be fighting with a cudgel, and wanted to take up the correct position *en quarte* or *en tierce*, to make a skilful thrust, *en prime* and so on, the cudgel of the people's war was raised in all its menacing and majestic power; and troubling itself about no question of any one's tastes or rules, about no fine distinctions, with stupid simplicity, with perfect consistency, it rose and fell and belaboured the French till the whole invading army had been driven out.

And happy the people that will not, as the French did in 1813, saluting according to the rules, gracefully and cautiously offer the sword hilt to the magnanimous conqueror. Happy the people who, in the moment of trial, asks no questions how others would act by the recognised rules in such cases, but with ease and directness picks up the first cudgel that comes handy and deals blows with it, till resentment and revenge give way to contempt and pity.

II

ONE of the most conspicuous and advantageous departures from the so-called rules of warfare is the independent action of men acting separately against men huddled together in a mass. Such independent activity is always seen in a war that assumes a national character. In this kind of warfare, instead of forming in a crowd to attack a crowd, men disperse in small groups, attack singly and at once fly, when attacked by superior forces, and then attack again, when an opportunity presents itself. Such were the methods of the guerillas in Spain; of the mountain tribes in the Caucasus, and of the Russians in 1812.

War of this kind has been called partisan warfare on the supposition that this name defined its special significance. But this kind of warfare does not follow any rules of war, but is in direct contradiction to a well-known rule of tactics, regarded as infallible. That rule lays it down that the attacking party must concentrate his forces in order to be stronger than his opponent at the moment of conflict.

Partisan warfare (always successful, as history testifies) acts in direct contradiction of this rule.

Military science assumes that the relative strength of forces is identical with their numerical proportions. Military science maintains that the greater the number of soldiers, the greater their strength. *Les gros bataillons ont toujours raison.*

To say this is as though one were in mechanics to say that forces were equal or unequal simply because the masses of the moving bodies were equal or unequal.

Force (the volume of motion) is the product of the mass into the velocity.

In warfare the force of armies is the product of the mass multiplied by something else, an unknown x.

Military science, seeing in history an immense number of examples in which the mass of an army does not correspond with its force, and in which small numbers conquer large ones, vaguely recognises the existence of this unknown factor, and tries to find it sometimes in some geometrical disposition of the troops, sometimes in the superiority of weapons, and most often in the genius of the leaders. But none of those factors yield results that agree with the historical facts.

One has but to renounce the false view that glorifies the effect of the activity of the heroes of history in warfare in order to discover this unknown quantity, x.

X is the spirit of the army, the greater or less desire to fight and to face dangers on the part of all the men composing the army, which is quite apart from the question whether they are fighting under leaders of genius or not, with cudgels or with guns that fire thirty times a minute. The men who have the greater desire to fight always put themselves, too, in the more advantageous position for fighting. The spirit of the army is the factor which multiplied by the mass gives the product of the force. To define and express the significance of this unknown factor, the spirit of the army, is the problem of science.

This problem can only be solved when we cease arbitrarily substituting for that unknown factor x the conditions under which the force is manifested, such as the plans of the general, the arming of the men and so on, and recognise this unknown factor in its entirety as the greater or less desire to fight and face danger. Then only by expressing known historical facts in equations can one hope from comparison of the relative value of this unknown factor to approach its definition. Ten men, or battalions or divisions are victorious fighting with fifteen men or battalions or divisions, that is, they kill or take prisoner all of them while losing four of their own side, so that the loss has been four on one side and fifteen on the other. Consequently, four on one side have been equivalent to fifteen on the other, and consequently $4x = 15y$. Consequently $\frac{x}{y} = \frac{15}{4}$. This equation does not give us the value of the unknown factors, but it does give us the ratio between their values. And from the reduction to such equations of various historical units (battles, campaigns, periods of warfare) a series of numbers are obtained, in which there must be and may be discovered historical laws.

The strategic principle, that armies should act in masses on the offensive, and should break up into smaller groups for retreat, unconsciously confirms the truth that the force of an army depends on its spirit. To lead men forward under fire needs more discipline (which can only be attained by marching in masses) than is needed for self-defence when attacked. But this rule, which leaves out of sight the spirit of the army, is continually proving unsound, and is strikingly untrue in practice in all national wars, when there is a great rise or fall in the spirit of the armies.

The French, on their retreat in 1812, though they should, by the laws of tactics, have defended themselves in detached groups, huddled together in a crowd, because the spirit of the men had sunk so low that it was only their number that kept them up. The Russians should, on the contrary, by the laws of tactics, have attacked them in a mass, but in fact attacked in scattered companies, because the spirit of the men ran so high that individual men killed the French without orders, and needed no compulsion to face hardships and dangers.

III

THE so-called "partisan" warfare had begun with the enemy's entrance into Smolensk. Before the irregular warfare was officially recognised by our government many thousands of the enemy's soldiers—straggling, marauding, or foraging parties—had been slain by Cossacks and peasants, who killed these men as instinctively as dogs set upon a stray mad dog. Denis Davydov was the first to feel with his Russian instinct the value of this terrible cudgel which belaboured the French, and asked no questions about the etiquette of the military art; and to him belongs the credit of the first step towards the recognition of this method of warfare.

The first detachment of irregulars—Davydov's—was formed on the 24th of August, and others soon followed. In the latter stages of the campaign these detachments became more and more numerous.

The irregulars destroyed the Grande Armée piecemeal. They swept up the fallen leaves that were dropping of themselves from the withered tree, and sometimes they shook the tree itself. By October, when the French were fleeing to Smolensk, there were hundreds of these companies, differing widely from one another in number and in character. Some were detachments that followed all the usual routine of an army, with infantry, artillery, staff-officers, and all the conveniences of life. Some consisted only of Cossacks, mounted men. Others were small bands of men, on foot and also mounted. Some consisted of peasants, or of landowners and their serfs, and remained unknown. There was a deacon at the head of such a band, who took several hundred prisoners in a month. There was the village elder's wife, Vassilisa, who killed hundreds of the French.

The latter part of October was the time when this guerilla warfare reached its height. That period of this warfare, in which the irregulars were themselves amazed at their own audacity, were every moment in dread of being surrounded and captured by the French, and never unsaddling, hardly dismounting, hid in the woods, in momentary expectation of pursuit, was already over. The irregular warfare had by now taken definite shape; it had become clear to all the irregulars what they could, and what they could not, accomplish with the French. By now it was only the commanders of detachments marching with staff-officers according to the rules at a distance from the French who considered much impossible. The small bands of irregulars who had been at work a long while, and were at close quarters with the French, found it possible to attempt what the leaders of larger companies did not dare to think of doing. The Cossacks and the peasants, who crept in among the French, thought everything possible now.

On the 22nd of October, Denisov, who was a leader of a band of irregulars, was eagerly engaged in a typical operation of this irregular warfare. From early morning he had been with his men moving about the woods that bordered the high road, watching a big convoy of cavalry baggage and Russian prisoners that had dropped behind the other French troops, and under strong escort—as he learned from his scouts and from prisoners—was making its way to Smolensk. Not only Denisov and Dolohov (who was also a leader of a small band acting in the same district) were aware of the presence of this convoy. Some generals in command of some larger detachments, with staff-officers also, knew of this convoy, and, as Denisov said, their mouths were watering for it. Two of these generals—one a Pole, the other a German—had almost at the same time sent to Denisov an invitation to join their respective detachments in attacking the convoy.

"No, friend, I wasn't born yesterday!" said Denisov, on reading these documents; and he wrote to the German that in spite of his ardent desire to serve under so brilliant and renowned a general, he must deprive himself of that happiness because he was already under the command of the Polish general. To the Pole he wrote the same thing, informing him that he was already serving under the command of the German.

Having thus disposed of that difficulty, Denisov, without communicating on the subject to the higher authorities, intended with Dolohov to attack and carry off this transport with his own small force. The transport was, on the 22nd of October, going from the village of Mikulino to the village of Shamshevo. On the left side of the road between Mikulino and Shamshevo there were great woods, which in places bordered on the road, and in places were a verst or more from the road. Denisov, with a small party of followers, had been the whole day riding about in these woods, sometimes plunging into their centre, and sometimes coming out at the edge, but never losing sight of the moving French. In the morning, not far from Mikulino, where the wood ran close to the road, the Cossacks of Denisov's party had pounced on two French waggonloads of saddles, stuck in the mud, and had carried them off into the wood. From that time right on to evening, they had been watching the movements of the French without attacking them. They wanted to avoid frightening them, and to let them go quietly on to Shamshevo, and then, joining Dolohov (who was to come that evening to a trysting-place in the wood, a verst from Shamshevo, to concert measures with them), from two sides to fall at dawn like an avalanche of snow on their heads, and to overcome and capture all of them at a blow.

Six Cossacks had been left behind, two versts from Mikulino, where the wood bordered the road. They were to bring word at once as soon as any fresh columns of French came into sight.

In front of Shamshevo, Dolohov was in the same way to watch the road to know at what distance there were other French troops. With the transport there were supposed to be fifteen hundred men. Denisov had two hundred men, and Dolohov might have as many more. But superiority in numbers was no obstacle to Denisov. There was only one thing that he still needed to know, and that was what troops these were; and for that object Denisov needed to take a "tongue" (that is, some man belonging to that column of the enemy). The attack on the waggons in the morning was all done with such haste that they killed all the French soldiers in charge of the waggons, and captured alive only a little drummer-boy, who had straggled away from his own regiment, and could tell them nothing certain about the troops forming the column.

To make another descent upon them, Denisov thought, would be to risk alarming the whole column, and so he sent on ahead to Shamshevo a peasant, Tihon Shtcherbatov, to try if he could capture at least one of the French quartermasters from the vanguard.

IV

It was a warm, rainy, autumn day. The sky and the horizon were all of the uniform tint of muddy water. Sometimes a mist seemed to be falling, and sometimes there was a sudden downpour of heavy, slanting rain.

Denisov, in a long cape and a high fur cap, both streaming with water, was riding a thin, pinched-looking, thoroughbred horse. With his head aslant, and his ears pricked up, like his horse, he was frowning at the driving rain, and anxiously looking before him. His face, which had grown thin, and was covered with a thick, short, black beard, looked wrathful.

Beside Denisov, wearing also a long cape and a high cap, and mounted on a sleek, sturdy Don horse, rode the esaul, or hetman of the Cossacks —Denisov's partner in his enterprises.

The esaul, Lovaisky, a third man, also in a cape, and a high cap, was a long creature, flat as a board, with a pale face, flaxen hair, narrow, light eyes, and an expression of calm self-confidence both in his face and his attitude. Though it was impossible to say what constituted the peculiarity of horse and rider, at the first glance at the esaul and at Denisov, it was evident that Denisov was both wet and uncomfortable; that Denisov was a man sitting on a horse; while the esaul seemed as comfortable and calm as always, and seemed not a man sitting on a horse, but a man forming one whole with a horse—a single being enlarged by the strength of two.

A little ahead of them walked a peasant-guide, soaked through and through in his grey full coat and white cap.

A little behind, on a thin, delicate Kirghiz pony, with a flowing tail and mane, and a mouth flecked with blood, rode a young officer in a blue French military coat. Beside him rode an hussar, with a boy in a tattered French uniform and blue cap, perched upon his horse behind him. The boy held on to the hussar with hands red with cold, and kept moving his bare feet, trying to warm them, and lifting his eyebrows, gazed about him wonderingly. This was the French drummer, who had been taken in the morning.

Along the narrow, muddy, cut-up forest-track there came hussars in knots of three and four at a time, and then Cossacks; some in capes, some in French cloaks; others with horse-cloths pulled over their heads. The horses, chestnut and bay, all looked black from the soaking rain. Their necks looked strangely thin with their drenched manes, and steam rose in clouds from them. Clothes, saddles, and bridles, all were sticky and swollen with the wet, like the earth and the fallen leaves with which the track was strewn. The men sat huddled up, trying not to move, so as to keep warm the water that had already reached their skins, and not to let any fresh stream of cold rain trickle in anywhere under their seat, or at their knees or necks. In the midst of the file of Cossacks two wag-gons, drawn by French horses, and Cossack saddle-horses hitched on in front, rumbled over stumps and branches, and splashed through the ruts full of water.

Denisov's horse, in avoiding a puddle in the track, knocked his rider's knee against a tree.

"Ah, devil!" Denisov cried angrily; and showing his teeth, he struck his horse three times with his whip, splashing himself and his comrades with mud. Denisov was out of humour, both from the rain and hunger (no one had eaten anything since morning); and, most of all, from hav-ing no news of Dolohov, and from no French prisoner having been caught to give him information.

"We shall never have such another chance to fall on the transport as to-day. To attack them alone would be risky, and to put it off to another day—some one of the bigger leaders will carry the booty off from under our noses," thought Denisov, continually looking ahead, and fancying he saw the messenger from Dolohov he expected.

Coming out into a clearing from which he could get a view to some distance on the right, Denisov stopped.

"There's some one coming," he said.

The esaul looked in the direction Denisov was pointing to.

"There are two men coming—an officer and a Cossack. Only I wouldn't be *prepositive* that is the colonel himself," said the esaul, who loved to use words that were unfamiliar to the Cossacks. The two fig-ures, riding downhill, disappeared from sight, and came into view again a few minutes later. The foremost was an officer, dishevelled looking, and soaked through, with his trousers tucked up above his knees; he was lashing his horse into a weary gallop. Behind him a Cossack trotted along, standing up in his stirrups. This officer, a quite young boy, with a broad, rosy face and keen, merry eyes, galloped up to Denisov, and handed him a sopping packet

"From the general," he said. "I must apologise for its not being quite dry. . . ."

Denisov, frowning, took the packet and broke it open.

"Why, they kept telling us it was so dangerous," said the officer, turning to the esaul while Denisov was reading the letter. "But Komarov"—and he indicated the Cossack—"and I were prepared. We have both two pisto . . . But what's this?" he asked, seeing the French drummer-boy. "A prisoner? You have had a battle already? May I talk to him?"

"Rostov! Petya!" Denisov cried at that moment, running through the packet that had been given him. "Why, how was it you didn't say who you were?" and Denisov, turning with a smile, held out his hand to the officer. This officer was Petya Rostov.

Petya had been all the way preparing himself to behave with Denisov as a grown-up person and an officer should do, making no reference to their previous acquaintance. But as soon as Denisov smiled at him, Petya beamed at once, blushed with delight, and forgetting all the formal demeanour he had been intending to preserve, he began telling him how he had ridden by the French, and how glad he was he had been given this commission, and how he had already been in a battle at Vyazma, and how a certain hussar had distinguished himself in it.

"Well, I am glad to see you," Denisov interrupted him, and his face looked anxious again.

"Mihail Feoklititch," he said to the esaul, "this is from the German again, you know. He" (Petya) "is in his suite." And Denisov told the esaul that the letter, which had just been brought, repeated the German general's request that they would join him in attacking the transport. "If we don't catch them by to-morrow, he'll snatch them from under our noses," he concluded.

While Denisov was talking to the esaul, Petya, disconcerted by Denisov's cold tone, and imagining that that tone might be due to the condition of his trousers, furtively pulled them down under his cloak, trying to do so unobserved, and to maintain as martial an air as possible.

"Will your honour have any instructions to give me?" he said to Denisov, putting his hand to the peak of his cap, and going back to the comedy of adjutant and general, which he had prepared himself to perform, "or should I remain with your honour?"

"Instructions? . . ." said Denisov absently. "Well, can you stay till to-morrow?"

"As, please . . . May I stay with you?" cried Petya.

"Well, what were your instructions from your general—to go back at once?" asked Denisov.

Petya blushed.

"Oh, he gave me no instructions. I think I may?" he said interrogatively.

"All right, then," said Denisov. And turning to his followers, he directed a party of them to go to the hut in the wood, which they had fixed on as a resting-place, and the officer on the Kirghiz horse (this officer performed the duties of an adjutant) to go and look for Dolohov, to find out where he was, and whether he were coming in the evening.

Denisov himself, with the esaul and Petya, intended to ride to the edge of the wood near Shamshevo to have a look at the position of the French, where their attack next day was to take place.

"Come, my man," he said to their peasant guide, "take us to Shamshevo."

Denisov, Petya, and the esaul, accompanied by a few Cossacks and the hussar with the prisoner, turned to the left and crossed a ravine towards the edge of the wood.

V

THE rain was over, but a mist was falling and drops of water dripped from the branches of the trees. Denisov, the esaul, and Petya, in silence, followed the peasant in the pointed cap, who, stepping lightly and noiselessly in his bast shoes over roots and wet leaves, led them to the edge of the wood.

Coming out on the road, the peasant paused, looked about him, and turned toward a thin screen of trees. He stood still at a big oak, still covered with leaves, and beckoned mysteriously to them.

Denisov and Petya rode up to him. From the place where the peasant was standing the French could be seen. Just beyond the wood a field of spring corn ran sharply downhill. On the right, across a steep ravine, could be seen a little village and a manor-house with the roofs broken down. In that village and in the house and all over the high ground in the garden, by the wells and the pond, and all along the road uphill from the bridge to the village, not more than five hundred yards away, crowds of men could be seen in the shifting mist. They could distinctly hear their foreign cries at the horses pulling the baggage uphill and their calls to one another.

"Give me the prisoner here," said Denisov, in a low voice, never taking his eyes off the French.

A Cossack got off his horse, lifted the boy down, and came with him to Denisov. Denisov, pointing to the French, asked the boy what troops they were. The boy, thrusting his chilled hands into his pockets and raising his eyebrows, looked in dismay at Denisov, and in spite of his unmistakable desire to tell all he knew, he was confused in his answers, and merely repeated Denisov's questions. Denisov, frowning, turned away from him, and addressing the esaul, told him his own views on the matter.

Petya, turning his head rapidly, looked from the drummer to Denisov, and from the esaul to the French in the village and on the road, trying not to miss anything of importance.

"Whether Dolohov comes or not, we must take them. . . . Eh?" said Denisov, his eyes sparkling merrily.

"It is a convenient spot," said the esaul.

"We will send the infantry down below, by the marshes," Denisov went on. "They will creep up to the garden; you dash down with the Cossacks from there"—Denisov pointed to the wood beyond the village —"and I from here with my hussars. And at a shot . . ."

"It won't do to go by the hollow; it's a bog," said the esaul. "The horses will sink in, you must skirt round more to the left. . . ."

While they were talking in undertones, there was the crack of a shot and a puff of white smoke in the hollow below near the pond, and the voices of hundreds of Frenchmen halfway up the hill rose in a ringing shout, as though in merry chorus. At the first minute both Denisov and the esaul darted back. They were so near that they fancied they were the cause of that shot and those shouts. But they had nothing to do with them. A man in something red was running through the marshes below. The French were evidently firing and shouting at him.

"Why, it's our Tihon," said the esaul.

"It's he! it's he!"

"The rogue," said Denisov.

"He'll get away!" said the esaul, screwing up his eyes.

The man they called Tihon, running up to the little river, splashed into it, so that the water spurted up round him, and disappearing for an instant, scrambled out on all fours, looking dark from the water, and ran on. The French, who had been pursuing him, stopped.

"Well, he's a smart fellow," said the esaul.

"The beast," said Denisov, with the same expression of vexation. "And what has he been about all this time?"

"Who is he?" asked Petya.

"It's our scout. I sent him to catch a 'tongue' for us."

"Ah, to be sure," said Petya, nodding at Denisov's first word, as though he knew all about it, though he did not understand a word.

Tihon Shtcherbatov was one of the most useful men among Denisov's followers. He was a peasant of the village of Pokrovskoe, near Gzhat. Denisov had come to Pokrovskoe early in his operations as a guerilla leader, and sending, as he always did, for the village elder, asked him what he knew about the French.

The village elder had answered, as all village elders always did answer, that he knew nothing about them, and had seen nothing of them. But when Denisov explained to him that his object was to kill the French, and inquired whether no French had strayed into his village, the village elder replied that there had been some *miroders* certainly, but that the only person who took any heed of such things was Tishka Shtcherbatov. Denisov ordered Tihon to be brought before him, and praising his activity, said in the presence of the elder a few words about the devotion to the Tsar and the Fatherland and the hatred of the French that all sons of the Fatherland must cherish in their hearts.

"We don't do any harm to the French," said Tihon, evidently scared at Denisov's words. "It's only, you know, just a bit of fun for the lads and me. The *miroders* now—we have killed a dozen or so of them, but we have done no harm else . . ."

Next day, when Denisov was leaving Pokrovskoe, having forgotten all about this peasant, he was told that Tihon was with his followers, and asked to be allowed to remain with them. Denisov bade them let him stay.

At first Tihon undertook the rough work of making fires, fetching water, skinning horses, and so on, but he soon showed great zeal and capacity for guerilla warfare. He would go after booty at night, and never failed to bring back French clothes and weapons, and when he was bidden, he would bring back prisoners too. Denisov took Tihon from his menial work, and began to employ him on expeditions, and to reckon him among the Cossacks.

Tihon did not like riding, and always went on foot, yet never lagged behind the cavalry. His weapons were a musket, which he carried rather as a joke, a pike, and an axe, which he used as skilfully as a wolf does its teeth—catching fleas in its coat and crunching thick bones with them equally easily. With equal precision Tihon swinging his axe split logs, or, taking it by the head, cut thin skewers or carved spoons. Among Denisov's followers, Tihon was on a special footing of his own. When anything particularly disagreeable or revolting had to be done—to put one's shoulder to a waggon stuck in the mud, to drag a horse out of a bog by the tail, to flay a horse, to creep into the midst of the French, to walk fifty versts in a day—every one laughed, and looked to Tihon to do it.

"No harm will come to him; the devil; he's a stalwart beast," they used to say of him.

One day a Frenchman he had captured wounded Tihon with a pistol-shot in the fleshy part of the back. This wound, which Tihon treated only by applications of vodka—internal and external—was the subject of the liveliest jokes through the whole party, and Tihon lent himself readily to their jests.

"Well, old chap, you won't do that again! Are you crook-backed!" laughed the Cossacks; and Tihon, assuming a doleful face, and grimacing to pretend he was angry, would abuse the French with the most comical oaths. The effect of the incident on Tihon was that he rarely afterwards brought prisoners in.

Tihon was the bravest and most useful man of the lot. No one discovered so many opportunities of attack, no one captured or killed so many Frenchmen. And consequently he was the favourite subject of all the gibes of the Cossacks and the hussars, and readily fell in with the position.

Tihon had been sent overnight by Denisov to Shamshevo to capture a "tongue." But either because he was not satisfied with one French prisoner, or because he had been asleep all night, he had crept by day into the bushes in the very middle of the French, and, as Denisov had seen from the hill, had been discovered by them.

VI

AFTER talking a little while longer with the esaul about the next day's attack, which Denisov seemed to have finally decided upon after seeing how near the French were, he turned his horse's head and rode back.

"Now, my boy, we will go and dry ourselves," he said to Petya.

As he came near the forester's hut, Denisov stopped, looking into the wood before him. A man in a short jacket, bast shoes, and a Kazan hat, with a gun across his shoulder, and an axe in his belt, was striding lightly through the forest with long legs and long arms swinging at his side. Catching sight of Denisov, he hastily flung something into the bushes, and taking off his sopped hat, the brim of which drooped limply, he walked up to his commanding officer.

This was Tihon. His pock-marked and wrinkled face, with little slits of eyes, beamed with self-satisfaction and merriment. He held his head high, and looked straight at Denisov as though he were suppressing a laugh.

"Well, where have you been?" said Denisov.

"Where have I been? I have been after the French," Tihon answered boldly and hastily, in a husky, but mellow bass.

"Why did you creep in in the daytime? Ass! Well, why didn't you catch one?"

"Catch one I did," said Tihon.

"Where is he, then?"

"I caught one at the very first at daybreak," Tihon went on, setting his feet down wider apart, in their flat, turned-up bast shoes; "and I took him into the wood too. I see he's no good. So, thinks I, better go and get another, rather more the proper article."

"Ay, the rogue, so that's how it is," said Denisov to the esaul. "Why didn't you bring that one?"

"Why, what was the use of bringing him in?" Tihon broke in, hurriedly and angrily. "A worthless fellow! Don't I know what sort you want?"

"Ah, you brute! . . . Well?"

"I went to get another," Tihon went on. "I crept up in this way in the wood, and I lay down." With a sudden, supple movement, Tihon lay down on his stomach, to show how he had done this. "One turned up," he went on, "I seized him like this," Tihon jumped up swiftly and lightly. " 'Come along to the colonel,' says I. He set up such a shouting; and then I saw four of them. And they rushed at me with their sabres. I went at them like this with my axe. 'What are you about?' says I. 'Christ be with you,' " cried Tihon, waving his arms and squaring his chest with a menacing scowl.

"Oh yes, we saw from the hill how you gave them the slip, through the pools," said the esaul, screwing up his sparkling eyes.

Petya had a great longing to laugh, but he saw that all the others re-

·frained from laughing. He kept looking rapidly from Tihon's face to the face of the esaul and Denisov, not knowing what to make of it all.

"Don't play the fool," said Denisov, coughing angrily. "Why didn't you bring the first man?"

Tihon began scratching his back with one hand and his head with the other, and all at once his countenance expanded into a beaming, foolish grin, showing the loss of a tooth that had given him his name, Shtcherbatov (*i.e.* lacking a tooth). Denisov smiled, and Petya went off into a merry peal of laughter, in which Tihon himself joined.

"Why, he was no good at all," said Tihon. "He was so badly dressed, how could I bring him? And a coarse fellow, your honour. Why, says he, 'I'm a general's son,' says he, 'I'm not going.' "

"Ugh, you brute!" said Denisov. "I wanted to question him . . ."

"Oh, I did question him," said Tihon. "He said he didn't know much. 'There are a lot of our men,' says he, 'but they are all poor creatures; that's all you can say for them. Give a good shout,' says he, 'and you can take them all,' " Tihon concluded, with a merry and determined look at Denisov.

"Mind, I'll give you a good hundred lashes that will teach you to play the fool," said Denisov sternly.

"Why be angry," said Tihon, "because I haven't seen your sort of Frenchmen? As soon as it gets dark, I'll catch whatever kind you like, three of them I'll bring."

"Well, come along," said Denisov, and all the way to the forester's hut he was silent, frowning angrily.

Tihon was walking behind, and Petya heard the Cossacks laughing with him and at him about a pair of boots that he had thrown into the bushes.

When the laughter roused by Tihon's words and smile had passed, and Petya understood for a moment that Tihon had killed the man, he had an uneasy feeling. He looked round at the boy prisoner, and there was a sudden pang in his heart. But that uneasiness only lasted a moment. He felt it incumbent on him to hold his head high, and with a bold and important air to question the esaul about the next day's expedition, that he might not be unworthy of the company in which he found himself.

The officer Denisov had sent to Dolohov met him on the way with the news that everything was going well with Dolohov, and that he was coming himself immediately.

Denisov at once became more cheerful, and beckoned Petya to him.

"Come, tell me about yourself," he said.

VII

On leaving Moscow, Petya had parted from his parents to join his regiment, and shortly afterwards had been appointed an orderly in attendance on a general who was in command of a large detachment. From the time of securing his commission, and even more since joining a regiment in active service, and taking part in the battle of Vyazma, Petya had been in a continual state of happy excitement at being grown-up, and of intense anxiety not to miss any opportunity of real heroism. He was highly delighted with all he had seen and experienced in the army, but, at the same time, he was always fancying that wherever he was not, there the most real and heroic exploits were at that very moment being performed. And he was in constant haste to be where he was not.

On the 21st of October, when his general expressed a desire to send some one to Denisov's company, Petya had so piteously besought him to send him, that the general could not refuse. But, as he was sending him off, the general recollected Petya's foolhardy behaviour at the battle of Vyazma, when, instead of riding by way of the road to take a message, Petya had galloped across the lines under the fire of the French, and had there fired a couple of pistol-shots. Recalling that prank, the general explicitly forbade Petya's taking part in any enterprise whatever that Denisov might be planning. This was why Petya had blushed and been disconcerted when Denisov asked him if he might stay. From the moment he set off till he reached the edge of the wood, Petya had fully intended to do his duty steadily, and to return at once. But when he saw the French, and saw Tihon, and learned that the attack would certainly take place that night, with the rapid transition from one view to another, characteristic of young people, he made up his mind that his general, for whom he had till that moment had the greatest respect, was a poor stick, and only a German, that Denisov was a hero, and the esaul a hero, and Tihon a hero, and that it would be shameful to leave them at a moment of difficulty.

It was getting dark when Denisov, with Petya and the esaul, reached the forester's hut. In the half-dark they could see saddled horses, Cossacks and hussars, rigging up shanties in the clearing, and building up a glowing fire in a hollow near, where the smoke would not be seen by the French. In the porch of the little hut there was a Cossack with his sleeves tucked up, cutting up a sheep. In the hut, three officers of Denisov's band were setting up a table made up of doors. Petya took off his wet clothes, gave them to be dried, and at once set to work to help the officers in fixing up a dining-table.

In ten minutes the table was ready and covered with a napkin. On the table was set vodka, a flask of rum, white bread, and roast mutton, and salt.

Sitting at the table with the officers, tearing the fat, savoury mutton with greasy fingers, Petya was in a childishly enthusiastic condition of tender love for all men and a consequent belief in the same feeling for himself in others.

"So what do you think, Vassily Fyodorovitch," he said to Denisov, "it won't matter my staying a day with you, will it?" And without waiting for an answer, he answered himself: "Why, I was told to find out, and here I am finding out . . . Only you must let me go into the middle . . . into the real . . . I don't care about rewards . . . But I do want

. . ." Petya clenched his teeth and looked about him, tossing his head and waving his arm.

"Into the real, real thing . . ." Denisov said, smiling.

"Only, please, do give me a command of something altogether, so that I really might command," Petya went on. "Why, what would it be to you? Ah, you want a knife?" he said to an officer, who was trying to tear off a piece of mutton. And he gave him his pocket-knife. The officer praised the knife.

"Please keep it. I have several like it . . ." said Petya, blushing. "Heavens! Why, I was quite forgetting," he cried suddenly. "I have some capital raisins, you know the sort without stones. We have a new canteen-keeper, and he does get first-rate things. I bought ten pounds of them. I'm fond of sweet things. Will you have some?" . . . And Petya ran out to his Cossack in the porch, and brought in some panniers in which there were five pounds of raisins. "Please take some."

"Don't you need a coffee-pot?" he said to the esaul; "I bought a famous one from our canteen-keeper! He has first-rate things. And he's very honest. That's the great thing. I'll be sure and send it you. Or perhaps your flints are worn out; that does happen sometimes. I brought some with me, I have got them here . . ." he pointed to the panniers. "A hundred flints. I bought them very cheap. You must please take as many as you want or all, indeed . . ." And suddenly, dismayed at the thought that he had let his tongue run away with him, Petya stopped short and blushed.

He began trying to think whether he had been guilty of any other blunders. And running through his recollections of the day the image of the French drummer-boy rose before his mind.

"We are enjoying ourselves, but how is he feeling? What have they done with him? Have they given him something to eat? Have they been nasty to him?" he wondered.

But thinking he had said too much about the flints, he was afraid to speak now.

"Could I ask about him?" he wondered. "They'll say: he's a boy himself, so he feels for the boy. I'll let them see to-morrow whether I'm a boy! Shall I feel ashamed if I ask?" Petya wondered. "Oh, well! I don't care," and he said at once, blushing and watching the officers' faces in dread of detecting amusement in them:

"Might I call that boy who was taken prisoner, and give him something to eat . . . perhaps . . ."

"Yes, poor little fellow," said Denisov, who clearly saw nothing to be ashamed of in this reminder. "Fetch him in here. His name is Vincent Bosse. Fetch him in."

"I'll call him," said Petya.

"Yes, do. Poor little fellow," repeated Denisov.

Petya was standing at the door as Denisov said this. He slipped in between the officers and went up to Denisov.

"Let me kiss you, dear old fellow," he said. "Ah, how jolly it is! how splendid!" And, kissing Denisov, he ran out into the yard.

"Bosse! Vincent!" Petya cried, standing by the door.

"Whom do you want, sir?" said a voice out of the darkness. Petya answered that he wanted the French boy, who had been taken prisoner that day.

"Ah! Vesenny?" said the Cossack.

His name Vincent had already been transformed by the Cossacks into Vesenny, and by the peasants and the soldiers into Visenya. In both names there was a suggestion of the spring—vesna—which seemed to them to harmonise with the figure of the young boy.

"He's warming himself there at the fire. Ay, Visenya! Visenya!" voices called from one to another with laughter in the darkness. "He is a sharp boy," said an hussar standing near Petya. "We gave him a meal not long ago. He was hungry, terribly."

There was a sound of footsteps in the darkness, and the drummer-boy came splashing through the mud with his bare feet towards the door.

"Ah, that's you!" said Petya. "Are you hungry? Don't be afraid, they won't hurt you," he added, shyly and cordially touching his hand. "Come in, come in."

"Thank you," answered the drummer, in a trembling, almost childish voice, and he began wiping the mud off his feet on the threshold. Petya had a great deal he longed to say to the drummer-boy, but he did not dare. He stood by him in the porch, moving uneasily. Then he took his hand in the darkness and squeezed it. "Come in, come in," he repeated, but in a soft whisper.

"Oh, if I could only do something for him!" Petya was saying inwardly, and opening the door he ushered the boy in before him.

When the drummer-boy had come into the hut, Petya sat down at some distance from him, feeling that it would be lowering his dignity to take much notice of him. But he was feeling the money in his pocket and wondering whether it would do to give some to the drummer-boy.

VIII

L'ENISOV gave orders for the drummer-boy to be given some vodka and mutton, and to be put into a Russian dress, so that he should not be sent off with the other prisoners, but should stay with his band. Petya's attention was diverted from the boy by the arrival of Dolohov. He had heard a great many stories told in the army of Dolohov's extraordinary gallantry and of his cruelty to the French. And therefore from the moment Dolohov entered the hut Petya could not take his eyes off him, and flinging up his head, he assumed a more and more swaggering air, that he might not be unworthy of associating even with a hero like Dolohov.

Dolohov's appearance struck Petya as strange through its simplicity. Denisov was dressed in a Cossack coat; he had let his beard grow, and had a holy image of Nikolay, the wonder-worker, on his breast. His whole manner of speaking and all his gestures were suggestive of his peculiar position. Dolohov, on the contrary, though in old days he had worn a Persian dress in Moscow, looked now like the most correct officer of the Guards. He was clean-shaven; he wore the wadded coat of the Guards with a St. George medal on a ribbon, and a plain forage cap, put on straight on his head. He took his wet cloak off in the corner and, without greeting any one, went straight up to Denisov and began at once asking questions about the matter in hand. Denisov told him of the designs the larger detachment had upon the French convoy, of the message Petya had brought, and the answer he had given to both generals. Then he told him all he knew of the position of the French.

"That's so. But we must find out what troops they are, and what are their numbers," said Dolohov; "we must go and have a look at them. We can't rush into the thing without knowing for certain how many there are of them. I like to do things properly. Come, won't one of you gentlemen like to come with me to pay them a call in their camp? I have an extra uniform with me."

"I, I . . . I'll come with you!" cried Petya.

"There's not the slightest need for you to go," said Denisov, addressing Dolohov; "and as for him I wouldn't let him go on any account."

"That's good!" cried Petya; "why shouldn't I go? . . ."

"Why, because there's no reason to."

"Oh, well, excuse me . . . because . . . because . . . I'm going, and that's all. You will take me?" he cried, turning to Dolohov.

"Why not? . . ." Dolohov answered, absently, staring into the face of the French drummer-boy.

"Have you had that youngster long?" he asked Denisov.

"We caught him to-day, but he knows nothing; I have kept him with us."

"Oh, and what do you do with the rest?" said Dolohov.

"What do I do with them? I take a receipt for them, and send them off!" cried Denisov, suddenly flushing. "And I make bold to say that I haven't a single man's life on my conscience. Is there any difficulty in your sending thirty, or three hundred men, under escort, to the town rather than stain—I say so bluntly—one's honour as a soldier?"

"It's all very well for this little count here at sixteen to talk of such refinements," Dolohov said, with a cold sneer; "but it's high time for you to drop all that."

"Why, I am not saying anything, I only say that I am certainly going with you," said Petya shyly.

"But for me and you, mate, it's high time to drop such delicacy," Dolohov went on, apparently deriving peculiar gratification from talking on a subject irritating to Denisov. "Why have you kept this lad," he said, "except because you are sorry for him? Why, we all know how much your receipts are worth. You send off a hundred men and thirty reach the town. They die of hunger or are killed on the way. So isn't it just as well to make short work of them?"

The esaul, screwing up his light-coloured eyes, nodded his head approvingly.

"That's not my affair, no need to discuss it. I don't care to have their lives on my conscience. You say they die. Well, let them. Only not through my doing."

Dolohov laughed.

"Who prevented their taking me twenty times over? But you know if they do catch me—and you too with your chivalrous sentiments—it will just be the same—the nearest aspen-tree." He paused. "We must be getting to work, though. Send my Cossack here with the pack. I have two French uniforms. Well, are you coming with me?" he asked Petya.

"I? Yes, yes, of course," cried Petya, blushing till the tears came into his eyes, and glancing at Denisov.

While Dolohov had been arguing with Denisov what should be done with prisoners, Petya had again had that feeling of discomfort and nervous hurry; but again he had not time to get a clear idea of what they were talking about. "If that's what is thought by grown-up men, famous leaders, then it must be so, it must be all right," he thought. "And the great thing is, that Denisov shouldn't dare to imagine that I must obey him, that he can order me about. I shall certainly go with Dolohov into the French camp. He can go, and so can I!"

To all Denisov's efforts to dissuade him from going, Petya replied that he too liked doing things properly and not in haphazard fashion, and that he never thought about danger to himself.

"For, you must admit, if we don't know exactly how many men there are there, it might cost the life of hundreds, and it is only we two, and so I very much wish it, and I shall certainly, most certainly go, and don't try to prevent me," he said; "it won't be any use . . ."

IX

PETYA and Dolohov, after dressing up in French uniforms and shakoes, rode to the clearing from which Denisov had looked at the French camp, and coming out of the wood, descended into the hollow in the pitch darkness. When they had ridden downhill, Dolohov bade the Cossacks accompanying him to wait there, and set off at a smart trot along the road towards the bridge. Petya, faint with excitement, trotted along beside him.

"If we are caught, I won't be taken alive. I have a pistol," whispered Petya.

"Don't speak Russian," said Dolohov, in a rapid whisper, and at that moment they heard in the dark the challenge: "Who goes there?" and the click of a gun.

The blood rushed into Petya's face, and he clutched at his pistol.

"Uhlans of the Sixth Regiment," said Dolohov, neither hastening nor slackening his horse's pace.

The black figure of a sentinel stood on the bridge.

"The password?"

Dolohov reined in his horse, and advanced at a walking pace.

"Tell me, is Colonel Gerard here?" he said.

"Password?" repeated the sentinel, making no reply and barring their way.

"When an officer makes his round, sentinels don't ask him for the password . . ." cried Dolohov, suddenly losing his temper and riding straight at the sentinel. "I ask you, is the colonel here?"

And not waiting for an answer from the sentinel, who moved aside, Dolohov rode at a walking pace uphill.

Noticing the black outline of a man crossing the road, Dolohov stopped the man, and asked where the colonel and officers were. The man, a soldier with a sack over his shoulder, stopped, came close up to Dolohov's horse, stroking it with his hand, and told them in a simple and friendly way that the colonel and the officers were higher up the hill, on the right, in the courtyard of the farm, as he called the little manor-house.

After going further along the road, from both sides of which they heard French talk round the camp-fires, Dolohov turned into the yard of the manor-house. On reaching the gate, he dismounted and walked towards a big, blazing fire, round which several men were sitting, engaged in loud conversation. There was something boiling in a cauldron on one side, and a soldier in a peaked cap and blue coat, kneeling in the bright glow of the fire, was stirring it with his ramrod.

"He's a tough customer," said one of the officers, sitting in the shadow on the opposite side of the fire.

"He'll make them run, the rabbits" (a French proverb), said the other, with a laugh.

Both paused, and peered into the darkness at the sound of the steps of Petya and Dolohov approaching with their horses.

"Bonjour, messieurs!" Dolohov called loudly and distinctly.

There was a stir among the officers in the shadow, and a tall officer with a long neck came round the fire and went up to Dolohov.

"Is that you, Clément?" said he. "Where the devil . . ." but becoming aware of his mistake, he did not finish, and with a slight frown greeted Dolohov as a stranger, and asked him what he could do for him. Dolohov told him that he and his comrade were trying to catch up with their regiment, and asked, addressing the company in general, whether the officers knew anything about the Sixth Regiment. No one could tell them anything about it; and Petya fancied the officers began to look at him and Dolohov with unfriendly and suspicious eyes.

For several seconds no one spoke.

"If you're reckoning on some soup, you have come too late," said a voice from behind the fire, with a smothered laugh.

Dolohov answered that they had had supper, and wanted to push on further that night.

He gave their horses to the soldier who was stirring the pot, and squatted down on his heels beside the officer with the long neck. The latter never took his eyes off Dolohov, and asked him again what regiment did he belong to.

Dolohov appeared not to hear the question. Making no answer, he lighted a short French pipe that he took from his pocket, and asked the officers whether the road ahead of them were safe from Cossacks.

"The brigands are everywhere," answered an officer from behind the fire.

Dolohov said that the Cossacks were only a danger for stragglers like himself and his comrade; "he supposed they would not dare to attack large detachments," he added inquiringly.

No one replied.

"Well, now he will come away," Petya was thinking every moment, as he stood by the fire listening to the talk.

But Dolohov took up the conversation that had dropped, and proceeded to ask them point-blank how many men there were in their battalion, how many battalions they had, and how many prisoners.

When he asked about the Russian prisoners, Dolohov added:

"Nasty business dragging those corpses about with one. It would be better to shoot the vermin," and he broke into such a strange, loud laugh, that Petya fancied the French must see through their disguise at once, and he involuntarily stepped back from the fire.

Dolohov's words and laughter elicited no response, and a French officer whom they had not seen (he lay rolled up in a coat), sat up and whispered something to his companion. Dolohov stood up and called to the men, who held their horses.

"Will they give us the horses or not?" Petya wondered, unconsciously coming closer to Dolohov.

They did give them the horses. *"Bonsoir, messieurs,"* said Dolohov.

Petya tried to say *"Bonsoir,"* but he could not utter a sound. The officers were whispering together. Dolohov was a long while mounting his horse, who would not stand still; then he rode out of the gate at a walking pace. Petya rode beside him, not daring to look round, though he was longing to see whether the French were running after him or not.

When they came out on to the road, Dolohov did not turn back towards the open country, but rode further along it into the village. At one spot he stood still, listening. "Do you hear?" he said. Petya recognised the sound of voices speaking Russian, and saw round the camp-fire the dark outlines of Russian prisoners. When they reached the bridge again, Petya and Dolohov passed the sentinel, who, without uttering a word, paced gloomily up and down. They came out to the hollow where the Cossacks were waiting for them.

"Well now, good-bye. Tell Denisov, at sunrise, at the first shot," said Dolohov, and he was going on, but Petya clutched at his arm.

"Oh!" he cried, "you are a hero! Oh! how splendid it is! how jolly! How I love you!"

"That's all right," answered Dolohov, but Petya did not let go of him, and in the dark Dolohov made out that he was bending over to him to be kissed. Dolohov kissed him, laughed, and turning his horse's head, vanished into the darkness.

X

ON reaching the hut in the wood, Petya found Denisov in the porch. He was waiting for Petya's return in great uneasiness, anxiety, and vexation with himself for having let him go.

"Thank God!" he cried. "Well, thank God!" he repeated, hearing Petya's ecstatic account. "And, damn you, you have prevented my sleeping!" he added. "Well, thank God; now, go to bed. We can still get a nap before morning."

"Yes . . . no," said Petya. "I'm not sleepy yet. Besides, I know what I am; if once I go to sleep, it will be all up with me. And besides, it's not my habit to sleep before a battle."

Petya sat for a long while in the hut, joyfully recalling the details of his adventure, and vividly imagining what was coming next day. Then, noticing that Denisov had fallen asleep, he got up and went out of doors.

It was still quite dark outside. The rain was over, but the trees were still dripping. Close by the hut could be seen the black outlines of the Cossacks' shanties and the horses tied together. Behind the hut there was a dark blur where two waggons stood with the horses near by, and in the hollow there was a red glow from the dying fire. The Cossacks and the hussars were not all asleep; there mingled with the sound of the falling drops and the munching of the horses, the sound of low voices, that seemed to be whispering.

Petya came out of the porch, looked about him in the darkness, and went up to the waggons. Some one was snoring under the waggons, and saddled horses were standing round them munching oats. In the dark Petya recognised and approached his own mare, whom he called Karabach, though she was in fact of a Little Russian breed.

"Well, Karabach, to-morrow we shall do good service," he said, sniffing her nostrils and kissing her.

"Why, aren't you asleep, sir?" said a Cossack, sitting under the waggon.

"No; but . . . Lihatchev—I believe that's your name, eh? You know I have only just come back. We have been calling on the French." And Petya gave the Cossack a detailed account, not only of his adventure, but also of his reasons for going, and why he thought it better to risk his life than to do things in a haphazard way.

"Well, you must be sleepy; get a little sleep," said the Cossack.

"No, I am used to it," answered Petya. "And how are the flints in your pistols—not worn out? I brought some with me. Don't you want any? Do take some."

The Cossack popped out from under the waggon to take a closer look at Petya.

"For, you see, I like to do everything carefully," said Petya. "Some men, you know, leave things to chance, and don't have things ready, and then they regret it. I don't like that."

"No, to be sure," said the Cossack.

"Oh, and another thing, please, my dear fellow, sharpen my sabre for me; I have blunt . . ." (but Petya could not bring out a lie) . . . "it has never been sharpened. Can you do that?"

"To be sure I can."

Lihatchev stood up, and rummaged in the baggage, and Petya stood and heard the martial sound of steel and whetstone. He clambered on to the waggon, and sat on the edge of it. The Cossack sharpened the sabre below.

"Are the other brave fellows asleep?" said Petya.

"Some are asleep, and some are awake, like us."

"And what about the boy?"

"Vesenny? He's lying yonder in the hay. He's sleeping well after his fright. He was so pleased."

For a long while after that Petya sat quiet, listening to the sounds. There was a sound of footsteps in the darkness, and a dark figure appeared.

"What are you sharpening?" asked a man coming up to the waggon.

"A sabre for the gentleman here."

"That's a good thing," said the man, who seemed to Petya to be an hussar. "Was the cup left with you here?"

"It's yonder by the wheel." The hussar took the cup. "It will soon be daylight," he added, yawning, as he walked off.

Petya must, one would suppose, have known that he was in a wood, with Denisov's band of irregulars, a verst from the road; that he was sitting on a waggon captured from the French; that there were horses fastened to it; that under it was sitting the Cossack Lihatchev sharpening his sabre; that the big, black blur on the right was the hut, and the red, bright glow below on the left the dying camp-fire; that the man who had come for the cup was an hussar who was thirsty. But Petya knew nothing of all that, and refused to know it. He was in a fairyland, in which nothing was like the reality. The big patch of shadow might be a hut certainly, but it might be a cave leading down into the very depths of the earth. The red patch might be a fire, but it might be the eye of a huge monster. Perhaps he really was sitting now on a waggon, but very likely he was sitting not on a waggon, but on a fearfully high tower, and if he fell off, he would go on flying to the earth for a whole day, for a whole month—fly and fly for ever and never reach it. Perhaps it was simply the Cossack Lihatchev sitting under the waggon; but very likely it was the kindest, bravest, most wonderful and splendid man in the world whom no one knew of. Perhaps it really was an hussar who had come for water and gone into the hollow; but perhaps he had just vanished, vanished altogether and was no more.

Whatever Petya had seen now, it would not have surprised him. He was in a land of fairies, where everything was possible.

He gazed at the sky. The sky too was an enchanted realm like the earth. It had begun to clear, and the clouds were scudding over the tree-tops, as though unveiling the stars. At times it seemed as though they were swept away, and there were glimpses of clear, black sky between them. At times these black patches looked like storm-clouds. At times the sky seemed to rise high, high overhead, and then again to be drop-ping down so that one could reach it with the hand.

Petya closed his eyes and began to nod. The branches dripped. There was a low hum of talk and the sound of some one snoring. The horses neighed and scuffled.

"Ozheeg, zheeg, ozheeg, zheeg . . ." hissed the sabre on the whet-stone; and all at once Petya seemed to hear harmonious music, an or-chestra playing some unfamiliar, solemnly sweet hymn. Petya was as musical by nature as Natasha, and far more so than Nikolay; but he had had no musical training, and never thought about music, so that the melody that came unexpectedly into his mind had a special freshness and charm for him. The music became more and more distinct. The melody grew and passed from one instrument to another. There was be-ing played what is called a fugue, though Petya had not the slightest idea of what was meant by a fugue. Each instrument—one like a violin, others like flutes, but fuller and more melodious than violins and flutes —played its part, and before it had finished the air, melted in with an-other, beginning almost the same air, and with a third and a fourth; and all mingled into one harmony, and parted again, and again mingled into solemn church music, and then into some brilliant and triumphant song of victory.

"Oh yes, of course I am dreaming," Petya said to himself, nodding forward. "It is only in my ears. Perhaps, though, it's my own music. Come, again. Strike up, my music! Come! . . ."

He closed his eyes. And from various directions the sounds began vi-brating as though from a distance, began to strike up, to part, and to mingle again, all joined in the same sweet and solemn hymn. "Ah how exquisite! As much as I want, and as I like it!" Petya said to himself. He tried to conduct this immense orchestra.

"Come, softly, softly, now!" And the sounds obeyed him. "Come, now fuller, livelier! More and more joyful!" And from unknown depths rose the swelling, triumphant sounds. "Now, voices, join in!" Petya commanded. And at first in the distance he heard men's voices, then women's. The voices swelled into rhythmic, triumphant fulness. Petya felt awe and joy as he drank in their marvellous beauty.

With the triumphant march of victory mingled the song of voices, and the drip of the branches and the zheeg, zheeg, zheeg of the sabre on the whetstone; and again the horses neighed and scuffled, not disturbing the harmony, but blending into it. How long it lasted, Petya could not tell; he was enjoying it, and wondering all the while at his own enjoyment, and regretting he had no one to share it with. He was waked by the friendly voice of Lihatchev.

"It's ready, your honour, you can cut the Frenchman in two now."

Petya waked up.

"Why, it's light already; it's really getting light," he cried. The horses, unseen before, were visible to the tails now; and through the leafless boughs there could be seen a watery light. Petya shook himself, jumped up, took a rouble out of his pocket, and gave it to Lihatchev, brandished his sabre to try it, and thrust it into the scabbard. The Cossacks were untying the horses and fastening the saddlegirths.

"And here is the commander," said Lihatchev.

Denisov came out of the hut, and calling to Petya, bade him get ready.

XI

RAPIDLY in the twilight the men picked out their horses, tightened saddlegirths, and formed into parties. Denisov stood by the hut, giving the last orders. The infantry of the detachment moved on along the road, hundreds of feet splashing through the mud. They quickly vanished among the trees in the mist before the dawn. The esaul gave some order to the Cossacks. Petya held his horse by the bridle, eagerly awaiting the word of command to mount. His face glowed from a dip in cold water and his eyes gleamed. He felt a chill running down his back, and a kind of rapid, rhythmic throbbing all over.

"Well, have you everything ready?" said Denisov. "Give us our horses."

They brought the horses up. Denisov was vexed with the Cossack because the saddlegirths were slack, and swore at him as he mounted his horse. Petya put his foot in the stirrup. The horse, as its habit was, made as though to nip at his leg; but Petya leaped into the saddle, unconscious of his own weight, and looking round at the hussars moving up from behind in the darkness, he rode up to Denisov.

"Vassily Fyodorovitch, you will trust me with some commission? Please . . . for God's sake . . ." he said. Denisov seemed to have forgotten Petya's existence. He looked round at him.

"One thing I beg of you," he said sternly, "to obey me and not to put yourself forward."

All the way Denisov did not say another word to Petya; he rode on in silence. By the time that they reached the edge of the wood, it was perceptibly getting light in the open country. Denisov whispered something to the esaul, and the Cossacks began riding by Petya and Denisov. When they had all passed on Denisov put his spurs to his horse, and rode downhill. Slipping and sinking back on their haunches, the horses slid down into the hollow with their riders. Petya kept beside Denisov. The tremor all over him was growing more intense. It was getting lighter and lighter, but the mist hid objects at a distance. When he had reached the bottom, Denisov looked back and nodded to the Cossack beside him.

"The signal," he said. The Cossack raised his arm, and a shot rang out. At the same moment they heard the tramp of horses galloping in front, shouts from different directions, and more shots.

The instant that he heard the first tramp of hoofs and shouts, Petya gave the rein to his horse, and lashing him on, galloped forward, heedless of Denisov, who shouted to him. It seemed to Petya that it suddenly became broad daylight, as though it were midday, at the moment when he heard the shot. He galloped to the bridge. The Cossacks were galloping along the road in front. At the bridge he jostled against a Cossack who had lagged behind, and he galloped on. In front Petya saw men of some sort—the French he supposed—running across the road from right to left. One slipped in the mud under his horse's legs.

Cossacks were crowding about a hut, doing something. A fearful scream rose out of the middle of the crowd. Petya galloped to this crowd, and the first thing he saw was the white face and trembling lower-jaw of a Frenchman, who had clutched hold of a lance aimed at his breast.

"Hurrah! . . . Mates . . . ours . . ." shouted Petya, and giving the rein to his excited horse, he galloped on down the village street.

He heard firing in front. Cossacks, hussars, and tattered Russian prisoners, running up from both sides of the road, were all shouting something loud and unintelligible. A gallant-looking Frenchman, in a blue coat, with a red, frowning face, and no cap, was keeping back the hussars with a bayonet. By the time that Petya galloped up, the Frenchman had fallen. "Too late again," flashed through Petya's brain, and he galloped to the spot where he heard the hottest fire. The shots came from the yard of the manor-house where he had been the night before with Dolohov. The French were ambushing there behind the fence in among the bushes of the overgrown garden, and firing at the Cossacks who were crowding round the gates. As he rode up to the gates, Petya caught a glimpse in the smoke of Dolohov's white, greenish face, as he shouted something to the men. "Go round. Wait for the infantry!" he was shouting, just as Petya rode up to him.

"Wait? . . . Hurrah! . . ." shouted Petya, and without pausing a moment, he galloped towards the spot where he heard the shots, and where the smoke was the thickest. There came a volley of shots with the sound of bullets whizzing by and thudding into something. The Cossacks and Dolohov galloped in at the gates after Petya. In the thick, hovering smoke the French flung down their arms and ran out of the bushes to meet the Cossacks, or fled downhill towards the pond. Petya was galloping on round the courtyard, but instead of holding the reins he was flinging up both arms in a strange way, and slanting more and more to one side in the saddle. The horse stepped on to the ashes of the fire smouldering in the morning light, and stopped short. Petya fell heavily on the wet earth. The Cossacks saw his arms and legs twitching rapidly, though his head did not move. A bullet had passed through his brain.

After parleying with the French senior officer, who came out of the house with a handkerchief on a sword to announce that they surrendered, Dolohov got off his horse and went up to Petya, who lay motion-less with outstretched arms.

"Done for," he said frowning, and walked to the gate to Denisov, who was riding towards him.

"Killed?" cried Denisov, even from a distance recognising the famil-iar, unmistakably lifeless posture in which Petya's body was lying.

"Done for," Dolohov repeated, as though the utterance of those words afforded him satisfaction; and he walked rapidly towards the prisoners, whom the Cossacks were hurriedly surrounding. "No quarter!" he shouted to Denisov. Denisov made no reply. He went up to Petya, got off his horse, and with trembling hands turned over the blood-stained, mud-spattered face that was already turning white.

"I'm fond of sweet things. They are capital raisins, take them all," came into his mind. And the Cossacks looked round in surprise at the sound like the howl of a dog, that Denisov uttered as he turned away, walked to the fence and clutched at it.

Among the Russian prisoners rescued by Denisov and Dolohov was Pierre Bezuhov.

XII

THE party of prisoners, of whom Pierre was one, was on the 22nd of October not with the troops and transport, in whose company they had left Moscow, though no fresh instructions in regard to them had been given by the French authorities. Half of the transport with stores of bis-cuit, which had followed them during the early stages of the march, had been carried off by the Cossacks, the other half had got away in front. Of the cavalry soldiers on foot, who had marched in front of the prison-ers, not one was left; they had all disappeared. The artillery, which the prisoners had seen in front during the early stages, was now replaced by the immense train of Marshal Junot's baggage, convoyed by an escort of Westphalians. Behind the prisoners came a transport of cavalry ac-coutrements.

The French had at first marched in three columns, but from Vyazma they had formed a single mass. The symptoms of lack of discipline, which Pierre had observed at the first halt outside Moscow, had by now reached their extreme limits.

The road along which they marched was strewn on both sides with the carcases of dead horses. The tattered soldiers, stragglers from different regiments, were continually changing, joining the column as it marched, and dropping behind it again. Several times there had been false alarms, and the soldiers of the convoy had raised their guns, and fired and fled, trampling one another underfoot. Then they had rallied again, and abused one another for their causeless panic.

These three bodies, travelling together—the cavalry transport, the convoy of prisoners, and Junot's baggage transport—still made up a complete separate whole, though each of its three parts was rapidly dwindling away.

Of the cavalry transport, which had at first consisted of one hundred and twenty waggons, only sixty were left; the rest had been carried off or abandoned. Several waggonloads of Junot's baggage, too, had been discarded or captured. Three waggons had been attacked and pillaged by stragglers from Davoust's regiment. From the talk he overheard among the Germans, Pierre learned that a more careful watch was kept over this baggage-train than over the prisoners, and that one of their comrades, a German, had been shot by order of the marshal himself because a silver spoon belonging to the marshal had been found in the soldier's possession.

The convoy of prisoners had dwindled even more than the other two convoys. Of the three hundred and thirty men who had started from Moscow there were now less than a hundred left. The prisoners were a burden even more irksome to the soldiers than the cavalry stores and Junot's baggage. The saddles and Junot's spoons they could understand might be of some use, but why cold and starving soldiers should stand as sentinels, keeping guard over Russians as cold and starving, who were continually dying and being left behind on the road, and whom they had orders to shoot—it was not only incomprehensible, but revolting. And the soldiers of the escort, apparently afraid in the miserable plight they were in themselves, to give way to the pity they felt for the prisoners, for fear of making their own lot harder, treated them with marked moroseness and severity.

At Dorogobuzh the soldiers of the escort had gone off to plunder their own stores, leaving the prisoners locked in a stable, and several prisoners had burrowed under the wall and run away, but they were caught by the French and shot.

The arrangement, made at the start from Moscow, that the officers among the prisoners should march separately from the common soldiers, had long since been given up. All who could walk marched together; and at the third stage Pierre had rejoined Karataev and the bow-legged, purple-grey dog, who had chosen Karataev for her master.

On the third day after leaving Moscow, Karataev had a return of the fever, which had kept him in the Moscow hospital, and as Karataev's strength failed, Pierre held more aloof from him. Pierre could not have said why it was, but from the time Karataev fell sick, he had to make an effort to force himself to go near him. And when he did go near him and heard the subdued moans, which Karataev often uttered, as he lay at the halting-places, and smelt the increasing odour from the sick man, Pierre moved further away from him and did not think about him.

In captivity in the shed that had been his prison, Pierre had learned not through his intellect, but through his whole being, through life, that man is created for happiness, that happiness lies in himself, in the satisfaction of his natural, human cravings; that all unhappiness is due, not to lack of what is needful, but to superfluity. But now, during the last three weeks of the march, he had learned another new and consolatory truth—he had learned that there is nothing terrible to be dreaded in the world. He had learned that just as there is no position in the world in which a man can be happy and perfectly free, so too there is no position in which he need be unhappy and in bondage. He had found out that there is a limit to suffering and a limit to freedom, and that that limit is very soon reached; that the man who suffered from a crumpled petal in his bed of roses, suffered just as much as he suffered now, sleeping on the bare, damp earth, with one side getting chilled as the other side got warm; that when in former days he had put on his tight dancing-shoes, he had suffered in just the same way as now, when he walked quite bare-foot (his foot-gear had long since fallen to pieces), with his feet covered with sores. He learned that when he had—by his own free-will, as he had fancied—married his wife, he had been no more free than now when he was locked up for the night in a stable. Of all that he did himself after-wards call sufferings, though at the time he hardly felt them so, the chief was the state of his bare, blistered, sore feet. The horse-flesh was savoury and nourishing, the saltpetre flavour given it by the gunpowder they used instead of salt was positively agreeable; there was no great degree of cold, it was always warm in the daytime on the march, and at night there were the camp-fires, and the lice that devoured him helped to keep him warm. One thing was painful in the earlier days—that was his feet.

On the second day of the march, as he examined his blisters by the camp-fire, Pierre thought he could not possibly walk on them; but when they all got up, he set off limping, and later on, when he got warm, he walked without pain, though his feet looked even more terrible that evening. But he did not look at them, and thought of something else.

Only now Pierre grasped all the force of vitality in man, and the sav-ing power innate in man, of transferring his attention, like the safety-valve in steam-engines, that lets off the superfluous steam so soon as its pressure exceeds a certain point.

He did not see and did not hear how the prisoners that lagged behind were shot, though more than a hundred of them had perished in that way. He did not think about Karataev, who was getting weaker every day, and would obviously soon fall a victim to the same fate. Still less did Pierre think about himself. The harder his lot became, the more ter-rible his future, the more independent of his present plight were the glad and soothing thoughts, memories, and images that occurred to him.

XIII

AT midday on the 22nd, Pierre was walking along the muddy, slippery road uphill, looking at his feet and at the unevenness of the road. From time to time he glanced at the familiar crowd around him, and then again at his feet. Both that crowd and those feet were alike his and fa-miliar to him. The purplish, bandy-legged, grey dog was running merrily along at the side of the road; sometimes picking up a hind leg, and skipping along on three paws as a sign of content and briskness, or barking at the crows that perched on the carrion. The grey dog was sleeker and merrier than in Moscow. All around lay the flesh of different animals—from men to horses—in different stages of decomposition, and the marching soldiers prevented wolves from coming near it, so that the grey dog could feast to her heart's content.

Rain had been falling since early morning; and it seemed continually as though in another minute it would cease and the sky would clear, when, after a short break, the rain came on again more heavily. The road, saturated with rain, could soak up no more, and streams flowed along the ruts.

Pierre walked, looking from side to side, counting his steps, and reckoning them off in threes on his fingers. Inwardly addressing the rain, he said to it, "Now then, come on then, pelt away!"

It seemed to him that he was thinking of nothing at all; but somewhere deep down his soul was pondering something grave and consolatory. That something was the subtlest, spiritual deduction arising from his talk the night before with Karataev.

Getting chilled by the dying fire on the previous night's halt, Pierre had got up and moved to the next fire, which was burning better. There Platon was sitting, with a coat put over his head, like a priest's chasuble. In his flexible, pleasant voice, feeble now from illness, he was telling the soldiers a story Pierre had heard already. It was past midnight, the time when Karataev's fever usually abated, and he was particularly lively. As he drew near the fire and heard Platon's weak, sickly voice, and saw his piteous mien in the bright firelight, Pierre felt a pang at heart. He was frightened at his own pity for this man, and would have gone away, but there was no other fire to go to, and trying not to look at Platon, he sat down by it.

"Well, how is your fever?" he asked.

"How is my fever? Weep over sickness, and God won't give you death," said Karataev, and he went back at once to the story he had begun.

"And so, brother," he went on with a smile on his thin, white face, and a peculiar, joyful light in his eyes, "And so, brother . . ."

Pierre had heard the story long before. Karataev had told it to him about six times already, and always with special joyful emotion. But well as Pierre knew the story, he listened to it now as though it were something new, and the subdued ecstasy, which Karataev evidently felt in telling it, infected Pierre too.

It was the story of an old merchant, who had lived in good works and in the fear of God with his family, and had made a journey one day with a companion, a rich merchant, to Makary.

Both the merchants had put up at an inn and gone to sleep; and next day the rich merchant had been found robbed, and with his throat cut. A knife, stained with blood, was found under the old merchant's pillow

The merchant was tried, sentenced to be flogged, and to have his nostrils slit—all according to the law in due course, as Karataev said—and sent to hard labour.

"And so, brother" (it was at this point in the story that Pierre found Karataev) "ten years or more passed by after that. The old man lives on in prison. He submits, as is fitting; he does nothing wrong. Only he prays to God for death. Very well. And so at night-time they are gathered together, the convicts, just as we are here, and the old man with them. And so they fall to talking of what each is suffering for, and how he has sinned against God. One tells how he took a man's life, another two, another had set fire to something, and another was a runaway just for no reason. So they began asking the old man, 'What,' they say, 'are you suffering for, grandfather?' 'I am suffering, dear brethren,' says he, 'for my own sins, and for other men's sins. I have not taken a life, nor taken other men's goods, save what I have bestowed on poorer brethren. I was a merchant, dear brethren, and I had great wealth.' And he tells them this and that, and how the whole thing had happened. 'For myself,' says he, 'I do not grieve. God has chastened me. The only thing,' says he, 'I am sorry for my old wife and my children.' And so the old man fell a-weeping. And it so happened that in that company there was the very man, you know, who had killed the merchant. 'Where did it happen, grandfather?' says he. 'When and in what month?' and so he asked him all about it. His heart began to ache. He goes up to the old man like this—and falls down at his feet. 'You are suffering for me, old man,' says he. 'It's the holy truth; this man is tormented innocently, for nothing, lads,' says he. 'I did that deed,' says he, 'and put the knife under his head when he was asleep. Forgive me, grandfather, for Christ's sake!' says he."

Karataev paused, smiling blissfully, and gazing at the fire, as he rearranged the logs.

"The old man, he says, 'God forgive you,' says he, 'but we are all sinners before God,' says he. 'I am suffering for my own sins.' And he wept with bitter tears. What do you think, darling?" said Karataev, his ecstatic smile growing more and more radiant, as though the great charm and whole point of his story lay in what he was going to tell now, "what do you think, darling, that murderer confessed of himself to the police. 'I have killed six men,' says he (for he was a great criminal), 'but what I am most sorry for is this old man. Let him not weep through my fault.' He confessed. It was written down, and a paper sent off to the right place. The place was far away. Then came a trial. Then all the reports were written in due course, by the authorities, I mean. It was brought to the Tsar. Then a decree comes from the Tsar to let the merchant go free; to give him the recompense they had awarded him. The paper comes; they fall to looking for the old man. Where was that old man who had suffered innocently? The paper had come from the Tsar, and they fell to looking for him." Karataev's lower jaw quivered. "But God had pardoned him already—he was dead! So it happened, darling!"

Karataev concluded, and he gazed a long while straight before him, smiling silently.

Not the story itself, but its mysterious import, the ecstatic gladness that beamed in Karataev's face as he told it, the mysterious significance of that gladness vaguely filled and rejoiced Pierre's soul now.

XIV

"To your places!" a voice shouted suddenly.

There was a cheerful stir among the prisoners and convoy soldiers, and an air of expecting something festive and solemn. Shouted commands could be heard on all sides, and a party of well-dressed cavalry soldiers on good horses came trotting up from the left, making a circuit round the prisoners. Every face wore the look of nervousness commonly seen at the approach of men in authority. The prisoners huddled together and were shoved out of the way. The convoy soldiers formed in ranks.

"The Emperor! The Emperor! The marshal! The duke! . . ." and the sleek cavalry soldiers had hardly ridden by when a carriage rattled up drawn by grey horses. Pierre had a passing glimpse of the serene, handsome, fat, white face of a man in a three-cornered hat. It was one of the marshals. The marshal's eye was caught by Pierre's big, striking figure; and in the expression with which he frowned and looked away Pierre fancied he saw pity and the desire to conceal it.

The general in charge of the transport whipped up his lean horse, and galloped after the carriage with a red, panic-stricken face. Several officers met in a group; the soldiers came round them. All had excited and uneasy faces.

"What did he say? What was it he said? . . ." Pierre heard.

While the marshal was driving by, the prisoners had been hustled together into one group, and Pierre caught sight of Karataev, whom he had not yet seen that morning. He was sitting, wrapped in his little military coat, leaning against a birch-tree. His face still wore the same look of joyous emotion as when he had been telling the story of the merchant, but it had another expression too, a look of subdued solemnity.

Karataev looked at Pierre with his kindly, round eyes, that were bright now with tears, and there was an unmistakable appeal in them. He evidently wanted to say something to him. But Pierre was in too great dread for himself. He made as though he had not seen that look, and hastily walked away.

When the prisoners set off again Pierre looked back. Karataev was sitting under the birch-tree by the edge of the road, and two Frenchmen were bending over him in conversation. Pierre did not look again. He went on limping up the hill.

There was the sound of a shot behind, at the spot where Karataev was sitting. Pierre heard that shot distinctly, but at the moment that he heard it, he recalled that he had not finished reckoning up how many stages were left to Smolensk, the calculation he had begun before the marshal rode by. And he began to reckon. Two French soldiers ran by Pierre, one holding a still smoking gun. They were both pale, and in the expression of their faces—one of them glanced timidly at Pierre—there was something like what he had seen in the young soldier at the execution in Moscow. Pierre looked at the soldier and remembered how, the day before yesterday, the man had burnt his shirt in drying it before the fire, and how the others had laughed at him.

The dog began to howl behind at the spot where Karataev was sitting. "Silly creature! what is she howling for?" thought Pierre.

The prisoners, his companions marching at his side, like him, refrained from looking back to the place whence came the sound of the shot and the dog's howl. There was a set look on all their faces.

XV

THE cavalry transport, and the prisoners, and the marshal's baggage-train, halted at the village of Shamshevo. All crowded together round the campfire. Pierre went up to a fire, ate some roast horse-flesh, lay down with his back to the fire, and at once fell asleep. He fell into the same sort of sleep that he had slept at Mozhaisk, after the battle of Borodino.

Again the facts of real life mingled with his dreams; and again some one, himself or some one else, was uttering thoughts in his ear, and the same thoughts, indeed, as had come in his dream at Mozhaisk.

Life is everything. Life is God. All is changing and moving, and that motion is God. And while there is life, there is the joy of the consciousness of the Godhead. To love life is to love God. The hardest and the most blessed thing is to love this life in one's sufferings, in undeserved suffering.

"Karataev!" flashed into Pierre's mind. And all at once there rose up, as vivid as though alive, the image, long forgotten, of the gentle old teacher, who had given Pierre geography lessons in Switzerland. "Wait a minute," the old man was saying. And he was showing Pierre a globe. This globe was a living, quivering ball, with no definite limits. Its whole surface consisted of drops, closely cohering together. And those drops were all in motion, and changing, several passing into one, and then one splitting up again into many. Every drop seemed striving to spread, to take up more space, but the others, pressing upon it, sometimes absorbed it, sometimes melted into it.

"This is life," the old teacher was saying.

"How simple it is and how clear," thought Pierre. "How was it I did not know that before? God is in the midst, and each drop strives to expand, to reflect Him on the largest scale possible. And it grows, and is

absorbed and crowded out, and on the surface it disappears, goes back
into the depths, and falls not to the surface again. That is how it is with
him, with Karataev; he is absorbed and has disappeared."

"You understand, my child," said the teacher.

"You understand, damn you!" shouted a voice, and Pierre woke up.
He raised his head and sat up. A French soldier was squatting on his
heels by the fire. He had just shoved away a Russian soldier, and was
roasting a piece of meat on the end of a ramrod. His sinewy, lean, hairy,
red hands, with short fingers, were deftly turning the ramrod. His
brown, morose face, with its sullen brows, could be clearly seen in the
light of the glowing embers.

"It's just the same to him," he muttered, quickly addressing a soldier
standing behind him. "Brigand! go!"

And the soldier, turning the ramrod, glanced gloomily at Pierre. The
latter turned away, gazing into the shadows. A Russian soldier, the one
who had been pushed away, was sitting near the fire, patting something
with his hand. Looking more closely, Pierre saw the grey dog, who was
sitting by the soldier, wagging her tail.

"Ah, she has come . . ." said Pierre. "And Plat . . ." he was beginning, but he did not go on. All at once, instantly in close connection,
there rose up the memory of the look Platon had fixed upon him, as he
sat under the tree, of the shot heard at that spot, of the dog's howl, of
the guilty faces of the soldiers as they ran by, of the smoking gun, of
Karataev's absence at that halting-place; and he was on the point of
fully realising that Karataev had been killed, but at the same instant, at
some mysterious summons, there rose up the memory of a summer evening he had spent with a beautiful Polish lady on the verandah of his
house at Kiev. And nevertheless, making no effort to connect the impressions of the day, and to deduce anything from them, Pierre closed
his eyes, and the picture of the summer night in the country mingled
with the thought of bathing and of that fluid, quivering globe, and he
seemed to sink deep down into water, so that the waters closed over his
head.

Before sunrise he was wakened by loud and rapid shots and outcries.
The French were flying by him.

"The Cossacks!" one of them shouted, and a minute later a crowd of
Russians were surrounding Pierre. For a long while Pierre could not
understand what had happened to him. He heard all about him his
comrades' wails of joy.

"Mates! our own folk! brothers!" the old soldiers cried, weeping, as
they embraced the Cossacks and the hussars. The hussars and the Cossacks crowded round the prisoners, pressing on them clothes, and boots,
and bread. Pierre sat sobbing in their midst, and could not utter one
word; he hugged the first soldier who went up to him, and kissed him,
weeping.

Dolohov was standing at the gates of a dilapidated house, letting the
crowd of unarmed Frenchmen pass by him. The French, excited by all

that had happened, were talking loudly among themselves; but as they passed before Dolohov, who stood switching his boots with his riding-whip, and watching them with his cold, glassy eyes, that boded nothing good, their talk died away. One of Dolohov's Cossacks stood on the other side, counting the prisoners, and marking off the hundreds with a chalk mark on the gate.

"How many?" Dolohov asked him.

"The second hundred," answered the Cossack.

"*Filez, filez*," said Dolohov, who had picked up the expression from the French; and when he met the eyes of the passing prisoners, his eyes gleamed with a cruel light.

With a gloomy face Denisov, holding his high Cossack hat in his hand, was walking behind the Cossacks, who were bearing to a hole freshly dug in the garden the body of Petya Rostov.

XVI

FROM the 28th of October, when the frosts began, the flight of the French assumed a more tragic aspect, from the men being frozen or roasted to death by the camp-fires, while the Emperor, and kings, and dukes, still drove on with their stolen booty in fur cloaks and closed carriages. But in its essentials, the process of the flight and disintegration of the French army went on unchanged.

From Moscow to Vyazma of the seventy-three thousands of the French army (not reckoning the Guards, who had done nothing but pillage all through the war), only thirty-six thousand were left, though only five thousand had been killed in battle. Here we have the first term of a progression, by which the remaining terms are determined with mathematical exactness. The French army went on melting away and disappearing in the same ratio from Moscow to Vyazma, from Vyazma to Smolensk, from Smolensk to the Berezina, from the Berezina to Vilna, apart from the greater or less degree of cold, the pursuit and barring of the way, and all other conditions taken separately. After Vyazma, instead of three columns, the French troops formed a single mass, and so they marched on to the end. This is how Berthier wrote to the Emperor (and we know that generals feel it permissible to depart rather widely from the truth in describing the condition of their armies):—

"I think it my duty to report to·your majesty the condition of the various corps under my observation on the march the last two or three days. They are almost disbanded. Hardly a quarter of the men remain with the flags of their regiments; the rest wander off on their own account in different directions, trying to seek food and to escape discipline. All think only of Smolensk, where they hope to recover. During the last few days many soldiers have been observed to throw away their cartridges and muskets.·In such a condition of affairs, whatever your further plans may be, the interests of your majesty's service make it essential to muster the army at Smolensk, and to rid them of ineffectives, such as cavalry men without horses, as well as of superfluous baggage and a part of the artillery, which is now out of proportion with the numbers of the effective army. Supplies and some days' rest are essential: the soldiers are exhausted by hunger and fatigue; during the last few days many have died by the roadside or in the bivouacs. This state of things is growing continually worse, and if steps are not quickly taken for averting the danger, we shall be exposed to the risk of being unable to control the army in the event of a battle.

"November 9. Thirty versts from Smolensk."

After struggling into Smolensk, the promised land of their dreams, the French killed one another fighting over the food there, sacked their own stores, and when everything had been pillaged, they ran on further. All hastened on, not knowing whither or for what end they were going; least of all knew that great genius, Napoleon, since there was no one to give him orders. But still he and those about him clung to their old habits: wrote commands, letters, reports, orders of the day; called each other your majesty, *mon frère, Prince d'Eckmühl, roi de Naples,* and so on. But the orders and reports were all on paper: no attempt was made to carry them out, because they could not be carried out. And although they addressed each other as "majesty," "highness," and *"mon cousin,"* they all felt that they were pitiful and loathsome creatures, who had done a great wrong, for which they had now to pay the penalty. And in spite of their pretence of caring for the army, each was thinking only of himself, and how to make his escape as quickly as possible to safety.

XVII

THE actions of the Russian and French armies during the retreat from Moscow to the Niemen resemble a game of Russian blindman's buff, in which there are two players, both with their eyes bandaged, and one rings a bell at intervals to let the other know of his whereabouts. At first he rings his bell with no fear of his opponent; but when he begins to find himself in a difficult position, he runs away as noiselessly as he can from his opponent, and often supposing he is running away from him, walks straight into his arms.

At first Napoleon's army made its whereabouts known—that was in the early period of the retreat along the Kaluga road—but afterwards, when they had taken to the Smolensk road, they ran holding the tongue of the bell; and often supposing they were running away, ran straight towards the Russians.

Owing to the rapidity of the flight of the French, and of the Russians after them, and the consequent exhaustion of the horses, the chief means of keeping a close watch on the enemy's position—by means of charges of cavalry—was out of the question. Moreover, in consequence of the frequent and rapid changes of position of both armies, what news did come always came too late. If information arrived on the second that the army of the enemy had been in a certain place on the first, by the third, when the information could be acted upon, the army was already two days' march further, and in quite a different position.

One army fled, the other pursued. From Smolensk, there were a number of different roads for the French to choose from; and one would have thought that, as they stayed there four days, the French might have found out where the enemy was, have thought out some advantageous plan, and undertaken something new. Yet, after a halt of four days, the crowds of them ran back; again not to right or to left, but, with no manœuvres or plans, along their old road—the worst one—by Krasnoe and Orsha, along their beaten track.

Expecting the enemy in their rear and not in front, the French ran. straggling out, and getting separated as far as twenty-four hours' march from one another. In front of all fled the Emperor, then the kings, then the dukes. The Russian army, supposing Napoleon would take the road to the right beyond the Dnieper—the only sensible course—turned also to the right, and came out on the high road at Krasnoe. And here, just as in the game of blindman, the French came bearing straight down on our vanguard. Seeing the enemy unexpectedly, the French were thrown into confusion, stopped short from the suddenness of the fright, but then ran on again, abandoning their own comrades in their rear. Then for three days, the separate parts of the French army passed, as it were, through the lines of the Russian army: first the viceroy's troops, then Davoust's, and then Ney's. They all abandoned one another, abandoned their heavy baggage, their artillery, and half their men, and fled, making semicircles to the right to get round the Russians by night.

Ney was the last, because in spite, or perhaps in consequence, of their miserable position, with a child's impulse to beat the floor that has bruised it, he lingered to demolish the walls of Smolensk, which had done nobody any harm. Ney, who was the last to pass with his corps of ten thousand, reached Napoleon at Orsha with only a thousand men, having abandoned all the rest, and all his cannons, and made his way by stealth at night, under cover of the woods, across the Dnieper.

From Orsha they fled on along the road to Vilna, still playing the same game of blindman with the pursuing army. At Berezina again, they were thrown into confusion, many were drowned, many surrendered, but those that got across the river, fled on.

Their chief commander wrapped himself in a fur cloak, and getting into a sledge, galloped off alone, deserting his companions. Whoever could, ran away too, and those who could not—surrendered or died.

XVIII

ONE might have supposed that the historians, who ascribe the actions of the masses to the will of one man, would have found it impossible to explain the retreat of the French on their theory, considering that they did everything possible during this period of the campaign to bring about their own ruin, and that not a single movement of that rabble of men, from their turning into the Kaluga road up to the flight of the commander from his army, showed the slightest trace of design.

But no! Mountains of volumes have been written by historians upon this campaign, and in all of them we find accounts of Napoleon's masterly arrangements and deeply considered plans; of the strategy with which the soldiers were led, and the military genius showed by the marshals.

The retreat from Maley Yaroslavets, when nothing hindered Napoleon from passing through a country abundantly furnished with supplies, and the parallel road was open to him, along which Kutuzov afterwards pursued him—this wholly unnecessary return by a road through devastated country is explained to us as due to various sagacious considerations. Similar reasons are given us for Napoleon's retreat from Smolensk to Orsha. Then we have a description of his heroism at Krasnoe, when he is reported to have prepared to give battle, and to take the command, and coming forward with a birch stick in his hand, to have said:

"Long enough I have been an emperor, it is time now to be a general!"

Yet in spite of this, he runs away immediately afterwards, abandoning the divided army in the rear to the hazards of destiny.

Then we have descriptions of the greatness of some of the marshals, especially of Ney—a greatness of soul that culminated in his taking a circuitous route by the forests across the Dnieper, and fleeing without his flags, his artillery, and nine-tenths of his men into Orsha.

And lastly, the final departure of the great Emperor from his heroic army is represented by the historians as something great—a stroke of genius.

Even that final act of running away—which in homely language would be described as the lowest depth of baseness, such as every child is taught to feel ashamed of—even that act finds justification in the language of the historians.

When it is impossible to stretch the elastic thread of historical argument further, when an action is plainly opposed to what all humanity is agreed in calling right and justice, the historians take refuge in the conception of greatness. Greatness would appear to exclude all possibility of applying standards of right and wrong. For the great man—nothing is wrong. There is no atrocity which could be made a ground for blaming a great man.

"*C'est grand!*" cry the historians; and at that word good and bad have ceased to be, and there are only "*grand*" and not "*grand.*" "*Grand*" is equivalent to good, and not "*grand*" to bad. To be *grand* is to their notions the characteristic of certain exceptional creatures, called by them heroes. And Napoleon, wrapping himself in his warm fur cloak and hurrying home away from men, who were not only his comrades, but (in his belief) brought there by his doing, feels *que c'est grand;* and his soul is content.

"Du sublime au ridicule il n'y a qu'un pas," he says (he sees something grand in himself). And the whole world has gone on for fifty years repeating: Sublime! Grand! Napoleon the Great.

"Du sublime au ridicule il n'y a qu'un pas."

And it never enters any one's head that to admit a greatness, immeasurable by the rule of right and wrong, is but to accept one's own nothingness and immeasurable littleness.

For us, with the rule of right and wrong given us by Christ, there is nothing for which we have no standard. And there is no greatness where there is not simplicity, goodness, and truth.

XIX

WHAT Russian reader has not known an irksome feeling of annoyance, dissatisfaction, and perplexity, when he reads the accounts of the latter period of the campaign of 1812? Who has not asked himself: How was it all the French were not captured or cut to pieces, when all the three Russian armies were surrounding them in superior numbers, when the French were a disorderly, starving, and freezing rabble, and the whole aim of the Russians (so history tells us) was to check, to cut off, and to capture all the French?

How was it that the Russian army, that with inferior numbers had fought the battle of Borodino, failed in its aim of capturing the French, when the latter were surrounded on three sides? Can the French be so immensely superior to us that we are not equal to beating them, when we have surrounded them with forces numerically superior? How could that have come to pass? History (what passes by that name) answers these questions by saying that that came to pass because Kutuzov, and Tormasov, and Tchitchagov, and this general and that failed to carry out certain manœuvres.

But why did they fail to carry them out? And how was it, if they really were responsible for not attaining the aim set before them, that they were not tried and punished for their shortcomings? But even if we admit that Kutuzov and Tchitchagov and the others were responsible for the non-success of the Russians, it is still impossible to understand why, in the position the Russian troops were in at Krasnoe and the Berezina, on both occasions with numerically superior forces, the French army and marshals were not taken prisoners, if that really was the aim of the Russians.

The explanation of this phenomenon given by the Russian military historians—that Kutuzov hindered the attack—is insufficient, because we know that Kutuzov was not able to restrain the troops from attacking at Vyazma and Tarutino. Why was it that the Russian army, that with inferior forces gained a victory at Borodino over the enemy in full strength, was unsuccessful at Krasnoe and the Berezina, when fighting in superior numbers against the undisciplined crowds of the French?

If the aim of the Russians really was to cut off Napoleon and his marshals, and to take them prisoners, and that aim was not only frustrated, but all attempts at attaining it were every time defeated in the most shameful way, this last period of the war is quite correctly represented by the French as a series of victories for them, and quite incorrectly represented by the Russians as redounding to our glory.

The Russian military historians, so far as they recognise the claims of logic, are forced to this conclusion, and in spite of their lyric eulogies of Russian gallantry and devotion, and all the rest of it, they are reluctantly obliged to admit that the retreat of the French from Moscow was a series of victories for Napoleon and of defeats for Kutuzov.

But putting patriotic vanity entirely aside, one cannot but feel that there is an inherent discrepancy in this conclusion, seeing that the series of French victories led to their complete annihilation, while the series of Russian defeats was followed by the destruction of their enemy, and the deliverance of their country.

The source of this discrepancy lies in the fact that historians, studying events in the light of the letters of the sovereigns and of generals, of narratives, reports, projects, and so on, have assumed quite falsely that the plan of that period of the campaign of 1812 was to cut off and capture Napoleon and his marshals and his army.

Such a plan never was, and could not have been, the aim of the Russian army, because it had no meaning, and its attainment was utterly out of the question.

There was no object in such a plan. In the first place, because Napoleon's army was flying in disorder at its utmost possible speed out of Russia; that is to say, doing the very thing that every Russian most desired. What object was there in conducting all sorts of operations against the French when they were running away as fast as they could already? Secondly, it would have been idle to stop men on the road, whose whole energies were bent on flight. Thirdly, it would have been absurd to lose men in destroying the French army when it was already, without external interference, perishing at such a rate that, without any obstruction of their road, not more than one hundredth of its original number succeeded in crossing the frontier in December.

Fourthly, it was absurd to desire to take prisoners the Emperor, kings, and dukes, since the possession of such prisoners would have greatly enhanced the difficulty of the Russian position, as was recognised by the most clear-sighted diplomatists of the time (J. Maistre and others). Still more absurd would have been the desire to capture the French army when it had dwindled to one-half before reaching Krasnoe, and a division of convoys had to be given up to guard a corps of prisoners, while the Russian soldiers themselves had not always full rations, and the prisoners they did take died of hunger.

Any plan of cutting off and capturing Napoleon and his army, however carefully thought out, would have been like the action of a gardener who, after driving out a herd of cattle that had been trampling his beds, should run out to belabour the cattle about the head. The only thing that could be said in justification of his proceeding would be that he was greatly incensed. But the authors of this supposed plan cannot plead even this excuse, since theirs were not the gardens that had been trampled.

And, besides being absurd, to cut off the retreat of Napoleon's army was also impossible.

It was impossible, in the first place, because, since experience shows that the movement of columns in a single battlefield at five versts' distance never coincides with the plan of their movements, the probability that Tchitchagov, Kutuzov, and Wittgenstein would all reach an appointed spot in time was so remote that it practically amounted to impossibility. As Kutuzov in fact regarded it when he said that manœuvres planned at great distances do not produce the results expected of them.

Secondly, it was impossible, because to paralyse the force of inertia with which Napoleon's army was rebounding back along its track, incomparably greater forces were needed than those the Russians had at their command.

Thirdly, it was impossible, because the military expression, to cut off, has really no meaning. One may cut off a slice of bread, but not an army. To cut off an army—that is, to bar its road—is impossible, because there are always many places by which the men can make a circuit to get out, and there is always the night, during which nothing can be done; a fact of which the military strategists might have been convinced by the examples of Krasnoe and Berezina. One can never take a prisoner unless he agrees to be taken, just as one can never catch a swallow, though of course it is possible if it settles on one's hand. One can take a prisoner who will surrender, as the Germans did, in accordance with the rules of strategy and tactics. But the French soldiers very wisely did not feel it incumbent on them to do so, since death from cold and hunger awaited them as much if taken prisoner, as if persisting in their flight.

The fourth and chief reason why it was impossible is that war was waged in 1812 under conditions more terrible than ever since the world has existed; and the Russian troops strained every nerve in the pursuit of the French, and could not have done more without perishing themselves.

The Russian army lost in its march from Tarutino to Krasnoe fifty thousand sick or stragglers, that is, a number equal to the population of a large provincial town. Half of the army was lost without a battle.

At this period of the campaign the soldiers were without boots or fur-lined coats, on half rations, without vodka, camping out at night for months in the snow with fifteen degrees of frost; while there were only seven or eight hours of daylight, and the rest was night; where discipline could not exert the same influence, and men were put in peril of death, not for a few hours, as on the field of battle, but for whole months together were keeping up a struggle every moment with death from cold and hunger. And of this period of the campaign, when half the army perished in one month, the historians tell us that Miloradovitch ought to have made an oblique march in one direction, and Tormasov in another, and Tchitchagov ought to have advanced to this point (the men advancing knee-deep in the snow), and that so and so pushed through and cut the French off, and so on, and so on.

The Russian soldiers did all that could or ought to have been done to attain an end worthy of the people, and half of them died in doing it. They are not to blame because other Russians, sitting in warm rooms at home, proposed that they should do the impossible.

All this strange discrepancy between the facts and the accounts of historians, so difficult to understand to-day, arises simply from this, that the historians wrote the history of the noble sentiments and fine speeches of various generals, and not the history of the events themselves.

They attach great consequence to the words of Miloradovitch, to the honours bestowed on this general or that, and the proposals made by them. But the question of the fifty thousand men who lay in the hospitals and graveyards does not even interest them, for it does not come within the scope of their researches.

And yet we have but to turn away from researches among the reports and plans of the generals, and to look into the movements of those hundred thousand men who took direct immediate part in the events; and all the questions that seemed insoluble before can be readily and certainly explained with extraordinary ease and simplicity.

The plan of cutting off Napoleon and his army never existed save in the imagination of some dozen men. It could not have existed because it was absurd and could not be carried out.

The people had a single aim: to clear their country of the invaders That aim was effected primarily of itself, since the French were flying, and all that was necessary was not to check their flight. It was promoted, too, by the irregular warfare kept up by the people destroying the French army piecemeal; and thirdly, by the great Russian army following in the rear of the French, ready to use force in case there were any pause in their retreat.

The Russian army had to act as a whip urging on a fleeing animal. And the experienced driver knew that it was better to keep the whip raised as a menace than to bring it down on the creature's back.

WHEN A man sees an animal dying, a horror comes over him. What he is himself—his essence, visibly before his eyes, perishes—ceases to exist. But when the dying creature is a man and a man dearly loved, then, besides the horror at the extinction of life, what is felt is a rending of the soul, a spiritual wound, which, like a physical wound, is sometimes mortal, sometimes healed, but always aches and shrinks from contact with the outer world, that sets it smarting.

After Prince Andrey's death, Natasha and Princess Marya both alike felt this. Crushed in spirit, they closed their eyes under the menacing cloud of death that hovered about them, and dared not look life in the face. Carefully they guarded their open wounds from every rough and painful touch. Everything—the carriage driving along the street, the summons to dinner, the maid asking which dress to get out; worse still —words of faint, feigned sympathy—set the wound smarting, seemed an insult to it, and jarred on that needful silence in which both were trying to listen to the stern, terrible litany that had not yet died away in their ears, and to gaze into the mysterious, endless vistas that seemed for a moment to have been unveiled before them.

Only alone together were they safe from such outrage and pain. They said little to one another. When they did speak, it was about the most trivial subjects. And both equally avoided all mention of anything connected with the future.

To admit the possibility of a future seemed to them an insult to his memory. Still more circumspectly did they avoid in their talk all that could be connected with the dead man. It seemed to them that what they had felt and gone through could not be expressed in words. It seemed to them that every allusion in words to the details of his life was an outrage on the grandeur and holiness of the mystery that had been accomplished before their eyes.

The constant restraint of speech and studious avoidance of everything that might lead to words about him, these barriers, fencing off on all sides what could not be spoken of, brought what they were feeling even more clearly and vividly before their minds.

But pure and perfect sorrow is as impossible as pure and perfect joy. From the isolation of her position, as the guardian and foster-mother of her nephew, and independent mistress of her own destinies, Princess Marya was the first to be called back to life from that world of mourning in which she lived for the first fortnight. She received letters from her relations which had to be answered; the room in which Nikolushka had been put was damp, and he had begun to cough. Alpatitch came to Yaroslavl with accounts. He had suggestions to make, and advised Princess Marya to move to Moscow to the house in Vozdvizhenka, which was uninjured, and only needed some trifling repairs. Life would not stand still, and she had to live. Painful as it was for Princess Marya to come out of that world of solitary contemplation, in which she had been living till then, and sorry, and, as it were, conscience-stricken, as she felt at leaving Natasha alone, the duties of daily life claimed her attention, and against her own will she had to give herself up to them. She went through the accounts with Alpatitch, consulted Dessalle about her little nephew, and began to make preparations for moving to Moscow.

Natasha was left alone, and from the time that Princess Marya began to busy herself with preparations for her journey, she held aloof from her too.

Princess Marya asked the countess to let Natasha come to stay with her in Moscow; and both mother and father eagerly agreed to her suggestion, for they saw their daughter's physical strength failing every day, and they hoped that change of scene and the advice of Moscow doctors might do her good.

"I am not going anywhere," answered Natasha, when the suggestion was made to her; "all I ask is, please let me alone," she said, and she ran out of the room, hardly able to restrain tears more of vexation and anger than of sorrow.

Since she felt herself deserted by Princess Marya, and alone in her grief, Natasha had spent most of her time alone in her room, huddled up in a corner of her sofa. While her slender, nervous fingers were busy twisting or tearing something, she kept her eyes fixed in a set stare on the first object that met them. This solitude exhausted and tortured her; but it was what she needed. As soon as any one went in to her, she got up quickly, changed her attitude and expression, and picked up a book or some needlework, obviously waiting with impatience for the intruder to leave her.

It seemed to her continually that she was on the very verge of understanding, of penetrating to the mystery on which her spiritual vision was fastened with a question too terrible for her to bear.

One day towards the end of December, Natasha, thin and pale in a black woollen gown, with her hair fastened up in a careless coil, sat perched up in the corner of her sofa, her fingers nervously crumpling and smoothing out the ends of her sash, while she gazed at the corner of the door.

She was inwardly gazing whither he had gone, to that further shore. And that shore, of which she had never thought in old days, which had seemed to her so far away, so incredible, was now closer to her, and more her own, more comprehensible than this side of life, in which all was emptiness and desolation or suffering and humiliation.

She was gazing into that world where she knew he was. But she could not see him, except as he had been here on earth. She was seeing him again as he had been at Mytishtchy, at Troitsa, at Yaroslavl.

She was seeing his face, hearing his voice, and repeating his words, and words of her own that she had put into his mouth; and sometimes imagining fresh phrases for herself and him which could only have been uttered in the past.

Now she saw him as he had once been, lying on a low chair in his velvet, fur-lined cloak, his head propped on his thin, pale hand. His chest looked fearfully hollow, and his shoulders high. His lips were firmly closed, his eyes shining, and there was a line on his white brow that came and vanished again. There was a rapid tremor just perceptible in one foot. Natasha knew he was struggling to bear horrible pain. "What was that pain like? Why was it there? What was he feeling? How did it hurt?" Natasha had wondered. He had noticed her attention, raised his eyes, and, without smiling, began to speak:

"One thing would be awful," he said: "to bind oneself for ever to a suffering invalid. It would be an everlasting torture." And he had looked with searching eyes at her. Natasha, as she always did, had answered without giving herself time to think; she had said: "It can't go on like this, it won't be so, you will get well—quite well."

She was seeing him now as though it were the first time, and going through all she had felt at that time. She recalled the long, mournful, stern gaze he had given her at those words, and she understood all the reproach and the despair in that prolonged gaze.

"I agreed," Natasha said to herself now, "that it would be awful if he were to remain always suffering. I said that then only because it would be so awful for him, but he did not understand it so. He thought that it would be awful *for me*. Then he still wanted to live, and was afraid of death. And I said it so clumsily, so stupidly. I was not thinking that. I was thinking something quite different. If I had said what I was thinking, I should have said: 'Let him be dying, dying all the time before my eyes, and I should be happy in comparison with what I am now.' Now . . . there is nothing, no one. Did he know that? No. He did not know, and never will know it. And now it can never, never be made up for."

And again he was saying the same words; but this time Natasha in her imagination made him a different answer. She stopped him, and said: "Awful for you, but not for me. You know that I have nothing in life but you, and to suffer with you is the greatest happiness possible for me." And he took her hand and pressed it, just as he had pressed it on that terrible evening four days before his death. And in her imagination she said to him other words of tenderness and love, which she might have said then, which she only said now. . "I love thee! . thee . I love, love thee . ." she said, wringing her hands convulsively, and setting her teeth with bitter violence . .

And a sweeter mood of sorrow was coming over her, and tears were starting into her eyes; but all at once she asked herself: "To whom was she saying that? Where is he, and what is he now?"

And again everything was shrouded in chill, cruel doubt, and again, frowning nervously, she tried to gaze into that world where he was. And

now, now, she thought, she was just penetrating the mystery . . . But
at that instant, when the incomprehensible, it seemed, was being unveiled before her eyes, a loud rattle at the door handle broke with a
painful shock on her hearing. Her maid, Dunyasha, rushed quickly and
abruptly into the room with frightened eyes, that took no heed of her

"Come to your papa, make haste," Dunyasha said, with a strange,
excited expression. "A misfortune . . . Pyotr Ilyitch . . . a letter,"
she gasped out, sobbing.

II

THE feeling of aloofness from all the world, that Natasha experienced at
this time, she felt in an even more marked degree with the members of
her own family. All her own family, her father and mother and Sonya,
were so near her, so everyday and ordinary that every word they
uttered, every feeling they expressed, was jarring in the world in which
she had lived of late. She felt more than indifference, positive hostility
to them. She heard Dunyasha's words of Pyotr Ilyitch, of a misfortune,
but she did not understand them.

"What misfortune could they have, what misfortune is possible to
them? Everything goes on in its old, regular, easy way with them," Natasha was saying inwardly.

As she went into the drawing-room, her father came quickly out of the
countess's room. His face was puckered up and wet with tears. He had
evidently run out of the room to give vent to the sobs that were choking
him. Seeing Natasha, he waved his arms in despair, and went off into
violent, miserable sobs, that convulsed his soft, round face.

"Pet . . . Petya . . . Go, go in, she's calling . . ." And sobbing
like a child, he tottered with feeble legs to a chair, and almost dropped
on to it, hiding his face in his hands.

An electric shock seemed to run all through Natasha. Some fearful
pain seemed to stab her to the heart. She felt a poignant anguish; it
seemed to her that something was being rent within her, and she was
dying. But with the pain she felt an instant release from the seal that
shut her out of life. At the sight of her father, and the sound of a fearful,
husky scream from her mother through the door, she instantly forgot
herself and her own sorrow.

She ran up to her father, but he feebly motioned her towards her
mother's door. Princess Marya, with a white face and quivering lower
jaw, came out and took Natasha's hand, saying something to her. Natasha neither saw nor heard her. With swift steps she went towards the
door, stopped for an instant as though struggling with herself, and ran
in to her mother.

The countess was lying down on a low chair in a strange awkward
attitude; she was beating her head against the wall. Sonya and some
maid-servants were holding her by the arms.

"Natasha. Natasha! . . ." the countess was screaming. "It's not true, not true . . . it's false . . . Natasha!" she screamed, pushing the maids away. "All you go away, it's not true! Killed! . . . ha, ha, ha! . . . not true! . . ."

Natasha knelt down on the low chair, bent over her mother, embraced her, with surprising strength lifted her up, turned her face to her, and pressed close to her.

"Mamma! . . . darling! . . . I'm here, dearest mamma," she whispered to her, never ceasing for a second.

She would not let her mother go; she struggled tenderly with her, asked for pillows and water, unbuttoned and tore open her mother's dress. "Dearest . . . my darling . . . mamma . . . my precious," she whispered without pausing, kissing her head, her hands, her face, and feeling the tears streaming in irrepressible floods over her nose and cheeks.

The countess squeezed her daughter's hand, closed her eyes, and was quieter for a moment. All at once she sat up with unnatural swiftness, looked vacantly round, and seeing Natasha, began hugging her head to her with all her might. Natasha's face involuntarily worked with the pain, as her mother turned it toward her, and gazed a long while into it. "Natasha, you love me," she said, in a soft, confiding whisper. "Natasha, you won't deceive me? You will tell me the whole truth?"

Natasha looked at her with eyes swimming with tears, and in her face seemed only imploring her love and forgiveness.

"Mamma . . . darling," she kept repeating, putting forth all the strength of her love to try somehow to take a little of the crushing load of sorrow off her mother on to herself.

And again in the helpless struggle with reality, the mother, refusing to believe that she could live while her adored boy, just blossoming into life, was dead, took refuge from reality in the world of delirium.

Natasha had no recollection of how she spent that day and that night, and the following day and the following night. She did not sleep, and did not leave her mother's side. Natasha's love, patient and persistent, seemed to enfold the countess on all sides every second, offering no explanation, no consolation, simply beckoning her back to life.

On the third night the countess was quiet for a few minutes, and Natasha closed her eyes, her head propped on the arm of the chair. The bedstead creaked; Natasha opened her eyes. The countess was sitting up in bed, and talking softly.

"How glad I am you have come home. You are tired, won't you have tea?" Natasha went up to her. "You have grown so handsome and manly," the countess went on, taking her daughter's hand.

"Mamma, what are you saying . . . ?"

"Natasha, he is gone, he is no more." And embracing her daughter, the countess for the first time began to weep.

III

PRINCESS MARYA put off her departure. Sonya and the count tried to take Natasha's place, but they could not. They saw that she was the only one who could keep the mother from the frenzy of despair. For three weeks Natasha never left her mother's side, slept on a lounge in her room, made her drink and eat, and without pause talked to her, talked because her tender, loving voice was the only thing that soothed the countess.

The wound in the mother's heart could never be healed. Petya's death had torn away half of her life. When the news of Petya's death reached her, she was a fresh-looking, vigorous woman of fifty; a month later she came out of her room an old woman, half dead and with no more interest in life. But the wound that half killed the countess, that fresh wound, brought Natasha back to life.

A spiritual wound that comes from a rending of the spirit is like a physical wound, and after it has healed externally, and the torn edges are scarred over, yet, strange to say, like a deep physical injury, it only heals inwardly by the force of life pushing up from within.

So Natasha's wound healed. She believed that her life was over. But suddenly her love for her mother showed her that the essence of her life —love—was still alive within her. Love was awakened, and life waked with it.

The last days of Prince Andrey had been a close bond between Natasha and Princess Marya. This fresh trouble brought them even closer together. Princess Marya put off her departure, and for the last three weeks she had been looking after Natasha, as though she were a sick child. Those weeks spent by Natasha in her mother's room had completely broken down her health.

One day Princess Marya noticed that Natasha was shivering with a feverish chill, and brought her away to her own room, and tucked her up in bed in the middle of the day. Natasha lay down, but when Princess Marya, having let down the blinds, was about to leave the room, Natasha called her to her.

"I'm not sleepy, Marie; stay with me."

"You are tired; try and go to sleep."

"No, no. Why did you bring me away? She will ask for me."

"She is much better. She was talking much more like herself to-day," said Princess Marya.

Natasha lay on the bed, and in the half-dark room she tried to make out Princess Marya's face.

"Is she like him?" Natasha wondered. "Yes; like and unlike. But she is original, different, a quite new, unknown person. And she likes me. What is there in her heart? Everything good. But what is it like? What are her thoughts like? How does she look on me? Yes; she is nice!"

"Masha," she said, shyly drawing her hand towards her. "Masha, you mustn't think I'm horrid. No? Masha, darling! How I love you! Let us be quite, quite friends." And embracing her, Natasha fell to kissing her hands and face.

Princess Marya was abashed and overjoyed at this demonstration of feeling.

From that day there sprang up between Princess Marya and Natasha one of those tender and passionate friendships which can only exist between women. They were continually kissing each other and saying tender things to one another, and they spent the greater part of their time together. If one went away, the other was uneasy and hastened to join her. They felt more harmony together with each other than apart, each with herself. There sprang up between them a feeling stronger than friendship; that was the feeling of life being only possible in each other's company.

Sometimes they did not speak for hours together. Sometimes, as they lay in their beds, they would begin to talk, and talked till morning. They talked, for the most part, of their own remote past. Princess Marya told her of her childhood, of her mother, of her father, of her dreams. And Natasha, who had in the past turned away with calm acceptance of her non-comprehension of that life of devotion and resignation, of the idealism of Christian self-sacrifice, grew to love Princess Marya's past, and to understand that side of life of which she had had no conception before. She had no thought of imitating that resignation and self-sacrifice in her own life, because she was accustomed to look for other joys in life; but she understood and loved in another that virtue that had been till now beyond her ken. Princess Marya, too, as she listened to Natasha's stories of her childhood and early girlhood, had a glimpse of a side of life she had known nothing of, of faith in life and in the enjoyment of life.

They still refrained from talking of *him*, that they might not, as it seemed to them, desecrate the exalted feeling in their hearts; but this reticence led them, though they would not have believed it, into gradually forgetting him.

Natasha had grown thin and pale, and was physically so weak that every one was continually talking about her health, and she was glad it was so. Yet sometimes she was suddenly seized, not simply by a dread of death, but by a dread of sickness, of ill-health, of losing her good looks; and sometimes she unconsciously examined her bare arm, marvelling at its thinness, or peeped in the looking-glass in the morning at her pinched face, and was touched by its piteous look. It seemed to her that this was as it should be, and yet she felt afraid and mournful at it.

One day she ran upstairs quickly, and was painfully short of breath. Immediately she made some pretext for going down again, and ran upstairs again, to try her strength and put herself to the test.

Another day she called Dunyasha, and her voice broke. She called her once more, though she heard her coming—called her in the deep chest-voice with which she used to sing, and listened to the sound.

She knew it not, and would not have believed it; yet though the layer of mould under which she fancied that her soul was buried seemed unbroken, the delicate, tender, young blades of grass were already pushing through it, and were destined to take root, and so to hide the grief that had crushed her under their living shoots that it would soon be unseen and forgotten. The wound was healing from within.

Towards the end of January Princess Marya set off for Moscow, and the count insisted on Natasha going with her to consult the doctors.

IV

AFTER the engagement at Vyazma, where Kutuzov could not restrain his troops in their desire to break through, to cut off and all the rest of it, the further march of the flying French, and of the Russians flying after them, continued as far as Krasnoe without a battle. The flight was so rapid that the Russian army racing after the French could not catch them up; the horses of the cavalry and artillery broke down, and information as to the movements of the French was always very uncertain.

The Russian soldiers were so exhausted by this unbroken march at the rate of forty versts a day that they were unable to quicken their pace.

To form an idea of the degree of exhaustion of the Russian army, one need only grasp clearly what is meant by the fact that while losing no more than five thousand killed and wounded, and not a hundred prisoners, the Russian army, which had left Tarutino a hundred thousand strong, numbered only fifty thousand on reaching Krasnoe.

The rapidity of the Russian pursuit had as disintegrating an effect on the Russian army as the flight of the French had on their army. The only difference was that the Russian army moved at its own will, free from the menace of annihilation that hung over the French, and that the sick and stragglers of the French were left in the hands of their enemy, while Russian stragglers were at home among their own people. The chief cause of the wasting of Napoleon's army was the rapidity of its movements, and an indubitable proof of that is to be seen in the corresponding dwindling of the Russian army.

Just as at Tarutino and at Vyazma, all Kutuzov's energies were directed to preventing—so far as it lay in his power—any arrest of the fatal flight of the French from being checked (as the Russian generals in Petersburg, and also in the army, wished it to be). He did all he could to urge on the flight of the French, and to slacken the speed of his own army.

In addition to the exhaustion of the men, and the immense losses due to the rapidity of their movements, Kutuzov saw another reason for slackening the pace, and not being in a hurry. The object of the Russian army was the pursuit of the French. The route of the French was uncertain, and therefore the more closely our soldiers followed on the heels of the French, the greater the distances they had to traverse. It was only by following at a considerable distance that they could take advantage of short cuts across the zig-zags made by the French in their course. All the skilful manœuvres suggested by the generals were based on forced marches at accelerated speed, while the only rational object to be aimed at was the diminution of the strain put on the men. And this was the object to which all Kutuzov's efforts were directed during the whole campaign from Moscow to Vilna,—not casually, not fitfully, but so consistently that he never once lost sight of it.

Not through reason, not by science, but with all his Russian heart and soul, Kutuzov felt and knew, as every Russian soldier felt it, that the French were vanquished, that their foes were in flight, and that they must see them off. But at the same time he felt with his soldiers, as one man, all the sufferings of that march, unheard of at such speed and in such weather.

But the generals, especially those not Russian, burning to distinguish themselves, to dazzle people, to take some duke or king prisoner for some incomprehensible reason—those generals thought that then, when any battle was sickening and meaningless, was the very time for fighting battles and conquering somebody. Kutuzov simply shrugged his shoulders when they came to him one after another with projects of manœuvres with the ill-shod, half-clothed, and half-starved soldiers, whose numbers had in one month dwindled to one-half without a battle, and who would even, under the most favourable circumstances, have a longer distance to traverse before they reached the frontier than they had come already.

This desire on the part of the generals to distinguish themselves, to execute manœuvres, to attack, and to cut off the enemy, was particularly conspicuous whenever the Russian army did come into contact with the French.

So it was at Krasnoe, where they had expected to find one of the three columns of the French, and stumbled upon Napoleon himself with sixteen thousand troops. In spite of all Kutuzov's efforts to avoid this disastrous engagement, and to keep his men safe for three days at Krasnoe, there was a slaughter of the disordered bands of the French by the exhausted soldiers of the Russian army.

Toll wrote out a disposition: first column to advance to this spot, and so on. And as always, what was done was not at all in accordance with that disposition. Prince Eugene of Würtemberg kept up a fire from the hills on the mob of French as they raced by, and asked for reinforcements, which did not come. In the nights the French dispersed to get round the Russians, hid themselves in the woods, and all that could struggled on again.

Miloradovitch, who declared that he had no wish to know anything about the commissariat arrangements of his detachment, who could never be found when he was wanted, that *chevalier sans peur et sans reproche*, as he called himself, always eager for parleys with the French, sent messengers to demand their surrender, wasted time, and did not carry out the orders given him.

"I make you a present of that column, lads," he said to his men, pointing out the French to his cavalry. And the cavalry, with spur and sabre, urged their broken-down horses into a trot, and with immense effort reached the column he had bestowed on them, that is to say, a mob of frozen, numb, and starving Frenchmen. And the column laid down their weapons and surrendered, which was what they had been longing to do for weeks past.

At Krasnoe there were taken twenty-six thousand prisoners, a hundred cannons, a stick of some sort, which was promptly dubbed a "marshal's baton." And the generals disputed among themselves who had gained most distinction in the action, and were delighted at it, though they were full of regret at not having captured Napoleon or some marshal and hero, and blamed one another, and above all Kutuzov, for failing to do so.

These men, drawn on by their own passions, were but the blind instruments of the most melancholy law of necessity; but they believed themselves heroes, and imagined that what they were doing was the noblest and most honourable achievement. They blamed Kutuzov, and declared from the very beginning of the campaign he had prevented them from conquering Napoleon; that he thought of nothing but his own sensual gratifications, and would not advance out of Polotnyany Zavody because he was comfortable there; that he had checked the advance at Krasnoe; that he had completely lost his head when he heard Napoleon was near; that one might really suppose he had a secret understanding with Napoleon, that he had been bought over by him, and so on and so on.

And not only contemporaries, misled by their own passions, have spoken thus. Posterity and history have accepted Napoleon as *grand*, while foreign writers[1] have called Kutuzov a crafty, dissolute, weak, intriguing old man; and Russians have seen in him a nondescript being, a sort of puppet, only of use owing to his Russian name . . .

V

IN 1812 and 1813 Kutuzov was openly accused of blunders. The Tsar was dissatisfied with him. And in a recent history[2] inspired by promptings from the highest quarters, Kutuzov is spoken of as a designing, intriguing schemer, who was panic-stricken at the name of Napoleon, and guilty through his blunders at Krasnoe and Berezina of robbing the Russian army of the glory of complete victory over the French. Such is the lot of men not recognised by Russian intelligence as "great men," *grands hommes;* such is the destiny of those rare and always solitary men who divining the will of Providence submit their personal will to it. The hatred and contempt of the crowd is the punishment of such men for their comprehension of higher laws.

Strange and terrible to say, Napoleon, the most insignificant tool of history, who never even in exile displayed one trait of human dignity, is

[1] Wilson's *Letters.*
[2] Bogdanovitch's *History of the Year 1812*: The character of Kutuzov, and criticism of the unsatisfactory results of Kutuzov's battles.

the subject of the admiration and enthusiasm of the Russian historians; in their eyes he is a *grand homme*.

Kutuzov, the man who from the beginning to the end of his command in 1812, from Borodino to Vilna, was never in one word or deed false to himself, presents an example exceptional in history of self-sacrifice and recognition in the present of the relative value of events in the future. Kutuzov is conceived of by the historians as a nondescript, pitiful sort of creature, and whenever they speak of him in the year 1812, they seem a little ashamed of him.

And yet it is difficult to conceive of an historical character whose energy could be more invariably directed to the same unchanging aim. It is difficult to imagine an aim more noble and more in harmony with the will of a whole people. Still more difficult would it be to find an example in history where the aim of any historical personage has been so completely attained as the aim towards which all Kutuzov's efforts were devoted in 1812.

Kutuzov never talked of "forty centuries looking down from the Pyramids," of the sacrifices he was making for the fatherland, of what he meant to do or had done. He did not as a rule talk about himself, played no sort of part, always seemed the plainest and most ordinary man, and said the plainest and most ordinary things. He wrote letters to his daughters and to Madame de Staël, read novels, liked the company of pretty women, made jokes with the generals, the officers, and the soldiers, and never contradicted the people, who tried to prove anything to him. When Count Rastoptchin galloped up to him at Yautsky bridge, and reproached him personally with being responsible for the loss of Moscow, and said: "Didn't you promise not to abandon Moscow without a battle?" Kutuzov answered: "And I am not abandoning Moscow without a battle," although Moscow was in fact already abandoned. When Araktcheev came to him from the Tsar to say that Yermolov was to be appointed to the command of the artillery, Kutuzov said: "Yes, I was just saying so myself," though he had said just the opposite a moment before. What had he, the one man who grasped at the time all the vast issues of events, to do in the midst of that dull-witted crowd? What did he care whether Count Rastoptchin put down the disasters of the capital to him or to himself? Still less could he be concerned by the question which man was appointed to the command of the artillery.

This old man, who through experience of life had reached the conviction that the thoughts and words that serve as its expression are never the motive force of men, frequently uttered words, which were quite meaningless—the first words that occurred to his mind.

But heedless as he was of his words, he never once throughout all his career uttered a single word which was inconsistent with the sole aim for the attainment of which he was working all through the war. With obvious unwillingness, with bitter conviction that he would not be understood, he more than once, under the most different circumstances, gave expression to his real thought. His first differed from all about him after the battle of Borodino, which he alone persisted in calling a victory, and this view he continued to assert verbally and in reports and to his dying day. He alone said that *the loss of Moscow is not the loss of Russia.* In answer to the overtures for peace, his reply to Lauriston was: *There can be no peace, for such is the people's will.* He alone during the retreat of the French said that *all our manœuvres are unnecessary; that everything is being done of itself better than we could desire; that we must give the enemy a "golden bridge"; that the battles of Tarutino, of Vyazma, and of Krasnoe, were none of them necessary; that we must keep some men to reach the frontier with; that he wouldn't give one Russian for ten Frenchmen.* And he, this intriguing courtier, as we are told, who lied to Araktcheev to propitiate the Tsar, he alone dared to face the Tsar's displeasure by telling him at Vilna that *to carry the war beyond the frontier would be mischievous and useless.*

But words alone would be no proof that he grasped the significance of events at the time. His actions—all without the slightest deviation—were directed toward the one threefold aim: first, to concentrate all his forces to strike a blow at the French; secondly, to defeat them; and thirdly, to drive them out of Russia, alleviating as far as was possible the sufferings of the people and the soldiers in doing so.

He, the lingerer Kutuzov, whose motto was always "Time and Patience," the sworn opponent of precipitate action, he fought the battle of Borodino, and made all his preparations for it with unwonted solemnity. Before the battle of Austerlitz he foretold that it would be lost, but at Borodino, in spite of the conviction of the generals that the battle was a defeat, in spite of the fact, unprecedented in history, of his army being forced to retreat after the victory, he alone declared in opposition to all that it was a victory, and persisted in that opinion to his dying day. He was alone during the whole latter part of the campaign in insisting that there was no need of fighting now, that it was a mistake to cross the Russian frontier and to begin a new war. It is easy enough now that all the events with their consequences lie before us to grasp their significance, if only we refrain from attributing to the multitude the aims that only existed in the brains of some dozen or so of men

But how came that old man, alone in opposition to the opinion of all, to gauge so truly the importance of events from the national standard, so that he never once was false to the best interests of his country?

The source of this extraordinary intuition into the significance of contemporary events lay in the purity and fervour of patriotic feeling in his heart

It was their recognition of this feeling in him that led the people in such a strange manner to pick him out, an old man out of favour, as the chosen leader of the national war, against the will of the Tsar And this feeling alone it was to which he owed his exalted position, and there he exerted all his powers as commander-in-chief not to kill and maim men, but to save them and have mercy on them.

This simple, modest, and therefore truly great figure, could not be cast into the false mould of the European hero, the supposed leader of men, that history has invented.

To the flunkey no man can be great, because the flunkey has his own
flunkey conception of greatness.

VI

THE 5th of November was the first day of the so-called battle of Krasnoe.

Many had been the blunders and disputes among the generals, who
had not reached their proper places, many the contradictory orders carried to them by adjutants, but towards evening it was clear that the
enemy were everywhere in flight, and that there would not and could
not be a battle. In the evening Kutuzov set out from Krasnoe towards
Dobroe, to which place the headquarters had that day been removed.

It had been a clear, frosty day. Kutuzov, mounted on his fat, white
little horse, was riding towards Dobroe, followed by an immense suite of
generals, whispering their dissatisfaction behind his back. Seven thousand French prisoners had been taken that day, and all along the road
they met parties of them, crowding to warm themselves round the camp-
fires. Not far from Dobroe they heard a loud hum of talk from an immense crowd of tattered prisoners, bandaged and wrapped up in rags of
all sorts, standing in the road near a long row of unharnessed French
cannons. At the approach of the commander-in-chief the buzz of talk
died away, and all eyes were fixed upon Kutuzov, who moved slowly
along the road, wearing a white cap with a red band, and a wadded overcoat, that set in a hunch on his round shoulders. One of the generals began explaining to Kutuzov where the prisoners and the guns had been
taken.

Kutuzov seemed absorbed in anxious thought, and did not hear the
general's words. He screwed up his eyes with an air of displeasure, and
gazed intently at the figures of the prisoners, who presented a particularly pitiable appearance. The majority of the French soldiers were disfigured by frost-bitten cheeks and noses, and almost all of them had red,
swollen, and streaming eyes.

One group of Frenchmen was standing close by the road, and two
soldiers, one with his face covered with sores, were tearing at a piece of
raw meat with their hands. There was something bestial and horrible in
the cursory glance they cast on the approaching generals, and the frenzied expression with which the soldier with the sore face, after a glance
at Kutuzov, turned away and went on with what he was doing.

Kutuzov looked a long while intently at those two soldiers; frowning
more than before, he half-closed his eyelids, and shook his head thoughtfully. Further on, he noticed a Russian soldier, who was saying something friendly to a French prisoner, laughing and clapping him on the
shoulder. Kutuzov shook his head again with the same expression.

"What do you say?" he asked the general, who was trying to draw
the commander-in-chief's attention to the French flags, that were set up
in front of the Preobrazhensky regiment.

"Ah, the flags!" said Kutuzov, rousing himself with evident difficulty from the subject absorbing his thoughts. He looked about him absently. Thousands of eyes were gazing at him from all sides, waiting for his words.

He came to a standstill before the Preobrazhensky regiment, sighed heavily and closed his eyes. One of the suite beckoned to the soldiers holding the flags to come up and set up the flagstaffs around the commander-in-chief. Kutuzov was silent for a few seconds. Then with obvious reluctance, yielding to the obligations of his position, he raised his head and began to speak. Crowds of officers gathered round him. He scanned the circle of officers with an attentive eye, recognising some of them.

"I thank you all!" he said, addressing the soldiers, and then again turning to the officers. In the deep stillness that prevailed all round him, his slowly articulated words were distinctly audible: "I thank you all for your hard and faithful service. The victory is complete, and Russia will not forget you. Your glory will be for ever!" He paused, looking about him.

"Lower; bow his head lower," he said to the soldier, who was holding the French eagle, and had accidentally lowered it before the Preobrazhensky standard.

"Lower, lower, that's it. Hurrah, lads!" he said, his chin moving quickly as he turned to the soldiers.

"Hurrah-rah-rah!" thousands of voices roared.

While the soldiers were shouting, Kutuzov, bending forward in his saddle, bowed his head, and his eyes gleamed with a mild and, as it were, ironical light.

"And now, brothers . . ." he said, when the shouts had died away.

And all at once his face and expression changed: it was not the commander-in-chief speaking now, but a simple, aged man, who plainly wanted to say something most important now to his comrades.

"And now, brothers. I know it's hard for you, but there's no help for it! Have a little patience; it won't last much longer. We will see our visitors off, and then we will rest. The Tsar won't forget your services. It's hard for you, but still you are at home; while they—you see what they have come to," he said, pointing to the prisoners. "Worse than the lowest beggars. While they were strong, we did not spare ourselves, but now we can even spare them. They too are men. Eh, lads?"

He looked about him. And in the unflinching, respectfully wondering eyes staring persistently at him, he read sympathy with his words. His face grew brighter and brighter with the gentle smile of old age, that brought clusters of wrinkles at the corners of his mouth and his eyes. He paused and dropped his head, as though in doubt.

"But after all is said and done, who asked them to come here? It serves them right, the b—— b——" he said suddenly, lifting his head. And swinging his riding-whip, he rode off at a gallop, accompanied for the first time during the whole campaign by gleeful guffaws and roars of hurrah from the men as they moved out of rank.

The words uttered by Kutuzov were hardly understood by the soldiers. No one could have repeated the field-marshal's speech at first of such solemnity, and towards the end of such homely simplicity. But the meaning at the bottom of his words, they understood very well, and the same feeling of solemn triumph in their victory, together with pity for the enemy and the sense of the justice of their cause—expressed, too, with precisely the same homely coarseness—lay at the bottom of every soldier's heart, and found a vent in delighted shouts, that did not cease for a long while. When one of the generals addressed the commander-in-chief after this, asking whether he desired his carriage, Kutuzov broke into a sudden sob in replying. He was evidently deeply moved.

VII

It was getting dusk on the 8th of November, the last day of the battle of Krasnoe, when the soldiers reached their halting-place for the night. The whole day had been still and frosty, with now and then a few light flakes of snow. Towards evening the sky began to grow clearer. Through the snowflakes could be seen a dark, purplish, starlit sky, and the frost was growing more intense.

A regiment of musketeers, which had left Tarutino three thousand strong, but had now dwindled to nine hundred, was among the first to reach the halting-place, a village on the high road. The quartermasters, on meeting the regiment, reported that all the cottages were full of sick and dead Frenchmen, cavalrymen, and staff-officers. There was only one cottage left for the colonel of the regiment.

The colonel went on to his cottage. The regiment passed through the village, and stacked their guns up at the furthest cottages along the road.

Like a huge, many-legged monster, the regiment set to work preparing its food and lodging for the night. One party of soldiers trudged off, knee-deep in the snow, into the birch copse, on the right of the village, and the ring of axes and cutlasses, the crash of breaking branches, and the sounds of merry voices were immediately heard coming thence. Another group were busily at work all round the regimental baggage-waggons, which were drawn up altogether. Some fed the horses, while others got out cooking-pots and biscuits. A third section dispersed about the village, getting the cottages ready for the staff-officers, carrying out the dead bodies of the French lying in the huts, and dragging away boards, dry wood, and straw from the thatch roofs, to furnish fuel for their fires and materials for the shelters they rigged up.

Behind the huts at the end of the village fifteen soldiers were trying with merry shouts to pull down the high wattle wall of a barn from which they had already removed the roof.

"Now then, a strong pull, all together!" shouted the voices; and in the dark the huge, snow-sprinkled boards of the wall began to give. The lower stakes of the wattle cracked more and more often, and at last the

wattle wall heaved over, together with the soldiers, who were hanging
onto it. A loud shout and the roar of coarse merriment followed.

"Work at it in twos! give us a lever here! that's it. Where are you
coming to?"

"Now, all together. . . . But wait, lads! . . . With a shout!" . . .

All were silent, and a low voice of velvety sweetness began singing a
song. At the end of the third verse, as the last note died away, twenty
voices roared out in chorus, "O-O-O-O-O! It's coming! Pull away!
Heave away, lads! . . ." but in spite of their united efforts the wall
hardly moved, and in the silence that followed the men could be heard
panting for breath.

"Hi, you there, of the sixth company! You devils, you! Lend us a
hand . . . We'll do you a good turn one day!"

Twenty men of the sixth company, who were passing, joined them,
and the wattle wall, thirty-five feet in length, and seven feet in breadth
was dragged along the village street, falling over, and cutting the shoulders of the panting soldiers.

"Go on, do. . . . Heave away, you there. . . . What are you stopping for? Eh, there?" . . .

The merry shouts of unseemly abuse never ceased.

"What are you about?" cried a peremptory voice, as a sergeant ran
up to the party. "There are gentry here; the general himself's in the hut
here, and you devils, you curs, you! I'll teach you!" shouted the sergeant, and sent a swinging blow at the back of the first soldier he could
come across. "Can't you go quietly?"

The soldiers were quiet. The soldier who had received the blow began
grumbling, as he rubbed his bleeding face, which had been scratched by
his being knocked forward against the wattle.

"Ay, the devil; how he does hit a fellow! Why, he has set all my face
bleeding," he said in a timid whisper, as the sergeant walked away
"And you don't enjoy it, eh?" said a laughing voice; and the soldiers,
moderating their voices, moved on. As they got out of the village, they
began talking as loudly again, interspersing their talk with the same
meaningless oaths.

In the hut by which the soldiers had passed there were assembled the
chief officers in command, and an eager conversation was going on over
their tea about that day's doings and the manœuvres proposed for the
next. The plan was to execute a flank movement to the left, cut off and
capture the viceroy.

By the time the soldiers had dragged the fence to its place they found
blazing fires, cooking supper on all sides. The firewood was crackling,
the snow was melting, and the black shadows of soldiers were flitting to
and fro all over the space between trampled down in the snow.

Axes and cutlasses were at work on all sides. Everything was done
without a word of command being given. Wood was piled up for a supply
of fuel through the night, shanties were being rigged up for the officers
pots were being boiled, and arms and accoutrements set to rights.

The wattle wall was set up in a semicircle to give shelter from the north, propped up by stakes, and before it was built a camp-fire. They beat the tattoo-call, counted over their number, had supper, and settled themselves round the fires—some repairing their foot-gear, some smoking pipes, others stripped naked trying to steam the lice out of their clothes.

VIII

ONE would naturally have expected that in the almost inconceivably wretched conditions in which the Russian soldiers were placed at that time—without thick boots, without fur coats, without a roof over their heads in the snow, with a frost of eighteen degrees, often without full rations—they must have presented a most melancholy and depressing spectacle.

It was quite the opposite. Never under the most favourable material conditions had the army worn a livelier and more cheerful aspect. This was due to the fact that every element that showed signs of depression or weakness was sifted every day out of the army. All the physically and morally weak had long ago been left behind. What was left was the pick of the army—in strength of body and of spirit.

The camp-fire of the eighth company, screened by their wattle fence, attracted a greater crowd than any. Two sergeants were sitting by it, and the fire was blazing more brightly than any of them. They insisted on logs being brought in return for the right of sitting under the screen.

"Hi, Makyev, hullo . . . are you lost, or have the wolves eaten you? Fetch some wood," shouted a red-faced, red-haired soldier, screwing up his eyes, and blinking from the smoke, but not moving back from the fire.

"You run, Crow, and fetch some wood," he cried, addressing another soldier. The red-headed man was not a non-commissioned officer, nor a corporal, but he was a sturdy fellow, and so he gave orders to those who were weaker than himself. A thin, little soldier, with a sharp nose, who was called the "Crow," got up submissively, and was about to obey; but at that moment there stepped into the light of the fire the slender, handsome figure of a young soldier, carrying a load of wood.

"Give it here. Well, that's something like!"

They broke up the wood and threw it on, blew up the fire with their mouths, and fanned it with the skirts of their coats, and the flame began to hiss and crackle. The soldiers drew nearer the fire and lighted their pipes. The handsome young soldier who had brought in the wood put his arms akimbo, and began a smart and nimble shuffle with his frozen feet as he stood.

"Ah, mother dear, the dew is cold, but yet it is fine, and a musketeer!" . . . he began singing, with a sort of hiccup at each syllable of the song.

"Hey, his soles are flying off!" cried the red-haired man, noticing that the dancer's soles were loose. "He's a rare devil for dancing!"

The dancer stopped, tore off the loose leather, and flung it in the fire.

"You're right there, brother," said he, and sitting down he took out of his knapsack a strip of French blue cloth, and began binding it round his foot. "It's the steam that warps them," he added, stretching his feet out to the fire.

"They'll soon serve us new ones. They say when we finish them off, we are all to have a double lot of stuff."

"I say, that son of a bitch, Petrov, has sneaked off, it seems," said a sergeant.

"It's a long while since I've noticed him," said the other.

"Oh, well, a poor sort of soldier . . ."

"And in the third company, they were saying, there were nine men missing at the roll-call yesterday."

"Well, but after all, when one's feet are frozen, how's one to walk?"

"Oh, stuff and nonsense!" said the sergeant.

"Why, do you want to do the same?" said an old soldier, reproachfully addressing the man who had talked of frozen feet.

"Well, what do you think?" the sharp-nosed soldier, called "Crow," said suddenly, in a squeaking and quavery voice, turning himself on one elbow behind the fire. "If a man's sleek and fat, he just grows thin, but for a thin man it's death. Look at me, now! I have no strength left," he said, with sudden resolution, addressing a sergeant. "Say the word for me to be sent off to the hospital. I'm one ache with rheumatism, and one only gets left behind just the same . . ."

"There, that's enough; that's enough," said the sergeant calmly.

The soldier was silent, and the conversation went on.

"There's a rare lot of these Frenchies have been taken to-day; but not a pair of boots or one of them, one may say, worth having; no, not worth mentioning," one of the soldiers began, starting a new subject.

"The Cossacks had stripped them of everything. We cleaned a hut for the colonel, and carried them out. It was pitiful to see them, lads," said the dancer. "We overhauled them. One was alive, would you believe it muttering something in their lingo."

"They're a clean people, lads," said the first. "White—why, as white as a birch-tree, and brave they are, I must say, and gentlemen too."

"Well, what would you expect? Soldiers are taken from all classes with them."

"And yet they don't understand a word we say," said the dancer, with a wondering smile. "I says to him, 'Of what kingdom are you?' and he mutters away his lingo. A strange people!"

"I'll tell you a wonderful thing, mates," went on the man who had expressed surprise at their whiteness. "The peasants about Mozhaisk were telling how, when they went to take away the dead where the great battle was, why, their bodies had been lying there a good month. Well, they lay there, as white and clean as paper, and not a smell about them."

"Why, from the cold, eh?" asked one.

"You're a clever one! Cold, indeed! Why, it was hot weather. If it had been from the cold, our men, too, wouldn't have rotted. But they say, go up to one of ours, and it would all be putrefied and maggoty. They tie handkerchiefs round their noses, and drag them off, turning their faces away, so they say. They can't help it. But they're white as paper; not a smell about them."

There was a general silence.

"Must be from the feeding," said the sergeant: "they are gorged like gentry."

No one replied.

"That peasant at Mozhaisk, where the battle was, was saying that they were fetched from ten villages round, and at work there for twenty days, and couldn't get all the dead away. A lot of those wolves, says he . . ."

"That was something like a battle," said an old soldier. "The only one worth mentioning; everything since . . . it's simply tormenting folks for nothing."

"Oh, well, uncle, we did attack them the day before yesterday. But what's one to do? They won't let us get at them. They were so quick at laying down their arms, and on their knees. *Pardon!*—they say. And that's only one example. They have said twice that Platov had taken Polion himself. He catches him, and lo! he turns into a bird in his hands and flies away and away. And as to killing him, no manner of means of doing it."

"You're a sturdy liar, Kiselov, by the look of you!"

"Liar, indeed! It's the holy truth."

"Well, if you ask me, I'd bury him in the earth, if I caught him. Yes, with a good aspen cudgel. The number of folk he has destroyed!"

"Any way, we shall soon make an end of him; he won't come again," said the old soldier, yawning.

The conversation died away; the soldiers began making themselves comfortable for the night.

"I say, what a lot of stars; how they shine! One would say the women had been laying out their linen!" said a soldier admiring the Milky Way.

"That's a sign of a good harvest, lads!"

"We shall want a little more wood."

"One warms one's back, and one's belly freezes. That's queer."

"O Lord!"

"What are you shoving for—is the fire only for you, eh? See . . . there he sprawls."

In the silence that reigned snoring could be heard from a few who had gone to sleep. The rest turned themselves to get warm by the fire, exchanging occasional remarks. From a fire a hundred paces away came a chorus of merry laughter.

"They are guffawing in the fifth company," said a soldier. "And what a lot of them there!"

A soldier got up and went off to the fifth company.

"There's a bit of fun!" he said, coming back. "Two Frenchies have

come. One's quite frozen, but the other's a fine plucky fellow! He's sing
ing songs."

"O-O! must go and look . . ." Several soldiers went across to the
fifth company.

IX

THE fifth company was bivouacking close up to the birch copse. An immense camp-fire was blazing brightly in the middle of the snow, lighting
up the rime-covered boughs of the trees.

In the middle of the night the soldiers had heard footsteps and the
cracking of branches in the copse.

"A bear, lads," said one soldier.

All raised their heads and listened; and out of the copse there stepped
into the bright light of the fire two strangely garbed human figures,
clinging to one another. These were two Frenchmen, who had been hid
ing in the wood. Hoarsely articulating something in a tongue incomprehensible to the soldiers, they approached the fire. One, wearing an offi·
cer's hat, was rather the taller, and seemed utterly spent. He tried to sit
down by the fire, but sank on to the ground. The other, a little, stumpy
man, with a kerchief bound round his cheeks, was stronger. He held his
companion up, and said something pointing to his mouth. The soldiers
surrounded the Frenchmen, laid a coat under the sick man, and brought
both of them porridge and vodka. The exhausted French officer was
Ramballe; the little man bandaged up in the kerchief was his servant,
Morel.

When Morel had drunk some vodka and eaten a bowl of porridge, he
suddenly passed into a state of morbid hilarity, and kept up an incessant
babble with the soldiers, who could not understand him. Ramballe refused food, and leaning on one elbow by the fire, gazed dumbly with red,
vacant eyes at the Russian soldiers. At intervals he uttered a prolonged
groan and then was mute again. Morel, pointing to his shoulders, gave
the soldiers to understand that this was an officer, and that he needed
warmth. A Russian officer, who had come up to the fire, sent to ask the
colonel whether he would take a French officer into his warm cottage.
When they came back and said that the colonel bade them bring the
officer, they told Ramballe to go to him. He got up and tried to walk,
but staggered, and would have fallen had not a soldier standing near
caught him.

"What? You don't want to, eh?" said a soldier addressing Ramballe
with a jocose wink.

"Eh, you fool! It's no time for your fooling. A peasant, a real peasant," voices were heard on all sides blaming the jocose soldier. The
others surrounded Ramballe. Two of them held him up under the arms
and carried him to the cottage. Ramballe put his arms round the soldiers' necks, and as they lifted him he began wailing plaintively.

"O you good fellows! O my kind, kind friends. These are men! O my brave, kind friends"; and like a child he put his head down on the soldier's shoulder.

Meanwhile Morel was sitting in the best place surrounded by the soldiers.

Morel, a little, thickset Frenchman, with swollen, streaming eyes, was dressed in a woman's jacket and had a woman's kerchief tied over his forage cap. He was evidently tipsy, and with one arm thrown round the soldier sitting next him, he was singing a French song in a husky, broken voice. The soldiers simply held their sides as they looked at him.

"Now then, now then, teach it me; how does it go? I'll catch it in no time. How was it?" said the soldier Morel was hugging, who was one of the singers and fond of a joke.

"*Vive Henri Quatre! Vive ce roi vaillant!* . . ." sang Morel, winking. "*Ce diable à quatre* . . ."

"*Vi-va-ri-ka! Viff-se-ru-va-ru! Si-dya-blya-ka!* . . ." repeated the soldier, waving his hand and catching the tune correctly.

"Bravo! Ho-ho-ho-ho!" a hoarse guffaw of delight rose on all sides. Morel, wrinkling up his face, laughed too.

"Come, strike up, more, more!"

"*Qui eut le triple talent de boire, de battre, et d'être un vert galant.*"

"That sounds well too. Now, Zaletaev! . . ."

"*Kyu,*" Zaletaev articulated with effort. "*Kyu-yu-yu* . . ." he sang, puckering up his lips elaborately; "*le-trip-ta-la-de-boo-de-ba-ce-detra-va-ga-la.*"

"That's fine! That's a fine Frenchman, to be sure! oy . . . ho-ho-ho. Well, do you want some more to eat?"

"Give him some porridge; it'll take him some time to satisfy his hunger."

They gave him more porridge, and Morel, laughing, attacked a third bowlful. There were gleeful smiles on the faces of all the young soldiers watching him. The old soldiers, considering it beneath their dignity to show interest in such trifles, lay on the other side of the fire, but now and then one would raise himself on his elbow and glance with a smile at Morel.

"They are men, too," said one, rolling himself up in his coat. "Even the wormwood has its roots."

"O Lord! What lots of stars! It's a sign of frost . . ." And all sank into silence.

The stars, as though they knew no one would see them now, were twinkling brightly in the black sky. Flaring up and growing dim again, and quivering, they seemed to be busily signalling some joyful mystery to each other.

X

THE French army went on melting away at a regularly increasing rate. And the crossing of the Berezina, of which so much has been written, was only one of the intermediate stages of the destruction of the army, and by no means the decisive episode of the campaign. The reason that so much has been written about Berezina on the French side is that at the broken-down bridge of Berezina the woes, which had till then come upon them in a sort of regular succession, were suddenly concentrated there in a single moment—in one tragic catastrophe, which remained printed on the memory of all. On the Russian side, the reason that so much has been made of Berezina was simply that at Petersburg, far away from the theatre of war, a plan had been devised (again by Pfuhl of all people) for catching Napoleon in a strategic snare on the banks of the Berezina. Every one was convinced that the plan would come off exactly as arranged, and so they insisted that Berezina had in any case been the scene of the final ruin of the French. In reality the results of Berezina were less ruinous to the French in loss of cannons and prisoners than was the fighting at Krasnoe, as statistics prove.

The sole significance of the disaster of Berezina lies in the fact that it proved obviously and unmistakably how misleading were all plans for cutting off the enemy's retreat; and the one possible course of action was that which was supported by Kutuzov and the mass of the Russian army—simply to follow on the enemy's track. The crowd of French soldiers fled with continually accelerating velocity, with all their energies directed to the attainment of their goal. It was fleeing like a wounded beast and could not be stopped on the way. This was proved, not so much by the construction of the crossing, as by what happened at the bridges. When the bridges were broken down, unarmed soldiers, camp-followers from Moscow, women with children, who were with the French transport, all under the influence of *vis inertiœ*, dashed forward for the boats, or rushed into the frozen water, instead of surrendering.

Their impulse was a reasonable one. The position of fugitives and of pursuers was equally wretched. By remaining with his own men, each hoped for the help of comrades in misfortune, for a definite place of his own among them. By surrendering to the Russians, he found himself in the same wretched circumstances, but placed on a lower level than others as regards the satisfaction of his vital needs. The French had no need of authentic evidence that half of the prisoners—whom the Russians were unable to look after, however much they desired to save them —were dying of cold and hunger. They felt that it could not but be so. The most humane Russian officers, even those naturally warmly disposed to the French, Frenchmen in the Russian service, could do nothing for the prisoners. They perished from the wretched plight in which the Russians were themselves placed. Bread and clothing could not be taken from the starving, insistent soldiers to give it to Frenchmen—

not hated, not obnoxious, nor in any way to blame—but simply super-fluous. Some did even do this; but it was only an exception.

Behind them lay certain destruction; before them lay hope. Their ships were burnt; there was no hope of safety but in keeping together and in flight, and all the forces of the French were bent on this united flight.

The more precipitate the flight of the French, and the more wretched the plight of those left behind (especially after Berezina, on which great hopes had been set, owing to the Petersburg plan), the more violent were the attacks made by the Russian generals on one another, and still more on Kutuzov. Assuming that the failure of the Petersburg plan would be ascribed to him, the dissatisfaction with him, contempt of him, and jeering at him became more and more pronounced. This contempt and jeering was of course expressed in respectful form—in such a form that Kutuzov could not even ask what he was accused of. They did not talk to him seriously; they submitted their reports and asked for his decisions with an air of performing a melancholy ceremony, while they winked behind his back, and at every step tried to deceive him. It was accepted as a recognized thing by all those men that it was useless talking to the old man, simply because they could not understand him. They took it for granted that he could never comprehend the deep significance of their plans, that he would answer them with his phrases (they fancied they were only meaningless phrases) about a golden bridge, and about the impossibility of going beyond the frontier with a crowd of barefoot beggars. And everything he said—for instance, that they must wait for provisions, or that the men had no boots—all was so simple; while everything they proposed was so complicated and so clever, that it was obvious to them that he was stupid and in his dotage, while they were military officers of genius, without authority to take the lead. The dissatisfaction and malicious gossip of the staff reached its utmost limits after the brilliant admiral, the favourite hero of Petersburg, Wittgenstein, had joined the army. Kutuzov saw it, and simply sighed and shrugged his shoulders. Only once, after Berezina, he lost his temper and wrote to Bennigsen, who was in private correspondence with the Tsar, the following note:

"I beg your Most High Excellency on the receipt of this letter to retire to Kaluga, on account of your attacks of ill-health, and there to await the further commands of His Majesty the Emperor."

But this dismissal of Bennigsen was followed by the arrival on the scene of the Grand Duke Konstantin Pavlovitch, who had received a command at the beginning of the campaign and had been removed from the army by Kutuzov. Now the Grand Duke on rejoining the army informed Kutuzov of the Tsar's dissatisfaction at the poor successes of our troops, and the slowness of their progress. The Tsar himself intended to be with the army in a few days.

The old man, as experienced in court methods as in warfare—who in the August of that year had been chosen commander-in-chief against the Tsar's will, who had dismissed the Grand Duke and heir-apparent from

the army, and acting on his own authority, in opposition to the Tsar's
will, had decreed the abandonment of Moscow—understood at once now
that his day was over, that his part was played out, and that his supposed power was no more. And not only from the attitude of the court
did he see this. On one side he saw the war—that war in which he had
played his part—was over, and he felt that his work was done. On the
other hand, at this very time, he began to be sensible of the physical
weariness of his aged frame, and the necessity of physical rest.

On the 29th of November, Kutuzov reached Vilna—his dear Vilna, as
he used to call it. Twice during his military career he had been governor
of Vilna.

In that wealthy town, which had escaped injury, Kutuzov found old
friends and old associations, as well as the comforts of which he had
been so long deprived. And at once turning his back on all military and
political cares, he plunged into the quiet routine of his accustomed life,
so far as the passions raging all round him would permit. It was as
though all that was being done, and had still to be done, in the world of
history, was no concern of his now.

Tchitchagov was one of the generals most zealous in advocating attack and cutting off the enemy's retreat; he had at first suggested making a diversion in Greece and then in Warsaw, but was never willing to
go where he was commanded to go. Tchitchagov, who was notorious for
the boldness of his remarks to the Tsar, considered Kutuzov was under
an obligation to him, because when he had been sent in 1811 to conclude
peace with Turkey over Kutuzov's head, and found on arriving that
peace had already been concluded, he had frankly admitted to the Tsar
that the credit of having concluded peace belonged to Kutuzov.

This Tchitchagov was the first to meet Kutuzov at Vilna, at the castle
where the latter was to stay. Wearing a naval uniform with a dirk, and
holding his forage cap under his arm, he handed the commander-in-chief
the military report and the keys of the town. The contemptuously respectful attitude of youth to old age in its dotage was expressed in the
most marked manner in all the behaviour of Tchitchagov, who was
aware of the disfavour into which Kutuzov had fallen.

In conversation with Tchitchagov, Kutuzov happened to say that his
carriages, packed with china, that had been carried off by the enemy at
Borisovo, had been recovered unhurt, and would be restored to him.

"You mean to say I have nothing to eat out of? On the contrary, I can
provide everything for you, even if you want to give dinner-parties,"
Tchitchagov protested, getting hot. Every word he had uttered had been
with the motive of proving his own rectitude, and so he imagined that
Kutuzov too was preoccupied with the same desire. Shrugging his shoulders and smiling his subtle, penetrating smile, Kutuzov answered:

"I mean to say to you what I do say to you. Nothing more."

In opposition to the Tsar's wishes, Kutuzov kept the greater part of
the troops in Vilna. He was said by all the persons about him to be getting much weaker, and breaking down physically during his stay in
Vilna. He took no interest in the business of the army, left everything to

his generals, and spent the time of waiting for the Tsar in social dissipation.

The Tsar, with his suite—Count Tolstoy, Prince Volkonsky, Araktcheev, and the rest—left Petersburg on the 7th of December, and reached Vilna on the 11th, and drove straight up to the castle in his travelling sledge. In spite of the intense cold there were some hundred generals and staff-officers in full parade uniform, and a guard of honour of the Semyonovsky regiment standing before the castle.

A courier, galloping up to the castle with steaming horses in advance of the Tsar, shouted: "He is coming!"

Konovnitsyn rushed into the vestibule to inform Kutuzov, who was waiting in the porter's little room within.

A minute later the big, heavy figure of the old man in full parade uniform, his breast covered with orders, and a scarf drawn tight about his bulky person, walked with a rolling gait on to the steps. He put his cocked hat on, with the flat side foremost, took his gloves in his hand, and going sideways with difficulty down the steps, took in his hand the report, that had been prepared to give the Tsar.

Bustle and hurry and whispering, another set of three horses dashing furiously up, and all eyes were turned on the approaching sledge, in which the figures of the Tsar and Volkonsky could already be distinguished.

From the habit of fifty years, all this had a physically agitating effect on the old man. He felt himself over with nervous haste, set his hat straight, and pulling himself together and standing erect at the very moment when the Tsar stepping out of the sledge, turned his eyes upon him, he handed him the report, and began speaking in his measured, ingratiating voice.

The Tsar scanned Kutuzov from head to foot in a rapid glance, frowned for an instant; but at once overcoming his feelings, went up to him, and opening his arms, embraced the old general. Again, through old habitual association of ideas, arousing some deep feeling in his own heart, this embrace had its usual effect on Kutuzov: he gave a sob.

The Tsar greeted the officers and the Semyonovsky guard of honour; and once more shaking hands with the old man, he went with him into the castle.

When he was alone with the commander-in-chief, the Tsar gave expression to his displeasure at the slowness of the pursuit of the enemy, and the blunders made at Krasnoe and the Berezina, and to his views as to the coming campaign abroad. Kutuzov made no observation or explanation. The same expression of unreasoning submission with which seven years before he had listened to the Tsar's commands on the field of Austerlitz remained fixed now on his face.

When Kutuzov had left the room, and with downcast head walked across the reception-hall with his heavy, waddling step, a voice stopped him.

"Your highness," said some one.

He raised his head, and looked into the face of Count Tolstoy, who stood facing him with a small object on a silver dish. Kutuzov seemed for some time unable to grasp what was wanted of him.

All at once he seemed to recollect himself; a faint smile gleamed on his pudgy face, and with a low, respectful bow, he picked up the object on the dish. It was the Order of St. George of the first rank.

XI

THE next day the commander-in-chief gave a dinner and a ball, which the Tsar honoured with his presence.

Kutuzov had received the Order of St. George of the first rank; the Tsar had shown him the highest marks of respect, but every one was aware that the Tsar was displeased with the commander-in-chief. The proprieties were observed, and the Tsar set the first example in doing so. But every one knew that the old man was in fault, and had shown his incapacity. When, in accordance with the old custom of Catherine's time, Kutuzov gave orders for the captured standards to be lowered at the Tsar's feet on his entering the ball-room, the Tsar frowned with vexation, and muttered words, which some heard as: "The old comedian."

The Tsar's displeasure was increased at Vilna by Kutuzov's obvious unwillingness or incapacity to see the importance of the approaching campaign.

When next morning the Tsar said to the officers gathered about him: "You have not only saved Russia, you have saved Europe," every one knew at once that the war was not over.

Kutuzov alone refused to see this, and frankly gave it as his opinion that no fresh war could improve the position of Russia, or add to her glory; that it could but weaken her position, and cast her down from that high pinnacle of glory at which in his view Russia was standing now. He tried to show the Tsar the impossibility of levying fresh troops, and talked of the hardships the people were suffering, the possibility of failure, and so on.

Such being his attitude on the subject, the commander-in-chief could naturally be looked upon only as a hindrance and a drag on the progress of the coming campaign.

To avoid friction with the old man, the obvious resource was—as with him at Austerlitz and with Barclay at the beginning of the war—to withdraw all real power from the commander-in-chief, without disturbing him by any open explanation on the matter, and to transfer it to the Tsar.

With this object, the staff was gradually transformed, and all the real power of Kutuzov's staff was removed and transferred to the Tsar. Toll, Konovnitsyn, and Yermolov received new appointments. Every one talked openly of the commander-in-chief's great weakness and failing health.

He was bound to be in failing health, so as to make way for his successor. And his health was, in fact, failing.

Just as naturally, as simply, and as gradually as Kutuzov had come to the Court of Exchequer at Petersburg out of Turkey to raise the militia, and then to take the command of the army just at the time when he was needed, did a new commander come now to replace him, when his part was played.

The war of 1812, in addition to its national significance, dear to every Russian heart, was to take a new European character.

The movement of men from west to east was to be followed by a movement from east to west, and this new war needed a new representative, with other aims and other qualities, and moved by impulses different from Kutuzov's.

For the movement from east to west, and the establishment of the position of peoples, Alexander was needed just as Kutuzov was needed for the deliverance and the glory of Russia.

Kutuzov did not see what was meant by Europe, the balance of power, and Napoleon. He could not understand all that.

After the enemy had been annihilated, Russia had been delivered and raised to the highest pinnacle of her glory, the representative of the Russian people, a Russian of the Russians, had no more left to do. Nothing was left for the representative of the national war but to die. And he did die.

XII

As is generally the case, Pierre only felt the full strain of the physical hardships and privations he had suffered as a prisoner, when they were over. After he had been rescued, he went to Orel, and two days after getting there, as he was preparing to start for Kiev, he fell ill and spent three months laid up at Orel. He was suffering, so the doctors said, from a bilious fever. Although they treated him by letting blood and giving him drugs, he recovered.

Everything that had happened to Pierre from the time of his rescue up to his illness had left hardly any impression on his mind. He had only a memory of dark grey weather, sometimes rainy and sometimes sunshiny, of internal physical aches, of pain in his feet and his side. He remembered a general impression of the misery and suffering of men, remembered the worrying curiosity of officers and generals, who questioned him about his imprisonment, the trouble he had to get horses and a conveyance; and more than all he remembered his own dullness of thought and of feeling all that time.

On the day of his rescue he saw the dead body of Petya Rostov. The same day he learned that Prince Andrey had lived for more than a month after the battle of Borodino, and had only a short time before died at Yaroslavl in the Rostovs' house. The same day Denisov, who had told Pierre this piece of news, happened to allude in conversation to the death of Ellen, supposing Pierre to have been long aware of it. All this had at the time seemed to Pierre only strange. He felt that he could not take in all the bearings of these facts. He was at the time simply in haste to get away from these places where men were slaughtering each other to some quiet refuge where he might rest and recover his faculties, and think over all the new strange things he had learned.

But as soon as he reached Orel, he fell ill. On coming to himself after his illness, Pierre saw waiting on him two of his servants, Terenty and Vaska, who had come from Moscow, and the eldest of his cousins, who was staying at Pierre's estate in Elets, and hearing of his rescue and his illness had come to nurse him.

During his convalescence Pierre could only gradually recover from the impressions of the last few months, which had become habitual. Only by degrees could he become accustomed to the idea that there was no one to drive him on to-morrow, that no one would take his warm bed from him, and that he was quite sure of getting his dinner, and tea, and supper. But for a long while afterwards he was always in his dreams surrounded by his conditions as a prisoner.

And only in the same gradual way did Pierre grasp the meaning of the news he had heard since his escape: of the death of Prince Andrey, of the death of his wife, and of the overthrow of the French.

The joyful sense of freedom—that full, inalienable freedom inherent in man, of which he had first had a consciousness at the first halting place outside Moscow—filled Pierre's soul during his convalescence. He was surprised that this inner freedom, independent as it was of all external circumstances, was now as it were decked out in a luxury, a superfluity of external freedom. He was alone in a strange town without acquaintances. No one made any demands on him; no one sent him anywhere. He had all he wanted; the thought of his wife, that had in old days been a continual torture to him, was no more, since she herself was no more.

"Ah, how happy I am! how splendid it is!" he said to himself, when a cleanly covered table was moved up to him, with savoury-smelling broth, or when he got into his soft, clean bed at night, or when the thought struck him that his wife and the French were no more. "Ah, how good it is! how splendid!" And from old habit he asked himself the question, "Well, and what then? what am I going to do?" And at once he answered himself: "I am going to live. Ah, how splendid it is!"

What had worried him in old days, what he had always been seeking to solve, the question of the object of life, did not exist for him now. That seeking for an object in life was over for him now; and it was not fortuitously or temporarily that it was over. He felt that there was no such object, and could not be. And it was just the absence of an object that gave him that complete and joyful sense of freedom that at this time made his happiness.

He could seek no object in life now, because now he had faith—not faith in any sort of principles, or words, or ideas, but faith in a living, ever-palpable God. In old days he had sought Him in the aims he set before himself. That search for an object in life had been only a seeking after God; and all at once in his captivity he had come to know, not through words or arguments, but by his own immediate feeling, what his old nurse had told him long before; that God is here, and everywhere. In his captivity he had come to see that the God in Karataev was grander, more infinite, and more unfathomable than the Architect of the Universe recognised by the masons. He felt like a man who finds what he has sought at his feet, when he has been straining his eyes to seek it in the distance. All his life he had been looking far away over the heads of all around him, while he need not have strained his eyes, but had only to look in front of him.

In old days he had been unable to see the great, the unfathomable, and the infinite in anything. He had only felt that it must be somewhere, and had been seeking it. In everything near and comprehensible, he had seen only what was limited, petty, everyday, and meaningless. He had armed himself with the telescope of intellect, and gazed far away into the distance, where that petty, everyday world, hidden in the mists of distance, had seemed to him great and infinite, simply because it was not clearly seen. Such had been European life, politics, freemasonry, philosophy, and philanthropy in his eyes. But even then, in moments which he had looked on as times of weakness, his thought had penetrated even to these remote objects, and then he had seen in them the same pettiness, the same ordinariness and meaninglessness.

Now he had learnt to see the great, the eternal, and the infinite in everything; and naturally therefore, in order to see it, to revel in its contemplation, he flung aside the telescope through which he had hitherto been gazing over men's heads, and looked joyfully at the ever-changing, ever grand, unfathomable, and infinite life around him. And the closer he looked at it, the calmer and happier he was. The terrible question that had shattered all his intellectual edifices in old days, the question: What for? had no existence for him now. To that question, What for? he had now always ready in his soul the simple answer: Because there is a God, that God without whom not one hair of a man's head falls.

XIII

PIERRE was hardly changed in his external habits. In appearance he was just the same as before. He was, as he had always been, absent-minded, and seemed preoccupied with something of his own, something apart from what was before his eyes. The difference was that in old days, when he was unconscious of what was before his eyes, or what was being said to him, he would seem with painfully knitted brows to be striving unsuccessfully to discern something far away from him. He was just as unconscious now of what was said to him, or of what was before him. But now with a faint, apparently ironical smile, he gazed at what was before him, or listened to what was said, though he was obviously seeing and hearing something quite different. In old days he had seemed a good-hearted man, but unhappy. And so people had unconsciously held a little aloof from him. Now a smile of joy in life was continually playing about his mouth, and his eyes were bright with sympathy for others, and the question: Were they all as happy as he? And people felt at ease in his presence.

In old days he had talked a great deal, and had got hot when he talked, and he had listened very little. Now he was rarely carried away in conversation, and knew how to listen, so that people were very ready to tell him the inmost secrets of their hearts.

The princess, who had never liked Pierre, and had cherished a particularly hostile feeling towards him, since after the old count's death she had felt herself under obligation to him, had come to Orel with the intention of proving to him that in spite of his ingratitude she felt it her duty to nurse him, but after a short time she felt, to her own surprise and annoyance, that she was growing fond of him. Pierre did nothing to try and win his cousin's favour; he simply looked at her with curiosity. In old days she had felt that there was mockery and indifference in his eyes, and she had shrunk into herself before him, as she did before other people, and had shown him only her aggressive side. Now she felt on the contrary as though he were delving into the most secret recesses of her life. It was at first mistrustfully, and then with gratitude, that she let him see now the latent good side of her character.

The most artful person could not have stolen into the princess's confidence more cunningly, by arousing her recollections of the best time of her youth, and showing sympathy with them. And yet all Pierre's artfulness consisted in seeking to please himself by drawing out human qualities in the bitter, hard, and, in her own way, proud princess.

"Yes, he is a very, very good-hearted fellow when he is not under bad influence, but under the influence of people like me," thought the princess.

The change that had taken place in Pierre was noticed in their own way by his servants too—Terenty and Vaska. They considered that he had grown much more good-natured. Often after undressing his master, and wishing him good night, Terenty would linger with his boots and his clothes in his hand, in the hope that his master would begin a conversation with him. And as a rule Pierre kept Terenty, seeing he was longing for a chat.

"Come, tell me, then . . . how did you manage to get anything to eat?" he would ask. And Terenty would begin his tales of the destruction of Moscow and of the late count, and would stand a long while with the clothes, talking away or listening to Pierre; and it was with a pleasant sense of his master's close intimacy with him and affection for him that he finally withdrew.

The doctor, who was attending Pierre, and came to see him every day, though he thought it his duty as a doctor to pose as a man every minute of whose time is of value for suffering humanity, used to sit on with him for hours together, repeating his favourite anecdotes and observations on the peculiarities of patients in general, and of ladies in particular.

"Yes, it's a pleasure to talk to a man like that; it's not what we are used to in the provinces," he would say.

In Orel there happened to be several French prisoners, and the doctor brought one of them, a young Italian officer, to see Pierre.

This officer became a frequent visitor, and the princess used to laugh at the tender feelings the Italian expressed for Pierre.

It was obvious that the Italian was never happy but when he could see Pierre, and talk to him, and tell him all about his own past, his home life, and his love, and pour out his indignation against the French, and especially against Napoleon.

"If all Russians are the least bit like you," he used to say to Pierre, "it is sacrilege to make war on a people like yours. You who have suffered so much at the hands of the French, have not even a grudge against them."

And Pierre had won the Italian's passionate devotion simply by drawing out what was best in his soul and admiring it.

During the latter part of Pierre's stay in Orel, he received a visit from an old acquaintance, Count Villarsky, the freemason, who had introduced him to the lodge in 1807. Villarsky had married a Russian heiress, who had great estates in the Orel province, and he was filling a temporary post in the commissariat department in the town.

Though Villarsky had never been very intimately acquainted with Bezuhov, on hearing that he was in Orel, he called upon him with those demonstrations of friendliness and intimacy that men commonly display on meeting one another in the desert. Villarsky was dull in Orel, and was delighted to meet a man of his own circle, who had, as he supposed, the same interests as he had.

But to his surprise, Villarsky noticed soon that Pierre had quite dropped behind the times, and had, as he defined it himself to Pierre, sunk into apathy and egoism.

"You are stagnating," he said to him.

But in spite of that, Villarsky felt much more at home with Pierre now than he had done in the past, and came every day to see him. As Pierre watched Villarsky, and listened to him now, it seemed strange and incredible to him to think that he had very lately been the same sort of person himself.

Villarsky was a married man with a family, whose time was taken up in managing his wife's property, in performing his official duties, and in looking after his family. He regarded all these duties as a drawback in his life, and looked on them all with contempt, because they were all directed to securing his own personal welfare and that of his family. Military, administrative, political, and masonic questions were continually engrossing his attention. And without criticising this view or attempting to change it, Pierre watched this phenomenon—so strange, yet so familiar to him—with the smile of gentle, delighted irony that was now habitual with him.

In Pierre's relations with Villarsky, with his cousin, with the doctor, and with all the people he met now, there was a new feature that gained him the good-will of all. This was the recognition of the freedom of every man to think, to feel, and to look at things in his own way; the recognition of the impossibility of altering a man's conviction by words. This legitimate individuality of every man's views, which had in old days troubled and irritated Pierre, now formed the basis of the sympathetic interest he felt in people. The inconsistency, sometimes the complete antagonism of men's views with their own lives or with one another, delighted Pierre, and drew from him a gentle and mocking smile.

In practical affairs Pierre suddenly felt now that he had the centre of gravity that he had lacked in former days. In the past every money question, especially requests for money, to which as a very wealthy man he was particularly liable, had reduced him to a state of helpless agitation and perplexity. "Ought I to give or not to give?" he used to ask himself. "I have money and he needs it. But some one else needs it more. Who needs it more? And perhaps both are impostors?" And of all these suppositions he had in old days found no satisfactory solution, and gave to all as long as he had anything to give. In old days he had been in the same perplexity over every question relating to his property when one person told him he ought to act in one way and another advised something else.

Now to his own surprise he found that he had no more doubt or hesitation on all such questions. Now there was a judge within him settling what he must do and what he must not, by some laws of which he was himself unaware.

He was just as unconcerned about money matters as before; but now he unhesitatingly knew what he ought to do and what he ought not to do. The first application of that new power within him was in the case of a prisoner, a French colonel, who called on him, talked very freely of his own great exploits, and finally delivered himself of a request that was more like a demand, that he should give him four thousand francs to send to his wife and children. Pierre refused to do so without the slightest difficulty or effort, and wondered himself afterwards that it had been so easy and simple to do what had in old days seemed so hopelessly difficult. At the same time as he refused the French colonel, he made up his mind that he must certainly resort to some stratagem when he left Orel to induce the Italian officer to accept assistance, of which he stood in evident need. A fresh proof to Pierre of his greater certainty in regard to practical matters was the settlement of the question of his wife's debts, and of the rebuilding of his Moscow house and villas in the suburbs.

His head steward came to him in Orel, and with him Pierre went into a general review of his financial position. The fire of Moscow had cost Pierre, by the steward's account, about two millions.

The chief steward to console him for these losses presented a calculation he had made, that Pierre's income, far from being diminished, would be positively increased if he were to refuse to pay the debts left by the countess—which he could not be forced to pay—and if he were not to restore his Moscow houses and the villa near Moscow, which had cost him eight thousand to keep up, and brought in nothing.

"Yes, yes, that's true," said Pierre, with a beaming smile.

"Yes, yes, I don't need any of them. I have been made much richer by the destruction of the city."

But in January Savelitch came from Moscow, talked to him of the position of the city, of the estimate the architect had sent in for restoring the house, and the villa in the suburbs, speaking of it as a settled matter. At the same time Pierre received letters from Prince Vassily and other acquaintances in Petersburg, in which his wife's debts were mentioned. And Pierre decided that the steward's plan that he had liked so much was not the right one, and that he must go to Petersburg to wind up his wife's affairs, and must rebuild in Moscow. Why he ought to do so, he could not have said; but he was convinced that he ought. His income was diminished by one-fourth owing to this decision. But it had to be so; he felt that.

Villarsky was going to Moscow, and they agreed to make the journey together.

During the whole period of his convalescence in Orel, Pierre had enjoyed the feeling of joyful freedom and life. But when he found himself on this journey on the open road, and saw hundreds of new faces, that feeling was intensified. During the journey he felt like a schoolboy in the holidays. All the people he saw—the driver, the overseer of the posting station, the peasants on the road, or in the village—all had a new significance for him. The presence and the observations of Villarsky, who was continually deploring the poverty and the ignorance and the backwardness of Russia, compared with Europe, only heightened Pierre's pleasure in it. Where Villarsky saw deadness, Pierre saw the extraordinary mighty force of vitality, the force which sustained the life of that homogeneous, original, and unique people over that immense expanse of snow. He did not contest Villarsky's opinions, and smiled gleefully, as he listened, appearing to agree with him as the easiest means of avoiding arguments which could lead to nothing.

XIV

JUST as it is difficult to explain why the ants hurry back to a scattered ant-hill, some dragging away from it bits of refuse, eggs, and corpses, while others run back again, and what is their object in crowding together, overtaking one another, fighting with each other, so it would be hard to give the reasons that induced the Russians, after the departure of the French, to flock back to the place which had been known as Moscow. But just as looking at the ants hurrying about a ruined ant-heap, one can see by the tenacity, the energy, and the multitude of the busy insects that though all else is utterly destroyed, there is left something indestructible and immaterial that was the whole strength of the colony, so too Moscow in the month of October, though without its governing authorities, without its churches, without its holy things, without its wealth and its houses, was still the same Moscow as it had been in

August. Everything was shattered except something immaterial, but mighty and indestructible.

The motives of the people, who rushed from all parts to Moscow after it was evacuated by the enemy, were of the most varied and personal kind, and at first mostly savage and brutal impulses. Only one impulse was common to all—the attraction to the place which had been called Moscow in order to set their energies to work there.

Within a week there were fifteen thousand persons in Moscow, within a fortnight twenty-five thousand; and so it went on. The number went on mounting and mounting till by the autumn of 1813 it had reached a figure exceeding the population of the city in 1812.

The first Russians to enter Moscow were the Cossacks of Wintzen-gerode's detachment, the peasants from the nearest villages and the residents who had fled from Moscow and concealed themselves in the environs. On entering the ruined city, and finding it pillaged, the Russians fell to pillaging it too. They continued the work begun by the French. Trains of peasants' waggons drove into Moscow to carry away to the villages all that had been abandoned in the ruined Moscow houses and streets. The Cossacks carried off what they could to their tents; the householders collected all they could out of other houses, and removed it to their own under the pretence that it was their property.

But the first pillaging parties were followed by others; and every day as the numbers pillaging increased, the work of plunder became more difficult and assumed more definite forms.

The French had found Moscow deserted but with all the forms of an organically normal town life still existent, with various branches of trades and crafts, of luxury, and political government and religion. These forms were lifeless but they still existed. There were markets, shops, stores, corn-exchanges, and bazaars—most of them stocked with goods. There were factories and trading establishments. There were palaces and wealthy houses filled with articles of luxury. There were hospitals, prisons, courts, churches, and cathedrals. The longer the French remained, the more these forms of town life perished, and at the end all was lost in one indistinguishable, lifeless scene of pillage.

The longer the pillaging of the French lasted, the more complete was the destruction of the wealth of Moscow and of the forces of the pillagers. The longer the pillaging lasted that was carried on by the Russians on their first return to the capital, and the more there were taking part in it, the more rapidly was the wealth of Moscow and the normal life of the town re-established.

Apart from those who came for plunder, people of all sorts, drawn thither, some by curiosity, some by the duties of office, some by self-interests—householders, priests, officials, high and low, traders, artisans, and peasants—flowed back to Moscow from all sides, as the blood flows to the heart.

Within a week the peasants who had come with empty carts to carry off goods were detained by the authorities, and compelled to carry dead bodies out of the town. Other peasants, who had heard of their companions' discomfiture, drove into the town with wheat, and oats, and hay, knocking down each others' prices to a figure lower than it had been in former days. Gangs of carpenters, hoping for high wages, were arriving in Moscow every day; and on all sides there were new houses being built, or old half-burnt ones being repaired. Tradesmen carried on their business in booths. Cook-shops and taverns were opened in fire-blackened houses. The clergy held services in many churches that had escaped the fire. Church goods that had been plundered were restored as offerings. Government clerks set up their baize-covered tables and pigeon-holes of papers in little rooms. The higher authorities and the police organised a distribution of the goods left by the French. The owners of houses in which a great many of the goods plundered from other houses had been left complained of the injustice of all goods being taken to the Polygonal Palace. Others maintained that the French had collected all the things from different houses to one spot, and that it was therefore unfair to restore to the master of the house the things found in it. The police were abused and were bribed; estimates for government buildings that had been burnt were reckoned at ten times their value; and appeals for help were made. Count Rastoptchin wrote his posters again.

XV

AT the end of January Pierre arrived in Moscow and settled in the lodge of his mansion, as that had escaped the fire. He called on Count Rastoptchin and several acquaintances, and was intending in three days to set off to Petersburg. Every one was triumphant at victory; the ruined and reviving city was bubbling over with life. Every one was glad to see Pierre; everybody was eager to see him, and to ask him about all he had seen. Pierre had a particularly friendly feeling towards every one he met. But unconsciously he was a little on his guard with people to avoid fettering his freedom in any way. To all the questions put to him —important or trivial—whether they asked him where he meant to live, whether he were going to build, when he was starting for Petersburg, or whether he could take a parcel there for someone, he answered, "Yes, very possibly," "I dare say I may," and so on.

He heard that the Rostovs were in Kostroma, and the thought of Natasha rarely came to his mind, and when it did occur to him it was as a pleasant memory of time long past. He felt himself set free, not only from the cares of daily life, but also from that feeling which, it seemed to him, he had voluntarily brought upon himself.

The third day after his arrival in Moscow he learnt from the Drubetskoys that Princess Marya was in Moscow. The death, the sufferings, and the last days of Prince Andrey had often engaged Pierre's thoughts, and now recurred to him with fresh vividness. He heard at dinner that Princess Marya was in Moscow, and living in her own house in Vosdvizhenka, which had escaped the fire, and he went to call upon her the same evening.

On the way to Princess Marya's Pierre's mind was full of Prince Andrey, of his friendship for him, of the different occasions when they had met, and especially of their last interview at Borodino.

"Can he possibly have died in the bitter mood he was in then? Was not the meaning of life revealed to him before death?" Pierre wondered. He thought of Karataev, of his death, and unconsciously compared those two men, so different, and yet alike, in the love he had felt for both, and in that both had lived, and both were dead.

In the most serious frame of mind Pierre drove up to the old prince's house. The house had remained entire. There were traces to be seen of the havoc wrought in it, but the character of the house was unchanged. The old footman met Pierre with a stern face, that seemed to wish to make the guest feel that the absence of the old prince did make no difference in the severe routine of the household, and said that the princess had retired to her own apartments, and received on Sundays.

"Take my name to her, perhaps she will see me," said Pierre.

"Yes, your excellency," answered the footman; "kindly walk into the portrait-gallery."

A few minutes later the footman returned accompanied by Dessalle. Dessalle brought a message from the princess that she would be very glad to see Pierre, and begged him, if he would excuse the lack of ceremony, to come upstairs to her apartment.

In a low-pitched room, lighted by a single candle, he found the princess, and some one with her in a black dress. Pierre recollected that the princess had always had lady-companions of some sort with her, but who those companions were, and what they were like, he did not remember. "That is one of her companions," he thought, glancing at the lady in the black dress.

The princess rose swiftly to meet him, and held out her hand.

"Yes," she said, scrutinising his altered face, after he had kissed her hand; "so this is how we meet again. He often talked of you at the last," she said, turning her eyes from Pierre to the companion with a sort of bashfulness that struck him.

"I was so glad to hear of your safety. It was the only piece of good news we had had for a long time."

Again the princess glanced still more uneasily at the companion, and would have spoken; but Pierre interrupted her.

"Only imagine, I knew nothing about him," he said. "I believed he had been killed. All I have heard has been through others, at third-hand. I only know that he fell in with the Rostovs. . . . What a strange stroke of destiny!"

Pierre talked rapidly, eagerly. He glanced once at the companion's face, saw attentively friendly, inquiring eyes fixed upon him; and as often happens, while talking, he vaguely felt that this lady-companion in the black dress was a good, kind, friendly creature, who need be no hindrance to his talking freely to Princess Marya.

But as he uttered the last words about the Rostovs, the embarrassment in Princess Marya's face became even more marked. Again her eyes shifted from Pierre's face to the face of the lady in the black dress, and she said:

"You don't recognise her?"

Pierre glanced once more at the pale, thin face of her companion, with its black eyes and strange mouth. Something very near to him, long forgotten, and more than sweet, gazed at him out of those intent eyes.

"But no, it cannot be," he thought. "That stern, thin, pale face that looks so much older? It cannot be she. It is only a reminder of it."

But at that moment Princess Marya said, "Natasha!"

And the face with the intent eyes—painfully, with effort, like a rusty door opening—smiled, and through that opened door there floated to Pierre a sudden, overwhelming rush of long-forgotten bliss, of which, especially now, he had no thought. It breathed upon him, overwhelmed him, and swallowed him up entirely. When she smiled, there could be no doubt. It was Natasha, and he loved her.

In that first minute Pierre unwittingly betrayed to her and to Princess Marya, and most of all to himself, the secret of which he had been himself unaware. He flushed joyfully, and with agonising distress. He tried to conceal his emotion. But the more he tried to conceal it, the more clearly—more clearly than if he had uttered the most definite words—he betrayed to himself, and to her, and to Princess Marya, that he loved her.

"No, it is nothing; it's the sudden surprise," Pierre thought. But as soon as he tried to go on with the conversation with Princess Marya, he glanced again at Natasha, and a still deeper flush spread over his face, and a still more violent wave of rapture and terror flooded his heart. He stammered in his speech, and stopped short in the middle of a sentence.

Pierre had not noticed Natasha because he had never expected to see her here; but he had not recognised her because the change that had taken place in her since he had seen her was immense. She had grown thin and pale. But it was not that that made her unrecognisable. No one would have recognised her at the moment when he entered, because when he first glanced at her there was no trace of a smile in the eyes that in old days had always beamed with a suppressed smile of the joy of life. They were intent, kindly eyes, full of mournful inquiry, and nothing more.

Pierre's embarrassment was not reflected in a corresponding embarrassment in Natasha, but only in a look of pleasure, that faintly lighted up her whole face.

XVI

"She has come to stay with me," said Princess Marya. "The count and the countess will be here in a few days. The countess is in a terrible state. But Natasha herself had to see the doctors. They made her come away with me."

"Yes. Is there a family without its own sorrow?" said Pierre, turning to Natasha. "You know it happened the very day we were rescued. I saw him. What a splendid boy he was!"

Natasha looked at him, and, in answer to his words, her eyes only opened wider and grew brighter.

"What can one say, or think, to give comfort?" said Pierre. "Nothing. Why had he to die, such a noble boy, so full of life?"

"Yes; in these days it would be hard to live without faith . . ." said Princess Marya.

"Yes, yes. That is true, indeed," Pierre put in hurriedly.

"How so?" Natasha asked, looking intently into Pierre's eyes.

"How so?" said Princess Marya. "Why, only the thought of what awaits . . ."

Natasha, not heeding Princess Marya's words, looked again inquiringly at Pierre.

"And because," Pierre went on, "only one who believes that there is a God guiding our lives can bear such a loss as hers, and . . . yours," said Pierre.

Natasha opened her mouth, as though she would say something, but she suddenly stopped.

Pierre made haste to turn away from her, and to address Princess Marya again with a question about the last days of his friend's life. Pierre's embarrassment had by now almost disappeared, but at the same time he felt that all his former freedom had vanished too. He felt that there was now a judge criticising every word, every action of his; a judge whose verdict was of greater consequence to him than the verdict of all the people in the world. As he talked now he was considering the impression his words were making on Natasha as he uttered them. He did not intentionally say what might please her; but whatever he said, he looked at himself from her point of view.

With the unwillingness usual in such cases, Princess Marya began telling Pierre of the position in which she had found her brother. But Pierre's questions, his eagerly restless glance, his face quivering with emotion, gradually induced her to go into details which she shrank, for her own sake, from recalling to her imagination.

"Yes, yes, . . ." said Pierre, bending forward over Princess Marya, and eagerly drinking in her words. "Yes, yes. So he found peace? He was softened? He was always striving with his whole soul for one thing only: to be entirely good, so that he could not dread death. The defects that were in him—if he had any—did not come from himself. So he was softened?" he said.

"What a happy thing that he saw you again," he said to Natasha, turning suddenly to her, and looking at her with eyes full of tears.

Natasha's face quivered. She frowned, and for an instant dropped her eyes. For a moment she hesitated whether to speak or not to speak.

"Yes, it was a great happiness," she said in a low, deep voice; "for me it was certainly a great happiness." She paused. "And he . . . he . . . he told me he was longing for it the very moment I went in to him . . ."

Natasha's voice broke. She flushed, squeezed her hands against her knees and suddenly, with an evident effort to control herself, she lifted her head and began speaking rapidly:

"We knew nothing about it when we were leaving Moscow. I did not dare ask about him. And all at once Sonya told me he was with us. I could think of nothing, I had no conception in what state he was; all I wanted was to see him—to be with him," she said, trembling and breathless. And not letting them interrupt her, she told all that she had never spoken of to any one before; all she had gone through in those three weeks of their journey and their stay in Yaroslavl.

Pierre heard her with parted lips and eyes full of tears fastened upon her. As he listened to her, he was not thinking of Prince Andrey, nor of death, nor of what she was saying. He heard her voice and only pitied her for the anguish she was feeling now in telling him.

The princess, frowning in the effort to restrain her tears, sat by Natasha's side and heard for the first time the story of those last days of her brother's and Natasha's love.

To speak of that agonising and joyous time was evidently necessary to Natasha.

She talked on, mingling up the most insignificant details with the most secret feelings of her heart, and it seemed as though she could never finish. Several times she said the same thing twice.

Dessalle's voice was heard at the door asking whether Nikolushka might come in to say good-night. "And that is all, all . . ." said Natasha. She got up quickly at the moment Nikolushka was coming in, and almost running to the door, knocked her head against it as it was hidden by the portière, and with a moan, half of pain, half of sorrow, she rushed out of the room.

Pierre gazed at the door by which she had gone out, and wondered why he felt suddenly alone in the wide world.

Princess Marya roused him from his abstraction, calling his attention to her nephew who had just come into the room.

The face of Nikolushka, so like his father, had such an effect on Pierre at this moment of emotional tension, that, after kissing the child, he got up himself, and taking out his handkerchief, walked away to the window. He would have taken leave, but Princess Marya would not let him go.

"No, Natasha and I often do not go to bed till past two, please stay a little longer. We will have supper. Go downstairs, we will come in a moment."

Before Pierre went down, the princess said to him: "It is the first time she has talked of him like this."

XVII

PIERRE was conducted into the big, lighted-up dining-room. In a few minutes he heard footsteps and the princess and Natasha came into the room. Natasha was calm, though the stern, unsmiling expression had come back again now into her face. Princess Marya, Natasha, and Pierre all equally experienced that feeling of awkwardness which usually follows when a serious and deeply felt conversation is over. To continue on the same subject is impossible; to speak of trivial matters seems desecration, and to be silent is unpleasant, because one wants to talk, and this silence seems a sort of affectation. In silence they came to the table. The footmen drew back and pushed up the chairs. Pierre unfolded his cold dinner napkin, and making up his mind to break the silence he glanced at Natasha and at Princess Marya. Both had plainly reached the same decision at the same moment; in the eyes of both there gleamed a satisfaction with life, and an admission that there was gladness in it as well as sorrow.

"Do you drink vodka?" said Princess Marya, and those words at once dispelled the shadows of the past.

"Tell us about yourself," said Princess Marya; "such incredibly marvellous stories are being told about you."

"Yes," answered Pierre, with the gentle smile of irony that had now become habitual with him. "I myself am told of marvels that I never dreamed of. Marya Abramovna invited me to come and see her and kept telling me what had happened to me, or ought to have happened. Stepan Stepanovitch too instructed me how I was to tell my story. Altogether I have noticed that to be an interesting person is a very easy position (I am now an interesting person); people invite me and then tell me all about it."

Natasha smiled and was about to say something.

"We have been told that you lost two millions in Moscow. Is that true?"

"Oh, I am three times as rich," said Pierre. In spite of the strain on his fortune, of his wife's debts, and the necessity of rebuilding, Pierre still said that he had become three times as rich.

"What I have undoubtedly gained," he said, "is freedom . . ." he was beginning seriously; but on second thoughts he did not continue, feeling that it was too egoistic a subject.

"And you are building?"

"Yes, such are Savelitch's orders."

"Tell me, you had not heard of the countess's death when you stayed on in Moscow?" said Princess Marya; and she flushed crimson at once, conscious that in putting this question to him after his mention of "freedom," she was ascribing a significance to his words which was possibly not intended.

"No," answered Pierre, obviously unconscious of any awkwardness in the interpretation Princess Marya had put on his allusion to his freedom. "I heard of it in Orel, and you cannot imagine how it affected me. We were not an exemplary couple," he said quickly, glancing at Natasha and detecting in her face curiosity as to how he would speak of his wife. "But her death affected me greatly. When two people quarrel, both are always in fault. And one becomes terribly aware of one's shortcomings towards any one who is no more. And then such a death . . . apart from friends and consolation. I felt very sorry for her," he concluded, and noticed with satisfaction a glad look of approval on Natasha's face.

"And so you are once more an eligible *parti*," said Princess Marya.

Pierre flushed suddenly crimson; and for a long while he tried not to look at Natasha. When he did venture to glance at her, her face was cold and severe, even, he fancied, disdainful.

"But did you really see and talk to Napoleon, as we have been told?" said Princess Marya.

Pierre laughed.

"Not once, never. Every one always imagines that to be a prisoner is equivalent to being on a visit to Napoleon. I never saw, never even heard anything about him. I was in much lower company."

Supper was over, and Pierre, who had at first refused to talk about his captivity, was gradually drawn into telling them about it.

"But it is true that you stayed behind to kill Napoleon?" Natasha asked him with a slight smile. "I guessed that at the time when we met you by the Suharev Tower: do you remember?"

Pierre owned that it was so; and from that question was led on by Princess Marya's, and still more by Natasha's, questions to give a detailed account of his adventures.

At first he told his story with that tone of gentle irony that he always had now towards men and especially towards himself. But as he came to describe the horrors and sufferings he had seen, he was drawn on unawares, and began to speak with the suppressed emotion of a man living again in imagination through the intense impressions of the past.

Princess Marya looked from Pierre to Natasha with a gentle smile. In all he told them she saw only Pierre and his goodness. Natasha, her head supported in her hand, and her face changing continually with the story, watched Pierre, never taking her eyes off him, and was in imagination passing through all he told her with him. Not only her eyes, but her exclamations and the brief questions she put showed Pierre that she understood from his words just what he was trying to convey by them. It was evident that she understood, not only what he said, but also what he would have liked to say and could not express in words. The episode of the child and of the woman in whose defence he was taken prisoner, Pierre described in this way. "It was an awful scene, children abandoned, some in the midst of the fire . . . Children were dragged out before my eyes . . . and women, who had their things pulled off them, earrings torn off . . ."

Pierre flushed and hesitated. "Then a patrol came up and all who were not pillaging, all the men, that is, they took prisoner. And me with them."

"I am sure you are not telling us all; I am sure you did something," said Natasha, and after a moment's pause, "something good."

Pierre went on with his story. When he came to the execution, he would have passed over the horrible details of it, but Natasha insisted on his leaving nothing out.

Pierre was beginning to tell them about Karataev; he had risen from the table and was walking up and down, Natasha following him with her eyes.

"No," he said, stopping short in his story, "you cannot understand what I learned from that illiterate man—that simple creature."

"No, no, tell us," said Natasha. "Where is he now?"

"He was killed almost before my eyes."

And Pierre began to describe the latter part of their retreat, Karataev's illness (his voice shook continually) and then his death.

Pierre told the tale of his adventures as he had never thought of them before. He saw now as it were a new significance in all he had been through. He experienced now in telling it all to Natasha that rare happiness given to men by women when they listen to them—not by *clever* women, who, as they listen, are either trying to remember what they are told to enrich their intellect and on occasion to repeat it, or to adapt what is told them to their own ideas and to bring out in haste the clever comments elaborated in their little mental factory. This rare happiness is given only by those real women, gifted with a faculty for picking out and assimilating all that is best in what a man shows them. Natasha, though herself unconscious of it, was all rapt attention; she did not lose one word, one quaver of the voice, one glance, one twitching in the facial muscles, one gesture of Pierre's. She caught the word before it was uttered and bore it straight to her open heart, divining the secret import of all Pierre's spiritual travail.

Princess Marya understood his story and sympathised with him, but she was seeing now something else that absorbed all her attention. She saw the possibility of love and happiness between Natasha and Pierre. And this idea, which struck her now for the first time, filled her heart with gladness.

It was three o'clock in the night. The footmen, with melancholy and severe faces, came in with fresh candles, but no one noticed them.

Pierre finished his story. With shining, eager eyes Natasha still gazed intently and persistently at him, as though she longed to understand something more, that perhaps he had left unsaid. In shamefaced and happy confusion, Pierre glanced at her now and then, and was thinking what to say now to change the subject. Princess Marya was mute. It did not strike any of them that it was three o'clock in the night, and time to be in bed.

"They say: sufferings are misfortunes," said Pierre. "But if at once, this minute, I was asked, would I remain what I was before I was taken prisoner, or go through it all again, I should say, for God's sake let me rather be a prisoner and eat horseflesh again. We imagine that as soon as we are torn out of our habitual path all is over, but it is only the beginning of something new and good. As long as there is life, there is happiness. There is a great deal, a great deal before us. That I say to you," he said, turning to Natasha.

"Yes, yes," she said, answering something altogether different, "and I too would ask for nothing better than to go through it all again."

Pierre looked intently at her.

"Yes, and nothing more," Natasha declared.

"Not true, not true," cried Pierre. "I am not to blame for being alive and wanting to live; and you the same."

All at once Natasha let her head drop into her hands, and burst into tears.

"What is it, Natasha?" said Princess Marya.

"Nothing, nothing." She smiled through her tears to Pierre. "Good-night, it's bedtime."

Pierre got up, and took leave.

Natasha, as she always did, went with Princess Marya into her bedroom. They talked of what Pierre had told them. Princess Marya did not give her opinion of Pierre. Natasha, too, did not talk of him.

"Well, good-night, Marie," said Natasha. "Do you know I am often afraid that we don't talk of him" (she meant Prince Andrey), "as though we were afraid of desecrating our feelings, and so we forget him."

Princess Marya sighed heavily, and by this sigh acknowledged the justice of Natasha's words; but she did not in words agree with her.

"Is it possible to forget?" she said.

"I was so glad to tell all about it to-day; it was hard and painful, and yet I was glad to . . . very glad," said Natasha; "I am sure that he really loved him. That was why I told him . . . it didn't matter my telling him?" she asked suddenly, blushing.

"Pierre? Oh, no! How good he is," said Princess Marya.

"Do you know, Marie," said Natasha, suddenly, with a mischievous smile, such as Princess Marya had not seen for a long while on her face. "He has become so clean and smooth and fresh; as though he had just come out of a bath; do you understand? Out of a moral bath. Isn't it so?"

"Yes," said Princess Marya. "He has gained a great deal."

"And his short jacket, and his cropped hair; exactly as though he had just come out of a bath . . . papa used sometimes . . ."

"I can understand how *he*" (Prince Andrey) "cared for no one else as he did for him," said Princess Marya.

"Yes, and he is so different from him. They say men are better friends when they are utterly different. That must be true; he is not a bit like him in anything, is he?"

"Yes, and he is such a splendid fellow."

"Well, good-night," answered Natasha. And the same mischievous smile lingered a long while as though forgotten on her face.

XVIII

For a long while Pierre could not sleep that night. He walked up and down his room, at one moment frowning, deep in some difficult train of thought, at the next shrugging his shoulders and shaking himself, and at the next smiling blissfully.

He thought of Prince Andrey, of Natasha, of their love, and at one moment was jealous of her past, and at the next reproached himself, and then forgave himself for the feeling. It was six o'clock in the morning, and still he paced the room.

"Well, what is one to do, if there's no escaping it? What is one to do? It must be the right thing, then," he said to himself; and hurriedly undressing, he got into bed, happy and agitated, but free from doubt and hesitation.

"However strange, however impossible such happiness, I must do everything that we may be man and wife," he said to himself.

Several days previously Pierre had fixed on the following Friday as the date on which he would set off to Petersburg. When he waked up next day it was Thursday, and Savelitch came to him for orders about packing the things for the journey.

"To Petersburg? What is Petersburg? Who is in Petersburg?" he unconsciously asked, though only of himself. "Yes, some long while ago, before this happened, I was meaning for some reason to go to Petersburg," he recalled. "Why was it? And I shall go, perhaps. How kind he is, and how attentive, how he remembers everything!" he thought, looking at Savelitch's old face. "And what a pleasant smile!" he thought.

"Well, and do you still not want your freedom, Savelitch?" asked Pierre.

"What should I want my freedom for, your excellency? With the late count—the Kingdom of Heaven to him—we got on very well, and under you, we have never known any unkindness."

"Well, but your children?"

"My children too will do very well, your excellency; under such masters one can get on all right."

"Well, but my heirs?" said Pierre. "All of a sudden I shall get married . . . It might happen, you know," he added, with an involuntary smile.

"And I make bold to say, a good thing too, your excellency."

"How easy he thinks it," thought Pierre. "He does not know how terrible it is, how perilous. Too late or too early . . . It is terrible!"

"What are your orders? Will you be pleased to go to-morrow?" asked Savelitch.

"No; I will put it off a little. I will tell you later. You must excuse the trouble I give you," said Pierre, and watching Savelitch's smile, he thought how strange it was, though, that he should not know there was no such thing as Petersburg, and that *that* must be settled before everything.

"He really does know, though," he thought; "he is only pretending. Shall I tell him? What does he think about it? No, another time."

At breakfast, Pierre told his cousin that he had been the previous evening at Princess Marya's, and had found there—could she fancy whom—Natasha Rostov.

The princess looked as though she saw nothing more extraordinary in that fact than if Pierre had seen some Anna Semyonovna.

"You know her?" asked Pierre.

"I have seen the princess," she answered, "and I had heard they were making a match between her and young Rostov. That would be a very fine thing for the Rostovs; I am told they are utterly ruined."

"No, I meant, do you know Natasha Rostov?"

"I heard at the time all about that story. Very sad."

"She does not understand, or she is pretending," thought Pierre. "Better not tell her either."

The princess, too, had prepared provisions for Pierre's journey.

"How kind they all are," thought Pierre, "to trouble about all this now, when it certainly can be of no interest to them. And all for my sake; that is what's so marvellous."

The same day a police officer came to see Pierre, with an offer to send a trusty agent to the Polygonal Palace to receive the things that were to-day to be restored among the owners.

"And this man too," thought Pierre, looking into the police officer's face, "what a nice, good-looking officer, and how good-natured! To trouble about such trifles *now*. And yet they say he is not honest, and takes bribes. What nonsense! though after all why shouldn't he take bribes? He has been brought up in that way. They all do it. But such a pleasant, good-humoured face, and he smiles when he looks at me."

Pierre went to Princess Marya's to dinner. As he drove through the streets between the charred wrecks of houses, he admired the beauty of those ruins. The chimneys of stoves, and the tumbledown walls of houses stretched in long rows, hiding one another, all through the burnt quarters of the town, and recalled to him the picturesque ruins of the Rhine and of the Colosseum. The sledge-drivers and men on horseback, the carpenters at work on the frames of the houses, the hawkers and shopkeepers all looked at Pierre with cheerful, beaming faces, and seemed to him to say: "Oh, here he is! We shall see what comes of it."

On reaching Princess Marya's house, Pierre was beset by a sudden doubt whether it were true that he had been there the day before, and had really seen Natasha and talked to her. "Perhaps it was all my own invention, perhaps I shall go in and see no one." But no sooner had he entered the room than in his whole being, from his instantaneous loss of freedom, he was aware of her presence. She was wearing the same black dress, that hung in soft folds, and had her hair arranged in the same way, but she was utterly different. Had she looked like this when he came in yesterday, he could not have failed to recognise her.

She was just as he had known her almost as a child, and later when betrothed to Prince Andrey. A bright, questioning light gleamed in her eyes; there was a friendly and strangely mischievous expression in her face.

Pierre dined, and would have spent the whole evening with them; but Princess Marya was going to vespers, and Pierre went with them.

Next day Pierre arrived early, dined with them, and stayed the whole evening. Although Princess Marya and Natasha were obviously glad to see their visitor, and although the whole interest of Pierre's life was now centred in that house, by the evening they had said all they had to say, and the conversation passed continually from one trivial subject to another and often broke off altogether. Pierre stayed so late that evening that Princess Marya and Natasha exchanged glances, plainly wondering whether he would not soon go. Pierre saw that, but he could not go away. He began to feel it irksome and awkward, but still he sat on because he *could not* get up and go.

Princess Marya, foreseeing no end to it, was the first to get up, and complaining of a sick headache, she began saying good-night.

"So you are going to-morrow to Petersburg?" she said.

"No, I am not going," said Pierre hurriedly, with surprise and a sort of resentment in his tone. "No . . . yes, to Petersburg. To-morrow, perhaps; but I won't say good-bye. I shall come to see if you have any commissions to give me," he added, standing before Princess Marya, turning very red, and not taking leave.

Natasha gave him her hand and retired. Princess Marya, on the contrary, instead of going away, sank into an armchair, and with her luminous, deep eyes looked sternly and intently at Pierre. The weariness she had unmistakably betrayed just before had now quite passed off. She drew a deep, prolonged sigh, as though preparing for a long conversation.

As soon as Natasha had gone, all Pierre's confusion and awkwardness instantly vanished, and were replaced by excited eagerness.

He rapidly moved a chair close up to Princess Marya. "Yes, I wanted to tell you," he said, replying to her look as though to words. "Princess, help me. What am I to do? Can I hope? Princess, my dear friend, listen to me. I know all about it. I know I am not worthy of her; I know that it is impossible to talk of it now. But I want to be a brother to her. No, not that, I don't, I can't . . ." He paused and passed his hands over his face and eyes. "It's like this," he went on, making an evident effort to speak coherently. "I don't know since when I have loved her. But I have loved her alone, only her, all my life, and I love her so that I cannot imagine life without her. I cannot bring myself to ask for her hand now; but the thought that, perhaps, she might be my wife and my letting slip this opportunity . . . opportunity . . . is awful. Tell me, can I hope? Tell me, what am I to do? Dear princess," he said, after a brief pause, touching her hand as she did not answer.

"I am thinking of what you have just told me," answered Princess Marya. "This is what I think. You are right that to speak to her of love now . . ." The princess paused. She had meant to say that to speak to her of love now was impossible; but she stopped, because she had seen during the last three days by the sudden change in Natasha that she would by no means be offended if Pierre were to avow his love, that, in fact, it was the one thing she desired.

"To speak to her now . . . is out of the question," she nevertheless said.

"But what am I to do?"

"Trust the matter to me," said Princess Marya. "I know . . ."

Pierre looked into her eyes.

"Well, well . . ." he said.

"I know that she loves . . . that she will love you," Princess Marya corrected herself.

She had hardly uttered the words, when Pierre leaped up, and with a face of consternation clutched at Princess Marya's hand.

"What makes you think so? You think I may hope? You think so? . . ."

"Yes, I think so," said Princess Marya, smiling. "Write to her parents. And leave it to me. I will tell her when it is possible. I desire it to come to pass. And I have a feeling in my heart that it will be so."

"No, it cannot be! How happy I am! But it cannot be! . . . How happy I am! No, it cannot be!" Pierre kept saying, kissing Princess Marya's hands.

"You should go to Petersburg; it will be better. And I will write to you," she said.

"To Petersburg? I am to go? Yes, very well, I will go. But I can come and see you to-morrow?"

Next day Pierre came to say good-bye. Natasha was less animated than on the preceding days; but sometimes that day, looking into her eyes, Pierre felt that he was vanishing away, that he and she were no more, that there was nothing but happiness. "Is it possible? No, it cannot be," he said to himself at every glance she gave, every gesture, every word, that filled his soul with gladness.

When, on saying good-bye, he took her thin, delicate hand he unconsciously held it somewhat longer in his own.

"Is it possible that that hand, that face, those eyes, all that treasure of womanly charm, so far removed from me, is it possible it may all one day be my own for ever, as close and intimate as I am to myself? No, it's surely impossible? . . ."

"Good-bye, count," she said to him aloud. "I shall so look forward to seeing you again," she added in a whisper.

And those simple words, and the look in the eyes and the face, that accompanied them, formed the subject of inexhaustible reminiscences, interpretations, and happy dreams for Pierre during two whole months. "I shall look forward to seeing you again." "Yes, yes, how did she say it? Yes. 'I shall so look forward to seeing you again.' Oh, how happy I am! How can it be that I am so happy!" Pierre said to himself.

XIX

THERE was nothing in Pierre's soul now like what had passed within him in similar circumstances during the time of his being betrothed to Ellen.

He did not go over, as he had then, with a sickening sense of shame the words he had uttered; he did not say to himself: "Oh, why did I not say that, and why, oh why, did I say then: I love you." Now, on the contrary, every word of hers and of his own, he went over in his imagination with every detail of look and smile, and wanted to add nothing, to take nothing away, he longed only to hear it over again. As for doubts —whether what he contemplated doing was right or wrong—there was never a trace of them now. Only one terrible doubt sometimes assailed his mind. Was it not all a dream? Was not Princess Marya mistaken? Am I not too conceited and self-confident? I believe in it; but all at once—and it's what is sure to happen—Princess Marya tells her; and she smiles and answers: "How queer! He has certainly made a mistake. Doesn't he know that he is a man, a mere man, while I? . . . I am something altogether different, higher."

This doubt alone often beset Pierre. He made no plans of any sort now. The happiness before him seemed to him so incredible that the only thing that mattered was to bring it to pass, and nothing could be beyond. Everything else was over.

A joyful, unexpected frenzy, of which Pierre had believed himself incapable, seized upon him. The whole meaning of life, not for him only, but for all the world, seemed to him centred in his love and the possibility of her loving him. Sometimes all men seemed to him to be absorbed in nothing else than his future happiness. It seemed to him sometimes that they were all rejoicing as he was himself, and were only trying to conceal that joy, by pretending to be occupied with other interests. In every word and gesture he saw an allusion to his happiness. He often surprised people by his significant and blissful looks and smiles, that seemed to express some secret understanding with them. But when he realised that people could not know of his happiness, he pitied them from the bottom of his heart, and felt an impulse to try to make them somehow understand that all that they were interested in was utter nonsense and trifles not deserving of attention.

When suggestions were made to him that he should take office under government, or when criticisms of any sort on general, political questions, or on the war, were made before him, on the supposition that one course of events or another would affect the happiness of all men, he listened with a gentle smile of commiseration, and astounded the persons conversing with him by his strange observations. But both those persons, who seemed to Pierre to grasp the true significance of life, that is, his feeling, and those luckless wretches who obviously had no notion of it—all at this period appeared to Pierre in the radiant light of his own glowing feeling; so that on meeting any one, he saw in him without the slightest effort everything that was good and deserving of love.

As he looked through his dead wife's papers and belongings, he had no feeling towards her memory but one of pity that she had not known the happiness he knew now. Prince Vassily, who was particularly haughty just then, having received a new post and a star, struck him as a pathetic and kind-hearted old man, very much to be pitied.

Often afterwards Pierre recalled that time of happy insanity. All the judgments he formed of men and circumstances during that period remained for ever true to him. Far from renouncing later on those views of men and things, on the contrary, in inner doubts and contradictions, he flew back to the view he had had during that time of madness; and that view always turned out to be a true one.

"Perhaps," he thought, "I did seem strange and absurd then; but I was not so mad then as I seemed. On the contrary, I was cleverer and had more insight then than at any time, and I understood everything worth understanding in life, because . . . I was happy."

Pierre's madness showed itself in his not waiting, as in old days, for those personal grounds, which he had called good qualities in people, in order to love them; but as love was brimming over in his heart he loved men without cause, and so never failed to discover incontestable reasons that made them worth loving.

XX

FROM that first evening, when Natasha had said to Princess Marya, with a gaily mocking smile, that he looked exactly, yes, exactly, as if he had come out of a bath with his short jacket and his cropped hair—from that minute something hidden and unrecognised by herself, yet irresistible, awakened in Natasha's soul.

Everything—face, gait, eyes, voice—everything was at once transformed in her. To her own surprise, the force of life and hopes of happiness floated to the surface and demanded satisfaction. From that first evening Natasha seemed to have forgotten all that had happened to her. From that time she never once complained of her position; she said not one word about the past, and was not afraid of already making lighthearted plans for the future. She spoke little of Pierre; but when Princess Marya mentioned him, a light that had long been dim gleamed in her eyes, and her lips curved in a strange smile.

The change that took place in Natasha at first surprised Princess Marya; but when she understood what it meant, that change mortified her. "Can she have loved my brother so little that she can so soon forget him?" thought Princess Marya, when she thought over it alone. But when she was with Natasha she was not vexed with her, and did not blame her. The awakened force of life that had regained possession of Natasha was obviously so irresistible and so unexpected by herself, that in Natasha's presence Princess Marya felt that she had no right to blame her even in her heart.

Natasha gave herself up with such completeness and sincerity to her new feeling that she did not even attempt to conceal that she was not now sorrowful, but glad and happy.

When Princess Marya had returned to her room that night after her interview with Pierre, Natasha met her on the threshold.

"He has spoken? Yes? He has spoken?" she repeated. And a joyful, and at the same time piteous, expression, that begged forgiveness for its joy, was in Natasha's face. "I wanted to listen at the door; but I knew you would tell me."

Ready as Princess Marya was to understand and to be touched by the expression with which Natasha looked at her, and much as she felt for her agitation, yet her words for the first moment mortified her. She thought of her brother and his love.

"But what is one to do? She cannot help it," thought Princess Marya; and with a sad and somewhat severe face she repeated to Natasha all Pierre had said to her. Natasha was stupefied to hear he was going to Petersburg. "To Petersburg!" she repeated, as though unable to take it in.

But looking at the mournful expression of Princess Marya's face she divined the cause of her sadness, and suddenly burst into tears.

"Marie," she said, "tell me what I am to do. I am afraid of being horrid. Whatever you say, I will do; tell me . . ."

"You love him?"

"Yes!" whispered Natasha.

"What are you crying for, then? I am very glad for you," said Princess Marya, moved by those tears to complete forgiveness of Natasha's joy.

"It will not be soon . . . some day. Only think how happy it will be when I am his wife and you marry Nikolay!"

"Natasha, I have begged you not to speak of that. Let us talk of you."

Both were silent.

"Only why go to Petersburg?" cried Natasha suddenly, and she hastened to answer herself. "No, no; it must be so . . . Yes, Marie? It must be . . ."

EPILOGUE

PART ONE

I

SEVEN YEARS had passed by. The storm-tossed, historic ocean of Europe was subsiding within its shores. It seemed to have grown calm; but the mysterious forces moving humanity (mysterious, because the laws controlling their action are unknown to us) were still at work.

Although the surface of the ocean of history seemed motionless, the movement of humanity was as uninterrupted as the flow of time. Various series of groups of men were joining together and separating; the causes were being prepared that would bring about the formation and the dissolution of empires and the migrations of peoples.

The ocean of history was not now, as before, tossed violently from one shore to the other; it was seething in its depths. Historical figures were not dashing abruptly from one side to the other; now they seemed to be rotating on the same spot. The historical figures, that had in the preceding years at the head of armies reflected the movement of the masses, commanding wars, and marches, and battles, now reflected that movement in political and diplomatic combinations, statutes, and treaties.

This tendency on the part of the figures of history, the historians call the reaction.

In describing the part played by these historical personages, the historians criticise them severely, supposing them to be the cause of what they call the *reaction*. All the celebrated persons of that period, from Alexander and Napoleon to Madame de Staël, Foty, Schelling, Fichte, Chateaubriand, and so on, receive the severest criticism at their hands, and are acquitted or condemned according as they worked for *progress* or for *reaction*.

In Russia, too, so they tell us, a reaction was taking place at that period, and the person chiefly to blame for that reaction was Alexander I.—the same Alexander who, by their own account, was chiefly responsible for the liberal movement at the beginning of his reign, and for the saving of Russia.

In modern Russian literature there is no one, from the schoolboy essay writer to the learned historian, who would not throw his stone at Alexander for the unprincipled acts of this later period of his reign.

"He should have acted in such and such a way. On that occasion he acted well, and on that other he acted ill. He behaved splendidly in the beginning of his reign and during 1812; but he did ill in giving a constitution to Poland, in making the Holy Alliance, in letting Arakcheev have power, in encouraging Golitsin and mysticism; and later on, in encouraging Shishkov, and Foty. He acted wrongly in interfering with the army on active service; he acted wrongly in cashiering the Semyonovsky regiment, and so on."

One might cover ten pages in enumerating all the faults found in him by the historians on the assumption that they possess a knowledge of what is for the good of humanity.

What do these criticisms mean?

Do not the very actions for which the historians applaud Alexander I., such as the liberalism of the early part of his reign, the struggle with Napoleon, the firmness shown in 1812, and the campaign of 1813, proceed from those very sources—the circumstances of birth and breeding and life that made Alexander's personality what it was—from which proceed also the acts for which he is censured by the historians, such as the Holy Alliance, the restoration of Poland, the reaction from 1820 onward?

What is the substance of the charge brought in these criticisms? It is a charge brought against an historical personage standing at the highest possible pinnacle of human power, as it were, in the focus where all the rays of history concentrated their blinding light upon him; a personage subjected to the strongest influences of intrigue, deceit, flattery, and self-deception, inseparable from power; a personage who felt himself at every moment of his life responsible for all that was being done in Europe; and a personage, not an invented character, but a live creature, like any other man, with his own personal idiosyncrasies, and passions and impulses towards goodness, beauty, and truth. And the charge brought against this personage is not that he was not virtuous (the historians have no reproach to make against him on this score), but that he, living fifty years ago, had not the same views as to the good of humanity as those held to-day by a professor who has, from his youth up, been engaged in study, *i.e.* in reading books, listening to lectures, and making notes of those books and those lectures in a note-book.

But even if we assume that Alexander I., fifty years ago, was mistaken in his view of what was for the good of peoples, we can hardly help assuming that the historian, criticising Alexander, will, after a certain lapse of time, prove to be also incorrect in his view of what is for the good of humanity. It is the more natural and inevitable to assume this because, watching the development of history, we see that with every year, with every new writer, the view of what is for the good of humanity is somewhat shifted; so that what did seem good, after ten years, is regarded as harmful, and *vice versa*. That is not all. We even find in history the views of contemporaries as to what was good, and what was harmful, utterly opposed to one another. Some regard the giving of a constitution to Poland, and the Holy Alliance, as highly to the credit of Alexander; while others regard the same actions as a slur on his name.

It is impossible to say of the careers of Alexander and of Napoleon that they were beneficial or harmful, seeing that we cannot say wherein the benefit or harm of humanity lies. If any one dislikes the career of either, he only dislikes it from its incompatibility with his own limited conception of what is the good of humanity. Even though I regard as good the preservation of my father's house in Moscow in 1812, or the glory of the Russian army, or the flourishing of the Petersburg or some other university, or the independence of Poland, or the supremacy of Russia, or the balance of European power, or a special branch of European enlightenment—progress—yet I am bound to admit that the activity of any historical personage had, apart from such ends, other ends more general and beyond my grasp.

But let us suppose that so-called science has the power of conciliating all contradictions, and has an invariable standard of good and bad by which to try historical personages and events.

Let us suppose that Alexander could have acted quite differently. Let us assume that, in accordance with the prescription of those who censure him, and who profess a knowledge of the final end of the movement of humanity, he could have followed that programme of nationalism, of freedom, of equality, and of progress (there seems to be no other) which his modern critics would have selected for him. Let us suppose that programme could have been possible, and had actually been formulated at that time, and that Alexander could have acted in accordance with it. What, then, would have become of the activity of all the persons who were opposing the tendency of the government of that day —of the activity which, in the opinion of the historians, was good and beneficial? There would have been none of that activity; there would have been no life; there would have been nothing.

Once admit that human life can be guided by reason, and all possibility of life is annihilated.

II

IF one admits, as historians do, that great men lead humanity to the attainment of certain ends, such as the aggrandisement of Russia or of France, or the balance of power, or the diffusion of the ideas of the revolution, or of general progress, or anything else you like, it becomes impossible to explain the phenomena of history apart from the conceptions of *chance* and *genius*.

If the object of the European wars of the beginning of this century had been the aggrandisement of Russia, that object might have been attained without any of the preceding wars, and without invasion of foreign territory.

If the object were the aggrandisement of France, that aim might have been attained apart from the revolution and the empire. If the object were the diffusion of ideas, the printing of books would have attained that object much more effectually than soldiers. If the object were the progress of civilisation, one may very readily assume that there are other more effectual means of diffusing civilisation than the slaughter of men and the destruction of their property.

Why did it come to pass in this way and no other? Because it happened so. *"Chance* created the position; *genius* took advantage of it,"* says history.

But what is *chance?* What is *genius?*

The words *chance* and *genius* mean nothing actually existing, and so cannot be defined. These words merely denote a certain stage in the comprehension of phenomena. I do not know how some phenomenon is brought about; I believe that 1 cannot know; consequently I do not want to know and talk of *chance.* I see a force producing an effect out of proportion with the average effect of human powers; I do not understand how this is brought about, and I talk about *genius.*

To a flock of sheep the sheep who is every evening driven by the shepherd into a special pen to feed, and becomes twice as fat as the rest, must seem to be a genius. And the circumstance that every evening that sheep does not come into the common fold, but into a special pen full of oats, and that that same sheep grows fat and is killed for mutton, must present itself to the minds of the other sheep as a singular conjunction of genius with a whole series of exceptional chances.

But the sheep need only cease to assume that all that is done to them is with a view to the attainment of their sheepish ends; they need only admit that the events that occur to them may have ends beyond their ken, and they will at once see a unity and a coherence in what happens with the fatted sheep. Even though they will not know for what end he is fattened, at least they will know that all that happens to him does not happen by chance, and they will have no need to resort to the conception of *chance,* nor to the conception of *genius.*

It is only by renouncing all claims to knowledge of an immediate comprehensible aim, and acknowledging the final aim to be beyond our ken, that we see a consistent whole in the life of historical persons. The cause is then revealed to us of that effect produced by them out of proportion with the common powers of humanity, and we have no need of the words *chance* and *genius.*

We have only to admit that the object of the convulsions of the European nations is beyond our knowledge, and that we know only the facts, consisting mainly of murders committed at first in France, then in Italy, then in Africa, in Prussia, in Austria, in Spain, and in Russia, and that the movements from west to east and from east to west constitute the essence and end of those events, and we shall not need to see something exceptional—*genius*—in the characters of Napoleon and of Alexander, and shall indeed be unable to conceive of those persons as being in any way different from everybody else. And far from having to explain as *chance* those petty events, which made those men what they were, it will be clear to us that all those petty details were inevitable.

When we give up all claim to a knowledge of the final end, we shall clearly perceive that just as we cannot invent any flower or seed more truly appropriate to a plant than those it produces, so we cannot imagine any two persons, with all their past in such complete congruity down to the smallest details, with the part they were destined to play

III

THE underlying essentially significant feature of the European events of the beginning of the present century is the military movement of masses of European peoples from west to east, and again from east to west. The original movement was that from west to east. That the peoples of the west might be able to accomplish the military march upon Moscow, which they did accomplish, it was essential (1) that they should be combined in a military group of such a magnitude as to be able to withstand the resistance of the military group of the east; (2) that they should have renounced all their established traditions and habits; and (3) that they should have at their head a man able to justify in his own name and theirs the perpetration of all the deception, robbery, and murder that accompany that movement.

And to start from the French Revolution, that old group of insufficient magnitude is broken up; the old habits and traditions are destroyed; step by step a group is elaborated of new dimensions, new habits, and new traditions; and the man is prepared, who is to stand at the head of the coming movement, and to take upon himself the whole responsibility of what has to be done.

A man of no convictions, no habits, no traditions, no name, not even a Frenchman, by the strangest freaks of chance, as it seems, rises above the seething parties of France, and without attaching himself to any one of them, advances to a prominent position.

The incompetence of his colleagues, the weakness and insignificance of his opponents, the frankness of the deception, and the dazzling and self-confident limitation of the man raise him to the head of the army. The brilliant personal qualities of the soldiers of the Italian army, the disinclination to fight of his opponents, and his childish insolence and conceit gain him military glory. Innumerable so-called *chance* circumstances attend him everywhere. The disfavour into which he falls with the French Directorate turns to his advantage. His efforts to avoid the path ordained for him are unsuccessful; he is not received into the Russian army, and his projects in Turkey come to nothing.

During the wars in Italy he was several times on the verge of destruction, and was every time saved in an unexpected fashion. The Russian troops—the very troops which were able to demolish his glory—owing to various diplomatic considerations, do not enter Europe until he is there.

On his return from Italy, he finds the government in Paris in that process of dissolution in which all men who are in the government are inevitably effaced and nullified. And an escape for him from that perilous position offers itself in the shape of an aimless, groundless expedition to Africa. Again the same so-called *chance* circumstances accompany him. Malta, the impregnable, surrenders without a shot being fired; the most ill-considered measures are crowned with success. The enemy's fleet, which later on does not let one boat escape it, now lets a whole army elude it. In Africa a whole series of outrages is perpetrated on the almost unarmed inhabitants. And the men perpetrating these atrocities, and their leader most of all, persuade themselves that it is noble, it is glory, that it is like Cæsar and Alexander of Macedon, and that it is fine.

That ideal of *glory* and of *greatness,* consisting in esteeming nothing one does wrong, and glorying in every crime, and ascribing to it an incomprehensible, supernatural value—that ideal, destined to guide this man and those connected with him, is elaborated on a grand scale in Africa. Whatever he does succeeds. The plague does not touch him. The cruelty of murdering his prisoners is not remembered against him. His childishly imprudent, groundless, and ignoble departure from Africa, abandoning his comrades in misfortune, does him good service; and again the enemy's fleet lets him twice slip through their hands. At the moment when, completely intoxicated by the success of his crimes and ready for the part he has to play, he arrives in Paris entirely without any plan, the disintegration of the Republican government, which might have involved him in its ruin a year before, has now reached its utmost limit, and his presence, a man independent of parties, can now only aid his elevation.

He has no sort of plan; he is afraid of everything; but all parties clutch at him and insist on his support.

He alone—with the ideal of glory and greatness he has acquired in Italy and Egypt, with his frenzy of self-adoration, with his insolence in crime, and his frankness in mendacity—he alone can justify what has to be accomplished.

He is needed for the place that awaits him, and so, almost apart from his own volition, and in spite of his uncertainty, the lack of plan, and the blunders he commits, he is drawn into a conspiracy that aims at seizing power; and that conspiracy is crowned with success.

He is dragged into the assembly of the rulers. In alarm he tries to flee, believing himself in danger; pretends to faint, says the most senseless things that should have been his ruin. But the rulers of France, once proud and discerning, now feeling their part is over, are even more panic-stricken than he, and fail to utter the words they should have pronounced to preserve their power and crush him.

Chance, millions of *chances,* give him power; and all men, as though in league together, combine to confirm that power. *Chance* circumstances create the characters of the rulers of France, who cringe before him; *chance* creates the character of Paul i., who acknowledges his authority; *chance* causes the plot against him to strengthen his power instead of shaking it. *Chance* throws the Duc d'Enghien into his hands and accidentally impels him to kill him, thereby convincing the crowd by the strongest of all arguments that he has the right on his side since he has the might. *Chance* brings it to pass that though he strains **every** nerve to fit out an expedition against England, which would unmistakably have led to his ruin, he never puts this project into execution, **and** happens to fall upon Mack with the Austrians, who surrender without a battle. *Chance* and *genius* give him the victory at Austerlitz; and by *chance* it comes to pass that all men, not only the French, but all the countries of Europe except England, which takes no part in the events that are to be accomplished, forget their old horror and aversion for his crimes, and now recognise the power he has gained by them, acknowledge the title he has bestowed upon himself, and accept his ideal of greatness and glory, which seems to every one something fine and rational.

As though practising and preparing themselves for the great movement before them, the forces of the west made several dashes—in 1805, 1806, 1807 and 1809—into the east, growing stronger and more numerous. In 1811 a group of men formed in France is joined by an enormous group from the peoples of Central Europe. As the numbers of the great mass increase, the power of justification of the man at the head of the movement gathers more and more force. During the ten years of the preparatory period preceding the great movement, this man forms relations with all the crowned heads of Europe. The sovereigns of the world, stripped bare by him, can oppose no rational ideal to the senseless Napoleonic ideal of *glory* and greatness. They vie with one another in demonstrating to him their insignificance. The King of Prussia sends his wife to sue for the good graces of the great man; the Emperor of Austria considers it a favour for this man to take the daughter of the Kaisers to his bed. The Pope, the guardian of the faith of the peoples, uses religion to aid the great man's elevation. Napoleon does not so much prepare himself for the part he is to play as all around him lead him on to take upon himself the responsibility of what is being done and is to be done. There is no act, no crime, no petty deceit which he would not commit, and which would not be at once represented on the lips of those about him as a great deed. The most suitable fête the Germans could think of in his honour was the celebration of Jena and Auerstadt. Not only is he great; his forefathers, his brothers, his step-children, and his brothers-in-law are great too. Everything is done to deprive him of the last glimmering of reason, and to prepare him for his terrible part. And when he is ready, his forces too are in readiness.

The invading army flows towards the east and reaches its final goal: Moscow. The ancient city is taken; the Russian army suffers greater losses than were ever suffered by the opposing armies in the previous wars from Austerlitz to Wagram. But all at once, instead of that *chance* and *genius,* which had so consistently led him hitherto by an uninterrupted series of successes to his destined goal, an immense number of *chance* circumstances occur of an opposite kind from the cold caught at Borodino to the spark that fired Moscow; and instead of *genius* there was shown a folly and baseness unexampled in history.

The invading army flees away, turns back and flees again; and all the chances now are consistently not for but against him.

Then there follows the opposing movement from east to west, with a remarkable similarity to the eastward movement from the west that had preceded it. There were similar tentative movements westward as had in 1805, 1807 and 1809 preceded the great eastward movement. There was the same cohesion together of all into one group of immense numbers; the same adherence of the peoples of Central Europe to the movement; the same hesitation midway, and the same increased velocity as the goal was approached.

Paris, the furthest goal, was reached. Napoleon's government and armies are shattered. Napoleon himself is of no further consequence; all his actions are obviously paltry and mean; but again inexplicable chance comes in. The allies detest Napoleon, in whom they see the cause of all their troubles. Stripped of his power and his might, convicted of frauds and villainies, he should have been seen by them as he had been ten years before, and was a year later—a brigand outside the pale of the law. But by some strange freak of chance no one sees it. His part is not yet played out. The man who ten years back, and one year later, was looked on as a miscreant outside the law, was sent by them to an island two days' journey from France, given to him as his domain, with guards and millions of money, as though to pay him for some service he had done.

IV

THE commotion among the peoples begins to subside. The waves of the great tempest begin to abate, and eddies begin to be formed about the calmer surface where diplomatists are busy, fancying the calm is their work.

But all at once the quiet sea is convulsed again. The diplomatists imagine that they, their disagreements, are the cause of this fresh disturbance; they look for wars between their sovereigns; the position seems insoluble. But the storm they feel brewing does not come from the quarter where they look for it. It rises again from the same starting point—Paris. The last backwash of the westward movement follows— the backwash which was to solve the seemingly inextricable diplomatic difficulties, and to put an end to the military unrest of the period.

The man who has devastated France comes back to France alone, with no project, and no soldiers. Any policeman can arrest him; but by a strange freak of chance no one does seize him, but all meet with enthusiasm the man they have been cursing but a day before, and will curse again within a month.

That man is needed for the last act winding up the drama.

The act is performed.

The last part is played. The actor is bidden to undress, and wash off his powder and paint; he will be needed no more.

And for several years this man, in solitude on his island, plays his pitiful farce to himself, intrigues and lies, justifying his conduct when a justification is no longer needed, and shows all the world what the thing was men took for power when an unseen hand guided it.

The stage manager, when the drama was over, and the puppet stripped, showed him to us.

"Look what you believed in! Here he is! Do you see now that it was not he but I that moved you?"

But blinded by the force of the movement men for long could not perceive that.

Even more coherence and inevitability is to be seen in the life of Alexander I., the personage who stood at the head of the counter-movement from east westward.

What was needed for the man who, to the exclusion of others, should stand at the head of that movement from the east westward?

There was needed a sense of justice, an interest in the affairs of Europe, but a remote one, not obscured by petty interests, a moral preeminence over his peers—the sovereigns of the time; there was needed a gentle and attractive personal character; there was needed too a personal grievance against Napoleon. And all that is to be seen in Alexander I.; it was all prepared beforehand by the innumerable so called *chance* circumstances of his previous life, by his education and the liberalism of the beginning of his reign, and the counsellors around, and Austerlitz, and Tilsit, and Erfurt.

During the war in defence of the country this personage is inactive; he is not needed. But as soon as a general European war becomes inevitable, at the given moment, he is in his place, and bringing the European peoples together he leads them to the goal.

The goal is reached. After the last war of 1815 Alexander finds himself at the highest possible pinnacle of human power. How does he use it?

While Napoleon in his exile was drawing up childish and lying schemes of the blessings he would have showered on humanity if he had had the power, Alexander, the pacifier of Europe, the man who, from his youth up, had striven for nothing but the good of the people, the first champion of liberal reforms in his country, now when he seemed to possess the greatest possible power, and consequent possibility of doing good to his people, felt his work was done, and God's hand was laid upon him, and recognising the nothingness of that semblance of power, turned from it, gave it up to despicable men, and men he despised, and could only say:

"Not to us, not to us, but to Thy Name! I too am a man like all of you; let me live like a man, and think of my soul and of God."

Just as the sun and every atom of ether is a sphere complete in itself, and at the same time is only a part of a whole inconceivable to man through its vastness, so every individuality bears within it its own ends, and yet bears them so as to serve general ends unfathomable by man.

A bee settling on a flower has stung a child. And the child dreads bees, and says the object of the bee is to sting people. A poet admires the bee, sipping honey from the cup of the flower, and says the object of the bee is to sip the nectar of the flower. A beekeeper, noticing that the bee gathers pollen and brings it to the hive, says that the object of the bee is to gather honey. Another beekeeper, who has studied the life of the swarm more closely, says the bee gathers honey to feed the young ones, and to rear a queen, that the object of the bee is the perpetuation of its race. The botanist observes that the bee flying with the pollen fertilises the pistil, and in this he sees the object of the bee. Another, watching the hybridisation of plants, sees that the bee contributes to that end also, and he may say that the bee's object is that. But the final aim of the bee is not exhausted by one or another, or a third aim, which the human intellect is capable of discovering. The higher the human intellect rises in the discovery of such aims, the more obvious it becomes that the final aim is beyond its reach.

All that is within the reach of man is the observation of the analogy of the life of the bee with other manifestations of life. And the same is true with the final aims of historical persons and of nations.

V

NATASHA'S marriage to Bezuhov, which took place in 1813, was the last happy event in the family of the old Rostovs. Count Ilya Andreivitch died the same year; and as is always the case, with the death of the father the family was broken up.

The events of the previous year: the burning of Moscow and the flight from that city; the death of Prince Andrey and Natasha's despair; the death of Petya and the grief of the countess fell like one blow after another on the old count's head. He seemed not to understand, and to feel himself incapable of understanding, the significance of all these events, and figuratively speaking, bowed his old head to the storm, as though expecting and seeking fresh blows to make an end of him. By turns he seemed scared and distraught, and then unnaturally lively and active.

Natasha's marriage for a time occupied him on its external side. He arranged dinners and suppers in honour of it, and obviously tried to be cheerful; but his cheerfulness was not infectious as in old days, but, on the contrary, aroused the commiseration of those who knew and liked him.

After Pierre and his wife had left, he collapsed and began to complain of depression. A few days later he fell ill and took to his bed. In spite of the doctor's assurances, he knew from the first days of his illness that he would never get up again. For a whole fortnight the countess sat in a low chair by his pillow, never taking off her clothes. Every time she gave him his medicine, he mutely kissed her hand, weeping. On the last day, sobbing, he begged forgiveness of his wife, and of his absent son, too, for squandering their property, the chief sin that lay on his conscience.

After receiving absolution and the last unction, he quietly died; and next day a crowd of acquaintances, came to pay the last debt of respect to the deceased, filled the Rostovs' hired lodgings. All those acquaintances, who had so often dined and danced in his house, and had so often laughed at his expense, were saying now with the same inward feeling of contrition and self-reproach, as though seeking to justify themselves: "Yes, whatever he may have been, he was a splendid man. One doesn't meet such men nowadays . . . And who has not his weaknesses? . . ."

It was precisely when the count's fortunes were so irretrievably embroiled that he could not conceive how, in another year, it would end, that he suddenly died.

Nikolay was with the Russian army in Paris when the news of his father's death reached him. He at once applied for his discharge, and without waiting for it, obtained leave and went to Moscow. Within a month after the count's death the financial position had been made perfectly clear, astounding every one by the immense sum of various petty debts, the existence of which no one had suspected. The debts were more than double the assets of the estate.

The friends and relations advised Nikolay to refuse to accept his inheritance. But Nikolay looked on such a refusal as a slur on the honoured memory of his father; and so he would not hear of such a course, and accepted the inheritance with the obligation of paying the debts.

The creditors, who had so long been silent, held in check during the old count's lifetime by the vague but powerful influence of his easy good-nature, all beset Nikolay at once. There seemed, as so often happens, a sort of rivalry among them, which should get paid first; and the very people, such as Mitenka and others, who held promissory notes, not received in discharge of debts, but as presents, were now the most importunate of the creditors. They would give Nikolay no peace and no respite, and those who had shown pity for the old man, who was responsible for their losses (if they really had lost money by him), were now ruthless in their persecution of the young heir, who was obviously guiltless as far as they were concerned, and had voluntarily undertaken to pay them.

Not one of the plans that Nikolay resorted to was successful: the estate was sold by auction at half its value, and half the debts remained still unpaid. Nikolay accepted a loan of thirty thousand roubles offered him by his brother-in-law Bezuhov; and paid that portion of the debts that he recognised as genuine obligations. And to avoid being thrown into prison for the remainder, as the creditors threatened, he once more entered the government service.

To return to the army, where at the next promotion he would have been colonel, was out of the question, because his mother now clung to her son as her one hold on life. And so in spite of his disinclination to remain in Moscow, in the midst of a circle of acquaintances who had known him in former days, in spite of his distaste for the civil service, he accepted a civilian post in Moscow, and taking off his beloved uniform, established himself in a little lodging in Sivtsevoy Vrazhok with his mother and Sonya.

Natasha and Pierre were living at this period in Petersburg, and had no very distinct idea of Nikolay's position. After having borrowed money from his brother-in-law, Nikolay did his utmost to conceal his poverty-stricken position from him. His situation was rendered the more difficult, as with his twelve hundred roubles of salary he had not only to keep himself, Sonya, and his mother, but to keep his mother in such a way that she would not be sensible of their poverty. The countess could not conceive of life being possible without the luxurious surroundings to which she had been accustomed from her childhood; and without any idea of its being difficult for her son, she was continually insisting on having a carriage, which they had not, to send for a friend, or an expensive delicacy for herself, or wine for her son, or money to buy a present, as a surprise for Natasha, for Sonya, or for Nikolay himself.

Sonya kept house, waited on her aunt, read aloud to her, bore with her caprices and her secret dislike, and helped Nikolay to conceal from the old countess their poverty-stricken position. Nikolay felt himself under a debt of gratitude to Sonya that he could never repay, for all she did for his mother; he admired her patience and devotion, but he tried to keep himself aloof from her.

In his heart he seemed to feel a sort of grudge against her for being too perfect, and for there being no fault to find with her. She had all the good qualities for which people are valued, but little of what would have made him love her. And he felt that the more he valued her the less he loved her. He had taken her at her word when she had written to him giving him his freedom, and now he behaved with her as though what had passed between them had been long, long ago forgotten, and could never under any circumstances be renewed.

Nikolay's position was becoming worse and worse. His hope of laying by something out of his salary proved to be an idle dream. Far from saving anything, he was even running up some small debts to satisfy his mother's exigencies. There seemed no means of escape from his position. The idea of marrying a rich heiress, which his female relatives suggested, was repulsive to him. The only other solution of his difficulties—the death of his mother—never entered his head. He desired nothing, and hoped for nothing; and at the bottom of his heart he took a stern and gloomy satisfaction in the unrepining endurance of his position. He tried to avoid his old acquaintances, with their commiseration and their mortifying offers of assistance; shunned every sort of entertainment and amusement; and even at home did nothing but play patience with his mother, pace silently about the room, and smoke pipe after pipe. He seemed studiously to maintain in himself that gloomy temper, which alone enabled him to bear his position.

VI

At the beginning of the winter Princess Marya arrived in Moscow. From the gossip of the town she heard of the position of the Rostovs, and of how "the son was sacrificing himself for his mother," as the gossips said. "It is just what I expected of him," Princess Marya said to herself, finding in it a delightful confirmation of her love for him. Remembering her intimate relations with the whole family—almost as one of themselves—she thought it her duty to call on them. But thinking of her relations with Nikolay in Voronezh, she was afraid of doing so. A few weeks after her arrival in Moscow, she did, however, make an effort, and went to see the Rostovs.

Nikolay was the first to meet her, since it was impossible to reach the countess's room without passing through his room. Instead of the expression of delight Princess Marya had expected to see on his face at the first glance at her, he met her with a look of chilliness, stiffness, and pride that she had never seen before. Nikolay inquired after her health, conducted her to his mother, and, after staying five minutes, went out of the room.

When Princess Marya left the countess, Nikolay again met her, and with marked formality and stiffness led her to the hall. He made no reply to her remarks about the countess's health. "What is it to you? Leave me in peace," his expression seemed to say.

"And why should she stroll in here? What does she want? I can't endure these ladies and all these civilities!" he said aloud before Sonya, obviously unable to restrain his vexation, after the princess's carriage had rolled away from the house.

"Oh, how can you talk like that, *Nicolas*," said Sonya, hardly able to conceal her delight. "She is so kind, and *maman* is so fond of her."

Nikolay made no reply, and would have liked to say no more about Princess Marya. But after her visit the old countess talked about her several times every day.

She sang her praises; insisted that her son should go and see her; expressed a wish to see more of her; and yet was always out of temper when she had been talking of her.

Nikolay tried to say nothing when his mother talked of Princess Marya, but his silence irritated her.

"She is a very good and conscientious girl," she would say, "and you must go and call on her. Anyway, you will see some one; and it is dull for you, I expect, with us."

"But I don't at all wish to, mamma."

"Why, you wanted to see people and now you don't wish it. I really don't understand you, my dear. At one minute you are dull, and the next you suddenly don't care to see any one."

"Why, I never said I was dull."

"Why, you said yourself you did not even wish to see her. She is a very good girl, and you always liked her; and now all of a sudden you have some reasons or other. Everything is kept a secret from me."

"Not at all, mamma."

"If I were to beg you to do something unpleasant, but as it is, I simply beg you to drive over and return her call. Why, civility demands it, I should suppose . . . I have begged you to do so, and now I will meddle no further since you have secrets from your mother."

"But I will go, if you wish it."

"It's nothing to me; it's for your sake I wish it."

Nikolay sighed, and bit his moustache, and dealt the cards, trying to draw his mother's attention to another subject.

Next day, and the third, and the fourth, the same conversation was repeated again and again.

After her visit to the Rostovs, and the unexpectedly cold reception she had met with from Nikolay, Princess Marya acknowledged to herself that she had been right in not wanting to be the first to call.

"It was just what I expected," she said to herself, summoning her pride to her aid. "I have no concern with him, and I only wanted to see the old lady, who was always kind to me, and to whom I am under obligation for many things."

But she could not tranquillise herself with these reflections: a feeling akin to remorse fretted her, when she thought of her visit. Although she was firmly resolved not to call again on the Rostovs, and to forget all about it, she was continually feeling herself in an undefined position. And when she asked herself what it was that worried her, she was obliged to admit that it was her relation to Rostov. His cold, ceremonious tone did not proceed from his feeling for her (of that she was convinced), but that tone covered something. What that something was, she wanted to see clearly, and till then she felt that she could not be at peace.

In the middle of the winter she was sitting in the schoolroom, supervising her nephew's lessons, when the servant announced that Rostov was below. With the firm determination not to betray her secret, and not to manifest any embarrassment, she summoned Mademoiselle Bourienne, and with her went into the drawing-room.

At the first glance at Nikolay's face, she saw that he had come merely to perform the obligations of civility, and she determined to keep to the tone he adopted towards her.

They talked of the health of the countess, of common acquaintances, of the latest news of the war, and when the ten minutes required by propriety had elapsed, Nikolay got up to say good-bye.

With the aid of Mademoiselle Bourienne, Princess Marya had kept up the conversation very well. But at the very last moment, just when he was getting up, she was so weary of talking of what did not interest her, and she was so absorbed in wondering why to her alone so little joy had been vouchsafed in life, that in a fit of abstraction, she sat motionless gazing straight before her with her luminous eyes, and not noticing that he was getting up.

Nikolay looked at her, and anxious to appear not to notice her abstraction, he said a few words to Mademoiselle Bourienne, and again glanced at the princess. She was sitting in the same immovable pose, and there was a look of suffering on her soft face. He felt suddenly sorry for her, and vaguely conscious that he might be the cause of the sadness he saw in her face. He longed to help her, to say something pleasant to her, but he could not think what to say to her.

"Good-bye, princess," he said. She started, flushed, and sighed heavily.

"Oh, I beg your pardon," she said, as though waking from sleep. "You are going already, count; well, good-bye! Oh, the cushion for the countess?"

"Wait a minute, I will fetch it," said Mademoiselle Bourienne, and she left the room.

They were both silent, glancing at each other now and then.

"Yes, princess," said Nikolay at last, with a mournful smile, "it seems not long ago, but how much has happened since the first time we met at Bogutcharovo. We all seemed in such trouble then, but I would give a great deal to have that time back . . . and there's no bringing it back."

Princess Marya was looking intently at him with her luminous eyes, as he said that. She seemed trying to divine the secret import of his words, which would make clear his feeling towards her.

"Yes, yes," she said, "but you have no need to regret the past, count. As I conceive of your life now, you will always think of it with satisfaction, because the self-sacrifice in which you are now . . ."

"I cannot accept your praises," he interrupted hurriedly; "on the contrary, I am always reproaching myself; but it is an uninteresting and cheerless subject."

And again the stiff and cold expression came back into his face. But Princess Marya saw in him again now the man she had known and loved, and it was to that man only she was speaking now.

"I thought you would allow me to say that," she said. "I have been such intimate friends with you . . . and with your family, and I thought you would not feel my sympathy intrusive; but I made a mistake," she said. Her voice suddenly shook. "I don't know why," she went on, recovering herself, "you used to be different, and . . ."

"There are thousands of reasons *why*." (He laid special stress on the word *why*.) "I thank you, princess," he added softly. "It is sometimes hard . . ."

"So that is why! That is why!" an inner voice was saying in Princess Marya's soul. "Yes, it was not only that gay, kind, and frank gaze, not only that handsome exterior I loved in him; I divined his noble, firm, and self-sacrificing soul," she said to herself.

"Yes, he is poor now, and I am rich . . . Yes, it is only that . . . Yes, if it were not for that . . ." And recalling all his former tenderness, and looking now at his kind and sad face, she suddenly understood the reason of his coldness.

"Why, count, why?" she almost cried all at once, involuntarily moving nearer to him. "Why, do tell me. You must tell me." He was mute. "I do not know, count, your *why*," she went on. "But I am sad, I . . . I will own that to you. You mean for some reason to deprive me of our old friendship. And that hurts me." There were tears in her eyes and in her voice. "I have had so little happiness in my life that every loss is hard for me . . . Excuse me, good-bye," she suddenly burst into tears, and was going out of the room.

"Princess! stay, for God's sake," he cried, trying to stop her. "Princess!"

She looked round. For a few seconds they gazed mutely in each other's eyes, and the remote and impossible became all at once close at hand, possible and inevitable.

VII

IN the autumn of 1813, Nikolay married Princess Marya, and with his wife, and mother, and Sonya, took up his abode at Bleak Hills.

Within four years he had paid off the remainder of his debts without selling his wife's estates, and coming into a small legacy on the death of a cousin, he repaid the loan he had borrowed from Pierre also.

In another three years, by 1820, Nikolay had so well managed his pecuniary affairs that he was able to buy a small estate adjoining Bleak Hills, and was opening negotiations for the repurchase of his ancestral estate of Otradnoe, which was his cherished dream.

Though he took up the management of the land at first from necessity, he soon acquired such a passion for agriculture, that it became his favourite and almost his exclusive interest. Nikolay was a plain farmer, who did not like innovations, especially English ones, just then coming into vogue, laughed at all theoretical treatises on agriculture, did not care for factories, for raising expensive produce, or for expensive imported seed. He did not, in fact, make a hobby of any one part of the work, but kept the welfare of the *estate* as a whole always before his eyes. The object most prominent to his mind in the estate was not the azote nor the oxygen in the soil or the atmosphere, not a particular plough nor manure, but the principal agent by means of which the azote and the oxygen and the plough and the manure were all made effectual —that is, the labourer, the peasant. When Nikolay took up the management of the land, and began to go into its different branches, the peasant attracted his chief attention. He looked on the peasant, not merely as a tool, but also as an end in himself, and as his critic. At first he studied the peasant attentively, trying to understand what he wanted, what he thought good and bad; and he only made a pretence of making arrangements and giving orders, while he was in reality learning from the peasants their methods and their language and their views of what was good and bad. And it was only when he understood the tastes and impulses of the peasant, when he had learned to speak his speech and to grasp the hidden meaning behind his words, when he felt himself in alliance with him, that he began boldly to direct him—to perform, that is, towards him the office expected of him. And Nikolay's management produced the most brilliant results.

On taking over the control of the property, Nikolay had at once by some unerring gift of insight appointed as bailiff, as village elder, and as delegate the very men whom the peasants would have elected themselves had the choice been in their hands, and the authority once given them was never withdrawn. Before investigating the chemical constituents of manure, or going into "debit and credit" (as he liked sarcastically to call book-keeping), he found out the number of cattle the peasants possessed, and did his utmost to increase the number. He kept the peasants' families together on a large scale, and would not allow them to split up into separate households. The indolent, the dissolute, and the feeble he was equally hard upon and tried to expel them from the community. At the sowing and the carrying of the hay and corn, he watched over his own and the peasants' fields with absolutely equal care. And few landowners had fields so early and so well sown and cut, and few had such crops as Nikolay.

He did not like to have anything to do with the house-serfs, he called them *parasites,* and everybody said that he demoralised and spoiled them. When any order had to be given in regard to a house-serf, especially when one had to be punished, he was always in a state of indecision and asked advice of every one in the house. But whenever it was possible to send a house-serf for a soldier in place of a peasant, he did so without the smallest compunction. In all his dealings with the peasants, he never experienced the slightest hesitation. Every order he gave would, he knew, be approved by the greater majority of them.

He never allowed himself either to punish a man by adding to his burdens, or to reward him by lightening his tasks simply at the prompting of his own wishes. He could not have said what his standard was of what he ought and ought not to do; but there was a standard firm and rigid in his soul.

Often talking of some failure or irregularity, he would complain of "our Russian peasantry," and he imagined that he could not bear the peasants.

But with his whole soul he did really love "our Russian peasantry," and their ways; and it was through that he had perceived and adopted the only method of managing the land which could be productive of good results.

Countess Marya was jealous of this passion of her husband's for agriculture, and regretted she could not share it. But she was unable to comprehend the joys and disappointments he met with in that world apart that was so alien to her. She could not understand why he used to be so particularly eager and happy when after getting up at dawn and spending the whole morning in the fields or the threshing-floor he came back to tea with her from the sowing, the mowing, or the harvest. She could not understand why he was so delighted when he told her with enthusiasm of the well-to-do, thrifty peasant Matvey Ermishin, who had been up all night with his family, carting his sheaves, and had all harvested when no one else had begun carrying. She could not understand why, stepping out of the window on to the balcony, he smiled under his moustaches and winked so gleefully when a warm, fine rain began to fall on his young oats that were suffering from the drought, or why, when a menacing cloud blew over in mowing or harvest time, he would come in from the barn red, sunburnt, and perspiring, with the smell of wormwood in his hair, and rubbing his hands joyfully would say: "Come, another day of this and my lot, and the peasants' too, will all be in the barn."

Still less could she understand how it was that with his good heart and everlasting readiness to anticipate her wishes, he would be thrown almost into despair when she brought him petitions from peasants or their wives who had appealed to her to be let off tasks, why it was that he, her good-natured Nikolay, obstinately refused her, angrily begging her not to meddle in his business. She felt that he had a world apart, that was intensely dear to him, governed by laws of its own which she did not understand.

Sometimes trying to understand him she would talk to him of the good work he was doing in striving for the good of his serfs; but at this he was angry and answered: "Not in the least; it never even entered my head; and for their good I would not lift my little finger. That's all romantic nonsense and old wives' cackle—all that doing good to one's neighbour. I don't want our children to be beggars; I want to build up our fortunes in my lifetime; that is all. And to do that one must have discipline, one must have strictness . . . So there!" he would declare, clenching his sanguine fist. "And justice too—of course," he would add, "because if the peasant is naked and hungry, and has but one poor horse, he can do no good for himself or me."

And doubtless because Nikolay did not allow himself to entertain the idea that he was doing anything for the sake of others, or for the sake of virtue, everything he did was fruitful. His fortune rapidly increased; the neighbouring serfs came to beg him to purchase them, and long after his death the peasantry preserved a reverent memory of his rule. "He was a master . . . The peasants' welfare first and then his own. And to be sure he would make no abatements. A real good master—that's what he was!"

VIII

THE one thing that sometimes troubled Nikolay in his government of his serfs was his hasty temper and his old habit, acquired in the hussars, of making free use of his fists. At first he saw nothing blameworthy in this, but in the second year of his married life his views on that form of correction underwent a sudden change.

One summer day he had sent for the village elder who had taken control at Bogutcharovo on the death of Dron. The man was accused of various acts of fraud and neglect. Nikolay went out to the steps to see him, and at the first answers the village elder made, shouts and blows were heard in the hall. On going back indoors to lunch, Nikolay went up to his wife, who was sitting with her head bent low over her embroidery frame, and began telling her, as he always did, everything that had interested him during the morning, and among other things about the Bogutcharovo elder. Countess Marya, turning red and pale and setting her lips, sat in the same pose, making no reply to her husband.

"The insolent rascal," he said, getting hot at the mere recollection. "Well, he should have told me he was drunk, he did not see . . . Why, what is it, Marie?" he asked all at once.

Countess Marya raised her head, tried to say something, but hurriedly looked down again, trying to control her lips.

"What is it? What is wrong, my darling? . . ." His plain wife always looked her best when she was in tears. She never wept for pain or anger, but always from sadness and pity. And when she wept her luminous eyes gained an indescribable charm.

As soon as Nikolay took her by the hand, she was unable to restrain herself, and burst into tears.

"Nikolay, I saw . . . he was in fault, but you, why did you! Nikolay!" and she hid her face in her hands.

Nikolay did not speak; he flushed crimson, and walking away from her, began pacing up and down in silence. He knew what she was crying about, but he could not all at once agree with her in his heart that what he had been used to from childhood, what he looked upon as a matter of course, was wrong. "It's sentimental nonsense, old wives' cackle—or is she right?" he said to himself. Unable to decide that question, he glanced once more at her suffering and loving face, and all at once he felt that she was right, and that he had known himself to be in fault a long time before.

"Marie," he said, softly, going up to her: "it shall never happen again; I give you my word. Never," he repeated in a shaking voice like a boy begging for forgiveness.

The tears flowed faster from his wife's eyes. She took his hand and kissed it.

"Nikolay, when did you break your cameo?" she said to change the subject, as she scrutinised the finger on which he wore a ring with a cameo of Laocoon.

"To-day; it was all the same thing. O Marie, don't remind me of it!" He flushed again. "I give you my word of honour that it shall never happen again. And let this be a reminder to me for ever," he said, pointing to the broken ring.

From that time forward, whenever in interviews with his village elders and foremen he felt the blood rush to his face and his fists began to clench, Nikolay turned the ring round on his finger and dropped his eyes before the man who angered him. Twice a year, however, he would forget himself, and then, going to his wife, he confessed, and again promised that this would really be the last time.

"Marie, you must despise me," he said to her. "I deserve it."

"You must run away, make haste and run away if you feel yourself unable to control yourself," his wife said mournfully, trying to comfort him.

In the society of the nobility of the province Nikolay was respected but not liked. The local politics of the nobility did not interest him. And in consequence he was looked upon by some people as proud and by others as a fool. In summer his whole time from the spring sowing to the harvest was spent in looking after the land. In the autumn he gave himself up with the same business-like seriousness to hunting, going out for a month or two at a time with his huntsmen, dogs, and horses on hunting expeditions. In the winter he visited their other properties and spent his time in reading, chiefly historical books, on which he spent a certain sum regularly every year. He was forming for himself, as he used to say, a serious library, and he made it a principle to read through every book he bought. He would sit over his book in his study with an important air; and what he had at first undertaken as a duty became an habitual pursuit, which afforded him a special sort of gratification in the feeling that he was engaged in serious study. Except when he went on business to visit their other estates, he spent the winter at home with his family, entering into all the petty cares and interests of the mother and children. With his wife he got on better and better, every day discovering fresh spiritual treasures in her.

From the time of Nikolay's marriage Sonya had lived in his house. Before their marriage, Nikolay had told his wife all that had passed between him and Sonya, blaming himself and praising her conduct. He begged Princess Marya to be kind and affectionate to his cousin. His wife was fully sensible of the wrong her husband had done his cousin; she felt herself too guilty toward Sonya; she fancied her wealth had influenced Nikolay in his choice, could find no fault in Sonya, and wished to love her. But she could not like her, and often found evil feelings in her soul in regard to her, which she could not overcome.

One day she was talking with her friend Natasha of Sonya and her own injustice towards her.

"Do you know what," said Natasha; "you have read the Gospel a great deal; there is a passage there that applies exactly to Sonya."

"What is it?" Countess Marya asked in surprise.

" 'To him that hath shall be given, and to him that hath not shall be taken even that that he hath,' do you remember? She is the one that hath not; why, I don't know; perhaps she has no egoism. I don't know; but from her is taken away, and everything has been taken away. I am sometimes awfully sorry for her. I used in old days to want Nikolay to marry her but I always had a sort of presentiment that it would not happen. She is a *barren flower,* you know, like what one finds among the strawberry flowers. Sometimes I am sorry for her, and sometimes I think she does not feel it as we should have felt it."

And although Countess Marya argued with Natasha that those words of the Gospel must not be taken in that sense, looking at Sonya, she agreed with the explanation given by Natasha. It did seem really as though Sonya did not feel her position irksome, and was quite reconciled to her fate as a *barren flower*. She seemed to be fond not so much of people as of the whole family. Like a cat, she had attached herself not to persons but to the house. She waited on the old countess, petted and spoiled the children, was always ready to perform small services, which she seemed particularly clever at; but all she did was unconsciously taken for granted, without much gratitude. . . .

The Bleak Hills house had been built up again, but not on the same scale as under the old prince.

The buildings, begun in days of straitened means, were more than simple. The immense mansion on the old stone foundation was of wood, plastered only on the inside. The great rambling house, with its un-stained plank floors, was furnished with the simplest rough sofas and chairs and tables made of their own birch-trees by the labor of their serf carpenters. The house was very roomy, with quarters for the house-serfs and accommodation for visitors.

The relations of the Rostovs and the Bolkonskys would sometimes come on visits to Bleak Hills with their families, sixteen horses and dozens of servants, and stay for months. And four times a year—on the namedays and birthdays of the master and mistress—as many as a hundred visitors would be put up for a day or two. The rest of the year the regular life of the household went on in unbroken routine, with its round of duties, and of teas, breakfasts, dinners, and suppers, all provided out of home-grown produce.

IX

It was on the eve of St. Nikolay's day, the 5th of December, 1820. That year Natasha with her husband and children had been staying at Bleak Hills since the beginning of autumn. Pierre was in Petersburg, where he had gone on private business of his own, as he said, for three weeks. He had already been away for six, and was expected home every minute.

On this 5th of December there was also staying with the Rostovs Nikolay's old friend, the general on half-pay, Vassily Fedorovitch Denisov.

Next day visitors were coming in celebration of his nameday, and Nikolay knew that he would have to take off his loose Tatar coat, to put on a frock coat, and narrow boots with pointed toes, and to go to the new church he had built, and there to receive congratulations, and to offer refreshments to his guests, and to talk about the provincial elections and the year's crops. But the day before he considered he had a right to spend as usual. Before dinner-time Nikolay had gone over the bailiff's accounts from the Ryazan estate, the property of his wife's nephew; written two business letters, and walked through the corn barns, the cattleyard, and the stables. After taking measures against the general drunkenness he expected next day among his peasants in hon-our of the fête, he came in to dinner, without having had a moment's conversation alone with his wife all day. He sat down to a long table laid with twenty covers, at which all the household were assembled, con-sisting of his mother, old Madame Byelov, who lived with her as a com-panion, his wife and three children, their governess and tutor, his wife's nephew with his tutor, Sonya, Denisov, Natasha, her three children, their governess, and Mihail Ivanitch, the old prince's architect, who was living out his old age in peace at Bleak Hills.

Countess Marya was sitting at the opposite end of the table. As soon as her husband sat down to the table, from the gesture with which he took up his table-napkin and quickly pushed back the tumbler and wine-glass set at his place, she knew that he was out of humour, as he sometimes was, particularly before the soup, and when he came straight in to dinner from his work. Countess Marya understood this mood in her husband very well, and when she was herself in a good temper, she used to wait quietly till he had swallowed his soup, and only then began to talk to him and to make him admit that he had no reason to be out of temper. But to-day she totally forgot this principle of hers; she had a miserable sense of his being vexed with her without cause, and she felt wretched. She asked him where he had been. He answered. She asked again whether everything were going well on the estate. He frowned disagreeably at her unnatural tone, and made a hasty reply.

"I was right then," thought Countess Marya, "and what is he cross with me for?" In the tone of his answer she read ill-will towards her and a desire to cut short the conversation. She felt that her words were un-natural; but she could not restrain herself, and asked a few more ques-tions.

The conversation at dinner, thanks to Denisov, soon became general and animated, and she did not say more to her husband. When they rose from table, and according to custom came up to thank the old countess, Countess Marya kissed her husband, offering him her hand, and asked why he was cross with her.

"You always have such strange ideas; I never thought of being cross," he said.

But that word *always* answered her: Yes, I am angry, and I don't choose to say.

Nikolay lived on such excellent terms with his wife that even Sonya and the old countess, who from jealousy would have been pleased to see disagreement between them, could find nothing to reproach them with; but there were moments of antagonism even between them. Sometimes, particularly just after their happiest periods, they had a sudden feeling of estrangement and antagonism; that feeling was most frequent during the times when Countess Marya was with child. They happened to be just now at such a period of antagonism.

"Well, *messieurs et mesdames*," said Nikolay loudly, and with a show of cheerfulness (it seemed to his wife that this was on purpose to mor-tify her), "I have been since six o'clock on my legs. To-morrow will be an infliction, so to-day I'll go and rest." And saying nothing more to Countess Marya, he went off to the little divan-room, and lay down on the sofa.

"That's how it always is," thought his wife. "He talks to everybody but not to me. I see, I see that I am repulsive to him, especially in this condition." She looked down at her high waist and then into the looking-glass at her sallow and sunken face, in which the eyes looked bigger than ever.

And everything jarred upon her: Denisov's shout and guffaw and Natasha's chatter, and above all the hasty glance Sonya stole at her.

Sonya was always the first excuse Countess Marya pitched on for her irritability.

After sitting a little while with her guests, not understanding a word they were saying, she slipped out and went to the nursery.

The children were sitting on chairs playing at driving to Moscow, and invited her to join them. She sat down and played with them, but the thought of her husband and his causeless ill-temper worried her all the time. She got up, and walked with difficulty on tiptoe to the little divan-room.

"Perhaps he is not asleep. I will speak plainly to him," she said to herself. Andryusha, her elder boy, followed her on tiptoe, imitating her. His mother did not notice him.

"Dear Marie, I believe he is asleep; he was so tired," said Sonya, meeting her in the next room (it seemed to Countess Marya that she was everywhere). "Andryusha had better not wake him."

Countess Marya looked round, saw Andryusha behind her, felt that Sonya was right, and for that very reason flushed angrily, and with evident difficulty restrained herself from a cruel retort. She said nothing, and, so as not to obey her, let Andryusha follow her, but signed to him to be quiet, and went up to the door. Sonya went out by the other door. From the room where Nikolay was asleep, his wife could hear his even breathing, every tone of which was so familiar. As she listened to it, she could see his smooth, handsome brow, his moustaches, the whole face she had so often gazed at in the stillness of the night when he was asleep. Nikolay suddenly stirred and cleared his throat. And at the same instant Andryusha shouted from the door, "Papa, mamma's here!" His mother turned pale with dismay and made signs to the boy. He was quiet, and there followed a terrible silence that lasted a minute. She knew how Nikolay disliked being waked. Suddenly she heard him stir and clear his throat again, and in a tone of displeasure he said:

"I'm never given a moment's peace. Marie, is it you? Why did you bring him here?"

"I only came to look . . . I did not see . . . I'm so sorry . . ."

Nikolay coughed and said no more. His wife went away, and took her son back to the nursery. Five minutes later little, black-eyed, three-year-old Natasha, her father's favourite, hearing from her brother that papa was asleep, and mamma in the next room, ran in to her father, unnoticed by her mother.

The black-eyed little girl boldly rattled at the door, and her fat, little feet ran with vigorous steps up to the sofa. After examining the position of her father, who was asleep with his back to her, she stood on tiptoe and kissed the hand that lay under his head. Nikolay turned round to her with a smile of tenderness on his face.

"Natasha, Natasha!" he heard his wife whisper in dismay from the door. "Papa is sleepy."

"No, mamma, he isn't sleepy," little Natasha answered with conviction. "He's laughing."

Nikolay set his feet down, got up, and picked his little daughter up in his arms.

"Come in, Masha," he said to his wife. She went in and sat down beside him.

"I did not see him run in after me," she said timidly. "I just looked in . . ."

Holding his little girl on one arm, Nikolay looked at his wife, and noticing her guilty expression, he put the other arm round her and kissed her on the hair.

"May I kiss mamma?" he asked Natasha. The little girl smiled demurely. "Again," she said, with a peremptory gesture, pointing to the spot where Nikolay had kissed her mother.

"I don't know why you should think I am cross," said Nikolay, replying to the question which he knew was in his wife's heart.

"You can't imagine how unhappy, how lonely, I am when you are like that. It always seems to me . . ."

"Marie, hush, nonsense! You ought to be ashamed," he said gaily.

"It seems to me that you can't care for me; that I am so ugly . . . at all times, and now in this . . ."

"Oh, how absurd you are! It's not those who are handsome we love, but those we love who are handsome. It is only Malvinas and such heroines who are loved because they are beautiful. And do you suppose I love my wife? Oh no, I don't love you, but only . . . I don't know how to tell you. When you are away, and any misunderstanding like this comes between us, I feel as though I were lost, and can do nothing. Why, do I love my finger? I don't love it, but only try cutting it off . . ."

"No, I don't feel like that, but I understand. Then you are not angry with me?"

"I am awfully angry!" he said, smiling, and getting up, and smoothing his hair, he began pacing up and down the room.

"Do you know, Marie, what I have been thinking?" he began, beginning at once now that peace was made between them, thinking aloud before his wife. He did not inquire whether she were disposed to listen; that did not matter to him. An idea occurred to him; and so it must to her, too. And he told her that he meant to persuade Pierre to stay with them till the spring.

Countess Marya listened to him, made some comments, and then in her turn began thinking her thoughts aloud. Her thoughts were of the children.

"How one can see the woman in her already," she said in French, pointing to little Natasha. "You reproach us women for being illogical. You see in her our logic. I say, papa is sleepy, and she says, no, he's laughing. And she is right," said Countess Marya, smiling blissfully.

"Yes, yes," said Nikolay, lifting up his little girl in his strong arm, raised her high in the air, sat her on his shoulder, holding her little feet, and began walking up and down with her. There was just the same look of thoughtless happiness on the faces of father and daughter.

"But do you know, you may be unfair. You are too fond of this one," his wife whispered in French.

"Yes, but what can I do? . . . I try not to show it . . ."

At that moment there was heard from the hall and the vestibule the sound of the block of the door, and footsteps, as though some one had arrived.

"Somebody has come."

"I am sure it is Pierre. I will go and find out," said Countess Marya, and she went out of the room.

While she was gone Nikolay allowed himself to gallop round the room with his little girl. Panting for breath, he quickly lowered the laughing child, and hugged her to his breast. His capers made him think of dancing; and looking at the childish, round, happy little face, he wondered what she would be like when he would be an old man, taking her out to dances, and he remembered how his father used to dance Daniel Cooper and the mazurka with his daughter.

"It is he, it is he, Nikolay!" said Countess Marya, returning a few minutes later. "Now our Natasha is herself again. You should have seen her delight, and what a scolding he came in for at once for having outstayed his time. Come, let us go; make haste; come along! You must part at last," she said, smiling, as she looked at the little girl nestling up to her father. Nikolay went out, holding his daughter by the hand.

Countess Marya lingered behind.

"Never, never could I have believed," she murmured to herself, "that one could be so happy." Her face lighted up with a smile; but at the same moment she sighed, and a soft melancholy came into her thoughtful glance. It was as though, apart from the happiness she was feeling there was another happiness unattainable in this life, which she could not help remembering at that moment.

X

NATASHA was married in the early spring of 1813, and by 1820 she had three daughters and a son. The latter had been eagerly desired, and she was now nursing him herself. She had grown stouter and broader, so that it was hard to recognise in the robust-looking young mother the slim, mobile Natasha of old days. Her features had become more defined, and wore an expression of calm softness and serenity. Her face had no longer that ever-glowing fire of eagerness that had once constituted her chief charm. Now, often her face and body were all that was to be seen, and the soul was not visible at all. All there was to be seen in her was a vigorous, handsome, and fruitful mother. Only on rare occasions now the old fire glowed in her again. That happened only when, as now, her husband returned after absence, when a sick child recovered, or when she spoke to Countess Marya of Prince Andrey (to her husband she never spoke of Prince Andrey, fancying he might be jealous of her love for him), or on the rare occasions when something happened to attract her to her singing, which she had entirely laid aside since her marriage. And at those rare moments, when the old fire glowed again, she was more attractive, with her handsome, fully-developed figure, than she had ever been in the past.

Since her marriage Natasha and her husband had lived in Moscow, in Petersburg, on their estate near Moscow, and at her mother's; that is to say, at Nikolay's. The young Countess Bezuhov was little seen in society, and those who had seen her there were not greatly pleased with her. She was neither charming nor amiable. It was not that Natasha was fond of solitude (she could not have said whether she liked it or not; she rather supposed indeed that she did not); but as she was bearing and nursing children, and taking interest in every minute of her husband's life, she could not meet all these demands on her except by renouncing society. Every one who had known Natasha before her marriage marvelled at the change that had taken place in her, as though it were something extraordinary. Only the old countess, with her mother's insight, had seen that what was at the root of all Natasha's wild outbursts of feeling was simply the need of children and a husband of her own, as she often used to declare, more in earnest than in joke, at Otradnoe. The mother was surprised at the wonder of people who did not understand Natasha, and repeated that she had always known that she would make an exemplary wife and mother.

"Only she does carry her devotion to her husband and children to an extreme," the countess would say; "so much so, that it's positively foolish."

Natasha did not follow the golden rule preached by so many prudent persons, especially by the French, that recommends that a girl on marrying should not neglect herself, should not give up her accomplishments, should think even more of her appearance than when a young girl, and should try to fascinate her husband as she had fascinated him before he was her husband. Natasha, on the contrary, had at once abandoned all her accomplishments, of which the greatest was her singing. She gave that up just because it was such a great attraction. Natasha troubled herself little about manners or delicacy of speech; nor did she think of showing herself to her husband in the most becoming attitudes and costumes, nor strive to avoid worrying him by being over-exacting. She acted in direct contravention of all those rules. She felt that the arts of attraction that instinct had taught her to use before would now have seemed only ludicrous to her husband, to whom she had from the first moment given herself up entirely, that is with her whole soul, not keeping a single corner of it hidden from him. She felt that the tie that bound her to her husband did not rest on those romantic feelings which had attracted him to her, but rested on something else undefined, but as strong as the tie that bound her soul to her body.

To curl her hair, put on a crinoline, and sing songs to attract her husband would have seemed to her as strange as to deck herself up so as to please herself. To adorn herself to please others might perhaps have been agreeable to her—she did not know—but she had absolutely no time for it. The chief reason why she could not attend to her singing, nor to her dress, nor to the careful choice of her words was that she simply had no time to think of those things.

It is well known that man has the faculty of entire absorption in one subject, however trivial that subject may appear to be. And it is well known that there is no subject so trivial that it will not grow to indefinite proportions if concentrated attention be devoted to it.

The subject in which Natasha was completely absorbed was her family, that is, her husband, whom she kept such a hold on so that he should belong entirely to her, to his home and her children, whom she had to carry, to bear, to nurse and to bring up.

And the more she put, not her mind only, but her whole soul, her whole being, into the subject that absorbed her, the more that subject seemed to enlarge under her eyes, and the feebler and the more inadequate her own powers seemed for coping with it, so that she concentrated them all on that one subject, and still had not time to do all that seemed to her necessary.

There were in those days, just as now, arguments and discussions on the rights of women, on the relations of husband and wife, and on freedom and rights in marriage, though they were not then, as now, called *questions*. But these questions had no interest for Natasha, in fact she had absolutely no comprehension of them.

Those questions, then as now, existed only for those persons who see in marriage only the satisfaction the married receive from one another, that is, only the first beginnings of marriage and not all its significance, which lies in the family.

Such discussions and the questions of to-day, like the question how to get the utmost possible gratification out of one's dinner, then, as now, did not exist for persons for whom the object of dinner is nourishment, and the object of wedlock is the family.

If the end of dinner is the nourishment of the body, the man who eats two dinners obtains possibly a greater amount of pleasure, but he does not attain the object of it, since two dinners cannot be digested by the stomach.

If the end of marriage is the family, the person who prefers to have several wives and several husbands may possibly derive a great deal of satisfaction therefrom, but will not in any case have a family. If the end of dinner is nourishment and the end of marriage is the family, the whole question is only solved by not eating more than the stomach can digest and not having more husbands or wives than as many as are needed for the family, that is, one wife and one husband. Natasha needed a husband. A husband was given her; and her husband gave her a family. And she saw no need of another better husband, and indeed, as all her spiritual energies were devoted to serving that husband and his children, she could not picture, and found no interest in trying to picture, what would have happened had things been different.

Natasha did not care for society in general, but she greatly prized the society of her kinsfolk—of Countess Marya, her brother, her mother, and Sonya. She cared for the society of those persons to whom she could rush in from the nursery in a dressing-gown with her hair down; to whom she could, with a joyful face, show a baby's napkin stained yellow instead of green, and to receive their comforting assurances that that proved that baby was now really better.

Natasha neglected herself to such a degree that her dresses, her un-tidy hair, her inappropriately blurted-out words, and her jealousy—she was jealous of Sonya, of the governess, of every woman, pretty and ugly —were a continual subject of jests among her friends. The general opin-ion was that Pierre was tied to his wife's apron strings, and it really was so. From the earliest days of their marriage Natasha had made plain her claims. Pierre had been greatly surprised at his wife's view—to him a completely novel idea—that every minute of his life belonged to her and their home. He was surprised at his wife's demands, but he was flattered by them, and he acquiesced in them.

Pierre was so far under petticoat government that he did not dare to be attentive, or even to speak with a smile, to any other woman; did not dare go to dine at the club, without good reason, simply for entertain-ment; did not dare spent money on idle whims, and did not dare to be away from home for any long time together, except on business, in which his wife included his scientific pursuits. Though she understood nothing of the latter, she attached great consequence to them. To make up for all this Pierre had complete power in his own house to dispose of the whole household, as well as of himself, as he chose. In their own home Natasha made herself a slave to her husband; and the whole household had to go on tiptoe if the master were busy reading or writ-ing in his study. Pierre had only to show the slightest preference, for what he desired to be at once carried out. He had but to express a wish and Natasha jumped up at once and ran for what he wanted.

The whole household was ruled by the supposed directions of the master, that is, by the wishes of Pierre, which Natasha tried to guess. Their manner of life and place of residence, their acquaintances and ties, Natasha's pursuits, and the bringing up of the children—all fol-lowed, not only Pierre's expressed wishes, but even the deductions Na-tasha strove to draw from the ideas he explained in conversation with her. And she guessed very correctly what was the essential point of Pierre's wishes, and having once guessed it she was steadfast in adher-ing to it: even when Pierre himself would have veered round she op-posed him with his own weapons.

In the troubled days that Pierre could never forget, after the birth of their first child, they had tried three wet nurses, one after another, for the delicate baby, and Natasha had fallen ill with anxiety. At the time Pierre had explained to her Rousseau's views on the unnaturalness and harmfulness of a child being suckled by any woman but its own mother, and told her he fully agreed with those views. When the next baby was born, in spite of the opposition of her mother, the doctors, and even of her husband himself, who all looked on it as something unheard of, and injurious, she insisted on having her own way, and from that day had nursed all her children herself. It happened very often in moments of irritability that the husband and wife quarrelled; but long after their dispute Pierre had, to his own delight and surprise, found in his wife's actions, as well as words, that very idea of his with which she had quarrelled. And he not only found his own idea, but found it purified of all that was superfluous, and had been evoked by the heat of argument in his own expression of the idea.

After seven years of married life, Pierre had a firm and joyful consciousness that he was not a bad fellow, and he felt this because he saw himself reflected in his wife. In himself he felt all the good and bad mingled together, and obscuring one another. But in his wife he saw reflected only what was really good; everything not quite good was left out. And this result was not reached by the way of logical thought, but by way of a mysterious, direct reflection of himself.

XI

Two months previously, Pierre was already settled at the Rostovs' when he received a letter from a certain Prince Fyodor, urging him to come to Petersburg for the discussion of various important questions that were agitating the Petersburg members of a society, of which Pierre had been one of the chief founders.

Natasha read this letter, as she did indeed all her husband's letters, and bitterly as she always felt his absence, she urged him herself to go to Petersburg. To everything appertaining to her husband's intellectual, abstract pursuits, she ascribed immense consequence, though she had no understanding of them, and she was always in dread of being a hindrance to her husband in such matters. To Pierre's timid glance of inquiry after reading the letter, she replied by begging him to go, and all she asked was that he would fix an absolutely certain date for his return. And leave of absence was given him for four weeks.

Ever since the day fixed for his return, a fortnight before, Natasha had been in a continual condition of alarm, depression, and irritability.

Denisov, a general on the retired list, very much dissatisfied at the present position of public affairs, had arrived during that fortnight, and he looked at Natasha with melancholy wonder, as at a bad likeness of a person once loved. A bored, dejected glance, random replies, and incessant talk of the nursery was all he saw and heard of his enchantress of old days.

All that fortnight Natasha had been melancholy and irritable, especially when her mother, her brother, Sonya, or Countess Marya tried to console her by excusing Pierre, and inventing good reasons for his delay in returning.

"It's all nonsense, all idiocy," Natasha would say; "all his projects that never lead to anything, and all those fools of societies," she would declare of the very matters in the immense importance of which she firmly believed. And she would march off to the nursery to nurse her only boy, the baby Petya.

No one could give her such sensible and soothing consolation as that little three months' old creature, when it lay at her breast, and she felt the movement of its lips and the snuffling of its nose. That little creature said to her: "You are angry, you are jealous, you would like to punish him, you are afraid, but here am I—I am he. Here, I am he . . ." And there was no answering that. It was more than true.

Natasha had so often during that fortnight had recourse to her baby for comfort, that she had over-nursed him, and he had fallen ill. She was terrified at his illness, but still this was just what she needed. In looking after him, she was able to bear her uneasiness about her husband better.

She was nursing the baby when Pierre's carriage drove noisily up to the entrance, and the nurse, knowing how to please her mistress, came inaudibly but quickly to the door with a beaming face.

"He has come?" asked Natasha in a rapid whisper, afraid to stir for fear of waking the baby, who was dropping asleep.

"He has come, ma'am," whispered the nurse.

The blood rushed to Natasha's face, and her feet involuntarily moved, but to jump up and run was out of the question. The baby opened its little eyes again, and glanced, as though to say, "You are here," and gave another lazy smack with its lips.

Cautiously withdrawing her breast, Natasha dandled him, handed him to the nurse, and went with swift steps towards the door. But at the door she stopped as though her conscience pricked her for being in such haste and joy to leave the baby, and she looked back. The nurse, with her elbows raised, was lifting the baby over the rail of the cot.

"Yes, go along, go along, ma'am, don't worry, run along," whispered the nurse, smiling with the familiarity that was common between nurse and mistress.

With light steps Natasha ran to the vestibule. Denisov, coming out of the study into the hall with a pipe in his mouth, seemed to see Natasha again for the first time. A vivid radiance of joy shed streams of light from her transfigured countenance.

"He has come!" she called to him, as she flew by, and Denisov felt that he was thrilled to hear that Pierre had come, though he did not particularly care for him. Running into the vestibule, Natasha saw a tall figure in a fur cloak fumbling at his scarf.

"He! he! It's true. Here he is," she said to herself, and darting up to him, she hugged him, squeezing her head to his breast, and then drawing back, glanced at the frosty, red, and happy face of Pierre. "Yes, here he is; happy, satisfied . . ."

And all at once she remembered all the tortures of suspense she had passed through during the last fortnight. The joy beaming in her face vanished; she frowned, and a torrent of reproaches and angry words broke upon Pierre.

"Yes, you are all right, you have been happy, you have been enjoying yourself . . . But what about me! You might at least think of your children. I am nursing, my milk went wrong . . . Petya nearly died of it. And you have been enjoying yourself. Yes, enjoying yourself . . ."

Pierre knew he was not to blame, because he could not have come sooner. He knew this outburst on her part was unseemly, and would be all over in two minutes. Above all, he knew that he was himself happy and joyful. He would have liked to smile, but dared not even think of that. He made a piteous, dismayed face, and bowed before the storm.

"I could not, upon my word. But how is Petya?"

"He is all right now, come along. Aren't you ashamed? If you could see what I am like without you, how wretched I am . . ."

"Are you quite well?"

"Come along, come along," she said, not letting go of his hand. And they went off to their rooms. When Nikolay and his wife came to look for Pierre, they found him in the nursery, with his baby son awake in his arms, and he was dandling him. There was a gleeful smile on the baby's broad face and open, toothless mouth. The storm had long blown over, and a bright, sunny radiance of joy flowed all over Natasha's face, as she gazed tenderly at her husband and son.

"And did you have a good talk over everything with Prince Fyodor?" Natasha was saying.

"Yes, capital."

"You see, he holds his head up" (Natasha meant the baby). "Oh, what a fright he gave me. And did you see the princess? Is it true that she is in love with that . . ."

"Yes, can you fancy . . ."

At that moment Nikolay came in with his wife. Pierre, not letting go of his son, stooped down, kissed them, and answered their inquiries. But it was obvious that in spite of the many interesting things they had to discuss, the baby, with the wobbling head in the little cap, was absorbing Pierre's whole attention.

"How sweet he is!" said Countess Marya, looking at the baby and playing with him. "That's a thing I can't understand, Nikolay," she said, turning to her husband, "how it is you don't feel the charm of these exquisite little creatures?"

"Well, I don't, I can't," said Nikolay, looking coldly at the baby. "Just a morsel of flesh. Come along, Pierre."

"The great thing is, that he is really a devoted father," said Countess Marya, apologising for her husband, "but only after a year or so . . ."

"Oh, Pierre is a capital nurse," said Natasha; "he says his hand is just made for a baby's back. Just look."

"Oh yes, but not for this," Pierre cried laughing, and hurriedly snatching up the baby, he handed him back to his nurse.

XII

As in every real family, there were several quite separate worlds living together in the Bleak Hills house, and while each of these preserved its own individuality, they made concessions to one another, and mixed into one harmonious whole. Every event that occurred in the house was alike important and joyful or distressing to all those circles. But each circle had its own private grounds for rejoicing or mourning at every event quite apart from the rest.

So Pierre's arrival was a joyful and important event, reflected as such in all the circles of the household.

The servants, the most infallible judges of their masters, because they judge them, not from their conversation and expression of their feelings, but from their actions and their manner of living, were delighted at Pierre's return, because they knew that when he was there, the count, their master, would not go out every day to superintend the peasants on the estate, and would be in better temper and spirits, and also because they knew there would be valuable presents for all of them for the fête day.

The children and their governesses were delighted at Bezuhov's return, because no one drew them into the general social life of the house as Pierre did. He it was who could play on the clavichord that écossaise (his one piece), to which, as he said, one could dance all possible dances; and he was quite sure, too, to have brought all of them presents.

Nikolinka Bolkonsky, who was now a thin, delicate, intelligent boy of fifteen, with curly light hair and beautiful eyes, was delighted because Uncle Pierre, as he called him, was the object of his passionate love and adoration. No one had instilled a particular affection for Pierre into Nikolinka, and he only rarely saw him. Countess Marya, who had brought him up, had done her utmost to make Nikolinka love her husband, as she loved him; and the boy did like his uncle, but there was a scarcely perceptible shade of contempt in his liking of him. Pierre he adored. He did not want to be an hussar or a Cavalier of St. George like his Uncle Nikolay; he wanted to be learned, clever, and kind like Pierre. In Pierre's presence there was always a happy radiance on his face, and he blushed and was breathless when Pierre addressed him. He never missed a word that Pierre uttered, and afterwards alone or with Dessalle recalled every phrase, and pondered its exact significance. Pierre's past life, his unhappiness before 1812 (of which, from the few words he had heard, he had made up a vague, romantic picture), his adventures in Moscow, and captivity with the French, Platon Karataev (of whom he had heard from Pierre), his love for Natasha (whom the boy loved too with quite a special feeling), and, above all, his friendship with his father, whom Nikolinka did not remember, all made Pierre a hero and a saint in his eyes.

From the phrases he had heard dropped about his father and Natasha, from the emotion with which Pierre spoke of him, and the circumspect, reverent tenderness with which Natasha spoke of him, the boy, who was only just beginning to form his conceptions of love, had gathered the idea that his father had loved Natasha, and had bequeathed her at his death to his friend. That father, of whom the boy had no memory, seemed to him a divine being, of whom one could have no clear conception, and of whom he could not think without a throbbing heart and tears of sorrow and rapture.

And so the boy too was happy at Pierre's arrival.

The guests in the house were glad to see Pierre, for he was a person who always enlivened every party, and made its different elements mix well together.

The grown-up members of the household were glad to see a friend who always made daily life run more smoothly and easily.

The old ladies were pleased both at the presents he brought them, and still more at Natasha's being herself again.

Pierre felt the various views those different sets of people took of him, and made haste to satisfy the expectations of all of them.

Though he was the most absent-minded and forgetful of men, by the help of a list his wife made for him, he had bought everything, not forgetting a single commission from his mother-in-law or brother-in-law, nor the presents of a dress for Madame Byelov and toys for his nephews.

In the early days of his married life his wife's expectation that he should forget nothing he had undertaken to buy had struck him as strange, and he had been impressed by her serious chagrin when after his first absence he had returned having forgotten everything. But in time he had grown used to this. Knowing that Natasha gave him no commissions on her own account, and for others only asked him to get things when he had himself offered to do so, he now took a childish pleasure, that was a surprise to himself, in those purchases of presents for all the household, and never forgot anything. If he incurred Natasha's censure now, it was only for buying too much, and paying too much for his purchases. To her other defects in the eyes of the world—good qualities in Pierre's eyes—her untidiness and negligence, Natasha added that of stinginess.

Ever since Pierre had begun living a home life, involving increased expenses in a large house, he had noticed to his astonishment that he was spending half what he had spent in the past, and that his circumstances, somewhat straitened latterly, especially by his first wife's debts, were beginning to improve.

Living was much cheaper, because his life was coherent; the most expensive luxury in his former manner of life, that is, the possibility of a complete change in it at any moment, Pierre had not now, and had no desire for. He felt that his manner of life was settled now once for all till death; that to change it was not in his power, and therefore that manner of life was cheaper.

With a beaming, smiling countenance, Pierre was unpacking his purchases.

"Look!" he said, unfolding a piece of material like a shopman. Natasha was sitting opposite him with her eldest girl on her knee, and she turned her sparkling eyes from her husband to what he was showing her.

"That's for Madame Byelov? Splendid." She touched it to feel the goodness of the material. "It must have been a rouble a yard?"

Pierre mentioned the price.

"Very dear," said Natasha. "Well, how pleased the children will be and *maman* too. Only you shouldn't have bought me this," she added, unable to suppress a smile, as she admired the gold and pearl comb, of a pattern just then coming into fashion.

"Adèle kept on at me to buy it," said Pierre.

"When shall I wear it?" Natasha put it in her coil of hair. "It will do when I have to bring little Masha out; perhaps they will come in again then. Well, let us go in."

And gathering up the presents, they went first into the nursery, and then in to see the countess.

The countess, as her habit was, was sitting playing patience with Madame Byelov when Pierre and Natasha went into the drawing-room with parcels under their arms.

The countess was by now over sixty. Her hair was completely grey, and she wore a cap that surrounded her whole face with a frill. Her face was wrinkled, her upper lip had sunk, and her eyes were dim.

After the deaths of her son and her husband that had followed so quickly on one another, she had felt herself a creature accidentally forgotten in this world, with no object and no interest in life. She ate and drank, slept and lay awake, but she did not live. Life gave her no impressions. She wanted nothing from life but peace, and that peace she could find only in death. But until death came to her she had to go on living—that is, using her vital forces. There was in the highest degree noticeable in her what may be observed in very small children and in very old people. No external aim could be seen in her existence; all that could be seen was the need to exercise her various capacities and propensities. She had to eat, to sleep, to think, to talk, to weep, to work, to get angry, and so on, simply because she had a stomach, a brain, muscles, nerves, and spleen. All this she did, not at the promptings of any external motive, as people do in the full vigour of life, when the aim towards which they strive screens from our view that other aim of exercising their powers. She only talked because she needed to exercise her lungs and her tongue. She cried like a child, because she needed the physical relief of tears, and so on. What for people in their full vigour is a motive, with her was obviously a pretext.

Thus in the morning, especially if she had eaten anything too rich the night before, she sought an occasion for anger, and pitched on the first excuse—the deafness of Madame Byelov.

From the other end of the room she would begin to say something to her in a low voice.

"I fancy it is warmer to-day, my dear," she would say in a whisper. And when Madame Byelov replied: "To be sure, they have come," she would mutter angrily: "Mercy on us, how deaf and stupid she is!"

Another excuse was her snuff, which she fancied either too dry, or too moist, or badly pounded. After these outbursts of irritability, a bilious hue came into her face. And her maids knew by infallible tokens when Madame Byelov would be deaf again, and when her snuff would again be damp, and her face would again be yellow. Just as she had to exercise her spleen, she had sometimes to exercise her remaining faculties; and for thought the pretext was patience. When she wanted to cry, the subject of her tears was the late count. When she needed excitement, the subject was Nikolay and anxiety about his health. When she wanted to say something spiteful, the pretext was the Countess Marya. When she required exercise for her organs of speech—this was usually about seven o'clock, after she had had her after-dinner rest in a darkened room —then the pretext was found in repetition of anecdotes, always the same, and always to the same listeners.

The old countess's condition was understood by all the household, though no one ever spoke of it, and every possible effort was made by every one to satisfy her requirements. Only rarely a mournful half-smile passed between Nikolay, Pierre, Natasha, and Countess Marya that betrayed their comprehension of her condition.

But those glances said something else besides. They said that she had done her work in life already, that she was not all here in what was seen in her now, that they would all be the same, and that they were glad to give way to her, to restrain themselves for the sake of this poor creature, once so dear, once as full of life as they. *Memento mori,* said those glances.

Only quite heartless and stupid people and little children failed to understand this, and held themselves aloof from her.

XIII

WHEN Pierre and his wife came into the drawing-room, the countess happened to be in her customary condition of needing the mental exercise of a game of patience, and therefore, although from habit she uttered the words, she always repeated on the return of Pierre or her son after absence: "It was high time, high time, my dear boy; we have been expecting you a long while. Well, thank God, you are here." And on the presents being given her, pronounced another stock phrase: "It's not the gift that is precious, my dear. . . . Thank you for thinking of an old woman like me. . . ." It was evident that Pierre's entrance at that moment was unwelcome, because it interrupted her in dealing her cards. She finished her game of patience, and only then gave her attention to the presents. The presents for her consisted of a card-case of fine

workmanship, a bright blue Sèvres cup with a lid and a picture of shep-
herdesses on it, and a gold snuff-box with the count's portrait on it,
which Pierre had had executed by a miniature-painter in Petersburg.
The countess had long wished to have this; but just now she had no inclination to weep, and so she looked unconcernedly at the portrait, and
took more notice of the card-case.

"Thank you, my dear, you are a comfort to me," she said, as she always did. "But best of all, you have brought yourself back. It has been
beyond everything; you must really scold your wife. She is like one
possessed without you. She sees nothing, thinks of nothing," she said as
usual. "Look, Anna Timofyevna," she added, "what a card-case my son
has brought us."

Madame Byelov admired the present, and was enchanted with the
dress material.

Pierre, Natasha, Nikolay, Countess Marya, and Denisov had a great
deal they wanted to talk about, which was not talked of before the old
countess; not because anything was concealed from her, but simply
because she had dropped so out of things, that if they had begun to
talk freely before her they would have had to answer so many questions
put by her at random, and to repeat so many things that had been
repeated to her so many times already; to tell her that this person was
dead and that person was married, which she could never remember.
Yet they sat as usual at tea in the drawing-room, and Pierre answered
the countess's quite superfluous questions, which were of no interest
even to her, and told her that Prince Vassily was looking older, and that
Countess Marya Alexeyevna sent her kind regards and remembrances,
etc.

Such conversation, of no interest to any one, but inevitable, was kept
up all tea-time. All the grown-up members of the family were gathered
about the round tea-table with the samovar, at which Sonya presided.
The children with their tutors and governesses had already had tea, and
their voices could be heard in the next room. At tea every one sat in
his own habitual place. Nikolay sat by the stove at a little table
apart, where his tea was handed him. An old terrier bitch, with a perfectly grey face, Milka, the daughter of the first Milka, lay on a chair
beside him. Denisov, with streaks of grey in his curly hair, moustaches,
and whiskers, wearing his general's coat unbuttoned, sat beside Countess Marya. Pierre was sitting between his wife and the old countess. He
was telling what he knew might interest the old lady and be intelligible
to her. He talked of external social events and of the persons who had
once made up the circle of the old countess's contemporaries, and had
once been a real living circle of people, but were now for the most part
scattered about the world, and, like her, living out their remnant of life,
gleaning up the stray ears of what they had sown in life. But they, these
contemporaries, seemed to the old countess to make up the only real
world that was worth considering. By Pierre's eagerness, Natasha saw
that his visit had been an interesting one, that he was longing to tell
them about it, but dared not speak freely before the countess. Denisov,

not being a member of the family, did not understand Pierre's circum-spectness, and, moreover, being dissatisfied with the course of events, took a very great interest in all that was going forward at Petersburg. He was continually trying to get Pierre to tell him about the recent scandal about the Semyonovsky regiment, or about Araktcheev, or about the Bible Society. Pierre was sometimes led on into beginning to talk about those subjects, but Nikolay and Natasha always brought him back to the health of Prince Ivan and Countess Marya Antonovna.

"Well, what is all this idiocy, Gossner and Madame Tatarinov," Denisov asked, "is that still going on?"

"Going on?" said Pierre. "Worse than ever. The Bible Society is now the whole government."

"What is that, *mon cher ami?*" asked the old countess, who, having drunk her tea, was obviously seeking a pretext for ill-humour after tak-ing food. "What are you saying about the government? I don't under-stand that."

"Why, you know, *maman,*" put in Nikolay, who knew how to trans-late things into his mother's language. "Prince Alexander Nikolaevitch Golitsin had founded a society, so he has great influence they say."

"Araktcheev and Golitsin," said Pierre incautiously, "are practically the government now. And what a government! They see conspiracy in everything, they are afraid of everything."

"What, Prince Alexander Nikolaevitch found fault with! He is a most estimable man. I used to meet him in old days at Marya Anton-ovna's," said the countess in an aggrieved tone. And still more aggrieved by the general silence, she went on, "Nowadays people find fault with every one. A Gospel Society, what harm is there in that?" and she got up (every one rose too), and with a severe face sailed out to her table in the adjoining divan-room.

In the midst of the mournful silence that followed, they heard the sound of children's voices and laughter from the next room. There was evidently some joyful excitement afoot among the children.

"Finished, finished!" the gleeful shriek of little Natasha was heard above all the rest. Pierre exchanged glances with Countess Marya and Nikolay (Natasha he was looking at all the time), and he smiled hap-pily.

"Delightful music!" he said.

"Anna Makarovna has finished her stocking," said Countess Marya.

"Oh, I'm going to have a look at them," said Pierre, jumping up. "You know," he said, stopping at the door, "why it is I so particularly love that music—it is what first lets me know that all's well. As I came to-day, the nearer I got to home, the greater my panic. As I came into the vestibule, I heard Andryusha in peals of laughter, and then I knew all was well . . ."

"I know, I know that feeling," Nikolay chimed in. "I mustn't come —the stockings are a surprise in store for me."

Pierre went into the children, and the shrieks and laughter were louder than ever. "Now, Anna Makarovna," cried Pierre's voice, "here in the middle of the room and at the word of command—one, two, and when I say three, you stand here. You in my arms. Now, one, two . . ." there was complete silence. "Three!" and an enthusiastic roar of children's voices rose in the room. "Two, two!" cried the children.

They meant the two stockings, which, by a secret only known to her, Anna Makarovna used to knit on her needles at once. She always made a solemn ceremony of pulling one stocking out of the other in the presence of the children when the pair was finished.

XIV

Soon after this the children came in to say good-night. The children kissed every one, the tutors and governesses said good-night and went away. Dessalle alone remained with his pupil. The tutor whispered to his young charge to come downstairs.

"No, M. Dessalle, I will ask my aunt for leave to stay," Nikolinka Bolkonsky answered, also in a whisper.

"*Ma tante*, will you let me stay?" said Nikolinka, going up to his aunt. His face was full of entreaty, excitement, and enthusiasm. Countess Marya looked at him and turned to Pierre.

"When you are here, there is no tearing him away . . ." she said.

"I will bring him directly, M. Dessalle. Good-night," said Pierre, giving his hand to the Swiss tutor, and he turned smiling to Nikolinka. "We have not seen each other at all yet. Marie, how like he is growing," he added, turning to Countess Marya.

"Like my father?" said the boy, flushing crimson and looking up at Pierre with rapturous, shining eyes.

Pierre nodded to him, and went on with the conversation that had been interrupted by the children. Countess Marya had some canvas embroidery in her hands; Natasha sat with her eyes fixed on her husband. Nikolay and Denisov got up, asked for pipes, smoked, and took cups of tea from Sonya, still sitting with weary pertinacity at the samovar, and asked questions of Pierre. The curly-headed, delicate boy, with his shining eyes, sat unnoticed by any one in a corner. Turning the curly head and the slender neck above his laydown collar to follow Pierre's movements, he trembled now and then, and murmured something to himself, evidently thrilled by some new and violent emotion.

The conversation turned on the scandals of the day in the higher government circles, a subject in which the majority of people usually find the chief interest of home politics. Denisov, who was dissatisfied with the government on account of his own disappointments in the service, heard with glee of all the follies, as he considered them, that were going on now in Petersburg, and made his comments on Pierre's words in harsh and in cutting phrases.

"In old days you had to be a German to be anybody, nowadays you have to dance with the Tatarinov woman and Madame Krüdner, to read . . . Eckartshausen, and the rest of that crew. Ugh! I would let good old Bonaparte loose again! He would knock all the nonsense out of them. Why, isn't it beyond everything to have given that fellow Schwartz the Semyonovsky regiment?" he shouted.

Though Nikolay had not Denisov's disposition to find everything amiss, he too thought it dignified and becoming to criticise the government, and he believed that the fact, that A. had been appointed minister of such a department, and B. had been made governor of such a province, and the Tsar had said this, and the minister had said that, were all matters of the greatest importance. And he thought it incumbent upon him to take an interest in the subject and to question Pierre about it. So the questions put by Nikolay and Denisov kept the conversation on the usual lines of gossip about the higher government circles.

But Natasha, who knew every thought and expression in her husband, saw that Pierre all the while wanted to lead the conversation into another channel, and to open his heart on his own idea, the idea which he had gone to Petersburg to consult his new friend Prince Fyodor about. She saw too that he could not lead up to this, and she came to the rescue with a question: How had he settled things with Prince Fyodor?

"What was that?" asked Nikolay.

"All the same thing over and over again," said Pierre, looking about him. "Every one sees that things are all going so wrong that they can't be endured, and that it's the duty of all honest men to oppose it to the utmost of their power."

"Why, what can honest men do?" said Nikolay, frowning slightly. "What can be done?"

"Why, this . . ."

"Let us go into the study," said Nikolay.

Natasha, who had a long while been expecting to be fetched to her baby, heard the nurse calling her, and went off to the nursery. Countess Marya went with her. The men went to the study, and Nikolinka Bolkonsky stole in, unnoticed by his uncle, and sat down at the writing-table, in the dark by the window.

"Well, what are you going to do?" said Denisov.

"Everlastingly these fantastic schemes," said Nikolay.

"Well," Pierre began, not sitting down, but pacing the room, and coming to an occasional standstill, lisping and gesticulating rapidly as he talked. "This is the position of things in Petersburg: the Tsar lets everything go. He is entirely wrapped up in this mysticism" (mysticism Pierre could not forgive in anybody now). "All he asks for is peace; and he can only get peace through these men of no faith and no conscience, who are stifling and destroying everything, Magnitsky and Araktcheev, and *tutti quanti* . . . You will admit that if you did not look after your property yourself, and only asked for peace and quiet, the crueller your bailiff were, the more readily you would attain your object," he said, turning to Nikolay.

"Well, but what is the drift of all this?" said Nikolay.

"Why, everything is going to ruin. Bribery in the law-courts, in the army nothing but coercion and drill: exile—people are being tortured, and enlightenment is suppressed. Everything youthful and honourable

—they are crushing! Everybody sees that it can't go on like this. The strain is too great, and the string must snap," said Pierre (as men always do say, looking into the working of any government so long as governments have existed). "I told them one thing in Petersburg."

"Told whom?" asked Denisov.

"Oh, you know whom," said Pierre, with a meaning look from under his brows, "Prince Fyodor and all of them. Zeal in educational and philanthropic work is all very good of course. Their object is excellent and all the rest of it; but in present circumstances what is wanted is something else."

At that moment Nikolay noticed the presence of his nephew. His face fell; he went up to him.

"Why are you here?"

"Oh, let him be," said Pierre, taking hold of Nikolay's arm; and he went on. "That's not enough, I told them; something else is wanted now. While you stand waiting for the string to snap every moment; while every one is expecting the inevitable revolution, as many people as possible should join hands as closely as they can to withstand the general catastrophe. All the youth and energy is being drawn away and dissipated. One lured by women, another by honours, a third by display or money—they are all going over to the wrong side. As for independent, honest men, like you and me—there are none of them left. I say: enlarge the scope of the society: let the *mot d'ordre* be not loyalty only, but independence and action."

Nikolay, leaving his nephew, had angrily moved out a chair, and sat down in it. As he listened to Pierre, he coughed in a dissatisfied way, and frowned more and more.

"But action with what object?" he cried. "And what attitude do you take up to the government?"

"Why, the attitude of supporters! The society will perhaps not even be a secret one, if the government will allow it. So far from being hostile to the government, we are the real conservatives. It is a society of *gentlemen*, in the full significance of the word. It is simply to prevent Pugatchov from coming to massacre my children and yours, to prevent Araktcheev from transporting me to a military settlement, that we are joining hands, with the sole object of the common welfare and security."

"Yes; but it's a secret society, and consequently a hostile and mischievous society, which can only lead to evil."

"Why so? Did the *Tugend-bund* which saved Europe" (people did not yet venture to believe that Russia had saved Europe) "lead to evil? A *Tugend-bund* it is, an alliance of virtue; it is love and mutual help; it is what Christ preached on the cross . . ."

Natasha, coming into the room in the middle of the conversation, looked joyfully at her husband. She was not rejoicing in what he was saying. It did not interest her indeed, because it seemed to her that it was all so excessively simple, and that she had known it long ago. She fancied this, because she knew all that it sprang from—all Pierre's soul. But she was glad looking at his eager, enthusiastic figure.

Pierre was watched with even more rapturous gladness by the boy with the slender neck in the laydown collar, who had been forgotten by all of them. Every word Pierre uttered set his heart in a glow, and his fingers moving nervously, he unconsciously picked up and broke to pieces the sticks of sealing-wax and pens on his uncle's table.

"It's not at all what you imagine, but just such a society as the German *Tugend-bund* is what I propose."

"Well, my boy, that's all very well for the sausage eaters—a *Tugend-bund*—but I don't understand it, and I can't even pronounce it," Denisov's loud, positive voice broke in. "Everything's rotten and corrupt; I agree there; only your *Tugend-bund* I don't understand, but if one is dissatisfied,—a *bunt* now" (*i.e.* riot or mutiny), *"je suis votre homme!"*

Pierre smiled, Natasha laughed; but Nikolay knitted his brows more than ever, and began arguing with Pierre that no revolution was to be expected, and that the danger he talked of had no existence but in his imagination. Pierre maintained his view, and as his intellectual faculties were keener and more resourceful, Nikolay was soon at a loss for an answer. This angered him still more, as in his heart he felt convinced, not by reasoning, but by something stronger than reasoning, of the indubitable truth of his own view.

"Well, let me tell you," he said, getting up and nervously setting his pipe down in the corner, and then flinging it away; "I can't prove it you. You say everything is all rotten, and there will be a revolution; I don't see it; but you say our oath of allegiance is a conditional thing, and as to that, let me tell you, you are my greatest friend, you know that, but you make a secret society, you begin working against the government—whatever it may be, I know it's my duty to obey it. And if Araktcheev bids me march against you with a squadron and cut you down, I shan't hesitate for a second, I shall go. And then you may think what you like about it."

An awkward silence followed these words. Natasha was the first to break it by defending her husband and attacking her brother. Her defence was weak and clumsy. But it attained its object. The conversation was taken up again, and no longer in the unpleasantly hostile tone in which Nikolay's last words had been spoken.

When they all got up to go in to supper, Nikolinka Bolkonsky went up to Pierre with a pale face and shining, luminous eyes.

"Uncle Pierre . . . you . . . no . . . If papa had been alive . . . he would have been on your side?" he asked.

Pierre saw in a flash all the original, complicated and violent travail of thought and feeling that must have been going on independently in this boy during the conversation. And recalling all he had been saying, he felt vexed that the boy should have heard him. He had to answer him, however.

"I believe he would," he said reluctantly, and he went out of the study.

The boy looked down, and then for the first time seemed to become aware of the havoc he had been making on the writing-table. He flushed hotly and went up to Nikolay.

"Uncle, forgive me; I did it—not on purpose," he said, pointing to the fragments of sealing-wax and pens.

Nikolay bounded up angrily. "Very good, very good," he said, throwing the bits of pens and sealing-wax under the table. And with evident effort mastering his fury, he turned away from him.

"You ought not to have been here at all," he said.

XV

AT supper no more was said of politics and societies, but a conversation turned on the subject most agreeable to Nikolay—reminiscences of 1812. Denisov started the talk, and Pierre was particularly cordial and amusing. And the party broke up on the friendliest terms. Nikolay, after undressing in his study, and giving instructions to his steward, who was awaiting him, went in his dressing-gown to his bedroom, and found his wife still at her writing-table: she was writing something.

"What are you writing, Marie?" asked Nikolay. Countess Marya flushed. She was afraid that what she was writing would not be understood and approved by her husband.

She would have liked to conceal what she was writing from him, and at the same time, she was glad he had caught her, and she had to tell him.

"It's my diary, Nikolay," she said, handing him a blue note-book, filled with her firm, bold handwriting.

"A diary!" . . . said Nikolay with a shade of mockery, and he took the note-book. He saw written in French:

"*December* 4.—Andryusha" (their elder boy) "would not be dressed when he waked up this morning, and Mademoiselle Louise sent for me. He was naughty and obstinate. I tried threatening him, but he only got more ill-tempered. Then I undertook to manage him, left him, and helped nurse get the other children up, and told him I did not love him. For a long while he was quiet, as though he were surprised. Then he rushed out to me in his night-shirt, and sobbed so that I could not soothe him for a long while. It was clear that what distressed him most was having grieved me. Then, when I gave him his report in the evening, he cried piteously again as he kissed me. One can do anything with him by tenderness."

"What is his report?" asked Nikolay.

"I have begun giving the elder ones little marks in the evening of how they have behaved."

Nikolay glanced at the luminous eyes watching him, and went on turning over, and read the diary. Everything in the children's lives was noted down in it that seemed to the mother of interest as showing the character of the children, or leading to general conclusions as to methods of bringing them up. It consisted mostly of the most trifling details; but they did not seem so either to the mother or the father, as he now, for the first time, read this record of his children's lives. On the 5th of December there was the note:

"Mitya was naughty at table. Papa said he should have no pudding. He had none; but he looked so miserably and greedily at the others while they were eating. I believe that punishing them by depriving them of sweet things only develops greediness. Must tell Nikolay."

Nikolay put the book down and looked at his wife. The luminous eyes looked at him doubtfully, to see whether he approved or not. There could be no doubt of Nikolay's approval, of his enthusiastic admiration of his wife.

Perhaps there was no need to do it so pedantically; perhaps there was no need of it all, thought Nikolay; but this untiring, perpetual spiritual effort, directed only at the children's moral welfare, enchanted him. If Nikolay could have analysed his feelings, he would have found that the very groundwork of his steady and tender love and pride in his wife was always this feeling of awe at her spirituality, at that elevated moral world that he could hardly enter, in which his wife always lived.

He was proud that she was so clever and so good, recognising his own insignificance beside her in the spiritual world, and he rejoiced the more that she, with her soul, not only belonged to him, but was a part of his very self.

"I quite, quite approve, my darling!" he said, with a significant air. "And," after a brief pause, he added, "And I have behaved badly to-day. You were not in the study. Pierre and I were arguing, and I lost my temper. I couldn't help it. He is such a child. I don't know what would become of him if Natasha didn't keep him at her apron-strings. Can you imagine what he went to Petersburg about? . . . They have made a . . ."

"Yes, I know," said Countess Marya. "Natasha told me."

"Oh, well, you know, then," Nikolay went on, getting hot at the mere recollection of the discussion. "He wants to persuade me that it's the duty of every honest man to work against the government when one's sworn allegiance and duty. . . . I am sorry you were not there. As it was, they all fell upon me, Denisov, and Natasha, too. . . . Natasha is too amusing. We know she twists him round her little finger, but when it comes to discussion—she hasn't an idea to call her own—she simply repeats his words," added Nikolay, yielding to that irresistible impulse that tempts one to criticise one's nearest and dearest. Nikolay was unaware that what he was saying of Natasha might be said word for word of himself in relation to his wife.

"Yes, I have noticed that," said Countess Marya.

"When I told him that duty and sworn allegiance come before everything, he began arguing God knows what. It was a pity you were not there. What would you have said?"

"To my thinking, you were quite right. I told Natasha so. Pierre says that every one is suffering, and being ill-treated and corrupted, and that it's our duty to help our neighbours. Of course, he is right," said Countess Marya; "but he forgets that we have other nearer duties, which God Himself has marked out for us, and that we may run risks for ourselves, but not for our children."

"Yes, yes, that's just what I told him," cried Nikolay, who actually fancied he had said just that. "And they had all their say out about loving one's neighbour, and Christianity, and all the rest of it, before Nikolinka, who had slipped in there, and was pulling all my things to pieces."

"Ah, do you know, Nikolay, I am so often worried about Nikolinka," said Countess Marya. "He is such an exceptional boy. And I am afraid I neglect him for my own. All of us have our children; we all have our own ties; while he has nobody. He is always alone with his thoughts."

"Well, I don't think you have anything to reproach yourself with on his account. Everything the fondest mother could do for her son you have done, and are doing, for him. And of course I am glad you do. He is a splendid boy, splendid! This evening he was lost in a sort of dream listening to Pierre. And only fancy, we got up to go in to supper. I look; and there he has broken everything on my table to fragments, and he told me of it at once I have never known him to tell a fib. He's a splendid boy!" repeated Nikolay, who did not in his heart like Nikolinka, but always felt moved to acknowledge that he was a splendid fellow.

"Still I am not the same as a mother," said Countess Marya. "I feel that it's not the same, and it worries me. He's a wonderful boy; but I am awfully afraid for him. Companionship will be good for him."

"Oh, well, it's not for long; next summer I shall take him to Petersburg," said Nikolay. "Yes, Pierre always was, and always will be, a dreamer," he went on, returning to the discussion in the study, which had evidently worked on his feelings. "Why, what concern is all that of mine—Araktcheev's misdoings, and all the rest of it—what concern was it of mine, when at the time of our marriage I had so many debts that they were going to put me in prison, and a mother who couldn't see it or understand it. And then you, and the children, and my work. It's not for my own pleasure I am from morning to night looking after the men, or in the counting-house. No, I know I must work to comfort my mother, repay you, and not leave my children in beggary, as I was left myself."

Countess Marya wanted to tell him that man does not live by bread alone; that he attached too much importance to this *work*. But she knew that she must not say this, and that it would be useless. She only took his hand and kissed it. He accepted this gesture on his wife's part as a sign of assent and approval of his words, and after a few moments of silent thought he went on thinking aloud.

"Do you know, Marie," he said, "Ilya Mitrofanitch" (this was a steward of his) "was here to-day from the Tambov estate, and he tells me they will give eighty thousand for the forest." And with an eager face Nikolay began talking of the possibility of buying Otradnoe back within a very short time. "Another ten years of life, and I shall leave the children . . . in a capital position."

Countess Marya listened to her husband, and understood all he said to her. She knew that when he was thus thinking aloud, he would sometimes ask what he had been saying, and was vexed when he noticed she had been thinking of something else. But she had to make a great effort to attend, because she did not feel the slightest interest in what he was saying to her. She looked at him, and though she would not exactly think of other things, her feelings were elsewhere. She felt a submissive, tender love for this man, who could never understand all that she understood; and she seemed, for that very reason, to love him the more, with a shade of passionate tenderness. Apart from that feeling, which absorbed her entirely, and prevented her from following the details of her husband's plans, thoughts kept floating through her brain that had nothing in common with what he was saying. She thought of her nephew (what her husband had said of his excitement over Pierre's talk had made a great impression on her), and various traits of his tender, sensitive character rose to her mind; and while she thought of her nephew, she thought, too, of her own children. She did not compare her nephew with her own children, but she compared her own feeling for him, and her feeling for her children, and felt, with sorrow, that in her feeling for Nikolinka there was something wanting.

Sometimes the idea had occurred to her that this difference was due to his age; but she felt guilty towards him, and in her soul vowed to amend, and to do the impossible, that is, in this life, to love her husband, and her children, and Nikolinka, and all her fellow-creatures, as Christ loved men. Countess Marya's soul was always striving towards the infinite, the eternal, and the perfect, and so she could never be at peace. A stern expression came into her face from that hidden, lofty suffering of the spirit, weighed down by the flesh. Nikolay gazed at her. "My God! What will become of us, if she dies, as I dread, when she looks like that?" he thought, and standing before the holy images, he began to repeat his evening prayer.

XVI

NATASHA, as soon as she was alone with her husband, had begun talking too, as only husband and wife can talk, that is, understanding and communicating their thoughts to each other, with extraordinary clearness and rapidity, by a quite peculiar method opposed to all the rules of logic, without the aid of premises, deductions, and conclusions. Natasha was so used to talking to her husband in this fashion that a logical sequence of thought on Pierre's part was to her an infallible symptom of something being out of tune between them. When he began arguing, talking reasonably and calmly, and when she was led on by his example into doing the same, she knew it would infallibly lead to a quarrel.

From the moment they were alone together and Natasha, with wide-open, happy eyes, crept softly up to him and suddenly, swiftly seizing his head, pressed it to her bosom, saying, "Now you're all mine, mine! You shan't escape!" that conversation began that contravened every rule of logic, especially because they talked of several different subjects at once. This discussion of all sorts of things at once, far from hindering clearness of comprehension, was the surest token that they understood one another fully.

As in a dream everything is uncertain, meaningless, and contradictory except the feeling that directs the dream, so in this communion of ideas, apart from every law of reason, what is clear and consecutive is not what is said, but the feeling that prompts the words.

Natasha talked to Pierre of the daily round of existence at her brother's; told him how she had suffered and been half-dead without him; and that she was fonder of Marie than ever, and Marie was better in every way than she was. In saying this Natasha was quite sincere in acknowledging Marie's superiority, but at the same time she expected Pierre to prefer her to Marie and all other women, and now, especially after he had been seeing a great many women in Petersburg, to tell her so anew. In response to Natasha's words, Pierre told her how intolerable he had found the evening parties and dinners with ladies in Petersburg.

"I have quite lost the art of talking to ladies," he said; "it was horribly tiresome. Especially as I was so busy."

Natasha looked intently at him, and went on. "Marie, now she is wonderful!" she said. "The insight she has into children. She seems to see straight into their souls. Yesterday, for instance, Mitenka was naughty . . ."

"And isn't he like his father?" Pierre put in.

Natasha knew why he made this remark about Mitenka's likeness to Nikolay. He disliked the thought of his dispute with his brother-in-law, and was longing to hear what she thought about it.

"It's a weakness of Nikolay's, that if anything is not generally accepted, he will never agree with it. And I see that that's just what you value to *ouvrir une carrière*," she said, repeating a phrase Pierre had once uttered.

"No, the real thing is that to Nikolay," said Pierre, "thoughts and ideas are an amusement, almost a pastime. Here he's forming a library and has made it a rule not to buy a new book till he has read through the last he has bought—Sismondi and Rousseau and Montesquieu," Pierre added with a smile. "You know how I——," he was beginning to soften his criticism; but Natasha interrupted, giving him thereby to understand that that was not necessary.

"So you say ideas to him are not serious . . ."

"Yes, and to me nothing else is serious. All the while I was in Petersburg, I seemed to be seeing every one in a dream. When I am absorbed by an idea, nothing else is serious."

"Oh, what a pity I didn't see your meeting with the children," said Natasha. "Which was the most pleased? Liza, of course?"

"Yes," said Pierre, and he went on with what interested him. "Niko-lay says we ought not to think. But I can't help it. To say nothing of the fact (I can say so to you) that in Petersburg I felt that the whole thing would go to pieces without me, every one pulled his own way. But I succeeded in bringing them all together; and then my idea is so clear and simple. I don't say we ought to work against so and so. We may be mistaken. But I say: let those join hands who care for the good cause, and let our one standard be energy and honesty. Prince Sergey is a capital fellow, and clever."

Natasha would have had no doubt that Pierre's idea was a grand idea, but that one thing troubled her. It was his being her husband. "Is it possible that a man of such value, of such importance to society, is at the same time my husband? How can it have happened?" She wanted to express this doubt to him. "Who are the persons who could decide positively whether he is so much cleverer than all of them?" she won-dered, and she went over in imagination the people who were very much respected by Pierre. There was nobody whom, to judge by his own ac-count, he had respected so much as Platon Karataev.

"Do you know what I am thinking about?" she said. "About Platon Karataev. What would he have said? Would he have approved of you now?"

Pierre was not in the least surprised at this question. He understood the connection of his wife's ideas.

"Platon Karataev?" he said, and he pondered, evidently trying sin-cerely to picture what Karataev's judgment would have been on the subject. "He would not have understood, and yet, perhaps, he would."

"I like you awfully!" said Natasha all at once. "Awfully! awfully!"

"No, he wouldn't have approved," said Pierre, musing. "What he would have approved of is our home life. He did so like to see seemli-ness, happiness, peace in everything, and I could have shown him all of us with pride. You talk about separation. But you would not believe what a special feeling I have for you after separation . . ."

"And, besides, . . ." Natasha was beginning.

"No, not so. I never leave off loving you. And one couldn't love more; but it's something special. . . ." He did not finish, because their eyes meeting said the rest.

"What nonsense," said Natasha suddenly, "it all is about the honey-moon and that the greatest happiness is at first. On the contrary, now is much the best. If only you wouldn't go away. Do you remember how we used to quarrel? And I was always in the wrong. It was always my do-ing. And what we quarrelled about—I don't remember even."

"Always the same thing," said Pierre smiling. "Jea . . ."

"Don't say it, I can't bear it," cried Natasha, and a cold, vindictive light gleamed in her eyes. "Did you see her?" she added after a pause.

"No; and if I had, I shouldn't have known her."

They were silent.

"Oh! do you know, when you were talking in the study, I was look-ing at you," said Natasha, obviously trying to drive away the cloud that had come between them. "And do you know you are as like him as two drops of water, like the boy." That was what she called her baby son. "Ah, it's time I went to him. . . . But I am sorry to go away."

They were both silent for some seconds. Then all at once, at the same moment, they turned to each other and began talking. Pierre was beginning with self-satisfaction and enthusiasm, Natasha with a soft, happy smile. Interrupting each other, both stopped, waiting for the other to go on.

"No, what is it? Tell me, tell me."

"No, you tell me, it wasn't anything, only nonsense," said Natasha.

Pierre said what he had been going to say. It was the sequel to his complacent reflections on his success in Petersburg. It seemed to him at that moment that he was destined to give a new direction to the progress of the whole of Russian society and of the whole world.

"I only meant to say that all ideas that have immense results are always simple. All my idea really is that if vicious people are united and form a power, honest men must do the same. It's so simple, you see."

"Yes."

"But what were you going to say?"

"Oh, nothing, nonsense."

"No, say it though."

"Oh, nothing, only silly nonsense," said Natasha, breaking into a more beaming smile than ever. "I was only going to tell you about Petya. Nurse came up to take him from me to-day, he laughed and puckered up his face and squeezed up to me—I suppose he thought he was hiding. He's awfully sweet. . . . There he is crying. Well, good-bye!" and she ran out of the room.

Meanwhile, below in Nikolinka Bolkonsky's bedroom a lamp was burning as usual (the boy was afraid of the dark and could not be cured of this weakness). Dessalle was asleep with his head high on his four pillows, and his Roman nose gave forth rhythmic sounds of snoring. Nikolinka had just waked up in a cold sweat, and was sitting up in bed, gazing with wide-open eyes straight before him. He had been waked by a fearful dream. In his dream his Uncle Pierre and he in helmets, such as appeared in the illustrations in his Plutarch, were marching at the head of an immense army. This army was made up of slanting, white threads that filled the air like those spider-webs that float in autumn and that Dessalle used to call *le fil de la Vierge*. Ahead of them was glory, which was something like those threads too, only somewhat more opaque. They—he and Pierre—were flying lightly and happily nearer and nearer to their goal. All at once the threads that moved them seemed to grow weak and tangled; and it was all difficult. And Uncle Nikolay stood before them in a stern and menacing attitude.

"Have you done this?" he said, pointing to broken pens and sticks of sealing-wax. "I did love you, but Araktcheev has bidden me, and I will kill the first that moves forward."

Nikolinka looked round for Pierre; but Pierre was not there. Instead of Pierre, there was his father—Prince Andrey—and his father had no shape or form, but he was there; and seeing him, Nikolinka felt the weakness of love; he felt powerless, limp, and relaxed. His father caressed him and pitied him, but his Uncle Nikolay was moving down upon them, coming closer and closer. A great horror came over Nikolinka, and he waked up.

"My father!" he thought. (Although there were two very good portraits of Prince Andrey in the house, Nikolinka never thought of his father in human form.) "My father has been with me, and has caressed me. He approved of me; he approved of Uncle Pierre. Whatever he might tell me, I would do it. Mucius Scaevola burnt his hand. But why should not the same sort of thing happen in my life? I know they want me to study. And I am going to study. But some day I shall have finished, and then I will act. One thing only I pray God for, that the same sort of thing may happen with me as with Plutarch's men, and I will act in the same way. I will do more. Every one shall know of me, shall love me, and admire me." And all at once Nikolinka felt his breast heaving with sobs, and he burst into tears.

"Are you ill?" he heard Dessalle's voice.

"No," answered Nikolinka, and he lay back on his pillow. "How good and kind he is; I love him!" He thought of Dessalle. "But Uncle Pierre! Oh, what a wonderful man! And my father? Father! Father! Yes, I will do something that even *he* would be content with . . ."

PART TWO

I

THE SUBJECT of history is the life of peoples and of humanity. To catch and pin down in words—that is, to describe directly the life, not only of humanity, but even of a single people, appears to be impossible.

All the ancient historians employed the same method for describing and catching what is seemingly elusive—that is, the life of a people. They described the career of individual persons ruling peoples; and their activity was to them an expression of the activity of the whole people.

The questions, In what way individual persons made nations act in accordance with their will, and by what the will of those individuals themselves was controlled, the ancients answered, By the will of God; which in the first case made the nation subject to the will of one chosen person, and, in the second, guided the will of that chosen monarch to the ordained end.

For the ancients these questions were solved by faith in the immediate participation of the Deity in the affairs of mankind.

Modern history has theoretically rejected both those positions. One would have thought that rejecting the convictions of the ancients of men's subjection to the Deity, and of a defined goal to which nations are led, modern history should have studied, not the manifestations of power, but the causes that go to its formation. But modern history has not done that. While in theory rejecting the views of the ancients, it follows them in practice.

Instead of men endowed with divine authority and directly led by the will of the Deity, modern history has set up either heroes, endowed with extraordinary, superhuman powers, or simply men of the most varied characteristics, from monarchs to journalists, who lead the masses. Instead of the old aim, the will of the Deity, that to the old historians seemed the end of the movements of peoples, such as the Gauls, the Greeks, and the Romans, modern history has advanced aims of its own —the welfare of the French, the German, or the English people, or its highest pitch of generalisation, the civilisation of all humanity, by which is usually meant the peoples inhabiting a small, northwestern corner of the great mother-earth.

Modern history has rejected the faiths of the ancients, without putting any new conviction in their place; and the logic of the position has forced the historians, leaving behind them the rejected, divine right of kings and fate of the ancients, to come back by a different path to the same point again: to the recognition, that is (1) that peoples are led by individual persons; and (2) that there is a certain goal towards which humanity and the peoples constituting it are moving.

In all the works of the more modern historians, from Gibbon to Buckle, in spite of their apparent differences and the apparent novelty of their views, these two old inevitable positions lie at the basis of the argument.

In the first place the historian describes the conduct of separate persons who, in his opinion, lead humanity (one regards as such only monarchs, military generals, and ministers of state; another includes besides monarchs, orators, scientific men, reformers, philosophers, and poets). Secondly, the goal towards which humanity is being led is known to the historian. To one this goal is the greatness of the Roman, or the Spanish, or the French state; for another, it is freedom, equality, a certain sort of civilisation in a little corner of the world called Europe.

In 1789 there was a ferment in Paris: it grew and spread, and found expression in the movement of peoples from west to east. Several times that movement is made to the east, and comes into collision with a counter-movement from east westwards. In the year 1812 it reaches its furthest limit, Moscow, and then, with a remarkable symmetry, the counter-movement follows from east to west; drawing with it, like the first movement, the peoples of Central Europe. The counter-movement reaches the starting-point of the first movement—Paris—and subsides.

During this period of twenty years an immense number of fields are not tilled; houses are burned; trade changes its direction; millions of men grow poor and grow rich, and change their habitations; and millions of Christians, professing the law of love, murder one another.

What does all this mean? What did all this proceed from? What induced these people to burn houses and to murder their fellow-creatures? What were the causes of these events? What force compelled men to act in this fashion? These are the involuntary and most legitimate questions that, in all good faith, humanity puts to itself when it stumbles on memorials and traditions of that past age of restlessness.

To answer these questions the common-sense of humanity turns to the science of history, the object of which is the self-knowledge of nations and of humanity.

Had history retained the view of the ancients, it would have said: The Deity, to reward or to punish His People, gave Napoleon power, and guided his will for the attainment of His own divine ends. And that answer would have been complete and clear. One might believe or disbelieve in the divine significance of Napoleon. For one who believed in it, all the history of that period would have been comprehensible, and there would have been nothing contradictory in it.

But modern history cannot answer in that way. Science does not accept the view of the ancients as to the direct participation of the Deity in the affairs of mankind, and therefore must give other answers.

Modern history, in answer to these questions, says: "You want to know what this movement means, what it arose from, and what force produced these events? Listen.

"Louis XIV. was a very haughty and self-willed man; he had such and such mistresses, and such and such ministers, and he governed France badly. Louis's successors, too, were weak men, and they, too, governed France badly. And they had such and such favourites, and such and such mistresses. Moreover, there were certain men writing books at this period. At the end of the eighteenth century there were some two dozen men in Paris who began to talk all about men being equal and free. This led people all over France to fall to hewing and hacking at each other. These people killed the king and a great many more. At that time there was in France a man of genius—Napoleon. He conquered every one everywhere, that is, he killed a great many people, because he was a very great genius. And for some reason he went to kill the Africans; and killed them so well, and was so cunning and clever, that on returning to France he bade every one obey him. And they all did obey him. After being made Emperor he went to kill people in Italy, Austria, and Prussia. And there, too, he killed a great many. In Russia there was an Emperor, Alexander, who was resolved to re-establish order in Europe, and so made war with Napoleon. But in 1807 he suddenly made friends with him, and in 1811 he quarrelled again, and again they began killing a great many people. And Napoleon took six hundred thousand men into Russia, and conquered Moscow, and then he suddenly ran away out of Moscow, and then the Emperor Alexander, aided by the counsels of Stein and others, united Europe for defence against the destroyer of her peace. All Napoleon's allies suddenly became his enemies; and the united army advanced against the fresh troops raised by Napoleon. The allies vanquished Napoleon; entered Paris; forced Napoleon to abdicate, and sent him to the island of Elba, not depriving him, however, of the dignity of Emperor, showing him, in fact, every respect, although five years before, and one year later, he was regarded by every one as a brigand outside the pale of the law. And Louis XVIII., who, till then, had been a laughing-stock to the French and the allies, began to reign. Napoleon shed tears before the Old Guard, abdicated the throne, and went into exile. Then the subtle, political people and diplomatists (conspicuous among them Talleyrand, who succeeded in sitting down in a particular chair before any one else, and thereby extended the frontiers of France) had conversations together at Vienna, and by these conversations made nations happy or unhappy. All at once the diplomatists and monarchs all but quarrelled; they were on the point of again commanding their armies to kill one another; but at that time Napoleon entered France with a battalion, and the French, who had been hating him, at once submitted to him. But the allied monarchs were angry at this, and again went to war with the French. And the genius, Napoleon, was conquered; and suddenly recognising that he was a brigand, they took him to the island of St. Helena. And on that rock the exile, parted from the friends of his heart, and from his beloved France, died a lingering death, and bequeathed all his great deeds to posterity. And in Europe the reaction followed, and all the sovereigns began oppressing their subjects again."

It would be quite a mistake to suppose that this is mockery—a caricature of historical descriptions. On the contrary, it is a softened-down picture of the contradictory and random answers, that are no answers, given by *all* history, from the compilers of memoirs and of histories of separate states to general histories, and the new sort of histories of the *culture* of that period.

What is strange and comic in these answers is due to the fact that modern history is like a deaf man answering questions which no one has asked him.

If the aim of history is the description of the movement of humanity and of nations, the first question which must be answered, or all the rest remains unintelligible, is the following: What force moves nations? To meet this question modern history carefully relates that Napoleon was a very great genius, and that Louis XIV. was very haughty, or that certain writers wrote certain books.

All this may very well be so, and humanity is ready to acquiesce in it; but it is not what it asks about. All that might be very interesting if we recognised a divine power, based on itself and always alike, guiding its peoples through Napoleons, Louis', and writers; but we do not acknowledge such a power, and therefore before talking about Napoleons, and Louis', and great writers, we must show the connection existing between those persons and the movement of the nations. If another force is put in the place of the divine power, then it should be explained what that force consists of, since it is precisely in that force that the whole interest of history lies.

History seems to assume that this force is taken for granted of itself, and is known to every one. But in despite of every desire to admit this new force as known, any one who reads through very many historical works cannot but doubt whether this new force, so differently understood by the historians themselves, is perfectly well known to every one.

II

WHAT is the force that moves nations?

Biographical historians, and historians writing of separate nations, understand this force as a power residing in heroes and sovereigns. According to their narratives, the events were entirely due to the wills of Napoleons, of Alexanders, or, generally speaking, of those persons who form the subject of historical memoirs. The answers given by historians of this class to the question as to the force which brings about events are satisfactory, but only so long as there is only one historian for any event. But as soon as historians of different views and different nationalities begin describing the same event, the answers given by them immediately lose all their value, as this force is understood by them, not only differently, but often in absolutely opposite ways. One historian asserts that an event is due to the power of Napoleon; another maintains that it is produced by the power of Alexander; a third ascribes it to the influence of some third person. Moreover, historians of this class contradict one another even in their explanation of the force on which the influence of the same person is based. Thiers, a Bonapartist, says that Napoleon's power rested on his virtue and his genius; Lanfrey, a Republican, declares that it rested on his duplicity and deception of the people. So that historians of this class, mutually destroying each other's position, at the same time destroy the conception of the force producing events, and give no answer to the essential question of history.

Writers of universal history, who have to deal with all the nations at once, appear to recognise the incorrectness of the views of historians of separate countries as to the force that produces events. They do not recognise this force as a power pertaining to heroes and sovereigns, but regard it as the resultant of many forces working in different directions. In describing a war on the subjugation of a people, the writer of general history seeks the cause of the event, not in the power of one person, but in the mutual action on one another of many persons connected with the event.

The power of historical personages conceived as the product of several forces, according to this view, can hardly, one would have supposed, be regarded as a self-sufficient force independently producing events. Yet writers of general history do in the great majority of cases employ the conception of power again as a self-sufficient force producing events and standing in the relation of cause to them. According to their exposition now the historical personage is the product of his time, and his power is only the product of various forces, now his power is the force producing events. Gervinus, Schlosser, for instance, and others, in one place, explain that Napoleon is the product of the Revolution, of the ideas of 1789, and so on; and in another plainly state that the campaign of 1812 and other events not to their liking are simply the work of Napoleon's wrongly directed will, and that the very ideas of 1789 were arrested in their development by Napoleon's arbitrary rule. The ideas of the Revolution, the general temper of the age produced Napoleon's power. The power of Napoleon suppressed the ideas of the Revolution and the general temper of the age.

This strange inconsistency is not an accidental one. It confronts us at every turn, and, in fact, whole works upon universal history are made up of consecutive series of such inconsistencies. This inconsistency is due to the fact that after taking a few steps along the road of analysis, these historians have stopped short halfway.

To find the component forces that make up the composite or resultant force, it is essential that the sum of the component parts should equal the resultant. This condition is never observed by historical writers, and consequently, to explain the resultant force, they must inevitably admit, in addition to those insufficient contributory forces, some further unexplained force that affects also the resultant action.

The historian describing the campaign of 1813, or the restoration of the Bourbons, says bluntly that these events were produced by the will of Alexander. But the philosophic historian Gervinus, controverting the view of the special historian of those events, seeks to prove that the campaign of 1813 and the restoration of the Bourbons was due not only to Alexander, but also to the work of Stein, Metternich, Madame de Staël, Talleyrand, Fichte, Chateaubriand, and others. The historian obviously analyses the power of Alexander into component forces. Talleyrand, Chateaubriand, and so on, and the sum of these component forces, that is, the effect on one another of Chateaubriand, Talleyrand, Madame de Staël, and others is obviously not equal to the resultant effect, that is, the phenomenon of millions of Frenchmen submitting to the Bourbons. Such and such words being said to one another by Chateaubriand, Madame de Staël, and others, only affects their relation to one another, and does not account for the submission of millions. And therefore to explain how the submission of millions followed from their relation to one another, that is, how from component forces equal to a given quantity A, there followed a resultant equal to a thousand times A. the historian is inevitably bound to admit that force of power, which he has renounced, accepting it in the resultant force, that is, he is obliged to admit an unexplained force that acts on the resultant of those components. And this is just what the philosophic historians do. And consequently they not only contradict the writers of historical memoirs, but also contradict themselves.

Country people who have no clear idea of the cause of rain say: The wind has blown away the rain, or the wind is blowing up for rain, according as they are in want of rain or of fair weather. In the same way, philosophic historians at times, when they wish it to be so, when it fits in with their theory, say that power is the result of events; and at times, when they want to prove something else, they say power produces the events.

A third class of historians, the writers of the so-called history of culture, following on the lines laid down by the writers of universal history who sometimes accept writers and ladies as forces producing events, yet understand that force quite differently. They see that force in so-called culture, in intellectual activity. The historians of culture are quite consistent as regards their prototypes—the writers of universal history—for if historical events can be explained by certain persons having said certain things to one another, why not explain them by certain persons having written certain books? Out of all the immense number of tokens that accompany every living phenomenon, these historians select the symptom of intellectual activity, and assert that this symptom is the cause. But in spite of all their endeavours to prove that the cause of events lies in intellectual activity, it is only by a great stretch that one can agree that there is anything in common between intellectual activity and the movement of peoples. And it is altogether impossible to admit that intellectual activity has guided the actions of men, for such phenomena as the cruel murders of the French Revolution, resulting from the doctrine of the equality of man, and the most wicked wars and massacres arising from the Gospel of love, do not confirm this hypothesis.

But even admitting that all the cunningly woven arguments with which these histories abound are correct, admitting that nations are governed by some indefinite force called an *idea*—the essential question of history still remains unanswered; or to the power of monarchs and the influence of counsellors and other persons, introduced by the philosophic historian, another new force is now joined—the *idea*, the connection of which with the masses demands explanation. One can understand that Napoleon had power and so an event came to pass; with some effort one can even conceive that Napoleon together with other influences was the cause of an event. But in what fashion a book, *Le Contrat Social*, led the French to hack each other to pieces cannot be understood without an explanation of the causal connection of this new force with the event.

There undoubtedly exists a connection between all the people living at one time, and so it is possible to find some sort of connection between the intellectual activity of men and their historical movements, just as one may find a connection between the movements of humanity and commerce, handicrafts, gardening, and anything you like. But why intellectual activity should be conceived of by the historians of culture as the cause or the expression of a whole historical movement, it is hard to understand. Historians can only be led to such a conclusion by the following considerations: (1) That history is written by learned men; and so it is natural and agreeable to them to believe that the pursuit of their calling is the basis of the movement of the whole of humanity, just as a similar belief would be natural and agreeable to merchants, agriculturists, or soldiers (such a belief on their part does not find expression simply because merchants and soldiers don't write history); and (2) that spiritual activity, enlightenment, civilisation, culture, ideas are all vague, indefinite conceptions, under cover of which they can conveniently use phrases having less definite signification, and so easily brought under any theory.

But to say nothing of the inner dignity of histories of this kind (possibly they are of use for some one or for something), the histories of culture, towards which all general histories tend more and more to approximate, are noteworthy from the fact that though they give a serious and detailed analysis of various religious, philosophic, and political doctrines as causes of events, every time they have to describe an actual historical event, as, for instance, the campaign of 1812, they unconsciously describe it as the effect of the exercise of power, frankly saying that that campaign was the work of Napoleon's will. In saying this, the historians of culture unconsciously contradict themselves, to prove that the new force they have invented is not the expression of historical events, and that the sole means of explaining history is by that power which they had apparently rejected.

III

A STEAM-ENGINE moves. The question is asked, How is it moved? A peasant answers, It is the devil moving it. Another man says, The steam-engine moves because the wheels are going round. A third maintains that the cause of the motion is to be found in the smoke floated from it by the wind.

The peasant's contention is irrefutable. To refute him some one must prove to him that there is no devil, or another peasant must explain that it is not a devil, but a German who moves the steamer. Then from their contradictory views they see that both are wrong. But the man who says the cause is the movement of the wheels refutes himself, seeing that having once entered on the path of analysis, he ought to proceed further and further along it; he ought to explain the cause of the wheels moving. And he has not to stop in his search for a cause till he finds the ultimate cause of the movement of the steam-engine in the steam compressed in the boiler. As for the man who explained the movement of the steam-engine as due to the smoke being blown back from it, he has simply noticed that the wheel explanation was insufficient, and pitching on the first accompanying symptom, gave that out as his cause.

The only conception which can explain the movement of the steamer is the conception of a force equal to the movement that is seen.

The only conception by means of which the movements of nations can be explained is a conception of a force equal to the whole movement of the nations.

Yet under this conception there are included by various historians forces of the most various kinds, and all unequal to the movement that is seen. Some see in it a force directly pertaining to heroes, as the peasant sees the devil in the steam-engine. Others, a force resulting from several other forces, like the movement of the wheels; a third class, intellectual influence, like the smoke.

So long as histories are written of individual persons—whether they are Cæsars and Alexanders, or Luthers and Voltaires—and not the history of *all*, without one exception, *all* the people taking part in an event, there is no possibility of describing the movement of humanity without a conception of a force impelling men to direct their activity to one end. And the only conception of this kind familiar to historians is power.

This conception is the sole handle by means of which the material of history, as at present expounded, can be dealt with; and the historian who should, like Buckle, break off this handle, without discovering any other means of dealing with historical material, would only be depriving himself of the last chance of dealing with it. The necessity of the conception of the exercise of power to explain the phenomena of history is most strikingly shown by the very writers of universal history and the history of culture, who, after professedly rejecting the conception of power, inevitably resort to it at every step.

Historical science in relation to the questions of humanity has hitherto been like money in circulation—paper notes and metal coins. The historical memoirs and histories of separate peoples are like paper money. They may pass and be accepted, doing their part without mischief to any one, and even being useful, so long as no question arises as to their value. One has only to forget the question how the will of heroes produces events, and Thiers's histories will be interesting, instructive, and will, moreover, not be devoid of a certain poetry. But just as a doubt of the stability of paper money arises, either because from the ease of making it, too much is put into circulation, or because of a desire to replace it by gold, so a doubt of the real value of history of this kind arises either because too many such histories appear, or because some one in the simplicity of his heart asks: By what force did Napoleon do that?—that is, wishes to change the current paper for the pure gold of a true conception.

The writers of general history and the history of culture are like men who, recognising the inconvenience of paper money, should decide to make instead of paper notes, jingling coin of metal not of the density of gold. And such coin would be jingling coin, and only jingling coin. A paper note might deceive the ignorant; but coin not of precious metal could deceive no one. Just as gold is only gold when it is of value, not only for exchange, but also for use, so the writers of universal history will only prove themselves of real value when they are able to answer the essential question of history: What is power? These historians give contradictory answers to this question, while the historians of culture altogether evade it, answering something quite different. And as counters in imitation of gold can only be used in a community of persons who agree to accept them for gold, or who are ignorant of the true character of gold, so do the historians who do not answer the essential questions of humanity serve for some objects of their own as current coin at the universities and with that crowd of readers—fond of serious reading, as they call it.

IV

SINCE history has abandoned the views of the ancients as to the divine subjection of the will of a people to one chosen vessel, and the subjection of the will of that chosen vessel to the Deity, it cannot take a single step without encountering contradictions. It must choose one of two alternatives: either to return to its old faith in the direct intervention of the Deity in the affairs of humanity; or to find a definite explanation of that force producing historical events that is called power.

To return to the old way is out of the question: the old faith is shattered, and so an explanation must be found of the meaning of power.

Napoleon commanded an army to be raised, and to march out to war. This conception is so familiar to us, we are so accustomed to this idea that the question why six hundred thousand men go out to fight when

Napoleon utters certain words seems meaningless to us. He had the
power, and so the commands he gave were carried out.

This answer is completely satisfactory if we believe that power has
been given him from God. But as soon as we do not accept that, it is
essential to define what this power is of one man over others.

This power cannot be that direct power of the physical ascendency of
a strong creature over a weak one, that ascendency based on the application or the threat of the application of physical force—like the
power of Hercules. Nor can it be based on the ascendency of moral
force, as in the simplicity of their hearts several historians suppose,
maintaining that the leading historical figures are heroes—that is, men
endowed with a special force of soul and mind called genius. This power
cannot be based on the ascendency of moral force; for, to say nothing of
historical heroes, like Napoleon, concerning whose moral qualities opinions greatly differ, history proves to us that neither Louis XI. nor Metternich, who governed millions of men, had any marked characteristics
of moral force, but that they were, on the contrary, in most respects
morally weaker than any one of the millions of men they governed.

If the source of power lies not in the physical and not in the moral
characteristics of the person possessing it, it is evident that the source of
this power must be found outside the person—in those relations in
which the person possessing the power stands to the masses.

That is precisely how power is interpreted by the science of law, that
cash bank of history, that undertakes to change the historical token
money of power for sterling gold.

Power is the combined wills of the masses, transferred by their expressed or tacit consent to the rulers chosen by the masses.

In the domain of the science of law, made up of arguments on how a
state and power ought to be constructed, if it were possible to construct
it, all this is very clear; but in its application to history this definition
of power calls for elucidation.

The science of law regards the state and power, as the ancients regarded fire, as something positively existing. But for history the state
and power are merely phenomena, just as for the physical science of
to-day fire is not an element, but a phenomenon.

From this fundamental difference in the point of view of history and
of the science of law, it comes to pass that the science of law can discuss
in detail how in the scientific writer's opinion power should be organised, and what is power, existing immovable outside the conditions of
time; but to historical questions as to the significance of power, undergoing visible transformation in time, it can give no answer.

If power is the combined will of the masses transferred to their rulers,
is Pugatchov a representative of the will of the masses? If he is not, how
then is Napoleon I. such a representative? Why is it that Napoleon III.,
when he was seized at Boulogne, was a criminal, and afterwards those
who had been seized by him were criminals?

In palace revolutions—in which sometimes two or three persons only

take part—is the will of the masses transferred to a new person? In international relations, is the will of the masses of the people transferred
to their conqueror? In 1808 was the will of the Rhine Alliance league
transferred to Napoleon? Was the will of the mass of the Russian people
transferred to Napoleon in 1809, when our army in alliance with the
French made war upon Austria?

These questions may be answered in three ways: (1) By maintaining
that the will of the masses is always unconditionally delegated over to
that ruler or those rulers whom they have chosen, and that consequently
every rising up of new power, every struggle against the power once
delegated, must be regarded as a contravention of the real power.

Or (2) by maintaining that the will of the masses is delegated to the
rulers, under certain definite conditions, and by showing that all re-
strictions on, conflicts with, and even abolition of power are due to non-
observance of the rulers of those conditions upon which power was delegated to them.

Or (3) by maintaining that the will of the masses is delegated to the
rulers conditionally, but that the conditions are uncertain and undefined, and that the rising up of several authorities, and their conflict and
fall, are due only to the more or less complete fulfilment of the rulers
of the uncertain conditions upon which the will of the masses is transferred from one set of persons to another.

In these three ways do historians explain the relation of the masses
to their rulers.

Some historians—those most distinctively biographers and writers of
memoirs, of whom we have spoken above—failing in the simplicity of
their hearts to understand the question as to the meaning of power,
seem to believe that the combined will of the masses is delegated to historical leaders unconditionally, and therefore, describing any such authority, these historians assume that that authority is the one absolute
and real one, and that every other force, opposing that real authority,
is not authority, but a violation of authority, and unlawful violence.

Their theory fits in well with primitive and peaceful periods of history; but in its application to complicated and stormy periods in the
life of nations, when several different authorities rise up simultaneously
and struggle together, the inconvenience arises that the legitimist historian will assert that the National Assembly, the Directorate, and
Bonaparte were only violations of real authority; while the Republican
and the Bonapartist will maintain, one that the Republic, and the other
that the Empire were the real authority, and that all the rest was a
violation of authority. It is evident that the explanations given by these
historians, being mutually contradictory, can satisfy none but children
of the tenderest age.

Recognising the deceptiveness of this view of history, another class of
historians assert that authority rests on the conditional delegation of the
combined will of the masses to their rulers, and that historical leaders
possess power only on condition of carrying out the programme which

the will of the people has by tacit consent dictated to them. But what this programme consists of, those historians do not tell us, or if they do, they continually contradict one another.

In accordance with his view of what constitutes the goal of the movements of a people, each historian conceives of this programme, as, for instance, the greatness, the wealth, the freedom, or the enlightenment of the citizens of France or some other kingdom. But putting aside the contradictions between historians as to the nature of such a programme, and even supposing that one general programme to exist for all, the facts of history almost always contradict this theory.

If the conditions on which power is vested in rulers are to be found in the wealth, freedom, and enlightenment of the people, how is it that kings like Louis xiv. and John iv. lived out their reigns in peace, while kings like Louis xvi. and Charles i. were put to death by their peoples? To this question these historians reply, that the effect of the actions of Louis xiv. contrary to the programme were reacted upon Louis xvi. But why not reflected on Louis xiv. and Louis xv.? Why precisely on Louis xvi.? And what limit is there to such reflection? To these questions there is and can be no reply. Nor does this view explain the reason that the combined will of a people remains for several centuries vested in its rulers and their heirs, and then all at once during a period of fifty years is transferred to a Convention, a Directory, to Napoleon, to Alexander, to Louis xviii., again to Napoleon, to Charles x., to Louis Philippe, to a republican government, and to Napoleon iii. To explain these rapid transferences of the people's will from one person to another, especially when complicated by international relations, wars, and alliances, these historians are unwillingly obliged to allow that a proportion of these phenomena are not normal transferences of the will of the people, but casual incidents, depending on the cunning, or the blundering, or the craft, or the weakness of a diplomatist or a monarch, or the leader of a party. So that the greater number of the phenomena of history—civil wars, revolutions, wars—are regarded by these historians as not being produced by the delegation of the free-will of the people, but as being produced by the wrongly directed will of one or several persons, that is, again by a violation of authority. And so by this class of historians, too, historical events are conceived of as exceptions to their theory.

These historians are like a botanist who, observing that several plants grow by their seed parting into two cotyledons, or seed-leaves, should insist that everything that grows only grows by parting into two leaves; and that the palm-tree and the mushroom, and even the oak, when it spreads its branches in all directions in its mature growth, and has lost all semblance to its two seed-leaves, are departures from their theory of the true law of growth. A third class of historians admit that the will of the masses is vested in historical leaders conditionally, but say that those conditions are not known to us. They maintain that historical leaders have power only because they are carrying out the will of the masses delegated to them.

But in that case, if the force moving the peoples lies not in their his-torical leaders, but in the peoples themselves, where is the significance of those historical leaders?

Historical leaders are, so those historians tell us, the self-expression of the will of the masses; the activity of the historical leaders serves as a type of the activity of the masses.

But in that case the question arises. Does all the activity of historical leaders serve as an expression of the will of the masses, or only a certain side of it? If all the life-activity of historical leaders serves as an ex-pression of the will of the masses, as some indeed believe, then the biographies of Napoleons and Catherines, with all the details of court scandal, serve as the expression of the life of their peoples, which is an obvious absurdity. If only one side of the activity of an historical leader serves as the expression of the life of a people, as other supposed philo-sophical historians believe, then to define what side of the activity of an historical leader does express the life of a people, one must know first what the life of the people consists of.

Being confronted with this difficulty, historians of this class invent the most obscure, intangible, and general abstraction, under which to class the greatest possible number of events, and declare that in this abstraction is to be found the aim of the movements of humanity. The most usual abstractions accepted by almost all historians are: freedom, equality, enlightenment, progress, civilisation, culture. Postulating some such abstraction as the goal of the movements of humanity, the histo-rians study those persons who have left the greatest number of memo-rials behind them—kings, ministers, generals, writers, reformers, popes, and journalists—from the point of view of the effect those persons in their opinion had in promoting or hindering that abstraction. But as it is nowhere proven that the goal of humanity really is freedom, equality, enlightenment, or civilisation, and as the connection of the masses with their rulers and with the leaders of humanity only rests on the arbitrary assumption that the combined will of the masses is always vested in these figures which attract our attention—the fact remains that the activity of the millions of men who move from place to place, burn houses, abandon tilling the soil, and butcher one another, never does find expression in descriptions of the activity of some dozen persons, who do not burn houses, never have tilled the soil, and do not kill their fellow-creatures.

History proves this at every turn. Is the ferment of the peoples of the west towards the end of last century, and their rush to the east, ex-plained by the activity of Louis xiv., Louis xv., and Louis xvi., or their mistresses and ministers, or by the life of Napoleon, of Rousseau, of Diderot, of Beaumarchais, and others?

The movement of the Russian people to the east, to Kazan and Siberia, is that expressed in the details of the morbid life of John iv. and his correspondence with Kurbsky?

Is the movement of the peoples at the time of the Crusades explained by the life and activity of certain Godfreys and Louis' and their ladies?

It has remained beyond our comprehension, that movement of the peoples from west to east, without an object, without leadership, with a crowd of tramps following Peter the Hermit. And even more incomprehensible is the cessation of that movement, when a rational and holy object for the expeditions had been clearly set up by historical leaders— that is, the deliverance of Jerusalem.

Popes, kings, and knights urged the people to set free the Holy Land. But the people did not move, because that unknown cause, which had impelled them before to movement, existed no longer. The history of the Godfreys and the Minnesingers evidently cannot be regarded as an epitome of the life of the peoples. And the history of the Godfreys and the Minnesingers has remained the history of those knights and those Minnesingers, while the history of the life of the peoples and their impulses has remained unknown.

Even less explanatory of the life of the peoples is the history of the lives of writers and reformers.

The history of culture offers us as the impelling motives of the life of the people the circumstances of the lives or the ideas of a writer or a reformer. We learn that Luther had a hasty temper and uttered certain speeches; we learn that Rousseau was distrustful and wrote certain books; but we do not learn what made the nations cut each other to pieces after the Reformation, or why men guillotined each other during the French Revolution.

If we unite both these kinds of history together, as do the most modern historians, then we shall get histories of monarchs and of writers, but not a history of the life of nations.

V

THE life of nations is not contained in the life of a few men, since the connection between those few men and the nations has not been found. The theory that this connection is based on the delegation of the combined will of a people to its historical leaders is an hypothesis, not supported by the testimony of history.

The theory of the delegation of the combined will of the masses to historical personages may perhaps explain a great deal in the domain of the science of law, and is possibly essential for its purposes. But in its application to history, as soon as revolutions, wars, civil disturbances arise, as soon as history begins in fact—this theory explains nothing.

This theory appears irrefutable, just because the act of delegating the will of the people can never be verified, since it has never existed.

Whatever event might take place, and whoever might be taking the lead in such an event, the theory can always say that such a person took the lead in bringing about that event because the combined will was vested in him.

The answers given by this theory to historical questions are like the answers of a man who, watching the movements of a flock, should pay no attention to the varying quality of the pasturage in different parts of the field, nor to the actions of the shepherd, but should look for the causes of the flock taking this or that direction simply in the animal that happened to be foremost in it.

"The flock moves in this direction because the animal in front leads it, and the combined will of all the other animals is delegated to the leader of the flock." Such is the answer given by the first class of historians, who suppose an unconditional delegation of will to the authority.

"If the animals leading the flock are changed for others, it is due to the fact that the combined will of all the beasts is transferred from one leader to another owing to the fact that the first leader did not follow the direction chosen by all the flock." Such is the reply of those historians who assume that the combined will of the masses is vested in their rulers on conditions which they regard as unknown. (With this method of observation it very often happens that the observer, judging from the direction chosen by him, reckons as leaders those who, when the direction of the masses is changed, are not in front, but on one side, and even sometimes the hindmost.)

"If the beasts that are foremost are constantly being changed, and the direction taken by the flock too is continually changing, that is due to the fact that to attain a certain direction known to us the beasts delegate their wills to those beasts which attract our attention, and to study the movements of the flock we ought to observe all the noticeable animals that are moving on all sides of the flock." So say the third class of historians, who accept all historical characters as the expression of their age from monarchs to journalists.

The theory of the transference of the will of the masses to historical characters is only a paraphrase—only a restatement of the question in other words.

What is the cause of historical events? Power.

What is Power? Power is the combined will of the masses vested in one person.

On what conditions are the wills of the masses vested in one person? On condition of that person's expressing the will of all men. That is, power is power. That is, power is a word the meaning of which is beyond our comprehension.

If the domain of human knowledge were confined to abstract reasoning alone, then, after subjecting the explanation of power given by science to criticism, humanity would come to the conclusion that power is only a word, and that it has no existence in reality. But for the knowledge of phenomena, man has besides abstract reasoning another instrument—experience—by which he verifies the results of reasoning. And experience tells him that power is not merely a word, but an actually existing phenomenon.

To say nothing of the fact that not a single account of the combined action of men can omit the conception of power, the reality of power is shown us, not only by history, but by observation of contemporary events.

Whenever an event takes place, a man or men appear by whose will the event is conceived to have been accomplished. Napoleon III. gives an order, and the French go to Mexico. The Prussian King and Bismarck give certain orders, and troops go to Bohemia. Napoleon I. gives a command, and soldiers march into Russia. Alexander I. gives a command, and the French submit to the Bourbons. Experience shows us that whatever takes place, it is always connected with the will of one or of several men, who decreed it should be so.

Historians, from the old habit of recognising divine intervention in the affairs of humanity, are inclined to look for the cause of events in the exercise of the will of the person endowed with power; but this conclusion is not confirmed either by reason or by experience.

On one side reason shows that the expression of the will of a man— his words, in fact, are only a part of the general activity expressed in an event, such as a revolution or a war, and therefore without the assumption of an incomprehensible, supernatural force—a miracle—it cannot be admitted that these words can be the immediate cause of the movements of millions of men.

On the other side, even if one admits that words may be the cause of an event, history shows us that the expression of the will of historical personages in the great majority of cases does not lead to any effect at all—that is, that their commands are often not carried out, and, in fact, sometimes the very opposite of what they have commanded is done.

Without admitting divine intervention in the affairs of humanity, we cannot accept power as a cause of events.

Power, from the point of view of experience, is only the dependence existing between the expression of the will of a person and the carrying out of that will by others.

To explain the conditions of that dependence, we have, first of all, to reinstate the conception of the expression of will, referring it to man, and not to the Deity.

If the Deity gives a command, expresses His will, as the history of the ancients tell us, the expression of that will is independent of time, and is not called forth by anything, as the Deity is not connected with the event. But when we speak of commands that are the expression of the will of men, acting in time and connected with one another, we must, if we are to understand the connection of the command with the event, restore (1) the conditions of all the circumstances that took place, the dynamic continuity in time both of the event and of the person commanding it; and (2) the condition of the inevitable connection in which the person commanding stands with those who carry out his command.

VI

ONLY the expression of the will of the Deity, not depending on time, can relate to a whole series of events that have to take place during several years or centuries; and only the Deity, acting by His will alone, not affected by any cause, can determine the direction of the movement of humanity. Man acts in time, and himself takes part in the event.

Restoring the first condition that was omitted, the condition of time, we perceive that no single command can be carried out apart from preceding commands that have made the execution of the last command possible.

Never is a single command given quite independently and arbitrarily, nor does it cover a whole series of events. Every command is the sequel to some other; and it never relates to a whole course of events, but only to one moment in those events.

When we say, for instance, that Napoleon commanded the army to go to fight, we sum up in one single expression a series of consecutive commands, depending one upon another. Napoleon could not command a campaign against Russia, and never did command it. He commanded one day certain papers to be written to Vienna, to Berlin, and to Petersburg; next day certain decrees and instructions to the army, the fleet, and the commissariat, and so on and so on—millions of separate commands, making up a whole series of commands, corresponding to a series of events leading the French soldiers to Russia.

Napoleon was giving commands all through his reign for an expedition to England. On no one of his undertakings did he waste so much time and so much effort, and yet not once during his reign was an attempt made to carry out his design. Yet he made an expedition against Russia, with which, according to his repeatedly expressed conviction, it was to his advantage to be in alliance; and this is due to the fact that his commands in the first case did not, and in the second did, correspond with the course of events.

In order that a command should certainly be carried out, it is necessary that the man should give a command that can be carried out. To know what can and what cannot be carried out is impossible, not only in the case of Napoleon's campaign against Russia, in which millions took part, but even in the case of the simplest event, since millions of obstacles may always arise to prevent its being carried out. Every command that is carried out is always one out of a mass of commands that are not carried out. All the impossible commands are inconsistent with the course of events and are not carried out. Only those which are possible are connected with consecutive series of commands, consistent with series of events, and they are carried out.

Our false conception that the command that precedes an event is the cause of an event is due to the fact that when the event has taken place and those few out of thousands of commands, which happen to be consistent with the course of events, are carried out, we forget those which were not, because they could not be carried out. Apart from that, the chief source of our error arises from the fact that in the historical account a whole series of innumerable, various, and most minute events, as, for instance, all that led the French soldiers to Russia, are generalised into a single event, in accordance with the result produced by that series of events; and by a corresponding generalisation a whole series of commands too is summed up into a single expression of will.

We say: Napoleon chose to invade Russia and he did so. In reality we never find in all Napoleon's doings anything like an expression of that design: what we find is a series of commands or expressions of his will of the most various and undefined tendency. Out of many series of innumerable commands of Napoleon not carried out, one series of commands for the campaign of 1812 was carried out; not from any essential difference between the commands carried out and those not carried out, but simply because the former coincided with the course of events that led the French soldiers into Russia; just as in stencil-work one figure or another is sketched, not because the colours are laid on this side or in that way, but because on the figure cut out in stencil, colours are laid on all sides.

So that examining in time the relation of commands to events, we find that the command can never in any case be the cause of the event, but that a certain definite dependence exists between them. To understand of what this dependence consists, it is essential to restore the other circumstance lost sight of, a condition accompanying any command issuing not from the Deity, but from man. That circumstance is that the man giving the command is himself taking part in the event.

That relation of the commanding person to those he commands is indeed precisely what is called power. That relation may be analysed as follows.

For common action, men always unite in certain combinations, in which, in spite of the difference of the objects aimed at by common action, the relation between the men taking a part in the action always remains the same.

Uniting in these combinations, men always stand in such a relation to one another that the largest number of men take a greater direct share, and a smaller number of men a less direct share in the combined action for which they are united. Of all such combinations in which men are organised for the performance of common action, one of the most striking and definite examples is the army.

Every army is composed of members of lower military standing—the private soldiers, who are always the largest proportion of the whole, of members of a slightly higher military standing—corporals and non-commissioned officers, who are fewer in number than the privates; of still higher officers, whose numbers are even less; and so on, up to the chief military command of all, which is concentrated in one person.

The military organisation may be with perfect accuracy compared to the figure of a cone, the base of which, with the largest diameter, consists of privates; the next higher and smaller plane, of the lower officers; and so on up to the apex of the cone, which will be the com mander-in-chief.

The soldiers, who are the largest number, form the lowest plane and the base of the cone. The soldier himself does the stabbing and hacking, and burning and pillaging, and always receives commands to perform these acts from the persons in the plane next above. He himself never gives a command. The non-commissioned officer (these are fewer in number) more rarely performs the immediate act than the soldier; but he gives commands. The officer next above him still more rarely acts directly himself, and still more frequently commands. The general does nothing but command the army, and hardly ever makes use of a weapon. The commander-in-chief never takes direct part in the action itself, and simply makes general arrangements as to the movements of the masses. A similar relation exists in every combination of persons for common action—in agriculture, commerce, and in every department of activity.

And so without artificially analysing all the converging planes of the cone and ranks of the army or classes or ranks of any department whatever, or public undertaking, from lower to higher, a law comes into existence, by which men always combine together for the performance of common action in such relation that the more directly they take part in the action, the less they command, and the greater their numbers; and the less direct the part they take in the common action, the more they command, and the fewer they are in number; passing in that way from the lower strata up to a single man at the top, who takes least direct share in the action, and devotes his energy more than all the rest to giving commands.

This is the relation of persons in command to those whom they command, and it constitutes the essence of the conception of what is called power.

Restoring the conditions of time under which all events take place, we found that a command is carried out only when it relates to a corresponding course of events. Restoring the essential condition of connection between the persons commanding and fulfilling the commands, we have found that by their very nature the persons commanding take the smallest part in the action itself, and their energy is exclusively directed to commanding.

VII

WHEN some event takes place, men express their opinions and desires in regard to the event, and as the event proceeds from the combined action of many men, some one of the opinions or desires expressed is certain to be at least approximately fulfilled. When one of the opinions expressed is fulfilled, that opinion is connected with the event as the command preceding it.

Men are dragging a log. Every man expresses his opinion as to how and where to drag it. The men drag the log off; and it turns out that it has been done just as one of them advised. He gave the command then. This is commanding and power in its primitive aspect.

The man who did most work with his arms could think least what he was doing, reflect least what might come of the common action, and so command least. The man who commanded most could obviously, from his greater verbal activity, act less vigorously with his arms. In a larger assembly of men, combining their energies to one end, the class of those persons who take the less direct share in the common work the more their energy is turned to command, is still more sharply defined.

When a man acts alone, he always carries within him a certain series of considerations, that have, as he supposes, directed his past conduct, and that serve to justify to him his present action, and to lead him to make projects for his future activity.

Assemblies of men act in the same way, only leaving to those who do not take direct part in the action to invent considerations, justifications, and projects concerning their combined activity.

For causes, known or unknown to us, the French begin to chop and hack at each other. And to match the event, it is accompanied by its justification in the expressed wills of certain men, who declare it essential for the good of France, for the cause of freedom, of equality. Men cease slaughtering one another, and that event is accompanied by the justification of the necessity of centralisation of power, of resistance to Europe, and so on. Men march from west to east, killing their fellow-creatures, and this event is accompanied by phrases about the glory of France, the baseness of England, and so on. History teaches us that those justifications for the event are devoid of all common-sense, that they are inconsistent with one another, as, for instance, the murder of a man as a result of the declaration of his rights, and the murder of millions in Russia for the abasement of England. But those justifications have an incontestable value in their own day.

They remove moral responsibility from those men who produce the events. At the time they do the work of brooms, that go in front to clear the rails for the train: they clear the path of men's moral responsibility. Apart from those justifications, no solution could be found for the most obvious question that occurs to one at once on examining any historical event; that is, How did millions of men come to combine to commit crimes, murders, wars, and so on?

Under the existing complex forms of political social life in Europe, can any event be imagined which would not have been prescribed, decreed, commanded by some sovereigns, ministers, parliaments, or newspapers? Is there any sort of combined action which could not find justification in political unity, or in patriotism, or in the balance of power, or in civilisation? So that every event that occurs inevitably coincides with some expressed desire, and receiving justification, is regarded as the result of the will of one or more persons.

Whichever way the ship steers its course, there will always be seen ahead of it the flow of the waves it cleaves. To the men in the ship the movement of those waves will be the only motion perceptible.

It is only by watching closely, moment by moment, the movement of that flow, and comparing it with the movement of the ship, that we are convinced that every moment that flowing by of the waves is due to the forward movement of the ship, and that we have been led into error by the fact that we are ourselves moving too.

We see the same thing, watching moment by moment the movement of historical personages (that is, restoring the inevitable condition under which all action takes place—the condition of the continuity of motion in time), and not losing sight of the necessary connection of historical figures with the masses.

Whatever happens, it always appears that that was foreseen and decreed. Whichever way the ship turns, the waves gurgle in front of it, and neither guiding nor accelerating its movement, will seem to us at a distance to be moving arbitrarily and guiding the course of the ship.

Examining only those expressions of the will of historical characters which related to events as commands, historians have assumed that the events were dependent on the commands. Examining the events themselves, and that connection in which the historical characters stand with the masses, we have found that historical characters and their commands are dependent on the events. An incontestable proof of this deduction is to be found in the fact that, however many commands may be given, the event does not take place if there is no other cause to produce it. But as soon as an event does take place—whatever it may be— out of the number of all the expressions of the will of different persons, there are always some which, from their meaning and time of utterance, are related to the events as commands.

Having reached this conclusion, we can directly and positively answer these two essential questions of history:—

1. What is power?

2. What force produces the movements of peoples?

1. Power is a relation of a certain person to other persons, in which that person takes the less direct share in an act, the more he expresses opinions, theories, and justifications of the combined action.

2. The movement of peoples is not produced by the exercise of power; nor by intellectual activity, nor even by a combination of the two, as historians have supposed; but by the activity of *all* the men taking part in the event, who are always combined in such a way that those who take most direct part in the action take the smallest share in responsibility for it, and *vice versa*.

In its moral aspect the cause of the event is conceived of as power; in its physical aspect as those who were subject to that power. But since moral activity is inconceivable apart from physical, the cause of the event is found in neither the one nor the other, but in the conjunction of the two.

Or, in other words, the conception of cause is not applicable to the phenomenon we are examining.

In our final analysis we are brought to the circle of infinity, to that utmost limit, to which the human intellect is brought in every department of thought, if it is not merely playing with its subject. Electricity produces heat; heat produces electricity. Atoms are attracted; atoms are repelled.

Speaking of the mutual relations of heat and of electricity and of atoms, we cannot say why it is so, and we say it is so because it is unthinkable otherwise; because it must be so; because it is a law. The same thing applies also to historical phenomena. Why does a war or a revolution come to pass? We do not know. We only know that to bring either result to pass, men form themselves into a certain combination in which all take part; and we say that this is so because it is unthinkable otherwise; because it is a law.

VIII

IF history had to deal with external phenomena, the establishment of this simple and obvious law would be sufficient, and our argument would be at an end. But the law of history relates to man. A particle of matter cannot tell us that it does not feel the inevitability of attraction and repulsion, and that the law is not true. Man, who is the subject of history, bluntly says: I am free, and so I am not subject to law.

The presence of the question of the freedom of the will, if not openly expressed, is felt at every step in history.

All seriously thinking historians are involuntarily led to this question. All the inconsistencies, and the obscurity of history, and the false path that science has followed, is due to that unsolved question.

If the will of every man were free, that is, if every man could act as he chose, the whole of history would be a tissue of disconnected accidents.

If one man only out of millions once in a thousand years had the power of acting freely, that is, as he chose, it is obvious that a single free act of that man in opposition to the laws governing human action would destroy the possibility of any laws whatever governing all humanity.

If there is but one law controlling the actions of men, there can be no free will, since men's will must be subject to that law.

In this contradiction lies the question of the freedom of the will, which from the most ancient times has occupied the best intellects of mankind, and has from the most ancient times been regarded as of immense importance.

Looking at man as a subject of observation from any point of view —theological, historical, ethical, philosophical—we find a general law of necessity to which he is subject like everything existing. Looking at him from within ourselves, as what we are conscious of, we feel ourselves free.

This consciousness is a source of self-knowledge utterly apart and independent of reason. Through reason man observes himself; but he knows himself only through consciousness.

Apart from consciousness of self, any observation and application of reason is inconceivable.

To understand, to observe, to draw conclusions, a man must first of all be conscious of himself as living. A man knows himself as living, not otherwise than as willing, that is, he is conscious of his free will. Man is conscious of his will as constituting the essence of his life, and he cannot be conscious of it except as free.

If subjecting himself to his own observation, a man perceives that his will is always controlled by the same law (whether he observes the necessity of taking food, or of exercising his brain, or anything else), he cannot regard this never-varying direction of his will otherwise than as a limitation of it. If it were not free, it could not be limited. A man's will seems to him to be limited just because he is not conscious of it except as free. You say: I am not free. But I have lifted and dropped my hand. Everybody understands that this illogical reply is an irrefutable proof of freedom.

This reply is an expression of a consciousness not subject to reason.

If the consciousness of freedom were not a separate source of self-knowledge apart from reason, it would be controlled by reasoning and experience. But in reality such control never exists, and is inconceivable.

A series of experiments and arguments prove to every man that he, as an object of observation, is subject to certain laws, and the man submits to them, and never, after they have once been pointed out to him, controverts the law of gravity or of impenetrability. But the same series of experiments and arguments proves to him that the complete freedom of which he is conscious in himself is impossible; that every action of his depends on his organisation, on his character, and the motives acting on him. But man never submits to the deductions of these experiments and arguments.

Learning from experience and from reasoning that a stone falls to the ground, a man unhesitatingly believes this; and in all cases expects the law he has learnt to be carried out.

But learning just as incontestably that his will is subject to laws, he does not, and cannot, believe it.

However often experience and reasoning show a man that in the same circumstances, with the same character, he does the same thing as before, yet on being led the thousandth time in the same circumstances, with the same character, to an action that always ends in the same way, he feels just as unhesitatingly convinced that he can act as he chooses, as ever. Every man, savage and sage alike, however incontestably reason and experience may prove to him that it is impossible to imagine two different courses of action under precisely the same circumstances, yet feels that without this meaningless conception (which constitutes the essence of freedom) he cannot conceive of life. He feels that, however impossible it may be, it is so; seeing that, without that conception of freedom, he would be not only unable to understand life, but could not live for a single instant.

He could not live because all men's instincts, all their impulses in life, are only efforts to increase their freedom. Wealth and poverty, health and disease, culture and ignorance, labour and leisure, repletion and hunger, virtue and vice, are all only terms for greater or less degrees of freedom.

To conceive a man having no freedom is impossible except as a man deprived of life.

If the idea of freedom appears to the reason a meaningless contradiction, like the possibility of doing two actions at a single moment of time, or the possibility of an effect without a cause, that only proves that consciousness is not subject to reason.

That unwavering, irrefutable consciousness of freedom, not influenced by experience and argument, recognised by all thinkers, and felt by all men without exception, that consciousness without which no conception of man is reliable, constitutes the other side of the question.

Man is the creation of an Almighty, All-good, and All-wise God. What is sin, the conception of which follows from man's consciousness of freedom? That is the question of theology.

Men's actions are subject to general and invariable laws, expressed in statistics. What is man's responsibility to society, the conception of which follows from his consciousness of freedom? That is the question of jurisprudence.

A man's actions follow from his innate character and the motives acting on him. What is conscience and the sense of right and wrong in action that follows from the consciousness of freedom? That is the question of ethics.

Man in connection with the general life of humanity is conceived as governed by the laws that determine that life. But the same man, apart from that connection, is conceived of as free. How is the past life of nations and of humanity to be regarded—as the product of the free or not free action of men? That is the question of history.

Only in our conceited age of the popularisation of knowledge, thanks to the most powerful weapon of ignorance—the diffusion of printed matter—the question of the freedom of the will has been put on a level, on which it can no longer be the same question. In our day the majority of so-called advanced people—that is, a mob of ignoramuses—have accepted the result of the researches of natural science, which is occupied with one side only of the question, for the solution of the whole question.

There is no soul and no free will, because the life of man is expressed in muscular movements, and muscular movements are conditioned by nervous activity. There is no soul and no free will, because at some unknown period of time we came from apes, they say, and write, and print. Not at all suspecting that thousands of years ago all religions and all thinkers have admitted—have never, in fact, denied—that same law of necessity, which they are now so strenuously trying to prove by physiology and comparative zoology. They do not see that natural science can do no more in this question than serve to illumine one side of it. The fact that, from the point of view of observation, the reason and the will are but secretions of the brain, and that man, following the general law of development, may have developed from lower animals at some unknown period of time, only illustrates in a new aspect the truth, recognised thousands of years ago by all religious and philosophic theories, that man is subject to the laws of necessity. It does not advance one hair's-breadth the solution of the question, which has another opposite side, founded on the consciousness of freedom.

If men have descended from apes at an unknown period of time, that is as comprehensible as that they were fabricated out of a clod of earth at a known period of time (in the one case the date is the unknown quantity, in the other the method of fabrication); and the question how to reconcile man's consciousness of free will with the law of necessity to which he is subject cannot be solved by physiology and zoology, seeing that in the frog, the rabbit, and the monkey we can observe only muscular and nervous activity, while in man we find muscular and nervous activity plus consciousness.

The scientific men and their disciples who suppose they are solving this question are like plasterers set to plaster one side of a church wall, who, in the absence of the chief superintendent of their work, should in the excess of their zeal plaster over the windows, and the holy images, and the woodwork, and the scaffolding, and rejoice that from their plasterers' point of view everything was now so smooth and even.

IX

THE question of free will and necessity holds a position in history different from its place in other branches of knowledge, because in history, the question relates, not to the essential nature of the will of man, but to the representation of the manifestations of that will in the past and under certain conditions.

History, in regard to the solution of this question, stands to the other sciences in the position of an experimental science to speculative sciences.

The subject of history is not the will of man, but our representation of its action.

And so the insoluble mystery of the union of the two antinomies of freedom and necessity does not exist for history as it does for theology, ethics, and philosophy. History deals with the representation of the life of man, in which the union of those two antinomies is accomplished.

In actual life every historical event, every human action, is quite clearly and definitely understood, without a sense of the slightest contradiction in it, although every event is conceived of partly as free, and partly as necessary.

To solve the problem of combining freedom and necessity and the question what constitutes the essence of those two conceptions, the

philosophy of history can and ought to go to work in a direction opposite to that taken by the other sciences. Instead of first defining the
ideas of freedom and necessity in themselves, and then ranging the phenomena of life under those definitions, history must form the definition
of the ideas of free will and necessity from the immense multitude of
phenomena in her domain that are always dependent on those two elements.

Whatever presentation of the activity of one man or of several persons we examine, we always regard it as the product partly of that man
or men's free will, partly of the laws of necessity.

Whether we are discussing the migrations of peoples and the inroads
of barbarians, or the government of Napoleon III., or the action of some
man an hour ago in selecting one direction for his walk out of several,
we see nothing contradictory in it. The proportion of freedom and necessity guiding the actions of those men is clearly defined for us.

Very often our conception of a greater or less degree of freedom dif-
fers according to the different points of view from which we regard the
phenomenon.

But every human action is always alike conceived by us as a certain
combination of free will and necessity.

In every action we investigate, we see a certain proportion of freedom
and a certain proportion of necessity. And whatever action we investigate, the more necessity we see, the less freedom, and the more freedom,
the less necessity.

The proportion of freedom to necessity is decreased or increased, according to the point of view from which the act is regarded; but there
always remains an inverse ratio between them.

A drowning man clutching at another and drowning him, or a hungry
mother starved by suckling her baby and stealing food, or a man trained
to discipline who at the word of command kills a defenceless man, all
seem less guilty—that is, less free and more subject to the law of necessity to one who knows the circumstances in which they are placed, and
more free to one who did not know that the man was himself drowning,
that the mother was starving, that the soldier was on duty, and so on.
In the same way a man who has twenty years ago committed a murder
and afterwards has gone on living calmly and innocently in society
seems less guilty, and his acts seem more subject to the law of necessity,
to one who looks at his act after the lapse of twenty years than to one
looking at the same act the day after it was perpetrated. And just in the
same way the act of a madman, a drunkard, or a man labouring under
violent excitement seems less free and more inevitable to one who knows
the mental condition of the man who performed the action, and more
free and less inevitable to one who does not know it. In all such cases
the conception of freedom is increased or diminished, and that of necessity correspondingly diminished or increased, according to the point of
view from which the action is regarded. So that the more necessity is
seen in it the less freedom. And *vice versa*.

Religion, the common-sense of humanity, the science of law, and his-tory itself understand this relation between necessity and free will.

All cases, without exception, in which our conception of free will and necessity varies depend on three considerations:

1. The relation of the man committing the act to the external world.
2. His relation to time.
3. His relation to the causes leading to the act.

In the first case the variation depends on the degree to which we see the man's relation to the external world, on the more or less clear idea we form of the definite position occupied by the man in relation to everything co-existing with him. It is this class of considerations that makes it obvious to us that the drowning man is less free and more sub-ject to necessity than a man standing on dry ground; and that makes the actions of a man living in close connection with other people in a thickly populated district, bound by ties of family, official duties, or business undertaking, seem undoubtedly less free than those of a man living in solitude and seclusion.

If we examine a man alone, apart from his relations to everything around him, every action of his seems free to us. But if we see any rela-tion of his to anything surrounding, if we perceive any connection be-tween him and anything else, a man speaking to him, a book read by him, the work he is employed in, even the air he breathes, or the light that falls on the objects around him, we perceive that every one of those circumstances has its influence on him, and controls at least one side of his activity. And the more we perceive of those influences, the smaller the idea we form of his freedom, and the greater our conception of the necessity to which he is subject.

2. The second cause of variation is due to the degree of distinctness with which the man's position in time is perceived, the clearness of the notion formed by us of the place the man's action fills in time. It is ow-ing to this class of considerations that the fall of the first man, leading to the origin of the human race, seems to us obviously less free than the marriage of any one of our contemporaries. It is owing to this class of considerations that the life and acts of men who lived years ago cannot seem to me as free as the life of my contemporaries, the consequences of whose acts are still unknown to me.

The variation in our conception of free will in this connection depends on the interval of time that has elapsed between the action and our criti-cism of it.

If I examine an act I have committed a moment ago in approximately the same circumstances as I am placed in now, my act appears to me indubitably free. But if I examine an act I have committed a month ago, then being placed in other circumstances, I cannot help recognising that had not that act been committed, much that is good and agreeable, and even inevitable, resulting from that act, could not have taken place. If I reflect on a still more remote action, performed ten years or more ago, the consequences of my act are even plainer to me, and it will be difficult for me to conceive what would have happened if that action had not taken place. The further back I go in my reminiscences, or what is the same thing, the further forward in my criticism of them, the more doubtful becomes my view of the freedom of my action.

We find precisely the same ratio of variation in our views of the element of free will in the general affairs of men in history. A contemporary event we conceive of as undoubtedly the doing of all the men we know of concerned in it. But with a more remote event, we see its inevitable consequences, which prevent our conceiving of anything else as possible. And the further back we go in the examination of events, the less arbitrary they seem to us.

The Austro-Prussian war appears to us to be undoubtedly the result of the crafty acts of Bismarck and so on.

The Napoleonic wars, though more doubtful, appear to us the effect of the free will of the leading heroes of those wars. But in the Crusades we see an event, filling its definite place in history, without which the modern history of Europe is inconceivable, although to the chroniclers of the Crusades, those events appeared simply due to the will of a few persons. In the migrations of peoples it never occurs to any one now that the renewal of the European world depended on a caprice of Attila's. The more remote in history the subject of our observations, the more doubtful we feel of the free will of the persons concerned in the event, and the more obvious is the law of necessity in it.

3. The third element influencing our judgment is the degree to which we can apprehend that endless chain of causation demanded by the reason, in which every phenomenon comprehended, and so every act of man, must have its definite place, as a result of past and a cause of future acts.

This is the element that causes our acts and those of others to appear to us on one side more free the less we know of the physiological, psychological, and historical laws deduced from observation, and the less thoroughly the physiological, psychological, or historical cause of the act has been investigated by us, and on the other hand the less simple the act observed and the less complex the character and mind of the man whose action we are examining.

When we have absolutely no understanding of the causes of an action —whether vicious or virtuous or simply non-moral—we ascribe a greater element of free will to it. In the case of a crime, we are more urgent in demanding punishment for the act; in the case of a virtuous act, we are warmer in our appreciation of its merits. In cases of no moral bearing, we recognise more individuality, originality, and independence in it. But if only one of the innumerable causes of the act is known to us, we recognise a certain element of necessity, and are less ready to exact punishment for the crime, to acknowledge merit in the virtuous act, or freedom in the apparent originality. The fact that the criminal was reared in vicious surroundings softens his fault in our eyes. The self-sacrifice of a father, of a mother, or self-sacrifice with the possibility of reward is more comprehensible than gratuitous self-sacrifice.

and so is regarded by us as less deserving of sympathy and less the work of free will. The founder of a sect, of a party, or the inventor impresses us less when we understand how and by what the way was paved for his activity. If we have a large range of experiments, if our observation is continually directed to seeking correlations in men's actions between causes and effects, their actions will seem to us more necessary and less free, the more accurately we connect causes and effects. If the actions investigated are simple, and we have had a vast number of such actions under observation, our conception of their inevitability will be even more complete. The dishonest conduct of the son of a dishonest father, the misbehaviour of women, who have been led into certain surroundings, the relapse of the reformed drunkard into drunkenness, and so on, are instances of conduct which seem to us to be less free the better we understand their cause. If the man himself whose conduct we are examining is on the lowest stage of mental development, like a child, a madman, or a simpleton, then when we know the causes of the act and the simplicity of the character and intelligence, we see so great an element of necessity, and so little free will, that we can foretell the act that will follow, as soon as we know the cause bound to bring it forth.

In all legislative codes the exoneration of crime or admission of mitigating circumstances rests only on those three classes of consideration. The guilt is conceived as greater or less according to the greater or lesser knowledge of the conditions in which the man judged is placed, the greater or less interval of time between the perpetration of the crime and the judgment of it, and the greater or less comprehension of the causes that led to the act.

X

AND thus our conception of free will and necessity is gradually diminished or increased according to the degree of connection with the external world, the degree of remoteness in time, and the degree of dependence on causes which we see in the phenomenon of man's life that we examine. So that if we examine the case of a man in which the connection with the external world is better known, the interval of time between the examination and the act greater, and the causes of the action easier to comprehend, we form a conception of a greater element of necessity and less free will. If we examine a man in a less close dependence on external conditions, if his action is committed at a moment nearer the present, and the causes leading him to it are beyond our ken, we form a conception of a less element of necessity and a greater element of free will in his action.

But in neither case, however we shift our point of view, however clear we make to ourselves the connection in which the man is placed with the external world, or however fully comprehensible it may appear to us, however long or short a period of time we select, however explicable or unfathomable the causes of the act may be to us, we can never conceive of complete free will, nor of complete necessity in any action.

1. However carefully we imagine a man excluded from the influence of the external world, we can never form a conception of freedom in space. Every act of man's is inevitably limited by what surrounds him and by his own body. I raise my arm and let it fall. My action seems to me free; but asking myself could I raise my arm in any direction, I see that I moved it in the direction in which there was least hindrance to the action arising from bodies around me or from the construction of my own body. I chose one out of all the possible directions, because in that direction I met with least hindrance. For my action to be entirely free, it would have to meet with no hindrance in any direction. To conceive a man quite free, we have to conceive him outside of space, which is obviously impossible.

2. However near we bring the time of criticism to the time of action, we can never form a conception of freedom in time. For if I examine an act committed a second ago, I must still recognise that it is not free, since the act is irrevocably linked to the moment at which it was committed. Can I lift my arm? I lift it; but I ask myself: Could I not have lifted my arm in that moment of time that has just passed? To convince myself of that, I do not lift my arm the next moment. But I am not abstaining from lifting it that first moment of which I asked myself the question. The time has gone by and to detain it was not in my power, and the hand which I then raised and the air in which I raised it are not the same as the hand I do not raise now or the air in which I do not now raise it. The moment in which the first movement took place is irrevocable, and in that moment I could only perform one action, and whatever movement I had made, that movement could have been the only one. The fact that the following moment I abstained from lifting my arm did not prove that I could have abstained from lifting it. And since my movement could only be one in one moment of time, it could have been no other. To conceive it to oneself as free, one must conceive it in the present on the boundary between the past and the future, that is, outside time, which is impossible.

3. However we increase the degree of difficulty of comprehending the causes of the act, we never reach a conception of complete free will, that is, absolute absence of cause. Though the cause of the expression of will in any act of our own or another's may be beyond our ken, it is the first impulse of the intellect to presuppose and seek a cause, without which no phenomenon is conceivable. I raise my arm in order to perform an act independent of any cause, but the fact that I want to perform an act independent of any cause is the cause of my action.

But even if by conceiving a man entirely excluded from external influence, and exercising only a momentary act in the present, not called forth by any cause, we were to reduce the element of necessity to an infinitesimal minimum equivalent to nil, we should even then not have reached a conception of complete free will in a man; for a creature, uninfluenced by the external world, outside of time, and independent of cause, is no longer a man.

In the same way we can never conceive a human action subject only to necessity without any element of free will.

1. However we increase our knowledge of the conditions of space in which a man is placed, that knowledge can never be complete since the number of these conditions is infinitely great, seeing that space is infinite. And so long as not *all* the conditions that may influence a man are defined, the circle of necessity is not complete, and there is still a loophole for free will.

2. Though we may make the period of time intervening between an act and our criticism of it as long as we choose, that period will be finite, and time is infinite, and so in this respect too the circle of necessity is not complete.

3. However easy the chain of causation of any act may be to grasp, we shall never know the whole chain, since it is endless, and so again we cannot attain absolute necessity.

But apart from that, even if, reducing the minimum of free will till it is equivalent to nil, we were to admit in some case—as, for instance, that of a dying man, an unborn babe, an idiot—a complete absence of free will, we should in so doing have destroyed the very conception of man, in the case we are examining; since as soon as there is no free will, there is no man. And therefore the conception of the action of a man subject only to the law of necessity, without the smallest element of free will, is as impossible as the conception of a completely free human action.

Thus to conceive a human action subject only to the law of necessity without free will, we must assume a knowledge of an *infinite* number of conditions in space, an *infinitely* long period of time, and an *infinite* chain of causation.

To conceive a man perfectly free, not subject to the law of necessity, we must conceive a man *outside of space, outside of time,* and *free from all dependence on cause.*

In the first case, if necessity were possible without free will, we should be brought to a definition of the laws of necessity in the terms of the same necessity, that is, to mere form without content.

In the second case, if free will were possible without necessity, we should come to unconditioned free will outside of space, and time, and cause, which by the fact of its being unconditioned and unlimited would be nothing else than content without form.

We should be brought in fact to these two fundamental elements, of which man's whole cosmic conception is made up—the incomprehensible essence of life and the laws that give form to that essence.

Reason says: 1. space with all the forms given it by its visibility—matter—is infinite, and is not thinkable otherwise.

2. Time is infinite movement without one moment of rest, and it is not otherwise thinkable.

3. The connection of cause and effect has no beginning, and can have no end.

Consciousness says: 1. I alone am, and all that exists is only *I*; consequently I include space.

2. I measure moving time by the unchanging moment of the present, in which alone I am conscious of myself living; consequently I am outside of time, and

3. I am outside of cause, since I feel myself the cause of every phenomenon of my life.

Reason gives expression to the laws of necessity. Consciousness gives expression to the reality of free will.

Freedom unlimited by anything is the essence of life in man's consciousness. Necessity without content is man's reason with its three forms of thought.

Free will is what is examined: Necessity is what examines. Free will is content: Necessity is form.

It is only by the analysis of the two sources of knowledge, standing to one another in the relation of form and content, that the mutually exclusive, and separately inconceivable ideas of free will and necessity are formed.

Only by their synthesis is a clear conception of the life of man gained.

Outside these two ideas—in their synthesis mutually definitive as form and content—no conception of life is possible.

All that we know of men's life is only a certain relation of free will to necessity, that is, of consciousness to the laws of reason.

All that we know of the external world of nature is only a certain relation of the forces of nature to necessity, or of the essence of life to the laws of reason.

The forces of the life of nature lie outside us, and not subject to our consciousness; and we call these forces gravity, inertia, electricity, vital force, and so on. But the force of the life of man is the subject of our consciousness, and we call it free will.

But just as the force of gravitation—in itself incomprehensible, though felt by every man—is only so far understood by us as we know the laws of necessity to which it is subject (from the first knowledge that all bodies are heavy down to Newton's law), so too the force of free will, unthinkable in itself, but recognised by the consciousness of every man, is only so far understood as we know the laws of necessity to which it is subject (from the fact that every man dies up to the knowledge of the most complex economic or historic laws).

All knowledge is simply bringing the essence of life under the laws of reason.

Man's free will is distinguished from every other force by the fact that it is the subject of man's consciousness. But in the eyes of reason it is not distinguished from any other force.

The forces of gravitation, of electricity, or of chemical affinity, are only distinguished from one another by being differently defined by reason. In the same way the force of man's free will is only distinguished by reason from the other forces of nature by the definition given it by reason. Free will apart from necessity, that is, apart from the laws of reason defining it, is in no way different from gravitation, or heat, or the force of vegetation; for reason, it is only a momentary, indefinite sensation of life.

And as the undefined essence of the force moving the heavenly bodies, the undefined essence of the force of heat, of electricity, or of chemical affinity, or of vital force, forms the subject of astronomy, physics, chemistry, botany, zoology, and so on, so the essence of the force of free will forms the subject matter of history. But even as the subject of every science is the manifestation of that unknown essence of life, yet that essence itself can only be the subject of metaphysics, so too the manifestation of the force of free will in space, and time, and dependence on cause, forms the subject of history, but free will itself is the subject of metaphysics.

In the experimental sciences, what is known to us we call the laws of necessity; what is unknown to us we call vital force. Vital force is simply an expression for what remains unexplained by what we know of the essence of life. So in history what is known to us we call the laws of necessity; what is unknown, we call free will. Free will is for history simply an expression for what remains unexplained by the laws of men's life that we know.

XI

HISTORY examines the manifestations of man's free will in connection with the external world in time and in dependence on cause, that is, defines that freedom by the laws of reason; and so history is only a science in so far as that freedom is defined by those laws.

To history the recognition of the free wills of men as forces able to influence historical events, that is, not subject to laws, is the same as would be to astronomy the recognition of free will in the movements of the heavenly bodies.

This recognition destroys the possibility of the existence of laws, that is, of any science whatever. If there is so much as one body moving at its free will, the laws of Kepler and of Newton are annulled, and every conception of the movement of the heavenly bodies is destroyed. If there is a single human action due to free will, no historical law exists, and no conception of historical events can be formed.

For history there exist lines of movement of human wills, one extremity of which vanishes in the unknowable, and at the other extremity of which in space, in time, and in dependence on cause, there moves men's consciousness of free will in the present.

The more this curve of movement is analysed before our eyes, the clearer are the laws of its movement. To discover and define those laws is the problem of history.

From the point of view from which the science of history now approaches its subject, by the method it now follows, seeking the causes of phenomena in the free will of men, the expression of laws by science is impossible; since however we limit the free will of men, so long as we recognise it as a force not subject to law, the existence of law becomes impossible.

Only limiting this element of free will to infinity, that is, regarding it as an infinitesimal minimum, we are convinced of the complete unattainability of causes, and then, instead of seeking causes, history sets before itself the task of seeking laws.

The seeking of those laws has been begun long ago, and the new lines of thought which history must adopt are being worked out simultaneously with the self-destruction towards which the old-fashioned history is going, forever dissecting and dissecting the causes of phenomena.

All human sciences have followed the same course. Reaching infinitesimals, mathematics, the most exact of the sciences, leaves the process of analysis and enters on a new process of approximating to summing up the unknown infinitesimals. Forsaking the conception of cause, mathematics seeks law, that is, properties common to all unknown, infinitesimal quantities.

The other sciences, too, have followed the same course, though under another form. When Newton formulated the law of gravity, he did not say that the sun or the earth has the property of attraction. He said that all bodies—from the greatest to the smallest—have the property of attracting one another; that is, leaving on one side the question of the cause of the movements of bodies, he expressed the property common to all bodies, from the infinitely great to the infinitely small. The natural sciences do the same thing; leaving on one side the question of cause, they seek for laws. History, too, is entered on the same course. And if the subject of history is to be the study of the movements of peoples and of humanity, and not episodes from the lives of individual men, it too is bound to lay aside the idea of cause, and to seek the laws common to all the equal and inseparably interconnected, infinitesimal elements of free will.

XII

EVER since the law of Copernicus was discovered and proved, the mere recognition that not the sun, but the earth moves, has destroyed the whole cosmography of the ancients. By disproving the law, it might have been possible to retain the old conception of the movements of the heavenly bodies; but without disproving it, it would seem to be impossible to continue studying the Ptolemaic worlds. But as a fact even after the discovery of the law of Copernicus, the Ptolemaic worlds long continued to be a subject of study.

Ever since the first person said and proved that the number of births or crimes is subject to mathematical laws, that certain geographical and politico-economical laws determine this or that form of government, that certain relations of the population to the soil lead to migrations of peoples—from that moment the foundations on which history was built were destroyed in their essence.

By disproving those new laws, the old view of history might have been retained. But without disproving them, it would seem impossible to continue studying historical events, merely as the arbitrary product of the free will of individual men. For if a certain type of government is established, or a certain movement of peoples takes place in consequence of certain geographical, ethnographical, or economic conditions, the free will of those persons who are described to us as setting up that type of government or leading that movement cannot be regarded as the cause.

And yet history goes on being studied as of old, side by side with laws of statistics, of geography, of political economy, of comparative philology and geology, that flatly contradict its assumptions.

The struggle between the new views and the old was long and stubborn in physical philosophy. Theology stood on guard over the old view, and accused the new view of violating revelation. But when truth gained the day, theology established itself as firmly as ever on a new basis.

As long and as obstinate is the conflict to-day between the old and the new view of history; and in the same way theology stands on guard over the old view, and accuses the new of attacking revelation.

In both cases on both sides, the struggle rouses evil passions and stifles truth. On one side there is dread and regret at demolishing the edifice that has been raised by the ages; on the other, the passion for destruction.

To the men who fought against the new truths of physical philosophy, it seemed that if they were to admit that truth, it would shatter faith in God, in the creation of the firmament, in the miracle of Joshua, the son of Nun. To the champions of the laws of Copernicus and Newton, to Voltaire, for instance, it seemed that the laws of astronomy were destructive of religion, and the latter made use of the law of gravity as a weapon against religion.

So now it seems that we have but to admit the law of necessity to shatter the conception of the soul, of good, of evil, and of the political and ecclesiastical edifices reared on the basis of those conceptions.

So too, like Voltaire in his day, the champions of the law of necessity use the law as a weapon against religion, though, like the law of Copernicus in astronomy, the law of necessity in history, far from destroying even strengthens the foundation on which political and ecclesiastical edifices are reared.

Just as then in the question of astronomy, now in the question of history, the whole difference of view rested on the recognition or non-recognition of an absolute unit as a measure of visible phenomena. For astronomy, this was the immobility of the earth; in history, the independence of personality—free will.

Just as in astronomy the difficulty of admitting the motion of the earth lay in the immediate sensation of the earth's stationariness and of the planets' motion, so in history the difficulty of recognising the subjection of the personality to the laws of space and time and causation lies in the difficulty of surmounting the direct sensation of the independence of one's personality. But just as in astronomy, the new view said, "It is true, we do not feel the movement of the earth, but, if we admit its immobility, we are reduced to absurdity, while admitting its movement, we are led to laws"; so in history, the new view says, "It is true, we do not feel our dependence, but admitting our free will, we are led to absurdity; admitting our dependence on the external world, time, and cause, we are led to laws."

In the first case, we had to surmount the sensation of an unreal immobility in space, and to admit a motion we could not perceive of by sense. In the present case, it is as essential to surmount a consciousness of an unreal freedom and to recognise a dependence not perceived by our senses.